the mists of avalon

The Mists of Avalon

MARION ZIMMER BRADLEY

alfred a. knopf   new york   1983

THIS IS A BORZOI BOOK
PUBLISHED BY ALFRED A. KNOPF, INC.

Copyright © 1982 by Marion Zimmer Bradley

Library of Congress Cataloging in Publication Data

Bradley, Marion Zimmer. The mists of Avalon.

1. Arthurian romances. 2. Great Britain—History—Anglo-Saxon period, 449-1066—Fiction. I. Title.
PS3552.R228M5   1983   813'.54   82-47810
ISBN 0-394-52406-3   AACR2

Manufactured in the United States of America

Published January 18, 1983
Reprinted Four Times
Fifth Printing, March 1983

"... Morgan le Fay was not married, but put to school in a nunnery, where she became a great mistress of magic."

—Malory, *Morte d'Arthur*

acknowledgments

ANY BOOK of this complexity drives its author to sources far too many to be listed in entirety. I should probably cite, first, my late grandfather, John Roscoe Conklin, who first gave me a battered old copy of the Sidney Lanier edition of the *Tales of King Arthur,* which I read so often that I virtually memorized the whole thing before I was ten years old. My imagination was also stirred by varied sources such as the illustrated weekly *Tales of Prince Valiant;* and in my fifteenth year I played hooky from school far oftener than anyone realized to hide in the library of the Department of Education in Albany, New York, reading my way through a ten-volume edition of James Frazer's *The Golden Bough* and a fifteen-volume set of books on comparative religions, including an enormous volume on the Druids and Celtic religions.

In direct research for the present volume, I should give thanks to Geoffrey Ashe, whose works suggested several directions for further research, and to Jamie George of the Gothic Image bookstore in Glastonbury, who, in addition to showing me the geography of Somerset and the sites of Camelot and Guinevere's kingdom (for the purposes of this book, I accept the current theory that Camelot was the Cadbury Castle site in Somerset), guided me through the Glastonbury pilgrimage. He also drew my attention to the persistent traditions surrounding Chalice Well in Glastonbury, and the long-standing belief that Joseph of Arimathea had planted the Holy Thorn on Wearyall Hill; I also saw there many materials exploring the Celtic tradition that Jesus Christ had been educated in the wisdom religion at the temple that once stood on Glastonbury Tor.

For material on pre-Augustinian Christianity, I have used, by permission, a privately circulated manuscript entitled "The Pre-Constantine Mass: A Conjecture," by Father Randall Garrett; I have also drawn upon materials from the Syro-Chaldean liturgies, including the Holy Orbana of St. Serapion, as well as liturgical materials from local groups of St. Thomas Christians and Pre-Nicene Catholic groups. The excerpts from Scripture, especially the Pentecost story and the Magnificat, were translated for me from the Greek Testaments by Walter Breen; I should also cite Christine Hartley's *The Western Mystery Tradition* and Dion Fortune's *Avalon of the Heart*.

Any attempt at recapturing the pre-Christian religion of the British Isles has been made conjectural by the determined efforts of their successors to extinguish all such traces; scholars differ so much that I make no apology for selecting, among varying sources, those that best fit the needs of fiction. I have read, though not slavishly followed, the works of Margaret Murray and several books on Gardnerian Wicca. For the feel of the ceremonies, I would like to express my grateful thanks to local neopagan groups; to Alison Harlow and the Covenant of the Goddess, to Otter and Morning-Glory Zell, to Isaac Bonewits and the New Reformed Druids, to Robin Goodfellow and Gaia Wildwoode, to Philip Wayne and *Crystal Well*, to Starhawk, whose book *The Spiral Dance* proved invaluable to me in helping deduce much about the training of a priestess; and, for much personal and emotional support (including comforting and backrubs) during the actual writing of this book, to Diana Paxson, Tracy Blackstone, Elisabeth Waters, and Anodea Judith, of the Darkmoon Circle.

Finally I must express loving gratitude to my husband, Walter Breen, who said, at a crucial moment in my career, that it was time to stop playing it safe by writing potboilers, and provided financial support so that I could do so: also to Don Wollheim, who always believed in me, and his wife, Elsie. Above all, and always, to Lester and Judy-Lynn del Rey, who helped me to outgrow categories in writing, always a scary business, my grateful love and thanks. And last but not least to my elder son, David, for his careful preparation of the final manuscript.

pROLOGUE

In my time I have been called many things: sister, lover, priestess, wise-woman, queen. Now in truth I have come to be wise-woman, and a time may come when these things may need to be known. But in sober truth, I think it is the Christians who will tell the last tale. For ever the world of Fairy drifts further from the world in which the Christ holds sway. I have no quarrel with the Christ, only with his priests, who call the Great Goddess a demon and deny that she ever held power in this world. At best, they say that her power was of Satan. Or else they clothe her in the blue robe of the Lady of Nazareth—who indeed had power in her way, too—and say that she was ever virgin. But what can a virgin know of the sorrows and travail of mankind?

And now, when the world has changed, and Arthur—my brother, my lover, king who was and king who shall be—lies dead (the common folk say sleeping) in the Holy Isle of Avalon, the tale should be told as it was before the priests of the White Christ came to cover it all with their saints and legends.

For, as I say, the world itself has changed. There was a time when a traveller, if he had the will and knew only a few of the secrets, could send his barge out into the Summer Sea and arrive not at Glastonbury of the monks, but at the Holy Isle of Avalon; for at that time the gates between the worlds drifted within the mists, and were open, one to another, as the traveller thought and willed. For this is the great secret, which was known to all educated men in our day: that by what men think, we create the world around us, daily new.

And now the priests, thinking that this infringes upon the power of their God, who created the world once and for all to be unchanging, have closed those doors (which were never doors, except in the minds of men), and the pathway leads only to the priests' Isle, which they have safeguarded with the sound of their church bells, driving away all thoughts of another world lying in the darkness. Indeed, they say that world, if it indeed exists, is the property of Satan, and the doorway to Hell, if not Hell itself.

I do not know what their God may or may not have created. In spite of the

*tales that are told, I never knew much about their priests and never wore the black
of one of their slave-nuns. If those at Arthur's court at Camelot chose to think me
so when I came there (since I always wore the dark robes of the Great Mother
in her guise as wise-woman), I did not undeceive them. And indeed, toward the
end of Arthur's reign it would have been dangerous to do so, and I bowed my head
to expediency as my great mistress would never have done: Viviane, Lady of the
Lake, once Arthur's greatest friend, save for myself, and then his darkest enemy
—again, save for myself.*

*But the strife is over; I could greet Arthur at last, when he lay dying, not
as my enemy and the enemy of my Goddess, but only as my brother, and as a dying
man in need of the Mother's aid, where all men come at last. Even the priests know
this, with their ever-virgin Mary in her blue robe; for she too becomes the World
Mother in the hour of death.*

*And so Arthur lay at last with his head in my lap, seeing in me neither sister
nor lover nor foe, but only wise-woman, priestess, Lady of the Lake; and so rested
upon the breast of the Great Mother from whom he came to birth and to whom
at last, as all men, he must go. And perhaps, as I guided the barge which bore
him away, not this time to the Isle of the Priests, but to the true Holy Isle in the
dark world behind our own, that Island of Avalon where, now, few but I could
go, he repented the enmity that had come between us.*

*AS I TELL THIS TALE I will speak at times of things which befell when I was too
young to understand them, or of things which befell when I was not by; and my
hearer will draw away, perhaps, and say:* This is her magic. *But I have always
held the gift of the Sight, and of looking within the minds of men and women;
and in all this time I have been close to all of them. And so, at times, all that
they thought was known to me in one way or another. And so I will tell this tale.*

*For one day the priests too will tell it, as it was known to them. Perhaps
between the two, some glimmering of the truth may be seen.*

*For this is the thing the priests do not know, with their One God and One
Truth: that there is no such thing as a true tale. Truth has many faces and the
truth is like to the old road to Avalon; it depends on your own will, and your own
thoughts, whither the road will take you, and whether, at the end, you arrive in
the Holy Isle of Eternity or among the priests with their bells and their death and
their Satan and Hell and damnation . . . but perhaps I am unjust even to them.
Even the Lady of the Lake, who hated a priest's robe as she would have hated a
poisonous viper, and with good cause too, chid me once for speaking evil of their
God.*

*"For all the Gods are one God," she said to me then, as she had said many
times before, and as I have said to my own novices many times, and as every
priestess who comes after me will say again, "and all the Goddesses are one*

Goddess, and there is only one Initiator. And to every man his own truth, and the God within."

And so, perhaps, the truth winds somewhere between the road to Glastonbury, Isle of the Priests, and the road to Avalon, lost forever in the mists of the Summer Sea.

But this is my truth; I who am Morgaine tell you these things, Morgaine who was in later days called Morgan le Fay.

BOOK ONE

Mistress
of
Magic

1

Even in high summer, Tintagel was a haunted place; Igraine, Lady of Duke Gorlois, looked out over the sea from the headland. As she stared into the fogs and mists, she wondered how she would ever know when the night and day were of equal length, so that she could keep the Feast of the New Year. This year the spring storms had been unusually violent; night and day the crash of the sea had resounded over the castle until no man or woman within could sleep, and even the hounds whimpered mournfully.

Tintagel . . . there were still those who believed the castle had been raised, on the crags at the far end of the long causeway into the sea, by the magic of the ancient folk of Ys. Duke Gorlois laughed at this and said that if he had any of their magic, he would have used it to keep the sea from encroaching, year by year, upon the shoreline. In the four years since she had come here as Gorlois's bride, Igraine had seen land, good land, crumble into the Cornish sea. Long arms of black rock, sharp and craggy, extended into the ocean from the coast. When the sun shone, it could be fair and brilliant, the sky and water as brilliant as the jewels Gorlois had heaped on her on the day when she told him she bore his first child. But Igraine had never liked wearing them. The jewel which hung now at her throat had been given her in Avalon: a moonstone which sometimes reflected the blue brilliance of sky and sea; but in the fog, today, even the jewel looked shadowed.

In the fog, sounds carried a long way. It seemed to Igraine, as she stood looking from the causeway back toward the mainland, that she could hear footfalls of horses and mules, and the sound of voices—human voices, here in isolated Tintagel, where nothing lived but goats and sheep, and the herdsmen and their dogs, and the ladies of the castle with a few serving women and a few old men to guard them.

Slowly, Igraine turned and went back toward the castle. As always, standing in its shadow, she felt dwarfed by the loom of these ancient stones at the end of the long causeway which stretched into the sea. The herdsmen believed that the castle had been built by the Ancient Ones from the lost

3

lands of Lyonnesse and Ys; on a clear day, so the fishermen said, their old castles could be seen far out under the water. But to Igraine they looked like towers of rock, ancient mountains and hills drowned by the ever encroaching sea that nibbled away, even now, at the very crags below the castle. Here at the end of the world, where the sea ate endlessly at the land, it was easy to believe in drowned lands to the west; there were tales of a great fire mountain which had exploded, far to the south, and engulfed a great land there. Igraine never knew whether she believed those tales or not.

Yes; surely she could hear voices in the fog. It could not be savage raiders from over the sea, or from the wild shores of Erin. The time was long past when she needed to startle at a strange sound or a shadow. It was not her husband, the Duke; he was far away to the North, fighting Saxons at the side of Ambrosius Aurelianus, High King of Britain; he would have sent word if he intended to return.

And she need not fear. If the riders were hostile, the guards and soldiers in the fort at the landward end of the causeway, stationed there by Duke Gorlois to guard his wife and child, would have stopped them. It would take an army to cut through them. And who would send an army against Tintagel?

There was a time—Igraine remembered without bitterness, moving slowly into the castle yard—when she would have known who rode toward her castle. The thought held little sadness, now. Since Morgaine's birth she no longer even wept for her home. And Gorlois was kind to her. He had soothed her through her early fear and hatred, had given her jewels and beautiful things, trophies of war, had surrounded her with ladies to wait upon her, and treated her always as his equal, except in councils of war. She could have asked no more, unless she had married a man of the Tribes. And in this she had been given no choice. A daughter of the Holy Isle must do as was best for her people, whether it meant going to death in sacrifice, or laying down her maidenhood in the Sacred Marriage, or marrying where it was thought meet to cement alliances; this Igraine had done, marrying a Romanized Duke of Cornwall, a citizen who lived, even though Rome was gone from all of Britain, in Roman fashion.

She shrugged the cloak from her shoulders; inside the court it was warmer, out of the biting wind. And there, as the fog swirled and cleared, for a moment a figure stood before her, materialized out of the fog and mist: her half-sister, Viviane, the Lady of the Lake, the Lady of the Holy Isle.

"Sister!" The words wavered, and Igraine knew she had not cried them aloud, but only whispered, her hands flying to her breast. "Do I truly see you here?"

The face was reproachful, and the words seemed to blow away in the sound of the wind beyond the walls.

Have you given up the Sight, Igraine? Of your free will?

Stung by the injustice of that, Igraine retorted, "It was you who decreed that I must marry Gorlois . . ." but the form of her sister had wavered into shadows, was not there, had never been there. Igraine blinked; the brief apparition was gone. She pulled the cloak around her body, for she was cold, ice cold; she knew the vision had drawn its force from the warmth and life of her own body. She thought, *I didn't know I could still see in that way, I was sure I could not* . . . and then she shivered, knowing that Father Columba would consider this the work of the Devil, and she should confess it to him. True, here at the end of the world the priests were lax, but an unconfessed vision would surely be treated as a thing unholy.

She frowned; why should she treat a visit from her own sister as the work of the Devil? Father Columba could say what he wished; perhaps his God was wiser than he was. Which, Igraine thought, suppressing a giggle, would not be very difficult. Perhaps Father Columba had become a priest of Christ because no college of Druids would have had a man so stupid among their ranks. The Christ God seemed not to care whether a priest was stupid or not, so long as he could mumble their mass, and read and write a little. She, Igraine herself, had more clerkly skills than Father Columba, and spoke better Latin when she wished. Igraine did not think of herself as well educated; she had not had the hardihood to study the deeper wisdom of the Old Religion, or to go into the Mysteries any further than was absolutely necessary for a daughter of the Holy Isle. Nevertheless, although she was ignorant in any Temple of the Mysteries, she could pass among the Romanized barbarians as a well-educated lady.

In the small room off the court where there was sun on fine days, her younger sister, Morgause, thirteen years old and budding, wearing a loose house robe of undyed wool and her old frowsy cloak about her shoulders, was spinning listlessly with a drop spindle, taking up her uneven yarn on a wobbly reel. On the floor by the fire, Morgaine was rolling an old spindle around for a ball, watching the erratic patterns the uneven cylinder made, knocking it this way and that with chubby fingers.

"Haven't I done enough spinning?" Morgause complained. "My fingers ache! Why must I spin, spin, spin all the time, as if I were a waiting-woman?"

"Every lady must learn to spin," rebuked Igraine as she knew she ought to do, "and your thread is a disgrace, now thick, now thin. . . . Your fingers will lose their weariness as you accustom them to the work. Aching fingers are a sign that you have been lazy, since they are not hardened to their task." She took the reel and spindle from Morgause and twirled it with careless ease; the uneven yarn, under her experienced fingers, smoothed out into a thread of perfectly even thickness. "Look, one could weave this yarn without snagging the shuttle . . ." and suddenly she tired of behaving as she ought. "But you may put the spindle away now; guests will be here before midafternoon."

Morgause stared at her. "I heard nothing," she said, "nor any rider with a message!"

"That does not surprise me," Igraine said, "for there was no rider. It was a Sending. Viviane is upon her way here, and the Merlin is with her." She had not known that last until she said it. "So you may take Morgaine to her nurse, and go and put on your holiday robe, the one dyed with saffron."

Morgause put away the spindle with alacrity, but paused to stare at Igraine. "My saffron gown? For my *sister?*"

Igraine corrected her, sharply. "Not for our sister, Morgause, but for the Lady of the Holy Isle, and for the Messenger of the Gods."

Morgause looked down at the patterned floor. She was a tall, sturdy girl, just beginning to lengthen and ripen into womanhood; her thick hair was reddish like Igraine's own, and there were splotches of freckles on her skin, no matter how carefully she soaked it in buttermilk and begged the herbwife for washes and simples for it. Already at thirteen she was as tall as Igraine, and someday would be taller. She picked up Morgaine with an ill grace and carried her away. Igraine called after her, "Tell Nurse to put a holiday gown on the child, and then you may bring her down; Viviane has not seen her."

Morgause said something ill-tempered to the effect that she didn't see why a great priestess would want to see a brat, but she said it under her breath so that Igraine had an excuse to ignore it.

Up the narrow stairs, her own chamber was cold; no fires were lighted there except in the dead of winter. While Gorlois was away, she shared the bed with her waiting-woman Gwennis, and his prolonged absence gave her an excuse to have Morgaine in her bed at night. Sometimes Morgause slept there too, sharing the fur coverlets against the bitter cold. The big marriage bed, canopied, curtained against draughts, was more than big enough for three women and a child.

Gwen, who was old, was drowsing in a corner, and Igraine forbore to wake her, stripping off her workaday dress of undyed wool and hurrying on her fine gown, laced at the neck with a silk ribbon Gorlois had brought her as a fairing from Londinium. She put on her fingers some little silver rings she had had since she was a little girl . . . they would go only on her two smallest fingers, now . . . and hung a necklace of amber which Gorlois had given her about her neck. The gown was dyed rust color, and had an overtunic of green. She found her carven horn comb, and began to pull it through her hair, sitting on a bench and working her comb patiently through the tangles. From another room she heard a loud yelling and decided that Morgaine was having her hair combed by her nurse and didn't like it. The yelling stopped suddenly, and she supposed that Morgaine had been slapped into silence; or perhaps, as sometimes happened when Morgause was in a good temper, Morgause had taken over the combing herself, with her clever, patient fingers. This was how Igraine knew that her young sister could spin well enough when she chose, her hands were so clever at everything else—at combing, at carding, at making Yule pies.

Igraine braided her hair, clasped it on top of her head with a gold clasp, and put her good gold brooch into the fold of her cloak. She looked at herself in the old bronze mirror her sister Viviane had given her at her wedding, brought, they said, all the way from Rome. She knew, lacing her gown, that her breasts were once again as they had been before: Morgaine had been weaned a year now, and they were only a little softer and heavier. She knew she had her old slimness back, for she had been married in this gown, and now the laces were not strained even a little.

Gorlois, when he returned, would expect to take her to his bed again. Last time he had seen her, Morgaine had still been at the breast, and he had yielded to her plea that she might continue to suckle the child through the summer season when so many little children died. She knew he was discontented because the baby had not been the son he craved—these Romans counted their lineage through the male line, rather than sensibly through the mother; it was silly, for how could any man ever know precisely who had fathered any woman's child? Of course, these Romans made a great matter of worrying over who lay with their women, and locked them up and spied on them. Not that Igraine needed watching; one man was bad enough, who would want others who might be worse?

But even though he was eager for a son, Gorlois had been indulgent, letting her have Morgaine in her bed and continue to suckle her, even keeping away from her and lying nights with her dressing-woman Ettarr so that she would not get with child again and lose her milk. He too knew how many children died if they were weaned before they could chew meat and hard bread. Children fed on gruel were sickly, and often there was no goat's milk in the summer, even if they would drink it. Children fed on cow's or mare's milk often got the vomit and died, or suffered with the flux in their bowels and died. So he had left Morgaine at her breast, thus postponing the son he wanted for at least another year and a half. For that at least she would always be grateful to him, and not murmur, however quickly he got her with child now.

Ettarr had gotten herself a belly from that visit, and gone about preening herself; would *she* be the one to have a son by the Duke of Cornwall? Igraine had ignored the girl; Gorlois had other bastard sons, one

of whom was with him now, in the camp of the war duke, Uther. But Ettarr
had fallen sick and miscarried, and Igraine had enough intuition not to ask
Gwen why she looked so pleased at the event. Old Gwen knew too much
of herbs for Igraine's perfect peace of mind. *Some day,* she resolved, *I will
make her tell me exactly what she put into Ettarr's beer.*

She went down to the kitchen, her long skirts trailing on the stone
steps. Morgause was there, in her finest gown, and she had put Morgaine
into a holiday dress, dyed saffron, so that the child looked dark as a Pict.
Igraine picked her up, holding her with pleasure. Small, dark, delicately
made, so small-boned it was like handling a little soft bird. How had that
child come by her looks? She herself and Morgause were tall and red-haired,
earth-colored like all of the Tribeswomen, and Gorlois, though dark, was
Roman, tall and lean and aquiline; hardened from years of battle against the
Saxons, too filled with his Roman dignity to show much tenderness to a
young wife, and with nothing but indifference for the daughter who came
in the place of the son she should have borne him.

But, Igraine reminded herself, these Roman men considered it their
divine right to have power of life and death over their children. There were
many, Christians or no, who would have demanded that a daughter not be
reared, so that their wives might be free at once to give them a son. Gorlois
had been good to her, he had let her keep her daughter. Perhaps, though
she did not give him credit for much imagination, he knew how she, a
woman of the Tribes, felt about a daughter.

While she was giving orders for the entertainment of guests, for wine
to be brought up from the cellars and for the roasting of meat—not rabbit,
but good mutton from the last slaughtering—she heard the squawk and
flutter of frightened hens in the court and knew that the riders had come
across the causeway. The servants looked frightened, but most of them had
become resigned to the knowledge that the mistress had the Sight. She had
pretended it, using clever guesses and a few tricks; it was just as well that
they should remain in awe of her. Now she thought, *Maybe Viviane is right,
maybe I still have it. Maybe I only believed it was gone—because in those months
before Morgaine was born, I felt so weak and powerless. Now I have come back
to myself. My mother was a great priestess till the day of her death, though she
bore several children.*

But, her mind answered her, her mother had borne those children in
freedom, as a Tribeswoman should, to such fathers as she chose, not as a slave
to some Roman whose customs gave him power over women and children.
Impatiently, she dismissed such thoughts; did it matter whether she had the
Sight or only seemed to have it, if it kept her servants properly in order?

She went slowly out to the courtyard, which Gorlois still liked to call
the atrium, though it was nothing like the villa where he had lived until

Ambrosius made him Duke of Cornwall. She found the riders dismounting, and her eyes went at once to the only woman among them, a woman smaller than herself and no longer young, wearing a man's tunic and woolen breeches, and muffled in cloaks and shawls. Across the courtyard their eyes met in welcome, but Igraine went dutifully and bent before the tall, slender old man who was dismounting from a raw-boned mule. He wore the blue robes of a bard, and a harp was slung across his shoulder.

"I bid you welcome to Tintagel, Lord Messenger; you bestow a blessing upon our roof and honor it with your presence."

"I thank you, Igraine," said the resonant voice, and Taliesin, Merlin of Britain, Druid, Bard, clasped his hands before his face, then extended them to Igraine in blessing.

Her duty done for the instant, Igraine flew to her half-sister and would have bent for her blessing too; but Viviane bent and prevented her.

"No, no, child, this is a family visit, time enough later to do me honors if you must. . . ." She clasped Igraine close and kissed her on the mouth. "And this is the babe? It is easy to see she has the blood of the Old People; she looks like our mother, Igraine."

Viviane, Lady of the Lake and of the Holy Isle, was at this time in her thirties; eldest daughter of the ancient priestess of the Lake, she had succeeded to her mother's holy office. She picked up Morgaine in her arms, dandling her with the experienced hands of a woman well accustomed to babies.

"She looks like *you,*" Igraine said, surprised, and then realizing that she should have realized this before. But it had been four years since she had seen Viviane, and then at her wedding. So much had happened, she had changed so much, since, a frightened girl of fifteen, she had been given into the hands of a man more than twice her age. "But come into the hall, Lord Merlin, sister. Come into the warm."

Freed of her enwrapping cloaks and shawls, Viviane, Lady of Avalon, was a surprisingly little woman, no taller than a well-grown girl of eight or ten. In her loose tunic with its wrapped belt, a knife sheathed at her waist, and bulky woolen breeches, legs wrapped with thick leggings, she looked tiny, a child put into adult clothes. Her face was small, swarthy and triangular, the forehead low beneath hair dark as the shadows beneath the crags. Her eyes were dark, too, and large in her small face; Igraine had never realized how small she was.

A serving-woman brought the guest cup: hot wine, mixed with the last of the spices Gorlois had had sent to her from the markets in Londinium. Viviane took it between her hands, and Igraine blinked at her; with the gesture with which she took the cup, she was suddenly tall and imposing; it might have been the sacred chalice of the Holy Regalia. She set it between

her hands and brought it slowly to her lips, murmuring a blessing. She tasted
it, turned, and laid it in the hands of the Merlin. He took it with a grave
bow and put it to his lips. Igraine, who had barely entered the Mysteries,
somehow felt that she too was part of this beautiful ritual solemnity as in
turn she took the cup from her guests, tasted it, and spoke formal words
of welcome.

Then she put the cup aside and her sense of the moment dropped away;
Viviane was only a small, tired-looking woman, the Merlin no more than
a stooped old man. Igraine led them both quickly to the fire.

"It is a long journey from the shores of the Summer Sea in these days,"
she said, remembering when she had travelled it, a new-made bride, frightened and silently hating, in the train of the strange husband who, as yet, was
only a voice and a terror in the night. "What brings you here in the spring
storms, my sister and my lady?"

*And why could you not have come before, why did you leave me all alone,
to learn to be a wife, to bear a child alone and in fear and homesickness? And
since you could not have come before, why do you come at all, when it is too late
and I am at last resigned into submission?*

"The distance is indeed long," Viviane said softly, and Igraine knew
that the priestess had heard, as she always heard, the unspoken words as well
as what Igraine had said. "And these are dangerous times, child. But you
have grown into womanhood in these years, even if they have been lonely,
as lonely as the years of isolation for the making of a bard—or," she added,
with the flicker of a reminiscent smile, "the making of a priestess. Had you
chosen that path, you would have found it equally lonely, my Igraine. Yes,
of course," she said, reaching down, her face softening, "you may come up
on my lap, little one." She picked up Morgaine, and Igraine watched with
wonder; Morgaine was, ordinarily, as shy as a wild rabbit. Half resentful,
half falling again under the old spell, she watched the child settle into
Viviane's lap. Viviane looked almost too small to hold her securely. A fairy
woman, indeed; a woman of the Old People. And indeed Morgaine would
perhaps be very like her.

"And Morgause, how has she prospered since I sent her to you a year
ago?" Viviane said, looking up at Morgause in her saffron gown, where she
hung back resentfully in the shadows of the fire. "Come and kiss me, little
sister. Ah, you will be tall like Igraine," she said, raising her arms to embrace
the girl, who came, sullen as a half-trained puppy, from the shadows. "Yes,
sit there at my knee if you want to, child." Morgause sat on the floor, leaning
her head against Viviane's lap, and Igraine saw that the sulky eyes were filled
with tears.

*She has us all in her hand. How can she have such power over us all? Or
is it that she is the only mother Morgause has ever known? She was a grown*

*woman when Morgause was born, she has always been mother, as well as sister,
to both of us.* Their mother, who had been really too old for childbearing,
had died giving birth to Morgause. Viviane had borne a child of her own,
earlier in the year; her child had died, and Viviane had taken Morgause to
nurse.

Morgaine had snuggled tightly into Viviane's lap; Morgause leaned her
silky red head on Viviane's knee. The priestess held the little one with one
arm while her free hand stroked the half-grown girl's long, silky hair.

"I would have come to you when Morgaine was born," Viviane said,
"but I was pregnant, too. I bore a son that year. I have put him out to nurse,
and I think his foster-mother may send him to the monks. She is a Christian."

"Don't you mind his being reared as a Christian?" Morgause asked. "Is
he pretty? What is his name?"

Viviane laughed. "I called him Balan," she said, "and his foster-mother
named her son Balin. They are only ten days apart in age, so they will be
reared as twins, no doubt. And no, I do not mind that he is reared a
Christian, his father was so, and Priscilla is a good woman. You said the
journey here was long; believe me, child, it is longer now than it was when
you were wedded to Gorlois. Not longer, perhaps, from the Isle of
the Priests, where their Holy Thorn grows, but longer, far longer, from
Avalon . . ."

"And that is why we came here," said the Merlin suddenly, and his
voice was like the tolling of a great bell, so that Morgaine sat up suddenly
and began to whimper in fright.

"I do not understand," said Igraine, suddenly uneasy. "Surely the two
lie close together. . . ."

"The two are *one,*" said the Merlin, sitting very erect, "but the followers of Christ have chosen to say, not that *they* shall have no other Gods
before their God, but that there *is* no other God save for their God; that
he alone made the world, that he rules it alone, that he alone made the stars
and the whole of creation."

Igraine quickly made the holy sign against blasphemy.

"But that cannot be," she insisted. "No single God can rule all things
. . . and what of the Goddess? What of the Mother . . . ?"

"They believe," said Viviane, in her smooth low voice, "that there is
no Goddess; for the principle of woman, so they say, is the principle of all
evil; through woman, so they say, Evil entered this world; there is some
fantastic Jewish tale about an apple and a snake."

"The Goddess will punish them," Igraine said, shaken. "And yet you
married me to one of them?"

"We did not know that their blasphemy was so all-encompassing,"

Merlin said, "for there have been followers of other Gods in our time. But they respected the Gods of others."

"But what has this to do with the length of the road from Avalon?" asked Igraine.

"We come, then, to the reason for our visit," said the Merlin, "for, as the Druids know, it is the belief of mankind which shapes the world, and all of reality. Long ago, when the followers of Christ first came to our isle, I knew that this was a powerful pivot in time, a moment to change the world."

Morgause looked up at the old man, her eyes wide in awe.

"Are you so old, Venerable One?"

The Merlin smiled down at the girl and said, "Not in my own body. But I have read much in the great hall which is not in this world, there the Record of All Things is written. And also, I *was* living then. Those who are the Lords of this world permitted me to come back, but in another body of flesh."

"These matters are too abstruse for the little one, Venerable Father," Viviane said, gently rebuking him. "She is not a priestess. What the Merlin means, little sister, is that he was living when the Christians first came here, and that he chose, and was allowed, to reincarnate at once, to follow his work through. These are Mysteries, which you need not try to understand. Father, go on."

"I knew that this was one of those moments where the history of all mankind would be changed," the Merlin said. "The Christians seek to blot out all wisdom save their own; and in that strife they are banishing from this world all forms of mystery save that which will fit into their religious faith. They have pronounced it a heresy that men live more than one life —which every peasant knows to be true—"

"But if men do not believe in more than one life," Igraine protested, shaken, "how will they avoid despair? What just God would create some men wretched, and others happy and prosperous, if one life were all that they could have?"

"I do not know," said the Merlin. "Perhaps they wish men to despair at the harshness of fate, so that they may come on their knees to the Christ who will take them to heaven. I do not know what the followers of Christ believe, or what they hope for." His eyes were closed for a moment, the lines of his face bitter. "But whatever it is that they believe, the views they hold are altering this world; not only in the spirit, but on the material plane. As they deny the world of the spirit, and the realms of Avalon, so those realms cease to exist for them. They still exist, of course; but not in the same world with the world of the followers of Christ. Avalon, the Holy Isle, is now no longer the same island as the Glastonbury where we of the Old Faith once allowed the monks to build their chapel and their monastery. For our wisdom and their wisdom—how much do you know of natural philosophy, Igraine?"

"Very little," said the young woman, shaken, looking at the priestess and the great Druid. "I have never been taught."

"A pity," said the Merlin, "for you must understand this, Igraine. I will try to make it simple for you. Look you," he said, and took the gold torque from his throat, then drew his dagger. "Can I put this bronze and this gold into the same place, at once?"

She blinked and stared, not understanding. "No, of course not. They can be side by side, but not in the same place unless you move one of them first."

"And so it is with the Holy Isle," said Merlin. "The priests swore an oath to us, four hundreds of years ago, before even the Romans came here and tried to conquer, that they would never rise against us and drive us forth with weapons; for we were here before them, and then they were suppliants, and weak. And they have honored that oath—so much I must give to them. But in spirit, in their prayers, they have never ceased to strive with us for their God to drive away our Gods, their wisdom to rule over our wisdom. In our world, Igraine, there is room enough for many Gods and many Goddesses. But in the universe of the Christians—how can I say this?—there is no room for our vision or our wisdom. In their world there is one God alone; not only must he conquer over all Gods, he must make it as if there were no other Gods, had never been any Gods but only false idols, the work of their Devil. So that, believing in him, all men may be saved in this one life. This is what they believe. And as men believe, so their world goes. And so the worlds which once were one are drifting apart.

"There are now two Britains, Igraine: their world under their One God and the Christ; and, beside it and behind it, the world where the Great Mother still rules, the world where the Old People have chosen to live and worship. This has happened before. There was the time when the fairy folk, the Shining Ones, withdrew from our world, going further and further into the mists, so that only an occasional wanderer now can spend a night within the elf-mounds, and if he should do so, time drifts on without him, and he may come out after a single night and find that his kinfolk are all dead and that a dozen years have gone by. And now, I tell you, Igraine, it is happening again. Our world—ruled by the Goddess and the Horned One, her consort, the world you know, the world of many truths—is being forced away from the mainstream course of time. Even now, Igraine, if a traveller sets out with no guide for the Isle of Avalon, unless he know the way very well, he cannot come there, but will find only the Isle of the Priests. To most men, our world is now lost in the mists of the Summer Sea. Even before the Romans left us, this was beginning to happen; now, as churches cover the whole of Britain, our world grows further and further away. That is why it took us so long to come here; fewer and fewer of the cities and roads of the Old People remain for our guide. The worlds still touch, still lie upon one another, close as lovers; but they are drifting apart, and if they are not stopped, one day there will be two worlds, and none can come and go between the two—"

"Let them go!" interrupted Viviane angrily. "I still think we should let them go! I do not want to live in a world of Christians, who deny the Mother—"

"But what of all the others, what of those who will live in despair?" The Merlin's voice was like a great soft bell again. "No, a pathway must remain, even if it is secret. Parts of the world are still one. The Saxons raid in both worlds, but more and more of our warriors are followers of Christ. The Saxons—"

"The Saxons are barbarians, and cruel," said Viviane. "The Tribes alone cannot drive them from these shores, and the Merlin and I have seen that Ambrosius is not long for this world, and that his war duke, the Pendragon—is it Uther they call him?—will succeed him. But there are many in this country who will not rally to the Pendragon. Whatever may befall our world in the spirit, neither of our worlds can long survive the fire and sword of the Saxons. Before we can fight the spiritual battle which will keep the worlds from moving further apart, we must save the very heart of Britain from being ravaged by Saxon fires. Not only the Saxons assault us, but Jutes, Scots, all the wild folk who are moving down from the North. Every place, even Rome itself, is being overpowered; there are so many of them. Your husband has been fighting all his life. Ambrosius, Duke of Britain, is a good man, but he can command loyalty only from those who once followed Rome; his father wore the purple, and Ambrosius too was ambitious to be emperor. But we must have a leader who will appeal to all the folk of Britain."

"But—Rome remains," Igraine protested. "Gorlois told me that when Rome had overcome her troubles in the Great City, the legions would return! Can we not look to Rome for help against the wild folk from the North? The Romans were the greatest fighters of the world, they built the great wall to the North to hold back the wild raiders—"

Merlin's voice took on the empty sound that was like the tolling of a great bell. "I have seen it in the Holy Well," he said. "The Eagle has flown, and shall never return to Britain."

"Rome can do nothing," Viviane said. "We must have our own leader, one who can command all of Britain. Otherwise, when they mass against us, all Britain will fall, and for hundreds and hundreds of years, we will lie in ruins beneath the Saxon barbarians. The worlds will drift irrevocably apart and the memory of Avalon will not remain even in legend, to give hope to mankind. No, we must have a leader who can command loyalty from all the people of both the Britains—the Britain of the priests, and the world of the mists, ruled from Avalon. Healed by this Great King"—her voice took on the clear, mystical ring of prophecy—"the worlds shall once again come together, a world with room for the Goddess and for the Christ, the cauldron and the cross. And this leader shall make us one."

"But where shall we find such a king?" Igraine asked. "Who shall give us such a leader?"

And then, suddenly, she was afraid, felt ice pouring down her back, as the Merlin and the priestess turned to look at her, their eyes seeming to hold her motionless as a small bird under the shadow of a great hawk, and she understood why the messenger-prophet of the Druids was called the Merlin.

But when Viviane spoke her voice was very soft.

She said, "You, Igraine. You shall bear this Great King."

2

the**RE** was silence in the room, except for the small crackle of the fire. At last Igraine heard herself draw a long breath, as if she had just wakened from sleep. "What is this that you are telling me? Do you mean that Gorlois is to be the father of this Great King?" She heard the words echoing in her mind and ringing there, and wondered why she had never suspected Gorlois of so great a destiny. She saw her sister and the Merlin exchange glances, and saw, too, the small gesture with which the priestess silenced the old man.

"No, Lord Merlin, a woman must say this to a woman. . . . Igraine, Gorlois is Roman. The Tribes will not follow any man born to a son of Rome. The High King they follow must be a child of the Holy Isle, a true son of the Goddess. Your son, Igraine, yes. But it is not the Tribes alone that will fight away the Saxons and the other wild folk from the North. We will need the support of Romans and Celts and Cymry, and they will follow only their own war duke, their Pendragon, son of a man they trust to lead them and rule. And the Old People, too, who seek the son of a royal mother. Your son, Igraine—but the father will be Uther Pendragon."

Igraine stared at them, understanding, until rage slowly broke through against the numbness. Then she flared at them, "No! I have a husband, and I have borne him a child! I will not let you play again at skipping-stones

with my life! I married as you bade me—and you will never know—" The
words choked in her throat. There would never be any way to tell them
of that first year; even Viviane would never know. She could say, *I was
afraid,* or *I was alone and terrified,* or *Rape would have been easier because I
could have run away to die afterward,* but any of those would have been only
words, conveying only the smallest part of what she had felt.

And even if Viviane had known the whole, touching her mind and
knowing all that she could not say, Viviane would have looked on her with
compassion and even a little pity, but would not have changed her mind
or demanded even a little less from Igraine. She had heard her sister say it
often enough when Viviane still believed Igraine would become priestess
of the Mysteries: *If you seek to avoid your fate or to delay suffering, it only
condemns you to suffer it redoubled in another life.*

So she did not say any of those things, only glared at Viviane with
the stifled resentment of the last four years, when she had done her duty
valiantly and alone, submitting to her fate with no more outcry than any
woman was allowed to make. But again? *Never,* Igraine told herself silently,
never. She shook her head stubbornly.

"Listen to me, Igraine," said the Merlin. "I fathered you, though that
gives me no rights; it is the blood of the Lady which confers royalty, and
you are of the oldest royal blood, descended from daughter to daughter of
the Holy Isle. It is written in the stars, child, that only a king who comes
of two royalties, one royalty of the Tribes who follow the Goddess, and
one royalty of those who look to Rome, will heal our land of all this strife.
A peace must come when these two lands can dwell side by side, a peace
long enough for the cross and the cauldron, too, to come to such a peace.
If there is such a reign as this, Igraine, even those who follow the cross will
have the knowledge of the Mysteries to comfort them in their bleak lives
of suffering and sin, and their belief in one brief life to choose forever
between Hell or Heaven for all eternity. Otherwise, our world will fade
into the mists, and there will be hundreds of years—thousands, perhaps—
where the Goddess and the Holy Mysteries will be forgotten by all mankind
except those few who can come and go between the worlds. Would you
let the Goddess and her work fade from this world, Igraine, you who were
born of the Lady of the Holy Isle, and the Merlin of Britain?"

Igraine bent her head, barricading her mind against the tenderness in
the old man's voice. She had always known, without being told, that
Taliesin, Merlin of Britain, had shared with her mother the spark of life
which had made her, but a daughter of the Holy Isle did not speak of such
things. A daughter of the Lady belonged only to the Goddess, and to that
man into whose hands the Lady chose to give its care—most often her
brother, only very rarely the man who had begotten it. There was a reason

for this: no pious man should claim fatherhood to a child of the Goddess, and all children born to the Lady were considered so. That Taliesin should use this argument now shocked her deeply, but it touched her, too.

Yet she said stubbornly, refusing to look at him, "Gorlois might have been chosen Pendragon. Surely this Uther cannot be so much beyond all sons of mankind as that. If you must have such a one, could you not have used your spells so that Gorlois would be acclaimed war duke of Britain, and Great Dragon? Then, when our son was born, you would have had your High King—"

The Merlin shook his head, but again it was Viviane who spoke, and this silent collusion further angered Igraine. Why should they act in concert this way against her?

Viviane said softly, "You will bear no son to Gorlois, Igraine."

"Are you the Goddess, then, that you dispense childbearing to women in her name?" Igraine demanded rudely, knowing the words childish. "Gorlois has fathered sons by other women; why should I not give him one born in wedlock, as he desires?"

Viviane did not answer. She only looked directly at Igraine and said, her voice very soft, "Do you love Gorlois, Igraine?"

Igraine stared at the floor. "That has nothing to do with it. It is a matter of honor. He was kind to me—" She broke off, but her thoughts ran on unchecked: *Kind to me when I had nowhere to turn, when I was alone and deserted, and even you had abandoned me to my fate. What is love to that?*

"It is a matter of honor," she repeated. "I owe him this. He let me keep Morgaine, when she was all I had in my loneliness. He has been kind and patient, and for a man of his years it cannot be easy. He wants a son, he believes it all-important to his life and honor, and I will not deny him this. If I bear a son, it will be the son of Duke Gorlois, and of no other man living. And this I swear, by fire and—"

"*Silence!*" Viviane's voice, like the loud clang of a great bell, shocked Igraine's words silent. "I command you, Igraine, swear no oath lest you be forever forsworn!"

"And why should you think I would not keep my oath?" Igraine raged. "I was reared to truth! I too am a child of the Holy Isle, Viviane! You may be my elder sister and my priestess and the Lady of Avalon, but you shall not treat me as if I were a babbling child like Morgaine there, who cannot understand a word of what is said to her, nor knows the meaning of an oath—"

Morgaine, hearing her name spoken, sat bolt upright in the Lady's lap. The Lady of the Lake smiled and smoothed the dark hair. "Do not think that this little one cannot understand. Babes know more than we imagine; they cannot speak their minds, and so we believe they do not think. As for your babe—well, that is for the future, and I will not speak of it before her; but who knows, one day she too will be a great priestess—"

"Never! Not if I must become a Christian to prevent it," Igraine raged. "Do you think I will let you plot against my child's life as you have plotted against mine?"

"Peace, Igraine," said the Merlin. "You are free, as every child of the Gods is free. We came to entreat you, not to command. No, Viviane—" he said, holding up his hand when the Lady would have interrupted him. "Igraine is no helpless plaything of fate. Yet I think when she knows all, she will choose rightly."

Morgaine had begun to fret in the Lady's lap. Viviane crooned softly to her, stroking her hair, and she quieted, but Igraine rose and took her child, angry and jealous at Viviane's almost magical power to quiet the girl. In her arms Morgaine felt strange, alien, as if the time she had spent in Viviane's arms had changed her, tainted her, made her somehow less Igraine's own. Igraine felt tears burning her eyes. Morgaine was all she had, and now she, too, was being cut off from her; Morgaine was falling victim, like everyone else, to Viviane's charm, that charm which could make everyone into a helpless pawn of her will.

She said sharply to Morgause, who was still lying with her head in Viviane's lap, "Get up at once, Morgause, and go to your room; you are almost a woman, you must not behave like a spoilt child!"

Morgause raised her head, putting back her curtain of red hair from her pretty, sulky face. She said, "Why should you choose Igraine for your plans, Viviane? She wants no part in them. But I am a woman, and I too am a daughter of the Holy Isle. Why have you not chosen me for Uther the Pendragon? Why should I not be the mother of the High King?"

The Merlin smiled. "Will you fly so recklessly in the face of fate, Morgause?"

"Why should Igraine be chosen and not I? I have no husband—"

"There is a king in your future and many sons; but with that, Morgause, you must be content. No man or woman can live another's fate. Your fate, and that of your sons, depends on this great High King. More than that I cannot say," said the Merlin. "Enough, Morgause."

Igraine, standing, Morgaine in her arms, felt more in command. She said in a dead voice, "I am remiss in hospitality, my sister, my lord Merlin. Let my servants take you to the guest chambers prepared for you, bring you wine, and water for washing, and at sundown a meal will be prepared."

Viviane rose. Her voice was formal and correct, and Igraine, for a moment, was relieved; she was again mistress of her own hearth, not a passive child but the wife of Gorlois, Duke of Cornwall.

"At sunset, then, my sister."

But Igraine saw the glance Viviane exchanged with the Merlin, and she could read it as clearly as words: *Leave it for now, I will manage her, as I have always done.*

And Igraine felt her face harden into iron. *That is what she has always done, indeed. But this time it shall not be so. I did her will once, when I was a child and knew no better. But now I am grown, I am a woman, not so easily led as the child she gave away to be Gorlois's bride. Now I will do my own will, and not that of the Lady of the Lake.*

Servants took her guests away; Igraine, in her own chamber, laid Morgaine in her bed and fussed around her nervously, her mind full of what she had heard.

Uther Pendragon. She had never seen him, but Gorlois was full of the tales of his valor. He was a close kinsman, sister's son, of Ambrosius Aurelianus, High King of Britain, but unlike Ambrosius, Uther was a Briton of Britons, with no taint of Roman blood, so that the Cymry and the Tribes did not hesitate to follow him. There was little doubt that one day Uther would be chosen High King. Ambrosius was not a young man; that day could not be so far.

And I would be queen. . . . What am I thinking of? Would I betray Gorlois and my own honor?

Behind her, as she took up the bronze mirror again, she saw her sister in the door. Viviane had taken off the breeches she wore for riding, and put on a loose gown of undyed wool; her hair hung down, soft and dark as the wool of a black sheep. She looked small and fragile and aging, and her eyes were the eyes of the priestess in the cave of initiation, years away and in another world. . . . Igraine cut off the thought, impatiently.

Viviane came close to her, reaching up to touch her hair.

"Little Igraine. Not so little, now," she said, tenderly. "Do you know, little one, I gave you your name: Grainné, for the Goddess of the Beltane fires. . . . How long has it been since you did service to the Goddess at Beltane, Igraine?"

Igraine's mouth only stretched a little; the smile went no deeper than her teeth. "Gorlois is a Roman, and a Christian. Do you truly believe his household keeps the rites of Beltane?"

"No, I suppose not," said Viviane, amused, "though, if I were you, I would not take oath that your servants do not slip out at Midsummer to burn fires and lie together under the full moon. But lord and lady of a Christian household cannot do so, not in the sight of their priests and their stern and unloving God. . . ."

Igraine said sharply, "You will not speak so of the God of my husband, who is a God of love."

"You say so. And yet he has made war upon all other Gods, and slain those who will not worship him," Viviane said. "Such love we might well pray to be spared in a God. I could call upon you in the name of vows you once made, to do what I have asked of you in the name of the Goddess and the Holy Isle—"

"Oh, rare," Igraine said sarcastically. "Now my Goddess demands of me that I shall play the harlot, and the Merlin of Britain and the Lady of the Lake will act as panders for me!"

Viviane's eyes blazed; she stepped one step forward, and for a moment Igraine believed the priestess would strike her in the face. "How do you dare!" Viviane said, and though her voice was soft, it seemed to raise echoes through the entire room, so that Morgaine, half asleep beneath Igraine's woolen plaid, sat up and cried out in sudden fright.

"Now you have wakened my babe—" Igraine said, and sat down on the edge of the bed, hushing the child. Gradually the angry color receded from Viviane's face. She sat down beside Igraine and said, "You have not understood me, Grainné. Do you think Gorlois immortal? I tell you, child, I have sought to read in the stars the destinies of those who are vital to Britain's wholeness in the years to come, and I tell you, the name of Gorlois is not written there."

Igraine felt her knees weaken and her whole body loosen at the joints. "Will Uther kill him?"

"I swear to you: Uther will have no part in his death, and when Gorlois dies, Uther will be far away. But think, child. Tintagel is a great castle; do you believe, when Gorlois can hold it no longer, that Uther Pendragon would be slow to say, *Take the castle, and the woman who holds it,* to one of his war dukes? Better Uther than one of his men."

Morgaine. What will become of my child; of Morgause, my little sister? Truly, the woman who belongs to any man must pray that he will live to protect her.

"Can I not return to the Holy Isle, and live out my life in Avalon as priestess?"

"That is not your destiny, little one," Viviane said. Her voice was tender again. "You cannot hide from your fate. It is given to you to play a part in the salvation of this land, but the road to Avalon is closed to you forever. Will you walk the road to your destiny, or must the Gods drag you to it unwilling?"

She did not wait for Igraine's answer. "It will not be long. Ambrosius Aurelianus is dying; for many years he has led the Britons, and now his dukes will meet to choose a High King. And there is none but Uther whom they can all trust. So Uther must be duke of war and High King, both. And he will need a son."

Igraine felt as if the walls of a trap were closing around her. "If you make so much of this, why do you not do this thing yourself? If there is so much power to be gained as the wife of Britain's war duke and High King, why do you not seek to attract Uther with your charms, and bear this ordained king yourself?"

To her surprise, Viviane hesitated for a long time before saying, "Do you think I had not thought of that? But you have forgotten how old I am, Igraine. I am older than Uther, and he is not young as warriors go. I was twenty-six when Morgause was born. I am nine-and-thirty, Igraine, and I am past childbearing."

In the bronze mirror, somehow still in her hand, Igraine saw her sister's reflection, distorted, misshapen, flowing like water, the image suddenly clearing then clouding and vanishing. Igraine said, "You think so? But I tell you that you will bear another child."

"I hope not," Viviane said. "I am older than our mother was when she died in bearing Morgause, and I could not now hope to escape that fate. This is the last year I shall take part in the rites at Beltane; after this I shall hand on my office to some woman younger than I, and become as the Ancient One, the wise-woman. I had hoped that one day I would hand on the place of the Goddess to Morgause—"

"Then why did you not keep her in Avalon and train her to be priestess after you?"

Viviane looked very sad. "She is not fit. She sees, under the mantle of the Goddess, only power, not the unending sacrifice and suffering. And so that path is not for her."

"It does not seem to me that you have suffered," Igraine said.

"You know nothing about it. You did not choose to walk that path either. I, who have given my life to it, say still it would be simpler to live the life of a peasant woman, beast of burden and brood mare in season. You see me robed and crowned as the Goddess, triumphant beside her cauldron; you do not see the darkness of the cave or the depths of the great sea. . . . You are not called to it, dear child, and you should thank the Goddess that your destiny is laid elsewhere."

Igraine said silently, *Do you think I know nothing of suffering and enduring in silence, after these four years?* but she did not say the words aloud. Viviane had bent over Morgaine, her face tender, stroking the little girl's silky-dark hair.

"Ah, Igraine, you cannot know how I envy you—all my life I have so longed for a daughter. Morgause was like my own to me, the Goddess knows, but always as alien to me as if she had been born of a stranger, not my own mother. . . . I longed for a daughter into whose hands I could resign my office." She sighed. "But I bore only one girl-child, who died, and my sons are gone from me." She shuddered. "Well, this is my destiny, which

I shall try to obey as you do yours. I ask nothing of you but this, Igraine, and the rest I leave to her who is mistress of us all. When Gorlois comes home again, he will go to Londinium for the choosing of a High King. Somehow you must contrive to go there with him."

Igraine burst out laughing. "Only this you ask me, and this is harder than all the rest! Do you truly think that Gorlois would burden his men with escorting a young wife to Londinium? I would like to go there, indeed, but Gorlois will take me thither when figs and oranges from the south grow in the garden of Tintagel!"

"Nevertheless, somehow you must contrive to go, and you must look upon Uther Pendragon."

Igraine laughed again. "And I suppose you will give me a charm so that he will fall so deep in love with me that he cannot resist it?"

Viviane stroked her curling red hair. "You are young, Igraine, and I do not think you have any idea how beautiful you are. I do not think Uther will have need of any charms."

Igraine felt her body contract in a curious frightened spasm. "Perhaps I had better have the charm so that I will not shrink from him!"

Viviane sighed. She touched the moonstone about Igraine's neck. She said, "This was not Gorlois's gift to you—"

"No; I had it from you at my wedding, you remember? You said it was my mother's."

"Give it to me." Viviane reached under the curling hair at Igraine's neck and unfastened the chain. "When this stone comes back to you, Igraine, remember what I said, and do as the Goddess prompts you to do."

Igraine looked at the stone in the hands of the priestess. She sighed, but she did not protest. *I have promised her nothing,* she told herself fiercely, *nothing.*

"Will you go to Londinium for the choosing of this High King, Viviane?"

The priestess shook her head. "I go to the land of another king, who does not yet know that he must fight at the side of Uther. Ban of Armorica, in Less Britain, is being made High King of his land, and in token, his Druids have told him that he must make the Great Rite. I am sent to officiate in the Sacred Marriage."

"I thought Brittany was a Christian land."

"Oh, it is so," Viviane said indifferently, "and his priests will ring their bells, and anoint him with their holy oils, and tell him that his God has made the sacrifice for him. But the people will not accept a king who is not himself vowed to the Great Sacrifice."

Igraine drew a deep breath. "I know so little—"

"In the old days, Igraine," Viviane said, "the High King was bound with his life to the fortunes of the land, and pledged, as every Merlin of Britain is pledged, that if the land comes upon disaster or perilous times, he will die that the land may live. And should he refuse this sacrifice, the land would perish. I—I should not speak of this, it is a Mystery, but in your own way, Igraine, you too are offering your life for the healing of this land. No woman knows, when she lies down to childbirth, whether her life will not be demanded of her at the hands of the Goddess. I too have lain bound and helpless, with the knife at my throat, knowing that if death took me, my blood would redeem the land. . . ." Her voice trembled into silence; Igraine, too, was silent, in awe.

"A part of Less Britain, too, has withdrawn into the mists, and the Great Shrine of Stones cannot now be found. The avenue leading to the shrine is empty stone, unless the Way to Karnak is known," Viviane said, "but King Ban has pledged to keep the worlds from drifting apart, and the gateways open to the Mysteries. And so he will make the Sacred Marriage with the land, in token that if there is need his very blood will be spilled to feed the crops. It is fitting that my last service to the Mother, before I take my place among the wise-women, shall be to bind his land to Avalon, and so I am to be the Goddess to him in this mystery."

She was silent, but for Igraine the room was filled with the echo of her voice. Viviane bent over and picked up the sleeping Morgaine in her arms, holding her with great tenderness.

"She is not yet a maiden, and I not yet a wise-woman," she said, "but we are the Three, Igraine. Together we make up the Goddess, and she is here present among us."

Igraine wondered why she had not named their sister Morgause, and they were so open to one another that Viviane heard the words as if Igraine had spoken them aloud.

She said in a whisper, and Igraine saw her shiver, "The Goddess has a fourth face, which is secret, and you should pray to her, as I do—as I do, Igraine—that Morgause will never wear that face."

3

It seemed to Igraine that she had been riding forever in the rain. The journey to Londinium was like a journey from the end of the world.

She had travelled but little before, except, long ago, from Avalon to Tintagel. She contrasted the frightened, despairing child of that first journey with herself today. Now she rode at Gorlois's side, and he went to some trouble to tell her something of the lands they passed through, and she laughed and teased him, and at night in their tent she went willingly to his bed. Now and again she missed Morgaine, wondering how the child would be faring—would she cry at night for her mother, would she eat at Morgause's bidding? But it was pleasant to be free again, riding in this great company of men, conscious of their admiring looks and their deference— none of them would dare to approach Gorlois's lady, except with an admiring glance. She was a girl again, but not, now, frightened and shrinking from the strange man who was her husband and whom she must somehow manage to please. She was a girl again without the childish awkwardness of her real girlhood, and she was enjoying it. She did not even mind the ceaseless rain that obscured the distant hills so that they rode within a little circle of mist.

We could lose our way in this mist, wander off into the realms of Fairy, and never return at all to this world, where the dying Ambrosius and the ambitious Uther plan for the salvation of Britain from the wild savages. Britain could sink like Rome, under the barbarians, and we need never know nor care. . . .

"Are you weary, Igraine?" Gorlois's voice was gentle and concerned. Really, he was not the ogre he had seemed during those first terrifying days four years ago! Now he was only an aging man, grey in his hair and beard (though he shaved himself carefully in Roman fashion), scarred from years of fighting, and touchingly eager to please her. Perhaps, if she had not been so frightened and rebellious in those days, she might have seen that he was eager to please her then, too. He had not been cruel to her, or if he was, it was only that he seemed to know little of women's bodies and how to use them. Now it seemed only clumsiness, not cruelty; and if she told him he hurt her, he would caress her more gently. The younger Igraine had thought it inevitable, the hurt and the terror. Now she knew better.

She smiled at him now, gaily, and said, "No, not at all; I feel I could go on riding forever! But with so much mist, how do you know that we will not lose our way and never come to Londinium at all!"

"You need not fear that," he said gravely. "My guides are very good, and they know every inch of the road. And before nightfall we will come to the old Roman road which leads into the very heart of the city. So we will sleep this night under a roof and in a proper bed."

"I shall be glad to sleep again in a proper bed," said Igraine demurely, and saw, as she had known she would see, the sudden heat rising in his face and eyes. But he turned his face away from her; it was almost as if he was afraid of her, and Igraine, having just discovered this power, delighted in it.

She rode on at his side, reflecting on the sudden kindness she felt for Gorlois, a kindness mixed with regret, as if he had become dear to her only now, when she knew she must lose him. One way or another, she knew her days at his side were numbered; and she remembered how she had first known that he would die.

She had had his messenger, warning her to prepare for his coming; he had sent one of his men, with suspicious eyes which peered everywhere, telling Igraine without words that if this man had had a young wife, he would have come home without warning, hoping to surprise some misconduct or extravagance. Igraine, knowing herself guiltless, her steward competent, her kitchen in order, had ignored the prying stares and bade the man welcome. Let him question her servants if he would, he would find that except for her sister and the Lord Merlin she had received no guests at Tintagel.

When the messenger had gone, Igraine, turning to cross the courtyard, had stopped, a shadow falling across her in full sunlight, stricken with causeless fear. And in that moment she saw Gorlois, wondering where was his horse, his entourage? He looked thinner and older, so that for a moment she hardly knew him, and his face was drawn and haggard. There was a sword cut on his cheek which she did not remember.

"My husband!" she cried. "Gorlois—" And then, stricken by the unspeakable grief in his face, she had forgotten her fear of him and the years of resentment, rushed toward him and spoken as she would have spoken to her child. "Oh, my dear, what has happened to you? What has brought you here like this, alone, unarmed—are you ill? Are you—" And then she stopped, her voice dying away among the echoes. For there was no one there, only the fitful light from clouds and sea and shadows, and the echo of her own voice.

She tried, all the rest of that day, to reassure herself that it was only a Sending, like the one that had warned her of Viviane's coming. But she knew better: Gorlois had not the Sight, would not have used it or believed in it if he had had it. What she had seen—and she knew it even though she had never seen anything like it before—was her husband's fetch, his double, the shadow and precursor of his death.

And when at last he arrived, whole and sound, she had tried to shrug away the memory, had told herself that it was only a trick of the light that made her see, behind him, the shadow she had seen, with the sword cut on his face and the unspeakable grief in his eyes. For Gorlois now was neither wounded nor disheartened; on the contrary, he was in high good humor, bringing gifts for her, and even a string of little coral beads for Morgaine. He had looked in the sacks of his Saxon plunder and given Morgause a red cloak.

"No doubt it belonged to some Saxon strumpet, some camp follower, or even one of the screaming swordswomen who fight alongside their men, half-naked on the field of war," he said, laughing and chucking the girl under the chin, "so it is just as well it should be worn by a decent British maiden. The color becomes you, little sister. When you have grown a bit, you will be as pretty as my wife." Morgause had simpered and giggled and tossed her head, posing in the new cloak, and later Gorlois had said sharply, as he and Igraine were making themselves ready for bed (Morgaine, howling, had been banished to Morgause's room), "We must have that girl married as soon as can be arranged, Igraine. She is a puppy bitch with eyes hot for anything in the shape of a man; did you see how she cast her eyes not only on me but on my younger soldiers? I will not have such a one disgracing my family, nor influencing my daughter!"

Igraine had given him a soft answer. She could not forget that she had seen Gorlois's death, and she would not argue with a condemned man. And she too had been annoyed by Morgause's behavior.

So Gorlois is to die. Well, it takes not much prophecy to foresee that a man of five-and-forty, who has been fighting Saxons much of his life, will not live to see his little children grown. I shall not let it make me believe all the rest of the nonsense she spoke to me, or I shall be expecting Gorlois to take me to Londinium!

But the next day, as they lingered over breaking their fast and she was mending a great rent in his best tunic, he spoke bluntly.

"Did you not wonder what brought me here so suddenly, Igraine?"

After the night past, she had the confidence to smile into his eyes. "Should I question fortune, which has brought my husband home after a year's absence? I hope it means that the Saxon Shores are free and in British hands again."

He nodded absently, and smiled. Then the smile was gone.

"Ambrosius Aurelianus is dying. The old eagle will soon be gone, and there is no hatchling to fly in his place. It is like the legions going again; he has been High King for all my days, and a good king for those of us who still hoped, as I did, for the return of Rome one day. Now I know that day will never come. The kings of Britain from near and far have been summoned to gather in Londinium to choose their High King and war leader, and I too must go. It was a long journey to stay so little time, for I must be off again within three days. But I would not come so near without seeing you and the child. It will be a great gathering, Igraine, and many of the dukes and kings will bring their ladies; would you like to come with me?"

"To Londinium?"

"Yes, if you will travel so far," he said, "and if you can bring yourself to leave that child. I do not know why you should not. Morgaine is healthy and sound and there are enough women here to look after a dozen like her; and if I have managed to get you with child again"—he met her eyes in a smile she could hardly have imagined on his face—"it will not yet hinder you in riding." There was a tenderness she had never guessed in his voice as he added, "I would rather not be parted from you again for a little while, at least; will you come, my wife?"

Somehow you must contrive to come to Londinium with him. Viviane had said it. And now Gorlois had made it unnecessary even to ask. Igraine had a sudden feeling of panic—as if she were on a runaway horse. She picked up a cup of beer and sipped at it, to cover her confusion. "Certainly I will come if you wish it." Two days later they were on the road, riding eastward to Londinium and the encampment of Uther Pendragon and the dying Ambrosius, for the choosing of a High King. . . .

In midafternoon they came to the Roman road, and could ride more swiftly; and late that day they could see the outskirts of Londinium, and smell the tidal river that washed its shores. Igraine had never guessed so many houses could be gathered together in one place; for a moment she felt, after the chill spaces of the southern moors, that she could not breathe, that the houses were closing in on her. She rode as if in a trance, feeling that the stone streets and walls cut her off from air and light and life itself. . . . How could people live behind walls this way?

"We will sleep this night at the home of one of my soldiers, who has a house in the city," Gorlois said, "and tomorrow we will present ourselves at the court of Ambrosius."

She asked him that night, seated before the fire (what luxury, she thought, a fire this near to Midsummer!), "Who, think you, will be the next High King?"

"What can it matter to a woman who rules the land?"

She smiled sidelong at him; she had taken down her hair for the night and she could feel him warming to the smile. "Even though I am a woman, Gorlois, I must live in this land, and I would like to know what manner of man my husband must follow in peace and war."

"Peace! There will be no peace in my lifetime at least," Gorlois said. "Not with all those wild folk coming to our rich shores; we must gather all our strength to defend ourselves. And there are many who would like to wear the mantle of Ambrosius and lead us in war. Lot of Orkney, for instance. A harsh man, but reliable, a strong leader, good at battle strategy. Still unmarried, though; no dynasty. He's young for a High King, but ambitious, never knew a man of that age so ambitious. And Uriens of North Wales. No problems with dynasty, he already has sons. But the man has no imagination; wants to do everything as it's always been done, says that it worked once and it will work again. And I suspect he's no good Christian."

"Which would be your choice?" Igraine asked.

He sighed. "Neither," he said. "I have followed Ambrosius all my life,

and I will follow the man Ambrosius has chosen; it's a matter of honor, and
Uther is Ambrosius' man. It's as simple as that. Not that I like Uther. He's
a lecherous man with a dozen bastards, no woman's safe around him. He
goes to mass because the army does, and because it's the thing to do. I'd
rather he was an honest pagan than a Christian for the benefits he can get
from it."

"Yet you support him—"

"Oh, yes. He's soldier enough for a Caesar; the men will follow him
through hell, if they have to. He spares no effort to be popular with the
army—you know the kind of thing, going around the camp and munching
on their rations to make sure they're fit to eat, spending a day when he could
be taking his ease in going to the quartermaster's to get a discharge for an
old toothless veteran, sleeping in the field with the men before a battle. The
men would die for him—and they do. And he has both brains and imagination. He managed to make peace with the treaty troops and get them to fight
alongside us last fall—he thinks a little too much like a Saxon for me, he
knows how their minds work. Yes, I'll support him. But that doesn't mean
I like the man."

Igraine, listening, thought that Gorlois had revealed more of himself
than of the other candidates for High King. She said at last, "Have you never
thought—you are Duke of Cornwall, and Ambrosius values you; could you
be chosen as High King?"

"Believe me, Igraine, I want no crown. Have you a wish to be queen?"

"I would not refuse it," she said, recalling the Merlin's prophecy.

"You say that because you are too young to know what it means,"
Gorlois said with a smile. "Would you truly like to rule a kingdom as you
must rule over your servants at Tintagel, at everyone's beck and call? There
was a time when I was younger—but I do not want to spend the rest of
my lifetime at war. Ambrosius gave me Tintagel years ago, Igraine; until
four years ago I had not spent enough time there to bring home a wife!
I will defend these shores as long as I can hold a sword, but I want a son
to play with my daughter, and some time to spend in peace, fishing from
the rocks, and hunting, and sitting in the sun watching the peasant folk bring
in their crops, and time perhaps to make my peace with God, so that he may
forgive me for all the things I have had to do in a life as a soldier. But even
when there is peace in the land, the High King has no peace, for when the
enemies leave our shore, why, then, his friends begin to fight, if only for
his favor. No, there will be no crown for me, and when you are my age,
you will be glad of it."

Igraine felt a pricking behind her eyes as Gorlois spoke. So this harsh
soldier, the somber man she had feared, now felt enough at ease with her
to reveal something of his wishes. With all her heart she wished that he

might have his last few years in the sun as he wished, his children playing about him; but even here, in the flickering of the fire, she thought she could see the ominous shadow of the doom that followed him.

It is my imagination, I have let the words of the Merlin make me imagine foolish things, she told herself, and when Gorlois yawned and stretched, saying that he was weary from riding, she went quickly to help him take off his clothes.

She hardly slept in the strange bed, turning and tossing as she listened to Gorlois's quiet breathing; now and again he reached out for her in his sleep, and she soothed him against her breast as she would have done with her child. *Perhaps,* she thought, *the Merlin and the Lady were frightened by their own shadows, perhaps Gorlois will indeed have time to grow old in the sun.* Perhaps before he slept he had indeed planted in her womb the seed of the son they said he would never father. But toward morning she fell into fitful sleep, dreaming of a world in the mist, of the shoreline of the Holy Isle receding further and further in the mists; it seemed to Igraine that she was rowing on a barge, heavy and exhausted, seeking for the Isle of Avalon where the Goddess, wearing Viviane's face, was waiting to ask her how well she had done what was required of her. But although the shoreline was familiar, and the groves of apple trees which had grown on the shore when she came up to the temple, a crucifix stood in the temple of her dream and a choir of the black-robed nuns of the Christians was singing one of their doleful hymns, and when she began to run, looking everywhere for her sister, the sound of church bells drowned out her cries. She woke with a stifled whimper, a sleeper's scream, and sat up to hear the sound of church bells everywhere.

Gorlois sat up in bed beside her. "It is the church where Ambrosius goes to mass. Make haste to dress yourself, Igraine, and we will go together."

While she was winding a woven silk girdle around her linen overdress, a strange serving-man knocked at the door, saying he would like to speak with the lady Igraine, wife of the Duke of Cornwall. Igraine went to the door and it seemed to her that she recognized the man. He bowed to her, and now she remembered that she had seen him, years ago, rowing Viviane's barge. It made her remember her dream, and she felt cold inside.

"Your sister sends you this from the Merlin," he said, "and bids you to wear it and remember your promise, no more." He gave her a small parcel wrapped in silk.

"What is this, Igraine?" asked Gorlois, frowning, coming up behind her. "Who is sending you gifts? Do you recognize the messenger?"

"He is one of my sister's men from the Isle of Avalon," said Igraine, unwrapping the package; but Gorlois said sternly, "My wife does not receive gifts from messengers unknown to me," and took it roughly from her. She opened her mouth in indignation, all her new tenderness for Gorlois vanishing in a single breath; how dared he?

"Why, it is the blue stone you wore when we were wedded," Gorlois said, frowning. "What is this of a promise? How did your sister, if it is truly from her, come by the stone?"

Gathering her wits quickly, Igraine lied to him deliberately for the first time in her life. "When my sister visited me," she said, "I gave her the stone and its chain to have the clasp put right; she knows of a goldsmith in Avalon who is better than any in Cornwall. And the promise she spoke of is that I will care better for my jewels, since I am now a grown woman and not a heedless child who cannot take proper care of precious things. May I have my necklace, my husband?"

He handed her the moonstone, frowning. "I have smiths in my employ who would have put it right for you without reading you a lesson your sister no longer has a right to give. Viviane takes too much upon herself; she may have stood in a mother's place to you when you were a child, but you are not now in her care. You must strive to be more a grown woman, and less dependent upon your home."

"Why, now I have had two lessons," said Igraine crossly, putting the chain about her neck. "One from my sister and one from my husband, as if I were an unlessoned child indeed."

Over his head it seemed that she could still see the shadow of his death, the dread fetch of the death-doomed. Suddenly she hoped, with a passionate hope, that he had not gotten her with child, that she did not bear a son to a doomed man . . . she felt icy cold.

"Come, Igraine," he coaxed, putting out his hand to stroke her hair, "do not be angry with me. I shall try to remember that you are a grown woman in your nineteenth year, not a mere child of fifteen! Come, we must be ready to go to the King's mass, and the priests do not like it if there is much coming and going after the mass has started."

The church was small, made of daub and wattle, and the lamps inside were lighted against the cold dankness; Igraine was glad of her thick woolen mantle. Gorlois whispered to her that the white-haired priest, venerable as any Druid, was Ambrosius' own priest who travelled with the army, and that this was a service of thanksgiving for the King's homecoming.

"Is the King here?"

"He is just coming into the church, at the seat over there before the altar," Gorlois muttered, inclining his head.

She knew him at once by the dark red mantle, worn over a dark, heavily embroidered tunic, and the jewelled sword belt at his side. Ambrosius Aurelianus must, she thought, have been about sixty; a tall, spare man, shaven in the Roman fashion, but stooped, walking with a careful crouch as if he had some inner hurt. Once, perhaps, he had been handsome; now his face was lined and yellow, his dark moustache drooping, nearly all grey, and his hair grizzled. Beside him were two or three of his councillors or fellow kings; she wanted to know who they were, but the priest, seeing the King enter, had begun reading from his great book, and she bit her lip and was silent, listening to the service which even now, after four years in Father Columba's instruction, she did not fully understand, nor care to. She knew it was ill-mannered to gaze about her in church, like a country bumpkin, but she peeped below the hood of her mantle at some of the men around the King: a man whom she supposed to be Uriens of North Wales, and a richly dressed man, slender and handsome, dark hair cut short in Roman fashion around his chin. She wondered if this was Uther, Ambrosius' companion and heir apparent. He stood attentively at Ambrosius' side all through the long service, and when the aging King stumbled, the slight dark man offered him an arm. He cast his eyes attentively on the priest; but Igraine, trained to read people's thoughts in their faces, knew that he was not really listening to the priest or to the service, but that his thoughts ran inward on their own purposes. He raised his head, once, and looked straight at Gorlois, and briefly met Igraine's eyes. His own eyes were dark beneath heavy dark brows, and Igraine felt an instantaneous shiver of revulsion. If this was Uther, she resolved, she would have nothing to do with him; a crown would be too dearly bought at his side. He must be older than he looked, for this man was surely no more than five-and-twenty.

Partway through the service there was a little stir near the door, and a tall, soldierly man, broad-shouldered but lanky, in a thick woven plaid like those the Northmen wore, came into the church, followed by four or five soldiers. The priest went on, unruffled, but the deacon who stood at his side raised his head from the Gospel book and scowled. The tall man uncovered his head, revealing fair hair already worn thin and balding on top. He moved through the standing congregation, the priest said, *Let us pray,* and as Igraine knelt she saw the tall, fair-haired man and his soldiers quite near them; his soldiers had knelt around Gorlois's men and the man himself was at her side. When he had gotten himself down on his knees he gave one quick look round to see that all of his men were placed, then bent his head piously to listen to the prayer.

Through all the long service he did not raise his head; even when the congregation began to approach the altar for the consecrated bread and wine, he did not go. Gorlois touched Igraine's shoulder, and she went at his side—the Christians held that a wife should follow her husband's faith, so that God of theirs could just blame Gorlois if she went to the communion ill prepared. Father Columba had argued with her a long time about proper prayer and preparation, and Igraine had decided that she was never properly prepared for it. But Gorlois would be angry with her, and after all she could not interrupt the silence of the service to argue with him, even in a whisper.

Returning to her place, her teeth on edge from the coarse bread and the sourness of wine on an empty stomach, she saw the tall man raise his head. Gorlois gave him a curt nod and passed on. The man looked at Igraine, and it seemed for a moment that he was laughing at her, and at Gorlois too; she felt herself smile. Then at Gorlois's repressive frown she followed him and knelt meekly at his side. But she could see the fair-haired man watching her. From his Northman's plaid she supposed that this could be Lot of Orkney, the one Gorlois had called young and ambitious. Some of the Northmen too were fair as Saxons.

The final psalm had begun; she listened to the words without paying much attention to them.

> *He has sent redemption among his people in accordance with his eternal covenant . . .*
> *His name is holy and terrible; the fear of the Lord is the beginning of wisdom.*

Gorlois bowed his head for the benediction. She was learning so much about her husband in these few days. She had known he was a Christian when she married him; indeed most folk were Christian, in these days, or if they were not, they kept it most scrupulously to themselves, except near the Holy Isle where the Old Faith reigned, or among the Northern barbarians, or the Saxons. But she had not known that he was genuinely pious.

The benediction was over; the priest and his deacons departed bearing their long cross and the Holy Book. Igraine looked to where the King stood. He looked yellow and tired, and as he turned to leave the church, he leaned heavily on the arm of the dark young man who had stood next to him and supported him all through the service.

"Lot of Orkney loses no time, does he, my lord of Cornwall," said the tall, fair-haired man in the Northman's plaid. "He is ever at Ambrosius' elbow these days, and not wanting in service!"

So, Igraine thought, *this is not the Duke of Orkney as I thought.*

Gorlois grunted assent.

"Your lady wife, Gorlois?"

Reluctantly, churlishly, Gorlois said, "Igraine, my dear, this is our war duke: Uther, whom the Tribes call Pendragon, from his banner."

She dropped him a curtsey, blinking with astonishment. Uther Pendragon, this ungainly man, fair as a Saxon? Was this the courtier intended to succeed Ambrosius—this bumbling man who blundered in to disturb holy mass? Uther was staring—not, Igraine realized, at her face, but at something lower down, and Igraine, wondering if she had spilled communion wine on her gown, saw that he was staring at the moonstone on the breast of her mantle. She wondered sharply if he had never seen one before.

Gorlois, too, had noted the direction of his gaze. He said, "I would like to present my lady to the King; a good day to you, my lord Duke," and left without waiting for Uther's farewell. When they were out of earshot he said, "I like not the way he looks at you, Igraine. He is no man for a decent woman to know. Avoid him."

Igraine said, "He was not looking at me, my husband, but at the jewel I wore. Is he greedy for riches?"

"He is greedy for all things," Uther said shortly. Walking so swiftly that Igraine's thin shoes stumbled on the stone street, they had overtaken the royal party.

Ambrosius, surrounded by his priests and councillors, looked like any other elderly sick man who had gone fasting to mass and was ready for his breakfast and a place to sit down. He walked with one hand held to his side, as if it hurt him. But he smiled at Gorlois with real friendliness, and Igraine knew why the whole of Britain had made up their quarrels to serve under this man and fight away the Saxons from their shores.

"Why, Gorlois, are you back so swiftly from Cornwall? I had little hope of seeing you here before the Council, or again in this world," he said. His voice was thin, breathy, but he held out his arms to Gorlois, who embraced the old man carefully, then blurted out, "You are ill, my lord, you should have kept your bed!"

Ambrosius said, with a little smile, "I will keep it soon enough, and long enough, I fear. The bishop said as much, and would have brought me the holy things in my bed if I wished, but I wanted to show myself among you again. Come and breakfast with me, Gorlois, and tell me how all goes in your quiet countryside."

The two men walked on, Igraine walking behind her husband. On the King's other side was the slight, dark man, scarlet-clad: Lot of Orkney, she remembered. When they came into the King's house and Ambrosius had been placed in a comfortable chair, the High King beckoned Igraine forward.

"Welcome to my court, lady Igraine. Your husband tells me you are a daughter of the Holy Isle."

"It is so, sir," Igraine said shyly.

"Some of your people are advisers at my court; my priests do not like it that your Druids should be placed on equal footing with them, but I tell them you both serve the Great Ones above us, by whatever name. And wisdom is wisdom, however come by. I sometimes think your Gods demand wiser men for their servants than our God for his," Ambrosius said, smiling at her. "Come, Gorlois, sit here beside me at table."

It seemed to Igraine, as she took her seat on the cushioned bench, that Lot of Orkney hovered near like a dog who has been kicked but who wants to slink back to his master. If Ambrosius had men about him who loved him, that was well. But did Lot love his king, or only wish to be near to the throne that its power might reflect on him? She noticed that Ambrosius, though he courteously urged his guests to eat the fine wheaten bread and honey and fresh fish set for his table, ate only sops of bread moistened in milk. She noticed, too, the faint yellow staining the whites of his eyes. Gorlois had said, *Ambrosius is dying.* She had seen enough dying men in her lifetime to know he spoke no more than simple truth, and Ambrosius, from his words, knew it too.

"Intelligence has reached me that the Saxons have made some sort of treaty, killed a horse and sworn on its blood or some such rubbish, with the Northmen," Ambrosius said, "and the fighting may move into Cornwall this time. Uriens, you may have to guide our armies in the West land; you and Uther, who knows the Welsh hills as he knows the hilt of his own sword. The war may even come into your peaceful countryside, Gorlois."

"But you are guarded, as we are in the North, by the coasts and the crags lying below your lands," said Lot of Orkney in his smooth voice. "I do not think a horde of wild folk could come at Tintagel unless they knew the rocks and the harbors. And even from the land side, Tintagel could be defended, with that long causeway."

"True," Gorlois said, "but there are harbors, and shores where a boat can be beached, and even if they cannot reach the castle, there are farmsteads and rich lands and crops. I can defend the castle, but what of the countryside? I am their duke because I can defend my people."

"It seems to me that a duke, or a king, should be something more than this," Ambrosius said, "but I do not know what. I have never had peace to find out. Perhaps our sons will do so. It may come in your time, Lot, you are the youngest of us."

There was a sudden stir in the outer room, and then the tall, fair-haired Uther came into the room. He had a pair of dogs on leash in his hand, and the leashes tangled as the dogs yapped and snarled. He stood at the door patiently untangling them, then gave the leashes to his servant and came into the room.

"You are disturbing us all this morning, Uther," said Lot venomously, "first the priest at holy mass and then the King at his breakfast."

"Have I disturbed you? I beg your forgiveness, my lord," Uther said, smiling, and the King stretched out his hand, smiling as at a favorite child.

"You are forgiven, Uther, but send the dogs away, I pray you. Well, come and sit here, my boy," Ambrosius said, rising clumsily, and Uther embraced the King; Igraine saw that he did so carefully, deferentially. She thought, *Why, Uther loves the King, it is not just ambition or a courtier's currying of favor!*

Gorlois would have given up his place next to Ambrosius, but the King motioned to him to sit still. Uther stretched his long leg across the bench and climbed across it, to slide into a seat beside Igraine. She drew her skirts aside, feeling awkward, as he stumbled—*how clumsy he was! Like a big, friendly puppy!* He had to put out a hand to save himself from falling directly on top of Igraine.

"Forgive my clumsiness, lady," he said, smiling down at her. "I am all too big to sit in your lap!"

Against her will, she laughed up at him. "Even your dogs are too big for that, my lord Uther!"

He helped himself to bread and fish, offering her the honey as he spooned it out of the jar. She refused courteously.

"I do not like sweets," she said.

"You have no need of them, my lady," he said, and she noticed that he was staring at her bosom again. Had he never seen a moonstone before? Or was he staring at the curve of her breast beneath it? She was suddenly, acutely conscious that her breasts were no longer quite as high and firm as they had been before she had suckled Morgaine. Igraine felt the heat rising in her face and quickly took a sip of the fresh cold milk.

He was tall and fair, his skin firm and unwrinkled. She could smell his sweat, clean and fresh as a child's. And yet he was not so very young, his light hair was already thinning over his sunburnt skull. She felt a curious unease, something she had never felt before; his thigh lay alongside hers on the bench and she was very conscious of it, as if it were a separate part of her own body. She cast her eyes down and took a nibble of buttered bread, listening to Gorlois and Lot talking about what would happen if the war were to come to the West country.

"The Saxons are fighters, yes," Uther said, joining in, "but they fight in something like civilized warfare. The Northmen, the Scots, the wild folk from the lands beyond—they are madmen, they rush naked and screaming into battle, and the important thing is to train troops to hold firm against them and not break in fear of their charge."

"That is where the legions had the advantage over our men," Gorlois said, "for they were soldiers by choice, and disciplined, trained to fight, not farmers and countrymen called up to fight without knowledge of that business, and going back to their farms when the danger is past. What we need are legions for Britain. Perhaps if we appealed again to the emperor—"

"The emperor," Ambrosius said, smiling a little, "has troubles enough of his own. We need horsemen, cavalry legions: but if we want legions for Britain, Uther, we will have to train them for ourselves."

"It cannot be done," Lot said positively, "for our men will fight in defense of their homes, and in loyalty to their own clan chiefs, but not for any High King or emperor. And what are they fighting for, if not to return to their homes and enjoy them in comfort afterward? The men who follow me, follow *me*—not some ideal of freedom. I have some trouble getting them to come this far south—they say with some justice that there are no Saxons where we are, so why should they fight away down here? They say, when the Saxons reach their homeland, time enough to fight then and defend it, but the lowlanders should look out for the defense of their own country."

"Can't they see, if they come to stop the Saxons here, the Saxons may never reach their country at all—" Uther began hotly, and Lot raised his slender hand, laughing.

"Peace, Uther! *I* know this—it is my men who do not know it! You will get no legions for Britain, nor any standing army, Ambrosius, from the men north of the great wall."

Gorlois said huskily, "Perhaps Caesar had the right idea, then; perhaps we should regarrison the wall. Not, as he did, to keep the wild Northmen from the cities, but to keep the Saxons from your homeland, Lot."

"We cannot spare troops for that," said Uther impatiently. "We cannot spare any trained troops at all! We may have to let the treaty people defend the Saxon Shores, and set up our stand in the West country, against the Scots and Northmen. I think we should make our main stand in the Summer Country; then in winter they will not be able to come down to sack our camps as they did three years ago, for they will not know their way around the islands."

Igraine listened sharply, for she had been born in the Summer Country and knew how, in winter, the seas moved inward and flooded the land. What was passable, though boggy, ground in summer, in the winter became lakes and long inland seas. Even an invading army would find it hard to come into that country, except in high summer.

"That is what the Merlin told me," Ambrosius said, "and he has offered us place for our people to establish camp for our armies in the Summer Country."

Uriens said in a rusty voice, "I do not like to abandon the Saxon Shores to the treaty troops. A Saxon is a Saxon, and he will keep an oath only while it suits him. I think the mistake of all our lives was when Constantine made compact with Vortigern—"

"No," Ambrosius said, "a dog who is part wolf will fight more hardily against other wolves than any other dog. Constantine gave Vortigern's

Saxons their own land, and they fought to defend it. That is what a Saxon wants: land. They are farmers, and they will fight to the death to make their land safe. The treaty troops have fought valiantly against the Saxons who came to invade our shores—"

"But now there are so many of them," Uriens said, "that they are demanding to enlarge their treaty lands, and they have threatened that if we will not give them more land, they will come and take it. So now, as if it were not enough to fight the Saxons from beyond the sea, we must fight those whom Constantine brought into our lands—"

"Enough," said Ambrosius, raising a thin hand, and Igraine thought he looked terribly ill. "I cannot remedy mistakes, if they were mistakes, made by men who died before I was born; I have enough to do remedying my own mistakes, and I will not live long enough to set them all right. But I will do what I can while I live."

"I think the first thing and best to do," said Lot, "would be to drive forth the Saxons within our own kingdoms, and then fortify ourselves against their returning."

Ambrosius said, "I do not think we can do that. They have lived here since their fathers' and grandfathers' and great-grandfathers' time, some of them, and unless we are willing to kill them all, they will not leave the land they have a right to call their own; nor should we violate the treaty. If we fight among ourselves here within the shores of Britain, how will we have strength and weapons to fight when we are invaded from without? Also, some of the Saxons on the treaty shores are Christians, and will fight alongside us against the wild men and their heathen Gods."

"I think," Lot said, smiling in wry amusement, "that the bishops of Britain thought truly when they refused to send missionaries to save the souls of the Saxons on our shores, saying that if the Saxons were to be admitted to Heaven, they wanted no part of it for themselves! We have enough trouble on this earth with the Saxons, must we have their uncouth brawling in Heaven as well?"

"I think you mistake the nature of Heaven," said a familiar voice, and Igraine felt a strange, hollow awareness within herself. She looked down the table at the speaker, who wore a plain grey robe, monkish in cut. She would not have recognized the Merlin in this garb, but his voice she would have known anywhere. "Do you really think mankind's quarrels and imperfections will be carried on in Heaven, Lot?"

"Why, as to that, I have never spoken with anyone who has been in Heaven," Lot said, "nor, I think, have you, Lord Merlin. But you are talking as wisely as any priest—have you taken Holy Orders in your old age, sir?"

The Merlin laughed and said, "I have one thing in common with your priests. I have spent much time trying to separate the things of man from those that belong to the Divine, and when I have done separating them, I find there is not so great a difference. Here on Earth, we cannot see that, but when we have put off this body we will know more, and know that our differences make no difference at all to God."

"Then why are we fighting?" asked Uther, and grinned as if he were humoring the old man. "If all our differences will be resolved in Heaven, why do we not lay down our arms and embrace the Saxons as brethren?"

The Merlin smiled again and said amiably, "When we are all perfected, it will be just so, Lord Uther, but they do not yet know it, any more than we do, and while human destiny provokes men to fight, well, we must do our part by playing the games of this mortal life. But we need peace in this land so that men may think of Heaven instead of battle and war."

Uther said, laughing, "I have little taste for sitting and thinking of Heaven, old man; I will leave that to you and the other priests. I am a man of battle, I have been so all my days, and I pray to live all my life in war, as befits a man and not a monk!"

"Be careful what you pray for," said Merlin, looking sharply at Uther, "for the Gods will certainly give it to you."

"I do not want to be old, and think of Heaven and peace," said Uther, "for they seem very dull to me. I want war and plunder and women—oh, yes, women—and the priests do not approve of any of those things."

Gorlois said, "Why, then, you are not much better than the Saxons, are you, Uther?"

"Your very priests say we must love our enemies, Gorlois," said Uther, laughing, and reaching across Igraine to clap her husband good-naturedly on the back, "and so I love the Saxon, for he gives me what I want from life! And so should you, for when we have peace like this for a little time, we can enjoy feasting and women, and then back to the fight, as befits a real man! Do you think women care for the kind of man who wants to sit by the fire and till his home acres? Do you think your beautiful lady here would be as happy with a plowman as she is happy with a duke and leader of men?"

Gorlois said soberly, "You are young enough to say so, Uther. When you are my age, you will be sick of war too."

Uther chuckled and asked, "Are you sick of war, my lord Ambrosius?"

Ambrosius smiled, but he looked very weary. He said, "It would not matter if I were sick of war, Uther; for God has chosen in his wisdom to send me war all my days, and so it shall be, according to his will. I will defend my people, and so must those who come after. Perhaps in your days, or the days of our sons, we will have enough time at peace to ask ourselves what we are fighting for."

Lot of Orkney broke in, in his smooth equivocal voice, "Why, we are philosophers here, my lord Merlin, my king; even you, Uther, you have taken to philosophy. But none of this tells us what we are to do against the wild men who come at us from east and from west, and from the Saxons on our own shores. I think we all know that we will have no help from Rome; if we want legions we must train them, and I think we needs must have our own Caesar as well, for just as soldiers need their own captains and their own king, so all the kings in this island need someone to rule over them."

"Why need we call our High King by the name of Caesar? Or think of him so?" asked a man Igraine had heard called by the name Ectorius. "The Caesars ruled Britain well enough in our day, but we see the fatal flaw of an empire thus—when there is trouble in their home city, they withdraw the legions and leave us to barbarians! Even Magnus Maximus—"

"He was no emperor," said Ambrosius, smiling. "Magnus Maximus wished to be emperor, when he commanded the legions here—it is a common ambition for a war duke." And Igraine saw the quick smile he gave Uther over their heads. "So he took his legions and marched on Rome, wishing to be proclaimed emperor—he would have been neither the first nor the last to do so, with the army to support him. But he never got so far as Rome, and all his ambitions came to nothing, except for some fine stories—in your Welsh hills, Uther, do they not talk still of Magnus the Great who will come again with his great sword, at the head of his legions, rescuing them from all invaders—"

"They do," said Uther, laughing, "they have put upon him the old legend from time out of mind, of the king who was and the king who will come again to save his people when the need is dire. Why, if I could find such a sword as that, I could myself go into the hills of my country and raise as many legions as I wanted."

"Perhaps," said Ectorius somberly, "that is what we need, a king out of legend. If the king come, the sword will not be far to seek."

"Your priest would say," the Merlin said evenly, "that the only king who was and is and will be, is their Christ in Heaven, and that, following in his holy cause, you need no other."

Ectorius laughed, a short harsh laugh. "Christ cannot lead us into battle. Nor—I intend no blasphemy, my lord King—would the soldiers follow a banner of the Prince of Peace."

"Perhaps we should find a king who will put them in memory of the legends," Uther said, and silence fell in the room. Igraine, who had never listened before to the councils of men, could still read enough thoughts to know what they were all hearing in the silence: the knowledge that the High King who sat before them now would not live to see another summer. Which of them would sit in his high seat, next year at this time?

Ambrosius leaned his head against the back of his chair, and that was Lot's signal to say, in his eager jealous voice, "You are weary, sire; we have tired you. Let me call your chamberlain."

Ambrosius smiled gently at him. "I will rest soon enough, cousin, and long enough—" but even the effort of speech was too much for him and he sighed, a long, shaking sound, letting Lot help him from the table. Behind him the men broke up into groups, talking, arguing in low tones.

The man called Ectorius came to join Gorlois. "My lord of Orkney loses no opportunity to plead his case, and disguise it as thoughtfulness for the King—now we are the evil men who have wearied Ambrosius and will shorten his life."

"Lot does not care who is named High King," Gorlois said, "so that Ambrosius has no opportunity to state his preference, by which many of us—I among them, I may as well tell you, Ectorius—would be bound."

Ectorius said, "How not? Ambrosius has no son and cannot name an heir, but his wish must guide us, and he knows it. Uther is far too eager for the purple of a Caesar to suit me, but all in all he is better than Lot, so if it should come to a choice of sour apples . . ."

Gorlois nodded, slowly. "Our men will follow Uther. But the Tribes, Bendigeid Vran and that crew, they will not follow any man so Roman as that; and we need the Tribes. They would follow Orkney—"

"Lot has not the stuff to make a High King," Ectorius said. "Better we lose the support of the Tribes than the support of the entire countryside. Lot's way is to split everyone up into warring factions so that only he has the confidence of all. Paugh!" He spat. "The man's a snake and that's all there is to it."

"And yet he's persuasive," Gorlois said. "He has brains, and courage, and imagination—"

"So has Uther. And whether or not Ambrosius gets the chance to say so formally, Uther's the man he wants."

Gorlois set his teeth grimly and said, "True. True. I'm in honor bound to do Ambrosius' will. Yet I wish his choice had fallen on a man whose moral character matched his courage and his leadership. I don't trust Uther, and yet—" He shook his head, glanced at Igraine. "Child, this can be of no possible interest to you. I will have my man-at-arms escort you back to the house where we lay last night."

Dismissed like a little girl, Igraine went homeward in the noontime without protest. She had a good deal to think about. So men too, even Gorlois, could be bound in honor to endure what they did not want to do. She had never thought of that before.

And Uther's eyes, fixed on her, haunted her thoughts. How he had stared at her—no; not at her, at the moonstone. Had the Merlin enchanted it somehow so that Uther should be smitten with the woman who bore it?

Must I do the Merlin's will, and Viviane's, must I be given to Uther resistless, as I was given to Gorlois? The thought repelled her. And yet . . . her mind perversely still felt Uther's touch on her hand, the intensity of his grey eyes meeting her own.

I might as well believe that the Merlin enchanted the stone so that my mind would turn to Uther! They had reached her lodging, and she went inside and took off the moonstone, thrusting it into the pouch tied at her waist. *How foolish,* she thought, *I do not believe in those old tales of love charms and love spells.* She was a woman grown, nineteen years, not a passive child. She had a husband, she might even now be bearing in her womb the seed that would become the son he desired. And if her fancy should light on some man other than her husband, if she should wish to play the wanton, surely there were other men more appealing than that great boor, with his untidy hair like a Saxon's and his Northman's manners, upsetting mass, interrupting the High King's breakfast. Why, she might as well take Gorlois's man-at-arms, who was at least young and clear-skinned and handsome, to her bed. Not that she, as a virtuous wife, had any interest in taking any man whatsoever to her bed except her lawful husband.

And again, if she did, it would not be Uther. Why, he would be worse than Gorlois, a great clumsy oaf, even if his eyes were grey as the sea and his hands strong and unwrinkled. . . . Igraine swore under her breath, took her distaff from the pack of her belongings, and sat down to spin. What was she doing daydreaming of Uther, as if she were seriously considering what Viviane had asked of her? Would Uther really be the next High King?

She had seen the way he looked at her. But Gorlois said he was a lecher; might he look that way at any woman? If she must lose herself in daydreams, she might as well wonder something sensible, such as how Morgaine was faring without her mother, and if the housekeeper was keeping a watchful eye on Morgause so that she did not cast sheep's eyes at the soldiers guarding the castle. Morgause, now, she might run about and lose her maidenhood to some handsome man without thought of honor and propriety; she hoped Father Columba would give the girl a good lecture.

My own mother chose what lovers she would, to father her children, and she was a great priestess of the Holy Isle. Viviane has done the same. Igraine let her spindle drop into her lap, frowning a little, thinking of Viviane's prophecy that her child by Uther could be the great king that would heal the land and bring the warring peoples together in peace. What she had heard this morning at the King's table convinced her that such a king was far to seek.

She took up her spindle, in exasperation. They needed such a king now, not when some child not yet even conceived should grow to manhood. The Merlin was obsessed with old legends about kings—what was it one of the kings, was it Ectorius, had said, about Magnus the Great, the great war leader who had deserted Britain in quest of an emperor's crown? Nonsense, to think a son of Uther could be this Magnus returned.

LATE THAT DAY a bell began to toll, and shortly after, Gorlois came into the house, looking sad and discouraged.

"Ambrosius died a few minutes ago," he said. "The bell tolls for his passing."

She saw the grief in his face and spoke to it.

"He was old," she said, "and he was much loved. I met him only this day, but I can see he was the kind of man whom all those around him would love and follow."

Gorlois sighed heavily. "True. And we have none such to come after him; he has gone and left us leaderless. I loved the man, Igraine, and I hated to see him suffer. If there were any successor worthy the name, I would rejoice that he has gone to his rest. But what will become of us now?"

A little later he asked her to set out his best clothing. "At sunset they will say a requiem mass for him, and I must be there. So should you, Igraine. Can you dress yourself with no woman to robe you, or shall I ask our host to send you a maid?"

"I can dress myself." Igraine set about putting on her other gown, finely spun wool with embroidery at hem and sleeve, and braiding her silk ribbon into her hair. She ate a little bread and cheese; Gorlois would eat nothing, saying that with his king before the throne of God where his soul would be judged, he would fast and pray till he was buried.

Igraine, who had been taught in the Holy Isle that death was no more than the gateway to new birth, could not understand this; how could a Christian have such fear and trembling at going to his eternal peace? She remembered Father Columba chanting some of his doleful psalms. Yes, their God was supposed to be a God of fear and punishment as well. She could understand how a king, for the good of his people, might have to do some things which would lie heavy on his conscience. If even she could understand and forgive that, how could a merciful God be more bigoted and vengeful than the least of his mortals? She supposed it was one of their Mysteries.

She was still pondering these things when she went at Gorlois's side to the mass, and listened to the priest singing dolefully about the judgment of God and the day of wrath when the soul should face eternal damnation. Halfway through this hymn she saw that Uther Pendragon, kneeling at the far end of the church, his face white above his pale tunic, lifted his hands to cover his face and conceal sobs; a few minutes later he got up and went out of the church. She realized that Gorlois was looking sharply at her, and lowered her eyes again to listen piously to the endless hymns.

But when the mass was over, the men clustered outside the church and Gorlois introduced her to the wife of King Uriens of North Wales, a plump, solemn matron, and to the wife of Ectorius, whose name was Flavilla, a smiling woman not a great deal older than Igraine. She chatted with the women for a moment, but their minds were all on what the death of Ambrosius would mean to the soldiers and to their husbands, and her mind wandered; she had little interest in women's chatter, and their pious demeanor wearied her. Flavilla was about six moons pregnant, her belly beginning to bulge under her Roman-style tunics, and after a time their talk drifted to their families. Flavilla had borne two daughters who had died of the summer flux last year and she was hoping, this year, for a son. Uriens' wife, Gwyneth, had a son about Morgaine's age. They asked about Igraine's child, and talked about the efficiency of bronze amulets against winter fevers, and the charm of laying a priest's mass book in the cradle against the rickets.

"It is bad food which causes rickets," Igraine said. "My sister, who is a healer-priestess, told me that no child who is suckled for two full years by a healthy mother ever suffers from rickets, but only if it is given to an ill-nourished wet nurse or weaned too soon and fed on gruel."

"I call that foolish superstition," Gwyneth said. "The mass book is holy and efficient against all illnesses, but particularly those of little children, who have been baptized against the sins of their fathers and have committed no sins of their own."

Igraine shrugged impatiently, unwilling to argue such nonsense. The women went on talking about charms against childhood sicknesses, while she stood casting her eyes this way and that, waiting for an opportunity to leave them. After a time another woman joined them, whose name Igraine never knew; she too was bulging in late pregnancy, and the women immediately drew the newcomer into their talk, ignoring Igraine. After a time she slipped quietly away, saying (unheard) that she was going in search of Gorlois, and walked toward the back of the church.

There was a little graveyard there, and behind it an apple orchard, the branches whitened with blossom, pale in the twilight. The scent of the apple trees was fresh and welcome to Igraine, who found the smells of the city intrusive; dogs, and men too, relieved themselves in the stone streets. Behind every door was a smelly kitchen midden with everything from dirty rushes smelling of urine and rotting meat, to the contents of night pots. At Tintagel there was kitchen refuse and night soil too, but she had it buried every few weeks, and the clean smell of the sea washed away everything.

She walked slowly through the orchard. Some of the trees were very old, gnarled, with low-bending boughs. Then she heard a slight sound, and saw that on one of the low branches a man was sitting. He did not see Igraine; his head was bent, and his face was covered with his hands. But she knew, by the pale hair, that it was Uther Pendragon. She was about to turn and steal quietly away, knowing he would not want her to see his grief, but he had heard her light step and raised his head.

"Is it you, my lady of Cornwall?" His face twisted and looked wry. "Now you may run to tell the brave Gorlois that the war duke of Britain has hidden away to weep like a woman!"

She went swiftly to him, troubled by his angry, defensive face. She said, "Do you think Gorlois does not grieve, my lord? How cold and heartless any man should be, not to weep for the king he has loved all his days! If I were a man, I would not wish to follow any leader into war who would not weep for the dead whom he had loved, for fallen comrades or even for brave enemies."

Uther drew a long breath, wiping his face with the embroidered sleeve of his tunic. He said, "Why, that's true; when I was a young man, I slew the Saxon chief Horsa in the field, after many battles where he had challenged me and then escaped, and I wept for his death, because he was a gallant man. Even though he was a Saxon, I felt sorrow that we must be foemen instead of brothers and friends. But in the years between I have come to feel that I am too old to weep for what cannot be mended. And yet—when I heard the holy father in there, prating of judgment and eternal damnation before the throne of God, and I remembered how good and how pious a man Ambrosius was, and how he loved and feared God, and never skimped to do a kind or an honorable thing—sometimes I find this God of theirs too much to endure, and I almost wish I could listen without damnation to the wise Druids, who talk of no judgment but what a man brings on himself by the way he lives. If the holy bishop speaks sooth, Ambrosius now lies in the fires of Hell, not to be redeemed until the end of the world. I know little of Heaven, but I could wish to think my king there."

She said, reaching out her hand to him, "I do not think the priests of Christ know any more of what comes after death than do any other mortal men. Only the Gods know. They tell us, in the Holy Isle where I was reared, that death is always the gateway to new life and further wisdom, and although I did not know Ambrosius well, I like to think he is now learning, at the feet of his God, what true wisdom can be. What wise God would consign a man to Hell for ignorance, instead of teaching him better in the afterlife?"

She felt Uther's hand touch hers, and he said into the darkness, "Why, it is so. What is it their Apostle said—'Now I see as in a glass, darkly, but then I shall see face to face.' Perhaps we do not know, not even the priests, what will befall beyond death. If God is all-wise, why should we imagine he will be less merciful than men? Christ, they say, was sent to us to show God's love, not his judgment."

They sat in silence for some time. Then Uther said, "Where did you learn such wisdom, Igraine? We have holy ladies in our church, but they are not married, nor do they move among us sinners."

"I was born in the Isle of Avalon; and my mother was a priestess in the Great Temple there."

"Avalon," he said. "It lies in the Summer Sea, does it not? You were at the Council this morning; you know we are to go there. The Merlin has promised me that he will take me to King Leodegranz and introduce me to his court, although if Lot of Orkney has his way, Uriens and I will go back to Wales like dogs howling, with our tails between our legs; or we will fight in his train and pay him homage, which I will do when the sun rises over the western coast of Ireland."

"Gorlois said you are sure to be the next High King," Igraine said, and it struck her with sudden wonder that she was sitting here on a tree branch with the next High King of Britain, talking about religion and matters of state. He felt it too, she could sense it in the tone of his voice, when he said, "I never thought to discuss such matters with the wife of the Duke of Cornwall."

"Do you truly think that women know nothing of state matters?" she asked. "My sister Viviane, like my mother before her, is the Lady of Avalon. King Leodegranz, and other kings, came often to consult with her about the fate of Britain—"

Uther said, smiling, "Perhaps I should consult with her on the best way to bring Leodegranz, and Ban of Less Britain, into my fellowship. For if they listen to her bidding, then all I must do is win her confidence. Tell me, is the Lady married, and is she handsome?"

Igraine giggled. "She is priestess, and priestesses of the Great Mother may not marry, nor make alliance with any mortal man. They belong to the Gods alone." And then she remembered what Viviane had told her, and that this man sitting on the tree branch beside her was part of the prophecy; she stiffened, frightened of what she had done—was she walking on her own feet into the trap Viviane and the Merlin had set for her?

"What is it, Igraine? Are you cold? Are you frightened of war?" Uther asked.

She said, grasping at the first thing she could think of to say, "I have been talking to the wives of Uriens and sir Ectorius—they do not seem much concerned with matters of state. I think perhaps that is why Gorlois does not believe that I can know anything of them, either."

Uther laughed. He said, "I know the ladies Flavilla and Gwyneth—

they do indeed leave all things to their husbands, save those dealing with spinning and weaving and childbearing and such women's things. Have you no interest in those things, or are you as young as you look, too young almost to be wedded, let alone have children to worry about?"

"I have been married four years," Igraine said, "and I have a daughter who is three years old."

"I could envy Gorlois that; every man wants children to succeed him. If Ambrosius had a son, we would not now be in this turmoil. Now—" Uther sighed. "I do not like to think of what will befall Britain if that toad of Orkney should come to be High King, nor Uriens, who thinks everything can be solved by sending a messenger to Rome." Again his voice broke in a sob. "Men say I am ambitious to be High King, but I would give all my ambitions for Ambrosius to be sitting here on this tree branch beside us, or even a son of his, to be crowned in that church tonight! Ambrosius was frightened of what would befall when he was gone. He might have died last winter, but he hoped to make us agree on who should follow him—"

"How was it that he had no sons?"

"Oh, he had sons, two of them. One was slain by a Saxon; Constantine was his name, like to the king who converted this island. The other died of a wasting fever when he was but twelve years old. He said, often and often, that I had become the son he wanted." He buried his face in his hands again, weeping. "He would have made me his heir as well, but that the other kings would not have it. They followed me as war duke, but others were jealous of my influence—Lot, damn him, was the worst. Not for ambition, Igraine, I swear it, but to finish what Ambrosius left undone!"

"I think everyone knows that," she said, stroking his hand. She felt immobilized by his grief.

"I do not think Ambrosius could be happy, even in Heaven, if he looks down and sees the sorrow and confusion here, the kings already plotting, each one seeking to seize power for himself! I wonder if it would have been his will that I should murder Lot to take power? Once he made us swear the oath of blood brothers; I would not violate that," Uther said. His face was wet with tears. Igraine, as she would have done with her child, took the light veil around her face and dried them.

"I know you will do what you must do in honor, Uther. No man Ambrosius trusted so much could do otherwise."

The flare of a lighted torch suddenly struck across their eyes; she froze on the tree branch, her veil still at Uther's face. Gorlois said sharply, "Is it you, my lord Pendragon? Have you seen—ah, madam, are you there?"

Igraine, feeling abashed and suddenly guilty at the sharpness of Gorlois's voice, slipped off the tree branch. Her skirt caught on a projecting limb, hauled up above her knee so that she was bare to her linen drawers; she twitched it hastily down, and heard the fabric rip.

"I thought you lost—you were not in our lodging," Gorlois said harshly. "What do you here, in Heaven's name?"

Uther slipped off the tree branch. The man she had seen revealed, weeping for his lost king and foster-father, dismayed at the burden laid on him, had vanished in a moment; his voice was loud and hearty. "Why, Gorlois, I grew impatient at all the gabbling of that priest, and came out to find clear air with no pious mumblings; and your lady, who had found the blitherings of the good ladies not much more to her taste, happened upon me here. Madam, I thank you," he said, with a distant bow, and strode away. She noticed he was careful to keep his face out of the torchlight.

Gorlois, alone with Igraine, looked at her with angry suspicion. He said, gesturing her to walk before him, "My lady, you should be more careful to avoid gossip; I told you to keep away from Uther. His reputation is such that no chaste woman should be seen in private conversation with him."

Igraine turned and said angrily, "Is that what you think of me, that I am the sort of woman who will slip away to couple with a strange man like a beast in the field? Do you think I was lying with him on the branch of that tree, like some bird of the bough? Would you like to inspect my gown to see whether it is rumpled from lying with him on the ground?"

Gorlois lifted his hand and struck her, not very hard, across the mouth. "You will not play the shrew with me, madam! I told you to avoid him; obey me! I think you honest and chaste, but I would not trust you to that man, nor hear you made the subject of the tongues of women!"

"Surely there is no more evil mind than that of a good woman—unless perhaps it is the mind of a priest," said Igraine wrathfully. She rubbed her mouth where Gorlois's blow had knocked her lip against her teeth. "How dare you lay hands upon me? When I betray you, you may beat the flesh from off my bones, but I won't be beaten for talk! Do you think, in the name of all the Gods, that we were talking of love?"

"And what *were* you talking about with that man, at this hour, in God's name?"

"We talked of many things," Igraine said, "and mostly of Ambrosius in Heaven, and—yes, of Heaven and what one could hope to find in the afterlife."

Gorlois regarded her with a skeptical glare. "That I find unlikely, when he could not show respect for the dead by staying through the holy mass."

"He was sickened—as I was—by all those doleful psalms, as if they were mourning the worst of men instead of the best of kings!"

"Before God all men are miserable sinners, Igraine, and in the eyes of Christ a king is no better than other mortals."

"Yes, yes," she said impatiently, "I have heard your priests say so, and also they spend much time and labor to tell us all that God is love and our goodly father in Heaven. Yet I notice they are very careful not to fall into his hands, and they mourn for those who go to their eternal peace, exactly as for those who go to be sacrificed on the blood altar of the Great Raven herself. I tell you, Uther and I were talking of what the priests know of Heaven, which I think is not very much!"

"If you and Uther spoke of religion, it is for certain the only time that man of blood ever did so!" Gorlois grumbled.

Igraine said, and now she was angry, "He was weeping, Gorlois; weeping for the king who had been as a father to him. And if it shows respect for the dead to sit and listen to the caterwauling of a priest, then may I never have such respect! I envied Uther, that he was a man and could come and go as he chose, and for sure, if I had been born a man, I would never have sat peacefully and hearkened to yonder foolishness in the church. But I was not free to go, being dragged thither at the word of a man who thinks more of priests and psalms than of the dead!"

They had reached the door of their lodging; Gorlois, his face turning dark with wrath, pushed her angrily within. "You will not speak to me in that voice, lady, or I shall beat you in earnest."

Igraine realized that she had actually bared her teeth like a hunting cat, and her voice hissed as she said, "Touch me at your peril, Gorlois, or I shall teach you that a daughter of the Holy Isle is no man's slave nor servant!"

Gorlois opened his mouth for an angry retort, and for a moment Igraine thought he would strike her again. Instead, with an effort, he mastered his anger and turned away from her. "It is not fitting that I stand here brawling when my king and my lord lies still unburied. You may sleep here tonight, if you are not afraid to be alone; if you are so, I shall have you escorted to the house of Ectorius, to sleep with Flavilla. My men and I will fast and pray until sunrise tomorrow, when Ambrosius will be laid in earth to rest."

Igraine looked at him with surprise and a curious, growing contempt. So, for fear of the dead man's shade—even though he called it by another name and thought of it as respect—he would not eat nor drink nor lie with a woman till his king was buried. Christians said they were free of the superstitions of the Druids, but they had their own, and Igraine felt that these were even more distressing, being separated from nature. Suddenly she was very glad that this night she need not lie with Gorlois. "No," she said, "I am not afraid to be alone."

4

aMBROSIUS was buried at sunrise. Igraine, escorted by a Gorlois still angry and silent, watched the ceremonies with a strange detachment. Four years she had struggled to compromise with the religion Gorlois followed. Now she knew that, while she would show his religion a courteous respect so as not to anger him—and indeed, her early teaching had taught her that all Gods were one, and no one should ever mock the name by which another found God—she would try no more to be as pious as he was. A wife should follow her husband's Gods, and she would pretend to do so in a seemly and proper fashion, but she would never again fall prey to the fear that their all-seeing, all-vengeful God could have power over her.

She saw Uther during the ceremonies; he looked haggard and worn, his eyes red-rimmed, as if he, too, had fasted, sleepless; and somehow the sight touched her heart. Poor man, with none to care if he fasted, or to tell him what nonsense it was, as if the dead loitered near the living to see how they fared, and could be jealous of their eating and drinking! She would wager that King Uriens had committed no such folly; he looked fed and rested, and suddenly she wished that she were as old and wise as Uriens' lady, who could speak to her husband and tell him what he should do in such matters.

After the burial Gorlois took Igraine back to their lodging and there broke his fast with her, but he was still silent and grim, and immediately afterward excused himself. "I must attend the Council," he said. "Lot and Uther will be at one another's throats, and somehow I must help them to recall what Ambrosius wanted. I am sorry to leave you alone here, but I will send a man to escort you around the city, if you wish." He gave her a piece of coined money and bade her to buy herself a fairing at the market if she chose, and told her that his man would bear a purse as well, if she wished to choose spices and other things for the household in Cornwall. "For there is no reason for you to come so far, without purchasing some of the things it is needful for you to have. I am not a poor man, and you may buy whatever you need to keep a proper household, without consulting me; remember I trust you, Igraine," he said, and laid his hands on either side of her face and kissed her. Although he did not say so, she knew he was in his own gruff way apologizing for his suspicions and his angry blow, and her heart warmed to him; she returned his kiss with real tenderness.

It was exciting to walk through the great markets of Londinium; dirty and smelly as the city was, it seemed like four or five harvest fairs all in one. The banner of Gorlois, borne by his man-at-arms, kept her from being jostled or pushed very much. Yet it was a little frightening to walk through the enormous market square, with a hundred vendors crying their wares. It seemed to her that everything she saw was new and beautiful, something she wished for, but she resolved to see all over the market before she made any purchases; and then she bought spices, and a length of fine woven wool from the islands, far finer than that of the Cornish sheep—Gorlois should have a new cloak this year; she would begin weaving a border for it as soon as she was back at Tintagel. And so she also bought for herself small hanks of dyed silks; it would be pleasant to weave on such brilliant colors, restful and fine to her hands after the coarseness of wool and flax. She would teach Morgause, too. And it would be high time, next year, to teach Morgaine to spin; if she indeed bore Uther another child, this time next year she would be heavy and ungainly and she could sit and teach her daughter to spin. Four years was certainly old enough to start learning to handle a spindle and twist the thread, even though the thread would not be good for much except tying up bundles of yarn for dyeing.

She also bought some colored ribbons; they would be handsome on Morgaine's holiday gown, and they could be taken off each dress as the child outgrew it, and sewed at neck and sleeves of the new gown. It was only fitting, now that she was big enough not to soil her clothing, that she should be dressed suitably for the daughter of the Duke of Cornwall.

The market was doing a lavish business; at a distance she saw the wife of King Uriens, and other well-dressed ladies, and she wondered if every man in the Council who had a wife had sent her out to do her shopping in the markets of Londinium this morning while the debate raged. Igraine bought silver buckles for her shoes, even though she was sure she could have bought some just as fine in Cornwall, simply because it seemed a fine thing to have buckles to her shoes which had come all the way from Londinium. But when the man would have sold her a brooch with silver filigree all round an amber stone, she refused, shocked at spending all this money. She was very thirsty, and the display of men selling cider and hot pies tempted her, but it seemed an ugly thing to sit and eat in the open market like a dog. She told her man to come along back to the lodging, and resolved that there she would have some bread and cheese and beer. The man looked sullen, so she gave him one of the tiny coins left from her marketing and told him to buy himself a pot of cider or ale if he chose.

When she got back to her lodging, she was tired and sat listlessly looking over her purchases. She would have liked to begin work at once on the borders, but that must wait till she got back to her small loom. She had some spinning with her, but she felt too dull to do it, so she sat looking at her things until Gorlois, looking weary, came in.

He tried to take an interest in what she had bought, commending her frugality, but she could easily see that his mind was elsewhere, though he admired the ribbons for Morgaine's dresses, and said that she had done well to buy the silver buckles. "You should have a silver comb, too, and perhaps a new mirror, your old bronze one is scratched. You can let Morgause have the old one, she is a grown girl now. Tomorrow you may go and choose one, if you will."

"Will there be another meeting of the Council?"

"I fear so, and probably another and another, until we can argue Lot and the others into doing Ambrosius' will and accepting Uther as High King." Gorlois grunted. "Stubborn donkeys, all of them! Would that Ambrosius had left a son, then we could all swear him loyalty as High King and choose a war duke for his prowess in the field. There'd be no question then, it would be Uther; even Lot knows that. But Lot is damned ambitious to be High King, and sees only that it would be a fine thing to wear a crown and take oath from all of us. And there are men in the North who would rather have one of their own, and so they back up Lot—indeed, I think if Uther is chosen in the end, all the kings of the North, except perhaps Uriens, will ride away North with no fealty sworn at all. But even to keep the loyalty of the kings of the North, I'll not swear to be Lot's man. I trust him no further than I could kick his arse on a muddy day!" He shrugged. "This is dull hearing for a woman's ears, Igraine. Set me some bread and cold meat, if you will. I slept not at all last night, and I am tired as if I had been on campaign all day; arguing is weary work."

She started to say that she found it interesting, then shrugged to herself and let it be. She would not stoop to coax tales from him, as if she were a child begging for a nursery tale at bedtime. If she must learn what fared from the gossip of men in the marketplace, so be it. He would be weary this night, and wish for nothing but sleep.

She lay wakeful at his side, very late, and found herself thinking of Uther. How did it feel, to know he was the choice of Ambrosius for High King, and to know he must enforce that choice, probably at sword point? She twisted impatiently, wondering if the Merlin had indeed laid an enchantment on her, that she could not leave off thinking of Uther. At last she drifted into sleep, and in the country of sleep she found herself standing in the orchard where she had spoken with Uther, where she had dried his tears with her veil. Now, in the dream, he seized the end of her veil and drew her close to him with it, and laid his mouth to hers; and there was a sweetness in that kiss, a sweetness that she had never felt in all her years with Gorlois, and she found herself giving herself up to that kiss, felt her whole body melting with it. She looked into his blue eyes, and thought in the dream, *I have always been a child, I have never known until this moment what it was to be a woman.* She said, "I have never known what it was to love." He drew her close to him, and laid his body over hers, and Igraine, feeling that warmth and sweetness suffusing her whole body, raised her lips to his again, and woke, with a start of amazement, to find that Gorlois had drawn her into his arms as he slept. The sweetness of the dream was still in her whole body, so that she put her arms round his neck with a drowsy compliance, but she quickly grew impatient, waiting till he should be done and had fallen again into a heavy, moaning sleep. And she lay awake, shaking, until dawn, wondering what had happened to her.

All that week the Council went on, and every night Gorlois came home pale and angry, worn out with wrangling. Once he burst out, "We sit here at talk, while on the shores the Saxon could be making ready to come to war against us! Don't the fools know that our safety depends on the treaty troops' holding the Saxon Shores, and that they will follow no man but Uther, or one of their own? Is Lot so prejudiced against Uther that he would rather follow a painted chief who serves the Horse God?"

Even the pleasures of the markets had paled; much of that week it rained, and Igraine, who had bought some needles on her second visit, sat and mended Gorlois's clothes and her own, and wished she had her loom to do some fine weaving. She took some of the cloth she had bought and began to make some towels by hemming them and edging them with colored threads. In the second week her moon flux came on her, and she felt dismal and betrayed; Gorlois had not, after all, gotten on her the son he wanted. She was not yet twenty, she could hardly be barren already! She thought of an old tale she had heard, about a wife married to an elderly husband, who bore him no son until she slipped out one night and lay with a shepherd in his field, and her old husband was mighty pleased with the fine healthy boy. If she was barren, Igraine thought resentfully, it was more like than not to be Gorlois's fault! *He* was the one who was old and his blood thinned with years of war and campaigns. And then she thought of her dream, between guilt and dismay. Merlin and Viviane had said it: she should bear a son to the High King, one who would heal the land of all this strife. Gorlois himself had said that if Ambrosius had left a son, there would not be all this wrangling. If Uther were chosen High King, it would indeed be needful for him to get a son at once.

And I am young and healthy, if I were his queen I could give him a son. . . . And when she came again to this point she would weep with a sudden, trapped despair. *I am married to an old man, and my life is over at nineteen. I might as well be an old, old woman, past caring whether I live or die, fit only to sit by the fire and think of Heaven!* She took to her bed and told Gorlois she was ill.

Once during this week the Merlin came to her lodging while Gorlois was at the Council. She felt like flinging her rage and misery at him—he had begun this, she had been content and resigned to her fate until he had sent to waken her out of it! But it was unthinkable to speak rudely to the Merlin of Britain, father or no.

"Gorlois tells me you are ill, Igraine; can I do anything to help you with my healing arts?"

She looked at him in despair. "Only if you can make me young. I feel so old, Father, so old!"

He stroked her shining copper curls and said, "I see no grey in your hair nor wrinkles in your face, my child."

"But my life is over, I am an old woman, the wife of an old man. . . ."

"Hush, hush," he soothed, "you are weary and ill, you will feel better when the moon changes again, surely. It is best like this, Igraine," he said, looking sharply at her, and she suddenly knew that he read her thoughts; it was as if he spoke directly to her mind, repeating what he had said to her at Tintagel: *You will bear Gorlois no son.*

"I feel—trapped," she said, and put her head down and wept and would not speak again.

He stroked her uncombed hair. "Sleep is the best medicine for your illness now, Igraine. And dreams are the true remedy for what ails you. I, who am master of dreams, will send one to cure you." He stretched his hand over her in blessing and went away.

She wondered if something he had done, or some spell set by Viviane, was responsible—perhaps after all she had conceived Gorlois's child and cast it from her; such things had happened. She could not imagine the Merlin sending to dose her beer with herbs or simples, but perhaps with his power he could ensure it with magic or spells. And then she thought perhaps it was for the best. Gorlois was old, she had seen the shadow of his death; did she want to rear a son of his to manhood alone? When Gorlois came back to their lodging that night, it seemed that once again she could see, hovering behind him, the shadow of the dreaded fetch, his death waiting, the sword cut over his eye, his face haggard with grief and despair; and she turned her face away from him, feeling, when he touched her, that she was embraced by a dead man, a corpse.

"Come, my dear one, you must not be so dismal," Gorlois soothed, sitting on the bed beside her. "I know you are sick and wretched, you must be longing for your home and your child, but it will not be long now. I have news for you, listen and I'll tell you."

"Is the Council any nearer to their kingmaking?"

"It may be," Gorlois said. "Did you hear a stir in the streets this afternoon? Well, Lot of Orkney and the kings of the North have departed;

they have quite accepted it now, that we will not choose Lot to be High King until the sun and the moon rise together in the west, and so they have gone forth, leaving the rest of us to do what we know Ambrosius would have willed. If I were Uther—and I told him so much—I would not walk alone after sunset; Lot went away looking like a cur who's had his tail cut off, and I wouldn't think him incapable of curing his wronged pride by sending someone with a dirk on Uther's heels."

She whispered, "Do you truly think Lot will try and kill Uther?"

"Well, he's no match for Uther in a fight. A knife in the back, that would be Lot's way. I'm as well pleased he's not one of us, though it would ease my mind if Lot were sworn to keep the peace. An oath on some holy relic he dare not flout—and even then I'd watch him," Gorlois said.

When they were in bed he turned to her, but she shook her head and pushed him away. "Yet another day," she said, and, sighing, he turned away and fell almost instantly asleep. She could not, she thought, put him off much longer; yet a horror had come upon her, now that she saw again the doom-fetch hanging over him. She told herself that, whatever came, she should remain a dutiful wife to this honorable man who had been kind to her. And that brought back memory of the room where Viviane and the Merlin had shattered her security and all her peace. She felt tears surging up inside her, but tried to quiet her sobs, not wanting to wake Gorlois.

The Merlin had said that he would send her a dream to cure her misery, and yet all this had begun with a dream. She was afraid to sleep, fearing another dream would come to shatter such little peace as she had found. For she knew that this thing would shatter her life, if she allowed it; lay her promised word in shreds. And, although she was not herself a Christian, she had listened enough to their preaching to know that this was, by their standards, grave sin.

If Gorlois were dead . . . Igraine caught her breath in a spasm of terror; for the first time, now, she had allowed herself to form that thought. How could she wish him dead—her husband, the father of her daughter? How could she know that, even if Gorlois were no longer standing between them, Uther would want her? How could she lie at one man's side and long for another?

Viviane spoke as if this kind of thing happens often . . . am I simply childish and naïve, not to know?

I will not sleep lest I dream. . . .

If she went on tossing about like this, Igraine thought, Gorlois would wake. If she wept, he would wish to know why. And what could she tell him? Silently Igraine slid from the bed, wrapped her long cloak about her naked body, and went to sit by the remnants of the dying fire. Why, she wondered, staring into the flames, should the Merlin of Britain, Druid priest, adviser of kings, Messenger of the Gods, meddle this way in the affairs of a young woman's life? For that matter, what was a Druid priest doing as king's councillor at a court supposedly Christian?

If I think the Merlin so wise, why am I not willing to do his will?

After a long time she felt her eyes tiring as she stared at the dying fire, and wondered if she should go back and lie down at Gorlois's side, or if she should get up and walk about, lest she sleep and risk the Merlin's promised dream.

She rose and walked silently across the room to the house door. In her present mood she was not altogether surprised to look back and see that her body still sat, cloak-wrapped, before the fire; she did not trouble to unbolt the door of the room, nor, later, the great front door of the house, but slipped through them both like a wraith.

And yet, outside, the courtyard of the house of Gorlois's friend was gone. She stood on a great plain, where a ring of stones stood in a great circle, just touched by the rising light of dawn . . . no; that light was not the sun, it was a great fire to the west, so that the sky stood all on fire.

To the west, where stood the lost lands of Lyonnesse and Ys and the great isle of Atlas-Alamesios, or Atlantis, the forgotten kingdom of the sea. There, indeed, had been the great fire, where the mountain had blown apart, and in a single night, a hundred thousand men and women and little children had perished.

"But the priests knew," said a voice at her side. "For the past hundred years, they have been building the star temple here on the plains, so that they might not lose count of the tracking of the seasons, or of the coming of eclipses of the moon and sun. These people here, they know nothing of such things, but they know we are wise, priests and priestesses from over the sea, and they will build for us, as they did before. . . ."

Igraine looked up, without surprise, at the blue-cloaked figure by her side, and although his face was very different, and he wore a strange high headdress crowned with serpents, and golden serpents about his arms— torques or bracelets—his eyes were the eyes of Uther Pendragon.

The wind grew cold over the high windswept plain where the stone ring awaited the sun, rising over the heel stone. With the eyes of her living body Igraine had never seen the Temple of the Sun at Salisbury, for the Druids would not go near it. Who, they demanded, could worship the Greater Gods behind the Gods in a temple built by human hands? And so they held their rites within groves of trees, planted by the hands of the Gods. But when she was a girl, Viviane had told her of it, precisely calculated, by arts lost today, so that even those who did not know the secrets of the priests could tell when eclipses were to come, and trace the movements of stars and seasons.

Igraine knew that Uther, at her side—or was it indeed Uther, this tall man in the robe of a priesthood drowned centuries ago in a land now called legend?—was looking westward at the flaming sky.

"So at last it has come as they told us," he said, and laid his arm about her shoulders. "I never truly believed it till this moment, Morgan."

For a moment, Igraine, wife of Gorlois, wondered why this man should call her by the name of her child; yet even as she formed the question in her mind she knew that "Morgan" was not a name, but the title of a priestess, meaning no more than "woman come from the sea," in a religion which even the Merlin of Britain would have found a legend and the shadow of a legend.

She heard herself say, without volition, "I too found it impossible, that Lyonnesse and Ahtarrath and Ruta should fall and vanish away as if they had never been. Do you believe it is true, that the Gods are punishing the land of Atlantis for their sins?"

"I do not believe the Gods work that way," the man at her side said. "The land trembles in the great ocean beyond the ocean we know, and although the people of Atlantis spoke of the lost lands of Mu and Hy-Brasil, still I know that in the greatest ocean beyond the sunset, the land shakes, and islands rise and disappear even where the folk know nothing of sin or evil, but live as the innocent ones before the Gods gave us knowledge to choose good or ill. And if the earth Gods wreak vengeance on the sinless and the sinful alike, then this further destruction cannot be punishment for sins, but is in the way of all nature. I do not know if there is purpose in this destruction, or whether the land is not yet settled into its final form, even as we men and women are not yet perfected. Perhaps the land too struggles to evolve its soul and perfect itself. I do not know, Morgan. These things are matters for the highest Initiates. I know only that we have brought away the secrets of the temples, which we were pledged never to do, and thus we are forsworn."

She said, shaking, "But the priests bade us to do so."

"No priest can absolve us for that oath breaking, for a word sworn before the Gods resonates throughout time. And so we will suffer for it. It was not right that all the knowledge of our temples should be lost beneath the sea, and so we were sent away to bring the knowledge out, in full knowledge that we should suffer, life to life, for the breaking of that vow. It had to be, my sister."

She said resentfully, "Why should we be punished beyond this life for what we were bidden to do? Did the priests think it right that we should suffer for obeying them?"

"No," said the man, "but remember the oath we swore—" and his voice suddenly broke. "Swore in a temple now lost under the sea, where great Orion shall rule no more. We swore to share the lot of him who stole fire from heaven, that man should not live in darkness. Great good came of that gift of fire, but great evil too, for man learned misuse and wickedness . . . and so he who stole the fire, even though his name is revered in every temple for bringing the light to mankind, suffers forever the torments where he is chained, with the vulture gnawing ever at his heart. . . . These things are mysteries: that man can obey the priests blindly, and the laws they make, and live in ignorance, or he can disobey willfully, following the bringer of Light, and bear the sufferings of the Wheel of Rebirth. And look—" He pointed upward, to where the figure of the Greater-than-Gods swung, the three stars of purity and righteousness and choice in his belt. "He stands there still, though his temple is gone; and look, there the Wheel swings through his revolving path, even though the earth below may writhe in torment and cast temples and cities and mankind into a fiery death. And we have built here a new temple, so that his wisdom need never die."

The man she knew to be Uther, within, laid his arm about her, and she knew that she was weeping. He pulled her face roughly up to his and kissed her, and she tasted salt from his own tears on his lips. He said, "I cannot regret it. They tell us in the temple that true joy is found only in freedom from the Wheel that is death and rebirth, that we must come to despise earthly joy and suffering, and long only for the peace of the presence of the eternal. Yet I love this life on Earth, Morgan, and I love you with a love that is stronger than death, and if sin is the price of binding us together, life after life across the ages, then I will sin joyfully and without regret, so that it brings me back to you, my beloved!"

Never in all her life had Igraine known a kiss such as this one, passionate, and yet it seemed as if some essence beyond mere lust held them bound to each other. At that moment memory flooded through her, of where she had first known this man—of the great marble pillars and golden stairs of the great Temple of Orion, and of the City of the Serpent below, with the avenue of sphinxes, beasts with bodies as of lions and faces of women, leading up the great road to the Temple . . . here they stood on a barren plain, with a ring of undressed stones, and a fire to the west that was the dying light of the land of their birth, where they had dwelt together in the Temple since they were little children, and where they had been joined together in the holy fire, never to be parted while they should live. And now they had done that which would join them beyond death, too. . . .

"I love this land," he said violently again. "Here we stand where the temples are made with unhewn stone, and not with silver and gold and orichalcum, but already I love this land, so that I willingly give my life to keep it safe, this cold land where the sun never shines . . ." and he shivered beneath his cloak; but Igraine pulled him round, turning their backs on the dying fires of Atlantis.

"Look to the east," she said, "for always, while the light dies in the west, there is the promise of rebirth from the east." And they stood, clasped together, as the sun blazed, rising behind the eye of the great stone.

The man whispered, "This is indeed the great cycle of life and death . . ." and even as he spoke, he drew her to him. "A day will come when people will forget, and this will be no more than a ring of stones. But I will remember, and I will come back to you, beloved, I swear it."

And then she heard the voice of the Merlin saying somberly, "Take care what you pray for, for you will certainly be given that."

And silence; and Igraine found herself, naked, wrapped only in her cloak, huddled before the last cold ashes of the fire in her room in their lodging; and Gorlois snoring softly in the bed.

Shaking, she wrapped herself tightly in the shawl and crept, chilled to the bone, back to the bed, burrowing for some remnants of warmth. Morgan. Morgaine. Had she given her child that name because it was truly one she had borne? Was it only a bizarre dream sent by the Merlin, to convince her that once she had known Uther Pendragon in some former life?

But that had been no dream—dreams were confused, bizarre, a world where all is foolishness and illusion. She knew that somehow she had wandered into the Land of Truth, where the soul goes when the body is elsewhere, and somehow she had brought back not a dream but a memory.

One thing at least was made clear. If she and Uther had known each other, loved each other, in the past, it explained why she had this tremendous sense of familiarity with him, why he did not seem a stranger, why even his boorish—or boyish—manners seemed not offensive, but simply part of the person which he was and had always been. She remembered the tenderness with which she had dried his tears with her veil, knowing now that she had thought: *yes, he was always so.* Impulsive, boyish, rushing toward what he wanted, never weighing costs.

Had they truly brought the secrets of a vanished wisdom to this land, generations ago when the lost lands were newly vanished under the western ocean, and together incurred the penalties for that oathbreaking? *Penalties?* And then, not knowing why, she remembered that rebirth itself— human life—was supposed to be the penalty, life in a human body rather than endless peace. She curved her lips in a smile, thinking, *Is it penalty, or reward, to live in this body?* For thinking of the sudden wakening of her body in the arms of the man who was, or would be, or once had been, Uther Pendragon, she knew as she had never known before that, whatever the priests said, life, whether birth or rebirth, in this body, was reward enough.

She burrowed her body down in the bed, and lay, not sleepy now, looking into the darkness, smiling. So Viviane and the Merlin had known, perhaps, what it was fated for her to know: that she was bound to Uther by a bond which made her tie to Gorlois merely superficial and momentary. She would do as they willed; it was part of her destiny. She and the man who now was Uther had bound themselves, many lives ago, to the fate of this land, where they had come when the Old Temple was buried. Now, when once again the Mysteries were imperilled, this time by hordes of barbarians and wild men from the North, they returned together. It was given to her to bring to birth one of the great heroes who, so it was said, came back to life when they were needed, the king who was, and is, and will come again to save his people . . . even the Christians had a version of the story, saying that when their Jesus was born, his mother had had warnings and prophecies that she would bear a king. She smiled in the darkness, thinking of the fate that was reuniting her with the man she had loved so many centuries before. Gorlois? What had Gorlois to do with her fate, except to make her ready? Otherwise, she might have been too young to understand what was to happen to her.

In this life I am not a priestess. Yet I know that I am still the obedient child of my fate; as all men and women must be.

And for the priests and the priestesses there is no tie of marriage. They give themselves as they must, in the will of the Gods, to bring forth those who are pivotal to the fates of mankind.

She thought of the great constellation called the Wheel, in the north. The peasants called it the Wain, or the Great Bear, shambling ever round and round the northernmost of the stars; but Igraine knew it symbolized, in its coming and going, the endless Wheel of Birth and Death and Rebirth. And the Giant who strode across the sky, the sword hanging from his belt . . . for a moment it seemed to Igraine that she saw the hero who was to come, with a great sword in his hand, the sword of the conqueror. The priests of the Holy Isle would make certain that he had a sword, a sword out of legends.

At her side Gorlois stirred and reached for her, and she went dutifully into his arms. Her revulsion had quite gone in tenderness and pity, nor did she have any fear that he would get her with his unwanted child. That was not her fate. Poor, doomed man, he had no part in that mystery. He was one of the once-born; or, if he was not, he did not remember, and she was glad he had the comfort of his simple faith.

Later, when they rose, she heard herself singing; and Gorlois watched her curiously.

"It seems that you are well again," he said, and she smiled.

"Why, yes," she said, "I have never been better."

"Then the Merlin's medicine did you good," Gorlois said, and she smiled, and did not answer.

5

It seemed that nothing else was talked of in the city for several days—that Lot of Orkney had withdrawn and gone away to the North. It was feared that this would delay the final choice; but only three days later, Gorlois returned to the lodging, where Igraine was putting the final stitches into a new gown from the woven cloth she had found in the market, to say that the Council of Ambrosius' advisers had done as they had known, all along, that Ambrosius would have wished, and chosen Uther Pendragon to rule over all Britain as High King among the kings of the land.

"But what of the North?" she asked.

"Somehow he will bring Lot to terms, or else he will fight him," Gorlois said. "I do not like Uther, but he is the best fighter we have. I am not afraid of Lot, and I am sure Uther does not fear him either."

Igraine felt the old stirring of the Sight, knowing that Lot had much to do in the years to come . . . but she kept her peace; Gorlois had made it obvious that he did not like to hear her speak of men's affairs, and she would rather not quarrel with a doomed man in the little time remaining to him.

"I see your new gown is finished. You shall wear it, if you will, when Uther is made High King in the church and crowned, and afterward he will hold court for all his men and all their ladies, before he goes to the West country for their kingmaking," he said. "He bears the name Pendragon, Greatest Dragon, from the banner he bears, and they have some superstitious ritual about dragons and kingship—"

"The dragon is the same as the serpent," Igraine volunteered. "A symbol of wisdom; a Druidical symbol."

Gorlois frowned, displeased, and said that he had no patience with such symbols in a Christian country. "The anointing by a bishop should be enough for them."

"But all people are not fitted for the higher Mysteries," Igraine said. She had learned this as a child on the Holy Isle, and since her dream of Atlantis it seemed to her that all the early teaching about the Mysteries, which she thought she had forgotten, had assumed a new meaning and depth in her mind. "Wise men know that symbols are not needed, but the common folk of the countryside, they need their dragons flying for the kingship, just as they need the Beltane fires, and the Great Marriage when a king is wedded to the land—"

"Those things are forbidden to a Christian," Gorlois said austerely. "The Apostle has said it, there is only one name under Heaven by which we may be saved, and all those signs and symbols are wicked. I would not be surprised to hear it of Uther, that unchaste man, that he entangles himself in these lewd rites of pagandom, pandering to the folly of ignorant men. One day I hope to see a High King in Britain who will keep to Christian rites alone!"

Igraine smiled and said, "I do not think either of us will live to see that day, my husband. Even the Apostle in your holy books wrote that there was milk for babes and meat for strong men, and the common folk, the once-born, have need for their Holy Wells and their spring garlands and dancing rites. It would be a sad day for Britain if no Yule fires burned and no garlands fell into the Holy Wells."

"Even the devils can quote the holy words amiss," Gorlois said, but not angrily. "Perhaps this is what the Apostle meant, when he said that women should keep silence in the churches, for they are prone to fall into those errors. When you are older and wiser, Igraine, you will know better. Meanwhile, you can make yourself as fine as you please for the services in the church and for the merrymaking afterward."

Igraine put on her new gown and brushed her hair until it shone like fine copper; and when she looked at herself in the silver mirror—Gorlois had sent to the market for it, after all, and had it brought to her—she wondered with a sudden fit of despondency whether Uther would even notice her. She was beautiful, yes, but there were other women, beautiful as she was, and younger, not married women who had borne children—why should he want *her*, old and used as she was?

All through the long ceremonies in the church, she watched intently as Uther was sworn and anointed by their bishop. For once the psalms were not doleful hymns of God's wrath and punishment, but joyful songs, praising and offering thanks, and the bells sounded joyous instead of wrathful. Afterward in the house which had been Ambrosius' headquarters, there were delicacies and wine and much ceremony, as one by one, Ambrosius' war chiefs swore allegiance to Uther.

Long before it was over, Igraine grew weary. But at last it was done, and while the chiefs and their ladies congregated around the wine and the food, she moved a little away, watching the bright gathering. And there, at last, as she had been half aware that he would, Uther found her.

"My lady of Cornwall."

She made a deep curtsey. "My lord Pendragon, my king."

He said roughly, "There is no need for such formalities between us now, lady," and caught her shoulders, so much as he had done in her dream that she stared, half expecting that she would see on his arms the golden serpent torques.

But he only said, "You are not now wearing the moonstone. It was so strange, that stone. When first I saw you wearing it, it was like to a dream I had. . . . I had fever, last spring, and the Merlin attended me, and I had a strange dream, and I know now it was in that dream I first beheld you, long before ever I laid eyes on your face. I must have stared like a country lout, Lady Igraine, for I found myself struggling again and again to remember my dream, and what part you played in that dream, and the moonstone at your throat."

She said, "I have been told that one of the virtues of the jewel, moonstone, is to awaken the true memories of the soul. I too have dreamed. . . ."

He laid a light hand on her arm. "I cannot remember. Why is it that I seem to see you wearing something gold about your wrists, Igraine? Have you a golden bracelet in the form of—of a dragon, perhaps?"

She shook her head. "Not now," she said, paralyzed at the awareness that he had, somehow and without her full knowledge, shared that strange memory and dream.

"You will be thinking me a boor and beyond all courtesy, my lady of Cornwall. May I offer you some wine?"

Silently she shook her head. She knew that if she tried to take a cup in her hand she would shake and spill it all over herself.

"I do not know what is happening to me," Uther said violently. "All that has happened in these days—the death of my father and king, the strife of all these kings, their choosing me for High King—it seems unreal, and you, Igraine, are the most unreal of all! Have you been to the West, where the great ring of stones stands on the plain? They say that in olden time it was a Druid temple, but the Merlin says not, it was built long before the Druids came to these lands. Have you been there?"

"Not in this life, my lord."

"I wish I could show it to you, for I dreamed once I was there with you—oh, don't think me a madman, Igraine, chattering always of dreams and prophecy," he said with that sudden, boyish smile. "Let us talk very sedately of ordinary things. I am a poor Northern chief who has suddenly wakened to find himself High King of Britain, and perhaps I am a little mad with the strain!"

"I shall be sedate and ordinary." Igraine agreed with a smile. "And if you were a wedded man I would ask you how your wife did and if your oldest son had trouble with—oh, what is the most ordinary thing I could ask you—whether he was done teething before the hot weather, or if he had a skin rash from his swaddling clothes!"

He chuckled. "You will be thinking I am old not to be a married man," he said. "I've had women enough, God knows. I should not say that, perhaps, to the wife of my most Christian of chiefs; Father Jerome would say I had had all too many women for the health of my soul! But I never saw one I cared for, when we rose from bedding, and I always feared that if I wedded some woman before we bedded, I would tire of her in such manner. It seemed to me always that there should be some tie stronger than that between man and women, though the Christians seem to think that is enough—what is it they say, it is better to marry than to burn? Well, I did not burn, for I slaked the fire, and when I had spent it, the fire went out, and yet I feel that there could be a burning which would not spend itself so quickly, and it should be such a one I could marry." Abruptly he asked her, "Do you love Gorlois?"

Viviane had asked her this, and she had said that it did not matter. She had not known what she was saying. Now she said quietly, "No. I was given to him when I was too young to care what man I married."

Uther turned away and paced angrily, saying at last, "And I can see you are no wench to tumble, and why in the name of all the Gods I must be bewitched by a woman who is wedded to one of my most loyal partisans—"

So the Merlin had worked his meddlesome magic on Uther too. But now Igraine did not resent it. It was their destiny, and what would come, must come. But she could not believe it was her destiny to betray Gorlois crudely, here like this. It was like a part of her dream of the great plain, so that she could almost see the shadow of the great ring of stones, when he laid his hand on her shoulder. But she was confused, *No, that was another world, and another life.* It seemed that her whole soul and body cried out within her for the reality of that kiss in their dream. She put her hands over her face and wept. He stared at her, dismayed and helpless, backing away a little.

"Igraine," he whispered. "What can we do?"

"I don't know," she said, sobbing, "I don't know." Her certainty had become a miserable confusion. Had the dream been sent only to bewitch her, by magic, into a betrayal of Gorlois and her own honor and sworn word?

A hand fell on her shoulder, heavy and disapproving. Gorlois looked angry and suspicious.

"What is this unseemly matter, my lady? What have you been saying, my king, that my wife looks so wretched? I know you a man of lewd manners and little piety, but even so, sire, common decency should restrain you from approaching a vassal's wife at your crowning!"

Igraine raised her face to him in anger. "Gorlois, I have not deserved this of you! What have I ever done that you should cast such an accusation at me in a public place?" For indeed heads were turning now, hearing angry words spoken.

"Then why, lady, do you weep, if he has said nothing unseemly to you?" His hand, gripping her wrist, felt as if he would crush it.

"As for that," Uther said, "you must ask the lady why she weeps, for I do not know. But loose her arm, or I will make you. Husband or no, no one shall handle any woman roughly in my house."

Gorlois let go of Igraine's arm. She could see the marks of his fingers already reddening into dark bruises; she rubbed the marks, tears streaming down her face. Before the many faces surrounding them she was appalled, as if she had been taken and shamed; she covered her face with her veil and wept harder than ever. Gorlois pushed her before him. She did not hear what he said to Uther; only when they were outside in the street did she stare at him, amazed.

He said in a rage, "I will not accuse you before all men, Igraine, but God is my witness I should be justified in doing so. Uther looked at you just now as a man looks at a woman he has known as no Christian man has a right to know any other man's wife!"

Igraine, feeling her heart pounding in her breast, knew it was true, and felt confusion and despair. In spite of the fact that she had seen Uther only four times, and dreamed twice of him, she knew that they had looked at each other and spoken to each other as if they had been lovers for many years, knowing all and more than all about each other, body and mind and heart. She recalled her dream, where it seemed that they had been bound for many years by a tie which, if it was not marriage, might as well have been so. Lovers, partners, priest to priestess—whatever it was called. How could she tell Gorlois that she had known Uther only in a dream, but that she had begun to think of him as the man she had loved so long ago that Igraine herself was not yet born, was a shadow; that the essence within her was one and the same with that woman who had loved that strange man who bore the serpents on his arms in gold. . . . How could she say this to Gorlois, who knew, and wished to know, nothing of the Mysteries?

He pushed her ahead of him into their lodging. He was ready, she knew, to strike her if she had spoken; but her silence frustrated him even more. He shouted, "Have you nothing to say to me, my wife?" and gripped her already bruised arm so strongly that she cried out anew with the pain of his hand. "Did you think I did not see how you looked at your paramour?"

She wrenched her arm away from him, feeling as if he would actually tear it out of the socket. "If you saw that, then you saw me turn away from him when he would have had no more than a kiss! And did you not hear him say to me that you were his loyal supporter and he would not take the wife of his friend—"

"If I was ever his friend, I am so no more!" Gorlois said, his face dark with fury. "Do you truly think I shall support a man who would take my wife from me, in a public place, shaming me before all his assembled chiefs?"

"He did not!" Igraine cried out, weeping. "I have never so much as touched his lips!" It seemed all the more vicious since she had indeed desired Uther but had kept herself scrupulously away from him. *Why, if I am to be accused of guilt when I am innocent of any wrongdoing even as he would call it so, why should I not have done what Uther wished?*

"I saw how you looked at him! And you have kept apart from my bed since first you set eyes on Uther, you faithless whore!"

"How do you *dare!*" she gasped, raging, and caught up the silver mirror he had given her, flinging it at his head. "Take back that word, or I swear I will throw myself into the river before ever you touch me again! You lie, and you know you lie!"

Gorlois ducked his head and the mirror crashed against the wall. Igraine snatched off her amber necklace—another new gift from her husband—and flung it after the mirror; with hasty fingers tore off the fine new gown and hurled it at his head. "How dare you call me such names, who have loaded me with gifts as if I were one of your camp followers and fancy women? If you think me a whore, where are the gifts I have received from my lovers? All the gifts I have are given me by my husband, the whoreson foul-mouthed cullion who tries to buy my goodwill for his own lusts because the priests have made him half a eunuch! From now on I will wear the weaving of my own fingers, not your disgusting gifts, you knave whose mouth and mind are as foul as your filthy kisses!"

"Be silent, you evil-minded scold!" Gorlois shouted, striking her so hard that she fell to the ground. "Now get up and cover yourself decently as a Christian woman should, not tearing off your clothes so that I will go mad with looking at you like that! Is that how you seduced my king into your arms?"

She scrambled to her feet, kicking the ruins of the gown as far as she could, and rushed at him, striking his face again and again. He grabbed her, trying to hold her motionless; crushed her into his arms. Igraine was strong, but Gorlois was a big man and a warrior, and after a moment her struggles subsided, knowing they were useless.

He whispered, pushing her toward the bed, "I will teach you better than to look at any man that way except your rightful husband!"

She flung her head back in contempt and said, "Do you think I would ever look at you again except with the loathing I would feel for a snake?

Oh, yes, you can take me to bed and force me to do your will, your Christian piety permits you to ravish your own wife! I do not care what you say to me, Gorlois, because I know in my own heart that I am innocent! Until this very moment I felt guilty that some witchcraft or spell had made me love Uther. Now I wish I had done what he begged of me, if only because you were as ready to believe lies of my guilt as the truth about my innocence, and while I was anxious for my own honor and yours, you were prepared to believe I would fling mine to the winds!"

The contempt in her voice made Gorlois drop his arms and stare at her. He said, his voice husky, "Do you mean that, Igraine? Are you truly innocent of wrongdoing?"

"Do you think I would stoop to lie about it? To *you?*"

"Igraine, Igraine," he said humbly, "I know well I am too old for you, that you were given to me without love and without your will, but I thought, perhaps, in these days, you have come to think a little better of me, and when I saw you weeping before Uther—" His voice choked. "I could not bear it, that you should look like that at that lustful and vicious man, and look on me only with duty and resignation—forgive me, forgive me, I do beg it of you—if indeed I wronged you—"

"You wronged me," she said, her voice stinging with ice, "and you do well to beg my pardon, which you shall not have until the hells rise and the Earth sinks beneath the western ocean! Better you should go and make your peace with Uther—do you truly think you can stand against the wrath of the High King of Britain? Or will you end by buying his favor as you sought to buy mine?"

"Be still!" Gorlois said angrily, his face flushing; he had humbled himself before her, and she knew he would never forgive her for that either. "Cover yourself!"

Igraine realized that she was still bare to the waist. She went to the bed where her old gown was lying and pulled it leisurely over her head, doing up the laces. He gathered up her amber necklace from the floor, and the silver mirror, and held them out to her, but she turned her eyes away and ignored them and after a while he laid them on the bed, where she let them lie without looking at them.

He stared at her for a moment, then pushed the door and went out.

Left alone, Igraine began to put her things into her saddlebags. She did not know what she meant to do; perhaps she would go and find the Merlin, take him into her confidence. It was he who had begun this train of events that had put her and Gorlois at such odds. At least she knew she would no longer dwell with complacency under Gorlois's roof. A pain struck at her heart: they had been wedded under Roman law and by that law Gorlois had absolute power over their daughter, Morgaine. Somehow she must contrive to dissemble until she could get Morgaine away to a place of safety! She could perhaps send her to Viviane, at the Holy Isle, for fostering.

She left the jewels Gorlois had given her lying on the bed, packing with her only the gowns she had woven with her own hands at Tintagel, and for jewels, only the moonstone Viviane had given her. Later she realized it was this moment or two of delay which had cost her escape, for while she was laying out the gifts he had given her on the bed, separating her own things from them, Gorlois came back into the room. He cast one swift glance at her packed saddlebags, and nodded curtly. "Good," he said, "you are making ready to ride. We will leave before sunset."

"What do you mean, Gorlois?"

"I mean that I have cast back my oath in Uther's face and told him what I should have told him at once. Henceforth we are enemies. I go now to organize the defense of the West against the Saxons and the Irish, should they come there; I have told him that if he seeks to bring his armies into my country I will hang him like the felon he is from any handy tree."

She stared at him; at last she said, "You are mad, my husband. The men of Cornwall cannot hold the West country alone if the Saxons should come there in force. Ambrosius knew that; the Merlin knows that; God help me, *I* know it, and I am no more than a home-keeping woman! Will you strike down in one moment of madness everything that Ambrosius lived for and spent his last years struggling for because of some insane quarrel with Uther over your own mad jealousy?"

"You are quick to care for Uther!"

"I should be quick to pity the Saxon chief himself, if he lost his hardiest supporters in a quarrel with no foundation! In God's name, Gorlois, for our very lives and the lives of the people who look to you for help if the Saxons come, I beg of you to amend this quarrel with Uther, and not to break up the alliance this way! Lot has already gone; if you go, there will be none but treaty troops and a few minor kings to follow him in the defense of Britain!" She shook her head in despair. "Would that I had thrown myself from the cliffs at Tintagel before ever I came to Londinium! I will take any oath you like, that I have never so much as touched Uther Pendragon's lips! Will you break the alliance for which Ambrosius died, because of a woman?"

Gorlois glowered at her and said, "Even had Uther never set eyes on you, my lady, I should not in conscience follow a man of lewdness, so bad a Christian; I trust Lot not at all, but I now know that I should trust Uther less. I should have listened from the first to the voice of my conscience, and I would never have agreed to support him at all. Put my clothing into the other saddlebag. I have sent for the horses and our men-at-arms."

She looked at his implacable face and knew that if she protested he would beat her again. Silently, with seething anger, she obeyed. Now she was trapped, she could not flee, not even to the Holy Isle under her sister's protection—not while Gorlois held her daughter at Tintagel.

She was still laying folded shirts and tunics into the saddlebags when she heard alarm bells begin to ring. Gorlois said curtly, "Stay here!" and hurried out of the house.

Angry, Igraine hurried after him, only to find herself faced by a burly man-at-arms, one of Gorlois's men she had not seen before. He thrust his pike sideways across the house door, preventing her from stepping across the sill. His Cornish dialect was so thick that she could hardly understand his words, but she made out that the Duke had commanded his lady was to keep safely within the house; he was there to see that she stayed so.

It would be beneath her dignity to struggle with the man, and she had a shrewd suspicion that if she did he would simply bundle her like a sack of meal across the threshold. In the end, she sighed and went back inside the house, finishing her packing. From the street she heard cries and clamor, the sounds of men running, bells ringing in the nearby church, although it was not the hour for services. Once she heard a clashing of swords and wondered if the Saxons were in the city and among them—it would indeed be a good time for an attack, when Ambrosius' chiefs were all at odds! Well, that would solve one of her problems, but what would become of Morgaine, alone at Tintagel?

The day wore on, and near nightfall Igraine began to be afraid. Were the Saxons at the gates of the city, had Uther and Gorlois quarreled again, was one or the other of them dead? When at last Gorlois thrust open the door of the room, she was almost glad to see him. His face was drawn and distant, his jaw clenched as if in great grief, but his words to Igraine were brief and uncompromising.

"We ride at nightfall. Can you keep your saddle, or shall I have one of my men carry you on a pillion? We shall have no time to delay for a lady's pace."

She wanted to batter at him with a thousand questions, but she would not give him the satisfaction of seeming to care. "While you can ride, my husband, I can keep to my saddle."

"See that you do, then, for we shall not halt long enough for you to change your mind. Wear your warmest cloak; it will be cold riding at night, and the sea fog is coming in."

Igraine tied up her hair into a knot and wrapped her thick cloak over the tunic and breeches she always put on for riding. Gorlois lifted her to the horse's back. The street was thickly clustered with the dark forms of men-at-arms with their long spears. Gorlois spoke in low tones to one of the captains, then strode back and mounted; there were a dozen horsemen and soldiers riding behind Gorlois and Igraine at their head. He took the reins of Igraine's horse himself and said with an angry jerk of his head, "Come."

She was not sure of the way; she rode in silence where Gorlois led, through the falling dusk. Somewhere against the sky there was fire, but Igraine did not know whether it was a soldier's watch fire, or a house somewhere in flames, or simply the cooking fires of the travelling peddlers encamped in the marketplace. She had never learned her way through the thickly clustered houses and streets to the river, but as the thick fog began to blow in wisps across their path, she supposed they were coming to the riverbank, and after a time she heard the creaking of the rope windlass which controlled the heavy planking rafts of the ferry.

One of Gorlois's men, dismounting, led her horse aboard; Gorlois rode at her side. A few of the men swam their horses. She realized it must be very late—at this time of year the light lingered long, and it was almost unheard of to ride at night. Then she heard a cry from the shore.

"They are going! They are going! First Lot, and then my lord of Cornwall, and we are unprotected!"

"All the soldiers are leaving the town! What will we do when the Saxons land on the south coast?"

"Cowards," someone yelled from the shore as the ferry, with a great creaking, began to move away. "Cowards, running away with the country-side aflame!"

A stone came whizzing out of the dark. It struck one of the men-at-arms on his leather breastplate. He swore, but Gorlois spoke to him in a sharp undertone and he grumbled into silence. There were a few other insults hurled from the shore and a few more stones, but they were quickly out of range. As her eyes grew accustomed to the dark Igraine could see Gorlois, his face pale and set like a marble statue. He did not speak to her all that night, although they rode till dawn, and even when the dawn came up red and dripping behind them, turning the world to crimson fog, they stopped only a little while for horses and men to rest. Gorlois laid a cloak for Igraine to lie down on for a little while, and brought her some hard bread and cheese and a cup of wine, soldier's rations, but still he did not speak to her. She was weary and bruised from riding, and confused; she knew that Gorlois had quarreled with Uther and withdrawn his men, but nothing more. Would Uther have let him go without protest? Well, Lot had been let go.

After a short rest, Gorlois brought the horses again and would have lifted her into the saddle, but here Igraine rebelled.

"I will ride no further until you tell me where we ride, and why!" She kept her voice down, not wanting to shame Gorlois before his men, but she faced him fearlessly. "Why do we steal from Londinium like thieves in the night? Now you will tell me what is happening, unless you wish to have me tied to my horse's back and carry me screaming aloud all the way to Cornwall!"

"Do you think I would not do that if I must?" Gorlois said. "Don't seek to cross me, you for whom I have forsworn a lifetime of honor and oaths kept, and set the memory of my king at nothing!"

"How can you dare to blame me for that," Igraine flung at him. "You did it not for me but for your own insane jealousy! I am innocent of whatever sins your evil mind believes I have committed—"

"Silence, woman! Uther, too, swore that you were innocent of wrong. But you are a woman and you put some enchantment on him, I suppose —I went to Uther, hoping to mend this quarrel, and do you know what proffer that evil and lustful man made to me? He demanded of me that I should divorce you and give you to him!"

Igraine stared at him with wide-open eyes. "If you think so evil of me, that I am adulteress, witch, all these ill things, why then did you not rejoice at the prospect of getting quit of me so simply?"

And inside her was a new rage, that even Uther should think of her as a woman to be given away without her own consent, that he went to Gorlois and besought him to give the unwanted woman, even as Gorlois himself had asked her of the Lady of Avalon! Was she a horse to be sold at the spring fair, then? One part of her quivered with a secret pleasure— Uther wanted her, he wanted her enough that he would quarrel with Gorlois and alienate his allies by this quarrel over a woman. And with another part of her being she was enraged. Why had he not besought her, of herself, that she should put away Gorlois and come to him of her free will?

But Gorlois was attending seriously to her question. "You swore to me that you were not an adulteress. And no Christian man may put his wife away save for the sole cause of adultery."

Between impatience and sudden compunction, Igraine held her peace. She could not be grateful to him, but at least he had listened to what she said. Yet it occurred to her that it was mostly his pride; even if he believed she had betrayed him, he would not want his soldiers to think that his young wife preferred another man to himself. Perhaps he would even rather condone the sin of adultery than let them think he could not keep the loyalty of a young woman.

She said, "Gorlois—" but he silenced her with a gesture.

"Enough. I have no patience to change many words with you. Once in Tintagel, there you may forget this folly at leisure. As for the Pendragon, he will have quite enough to do at war on the Saxon Shores. If you were glamoured by him, well, you are young and a woman, with small knowledge of the world or of men. I will reproach you no more; within a year or two, you will have a son to take your mind from this man who has struck your fancy."

In silence, Igraine allowed Gorlois to lift her to her horse. He must believe whatever it was that he believed, there was nothing she could say to penetrate that iron surface. Yet her mind went back stubbornly to what Viviane and the Merlin had said: that her destiny and Uther's were bound. After her dream she believed it, she *knew* why they had come back together. She had begun to accept that this was the will of the Gods. Yet here she was, riding away from Londinium with Gorlois, the alliance in ruins, and Gorlois evidently determined that Uther never set eyes on her again. Certainly with a war on the Saxon Shores Uther would have no leisure to journey to the world's end at Tintagel, and even if he could, there was no way he could make his way into that castle, which could be defended by only a few men until the sky fell. Gorlois could leave her there, and there she would stay till she was an old woman, shut up bleakly behind walls and the great chasms and crags of rock. Igraine put her cloak over her face and wept.

She would never see Uther again. All the plans of the Merlin were in wreck and ruin; she was bound to an old man she hated—she knew, now, that she hated him, which she had never before allowed herself to know—and the man she loved could think of nothing better to do than to try and bully the proud Gorlois into giving her up of his own free will! Later, she thought she must have wept all through the long journey, all the days and nights which they travelled across the moors and down through the valleys of Cornwall.

On the second night they camped and pitched tents for a proper rest. She welcomed hot food and a chance to sleep within a tent, even though she knew she could no longer avoid Gorlois's bed. She could not cry out and struggle with him, not when they slept in a tent ringed about by his soldiers. She had been his wife four years; no one alive would believe a tale of ravishment. She would not have the strength to fight him, nor would she want to lose her dignity in a sordid struggle. She set her teeth and resolved to let him do as he would—although she wished she had some of the charms which were said to protect the maidens of the Goddess. When they lay with men at the Beltane fires, they conceived only when they willed it so. It seemed too bitter, that he should beget the son he wanted when she was humbled this way, beaten down utterly.

The Merlin had said it: *You will bear Gorlois no son.* But she did not trust to the Merlin's prophecy, not now when she saw the wreck of all his plans. Cruel, scheming old man! He used her as men had always used their daughters since the Romans came, pawns who should marry this man or that as their fathers desired, chattels like a horse or a milk goat! She had found some peace with Gorlois, and that peace had been broken, cruelly and for nothing! She wept silently as she made ready for bed, resigned, despairing, not even confident enough of her own power to drive him away with angry words—she could see from his manner that he was ready to prove himself in possession of her, to drive away memories of any other man by forcing her to take heed of him in the only way he could enforce himself upon her.

His familiar hands on her, his face over her in the dark, were like those of a stranger. And yet, when he drew her to him, he was unable; limp and powerless, and although he pulled and clasped her, trying desperately to rouse himself, it came to nothing, and at last he let her go with a furious whispered curse.

"Have you put some spell upon my manhood, you accursed bitch?"

"I have not," she said, low, with contempt, "although indeed, if I knew such spells I would have been glad to do so, my strong and gallant husband. Do you expect me to weep because you cannot take me by force? Try it, and I shall lie here and laugh into your face!"

For a moment he raised himself, clenching his fist.

"Yes," she said, "strike me. It will not be the first time. And perhaps it will make you feel enough like a man that your spear will rise into action!"

With a furious oath, he turned his back on her and lay down again, but Igraine lay awake, shaking, knowing that she had had her revenge. And indeed, all the way to Cornwall, no matter how he tried, Gorlois found himself powerless to touch her, until at last Igraine began to wonder if indeed, without being aware of it, her very righteous wrath had indeed cast some enchantment on his manhood. Even then she knew, with the sure intuition of the priestess-trained, that he would never be potent with her again.

6

CORNWALL seemed more than ever at the very end of the world. In those first days, after Gorlois had left her there under guard—coldly silent now, and without a word for her, good or bad—Igraine had found herself wondering whether Tintagel existed at all in the real world anymore, or whether, like Avalon, it existed only in the mist kingdom, the fairy kingdom, bearing no relationship to the world she had visited in her one brief venture outside.

Even during this brief absence it seemed that Morgaine had grown from babe to small girl, a serious, quiet, small girl who questioned incessantly everything she saw. Morgause too had grown, her body rounding, her childish face taking on definition with its high cheekbones and long-lashed eyes under dark brows; she was, Igraine thought, beautiful, not aware that Morgause was the twin of herself at fourteen. Morgause was ecstatic with the gifts and fairings Igraine had brought her; she frisked around Igraine like a playful puppy, and around Gorlois too. She chattered to him excitedly, practiced sidelong looks, and tried to sit in his lap as if she were a child Morgaine's age. Igraine saw that Gorlois did not laugh and push her off like a puppy, but stroked the long red hair, smiling, and pinched her cheek.

"You are too big for such foolishness, Morgause," she said sharply. "Say your thanks to my lord of Cornwall and take your fairings to your room. And put away the silks, for you will not wear such things till you are grown. Don't think to play the lady here just yet!"

Morgause gathered up the pretty things and went weeping to her room. Igraine saw that Gorlois followed the girl with his eyes. She thought, appalled, *Morgause is only fourteen,* then remembered in dismay that she herself had been but a year older when she was given to Gorlois as his bride.

Later she saw them together in the hall, Morgause laying her head confidingly on Gorlois's shoulder, and saw the look in her husband's eyes. Hard anger struck her, not so much for the girl as for Gorlois. She saw that they moved uneasily apart as she came into the hall, and when Gorlois had gone away, she looked at Morgause, her eyes unsparing, until Morgause giggled uneasily and stared at the floor.

"Why are you looking at me like that, Igraine? Are you afraid that Gorlois likes me better than you?"

"Gorlois was too old for me; is he not that much older than you? With you, he thinks he would have me back as he first knew me, too young to say him nay or to look at another man. I am no longer a pliant girl but a woman with a mind of her own, and perhaps he thinks you would be easier to deal with."

"Perhaps, then," Morgause said, insolent now, "you should look to keeping your own husband content, instead of complaining that some other woman can do for him what you cannot."

Igraine raised her hand to slap the girl, then by sheer force of will, kept herself still. She said, summoning all her self-discipline, "Do you think it matters to me whom Gorlois takes to his bed? I am certain he has had his share of trollops, but I would rather my sister was not among them. I have no wish for his embraces, and if I hated you, I would give you to him willingly. But you are too young. As I was too young. And Gorlois is a Christian man; if you let him lie with you and he gets you with child, he will have no choice but to marry you off in haste to whatever man-at-arms will have used goods—these Romans are not like our own people, Morgause. Gorlois may be smitten with you, but he will not put me away and take you to wife, believe me. Among our own people, maidenhood is of no great consequence—a woman of proven fertility, swelling with a healthy child, is a most desirable wife. But it is not so with these Christians, I tell you; they will treat you as one shamed, and the man he persuades to marry you will make you suffer all your life long that he did not have the planting of the child you bear. Is that what you want, Morgause, who could marry a king if you chose? Will you throw yourself away, sister, to spite me?"

Morgause went pale. "I had no idea—" she whispered. "Oh, no, I do not want to be shamed—Igraine, forgive me."

Igraine kissed her and gave her the silver mirror and the amber necklace, and Morgause stared at her.

"But these are Gorlois's gifts—"

"I have sworn I will never again wear his gifts," she said. "They are yours, for that king the Merlin saw in your future, sister. But you must keep yourself chaste till he comes for you."

"Have no fear," Morgause said and smiled again. Igraine was glad that this reminder had caught Morgause's ambition; Morgause was cool and calculating, she would never be swayed by emotion or impulse. Igraine wished, watching her, that she too had been born without the capacity to love.

I wish I could be content with Gorlois, or that I could seek coldly—as Morgause would surely do—to rid myself of Gorlois and be Uther's queen.

Gorlois stayed at Tintagel only four days, and she was glad to see him go. He left a dozen men-at-arms at Tintagel, and when he left, he called her to him.

"You and the child will be safe here, and well guarded," he said curtly. "I go to gather the men of Cornwall against Irish raiders or Northmen— or against Uther, should he seek to come and take what is not his own, woman or castle."

"I think Uther will have too much to do in his own country for that," Igraine said, tightening her mouth against despair.

"God grant it," Gorlois said, "for we have enough enemies without him, too. But I could wish him to come, so that I might show him Cornwall is not his, as he thinks all else is his own for the taking!"

To that Igraine said nothing. Gorlois rode away with his men, and Igraine was left to set her house in order, to recover her old closeness with her child, to try to mend her broken friendship with her sister Morgause.

But the thought of Uther was always with her, busy herself as she might with domestic tasks. It was not even the real Uther who haunted her, the man she had seen in orchard and court and in the church, impulsive and a little boyish, even somewhat boorish and clumsy. *That* Uther, the Pendragon, the High King, frightened her a little—she thought she might even be a little afraid of him, as she had once been of Gorlois. When she thought of Uther the man, thought of kisses and embraces and what more he might desire of her, at times she felt that melting sweetness she had known in her dream, but at other times she was seized with a panic terror, like the ravished child who had risen the morning after her wedding, cold with fear and dread. The thought of the act of marriage seemed terrifying and even grotesque to her, as it had seemed then.

What came back to her, again and again, in the silence of the night when she lay with Morgaine sleeping at her side, or when she sat on the terrace by the sea and guided her daughter's hands in her first clumsy attempts to spin, was the *other* Uther, the Uther she had known at the ring of stones outside time and ordinary place; the priest of Atlantis, with whom she had shared the Mysteries. *That* Uther she knew she would love as her own life, that she could never fear him or dread him, and whatever happened between them, it would be a sweetness, a joy greater than she had ever known. Quite simply, when she came near him, she knew that she had discovered some lost part of herself; with him she was whole. Whatever might happen between them as ordinary man and woman, something lay beyond it which would never die or lessen in its intensity. They shared a destiny, and somehow they must fulfill it together . . . and often when she had come so far in her thoughts she would stop and stare at herself in disbelief. Was she mad, with her fancies of shared destiny and the other half of her soul? Surely the facts were simpler and less pretty. She, a married woman, a decent matron and the mother of a child, had simply grown besotted with a younger and handsomer man than her lawful husband, and had fallen into a daydream of him and thereby quarreled with the good and honorable man to whom she had been given. And she would sit and spin, gritting her teeth with frantic guilt, and wonder if her whole life was to be spent in atonement for a sin only half-consciously committed.

The spring wore away into summer, and the Beltane fires were long past. Heat spread its haze over the land, and the sea lay blue and so clear that it seemed, at times, that far away in the clouds Igraine could see the forgotten cities of Lyonnesse and Atlantis. The days had begun to shorten, and there was sometimes frost in the nights again, when Igraine heard the first far rumblings of war—the men-at-arms brought news from the market town that there had been Irish raiders on the coast, that they had burnt a village and a church and carried off one or two women, and there were armies, not those commanded by Gorlois, marching west into the Summer Country and north to Wales.

"What armies?" Igraine asked the man, and he said, "I don't know, lady, for I didn't see them; those who did said they bore eagles like the Roman legions of the old days, which is impossible. But he said, also, that they bore a red dragon on their banner."

Uther! thought Igraine, with a pang, *Uther is near, and he will not even know where I am!* Only then did she ask for news of Gorlois, and the man told her that her husband, too, was in the Summer Country, and that the armies were making some sort of council there.

She gazed long into her old bronze mirror that night, wishing that it were the scrying glass of a priestess, that could see what was happening far away!

She longed to take counsel with Viviane, or with the Merlin. They had wrought all this trouble—had they abandoned her now? Why did they not come to see how their plans lay all in wreck? Had they found some other woman of the correct lineage, to throw *her* into Uther's path, to bear this king who would one day heal all the land and all the warring peoples?

But no word or message came from Avalon, and Igraine was not allowed by the men-at-arms even to ride to the market town; Gorlois, so the men said respectfully, had forbidden it because of the state of the country. Once, looking from the high window, she saw a rider approaching, and on the inner causeway stop to parley with the head man of the guards. The rider looked angry, and seemed to Igraine to look up at the walls in frustration, but finally he turned his back and rode away, and Igraine wondered if this had been a messenger sent to her whom the guardsman would not allow access.

She was, then, a prisoner in her husband's castle. He might say, or even believe, that he had placed her there for her own protection, against the turmoil in the land, but the truth was otherwise: his jealousy had led him to imprison her here. She tested her theory a few days later, calling the head of the guards to her.

"I wish to send a message to my sister, asking her to come and visit," she said. "Will you send a man with a message to Avalon?"

It seemed to her that the man avoided her eyes. He said, "Well, now, lady, I can't do that. My lord of Cornwall said very explicitly that all of us were to stay right here and protect Tintagel in case of a siege."

"Can't you hire a rider in the village then, to make the journey, if I paid the man well?"

"My lord wouldn't like that, lady. I'm sorry."

"I see," she said, and sent him away. She had not yet come to the point of desperation at which she would try to bribe one of the men. But the more she pondered this, the angrier she grew. How dared Gorlois imprison her here, she who was sister to the Lady of Avalon? She was his wife, not his slave or servant! At last she resolved on a desperate step.

She had not been trained in the Sight; she had used it a little, spontaneously, as a girl, but except for her brief vision of Viviane, she had never used it at all as a grown woman, and since her vision of Gorlois as death-doomed she had closed herself firmly to further visions. *That* one, the Gods knew, had come to nothing, for Gorlois was still very much alive. Yet somehow, she supposed, she might now manage to see what was to happen. It was a dangerous step—she had been reared on tales of what befell those who meddled in arts to which they were not trained, and at first she sought to compromise. As the first leaves began to turn yellow, she called the chief of the men-at-arms to her again.

"I cannot stay here forever, shut like a rat in a trap," she said. "I must go to the market fair. We must buy dyes and there is need of a new milk goat, and of needles and pins, and many things for the winter which comes."

"Lady, I have no orders to let you go abroad," he said, and turned his eyes from her. "I take my orders from my lord, and I have heard nothing from him."

"Then I will stay here and send one of my women," she said. "Ettarr or Isotta shall go, and the lady Morgause with her—will that suffice?"

He looked relieved, as she had hit upon a solution to save him from disobeying his lord; for indeed it was necessary that someone from the household should visit a fair before the winter, and he knew it as well as she did. It was outrageous to keep the lady of the house from what was, after all, one of her proper duties.

Morgause was wildly happy when Igraine told her she was to go. *Small wonder,* Igraine thought. *None of us has been abroad all this summer. The very shepherds are freer than we, for they at least take the sheep to graze on the mainland!* She watched, frankly envious, as Morgause put on the crimson cloak Gorlois had given her, and, with the chaperonage of two men-at-arms as well as both Ettarr and Isotta and two of the kitchen women to carry packages and goods, set forth on her pony. She watched from the causeway, holding Morgaine by the hand, until they were out of sight, and felt that she could not endure to reenter the castle which had become a prison to her.

"Mother," Morgaine asked at her side, "why can we not go to the market with Auntie?"

"Because your father does not wish us to go, my poppet."

"Why does not he want us to go? Does he think we will be naughty?"

Igraine laughed and said, "Indeed, I think that is what he believes, daughter."

Morgaine was silent—a small, quiet, self-possessed little creature, her dark hair now long enough to plait into a little braid halfway down her shoulder blades, but so fine and straight that it slipped out into loose elf locks around her shoulders. Her eyes were dark and serious, and her eyebrows straight and level, so heavy already that they were the most definite feature of her face. *A little fairy woman,* Igraine thought, *not human at all; a pixie.* She was no larger than the shepherd girl's babe who was not yet quite two, though Morgaine was nearing four, and spoke as clearly and thoughtfully as a great girl of eight or nine. Igraine caught up the child in her arms and hugged her.

"My little changeling!"

Morgaine suffered the caress, and even kissed her mother in return, which surprised Igraine, for Morgaine was not a demonstrative child, but soon she began to stir fretfully—she was not the kind of child who wished to be held for long; she would do everything for herself. She had even begun to dress herself and buckle her own shoes on her feet. Igraine set her down and Morgaine walked sedately at her side back into the castle.

Igraine sat down at her loom, telling Morgaine to take her spindle and sit beside her. The little girl obeyed, and Igraine, setting her shuttle in motion, stopped for a moment to watch her. She was neat-handed and precise; her thread was clumsy, but she twirled the spindle deftly as if it were a toy, twisting it between her small fingers. If her hands were bigger, she would already spin as well as Morgause. After a time Morgaine said, "I do not remember my father, Mother. Where is he?"

"He is away with his soldiers in the Summer Country, daughter."

"When will he come home?"

"I do not know, Morgaine. Do you want him to come home?"

She considered a moment. "No," she said, "because when he was here—I remember it just a little—I had to go sleep in Auntie's room and it was dark there and I was afraid at first. Of course I was very little then," she added solemnly, and Igraine concealed a smile. After a minute she went on, "And I do not want him to come home because he made you cry."

Well, Viviane had said it; women did not give babes enough credit for understanding what was going on around them.

"Why do you not have another baby, Mother? Other women have a baby as soon as the older one is weaned, and I am already four. I heard Isotta say you should have given me a baby brother. I think I would like to have a little brother to play with, or even a little sister."

Igraine actually started to say, "Because your father Gorlois—" and then stopped herself. No matter how adult Morgaine might sound, she was only four years old, and Igraine could not confide such things to her. "Because the Mother Goddess did not see fit to send me a son, child."

Father Columba came out on the terrace. He said austerely, "You should not talk to the child of Goddesses and superstition. Gorlois wishes her to be reared as a good Christian maiden. Morgaine, your mother did not have a son because your father was angry with her, and God withheld a son to punish her for her sinful will."

Not for the first time, Igraine felt that she would like to throw her shuttle at this black crow of ill omen. Had Gorlois confessed to this man, was he aware of all that had passed between them? She had often wondered that, in the moons that had passed, but she had never had any excuse to ask and knew he would not tell her if she did. Suddenly Morgaine stood up and made a face at the priest, "Go away, old man," she said clearly. "I don't like you. You have made my mother cry. My mother knows more than you do, and if she says that it is the Goddess who did not send her a child, I will believe what she says, and not what you say, because my mother does not tell lies!"

Father Columba said angrily to Igraine, "Now you see what comes of your willfulness, my lady? That child should be beaten. Give her to me and I will punish her for her disrespect!"

And at this all Igraine's rage and rebelliousness exploded. Father Columba had advanced toward Morgaine, who stood without flinching. Igraine stepped between them. "If you lay a hand on my daughter, priest," she said, "I will kill you where you stand. My husband brought you here, and I cannot send you away, but on the day you come into my presence again, I will spit on you. Get out of my sight!"

He stood his ground. "My lord Gorlois entrusted me with the spiritual well-being of this entire household, my lady, and I am not given to pride, so I will forgive what you have said."

"I care as little for your forgiveness as for that of the billy goat! Get out of my sight or I will call my serving-women and have you put out. Unless you want to be carried out of here, old man, get from here and do not presume to come into my presence until I send for you—and that will be when the sun rises over western Ireland! *Go!*"

The priest stared at her blazing eyes, at her uplifted hand, and scuttled out of the room.

Now that she had committed an act of open rebellion, she was paralyzed at her own temerity. But at least it had freed her from the priest, and freed Morgaine, too. She would not have her daughter brought up to feel shame at her own womanhood.

Morgause came back late that night from the fair, having chosen all her purchases carefully—Igraine knew she could not have done better herself—with a lump of loaf sugar for Morgaine to suck, which she had bought with her own pocket money, and full of tales from the marketplace. The sisters sat until midnight in Igraine's room, talking long after Morgaine had fallen asleep, sucking on her sugar candy, her small face sticky and her hands still clutching it. Igraine took it away and wrapped it for her, and came back to ask further news of Morgause.

This is ignoble, that I must hear news from the marketplace about the doings of my own husband!

"There is a great gathering in the Summer Country," Morgause said. "They say that the Merlin has made peace between Lot and Uther. They say, too, that Ban of Less Britain has allied with them, and is sending them horses brought from Spain—" She stumbled a little over the name. "Where is that, Igraine? Is it in Rome?"

"No, but it is far in the south, nearer than we to Rome by many, many leagues," Igraine told her.

"There was a battle with the Saxons, and Uther was there with the dragon banner," Morgause told her. "I heard a harper telling it like a ballad, how the Duke of Cornwall had imprisoned his lady in Tintagel—" In the darkness Igraine could see that the girl's eyes were wide, her lips parted. "Igraine, tell me true, *was* Uther your lover?"

"He was not," Igraine said, "but Gorlois believed he was, and that is why he quarreled with Uther. He did not believe me when I told him the truth." Her throat choked tight with tears. "I wish now that it had been the truth."

"They say King Lot is handsomer than Uther," Morgause said, "and that he is seeking a wife, and it is whispered in gossip that he would challenge Uther to be High King, if he thought he could do so safely. Is he handsomer than Uther? Is Uther as godlike as they say, Igraine?"

She shook her head. "I don't know, Morgause."

"Why, they say he was your lover—"

"I do not care what they say," Igraine interrupted her, "but as for that, I suppose as the world reckons such things, both of them are fine-looking men, Lot dark, and Uther blond like a Northman. But it was not for his fair face that I thought Uther the better man."

"What was it then?" asked Morgause, bright and inquisitive, and Igraine sighed, knowing the young girl would not understand. But the hunger to share at least a little of what she felt, and could never say to anyone, drove her to say, "Why—I hardly know. Only—it was as if I had known him from the beginning of the world, as if he could never be strange to me, whatever he did or whatever befell between us."

"But if he never so much as kissed you . . ."

"It does not matter," Igraine said wearily, and then at last, weeping, said what she had known for a long time now, and had been unwilling to admit. "Even should I never again look upon his face in this life, I am bound to him and I shall be so bound until I die. And I cannot believe the Goddess would have wrought this upheaval in my life, if I was meant never again to see him."

By the dim light she could see that Morgause was looking at her with awe and a measure of envy, as if in the younger girl's eyes Igraine had suddenly become the heroine of some old romantic tale. She wanted to say to her, no, it is not like that, it is not romantic at all, it is simply what has happened, but she knew there was no way to say that, for Morgause had not the experience to tell romance from this sort of ultimate reality, rock-hard at the bottom of imagination or fantasy. *Let her think it romance, then, if it pleases her,* Igraine thought, and realized that this kind of reality would never come to Morgause: it was a different world she lived in.

Now she had taken the step of alienating the priest who was Gorlois's man, and another step in confessing to Morgause that she loved Uther. Viviane had said something of worlds drawing apart one from the other, and it seemed to Igraine as if she had begun to dwell on some world apart from the ordinary one in which Gorlois perhaps had a right to expect that she be his faithful chattel, servant, slave—his wife. Only Morgaine now bound her to that world. She looked at the sticky-handed, sleeping child, her dark hair scattered wildly around her, and at her wide-eyed younger sister, and wondered if, at the call of this thing that had happened to her, she would abandon even these last hostages which held her to the real world.

The thought gave great pain, but inside herself she whispered, "Yes. Even that."

AND SO THE NEXT STEP, which she had feared so greatly, became simple to her.

She lay awake that night between Morgause and her child, trying to decide what she must do. Should she run away and trust to Uther's part in the vision to find her? Almost at once she rejected that thought. Should she send Morgause, with secret instructions to flee to Avalon and bear a message that she was imprisoned? No; if it was common talk—a ballad in the marketplace—that she was imprisoned, her sister would have come to her if she thought that it would help. And ever at her heart gnawed the silent voice of doubt and despair. Her vision had been a false one . . . or perhaps, when she had not flung all aside for Uther, they had abandoned the plan, found another woman for Uther, and the saving of Britain, as, should the high priestess be ill for the great Celebration, they would choose another for her part.

Toward morning, as the sky was already paling, she fell into a dazed sleep. And there, when she had ceased to hope for it, she found guidance. Just as she woke, it was as if a voice said inside her mind, *Rid yourself for this one day of the child, and the maiden, and you will know what to do.*

The day dawned clear and shining, and as they broke their fast on goat's cheese and new-baked bread, Morgause looked at the shining sea and said, "I am so weary of staying withindoors—I did not know till yesterday at the market how weary I am grown of this house!"

"Take Morgaine, then, and go out for the day with the shepherd women," Igraine suggested. "She too would like to go abroad, I imagine."

She wrapped up slices of meat and bread for them; to Morgaine it was like a festival. Igraine saw them go, hoping now for some way to evade the watchful eyes of Father Columba, for, although he followed her will and had not spoken to her, his eyes followed her everywhere. But at midmorning, as she sat weaving, he came into her presence and said, "Lady—"

She did not look up at him. "I bade you stay away from me, priest. Complain of me to Gorlois when he comes home if you will, but do not speak to me."

"One of Gorlois's men has been hurt in a fall from the cliffs. His comrades think he is dying, and have bidden me to come to him. You need not be afraid; you will be properly guarded."

She had known that—it had never occurred to her that, if she could get rid of the priest, she might somehow make her escape. In any case, where could she go? This was Gorlois's country and none of his people would shelter an escaped wife from his wrath. Simple flight had never been her intention. "Go and the Devil take you, so that you come not into my presence," and turned her back.

"If you presume to curse me, woman—"

"Why should I waste my breath with a curse? I would as willingly bid you Godspeed to your own heaven, and may your God find more pleasure in your company than I do."

Once he had gone, hurrying on his little donkey across the causeway, she knew why she had felt she must rid herself of the priest. In his own way he was an initiate of the Mysteries, though they were not her Mysteries, and he would be quick to know and to disapprove of what she meant to do. She went to Morgause's room and found the silver mirror. Then she went down to the kitchens to ask the serving-women to make a fire in her room. They stared, for the day was not cold, but she repeated it as if it were the most normal thing in the world, and fetched herself a few other things from the kitchen: salt and a little oil, a bit of bread and a small flask of wine— these, no doubt, the women thought she wanted for her noon meal—and she took a bit of cheese too to conceal her intent, and later flung it to the sea gulls.

Outside in the garden she found lavender flowers and managed to find a few wild-rose hips. Boughs of juniper, too, she cut with her own small knife, only a few symbolic branches, and a small piece of hazel. Once in her room again she drew the bolt and stripped off her garments, standing naked and shivering before the fire. She had never done this, and knew Viviane would not approve, for those who were unskilled in the arts of sorcery could cause trouble for themselves by meddling with it. But with these things, she knew, she could conjure the Sight even if she had it not.

She cast the juniper on the fire, and as the smoke rose, bound the branch of hazel to her forehead. She laid fruit and flowers before the fire, then touched salt and oil to her breast, took a bite of the bread and a sip of the wine, then, trembling, laid the silver mirror where the firelight shone on it and, from the barrel which was kept for washing the women's hair, poured clear rainwater across the silver surface of the mirror.

She whispered, "By common things and by uncommon, by water and fire, salt and oil and wine, by fruit and flowers together, I beg you, Goddess, let me see my sister Viviane."

Slowly, the surface of the water stirred. Igraine, in a sudden icy wind, shivered, wondering for a moment if the spell would fail, if her sorcery were blasphemy as well. The blurred face forming in the mirror was first her own, then slowly it shifted, changed, was the awesome face of the Goddess, with the rowanberries bound about her brow. And then, as it cleared and steadied, Igraine saw; but not, as she had hoped and foreseen, into a living, speaking face. She looked into a room which she knew. It had once been the chamber of her mother at Avalon, and there were women there, in the dark robes of priestesses, and at first she looked in vain for her sister, for the women were coming and going, and moving back and forth, and there was confusion in the chamber. And then she saw her sister, Viviane; she looked weary and ill and drawn, and she was walking, walking back and forth, leaning on the arm of one of the other priestesses, and Igraine knew, in horror, what she saw. For Viviane, in her pale robe of undyed wool, was heavy with child, her belly swollen, her face dragged down with suffering, and ever she walked and walked, as, Igraine remembered, the midwives had made her do when she was in labor with Morgaine. . . .

No, no! Oh, Mother Ceridwen, blessed Goddess, no . . . our mother so died, but Viviane was so sure she was past childbearing . . . and now she will die, she cannot bear a child at her age and live . . . why, when she knew she had conceived, did she not take some potion to rid her of the child? This is the wreck of all their plans, then, it is the end. . . .

I too have thrown my life into ruin with a dream . . . and then Igraine was ashamed of herself that she could think of her own misery when Viviane was to lie down in childbed from which it could hardly be hoped that she would ever rise again. In horror, weeping in dread, she could not even turn from the mirror, and then Viviane raised her head, looking past the head of the priestess on whose arm she leaned, and into her dulled eyes, drawn with anguish, came recognition and tenderness. Igraine could not hear her, but it was as if Viviane spoke directly to her mind.

Little girl . . . little sister . . . Grainné . . .

Igraine wanted to cry out to her, in sorrow and grief and fear, but she could not lay her own weight of sorrows upon Viviane now. She poured all her heart into a single outcry.

I hear you, my mother, my sister, my priestess, and my goddess. . . .

Igraine, I tell you, even in this hour do not lose hope, do not despair! There is a pattern to all our sufferings, I have seen it . . . do not despair . . . and for a moment, her hair rising on her forearms, Igraine actually felt on her cheek a light touch, like the lightest of kisses, and Viviane whispered, "Little sister . . ." and then Igraine saw her sister's face contorted with pain and she fell as if swooning into the arms of the priestess, and a wind ruffled the water of the mirror, and Igraine saw her own face, blurred with weeping, looking out through the water. She shivered, clutching some garment, anything to warm her, and flung the sorcerous mirror into the fire; then she threw herself down on her bed and wept.

Viviane told me not to despair. But how can I do other than despair, when she is dying?

She lay there, weeping herself into a stupor. At last, when she could not cry another tear, she rose wearily and washed her face in cold water. Viviane was dying, perhaps even dead. But her last words had been to bid Igraine not lose hope. She dressed herself and hung about her throat the moonstone Viviane had given her. And then, with a little stirring of the air before her, she saw Uther.

This time she knew it was a Sending, and not the man himself. Nothing human, certainly not Uther Pendragon, could have come into her guarded chamber without some man seeing and stopping him. He wore a heavy plaid about him, but on his arms—and this is why she knew it no dream—he wore the serpents she had seen when she dreamed of his life in Atlantis. Only they were not now golden torques, but live serpents, which raised their heads, hissing; only she did not fear them.

"My beloved," he said, and although it was the very tone of his voice, the room was silent in the light of the flickering fire, and through the whispered voice she heard the small crackling of the juniper twigs. "I will come to you at Midwinter. I swear it, I will come to you, whatever may bar the way. Make ready for me at Midwinter—"

And then she was alone, with only the sun in the room, and the reflection of the sea outside, and in the courtyard below, the laughing voices of Morgause and her little daughter.

Igraine drew a long breath, calmly drank the rest of the wine. On an empty stomach, fasting, she felt it rise to her head with a sort of dizzy elation. Then she went quietly down the stairs to await the news she knew would come.

7

What happened first was that Gorlois came home.

Still flustered with the elation of that moment of vision—and frightened, for she had never really thought that Viviane could die, and in spite of the words of hope, she could not imagine, now, that Viviane could live—Igraine had expected something else; some magical news of Uther, or word that Gorlois was dead and that she was free. Gorlois himself, dust-covered and hungry and scowling, was half calculated to make Igraine think her vision no more than self-deception or a delusion of the Evil One.

Well, if it is so, there is good in that too, for it would mean that my sister lives and my vision of her was a delusion born of my own fears. And so she welcomed Gorlois calmly, with food and a bath and clean dry clothes, and only pleasant words. Let him think, if he would, that she was repenting her harshness and trying to curry his favor again. It no longer mattered to her what Gorlois thought or what he did. She no longer hated him or resented the early years of misery and despair. Her sufferings had made her ready for what would come after. She served Gorlois his food and drink, saw to the housing of his men as was suitable, and forbore to question him. She brought Morgaine for a moment, washed and combed and pretty, for her curtsey to her father, then had Isotta take her away to bed.

Gorlois sighed, pushing away his plate. "She grows good-looking; but she is like a fairy child, one of the folk of the hollow hills. Where came she by such blood? There is none of it among my people."

"But my mother was of the old blood," Igraine said, "and Viviane, too. I think her father must have been one of the fairy folk."

Gorlois shivered and said, "And you don't even know who fathered her—one thing that the Romans did well was to make an end of those folk. I fear no armed man that I can slay, but I fear those underground folk of the hollow hills, with their enchanted circles and their food that can lead you to wander a hundred years in enchantment, and their elf bolts which come out of the dark and strike a man down, unshriven, to send him to the hells. . . . The Devil made them for the death of Christians, and it is the work of God to kill them, I think!"

Igraine thought of the herbs and simples which the women of the fairy folk brought even to their conquerors for healing; of the poison arrows that could bring down game which could be taken no other way; of her own mother, born of the fairy people, and of Viviane's unknown father. And Gorlois, like the Romans, would make an end of these simple people in the name of his God? "Well," she said, "that must be as God wills, I suppose."

"Morgaine perhaps should be brought up in a convent of holy women, so that the great evil she has inherited from your old blood will never taint her," Gorlois mused. "When she is old enough, we will see to it. A holy man told me once that women bear the blood of their mothers, and so it has been since the days of Eve, that what is within women, who are filled with sin, cannot be overcome by a woman-child; but that a son will bear his father's blood even as Christ was made in the image of God his father. So if we have a son, Igraine, we need not fear that he will show the blood of the old evil folk of the hills."

A surge of anger rippled through Igraine, but she had pledged herself not to anger him. "That too must be as your God wills." For she knew, if he had forgotten, that he would never touch her again as a man touches a woman. It did not matter now what he said or did. "Tell me what has brought you home so unexpectedly, my husband."

"Uther, of course," Gorlois said. "There has been a great kingmaking on Dragon Island, which is near to Glastonbury of the priests—I know not why the priests allow it to stand there, for it is a heathen place, and there they have paid homage to their Horned One of the woods, and raised serpents, and such foolishness as it is not fitting should be done in a Christian land. King Leodegranz, who is king of the Summer Country, stands with me and has refused to make compact with Uther. Leodegranz likes Uther no more than I, but he will not make war on the Pendragon now; it is not fitting that we should war among ourselves with the Saxons gathering on the eastern shores. If the Scots come this summer, we will be caught between hammer and anvil. And now Uther has sent an ultimatum—that I must put my Cornishmen under his command, or he will come and force me to. And so I am here—we can hold Tintagel forever, if we must. But I have warned Uther that if he sets foot in Cornwall I will fight him. Leodegranz has made truce with Uther, until the Saxons are gone from this country, but I would not."

"In God's name, that is folly," Igraine said, "for Leodegranz is right —the Saxons could not stand, if all men of Britain stood together. If you quarrel among yourselves, the Saxons can attack you one kingdom at a time, and before long all Britain will serve the Horse Gods!"

Gorlois pushed his dishes aside. "I do not expect a woman to know anything of honor, Igraine. Come to bed."

SHE HAD THOUGHT it would not matter now what he did to her, that she was past caring; but she had not been prepared for the despairing struggle of Gorlois's pride. At the last he had beaten her again, cursing. "You have put an enchantment on my manhood, you damned witch!"

When he had fallen into exhausted sleep, Igraine, her bruised face throbbing, lay awake, weeping quietly at his side. So this was the reward of her meekness, just as it had been the reward of her hard words? Now indeed she was justified in hating him, and in a way she was relieved to feel no guilt for her loathing. Suddenly, and with violence, she hoped Uther would kill him.

He rode away the next morning at daylight, taking all but a scant half-dozen men who were left to defend Tintagel. From the talk she heard in the hall before they went, she knew he was hoping to ambush Uther's invading army as it came down from the moors into the valley. And all this for what he called honor; he would deprive all Britain of her High King, leave the land naked like a woman to be ravished by the Saxon hordes—all because he was not man enough for his wife and feared that Uther would be.

When he had gone, the days dragged along, rainy and silent. Then the first frosts came, with snow sweeping across the moors, and even the moors themselves were out of sight except on the clearest of days. She longed for news; she felt like a badger trapped in a winter burrow.

Midwinter. Uther had said he would come to her at Midwinter—but now she began to wonder if it had been only a dream. As the autumn days lagged by, dark and cold, she began to doubt the vision, yet she knew that any attempt to repeat it, to bring herself reassurance, would not help. She had been taught in her childhood that such dependence on magical art was wrong. It was allowed to search for a glimpse of light in the darkness, and that she had done; but magic must not become a child's leading strings for walking, lest she become unable to take a single step without the need for supernatural guidance.

I have never been able to rely on myself, she thought bitterly. When she had been a child, she had looked for guidance to Viviane; but no sooner than she was grown to womanhood, she had been married to Gorlois, and he felt that she should look to him in all things, or in his absence turn to Father Columba for constant counsel.

So now, knowing she had the chance to begin to do her own thinking, she turned inward upon herself. She schooled her daughter in spinning, and began to teach her sister Morgause how to weave in colors; hoarded her supply of food, for it began to look as if the winter might be colder and longer than usual; and listened ravenously to such small scraps of news as came to her from the shepherds when they went to market, or from any travellers—but there were few of these, as the winter closed down over Tintagel.

It was past Samhain when a peddler woman came to the castle, wrapped in rags and torn shawls, weary and footsore. Her feet were bound in rags and she herself was none too clean, but Igraine brought her in and gave her a place by the fire and a ladle of rich goat's-meat stew with the stale bread which would have been her ordinary portion. When she saw that the woman was limping from a stone bruise, she asked the cook to heat some water, and found a cleaner rag to bind it. She bought two needles from the woman's pack—they were coarse enough, she had better ones, but they would do to teach Morgaine her first stitches. Then, feeling she had earned it, she asked the woman if there was any news from the North.

"Soldiers, lady," said the old woman, sighing, "and Saxons gathering on the northern roads, too, and a battle . . . and Uther with his dragon banner, Saxons to the north of him, and, they say, the Duke of Cornwall against him to the south. Battle everywhere, even to the Holy Isle—"

Igraine demanded, "You have come from the Holy Isle?"

"Yes, lady, I was benighted by the lakes there, and lost in the mist. . . . The priests gave me dry bread and bade me come to mass and be shriven, but what sins has an old woman like me? My sins are all done and over, all forgotten and forgiven and not even regretted anymore," she said with her thin laughter; it seemed to Igraine that she had not much wit, and what little she had, had been scattered by hardship and solitude and long wandering. "And indeed there is little opportunity for the old and poor to sin, except to doubt God's goodness, and if God cannot understand why we doubt that, then he is not as wise as his priests think, heh heh heh . . . but I had no taste to listen to mass and it was colder inside their church than without, so I wandered in the mist and the fog, and then I saw a boat, and somehow I came to the Holy Isle, and there the women of the Lady gave me food and fire, like you . . . heh heh heh. . . ."

"You saw the Lady?" Igraine demanded, leaning forward and looking into the woman's face. "Oh, give me news of her, she is my sister. . . ."

"Aye, she said as much to me, that her sister was wife to the Duke of Cornwall, if the Duke of Cornwall still lived, which she did not know about, heh heh heh. . . . Oh, aye, she gave me a message for you, that is why I came here through moors and rocks where my poor feet were mangled by all the stones, heh heh heh . . . now what did she say to me, poor me, I can't remember, I think I lost the message in the mists around the Holy Isle, the priests, you know, they told me there was no Holy Isle, not never no more, they said, God had sunk it in the sea and if I thought I had been entertained there it was only witchcraft and the delusions of the devil. . . ." She paused, bent and cackling; Igraine waited.

Finally she asked, "Tell me of the Lady of Avalon. Did you see her?"

"Oh, aye, I saw her, not like you she is, but like a fairy woman, little and dark. . . ." The woman's eyes brightened and then cleared. "Now I mind the message. She said, tell my sister Igraine that she should remember her dreams and not lose hope, and I laughed at that, heh heh heh, what good are dreams, except perhaps to you ladies in your great houses, not much good to those of us who wander the roads in the fog. . . . Ah, yes, this too: she was delivered of a fine son at harvesttime, and she bade me say that she was well beyond all hopes and expectations, and that she had named the boy Galahad."

Igraine let out a long sigh of relief. So Viviane had indeed, against all hope, survived childbed.

The peddler woman went on, "She also said, heh heh heh, that he was a king's son and that it was fitting that one king's son should serve another. . . . Does this mean anything to you, my lady? It sounds like more dreams and moon shadows, heh heh heh. . . ." And she collapsed into giggling, hunched in her rags, spreading her thin hands to the warmth of the fire.

But Igraine knew the meaning of the message. *One king's son should serve another.* So Viviane had indeed borne a son to King Ban of Less Britain, after the rite of the Great Marriage. And if, in the prophecy she and the Merlin had made, Igraine should bear a son to Uther, High King of Britain, one should serve the other. For a moment she felt herself trembling on the edge of the same hysterical laughter as the demented old woman's. *The bride is not yet brought to bed and here we make arrangement for the fostering of the sons!*

In her heightened state, Igraine saw these children, the born and the unborn, crowding round her like shadows; was Viviane's son Galahad to be the dark twin, the bane of her unborn son by Uther? It seemed to Igraine that she could see them in the flickering of the fire: a dark, slender lad with Viviane's eyes; a stripling with shining hair like a Northman's . . . and then, flashing in the firelight, she saw the Holy Regalia of the Druids, kept now at Avalon since the Romans burned the sacred groves—dish and cup and sword and spear, gleaming and flashing to the four elements: dish of earth, cup of water, sword of fire, and the spear or wand of air . . . she thought, drowsily, stirring as the fire flashed and flickered, that there was a piece of the regalia for each of them. *How fortunate.*

Fiercely she blinked, drawing herself upright. The fire had died to coals; the old peddler woman slept, her feet tucked under the shawls and rags, as close as she could roll herself to the fire. The hall was all but empty. Her waiting-woman drowsed on a bench, wrapped tightly in shawl and cloak; the other serving folk had gone to bed. Had she slept here half the night by the fire and dreamed it all? She roused the sleeping waiting-woman, who grumbled off to her own bed. Leaving the old peddler woman to sleep by the fire, Igraine crept shivering to her own room, crawling in beside Morgaine and clutching the child tight, as if to ward off fantasies and fear.

WINTER SET IN, then, in earnest. There was not much wood for fuel at Tintagel, only a kind of rock which would burn, but it smoked evilly and blackened doors and ceilings. Sometimes they had to burn dried seaweed, which made the whole castle stink of dead fish like the sea at low tide. And at last rumor began to speak of Uther's armies, drawing near to Tintagel, ready to cross the great moors.

Under ordinary conditions, Uther's army could beat Gorlois's men into submission. *But if they are ambushed? Uther does not know the country!* He would feel himself threatened enough by the rocky and unfamiliar terrain, knowing Gorlois's armies would be massed near Tintagel. Uther would not be expecting a nearer ambush!

She could do nothing but wait. It was a woman's fate to sit at home, in castle or cot—it had been so since the Romans came. Before that, the Celtic Tribes had followed the counsel of their women, and far to the north there had been an island of women warriors who made weapons and tutored the war chiefs in the use of arms. . . .

Igraine lay awake night after night, thinking of her husband and of her lover. *If,* she thought, *you can call a man your lover when you have never exchanged a single kiss.* Uther had sworn he would come to her at Midwinter, but how could he cross the moors and break through the trap of Gorlois, lying in wait for him . . . ?

If only she were a trained sorceress or a priestess like Viviane. She had been reared on tales of the evil involved in using sorcery to enforce one's own will on the Gods. Was it, then, a good thing to allow Uther to be waylaid and his men murdered? She told herself Uther would have spies and scouts and needed no woman's help. Still she felt, disconsolate, that there must be something better for her to do than to sit and wait.

A few days before Midwinter-night, a storm blew up and raged for two days, so fiercely that Igraine knew that northward, on the moors, nothing which was not burrowed like a rabbit in its hole could possibly live. Even safely within the castle, people crouched near the few fires and listened, trembling, to the raging of the wind. During the day it was so dark, with snow and sleet, that Igraine could not even see to spin. The supply of rushlights was so limited that she did not dare exhaust it further, for there was still a long weight of winter to bear, so most of the time they sat in the dark, and Igraine tried to remember old stories from Avalon, to keep Morgaine amused and quiet and Morgause from fretting with boredom and weariness.

But when at last the child and the young girl had fallen asleep, Igraine sat wrapped in her cloak before the remnants of the small fire, too tense to lie down, knowing that if she did, she would lie wakeful, staring with aching eyes into the darkness, trying to send her thoughts over the leagues that lay between . . . where? To Gorlois, to find where his treachery had led? For it was treachery: he had sworn alliance with Uther as his High King, and then, because of his own jealousy and mistrust, broken his word.

Or to Uther, trying to make camp on these unfamiliar moors, battered by the storm, lost, blinded?

How could she reach Uther? She gathered to herself all the memories of what small training she had had in magic when she was a girl in Avalon. Body and soul, she had been taught, were not firmly bonded; in sleep the soul left the body and went to the country of dreams, where all was illusion and folly, and sometimes, in the Druid-trained, to the country of truth, where Merlin's leading had taken her in dream that one time.

. . . Once, when Morgaine was being born, and the pains seemed to have gone on forever, she had briefly left her body, seen herself lying down below, a racked thing fussed over by the midwives and encouraged by her women, while she floated, free of pain and elated, somewhere above; then someone had bent over her, urgently telling her that now she must work harder, for they could see the crown of the baby's head, and she had come back to renewed pain and fierce effort, and she had forgotten. But if she could do it then, she could do it now. Shivering in her cloak, Igraine stared at the fire, and willed herself, abruptly, to be *elsewhere*. . . .

She had done it. She seemed to stand before herself, her whole awareness sharply focused. The main change was that she could no longer hear the wild wailing of the storm outside the walls of the castle. She did not look back—she had been told that when you left your body, you must never look back, for the body will draw back the soul—but somehow she could see without eyes, all round her, and knew that her body was still sitting motionless before the dying fire. Now that she had done it she felt frightened, thinking, *I should mend the fire first*—but she knew if she went back into her body she would never have the courage to try this again.

She thought of Morgaine, the living bond between herself and Gorlois —even though he now rejected it, spoke scathingly of the child, still the bond was there, and she could find Gorlois if she sought him. Even as the thought formed in her mind, she was . . . elsewhere.

. . . Where was she? There was the flare of a small lamp, and by its fitful light she saw her husband, surrounded by a cluster of heads: men huddled together in one of the small stone huts on the moors.

Gorlois was saying, "I have fought beside Uther for many years, under Ambrosius, and if I know him at all, he will count on courage and surprise.

His people do not know our Cornish weather, and it will not occur to them that if the sun sets in raging storm, it will clear soon after midnight; so they will not move till the sun rises, but he will be out and about the moment the sun is above the horizon, hoping to fall on us while it is still early. But if we can surround his camp in those hours between the clearing of the sky and the sunrise, then as they break camp we can surprise them. They will be prepared for a march, not a battle. With just a little luck we can take them before they have their weapons well out of the sheath! Once Uther's army is cut to pieces, if he himself is not killed, he will at least turn tail and get out of Cornwall, never to return." By the dim lamp, Igraine saw Gorlois bare his teeth like an animal. "And if he is killed, his armies will scatter like a beehive when someone kills their queen!"

Igraine felt herself shrink back; even bodiless, a wraith, it seemed that Gorlois *must* see her hovering there. And indeed, he raised his head and frowned, brushing at his cheek. "I felt a draught—it's cold in here," he muttered.

"And how could it be otherwise? It's cold here as the pit, with the snow raging like this," one of his men growled—but even before he got the words out, Igraine was away from there, hovering in bodiless limbo, shivering, resisting the strong pull to return to Tintagel. She longed for the feel of flesh, of fire, not to go wandering between worlds, like some flittering wraith of the dead. . . .

How could she come to Uther, to warn him? There was no bond between them; she had never exchanged with him so much as a kiss of passion, which would bind their bodies of flesh and so bind the bodiless spirit she was now. Gorlois had accused her of adultery; frantic, Igraine wished again that it were so. She was blind in the dark, bodiless, nowhere; she knew that the flicker of a thought would take her back to the room at Tintagel where her body, cramped and icy cold, slumped before the dead fire. She fought to remain in this deathly blind darkness, struggling, praying wordlessly, *Let me come to Uther,* while knowing that the curious laws of the world she was in now made it impossible; in this body she had no bond with Uther.

But my bond with Uther is stronger than the bond of flesh because it has endured for more lives than one, Igraine felt herself arguing with something impalpable, as if appealing to a higher judge than whatever it was that made the laws for this life. The darkness seemed to press on her now, and she felt that she could not breathe, that somewhere below her the body she had abandoned was chilled, iced over, breath failing. Something in her cried out, *Return, return, Uther is a grown man, he does not need you to care for him,* and she answered herself, struggling, fighting to stay out where she was, *He is only a man, he is not proof against treachery!*

Now in the pressing darkness there was a deeper darkness, and Igraine knew she looked not on her own invisible self, but on some Other. Chilling, trembling, racked, she did not hear with her bodily ears, but felt in every nerve of her whole being the command: "Go back. You must go back. You have no right to be here. The laws are made and fixed; you cannot remain here without penalty."

She heard herself say to the strange darkness, "If I must, I will pay the penalty that is exacted."

"Why do you seek to go where it is forbidden to go?"

"I must warn him," she said frantically, and then, suddenly, like a moth spreading its wings over the cocoon, something in Igraine that was greater than herself opened and spread its wings and the darkness around her was gone, and the fearsome shape warning her was no more than a veiled shape, a woman like herself, a priestess, certainly not a Goddess nor the Old Death-crone. Igraine said steadily, "We are bound and sworn, life to life and beyond; you have no right to forbid." Suddenly Igraine saw that about her arms were twining the golden serpents which she had worn in her strange dream of the ring stones. She raised her arms and cried out a word in a strange language. She could never, afterward, remember more than half a syllable, only that it began with a great "Aaahhh . . ." and that it was a word of power; nor did she know how the word had come to her in this extremity, to her who was not even a priestess in this life. The forbidding shape before her was gone, and Igraine saw light, light like the rising sun. . . .

No, it was the dimmest of lantern lights, a rushlight shielded crudely with a thin slice of horn in a wooden box, no more than a glimmer in the icy shadows of a small, stone-walled hut, tumbledown and roughly repaired with bundles of reeds. But by some curious, nonexistent light—or did she, bodiless, see in the dark without eyes?—she could make out a few faces in the shadows, faces she had seen around Uther in Londinium: kings and chiefs and soldiers. Exhausted and icy cold, they crouched around the tiny lantern as if its flickering fire could somehow warm them. And Uther was among them, gaunt and exhausted, his hands bleeding with chilblains, his woolen plaid drawn up closely over his head and around his chin. This was not the proud and kingly priest-lover she had seen in her first vision, not even the clumsy and boorish young man who had come into church disturbing them all; but this weary, haggard man, damp hair straggling around his nose, reddened with the cold, somehow seemed to her more real, more handsome than ever before. Igraine, aching with pity, longing to take him in her arms and warm him, felt as if she had cried out *Uther!*

She knew he heard, for she saw him raise his head and look all about the cold shelter, shivering as if some colder wind stirred there; and then she *saw,* through the cloaks and plaids huddled around his body, the serpents twining about his arms. They were not real; they writhed like living snakes where no snake ever known to humanity would leave its burrow in such weather. But she saw them, and somehow Uther saw her, and opened his mouth to speak. Imperatively, she gestured him to silence.

You must arouse, and make ready to march, or you are doomed! The message did not form itself in her mind as words, but she knew that it moved directly from her thoughts to his. *The snow will cease soon after midnight. Gorlois and his soldiers think you are pinned down where you are now, and they will fall upon you and cut you to pieces! You must be ready to meet their attack.*

The words pressed upon him, soundless, with her last remnant of strength. And even as they formed, she knew that the strength of will which had brought her here across the gulf, against the laws of this world, was fading. She was not accustomed to this work, and she struggled, not wanting to leave with her warning unspoken. Would they believe him, would they be ready to meet Gorlois? Or would they stay there, motionless in the darkness after the storm, and Gorlois find them like hens huddled on their roost for the fox? But she could do no more. A deathly cold, the faintness of utter exhaustion, came over her; she felt herself fading into icy cold and darkness, as if the storm were raging through her entire body . . .

. . . she was lying on the stone floor, before the cold ashes of the fire. Over her an icy wind was blowing, as if the storm which had followed her all through her vision was raging here too, inside her body. . . . No, it was not that. The wooden shutters of the room had blown open in the dying frenzy of the storm; they were slamming back and forth, and slashes of icy rain were blowing into the room.

She was cold. She was so cold she felt she would never move again, that she would lie there and freeze and that the cold of her body would gradually change to the sleep of death. At the moment she did not care.

There must be punishment for breaking a taboo; that is the law. I have done the forbidden thing, and I cannot emerge scatheless from it. If Uther is safe, I accept it, even if my punishment be death . . . and indeed, Igraine, huddling and trying to cover herself with the inadequate warmth of her cloak, felt that death would be merciful. At least she would not feel the cold. . . .

But Morgaine, Morgaine who slept in the bed near to that window, if the window were not closed she would take a chill and perhaps have the lung fever. . . . Igraine would not, for her own sake, have moved. But for her child and her innocent sister she forced herself painfully to stir, to make her numbed hands and feet move. Clumsy, moving as if drunken, she stumbled to the window and fumbled with her frozen hands to draw it closed. The wind twice tore it from her fingers, and she heard herself sobbing as she wrestled with it. She could not feel, but she knew she had torn away a fingernail in the struggle with the shutter, which fought her like a living thing. At last, capturing the clasp between her hands, she drew it shut by main force, pinching a finger, cold and blue, in the frame, as she managed to fasten the wooden hasp.

It was still cold in the room, cold as ice, and she knew that without the fire, Morgaine, and Morgause too, would be ill . . . she wanted nothing more than to creep into bed between them, still wrapped in her cloak, warm herself between their young warm bodies, but it was hours till morning, and she had been the one who left the fire untended. Shivering, pulling her cloak close, she took a fire pan from the hearth and stole down the stairs, feeling her icy feet bruised as they stumbled on the stone. In the kitchen, three serving women curled close like dogs in front of the banked fire; it was warm there, and a steaming pot hung on a long hook over the fire—gruel for the morning meal, no doubt. Well, it was her own kitchen and her own gruel. Igraine dipped a cup into the pot and drank the hot, unsalted oatmeal broth, but even that could not warm her. Then she filled the fire pan with red-hot coals and covered the fire, covered the fire pan, and, holding it in a fold of her skirt, went up the stairs again. She was weak and shaking, and, despite the hot drink, shuddering so hard she feared she would fall. *I must not fall, for if I fall I will never get up again, and the fire pan will set something afire.* . . .

She knelt before the cold hearth in her room, feeling the great shudders take her body and rack her with pain in her chest; but she was not cold now, she felt hot throughout her body. She fed the coals patiently with bits of tinder from the bin, then with small sticks; at last the log caught and roared up toward the ceiling. Igraine was so hot now that she flung off her cloak, stumbling toward the bed; lifted Morgaine and lay down with the child in her arms; but she did not know whether she slept or died.

No, SHE WAS NOT DEAD. Death would not bring this racking, shuddering heat and cold. . . . She knew that she lay a long time, wrapped in steaming cloths, which grew cold and were taken away and renewed; she knew that they forced hot drinks down her throat, sometimes nauseous herbal mixtures against fever and sometimes strong spirits mixed with hot water. Days, weeks, years, centuries, passed over her while she lay and burned and shivered and suffered the horrid stuff they poured down her throat when she was too weak even to vomit it up. Once Morgause came and asked her fretfully, "If you were ill, Igraine, why did you not wake me and send me to mend the fire?" The dark shape who had forbidden her the road was standing in one corner of the room, and now Igraine could see her face: it was the Death-crone who guards the doors of the forbidden, and now would punish her. . . . Morgaine came and looked down at her, her small, somber face frightened, and Igraine wanted to reassure her daughter, but she was too weak to speak aloud. And Uther was there too, but she knew that no one else could see him, and it was not seemly to call out any man's name save that of her own wedded husband . . . no one would think worse of her if she should call out Gorlois's name. But even if she was dying, she did not want to call out the name of Gorlois, she wanted no more of him, in life or in death.

Had she betrayed Gorlois, with her forbidden sorcery? Or had that been only a dream, no more real than her attempt to warn Uther? Had she saved him? It seemed that she was wandering in the icy spaces again, trying blindly to force herself through the storm to give her warning, and once Father Columba came and mumbled Latin at her, and she was frantic. By what right did he come to worry her with the last rites when she could not defend herself? She had meddled in sorcery, by his standards she was an evil woman, and he would condemn her for betraying Gorlois, he would come to avenge his master. The storm was back again, raging through her, she was wandering endlessly in the storm, trying to find Morgaine who was lost in it, only Morgause was there, wearing a crown, the crown of the High Kings of all Britain. Then Morgaine was standing at the prow of the barge which passed over the Summer Sea to the shores of Avalon, Morgaine wearing the robes of a priestess, the robes Viviane wore . . . and then all was darkness and silence.

And then there was sunlight in the room and Igraine stirred, only to discover that she could not sit up.

"Lie still, my lady," said Isotta, "in a little while I will bring you your medicine."

Igraine said, and was surprised to find herself whispering, "If I have lived through your herb drinks, I will probably live through this, too. What day is this?"

"Only ten days till Midwinter-night, my lady, and as for what happened, well, all we know is that the fire in your room must have gone out during the night, and your window blown open. The lady Morgause said she woke to see you closing it, and that you went out afterward, and came back with a fire pan. But you did not speak, and mended the fire, so she did not know you were ill till morning, when you were burning with fever and did not know her, or the child."

That was the simple explanation. Only Igraine knew that her illness was more, was punishment for attempting sorcery far beyond her strength, so that body and spirit were drained almost past returning.

"What of—" Igraine stopped herself; she could not inquire of Uther, what was she thinking of? "Is there news of my lord Duke?"

"None, my lady. We know there was a battle, but no news will come until the roads are cleared after the great storm," the serving-woman said. "But now you must not talk anymore, lady, you must have some hot gruel and lie down to sleep."

Patiently Igraine drank the hot broth they brought her, and slept. News would come when the time was ripe.

8

On MIDWINTER-EVE, the weather broke again and turned fine. All day snow was melting and dripping, the roads ran mud, and fog came in and lay softly over the sea and courtyard, so that voices and whispers seemed to echo endlessly when anyone spoke. For a little while in the early afternoon, the sun came out, and Igraine went into the courtyard for the first time since her illness. She felt quite recovered now, but she fretted, as they all did, for news.

Uther had sworn he would come at Midwinter-night. How would he manage it, with Gorlois's army lying between? All day she was silent and abstracted; she even spoke sharply to Morgaine, running about like a wild thing with the joy of being free after the confinement and cold of the winter weather.

I should not be harsh with my child because my mind is with my lover! Igraine thought, and, angry with herself, called Morgaine to her and kissed her. A chill went through her as she laid her lips to the soft cheek; by her forbidden sorcery, warning her lover of Gorlois's ambush, she might have condemned the father of her child to death . . .

. . . but no. Gorlois had betrayed his High King; whatever she, Igraine, had done or left undone, Gorlois was marked for death, and by his treason he had deserved it. Unless, indeed, he should compound his betrayal by killing that man whom his sworn king, Ambrosius, had marked for the defense of all Britain.

Father Columba came to her, insisting that she forbid her women and serving-men to light Midwinter fires. "And you yourself should set them a good example by coming tonight to mass," he insisted. "It has been long, my lady, since you received the sacraments."

"I have been ill," she said indifferently, "and as for the sacraments, I seem to remember that you gave me the last rites when I lay sick. Although I may have dreamed it—I dreamed many things."

"Many of them," said the priest, "such things as no Christian woman should dream. It was for my lord's sake, lady, that I gave you the sacraments when you had had no opportunity to confess yourself and receive them worthily."

"Aye—I know well it was not for my own sake," said Igraine, with a faint curl of her lip.

"I do not presume to set limits on God's mercy," the priest said, and Igraine knew the unspoken part of his thought: he would err if needed on the side of mercy, because Gorlois, for some reason, cared about this woman, and leave it to God to be harsh with her, as no doubt God would be. . . .

But at last she said that she would come to mass. Little as she liked this new religion, Ambrosius had been a Christian, Christianity was the religion of the civilized people of Britain and would inevitably become more so; Uther would bow to the public observance, whatever his private views on religion. She did not really know—she had had no opportunity to know how he really felt about matters of conscience. Would she ever know? *He swore he would come to me at Midwinter.* But Igraine lowered her eyes and tried to pay strict attention to the mass.

Dusk had fallen, and Igraine was speaking in the kitchen house to her women, when she heard a commotion at the end of the causeway and the sound of riders, then a cry in the courtyard. She flung her hood over her shoulders and ran out, Morgause behind her. At the gateway were men in Roman cloaks such as Gorlois wore, but the guards were barring their way with the long spears they carried.

"My lord Gorlois left orders; no one but the Duke himself to go inside in his absence."

One of the men at the center of the group of newcomers drew himself up, immensely tall.

"I am the Merlin of Britain," he said, his resounding voice ringing through the dusk and fog. "Stand back, man, will you deny passage to *me?*"

The guardsman drew back in instinctive deference, but Father Columba stepped forward, with an imperative gesture of refusal.

"I will deny you. My lord the Duke of Cornwall has said particularly that you, old sorcerer, are to have no entrance here at any time." The soldiers gaped, and Igraine, despite her anger—stupid, meddlesome priest!—had to admire his courage. It was not an easy thing to defy the Merlin of all Britain.

Father Columba held up the big wooden cross at his belt. "In the name of the Christ, I bid you begone! In God's name, return to the realms of darkness whence you came!"

The Merlin's ringing laugh raised echoes from the looming walls. "Good brother in Christ," he said, "your God and my God are one and the same. Do you really think I will vanish away at your exorcism? Or do you think I am some foul fiend from the darkness? No, not unless you call the falling of God's night the coming of darkness! I come from a land no darker than the Summer Country, and look, these men with me bear the ring of his lordship the Duke of Cornwall himself. Look." The torchlight flashed as one of the cloaked men thrust out a bare hand. On the first finger glinted Gorlois's ring.

"Now let us in, Father, for we are not fiends, but mortal men who are cold and weary, and we have ridden for a long way. Or must we cross ourselves and repeat a prayer to prove that to you?"

Igraine came forward, wetting her lips with nervousness. What was happening here? How did they come to bear Gorlois's ring, unless they were his messengers? Certainly one of them would have appealed to her. She saw no one she recognized, nor would Gorlois have chosen the Merlin for his messenger. Was Gorlois dead then, and was it news of his death being brought to her in this fashion? She said abruptly, her voice sounding harsh, "Let me see the ring. Is this truly his token or a forgery?"

"It is truly his ring, lady Igraine," said a voice she knew, and Igraine, bending her eyes to see the ring in the torchlight, saw familiar hands, big, broad and callused; and above them, what she had seen only in vision. Around Uther's hairy arms, tattooed there in blue woad, writhed two serpents, one on either wrist. She thought that her knees would give way and that she would sink down on the stones of the courtyard.

He had sworn it: *I will come to you at Midwinter.* And he had come, wearing Gorlois's ring!

"My lord Duke!" said Father Columba impulsively, stepping forward, but the Merlin raised a hand to forbid the words.

"Hush! The messenger is secret," he said. "Speak no word." And the priest fell back, thinking the cloaked man was Gorlois, puzzled but obedient.

Igraine dropped a curtsey, still struggling against disbelief and dismay. She said, "My lord, come in," and Uther, still concealing his face beneath the cloak, reached out with the ringed hand and gripped her fingers. Her own felt like ice beneath them, but his hand was warm and firm and steadied her as they stepped into the hall.

She took refuge in banalities. "Shall I fetch some wine, my lord, or send for food?"

He murmured close to her ear, "In God's name, Igraine, find some way we can be alone. The priest has sharp eyes, even in the dark, and I want it thought it is Gorlois, indeed, who has come here."

She said to Isotta, "Bring food and some beer to the soldiers here in the hall, and to the Lord Merlin. Bring them water for washing, and all they desire. I will speak with my lord in our chambers. Have food and wine sent there at once."

The servants went scurrying in all directions to do her will. The Merlin let a man take his cloak, and set his harp carefully on one of the benches. Morgause came into the doorway, peering boldly at the soldiers. Her eyes fell on Uther's tall form, and she dropped a curtsey.

"My lord Gorlois! Welcome, dear brother!" she said, and started toward him. Uther made a slight forbidding movement and Igraine stepped quickly in front of him. She thought, frowning, *This is ridiculous; even cloaked, Uther looks no more like Gorlois than do I!*

She said sharply, "My lord is weary, Morgause, and in no mood for the chatter of children. Take Morgaine to your chamber and keep her; she will sleep there with you this night."

Frowning, sullen, Morgause picked up Morgaine and carried her away up the stairs. Keeping well behind them, Igraine reached for Uther's hand and held it as they climbed. What manner of trickery was this, and why? Her heart was pounding until she thought she would faint away as she led him into the chamber she had shared with Gorlois and shut the door.

Inside, his arms were stretched to sweep her into his embrace; he shoved back the hood and stood there, his hair and beard wet with fog, holding out his arms, but she did not move toward him.

"My lord King! What is this, why do they think you are Gorlois?"

"A small magic of the Merlin," Uther said, "mostly a matter of a cloak and a ring, but a small glamour too; nothing that would hold if they should see me in full light, or uncloaked. I see that you were not deceived; I had not expected it. It is a seeming, not a Sending. I swore I would come to you, Igraine, at Midwinter, and I have kept my vow. Do I not even get a kiss for all my travail?"

She came and took the cloak from him, but she evaded his touch. "My lord King, how came you by Gorlois's ring?"

His face hardened. "That? I cut it from his hand in battle, but the oathbreaker turned tail and fled. Mistake me not, Igraine, I come here by right, not as a thief in the night; the glamour is to save your reputation in the eyes of the world, no more. I would not have my promised wife branded adulteress. But I come here by right; the life of Gorlois is forfeit to me. He held Tintagel as the sworn vassal of Ambrosius Aurelianus; that oath he renewed to me, and now that, too, is forfeit. Surely you understand this, Lady Igraine? No king can stand if his sworn men may break oath with impunity and stand under arms against their king."

She bowed her head in acknowledgment.

"Already he has cost me the wreck of a year's work against the Saxon. When he left London with his men I could not stand against them, and I had to step aside, flee, and let them pillage the town. My people, whom I am sworn to defend." His face was bitter. "Lot, I can forgive; he refused to take the oath. A score I have to settle with Lot, indeed—he will make peace with me or I will see him off his throne and hanged—but he is not oathbreaker or betrayer. Gorlois I trusted; he took oath and forswore it, and so I am left in the wreck of the work Ambrosius spent his life to accomplish, with all of it to do again. Gorlois cost me that, and I am come to have Tintagel at his hands. And I will have his life, too, and he knows it."

His face was like stone.

Igraine swallowed hard. "And you will have his lady, too—by conquest and by right, as you have Tintagel?"

"Ah, Igraine," he said, drawing her to him with his two hands, "I know well what choice you made, when I saw you the night of the great storm. If you had not warned me, I would have lost my best men, and, no doubt, my life as well. Thanks to you, when Gorlois came against me, I was ready for him. It was then I took the ring from his finger, and would have taken the hand, and the head too, but he escaped me."

"I know well you had no choice as to that, my lord King," Igraine said, but at that moment there was a knock on the door. One of the serving-women brought in a tray with food and a jug of wine, and muttered "My lord," dropping a curtsey. Mechanically Igraine freed herself from Uther's hands, took the food and wine, shut the door behind the woman. She took Uther's cloak, which was, after all, not so very different from the one Gorlois wore, and hung it on the bedpost to dry; bent and helped him off with his boots; took his sword belt from him, *Like a dutiful lady and wife,* a voice remarked in her mind, but she knew she had made her choice. It was even as Uther said: Tintagel belonged to the High King of Britain; so did its lady, and it was at her own will. She had given her allegiance to the King's own self.

The women had brought dried meat seethed with lentils, a loaf of new-baked bread, some soft cheese, and wine. Uther ate like a man starving, saying, "I have been in the field these two moons past, thanks to that damnable traitor you call husband; this is the first meal I have eaten under a roof since Samhain—the good Father down there, no doubt, would remind me to say All Souls."

"It is only what was cooking for the servants' supper and mine, my lord King, not at all fitting—"

"It seems to me good enough for the keeping of Christmas, after what I have been eating in the cold," he said, chewing noisily, tearing the bread asunder with strong fingers and cutting a chunk of cheese with his knife. "And am I to have no word from you save *my lord King?* I have dreamed so of this moment, Igraine," he said, laying down the cheese and staring up at her. He took hold of her round the waist and drew her close to his chair.

"Have you no word of love for me? Can it be that you are still loyal to Gorlois?"

Igraine let him draw her against him. She said it aloud. "I have made my choice."

"I have waited so long—" he whispered, pulling her down so that she half-knelt against his knee, and tracing the lines of her face with his hand. "I had begun to fear it would never come, and now you have no word of love or look of kindness for me—Igraine, Igraine, did I dream it, after all, that you loved me, wanted me? Should I have left you in peace?"

She felt cold, she was shaking from head to foot. She whispered, "No, no—or if it was a dream, then I too dreamed." She looked up at him, not knowing what else to say or do. She did not fear him, as she had feared Gorlois, but now that the moment was at hand she wondered, with a sudden wild panic, why she had come so far. He still held her within the curve of his arm. Now he pulled her down on his knee, and she let him draw her back, her head against his breast.

He said, encircling her narrow wrist in his big hand, "I had not realized how slight you were. You are tall; I thought you a big woman, queenly —and after all you are a little thing, I could break you with my two hands, little bones like a bird's—" He closed the fingers around her wrist. "And you are so young—"

"I am not so young as all that," she said, laughing suddenly. "I have been married five years and I have a child."

"You seem too young for that," Uther said. "Was that the little one I saw downstairs?"

"My daughter. Morgaine," Igraine said. And suddenly she realized that he, too, was ill at ease, delaying. Instinctively she realized that for all his thirty-odd years, his experience of women was only with such women as could be had for the asking, and that a chaste woman of his own station was something new to him. She wished, with a sudden ache, that she knew the right thing to do or say.

Still temporizing, she drew her free hand along the tattooed serpents twining around his wrists. "I had not seen these before. . . ."

"No," he said, "they were given me at my kingmaking on Dragon Island. I would you could have been with me, my queen," he whispered, and took her face between his hands, tilting it back to kiss her on the lips.

"I do not want to frighten you," he whispered, "but I have dreamed so long of this moment, so long . . ."

Shaking, she let him kiss her, feeling the strangeness of it stirring something deep in her body. It had never been like this with Gorlois . . . and suddenly she was afraid again. With Gorlois it had always been something done to her in which she had no part, something from which she could stand aside, watching with detachment. She had always been herself, Igraine. Now, with the touch of Uther's lips, she knew she could no longer remain apart, that she would never again be the self she had known. The thought terrified her. And yet the knowledge of how much he wanted her was racing through her veins. Her hand tightened about the blue serpents at his wrists. "I saw these in a dream . . . but I thought it was only a dream."

He nodded soberly. "I dreamed of them before ever I wore them. And it was in my mind that you had something like to them, too, about your arms . . ." He picked up her slender wrist again and traced along it. "Only they were golden."

She felt the hairs rise on her back. Indeed it had been no dream, but a vision from the Country of Truth.

"I cannot remember all the dream," Uther said, staring over her shoulder. "Only that we stood together on a great plain, and there was something like to the ring stones. . . . What does it mean, Igraine, that we share one another's dreams?"

She said, feeling her voice catch in her throat as if she were about to weep, "Perhaps it means only that we are fated for one another, my king . . . and my lord . . . and my love."

"My queen, and my love . . ." He met her eyes suddenly, a long look and a long question. "Surely the time for dreaming is over, Igraine." He thrust his hands into her hair, pulling out the pins, letting it tumble down over her embroidered collar and over his face; smoothed the long locks down with trembling hands. He rose to his feet, still holding her in his arms. She had never guessed at the strength in his hands. He crossed the room in two great strides, and laid her down on the bed. Kneeling at her side, he bent and kissed her again.

"My queen," he murmured. "I would you could have been crowned at my side at my kingmaking. . . . There were rites there such as no Christian man should know; but the Old People, who were here long before ever the Romans came to these isles, would not acknowledge me king without them. It was a long road I took to come there, and some of it, I am sure, was not anywhere in this world I know."

This reminded her of what Viviane had told her about the drifting of the worlds, apart in the mists. And thinking about Viviane brought to mind what Viviane had asked of her, and how reluctant she had been.

I did not know. I was so young then, and untried, I knew nothing, I did not know how all of me could be dissolved, torn, swept away. . . .

"Did they ask of you that you should make the Great Marriage with the land, as was done in the old days? I know that King Ban of Benwick in Less Britain was so required . . ." and a sudden, violent stab of jealousy went through her, that some woman or priestess might have symbolized for him the land he was sworn to defend.

"No," he said. "And I am not sure I would have done so, but it was not asked of me. The Merlin said, too, that it is he, as with every Merlin of Britain, who is sworn to die if need be, in sacrifice for his people—" Uther broke off. "But this can mean little to you."

"You have forgotten," she said, "I was reared in Avalon; my mother was priestess there and my eldest sister is now the Lady of the Lake."

"Are you a priestess too, Igraine?"

She shook her head, starting to say a simple no; then said, "Not in this life."

"I wonder . . ." Again he traced the line of the imaginary serpents, touching his own with his other hand. "I have always known, I think, that I lived before—it seems to me that life is too great a thing to live it only once and then be snuffed out like a lamp when the wind blows. And why, when first I looked upon your face, did I feel that I had known you before the world was made? These things are mysteries, and I think it may be that you know more of them than I. You say you are no priestess, yet you had sorcery enough to come to me, the night of the great storm, and warn me. . . . I think perhaps I should ask no more, lest I might hear from you what no Christian man should know. As for these"—again, with a fingertip, he touched the serpents—"if I wore them before this life, then perhaps that is why the old man, when he pricked them into my wrists the night of my kingmaking, told me that they were mine by right. I have heard that the Christian priests have driven all such serpents from our isles . . . but I do not fear the dragons, and I wear them in token that I will spread my protection over this land like the dragon's wings."

"In that case," she whispered, "surely you will be the greatest of kings, my lord."

"Call me not so!" he interrupted fiercely, bending over her where she lay and covering her mouth with his.

"Uther," she whispered, as if in a dream.

His hands moved at her throat, and he bent to kiss her bare shoulder. But when he began to pull off her gown, she flinched and shrank away. Tears flooded her eyes and she couldn't speak, but he laid his hands on her shoulders and looked into her eyes.

He said softly, "Have you been so mishandled, my beloved? God strike me if you ever have anything to fear from me, now or ever. I wish with all my heart that you had never been Gorlois's wife. Had I found you first . . . but what is done is done. But I swear to you, my queen: you will never have anything to fear from me." In the flickering light of the lamp, his eyes seemed dark, although she knew they were blue. "Igraine, I have—I have taken this for granted, because somehow I believed you must know how I feel. I know very little about your kind of woman. You are my love, my wife, my queen. I swear to you by my crown and by my manhood, you shall be my queen and I will never take another woman before you, or put you aside. Did you think I was treating you as a wanton?" His voice was trembling, and Igraine knew that he was stricken with fear—the fear of losing her. Knowing that he could fear too, knowing that he too was vulnerable, her own fear was gone. She put her arms around his neck and said clearly, "You are my love and my lord and my king, and I will love you as long as I live, and as long thereafter as God wills."

And this time she let him pull away her gown, and, naked, came willingly into his arms. Never, never had she guessed that it could be like this. Until this moment, despite five years of marriage and the birth of a child, she had been an innocent, a virgin, an unknowing girl. Now body and mind and heart blended, making her one with Uther as she had never been with Gorlois. She thought, fleetingly, that not even a child in its mother's womb could be so close. . . .

He lay weary on her shoulder, his coarse fair hair tickling her breasts. He murmured, "I love you, Igraine. Whatever comes of this, I love you. And if Gorlois should come here, I will kill him before he can touch you again."

She did not want to think of Gorlois. She smoothed the light hair across his brow and murmured, "Sleep, my love. Sleep."

She did not want to sleep. Even after his breathing became heavy and slow, she lay wakeful, caressing him softly so as not to wake him. His chest was almost as smooth as her own, with only a little light, fair hair; she had somehow thought all men were heavy and hairy. The scent of his body was sweet, though heavy with sweat and the juices of love. She felt she could never have enough of touching him. At one and the same time she longed for him to waken and take her again in his arms, and jealously guarded his exhausted sleep. She felt no fear now, and no shame; what had been with Gorlois duty and acceptance had become delight almost unendurable, as if she had been reunited with some hidden part of her own body and soul.

At last she did sleep a little, fitfully, curled into the curve of his body. She had slept perhaps an hour when she was roused abruptly by commotion in the courtyard. She sat up, flinging her long hair back. Uther pulled her sleepily down.

"Lie still, dear love, dawn is still far away."

"No," she said, with sure instinct, "we dare not linger now." She flung on a gown and kirtle, twisting her hair up with shaking hands. The lamp had gone out and she could not find the pin in the darkness. At last she caught up a veil to throw over it, slid her feet into her shoes, and ran down the stairs. It was still far too dark to see clearly. In the great hall there was only a little glimmer of light from the banked fire. And then she came up sharp before a little stirring of the air, and stopped dead.

Gorlois stood there, a great sword cut on his face, looking upon her with unutterable grief and reproach and dismay. It was the Sending she had seen before, the fetch, the death-doom; he raised his hand, and she could see that the ring and three fingers had been cut away. His face bore a ghastly pallor, but he looked at her with grief and love, and his lips moved in what she knew was her name, although she could not hear in the frozen silence around them. And in that moment she knew that he, too, had loved her, in his own harsh way, and whatever he had done to hurt her had been done for love. Indeed, for her love he had quarreled with Uther, flung away honor and dukedom both. And she had returned his love with nothing but hatred and impatience; only now could she understand that even as she felt for Uther, so Gorlois had felt for her. Her throat cramped with anguish and she would have cried out his name, but the dead air moved and he was gone; had never been there at all. And at that moment the frozen silence around her was lifted and she heard men shouting in the courtyard.

"Make way!" they were crying. "Make way! Lights, here, lights!"

Father Columba came into the hall, thrust a torch into the banked fire and set it ablaze. He hastened to fling the door wide.

"What is this outcry—"

"Your duke is slain, men of Cornwall," someone shouted. "We bring the Duke's body! Make way! Gorlois of Cornwall lies dead and we bring his body for burying!"

Igraine felt Uther's arms holding her up from behind, else she would have fallen. Father Columba protested loudly, "No! This cannot be! Why, the Duke came home last night with a few of his men, he's asleep upstairs now in his lady's chamber—"

"No." It was the voice of the Merlin, quiet, but ringing to the farthest corners of the court. He took one of the torches and thrust it against Father Columba's torch, then gave it to one of the soldiers to hold. "The oath-breaker Duke came never to Tintagel as a living man. Your lady stands here with your overlord and your High King, Uther Pendragon. You shall marry them today, Father."

There were cries and mutterings among the men, and the servants who had come running stood numbly watching as the rough bier, animal skins sewn into a litter, was borne into the hall. Igraine shrank away from the covered face and body. Father Columba bent over, briefly uncovered the face, made the sign of the cross, then turned away again. His face was grieved and angry.

"This is sorcery, this is witchcraft." He spat, brandishing the cross

between them. "This foul illusion was your doing, old wizard!"
Igraine said, "You will not speak so to my father, priest!"

Merlin lifted his hand. "I need no woman's protection—nor no man's, my lord Uther," he said. "And it was no sorcery. You saw what you willed to see—your lord come home. Only your lord was not the oathbreaker Gorlois, who had forfeited Tintagel, but the true High King and lord who came here to take what was his own. Keep you to your priestcraft, Father, there is need of a burying, and when that is done, of a nuptial mass for your king and for my lady whom he has chosen queen."

Igraine stood within the curve of Uther's arm. She met the resentful, contemptuous look in Father Columba's eyes; she knew that he would have turned on her, called her harlot and witch, but his fear of Uther kept him silent. The priest turned away from her and knelt beside Gorlois's body; he was praying. After a moment Uther knelt too, his fair hair gleaming in the torchlight. Igraine went to kneel at his side. *Poor Gorlois.* He was dead, he had met a traitor's death; he had richly deserved it, but he had loved her, and he had died.

A hand on her shoulder prevented her. The Merlin looked into her eyes for a moment, and said gently, "So it has come, Grainné. Your fate, as it was foretold. See that you meet it with such courage as you may."

Kneeling at Gorlois's side, she prayed—for Gorlois, and then, weeping, for herself; for the unknown fate that lay before them now. Had it indeed been ordained from the beginning of the world, or had it been brought about by the sorcery of the Merlin, and of Avalon, and by her own use of sorcery? Now Gorlois lay dead, and as she looked on Uther's face, already beloved and dear, she knew that soon others would come and he would take up the burdens of his kingdom, and that never again would he be wholly hers as he had been on this one night. Kneeling there between her dead husband and the man she would love all her life, she fought the temptation to play upon his love for her, to turn him, as she knew she could do, from thoughts of kingdom and state to think only of her. But the Merlin had not brought them together for her own joy. She knew that if she sought to keep it, she would rebel against the very fate that had brought them together, and thus destroy it. As Father Columba rose from the dead man's side and signalled to the soldiers to carry the body into the chapel, she touched his arm. He turned impatiently.

"My lady?"

"I have much to confess to you, Father, before my lord the Duke is laid to rest—and before I am married. Will you hear my confession?"

He looked at her, frowning, surprised. At last he said, "At daybreak, lady," and went away. The Merlin followed Igraine with his eyes as she came back to him. She looked into his face and said, "Here and now, my father, from this moment, be witness that I have done forever with sorcery. What God wills be done."

The Merlin looked tenderly into her ravaged face. His voice was gentler than she had ever heard it. "Do you think that all our sorcery could bring about anything other than God's will, my child?"

Catching at some small self-possession—if she did not, she knew, she would weep like a child before all these men—she said, "I will go and robe myself, Father, and make myself seemly."

"You must greet the day as befits a queen, my daughter."

Queen. The word sent shudders through her body. But it was for this that she had done all that she had done, it was for this that she had been born. She went slowly up the stairs. She must waken Morgaine and tell her that her father was dead; fortunately the child was too young to remember him, or to grieve.

And as she called her women, and had them bring her finest robes and jewelry and dress her hair, she laid her hand wonderingly over her belly. Somehow, with the last fleeting touch of magic before she renounced it forever, she knew that from this one night, when they had been only lovers and not yet king and queen, she would bear Uther's son. She wondered if the Merlin knew.

MORGAINE SPEAKS . . .

I think that my first real memory is of my mother's wedding to Uther Pendragon. I remember my father only a little. When I was unhappy as a little girl, I seemed to remember him, a heavyset man with a dark beard and dark hair; I remember playing with a chain he wore about his neck. I remember that as a little maiden when I was unhappy, when I was chidden by my mother or my teachers, or when Uther—rarely—noticed me to disapprove of me, I used to comfort myself by thinking that if my own father were alive, he would have been fond of me and taken me on his knee and brought me pretty things. Now that I am older and know what manner of man he was, I think it more likely he would have put me into a nunnery as soon as I had a brother, and never thought more about me.

Not that Uther was ever unkind to me; it was simply that he had no particular interest in a girl child. My mother was always at the center of his heart, and he at hers, and so I resented that—that I had lost my mother to this great fair-haired, boorish man. When Uther was away in battle—and there was battle a good deal of the time when I was a maiden—my mother Igraine cherished me and petted me, and taught me to spin with her own hands and to weave in colors. But when Uther's men were sighted, then I went back into my rooms and was forgotten until he went away again. Is it any wonder I hated him and resented, with all my heart, the sight of the dragon banner on any horsemen approaching Tintagel?

And when my brother was born it was worse. For there was this crying thing, all pink and white, at my mother's breast; and it was worse that she expected me to care as much for him as she did. "This is your little brother," she said, "take good care of him, Morgaine, and love him." Love him? I hated him with all my heart, for now when I came near her she would pull away and tell me that I was a big girl, too big to be sitting in her lap, too big to bring my ribbons to her for tying, too big to come and lay my head on her knees for comfort. I would have pinched him, except that she would have hated me for it. I sometimes thought she hated me anyhow. And Uther made much of my brother. But I think he always hoped for another son. I was never told, but somehow I knew—maybe I heard the women talking, maybe I was gifted even then with more of the Sight than I realized —that he had first lain with my mother when she was still wedded to Gorlois, and there were still those who believed that this son was not Uther's but the son of the Duke of Cornwall.

How they could believe that, I could not then understand, for Gorlois, they said, was dark and aquiline, and my brother was like Uther, fair-haired, with grey eyes.

Even during the lifetime of my brother, who was crowned king as Arthur, I heard all kinds of tales about how he came by his name. Even the tale that it was from Arth-Uther, Uther's bear; but it was not so. When he was a babe, he was called Gwydion—bright one—because of his shining hair; the same name his son bore later—but that is another story. The facts are simple: when Gwydion was six years old he was sent to be fostered by Ectorius, one of Uther's vassals in the North country near Eboracum, and Uther would have it that my brother should be baptized as a Christian. And so he was given the name of Arthur.

But from his birth until he was six years old, he was forever at my heels; as soon as he was weaned, my mother, Igraine, handed him over to me and said, "This is your little brother and you must love him and care for him." And I would have killed the crying thing and thrown him over the cliffs, and run after my mother begging that she should be all mine again, except that my mother cared what happened to him.

Once, when Uther came and she decked herself in her best gown, as she always did, with her amber and moonstone necklaces, and looked down on me with a careless kiss for me and one for my little brother, ready to run down to Uther, I looked at her glowing cheeks—heightened with color, her breathing quickened with delight that her man had come—and hated both Uther and my brother. And while I stood weeping at the top of the stairs, waiting for our nurse to come and take us away, he began to toddle down after her, crying out, "Mother, Mother" —he could hardly talk, then—and fell and cut his chin on the stair. I screamed for my mother, but she was on her way to the King, and she called back angrily, "Morgaine, I told you, look after the baby," and hurried on.

I picked him up, bawling, and wiped his chin with my veil. He had cut his *lip on his tooth—I think he had only eight or ten, then—and he kept on wailing and calling out for my mother, but when she did not come, I sat down on the step with him in my lap, and he put up his little arms around my neck and buried his face in my tunic and after a time he sobbed himself to sleep there. He was heavy on my lap, and his hair felt soft and damp; he was damp elsewhere, too, but I found I did not mind much, and in the way he clung to me I realized that in his sleep he had forgotten he was not in his mother's arms.* I thought, Igraine has forgotten both of us, abandoned him as she abandoned me. Now I must be his mother, I suppose.

And so I shook him a little, and when he woke, he put up his little arms around my neck to be carried, and I slung him across my hip as I had seen my nurse do.

"Don't cry," I said, "I'll take you to nurse."

"Mother," he whimpered.

"Mother's gone, she's with the King," I said, "but I'll take care of you, brother." *And with his chubby hand in mine I knew what Igraine meant; I was too big a girl to cry or whimper for my mother, because I had a little one to look after now.*

I think I was all of seven years old.

WHEN MY MOTHER'S SISTER Morgause *was married to King Lot of Orkney, I knew only that I had my first grown-up gown, and an amber necklace with silver. I loved Morgause well, for she often had time for me when Mother did not, and she told me stories of my father—after his death, I think Igraine never spoke his name. But even though I loved Morgause, I feared her, for sometimes she would pinch me and tug my hair and call me tiresome brat, and it was she who first taunted me with the taunt which then made me weep, though now I take pride in it: "You are born of the fairy folk. Why not paint your face blue and wear deerskins, Morgaine of the Fairies!"*

I knew only a little about the reasons for the wedding, or why Morgause was to be married so young. I knew my mother was glad to have her married and away, for she fancied Morgause looked on Uther lustfully; she was probably not aware that Morgause looked lustfully on all men she came by. She was a bitch dog in heat, though indeed I suppose it was because she had no one to care what she did. At the wedding, in my new holiday gown, I heard them speak of how fortunate it was that Uther had made haste to amend his quarrel with Lot of Orkney, even giving him his own sister-in-law in marriage. I found Lot charming; only Uther, I think, was ever immune to that charm. Certainly Morgause seemed to love him —or perhaps only found it expedient to act as if she did.

It was there, I think, that I first remember meeting with the Lady of Avalon. Like Morgause, she was my aunt, my mother's sister, and she was also of the ancient folk—small, and dark, and glowing, with crimson ribbons braided in her dark hair. She was not young, even then, but I thought her, as I always thought her, beautiful; and her voice was rich and low. What I liked best about her was that she spoke to me always as if I were a woman of her own age, not with the cooing falsity with which most grown-up people spoke to a child.

I came into the hall a little late, for my nurse had not been able to manage braiding my hair with ribbons, and in the end I did it myself; I have always been neat-handed, and could do well and swiftly things which grown-up people did only slowly. Already I could spin as well as my mother and better than Morgause ever did. I was very proud of myself, in my saffron gown with ribbons edged with gold, and an amber necklace instead of the baby corals I had outgrown. But there was no seat at the high table, and I circled it in disappointment, knowing that any moment now Mother would banish me to a lower table, or call my nurse to take me away, or call attention to me by sending a serving-woman to fetch a chair. And while I was a princess in Cornwall, at Uther's court in Caerleon I was only the Queen's daughter by a man who had been traitor to his High King.

And then I saw a small, dark woman—so small, in fact, that at first I thought she was a girl only a little older than I—sitting on an embroidered stool. She put out her arms and said, "Come here, Morgaine. Do you remember me?"

I did not, but I looked at the dark, glowing face, and felt as if I had known her from the beginning of time.

But I pouted a little, because I was afraid she would tell me to come and sit on her lap, as if I were a baby. Instead, she smiled and moved to one side of her stool. I could see now that she was not a girl, but a lady.

"We are neither of us very big," she said. "I think this one stool will hold us both, since it was made for bigger people."

From that moment I loved her, so much I sometimes felt guilty because Father Columba, my mother's confessor, told me I should honor my mother and my father above all others.

So I sat beside Viviane through the wedding feast, and I learned that she was Morgause's foster-mother—their mother had died at Morgause's birth and Viviane suckled her as her own. Which fascinated me, because I had been angry when Igraine refused to give my new brother up to a wet nurse and fed him from her own breasts. Uther said it was unseemly for a queen, and I had agreed with him; I had hated seeing Gwydion at Igraine's breasts. I suppose the truth is that I was jealous, though I would have been ashamed to say so.

"Was your mother, and Igraine's, a queen, then?" For she was robed as richly as Igraine, or any of the queens of the North.

"No, Morgaine, she was not a queen, but a great priestess, the Lady of the Lake; and I am Lady of Avalon in her place. One day, perhaps, you will be a priestess too. You have the old blood, and perhaps you have the Sight."

"What is the Sight?"

She frowned. "Igraine has not told you? Tell me, Morgaine, do you ever see things that others cannot see?"

"All the time," I said, realizing that this lady understood all about me. "Only Father Columba says it is the work of the Devil. And Mother says that I should be silent about it, and never speak of it to anyone, even to her, because these things are not suitable for a Christian court and if Uther knew of them he would send me into a nunnery. I do not think I want to go into a nunnery and wear black clothes and never laugh again."

Viviane said a word for which nurse had washed my mouth out with the harsh lye soap the kitchen people used for scrubbing floors. "Listen to me, Morgaine. Your mother is right that you should never speak of these things to Father Columba—"

"But God will be angry with me if I lie to a priest."

She said the bad word again. "Listen, dear child: a priest will be angry if you lie to him, and say it is his God who is angry. But the Great Creator has better things to do than to be angry with young people, and this is a matter for your own conscience. Trust me, Morgaine: never say any more to Father Columba than you must, but always believe what the Sight tells you, for it comes to you directly from the Goddess."

"Is the Goddess the same as the Virgin Mary, Mother of God?"

She frowned. "All the Gods are one God and all the Goddesses are one Goddess. The Great Goddess will not be angry if you call her by the name of Mary, who was good and loved mankind. Listen, my dear, this is no talk for a festival. But I swear you shall never go into a nunnery while there is life and breath in my body, no matter what Uther may say. Now that I know you have the Sight, I will move Heaven and Earth if I must, to bring you to Avalon. Shall this be a secret between us, Morgaine? Will you promise me?"

"I promise," I said, and she leaned down and kissed my cheek. "Listen, the harpers are beginning to play for the dancing. Is Morgause not beautiful in her blue gown?"

9

On a spring day in the seventh year of the reign of Uther Pendragon at Caerleon, Viviane, priestess of Avalon and Lady of the Lake, went out at twilight to look into her magic mirror.

Although the tradition in which the Lady was priestess was older than the Druids, she shared one of the great tenets of the Druid faith: that the great forces which created the Universe could not be fitly worshipped in a house made with human hands, nor the Infinite contained within any man-made thing. And therefore the Lady's mirror was not of bronze or even silver.

Behind her rose the grey stone walls of the ancient Temple of the Sun, built by the Shining Ones who had come there from Atlantis, centuries before. Before her lay the great lake, surrounded by tall, waving reeds, and swathed in the mist which, even on fine days, lay now across the land of Avalon. But beyond the Lake lay islands and more lakes, all through the whole of what was called the Summer Country. It lay mostly underwater, bog and salt marsh, but in the height of summer, the pools and some of the brackish lakes would dry in the sun and the lands would lie there, fertile for grazing and rich with grass and weeds.

Here, in fact, the inland sea was receding, year by year giving way to dry land; one day this would all be rich farmland . . . but not in Avalon. Avalon now lay eternally surrounded in the mists, hidden from all but the faithful, and when men came and went in pilgrimage to the monastery which the Christian monks called Glass Town, the Temple of the Sun was invisible to them, lying in some strange otherworld; Viviane could see, when she bent her Sight upon it, the church they had built there.

It had been there for a long time, she knew, though she had never set foot upon its grounds. Centuries ago—so the Merlin had told her, and she believed him—a little band of priests had come here from the south, and with them had been their Nazarene prophet for schooling; and the story went that Jesus himself had been schooled there, in the dwelling place of the Druids where once the Temple of the Sun had risen, and had learned all of their wisdom. And years later, when—so the story ran—their Christ had been brought to sacrifice, playing out in his life the old Mystery of the Sacrificed God which was older than Britain's very self, one of his kinsmen returned here, and struck his staff into the ground on the Holy Hill, and it had blossomed forth into the thorn tree which blossoms, not only with the other thorn, in Midsummer, but in the depth of the winter snow. And the Druids, in memory of the gentle prophet whom they too had known and loved, consented that Joseph of Arimathea should build, in the very grounds of the Holy Isle, a chapel and a monastery to their God; for all the Gods are one.

But that had been long ago. For a time, Christian and Druid had dwelt side by side, worshipping the One, but then the Romans had come to the Isle, and, although they were widely known for tolerating local deities, against the Druids they had been ruthless, cutting and burning down their sacred groves, trumping up lies that the Druids committed human sacrifice. Their real crime, of course, had been that they heartened the people not to accept the Roman laws and the Roman peace. And then, in one great act of Druid magic, to protect the last precious refuge of their school, they had made the last great change in the world; that change which removed the Island of Avalon from the world of mankind. Now it lay hidden in the mist which concealed it, except from those initiates who had been schooled there or those who were shown the secret ways through the Lake. The Tribesmen knew it was there, and there they worshipped. The Romans, Christian since the days of Constantine, who had converted his legions wholesale on the grounds of some vision he had seen in a battle, believed that the Druids had been vanquished by their Christ, not knowing that the few remaining Druids lived and passed on their ancient wisdom in the hidden land.

Viviane could see, if she chose, with doubled Sight, for she was High Priestess of Avalon. When she chose she could see the tower they had built atop the very Tor, on the Holy Mountain of Initiation; a tower dedicated to Michael, one of their Jewish angels whose ancient function was to keep down the inferior world of demons. This struck Viviane as a blasphemy, even now, but she comforted herself with the thought that it was not in *her* world at all; if the narrow-minded Christians wished to think of the great old Gods as demons, the Christians would be the poorer for it. The Goddess lived, whatever the Christians thought of her. She turned her thoughts to her own business, which was to look into her magic mirror while the new moon still stood in the sky.

Although it was still light enough to see perfectly well, the Lady had carried with her a little lamp with a tiny flickering flame. She turned her back on the reeds and salt marsh, and walked inland along the path, climbing slowly along the reedy shore, passing the ancient rotted pilings of the dwellers who had built their houses there at the edge of the Lake in time long past.

Her small lamp flickered, becoming more and more visible in the darkness, and above the trees the pure, slim crescent of the virgin moon, barely visible, shone like the silver torque about the Lady's throat. She went along the ancient processional way, climbing slowly—for, although she was still strong and vigorous, she was not a young woman—until she came to the mirror pool, lying clear between standing stones of enormous antiquity.

The water was clear, reflecting the moonlight and, as she bent over it, springing into flame at the Lady's tiny lamp. She bent, dipped her hand in the water, and drank—it was forbidden to dip any man-made object into the pool, though above them, where the water bubbled into a spring, pilgrims might come with bottles and jugs and take away what they would from the flow. She tasted the clear, metallic-tasting water, and as always felt the stir of awe: this spring had been flowing since the beginning of the world, and it would flow forever, generous and magical, and free to all people. Surely such a spring as this was the gift of the Great Goddess, and Viviane knelt as she drank, raising her face to the slender crescent in the sky.

But after that momentary renewal of awe, which she had observed since first she came here, a novice of the House of Maidens, she turned back to her business. She set the lamp on a flat rock near the lip of the mirror pool, so that its light would reflect, as would the crescent moon, into the water. Now there were present the four elements: fire, in her lamp; water, from which she had drunk; the earth where she stood; and as she invoked the powers of air, she saw, as always during this invocation, a vagrant breeze ripple across the surface.

She sat for a moment in meditation. Then at last she formulated to herself the question for which she would consult the magical mirror.

How is it with Britain? How is it with my sister, and her daughter who is priestess-born, and with the son who is the hope of Britain?

For a moment, as the wind stirred the surface of the mirror pool, she saw only confused images, flowing—were they within her mind, or on the restless surface of the pool? She caught glimpses of battles, blurred by the restless water; she saw Uther's dragon banner and saw her Tribesmen fighting at his side. She saw Igraine robed and crowned, as she had seen her in the flesh. And then, in a flash that made her heart pound faster, she saw Morgaine weeping; and in a second and terrifying flash of Sight, she saw a fair-haired child lying senseless, motionless—dead or alive?

Then the moon sank out of sight beyond the mist, and the vision was gone, and try as she might, Viviane could summon nothing back except mocking glimpses: Morgause holding her second son, Lot and Uther pacing in a great hall and hurling angry words, and the confused memory of the bruised and dying child. But had these things been, or were they only a warning of things yet to come?

Biting her lip, Viviane bent and picked up her mirror. She cast the remaining drops of pure oil into the surface of the pool—oil burned for the Sight must never be used for mundane purpose—and went swiftly in the falling darkness along the processional way and to the dwelling of the priestesses.

Once there, she summoned her waiting-woman.

"Make all ready to ride at first dawn," she said, "and let my novice make ready to serve at full moon, for before it waxes another day, I must be in Caerleon. Send to tell the Merlin."

10

they travelled mostly in the early hours, lying hidden at midday and riding again at dusk. The country was for the moment peaceful—the war was away to the east. But stray bands of marauding Northmen or Saxons had been known before this to fall upon villages or isolated country villas. Travellers, too, unless protected by armed men, went warily and trusted no one.

Viviane had half expected to find Uther's court deserted, abandoned to women and children and those who could not fight, but from a distance she saw the dragon banner flying, which meant that the King was in residence. Her lips tightened; Uther neither liked nor trusted the Druids of the Holy Isle. Yet she had set this man whom she disliked on his throne, because he was the best of the leaders who had risen in the island, and now, somehow, she must work with him. At least he was not such a dedicated Christian that he would set himself to the task of wiping out other religions. *Better,* she thought, *to have an ungodly man for High King than a religious fanatic.*

Since she had been last at Uther's court the fortified wall had risen higher, and there were sentries on the wall, who called out to challenge her party. She had instructed her men to use none of her titles, but to say only that the Queen's sister had come. It was not the time to demand that they give respect to her as the Lady of Avalon; her present mission was too urgent for that.

They were led through the grass-grown enclosure, past all the clutter of an enclosed fort. She could hear somewhere the sound of an armorer or blacksmith beating on his anvil. Some herdswomen clad roughly in skin tunics were driving sheep inside for the night. Viviane, recognizing all these preparations for a siege, raised her eyelids slightly.

A scant few years before, Igraine had run to meet her in the courtyard at Tintagel. Now a solemn chamberlain, richly clad, and having but one arm —no doubt, a veteran of Uther's service—welcomed her with a solemn bow and conducted her to an upper chamber. "I am sorry, Lady," he said, "we are short of living space here. You must share this room with two of the Queen's ladies."

"I shall be honored," she said gravely.

"I will send you a serving-woman. You have only to ask her for anything you require."

"All I require," said Viviane, "is a little water for washing, and to know when I can see my sister."

"Lady, I am certain the Queen will receive you at the proper time. . . ."

"Does Uther keep state like the Caesars, then? Listen to me, fellow, I am the Lady of Avalon, and I am not accustomed to be kept waiting. But if Igraine has grown to such high state as all this, then I beg you to send the lady Morgaine to me as quickly as is possible!"

The one-armed veteran shrank back, but when he spoke his voice was less formal and more human. "Lady, I am sure the Queen would receive you willingly, at once, but you have come at a time of trouble and danger. The young prince Gwydion fell this morning from a horse no one should have let him ride, and the Queen won't leave his side, not for an instant."

"By the Goddess! I came too late, then!" Viviane whispered to herself. Aloud, she said, "Take me to them, at once. I am skilled in all the healing arts, and I am sure Igraine would have sent for me if she knew I were here."

He bowed and said, "Come this way, Lady."

Following him, Viviane realized that she had not even had time to remove her cloak or the men's breeches she wore for riding; and she had meant to present herself in all the dignity of Avalon. Well, this was more important.

Outside the door, the chamberlain paused. "It would be as much as my head's worth to disturb the Queen. She won't even let her ladies bring her food or drink—"

Viviane pushed the heavy door and went into the room. Dead silence; it was uncannily like a death chamber. Igraine, pale and wan, her headcloth rumpled, knelt like a stone figure beside the bed. A black-robed priest stood motionless, muttering prayers under his breath. Softly as she moved, Igraine heard her.

"How dare you—" she began in a furious whisper, and broke off. "Viviane! God must have sent you to me!"

"I had a warning that you might need me," said Viviane. This was no time to speak of magical visions. "No, Igraine, you can do no good by weeping," she added. "Let me look at him and see how serious this is."

"The King's physician—"

"Is probably an old fool who knows nothing but potions of goat's dung," said Viviane calmly. "I was healing wounds of this kind before you were out of swaddlings, Igraine. Let me see the child."

She had seen Uther's son only once, briefly; he had been about three years old, and looked like any other fair-haired, blue-eyed toddler. Now he had stretched out to unusual tallness for his age—thin, but well-muscled arms and legs, much scratched by briars and brambles like any active boy's. She put aside the covers and saw the great livid bruises on his body.

"Did he cough any blood at all?"

"Not even a little. The blood on his mouth was where a tooth was knocked out, but it was loose anyway."

And indeed Viviane could see the contused lip and the extra gap in his mouth. More serious was the bruise on the temple, and Viviane knew a moment of real fear. Had all their planning come to this?

She ran her small fingers across his head. She could see him flinch when she touched the bruise, and that was the best sign she could possibly have had. If he had been bleeding inside the skull, he would by this time have been so deep in coma that no possible pain could reach him. She reached down and pinched his thigh, very hard, and he whimpered in his sleep.

Igraine protested. "You are hurting him!"

"No," Viviane said, "I am trying to find out if he will live or die. Believe me, he will live." She slapped his cheek gently and he opened his eyes for a moment.

"Bring me the candle," Viviane said, and moved it slowly across his field of vision. He followed it for a moment before his eyes fell shut again, with a whimper of pain.

Viviane rose from his side. "Make sure he's kept quiet, and nothing but water or soup, nothing solid to eat for a day or two. And don't sop his bread in wine; only in soup or milk. He'll be running all over the place in three days."

"How do you know?" demanded the priest.

"Because I am trained in healing, how do you think?"

"Are you not a sorceress from the Island of Witches?"

Viviane laughed softly. "By no means, Father. I am a woman who, like yourself, has spent her life in the study of holy things, and God has seen fit to give me skill at healing." She could, she reflected, turn their own jargon against them; she knew, if he did not, that the God they both worshipped was greater and less bigoted than any priesthood.

"Igraine, I must talk to you. Come away—"

"I must be here when he wakes again, he will want me—"

"Nonsense; send his nurse to him. This is a matter of importance!"

Igraine glared at her. "Bring Isotta to sit beside him," she said to one of the women, with an angry look, and followed Viviane into the hall.

"Igraine, how did this happen?"

"I am not sure—some tale about riding his father's stallion—I am confused. I only know that they carried him in like one dead—"

"And it was only your good fortune that he was *not* dead," Viviane said bluntly. "Is it thus that Uther safeguards the life of his only son?"

"Viviane, don't reproach me—I have tried to give him others," Igraine said, and her voice shook. "But I think I am being punished for my adultery, that I can give Uther no other son—"

"Are you mad, Igraine?" Viviane burst out, then stopped herself. It was not fair to upbraid her sister when she was distracted from watching at the bedside of her sick child. "I came because I foresaw some danger to you or the child. But we can talk of that later. Call your women, put on fresh clothing—and when did you last eat anything?" she asked shrewdly.

"I can't remember—I think I had a little bread and wine last night—"

"Then call your women, and break your fast," Viviane said impatiently. "I am still dusty from riding. Let me go and wash off the dirt of travel, and clothe myself as is seemly for a lady inside the walls, and then we will talk."

"Are you angry with me, Viviane?"

Viviane patted her on the shoulder. "I am angry, if it is anger, only at the way fate seems to fall, and that is foolish of me. Go and dress, Igraine, and eat something. The child's come to no harm this time."

Inside her room a fire had been built, and on a small stool before it, she saw an undersized female, dressed in a robe so dark and plain that for a moment Viviane thought it was one of the serving wenches. Then, she saw that the simple gown was of the finest stuff, the headcloth embroidered linen, and she recognized Igraine's daughter.

"Morgaine," she said, and kissed her. The girl was almost as tall now as Viviane herself. "Why, I think of you as a child, but you are almost a woman. . . ."

"I heard you had come, Aunt, and came to welcome you, but they told me you had gone at once to my brother's bedside. How does he, Lady?"

"He's badly bruised and banged about, but he'll be well again with no treatment but rest," Viviane said. "When he wakes, I must somehow convince Igraine and Uther to keep the physicians and their stupid potions away from him; if they make him vomit, he'll be worse. I got nothing from your mother but weeping and wailing. Can you tell me how this came to happen? Is there no one here who can guard a child properly?"

Morgaine twisted her small fingers together. "I am not sure how it happened. My brother's a brave child and always wants to ride horses which are too fast and too strong for him, but Uther has given orders that he's only to ride with a groom. His pony was lame that day, and he asked for another horse, but how he came to take out Uther's stallion, no one knows; all the grooms know that he's never allowed to go near Thunder, and everyone denied seeing him. Uther swore he'd hang the groom who allowed it, but that groom has put the river between Uther and himself by now, I should imagine. Still, they say Gwydion stuck on Thunder's back like a sheep in a thorn thicket until someone loosed a breeding mare in the stallion's path, and we cannot find out who loosed the mare, either. So of course the stallion was off after the mare, and my brother was off the stallion, in the blink of an eyelash!" Her face, small and dark and plain, quivered. "He's really going to live?"

"He's really going to live."

"Has anyone yet sent word to Uther? Mother and the priest said he could do no good in the sickroom—"

"No doubt Igraine will attend to that."

"No doubt," Morgaine said, and Viviane surprised a cynical smile on her face. Morgaine, evidently, bore no love to Uther, and thought no more of her mother for her love to her husband. Yet she had been conscientious enough to remember that Uther should be sent word about his son's life. This was no ordinary young girl.

"How old are you now, Morgaine? The years go by so fast, I no longer remember, as I grow old."

"I shall be eleven at Midsummer."

Old enough, Viviane thought, *to be trained as a priestess.* She looked down and realized she was still wearing her travel-stained clothing. "Morgaine, will you have the serving-women bring me some water for washing, and send someone to help me robe myself properly to appear before the King and Queen?"

"Water I have sent for; it is there, in the cauldron by the fire," Morgaine said, and then hesitated and added shyly, "I would be honored to attend on you myself, Lady."

"If you wish." Viviane let Morgaine help her remove her outer garments and wash off the dust of travel. Her saddlebags had been sent up too, and she put on a green gown; Morgaine touched the cloth with admiring fingers.

"This is a fine green dye. Our women can make no green as fine as this. Tell me, what do you use to make it?"

"Woad, no more."

"I thought that made only blue dyes."

"No. This is prepared differently, boiled and fixed—I will talk of dyes with you later, if you are interested in herb lore," Viviane said. "Now we have other matters on our mind. Tell me, is your brother given to escapades like this?"

"Not really. He is strong and hardy, but he's usually biddable enough," Morgaine said. "Once someone taunted him about riding so small a pony, and he said that he was to be a warrior and a soldier's first duty is to obey orders, and that his father had forbidden him to ride a horse beyond his strength. So I can't imagine how he came to ride Thunder. But still, he wouldn't have been hurt unless . . ."

Viviane nodded. "I would like to know who loosed that mare, and why."

Morgaine's eyes widened as she took in the implications of this. Watching her, Viviane said, "Think. Has he had any other narrow escapes from death, Morgaine?"

Morgaine said, hesitating, "He had the summer fever—but then, all the children had that last year. Uther said he should not have been allowed to play with the shepherd's boys. He caught the fever from them, I think —four of them died. But there was the time when he was poisoned—"

"Poisoned?"

"Isotta—and I would trust her with my life, Lady—swears that she put only wholesome herbs into his soup. Yet he was as sick as if a death-cup mushroom had found its way into his porridge. And yet how could that be? She knows wholesome ones from the poisonous, and she is not yet old and her eyesight is good." Again Morgaine's eyes widened. "Lady Viviane, do you think there are people plotting against my brother's life?"

Viviane drew the girl down to her side. "I came here because I had a warning of this. I have not yet inquired whence the danger comes, I had no time. Do you have the Sight still, Morgaine? When last I spoke with you, you said—"

The girl colored and looked down at her shoes. "You bade me not speak of it. And Igraine says I should turn my thoughts to real things and not daydreams, and so I have tried. . . ."

"Igraine is right thus far: that you should not speak idly of these things to the once-born," Viviane said. "But to me, you may always speak freely, I promise you. My Sight can show me only such things as are relevant to the safety of the Holy Isle and the continuance of Avalon, but Uther's son is your own mother's son, and by that tie, your Sight will find him and be able to tell who is trying to compass his death. Uther has enemies enough, all the Gods know."

"But I do not know how to use the Sight."

"I will show you, if you wish it," said Viviane.

The girl looked up at her, her face taut with fear. "Uther has forbidden sorceries in his court."

"Uther is not my master," Viviane said slowly, "and no one can rule over another's conscience. Yet—do you think it an offense to God, to try to discover whether someone is plotting against your brother's life, or whether it is only bad luck?"

Morgaine said unsteadily, "No, I don't think it wicked." She stopped and swallowed and finally said, "And I do not think you would lead me into anything that was wrong, Aunt."

A sudden pain clutched at Viviane's heart. What had she done to earn this trust? With all her heart she wished that this small solemn girl was her own daughter, the daughter she owed the Holy Isle and had never been able to bear. Even though she had risked a belated childbearing, of which she had nearly died, she had borne only sons. And here, it seemed, was the successor the Goddess had sent her, a kinswoman with the Sight, and the girl was looking up at her with complete trust. For a moment she could not speak.

Am I prepared to be ruthless with this girl too? Can I train her, never sparing, or will my love make me less harsh than I must be to train a High Priestess?

Can I use her love for me, which I have in no way deserved, to bring her to the feet of the Goddess?

But with the discipline of years, she waited until her voice was clear and perfectly steady. "Be it so, then. Bring me a silver or bronze basin, perfectly clean and scoured with sand, and fill it with fresh rainwater, not water drawn from the well. Be sure that you speak to no man or woman after you have filled the basin."

She waited, composed, seated by her fire, until at last Morgaine returned.

"I had to scrub it myself," she said, but the basin she held out was shining and brilliant, filled to the brim with clear water.

"Now, unbind your hair, Morgaine."

The girl looked at her curiously, but Viviane said, low and stern, "No questions."

Morgaine pulled out the bone hairpin, and her long locks, dark and coarse and perfectly straight, came tumbling down around her shoulders.

"Now, if you are wearing any jewelry, take it off, and set it over there, so that it will not be near the basin."

Morgaine tugged off two little gilt rings she had on her finger, and unpinned the brooch from her overdress. Without the pin holding it, the overdress fell around her shoulders, and without comment, Viviane helped her pull it off, so that she stood in her undergown alone. Then Viviane opened a little bag she wore about her neck and took out a small quantity of crushed herbs, which wafted a sweetish-musty scent through the chamber. She sifted only a few grains into the basin of water before saying in a low, neutral voice, "Look into the water, Morgaine. Make your mind perfectly still, and tell me what you see."

Morgaine came and knelt before the basin of water, looking intently into its clear surface. The room was very silent, so still that Viviane could hear the small chirping of some insect outside. Then Morgaine said, in a wandering, unfocused voice, "I see a boat. It is draped with black and there are four women in it . . . four queens, for they wear crowns . . . and one of them is you . . . or is it me?"

"It is the barge of Avalon," Viviane said, low. "I know what you see."

She passed her hand lightly over the water and saw the ripples follow her hand. "Look again, Morgaine. Tell me what you see."

This time the silence was longer. Finally the girl said, in that same strange tone, "I see deer—a great herd of deer, and a man among them with his body painted—they put the antlers on him—oh, he is down, they will kill him—" Her voice trembled and again Viviane passed her hand above the surface of the water, and the ripples passed over the surface.

"Enough," she commanded. "Now see your brother."

Silence, again, a silence that stretched and dragged; Viviane felt her body cramped with the tension of stillness but she did not move, with the long discipline of her training. At last Morgaine murmured, "How still he lies . . . but he is breathing, soon he will wake. I see my mother . . . no, it is not Mother, it is my aunt Morgause, and all of her children are with her . . . there are four of them . . . how strange, they are all wearing crowns . . . and there is another, he is holding a dagger . . . why is he so young? Is he *her* son? Oh, he will kill him, he will kill him—ah, no!" Her voice rose to a shriek. Viviane touched her shoulder.

"Enough," she said. "Wake, Morgaine."

The girl shook her head like a puppy stretching after sleep. "Did I see anything?" she asked.

Viviane nodded. "Some day you will learn to see and to remember," she said. "For now it is enough."

Now she was armed to confront Uther and Igraine. Lot of Orkney was, as far as she knew, an honorable man, and had taken oath to support Uther. But should Uther die without an heir . . . Morgause had borne two sons already and there were likely to be more—Morgaine had seen four, and there was no way in which the little Kingdom of Orkney would support four princes. The brothers, when they grew to manhood, were likely to be at one another's throats. And Morgause . . . sighing, Viviane remembered Morgause's vaulting ambition. If Uther died without an heir, then Lot, married to the Queen's own sister, would be a logical choice for the throne. And the succession would be Lot as High King, Lot's sons heirs to the smaller kingdoms. . . .

Would Morgause stoop to plot against the life of a child?

Viviane did not like to think that of the girl she had nursed at her own breasts. But Morgause and Lot, together, with their ambitions!

Easy enough, perhaps, to bribe a groom or insinuate one of her own men into Uther's court, with orders to lead the child into danger as often as possible. Not so easy, of course, to get past a faithful nurse who was his own mother's faithful waiting-woman, but she could be drugged, or given stronger drink than usual, to make her confused, so that something deadly found its way past her vigilance. And no matter how well a child rode, it

would take more strength than any six-year-old had to hold a stallion who
scented a mare in season.

All our plans could have come to ruin in a moment. . . .

At suppertime she found Uther alone at the high table, while the vassals
and serving-men ate their bread and bacon at a lower table in the hall. He
rose and saluted her courteously.

"Igraine is still at her son's side, sister-in-law; I begged her to go and
sleep, but she said she would sleep after he wakened and knew her."

"I have already spoken with Igraine, Uther."

"Oh, yes, she told me, she said you have given your word that he
would live. Was that wise? If he dies after that—"

Uther's face was drawn and worried. He looked no older than when
he had married Igraine; his hair was so fair, Viviane thought, that no one
could see whether it was greyed or not. He was richly dressed in the Roman
fashion, and he was clean-shaven, too, like a Roman. He wore no crown,
but around his upper arms he had two torques of pure gold, and a rich gold
collar.

"He won't die this time. I have some experience with head wounds.
And the injuries to the body haven't penetrated the lungs. He'll be running
around in a day or two."

Uther's face relaxed somewhat. "If I ever find out who loosed that
mare . . . I should beat the boy senseless for riding Thunder!"

"There would be no point in that. He has already paid the price of
his rashness, and I am sure it will teach him whatever lesson is needed,"
Viviane said. "But you should set better guard on your son."

"I cannot guard him night and day." Uther's face was haggard. "I am
away so often at the wars, and I cannot keep so big a boy tied to his nurse's
apron! And we have come near to losing him before this—"

"Morgaine told me."

"Bad luck, bad luck. The man with only one son walks always at the
mercy of any stroke of bad luck," said Uther. "But I am remiss in courtesy,
kinswoman. Here, sit beside me, share my dish if you will. I know Igraine
longed to send to you, and I gave her leave to send a messenger, but you
have come more swiftly than any of us dreamed—is it true, then, that the
witches of the Holy Islands can fly?"

Viviane chuckled. "Would that I could! I would not have spoiled two
pair of good shoes in the mire! Alas, the folk of Avalon, and the Merlin
himself, must walk or ride, even as common folk." She took a piece of the
wheaten loaf and helped herself to butter from a small wooden cask. "You
who wear the serpents at your wrists should know better than to credit those
old fables! But there is a bond of blood between us. Igraine is my mother's
daughter, and I know when she has need of me."

Uther set his lips tight. "I have had dreams and sorceries enough, I want no more of them in my life."

This, as it was intended to do, silenced Viviane. She allowed one of the serving-men to help her to salted mutton, and spoke amiably about the fresh boiled herbs, the first of the year. When she had eaten sparingly, she set down her knife and said, "However I came here, Uther, it was by good fortune, and a sign to me that your child is guarded by the Gods, for he is needed."

"I cannot bear much more of such fortune," Uther said, and his voice was taut. "If you are a sorceress indeed, sister-in-law, I would beg you to give Igraine a charm against barrenness. I thought when we were wedded that she would give me many children, since she had already borne a daughter to old Gorlois, but we have only one, and already he is six years old."

It is written in the stars that you shall have no other son. But Viviane forbore to say this to the man before her. Instead she said, "I will speak with Igraine, and be sure whether it is not some sickness in her which keeps her from conceiving."

"Oh, she conceives right enough, but she can carry the child no more than a moon or two, and the one she brought to birth bled to death when his navel string was cut," Uther said grimly. "He was misshapen, so perhaps it was as well, but if you could give her some charm for a healthy child —I do not know whether I believe in such things, but I am ready to grasp at any straw!"

"I have no such charms," Viviane said, honestly pitying him. "I am not the Great Goddess, to give or withhold children from you, and I would not if I could. I cannot meddle with what the fates have decreed. Does not your own priest say as much to you?"

"Oh, aye, Father Columba speaks about submitting myself to the will of God; but the priest has not a kingdom to rule, which will fall into chaos if I die without an heir," Uther said. "I cannot believe that is what God wants!"

"None of us knows what God wants," Viviane said, "not you, nor I, nor even Father Columba. But it seems certain to me, and it needs neither magic nor sorcery to see it, that you must guard the life of this little one, since he must come to the throne."

Uther's mouth tightened. "God avert that fate," he said. "I should grieve for Igraine's sake if her son died, and even for my own—he is a fine and promising child—but he cannot be heir to the High King of Britain. There is no man in all the length and breadth of this kingdom who does not know that he was begotten while Igraine was still wife to Gorlois, and he came to birth a whole moon sooner than he should have been born, to be my son. True, he was small and puny, and babes *are* cast forth from the womb before their proper time, but I cannot go around and tell all those in the kingdom who were counting on their fingers, can I? He will be Duke of Cornwall when he is grown, but I cannot hope to make him High King after me. Even if he lives to grow up, which with his luck is unlikely."

"He looks enough like you," Viviane said. "Do you think everyone at court is blind?"

"But what of all those who have never come to court? No, I must get myself an heir on whose birth there can be no stain. Igraine *must* bear me a son."

"Well, God grant it be so," Viviane said, "but you cannot force your will on God either, nor allow Gwydion's life to be thrown away. Why not send him to fosterage at Tintagel? That is so remote, and if you put him in charge of your most trusted vassal, sending him there would convince everyone that he was truly Cornwall's son and you have no intention of making him High King; perhaps then they would not bother to plot against him."

Uther frowned. "His life would not be safe till after Igraine had borne me another son," he said, "even if I sent him as far as Rome, or to the country of the Goths!"

"And with the hazards of the road, that is not practical," Viviane agreed. "I have, then, another suggestion. Send him to me, to be fostered in Avalon. None can come there except the faithful who serve the Holy Isle. My own youngest son is already seven, but soon he will be sent to King Ban in Less Britain, to be fostered as suits a nobleman's son. Ban has other sons, so Galahad is not his heir, but Ban acknowledges him, and has given him lands and estates, and will have him at court as a page, and a soldier when he is grown. At Avalon, your son will learn all that he needs to know about the history of his land, and his destiny . . . and the destiny of Britain. Uther, none of your enemies knows where Avalon lies, and no harm could come near him."

"It would keep him safe. But for practical reasons, it is not possible. My son must be reared as a Christian; the church is powerful. They would never accept any king—"

"I thought you said he could not be king after you," Viviane said dryly.

"Well, there is always the possibility," Uther said in despair, "if Igraine should have no other son. If he has been fostered among the Druids and their magic—the priests would call that evil."

"Do I seem evil to you, Uther? Or does the Merlin?" She looked straight into his eyes and Uther let his gaze fall.

"No, of course not."

"Then why will you not entrust Igraine's son to his wisdom and mine, Uther?"

"Because I too distrust the magic of Avalon," said Uther at last. With a nervous gesture he touched the tattooed serpents around his arms. "I saw such things on yonder island as would make any good Christian turn pale —and by the time my son is grown, this isle will be all Christian. There will be no need for a king to deal in such things."

Viviane felt like raging, *Fool, it was the Merlin and I who set you on that throne, not your Christian priests and bishops.* But there was no good to be gained in arguing with Uther.

"You must do as your own conscience bids you, Uther. But I beg you to send him somewhere for fostering, and let that place be secret. Give it out that you are sending him out to be brought up in obscurity, away from the flattery of a prince at court—that's common enough—and let people think he's going to Less Britain, where he has cousins at Ban's court. Then send him to one of your poorer vassals—one of Ambrosius' old courtiers, perhaps: Uriens, Ectorius, someone very obscure and very trustworthy."

Uther nodded slowly. "It will be a wrench to Igraine to part with the child," he said, "but a prince must be fostered as suits his future destiny, and schooled in military strength. I will not tell even you, sister-in-law, where he is to go."

Viviane smiled to herself, thinking, *Do you really think you can keep it secret from me, Uther, if I wish to know?* But she was too diplomatic to say it aloud.

"I have another boon to ask of you, brother-in-law," she said. "Give me Morgaine to foster in Avalon."

Uther stared a moment, then shook his head. "Impossible."

"What is impossible to a High King, Pendragon?"

"There are only two fates for Morgaine," said Uther. "She must marry a man completely sworn to me, one I trust. Or if I can find no such strong ally to give her, she's for the nunnery and the veil. She'll raise up no Cornwall party in this kingdom."

"She does not seem pious enough for a good nun."

Uther shrugged. "For the dower I can give her, any convent will be glad to take her."

And suddenly Viviane was angry. She fixed Uther with her gaze and said, "And do you think you can keep this kingdom long without the good will of the Tribes, Uther? They care nothing for your Christ or your religion. They look to Avalon, and when these—" She put out a finger and touched his tattooed wrists. He drew nervously away, but she went on. "When these were set on your arms, they swore to obey the Pendragon. If

Avalon withdraws its support from you—as high as we set you, Uther, that low can we bring you."

"Fine words, Lady. But can you do as you threaten?" Uther retorted. "Would you do that for a girl and Cornwall's daughter at that?"

"Test me." Her gaze was unflinching. This time he did not lower his eyes from her; he was angry enough to meet her stare equally, and she thought, *Goddess! Had I been ten years younger, how this man and I could have ruled!* In all her life she had known but one or two men who were her equal in strength; but Uther was an antagonist worthy of her steel. And he would need to be, to keep this kingdom together until the predestined king should grow to manhood. Even for Morgaine she could not endanger that. But she thought she could make him see reason.

"Uther, listen to me. The girl has the Sight; she was born to it. There's no way she can escape the Unseen, it will follow her wherever she goes, and in playing about with such things, she'll come to be shunned for a witch, and despised. Is that what you want for a princess at your court?"

"Do you doubt Igraine's ability to rear her daughter as befits a Christian woman? At worst, she could do no harm behind convent walls—"

"No!" Viviane said, so loudly that some of the folk in the lower hall raised their heads and stared round at her. "Uther, the girl's priestess-born. Put her behind convent walls and she'll pine like a caged skua gull. Could you send Igraine's child to death or lifelong misery? I truly believe—and I've spoken with the girl—that she'd kill herself there."

She could see that argument had reached him, and quickly pressed her point.

"She's born to it. Let her be properly trained to her gifts. Uther, is she so happy here, or such an ornament to your court, that you would be sorry to see her leave it?"

Slowly, he shook his head. "I have tried to love her for Igraine's sake. But she's—uncanny," he said. "Morgause used to tease her and say she was one of the fairy folk, and if I did not know her parentage I'd well believe it."

Viviane's smile was taut. "True. She is like me, and like our mother. She's not for the convent or the church bell."

"Yet how can I take both Igraine's children from her at once?" Uther demanded, despairing. That struck Viviane as well with a pang of grief, almost of guilt, but she shook her head.

"Igraine too is priestess-born. She will abide her destiny as you, Uther, abide yours. And if you fear the anger of your house priest," she added, striking shrewdly at a guess and saw, in his eyes, that she had hit home, "then tell no one where you have sent her. Put it about, if you wish, that you have sent her for schooling in a nunnery. She is too wise and sober for the ways of the court, small flirtations and womanish gossip. And Igraine, if she knows her children are safe and happy, growing toward their own fates, will be content while she has you."

Uther bowed his head. "So be it," he said. "The boy to be fostered with my trustiest and most obscure vassal—but how can I send him there unknown? Will the danger not follow him?"

"He can be sent by hidden ways, and under a glamour, as you yourself came to Tintagel," Viviane said. "You trust me not, but will you trust the Merlin?"

"With my very life," Uther said. "Let the Merlin take him. And Morgaine, then, to Avalon." He leaned his head in his hands, as if the burden he bore were too great for endurance. "You are wise," he said, then raised his head and stared at her with unflinching hatred. "I wish you were a foolish woman I could despise, damn you!"

"If your priests are right," said Viviane calmly, "I am already thoroughly damned and you may save your breath."

11

the sun was setting as they came to the Lake. Viviane twisted on her pony to look at Morgaine, who rode a little behind her. The girl's face was drawn with weariness and hunger, but she had not complained, and Viviane, who had deliberately set a hard pace to try her stamina, was satisfied. The life of a priestess of Avalon was not an easy one, and she needed to know that Morgaine could endure fatigue and hardship. She slowed her pony now, and let Morgaine draw abreast of her.

"There lies the Lake," she said. "In a little while we will be within walls, and there will be fire, and food and drink."

"I shall be glad of all three," Morgaine said.

"Are you tired, Morgaine?"

"A little," the girl said diffidently, "but I am sorry to see this journey end. I like seeing new things, and I have never gone anywhere before."

They halted their horses at the water's edge, and Viviane tried to see the familiar shore as it would appear to a stranger—the dull greyed waters of the Lake, the tall reeds edging the shore, silent, low-hanging clouds, and tufts of weed in the water. It was a silent scene, and Viviane could hear the girl's thoughts: *It is lonely here, and dark, and dismal.*

"How do we get to Avalon? There is no bridge—surely we do not have to swim the horses?" Morgaine asked her, and Viviane, remembering how they had had to do just that at a ford swollen by spring rains, reassured her quickly.

"No; I will call the boat."

She raised her two hands to cover her face, shut out unwanted sight and sound, and sent out the silent call. Within moments, over the greying surface of the Lake, a low barge appeared. Draped at one end in black and silver, it glided so silently that it seemed to skim over the water like some waterfowl—there was no sound of oars, but as it came nearer they could see the silent oarsmen, wielding their paddles without the slightest splash or sound. They were dark little men, half naked, their skins tattooed with blue woad in magical patterns, and Viviane saw Morgaine's eyes widen at the sight; but she said nothing.

She accepts all this too calmly, Viviane thought. *She is young enough that she does not see the mystery of what we do; somehow I must make her aware of it.*

The silent little men moored the boat, securing it with a curiously woven rope of plaited reed. Viviane signalled to the girl to dismount, and the horses were led on board. One of the tattooed men held out his hand to Morgaine to help her step on board, she half expected it to be insubstantial, a vision like the boat, but instead his hand felt callused, hard as horn. Last, Viviane took her place at the prow, and the barge moved out, slowly and silently, into the Lake.

Ahead of them rose the Isle and the Tor with its tall tower to Saint Michael; over the silent water, the sound of church bells rang a soft Angelus. Morgaine, from habit, crossed herself, and one of the little men gave her so sharp a frown that she flinched and dropped her hand. As the boat skimmed over the water through the overgrown reeds she could make out the walls of the church and the monastery. Viviane could sense the young girl's sudden fear—were they going, after all, to the Isle of the Priests, where convent walls would close about her forever?

"Are we going to the Island church, Aunt?"

"We will not come to the church," Viviane replied tranquilly, "though it is true that an ordinary traveller, or you yourself, if you set out upon the Lake alone, would never come to Avalon. Wait and see, and ask no questions; that is to be your lot while you are in training."

Rebuked, Morgaine fell silent. Her eyes were still dilated with fear. She said in a low voice, "It is like the folktale of the fairy barge, which sets sail from the islands to the Land of Youth. . . ."

Viviane paid no attention. She stood in the prow of the boat, breathing deeply, summoning her strength for the magical act she was about to perform; for a moment she wondered if she still had the strength for it.

I am old, she thought with momentary panic, *yet I must live until Morgaine and her brother are grown. The peace of all this land depends on what I can do to safeguard them!*

She cut off the thought; doubt was fatal. She reminded herself that she had done this almost every day of her adult life and by now it was so natural to her that she could have done it in her sleep or if she were dying. She stood still, rigid, locked into the tension of magic, then stretched out her arms, extending them full length, raising them high above her head, palms toward the sky. Then, with a swiftly exhaled breath, she brought them down —and with them fell the mists, so that the sight of the church was wiped out, and the shores of the Isle of the Priests, and even the Tor. The boat glided through thick, impenetrable fog, dark as night around them, and in the darkness she could hear Morgaine, breathing quickly like a small, scared animal. She began to speak—to reassure the girl that there was nothing to fear—then, deliberately, held her peace. Morgaine was now a priestess in training and must learn to conquer fear as she conquered fatigue and hardship and hunger.

The boat began to glide through the mists. Swiftly and surely—for there were no other boats on this Lake—the boat poled through the thick, clinging damp; Viviane felt it on her hair and eyebrows, soaking through her woolen shawl. Morgaine was shivering with the sudden cold.

Then, like a curtain being pulled back, the mist vanished, and before them lay a sunlit stretch of water and a green shore. The Tor was there, but Viviane heard the young girl in the boat catch her breath in shock and astonishment. Atop the Tor stood a circle of standing stones, brilliant in the sunlight. Toward it led the great processional way, winding upward in a spiral around the immense hill. At the foot of the Tor lay the buildings where the priests were housed, and on the slope she could see the Sacred Well and the silver flash of the mirror pool below. Along the shore were groves of apple trees and beyond them great oaks, with the golden shoots of mistletoe clinging to their branches in midair.

Morgaine whispered, "It is beautiful . . ." and Viviane could hear the awe in her voice. "Lady, is it real?"

"It is more real than any other place you have ever seen," Viviane told her, "and soon you will know it."

The barge moved toward the shore and scraped heavily on the sandy edge; the silent oarsmen moored it with a rope, and assisted the Lady to step on shore. Then they led the horses to land, and Morgaine was left to step on shore by herself.

She was never to forget that first sight of Avalon in the sunset. Green lawns sloped down to the edge of the reeds along the Lake, and swans glided, silent as the barge, over the waters. Beneath the groves of oak and apple trees rose a low building of grey stone, and Morgaine could see white-robed forms pacing slowly along the colonnaded walk. From somewhere, very softly, she could hear the sound of a harp. The low, slanting light—could it be the same sun she knew?—flooded the land with gold and silence, and she felt her throat tighten with tears. She thought, without knowing why, *I am coming home,* even though all the years of her life had been spent at Tintagel and at Caerleon and she had never seen this fair country before.

Viviane finished giving directions about the horses, and turned to Morgaine again. She saw the look of wonder and awe on the girl's face, and forbore to speak until Morgaine drew a shaking breath, as if waking from sleep. Women, robed in dark-dyed dresses with overtunics of deerskin, some of them with a crescent moon tattooed in blue between their brows, came down the path toward them; some were like Morgaine and Viviane herself, small and dark, of the Pictish people, but a few were tall and slender, with fair or reddish-brown hair, and there were two or three who bore the unmistakable stamp of Roman ancestry. They bent before Viviane in silent respect and she raised her hand in a gesture of benediction.

"This is my kinswoman," Viviane said. "Her name is Morgaine. She will be one of you. Take her—" Then she looked at the young girl, who stood shivering as the sun sank and darkness dropped grey, draining the fantastic colors from the landscape. The child was weary and frightened. There were enough trials and ordeals before her; she need not begin them at this moment.

"Tomorrow," she said to Morgaine, "you will go to the House of Maidens. It will make no difference there that you are my kinswoman and a princess, you will have no name and no favors except what you can earn for yourself. But for tonight only, come with me; we have had little time to talk together on this journey."

Morgaine felt her knees wobbling with the sudden relief. The women facing her, all strange and with their alien dress and the blue markings on their brows, frightened her more than the whole court of Uther assembled. She saw Viviane make a little dismissing motion, and the priestesses—for so she supposed they were—turned and went away. Viviane held out her hand, and Morgaine took it, feeling the fingers reassuringly cool and solid.

Once again Viviane was the kinswoman she knew, yet at the same time she was the awesome figure who had brought down the mists. Once again Morgaine felt the impulse to make the sign of the cross, and wondered if all this country would vanish away as Father Columba said all demonwork and sorceries must vanish at that sign.

But she did not cross herself; she knew suddenly that she would never do so again. *That* world lay behind her forever.

At the edge of the apple grove, between two trees just coming into blossom, stood a little house of wattle and daub. Inside, a fire was burning, and a young woman—like the others she had seen, in dark dress and deerskin tunic—welcomed them with a silent bow.

"Do not speak to her," said Viviane. "She is, at present, under a vow of silence. She is a priestess in her fourth year, and her name is Raven."

In silence, Raven stripped off Viviane's outer garments and her muddy and travel-worn shoes; at a sign from Viviane she did the same for Morgaine. She brought them water for washing, and later, food: barley bread and dried meat. For drink there was only cold water, but it was fresh and delicious, unlike any water Morgaine had ever tasted.

"It is the water of the Sacred Well," Viviane said. "We drink nothing else here; it brings vision and clear sight. And the honey is from our own hives. Eat your meat and enjoy it, for you will taste no more for years; the priestesses eat no meat until they have finished their training."

"Why is that, Lady?" Morgaine could not say "Aunt" or "kins-woman." Standing between her and the familiar names was the memory of the Goddess-like figure summoning the mists. "Is it wrong to eat meat?"

"Surely not and a day will come when you may eat whatever food comes to you. But a diet free of animal flesh produces a high level of consciousness, and this you must have while you are learning to use the Sight and to control your magical powers rather than letting them control you. Like the Druids in the early years of their training, the priestesses eat only bread and fruit, and sometimes a little fish from the lake, and drink only water from the Well."

Morgaine said shyly, "You drank wine at Caerleon, Lady."

"Certainly, and so may you, when you know the proper times to eat and drink, and the proper times to abstain," said Viviane curtly. That silenced Morgaine, and she sat nibbling at her bread and honey. But al-though she was hungry, it seemed to stick in her throat.

"Have you had enough to eat?" Viviane asked. "Good, then let Raven take the dishes—you should sleep, child. But sit here beside me before the fire and talk a little, for tomorrow Raven will take you to the House of Maidens, and you will see me no more, save at the rites, until you are trained to take your turn with the older priestesses, to sleep in my house and care for me as a serving-woman. And at that time you too may well be under a vow of silence, neither to speak nor answer. But for tonight, you are only my kinswoman, not yet vowed to the service of the Goddess, and you may ask me whatever you will."

She held out her hand, and Morgaine came to join her on the bench before the fire. Viviane turned and said, "Will you take the pin from my hair, Morgaine? Raven has gone to her rest, and I do not want to disturb her again."

Morgaine pulled the carven pin of bone from the older woman's hair, and it came down with a rush, long and dark with a streak of white at one temple. Viviane sighed, stretching her bare feet to the fire.

"It is good to be home again—I have had to travel overmuch in late years," she said, "and I am no longer strong enough to find it a pleasure."

"You said I might ask you questions," Morgaine said timidly. "Why do some of the women have blue signs on their brows, and others not?"

"The blue crescent is a sign that they are vowed to the service of the Goddess, to live and die at her will," Viviane said. "Those who are here only for some schooling in the Sight do not take such vows."

"Am I to take vows?"

"That will be your own choice," Viviane said. "The Goddess will tell you whether she wishes to set her hand upon you. Only the Christians use the cloister as a kitchen midden for their unwanted daughters and widows."

"But how will I know if the Goddess wants me?"

Viviane smiled in the darkness. "She will call you in a voice you cannot fail to understand. If you have heard that call, there will be nowhere in the world to hide from her voice."

Morgaine wondered, but was too timid to ask, if Viviane had been vowed so. *Of course! She is the High Priestess, the Lady of Avalon. . . .*

"I was so vowed," Viviane said quietly, with the trick she had of answering an unspoken question, "but the mark has worn away with time . . . if you look closely, I think you can still see a little of it at the edge of my hair, there."

"Yes, a little . . . what does it mean to be vowed to the Goddess, Lady? Who is this Goddess? I asked Father Columba once if God had any other name, and he said, no, there was only one Name by which we could be saved and that was Jesus the Christ, but—" She broke off, abashed. "I am very ignorant about such things."

"To know you are ignorant is the beginning of wisdom," Viviane said. "Then, when you begin to learn, you will not have to forget all the things you think you know. God is called by many names, but is everywhere One; and so, when you pray to Mary, mother of Jesus, you pray, without knowing it, to the World Mother in one of her many forms. The God of the priests and the Great One of the Druids is the same One, and that is why the Merlin sometimes takes his place among the Christian councillors of the High King; he knows, if they do not, that God is One."

"Your mother was priestess here before you, my mother said—"

"That is true, but it was not a matter of blood alone. Rather that I had inherited her gift of the Sight, and vowed myself to the Goddess of my free will. The Goddess did not call your mother, nor Morgause. So I sent Igraine to be married to your father and then to Uther, and Morgause to be married as the King should decree. Igraine's marriage served the Goddess; over Morgause, she had no power and no call."

"Are the priestesses called by the Goddess never married then?"

"Usually not. They do not vow themselves to any man, except for the Great Marriage, where priest and priestess join in symbol of God and Goddess, and children so born are children to no mortal man, but to the Goddess. This is a Mystery, and you will learn it at the proper time. I was so born, and have no earthly father. . . ."

Morgaine stared at her and whispered, "Do you mean that—that your mother lay with a God?"

"No, of course not. Only a priest, overshadowed by the power of the God; probably a priest whose name she never knew, because at that moment or in that time, the God came into him and possessed him so that the man was forgotten and unknown." Her face was distant, remembering strange things; Morgaine could see them moving across her brow. It seemed that the fire made pictures in the room, a great figure of a Horned One. . . . She shivered suddenly and pulled her cloak about her.

"Are you weary, child? You should sleep—"

But Morgaine was curious again. "Were you born in Avalon?"

"Yes, though I was fostered on the Druid Isle, far to the north, in the Islands. And when I was grown to womanhood, the Goddess set her hand upon me—the blood of the priestess-born ran true in me, as I think it does in you, my child." Her voice was distant; she rose and stood looking into the fire.

"I am trying to remember how many years ago it was that I came here with the old woman . . . the moon was farther south then, for it was harvesttime, and the dark days of Samhain coming on, in the dying of the year. It was a bitter winter, even at Avalon; we heard wolves in the night, and snow lay deep, and we hungered here, for no one could make the passage through the storms, and some of the little children at the breast died when milk failed. . . . Then the Lake froze, and they brought us food on sledges. I was a maiden then, my breasts had not grown, and now I am old, an old woman, a crone . . . so many years, child."

Morgaine could feel the older woman's hand trembling; she held it hard in her own. After a moment Viviane drew the girl to her side and stood, her arm around her waist.

"So many moons, so many Midsummers . . . and now it seems that Samhain follows hard upon Beltane-eve more swiftly than the moon waxed from maiden to full when I was young. And you too will stand here before the fire, and grow old as I have grown old, unless the Mother has other tasks for you . . . ah, Morgaine, Morgaine, little one, I should have left you in your mother's house. . . ."

Morgaine flung her arms fiercely around the priestess. "I could not stay there! I would rather have died. . . ."

"I knew that," Viviane said, sighing. "I think the Mother has laid her hand on you too, child. But you have come from a life of ease into a hard life and a bitter one, Morgaine, and it may be that I will have tasks for you as cruel as those the Great Mother has laid on me. Now you think only of learning to use the Sight, and of living in the beautiful land of Avalon, but it is no easy thing to serve the will of Ceridwen, my daughter; she is not only the Great Mother of Love and Birth, she is also the Lady of Darkness and Death." Sighing, she stroked the girl's soft hair. "She is also the Morrigán, the messenger of strife, the Great Raven . . . oh, Morgaine, Morgaine, I would you had been my own child, but even so I could not spare you, I must use you for her purposes as I was myself used." She bowed her head, laid it for a moment on the young girl's shoulder. "Believe that I love you, Morgaine, for a time will come when you will hate me as much as you love me now—"

Morgaine fell impulsively to her knees. "Never," she whispered. "I am in the hands of the Goddess . . . and in yours . . ."

"May she grant that you never regret those words," Viviane said. She stretched out her hands to the fire. They were small, and strong, and a little swollen with age. "With these hands I have brought children to birth; and I have seen a man's lifeblood flow from them. Once I betrayed a man to his death, a man who had lain in my arms and I had sworn to love. I destroyed your mother's peace, and now I have taken her children from her. Do you not hate me and fear me, Morgaine?"

"I fear you," said the girl, still kneeling at her feet, her dark, intense, small face glowing with firelight, "but I could never hate you."

Viviane sighed deeply, thrusting away foresight and dread. "And it is not me you fear," she said, "but her. We are both in her hands, child. Your virginity is sacred to the Goddess. See you keep it so till the Mother makes her will known."

Morgaine laid her small hands over Viviane's. "Be it so," she whispered. "I swear it."

The next day she went to the House of the Maidens, and there she remained for many years.

MORGAINE SPEAKS . . .

How do you write of the making of a priestess? What is not obvious is secret. Those who have walked that road will know, and those who have not will never know though I should write down all the forbidden things. Seven times Beltane-eve came and went; seven times the winters shrivelled us all with cold. The Sight came easily; *Viviane had said I was priestess-born. It was not so easy to bid it come when I willed and only when I willed, and to close the gates of the Sight when it was not fitting I should see.*

It was the small magics which came hardest, forcing the mind first to walk in unaccustomed paths. To call the fire and raise it at command, to call the mists, to bring rain—all these were simple, but to know when to bring rain or mist and when to leave it in the hands of the Gods, that was not so simple. Other lessons there were, at which my knowledge of the Sight helped me not at all: the herb lore, and the lore of healing, the long songs of which not a single word might ever be committed to writing, for how can the knowledge of the Great Ones be committed to anything made by human hands? Some of the lessons were pure joy, for I was allowed to learn to play upon the harp and to fashion my own, using sacred woods and the gut of an animal killed in ritual; and some lessons were of terror.

Hardest of all, perhaps, to look within myself, under the spell of the drugs which loosed the mind from the body, sick and retching, while the mind soared free past the limits of time and space, and to read in the pages of the past and the future. But of that I may say nothing. At last, the day when I was cast out of Avalon, clad only in my shift, and unarmed save for the little dagger of a priestess, to return—if I could. I knew that if I did not, they would mourn me as one dead, but the gates would never again be opened to me unless I could bid them open at my own will and command. And when the mists closed around me, I wandered long on the shores of the alien Lake, hearing only the bells and the doleful chanting of the monks. And at last I broke through the mists, and called upon her, my feet upon the earth and my head among the stars, stretching from horizon to horizon, and cried aloud the great word of Power. . . .

And the mists parted and I saw before me the same sunlit shore where the Lady had brought me seven years before, and I set my feet on the solid earth of my own home, and I wept as I had done when first I came there as a frightened child. And then the mark of the crescent moon was set between my brows by the hand of the Goddess herself . . . but this is a Mystery of which it is forbidden to write. Those who have felt their brow burned with the kiss of Ceridwen will know whereof I speak.

It was in the second spring after that, when I had been released from the silence, that Galahad, who was already skilled at fighting the Saxons under his own father, King Ban of Less Britain, returned to Avalon.

the priestesses above a certain grade took it in turns to serve the Lady of the Lake, and at this season when the Lady was very busy with preparations for the approaching Midsummer festival, one of them always slept in the little wattled house, so that the Lady might have someone at her call night and day. It was so early that the sun still hid in the mist at the edge of the horizon when Viviane stepped into the room beyond her own, where her attendant slept, and beckoned quietly to awaken her.

The woman sat up in bed, flinging her deerskin tunic over her undergown.

"Tell the bargemen to be ready. And go and ask my kinswoman Morgaine to attend upon me."

A few minutes later, Morgaine paused respectfully before the entrance where Viviane was kneeling to build up her fire. She made no sound; after nine years of training in the priestess arts, she moved so silently that no footfall or even a breath of air marked her passing. But after those years, too, the ways of the priestesses were so well known to her that she was not surprised when Viviane turned as she reached the door, and said, "Come in, Morgaine."

Rather contrary to her usual custom, however, Viviane did not invite her kinswoman to sit, but kept her standing there, regarding her evenly for a moment.

Morgaine was not tall; she would never be that, and in these years in Avalon she had grown as tall as she would ever be, a scant inch taller than the Lady. Her dark hair was plaited down the back of her neck and wrapped with a deerskin thong; she wore the dark-dyed blue dress and deerskin overtunic of any priestess, and the blue crescent shone darkly between her brows. Nevertheless, smooth and anonymous as she was among them, there was a glint in her eyes which answered to Viviane's cool stare, and Viviane knew from experience that, small and delicately made as she was, when she wished she could throw a glamour over herself that made her appear not only tall but majestic. Already she appeared ageless, and she would, Viviane knew, look much the same even when white appeared in her dark hair.

She thought, with a flicker of relief, *No, she is not beautiful,* then wondered why it should matter to her. No doubt Morgaine, like all young women, even a priestess vowed lifelong to the service of the Goddess, would prefer to be beautiful, and was intensely unhappy because she was not. She thought, with a slight curl of her lip, *When you are my age, my girl, it will not matter whether or no you are beautiful, for everyone you know will believe that you are a great beauty whenever you wish them to believe it; and when you do not, you can sit back and pretend to be a simple old woman long past such thoughts.* She had fought her own battle more than twenty years ago, when she saw Igraine growing to womanhood with the tawny and russet beauty for which Viviane, still young, would gladly have bartered her soul and all her power. Sometimes, in moments of self-doubt, she wondered if she had thrust Igraine into marriage with Gorlois so that she need not be endlessly taunted with the younger woman's loveliness, mocking her own dark severity. *But I brought her to the love of the man destined for her before the ring stones of Salisbury plain were piled one upon another,* she thought.

She realized that Morgaine was still standing quietly, awaiting her word, and smiled.

"Truly I grow old," she said. "I was lost, for a moment, in memories. You are not the child who came here many years ago; but there are times when I forget it, my Morgaine."

Morgaine smiled and the smile transformed her face, which in repose was rather sullen. *Like Morgause,* Viviane thought, *though otherwise they are nothing alike. It is Taliesin's blood.*

Morgaine said, "I think you forget nothing, kinswoman."

"Perhaps not. Have you broken your fast, child?"

"No. But I am not hungry."

"Very well. I want you to go in the barge."

Morgaine, who had grown used to silence, answered only with a gesture of respect and assent.

It was not, of course, a request unusual in any way—the barge from Avalon must always be guided by a priestess who knew the secret way through the mists.

"It is a family mission," Viviane said, "for it is my son who is approaching the island, and I thought it well to send a kinswoman to welcome him here."

Morgaine smiled. "Balan?" she said. "Will his foster-brother Balin not fear for his soul if he goes beyond the sound of church bells?"

A glint of humor lighted Viviane's eyes, and she said, "Both of them are proud men and dedicated warriors, and they live blameless lives, even by the standards of the Druids, harming none and oppressing none, and ever seeking to right a wrong when they find it. I doubt not that the Saxons find them four times as fearsome when they fight side by side. In fact, they are afraid of nothing, except the evil magic of that wicked sorceress who is mother to one of them . . ." and she giggled like a young woman, and Morgaine giggled with her.

Then, sobering, she said, "Well, I do not regret sending Balan to fosterage in the outer world. He had no call to become a Druid, and he would have made a very bad one, and if he is lost to the Goddess, no doubt she will watch over him in her own way, even if he prays to her with beads and calls upon her as Mary the Virgin. No, Balan is away on the coast, fighting against the Saxons at Uther's side, and I am content to have it so. It is of my younger son I spoke."

"I thought Galahad still in Brittany."

"So did I, but last night with the Sight I saw him . . . he is here. When last I saw him, he was but twelve years old. He is grown considerably, I should say; he must now be sixteen or more, and ready for his arms, but I do not know for certain that he is to bear arms at all."

Morgaine smiled, and Viviane remembered that when Morgaine had first come here, a lonely child, she had sometimes been allowed to spend her free time with the only other child fostered here, Galahad.

"Ban of Benwick must be old now," Morgaine remarked.

"Old, yes; and he has many sons, so that *my* son, among them, is just one more of the king's unregarded bastards. But his half-brothers fear him and would rather he went elsewhere, and a child of the Great Marriage cannot be treated like any other bastard." Viviane answered the unspoken question. "His father would give him land and estates in Brittany, but I saw to it before he was six years old that Galahad's heart would always be here, at the Lake." She saw the glint in Morgaine's eyes and answered, again, the unspoken.

"Cruel, to make him ever discontent? Perhaps. It was not I that was cruel, but the Goddess. His destiny lies in Avalon, and I have seen him with the Sight, kneeling before the Holy Chalice. . . ."

Again, with an ironic inflection, Morgaine made the little gesture of assent with which a priestess under vows of silence would have acquiesced to a command.

Suddenly Viviane was angry with herself. *I sit here justifying what I have done with my life, and the lives of my sons, to a chit of a girl! I owe her no explanations!* She said, and her voice was chilled with sudden distance, "Go with the barge, Morgaine, and bring him to me."

A third time the silent gesture of assent and Morgaine turned to go.

"One moment," Viviane said. "You will break your fast here with us when you bring him back to me; he is your cousin and kinsman too."

When Morgaine smiled again, Viviane realized that she had been trying to make the girl smile, and was surprised at herself.

MORGAINE WENT down along the path toward the edge of the Lake. Her heart was still beating faster than usual; often, these days, when she spoke with the Lady, anger was mixed with affection, to neither of which she was allowed to give voice, and this did strange things to her mind. She wondered at herself, because she had been taught to control her emotions as she controlled her words and even her thoughts.

Galahad she remembered from her first years in Avalon—a scrawny, dark, intense boy. She had not liked him much, but because her heart hungered for her own small brother, she had let the lonely boy run about after her. Then he had been sent away to fosterage and she had seen him only once since, when he was twelve years old, all eyes and teeth and bones thrusting through outgrown clothes. He had grown into an intense disdain of anything female, and she had been occupied with the most difficult part of her training, so she had paid him little heed.

The small, dark men who poled the barge bent before her in silent respect to the Goddess whose form the higher priestesses were supposed to wear, and she signed to them without speaking and took her place in the prow.

Swiftly and silently the draped barge glided out into the mist. Morgaine felt the dampness coalescing on her brow and clinging to her hair; she was hungry, and chilled to the bone, but she had been taught to ignore that too. When they came out of the mist, the sun had risen on the far shore, and she could see a horse and rider waiting there. The barge continued its slow strokes forward, but Morgaine, in a rare moment of self-forgetfulness, stood unguarded, looking at the horseman there.

He was slightly built, his face aquiline and darkly handsome, set off by the crimson cap with an eagle feather in its band and the wide crimson cloak that fell gracefully around him. When he dismounted, the natural grace with which he moved, a dancer's grace, took her breath away. Had she ever wished to be fair and rounded, when dark and slender could show this beauty? His eyes were dark too, glinting with a touch of mischief— mischief which alone gave Morgaine awareness of who this must be, although, otherwise, not a single feature remained of the scrawny boy with the bony legs and enormous feet.

"Galahad," she said, pitching her voice low to keep it from trembling —a priestess-trick. "I would not have recognized you."

He bowed smoothly, the cape swirling as he moved—had she ever despised that as an acrobat's trick? Here it seemed to grow from his body. "Lady," he said.

He has not recognized me either. Keep it so.

Why at this moment did she remember Viviane's words? *Your virginity is sacred to the Goddess. See you keep it so till the Mother makes her will known.* Startled, Morgaine recognized that for the first time in her life, she had looked on a man with desire. Knowing that such things were not for her, but that she was to use her life as the Goddess should decree, she had looked on men with scorn as the natural prey of the Goddess in the form of her priestesses, to be taken or denied as seemed right at the moment. Viviane had commanded that this year she need not take part in the Beltane fire rituals, from which some of her fellow priestesses emerged with child by the will of the Goddess, children who were either born, or cast forth by the knowledge of herb lore and drugs she had been taught—an unpleasant process, which if not followed inevitably brought on the even more unpleasant and dangerous process of birth, and tiresome children who were reared or sent to fosterage as the Lady decreed. Morgaine had been glad enough to escape this time, knowing that Viviane had other plans for her.

She gestured him to step on board. *Never lay hands upon an outsider—* the words of the old priestess who had schooled her; *a priestess of Avalon must be even as a visitor from the otherworld.* She wondered why she had to stop her hand from reaching out to touch his wrist. She knew, with a sureness that made the blood beat hard in her temples, that under the smooth skin would lie hard muscle, pulsing with life, and she hungered to meet his eyes again. She turned away, trying to master herself.

His voice was deep and musical as he said, "Why, now you move your hands, I know you—everything else about you has changed. Priestess, were you not once my kinswoman, called Morgaine?" The dark eyes glinted. "Nothing else is the same as when I used to call you Morgaine of the Fairies. . . ."

"I was, and I am. But years have passed," she said, turning away, gesturing to the silent servants of the barge to pole it away from the shore.

"But the magic of Avalon never changes," he murmured, and she knew he was not speaking to her. "The mist and the reeds and the cry of water birds . . . and then the barge, like magic, gliding from the silent shore . . . I know there is nothing for me here, and yet, somehow, I always return. . . ."

The barge moved silently across the Lake. Even now, after years of knowing that it was no magic, but intensive training in silencing the oars, Morgaine was still impressed by the mystical silence through which they moved. She turned to call the mists, and was conscious of the young man behind her. He stood, easily balanced beside his horse, one arm flung across the saddle blanket, shifting his weight easily without motion, so that he did not visibly sway or lose balance as the boat moved and turned. Morgaine did this herself from long training, but he managed it, it seemed, by his own natural grace.

It seemed that she could feel his dark eyes like a palpable warmth on her back as she stepped to the prow and raised her arms, the long sleeves trailing. She drew a deep breath, charging herself for the magical act, knowing she must concentrate all her strength, intensely angry at herself for her own awareness of the man's eyes on her.

Let him see, then! Let him fear me and know me as the Goddess-self! She knew some rebel part of herself, long stifled, was crying out, *No, I want him to see the woman, not the Goddess, not even the priestess,* but another deep breath and even the memory of that wish was exhaled.

Up went her arms into the arch of the sky; down, with the mists following the sweep of her trailing sleeves. Mist and silence hung dark around them. Morgaine stood motionless, feeling the young man's body warmth very close to her. If she moved even a little, she would touch his hand, and knew how his hand would feel, scalding against her own. She moved away with a little swirling of her robes, and collected distance about herself as with a veil. And all the time she was astonished at herself, saying within her mind somewhere, this is only my cousin, it is Viviane's son who used to sit in my lap when he was little and lonely! Deliberately she summoned the picture of that awkward boy covered with bramble scratches, but when they sailed out of the mist the dark eyes were smiling at her, and she felt dizzy.

Of course I am faint, I have not yet broken my fast, she told herself, and watched the hunger in Galahad's eyes as he looked on Avalon. She saw him cross himself. Viviane would be angry if she had seen that.

"It is indeed the land of the fairy folk," he said, low, "and you are Morgaine of the Fairies, as always . . . but you are a woman, now, and beautiful, kinswoman."

She thought, impatient, *I am not beautiful, what he sees is the glamour of Avalon.* And something rebellious in her said, *I want him to think me beautiful—myself, not the glamour!* She set her mouth tightly and knew that she looked stern, forbidding, all priestess again.

"This way," she said curtly and, as the barge's bottom scraped silently on the sandy edge, signalled for the bargemen to attend to his horse.

"By your leave, lady," he said, "I will attend to it myself. It is not an ordinary saddle."

"As you like," Morgaine said, and stood and watched while he unsaddled his horse himself. But she was too intensely curious about everything concerning him to stand silent.

"Why, it is indeed a strange saddle . . . what are the long leather strappings?"

"The Scythians wear them—they are called stirrups. My foster-father took me on pilgrimage, and I saw them in their country. Even the Roman legions had no such cavalry, for the Scythians with these can control and stop their horses in mid charge, and that way they can fight from horseback," he said, "and even in the light armor the horsemen wear, an equestrian knight is invincible against anyone on foot." He smiled, the dark, intense face lighting up. "The Saxons call me Alfgar—the elf-arrow which comes out of darkness and strikes unseen. At Ban's court they have taken up the name and call me Lancelet, which is as near as they can come to it. Some day I will have a legion of horses equipped this way, and then let the Saxons beware!"

"Your mother told me you were already a warrior," Morgaine said, forgetting to pitch her voice low, and he smiled again at her.

"And now I know your voice, Morgaine of the Fairies . . . how dare you come upon me as a priestess, kinswoman? Well, I suppose it is the Lady's will. But I like you better like this than solemn as a Goddess," he said, with the familiar mischief, as if they had parted but the day before.

Clasping at shreds of her dignity, Morgaine said, "Yes, the Lady awaits us, and we must not keep her waiting."

"Oh yes," he mocked, "always we must scurry to do her will. . . . I suppose you are one of those who hurry to fetch and carry, and hang trembling on her every word."

For that Morgaine found no answer except to say, "Come this way."

"I remember the way," he said, and walked quietly at her side instead of following behind with proper respect. "I too used to run to her and wait upon her will and tremble at her frown, until I found she was not just my mother, but thought herself greater than any queen."

"And so she is," Morgaine said sharply.

"No doubt, but I have lived in a world where men do not come and go at a woman's beckoning." She saw that his jaw was set and that the mischief was gone from his eyes. "I would rather have a loving mother than a stern Goddess whose every breath bids men live and die at her will."

To that Morgaine found nothing whatever to say. She set a swift pace that meant he must scurry at her heels to keep up.

Raven, still silent—for she had bound herself by vows of perpetual silence, save when she spoke tranced as a prophetess—let them into the dwelling with an inclination of the head. As her eyes adjusted to the dimness, Morgaine saw that Viviane, seated by the fire, had chosen to greet her son not in the ordinary dark dress and deerskin tunic of a priestess, but had put on a dress of crimson and done her hair high on her forehead with gems glittering there. Even Morgaine, who knew the tricks of glamour for herself, gasped at the magnificence of Viviane. She was like the Goddess welcoming a petitioner to her underworld shrine.

Morgaine could see that Galahad's chin was set and that the cords in his knuckles stood out, white, against his dark fists. She could hear him breathing, and guessed at the effort with which he steadied his voice, as he rose from his bow.

"My lady and mother, I give you greeting."

"Galahad," she said. "Come, sit here beside me."

He took a seat across from her instead. Morgaine hovered near the door and Viviane beckoned her to come and seat herself too.

"I waited to breakfast with you both. Here, join me."

There was fresh-cooked fish from the Lake, scented with herbs and dripping butter; there was hot, fresh barley bread, and fresh fruit, such food as Morgaine seldom tasted in the austere dwelling of the priestesses. She, and Viviane too, ate sparingly, but Galahad helped himself to everything with the healthy hunger of a youth still growing. "Why, you have set a meal fit for a king, Mother."

"How does your father, and how does Brittany?"

"Well enough, though I have not spent much time there in the last year. He sent me on a far journey, to learn for his court about the new cavalry of the Scythian peoples. I do not think even the soldiers of Rome, such as they are, have any such horsemen now. We have herds of Iberian horses—but you are not interested in the doings of the stud farms. Now I have come to bring word to the Pendragon's court of a new massing of Saxon armies; I doubt not they will strike in full force before Midsummer. Would that I had time and enough gold to train a legion of these horsemen!"

"You love horses," Viviane said in surprise.

"Does that surprise you, madam? With beasts you always know precisely what they think, for they cannot lie, nor pretend to be other than they are," he said.

"The ways of nature will all be open to you," Viviane said, "when you return to Avalon in the life of a Druid."

He said, "Still the same old song, Lady? I thought I gave you my answer when last I saw you."

"Galahad," she said, "you were twelve years old. That is too young to know the better part of life."

He moved his hand impatiently. "No one calls me Galahad now, save you alone, and the Druid who gave me that name. In Brittany and in the field I am Lancelet."

She smiled and said, "Do you think I care for what the soldiers say?"

"So you would bid me sit still in Avalon and play the harp while outside in the real world the struggle goes on for life and death, my lady?"

Viviane looked angry. "Are you trying to say this world is not real, my son?"

"It is real," said Lancelet, with an impatient movement of his hand, "but real in a different way, cut off from the struggle outside. Fairyland, eternal peace—oh, yes, it is home to me, you saw to that, Lady. But it seems that even the sun shines differently here. And this is not where the real struggles of life are taking place. Even the Merlin has the wit to know that."

"The Merlin came to be as he is through years when he learned to know the real from the unreal," said Viviane, "and so must you. There are warriors enough in the world, my son. Yours is the task to see farther than any, and perhaps to bid the warriors come and go."

He shook his head. "No! Lady, say no more, that path is not mine."

"You are still not grown to know what you want," Viviane said flatly. "Will you give us seven years, as you gave your father, to know whether this is your road in life?"

"In seven years," said Lancelet, smiling, "I hope to see the Saxons driven from our shores, and I hope to have a hand in their driving. I have no time for the magics and mysteries of the Druids, Lady, and would not if I could. No, my mother, I beg you to give me your blessing and send me forth from Avalon, for to tell the truth, Lady, I will go with your blessing or without it. I have lived in a world where men do not wait for a woman's bidding to go and come."

Morgaine shrank away as she saw the white of rage sweep over Viviane's face. The priestess rose from her seat, a small woman but given height and majesty by her fury.

"You defy the Lady of Avalon, Galahad of the Lake?"

He did not shrink before her. Morgaine, seeing him pale under the dark tanning of his skin, knew that inside the softness and grace was steel to match the Lady's own. He said quietly, "Had you bidden me this when I still starved for your love and approval, madam, no doubt I would have done even as you commanded. But I am not a child, my lady and mother, and the sooner we acknowledge that, then the sooner we shall be in harmony and cease from quarrelling. The life of a Druid is not for me."

"Have you become a Christian?" she asked, hissing with anger.

He sighed and shook his head. "Not really. Even that comfort is denied me, though in Ban's court I could pass as one when I wished. I think I have no faith in any God but this." He laid his hand on his sword.

The Lady sank down on her bench and sighed. She drew a long breath and then smiled.

"So," she said, "you are a man and there is no compelling you. Although I wish you would speak of this to the Merlin."

Morgaine, watching unregarded, saw the tension relax in the young man's hands. She thought, *He thinks she has given way; he does not know her well enough to know that she is angrier than ever.* Lancelet was young enough to let the relief show in his voice. "I'm grateful to you for understanding, madam. And I will willingly seek counsel of the Merlin, if it pleases you. But even the Christian priests know that a vocation to the service of God is God's gift and not anything that comes because one wants it or does not. God, or the Gods if you will, has not called me, or even given me any proof that He—or They—exist."

Morgaine thought of Viviane's words to her, many years ago: *it is too heavy a burden to be borne unconsenting.* But for the first time she wondered, *What would Viviane really have done if at any time during these years I had come to her and told her that I wished to depart? The Lady is all too sure that she knows the will of the Goddess.* Such heretical thoughts disturbed her, and quickly she thrust them from her mind, resting her eyes again on Lancelet. At first she had only been dazzled by his dark handsomeness, the grace of his body. Now she saw specific things: the first down of beard along his chin—he had not time, or had not chosen, to shave his face in the Roman fashion; his slender hands, exquisitely shaped, fashioned for harp strings or weapons, but callused just a little across palm and the insides of the fingers, more on the right hand than the left. There was a small scar on one forearm, a whitish seam that looked as if it had been there for many years, and another, crescent-shaped, on the left cheek. His lashes were as long as a girl's. But he did not have the androgynous, boy-girl look of many boys before their beards have grown; he was like a young stag. Morgaine thought she had never seen so masculine a creature before. Because her mind had been trained to such thoughts, she thought, *There is nothing of the softness of a woman's training in him, to make him pliable to any woman. He has denied the touch of the Goddess in himself; one day he will have trouble with her. . . .* And again her mind leaped, thinking that one day she would play the role of the Goddess at one of the great festivals, and she thought, feeling a pleasant heat in her body, *Would that he might be the God. . . .* Lost in her daydream, she did not hear what Lancelet and the Lady were saying until she was recalled by hearing Viviane speak her name, and she came back to herself as if she had been wandering somewhere out of the world.

"Morgaine?" the Lady repeated. "My son has been long away from Avalon. Take him away, spend the day on the shores if you will, you are freed for this day from duties. When you were children both, I remember, you liked it well, to walk on the shores of the Lake. Tonight, Galahad, you shall sup with the Merlin, and shall be housed among the young priests who are not under the silence. And tomorrow, if you still wish for it, you shall go with my blessing."

He bowed profoundly, and they went out.

The sun was high, and Morgaine realized that she had missed the sunrise salutations; well, she had the Lady's permission to absent herself, and in any case she was no longer one of the younger priestesses for whom the missing of such a service was a matter for penances and guilt. Today she had intended to supervise a few of the younger women in preparing dyes for ritual robes—nothing that could not wait another day or a handful of days.

"I will go to the kitchens," she said, "and fetch us some bread to take with us. We can hunt for waterfowl, if you like—are you fond of hunting?"

He nodded and smiled at her. "Perhaps if I bring my mother a present of some waterfowl she will be less angry with me. I would like to make my peace with her," he said, almost laughing. "When she is angry she is still frightening—when I was little, I used to believe that when I was not with her she took off her mortality and was the Goddess indeed. But I should not speak like that about her—I can see that you are very devoted to her."

"She has been as devoted to me as a foster-mother," Morgaine said slowly.

"Why should she not be? She is your kinswoman, is she not? Your mother—if I recall rightly—was the wife of Cornwall, and is now the wife of the Pendragon . . . is it so?"

Morgaine nodded. It had been so long that she could only half remember Igraine, and now sometimes it seemed to her that she had been long motherless. She had learned to live without need of any mother save the Goddess, and she had many sisters among the priestesses, so she had no need of any earthly mother. "I have not seen her for many years."

"I saw Uther's queen but once, from a distance—she is very beautiful, but she seems cold and distant too." Lancelet laughed uneasily. "At my father's court I grew used to women who were interested only in pretty gowns and jewels and their little children, and sometimes, if they were not married, in finding a husband. . . . I do not know much about women. You are not like them either. You seem unlike any woman I have ever known."

Morgaine felt herself blushing. She said low, reminding him, "I am a priestess like your mother—"

"Oh," he said, "but you are as different from her as night from day. She is great and terrible and beautiful, and one can only love and adore and fear her, but you, I feel you are flesh and blood and still real, in spite of all these mysteries around you! You dress like a priestess, and you look like one of them, but when I look into your eyes I see a real woman there whom I could touch." He was laughing and intense, and she thrust her hands into his, and laughed back at him.

"Oh, yes, I am real, as real as the ground under your feet or the birds in that tree. . . ."

They walked together down by the waterside, Morgaine leading him along a little path, carefully skirting the edges of the processional way.

"Is it a sacred place?" he asked. "Is it forbidden to climb the Tor unless you are a priestess or a Druid?"

"Only at the great festivals is it forbidden," she said, "and you may certainly come with me. I may go where I will. There is no one on the Tor now except sheep grazing. Would you like to climb it?"

"Yes," he said. "I remember once when I was a child I climbed it. I thought it was forbidden, and so I was sure that if anyone knew I had been there I would be punished. I still remember the view from the height. I wonder if it was as enormous as it seemed to me when I was a little lad."

"We can climb the processional way, if you will. It is not so steep, because it winds round and round the Tor, but it is longer."

"No," he said. "I would like to climb straight up the slope—but"— he hesitated—"is it too long and steep for a girl? I have climbed in rougher country, hunting, but can you manage in your long skirts?"

She laughed and told him that she had climbed it often. "And as for the skirts, I am used to them," she said, "but if they get into my way I will not hesitate to tuck them up above my knees."

His smile was slow and delightful. "Most women I know would think themselves too modest to show their bare legs."

Morgaine flushed. "I have never thought modesty had much to do with bared legs for climbing—surely men know that women have legs like their own. It cannot be so much of an offense of modesty to see what they must be able to imagine. I know some of the Christian priests speak so, but they seem to think the human body is the work of some devil, not of God, and that no one could possibly see a woman's body without going all into a rage to possess it."

He looked away from her, and she realized that beneath the outward assurance he was still shy, and that pleased her. Together they set off upward, Morgaine, who was strong and hardy from much running and walking, setting a pace which astonished him and which, after the first few moments, he found it difficult to match. About halfway up the slope Morgaine paused, and it was a definite satisfaction to her to hear him breathing hard when her own breath still came easily, unforced. She wound the loose folds of her skirt up around her waist, letting only a single drape hang to her knees, and went on along the steeper, rockier part of the slope. She had never before had the slightest hesitation in baring her legs, but now, when she knew he was looking at them, she could not keep from remembering that they were shapely and strong, and she wondered if he really thought her immodest after all. At the top, she climbed up over the rim of the hill and sat down in the shadow of the ring stones. A minute or two later he came over the edge behind her and flung himself down, panting.

When he could speak again, he said, "I suppose I have been riding too much and not walking and climbing enough! You, you are not even short of breath."

"Well, but I am accustomed to coming up here, and I do not always stop to go round by the processional way," she said.

"And on the priests' Isle there is not even a shadow of the ring stones," he said, and pointed.

"No," she said. "In their world there is only their church and its tower. If we wanted to listen with the ears of the spirit we could hear the church bells . . . they are shadows here, and in their world, we should be shadows. I sometimes wonder if that is why they avoid the church and keep great fasts and vigils on our holy days—because it would be too uncanny to feel all around them the shadow of the ring stones and perhaps even, for those who still had some shadow of the Sight, to feel and sense all around them the comings and goings of the Druids and hear the whisper of *their* hymns."

Lancelet shivered and it seemed that a cloud covered the sun for a moment. "And you, you have the Sight? You can see beyond the veil that separates the worlds?"

"Everyone has it," Morgaine said, "but I am trained to it beyond most women. Would you see, Galahad?"

He shivered again and said, "I beg you, do not call me by that name, cousin."

She laughed. "So even though you live among Christians, you have that old belief of the fairy folk, that one who knows your true name can command your spirit if he will? You know *my* name, cousin. What would you have me call you? Lance, then?"

"What you will, save for the name my mother gave me. I still fear her voice when she speaks that name in a certain tone. I seem to have drunk in that fear from her breasts. . . ."

She reached over to him and laid her fingertip over the spot between his brows which was sensitive to the Sight. She breathed softly on it, and heard his gasp of astonishment, for the ring stones above them seemed to melt away into shadows. Before them now the whole top of the Tor stretched, with a little wattle-and-daub church rising beneath a low stone tower which bore a crude painting of an angel.

Lancelet crossed himself swiftly as a line of grey-clad forms came toward them, as it seemed.

"Can they see us, Morgaine?" His voice was a rough whisper.

"Some of them, perhaps, can see us as shadows. A few may think we are some of their own people, or that their eyes are dazzled with the sun and they see what is not there," she said, with a catch of breath, for what she told him was a Mystery which she really should not have spoken to an uninitiated person. But she had never in her life felt so close to anyone; she felt she could not bear it, to keep secrets from him, and made him this gift, telling herself that the Lady wanted him for Avalon. What a Merlin he would make!

She could hear the soft sound of singing: *O thou lamb of God, who drawest away from us all evil of this world, Lord Christ, show us thy mercy. . . .*

He was singing it softly under his breath, as the church vanished and the ring stones towered again above them.

She said quietly, "Please. It is an offense to the Great Goddess to sing that here; the world she has made is not evil, and no priestess of hers will allow man to call it so."

"As you will." He was silent, and again the shadow of cloud passed over his face. His voice was musical, so sweet that when he ceased singing she longed to hear it again.

"Do you play the harp, Lance? Your voice is beautiful enough for a bard."

"As a child, I was taught. After, I had only the usual training befitting a nobleman's son," said Lancelet. "I learned only so great a love of music as to be discontented with my own sounds."

"Is it so? A Druid in training must be a bard before he is a priest, for music is one of the keys to the laws of the universe."

Lancelet sighed. "A temptation, that; one of the few reasons I can see for embracing that vocation. But my mother would have me sit in Avalon and play the harp while the world falls apart around us and the Saxons and the wild Northmen burn and ravage and pillage—have you ever seen a village sacked by the Saxons, Morgaine?" Quickly, he answered his own question. "No, you have not, you are sheltered here in Avalon, outside of the world where these things are happening, but I must think of them. I am a soldier, and it seems to me that in these times, defending this beautiful land against their burning and looting is the only work befitting a man." His face was indrawn, looking on dreadful things.

"If war is so evil," Morgaine said, "why not shelter from it here? So many of the old Druids died in that last of great magics which removed this holy place from profanation, and we have not enough sons to train in their place."

He sighed. "Avalon is beautiful, and if I could make all kingdoms as peaceful as Avalon, then I would gladly stay here forever, and spend my days in harping and making music and speaking with the spirits of the great trees . . . but it seems to me no work for a man, to skulk here in safety when others outside must suffer. Morgaine, let us not speak of it now. For today, I beg you, let me forget. The world outside is filled with strife, and I came here for a day or two of peace; will you not give it to me?" His voice, musical and deep, trembled a little, and the pain in it hurt her so profoundly she thought for a moment that she would weep. She reached for his hand and pressed it.

"Come," she said. "You wanted to see if the view was as you remembered. . . ."

She led him from the ring stones and they looked out over the Lake. Bright water, rippling softly in the sunlight, stretched all around the Island; far below, a little boat, no larger at this height than a fish leaping, streaked the surface. Other islands, indistinct in the mist, rose as dim shapes, blurred by distance and by the magical veil which removed Avalon from the world.

"Not very far from here," he said, "there is an old fairy fort at the top of a hill, and the view from the wall is such that standing there, a man can see the Tor, and the Lake, and there is an island which is like the shape of a coiled dragon—" He gestured with his shapely hand.

"I know the place," Morgaine said. "It is on one of the old magical lines of power which crisscross the earth; I was brought there once to feel the earth powers there. The fairy people knew those things—I can sense them a little, feel the earth and the air tingling. Can you feel it? You too are of that blood, being Viviane's son."

He said in a low voice, "It is easy to feel the earth and air tingling with power, here in this magical isle."

He turned away from the view, saying as he yawned and stretched, "That climb must have taxed me more than I thought; and I rode much of the night. I am ready to sit in the sun and eat some of that bread you carried here for us!"

Morgaine led him into the very center of the ring stones. If he was sensitive at all, she thought, he would be aware of the immense power here.

"Lie back on the earth and she will fill you with her strength," she said, and handed him a piece of the bread, which she had spread thickly with butter and comb honey before wrapping it in a bit of deerskin. They ate slowly, licking their fingers free of the honey, and he reached for her hand, taking it up playfully and sucking a bit of honey off her finger.

"How sweet you are, cousin," he said, laughing, and she felt her whole body alive with the touch. She picked up his hand to return the gesture, and suddenly dropped it as if it had burned her; to him it was only a game, perhaps, but it could never be so to her. She turned away, hiding her burning face in the grass. Power from the earth seemed to flow up through her, filling her with the strength of the very Goddess herself.

"You are a child of the Goddess," she said at last. "Do you know nothing of her Mysteries?"

"Very little, though my father once told me how I was begotten— a child of the Great Marriage between the king and the land. And so, I suppose, he thought I should be loyal to the very land of Brittany which is mother and father to me. . . . I have been at the great center of the old Mysteries, the great Avenue of Stones at Karnak, where once was the ancient Temple; that is a place of power, like to this one. I can feel the power here," he said. He turned over and looked up into her face. "You are like the Goddess of this place," he said wonderingly. "In the old worship, I know, men and women come together under her power, though the priests would like to forbid it, as they would like to tear down all the ancient stones like these above us, and the great ones of Karnak. . . . They have already torn down a part of them, but the task is too great."

"The Goddess will prevent them," said Morgaine simply.

"Maybe so," Lancelet said, and reached up to touch the blue crescent on her forehead. "It is here that you touched me when you made me see into the other world. Has this to do with the Sight, Morgaine, or is that another of your Mysteries of which you may not speak? Well, I'll not ask you, then. But I feel as if I had been ravished into one of the old fairy forts where, they say, a hundred years can pass in a night."

"Not so long as that," Morgaine said, laughing, "though it is true that time runs differently there. But some of the bards, I have heard, can still come and go from the elf country . . . it has moved further than Avalon into the mists, that is all." And as she spoke, she shivered.

Lancelet said, "Maybe when I go back to the real world, the Saxons will all have been vanquished . . . and gone."

"And will you weep because there is no longer any reason for your life?"

He laughed and shook his head, holding her hand in his. After a minute he said in a low voice, "Have you, then, gone to the Beltane fires to serve the Goddess?"

"No," said Morgaine quietly. "I am virgin while the Goddess wills; most likely I am to be kept for the Great Marriage . . . Viviane has not made her will or the will of the Goddess known to me." She bent her head and let her hair fall across her face, feeling shy before him, as if he could read her thoughts and know the desire which swept through her like a sudden flame. Would she indeed lay down that guarded virginity if he should ask it of her? Never before had the prohibition seemed a hardship; now it seemed that a sword of fire was laid between them. There was a long silence, while the shadows passed across the sun, and there was no sound except the chirping of small insects in the grass. At last Lancelet reached up and drew her down, laying a soft kiss, which burned like fire, on the crescent on her brow. His voice was soft and intense.

"All the Gods together forbid I should trespass where the Goddess has marked you for her own, my dear cousin. I hold you sacred as the Goddess herself." He held her close; she could feel that he was shaking, and a happiness so intense that it was pain flooded through her.

She had never known what it was to be happy, not since she was a small and heedless child; happiness was something she dimly remembered before her mother had burdened her with the weight of her little brother. And here in the Island, life had soared into the free spaces of the spirit and she had known exaltation and the delights of power as well as the suffering and struggle of the pain and the ordeals; but never the pure happiness she knew now. The sun seemed to burn more brightly, the clouds to move through the sky like great wings against the dazzling, sparkling air, every bud of clover in the grass shimmered with its own interior light, a light that seemed to shine out from her as well. She saw herself mirrored in Lancelet's eyes and knew that she was beautiful, and that he desired her, and that his love and respect for her were so great that he would even hold his own desire within bounds. She felt she would burst with her joy.

Time stopped. She swam in delight. He did no more than stroke her cheek with the gentlest of feather-light caresses, and neither of them wanted more. She played softly with his fingers, feeling the calluses on his palms.

After a long time, he drew her against him and spread the edges of his cloak over her. They lay side by side, barely touching, letting the power of the sun and the earth and the air move through them in harmony, and she dropped into a dreamless sleep through which she was still conscious of their intertwined hands. It seemed that some time, a very long time ago, they had lain like this, content, timeless, in an endless joyful peace, as if they were part of the standing stones which had stood here forever; as if she both experienced and remembered being with him here. Later she woke and saw him sleeping, and sat memorizing every line of his face with a fierce tenderness.

The sun had declined from noon when he woke, smiling into her eyes, and stretched like a cat. Still enclosed in the bubble of her joy, she heard him say, "We were going down to hunt waterfowl. I would like to make peace with my mother—I am so happy I cannot bear to think of being at odds with any living thing today, but perhaps the spirits of nature will send us some waterfowl whose given destiny is to make us a happy meal. . . ."

She laughed, clasping his hand. "I will take you where the water birds hunt and fish, and if it is the will of the Goddess, we will catch nothing, so we need not feel guilt about disturbing their destiny. But it is *very* muddy, so you must take off those boots you have for riding, and I will have to tuck up my dress again. Do you use a throwing stick like the Picts, or their little arrows with poison, or do you snare them and wring their necks?"

"I think they suffer less when they are quickly netted and their necks broken at once," Lancelet said thoughtfully, and she nodded.

"I will bring a net and snare—"

They saw no one as they climbed down the Tor, sliding in a few minutes down what had taken them more than an hour to climb. Morgaine slipped into the building where nets and snares were kept and brought out two; they went quietly along the shore and found the reeds at the far side of the Island. Barefoot, they waded into the water, hiding in the reeds and spreading the nets. They were in the great shadow of the Tor, and the air felt chill; the water birds were already beginning to descend in numbers to feed. After a moment a bird began to struggle and flap, its feet caught in Morgaine's snare; she moved swiftly, seized it and, within seconds, broke its neck. Soon Lancelet caught one, then another; he tied their necks together with a band of reeds.

"That is enough," he said. "It is good sport, but on such a day as this I would rather not kill anything needlessly, and there is one for my mother and two for the Merlin. Do you want one for yourself?"

She shook her head. "I eat no flesh," she said.

"You are so tiny," he said, "I suppose you need little food. I am big and I hunger quickly."

"Are you hungry now? It is too early for most berries, but we might find some haws from the winter—"

"No," he said, "not now, not really; my supper will be all the more welcome for a little hunger." They came up on the shore, soaked. Morgaine pulled off her deerskin overtunic to dry it on a bush, for it would stiffen, and pulled off her skirt too, wringing out the water, standing unselfconsciously in her undershift of unbleached linen. They found where they had left their shoes, but they did not put them on, only sitting on the grass, holding hands quietly and watching the waterfowl swimming, suddenly upending their tails and diving for small fish.

"How still it is," Lancelet said. "It is as if we were the only people alive in all the world today, outside time and space and all cares and troubles, or thoughts of war or battle or kingdoms or strife. . . ."

She said, her voice shaking as the thought struck her that this golden time must end, "I wish this day could last forever!"

"Morgaine, are you weeping?" he asked in sudden solicitude.

"No," she said fiercely, shaking a single rebellious drop from her lashes, seeing the world burst into prism colors. She had never been able to weep; had never shed a single tear in fear or pain, through all the years of ordeals in the making of a priestess.

"Cousin, kinswoman . . . Morgaine," he said, holding her against him, stroking her cheek. She turned and clung to him, burying her face in the front of his tunic. He felt warm; she could feel the steady beat of his heart.

After a moment he bent and laid one hand under her chin, raising her face, and their lips met.

He whispered, "I would you were not pledged to the Goddess."

"I, too," she said softly.

"Come here, come here—let me hold you, like this—I have sworn I will not . . . trespass."

She closed her eyes; she no longer cared. Her oath seemed a thousand leagues and a thousand years distant, and not even the thought of Viviane's anger could have deterred her. Years afterward, she wondered what would have happened if they had stayed like that even a few more minutes; no doubt the Goddess in whose hands they lay would have had her will with them. But even as their lips joined again, Lancelet stiffened a little, as if hearing something just outside the range of hearing.

Morgaine pulled away and sat up.

"Morgaine, what is that?"

"I hear nothing," she said, straining to hear beyond the sound of soft water lapping in the Lake, wind rustling in the reeds, and the occasional sound of a fish jumping. And then it came again, like a soft sighing . . . like someone weeping.

"Someone is crying," said Lancelet, and unfolded his long legs quickly to stand up. "Over there . . . someone is hurt or lost, it sounds like a little girl. . . ."

Morgaine followed quickly, barefoot, leaving her skirt and tunic on the bush. It was just possible that one of the younger priestesses might have become lost here, though they were not supposed to leave the enclosure near the House of Maidens. Still, young girls were young girls, and could not yet be trusted not to break rules; one of the old priestesses had once said that the House of Maidens was for little girls whose whole duty in life was to spill things, break things, and forget things, the rules of their daily life among them, until they had spilled, broken, and forgotten everything they could, and thus made room in their lives for a little wisdom. And now that Morgaine was a full priestess, she had begun to instruct the young, and sometimes she felt the old priestess had been right: surely she had never been so silly and empty-headed as the girls who were now in the House of Maidens.

They followed the sound. It was hazy, now fading out for minutes altogether, and then coming back, quite clear. Mist was beginning to drift in from the Lake in thick tendrils, and Morgaine was not quite sure whether it was ordinary fog born of the dampness and the approaching sunset, or whether it was the outlying mist of the veil surrounding the magical realm.

"There," said Lancelet, plunging suddenly into the mist. Morgaine followed him and saw dimly, fading from shadow into reality and back again, the figure of a young girl standing in the water up to her ankles, and crying.

Yes, Morgaine realized, *she's really there;* and, *No, this is no priestess.* She was very young and dazzlingly pretty; she seemed all white and gold, her skin pale as ivory just stained with coral, her eyes palest sky-blue, her hair long and pale and shining through the mist like living gold. She wore a white dress which she was trying unsuccessfully to hold out of the water. And somehow she seemed to shed tears without any ugly distortion of her face, so that, weeping, she only looked prettier than ever.

Morgaine said, "What is the matter, child? Are you lost?"

She stared at them as they came closer, and whispered, "Who are you? I didn't think anyone could hear me here—I called out to the sisters, but none of them could hear me, and then the land started to move, and where it had been all solid, suddenly I was standing here in the water and the reeds were all around me and I was afraid. . . . What is this place? I never saw it before, and I have been in the convent for almost a year now. . . ." And she crossed herself.

Suddenly Morgaine knew what had happened. The veil had thinned, as it did occasionally in spots of such concentrated power, and somehow this girl had had enough sensitivity to be aware of it. This happened, sometimes, as a momentary vision, so that someone could see the other world as a shadow or a brief vision; but to move through *into* the other world was rare.

The girl took a step toward them, but under her feet the marshy surface swayed, and she stopped in panic.

"Stand still," Morgaine said gently. "The ground is a little unsafe here. I know the paths. I'll help you out, dear."

But even as she moved forward, her hand extended, Lancelet stepped in front of her, picked up the young girl, and carried her to dry land, setting her down.

"Your shoes are wet," he said, for they squelched as she moved. "Take them off and you can dry them."

She looked at him in wonder; she had stopped crying. "You're very strong. Not even my father is as strong as that. And I think I have seen you somewhere, haven't I?"

"I don't know," Lancelet said. "Who are you? Who is your father?"

"My father is King Leodegranz," she said, "but I am here at school in the convent. . . ." Her voice began to shake again. "Where is it? I cannot even see the building anywhere, or the church—"

"Don't cry," Morgaine said, stepping forward, and the young girl drew back a little.

"Are you one of the fairy people? You have that blue sign on your forehead—" and she raised her hand and crossed herself again. "No," she said doubtfully, "you cannot be a demoness, you do not vanish when I cross myself, as the sisters say any demon must do—but you are little and ugly like the fairy people—"

Lancelet said firmly, "No, of course neither of us is a demon, and I think we can find the way back to your convent for you." Morgaine, her heart sinking, saw that he now looked upon the stranger as he had looked on her only minutes before, with love, desire, almost worship. As he turned back to Morgaine, saying eagerly, "We can help her, can't we?" Morgaine saw herself as she must look to Lancelet and to the strange golden maiden —small, dark, with the barbarian blue sign on her forehead, her shift muddy to the knees, her arms immodestly bare and her feet filthy, her hair coming down. *Little and ugly like one of the fairy folk. Morgaine of the Fairies.* So they had taunted her since childhood. She felt a surge of self-hatred, of loathing for her small, dark body, her half-naked limbs, the muddy deerskin. She snatched her damp skirt off the bush and put it on, conscious suddenly of her bare limbs; she wound the filthy deerskin tunic over it. For a moment, as Lancelet looked at her, she felt that he too must think her ugly, barbarian, alien; this exquisite golden creature belonged to his own world.

He came and gently took the stranger girl's hand, with a respectful bow. "Come, we can show you the way back."

"Yes," said Morgaine dully, "I will show you the way. Follow me, and stay close, because the ground is treacherous and you could mire yourself and not get out for a long time." For a furious moment she was tempted to lead them both into the impassable mire—she could do it, she knew the way—lead them out there and leave them to drown or wander forever in the mists.

Lancelet asked, "What is your name?"

The fair girl said, "My name is Gwenhwyfar," and she heard Lancelet murmuring, "What a lovely name, fitting to the lady who bears it." Morgaine felt a surge of hatred so great she thought that she would faint with its force. She felt it would be with her until she died, and in that molten instant she actually longed for death. All the color had gone from the day, into the mist and the mire and the dismal reeds, and all her happiness had gone with it.

"Come," she repeated in a leaden voice, "and I will show you the way."

As she turned to go she heard them laughing together behind her and wondered, through the dull surge of hatred, if they were laughing at her. She heard Gwenhwyfar's girlish voice saying, "But *you* don't belong to this horrible place, do you? *You* don't look like one of the fairy folk, you're not little and ugly."

No, she thought, no, he was beautiful, and she—*little and ugly.* The words burned into her heart; she forgot that she looked like Viviane, and that, to her, Viviane was beautiful. She heard Lancelet saying, "No, no, I would love to come back with you—really, I would—but I am promised to dine with a relative this night, and my mother is angry enough with me already; I don't want to make the old gentleman angry too. But no, I don't belong to Avalon . . ." and, after a minute, "No, she's—well, a cousin of my mother's, or something like that, we knew each other when we were children, that's all." And now she knew that he was speaking of her. So quickly, then, all that had been between them had been reduced to a distant family tie. Fiercely fighting back a surge of tears that made her throat ache, knowing that weeping would make her uglier than ever in their eyes, she stepped on dry land. "There lies your convent, Gwenhwyfar. Be careful to keep to the path, or you may lose yourself in the mists again."

She saw that the girl had been holding Lancelet's hand. It seemed to Morgaine that he let it go reluctantly. The girl said, "Thank you, oh, thank you!"

"It is Morgaine you should thank," Lancelet reminded her. "It is she who knows the paths in and out of Avalon." The girl gave her a shy sidelong look. She dropped a little polite curtsey. "I thank you, mistress Morgaine."

Morgaine drew a deep breath, drawing the mantle of a priestess around her again, the glamour she could summon when she would; despite her filthy and torn clothing, her bare feet, the hair that straggled in wet locks around her shoulders, she knew that suddenly she looked tall and imposing. She made a remote gesture of blessing and turned, silent, summoning Lancelet with another gesture. She knew, even though she did not see, that the awe and fright had returned to the girl's eyes, but she moved silently away, with the noiseless gliding of a priestess of Avalon, Lancelet's steps, reluctant, following her own silent ones.

After a moment she looked back, but the mists had closed and the girl had vanished within them. Lancelet said, shaken, "How did you do that, Morgaine?"

"How did I do what?" she asked.

"Suddenly look so—so—like my mother. All tall and distant and remote and—and not quite real. Like a female demon. You frightened the poor girl, you shouldn't have done it!"

Morgaine bit her tongue with her sudden wrath. She said in a remote and enigmatic voice, "Cousin, I am what I am," and turned, hurrying up the path ahead of him. She was cold and weary and sick with an inner sickness; she longed for the solitude of the House of Maidens. Lancelet seemed a long way behind her, but she no longer cared. He could find his own way from here.

13

In the spring of the year after this, through a drenching late-winter storm, the Merlin came late one night to Avalon. When word was brought to the Lady, she stared in astonishment.

"A night such as this would drown the very frogs," she said. "What brings him out in such weather?"

"I do not know, Lady," said the young apprentice Druid who had brought the word. "He did not even send for the barge, but made his own way by the hidden paths, and said that he must see you this night before you slept. I sent him for dry clothing—his own was in such a state as you can imagine. I would have brought him food and wine as well, but he asked if he might sup with you."

"Tell him he is welcome," Viviane said, keeping her face carefully neutral—she had learned very well the art of concealing her thoughts—but when the young man had gone, she allowed herself to stare in amazement, and to frown.

She sent for her attendant women, and bade them bring not her usual spare supper, but food and wine for the Merlin, and to build up the fire anew.

After a time she heard his step outside, and when he came in, he went directly to the fire. Taliesin was stooped now, his hair and beard all white, and he looked somewhat incongruous in the green robe of a novice bard, far too short for him, so that his scrawny ankles protruded from the lower edge of the garment. She seated him near the fire—he was still, she noticed, shivering—and set a plate of food and a cup of wine, good apple wine from Avalon itself, in a chased silver cup, at his side.

Then she seated herself on a small stool nearby and tasted her bread and dried fruit as she watched him eat. When he had pushed the plate aside and sat sipping at the wine, she said, "Now tell me everything, Father."

The old man smiled at her. "I never thought to hear you call me so, Viviane. Or do you think I have taken the holy orders of the church in my dotage?"

She shook her head. "No," she said, "but you were the lover of my mother who was Lady here before me, and you fathered two of my sisters. Together we have served the Goddess and Avalon for more years than I can number, and perhaps I long for the comfort of a father's voice this night . . . I do not know. I feel very old this night, Fa—Taliesin. Is it that you think me too old to be your daughter?"

The old Druid smiled. "Never that, Viviane. You are ageless. I know how old you are—or I could reckon up your age if I chose—but still you seem a girl to me. You might even now have as many lovers as you chose, if you willed it."

She dismissed that with a gesture. "Be sure I have never found any man who meant more to me than necessity, or duty, or a night's pleasure," she said. "And only once, I think, any man save yourself who came near to matching me in strength—" She laughed. "Though, had I been ten years younger—how, think you, would I have befitted the throne as the High King's queen, and my son the throne?"

"I do not think Galahad—what is it he would have you call him now? Lancelet?—I do not think he is the stuff of which kings are made. He is a visionary, a reed shaken by the wind."

"But if he had been fathered by Uther Pendragon—"

Taliesin shook his head. "He is a follower, Viviane, not a leader."

"Even so. That comes from being reared at Ban's court, as a bastard. Had he been reared as a king's son . . ."

"And who would have ruled Avalon in those years, had you chosen a crown in the Christian lands outside?"

"If I had ruled them at Uther's side," she said, "they would not have been Christian lands. I thought Igraine would have power over him, and use it for Avalon. . . ."

He shook his head. "There is no use in fretting after last winter's snow, Viviane. It is of Uther I came to speak. He is dying."

She raised her head and stared at him. "So it has come already." She felt her heart racing. "He is too young to die. . . ."

"He leads his men into battle, where a wiser man of his years might leave it to his generals; he took a wound, and fever set in. I offered my services as healer, but Igraine forbade it, as did the priests. I could have done nothing anyway; his time has come. I saw it in his eyes."

"How does Igraine as queen?"

"Very much as you would have foreseen," said the old Druid. "She is beautiful, and dignified, and pious, and goes always in mourning for the children she has lost. She bore another son at All Hallows; he lived four days, no more. And her house priest has convinced her it is the punishment for her sins. No breath of scandal has ever touched her since she married Uther —save for the birth of that first child, so soon. But that was enough. I asked her what would become of her after Uther's death, and when she had done weeping for that, she said she would retire into a convent. I offered her the shelter of Avalon, where she could be near to her daughter, but she said it would not be seemly for a Christian queen."

Viviane's smile hardened a little. "I never thought to hear that of Igraine."

"Viviane, you must not blame her, even in thought, for what you yourself have wrought. Avalon cast her out when most she needed it; would you chide the girl because she has found comfort in a simpler faith than ours?"

"I doubt it not—you are the only man in all of Britain who could speak of the High Queen as a girl!"

"To me, Viviane, even you are a little girl at times—that same little girl who used to climb on my knee and touch the strings of my harp."

"And now I can hardly play. My fingers lose their suppleness with the years," Viviane said.

He shook his head. "Ah, no, my dear," he said, holding out his own thin, gnarled old fingers. "Next to this, your hands are young, yet daily I speak to my harp with them, and you could have done so as well. Your hands chose to wield power, not song."

"And what would have become of Britain if I had not?" she flared at him.

"Viviane," he said, with a touch of sternness, "I did not censure you. I merely spoke the thing which is."

She sighed and leaned her chin in her hands. "I spoke well when I said that this night I was in need of a father. So it has come upon us already, the thing we feared and have wrought for all these years. What of Uther's son, my father? Is he ready?"

"He *must* be ready," said the Merlin. "Uther will not live till Midsummer-day. And already the carrion crows gather, as they did when Ambrosius lay dying. As for the boy—have you not seen him?"

"Now and again, I see a glimpse of him in the magic mirror," she said. "He looks healthy and strong, but that tells me nothing except that he can look the part of a king when it comes to that. You have visited him, have you not?"

"At Uther's will, I went now and again to see how he grew. I saw that he had those same books in Latin and Greek which taught your son so much of strategy and warfare; Ectorius is Roman to the core, and the conquests of Caesar and the exploits of Alexander are part of his very being. He is an educated man, and has trained both his sons for warfare. Young Caius was blooded in battle last year; Arthur fretted that he could not go, but he is an obedient son to Ectorius and did as he was told."

"If he is so much Roman," Viviane asked, "will Arthur be willing to be subject to Avalon? For he must rule the Tribes, as well, and the Pictish folk, remember."

"I saw to that," said the Merlin, "for I induced him to meet some of the little people, saying that they were the allies of Uther's soldiers in this war to defend our island. With them he has learned to shoot their elf bolts, and to move silently in the heather and over the moors, and—" He hesitated and said significantly, "He can stalk the deer and does not fear to go among them."

Viviane closed her eyes for a moment. "He is so young . . ."

"The Goddess chooses always the youngest and strongest of men to lead her warriors," said Taliesin.

Viviane bowed her head. "Be it so," she said. "He shall be tested. Bring him here if you can before Uther dies."

"Here?" The Merlin shook his head. "Not till the testing is done. Only then can we show him the road to Avalon and the two realms over which he must rule."

Again Viviane bowed her head. "To Dragon Island, then."

"It will be the ancient challenge? Uther was not tested so at his king-making—"

"Uther was a warrior; it was enough to make him lord over the dragon," Viviane said. "This boy is young and unblooded. He must be tested and proven."

"And if he fails . . ."

Viviane gritted her teeth. "He must not fail!"

Taliesin waited until she met his eyes again and repeated, "And if he fails . . ."

She sighed. "No doubt Lot is ready, if that should come."

"You should have taken one of Morgause's sons and fostered him here at Avalon," the Merlin said. "Gawaine is a likely boy. Hotheaded, quarrel-some—a bull, where Uther's boy is a stag. But there is the stuff of a king in Gawaine, I think, and he also is Goddess-born—Morgause too was your mother's daughter, and her sons have the royal blood."

"I do not trust Lot," said the Lady vehemently, "and I trust Morgause less than that!"

"Yet Lot holds the clansmen to the north, and I think the Tribes would accept him—"

"But those who hold to Rome—never," said the Lady, "and then there would be two kingdoms in Britain, ever warring, and neither strong enough to hold off the Saxons and the wild Northmen. No. Uther's son it must be, he must not fail!"

"That must be as the Goddess wills," said the Merlin sternly. "See you mistake not your own will for hers."

Viviane covered her face with her hands. "If he fails—if he fails it will all have been for nothing," she said wildly, "—all that I have done to Igraine, all I have done to all those I love. Father, have you foreseen that it will fail?"

The old man shook his white head and his voice was compassionate.

"The Goddess does not make her will known to me," he said, "and it was you who foresaw that this boy would have the powers to lead all of Britain. I caution you against pride, Viviane—thinking you know the best for every man and woman living. You have ruled well in Avalon—"

"But I am old," she said, raising her face, and she could see the pity in his eyes, "and one day soon . . ."

The Merlin bowed his head; he too lived under that law. "When that time comes, you will know; it is not yet, Viviane."

"No," she said, struggling against the sudden despair which had come, as it sometimes did now, a heat in her body, a torment in her mind, "when it comes, when I can no longer see what lies ahead, then I will know it is time to give over the rulership of Avalon to another. Morgaine is still young, and Raven, whom I love well, has given herself to silence and the voice of the Goddess. It has not yet come; but if it comes too soon—"

"Whenever it comes, Viviane, that will be the right time," the Merlin said. He stood up, tall and unsteady, and Viviane saw that he leaned heavily on his stick. "I will bring the boy to Dragon Island then, at the spring thaw, and we will see whether he is ready to be made king. And then you will give him the sword and the cup, in token that there is an eternal link between Avalon and the world outside—"

"The sword, at least," Viviane said. "The cup—I do not know."

The Merlin bowed his head. "That I leave to your wisdom. You, not I, are the voice of the Goddess. Yet you will not be the Goddess for him—"

Viviane shook her head. "He will meet the Mother when he is triumphant," she said, "and from her hand he will take the sword of victory. But first he must prove his own, and must meet first with the Maiden Huntress. . . ." A flicker of a smile crossed her face. "And no matter what happens after that," she said, "we will take no such chance as we did with Uther and Igraine. We shall make certain of the royal blood, whatever comes of it later."

WHEN THE MERLIN had gone away, she sat for a long time, watching pictures in the fire, seeing into the past alone, not seeking to look through the mist of time toward the future.

She too, years ago, so many years that she could not now remember how many, had laid down her maidenhood to the Horned God, the Great Hunter, the Lord of the living spiral dance. She hardly spared a thought for the virgin who would take this part in the kingmaking which was to come, but she let her mind stray into the past, and the other times she had played the part of the Goddess in the Great Marriage . . .

. . . never had it been more to her than duty; sometimes pleasant, sometimes distasteful, but always bidden, possessed by the Great Mother who had ruled her life since first she had come here. Suddenly she envied Igraine, and a detached part of her mind wondered why she envied a woman who had lost all her children to death or fosterage, and now was to suffer widowhood and end her life behind convent walls.

What I envy her is the love she has known. . . . I have no daughters, my sons are strangers and alien to me. . . . I have never loved, she thought. *Nor have I known what it is to be loved. Fear, awe, reverence . . . these have been given me. Never love. And there are times when I think I would give it all for one look from any human being such as Uther gave Igraine at their wedding.*

She sighed bleakly, repeating half aloud what the Merlin had said. "Well, there is no use fretting after last year's snowfall." She raised her head, and her attendant came on noiseless feet.

"Lady—?"

"Bring me—no," she said, changing her mind abruptly; let the girl sleep. *It is not true that I have never loved or been loved. I love Morgaine beyond all measuring, and she loves me.*

Now that, too, might come to an end. But that too must be as the Goddess willed it.

14

the palest splinter of new moon stood to the west of Avalon. Morgaine paced slowly upward, her bare feet treading out the spiral pathway, noiseless and pale as the virgin moon. Her hair was unbound, her single garment uncinctured. She knew that guards and priestesses watched her, silent, lest some unauthorized person disturb her silence with an unconsecrated word. Behind the dark curtain of her hair, her eyelids were lowered. She moved unerringly on the path, without need for sight. Raven moved silently behind her, like Morgaine barefoot, ungirdled, her unbound hair curtaining her face.

Upward and upward in the darkening twilight, with a few stars pale in the indigo dome above them. The ring stones were grey and shadowy, a single pallid flicker within them—not fire; some will-o'-the-wisp, witch fire, sorcery, gleaming out from within the magical circle.

By the last flicker of the setting moon, reflected for a moment in the shining Lake below, a silent maiden priestess moved toward them, only a little girl, robed in undyed wool, her shorn hair no more than a wisp of darkness. She offered Morgaine a cup and Morgaine accepted it and drank in silence, then handed the cup to Raven, who drained its last drops. Silver and gold gleamed in the dying light. Morgaine took, from unseen hands, the great cross-handled sword, gasping a little at the unexpected weight. Barefoot, cold but not aware of it, she traced out the circle under the ring stones. Behind her, Raven took the long spear, thrust it into the heart of the witch fire. Light sprang up on the bit of tow there and she carried it, after Morgaine, all around the circle, a dim line of pale witch fire springing up around the dimness. Returning to the center by the dimmest of pale lights, they saw the face of Viviane; ageless, timeless, floating in midair disembodied—the face of the Goddess, shining. Although Morgaine knew that the effect was produced by a luminous substance smeared on cheeks and brow against the darkness of the circle and the dark garments, it never failed to make her catch her breath.

Bodiless, shining hands laid something in Morgaine's hands, then in Raven's. Morgaine bit into the sharp wooden bitterness, forced herself, past sickness, to swallow. Silence descended. Eyes gleamed in the dark, but no faces could be seen. She felt as if she were standing among multitudes beyond multitudes thronging the top of the Tor, but she could see no single face among them. Even Viviane's bodiless face had vanished into the dark. She could feel the warmth of Raven's body near hers, though they nowhere touched one another. She tried to keep her mind still, in meditation, moving into the schooled silence, not sure why she had been brought here.

Time passed; stars brightened against the ever-darkening sky. *Time, Morgaine thought, time runs differently in Avalon, or perhaps it does not exist.* Many nights during the long years she had traced out the spiral paths up the Tor, probing the mysteries of time and space within the circle of the ring stones. Yet tonight seemed stranger, darker, somehow more weighted with mystery; never before had she been called out from the other priestesses to play the major part in ritual. She knew that what she had been given, the magical feast, was an herb used to strengthen the sight; that did not diminish its power or its magic.

After a time, in the darkness, she began to see pictures in her mind, small colored pictures as if at a very great distance. She saw a herd of deer running. She saw again the great darkness that had descended upon the land when the sun went out and a cold wind blew, and she had been afraid that the world was ending; but the older priestesses had explained to her, as they gathered in the courtyard, that the Moon God was effacing the brightness of the Goddess, and she ran out with them joyously to join in the shrieks of the women to frighten him away. Later it had been explained to her how the sun and moon moved, and why, now and again, one of them crossed the face of the other; that it was in the way of nature, and the common people's beliefs about the face of the Gods were symbols which these people, at the current state of their evolution, needed to visualize the great truths. Some day all men and women would know the inner truths, but now they needed them not.

She watched in the inner Sight, as she had done in life, while again and again the cycles of the year swung around the great ring stones; she watched the birth and fecundity and at last the dying of the God; she saw the great processions winding up the spiral toward the oak grove before the ring stones had been set here . . . time was transparent, it ceased to have meaning as the little painted people came and ripened and were cut down, and then the Tribes, and after them the Romans in their turn, and tall strangers from the coast of Gaul, and after them . . . time ceased, and she only saw the movement of peoples and the overgrowth of the world, ice came and receded and came again, she saw the great temples of Atlantis now drowned forever between the covering oceans, saw new worlds rising and setting . . . and silence and beyond the night the great stars wheeled and swung. . . .

Behind her she heard an eerie wailing cry and her skin iced. Raven cried out, Raven whose voice she had never heard; Raven, who once, when they were serving together in the Temple, had caught a lamp about to overflow, and, scalded with the burning oil, had sat smothering her screams with her two hands while her burns were bandaged, that she might not break the vow which had given her voice to the Goddess. She would always bear the scars; once, looking at her, Morgaine had thought, *The vow I made was a little thing next to that, and yet I came so near to breaking it for a dark and sweet-voiced man.*

And now Raven, in the moonless night, screamed aloud, a high, eldritch crying, like a woman in childbed. Three times the shrill cry trembled over the Tor, and Morgaine shivered again, knowing that even the priests on the other island that lay corresponding to their own must waken in their solitary cells and cross themselves, hearing that haunted cry that rang between the worlds.

After the cry, silence, a silence which seemed to Morgaine filled with breathing, with held breath even, from the unseen initiates who now surrounded the dreadful solitude inhabited only by the three motionless priestesses. Then, gasping and choking, as if her voice were long disabled from the silence, Raven cried out:

"Ah—seven times the Wheel, the Wheel with thirteen spokes, has turned about in the sky . . . seven times the Mother has given birth to her dark son. . . ."

Again the silence, deepening in contrast, except for the choking gasps of the entranced prophetess. She cried out, "Ah—ah—I burn—I burn—it

is time, it is time . . ." and lapsed again into the clotted silence, pregnant
with terror.

"They run! They run in the spring rutting, they run—they fight, they
choose their king—ah, the blood, the blood—and the greatest of them all,
he runs, and there is blood on the antlers of his pride. . . ."

Again the silence lengthened, and Morgaine, seeing in the darkness
behind her eyelids the spring running of the deer, saw again what she had
seen in a half-forgotten glimpse in the silver bowl—a man among the deer,
struggling, fighting. . . .

"It is the child of the Goddess, he runs, he runs . . . the Horned One
must die . . . and the Horned One must be crowned . . . the Virgin Huntress
must call the king to her, she must lay down her maidenhood to the God
. . . ah, the old sacrifice, the old sacrifice . . . I burn, I burn . . ." and the
words began to choke over one another and die in a long, sobbing scream.
Behind her, through her closed eyes, Morgaine saw Raven fall senseless to
the ground and lie there, gasping, her gasps the only sound in the deepening
silence.

Somewhere an owl called; once, twice, three times.

Out of the darkness, priestesses came, silent and dark, blue gleams on
their brow. They lifted Raven tenderly and bore her away. They lifted
Morgaine too, and she felt her throbbing head tenderly held to a woman's
breast as they carried her away. Then she knew no more.

THREE DAYS LATER, when she had recovered her strength somewhat, Viviane
sent for her.

Morgaine rose and tried to dress herself, but she was still weak, and
accepted the help of one of the young priestesses, grateful that the girl was
under silence and did not speak to her. The long fasting, the terrible sickness
brought on by the ritual herbs, the strung tension of the ritual, still gripped
at her body; she had eaten a little soup the night before, and some bread
soaked in milk this morning, but she still felt sick and empty after the long
strain, and her head throbbed, and her moon-dark bleeding had seized her
with a violence never felt before; this too, she knew, might be the aftereffect
of the sacred herbs. Sick and incurious, she wished that Viviane had left her
to recover in peace, but she did Viviane's will as she would have done that
of the Goddess, had the Goddess leaned down from Heaven and spoken a
wish aloud. When she was dressed, and had braided her hair and wound it
with a deerskin thong, and painted the blue crescent on her forehead with
fresh blue dye, she went along the trail to the house where the High Priestess
lived.

As was now her privilege, she entered without knocking or announcing her presence. Somehow in this house she always visualized Viviane waiting for her, seated in the thronelike chair as if she were the Goddess on her dark throne, but today Viviane was moving about at the back of the room, and the fire was not lighted, but dark and cold. Viviane wore her simple robe of undyed wool with a hood tied over her hair, and for the first time it came sharply on Morgaine that Viviane was priestess, not now of the Maiden or of the Mother, but of the ancient wise-woman—who was also the Old Death-crone. Her face looked lined and haggard, and Morgaine thought, *Of course, if the rites made Raven ill, and myself, and we are both young and strong, what must it have done to Viviane, who has grown old in the service of her whom we serve?*

Then Viviane turned and smiled at her, a loving smile, and Morgaine felt again the old surge of love and tenderness. But as was fitting a younger priestess in the presence of the Lady, she waited for Viviane to speak first.

Viviane gestured to her to sit. "Have you recovered, child?"

Morgaine let herself drop to the bench, and knew that even from the short walk she was exhausted. She shook her head.

"I know," Viviane said. "Sometimes, when they do not know how you will react, they give you too much. Next time, do not take all they give you—judge how much you can take—enough to give you the Sight, but not enough to make you so very ill. You have that right, now; you have reached a stage where obedience may be tempered with your own judgment."

For some reason those words rang again and again in Morgaine's mind: *tempered with your own judgment, tempered with your own judgment.* She thought, I am still sick from the drugs they gave me, and shook her head, impatient, to clear away the sound and listen to Viviane.

"How much did you understand of Raven's prophecy?"

"Very little," Morgaine confessed. "It was mysterious to me. I am not sure why I was there."

"Partly," Viviane said, "to lend your strength to her; she is not strong. She is still abed, and I am concerned about her. She knows how much of the herb she can take, yet even that little seemed to be too much; she vomited blood, and is passing more. But she will not die."

Morgaine put out a hand to steady herself; she felt hollow, and a sudden wave of sickness passed over her again, leaving her pale and giddy. Without excuse she stood up, staggered outside and vomited, bringing up the bread and milk she had swallowed that morning. She heard Viviane speak her name, and when she had done and stood clutching the doorframe, retching, she found one of the young attendant priestesses there with a cloth to wipe her face; it was wet and smelled faintly of sweet herbs. Viviane steadied her step as she came back inside, then handed her a small cup.

"Sip it slowly," she said.

It burned her tongue and for a moment exaggerated the feeling of sickness—it was the strong spirit distilled by the northern Tribes, water-of-life they called it. She had tasted it only once or twice. But when it was down she felt a strong warmth spreading out from her empty stomach, and after a few minutes she felt better, steadier, almost euphoric.

"A little more," Viviane said. "It will strengthen your heart. Now, do you feel better?"

Morgaine nodded. "Thank you."

"Tonight you will be able to eat," said Viviane, and in Morgaine's strange state it sounded like a command, as if Viviane could command her very stomach to behave itself. "So. Let us talk of Raven's prophecy. In the ancient days, long before the wisdom and the religion of the Druids came here from the sunken temples in the western continent, the fairy people— of whom we are both born, you and I, my Morgaine—lived here on the shores of the inland sea, and before they learned how to plant the barley and reap it again, they lived by gathering the fruits of the land, and by hunting the deer. And in those days there was no king among them, but only a queen who was their mother, though they had not yet learned to think of her as the Goddess. And since they lived by hunting, their queen and priestess learned to call the deer to her, and ask of their spirits that they sacrifice themselves and die for the life of the Tribe. But sacrifice must be given for sacrifice—the deer died for the Tribe, and one of the Tribe must in turn die for the life of the deer, or at least take the chance that the deer could, if they chose, take his life in exchange for their own. So the balance was kept. Do you understand this, my darling?"

Morgaine heard the unaccustomed endearment, and wondered dimly in her sick and drunken state, *Is she telling me that I am to be the sacrifice? Is my life chosen for the Tribe?*

It does not matter. I am given to the Goddess for life or for death.

"I understand, Mother. At least, I think I do."

"So the Mother of the Tribe chose, every year, her consort. And since he had agreed to give his life for the Tribe, the Tribe gave him of their lives. Even if little children at the breast starved, he always had abundance, and all the women of the Tribe were his to lie with, so that he, the strongest and best, might sire their children. Besides, the Mother of the Tribe was often old past childbearing, and so he must have the choice of the young maidens, too, and no man of the Tribe would interfere with what he wanted. And then, when the year was past—every year in those times—he would put on the antlers of the deer, and wear a robe of untanned deerskin so that the deer would think him one of their own, and he would run with the herd as the Mother Huntress put the spell upon them to run. But by this time the herd had chosen their

King Stag, and sometimes the King Stag would smell a stranger, and turn on him. And then the Horned One would die."

Morgaine felt again the ice down her spine that she had felt when, on the Tor, this ritual had been enacted before her eyes. *The year's king is to die for the life of his people.* Was the drug still working in her mind, that she could see it all so clearly?

"Well, time has moved on, Morgaine," Viviane told her quietly, "and now those old rites are no longer needed, for the barley grows and the sacrifice is bloodless. Only in times of great peril does the Tribe demand such a leader. And Raven has foreseen that this is a time of such peril. So once again there will be a testing of one who runs the risk of death for his chosen people, so that they will follow him unto death.

"You have heard me speak of the Great Marriage?"

Morgaine nodded; of this, Lancelet had been born.

"The Tribes of the fairy folk, and all the Tribes of the North, have been given a great leader, and the chosen one will be tested by the ancient rite. And if he survives the testing—which will, to some extent, depend on the strength with which the Maiden Huntress can enchant the deer—then he will become the Horned One, the King Stag, consort of the Virgin Huntress, crowned with the antlers of the God. Morgaine, I told you years ago that your maidenhood belongs to the Goddess. Now she calls for it in sacrifice to the Horned God. You are to be the Virgin Huntress, and the bride of the Horned One. You have been chosen for this service."

It was very still in the room, as if they stood again in the center of the ring stones in ritual. Morgaine dared not break the silence. At last, knowing that Viviane was waiting for some word of consent—what had the words been, so long ago? *It is too heavy a burden to be borne unconsenting* —she bowed her head.

"My body and my soul belong to her, to do with as she will," she whispered. "And your will is her will, Mother. Let it be so."

15

Since she had come there, Morgaine had left Avalon only two or three times, and then only for short journeys into the countryside at the edges of the Summer Sea, so that she could become aware of the nearby sites which retained, despite disuse, their old power.

Time and place were now none of her concern. She had been taken from the Island at dawn in silence, cloaked and veiled so that no unpriestly eye might see the consecrated one, and carried in a closed litter so that not even the sun might shine on her face. In less than a day's journeying from the enclosure of the sacred island she had lost all awareness of time and space and direction, lost in meditation, dimly aware of the beginning of the magical trance. There had been times when she had fought against the onset of the ecstatic state. Now she welcomed it, opening her mind full to the Goddess, inwardly imploring the Goddess to come into herself, the instrument, and possess her, body and soul, so that she might act in all things as the Goddess herself.

Nightfall; a moon nearly at full came dimly between the curtains of the litter. When the runners stopped, she felt it bathing her in cold light, like the kiss of the Goddess, and felt faint with the beginnings of ecstasy. She did not know where she was, nor did she care. She went where they led her, passive, blinded, tranced, knowing only that she went to meet her destiny.

She was inside a house, then she was put into the hands of a strange woman, who brought her bread and honey, which Morgaine did not touch —she would not break her fast again until she did so with the ritual meal —and water, which she drank thirstily. There was a bed, so placed that the moon fell upon her; the strange woman moved to draw the wooden shutters closed and Morgaine stopped her with an imperious gesture. She lay much of the night tranced, feeling the moonlight like a visible touch. At last she slept, but fitfully, wandering in and out of sleep like an uneasy traveller, strange images flickering in her mind—her mother, bending over the fair hair of the intruder Gwydion, her white breasts and coppery hair somehow forbidding instead of welcoming; Viviane, only somehow she was a sacrificial beast and the Lady of Avalon was leading her somewhere on the end of a rope, and she heard herself say fretfully, *You needn't pull, I am coming;* Raven, soundlessly screaming. A great horned figure, half man, half animal, suddenly thrusting aside a curtain and striding into her room—she woke and half sat up, but there was no one there, only the moonlight, and the stranger woman sleeping quietly at her side. Quickly she lay down again and slept, this time dreamlessly and deep.

About an hour before dawn they awakened her. Now, in contrast to the tranced unawareness of the previous day, she was wide awake and sharply aware of everything—the cold fresh air, the mists stained with pink where soon the sun would rise, the strong smell of the little dark women in their garments of badly tanned skins. Everything was clean-edged and brilliantly colored, as if fresh this moment from the hand of the Goddess. The dark women whispered among themselves, not presuming to disturb the strange priestess; she heard them, but she knew only a few words of their language.

After a time the eldest of them—the one who had welcomed her and led her inside on the previous night, and whose bed she had shared—came to Morgaine and brought her fresh water. Morgaine bowed to thank her, the salute, priestess to priestess, and then wondered why. The woman was old; her hair, long and tangled and fastened with a clasp of bone, was almost all white, and her dark skin bore faded blue stains. Her garment was of the same imperfectly dyed skin of the others, but over it she wore a cloak of deerskin, the hair still clinging to it, painted with magical symbols; and about her neck were two necklaces, one of beautiful amber beads—Viviane herself owned none finer—and the other of bits of horn alternating with exquisitely chased gold bars. She carried herself with the authority of Viviane herself, and Morgaine knew that this was the tribal Mother and priestess of the people.

With her own hands, the woman began to prepare Morgaine for the ritual. She stripped her naked, and painted the soles of her feet and the palms of her hands with blue dye, and renewed the crescent moon on her brow; on her breast and belly she outlined the full moon, and just above the dark patch of Morgaine's body hair she painted the dark moon. Briefly, almost perfunctorily, she parted the girl's legs and probed a little: Morgaine, beyond embarrassment, knew why she was searching. For this rite, the priestess must be a virgin. But the tribal priestess would find nothing wrong; Morgaine was untouched, but she felt a sudden half-pleasurable moment of fear, and at the same moment she was conscious that she was almost fiercely hungry. Well, she was trained to ignore hunger, and after a time the hunger left her.

The sun was rising as they led her outdoors, robed in a cloak like the old woman's, with the magical signs painted on it—the moon, the antlers of the deer. She was aware of the stiff astringency of her painted body, and some part of her mind, very far away, stared with amazement and a moment's contempt at these symbols of a mystery far older than the Druidic wisdom in which she had been so carefully schooled. That was momentary and vanished at once; the belief of generations ancient past knowing invested this rite with its own power and holiness. She saw the round stone house behind her; across from her was another, and they were leading forth a young man. She could not see him clearly; the rising sun was in her eyes, and she could see only that he was tall, with a shock of fair hair, and strongly built. *He is not one of their own people, then?* But it was not for her to question. The men of the tribe—and especially an old man, with the gnarled swollen muscles of a smith, blackened like his own forge—were painting the youth's body from head to foot with the blue woad, covering him with a cloak of untanned raw skins, smearing his body with the deer fat. On his head they fixed antlers; at a low word of command, he swung his head to make certain they could not be dislodged, no matter how he moved.

Morgaine looked up to see the proud swing of that young head, and suddenly she felt a ripple of awareness run down her body, cramping her calves, running into the secret parts of her body.

This is the Horned One, this the God, this the consort of the Virgin Huntress. . . .

They wound her hair in a garland of crimson berries and crowned her with the first of the spring flowers. The precious necklace of gold and bone was reverently taken from the neck of the Mother of the tribe and placed around her own; she felt its weight like the very weight of magic. Her eyes were dazzled with the rising sun. They placed something in her hand—a drum, taut skin stretched over a hooped frame. As if it came from somewhere else, she heard her own hand strike it.

They stood on a hillside, overlooking a valley filled to the brim with thick forest, empty and silent, but within it she could sense the life in the forest—the deer moving on silent, slender feet, the animals climbing in the trees, and the birds nesting, darting, moving, asurge with the life of the first running tide of the full moon of spring. She turned for a moment and looked behind, on the hillside. Above them, carved white in the chalk, was a monstrous figure, human or animal she could not tell, her eyes were blurred; was it a running deer, was it a striding man, phallus erect and filled with the spring tide, too?

She could not see the young man at her side, only the surge of the life in him. There was a solemn, waiting hush all over the hillside. Time ceased, was again transparent, something in which she moved, bathed, stepped freely. The drum was in the old crone's hands again, but she had no awareness of having given it over to her. Her eyes were dazed with sun as she felt the God's head between her hands, blessing him. Something in the face . . . of course: before these hills were raised, she had known this face, this man, her consort, from before the beginning of the world. . . . She did not hear her own ritual words, only the surge of force behind them: *Go forth and conquer . . . run with the deer . . . swift and strong as the very tides of the spring . . . forever blessed be the feet that brought you here. . . .* She was not conscious of speech, only of the power, of her own hands blessing, of the force that streamed out of her body, *through* her body as if the very strength of the sun poured through her and into the man before her. *Now the power of the winter is broken and the new life of the spring shall go with you and bring you to victory . . . life of the Goddess, life of the world, blood of the earth our Mother, shed for her people. . . .*

She raised her hands, casting the blessing on the forest, on the earth, feeling the surges of power rushing through her hands like visible light. The young man's body was glowing like her own in the sunlight; around them none dared speak until, pulling her hands back with a rush, she felt the surge of power flung over them all, releasing the chant that rose around them. She could not hear the words, only the thrum of power within them:

Life surges in the spring, the deer run in the forest, and our life runs with them. The King Stag of the world shall bring them down, the King Stag, the Horned One blessed by the Mother shall triumph. . . .

She was drawn to the last notch of tension, a strung bow pregnant with the arrow of power that must be sped. She touched the Horned One, releasing the power, and as if it sped through them all, they were off, running like the wind down the hillside, racing as if the very spring tides bore them. Behind them, feeling the power leave her, Morgaine crumpled and lay silent on the earth, feeling its damp chill strike up through her body. But she was unaware, tranced in the Sight.

She lay as if lifeless, but a part of her went with them, raced with them, speeding down the hillside, racing with the men of the tribe, flooding after the Horned One. Barking cries, as if they were hounds, sped after them, and a part of her knew that the women were crying out, speeding on the chase.

Higher in the sky the sun rose, the great Wheel of Life spinning in the heavens, fruitlessly speeding after her divine consort, the Dark Son. . . .

The life of the earth, the pounding tides of the spring, flooded and pounded in the hearts of the running men. Then, as the ebb followed the flow, from the sunlit hillside the darkness of forest closed over them and swallowed them, and from running they moved swiftly on noiseless feet, imitating the delicate step of the deer; they *were* the deer, following the antlers of their Horned One, wearing the cloaks which held the deer spellbound, the necklaces signifying life as endless chain, live and feed and bear and die and be eaten in turn to feed the children of the Mother.

. . . *hold thy children, Mother, thy King Stag must die to feed the life of her Dark Son* . . .

Darkness, the inner life of the forest closing around them; silence, the silence of the deer. . . . Morgaine, aware now of the forest as life and the deer as the heart of the forest, cast her power and her blessing through and over the forest. A part of her lay on the sunlit hillside, tranced, exhausted, letting the life of the sun flood through her, body and blood and inner being, and a part of her ran with deer and men until both were one . . . blending into one . . . the surges of life that were the quiet deer in their thicket, the little does, smooth and slender, the life racing in them as it raced in her body, the surges of life that were the men, slipping silent and intent through the shadows. . . .

Somewhere in the forest she felt the King Stag fling up his head, sniffing the wind, aware for the scent of an enemy, one of his own, one of the alien tribe of life . . . she did not know whether it was the four-footed

King Stag or the two-legged one she had blessed, they were one in the life of the Mother Earth, and their lot was in the hands of the Goddess. Antlers answered the toss of antlers, the sniffing breath taking in the life of the forest, searching it for alien, for prey, for predator, for rival where there could be none.

Ah, Goddess . . . they were off, crashing through the underbrush, men fleet behind them only more silent, running, running . . . run till the heart throbs like bursting in the chest, run till the life of the body overwhelms all knowledge and thought, fleet, searching and being sought, run with the deer who flee and the men who pursue, run with the spinning life of the great sun and the surge of the spring tides, run with the flow of life. . . .

Lying motionless, her face pressed into the earth and the flooding sun burning her back, time crawling and racing by turns, Morgaine began to see—and from very far off it seemed that she had seen this before, in vision, sometime, somewhere, a very long time ago—the tall, sinewy youth, gripping his knife, falling, falling among the deer, among the slashing hooves—she knew she screamed aloud, and simultaneously knew that her cry had rung everywhere, so that even the King Stag paused in mid charge, appalled, hearing the shriek. There was a moment when everything stopped, and in that terrible moment of silence she saw that he scrambled to his feet, panting, charging with his head down, swinging his antlers, locking head-on, as he swayed and struggled, wrestling the deer with his strong hands and young body . . . a knife slashed upward; blood spilled on the earth, and he was bleeding too, the Horned One, blood on his hands, blood from a long slash on his side, the blood spilling on the earth, sacrifice spilled to the Mother that life should feed on her blood . . . and then the blood of the King Stag went over him in a gush as his blade found the heart, and the men around him rushed in with their spears. . . .

She saw him carried back, covered in the blood of his twin and rival, the King Stag. All around him the little dark men were slashing, putting the raw, warm hide over his shoulders. Back they came in triumph, fires rising in the gathering dusk, and when the women lifted Morgaine she saw without surprise that the sun was setting, and she staggered, as if she too had run all day with the hunt and the deer.

They crowned her again with the crimson of triumph. The Horned One was brought before her, bleeding, and she blessed him and marked his forehead with the blood of the deer. The head was taken with the antlers which would bring down the next King Stag; the antlers which the Horned One had worn this day, broken and splintered, were cast into the fire. Soon there was a smell of burning flesh and she wondered if it was the flesh of man or stag. . . .

They seated them side by side, and brought the first meats to them, dripping still with blood and the fat juices. Morgaine felt her head swimming, the rich taste of the meat overpowering her after her long fast; she was afraid for a moment that she would be sick again. Next to her he was eating hungrily, and she noticed by firelight that he had fine strong hands . . . she blinked, seeing in a strange moment of doubled vision that serpents twined around them, then they were gone again. All around them the men and women of the Tribe were sharing in the ritual feast, the hymn of triumph, sung in an old language Morgaine could only half understand;

"He has triumphed, he has slain . . .
. . . the blood of our Mother is shed upon the earth . . .
. . . the blood of the God is spilled upon the earth . . .
. . . and he shall rise and reign forever . . .
. . . he has triumphed, he shall triumph forever, until the
end of the world . . ."

The old priestess who had painted and decked her this morning held a silver cup to her lips; she felt the strong liquor sting her throat and burn all the way down. Fire, with a strong taste of honey behind it. Already she was drunk with the blood of the meat—she had tasted meat only a few times in the last seven years. Her head was swimming as they bore her away, stripped her and bedecked her naked body with more paint and garlands, marking her nipples and brow with the blood of the slain deer.

The Goddess receives her consort and she will slay him again at the end of time, she shall give birth to her Dark Son who will bring the King Stag down. . . .

A little girl, painted blue from head to foot and bearing a broad dish, ran across the plowed fields, scattering dark drops as she ran, and Morgaine heard the great cry that went up behind her.

"The fields are blessed; give us food, O our Mother!"

And for an instant, some small part of Morgaine, dizzy and drunk and only half in her body at all, remarked coldly that she certainly must be mad; she, a civilized and educated woman, princess and priestess and kin to the royal line of Avalon, Druid-taught, here painted like a savage and smelling of freshly shed blood, enduring this barbarian mummery . . .

. . . then it was all gone again, as the full moon, serene and proud, rose over the clouds that had barriered it from sight. Bathed naked in the moonlight, Morgaine felt the light of the Goddess streaming over, *through* her . . . she was Morgaine no more, she was nameless, priestess and maiden and mother . . . they strung a garland of crimson berries about her loins; the crude symbolism struck her with sudden fear, and she felt the full weight of virginity pouring and flooding through her like the spring tide. A torch flared in her eyes and they led her into darkness, echoing silences above and beyond her, a cave. All round her, on the walls, she could see the sacred symbols, painted there from the beginnings of time, the stag and antlers, the man with the horns on his brow, the swollen belly and full breasts of She Who Gives Life. . . .

The priestess laid Morgaine on the couch of deerskins. For a moment she felt cold and frightened, and she shivered, and the old woman's brow wrinkled in compassion; she drew Morgaine into her arms and kissed her on the lips, and Morgaine clung for a moment to the old woman, hugging her in sudden terror, as if the woman's sheltering arms were her mother's own . . . then the woman smiled at her and kissed her again and touched her breasts in blessing and went away.

She lay there, feeling the life of the earth around her; she seemed to expand, to fill all the cave, the little scribbled drawings were painted on her breasts and her belly, and above her the great chalk figure, man or deer, strode with erect phallus . . . the invisible moon outside the cave flooding her body with light as the Goddess surged inside her, body and soul. She stretched out her arms, and at her command she knew that outside the cave, in the light of the fecundating fires, man and woman, drawn one to the other by the pulsating surges of life, came together. The little blue-painted girl who had borne the fertilizing blood was drawn down into the arms of a sinewy old hunter, and Morgaine saw her briefly struggle and cry out, go down under his body, her legs opening to the irresistible force of nature in them. She saw without sight, her eyes closed against the glare of the torch, hearing the cries.

Now he was in the door of the cave, the antlers gone from his brow, his hair streaked, his body smeared blue and stained with blood, white skin like the white chalk of the body of the huge figure above the cave . . . the Horned One, the consort. He moved dizzily, too, naked, except for a garland like her own about his loins, and she could see the erect life surging in him like that of the chalk figure. He knelt by her side, and by the torchlight, dazzled, she could see that he was no more than a boy, not one of the little dark people, but tall and fair. . . . *Why have they chosen a king who is not one of their own?* The thought darted across her mind like a moonbeam and was gone; she was not thinking at all.

Now it is the time for the Goddess to welcome the Horned One—he was kneeling at the edge of the deerskin couch, swaying, blinking by the light of the torch. She reached up to him, gripped his hands, drew him down to her, feeling the soft warmth and weight of his body. She had to guide him. *I am the Great Mother who knows all things, who is maiden and mother and all-wise, guiding the virgin and her consort* . . . dazed, terrified, exalted, only half conscious, she felt the life force take them both, moving her body without volition, moving him too, guiding him fiercely into her, till they were both moving without knowledge of what force gripped them. She heard herself crying out as if from a great distance, heard his voice high and shaken in the silence, never knowing what either of them cried out at that moment. The torch guttered and went out in the darkness as all the fierce fury of his young life burst and spurted into her womb.

He moaned and fell forward across her, lifeless except for his hoarse breathing. She eased him away, cradling his weight in her arms, holding him with weary warmth. She felt him kiss her naked breast. Then slowly, tiredly, his breathing quieted to normal, and after a moment she knew that he slept in her arms. She kissed his hair and his soft cheek with a wild tenderness, and then she too slept.

WHEN SHE WOKE the night was far advanced; moonlight had crept into the cave. She was utterly weary, her whole body aching, and she felt between her legs and knew that she was bleeding. She flung her damp hair back, looking down by the moonlight at the sprawled pale body still sleeping the sleep of long exhaustion beside her. He was tall and strong and beautiful, though by moonlight she could not see his features clearly, and the magical Sight had deserted her; now there was only the moon's light and brilliance, no longer the compelling face of the Goddess. She was Morgaine again, not the shadow of the Great Mother; she was herself again, clear in her mind about what had happened.

She thought for a moment of Lancelet, whom she had loved, and to whom she had hungered to give this gift. Now it had come, not to a lover but to a faceless stranger . . . no, she must not think like that. She was not a woman, she was a priestess, and she had given the force of the Virgin to the Horned One, as had been ordained for her fate before the walls of the world were laid. She had accepted her destiny as a priestess of Avalon must do, and she sensed that something of shattering importance had happened here in the night past.

She was cold and lay down, covering herself with the deerskin coverlet. She wrinkled her nose a little at its rankness; they had strewn it with sweet herbs, so at least there would not be fleas. Experienced at judging the tides, she guessed it was about an hour before sunrise. At her side the boy felt her stir and sat up sleepily.

"Where are we?" he asked. "Oh yes, I remember. In the cave. Why, it's already getting light." He smiled and reached for her; she let him pull her down and kiss her, wrapping her in strong arms. "Last night you were the Goddess," he murmured, "but I wake and I find you are a woman."

She laughed softly. "And you are not the God, but a man?"

"I think I have had enough of being a God, and besides, it seems to me that it is presumptuous for a man of flesh and blood," he said, holding her against him. "I am content to be no more than a man."

She said, "Perhaps there is a time to be Goddess and God, and a time to be no more than flesh and blood."

"I was afraid of you last night," he confessed. "I thought you the Goddess, all larger than life . . . and you are such a little thing!" Suddenly he blinked and said, "Why, you speak my language, I had not noticed—you are not one of this tribe, then?"

"I am a priestess from the Holy Isle."

"And the priestess is a woman," he said, his hands gently exploring her breasts, which stirred into sudden life and hunger at his touch. "Do you think the Goddess will be angry with me if I like the woman better?"

She laughed and said, "The Goddess is wise in the ways of men."

"And is her priestess?"

Suddenly she felt shy. "No—I have never known a man before this," she said, "and it was not I, but the Goddess—"

He said in the dimness, drawing her close to him, "Since the God and the Goddess have known pleasure, should not the man and the woman know it also?" His hands were growing bolder, and she pulled him down to her. "It seems only fitting," she said.

This time in full awareness she could savor it, the softness and hardness, the strong young hands and the surprising gentleness behind his bold approach. She laughed in delight at the unexpected pleasure, fully open to him, sensing his enjoyment as her own. She had never been so happy in her life. Spent, they lay, limbs twined, caressing each other in a pleasant fatigue.

At last, in the growing light, he sighed.

"They will be coming for me soon," he said, "and there is much more of this—I am to be taken somewhere and given a sword, and many other things." He sat up and smiled at her. "And I would like to wash, and have clothes befitting a civilized man, and free myself of all this blood and blue dye . . . how everything passes! Last night I did not even know I was all smeared with blood—look, you too are covered with the stag's blood where I lay on you—"

"I think when they come for me, they will bathe me and give me fresh garments," she said, "and you too, in a running stream."

He sighed with a gentle, boyish melancholy. His voice was breaking, an uncertain baritone; how could he be so young, this young giant who had fought the King Stag and killed him with his flint knife?

● "I do not suppose I will ever meet you again," he said, "for you are a priestess and dedicated to the Goddess. But I want to say this to you—" and he leaned down and kissed her between her breasts. "You were the very first. No matter how many women I may have, for all my life I will always remember you and love you and bless you. I promise you that."

There were tears on his cheek. Morgaine reached for her garment and tenderly dried the tears, cradling his head against her.

At the gesture he seemed to stop breathing.

"Your voice," he whispered, "and what you just did—why do I seem to know you? Is it because you are the Goddess, and in her all women are the same? No—" He stiffened, raised himself, took her face between his hands. In the growing light she saw the boyish features strengthened into the lines of a man. Still only half aware of why she seemed to know him, she heard his hoarse cry. "Morgaine! You are Morgaine! Morgaine, my sister! Ah, God, Mary Virgin, what have we done?"

She put her hands up to her eyes, slowly. "My brother," she whispered. "Ah, Goddess! Brother! Gwydion—"

"Arthur," he muttered.

She held him tight, and after a moment he sobbed, still holding her. "No wonder it seemed to me that I have known you since before the world was made," he said, weeping. "I have always loved you, and this—ah, God, what have we done—"

"Don't cry," she said, helplessly, "don't cry. We are in the hands of her who brought us here. It doesn't matter. We are not brother and sister here, we are man and woman before the Goddess, no more."

And I never knew you again. My brother, my baby, the one who lay on my breast like a little child. Morgaine, Morgaine, I told you to take care of the baby, as she went away and left us, and he cried himself to sleep in my arms. And I did not know.

"It's all right," she said again, rocking him, "don't cry, my brother, my beloved, my little one, don't cry, it's all right."

But even as she soothed him, despair beat at her.

Why did you do this to us? Great Mother, Lady, why?

And she did not know whether she was calling to Viviane, or to the Goddess.

16

ALL the long road to Avalon, Morgaine lay in her litter, her head throbbing, and that question beating in her mind: *Why?* She was exhausted after the three days of fasting and the long day of ritual. She knew vaguely that the night's feasting and lovemaking had been intended to release that force, and they would have done so, returning her to normal, except for the morning's shock.

She knew herself well enough to know that when the shock and exhaustion wore off, they would be followed by rage, and she wished that she could reach Viviane before the rage exploded, while she could still maintain some semblance of calm.

They took the Lake route this time, and she was allowed, at her own earnest request, to walk a part of the way; she was no longer the ritually shielded Maiden of the ceremony, but only one of the priestess attendants of the Lady of the Lake. Returning with the barge across the Lake, she was asked to summon the mists for the making of the gateway to Avalon; she rose to do so almost perfunctorily, so much had she come to take this Mystery for granted as a part of her life.

Yet as she raised her arms for the summoning, she had a sudden, paralyzing moment of doubt. The change within her seemed so great, did she still retain the force to make the gateway? So great was her rebellion that for an instant she hesitated, and the men in the boat looked at her in polite concern. She felt pierced by their eyes, and by a moment of intense shame, as if all that had befallen her the night before must somehow be printed on her face in the language of lust. The sound of church bells rang out quietly over the Lake, and suddenly Morgaine was back in childhood, listening to Father Columba speaking earnestly of chastity as the greatest approach to the holiness of Mary, Mother of God, who by miracle had borne her Son without even a momentary stain of the world's sin. Even at the time, Morgaine had thought, *What great nonsense that is, how could any woman bear a child without knowing a man?* But at the sound of the holy bells, something within her seemed to crumple and fold itself away, and she felt tears suddenly streaming down her face.

"Lady, are you ill?"

She shook her head, saying firmly, "No, I felt faint for a moment." She drew a deep breath. Arthur was not in the boat—no, of course not, he had been taken by the Merlin on the Hidden Way. *The Goddess is One— Mary the Virgin, the Great Mother, the Huntress . . . and I have a part in Her greatness.* She made a banishing gesture and raised her arms again, swiftly drawing down the curtain of the mist through which they would reach Avalon.

Night was falling, but, although Morgaine was hungry and weary, she made her way at once toward the Lady's house. But at the door, a priestess stopped her when she would have entered.

"The Lady can see no one at present."

"Nonsense," Morgaine said, feeling the beginnings of anger through the merciful numbness and hoping it would hold until she had confronted

Viviane. "I am her kinswoman; ask if I may come to her."

The priestess went away and quickly returned, saying, "The Lady said: 'Tell Morgaine to go at once to the House of Maidens, and I will speak to her when the proper time comes.'"

For a moment, anger surged in Morgaine so great that she came near to shoving the woman out of the way and forcing herself into Viviane's house. But awe still held her. She did not know what the penalty would be for a priestess who defied her sworn obedience, but through her flooding anger, a small, cold rational voice told her that she really did not want to find out this way. She drew a long breath, composing her face into the proper demeanor for a priestess, bowed obediently, and went away. The tears she had forced back, hearing church bells on the Lake, were beginning to break through, and for a moment she wished, wearily, that she could let them come. Now at long last, alone in the House of Maidens, in her own quiet room, she could weep if she must; but the tears would not come, only bafflement and pain and the anger which she had no way to express. It was as if her entire body and soul were locked into one great knot of anguish.

IT WAS TEN DAYS before Viviane sent for her; the full moon that had shone on the triumph of the Horned One had dwindled in the sky to a sickly dying splinter. By the time one of the young priestesses brought a message that Viviane required her presence, Morgaine had given way to smoldering anger.

She has played upon me as I would play upon the harp. The words rang so in her mind that at first, hearing harp music from inside Viviane's dwelling, she thought it the echo of her own bitter thoughts. Then she thought that Viviane was playing. But in the years she had been in Avalon she had learned much of music, and she knew the sound of Viviane's harp; the older woman was, at best, an indifferent player.

She listened now, wondering in spite of herself who the musician was. Taliesin? Before he was the Merlin, she knew, he had been the greatest of bards, renowned throughout the length of Britain. She had heard him play often enough on the great feast days, and for the most solemn of rituals; but now his hands were old. Their skill was not diminished, but even at his best he had never made such sounds as these—this was a new harper, one she knew she had never heard before. And she knew, even before she saw it, that this was a larger harp than even Taliesin played, and the strange musician's fingers spoke to the strings as if he had enchanted them.

Viviane had once told her some old tale from a far-off country, a tale of a bard whose strings had made the ring stones circle in their own dance and the trees drop their leaves in mourning, and when he went down into the country of the dead, the stern judges there relented and let his beloved dead go forth. Morgaine stood motionless outside the door as everything that was in her faded into the music. Suddenly she felt that all the weeping she had held back in the ten days past might come upon her again, that her rage might dissolve, if she let it, into tears which would wash it all away, leaving her weak as any girl. Abruptly she thrust the door back and entered without ceremony.

Taliesin the Merlin was there, but he was not playing; his hands were clasped attentively in his lap as he bent forward, listening. Viviane too, in her simple house robes, was seated, not in her accustomed seat, but further from the fire; she had given the seat of honor to the strange harper.

He was a young man, in the green robe of a bard; smooth-shaven in the Roman fashion, his curling hair darker than rusted iron. His eyes were deep-set under a forehead which seemed almost too big for him, and though Morgaine for some reason had expected them to be dark, they were instead an unexpected piercing blue. He frowned at the interruption, his hands stopping in the middle of a chord.

Viviane too looked displeased, but ignored the discourtesy. "Come here, Morgaine, and sit by me. I know you are fond of music, and I thought you would like to hear Kevin the Bard."

"I was listening outside."

The Merlin smiled. "Come and listen, then. He is new to Avalon, but I think perhaps he may have much to teach us."

Morgaine went and sat on the little seat beside Viviane. The Lady of the Lake said, "My kinswoman Morgaine, sir; she too is of the royal line of Avalon. You see before you, Kevin, she who will be Lady here in years to come."

Morgaine made a startled movement; never before had she known that this was what Viviane planned for her. But anger drowned out her rush of gratification. *She thinks she can say a kind or flattering word and I will rush to lick her feet like a bitch puppy!*

"May that day be far distant, Lady of Avalon, and may your wisdom long continue to guide us," said Kevin smoothly. He spoke their language as if he had learned it well—she could just tell that it was not his own; a little hesitation and thought before the words, although the accent was almost flawless. Well, he had a musician's ear, after all. He was, Morgaine surmised, about thirty, perhaps a little more. But she did not look too closely at him after that first quick surprise at the blueness of his eyes; her gaze was bent on the great harp at his knee.

As she had guessed, it was somewhat larger than even the harp Taliesin played at the great festivals. It was made of a dark-reddish, gleaming wood, completely unlike the pale willow wood from which the harps of Avalon were fashioned, and she wondered if it was this which had given it the silken brilliant tone. The bowed edge curved in a line as graceful as a cloud, the pegs were carved of a curious pale bone, and it was painted and adorned with runic letters strange to Morgaine, who had learned, like any educated woman, to read and write in Greek characters. Kevin followed her close scrutiny and looked somewhat less displeased as he said, "You are admiring my lady." He ran his hands caressingly over the dark wood. "I named her so when she was built for me—she was the gift of a king. She is the only woman, whether maiden or matron, whose caresses never weary me and of whose voice I never tire."

Viviane smiled at the harper. "Few men can boast of so loyal a mistress."

His smile was a cynical twist. "Oh, like all women, she will respond to whatever hand caresses her, but I think she knows that I can best make her thrill to my touch, and being like all women lecherous, I am sure she loves me best."

Viviane said, "It sounds to me as if you had no good opinion of women who are flesh and blood."

"Why, so I have not, Lady. Save for the Goddess—" He spoke the words with a faint lilt, not quite mockery. "I am content to have no mistress but My Lady here, who never chides me if I neglect her, but is always the same sweet paramour."

"Perhaps," said Morgaine, raising her eyes, "you treat her rather better than you treat a woman of flesh and blood, and she rewards you as is your due."

Viviane frowned, and Morgaine knew she had trespassed by this bold speech. Kevin raised his head suddenly from the harp and met Morgaine's eyes. For a moment he held her gaze, and she was astonished at his bitter hostility and with it, the sense that he understood something of her rage, had known his own and fought through it.

He might have spoken, but Taliesin nodded to him, and he bent his face again over the harp. Now she noticed that he played it differently from most harpers, who held their small instruments across their body, playing with the left hand. He set his harp between his knees, and leaned forward to it. It startled her, but as the music began to fill the room, like moonlight rippling from the strings, she forgot the strangeness of it, saw his face change and grow quiet and distant, without the mockery of his words. She decided that she liked him better when he played than when he spoke.

There was no other sound in the room, only the harping that filled it to the rafters, as if the listeners had stilled even their breathing. The sound swept away all else, and Morgaine dropped her veil over her face and let the tears come. It seemed that in the music she could hear the flooding of the spring tides, the sweet awareness that had filled her body as she lay that night in the moonlight, awaiting the coming of the dawn. Viviane reached out to her and, as she had done when Morgaine was only a child, took her hand, gently stroking her fingers one after another. Morgaine could not stop her tears. She raised Viviane's hand to her lips and kissed it. She thought, with a crushing sense of loss, *Why, she is old, she has grown old since I came here* . . . always before this, Viviane had seemed to her ageless, unchanging, like the very Goddess herself. *Ah, but I too have changed, I am no longer a child* . . . *once she told me, when I came here, that a day would come when I would hate her as much as I loved her, and I could not believe it then.* . . . She struggled against her weeping, afraid she would make some sound which would betray her and, even more, interrupt the flood of music. She thought, *No, I cannot hate Viviane,* and all her rage melted into sorrow so great that for a moment she thought she would break into the fiercest weeping. For herself, for the changes in herself, for Viviane who had been so beautiful, the very face of the Goddess, and who was now nearer to the Death-crone, and for the knowledge that she too, like Viviane, with the relentless years would one day herself come to stand as the crone; for the day she had climbed the Tor with Lancelet and lain there in the sun, hungering for his touch without clearly knowing what it was she wanted; and for something which had gone from her, irrevocably. Not virginity alone, but a trust and belief she would never know again. And Morgaine knew that beside her Viviane, too, was weeping silently behind her veil.

She glanced up. Kevin was motionless, only his fingers alive on the strings; then the sighing madness of the music shivered into silence, he raised his head, and his fingers swept the strings, plucking them gaily to a merry tune, one sung by the barley sowers in the fields, with a dancing rhythm, and words that were far from decorous. This time he sang. His voice was strong and clear, and Morgaine, under cover of the dancing music, sat up and began to watch his hands, pushing her veil aside and contriving to wipe away the betraying tears as she did so.

Then she noticed that for all their skill, there was something strangely amiss with his hands. They seemed somehow misshapen, and studying them, she noted that one or two of the fingers lacked a second joint, so that he played deftly with the stubs, and that the little finger was missing entirely from his left hand; and all along the hands, beautiful and supple as they seemed when he moved them, were odd discolorations. As he set down the harp, leaning to steady it, his sleeve fell away from his wrist, and she could see hideous white patches there, like the scars of burns or some ghastly mutilating wounds. Now that she looked on him closely, she could see that his face had a fine network of scars along chin and jawline. He saw her staring and raised his head, meeting her eyes again and holding them with a hard, angry stare. Morgaine looked away, flushing; after the music which had searched her very soul, she would not have wounded his feelings.

"Well," Kevin said abruptly, "My lady and I are always glad to sing to those who love her voice, but I do not suppose you called me here entirely to entertain you, madam; nor you, my lord Merlin."

"Not entirely," said Viviane in her rich, low voice, "but you have given us a delight I shall remember for many years."

"And I," Morgaine said. She felt as shy now before him as she had been bold before. Nevertheless she went forward, to look more closely at the great harp, and said, "I have never seen one made after this fashion."

"That I can well believe," Kevin said, "for I had it made after my own design. The harper who taught me my craft threw up his hands in horror as if I had blasphemed his Gods, and swore it would make an unholy clamor, fit only to frighten away enemies. Like the great war harps, twice as tall as a man, that were dragged on carts up the hills in Gaul, and left there in the wind to make ghostly noises, so that they say even the legions of Rome were frightened. Well, I played one of those war harps, and a grateful king gave me leave to have a harp made exactly as I chose—"

Taliesin broke in. "He speaks the truth," he said to Viviane, "though I did not believe it when I heard it first—what man and mortal could play one of those monsters?"

"I did it," Kevin said, "and so the king had my lady made for me. I have a smaller one to the same design, but not so fine."

"Indeed it is beautiful," Morgaine said. "What are the pegs? Are they seal bone?"

He shook his head. "They are carved, so I am told, from the teeth of a great beast that lives in the warm countries far to the south," he said. "I only know that the material is fine and smooth, yet hard and durable. It is more costly than gold, though less gaudy."

"You do not hold it as I have ever seen a harp played—"

"No," Kevin said with his twisted smile, "I have but small strength in my arms, and I had to experiment to find how I could best do so. I saw you look at my hands. When I was six years old, the house where I lived was burned over my head by the Saxons, and I was pulled out too late. No one thought I would live, but I surprised them all, and since I could neither walk nor fight, they set me in a corner and decided that with my broken hands"—he spread them out quite dispassionately before him—"perhaps I could learn to spin and weave among the women. But I showed small disposition for that, and so one day an old harper came by, and in return for a bowl of soup, set himself to amuse a cripple. When he showed me the strings, I tried to play. And I did make music, after a fashion, so he got his bread that winter and the next by schooling me to play and sing, and said he could put me in the way of earning a livelihood with my music. And so for ten years I did nothing but sit in the corner and play, until my legs at length grew strong enough that I could learn to walk again." He shrugged, and pulled a length of cloth from behind him, wrapping up the harp in it and sliding it into a leather case embroidered with signs. "And then I became harper to a village, and at length to a king. When the old king died, his son had no ear for music, and I thought it best to get well out of the kingdom before he began to look covetously at the gold on my harp. Then I came to the Druid isle, and there I studied bardcraft, and at last I was sent to Avalon—and here I find myself," he added, with a final shrug, "but still you have not told me why you bade me attend you, Lord Merlin, nor these ladies."

"Because," said the Merlin, "I am old, and the events we set in motion this night may not come into their full flower for another generation. And when that time comes, I shall be gone."

Viviane leaned forward and said, "Have you had warning, Father?"

"No, no, my dear. I would not waste the Sight on such a matter; we do not consult the Gods to tell if the next winter will bring snowfalls. And as you brought Morgaine here, so I brought Kevin the Bard, so that there may be one younger than myself to follow what may happen when I am gone. So hear my news: Uther Pendragon lies dying at Caerleon, and where the lion falls, there the kites will gather. And we have had word brought to us that there is a great army massing in the Kentish countries, where the treaty people have decided that now is the moment to rise and take the rest of Britain from us. They have sent for mercenaries from the mainland, north of Gaul, to join them in overthrowing our people and undoing what Uther has done. And this is the time for all our people to fight behind the banner we have worked so many years to raise. There is not much time—they must have their king and have him now. There is not another moon to waste, or they will be upon us. Lot wants the throne, but the Southmen will not follow him. There are others—Duke Marcus from Cornwall, Uriens in North Wales—but not one of them can gain the support outside his own lands, and we could well be like the donkey who starved to death between two bales of fodder, not knowing which to eat first. . . . We must have the Pendragon's son, young though he is."

Kevin said, "I had never heard that the Pendragon had a son. Or has he recognized that son his wife bore to Cornwall, soon after they were married? Uther must have been in unseemly haste to marry, if he could not even wait until she bore her child before taking her to his bed—"

Viviane raised her hand. "The young prince is the son of Uther," she said, "none may doubt it, nor will doubt it when they see him."

"Is it so? Then Uther did well to hide him away," Kevin said, "for his son by another man's wife—"

Viviane gestured him to silence. "Igraine is my sister, and she is of the royal line of Avalon. This son of Uther and Igraine is the one whose coming was foretold, the king who was and will be. Already he has taken the antlers and been crowned over the Tribes—"

"What king in Britain, do you think, will accept some boy of seventeen to be High King?" Kevin asked skeptically. "He could be brave as the fabled Cuchulain and they would want a warrior of greater skill."

"As for that, he has been schooled to war, and to the work of a king's son," Taliesin said, "though he knows not that his blood is royal. But I think the full moon just past gave him a sense of his destiny. Uther was honored above any king before his time; this lad Arthur will set his state even higher. I have seen him on the throne. The question is not, will they accept him, but what can we do to set him about with all the majesty of the High King, so all the warring kings will join hands against the Saxon instead of against one another!"

"I have found the way to do that," Viviane said, "and at the new moon it shall be done. I have a sword for him, a sword out of legend, never before wielded by a living hero." She paused a moment, then said slowly, "And for that sword, I shall exact from him a pledge. I shall swear him to be true to Avalon, despite whatever the Christians may do. Then perhaps the tide will turn, and Avalon will return from the mists, and it is the monks and their dead God who will go into the shadows and the mists, while Avalon shines again in the light of the outer world."

"An ambitious plan," said Kevin, "but if in truth the High King of Britain were sworn to Avalon—"

"This has been planned since before he was born."

Taliesin said slowly, "The boy has been fostered a Christian. Will he take such an oath?"

"How real is the talk of Gods to a boy, compared to a legendary sword with which to lead his people, and the fame of great deeds?" Viviane shrugged. "Whatever may come of it, we have gone too far to stop now; we are all committed. In three days the moon will be new again, and at that auspicious time he shall have the sword."

THERE WAS LITTLE MORE to say. Morgaine sat quietly listening, both excited and appalled. She had been in Avalon too long, she thought, too long concealed among the priestesses with her mind on holy things and the secret wisdom. She had forgotten that there was a world outside. Somehow it had never really come home to her that Uther Pendragon, her mother's husband, was High King of all Britain, and that her brother would be so some day. *Even,* she thought with a twist of that new cynicism, *with the stain of doubt on his birth.* Perhaps the rival kings would even welcome a candidate who had no loyalty to any of their parties and factions, a son of the Pendragon, handsome and modest, who could serve as a symbol round whom they all rallied. A candidate, for High King moreover, who had already been accepted by the Tribes, and by the Pict folk, and by Avalon . . . and then Morgaine flinched, remembering the part she had had in that. This brought her anger back, so that when Taliesin and Kevin rose to go, she remembered why she had wanted, ten days ago, when it was fresh in her mind, to confront Viviane with her rage.

Kevin's harp in its ornamented leather bag was difficult to carry, being so much larger than other harps, and when he was burdened with its weight he looked awkward, one knee stiff and a foot dragging. *Ugly,* she thought, *an ugly grotesque man; but when he plays, who would think so? There is more to this man than any of us knows.* And then she remembered what Taliesin had said; she knew that she looked on the next Merlin of Britain, as Viviane had called her next Lady of the Lake. The pronouncement brought no elation, although if Viviane had said it before that journey which had changed her life, she would have been proud and excited. Now it seemed shadowed by the thing which had happened to her.

⚹ *With my brother, my brother. It did not matter when we were priest and priestess, God and Goddess joining under the power of ritual. But in the morning, when we wakened and were man and woman together . . . that was real, that was sin. . . .*

Viviane was standing at the door, watching them move away. "For a man with such injuries, he moves well. It is fortunate for the world that he survived them and that he was not set as a beggar in the street, or to weaving rush mats in the market. Such skill as that one has should not be hidden in obscurity, or even in the court of a king. A voice and hands like that belong to the Gods."

"He is gifted, certainly," Morgaine said, "but I wonder—is he wise? The Merlin of Britain must be not only learned and gifted but wise as well. And—virtuous."

"I leave that to Taliesin," Viviane said. "What shall be, must be; it is not mine to order."

And suddenly Morgaine's wrath overflowed. "Are you truly acknowledging that there is anything on the face of this earth which you feel is not yours to order, Lady? I thought you believed that your will was the will of the Goddess, and all of us puppets to serve you!"

"You must not talk this way, my child," Viviane said, looking at her in astonishment. "You can hardly mean to be so insolent to me."

If Viviane had responded to her words with arrogance, it would have hardened Morgaine's anger into explosion; the gentleness baffled her. She said, "Viviane, *why?*" and felt, shamefully, that tears would rise again to choke her.

Now Viviane's voice was cold. "Did I leave you for too long among the Christians, after all, with their talk of sin?" she said. "Think, child. You are of the royal line of Avalon; so too is he. Could I have given you to a commoner? Or, could the High King to come be so given?"

"And I believed you when you said—I believed it was the doing of the Goddess—"

"Why, so it was," said Viviane gently, not understanding, "but even so, I could not give you to anyone unworthy of you, my Morgaine." Her voice was tender. "He was so young when you parted—I thought he would never have recognized you. I regret that you recognized him, but after all, you would have had to know sooner or later. And he need not know for a long time."

Morgaine said, tightening her body against rage, "He knows already. He knows. And he was more horrified, I think, than I was."

Viviane sighed. "Well, there is nothing we can do about that now," she said. "Done is done. And at this moment the hope of Britain is more important than your feelings."

Morgaine turned away and did not wait to hear more.

17

the moon was dark in the sky; at this time, so the young priestesses were told in the House of Maidens, the Goddess veils her face from mankind, taking counsel of the heavens themselves and the Gods which lie behind the Gods we know. Viviane too kept seclusion at moon-dark, her privacy guarded by two young priestesses.

Most of that day she kept her bed, lying with closed eyes, and wondering if she was, after all, what Morgaine thought her—drunk with power, believing that all things were at her command to play with as she thought good.

What I have done, she thought, *I have done to save this land and its people from rapine and destruction, a reversion to barbarism, a sacking greater than Rome suffered from of the Goths.*

She longed to send for Morgaine, hungering for their old closeness. If indeed the girl came to hate her, it would be the heaviest price she would ever pay for anything she had done. Morgaine was the one human being she had ever wholly loved. *She is the daughter I owed the Goddess. But, done is done and cannot be called back. The royal line of Avalon must not be contaminated by commoner blood.* She thought of Morgaine with a sorrowful hope that one day the young woman would understand; but whether or no, Viviane knew she had done what she must, no more.

She slept little that night, sliding off into chaotic dreams and visions, thinking of the sons she had distanced from her, of the world outside into which the young Arthur had ridden at Merlin's side; had he come in time to his dying father? For six weeks Uther Pendragon had lain ill in Caerleon, sinking, then rallying; but it seemed unlikely that he could live much longer.

As the dawn neared, she rose and dressed herself, so silently that neither of her attendant priestesses stirred. Did Morgaine sleep in the House of Maidens, or did she too lie awake with heavy heart, or weep? Morgaine had never wept before her, until that day when Kevin's harp had stirred their hearts, and even then she had concealed her tears.

Done is done! I cannot spare her. But with all my heart I wish there had been some other way. . . .

She went out silently into the garden behind her dwelling. Birds were waking; apple blossoms, soft and sweet-scented, drifted from the trees which had given Avalon its name.

They will bear fruit in time to come, as what I do now will bear fruit in its own season. But I shall blossom nor bear fruit no more. The burden of the years lay heavy on her mind. *I grow old; even now, at times, the Sight fails me, the Sight I am given to guide this land.*

Her own mother had not lived to be so old. The time would come —indeed, was almost upon her—when she must lay down her burden and her holy office, giving over the real rulership of Avalon to the next Lady, standing behind her in shadows as the wise-woman—or the Old Death-crone herself.

Morgaine is not yet ready. She still lives by the world's time, and she can still tremble and weep for what cannot be avoided. Her mind ran over the roster of priestesses, the young and the old, in Avalon. There was none to whom she could entrust the rulership of this land. Morgaine would some day grow to that stature; but not yet. Raven—Raven might have had that strength. But Raven had given her voice to the Gods; Raven was for the divine madness of the worlds beyond, not for the sober counsel and judgment of this one. What would come to Britain, if she should die before Morgaine was grown to her full powers?

Overhead the sky was still dark, although in the east the mist was lightening with the dawn. As she watched, the light grew; the red clouds formed slowly, twisting into the shape of a red dragon, coiling along the whole horizon. Then a great shooting star flamed along the sky, paling the form of the red dragon; its brilliance blinded Viviane for a moment, and when she could see again, the red dragon was gone and the shifting clouds were white with the rising sun.

Viviane felt shivers raking her spine. A portent like this was not seen twice in a lifetime—the whole of Britain must be alive with it. *So passes Uther,* she thought. *Farewell to the dragon who has spread his wings over our coast. Now will the Saxons be loosed upon us.*

She sighed and then, without warning, there was a ripple in the air, and a man stood before her in the garden. She trembled, not with the fear which a house-bred woman might feel of an intruder—Viviane had no fear of any man living—but because it had been long since she had experienced a true Sending of this kind. A vision which intruded on her, unsummoned, must be of great power.

Power like the shooting star, a portent such as has not been seen in my lifetime . . .

For a moment she did not recognize the man who stood before her; wasting illness had greyed the fair hair, shrunk the broad shoulders, and stooped the spine; the skin was yellowed and the eyes sunken with pain. Even thus, Uther Pendragon seemed, as always, larger than most men; and though there was little sound in the enclosed garden, so that she heard the twittering birds through his voice—yes, and saw the blossoming trees through his body—it seemed that he spoke as always to her, harshly, without warmth.

So, Viviane, we meet for the last time. There is a bond between us, not one I would have desired; we have not been friends, sister-in-law. But I trust to your vision, for what you spoke came always true. And you are the only one to make it sure that the next High King of Britain can take what is rightfully his.

Now she saw that across his breast was the mark of a great wound. How had it come about that Uther Pendragon, lying sick in Caerleon, had died of a wound and not of his long illness?

I died as a warrior would die; the treaty troops broke their faith again, and my armies could not stand against them until I had myself carried, to show myself on the field. Then they rallied, but Aesc, the Saxons' chief—I will not grant that wild savage the name of king—broke through, and slew three of my guard; and I killed him before his bodyguard could kill me. But we won that battle. The next battle will be for my son. If he comes to the throne.

Viviane heard herself say aloud, through the silence, "Arthur is King through the old royal line of Avalon. He needs no Pendragon blood to take his rightful place as High King."

But this, which would have made the living Uther burst out in wrath, only called forth the wry smile, and for the last time she seemed to hear his voice.

I doubt not it would take more even than your magic, sister-in-law, to make the lesser kings of Britain see that. You may think scorn of the Pendragon's blood, but it is upon that Merlin must call to put Arthur on my throne.

And then, before her eyes, the form of Uther Pendragon faded, and before her stood another man whom the living Viviane had seen only in dreams. And in a searing moment, Viviane knew why no man had ever been more to her than duty, or a path to power, or a night's pleasure; for a moment she stood in a land drowned before the ring stones on the Tor were raised, and about her arms she wore twining golden serpents . . . the faded crescent burned like a great horned moon between her brows, and she *knew* him, with a knowledge that went beyond time or space. . . . She cried aloud, with a great mourning cry for all that she had never known in this life, and the agony of a bereavement unguessed till this moment. Then the garden was empty and birds twittered mindlessly in the damp silence of the mists that concealed the rising sun.

And far away in Caerleon, Igraine, knowing herself widowed, cries out for her love . . . it is hers to mourn him now. . . . Viviane caught for support against the dew-drenched bark of the great tree, and leaned against it, wrung with unexpected sorrow. He had never known her. He had disliked her, had never trusted her until the very moment of his death, when the mortal disguise of one lifetime fell away. *Goddess be merciful . . . a lifetime gone and I never knew him . . . gone, gone again, and will I know him again when we meet or will we walk blinded again, passing each other by as strangers?* But there was no answer, only silence, and Viviane could not even weep.

Igraine will weep for him . . . I cannot. . . .

Quickly she collected herself. This was no time to stand and mourn for a love like a dream within a dream; time began to move for her again, and she looked back on the vision with a faint dismay. She could find no grief in her now for the dead man, nor anything except exasperation; she might have known that he would manage to die at the most inconvenient time possible, before he had time to proclaim his son to the rival kinglets all striving for the crown of the High King. Why had he not stayed in Caerleon, why had he given in to the pride which had led him to show himself one more time in battle? Had he even seen his son, had the Merlin arrived in time?

The Sending had gone beyond recall; there was no way to summon it back and ask mundane questions. Uther had indeed come to her at the moment of his death—it was just as well Igraine would never know that. But he was gone.

Viviane glanced skyward. There was no sign yet of the crescent moon in the sky; perhaps she still might see something in her mirror. Should she call Raven? No, there was no time for that, and Raven might not consent to break her silence for a vision of affairs in the world outside. Morgaine? She shrank from meeting Morgaine's eyes.

Will she live all her life as I have done, with a heart dead inside her body?

She drew a long shuddering breath and turned to leave the garden. It was still very damp and cold; the sunrise was still hidden in mist. There was none to see as she walked swiftly up the secret way toward the Holy Well where she bent to drink, flinging her hair back, cupping her hands to the water. Then she went to the mirror pool. For so many years she had served the shrine here that she had come to take for granted her power of vision; but now, unlike herself, she prayed.

Goddess, do not take the power from me, not yet, not for a little while. Mother, you know I do not ask it for myself, only that this land may be safe until I can place it into the hands which I have prepared to safeguard it.

For a moment, she saw only the ripples across the pool's water and clenched her hands as if she could force vision. Then, slowly, images began to form: she saw the Merlin going up and down the length of the land on his hidden ways, now as a Druid and Bard, as befitted the Messenger of the Gods; now as an old beggar or peddler, or as a simple harper. The face began to shift and change, and she saw Kevin the Bard, now in the white robes of the Messenger of Avalon, now in a nobleman's dress, confronting the Christian priests . . . and there was a shadow behind his head, he was circled in shadows, the shadow of the oak grove, the shadow of the cross; she saw him with the sacred cup of the Druid regalia . . . she saw the young Arthur, his brow still stained with the blood of the stag he had fought and slain, and Morgaine laughing, crowned with flowers, her face marked with blood. . . . She did not want to see it, and willed ferociously to turn her eyes away, but dared not break the flow of the visions. She saw a Roman villa, and Arthur standing between two boys—one was her own Lancelet, her younger son; she supposed the older was Arthur's foster-brother, Caius, the son of Ectorius . . . she saw Morgause surrounded by her sons; one by one they knelt at Arthur's feet. Then she saw the Avalon barge, draped in black like a pall, and Morgaine in the prow, only Morgaine was older . . . older, and weeping.

Impatiently, Viviane passed her hand over the surface of the water. This was no time to stand here, seeking guidance from visions which seemed to bear no meaning for the moment. She walked quickly down the hill toward her dwelling and summoned her attendant priestesses.

"Dress me," she said curtly, "and send for the Merlin; he must ride for Caerleon, and bring the young Arthur to me here before the moon is more than a day old in the sky. There is no time to waste."

18

But Arthur did not come with the new moon to Avalon.

Morgaine, in the House of Maidens, saw the new moon born, but she did not break the moon-dark fast. She felt faint, and knew that if she ate she would only be sick. Well, perhaps it was to be expected. She sometimes felt this way when her monthly courses were about to begin; later she would feel better. And later in the day she did feel better, and drank a little milk, and ate some bread; and that afternoon, Viviane sent for her.

"Uther lies dead in Caerleon," she said. "If you feel you must go to your mother—"

For a short time Morgaine considered that, but at last she shook her head. "I had no love for Uther," she said, "and Igraine knows it well. The Goddess grant that some of her priestly counselors may comfort her better than I could."

Viviane sighed. She looked tired and worn, and Morgaine wondered if she, too, felt sick with the aftermath of the stressful time of the moon's darkening. Viviane said, "Sorrow that I must say it, but I fear you are right. I would have spared you to her, if need be. There would be time for you to return to Avalon, before—" She broke off and then said, "You know that Uther, in his lifetime, kept the Saxons at bay, though with constant battle; we have not had more than a few moons of peace at any time. Now, I fear, it will be worse; they may come even to the doors of Avalon. Morgaine, you are full priestess, you have seen the sacred weapons—"

Morgaine replied with a sign, and Viviane nodded and said, "A day may come when that sword must be lifted in defense of Avalon and of all of Britain too."

Morgaine thought, *Why say this to me? I am priestess, not warrior; I cannot take the sword in defense of Avalon.*

"You remember the sword."

Barefoot, cold, tracing the circle with the weight of the sword in her hand, hearing Raven, the silent, cry aloud in terror . . .

"I remember."

✎ "Then I have a task for you," Viviane said. "When that sword is carried into battle, it must be circled with all the magic we have. You are to fashion a scabbard for the sword, Morgaine, and set into it every spell you know, that he who bears it into battle shall lose no blood. Can you do that?"

I had forgotten, Morgaine thought, that there might be a task for a priestess as well as a warrior. And, with her trick of following a thought, Viviane said, "So you, too, shall have a part in the battle to defend our country."

"So be it," Morgaine said, wondering why Viviane, who was the great priestess of Avalon, did not take this task for herself. The older woman gave her no answer, but said, "For this you must work with the sword before you; come, and Raven shall serve you, within the silence of magic."

Although she tried to remember that she was only a vessel of power and not the power itself, that the power itself came from the Goddess, Morgaine was young enough to feel exalted when she was conducted in silence to the secret place where work like this must be done, and surrounded by the priestesses who were to anticipate her every need so that she might not break the silence which would build the necessary power for the setting of spells. The sword was laid on a linen cloth before her; beside it, the low-brimmed chalice, fashioned of silver with gold beading around the edge. It was filled with water from the Holy Well; not for drinking—food and water were set aside for her—but that she might look into it and see within it such things as were needful for the work she must do.

On the first day, she cut, using the sword itself, an undersheath of thin doeskin. It was the first time she had had fine tools to work with, and she took pleasure in the special iron needle she had been given to stitch the sheath together; she took a pride which she knew was childish in that when she pricked her finger once or twice she did not utter even a momentary cry. She could not restrain a little caught breath of pure pleasure when she was shown the priceless piece of deepest crimson velvet, dyed with colors which, she had once been told, cost more money for an ounce than would buy a villa and hire men to work the land on it for a year. This would cover the doeskin, and on it she must work, in the golden and silken threads provided, the magical spells and their symbols.

Fashioning the shapes of doeskin sheath and velvet to cover it, she spent the first day; and before she slept, deep in the meditation of what she must do, almost in trance, she cut her arm a little and smeared the doeskin with her blood.

Goddess! Great Raven! Blood has been shed upon this scabbard, so that none need be spilt upon it when it is carried into battle.

She slept fitfully, dreaming that she sat on a high hill overlooking all of Britain and stitched spells, weaving them like visible light into the fabric of the earth itself. Below her the King Stag was running, and a man came striding up the hill to her, and took the sword from her hand. . . .

She woke with a start, thinking: *Arthur! It is Arthur who will bear the sword, he is the son of Pendragon . . .* and as she lay in the darkness, she thought that was why Viviane had given it to her, to make the magical scabbard for the sword he should bear in symbol of all his people. It was Arthur who had shed the blood of her virginity, and it was she, also of the sacred line of Avalon, who must fashion the spell-scabbard of his safety, guarding the royal blood.

All that day, in silence, she worked, gazing into the chalice, letting the images rise, now and then stopping to wait for inspiration in the meditative flow; she worked the horned moon, so that the Goddess should always watch over the sword and guard the sacred blood of Avalon. She was so wrapped in the magical silence that every object on which her eyes gazed, every movement of her consecrated hands, became power for the spell; it seemed at times as if visible light followed her fingers as she followed the horned moon with the full moon, and then with the dark moon, for all things must follow in season. Then, because she knew that a High King in Britain must rule in a Christian land, and because when first the followers of the Christ had come to Britain they had come here to the Druids, she worked in the symbol of Christian and Druid in friendship, the cross within the three-winged circle. She worked into the crimson velvet the signs of the magical elements, of earth and air and water and fire, and then figured the low-handled cup before her, in which visions moved and entwined, coming in and out of darkness: wand and earth platter, serpent of healing and wings of wisdom and the flaming sword of power . . . there were times when it seemed that needle and thread moved through her own flesh or through the flesh of the land, piercing earth and sky and her own blood and body . . . sign upon sign and symbol upon symbol, each marked with her blood and with the water of the Holy Well. Three days in all she worked, sleeping little, eating only a few bites of dried fruit, drinking only the water of the Well. There were times when, from a great distance within her own mind, she seemed to look out on her fingers working without any conscious choice, the spells wove themselves, blood and bone of the land, blood of her maidenhood, strength of the King Stag who had died and shed his blood so that the champion might not die. . . .

By sunset of the third day it was finished, every inch of the scabbard covered with twining symbols, some of which she did not even recognize; surely they had come directly from the hand of the Goddess through her hands? She lifted it, slid the sword into it; weighted it in her hands; then said aloud, breaking the ritual silence, "It is done."

Now that the long tension was broken she was aware that she was exhausted, shaken and sick. Ritual and prolonged use of the Sight could do this; it had, no doubt, interrupted her courses too, for they usually came on at moon-dark. This was said to be lucky, for the priestesses went apart to shield their power at this time, and it was the same as the ritual seclusion of the dark moon, when the Goddess herself secluded herself to safeguard the source of power.

Viviane came and took the scabbard. She could not suppress a little cry of astonishment as she looked upon it, and indeed it seemed even to Morgaine, who knew her own hands had fashioned it, to be a thing surpassing human work, pregnant with magic. Viviane touched it only briefly before wrapping it in a long, white silken cloth.

"You have done well," she said, and Morgaine thought, her mind spinning, *How is it that she thinks she can judge me? I too am a priestess, I have gone beyond her teaching* . . . and was shocked at her own thought.

Viviane touched her cheek gently. "Go and sleep, my dearest; you have wearied yourself in this great work."

Morgaine slept deeply and long, without dreams; but after midnight, suddenly, she woke to the sudden wild clamor of alarm bells, alarm bells, church bells, a terror out of childhood, *The Saxons are upon us! Get up and arm yourselves!*

It seemed that she woke out of a start, and she was not in the House of Maidens, but in a church, and on the altar stone of the church lay a set of weapons; and on a trestle nearby lay a man in armor, covered with a pall. Above her head the warning was still pealing and clamoring, fit to wake the dead . . . no, for the dead knight did not stir, and with a sudden prayer for forgiveness, she snatched up the sword . . . and woke fully this time, to light in her room, and quiet. Not even the church bells from the other island penetrated the quiet of her stone-floored chamber. She had dreamed the bells, the dead knight, and the chapel with burning tapers, the arms on the altar, the sword, all of it. *How did I come to see that? The Sight never comes upon me undesired* . . . *was it just a dream then?*

Later that day, she was summoned; with her conscious mind, she remembered some of the visions which had floated half-seen through her mind as she wrought the scabbard with the sword before her. Fallen to earth in a falling star, a clap of thunder, a great burst of light; dragged still smoking to be forged by the little dark smiths who had dwelled on the chalk before the ring stones were raised; powerful, a weapon for a king, broken and reforged this time into the long, leaf-shaped blade, tooled and annealed in blood and fire, hardened . . . *a sword three times forged, never ripped out of the earth's womb, and thus twice holy.* . . .

She had been told the name of the sword: Excalibur, which meant cut steel. Swords of meteorite iron were rare and precious; this one might well be the price of a kingdom.

Viviane bade her cover herself with her veil and come. As they moved slowly down the hillside, she saw the tall figure of Taliesin, the Merlin, Kevin the Bard at his side, moving with his hesitant, grotesque walk. He seemed more than ever clumsy and ugly, as out of place as a lump of tallow clinging to the edge of a fine-wrought silver candlestick. And at their side —Morgaine froze, recognizing that slender muscular body, that shining silver-gilt hair.

Arthur. But of course she had known the sword was for him. What was more natural than that he should come here to receive it?

He is a warrior, a king. The little brother I held upon my lap. It seemed unreal to her. But through that Arthur, and the solemn-faced boy who walked now between the two Druids, she saw some trace of the youth who had taken upon himself the antlers of the Horned God; quiet and grave as he was, she saw the swing of the antlers, the deadly desperate fight, and how he had come to her bloodied with the stag's blood—no child but a man, a warrior, a king.

At a whisper from the Merlin he bent the knee before the Lady of the Lake. His face was reverential. *No, of course,* she thought, *he has not seen Viviane before, only me, and I was in darkness.*

But he saw Morgaine next; she saw recognition move across his mobile features. He bowed to her too—*at least,* she thought irrelevantly, *where he was fostered they taught him manners befitting a king's son*—and murmured, "Morgaine."

She bowed her head to him. He had known her even through the veil. Perhaps she should kneel to the King. But a Lady of Avalon bends the knee to no human power. Merlin would kneel, and so would Kevin if he were asked; Viviane, never, for she was not only the priestess of the Goddess, but incorporated the Goddess within herself in a way the man-priests of male Gods could never know or understand. And so Morgaine also would never kneel again.

The Lady of the Lake held out her hand to him, bidding him rise. "You have had a long journey," she said, "and you are wearied. Morgaine, take him to my house and give him something to eat before we do this."

He smiled then, not a king in the making, nor a Chosen One, but just a hungry boy. "I thank you, Lady."

Inside Viviane's house he thanked the priestesses who brought him food, and fell to hungrily. When he had satisfied his first hunger, he asked Morgaine, "Do you live here too?"

"The Lady dwells alone, but she is attended by the priestesses who serve her in turns. I have dwelt here with her when it was my turn to serve."

"You, a queen's daughter! You *serve?*"

She said austerely, "We must serve before we command. She herself served in her youth, and in her I serve the Goddess."

He considered that. "I do not know this Great Goddess," he said at last. "The Merlin told me that the Lady was your . . . our . . . kinswoman."

"She is sister to Igraine, our mother."

"Why then, she is my aunt," Arthur said, trying the words out on his tongue as if they didn't quite fit. "All of this is so strange to me. Somehow I always tried to think of Ectorius as my father and Flavilla my mother. Of course I knew there was some secret; and because Ectorius wouldn't talk to me about it, I thought it must be something shameful, that I was a bastard or worse. I don't remember Uther—my father; not at all. Nor my mother, not really, though sometimes, when Flavilla punished me, I used to dream I lived somewhere else, with a woman who petted me, then pushed me away —is Igraine our mother much like you?"

"No, she is tall, red-haired," Morgaine said.

Arthur sighed. "Then I suppose I do not remember her at all. For in my dreams it was someone like you—it *was* you—"

He broke off, his voice had been trembling. *Dangerous ground,* Morgaine thought, *we dare not talk about that.* She said calmly, "Have another apple; they are grown on the island."

"Thank you." He took one and bit into it. "It's all so new and strange. So many things have happened to me since—since—" His voice faltered. "I think of you all the time. I cannot help myself. It was true what I said, Morgaine—that all my life I shall remember you because you were the first, and I shall always think of you and love you—"

She knew she should say something hard and hurtful. Instead she made her words kind, but distant. "You must not think of me in that way. For you I am not a woman, but a representative of the Goddess who came to you, and it is blasphemy to remember me as if I were only a mortal woman. Forget me and remember the Goddess."

"I have tried—" He broke off, clenching his fists, then said gravely, "You are right. That is the way to think of it—only one more of the strange things that have come to me since I was sent for from Ectorius' house. Mysterious, magical things. Like the battle with the Saxons—" He held out his arm, rolling back the tunic to reveal a bandage thickly smeared with pine-pitch already blackened. "I was wounded there. Only it was like a dream, my first battle. King Uther—" He looked down and swallowed. "I came too late. I never knew him. He lay in state in the church, and I saw him dead, his weapons lying on the altar—they told me it was the custom, that when a brave knight lay dead, his arms should watch with him. And then, even while the priest was chanting the Nunc Dimittis, all the alarm bells rang, there was a Saxon attack—the watchmen came right into the church and snatched the bell ropes out of the hands of the monk who was tolling the passing bell to ring the alarm, and all the King's men caught up their arms and ran out. I had no sword, only my dagger, but I snatched up a spear from one of the soldiers. My first battle, I thought, but then Cai—my foster-brother,

Caius, Ectorius' son—he told me he had left his sword behind at their lodging, and I should run and fetch it for him. And I knew this was just a way to get me out of the battle; Cai and my foster-father said I was not yet ready to be blooded. So instead of running back to the lodging house I went into the church and snatched the King's sword off the stone bier. . . . Well," he defended himself, "he fought Saxons with it for twenty years, he'd certainly be glad to have it fight them again, instead of lying useless on an old stone! So I ran off and was going to give it to Cai as we were all gathering against the attack, and then I saw the Merlin, and he said in the biggest voice I have ever heard, 'Where got you that sword, boy?'

"And I was angry because he'd called me *boy*, after what I'd done on Dragon Island, and I told him it was a sword for fighting Saxons, not for lying around on old stones, and then Ectorius came up and saw me with the sword in my hand, and then he and Cai both knelt down in front of me, just like that! I felt so strange—I said to him, 'Father, why are you kneeling, why do you make my brother kneel like that? Oh, get up, this is terrible,' and the Merlin said in that awful voice, 'He is the King, it is right he should have the sword.' And then the Saxons came óver the wall—we heard their horns—and there was no time to talk about swords or anything else; Cai grabbed up the spear and I hung on to the sword and off we went. I don't remember much about the battle—I suppose you never do. Cai was hurt—badly hurt in the leg. Afterward, while the Merlin was bandaging up my arm, he told me who I really was. Who my father had been, that is. And Ectorius came and knelt and said he would be a good knight to me as he had to my father and to Ambrosius, and I was so embarrassed . . . and the only thing he asked me was that I'd make Cai my chamberlain when I had a court. And of course I said I'd be glad to—after all, he's my brother. I mean, I'll always think of him as my brother. There was a lot of fuss about the sword, but the Merlin told all the kings that it was fate that had made me take it from the stone, and I tell you, they listened to him." He smiled, and Morgaine felt a surge of love and pity at his confusion.

The bells that had waked her . . . she had seen, but she had not known what she saw.

She dropped her eyes. There would always be a bond between them now. Would any blow which struck him always fall like this, a sword into her naked heart?

"And now it seems I am to get another sword," Arthur said. "From having no sword at all, suddenly I have two special ones!" He sighed and said almost plaintively, "I don't see what all this has to do with being a king."

As OFTEN AS she had seen Viviane in the robes of the High Priestess of Avalon, Morgaine had never grown used to the sight. She saw Arthur look

back and forth between them, and saw the likeness mirrored in his eyes. He
was silent, awed once more. At least, thought Morgaine, feeling an empty
sickness again, they did not make him keep the magical fast. Perhaps she
should have eaten with him, but the thought of food made her feel queasy.
Prolonged work with magic could do that; no wonder Viviane was so
emaciated.

"Come," Viviane said, and leading the way—the Lady of Avalon, in
her own place, preceded even a king—she passed from the house and along
the shores of the Lake and into the building where the priests were housed.
Arthur walked quietly at Morgaine's side, and for an instant she half
expected him to reach out his hand as he had done when he was very little,
clinging to hers . . . but now that little hand she had held was a warrior's
hand, bigger than her own, hardened with long practice at sword play and
with other weapons. Behind Arthur and Morgaine came the Merlin, and at
his side Kevin.

Down a narrow flight of steps they went, and the dank smell of
underground surrounded them. Morgaine did not see anyone strike a light,
but suddenly there was a tiny glow in the darkness and a pale light flared
around them. Viviane stopped, so abruptly that they jostled into her, and
for an instant Morgaine was surprised that she felt simply soft and small,
an ordinary woman's body, not a remote image of the Goddess. The Lady
reached out and took Arthur's wrist in her small dark hand; it did not come
near to reaching around his.

"Arthur, son of Igraine of Avalon and of Pendragon, rightful King of
all Britain," she said, "behold the most sacred things in all your land."

The light flared on gold and jewels in cup and platter, the long spear,
the crimson and gold and silver threads of the scabbard. And from the
scabbard, Viviane drew forth the long, dark blade. Dimly, stones glinted in
its hilt.

"The sword of the Sacred Regalia of the Druids," she said quietly.
"Swear now to me, Arthur Pendragon, King of Britain, that when you come
to your crown, you will deal fairly with Druid as with Christian, and that
you will be guided by the sacred magic of those who have set you on this
throne."

Arthur reached for the sword, his eyes wide; Morgaine could see it in
his eyes—that he knew what manner of sword this was. Viviane made a
quick gesture, preventing him.

"It is death to touch the holy things unprepared," she said. "Arthur,
swear. With this sword in your hand, there is no chieftain or king, pagan
or Christian, who will stand against you. But this is no sword for a king
who is bound to hear only the Christian priests. If you will not swear, you
may depart now, bearing such weapons as you can get from your Christian
followers, and the folk who look to Avalon for their rule shall follow you

only when we bid them to do so. Or will you swear, and have their allegiance through the sacred weapons of Avalon? Choose, Arthur."

He stared at her, frowning a little, the pale light glinting on his hair, which looked almost white. He said, "There can be only one ruler in this land; I must not be ruled from Avalon."

"Nor must you be ruled by the priests who would make you a pawn of their dead God," said Viviane quietly. "But we will not urge you. Choose whether or no you will take this sword, or refuse it and rule in your own name, despising the help of the Old Gods."

Morgaine saw that strike home—the day when he had run among the deer and the Old Gods had given him victory, so that he was acclaimed king among these people, the first to acclaim him. He said quickly, "God forbid I should despise—" and stopped, swallowing hard. "What must I swear, Lady?"

"Only this: to deal fairly with all men, whether or no they follow the God of the Christians, and always to reverence the Gods of Avalon. For whatever the Christians say, Arthur Pendragon, and whatever they may call their God, all the Gods are as one God, and all the Goddesses but one Goddess. Swear only to be true to that truth, and not to cling to one and despise another."

"You have seen," said the Merlin, his voice deep and resonant in the silence, "that I do truly reverence the Christ and that I have knelt at the altar and shared their sacred meal."

Arthur said, troubled, "Why, that's true, my lord Merlin. And you, I think, are the councillor I shall trust more than any other. Do you bid me swear, then?"

"My lord and king," said Taliesin, "you are young for this rule, and perhaps your priests and bishops would presume to keep the conscience even of a king. But I am not a priest; I am a Druid. And I say only that wisdom and truth are not the special property of any priest. Ask your own conscience, Arthur, if it would be wrong to swear to deal fairly with all men and whatever Gods they worship, instead of swearing allegiance to one only."

Arthur said quietly, "Well then, I will swear, and take the sword."

"Kneel, then," Viviane said, "in token that a king is but a man, and a priestess, even a high priestess, no more than a woman, but that the Gods are over us all."

Arthur knelt. The light on his fair hair, Morgaine thought, was like a crown. Viviane laid the sword in his hand; his fists closed around the hilt. He drew a long breath.

"Take this sword, my king," Viviane said, "and bear it in justice. This sword was not made of iron raped from the body of the earth, our mother;

it is holy, forged of metal which fell from the heavens, so long ago that even the tradition of the Druids keeps no accurate account of the years, for it was forged before there were Druids in these islands."

Arthur rose, the sword in his hand.

"Which do you like better?" asked Viviane. "The sword or the scabbard?"

Arthur looked admiringly at the richly worked scabbard, but he said, "I am a warrior, my lady. The scabbard is beautiful, but I like the sword better."

"Even so," Viviane said, "keep the scabbard always by you; it was wrought with all the magic of Avalon. While you bear that scabbard, even though you take a wound, you will not shed enough blood to endanger your life; it is set about with blood-stanching spells. It is a rare and precious thing, and magical."

He smiled, saying—almost laughing with the breaking of the long tension—"Would I had had it when I took this wound against the Saxons; I bled like a sheep in the slaughterhouse!"

"You were not then a king, my lord. But now the magical scabbard will protect you."

"Even so, my king," said the melodious voice of Kevin the Bard, shadowed behind the Merlin, "however much you trust in the scabbard, I advise you to get yourself arms masters and cease not to practice with weapons!"

Arthur chuckled as he belted on sword and scabbard. "Never doubt it, sir. My foster-father had me taught to read by an old priest who read to me from one of the Gospels, how the Devil tempted the Lord Jesus, telling him that God had given him angels to watch over him; and Jesus said that it was ill done to tempt God. And a king is no more than flesh and blood—remember, I took my first sword from where Uther was lying dead. Don't think I shall tempt God that way, Lord Druid."

Somehow, with the sword of the Sacred Regalia belted at his waist, Arthur seemed taller, more impressive. Morgaine could see him crowned and robed as a king, seated upon his high seat . . . and for a moment, around him, it seemed that the small room was thronged with other men, shadowy, armed, richly clad, noble, standing around him closely, his Companions . . . then they were gone, and he was only a young man again, smiling uncertainly, wearing his rank a little uneasily as yet.

They turned and left the underground chapel. But before they passed completely out of the room, Arthur turned back for a moment to look at the other things of the regalia, lying in shadow. His uncertainty could be seen on his face, the almost visible question, *Did I do right, am I blaspheming the God I was taught to worship as the only One?*

The voice of Taliesin was low and gentle. "Know you my dearest wish, my lord and king?"

"What, Lord Merlin?"

"That one day—not now, for the land is not yet ready for it, and neither are those who follow Christ—but one day, Druid and priest should worship as one; that within their great church, their sacred Eucharist should be celebrated with yonder cup and dish to hold their bread and wine, in token that all the Gods are as One."

Arthur crossed himself, and said, almost in a whisper, "Amen to that, Lord Merlin, and Holy Jesus make it possible one day in these islands."

Morgaine felt the prickling up and down her forearms, and heard herself say, without knowing that she spoke until the Sight spoke through her, "That day will come, Arthur, but not as you think. Beware about how you bring that day to pass, for it may be a sign to you that your work is done."

Arthur said, in a hushed voice, "If that day should ever come to pass, Lady, then indeed it will be a sign to me that I have done what I came to the throne to do, and I am content to have it so."

"Beware what you speak," said the Merlin very softly, "for indeed the words we speak make shadows of what is to come, and by speaking them we bring them to pass, my king."

Morgaine blinked as they came into the sunlight. She swayed on her feet and Kevin reached out a hand to steady her.

"Are you ill, my lady?"

She shook her head impatiently, willing the blurring behind her eyes to vanish. Arthur looked at her, troubled. But then they were all in the sunshine, and his mind returned to the business at hand.

"I am to be crowned at Glastonbury, on the Isle of the Priests. If it is possible for you to leave Avalon, Lady, will you be there?"

Viviane smiled at him and said, "I think not. But the Merlin shall go with you. And Morgaine shall see your crowning if you wish, and she wishes," she added, and Morgaine wondered why the Lady spoke so, and why she was smiling. "Morgaine, my child, will you go with them in the barge?"

Morgaine bowed. She stood in the prow as the boat moved toward shore, bearing now only Arthur and the Merlin, and as it neared shore, she saw several armed men awaiting him. She saw the awe in their eyes as the draped boat of Avalon appeared quite suddenly from the mists, and one of them she recognized. Lancelet had not changed from that day two years ago, only he was taller, more handsome, dressed richly in dark crimson, bearing sword and shield.

He recognized her as well, and bowed. "Cousin," he said.

"You know my sister, the lady Morgaine, Duchess of Cornwall, priestess of Avalon," said Arthur. "Morgaine, this is my dearest friend, our cousin."

"We have met." Lancelet bent over her hand, and again, through the uneasy sickness in her, Morgaine felt a sudden thrust of that longing that would never really leave her.

He and I were meant, one for the other; I should have had the courage that day, even though it meant the breaking of a vow . . . she could see in his eyes that he remembered, in the tenderness with which he touched her hand.

Then she sighed, raised her eyes, and was introduced to the others. "My foster-brother Cai," Arthur said. Cai was big and dark and Roman to the core, and she saw as he spoke to Arthur, with natural deference and affection, that here indeed Arthur had two strong chiefs to lead his armies. The other knights were introduced as Bedwyr, Lucan, and Balin, which name made Morgaine, and the Merlin too, lift their eyes in surprise: this was foster-brother to Viviane's older son, Balan. Balin was fair-haired and broad-shouldered, in ragged clothing, but he moved as gracefully as his half-brother Lancelet. His dress was poor but his weapons and armor were bright and well kept, and looked well used.

Morgaine was content to leave Arthur to his knights; but first he raised her hand to his lips ceremoniously and kissed it.

"Come to my crowning if you can, sister," he said.

19

A **few** days later Morgaine went forth, with a few of the people of Avalon, to the crowning of Arthur. Never, in all her years upon Avalon —except for the few moments when she had opened the mists to allow Gwenhwyfar to find her convent again—had she set foot on the earth of the Isle of the Priests, Ynis Witrin, the Isle of Glass. It seemed to her that the sun shone with a curious harshness, unlike the soft and misty sunlight of Avalon. She had to remind herself that to almost all the people of Britain, *this* was the real world, and the land of Avalon only an enchanted dream, as if it were the very kingdom of fairy. To her, Avalon alone was real, and this last but a harsh dream from which, for some reason, she did not now waken.

All the space before the church seemed to have sprouted colorful tents and pavilions, like strange mushrooms. To Morgaine it seemed that the bells of the churches rang day and night, hour upon hour, a jangling sound that oppressed her nerves. Arthur greeted her, and for the first time she met Ectorius, the good knight and warrior who had fostered her brother and his wife, Flavilla.

For this venture into the world outside, at Viviane's advice, Morgaine had laid aside the blue robes of an Avalon priestess and the spotted deerskin overtunic, and had put on a simple dress of black wool, with linen underdress in white, and a white veil over her braided hair. Soon she realized that this made her look like a matron; among the British women, young maidens went with their hair unbound and wore dresses dyed in bright colors. They all took her for one of the women from the nunnery on Ynis Witrin, near to the church, where the sisters wore such somber robes; Morgaine said nothing to undeceive them. Nor, although he lifted his eyebrows and grinned at her, did Arthur.

To Flavilla he said, "Foster-mother, too many things are to be done —the priests want to speak to me of my soul, and the King of Orkney and the King of North Wales want audience with me. Will you take my sister to our mother, then?"

To our mother, Morgaine thought; *but that mother has become a stranger to us both.* She looked in her mind for any joy in this meeting and found none. Igraine had been content to let both her children go, the child of her first joyless marriage, the love child of her second; what manner of woman could she be then? Morgaine found that she was stiffening her mind and heart against the first sight of Igraine. *I do not,* she thought, *even remember her face.*

Yet when she did see Igraine, she realized that she would have known her anywhere.

"Morgaine!" She had forgotten, or remembered only in dreams, how rich and warm was Igraine's voice. "My darling child! Why, you are a woman grown, I see you always in my heart as a little maiden—and how worn and sleepless you look—has all this ceremony been heavy on you, Morgaine?"

Morgaine kissed her mother, again feeling tears choking at the back of her throat. Igraine was beautiful, and she herself—again words from a half-memory flooded her mind: *little and ugly like one of the fairy folk*—did Igraine think her ugly too?

"But what is this?" Igraine's light hands touched the crescent on her brow. "Painted like one of the fairy people—is this seemly, Morgaine?"

Morgaine's voice was stiff. "I am a priestess of Avalon, and I wear the mark of the Goddess with pride."

"Fold your veil over it then, child, or you will offend the abbess. You are to lodge with me in the nunnery."

Morgaine set her mouth hard. *Would the abbess, if she came to Avalon, keep her cross out of sight for fear of offending me, or the Lady?* "I do not wish to offend *you,* Mother, but it would not be suitable for me to lodge within the walls of a nunnery; the abbess would not like it, nor would the Lady, and I am under the Lady's orders and live under her laws." The thought of dwelling within those walls even for the three nights of the crowning, called to come and go, night and day, by the hellish jangling of those bells, made her blood run cold.

Igraine looked troubled. "Well, it shall be as you wish. Perhaps you could be lodged with my sister, the Queen of Orkney. Do you remember Morgause?"

"I will be glad to have my kinswoman Morgaine," said a soft voice, and Morgaine looked up to see the very image of her own mother as she remembered her from her own childhood: stately, robed richly in bright silks, with jewels and hair braided into a bright coronal on her brow. "Why, you were such a little girl, and now you are grown, and a priestess!" Morgaine was folded into a warm and scented embrace. "Welcome, kinswoman, come here and sit by me. How does our sister Viviane? We hear great things of her, that she is the moving force behind all the great events which have brought Igraine's son to the throne. Even Lot could not stand against one backed by the Merlin and the fairy folk and all the Tribes and all the Romans. And so your little brother is to be king! Will you come to court, Morgaine, and advise him, as Uther would have been well advised to have the Lady of Avalon do?"

Morgaine laughed, relaxing into Morgause's embrace. "A king will do as seems good to him, that is the first lesson which all who come near him must know. I suppose Arthur is like enough to Uther to learn that without much lessoning."

"Aye, there is not much doubt who had his fathering now, for all the talk there was about it then," Morgause said, and drew breath in swift compunction. "No, Igraine, you must not weep again—it should be joy to you, not sorrow, that your son is so much like his father, and accepted everywhere in all of Britain because he has pledged himself to rule all the lands and peoples."

Igraine blinked; she had, Morgaine thought, been doing overmuch weeping in the last days. She said, "I am happy for Arthur—" but her voice choked and she could not speak again. Morgaine stroked her mother's arm, but she felt impatient; always, always, ever since she could remember, her mother had had no thought for her children, only for Uther, Uther. . . . Even now when he was dead and lay in his grave, her mother would push her and Arthur aside for the memory of the man she had loved enough to make her forget everything else. With relief she turned back to Morgause.

"Viviane said you had sons—"

"True," Morgause said, "though most of them are still young enough to be here among the women. But the oldest is here to pledge loyalty to his king. Should Arthur die in battle—and not even Uther was immune to that fate—my Gawaine is his nearest kinsman, unless *you* already have a son, Morgaine—no? Have the priestesses of Avalon embraced chastity like nuns, then, that at your age you have given the Goddess neither son nor daughter? Or have you shared your mother's fate and lost many children at birth? Forgive me, Igraine—I did not mean to remind you—"

Igraine blinked back tears. "I should not weep against God's will; I have more than many women. I have a daughter who serves the Goddess to whom I was reared, and a son who will tomorrow be crowned with his father's crown. My other children are in the bosom of Christ."

Name of the Goddess, thought Morgaine, *what a way to think of a God, with all the generations of the dead clinging to him!* She knew it was only a way of speaking, a comfort to a sorrowing mother, yet the blasphemy of the idea troubled her. She remembered that Morgause had asked her a question and shook her head.

"No, I have borne no children, Morgause—until this year at Beltane I was kept virgin for the Goddess." She stopped abruptly; she should say no more. Igraine, who was more Christian than Morgaine could have believed, would have been horrified at the thought of the rite in which she had played the part of the Goddess for her own brother.

And then a second horror swept over her, worse than the first, so that she felt a wave of sickness follow in its wake. It had come about at full moon, and though the moon had waned and filled and waned again, her moon-dark bleeding had not yet come upon her, nor showed any sign it was about to do so. She had been relieved that she would not have this nuisance at the crowning, and had thought it was reaction to the great magic; no other explanation had suggested itself to her until this moment.

A rite for the renewal and fertility of crops and land, and of the wombs of the women of the tribe. She had known that. Yet such had been her blindness and her pride, she had thought that perhaps the priestess, the Goddess, would be exempted from the purpose of this ritual. Yet she had seen other young priestesses sicken and grow pale after these rites, until they began to bloom with their own ripening fruit; she had seen the children born, had brought some of them to birth with her own trained priestess-hands. Yet never once, in her stupid blindness, had it entered her mind that she too might come away from the ritual with a womb grown heavy.

She saw Morgause's sharp eyes on her, and deliberately drew a long breath and yawned to cover her silence. "I have been travelling since daybreak," she said, "and have not breakfasted; I am hungry." And Igraine apologized and sent her women for bread and barley beer which Morgaine forced herself to eat, though the food made her feel faintly sick and now she knew why.

Goddess! Mother Goddess! Viviane knew this might come about, yet she did not spare me! She knew what must be done, and done as quickly as possible; yet it could not be done in the three days of Arthur's crowning, for she had no access to the roots and herbs she could find in Avalon, and furthermore she dared not be sick now. She felt herself shrinking from the violence and sickness, yet it must be done, and done without delay, or in Midwinter she would bear a son to her own mother's son. Furthermore, Igraine must know nothing of it—the thought would strike her as evil beyond imagining. Morgaine forced herself to eat, and to talk of small things, and gossip like any woman.

But her mind did not rest as she talked. Yes, the fine linen she wore had been woven in Avalon, there was no linen anywhere like it, perhaps it was the flax of the Lake, which grew stronger, longer fibers, and whiter than anywhere else. But in her heart she was thinking, *Arthur, he must never know, he has enough to weigh his heart at this crowning. If I can bear this burden and keep silence to give his heart ease, I will do so.* Yes, she had been taught to play the harp—why, how foolish, Mother, to think it was wrong for a woman to make music. Even if one of the Scriptures did say that women were to keep silence in the church, it was shocking to think that the ears of God could be offended with the voice of a woman singing his praises; had not his own Mother lifted up her voice to sing praises when she knew she was to bear a child by the Holy Spirit? Then, when Morgaine took the harp in her hands and sang for her mother, beneath the refrain lay despair, for she knew as well as Viviane that she was to be the next Lady of Avalon, and she owed the Goddess a daughter at least. It was impious to cast out a child conceived under the Great Marriage. But how could she do anything else? The Mother of the Christian God had rejoiced in the God that had given her a child, but Morgaine could only rage in silent bitterness against the God who had taken the form of her unknown brother. . . . She was used to living her life on two levels at once, but even so the effort made her lips pale and her voice strained, and she was glad when Morgause cut her short.

"Morgaine, your voice is lovely, I hope to hear it at my own court. And Igraine, I hope to see you many times before the crowning feast is ended, but I must return and see how my babe is cared for. I have no love for convent bells and much praying, either, and Morgaine looks weary with travelling. I think I shall take her away to my tents and make her lie down, so she will be fresh in the morning to see Arthur crowned."

Igraine hardly troubled to conceal her relief. "Yes, I should be at the noonday office," she said. "You know, both of you, that when Arthur is crowned I shall dwell in the nunnery at Tintagel in Cornwall. Arthur asked me to remain with him, but soon, I hope, he will have a queen of his own, and no need of me."

Yes, they would insist that Arthur be wedded, and soon. Morgaine wondered which of these petty kings would manage the honor of being the king's father-in-law. *And my son might have been the heir to a crown . . . no. No, I will not even think of that.*

And again bitter anger overcame her, like choking; why, why had Viviane done this to her? To set all this in motion, so that they two, Arthur and Morgaine, might play out some mummery of Gods and Goddesses . . . was it no more than that?

Igraine kissed and embraced them both, promising to see them again afterward. As they walked along the path toward the brilliant array of pavilions, Morgause said, "Igraine is so changed I would not have known her—who would ever have thought she would grow so pious? No doubt she will end her days as the terror of a whole sisterhood of nuns, and, although I grieve to say it, I must rejoice I am not one of them. I have no call to a nunnery."

Morgaine forced herself to smile and say, "No, I suppose not; marriage and motherhood seem to have agreed with you. You blossom like the wild roses of the hedge, Aunt."

Morgause smiled lazily. "My husband is good to me, and it suits me well to be a queen," she said. "He is one of the Northmen, and so he does not think it wrong to take counsel of a woman, as these fools of Romans do. I hope Arthur has not been all spoilt by dwelling in a Roman household —it might have made him mighty in war, but if he despises the Tribes he will not rule. Even Uther was wise enough to know that and to have himself crowned on Dragon Island."

"So was Arthur," said Morgaine. It was all she could say.

"True. I have heard something of that, and I think he is wise. As for me, I am ambitious; Lot seeks my counsel, and all goes well in our land. The priests are very sour about me and say I do not keep my place as befits a woman—no doubt they think I am some kind of evil sorceress or witch, because I do not sit modestly at my spinning and weaving. But Lot thinks little of the priests though his people are Christian enough . . . to tell the truth, most of them care not whether the God of this land is the white Christ, or the Goddess, or the Horned One, or the Horse God of the Saxons, so long as their crops grow and their bellies are full. I think that is just as well —a land ruled by priests is a land filled with tyrants on Earth and in Heaven. Uther leaned a bit too far in that direction these last years, if you ask me. The Goddess grant that Arthur has more sense."

"He swore to deal justly by the Gods of Avalon, before Viviane gave him the sword of the Druids."

"Did she so?" Morgause said. "Now I wonder what brought that to her mind? But enough of Gods and kings and all of that—Morgaine, what ails you?" And, when Morgaine did not answer, "Do you think I can't tell a breeding woman when I see one? Igraine did not see it, but she has eyes now only for her grief."

Morgaine forced herself to say lightly, "Well, it might be so; I went to the rites at Beltane."

Morgause chuckled. "If that was your first time, you might not know for a moon or so, but good fortune to you. You are already past your best childbearing years—at your age I had three. I would not advise telling Igraine—she is far too Christian to accept a child to the Goddess now. Ah well, I suppose all women grow old in time. Viviane too must be well on in years now. I have not seen her since Gawaine was born."

"She seems much the same to me as always," Morgaine said.

"And so she did not come to Arthur's crowning. Well, we can manage without her. But I do not think she will be content to stay long in the background. One day, I doubt it not, she will put her will to seeing the cauldron of the Goddess rather than the sharing-cup of the Christian's love feast on our altar at court, and I won't weep when that day comes, either."

Morgaine felt a prophetic shiver as she saw in her mind the robed priest raising the cup of the Mysteries before the altar of Christ; and clearly before her eyes then she saw Lancelet, kneeling, a light on his face such as she had never seen . . . she shook her head to clear it of the unwanted Sight.

THE DAY OF ARTHUR'S CROWNING dawned brilliant and shining. All night they had come, from the length and breadth of Britain, to see the High King crowned here on the Isle of the Priests. There were crowds of the little dark people; Tribesmen clad in skins and checkered cloth and adorned with the dull-colored stones from the North, red-haired and tall and bearded; and more than any other, the Roman peoples of the civilized lands. And there were tall, fair, broad-shouldered men, Angles and Saxons from the treaty troops who had been settled south in Kent, and had come to renew the broken allegiance. The slopes were lined solid; even at Beltane festivals Morgaine had never seen so many people in one place, and she felt frightened.

She herself had a privileged place, with Igraine, Lot, Morgause and her sons, and the family of Ectorius. King Lot, slender and dark and charming, bent over her hand and embraced her and made a great show of calling her "kinswoman" and "niece," but Morgaine, looking behind the superficial smile, saw the sullen bitterness in Lot's eyes. He had schemed and intrigued to prevent this day. Now his son Gawaine was to be proclaimed Arthur's nearest heir; would that satisfy his ambition, or would he continue to work to undermine the authority of the High King? Morgaine slitted her eyes at Lot and discovered she did not like him at all.

Then the bells rang from the church and a cry went up all along the slopes overlooking the flat land before the church, and out of the church door a slender youth was walking, the sun glinting on his shining hair. *Arthur,* thought Morgaine. *Their young king, like a hero out of legend, with that great sword in his hand.* Although she could hear no words from where she sat, she saw the priest place on his head Uther's slender golden circlet.

Arthur raised the sword in his hand and said something she could not hear. But it was repeated from mouth to mouth, and when she heard it, Morgaine felt the same thrill she had felt, seeing him come victorious and crowned from the victory over the King Stag.

For all the peoples of Britain, he had said, *my sword for your protection, and my hand for justice.*

The Merlin came forward in his white robes of state; next to the venerable Bishop of Glastonbury, he looked mild and gentle. Arthur bowed briefly to them both, taking each of them by the hand. *The Goddess put it into his head to do that,* Morgaine thought—and in a moment she heard Lot saying as much.

"Damned clever, that, to set the Merlin and the Bishop side by side, in token that he'll be advised by both!"

Morgause said, "I don't know who had the teaching of him, but believe me, Uther had no foolish son."

"It is our turn," Lot said, rising to his feet, holding out his hand to Morgause. "Come, Lady; don't mind worrying that old crew of greybeards and priests. I've no shame to confess you sit at my side as my equal in all things. Shame to Uther that he didn't do likewise with your sister."

Morgause's smile twisted. "Perhaps it is our good fortune that Igraine had not the strength of will to insist on it."

Morgaine rose to her feet, driven by a sudden impulse, and went forward with them. Lot and Morgause motioned her courteously to precede them. Though she did not kneel, she bowed her head slightly. "I bring you the homage of Avalon, my lord Arthur, and of those who serve the Goddess." Behind her she could hear the priests murmuring, see Igraine among the black-robed sisters from the convent. She heard Igraine as if her mother had spoken: *Bold, forward, she was headstrong even as a child.* She forced herself not to hear. She was a priestess of Avalon, not one of those housebound hens of God!

"I welcome you, for yourself and for Avalon, Morgaine." Arthur took her by the hand, and placed her near where he stood. "I do you all honor as the only other child of my mother, and Duchess of Cornwall in your own right, dear sister." He released her hand and she bent her head to keep herself from fainting, because her eyes had blurred and her head swam. *Why must I feel like this now? Arthur's doing. No, not his, the doing of the Goddess. It is her will, not ours.*

Lot stepped forward, kneeling before Arthur, and Arthur raised him. "Welcome, dear Uncle."

That same dear Uncle, Morgaine thought, *who if I am not mistaken would gladly have seen him die as an infant.*

"Lot of Orkney, will you keep your shores against the Northmen, and come to my aid if the shores of Britain are threatened?"

"I will, kinsman, I swear it."

"Then I bid you keep the throne of Orkney and Lothian in peace, and never will I claim it or fight against you for it," said Arthur, and bent slightly to kiss Lot on the cheek. "May you and your lady rule well and long in the North, kinsman."

Lot, rising, said, "I beg leave to present you a knight for your company; I beg you to make him one of your Companions, Lord Arthur. My son Gawaine—"

Gawaine was big, tall and strongly built, rather like a male version of Igraine and Morgause herself. Red curls crowned his head, and though he was not much older than Arthur himself—in fact, Morgaine thought, he must have been a little younger, for Morgause had not wedded Lot until Arthur was born—he was already a young giant, six feet tall. He knelt before Arthur, and Arthur raised him and embraced him.

"Welcome, cousin. I will gladly make you the first of my Companions; I hope you will join and be welcomed by my dearest friends," he said, and nodded to the three young men standing at one side. "Lancelet, Gawaine is our cousin. This is Cai, and this Bedwyr; they are my foster-brothers. Now I have Companions, even as did that Alexander of the Greeks."

Morgaine stood and watched all that day as kings from all over Britain came to pledge fealty to the throne of the High King and swear to join him in war and to defend their shores. Fair-haired King Pellinore, lord of the Lake Country, came to bend the knee before Arthur and beg to take leave even before the end of the feasting.

"What, Pellinore?" said Arthur, laughing. "You, who I thought would be my staunchest supporter here, to desert me so soon?"

"I have had news from my homeland, Lord, that a dragon is raging there; I would swear to follow it until I have killed it."

Arthur embraced him and handed him a gold ring. "I will keep no king from his own people when they have need of him. Go and see to the killing of the dragon, then, and bring me its head when you have killed it."

It was nearing sunset when at last all the kings and nobles who had come to swear allegiance to their High King had finished. Arthur was no more than a boy, but he stood through the long afternoon with unflagging courtesy, speaking to each person who came as if he had been the first. Only Morgaine, trained in Avalon to read faces, could see the traces of weariness. But at last it was over, and servants began to bring the feast.

Morgaine had expected Arthur to sit down to dine among the circle of youths he had appointed as his Companions; it had been a long day, he was young, and he had done his duty with concentrated attention all day. Instead, he sat among the bishops and elder kings of his father's Council—Morgaine was pleased to see that the Merlin was among them. After all, Taliesin was his own grandsire, although she was not sure that Arthur knew that. When he had eaten (and he stuffed himself like a hungry boy who was still growing)—he rose and began to make his way among the guests.

In his plain white tunic, adorned only with the slender gold coronet, he stood out among the brightly dressed kings and nobles like a white deer in the dark forest. His Companions came at his side: the huge young Gawaine, and Cai, dark, with Roman, hawklike features and a sardonic smile—as he came closer Morgaine saw that he had a scar at the corner of his mouth, still red and ugly, which drew his face up into an ugly leer. It was a pity; he had probably been good-looking before that. Lancelet, next to him, looked pretty as a girl—no; something fierce, masculine and beautiful, perhaps a wild cat. Morgause looked at him with a greedy eye.

"Morgaine, who is that beautiful young man—the one beside Cai and Gawaine, the one in crimson?"

Morgaine laughed. "Your nephew, Aunt; Viviane's son Galahad. But the Saxons named him Elf-arrow, and mostly he is called Lancelet."

"Who would have thought that Viviane, who is so plain, should have such a handsome son! Her older son Balan—now *he* is not handsome; rugged, strong and hearty, and trustworthy as an old dog, but he is like Viviane. No one alive could call *her* beautiful!"

The words cut Morgaine to the heart. *I am said to be like Viviane; does everyone think me ugly, then? That girl said, little and ugly as one of the fairy folk.* She said coldly, "I think Viviane very beautiful."

Morgause snickered. "It is easy to see you have been reared in Avalon, which is even more isolated than most nunneries. I do not think you know what men desire for beauty in a woman."

"Come now," said Igraine soothingly, "there are virtues other than beauty. This Lancelet has his mother's eyes, and no one has ever denied that Viviane's eyes are beautiful; Viviane has so much charm that no one knows or cares whether or no she is beautiful, only that she has pleased them with her beautiful eyes and her fine voice. Beauty is not only in queenly stature and a fair complexion and golden curls, Morgause."

Morgause said, "Ah, you too are unworldly, Igraine. You are a queen, and everyone thinks a queen is beautiful. And you were married to the man you loved well. Most of us are not so fortunate, and it's a comfort to know that other men admire one's beauty. If you had lived all your life with old Gorlois, you too would be glad of your fair face and beautiful hair, and take pains to outshine those women who have nothing but charm and nice eyes and a sweet voice. Men are like babies—they see only the first thing they want, a full breast—"

"Sister!" said Igraine, and Morgause said, with a wry smile, "Ah well, it has been easy for you to be virtuous, sister, since the man you loved was a king. Most of us are not so fortunate."

"Do you not love Lot after all these years, Morgause?"

Morgause shrugged. "Love is a diversion for the bower and the winter fireside. Lot takes counsel of me in all things, and leaves the ruling of his household to me in time of war; and whenever he has plunder of gold or jewels or fine garments, I have first choice. So I am grateful to him, and he has never had the shadow of cause to think he rears another man's son. But that does not mean I must be blind when a young man has fine features and shoulders like a young bull, either—or an eye for his queen."

I doubt not, thought Morgaine, faintly disgusted, *that to Morgause this seems great virtue and she thinks of herself as a very virtuous queen.* For the first time in many years she felt confused, knowing that virtue could not be so simply defined. The Christians valued chastity above all other virtues, while on Avalon the highest virtue was to give over your body to the God or Goddess in union with all of the flow of nature; to each, the virtue of the other was the blackest sin and ingratitude to their own God. If one of them was right, the other was of necessity evil. It seemed to her that the Christians were rejecting the holiest of the things under heaven, but to them, she would not be considered much better than a harlot. If she should speak of the Beltane fires as a sacred duty to the Goddess, even Igraine, who had been reared in Avalon, would stare and think that some fiend spoke through her.

She turned her eyes back to the young men approaching: Arthur, fair and grey-eyed; Lancelet, slender, graceful; and the huge, red-haired Gawaine, who towered over the others like a bull over a pair of fine Spanish horses. Arthur came and bowed to his mother.

"My lady." He recollected himself. "Mother, has this day been long for you?"

"No longer than for you, my son. Will you sit here?"

"For a moment, Mother." As he seated himself, Arthur, though he had eaten well, absentmindedly took a handful of the sweets that Morgaine had put aside from her plate. It made Morgaine realize again how very young Arthur was. Still munching on almond paste, he said, "Mother, do you want to marry again? If you do, I will find the very richest—and the very kindest —of the kings to marry you. King Uriens of Northern Wales is widowed; I have no doubt he would be happy to have a good wife."

Igraine smiled. "Thank you, dear son. But after being wife to the High King, I do not want to be wife to a lesser man. And I loved your father well; I have no wish to replace him."

"Well, Mother, let it be as you wish," said Arthur, "only I was afraid you would be lonely."

"It is hard to be lonely in a nunnery, son, with other women. And God is there."

Morgause said, "I would rather dwell in a hermitage in the forest than in a house full of chattering ladies! If God is there, it must be hard for him to get a word in edgewise!"

For a moment Morgaine saw the sprightly mother of her own childhood as Igraine retorted, "I imagine, like any henpecked husband, he spends more time in listening to his brides than in speaking to them—but if one listens hard enough for the voice of God it is not far away. But have you ever been quiet enough to listen and hear him, Morgause?"

Laughing, Morgause made a gesture, as a fighter who acknowledges a hit. "And what of you, Lancelet?" she asked, smiling enticingly. "Are you betrothed yet, or even married?"

He laughed and shook his head. "Ah, no, Aunt. No doubt my father, King Ban, would find me a wife. But as yet I wish to follow my king and serve him."

Arthur, smiling up at his friend, clapped a hand on his shoulder. "With my two strong cousins here, I am guarded as well, I make no doubt, as any of those old Caesars themselves!"

Igraine said softly, "Arthur, I think Cai is jealous; say something kind to him," and Morgaine, hearing this, looked up at the sullen-looking, scarred Cai. Hard for him, indeed; after years of thinking Arthur his father's unregarded fosterling, now to be supplanted by a younger brother—a younger brother become king—and to find that brother surrounded by two new friends to whom his heart was given.

Arthur said, "When this land is at peace we shall find wives and castles for all of you, no doubt. But you, Cai, shall keep mine for me as my own chamberlain."

"I am content with that, foster-brother—forgive me, I should say, my lord and king—"

"No," said Arthur, turning right round to embrace Cai. "God strike me if I ever ask that you, brother, should call me any such thing!"

Igraine swallowed hard. "Arthur, when you speak so, sometimes it seems to me that I hear your father's very voice."

"I wish for my own sake, madam, that I could have known him better. But I know, too, that a king cannot always do as he chooses, nor a queen." He lifted Igraine's hand and kissed it, and Morgaine thought: *So he has already learned that much of king craft.*

"I suppose," Igraine said, "that they have already set about telling you that you should be married."

"Oh, I suppose so," Arthur said, with a shrug. "Every king, I suppose, has a daughter he would like to marry to the High King. I think I will ask the Merlin which one I ought to marry." His eyes sought Morgaine's and for a moment it seemed they held a terrible vulnerability. "I don't know so very much about women, after all."

Lancelet said gaily, "Why then, we must find you the most beautiful woman in the kingdom, and the highest born."

"No," Cai said slowly, "since Arthur says very sensibly that all women are alike to him, find him the one with the best dowry."

Arthur chuckled. "I'll leave it to you then, Cai, and I've no doubt I'll be as well wed as I am crowned. I'd suggest you take counsel of the Merlin and no doubt His Holiness the Archbishop will want some say in the matter. And what of you, Morgaine? Shall I find you a husband, or will you be one of my queen's ladies-in-waiting? Who should be higher in the kingdom than the daughter of my mother?"

Morgaine found her voice. "My lord and king, I am content in Avalon. Pray don't trouble yourself with finding me a husband." *Not even,* she thought fiercely, *not even if I am with child! Not even then!*

"So be it, sister, though I doubt not. His Holiness will have something to say about it—he will have it that the women of Avalon are evil sorceresses or harpies, all."

Morgaine did not answer, and Arthur glanced back almost guiltily at the other kings and councillors; the Merlin was looking at him, and he said, "I see, I have spent all the time I am allowed with my mother and my sister and my Companions; I must go back to the business of being a king again. Madam." He bowed to Igraine, more formally to Morgause, but as he approached Morgaine he leaned forward and kissed her on the cheek. She stiffened.

Mother, Goddess, what a tangle we have made. He says he will always love me and long for me, and that is the one thing he must not do! If Lancelet only felt so . . . She sighed, and Igraine came and took her hand.

"You are tired, daughter. That long standing in the sun this morning has wearied you. You are sure you would not rather come back with me

to the convent where it is so quiet? No? Well, then, Morgause, take her back
to your tent, if you will."

"Yes, dear sister, go and rest." She watched the young men walk away,
Arthur tactfully tempering his pace to Cai's halting step.

MORGAINE RETURNED with Morgause to their tent; she was weary, but she
had to remain alert and courteous while Lot talked of some plan Arthur had
spoken of—fighting on horseback, with attack tactics which could strike
down armed bands of Saxon raiders and foot soldiers, most of whom were
not trained battle troops.

"The boy's a master of strategy," Lot said. "It might well work; after
all, it was bands of Picts and Scots, and the Tribes, fighting from cover, who
could demoralize the legions, so I am told—the Romans were so used to
orderly fighting by the rules, and to foes who stood to give battle. Horsemen
always have an advantage over any foot soldiers; the Roman cavalry units,
I have been told, were always the ones who had the greater victories."

Morgaine remembered Lancelet, talking with passion of his theories of
fighting. If Arthur shared that enthusiasm and was willing to work with
Lancelet to build cavalry units, then a time might come, indeed, when all
the Saxon hordes were driven from this land. Then peace would reign,
greater than the legendary two hundred years of the Pax Romana. And if
Arthur bore the sword of Avalon and the Druid regalia, then indeed the
ensuing time might be a reign of wonder. . . . Viviane had spoken once of
Arthur as a king come out of legend, bearing a legendary sword. *And the
Goddess might rule again in this land, not the dead God of the Christians with
his suffering and death. . . .* She drifted into daydream, waking to reality only
when Morgause shook her shoulder lightly.

"Why, my dear, you are half asleep, go to your bed; we will excuse
you," she said, and sent her own waiting-woman to help Morgaine from
her garments, to wash her feet and braid her hair.

She slept long and deeply, without dreams, the weariness of many days
suddenly descending on her. But when she waked, she hardly knew where
she was or what had happened, only that she was deathly sick and must
stumble outside the tent to vomit. When she straightened up, her head
ringing, Morgause was there, a firm and kindly hand to help her back inside.
So Morgaine remembered her from earliest childhood, Morgause intermit-
tently kind and sharp. Now she wiped Morgaine's sweating forehead with
a wet towel and then sat beside her, telling the waiting-woman to bring her
kinswoman a cup of wine.

"No, no, I don't want it, I shall be sick again—"

"Drink it," Morgause said sternly, "and try to eat this piece of bread, it is hard and won't sicken you—you need something in your belly at these times." She laughed. "Indeed, something in the belly is what brings all this trouble on you."

Humiliated, Morgaine looked away from her.

Morgause's voice was kind again. "Come, girl, we've all been through it. So you're breeding—what of it? You're not the first or the last. Who is the father, or shouldn't I ask? I saw you looking at Viviane's handsome son—was he the lucky one? Who could blame you? No? A child of the Beltane fires, then? I'd have thought as much. And why not?"

Morgaine clenched her fists against Morgause's well-meant briskness. "I won't have it; when I return to Avalon, I know what to do."

Morgause looked at her, troubled. "Oh, my dear, must you? In Avalon they would welcome a child to the God, and you're of the royal Avalon line. I won't say I've never done the same—I told you I had been very careful never to bear a child which was not Lot's, which does not mean I slept alone all the time when he was away on his wars. Well, why should I? I don't suppose he always lay down alone! But an old midwife told me once, and she knew her business well, I must say—she told me that a woman should never try to cast out the first child she conceives, for if she did, it might injure her womb so that she could never bear another."

"I am a priestess, and Viviane grows old; I do not want it to interfere with my duties in the temple." And even as she spoke, she knew she was hiding her truth; there were women in Avalon who pursued their work to the last few months of their pregnancies, and then the other women cheerfully divided their tasks so that they could rest before the birth; and afterward, they even had time to nurse their babies before they were sent to fostering. Indeed, some of their daughters were priestess-reared, as Igraine had been. Morgause herself had been reared to her twelfth year in Avalon as Viviane's foster-daughter.

Morgause looked at her shrewdly. "Yes, I think every woman feels like that when first she carries a babe in her womb—trapped, angry, something she can't change and is afraid of. I know it was so with Igraine, it was so with me, I suppose it is so with every woman." Her arms went out and circled Morgaine, holding her close. "But, dear child, the Goddess is kind. As the child grows quick within you, the Goddess will put love in your heart for him, even if you care nothing for the man who put him there. Child, I was married at fifteen to a man far older; and on the day I knew I was with child I was ready to cast myself into the sea—it seemed the end of my youth, the end of my life. Ah, don't cry," she added, stroking Morgaine's soft hair, "you'll feel better soon. I have no liking for going about with a big belly and piddling like a babe in breechclouts all the day long, but the time will pass, and a babe at the breast is as much pleasure as

the bearing is pain. I have borne four and would willingly have another—
so often I had wished one of my sons had been a daughter. If you'd rather
not foster your babe in Avalon, I'll foster him for you—what do you think
of that?"

Morgaine drew a long, sobbing breath, raising her head from Morgause's shoulder. "I am sorry—I have wept all over your fine gown."

Morgause shrugged. "If nothing worse should happen to it, it is well.
See? The sickness passes and for the rest of the day you will feel well. Do
you think Viviane would spare you for a visit to me? You can return to
Lothian with us, if you will—you have not seen the Orkneys, and a change
will do you good."

Morgaine thanked her, but said that she must return to Avalon, and
that before she went, she must go and pay her respects to Igraine.

"I would not counsel you to confide in her," Morgause said. "She has
grown so holy she would be shocked, or think it her duty to be so."

Morgaine smiled weakly—she had no intention of confiding in
Igraine, nor for that matter in anyone else. Before Viviane could know,
there would no longer be anything for her to know. She was grateful for
Morgause's advice, and for her goodwill and good advice, but she did not
intend to heed it. She told herself fiercely that it was her own privilege to
choose: she was a priestess, and whatsoever she did should be tempered with
her own judgment.

All through the leavetaking with Igraine, which was strained—and
interrupted, more than once, by that damnable bell calling the nuns to their
duties—she was thinking that Morgause was more like the mother she
remembered than Igraine herself. Igraine had grown old and hard and pious,
it seemed to Morgaine, and she bade her farewell with relief. Returning to
Avalon, she knew, she was returning home; now she had no other home
anywhere in the world.

But if Avalon was no longer home to her, what then?

20

It was early in the day when Morgaine slipped quietly out of the
House of Maidens and into the wild marsh behind the Lake. She skirted the
Tor and came out into the patch of forest; with luck she could find what
she wanted here without wandering into the mists.

She knew the things she needed—a single root and then the bark of
a bush, and two herbs. They were all to be found in Avalon. She could have

taken them from the storerooms in the House of the Maidens, but she would have had to explain why she wanted them, and she shrank from that. She wanted neither the teasing nor the sympathy of the other women; better to find them herself. She knew something of herb lore, and of the midwife's skill. She need not place herself, for this, at the mercy of any other person.

One herb she wanted grew in the garden in Avalon; she had picked it unnoticed. For the others she must go afield, and she went a considerable distance before she noticed that she had not yet gone into the mists. Looking about, she realized that she had wandered into a part of Avalon she did not know—and that was utter madness. She had lived in Avalon for ten years or more, she knew every rise and knoll, every path and almost every tree. It was impossible that she could be lost in Avalon, and yet it was true; she had wandered into a thicker patch of forest, where the trees were older and closer than any she had seen, and there were bushes and herbs and trees on which she had never laid eyes.

Could it be that she had somehow strayed through the mists without knowing it, and was now on the mainland surrounding the Lake and the Island? No; she mentally retraced every step of her journey. There had been no mist. In any case, Avalon was almost an island, and if she had trespassed its borders, she would have come only to the water of the Lake. There was the hidden, almost dry, horse path, but she was nowhere near to that.

Even on that day when she and Lancelet had found Gwenhwyfar in the mists, they had been surrounded by marsh, not forest. No, she was not on the Isle of the Priests, and unless she had somehow developed the magical ability to walk over the Lake without swimming, she was not on the mainland either. Nor was she in any part of Avalon. She glanced up, looking to take her bearings by the sun, but she could not see the sun anywhere; it was full day now, but the light was like a soft radiance in the sky, seeming to come from everywhere at once.

Morgaine began to feel the coldness of fear. She was nowhere, then, in the world she knew. Was it possible that within the Druid magic which had removed Avalon from the very world, there was a further unknown country, a world around or past Avalon? Glancing at the thick trees, the ancient oaks and hazel, fern and willow, she knew she was not in any world she had ever seen. There was a single gnarled oak, old past guessing, that she could not possibly have failed to see and know. Certainly, so old and venerable a tree would have been marked as holy by the Druids. "By the Goddess! Where am I?"

Wherever she might be, she could not simply stay. Either she would wander into a part of the world that was familiar to her again, find some landmark back to where she intended to go, or she would come to a place where the mists began and she could return to her own place that way.

She moved slowly in the thickening forest. There seemed to be a clearing ahead which she moved toward. It was surrounded by hazel trees, none of which, she knew instinctively, had ever been touched, even by the metal of a Druid knife, to cut the divining wands which could find water, hidden treasure, or poisonous things. There was a hazel grove on the island of Avalon, but she knew the trees there; had cut her own divining stick there, years ago when she was first learning such things. This was not the place. At the very edge of the grove she saw a small patch of one of the herbs she wanted. Well, she might as well take it now, she might as well get some good for coming here. She went and knelt, folding her skirts to make a pad under her knees for working, and began digging for the root.

Twice, as she grubbed in the earth, she had the sense that she was being watched, that little prickle in her back which comes to all who have lived among wild things. But when she raised her eyes, although there was a shadow of movement in the trees, she could see no one watching.

The third time she delayed raising her eyes as long as she could, telling herself that no one would be there. She wrested the herb free from the earth and began stripping the root, murmuring the charm appointed for this use —a prayer to the Goddess to restore life to the bush uprooted, that while she took this one bush, others might grow in its place always. But the sense of being watched grew stronger, and at last Morgaine raised her eyes. Almost invisible at the edge of the trees, standing in shadow, a woman was watching her.

She was not one of the priestesses; she was not anyone Morgaine had ever seen before. She wore a gown of shadowy grey-green, the color of willow leaves when they grow old and dusty in late summer, and some kind of dark cloak. There was a tiny glimmer of gold at her throat. At first glance Morgaine thought she was one of the little dark people with whom she had awaited the killing of the King Stag. But the woman's bearing made her look quite unlike those small hunted people; she carried herself like a priestess or a queen. Morgaine had no idea of her age, but the deep-set eyes and the lines around them told her that the woman was not young.

"What are you doing, Morgaine of the Fairies?"

Ice prickled all along her spine. How did the woman know her name? But, concealing her fear with the skill of a priestess, she said, "If you know my name, lady, surely you can see what I am doing." Firmly she wrenched her eyes away from the dark gaze bent on her own, and returned to peeling the bark. Then she looked up again, half expecting that the strange woman would have disappeared as quickly as she had come, but she was still there, regarding Morgaine's work dispassionately. She said, her eyes now resting on Morgaine's grubby hands, the nail she had broken in her rooting, "Yes, I can see what you are doing, and what you intend to do. Why?"

"What is that to you?"

"Life is precious to my people," the woman said, "though we neither bear nor die as easily as your kind. But it is a marvel to me that you, Morgaine, who bear the royal line of the Old People, and thus are my far kinswoman, would seek to cast away the only child you will ever bear."

Morgaine swallowed hard. She scrambled to her feet, conscious of her grubby earth-covered hands, the half-stripped roots in her hand, her skirt wrinkled with kneeling on the damp muddy earth—like a goose girl before a High Priestess. She said defiantly, "What makes you say that? I am still young. Why do you think that if I cast this child forth I should not bear a dozen others?"

"I had forgotten that where the fairy blood is dilute, the Sight comes down to you maimed and incomplete," the stranger said. "Let it be enough to say: I have seen. Think twice, Morgaine, before you refuse what the Goddess sent you from the King Stag."

Suddenly Morgaine began to weep again. She said, stammering, "I don't want it! I didn't want it! Why did the Goddess do this to me? If you come from her, can you answer that, then?"

The strange woman looked at her sadly. "I am not the Goddess, Morgaine, nor even her emissary. My kind know neither Gods nor Goddesses, but only the breast of our mother who is beneath our feet and above our heads, from whom we come and to whom we go when our time is ended. Therefore we cherish life and weep to see it cast aside." She stepped forward and took the root from Morgaine's hand. She said, "You do not want this," and cast it aside on the ground.

"What is your name?" Morgaine cried. "What is this place?"

"You could not say my name in your language," said the lady, and suddenly Morgaine wondered what language they were speaking. "As for this place, it is the hazel grove, and it is what it is. It leads to my place, and the path yonder—" she pointed—"will lead you to your own place, in Avalon."

Morgaine followed her pointing finger with her eyes. Yes, there was a path there; she would have taken oath it had not been there when she came first into the grove.

The lady was still standing near her. There was a strange smell to her, not the strong smell of an unwashed body as it had been with the old tribal priestess, but a curious indefinable fragrance, as of some unfamiliar herb or leaf, a strange, fresh, almost bitter scent. Like the ritual herbs for the Sight, it made Morgaine feel as if there was some spell on her eyes so that she saw more than she saw at any other time, as if everything was new and clean, not the ordinary things of every day.

The lady said in a low, mesmerizing voice, "You can stay here with

me if you will; I will make you sleep so that you will bear your child
without pain, and I will take him for the strong life that is in him, and he
will live longer than he would with your kind. For I see a destiny for him,
in your world—he will try to do good, and like most of your kind, he will
do only harm. But if he stays here among my people, he will live long and
long—almost, *you* would say, forever—perhaps a magician or enchanter
among us, living with trees and wild things that were never tamed by man.
Stay here, little one; give me the babe you do not want to bear, then return
to your people, knowing he is happy and will come to no harm."

Morgaine felt a sudden deathly chill. She knew that this woman
confronting her was not wholly human; she herself bore some such taint of
this ancient elf-blood—*Morgaine of the Fairies,* the old name with which
Lancelet had taunted her. She pulled away from the fairy woman's hand and
ran, ran toward the path she had pointed out, ran wildly as if pursued by
a demon. Behind her the woman called, "Cast out your child, then, or
strangle him at birth, Morgaine of the Fairies, for your people have their
own fate, and what befalls the son of the King Stag? The king must die and
be cast down in his turn . . ." But her voice died away as Morgaine plunged
into the mists, racing, stumbling, briars catching at her and pulling her down
as she fled in panic flight, until she broke through the mists into glaring sun
and silence and knew that she stood again on the familiar shores of Avalon.

THE MOON WAS DARK in the sky again. Avalon was covered in mist and
summer fog, but Viviane had been priestess for so many years that she knew
the moon's changes as if they ran in the tides of her own blood. She paced
the floor of her house silently, and after a time told one of the priestesses,
"Bring me my harp." But when she sat with the pale willow-wood harp
on her knee, she only touched the strings idly, without the will or the heart
to make music.

As the night began to pale toward morning, Viviane rose and took a
tiny lamp. Her attendant priestess came swiftly from the inner room where
she slept, but Viviane shook her head without speaking and gestured the
woman to return to her bed. She went, silent as a wraith, down the pathway
to the House of Maidens, and stole inside, treading more silently than any
cat.

In the room where Morgaine slept, she went to the bedside and looked
down on the sleeping face so like her own. Morgaine, sleeping, had the face
of the little girl who had come to Avalon so many years ago and who had
entered into Viviane's inmost heart. Under the dark lashes, there were
patches of darkness like bruises, and the edges of the eyelids were red, as if
Morgaine had wept before sleeping.

Holding the lamp high, she looked long on her young kinswoman. She loved Morgaine as she had never loved Igraine, or Morgause whom she had nursed at her own breasts; as she had never loved any of the men who had shared her bed for a night or for a season. Not even Raven, whom she had schooled to the ways of a priestess since the age of seven, had she loved like this. Only once had she felt this fierce love, this inner pain as if every breath of the beloved were agony—for the daughter she had borne in her first year as sworn priestess, who had lived a scant six months and whom, weeping for the last time, Viviane had buried before she had completed her fifteenth year. From the moment they had laid that daughter in her arms, until the frail child's last breath had ceased, Viviane had drawn her every breath in a kind of mingled delirium of love and pain, as if the beloved child were a part of her own body, whose every moment of contentment or suffering was her own. That had been a lifetime ago, and Viviane knew that the woman she had been born to be had been buried within the hazel grove in Avalon. The woman who walked tearlessly away from that tiny grave had been another person altogether, holding herself aloof from every human emotion. Kind, yes; content, even happy, at times; but not the same woman. She had loved her sons, but from the moment of their birth she had been resigned to the thought of giving them up to foster-mothers.

Raven she had let herself love a little . . . but there were times when Viviane had felt in the innermost depths of her heart that her own dead daughter had been sent back to her by the Goddess in the form of Igraine's child.

Now she weeps, and it is as if every tear burns into my heart. Goddess, you gave me this child to love, and yet I must give her up to this torment. . . . All of mankind suffers, the Earth herself cries out under the torment of her sons. In our suffering, Mother Ceridwen, we grow nearer to thee. . . . Viviane raised her hand swiftly to her eyes, shaking her head so that the single tear vanished without trace. *She too is vowed to what must be; her suffering has not yet begun.*

Morgaine stirred and turned on her side, and Viviane, suddenly fearful that Morgaine would wake and that she must confront again the accusation of those eyes, stole quickly out of the room and silently returned to her own dwelling.

She lay down on her bed and tried to sleep, but she did not close her eyes. Once, toward morning, she saw a shadow move across the wall, and in the dimness she made out a face; it was the Death-crone, waiting for her, in the form of an old woman clothed in rags and tatters of shadow.

Mother, have you come for me?

Not yet, my daughter and my other self, I wait here that you may remember I await you, as I await every other mortal. . . .

Viviane blinked, and when she opened her eyes again the corner was dark and empty. *Surely I need no reminding that she awaits me now. . . .*

She lay silent, waiting as she had been trained to wait, until at last the dawn stole into the room. Even then she waited until she had dressed herself, though she would not break the moon-dark fast until the crescent could be seen tonight in the evening sky. Then she called her attendant priestess and said, "Bring the lady Morgaine to me."

When Morgaine came, she noted that the younger woman had dressed herself in the garb of a priestess of the highest rank, her hair high and braided, the small sickle-shaped knife hanging from its black cord. Viviane's mouth moved in a dry smile, and when they had greeted each other and Morgaine sat beside her, she said, "Twice now the moon has darkened; tell me, Morgaine, has the Horned One of the grove quickened your womb?"

Morgaine looked quickly at her, the glance of some small frightened thing in a snare. Then the younger woman said, angry and defiant, "You told me yourself that I should use my own judgment; I have cast it forth."

"You have not," said Viviane, steadying her voice to complete detachment. "Why should you lie to me? I say you shall not."

"I will!"

Viviane felt the power in the girl; for a moment, as Morgaine rose swiftly from the bench, it seemed to her that she had grown suddenly tall and imposing. But it was a priestess-trick and Viviane knew it too.

She has outstripped me, I cannot overawe her any longer. Nevertheless she said, summoning all her old authority, "You *shall* not. The royal blood of Avalon is not to be cast aside."

Suddenly Morgaine fell to the ground, and for an instant Viviane feared the girl would break into wild sobbing. "Why did you do this to me, Viviane? Why did you use me this way? I thought you loved me!" Her face worked, though she did not weep.

"The Goddess knows, child, I love you as I have never loved any other human being on earth," Viviane said steadily, through the knifing pain in her heart. "But when I brought you here, I told you: a time would come when you might hate me as much as you loved me then. I am Lady of Avalon; I do not give reasons for what I do. I do what I must, no more and no less, and so will you when the day comes."

"That day will never come!" Morgaine cried out, "for here and now, I tell you that you have worked upon me and played with me like a puppet for the last time! Never again—never!"

Viviane kept her voice even, the voice of the trained priestess who would remain calm though the heavens should fall upon her. "Take care how you curse me, Morgaine; words flung in anger have an evil way of returning when you love them least."

"Curse you—I thought not of it," Morgaine said quickly. "But I will no longer be your toy and plaything. As for this child which you moved Heaven and Earth to bring to the light, I will not bear him in Avalon for you to gloat at what you have done."

"Morgaine—" Viviane said, holding out her hand to the younger woman, but Morgaine stepped back. She said into the silence, "May the Goddess deal with you as you have done with me, Lady."

Without another word she turned and left the room, not waiting for dismissal. Viviane sat frozen, as if Morgaine's parting words had been a curse indeed.

When finally she could think clearly, she summoned one of the priestesses; already it was late in the day, and the moon, the thinnest paring of a crescent, was visible, slim and silver-edged, in the western sky. "Tell my kinswoman, the lady Morgaine, to attend upon me; I did not give her leave to go."

The priestess went away, but she did not return for a long time; it was already dark, and Viviane had summoned the other attendant to bring food to break her long fast, when the first returned.

"Lady," she said and bowed, and her face was white.

Viviane's throat tightened, and for some reason she remembered how a long time ago a priestess in deep despair, after the birth of a child she had not wanted, had hanged herself by her girdle from one of the trees in the oak grove. *Morgaine! Was it of this the Death-crone came to warn me? Would she lay hands on her own life?* She said through dry lips, "I bade you bring the lady Morgaine to me."

"Lady, I cannot."

Viviane rose from the seat and her face was terrible; the young priestess backed away so swiftly that she almost fell over her skirt. "What has happened to the lady Morgaine?"

"Lady—" the young woman said stammering, "she—she was not in her room, and I asked everywhere. I found—I found this in her room," she said, holding out the veil and deerskin tunic, the silver crescent and the little sickle knife which Morgaine had been given at her initiation. "And they told me on the shore that she had summoned the barge and gone away to the mainland. They thought she went by your orders."

Viviane drew a long breath, reached out and took the dagger and crescent from the priestess. She looked at the food on the table and a terrible sense of weakness assailed her; she sat down and quickly ate some bread and drank a cup of water from the Holy Well. Then she said, "It is not your fault, I am sorry I spoke harshly to you." She stood with her hand on Morgaine's little knife and for the first time in her life, as she looked down at her hand, she saw the pulsing of the vein there and thought how easily she could draw the knife across it and watch her life spurt forth. *Then would* the Death-crone have come for me, and not for Morgaine. *If she must have blood, let her have mine.* But Morgaine had left the knife; she would not hang herself or cut her wrists. She had, no doubt, gone to her mother for comfort and counsel. She would come back one day, and if not, it was in the hands of the Goddess.

When she was alone again, she went out of her house and, by the pale shimmer of the newborn moon, climbed along the path to her mirror.

Arthur is crowned and a king, she thought; *all that I have wrought for in the last twenty years has come to pass. Yet I am here alone and bereft. Let it be as the Goddess wills with me, but let me see once again the face of my daughter, my only child, before I die; let me know that it will be well with her. Mother, in your name.*

But the face of the mirror showed only silence, and shadows, and behind and through it all, a sword in the hands of her own son, Balan.

MORGAINE SPEAKS . . .

The little dark oarsmen had not looked twice at me; they were used to Viviane's comings and goings in such garb as she chose, and whatever a priestess chose to do was good in their eyes. None of them presumed to speak to me, and as for me, I kept my face resolutely turned to the outside world.

I could have stolen from Avalon by the hidden path. This way, taking the boat, Viviane was sure to hear that I had gone forth . . . but even to myself I was afraid to admit the fear that kept me from the hidden path, that my steps would take me not to the mainland, but to that unknown country where strange flowers and trees grew untouched by mankind, and the sun shone never, and the mocking eyes of the fairy woman saw clearly into my very soul. I still bore the herbs, tied in a little pouch at my waist, but as the boat moved on silent oars into the mists of the Lake, I untied the bag and let it fall into the water. It seemed that something gleamed there under the surface of the Lake, like a shadow . . . a glimmer of gold, perhaps jewels; but I looked away, knowing that the oarsmen were waiting for me to raise the mists.

Avalon lay behind me, renounced; the Island lay fair in the rising sun, but I did not turn to look my last on the Tor or the ring stones.

  ❂ *I would not be a pawn for Viviane, giving a son to my brother for some secret purpose of the Lady of the Lake. Somehow I never doubted that it would be a son. Had I believed I would bear a daughter, I would have stayed in Avalon, giving the Goddess the daughter I owed to her shrine. Never, in all the years since, have I ceased to regret that the Goddess sent me a son, rather than a daughter to serve her in temple and grove.*

And so I spoke the magical words for the last time, as I believed then, and the mists drew back, and we came to the shores of the Lake. I felt as if I were waking from a long dream. I had asked, looking for the first time upon Avalon, "Is it real?" and I remembered what Viviane had answered me: "It is more real than any other place." But it was real no more. I looked on the dismal reeds and thought, this only is real, and the years in Avalon no more than a dream which will fade and be gone as I wake.

Rain was falling; the drops splashed coldly into the Lake. I put my heavy cloak over my head and stepped onto the real shore, watching for a moment as the boat faded again into the mists, then resolutely turning away.

I never doubted where I should go. Not to Cornwall, though my whole soul longed for the country of my childhood, the long arms of rock stretching into the dark sea, the deep and shadowed valleys lying between slate cliffs, the beloved and half-forgotten shoreline of Tintagel. Igraine would have welcomed me there. But she was content within convent walls, and it seemed good to me that she should stay there untroubled. Nor did I ever think of going to Arthur, although I have no doubt he would have pitied and sheltered me.

The Goddess had had her way with us. I felt some of the shared regret for what had happened that morning—what we had done as Goddess and God had been ordained by ritual, but what had happened at sunrise, that had been for ourselves. But that, too, was as the Goddess would have it. It is only humankind who make these distinctions of blood times and kindred; the beast-kind know nothing of such things, and after all, man and woman are of the beast-kind. But in kindness to Arthur, who had been reared as a Christian, he should never know that he had fathered a son in what he would call grievous sin.

As for me, I was not priest-bred or priest-ridden. The child now in my womb —I resolved this firmly—had not been gotten by any mortal man. He had been sent to me by the King Stag, the Horned One, as was lawful for the first child of a sworn priestess.

So I turned my steps toward the North, without fear of the long journey over moorland and fell which would bring me at last to the kingdom of Orkney, and to my kinswoman Morgause.

BOOK TWO

The high
Queen

1

*f*AR to the north, where Lot was king, the snow lay deep on the fells, and even at midday there was often no more than a twilit fog. On the rare days when the sun shone, the men could get out for some hunting, but the women were imprisoned in the castle. Morgause, idly twirling her spindle—she hated spinning as much as ever, but the room was too dark for any finer work—felt an icy draft from the opened door and looked up. She said in mild reproof, "It is too cold for that, Morgaine, and you have been complaining of the cold all day; now would you turn us all into icicles?"

"I was not complaining," said Morgaine. "Did I say a word? The room is as stuffy as a privy, and the smoke stinks. I want to breathe—no more!" She pushed the door shut and went back to the fire, rubbing her hands and shivering. "I have not once been warm since Midsummer."

"I doubt that not at all," said Morgause. "Your little passenger in there steals all the heat from your bones—he is warm and snug, and his mother shivers. It is always so."

"At least Midwinter is now past, the light comes earlier and stays later," said one of Morgause's women. "And perhaps in another fortnight, you will have your babe with you. . . ."

Morgaine did not answer but stood shivering near the fire, chafing her hands as if they ached. Morgause thought that the girl looked like her own ghost, her face sharpened and fined to deathly thinness, her hands bony as skeleton sticks contrasted with the huge bulging of her pregnant belly. There were great dark circles under her eyes, and the lids were red as if sore with long weeping; but in all the moons Morgaine had been in this house, Morgause had not seen the younger woman shed a single tear.

I would comfort her, but how can I, if she does not weep?

Morgaine was wearing an old gown of Morgause's own, a faded and threadbare kirtle of dark blue, grotesquely too long. She looked clumsy, almost slatternly, and it exasperated Morgause that her kinswoman had not even troubled to take needle and thread and shorten the dress somewhat. Her ankles, too, were swollen so that they bulged over her shoe tops; that was from having only salt fish and coarse vegetables to eat at this time of year. They all needed fresh food, which was not easy to come by in this weather. Well, perhaps the men would have some luck at hunting and she could induce Morgaine to eat some of the fresh meat; after four pregnancies of her own, Morgause knew the near-starvation of late pregnancy. Once, she remembered, when she was pregnant with Gawaine, she had gone into the dairy and eaten some of the clay they kept for whitening it. An old midwife had told her that when a pregnant woman cannot keep herself from eating such strange things, it is the child that hungers and she should feed him whatever he wishes for. Maybe tomorrow there would be fresh herbs by the mountain stream—that was something every pregnant woman craved, especially in late winter like this.

Morgaine's beautiful dark hair was tangled, too, in a loose braid—it looked as if she hadn't combed or rebraided it for weeks. She turned from the fire now, took down a comb that was kept on the shelf, picked up one of Morgause's little lapdogs and began combing it. Morgause thought, *You would be better occupied at combing your own hair,* but she held her peace; Morgaine had been so edgy lately that there was no speaking to her at all. It was natural enough, so near her time, she thought, watching the younger woman's bony hands pulling the comb through the matted hair; the little dog yelped and whined, and Morgaine hushed him in a softer voice than she ever used to anything human these days.

"It cannot be long now, Morgaine," Morgause said gently. "By Candlemas, surely, you will be delivered."

"It cannot be too soon for me." Morgaine gave the dog a final pat and set him on the floor. "There, now you are decent to be among ladies, puppy . . . how fine you are, with your hair all smooth!"

"I will make up the fire," said one of the women, whose name was Beth, putting aside her spindle and thrusting the distaff into a basket of loose wool. "The men will be home, surely—it is already dark." She went over to the fire, tripped on a loose stick, and half fell on the hearth. "Gareth, you little wretch, will you clear away this rubbish?" She flung the stick into the fire, and five-year-old Gareth, who had been pushing the sticks about and prattling to them in an undertone, set up a howl of outrage—the sticks were his armies!

"Well, Gareth, it is night, and your armies must go to their tents," said Morgause briskly. Pouting, the little boy pushed the array of small sticks into a corner, but one or two he put carefully into a fold of his tunic—they were thicker ones, which Morgaine, earlier that year, had carved into the crude likeness of men in helmets and armor, dyed with berry juice for their crimson tunics.

"Will you make me another Roman knight, Morgaine?"

"Not now, Gareth," she said. "My hands ache with the cold. Tomorrow, perhaps."

He came and scowled, standing at her knee, demanding, "When will I be old enough to go hunting with Father and Agravaine?"

"It will be a few years still, I suppose," said Morgaine, smiling. "Not until you are tall enough not to be lost in a snowdrift!"

"I'm big!" he said, drawing himself up to his full height, "Look, when you're sitting down I'm taller than you are, Morgaine!" He kicked restlessly at the chair. "There's nothing to do in here!"

"Well," said Morgaine, "I could always teach you to spin, and then you need not be idle." She picked up Beth's abandoned distaff and held it out to him, but he made a face and started back.

"I'm going to be a knight! Knights don't have to spin!"

"That's a pity," Beth said sourly. "Perhaps they would not wear out so many cloaks and tunics if they knew what toil it is to spin them!"

"Yet there was a knight who did spin, so the tale says," Morgaine said, holding out her arms to the little boy. "Come here. No, sit on the bench, Gareth, you are all too heavy now for me to hold you on my lap like a sucking babe. There was in the old days, before the Romans came, a knight named Achilles, and he was under a curse; an old sorceress told his mother that he would die in battle, and so she put him into skirts and hid him among the women, where he learned to spin and to weave and do all that was fitting for a maiden."

"And did he die in battle?"

"He did indeed, for when the city of Troy was besieged, they called on all the knights and warriors to come and take it, and Achilles went with the rest, and he was the best of all the knights. It was told of him that he was offered a choice, he could live long in safety, then die an old man in his bed and be forgotten, or he could live a short life and die young with great glory, and he chose the glory; so men still tell of his story in the sagas. He fought with a knight in Troy called Hector—Ectorius, that is, in our tongue—"

"Was it that same sir Ectorius who fostered our king Arthur?" asked the little boy, wide-eyed.

"To be sure it was not, for it was many hundred years ago, but it might have been one of his forefathers."

"When I am at court, and one of Arthur's Companions," said Gareth, his eyes round as saucers, "I will be the best fighter in war, and I will win all the prizes when there are games. What happened to Achilles?"

"I remember it not—it was long ago, at Uther's court, I heard the tale," Morgaine said, pressing her hands against her back as if it hurt her.

"Tell me about Arthur's knights, Morgaine. You have really seen Lancelet, have you not? I saw him, that day at the King's crowning—has he killed any dragons? Tell me, Morgaine—"

"Don't plague her, Gareth, she's not well," said Morgause. "Run out to the kitchens and see if they can find you some bannock."

The child looked sulky, but he took his carved knight out of his tunic and went off, talking to it in an undertone. "So, sir Lancelet, we will go out and we will kill all the dragons in the Lake. . . ."

"That one, he talks only of war and fighting," said Morgause impatiently, "and his precious Lancelet, as if it were not enough to have Gawaine away with Arthur at the wars! I hope that when Gareth is old enough, there will be peace in the land!"

"There will be peace," Morgaine said absently, "but it will not matter, for he will die at the hands of his dearest friend—"

"What?" cried Morgause staring, but the younger woman's eyes were vacant and unfocused; Morgause shook her gently and demanded, "Morgaine! Morgaine, are you ill?"

Morgaine blinked and shook her head. "I am sorry—what did you say to me?"

"What did I say to you? What, rather, did you say to *me?*" Morgause demanded, but at the look of distress in Morgaine's eyes, her skin prickled. She stroked the younger woman's hand, dismissing the grim words as delirium. "I think you must have been dreaming with your eyes wide open." She found that she did not want to think that Morgaine might have had a moment of the Sight. "You must care for yourself better, Morgaine, you hardly eat, you don't sleep—"

"Food sickens me," Morgaine said, sighing. "Would it were summer, that I might have some fruit . . . last night I dreamed I ate of the apples of Avalon—" Her voice trembled, and she lowered her head so that Morgause would not see the tears hanging from her lashes; but she clenched her hands and did not weep.

"We are all weary of salt fish and smoked bacon," said Morgause, "but if Lot has had good hunting, you must eat some of the fresh meat." Morgaine, she thought, had been trained in Avalon to ignore hunger and thirst and fatigue; now, pregnant, when she should relax her austerities somewhat, she took pride in enduring everything without complaint.

"You are priestess-trained, Morgaine, hardened to fasting, but your child cannot endure hunger and thirst, and you are far too thin—"

"Don't mock me!" Morgaine said angrily, gesturing at her enormously swollen belly.

"But your hands and face are like bare bone," said Morgause. "You must not starve yourself like this, you have a child and you must consider him!"

"I will consider his welfare when he considers mine!" Morgaine said, rising abruptly, but Morgause took her hands and drew her down again. "Dear child, I know what you are going through, I have borne four children, remember? These last few days are worse than all the long months combined!"

"I should have had the sense to be rid of it while there was time!"

Morgause opened her mouth for a sharp answer, then sighed and said, "It's too late to say you should have done so or so; ten days more will bring it to an end." She took her own comb from her tunic folds and began to unravel Morgaine's tangled braid.

"Let it be—" said Morgaine restlessly, pulling her head away from the comb. "I will do it myself tomorrow. I have been too weary to think of it. But if you are sick of looking at me all bedraggled like this—well, give me the comb!"

"Sit still, *lennavan*," said Morgause. "Don't you remember, when you were a little girl at Tintagel, you used to cry for me to comb your hair because your nurse—what was her name? . . . Now I remember: Gwennis, that was it—she used to pull your hair so, and you would say, 'Let Aunt Morgause do it?' " She teased the comb through the tangles, smoothing out strand after strand, and stroked Morgaine's head affectionately. "You have lovely hair."

"Dark and coarse as a pony's mane in winter!"

"No, fine as the wool of a black sheep, and shining like silk," Morgause said, still stroking the dark strands. "Hold still, I will plait it for you. . . . Always I have wished for a girl-child, so that I could dress her finely and plait her hair like this . . . but the Goddess sent me only sons, and so you must just be my little daughter now when you need me. . . ." She pulled the dark head against her breast, and Morgaine lay there, shaking with the tears she could not shed. "Ah, there, there, my little one, don't cry, it won't be long now, there, there . . . you have not been taking good care of yourself, you need a mother's care, my little girl. . . ."

"It is only . . . it is so dark here . . . I long so for the sun. . . ."

"In the summer we have more than our share of sunlight, it is light even to midnight," said Morgause, "and so in winter we get so little." Morgaine was still shaking with uncontrollable sobs, and Morgause held her close, rocking her gently. "There, little one, *lennavan*, there, I know how you feel . . . I bore Gawaine in the darkest time of winter. It was dark and stormy like this, and I was only sixteen years old then, and very frightened, I knew so little of bearing children. I wished then that I had stayed to be priestess at Avalon, or at Uther's court, or anywhere but here. Lot was away at the wars, I hated my big body, I was sick all the time and my back hurt, and I was all alone with only strange women. Would you believe, all that winter, I kept my old doll secretly in my bed, and held her, and cried myself every night to sleep? Such a baby I was! You at least are a woman grown, Morgaine."

Morgaine said, choking, "I know I am too old to be such a baby . . ." but still she clung to Morgause, while the older woman petted and stroked her hair.

"And now that same babe I bore even before I was a grown woman is away fighting with the Saxons," she said, "and you, whom I held on my lap like a doll, you are to have a babe of your own. Ah, yes, I knew there was news I meant to tell you; the cook's wife Marged has borne hei child—no doubt that was why the porridge was so full of husks this morning—so there will be a wet nurse ready at hand for yours. Though indeed, when you see him, I doubt not you will want to suckle him yourself."

Morgaine made a gesture of revulsion, and Morgause smiled. "So I felt myself, before each of my sons was born, but when I looked once on their faces, I felt I could never let them out of my arms." She felt the younger woman flinch. "What is it, Morgaine?"

"My back aches; I have been sitting too long, that is all," Morgaine said, rising restlessly and wandering around the room, her hands clasped at the small of her back. Morgause narrowed her eyes thoughtfully; yes, in the last few days the girl's bulging belly was carried lower, it could not be long now. She should have the women's hall filled with fresh straw and speak to the midwives to be at hand for the lying-in.

LOT'S MEN HAD FOUND a deer on the hills; skinned and cleaned, the smell roasting over the great fire filled the whole of the castle, and even Morgaine did not refuse a slice of the raw liver, dripping blood—by custom this food was saved for such of the women as were with child.

Morgause could see her grimace with revulsion, as she herself had done when such things were given to her in her own pregnancies, but Morgaine, as Morgause had done, sucked at it with avidity, her body demanding the nourishment even as her mind revolted. Later, though, when the meat was cooked and carvers were slicing it and carrying it around, she gestured refusal. Morgause took a slice of meat and laid it on Morgaine's dish.

"Eat it," she commanded. "No, Morgaine, I will be obeyed, you cannot starve yourself and your child this way."

"I cannot," said Morgaine in a low voice. "I will be sick—put it by and I will try to eat it later."

"What is wrong?"

Morgaine lowered her head and muttered, "I cannot eat—the meat of deer—I ate it at Beltane when—and now the very smell sickens me—"

And this child was gotten at Beltane at the ritual fires. What is it that troubles her so? That memory should be a pleasant one, Morgause thought, smiling at the memory of the Beltane license. She wondered if the girl had fallen into the hands of some particularly brutish man and had undergone something like rape—that would account for her rage and despair at this pregnancy. Still, done was done, and Morgaine was old enough to know that not all men were brutes, even if she had once fallen into the hands of one who was neither gentle nor skilled with women.

Morgause took a slice of oatcake and sopped it in the meat juice in the dish. "Eat this, then—you will get the good of the meat so," she said, "and I have made you some tea with the hips of roses; it is sour and will taste good to you. I remember how I craved sour things when I was breeding."

Morgaine ate obediently, and it seemed to Morgause that a little color came into her face. She made a face at the sourness of the drink, but drank it down thirstily nonetheless. "I do not like it," she said, "but how strange, I cannot stop drinking it."

"Your child craves it," said Morgause seriously. "Babes in the womb know what is good for them, and they demand it of us."

Lot, sitting at his ease between two of his huntsmen, smiled amiably at his sister-in-law. "An old skinny animal, but a good dinner for late winter," he said, "and I'm just as glad we didn't get a breeding doe. We saw two or three of them, but I told my men to let them be, and even called off the dogs—I want the deer to drop their fawns in peace, and I could see that time is near, so many of them were heavy." He yawned, taking up small Gareth, whose face was greasy and shining with the meat. "Soon you'll be big enough to go hunting with us," he said. "You and the little Duke of Cornwall, no doubt."

"Who is the Duke of Cornwall, Father?" Gareth asked.

"Why, the babe Morgaine carries," Lot replied, smiling, and Gareth stared at Morgaine. "I don't see any baby. Where is your baby, Morgaine?"

Morgaine chuckled uneasily. "Next month at this time I shall show him to you."

"Will the spring maiden bring it to you?"

"You could say so," Morgaine said, smiling despite herself.

"How can a baby be a duke?"

"My father was Duke of Cornwall. I am his only child in marriage. When Arthur came to reign, he gave Tintagel back to Igraine; it will pass from her to me and to my sons, if I have any."

Morgause, looking at the young woman, thought: *Her son stands nearer the throne than my own Gawaine. I am full sister to Igraine, and Viviane but her half-sister, so Gawaine is nearer kin than Lancelet. But Morgaine's son will be Arthur's nephew. I wonder if Morgaine has thought of that?*

"Certainly, then, Morgaine, your son is Duke of Cornwall—"

"Or Duchess," said Morgaine, smiling again.

"No, I can tell by the way you carry, low and broad, that it will be a son," said Morgause. "I have borne four, and I have watched my women through pregnancies. . . ." She grinned maliciously at Lot and said, "My husband takes very seriously that old writing which says that a king should be father to his people!"

Lot said good-naturedly, "I think it only right for my true-born sons by my queen to have many foster-brothers; bare is back, they say, without brother, and my sons are many. . . . Come, kinswoman, will you take the harp and sing for us?"

Morgaine pushed aside the remnant of gravy-soaked oatcake. "I have eaten too much for singing," she said, frowning, and began to pace the hall again, and Morgause again saw her hands pressed to her back. Gareth came and tugged at her skirt.

"Sing to me. Sing me that song about the dragon, Morgaine."

"It is too long for tonight—you must be away to your bed," she said, but she went to the corner, took up the small harp that stood there, and sat on a bench. She plucked a few notes at random, bent to adjust one of the strings, then broke into a rowdy drinking song of the armies.

Lot joined in the chorus, as did his men, their raucous voices ringing up to the smoky beams:

"The Saxons came in dark of night,
With all the folk asleep,
They killed off all the women, for—
They'd rather rape the sheep!"

"You never learned that song in Avalon, kinswoman," Lot said, grinning, as Morgaine rose to replace the harp.

"Sing again," Gareth teased, but she shook her head.

"I am too short of breath now for singing," she said. She put the harp down and took up her spindle, but after a moment or two put it aside and once more began pacing the hall.

"What ails you, girl?" Lot asked. "You're restless as a caged bear!"

"My back aches with sitting," she said, "and that meat my aunt would have me eat has given me a bellyache after all." She held her hands again to her back and bent over suddenly as if with a cramp; then, suddenly, she gave a startled cry, and Morgause, watching, saw the too-long kirtle turn dark and wet, soaking her to the knees.

"Oh, Morgaine, you've wet yourself," Gareth cried out. "You're too big to wet your clothes—my nurse would beat me for that!"

"Hush, Gareth!" Morgause said sharply, and hurried to Morgaine, who stood bent over, her face crimson with astonishment and shame.

"It's all right, Morgaine," she said, taking her by the arm. "Does it hurt you here—and here? I thought as much. You are in labor, that is all, didn't you know?" But how should the girl know? It was her first, and she was never one for listening to women's gossip, so she would not know the signs. For much of this day she must have been feeling the first pains. She called Beth and said, "Take the Duchess of Cornwall to the women's hall and call Megan and Branwen. And take down her hair; she must have nothing knotted or bound about her or her clothing." She added, stroking Morgaine's hair, "I would that I had known this sooner this day when I braided your hair—I will come down soon and stay with you, Morgaine."

She watched the girl go out, leaning heavily on the nurse's arm. She said to Lot, "I must go and stay with her. It is her first time, and she will be frightened, poor girl."

"There's no hurry," Lot said idly. "If it's her first, she'll be in labor all this night, and you'll have time to hold her hand." He gave his wife a good-natured smile. "You are quick to bring our Gawaine's rival into the world!"

"What do you mean?" she asked, low.

"Only this—that Arthur and Morgaine were born of one womb, and *her* son stands nearer the throne than ours."

"Arthur is young," Morgause said coldly, "and has time enough to father a dozen sons. Why should you think he has need of an heir?"

Lot shrugged. "Fate is fickle," he said. "Arthur bears a charmed life in battle—and I doubt not that the Lady of the Lake had something to do with that, damn her—and Gawaine is all too loyal to his king. But fate may turn away from Arthur, and if that day should come, I would like to know that Gawaine stood closest to the throne. Think well, Morgause; the life of an infant is uncertain. You might do well to beseech your Goddess that the little Duke of Cornwall should not draw a second breath."

"How could I do that to Morgaine? She is like my own daughter!"

Lot chucked his wife affectionately under the chin. He said, "You are a loving mother, Morgause, and I wouldn't have you otherwise. But I doubt if Morgaine is so eager to have a child in her arms. I have heard her say that she wished she had cast forth her child—"

"She was ill and weary," said Morgause angrily. "Do you think I did not say as much, when I was weary of dragging around a great belly? Any woman says such things in the last few moons of her pregnancy."

"Still, if Morgaine's child should be born without breath, I do not think she would grieve overmuch. Nor—this is what I am saying—should you."

Morgause defended her kinswoman: "She is good to our Gareth, she has made him toys and playthings and told him tales. I am sure she will be just as good a mother to her own."

"Yet, it is not to our interest or our son's that Morgaine should think of *her* son as Arthur's heir." He put his arm around his wife. "Look, sweeting, you and I have four sons, and no doubt when they're all grown, they'll be at one another's throats—Lothian is not so big a kingdom as all that! But if Gawaine were High King, then there would be kingdoms enough for them all."

She nodded slowly. Lot had no love for Arthur, as he had had none for Uther; but she had not thought him quite so ruthless as this. "Are you asking me to kill her child as it comes forth?"

"She is our kinswoman and my guest," Lot said, "and thus sacred. I would not invoke the curse of a kinslayer. I said only—the lives of newborn babes are frail, unless they are very carefully tended, and if Morgaine has a difficult time of it, it might be well that none has leisure to tend the babe."

Morgause set her teeth and turned away from Lot. "I must go to my kinswoman."

Behind her Lot smiled. "Think well on what I have said, my wife."

Down in the little hall, a fire had been lighted for the women; a kettle of gruel was boiling on the hearth, for it would be a long night. Fresh straw had been spread. Morgause had forgotten, as women happy with their children do, the dread of birth, but the sight of the fresh straw made her teeth clench and a shudder go down her back. Morgaine had been put into a loose shift, and her hair, unbound, was hanging loose down her back; she was walking up and down in the room, leaning on Megan's arm. It all had the air of a festival, and so indeed it was for the other women. Morgause went up to her kinswoman and took her arm.

"Come now, you can walk with me a bit, and Megan can go and prepare the swaddlings for your child," she said. Morgaine looked at her, and Morgause thought the younger woman's eyes were like those of a wild animal in a snare, awaiting the hunter's hand which will cut its throat.

"Will it be long, Aunt?"

"Now, now, you must not think ahead," said Morgause tenderly. "Think, if you must, that you have been in labor most of this day, so it will go all the faster now." But to herself she thought, *It will not be easy for her, she is so small, and she is reluctant to bear this child; no doubt there is a long, hard night ahead of her. . . .*

And then she remembered that Morgaine had the Sight, and that it was useless to lie to her. She patted Morgaine's pale cheek. "No matter, child, we will take good care of you. It is always long with a first child—they are loath to leave their snug nest—but we will do all we can. Did anyone bring a cat into the room?"

"A cat? Yes, she is there, but why, Aunt?" Morgaine asked.

"Because, little one, if you have seen a cat kittening, you know that the cat bears her children purring, not crying out in pain, and so perhaps her pleasure in bearing will help you to feel the pains less," Morgause said, stroking the small furry creature. "It is a form of birth magic that perhaps you do not know in Avalon. Yes, you may sit down now, and rest for a little, and hold the cat in your lap." She watched Morgaine stroking the cat in a moment of respite, but then she doubled over again with the sharp cramps, and Morgause urged her to get up again and keep walking. "As long as you can bear it—it goes quicker so," she said.

"I am so tired, so tired . . ." Morgaine said, moaning a little.

You will be more tired before this is over, Morgause thought, but she only came and put her arms around the younger woman. "Here. Lean on me, child. . . ."

"You are so like my mother . . ." Morgaine said, clinging to Morgause, her face contorted as if she were about to cry. "I wish my mother were here . . ." and then she bit her lip as if she regretted her moment of weakness, and began slowly walking, walking up and down the crowded room.

The hours dragged slowly by. Some of the women slept, but there were plenty to take their turn in walking with Morgaine, who grew more and more frightened and pale as time wore on. The sun rose, and still the midwives had not said Morgaine might lie down in the straw, though she was so weary that she stumbled and could hardly put one foot before another. One moment she said she was cold and clutched her warm fur cloak about her; another time she thrust it from her, saying that she was burning up. Again and again she retched and vomited, at last bringing up nothing but green bile; but she could not seem to stop retching, though they forced her to drink hot herb drinks, which she gulped down thirstily. But then she would begin retching again, and Morgause, watching her, her mind full of what Lot had said, wondered if it would make any difference what she did or did not do . . . it might well be that Morgaine could not survive this birth.

At last she could walk no more, and they let her lie down, gasping and biting her lips against the recurrent pains; Morgause knelt beside her, holding her hand as the hours wore on. A long time past noon, Morgause asked her quietly, "Was he—the child's father—much bigger than you?

Sometimes when a baby takes so long to be born, it means the child takes after his father and is too big for the mother."

She wondered, as she had wondered before, who was this child's father? She had seen Morgaine looking on Lancelet at Arthur's crowning; if Morgaine had gotten herself with child by Lancelet, that might well explain why Viviane had been so angered that poor Morgaine had had to flee from Avalon. . . . In all of these months, Morgaine had said nothing of her reasons for leaving the temple, and of her child, no more than that it was gotten at Beltane fires. Viviane was so tender of Morgaine, she would not have allowed her to bear a child to just anyone. . . .

But if Morgaine, rebelling against her chosen destiny, had taken Lancelet for lover, or had seduced him into the Beltane grove, then it might explain why Viviane's chosen priestess, her successor as Lady of the Lake, fled from Avalon.

But Morgaine said only, "I did not see his face; he came to me as the Horned One," and Morgause knew, with her own faint trace of the Sight, that the younger woman was lying. Why?

THE HOURS DRAGGED BY. Once Morgause went into the main hall, where Lot's men were playing at knucklebones. Lot sat watching, one of Morgause's younger waiting-women on his lap and his hand playing casually with her breasts; as Morgause came in, the woman looked up apprehensively and started to slide from his knees, but Morgause shrugged. "Stay where you are; we have no need of you among the midwives, and tonight at least I shall be with my kinswoman and have no leisure to argue with you over a place in his bed. Tomorrow it might be another matter." The young woman bent her head, blushing. Lot said, "How goes it with Morgaine, sweeting?"

"Not well," Morgause said. "It was never so hard for me." Then she cried out in a rage, "Did you ill-wish my kinswoman that she might never rise from childbed?"

Lot shook his head. "You have the charms and magic in this kingdom, lady. I wish Morgaine no ill. God knows, that would be grievous waste of a pretty woman—and Morgaine's handsome enough, for all her sharp tongue! Though that she comes by honest enough from your side of the family, does she not, sweeting, and it adds salt to the dish. . . ."

Morgause smiled affectionately at her husband. Whatever pretty toys he might choose for his bed—and the girl on his lap was just one more of them—she knew that she suited him well.

"Where is Morgaine, Mother?" Gareth asked. "She said that today she would carve me another knight to play with!"

"She is sick, little son." Morgause drew a long breath, the weight of anxiety settling over her again.

"She will be well soon," Lot said, "and then you will have a little cousin to play with. He shall be your foster-brother and your friend—we have a saying that kin ties last for three generations and foster ties for seven, and since Morgaine's son will be both to you, he will be more than your own brother."

"I will be glad to have a friend," said Gareth. "Agravaine mocks me and calls me a silly baby, saying I am too old for wooden knights!"

"Well, Morgaine's son will be your friend, when he is grown a bit," said Morgause. "At first he will be like a puppy with his eyes not open, but in a year or two he will be old enough to play with you. But the Goddess hears the prayers of little children, son, so you must pray to the Goddess that she will hear you and bring Morgaine a strong son and health, and not come to her as the Death-crone—" and suddenly she began to cry. With astonishment, Gareth watched his mother weep, and Lot said, "As bad as that, sweetheart?"

Morgause nodded. But there was no need to frighten the child. She wiped her eyes with her kirtle.

Gareth looked upward and said, "Please, dear Goddess, bring my cousin Morgaine a strong son, so we can grow up and be knights together."

Against her will, Morgause laughed and stroked the chubby cheek. "Such a prayer I am sure the Goddess will hear. Now I must go back to Morgaine."

But she felt Lot's eyes on her as she left the hall, and remembered what he had said to her earlier—that it might be better for them all if Morgaine's son did not survive.

I shall be content if Morgaine comes alive through this, she thought, and almost for the first time, she regretted that she had learned so little of the great magics of Avalon, now, when she needed some charm or spell that could ease this struggle for Morgaine. It had gone so hard, so frightfully hard with the girl, her own childbed had been nothing to this. . . .

She came back into the women's hall. The midwives had Morgaine kneeling upright in the straw now, to help the child slip from the womb; but she was slumping between them like a lifeless thing, so that two of them had to hold her upright. She was crying out now in gasps, then biting her lip against the cries, trying to be brave. Morgause went and knelt before Morgaine in the blood-flecked straw; she held out her hands, and Morgaine gripped them, looking at Morgause almost without recognition.

"Mother!" she cried out. "Mother, I knew you would come—"

Then her face convulsed again and she flung back her head, her mouth squared with unvoiced screams. Megan said, "Hold her, my lady—no, behind her like that, hold her upright—" and Morgause, gripping Morgaine beneath the arms, felt the girl shaking, retching, sobbing as she fought and struggled, blindly, to get away from them. She was no longer capable of helping them or even letting them do what they must, but screamed aloud when they touched her. Morgause shut her eyes, unwilling to see, holding Morgaine's frail convulsing body with all her strength. She screamed again, "Mother! Mother!" but Morgaine did not know whether she was calling on Igraine or on the Goddess. Then she slumped backward into Morgaine's arms, all but unconscious; there was the sharp smell of blood in the room, and Megan held up something dark and shrivelled-looking.

"Look, lady Morgaine," she said, "you have a fine son—" then she bent over him, breathing into the little mouth. There was a sharp, outraged sound, the cry of a newborn shrieking with fury at the cold world into which he had come.

But Morgaine lay collapsed in Morgause's arms, utterly exhausted, and could not even open her eyes to look at her child.

THE BABE HAD BEEN washed and swaddled; Morgaine had swallowed a cup of hot milk with honey in it, and herbs against the bleeding, and now she lay drowsing, weary, not even stirring as Morgause bent to kiss her lightly on the brow.

She would live and heal, though Morgause had never seen a woman struggle so hard, and yet live, with a living child. And the midwife said that after all they had had to do to deliver this one alive, it was unlikely Morgaine would ever bear another. Which, Morgause thought, was just as well. She realized now that her own birthings, which had not been easy, had been nothing to this.

She picked up the swaddled child, looking down at the small features. He seemed to be breathing well enough, though sometimes, when a child did not cry at once and it was necessary to breathe into his mouth, the breathing would fail again later and he would die. But he was a healthy pink, even the tiny nails rosy. Dark hair, perfectly straight, dark, fine down on the small arms and legs—yes, this one was fairy-born, like Morgaine herself. It might indeed be Lancelet's son, and so doubly near to Arthur's throne.

The child should be given to a wet nurse at once . . . and then Morgause hesitated. No doubt, when she was a little rested, Morgaine would want to hold and suckle her child; it always happened that way, no matter how difficult the birth. And the harder the birth, the more joy the mother seemed to have in nursing her babe; the worse the struggle, the more was the love and delight when the babe was actually put to her breast.

And then she thought, against her will, of Lot's words. *If I want to see Gawaine on the throne, this child stands in his way.* She had not wanted to listen when Lot said it, but with the child actually in her hands, she could not help thinking it would not be so evil a thing if this child were overlaid by his nurse, or too weak to take suck. And if Morgaine had never held him or suckled him, she would not feel as much grief; if it was the will of the Goddess that he should not live . . .

I want only to spare her sorrow. . . .

Morgaine's child, probably by Lancelet, both of the old royal line of Avalon . . . should harm come to Arthur, the people would accept this child for his throne.

But she was not even sure it was Lancelet's child.

And although Morgause had borne four sons, Morgaine was the little girl she had petted and cared for like a doll, carried in her arms; she had brushed her hair and washed her and brought her gifts. Could she do this to Morgaine's own child? Who was to say Arthur would not have a dozen sons by his queen, whoever she was?

But Lancelet's son . . . yes, Lancelet's son she could abandon to death without a qualm. Lancelet was no closer kin to Arthur than Gawaine, yet Arthur preferred him, turned to Lancelet in everything. Just as she herself had always stood in Viviane's shadow, the unregarded sister, passed over for High Queen—she had never forgiven Viviane that she had chosen Igraine for Uther—just so, the loyal Gawaine would always stand in the shadow of the more flamboyant Lancelet. If Lancelet had played with Morgaine or dishonored her, all the more reason to hate him.

For there was no reason Morgaine should bear Lancelet's bastard child in secrecy and sorrow. Did Viviane think her precious son too good for Morgaine, perhaps? Morgause had seen that the girl wept in secret all during these long months; was she sick with love and abandonment?

Viviane, damn her, uses lives like knucklebones to be cast in play! She flung Igraine into Uther's arms without thought for Gorlois, she claimed Morgaine for Avalon; will she make wreck of Morgaine's life too?

If she could only be sure it was Lancelet's child!

As she had regretted, when Morgaine was in labor, that she had not enough magic to ease the birth, so now she regretted how little she knew of magic. She had not, when she dwelt in Avalon, had the interest nor the persistence to study the Druid lore. But still, as Viviane's fosterling, she had learned one thing and another from the priestesses, who had petted and spoilt her; offhand and good-naturedly, as one indulges a child, they had shown her certain simple spells and magics.

Well, now she would use them. She shut the doors of the chamber and lighted a new fire; she clipped three hairs from the silky down on the child's head, and bending over the sleeping Morgaine, cut a few of her hairs too. She pricked the child's finger with her bodkin, rocking him after to hush the fitful squalling; then, casting secret herbs on the fire with the hairs and blood, she whispered a word she had been taught, and stared into the flames.

And caught her breath in silence as the flames swirled, died, and for a moment a face looked out at her—a young face, crowned with fair hair and shadowed by antlers casting a darkness over the blue eyes that were like Uther's. . . .

Morgaine had spoken truth when she said he had come to her as the Horned God; yet she had lied. . . . Morgause should have known; they had made the Great Marriage for Arthur, then, before his crowning. Had Viviane planned this too, a child that should be born of the two royal lines?

There was a small sound behind her and she looked up, to see that Morgaine had struggled to her feet and was standing there, clinging to the bed frame, her face white as death.

Her lips hardly moved; only her dark eyes, sunken deep in her head with suffering, flickered from the fire to the sorcerous things on the floor before the hearth. "Morgause," she said, "swear to me—if you love me, swear to me—that you will speak nothing of this to Lot or to any other! Swear it, or I will curse you with all the curses I know!"

Morgause laid the child in the cradle and turned to Morgaine, taking her arm and leading her back to the bed.

"Come, lie down, rest, little one—we must talk about this. Arthur! Why? Was it Viviane's doing?"

Morgaine repeated, even more agitated, "Swear to say nothing! Swear never to speak of it again! Swear it! Swear it!" Her eyes glittered wildly. Morgause, looking at her, was afraid she would work herself into a fever.

"Morgaine, child—"

"Swear! Or I curse you by wind and fire, sea and stone—"

"No!" Morgause interrupted her, taking her hands to try to calm her. "See, I swear it, I swear."

She had not wanted to swear. She thought, *I should have refused, I should talk of this with Lot* . . . but it was too late, now she had sworn . . . and Morgause had no wish to be cursed by a priestess of Avalon.

"Lie still, now," she said quietly. "You must sleep, Morgaine." The younger woman closed her eyes, and Morgause sat petting her hand and thinking. *Gawaine is Arthur's man, whatever happens. Lot would get no good from Gawaine on the throne. This—no matter how many sons Arthur may have, this is his first. Arthur was reared Christian and makes much of being king over Christians; he would think this child of incest his shame. It is just as well to know some evil secret of a king. Even of Lot, though I love him well, I have made it my business to know certain details of his sins and lecheries.*

The cradled child woke and squalled. Morgaine, as all mothers when a child cries, opened her eyes at the sound. She was almost too weak to move, but she whispered, "My baby—is that my baby? Morgause, I want to hold my baby."

Morgause bent and started to put the swaddled bundle into her arms. Then she hesitated; if Morgaine once held the child, she would wish to suckle him, she would love him, she would concern herself about his welfare. But if he was put to a wet nurse before she ever looked on his face . . . well, then, she would not feel anything much for him, and he would be truly the child of his foster-parents. It was just as well to have Arthur's firstborn son, the son he dared not acknowledge, feel the highest loyalty to Lot and Morgause as his truest parents; that Lot's sons should be his brothers, rather than any sons Arthur might have when he should marry.

Tears were sliding weakly down Morgaine's face. She begged, "Give me my baby, Morgause, let me hold my baby, I want him—"

Morgause said tenderly but relentlessly, "No, Morgaine; you are not strong enough to hold him and suckle him, and"—she groped quickly for a lie which the girl, unskilled in midwifery, would believe—"if you hold him even once, he will not suck from his wet nurse's breasts, so he must be given to her right away. You can hold him when you are a little stronger and he is feeding well." And, though Morgaine began to cry and held out her arms, sobbing, Morgause carried the child out of the room. *Now,* she thought, *this will be Lot's fosterling, and we will always have a weapon against the High King. And now I have made certain that Morgaine, when she is well enough, will care little for him and be content to leave him to me.*

2

Gwenhwyfar, daughter of King Leodegranz, sat on the high wall of the enclosed garden, clinging to the stones with both hands and watching the horses in the paddock below.

Behind her was the sweet smell of kitchen herbs and pot herbs, the still-room herbs her father's wife used to make medicines and simples. The garden was one of her favorite places, perhaps the only outdoor place Gwenhwyfar really liked. She felt safer indoors, as a rule, or when securely enclosed—the walls around the kitchen garden made it nearly as safe as inside the castle. Up here, on top of the wall, she could see out over the valley, and there was so much of it, stretching farther than the eye could see. . . . Gwenhwyfar turned her look back to the safety of the garden for a moment, for her hands were beginning to tingle with the numbness again, and her breath felt tight in her throat. Here, right on the very wall which enclosed her own garden, here it was safe; if she began to feel the strangling panic again she could turn and slide down the wall and be safe again inside the garden.

Her father's wife, Alienor, had asked her once in exasperation, when she said something like this, "Safe from *what,* child? The Saxons never come so far west as this. Where we are on the hill, we could see them three leagues off if they should come—it's the long view we have here that makes us safe, in heaven's name!"

Gwenhwyfar could never explain. Put like that it sounded sensible. How could she tell the sensible, practical Alienor that it was the very weight of all that sky and the wide lands which frightened her? There was nothing to be frightened *of,* and it was foolish to be frightened.

But that did not stop her from gasping and breathing hard and feeling the numbness rising up from her belly into her throat, her sweating hands losing all feeling. They were all exasperated with her—the house priest telling her that there was nothing out there but God's good green lands, her father shouting that he'd have none of that womanish nonsense in his house —and so she had learned never to whisper it aloud. Only in the convent had anyone understood. Oh, the dear convent where she had felt as snug as a mouse in her hole, and never, never having to go out of doors at all, except into the enclosed cloister garden. She would like to be back there, but now she was a woman grown, and her stepmother had little children and needed Gwenhwyfar.

The thought of marrying made her afraid, too. But then she should have her own house where she could do as she would and she would be the mistress; no one would dare to make fun of her!

Down below, the horses were running, but Gwenhwyfar's eyes were focused on the slender man in red, with dark curls shading his tanned brow, who moved among them. As swift he was as the horses themselves; she could well understand the name his Saxon foes gave him: Elf-arrow. Someone had whispered to her that he himself had fairy blood. Lancelet of the Lake, he called himself, and she had seen him in the magical Lake, that dreadful day when she had been lost, in the company of the terrible fairy woman.

Lancelet had caught the horse he wanted; one or two of her father's men shouted a warning, and Gwenhwyfar drew a breath of terror, herself wanting to cry out in dismay; that horse not even the king rode, only one or two of his best trainers. Lancelet, laughing, gestured disdain of their warning; he let the trainer come and hold the horse while he strapped the saddle on it. She could just hear his laughing voice.

"What good would it do to ride a lady's palfrey, which anyone could ride with a bridle of plaited straw? I want you to see—with leathers fitted like this, I can control the fiercest horse you have, and make him into a battle steed! Here, this way—" He gave a tug to a buckle somewhere under the horse, then swung himself up one-handed. The horse reared up; Gwenhwyfar watched with her mouth open as he leaned into it, forcing the horse down and under control, making it walk sedately. The spirited animal fidgeted, stepping sideways, and Lancelet gestured for one of the king's foot soldiers to give him a long pike.

"Now see—" he shouted. "Supposing that bale of straw there is a Saxon coming at me with one of those great blunt swords of theirs . . ." and he let the horse go, pounding hard across the paddock; the other horses scattered as he came sweeping down on the straw bale and impaling it on the long pike, then snatching his sword from its scabbard as he whirled, checking the horse in mid gallop, swinging the sword about him in great circles. Even the king stepped back as he thundered toward them. He brought the animal to a full stop before the king, slid off and bowed.

"My lord! I ask for leave to train horses and men, so that you may lead them into battle when the Saxons come again, to defeat them as he did at Celidon Wood last summer. We have had victories, but one day there will be a mighty battle which will decide for all time whether Saxon or Roman will rule this land. We are training all the horses we can get, but yours are better than those we can buy or breed."

"I have not sworn allegiance to Arthur," her father said. "Uther was another matter; he was a tried soldier and Ambrosius' man. Arthur is little more than a boy—"

"You still believe that, after the battles he has won?" Lancelet asked. "He has held his throne now for more than a year, he is your High King, sir. Whether you have sworn or not, every battle he fights against the Saxons protects you, too. Horses and men—that is little enough to ask."

Leodegranz nodded. "This is no place to discuss the strategy of a kingdom, sir Lancelet. I have seen what you can do with the horse. He is yours, my guest."

Lancelet bowed low and thanked King Leodegranz formally, but Gwenhwyfar saw his eyes shine like those of a delighted boy. Gwenhwyfar wondered how old he was.

"Come within my hall," her father said, "we will drink together, and I will make you an offer."

Gwenhwyfar slid down from the wall and ran through the garden to the kitchens, where her father's wife was supervising the baking women. "Madam, my father will be coming in with the High King's emissary, Lancelet; they will want food and drink."

Alienor gave her a startled glance. "Thank you, Gwenhwyfar. Go and make yourself tidy and you may serve the wine. I am far too busy."

Gwenhwyfar ran to her room, pulled her best gown on over the simple kirtle she wore, and hung a string of coral beads about her neck. She unbraided her fair hair and let it fall, rippled from the tight braiding. Then she put on the little gold maiden's circlet she wore, and went down, composing her steps and moving lightly; she knew the blue gown became her as no other color, no matter how costly, could do.

She fetched a bronze basin, filled it with warmed water from the kettle hanging near the fire, and strewed rose leaves in it; she came into the hall as her father and Lancelet were entering. She set down her basin, took their cloaks and hung them on the peg, then came and offered them the warmed, scented water to wash their hands. Lancelet smiled, and she knew he had recognized her.

"Did we not meet on the Isle of the Priests, lady?"

"You have met my daughter, sir?"

Lancelet nodded, and Gwenhwyfar said, in her shyest little voice—she had found, long ago, that it displeased her father if she spoke out boldly —"Father, he showed me the way to my convent door when I was lost."

Leodegranz smiled at her indulgently. "My little featherhead, if she goes three steps from her own doorway, she is lost. Well, sir Lancelet, what do you think of my horses?"

"I have told you—they are better than any we can buy or breed," he said. "We have some from the Moorish realms down in Spain, and we have bred them with the highland ponies, so we have horses that are sturdy and can endure our climate, but are swift and brave. But we need more. We can breed only so many. You have more than enough, and I can show you how to train them so you can lead them into battle—"

"No," the king interrupted, "I am an old man. I have no desire to learn new battle methods. I have been four times married, but all my former wives bore only sickly girls who die before they are weaned, sometimes before they are baptized. I have daughters; when the eldest marries, her husband will lead my men into battle, and can train them as he will. Tell your High King to come here, and we will discuss the matter."

Lancelet said, a little stiffly, "I am my lord Arthur's cousin and his captain, sire, but even I do not tell him to come and go."

"Beseech him, then, to come to an old man who does not want to ride out from his own fireside," the king said, a little wryly. "If he will not come for me, perhaps he will come to know how I will dispose of my horses and the armed men to ride them."

Lancelet bowed. "No doubt he will."

"Enough of this, then; pour us some wine, daughter," the king said, and Gwenhwyfar came shyly and poured wine into their cups. "Now run along, my girl, so that my guest and I may talk together."

Gwenhwyfar, dismissed, waited in the garden until a servant came out and called for the lord Lancelet's horse and armor. The horse he had ridden here and the horse her father had given him were brought to the door, and she watched from the shadow of the wall until she saw him ride away; then she stepped out and stood waiting. Her heart pounded—would he think her too bold? But he saw her and smiled, and the smile seized her very heart.

"Are you not afraid of that great fierce horse?"

Lancelet shook his head. "My lady, I do not believe the horse was ever foaled that I cannot ride."

She said, almost whispering, "Is it true that you control horses with your magic?"

He threw back his head with a ringing laugh. "By no means, lady; I have no magic. I like horses and I understand their ways and the way their minds work—that is all. Do I look to you like a sorcerer?"

"But—they say you have fairy blood," she said, and his laughter grew grave. He said, "My mother was indeed one of the old race who ruled this land before the Roman people ever came here, or even the northern Tribesmen. She is priestess on the Isle of Avalon, and a very wise woman."

"I can see that you would not want to speak ill of your mother," Gwenhwyfar said, "but the sisters on Ynis Witrin said that the women of Avalon were evil witches and served the devils. . . ."

He shook his head, still grave. "Not so," he said. "I do not know my mother well; I was fostered elsewhere. I fear her, as much as I love. But I can tell you she is no evil woman. She brought my lord Arthur to the throne, and gave him his sword to stand against the Saxons—does that sound so evil to you? As for her magic—it is only the ignorant among them who say she is a sorceress. I think it well that a woman should be wise."

Gwenhwyfar hung her head. "I am not wise; I am very stupid. Even among the sisters, I learned only enough to read my way through the mass book, which they said was all I needed of learning, and then such things as women learn—cookery and herbs and simples and the binding of wounds—"

"For me, all that would be a greater mystery than the training of horses, which you think magic," Lancelet said, with his wide smile. Then he leaned down from his horse and touched her cheek. "If God is good and the Saxons hold off a few moons yet, I will see you again, when I come here in the High King's train. Say a prayer for me, lady."

He rode away, and Gwenhwyfar stood watching, her heart pounding, but this time the sensation was almost pleasant. He would come again, he *wanted* to come again. And her father had said she should be married to someone who could lead horses and men into battle; who better than the

High King's cousin and his captain of horse? Was he thinking, then, to marry her to Lancelet? She felt herself blush with delight and happiness. For the first time she felt pretty and bold and brave.

But inside the hall, her father said, "A handsome man, this Elf-arrow, and good with horses, but far too handsome to be reckoned more than that."

Gwenhwyfar said, surprised at her own boldness, "If the High King has made him his first of captains, he must be the best of fighters!"

Leodegranz shrugged. "The King's cousin, he could hardly be left without some post in his armies. Has he tried to win your heart—or," he added, with the scowl that frightened her, "your maidenhead?"

She felt herself blushing again and was hopelessly angry at herself. "No, he is an honorable man, and what he has said to me is no more than he could have said in your presence, Father."

"Well, don't get any ideas into that featherhead of yours," Leodegranz said gruffly. "You can look higher than that one. He's no more than one of King Ban's bastards by God-knows-who, some damsel of Avalon!"

"His mother is the Lady of Avalon, the great High Priestess of the Old People—and he is himself a king's son—"

"Ban of Benwick! Ban has half a dozen legitimate sons," said her father. "Why marry a king's captain? If all goes as I plan, you'll wed the High King himself!"

Gwenhwyfar shrank away, saying, "I'd be afraid to be the High Queen!"

"You're afraid of everything, anyway," her father said brutally. "That's why you need a man to take care of you, and better the King than the King's captain!" He saw her mouth trembling and said, genial again, "There, there, my girl, don't cry. You must trust me to know what's best for you. That's what I'm here for, to look after you and make a good marriage with a trusty man to look after my pretty little featherhead."

If he had raged at her, Gwenhwyfar could have held on to her rebellion. *But how,* she thought wildly, *can I complain of the best of fathers, who has only my own welfare at heart?*

3

O n a day in early spring, in the year following Arthur's crowning, the lady Igraine sat in her cloister, bent over a set of embroidered altar linens.

All her life she had loved this fine work, but as a young girl, and later, married to Gorlois, she had been kept busy—like all women—with the weaving and spinning and sewing of clothes for her household. As Uther's queen, with a household of servants, she had been able to spend her time on fine broideries and weaving of borders and ribbons in silk; and here in the nunnery she put her skill to good use. Otherwise, she thought a little ruefully, it would be for her as it was with so many of the nuns, the weaving only of the dark plain woolen dresses which all of them, including Igraine herself, wore, or the smooth, but boring, white linens for veils and coifs and altar cloths. Only two or three of the sisters could weave with silks or do fine embroidering, and of them Igraine was the cleverest.

She was a little troubled. Again, as she sat down at her frame this morning, she thought she heard the cry, and jerked around before she could stop herself; it seemed to her that somewhere Morgaine cried out "Mother!" and the cry was one of agony and despair. But the cloister was quiet and empty around her, and after a moment Igraine made the sign of the cross and sat down again to her work.

Still . . . resolutely she banished the temptation. Long ago she had renounced the Sight as the work of the fiend; with sorcery she would have no doings. She did not believe Viviane was evil in herself, but the Old Gods of Avalon were certainly allied to the Devil or they could not maintain their force in a Christian land. And she had given her daughter to those Old Gods.

Late last summer Viviane had sent her a message saying, *If Morgaine is with you, tell her that all is well.* Troubled, Igraine had sent a reply that she had not seen Morgaine since Arthur's crowning; she had thought her still safe at Avalon. The Mother Superior of the convent had been dismayed at the thought of a messenger from Avalon to one of her ladies; even when Igraine explained that it was a message from her sister, the lady had still been displeased and said firmly that there could be no coming and going, even of messages, with that ungodly place.

Igraine, then, had been deeply troubled—if Morgaine had left Avalon, she must have quarrelled with Viviane. It was unheard of for a sworn priestess of the highest rank to leave the Island except upon the business of Avalon. For Morgaine to leave without the knowledge or permission of the Lady was so unprecedented that it made her blood run cold. Where could she have gone? Had she run away with some paramour, was she living a lawless life without the rites either of Avalon or the church? Had she gone to Morgause? Was she lying somewhere dead? Nevertheless, although she prayed continually for her daughter, Igraine had resolutely refused the constant temptation to use the Sight.

Still, much of this winter, it seemed that Morgaine had walked at her side; not the pale, somber priestess she had seen at the crowning, but the little girl who had been the only comfort, those desperate, lonely years in Cornwall, of the frightened child-wife, child-mother she had been. Little Morgaine, in a saffron gown and ribbons, a solemn child, dark-eyed in her crimson cloak; Morgaine with her little brother in her arms—her two children sleeping, dark head and golden close together on the one pillow. How often, she wondered, had she neglected Morgaine after she had come to her beloved Uther, and had borne him a son and heir to his kingdom? Morgaine had not been happy at Uther's court, nor had she ever had much love for Uther. And it was for that reason, as much as from Viviane's entreaty, that she had let Morgaine go to be fostered at Avalon.

Only now she felt guilty; had she not been overquick to send her daughter away, so that she might give all her thought to Uther and *his* children? Against her will, an old saying of Avalon rang in Igraine's mind: *the Goddess does not shower her gifts on those who reject them* . . . in sending her own children away, one to fosterage (for his own safety, she reminded herself, remembering Arthur lying white as death after the fall from the stallion) and the other to Avalon—in sending them away, had she herself sown the seed of loss? Was the Goddess unwilling to give her another child when she had let the first go so willingly? She had discussed this with her confessor, more than once, and he had reassured her that it was just as well to send Arthur away, every boy must go for fostering sooner or later; but, he said, she should not have sent Morgaine to Avalon. If the child was unhappy in Uther's court, she should have been sent to school in a nunnery somewhere.

She had thought, after hearing that Morgaine was not in Avalon, of sending a messenger to King Lot's court, to find out if she was there; but then the winter settled in in earnest, and every day was a new battle against cold, chilblains, the vicious dampness everywhere; even the sisters went hungry in the depths of winter, sharing what food they had with beggars and peasants.

And once in the hard weeks of winter, she thought she heard Morgaine's voice, crying—crying out for her in anguish: "Mother! Mother!" *Morgaine, alone and terrified—Morgaine dying? Where, ah God, where?* Her fingers clenched the cross which, like all the sisters of the convent, she wore at her belt. *Lord Jesus, keep and guard her, Mary, Mother divine, even if she is a sinner and a sorceress . . . pity her, Jesus, as you pitied the dame of Magdala who was worse than she. . . .*

In dismay, she realized that a tear had dripped down on the fine work she was doing; it might spot the work. She wiped her eyes with her linen veil and held the embroidery frame further away, narrowing her eyes to see better—ah, she was getting old, her sight blurred a little from time to time; or was it tears that blurred her vision?

She bent resolutely over her embroidery again, but Morgaine's face seemed again to be before her, and she could hear in her imagination that despairing shriek, as if Morgaine's soul were being torn from her body. She herself had cried out like that, for the mother she could hardly remember, when Morgaine was born . . . did all women in childbirth cry out for their mothers? Terror gripped her. Morgaine in that desperate winter, giving birth somewhere . . . Morgause had made some such jest at Arthur's crowning, saying Morgaine was as squeamish with her food as a breeding woman. Against her will, Igraine found herself counting on her fingers; yes, if it had been so with her, Morgaine would have borne her child in the dead of winter. And now, even in that soft spring, she seemed to hear again that cry; she longed to go to her daughter, but where, where?

There was a step behind her and a tentative cough, and one of the young girls fostered in the nunnery said, "Lady, there are visitors for you in the outer room; one of them is a churchman, the Archbishop himself!"

Igraine put her embroidery aside. After all, it was not spotted; *all the tears women shed, they leave no mark on the world,* she thought in bitterness. "Why does the Archbishop, of all men living, wish to see me?"

"He did not tell me, lady, and I do not think he told the Mother Superior either," said the little girl, not at all unwilling to gossip for a minute, "but did you not send gifts to the church there at the time of the High King's crowning?"

Igraine had, but she did not think the Archbishop would have come here to speak of a past charity. Perhaps he wanted something more. Priests were seldom greedy for themselves but all priests, especially those from rich churches, were greedy for silver and gold for their altars.

"Who are the others?" she asked, knowing that the young girl was eager to talk.

"Lady, I do not know, but I do know that the Mother Superior wanted to forbid one of them, because"—her eyes grew wide—"he is a wizard and sorcerer, so she said, and a Druid!"

Igraine rose. "It is the Merlin of Britain, for he is my father, and he is no wizard, child, but a scholar trained in the crafts of the wise. Even the church fathers say that the Druids are good and noble men, and worship with them in harmony, since they acknowledge God in all things, and Christ as one of many prophets of God."

The little girl dropped a small curtsey, acknowledging correction, as Igraine put away the embroidery work and adjusted her veil smoothly around her face.

When she came into the outer room, she saw not only the Merlin and a strange, austere man in the dark dress which churchmen were beginning to adopt to set them off from seculars, but a third man she hardly recognized, even when he turned; for a moment it was as if she looked into Uther's face.

"Gwydion!" she exclaimed, then, quickly amending, "Arthur. Forgive me; I forgot." She would have knelt before the High King but he reached out quickly and prevented her.

"Mother, never kneel in my presence. I forbid it."

Igraine bowed to the Merlin and to the dour, austere-looking Archbishop.

"This is my mother, Uther's queen," Arthur said, and the Archbishop responded, stretching his lips in what Igraine supposed was meant for a smile. "But now she has a higher honor than royalty, in that she is a bride of Christ."

Hardly a bride, Igraine thought, *simply a widow who has taken refuge in his house.* But she did not say so, and bowed her head.

Arthur said, "Lady, this is Patricius, Archbishop of the Isle of the Priests, now called Glastonbury, who has newly come there."

"Aye, by God's will," the Archbishop said, "having lately driven out all the evil magicians from Ireland, I am come to drive them forth from all Christian lands. I found in Glastonbury a corrupt lot of priests, tolerating among them even the common worship with the Druids, at which our Lord who died for us would have wept tears of blood!"

Taliesin the Merlin said in his soft voice, "Why, then, you would be harsher than Christ himself, brother? For he, I seem to remember, was greatly chided that he consorted with outcasts and sinners and even tax collectors, and such ladies as the Magdalen, when they would have had him a Nazarite like to John the Baptizer. And at last, even when he hung dying on his cross, he did promise the thief that that same night he would join him in Paradise—no?"

"I think too many people presume to read the divine Scriptures, and fall into just such errors as this," said Patricius sternly. "Those who presume on their learning will learn, I trust, to listen to their priests for the true interpretations."

The Merlin smiled gently. "I cannot join you in that wish, brother. I am dedicated to the belief that it is God's will that all men should strive for wisdom in themselves, not look to it from some other. Babes, perhaps, must have their food chewed for them by a nurse, but men may drink and eat of wisdom for themselves."

"Come, come!" Arthur interrupted with a smile. "I will have no controversies between my two dearest councillors. Lord Merlin's wisdom is indispensable to me; he set me on my throne."

"Sir," said the Archbishop, "God set you there."

"With the help of the Merlin," said Arthur, "and I pledged to him I would listen to his counsel always. Would you have me forsworn, Father Patricius?" He spoke the name with the North country accent of the lands where he had been fostered. "Come, Mother, sit down and let us talk."

"First let me send for wine to refresh you after your long ride here."

"Thank you, Mother, and if you will, send some, too, to Cai and Gawaine, who rode hither with me. They would not have me come unguarded. They insist on doing for me the service of chamberlains and grooms, as if I could not lift a hand for myself. I can do for myself as well as any soldier, with only the help of an ordinary groom or two, but they will not have it—"

"Your Companions shall have the best," Igraine said, and went to give orders for food and wine to be served the strangers and all their retinue. Wine was brought for the guests, and Igraine poured it.

"How is it with you, my son?" Looking him over, he seemed ten years older than the slightly built boy who had been crowned last summer. He had grown, it seemed, half a hand's span, and his shoulders were broader. There was a red seam on his face; it was already drawing cleanly together, God be praised . . . well, no soldier could escape a wound or two.

"As you see, Mother, I have been fighting, but God has spared me," he said. "And now I come here on a peaceful mission. But how is it with you here?"

She smiled. "Oh, nothing happens here," she said. "But I had word from Avalon that Morgaine had left the Island. Is she at your court?"

He shook his head. "Why, no, Mother, I've hardly a court worth the name," he said. "Cai keeps my castle—I had to force it on him, he'd rather ride with me to war, but I bade him stay and keep my house secure. And two or three of Father's old knights, too old to ride, are there with their wives and youngest sons. Morgaine's at the court of Lot—Gawaine told me as much when his brother came south to fight in my armies, young Agravaine. He said Morgaine had come to attend on his mother; he'd only seen her a time or two, but she was well and seemed in good spirits; she plays on the harp for Morgause, and keeps the keys of her spice cupboard. I gather Agravaine was quite charmed with her." A look of pain passed over his face, and Igraine wondered at it but said nothing.

"God be thanked that Morgaine is safe among kindred. I have been frightened for her." This was not the time, certainly not with churchmen present, to inquire whether Morgaine had borne a child. "When did Agravaine come south?"

"It was early in the fall, was it not, Lord Merlin?"

"I believe it was."

Then Agravaine would have known nothing; she herself had seen Morgaine and never guessed. If indeed it had been so with Morgaine, and not a fantasy born of her own imaginings.

"Well, Mother, I came to speak of women's affairs, at that—it seems I should be married. I have no heir but Gawaine—"

"I like not that," Igraine said. "Lot has been waiting for that all these many years. Don't trust his son behind you."

Arthur's eyes blazed with anger. "Even you shall not speak so of my cousin Gawaine, Mother! He is my sworn Companion, and I love him as the brother I never had, even as I love Lancelet! If Gawaine wished for my throne, he need only have relaxed his vigilance for five minutes, and I would have a split neck, not this slash on my face, and Gawaine *would* be High King! I would trust him with life and honor!"

Igraine was amazed at his vehemence. "Then I am glad you have so loyal and trusty a follower, my son." She added, with a caustic smile, "That must be a grief indeed to Lot, that his sons love you so well!"

"I know not what I have done that they should wish me so well, but they do, for which I consider myself blessed."

"Aye," Taliesin said, "Gawaine will be staunch and loyal to death, Arthur, and beyond if God wills."

The Archbishop said austerely, "Man cannot presume to know God's will—"

Taliesin ignored him and said, "More trusty even than Lancelet, Arthur, though it grieves me to say so."

Arthur smiled, and Igraine thought, with a pang at heart, he has all of Uther's charm, he too can inspire great loyalty in his followers! How like his father he is! Arthur said, "Come, I will chide even you, Lord Merlin, if you speak so of my dearest friend. Lancelet too I would trust with my life and my honor."

Merlin said, with a sigh, "Oh, yes, with your life you may trust him, I am sure. . . . I am not sure he will not break in the final test, but certainly he loves you well and would guard your life beyond his own."

Patricius said, "Certainly Gawaine is a good Christian, but I am not so sure about Lancelet. A time will come, I trust, when all these folk who call themselves Christian and are not may be revealed as the demon worshippers they are in truth. Whosoever will not accept the authority of Holy Church about the will of God are even as Christ says—'Ye who are not for me are against me.' Yet all over Britain there are those who are little better than pagans. In Tara I dealt with these, when I lighted the Paschal fires for Easter on one of their unholy hills, and the king's Druids could not stand against me. Yet even in the hallowed Isle of Glastonbury, where the sainted Joseph of Arimathea walked, I find the very priests worshipping a sacred well! This is heathendom! I will close it if I must appeal to the Bishop of Rome himself!"

Arthur smiled and said, "I cannot imagine that the Bishop of Rome would have the slightest idea what is going on in Britain."

Taliesin said gently, "Father Patricius, you would do a great disservice to the people of this land if you close their sacred well. It is a gift from God—"

"It is a part of pagan worship." The eyes of the Archbishop glowed with the austere fire of the fanatic.

"It comes from God," the old Druid insisted, "because there is nothing in this universe which does not come from God, and simple people need simple signs and symbols. If they worship God in the waters which flow from his bounty, how is that evil?"

"God cannot be worshipped in symbols which are made by man—"

"There you are in total agreement with me, my brother," said the Merlin, "for a part of the Druid wisdom lies in the saying that God, who is beyond all, cannot be worshipped in any dwelling made by human hands, but only under his own sky. And yet you build churches and deck them richly with gold and silver. Wherefore, then, is the evil in drinking from the sacred springs which God has made and blessed with vision and healing?"

"The Devil gives you your knowledge of such things," Patricius said sternly, and Taliesin laughed.

"Ah, but God makes doubts and the Devil too, and in the end of time they will all come to him and obey his will."

Arthur interrupted, before Patricius could answer, "Good fathers, we came here not to argue theology!"

"True," said Igraine, relieved. "We were speaking of Gawaine, and Morgause's other son—Agravaine, is it? And of your marriage."

"Pity," Arthur said, "that since Lot's sons love me well, and Lot—I doubt it not—is eager to have his household heir with me to the High Kingship, that Morgause has not a daughter, so that I could be his son-in-law and he would know that his daughter's son was my heir."

"That would suit well," Taliesin said, "for you are both of the royal line of Avalon."

Patricius frowned. "Is not Morgause your mother's sister, my lord Arthur? To wed with her daughter would be little better than bedding your own sister!"

Arthur looked troubled. Igraine said, "I agree; even if Morgause had a daughter, it is not even to be thought of."

Arthur said, plaintively, "I should find it easy to be fond of a sister of Gawaine. The idea of marrying a stranger doesn't please me all that much, and I wouldn't think the girl would be pleased either!"

"It happens to every woman," Igraine said, and was surprised to hear herself—was she still bitter over what was so long past? "Marriages must be arranged by those with wiser heads than any young maiden could have."

Arthur sighed. He said, "King Leodegranz has offered me his daughter —I forget her name—and has offered, too, that her dowry shall be a hundred of his best men, all armed and—hear this, Mother—each with the good horses he breeds, so that Lancelet may train them. This was one of the secrets of the Caesars, that their best cohorts fought on horseback; before them, none but the Scythians ever used horses except to move supplies and sometimes for riders to send messages. If I had four hundred men who could fight as cavalry—well, Mother, I could drive the Saxons back to their shores yelping like their own hounds!"

Igraine laughed. "That hardly seems reason to marry, my son. Horses can be bought, and men hired."

"But," Arthur said, "Leodegranz is of no mind to sell. I think he has it in his mind that in return for this dowry—and it is a kingly dowry, doubt not—he would like it well to be bound by kinship's ties to the High King. Not that he is the only one, but he has offered more than any other will offer.

"What I wished to ask you, Mother—I am unwilling to send any ordinary messenger to tell the king that I'll take his daughter and he should bundle her up like a package and send her to my court. Would you go and give my answer to the king, and escort her to my court?"

Igraine started to nod her agreement, then remembered that she had taken vows in this place. "Can you not send one of your trusty men, Gawaine or Lancelet?"

"Gawaine is a wencher. I am not so sure I want him within reach of my bride," Arthur said, laughing. "Let it be Lancelet."

The Merlin said somberly, "Igraine, I feel you should go."

"Why, Grandfather," Arthur said, "has Lancelet such charms that you fear my bride will love him instead?"

Taliesin sighed. Igraine said quickly, "I will go, if the abbess of this place gives me leave." The Mother Superior, she thought, could not refuse her leave to attend her son's wedding. And she realized that after years of being a queen, it was not easy to sit quietly behind walls and await tidings of the great events moving in the land. That was, perhaps, every woman's lot, but she would avoid it as long as she could.

4

GwenhwyfaR felt the familiar nausea gripping the pit of her stomach; she began to wonder if before they set forth she would have to run at once to the privy. What would she do if the need came on her *after* she had mounted and ridden out? She looked at Igraine, who stood tall and composed, rather like the Mother Superior of her old convent. Igraine had seemed kind and motherly on that first visit, a year ago, when the marriage had been arranged. Now, come to escort Gwenhwyfar to her bridal, she seemed stern and demanding, with no trace of the terror that gripped at Gwenhwyfar. How could she be so calm? Gwenhwyfar ventured, in a small voice, peering at the waiting horses and litter, "Aren't you afraid? It's so far—"

"Afraid? Why, no," said Igraine, "I have been to Caerleon many times, and it's not likely the Saxons are on the road to war this time. Travelling in winter is troublesome, with mud and rain, but better that than fall into the hands of the barbarians."

Gwenhwyfar felt the shock and shame gripping her, and clenched her fists, looking down at her sturdy, ugly travelling shoes.

Igraine reached out and took her hand, smoothing the small fingers. "I had forgotten, you have never been from home before, except to and from your convent. You were in Glastonbury, were you not?"

Gwenhwyfar nodded. "I wish I were going back there—"

She felt Igraine's sharp eyes on her for a moment, and quailed; perhaps the lady would know she was unhappy at marrying her son, and come to dislike her . . . but Igraine only said, holding her hand firmly, "I was not happy when I went first to be wedded to the Duke of Cornwall, I was not happy until I held my daughter in my arms. But I had scarce completed my fifteenth year; you are almost eighteen, are you not?"

Clinging to Igraine's hand, Gwenhwyfar felt a little less panic; but even so, as she stepped outside the gate, it seemed that the sky overhead was a vast menace, threatening, low, filled with rainclouds. The path before the house was a sea of mud where the horses had been trampling. Now they were being drawn up into riding order with more men, it seemed to Gwenhwyfar, than she had ever seen together in her life, shouting and calling to each other, the horses neighing and the yard full of confusion. But Igraine held her hand tightly and Gwenhwyfar, shrinking, followed her.

"I am grateful that you came to escort me, lady—"

Igraine smiled. "I am all too worldly—I like a chance to travel beyond convent walls." She made a long step to avoid a pile of horse dung which steamed in the mud. "Mind your step, there, child—look, your father has set aside these two fine ponies for us. Do you like riding?"

Gwenhwyfar shook her head, and whispered, "I thought I could ride in a litter—"

"Why, so you can, if you wish," Igraine said, looking at her wonderingly, "but you will grow very weary of it, I should think. When my sister Viviane went on her travels, she used to wear men's breeches. I should have found you a pair, though at my age it would hardly be seemly."

Gwenhwyfar blushed scarlet. "I couldn't," she said, shaking, "it's forbidden for a woman to put on the clothes of a man, so it says in Holy Writ—"

Igraine chuckled. "The Apostle seemed to know little of the North country. It is hot where he lived," she said, "and I have heard that the men in that country where our Lord lived knew nothing of breeches, but wore long gowns as some Roman men did and do still. I think it meant only that women were not to wear the garb of some particular man, not that they were not to wear clothing fashioned in a man's style. And certainly my sister Viviane is the most modest of women; she is a priestess of Avalon."

Gwenhwyfar's eyes were wide. "Is she a witch, madam?"

"No, no, she is a wise-woman, learned in herbs and medicines, and having the Sight, but she has sworn a vow never to hurt man nor beast. She does not even eat flesh food," Igraine said. "She lives as austerely as any abbess. Look," she said, and pointed, "there is Lancelet, Arthur's chief Companion. He has come to escort us, and to bring back the horses and men—"

Gwenhwyfar smiled, feeling a blush spread to her cheeks. She said, "I know Lancelet, he came to show my father what he could do with the horses."

Igraine said, "Aye; he rides like one of those centaurs the ancients used to speak of, half horse and half man!"

Lancelet swung down from his horse. His cheeks were as crimson with the cold as the Roman cloak he wore; the collar was turned high around his face. He bowed to the ladies.

"Madam," he said to Igraine, "are you ready to ride?"

"I think so. The princess's luggage is already loaded on that cart, I think," Igraine said, looking at the bulky wagon loaded high and covered with skins: a bed frame and furnishings, a great carved chest, a large and a small loom, pots and kettles.

"Aye. I hope it does not get mired in all this mud," Lancelet said, looking at the yoke of oxen hauling it. "It is not that wagon I am worried about, but the other—the king's wedding gift to Arthur," he added, without enthusiasm, looking at the second, much larger cart. "I would have thought it better to have a table built for the King's house in Caerleon, if Uther had not left tables and furniture enough—not that I begrudge my lady her bride furniture," he added, with a quick smile at Gwenhwyfar that made her cheeks glow, "but a table, as if my Lord Arthur had not enough furniture for his hall?"

"Ah, but that table is one of my father's treasures," said Gwenhwyfar. "It was a prize of war from one of the kings of Tara, where my grandsire fought him and carried off his best mead-hall table . . . it is round, you see, so a bard can sit at the center to sing to them, or the servants pass round to pour wine or beer. And when he entertained his fellow kings he need not set one higher than another . . . so my father thought it fitting for a High King, who must also seat his well-born Companions without preferring one above the other."

"It is truly a king's gift," Lancelet said politely, "but it takes three yoke of oxen to haul it, lady, and God alone knows how many joiners and carpenters to put it together again when we have come there, so that instead of travelling at the pace of a company of horse we must plod along at the pace of the slowest ox. Ah well, the wedding cannot begin until you get there, my lady." He cocked up his head, listened and shouted, "I will come in a minute, man! I cannot be everywhere at once!" He bowed. "Ladies, I must get this army moving! Can I help you to your horses?"

"I think Gwenhwyfar wants to travel in the litter," said Igraine.

Lancelet said, with a smile, "Why, it is as if the sun went behind a cloud then—but you do as you will, lady. I hope you will shine out on us again another day perhaps."

Gwenhwyfar felt pleasantly embarrassed, as she always did when Lancelet made his pretty speeches. She never knew whether he was serious or whether he was teasing her. Suddenly, as he rode away, she felt afraid again. The horses towering around her, the hordes of men coming and going —it was as if they really were the army Lancelet had called them, and she no more than an unregarded piece of luggage, almost a prize of war. Silent, she let Igraine help her into the litter, which was covered with cushions and a fur rug, and she curled up in a corner of it.

"Shall I leave the curtains of the litter open so we can have some light and air?" Igraine asked, settling herself comfortably in the cushions.

"No!" said Gwenhwyfar in a choking voice. "I—I feel better with them closed."

With a shrug, Igraine closed the curtains. She looked out through a crack, watching the first of the horsemen ride out, the wagons swing into line. A kingly dowry, indeed, all these men. Armed horsemen, with weapons and gear, to be added to Arthur's armies—it was almost like what she had heard of a Roman legion.

Gwenhwyfar's head was on the pillows, her face white, her eyes shut. "Are you sick?" Igraine asked in wonder.

Gwenhwyfar shook her head. "It's just—so big—" she said. "I'm— I'm afraid," she whispered.

"Afraid? But my dear child—" Igraine broke off, and after a moment said, "Well, you'll feel better soon."

Gwenhwyfar, her arms crossed over her eyes, hardly knew it when the litter began moving; she had willed herself into a state of half-sleep in which she could hold the panic at bay. Where was she going, under that huge all-covering sky, over the wide moors and through so many hills? The knot of panic in her belly pulled tighter and tighter. All round her she heard the sounds of horses and men, an army on the march. She was merely part of the furniture of the horses and men and their gear and a mead table. She was only a bride with all that properly belonged to her, clothes and gowns and jewels and a loom and a kettle and some combs and hackles for spinning flax. She was not herself, there was nothing for herself, she was only some property of a High King who had not even bothered to come and see the woman they were sending along with all the horses and gear. She was another mare, a brood mare this time for the High King's stud service, hopefully to provide a royal son.

Gwenhwyfar thought she would smother with the rage that was choking her. But no, she must not be angry, it was not seemly to be angry; the Mother Superior had told her in the convent that it was a woman's proper business to be married and bear children. She had wanted to be a nun and stay in the convent and learn to read and make beautiful letters with her clever pen and brush, but that was not suitable for a princess; she must obey her father's will as if it were the will of God. Women had to be especially careful to do the will of God because it was through a woman that mankind had fallen into Original Sin, and every woman must be aware that it was her work to atone for that Original Sin in Eden. No woman could ever be really good except for Mary the Mother of Christ; all other women were evil, they had never had any chance to be anything but evil. This was her punishment for being like Eve, sinful, filled with rage and rebellion against the will of God. She whispered a prayer and willed herself into semiconsciousness again.

Igraine, resigning herself to riding behind closed curtains although craving fresh air, wondered what in the world was wrong with the girl. She had not said a word against the marriage—well, she, Igraine, had not rebelled against her marriage to Gorlois, either; remembering the angry and terrified child she had been, she sympathized with Gwenhwyfar. But, why should the girl huddle behind curtains instead of going with her head up to meet her new life? What was she afraid of? Did Arthur seem such a monster? It was not as if she were marrying an old man, three times her age; Arthur was young, quite ready to give her honor and respect.

They slept that night in a tent pitched on a carefully chosen dry spot, listening to the winds and the rain moaning and pelting down. Igraine woke once in the night to hear Gwenhwyfar whimper.

"What is the matter, child? Are you sick?"

"No—lady, do you think Arthur will like me?"

"There is no reason he should not," Igraine said gently. "You certainly know you are beautiful."

"Am I?" In her soft voice, it sounded only naïve, not the self-conscious or coy plea for compliment or reassurance that it would have been in another. "Lady Alienor said my nose was too big, and that I had freckles like a cowherd."

"Lady Alienor—" Igraine reminded herself to be charitable; Alienor was not much older than Gwenhwyfar, and had borne four children in six years. "I think perhaps she is a little shortsighted. You are lovely indeed. You have the most beautiful hair I have ever seen."

"I don't think Arthur cares for beauty," Gwenhwyfar said. "He did not even send to inquire if I were cross-eyed or one-legged or had a squint or a harelip."

"Gwenhwyfar," said Igraine gently, "every woman is wedded for her dowry, but a High King, too, must marry as his councillors bid him. Do you not think he is lying wakeful of nights, wondering what fortune the lottery has cast him, and that he will not greet you with gratitude and joy because you bring him beauty and good temper and learning as well? He was resigned to taking whatever he must, but he will be all the happier when he discovers that you are not—what was it?—harelipped or pockmarked or cross-eyed. He is young, and has not much experience with women. And Lancelet, I am sure, has told him that you are beautiful and virtuous."

Gwenhwyfar let out her breath. "Lancelet is Arthur's cousin, is he not?"

"True. He is son to Ban of Benwick by my sister, who is the Great Priestess of Avalon. He was born in the Great Marriage—know you anything of that? In Less Britain, some of the people call for the old pagan rites," Igraine said. "Even Uther, when he was made High King, was taken to Dragon Island and crowned by the old rites there, though they did not demand of him that he marry the land; in Britain, that is done by the Merlin, so that he is sacrifice for the King if need be. . . ."

Gwenhwyfar said, "I did not know these old pagan rites were still known in Britain. Was—was Arthur crowned so?"

"If he was," said Igraine, "he has not told me. Perhaps by now things have changed, and he is content that the Merlin should be only his chiefest of councillors."

"Do you know the Merlin, lady?"

"He is my father."

"Is it so?" Gwenhwyfar stared at her in the dark. "Lady, is it true that when Uther Pendragon came to you before you were wedded to him, he came to you by the Merlin's arts in the magical disguise of Gorlois, so that you lay with him thinking he was Duke of Cornwall and you still a chaste and faithful wife?"

Igraine blinked; she had heard rumors of tales that she had borne

Uther's son with unseemly haste, but this story she had never heard. "They say that?"

"Sometimes, lady. There are bards' tales about it."

"Well, it is not true," said Igraine. "He wore Gorlois's cloak and bore Gorlois's ring which he had taken when they fought—Gorlois was traitor to his High King and his life forfeit. But whatever tales they tell, I knew perfectly well that it was Uther and no other." Her throat closed; even now, it seemed only as if Uther were still alive somewhere, away on campaign.

"You loved Uther? It was not, then, the Merlin's magic?"

"No," Igraine said, "I loved him well, though I think at first he chose to marry me because I was of the old royal line of Avalon. And so, you see, a marriage made for the good of the kingdom can come to be happy. I loved Uther; I could wish just such good fortune for you, that you and my son may come to love one another that way."

"I hope that too." Gwenhwyfar clutched again at Igraine's hand. To Igraine the fingers felt small and soft, easily crushed, unlike her own strong, competent ones. This was not a hand for tending babes or wounded men, but for fine needlework or prayer. Leodegranz should have left this child in her convent, and Arthur sought elsewhere for a bride. Things would go as God had ordained; she was sorry for Gwenhwyfar's fright, but she was also sorry for Arthur, with a bride so childish and unwilling.

Yet, she herself had been no better when she was sent to Gorlois; perhaps the girl's strength would grow with the years.

With the first rays of the sun the camp was astir, making ready for the day's march that would bring them to Caerleon. Gwenhwyfar looked white and weak and when she tried to get up, she turned on her side and retched. For a moment Igraine entertained an uncharitable suspicion, then put it aside; the girl, cloistered and timid, was ill with fright, no more. She said briskly, "I told you the closed litter would make you queasy. Today you must get on your horse and take the fresh air, or we shall have you coming to your bridal with pale cheeks instead of roses." She added to herself, *And if I must ride behind closed curtains for another day I shall certainly go mad; that would be a wedding to remember indeed, with a bride sick and pale, and the mother of the bridegroom raving.* "Come, if you will get up and ride, Lancelet shall ride with you, to gossip with you and cheer you."

Gwenhwyfar braided her hair, and even gave some thought to the arranging of her veil; she ate little, but she did sip a little barley beer and put a bit of bread in her pocket, saying that she would eat it later, as she rode.

Lancelet had been out and about since first light. When Igraine suggested, "You must ride with my lady. She is moping, she has never been from home before," his eyes lighted up and he smiled. "It will be my pleasure, madam."

Igraine rode alone behind the young people, glad of the solitude for her own thoughts. How handsome they were—Lancelet so dark and spirited and Gwenhwyfar all golden and white. Arthur was fair, too, their children would be dazzling. She realized with some surprise that she was looking forward to being a grandmother. It would be pleasant to have little children about, to pet them and play with them, but children who were not her own, over whom she need not worry and fret and trouble herself. She rode in a pleasant daydream; she had grown used to daydreaming a great deal in the convent. Looking ahead to the young people riding side by side, she saw that the girl sat her horse upright and had some color in her face and was smiling. Igraine had done right, to get her out into the air.

And then she saw how they were looking at each other.

Dear God! Uther looked so at me when I was Gorlois's wife—as if he were starving and I were food high out of his reach. . . . What can possibly come of it if they love one another? Lancelet is honorable, and Gwenhwyfar, I would swear, virtuous, so what can possibly come of it except misery? Then she reproved herself for her suspicions; they were riding at a decent distance from one another, they did not seek to touch hands, they were smiling because they were young and it was a fair day; Gwenhwyfar rode to her wedding, and Lancelet brought horses and men to his king, his cousin, and friend. *Why should they not be happy and talk with one another gaily and joyously? I am an evil-minded old woman.* But she still felt troubled.

What will come of this? Dear God, would it be traitorous to you to pray for a moment of the Sight? And then she wondered—was there yet any honorable way for Arthur to get out of this marriage? For the High King to wed a woman whose heart was already given, *that* would be a tragedy. Britain was filled with maidens ready to love him and wed him. But the dowry price was paid, the bride had left her father's house, the subject kings and liegemen were assembling to see their young King married.

Igraine resolved to speak to the Merlin. As Arthur's chiefest councillor, perhaps he could yet prevent this marriage—but could even he prevent it without war and ruin? It would be a pity, too, for Gwenhwyfar to be publicly rejected like this, in the presence of all Britain. No, it was too late, the wedding must take place as it was fated. Igraine sighed and rode on, her head lowered and all the beauty gone from the bright day. She told herself, angrily, that all her doubts and fears were meaningless, an idle old woman's imaginings; or that all of these fantasies were sent of the Devil to tempt her into using the Sight she had renounced, and becoming again a tool of wickedness and sorcery.

Yet as she rode, her eyes kept returning to Gwenhwyfar and Lancelet, and to the almost visible haze that seemed to hover between them, an aura of hunger and desire and longing.

They arrived at Caerleon shortly before sunset. The castle stood on a hill, the site of an old Roman fort, and some of the old Roman stonework was still in place—it looked, Igraine thought, very much as it must have looked in Roman days. For a moment, seeing the slopes covered with tents and people, she wondered dizzily if the place were under siege, but then she realized that all these folk must have come to see the High King married. Seeing the crowd, Gwenhwyfar had turned pale and terrified again; Lancelet was trying to arrange the long draggled column into some vestige of dignity, and Gwenhwyfar put her veil down over her face and rode silent by Igraine.

"It is a pity they must all see you worn and travel-weary," Igraine agreed, "but look, there is Arthur, come out to meet us."

The girl was so weary she hardly raised her head. Arthur, in a long blue tunic, his sword in its preciously worked crimson scabbard swinging at his side, had stopped to speak for a moment to Lancelet, at the head of the column; then, the crowding men and riders separating as he walked through them, he came toward Igraine and Gwenhwyfar.

He bowed to his mother. "Had you a good journey, madam?" But he had raised his eyes to Gwenhwyfar, and Igraine saw his eyes widen at her beauty, and could almost read the younger girl's thoughts.

Yes, I am beautiful, Lancelet thinks me beautiful, will my lord Arthur be pleased with me?

Arthur held out his hand to support her as she dismounted; she tottered a little, and he stretched out both arms to her.

"My lady and wife, welcome to your home and to my house. May you be happy here, and may this day be as joyous for you as for me."

Gwenhwyfar felt the crimson rising in her cheeks. Yes, Arthur was handsome, she told herself fiercely, with that fair hair and the serious, level grey eyes. How different he seemed from Lancelet's madcap gaiety and mischief! And how differently he looked at her—Lancelet looked at her as if she were the statue of the Virgin on the altar at church, but Arthur was looking at her soberly, tentatively, as if she were a stranger and he was not yet sure whether friend or foe.

She said, "I thank you, my husband and my lord. As you can see, I have brought you the promised dowry of men and horses—"

"How many horses?" he asked quickly. Gwenhwyfar was confused. What did she know about his precious horses? Did he have to make it so clear that it was the horses and not herself which he awaited in this wedding business? She drew herself to her full height—she was taller than some men, and for a woman she was a good height—and said with dignity, "I do not know, my lord Arthur, I have not counted them. You must ask your captain of horse. I am sure the lord Lancelet could tell you their number, to the last mare and the last foal at suck."

Oh, good girl, Igraine thought, seeing the color rise in Arthur's pale cheeks at the reproof. He smiled, ruefully. "Forgive me, my lady, no one expects of you that you should concern yourself with such things. I am sure Lancelet will tell me all of this at the proper time. I was thinking, also, of the men who came with you—it seems fit that I should welcome them as my new subjects, as well as welcoming their lady and my queen." For a moment he looked almost as young as he was. He looked around at the milling crowd of men, horses, carts, oxen, and drovers, and spread his hands helplessly. "In all this hullabaloo, I doubt they could hear me anyway. Allow me to conduct you to the castle gates." He took her hand and led her along the path, searching for the driest places. "I am afraid this is a dismal old place. It was my father's stronghold, but I never lived here after I was old enough to remember. Perhaps some year, if the Saxons let us alone for a time, we can find some place better suited for our home, but for the moment this must suit."

As he led her through the gates Gwenhwyfar reached out and touched the wall. It was thick, secure Roman stone, piled high and standing as if it had been there since the beginning of the world; here all was safe. She ran her finger almost lovingly along the wall. "I think it is beautiful. I am sure it will be safe—I mean, I am sure I will be happy here."

"I hope so, lady—Gwenhwyfar," he said, using her name for the first time, speaking it with a strange accent. She wondered suddenly where he had been reared. "I am very young to be in charge of all these—all these men and kingdoms. I will be glad to have a helpmeet." She heard his voice tremble as if he were afraid—but what in the world could a man have to be afraid of? "My uncle by marriage—Lot, King of Orkney—he is married to my mother's sister, Morgause, and Lot has said that his wife rules as well as he, when he is absent in war or council. I am willing to do you such honor, lady, and let you rule at my side."

Panic clutched again at Gwenhwyfar's stomach. How could he expect that of her? How could it be a woman's place to rule? What did she care what the wild barbarians, these northern Tribesmen, did, or their barbarian women? She said, in a shaky little voice, "I could never presume so far, my lord and my king."

Igraine said firmly, "Arthur, my son, what are you thinking of? The girl has been riding for two days and she is exhausted! This is no time to plot the strategy of kingdoms, with the mud of the road still on our shoes! I beg you, turn us over to your chamberlains, and there will be time enough to acquaint yourself with your bride tomorrow!"

Arthur's skin, Gwenhwyfar thought, was fairer than her own; this was the second time she had seen him blush like a scolded child. "I am sorry, Mother; and you, my lady." He raised his arm, signalling, and a dark, slender young man, with a scarred face and a pronounced limp, came unevenly toward them.

"My foster-brother, Cai, and my chamberlain," Arthur said. "Cai, this is Gwenhwyfar, my lady and queen."

Cai bowed to her, with a smile. "I am at your service."

"As you can see," Arthur said, "my lady has brought her furniture and belongings. Lady, I welcome you to your own house. Give Cai whatever orders seem good to you, about where to bestow your things. For now, I beg you give me leave to go; I must see to the men and horses and gear." He bowed low again, and it seemed to Gwenhwyfar that she could see relief on his face. She wondered if he was disappointed in her, or whether his only interest in this marriage was really in the dowry of horses and men, as she had thought. Well, she had been prepared for that; but still, some welcome for her personally would have been pleasant. She realized that the dark, scarred young man he called Cai was waiting expectantly for her word. He was gentle and deferential—she need not be afraid of him.

She sighed, reaching out again to touch the strong walls around her as if for reassurance and to steady her voice, so that when she spoke she would sound like a queen. "In the greatest of carts, sir Cai, there is an Irish mead-hall table. It is my father's wedding gift to my lord Arthur. It is a prize of war, and very old and very valuable. See to it that it is assembled in Arthur's largest feasting hall. But before that, please see to it that a room is made ready for my lady Igraine, and someone to wait on her tonight." Distantly she was surprised—she thought to herself that she sounded quite like a queen. Nor did Cai sound at all reluctant to accept her as one. He bowed very low, and said, "It shall be done at once, my lady and queen."

5

ALL through the night, groups of travellers had been assembling before the castle; it was barely daylight when Gwenhwyfar looked out to see the whole slope of the hill, leading up to the castle, covered with horses and tents and with crowds of men and women.

"It looks like a festival," she said to Igraine, who had shared her bed on this last night of her maidenhood, and the older woman smiled.

"When the High King takes a wife, child, that is as much a festival as anything happening in this island. Look, those men are the followers of Lot of Orkney." She thought, but did not say aloud, *Perhaps Morgaine will be with them.* As a young woman she had voiced every thought that crossed her mind, but no longer.

How strange it was, Igraine thought; all through the childbearing years, a woman is taught to think first and only of her sons. If she thinks of her daughters at all, it is only that when they are grown, they will go forth into the hands of another, they are being reared for another family. Was it only that Morgaine had been her firstborn, always closest to her heart? Arthur had returned physically after his long absence, but as all men do, he had grown so far from her that there was no longer any way to reach across that distance. But to Morgaine—she had discovered this at Arthur's crowning—she was bound with a tie of the soul which would never break. Was it only that Morgaine had shared her own heritage of Avalon? Was this why every priestess longed to bear a daughter, who would follow in her footsteps and never be lost to her?

"There are so many people," Gwenhwyfar said. "I did not know there were so many people in all of Britain."

"And you to be High Queen over them all—it is frightening, I know," said Igraine. "I felt so when I was married to Uther."

And for a moment it seemed to her that Arthur had chosen ill in his queen. Gwenhwyfar had beauty, yes, and good temper, and learning, but a queen must be able to take her place at the forefront of the court. Perhaps Gwenhwyfar was all too shy and retiring.

When you put it into the simplest terms, the queen was the king's lady; not only his hostess and keeper of his house—any chamberlain or housekeeper could do that—but, like the priestess of Avalon, a symbol of all the realities of life, a reminder that life was more than fighting and war and dominion. A king, when all was said and done, fought for the protection of those who were unable to fight for themselves, the childbearing women and little children and old people, aged men and grandmothers. Among the Tribes, indeed, the stronger women had fought at the side of the men—there had been, of old, a battle-college kept by women—but from the beginning of civilization it had been the work of men to hunt for food and to keep off invaders from the hearth-fire where their pregnant women and little children and old folk were sheltered; and the work of women to keep that hearth safe for them. As the King was joined to the High Priestess in the symbolic marriage to the land in token that he would bring strength to his kingdom, so the Queen, in a similar joining to the King, created a symbol of the central strength behind all the armies and the wars—the home and the center for which the men rallied their strength. . . . Igraine shook her head impatiently. All this of symbols and inner truths was fit, perhaps, for a priestess of Avalon, but she, Igraine, had been queen enough without any such thoughts, and there would be time enough for Gwenhwyfar to think of these things when she was an old woman and no longer needed them! In these civilized days, a queen was not a priestess over villagers tending their barley fields, any more than a king was the great hunter who ranged among the deer!

"Come, Gwenhwyfar, Cai left serving-women to wait on you, but as your husband's mother it is suitable that I should dress you for your wedding, since your own mother cannot be here to make you ready on this day."

The younger woman looked like an angel when she was clothed; her fine hair floated like spun gold in the sunlight, almost dimming the radiance of the golden garland she had put on. Her dress was of a white woven stuff, as fine as spiderweb; Gwenhwyfar told Igraine, with shy pride, that the fabric had been brought from a far country, further even than Rome, and was more costly than gold. Her father had gotten a length for the altar stone of their church and a little piece to hold a holy relic, and he had given her a piece, too, of which she had made her wedding gown. There was more for a holiday tunic for Arthur—it was her own wedding gift to him.

Lancelet came to conduct them to the early mass which would precede the wedding; afterward all the day could be given to feasting and revelry. He was resplendent in the crimson cloak he had worn before, but he was dressed for riding.

"Do you go from us, Lancelet?"

"No," he said soberly, but he was looking only at Gwenhwyfar. "As one of the entertainments of this day, the new horsemen—and Arthur's cavalry—will display what they can do: I am one of the horsemen who will show you these games this afternoon. Arthur feels it is time to make his plans known to his people."

And again Igraine saw that hopeless, transfixed look in his eyes when he looked on Gwenhwyfar, and the brilliance of the girl's smile as she looked up to him. She could not hear now what they were saying to each other —she had no doubt it was innocent enough. But they needed no words. Igraine felt again the despairing awareness that this would come to no good, but only to misery.

They walked down through the corridors, joined as they went by serving-people, noblemen, all those clustering to the early mass. On the steps of the chapel they were joined by two young men who wore, like Lancelet himself, long black feathers in their caps; Cai, she recalled, had worn one too. Was it some badge of Arthur's Companions?

Lancelet asked, "Where is Cai, brother? Should he not be here to escort my lady to the church?"

One of the newcomers, a big, sturdy man who, Gwenhwyfar thought, had nevertheless a look of Lancelet, said, "Cai, and Gawaine too, are dressing Arthur for his wedding. Indeed, I had thought you would be among them, you three are like brothers to Arthur. He sent me to take their place, as the lady Igraine's kinsman—madam," he said to Igraine, bowing, "can it be that you do not recognize me? I am the son of the Lady of the Lake. My name is Balan, and this is our foster-brother Balin."

Gwenhwyfar nodded courteously to them. She thought: *Can this big, coarse Balan truly be Lancelet's brother? It is as if a bull should call himself brother to the finest of southern stallions!* Balin, his foster-brother, was short and red-faced, with hair as yellow as a Saxon's, and bearded like a Saxon too. She said, "Lancelet, if it is your will to be with my lord and king—"

"I think you ought to go to him, Lancelet," said Balan with a laugh. "Like all men about to wed, Arthur is mad with nervousness. Our lord may fight like Pendragon himself on the field of battle, but this morning when he is being readied for his bride, he seems no more than the boy he is!"

Poor Arthur, thought Gwenhwyfar, *this marriage is more of an ordeal for him than for me—at least I have nothing to do but obey the will of my father and king!* A ripple of amusement went over her, quickly stifled; poor Arthur, he would have had to take her for the good of his kingdom, even if she really had been old or ugly or pockmarked. It was just another of his painful duties, like leading his men into battle against the Saxons. At least he knew what he could expect of the Saxons! She said gently, "My lord Lancelet, would you rather be at my lord Arthur's side?"

His eyes told her clearly that he did not want to leave her; she had become, in only a day or two, adept at reading those messages unspoken. She had never exchanged with Lancelet one word that could not have been shouted aloud in the presence of Igraine and her father and all the bishops of Britain assembled. But for the first time he seemed torn by conflicting desires.

"The last thing I wish is to leave your side, madam, but Arthur is my friend and my cousin—"

"God forbid that I should ever come between you kinsman," she said, and held out her small hand to him to kiss. "By this marriage you are my loyal kinsman too, and my cousin. Go to my lord the king and tell him—" She hesitated, startled at her own boldness; would it be seemly to say this? God help them all, within the hour she would be Arthur's wife, what did it matter if it sounded overbold, when what she spoke were words of proper concern for her own lord? "Tell him I gladly return to him his most loyal captain, and that I await him with love and obedience, sir."

Lancelet smiled. It seemed that smile stretched a string somewhere deep inside her, that she felt her own mouth moving with it. How could she feel so much a part of him? Her whole life seemed to have filtered down into the touch of his lips on her fingers. She swallowed, and suddenly she knew what it was she felt. In spite of her dutiful messages of love and obedience to Arthur, it seemed that she would sell her soul if time would only turn back and she could tell her father that she would marry no man but Lancelet. That was something as real as the sun around her and the grass under her feet, as real—she swallowed again—as real as Arthur, now being readied for the wedding, for which she must go to Holy Mass to prepare herself.

Is it one of God's cruel jokes that I did not know this was what I felt until it was too late? Or is this some wicked trick of the fiend, to seduce me from my duty to my father and to my husband? She did not hear what Lancelet said; she was only conscious that his hand had released hers and that he had turned his back and was walking away. She hardly heard the polite words of those two foster-brothers, Balin and Balan—which of them was the son of the priestess of the Lake, then? Balan; Lancelet's brother, but no more like him than a raven is like a great eagle.

She became aware that Igraine was speaking to her.

"I leave you to the Companions, my dear. I wish to speak with the Merlin before the mass."

Belatedly, it occurred to Gwenhwyfar that Igraine was awaiting her permission to go. Already her rank as High Queen was a reality. She hardly heard her own words to Igraine as the older woman withdrew.

Igraine crossed the courtyard, murmuring excuses to the people she jostled, trying to reach Taliesin through the crowd. Everyone was clad in bright festival clothing, but he wore his usual somber grey robes.

"Father—"

"Igraine, child." Taliesin looked down at her, and Igraine found it obscurely comforting that the old Druid spoke to her as he would have spoken to her when she was fourteen. "I had thought you would be in attendance upon our bride. How beautiful she is! Arthur has found himself a treasure. I have heard that she is clever, too, and learned, and also that she is pious, which will please the bishop."

"Father," Igraine appealed, lowering her voice so that no one in the crowd would hear, "I must ask you this—is there any honorable way for Arthur to avoid this marriage?"

Taliesin blinked in consternation. "No, I do not think so. Not when all is readied to join them together after the mass. God help us, have we all been deceived, is she barren, or unchaste, or—" The Merlin shook his head in dismay. "Unless she were secretly a leper, or actually with child by another man, there could be no way at all to stop it; and even then, no way without scandal or offense, or making an enemy of Leodegranz. Why do you ask, Igraine?"

"I believe her virtuous. But I have seen the way she looks at Lancelet and he at her. Can anything come of it but misery, when the bride is besotted with another, and that other the groom's dearest friend?"

The Merlin looked at her sharply; his old eyes were as seeing as ever. "Oh, it is like that, is it? I have always thought our Lancelet had too much good looks and charm for his own welfare. Yet he is an honorable lad, after all; it may be nothing but youthful fancies, and when the bridal pair are wedded and bedded, they will forget it, or think of it only with a little sadness, as something that might have been."

"In nine cases out of ten, I would say you were right," Igraine said, "but you have not seen them, and I have."

The Merlin sighed again. "Igraine, Igraine, I do not say you are wrong, but when all's done, what can we do about it? Leodegranz would find it such an insult that he would go to war against Arthur, and Arthur has already enough to challenge his kingship—or have you not heard of yonder northern king who sent word to Arthur that he had skinned the beards of eleven kings to make himself a cloak, and Arthur should send him tribute or he would come and take Arthur's beard too?"

"What did Arthur do?"

The Merlin said, "Why, he sent the older king word that as for his beard, it was scarce grown yet, and it would do him no good for his cloak; but that if he wanted it, he could come and try to take it, if he could find his way through the bodies of dead Saxons. And he sent him the head of one of the Saxons—he had just come back from a raiding party—and said *its* beard was better for lining a cloak than the beard of a friend at whose side he would rather be fighting. And finally he said he would send a fellow king a present, but he exacted no tribute from his friends, and paid none. So that all came to nothing; but as you can see, Arthur cannot afford more enemies, and Leodegranz would be a bad one. He'd better marry the girl, and I think I would say the same even if he'd found her in bed with Lancelet —which he hasn't and isn't likely to."

Igraine discovered that she was twisting her hands together. "What shall we do?"

The Merlin touched her cheek, very lightly. "We will do what we have always done, Igraine—what we must, what the Gods order. We will do the best we can. We are none of us embarked on this course for our own happiness, my child. You, who were reared in Avalon, you know that. Whatever we may do to try and shape our destiny, the end is with the Gods —or, as the bishop would no doubt prefer me to say, with God. The older I grow, the more I become certain that it makes no difference what words we use to tell the same truths."

"The Lady would not be pleased to hear you speak such words," said a dark, thin-faced man behind him, in dark robes which could have been those of a priest or a Druid. Taliesin turned half round and smiled.

"Nevertheless, Viviane knows they are true, as I do. . . . Igraine, I do not think you know our newest of chief bards—I have brought him hither to sing and play for Arthur's wedding. Kevin, madam."

Kevin bowed low. Igraine noticed that he walked leaning on a carven stick; his harp in its case was carried by a boy of twelve or thirteen. Many bards or harpers who were not Druids were blind or lamed—it was rare that any ablebodied lad would be given time and leisure to learn such arts, in these days of war—but usually the Druids chose among those who were sound of body as well as being keen of mind. It was rare for a man with any deformity to be allowed into the Druid teachings—it was felt that the Gods marked inner faults in this way. But it would have been inexcusably rude to speak of this; she could only imagine that his gifts were so great that he had been accepted in despite of all else.

He had diverted her mind from her purpose, but when she thought back, Taliesin was right. There was no way to stop this wedding without scandal and probably war. Inside the wattle-and-daub building that was the church, lights blazed and the bell had begun to ring. Igraine walked into the church. Taliesin knelt stiffly down; so did the boy carrying Kevin's harp, but Kevin himself did not kneel—for a moment Igraine wondered if, not being a Christian, he was defying the services, as Uther had once seemed to do. Then she decided, seeing the awkwardness of his gait, that he probably had a stiff leg and could not bend the knee at all. She saw the bishop look his way, frowning.

"Listen to the words of Jesus Christ our Lord," the bishop began. "Behold, where two or three are gathered together in my name, there am I among ye, and whatsoever thing ye ask in my name, so it shall be done. . . ."

Igraine knelt, drawing her veil around her face, but she was conscious, nevertheless, of Arthur, who had come into the church with Cai and Lancelet and Gawaine, wearing a fine white tunic and a blue cloak, with no ornament but the slender golden coronet of his crowning, and the crimson and jewels in the scabbard of his great sword. It seemed as if, without eyes, she could see Gwenhwyfar, in her fragile white gown, like Arthur all white and gold, kneeling between Balin and Balan. Lot, greying and thin, knelt between Morgause and one of his younger sons; and behind him—it was as if a harp had sounded some high, forbidden note through the chanting of the priest. She raised her head, cautiously, and tried to see, knowing who knelt there. The face and form of Morgaine were hidden behind Morgause.

Yet it seemed that she could *sense* her there, like a wrong note in the harmony of the sacred service. After all these years, was she reading thoughts again? In any case, what was a priestess of Avalon doing in the church? When Viviane had visited her and Uther in the years of their marriage, the priestess had either absented herself from divine service, or attended, listening and watching with the polite, grave attention she would have given to a child playing at a feast for her dolls. Yet now she could see Morgaine— she had changed, she was thinner, more beautiful, simply clad in a dress of fine dark wool, with a proper white coif around her head. She was not doing anything; she knelt with her head bent and her eyes lowered, the picture of respectful attention. Yet even the priest, it seemed, could sense the disruption and impatience emanating from her; he stopped twice and looked at her, although there was no way he could have accused her of doing anything that was not completely seemly and proper, and so after a moment he went on with the service.

But Igraine's attention, too, had been distracted. She tried to keep her mind on the service, she murmured the proper responses, but she could not think about the priest's words, nor of her son who was being married, nor of Gwenhwyfar who was, she could sense without seeing, looking around under the cover of her veil for Lancelet at Arthur's side. Now she could think only of her daughter. When the service was over, and the wedding, she would see her, and know where she had gone and what had befallen her.

Then, raising her eyes just a moment, as the priest's man was reading aloud the story of the wedding in Cana, she looked round at Arthur; and she saw that his eyes, too, were fixed on Morgaine.

6

Seated among Morgause's ladies, Morgaine listened quietly to the services, her head bent and her face wearing a polite mask of respect. Inwardly she was all impatience. Such nonsense—as if a house built by the hands of man could be converted by the words of some priest into an abiding place for the Spirit which was not of man's making at all. Her mind ran unruly. She was weary of Morgause's court; now she was back in the mainstream of events, and it was as if she had been cast from a backwater of stagnant pond-water into the channel of a racing river. She felt alive again. Even at Avalon, quiet and secluded as it was, she had had the sense of being in touch with the flow of life; but among the women of Morgause she felt she was idle, stagnant, useless. Now she was moving once more, whereas since the birth of her son she had been standing still. She thought for a moment of her little son, Gwydion. He hardly knew her now; when she would have picked him up and petted him, he fought and struggled to go to his foster-mother. Even now, the memory of his small arms winding about her neck made her feel weak and regretful, but she forced the memory away. He did not even know he was her son, he would grow up to think himself one of Morgause's brood. Morgaine was content to have it so, but she could not stifle her reluctant sorrow.

Well, she supposed that all women felt such regret when they must leave their child; but all women must endure it, except for homekeeping women who were content to do for their babes what any foster-mother or servant girl could do, and have no greater work measured to their hands. Even a cowherd must leave her babes to tend her flocks; how much more so a queen or a priestess? Even Viviane had given up her children. As had Igraine.

Arthur looked manly and handsome; he had grown, his shoulders broadened—he was no longer the slender boy who had come to her with the deer's blood on his face. *There* had been power, not these tame mouthings of the doings of their God who had meddled about, turning water into wine, which would be blasphemy anyway to the gifts of the Goddess. Or did the tale mean that to the joining of man and woman in wedlock, the ferment of the Spirit would transform their coupling into a sacred thing, as in the Great Marriage? For Arthur's sake she hoped it would be so with this woman, whoever she was; she could see, from where she knelt behind Morgause, only a cloud of pale golden hair, crowned with the paler gold of a bridal coronet, and a white robe of some fine and precious fabric. Arthur raised his eyes to look on his bride, and his gaze fell on Morgaine. She saw his face change, and thought, with a stir of awareness, *So, he recognized me. I cannot have changed so much as he has changed; he has grown from boy to man, and I—I was already a woman, and it has not changed me as much as that.*

She hoped that Arthur's bride would love him, and that he would love her well. In her mind rang Arthur's desolate words, *For all my life I will always remember you and love you and bless you.* But it must not be so. He must forget, he must come to see the Goddess only in his chosen wife. There stood Lancelet beside him. How could the years have changed and sobered Arthur so much, and left Lancelet untouched, unchanged? No, he had changed too: he looked sad, there was a long scar on his face which ran up into his hair and left a small white streak in it. Cai was thinner and more stooped, his limp more pronounced; he looked on Arthur as a devoted hound looks at his master. Half hoping, half fearing, Morgaine looked about to see if Viviane had come to see Arthur wedded as she had seen him crowned. But the Lady of the Lake was not here. There was the Merlin, his grey head bent in what almost looked like prayer, and behind him, standing—a tall shadow with too much of sense to bend the knee to this stupid mummery—was Kevin the Bard; good for him!

The mass concluded; the bishop, a tall, ascetic-looking man with a sour face, was pronouncing the words of dismissal. Even Morgaine bent her head —Viviane had taught her to show at least outward respect to the manifestations of another's faith, since, as she said, all faith was of the Gods. The only head unbent in the church was that of Kevin, standing proudly erect. Morgaine wished she had the courage to get up and stand beside him, head unbowed. Why was Arthur so reverential? Had he not sworn a solemn oath to regard Avalon as well as the priests? Must a day come when she, or Kevin, must remind Arthur of the vow? Surely that white, pious church angel he was marrying would do nothing to help. They should have married Arthur to a woman of Avalon; it would not be the first time a sworn priestess had been joined to a king. The idea shook her, and she stifled her unease with a quick picture of Raven as High Queen. At least she would have the Christian virtue of silence . . . Morgaine bent her head and bit her lip, suddenly afraid she would giggle aloud.

The mass came to an end; the people began to stream toward the doorway. Arthur and his Companions stayed where they were, and, at a gesture from Cai, Lot and Morgause approached him, Morgaine moving along behind them. She saw that Igraine and the Merlin and the silent harper remained as well. She raised her eyes and met her mother's glance; she knew, with something as poignant as the Sight, that except for the presence of the bishop she would even now be clasped in Igraine's arms. She flushed a little, turning away from Igraine's eager eyes.

She had thought as little as she could of Igraine, conscious only that in her presence she must guard the one thing Igraine must never know, who had fathered her child. . . . Once, in that long desperate struggle which she could hardly remember, she thought she had cried aloud, like a child, for her mother, but she had never been sure. Even now, she feared any contact with the mother who had once had the Sight, who knew the ways of Avalon; Morgaine might manage to put aside all her childhood training and guilt, but would Igraine chide her for what had not, after all, been her own choice?

Lot now came to bend the knee before Arthur, and Arthur, his young face serious and kindly, raised Lot and kissed him on both cheeks. "I am glad you could come to my wedding, Uncle. I am glad I have so faithful a friend and kinsman to guard my northern shores, and your son Gawaine is my dear friend and closest Companion. And you, Aunt. I owe you a debt of thanks for giving me your son for so loyal a Companion."

Morgause smiled. She was, Morgaine thought, still beautiful—far more so than Igraine. "Well, sire, you will have cause to thank me again soon enough, for I have younger sons who talk of nothing but the time when they may come to serve the High King."

"They will be as welcome as their elder brother," Arthur said courteously, and looked past Morgause to where Morgaine knelt.

"Welcome, sister. At my crowning I made you a promise, which now I shall redeem. Come." He stretched out his hand to her. Morgaine rose, feeling the clasp of his hand and the tension in it. He did not meet her eyes, but led her past the others to where the white-clad woman knelt in the cloud of her golden hair.

"My lady," he said softly, and for a moment Morgaine was not sure to which of them he was speaking; he looked from one to the other, and as Gwenhwyfar rose and looked up, her eyes met Morgaine's in a moment of shocked recognition.

"Gwenhwyfar, this is my sister Morgaine, Duchess of Cornwall. It is my wish that she should be first among your ladies-in-waiting, as she is highest in rank here among them."

Morgaine saw Gwenhwyfar moisten her lips with her small pink tongue, like a kitten's. "My lord and king, the lady Morgaine and I have met."

"What? Where?" Arthur demanded, smiling.

Morgaine said, just as stiffly, "It was while she was at school in a nunnery on Glastonbury, my lord. She lost her way in the mists and blundered onto the shores of Avalon." As on that faraway day, it seemed suddenly as if something grey and dismal, like ash, had covered and choked the fine day. Morgaine felt, in spite of her fine decent gown and beautifully woven veil, as if she were some gross, dwarfish, earthly creature before the ethereal whiteness and precious gold of Gwenhwyfar. It lasted only a moment, then Gwenhwyfar stepped forward and embraced her, kissing her on the cheek as was seemly for a kinswoman. Morgaine, returning the embrace, felt that Gwenhwyfar was fragile as precious glass, unlike her own gnarled-wood solidness; felt herself shrinking back, shy and stiff, so that she might not feel Gwenhwyfar shrink from *her*. Her lips felt coarse against the rose-leaf softness of the other girl's cheek.

Gwenhwyfar said softly, "I shall welcome the sister of my lord and husband, my lady of Cornwall—may I call you Morgaine, sister?"

Morgaine drew a long breath and muttered, "As it pleases you, my lady." When she had said it, she knew that she sounded ungracious, but she did not know what she should have said instead. Standing next to Arthur, she looked up to see Gawaine regarding her with a faint frown. Lot was a Christian only because it was expedient, but Gawaine was genuinely devout in his blunt way. His disapproving glance stiffened Morgaine's back;

she had as good a right to be here as Gawaine himself. It would be amusing to see some of these stiff-necked Companions of Arthur lose their proper manners around a Beltane fire! Well, Arthur had sworn to honor the people of Avalon as well as the Christians that might yet come about here at Arthur's court. Perhaps that was why she herself was here.

Gwenhwyfar said, "I hope we shall be friends, lady. I remember that you and the lord Lancelet set me on my way when I was lost in those dreadful mists—even now I shudder at the memory of that terrible place," she said, and raised her eyes to Lancelet, where he stood behind Arthur. Morgaine, attuned to the mood around them, followed her eyes and wondered why Gwenhwyfar spoke to him now; then realized that the other woman could not help it, she was bound as if on a string by Lancelet's eyes . . . and Lancelet was looking at Gwenhwyfar as a hungry dog looks at a dripping bone. If Morgaine had to meet this pink-and-white precious creature again in Lancelet's presence, it was well for them both that it was just as Gwenhwyfar was about to be married to someone else. She sensed Arthur's hand still in hers, and that troubled her too; that bond, too, would be broken, when he had taken Gwenhwyfar to bed. Gwenhwyfar would become the Goddess to Arthur and he would not look at Morgaine anymore in that way that troubled her so. She was Arthur's sister, not his lover; she was the mother not of his son, but the son of the Horned One, and so it must be.

But I have not broken that bond, either. True, I was ill after my son was born, and I had no will to fall like a ripe apple into Lot's bed, so I played Lady Chastity herself wherever Lot could see me. But she looked at Lancelet, hoping to intercept the glance between his eyes and Gwenhwyfar's.

He smiled, but he looked past her. Gwenhwyfar took Morgaine's hand in one of hers, reached to Igraine with the other. "Soon you will be as my own sister and my own mother," she said, "for I have neither mother nor sister living. Come and stand beside me as we are joined in marriage, mother and sister."

Stiffen her heart as she might against Gwenhwyfar's charm, Morgaine was warmed by those spontaneous words, and she returned the pressure of the girl's warm little fingers. Igraine reached past Gwenhwyfar to touch Morgaine's hand, and Morgaine said, "I have not had time to greet you properly, my mother," and let go of Gwenhwyfar's hand for a moment to kiss Igraine. She thought, as for a moment the three of them stood in a brief embrace, *All women, indeed, are sisters under the Goddess.*

"Well, come then," said the Merlin pleasantly. "Let us have the marriage signed and witnessed, and then for feasting and revelry."

Morgaine thought the bishop looked sober, but he too said amiably enough, "Now that our spirits are all lifted up and in charity, indeed, let us make merry as is suitable for Christian folk on such a day of good omen."

Standing beside Gwenhwyfar at the ceremony, Morgaine sensed that the girl was trembling. Her mind went back to the day of the deer hunting. At least she herself had been stimulated and exalted by ritual, but even so she had been frightened, she had clung to the old priestess. Suddenly, with an impulse of kindness, she wished she could give to Gwenhwyfar, who after all had been convent-reared and had none of the old wisdom, some of the instruction given to the younger priestesses. Then she would know how to let the life currents of sun and summer and earth and life flood through her. She could truly become the Goddess to Arthur and he the God to her, so that their marriage would not be an empty form, but a true inner binding on all the levels of life. . . . She almost found herself searching for the words, then remembered that Gwenhwyfar was a Christian, and would not thank Morgaine for such teaching. She sighed, frustrated, knowing she would not speak.

She raised her eyes and met Lancelet's, and for a moment he held her glance; she found herself remembering that sun-flooded moment on the Tor, when they should have been bound as man and woman, Goddess to God . . . she knew he was remembering too. But he dropped his eyes and looked away, signing himself, as the priest had done, with the cross.

The simple ceremony was over. Morgaine affixed her name as witness to the marriage contract, noting how smooth and flowing her own hand was next to Arthur's sprawling signature, Gwenhwyfar's clumsy and childish letters—had the nuns of Glastonbury so little learning? Lancelet signed, too, and Gawaine, and King Bors of Brittany, who had come as witness, and Lot, and Ectorius, and King Pellinore, whose sister had been Gwenhwyfar's mother. Pellinore had a young daughter with him, whom he solemnly beckoned forward.

"My daughter, Elaine—your cousin, my lady and queen. I beg you to accept her service."

"I shall be happy for her company among my ladies," Gwenhwyfar said, smiling. Morgaine thought that Pellinore's daughter was very like Gwenhwyfar, pink and golden, though a little dimmer than Gwenhwyfar's bright radiance, and wearing simple linen dyed with saffron, which dulled the coppery gold of her hair. "What is your name, cousin? How old are you?"

"Elaine, my lady, and I am thirteen years old." She dropped a deep curtsey, so deep that she stumbled and Lancelet caught her to steady her. She blushed deeply and hid her face behind her veil. Lancelet smiled indulgently, and Morgaine felt a sickening pang of jealousy. He would not look at her, he would look only at these pale gold-white angels; no doubt he too thought her little and ugly. And at that moment all her kindness for

Gwenhwyfar faded into anger, and she had to turn her face away.

Gwenhwyfar had to spend the next hours welcoming, it seemed, every king in the whole of Britain, and being presented to their wives, sisters, and daughters. When it came time to sit at the feast, in addition to Morgaine and Elaine and Igraine and Morgause, she had to show courtesy and graciousness to Flavilla, Arthur's foster-mother and mother of Sir Cai; to the queen of North Wales, who had her own name, Gwenhwyfar, but was dark and Roman-looking; and to half a dozen others. She whispered to Morgaine, "I do not know how I am ever to remember all their names! Shall I simply call them all 'my lady' and hope they don't know why?"

Morgaine whispered back, momentarily sharing the sense of fun in her voice, "That is one thing about being a High Queen, madam, no one will dare to ask you why! Whatever you do, they will think it well done! Or if they do not, they will not dare to tell you so!"

Gwenhwyfar giggled a little. "But you must call me by my name, Morgaine—not just *madam*. When you say *madam,* I look about for some stout old lady like Dame Flavilla, or King Pellinore's queen!"

At last the feast began. Morgaine had more appetite now than she had had at Arthur's crowning. She sat between Gwenhwyfar and Igraine, and ate with a good appetite; the abstemious ways of Avalon seemed far behind her. She even ate some meat, though she did not like it, and, since there was no water on the table and beer mostly for the servants, drank the wine she really disliked. It made her head swim a little, though it was not as fiery as the strong barley liquors common at the court of Orkney, which she hated and never touched.

After a time Kevin came forward to play, and the conversation died. Morgaine, who had not heard a fine harper since leaving Avalon, listened, letting the past slip away. Suddenly she longed for Viviane. Even when she raised her eyes and saw Lancelet—who, as Arthur's closest Companion, sat nearer to him than any other, even Gawaine his heir, and shared his dish —she thought of him only as the companion of those years at the Lake.

Viviane, not Igraine, is my real mother, and it was for her I cried out. . . . She bent her head, blinking back tears she did not know how to shed.

The music died away, and she heard Kevin's rich voice. "We have another musician here," he said. "Will the lady Morgaine sing for this company?"

How, she wondered, *did he know I was pining for the touch of my harp?* "It will be a pleasure to play your harp, sir. But I have not touched a fine one for many years, only a makeshift at Lot's court."

Arthur said, and sounded ill-pleased, "What, my sister, sing like a hired musician for all these people?"

Kevin looked offended, as well he might, thought Morgaine. In a
sudden rage, she rose from her seat, saying, "What the Master Harper of
Avalon condescends to do, I am honored to do! In music, the Gods only
are served!" She took the harp from his hand, seating herself on a bench.
It was larger than her own harp and for a moment her hands fumbled on
the strings; then she found the set and her hands moved more surely, playing
a northern song she had heard at Lot's court. She was suddenly grateful for
the wine that had cleared her throat; she heard her own voice rich and sweet
—it had come back as strong as ever, though she had not recognized it till
this moment. Her voice was contralto, deep and strong, trained by the bards
at Avalon, and she was proud, again. *Gwenhwyfar may be beautiful, but I have
the voice of a bard.*

And even Gwenhwyfar crowded close when she was done, to say,
"Your voice is very lovely, sister. Did you learn to sing so well in Avalon?"

"Why yes, madam, music is sacred—did you not learn the harp in your
nunnery?"

Gwenhwyfar shrank. "No, it is unseemly for a woman to raise her
voice before the Lord. . . ."

Morgaine chuckled. "You Christians are overfond of that word *unseemly,* especially when it relates to women," she said. "If music is evil, then
it is evil for men as well; and if it is a good thing, should not women do
all the good things they can do, to make up for their supposed sin at the
beginning of the world?"

"Still, I would not have been allowed—once I was beaten for touching
a harp," said Gwenhwyfar wistfully. "But you have cast a spell over us, and
I cannot think but this magic is good."

Kevin said, "All the men and women of Avalon learn something of
music; but few have such gifts as the lady Morgaine. A fine voice is born,
not trained. And if it is a gift of God, then seems it to me that it is arrogant
to look down and think little of such a gift, be it given to man or woman.
We cannot believe God has made a mistake in giving such a gift to a woman,
since God makes no mistakes, so we must accept it wherever it is found."

"I cannot argue theology with a Druid," said Ectorius, "but if I had
a daughter born with such a gift, I would hold it a temptation, that she
would be tempted to step beyond the place appointed to a woman. We are
not told that Mary, the Mother of our Lord, sang or danced—"

The Merlin said softly, "Though we are told that when the Holy Ghost
descended upon her, she lifted up her voice and sang, *My soul hath magnified
the Lord . . .*" But he said it in Greek: *Megalýnei hē psychē mou tòn
Kýrion. . . .*

Only Ectorius and Lancelet and the bishop recognized the Greek
words, although Morgaine too had heard them more than once. The bishop

said firmly, "But she sang in the presence of God alone. Only Mary the Magdalene is said to have sung or danced before men, and only before our Redeemer saved her soul for God, for it was part of her wicked ways."

Igraine said with a flicker of mischief, "King David was a singer and played, we are told, upon the harp. Do you suppose he beat any of his wives or daughters for playing on the harp?"

Morgaine flashed, "If Mary of Magdala—I mind the story—played on the harp and danced, still she came to be· saved, and we are nowhere told that Jesus told her to sit meekly and be silent! If she poured precious balm on the head of Jesus and he would not let his Companions rebuke her, he may well have enjoyed her other gifts as well! The Gods give of their best, not their worst, to men!"

Patricius said stiffly, "If this is the form of religion which is known here in Britain, we are well in need of such councils as our church has called together!" He scowled, and Morgaine, already regretting her hasty words, lowered her head—it was hardly suitable to pick a quarrel between Avalon and the church at Arthur's wedding. But why did Arthur not speak out? All at once everyone began to talk all together, and Kevin, taking the harp again, began to play a lively air, under cover of which the servants went around with fresh delicacies which nobody wanted by now.

After a time Kevin put by the harp, and Morgaine, as she would have done in Avalon, poured him wine and knelt to offer it to him. He smiled and took it, gesturing to her to rise and sit by him.

"Lady Morgaine, my thanks."

"It is my duty and my pleasure to serve such a bard, Master Harper. Are you recently come from Avalon? Is my kinswoman Viviane well?"

"Well, but much aged," he said quietly. "And, I think, pining for you —you should return."

Morgaine felt again the surge of unforgotten despair; she looked away from him. "I cannot. But give me news of my home."

"If you wish more news of Avalon you will have to go there. I have not returned myself for a year, since I am required to give news of all the kingdom to the Lady—Taliesin is too old now for a Messenger of the Gods."

"Well," Morgaine said, "you will have something to tell her of this marriage."

"I will tell her that you are alive and well," said Kevin, "since she has mourned you. She has not now the Sight to see for herself. And I shall tell her of her younger son who is Arthur's chiefest Companion; indeed," he said, his lips curving in a sarcastic smile, "watching him with Arthur, I think him like that youngest disciple who leaned at dinner upon the bosom of Christ. . . ."

Morgaine could not keep back a small chuckle. "Yonder bishop would have you whipped for blasphemy, no doubt, if he heard you say so."

"Well, there sits Arthur like to Jesus with his Apostles, defending Christianity to all the land," Kevin said. "As for yonder bishop, he is an ignorant man."

"What, because he has no ear for music?" Morgaine had not realized how she had starved for the banter of casual equals like this; Morgause and the gossip of her ladies were so small, so bound by little things!

"I would say that any man without an ear for music is an ignorant ass indeed, since without it he does not speak but brays," Kevin retorted, "but it is more than that. Is this any time for a wedding?"

Morgaine had been so long away from Avalon that for a moment she did not know what he meant; but he pointed to the sky.

"The moon is waning from the full. This augurs ill for a wedding, and the lord Taliesin told them so. But the bishop would have it a little after the full so that all these people would have light to travel to their homes, and because it is the feast of one of their saints—I know not which! The Merlin spoke to Arthur as well, to tell him this marriage would bring him no joy—I know not why. But there was no honorable way to stop it, it seemed, all had gone too far."

Morgaine knew instinctively what the old Druid had meant; she too had seen the way in which Gwenhwyfar looked upon Lancelet. Was it a flash of the Sight which had caused her to shrink from Gwenhwyfar, that day upon Avalon?

She took Lancelet from me forever on that day, Morgaine thought, then, remembering that she had been under a vow to keep her maidenhood for the Goddess, looked within, in dull astonishment. Would she have been forsworn for his sake? She lowered her head in shame, almost fearing, for a moment, that Kevin could read her thoughts.

Viviane had said to her that a priestess must temper everything with her own judgment. It had been a right instinct, vows or no vows, which had led her to desire Lancelet . . . *I would have done better, even by Avalon, to take Lancelet then; then would Arthur's queen have come to him with her heart untouched, for Lancelet would have formed that mystical bond with me, and the child I bore would have been born of the ancient royal line of Avalon. . . .*

But they had had other plans for her, and in the wreck of that she had left Avalon forever, borne a child who had destroyed any hope that she could ever give the Goddess a daughter to her shrine: after Gwydion, she could carry no other to life. If she had trusted her own instinct and judgment, Viviane would have been angry, but they would have found someone suitable for Arthur, somehow. . . .

By doing right I did wrong; by obeying Viviane's word I helped with the wreck and disaster of this marriage, for wreck I now know it will be. . . .

"Lady Morgaine," Kevin said gently, "you are troubled. Can I do anything to help you?"

Morgaine shook her head, biting back tears again. She wondered if he knew she had been given to Arthur in the kingmaking. She could not accept his pity. "Nothing, lord Druid. Perhaps I share your fears for this marriage made in a waning moon. I am concerned for my brother, no more. And I do pity the woman he has wedded." And as she spoke the words she knew they were true; for all her fear of Gwenhwyfar, not unmixed with hatred, she knew that she did pity her—marrying a man who did not love her, loving a man she could not wed.

If I take Lancelet from Gwenhwyfar, then I do my brother a service, and his wife as well, for if I take him away she will forget him. She had been trained to examine her own motives in Avalon, and now she cringed inwardly; she was not being honest with herself. If she took Lancelet from Gwenhwyfar, it would not be for her brother's sake nor for the sake of the kingdom, but purely and solely because she desired Lancelet herself.

Not for yourself. For the sake of another you could use your magic; but you must not deceive yourself. She knew love charms enough. It would be for Arthur's good! It *would* work to the advantage of the kingdom, she told herself repeatedly, if she took Lancelet from her brother's wife; but the unsparing conscience of a priestess kept saying: *This you may not. It is forbidden to use your magic to make the universe do your will.*

So, still, she would try; but she must do it unassisted, with no more than her own woman's wiles. She told herself fiercely that Lancelet had desired her once, without the aid of magic; she could certainly make him desire her again!

GWENHWYFAR WAS WEARY of the feasting. She had eaten more than she wanted, and although she had sipped only one glass of wine, she felt overly hot, and slid her veil back, fanning herself. Arthur had come to speak to many of his guests, moving slowly toward the table where she sat with the ladies, and finally reaching her; with him, Lancelet and Gawaine. The women slid along the benches, making room, and Arthur sat beside her.

"It is the first moment I have really had to speak to you, my wife." She held out her small hand to him. "I understand. This is more like a council than a wedding feast, my husband and my lord."

He laughed, somewhat ruefully. "All events in my life now seem to become so. A king does nothing in private. Well," he amended, smiling, seeing the flush that spread over her face, "*almost* nothing—I think there will be a few exceptions, my wife. The law requires that they must see us put to bed together, but what happens after that need concern no one but ourselves, I trust."

She lowered her eyes, knowing that he had seen her blush. Once again, with the flood of shame, she realized that she had forgotten him again, that she had been watching Lancelet and thinking, with the drowsy sweetness of a dream, how very much she wished it had been to him she had been joined in marriage this day—what damnable fate had made her a High Queen? His eyes fell on her with that hungry look, and she dared not look up at him. She saw him turn his eyes from her even before the shadow fell over them and the lady Morgaine stood there; Arthur made room for her at his side.

"Come and sit with us, my sister, there is always room for you here," he said, his voice so languorous that Gwenhwyfar wondered for a moment how much he had drunk. "When the feast has worn away a little, see, we have prepared something more for entertainment, perhaps something more stirring than the bard's music, beautiful though it is. I did not know you were a singer, my sister. I knew you were an enchantress, but not that you were a musician as well. Have you enchanted us all?"

"I hope not," Morgaine said, laughing, "else I would never dare sing again—what is that old saga, about the bard who sang the evil giants into a circle of ring stones, and there they stand, cold and stone to this day?"

"That one I have never heard," said Gwenhwyfar, "though in my convent there was a tale that these were evil folk who mocked the Christ on his way to his cross, and a saint raised his hand and turned them into crows who fly over the world crying out wailing jests forever . . . and another tale of a saint who transformed a circle of sorceresses, at their evil rites, into a circle of stones."

Lancelet said lazily, "If I had leisure to study philosophy instead of being warrior or councillor or horseman, I think I would try to find who built the ring stones and why."

Morgaine laughed. "That is known in Avalon. Viviane could tell you if she would."

"But," said Lancelet, "what the priestesses and the Druids say may be no more truth than your pious nun's fables, Gwenhwyfar—forgive me, I should say, my lady and queen. Arthur, forgive me, I meant no disrespect to your lady, but I called her by her name when she was younger and not yet a queen—" but Morgaine knew that he was simply seeking an excuse to speak her name aloud.

Arthur yawned. "My dear friend, I do not mind if my lady does not. God forbid I should be the kind of husband who wishes to keep his wife locked away in a cage from all other human beings. A husband who cannot keep his wife's kind regards and faithfulness probably does not deserve them." He leaned over and took Gwenhwyfar's hand in his own. "I think this feasting long. Lancelet, how long before the riders are ready?"

"I think they will be ready soon," Lancelet said, deliberately looking away from Gwenhwyfar. "Does my lord and king wish me to go and see?"

Morgaine thought, *He is torturing himself, he cannot bear to look on Gwenhwyfar with Arthur, he cannot bear to leave her alone with him.* She said, deliberately making a joke of a truth, "I think, Lancelet, our bridal couple wishes to have a few moments to talk together alone. Why do we not leave them here and go down and see ourselves whether the riders are ready."

Lancelet said, "My lord—" and as Gwenhwyfar opened her mouth to protest, he said roughly, "Give me leave to go."

Arthur nodded permission, and Morgaine took his hand. He let her draw him along, but she saw him turn his head halfway, as if he could not take his eyes from Gwenhwyfar. Her heart was wrung; at one and the same time it seemed that she could not bear his pain, and that she would do anything to get him away so that she need not see him look at Gwenhwyfar. Behind her she heard Arthur say, "Until yesterday evening I had no idea that the fates, in sending me a bride, had sent me a beautiful one," and Gwenhwyfar answer, "But it was not the fates, my lord, it was my father." Before Morgaine could hear what Arthur answered, they were out of earshot.

"I remember," Morgaine said, "once, years ago, at Avalon, you spoke of cavalry as the key to victory over the Saxons—that and a disciplined army, like to the Romans. I suppose that is what you plan for these horsemen."

"It is true that I have been training them. I had not imagined that a woman would remember a point of military strategy, cousin."

Morgaine laughed. "I live under fear of the Saxons, like every other woman in these islands. I passed through a village once where a band of them had passed over, and every woman from little girls of five years old to old grandmothers in their nineties with no teeth and no hair had been raped. Whatever offers hope to rid us of them once and for all is meaningful to me, perhaps more than to men and soldiers, who need to fear only death."

"I had not thought of that," Lancelet said soberly. "Uther Pendragon's troops were not above scouring the countryside for willing women—nor are Arthur's—but in general, there is no rape. And I had forgotten, Morgaine, you were trained at Avalon and you think often on things which mean little or nothing to other women." He looked up and clasped her hand in his. "I had forgotten the harps of Avalon. I thought I hated the place, that I never wished to go back. And yet—sometimes—some little thing will take me back there. The sound of a harp. Sunlight on ring stones. The scent of apples and the sound of bees in the sun. Fish splashing in the lake, and the cries of water birds at sunset—"

"Do you remember," she asked softly, "the day we climbed the Tor?"

"I remember." With sudden bitterness he said, "I would to God you had not been sworn to the Goddess, that day."

She said in a low voice, "I have wished it almost as long as I can remember." Her voice suddenly broke, and Lancelet looked with apprehension into her eyes.

"Morgaine, Morgaine—kinswoman, I have never seen you weep."

"Are you like so many men, afraid of a woman's tears?"

He shook his head, and his arm went around her shoulders. "No," he confessed in a low voice, "it makes them seem so much more real, so much more vulnerable—women who never weep frighten me, because I know they are stronger than I, and I am always a little afraid of what they will do. I was always afraid of—Viviane." She sensed that he had been about to say *my mother,* and had shrunk from the words.

They were passing under the low lintel of the stables; the long line of horses, tied there, shadowed the day. There was a pleasant smell of hay and straw. Outside, she saw men moving back and forth, erecting piles of hay, standing up mannikins of stuffed leather, and men were coming in and out, saddling their horses.

Someone caught sight of Lancelet and shouted, "Will the High King and their lordships be ready for us soon, sir? We don't want to bring the horses out and keep them standing to get restless."

"Soon," Lancelet called back.

The soldier behind the horse resolved himself into Gawaine. "Ah, cousin," he said to Morgaine. "Lance, don't bring her in here, it's no place for a lady, a few of these damned beasts are still unbroken. Are you still resolved to take out that white stallion?"

"I'm resolved to have him ready for Arthur to ride into battle next time, if I break my own neck for it!"

"Don't jest about things like that," Gawaine said.

"Who says I am jesting? If Arthur can't ride him, I'll ride him myself in battle, and I'll show him this afternoon in honor of the Queen!"

"Lancelet," Morgaine said, "don't risk your neck for that. Gwenhwyfar doesn't know one horse from another, she'd be as impressed if you rode a hobbyhorse from one end of the yard to another as by the feats of the centaur himself!"

The look he gave her was, for a moment, almost contemptuous, but she could read it clearly: *How could she understand his need to show himself undamaged by this day?*

"Go and get saddled, Gawaine, and give the word on the field, we'll be ready in half an hour," said Lancelet, "and ask Cai if he wants to start."

"Don't tell me Cai's going to ride, wi' that crippled leg o' his?" demanded one of the men who spoke in a strange accent. Gawaine turned on the stranger and said fiercely, "Would you grudge him that—the one military exercise where that leg makes no difference and he's not tied to the kitchens and the ladies' bowers?"

"Na, na, I see what ye mean," said the strange soldier, and turned to saddling his own horse. Morgaine touched Lancelet's hand; he looked down at her, the mischief back in his eyes. *Here,* she thought, *arranging something, risking his neck, doing something for Arthur, he has forgotten about love, he is happy again. If he could only keep himself busy here, he would not need to moon after Gwenhwyfar or any other woman.*

She said, "Show me this dangerous horse you are going to ride."

He led her down between the rows of tied steeds. She saw the pale silvery nose, the long mane like linen floss—a big horse, tall as Lancelet himself across the shoulders. The creature tossed his head, and the snort was like a dream of dragons breathing fire.

"Oh, you beauty," said Lancelet, laying his hand alongside the horse's nose; he sidled and stepped away. He said to Morgaine, "This one I trained with my own hands to bit and stirrup—it was my wedding present to Arthur, who has no leisure to break a horse for his own use. I swore it would be ready on his wedding day, for him to ride, and gentle as a house pet."

"A thoughtful gift," said Morgaine.

"No, the only thing I could give," Lancelet said. "I am not rich. And anyway, he has no need of jewels or gold, he is showered with those things. This was a gift only I could give him."

"A gift of yourself," said Morgaine, and thought, *How he loves Arthur; this is why he is so tormented. It is not that he desires Gwenhwyfar that tortures him; it is that he loves Arthur no less. If he were simply a wencher like Gawaine I would not even pity him; Gwenhwyfar is virtuous, and I could take pleasure in seeing her turn him away.*

She said, "I would like to ride him. There is no horse I fear."

He laughed. "Morgaine, you fear nothing, do you?"

"Oh, no, my kinsman," she said, suddenly sober, "I fear many things."

"Well, I am not as fearless even as you, I am afraid of battle and I fear the Saxons and I fear I will be killed before I have tasted all there is to life," he said. "And so I never dare shrink from any challenge. . . . And I fear lest both Avalon and the Christians are wrong, and there should be no Gods and no Heaven and no afterlife, so that when I die I will perish forever. So I fear to die before I have savored my fill of life."

"It does not seem to me you have left much untasted," Morgaine said.

"Ah, but I have, Morgaine, there are so many things I long for, and whenever I pass one by I regret it so bitterly, and wonder what weakness or folly prevents me from doing what I will . . ." he said, and suddenly he turned in the horse lanes and put his arms hungrily round her, pulling her close.

Desperation, she thought bitterly; *it is not me he wants, it is a moment of forgetfulness of Arthur and Gwenhwyfar in one another's arms this night.* His hands moved, with a detached, practiced deftness, over her breasts; he pressed his lips to hers, and she could feel the whole hard length of his body pushing against her. She stood in his arms, motionless, feeling languor and a rising hunger that was like pain; she was hardly conscious of her small movements, to fit her body against his. Her mouth opened under his lips, his hands were over her. But when he moved with her toward one of the piles of hay, she roused to a dim protest.

"My dear, you are mad, there are half a hundred of Arthur's soldiers and riders swarming in this stable—"

"Do you mind," he whispered, and she murmured, shaking with excitement, "No. *No!*" She let him push her down. Through the back of her mind, in bitterness, was the thought, *a princess, Duchess of Cornwall, a priestess of Avalon, tumbled in the stables like some dairymaid, without even the excuse of the Beltane fires.* But she closed it away from her mind and let his hands move on her as they would, unresisting. *Better this than break Arthur's heart.* She did not know whether it was her own thought or that of the man whose body was somehow all over hers, whose fierce furious hands were bruising her; his kisses were almost savage, driving into her mouth in a rage. She felt him pull at her dress and moved to loosen it for him.

And then there were voices, clamoring, shouting, a noise like hammering, a frightened scream, and suddenly a dozen voices were all yelling. "Captain! Lord Lancelet! Where is he? Captain!

"Down here, I thought—" One of the younger soldiers ran down between the horse lines. Swearing savagely under his breath, Lancelet thrust his body between Morgaine and the young soldier, while she buried her face in her veil and hunched herself, half-naked already, into the straw so that she would not be seen.

"Damnation! Can't I be out of the way for a moment—"

"Oh, sir, come quickly, one of the strange horses—there was a mare in season, and two of the stallions began fighting, and I think one of them's broken a leg—"

"Hell and furies!" Lancelet was swiftly tucking garments into place, rising and towering over the lad who had interrupted them. "I'll come—"

The young man had caught sight of Morgaine; she hoped in a moment of horror that he had not recognized her—that would be a fine juicy morsel of gossip for the court indeed. *Not as bad as what they do not know . . . that I bore my brother's child.*

"Did I interrupt anything, sir?" the young man said, trying to peer around Lancelet, almost sniggering. Morgaine wondered disconsolate, *What will this do to* his *reputation? Or is it to a man's credit to be caught in the hay?* Lancelet did not even answer; he shoved the youngster along before him, so that he almost fell. "Go and find Cai, and the farrier, get along with you." He came swiftly back, a whirlwind, kissed Morgaine who had staggered somehow to her feet. "Gods! Of all the damnable——" He pressed her hard against him, with hungry fingers, kissed her so hard that she felt the brand of it was scalding red on her face. "Gods! Tonight—swear it! Swear!"

She couldn't speak. She could only nod, dazed, numb, her whole body screaming for the interrupted fulfillment, as she saw him rush away. A minute or two later a young man came up to her deferentially and bowed, while soldiers began rushing back and forth and somewhere there was the terrible, almost human scream of a dying animal.

"Lady Morgaine? I am Griflet. The lord Lancelet sent me to escort you to the pavilions. He told me he had brought you down here to see the horse he is training for my lord the king, but that you had slipped and fallen in the hay, and that he was trying to see if you had hurt yourself when they began shrieking for him—when this fight broke out with King Pellinore's horse. And he begs you to excuse him and return to the castle——"

Well, she thought, at least it explained her kirtle crushed and stained with hay and her hair and headcloth filled with hayseed. She need not go before Gwenhwyfar and her mother looking like the woman in Scriptures, the one taken in adultery; young Griflet held out his arm and she leaned on it heavily, saying, "I think my ankle is twisted," and limped all the way up to the castle. It would explain the hay, if she had had a hurt and fallen hard. One part of her was glad of Lancelet's quick thinking; the other, desolate, cried out for him to acknowledge and shelter her.

Arthur had gone off with Cai to the stables, distressed at the accident to the horses. She let Gwenhwyfar fuss over her and Igraine send for cold water and linen strips to bandage her ankle, and she accepted a place at Igraine's side, in the shade, when horses and men rode out to display their exercises. Arthur made a little speech about the new legion of Caerleon which would revive the glories of the days of Rome, and save the country-side. His foster-father, Ectorius, was beaming. Then a dozen riders rode out, displaying the new skills with which the horses could stop in mid gallop, pull up, wheel, move together.

"After this," Arthur declared grandly, "no one will ever again say that horses are fit for nothing but to move wagons!" He smiled at Gwenhwyfar. "How do you like my knights, my lady? I have called them after the old

Roman *equites*—noblemen who could own and fit out their own horse."

"Cai rides as well as a centaur," Igraine said to Ectorius, and the old man smiled with pleasure. "Arthur, you never did a kinder thing than when you gave Cai one of the best of the horses."

"Cai is too good a soldier, and too good a friend, to wither in the house," said Arthur decisively.

Gwenhwyfar said, "Is he not your foster-brother?"

"True. He was wounded in his first battle, and feared he would skulk at home with the women forever after that," said Arthur. "A frightful fate for a soldier. But on horseback he fights as well as any."

"Look," exclaimed Igraine, "the legion has smashed down that whole series of targets—I have never seen such riding!"

"I don't think anything could stand against that attack," said King Pellinore. "What a pity Uther Pendragon could not live to see this, my boy —excuse me—my lord and king—"

Arthur said warmly, "My father's friend may call me whatever he wishes, dear Pellinore! But the credit must go to my friend and captain, Lancelet."

Morgause's son Gaheris bobbed in a bow to Arthur. "My lord, may I go down to the stables and see them unsaddled?" He was a bright, merry-looking boy of fourteen or so.

"You may," said Arthur. "When will he come to join Gawaine and Agravaine at our side, Aunt?"

"This year, perhaps, if his brothers can teach him soldierly arts and keep him close," Morgause said, then raised her voice: "No! Not you, Gareth!" and made a snatch at the chubby six-year-old. "Gaheris! Bring him back here!"

Arthur spread his hands with a laugh. "Don't worry about it—boys run to stables like fleas to dogs. I have been told how I rode my father's stallion when I was scarce six years old! I don't remember; it was only a little before I went to be fostered with Ectorius," he said, and Morgaine shivered suddenly, remembering a fair-haired child lying like death and something like a shadow in a bowl of water—no, it was gone.

"Does your ankle pain you much, sister?" Gwenhwyfar asked solicitously. "Here, lean against me—"

"Gawaine will look after him," Arthur said offhandedly. "I think he's the best man we have at training the young knights and riders."

"Better than the lord Lancelet?" asked Gwenhwyfar.

Morgaine thought, *She only wants to speak his name. But it is me he wanted, not long ago, and tonight it will be too late . . . better that than break Arthur's heart. I will tell Gwenhwyfar if I must.*

Arthur said, "Lancelet? He's our best rider, though too much of a daredevil for my taste. The lads all adore him, of course—look, there's your little Gareth, Aunt, tagging after him like a puppy—they'll do anything for a kind word from him. But he's not as good at teaching the boys their business as Gawaine; he's too flamboyant and he likes to show off. Gawaine takes them slow and easy and makes them learn the art step by step, and they never get hurt through carelessness—Gawaine's my best arms master. Look, there's Lancelet on that horse he's training for me—" He burst into a laugh, and Igraine said, "That little devil!"

For Gareth had swung like a monkey from the saddle leather, and Lancelet, laughing, scooped up the boy in front of him on his saddle and broke into a fast gallop, racing directly up the hill toward the sheltered place where the royal party sat watching. They raced at breakneck speed straight toward them, so that even Arthur gasped and Igraine stepped back, her face white. Lancelet pulled up the horse so that it reared into the air and wheeled it round.

"Your horse, lord Arthur," he said with a flourish, holding the reins with one hand, "and your cousin. Aunt Morgause, take this little scapegrace and tan his breeches for him!" he added, letting Gareth slide down almost into Morgause's lap. "He could have been killed under the stallion's feet like that!"

Gareth heard not a word of Morgause's scolding, looking up at Lancelet, his blue eyes wide with adoration.

"When you get older," Arthur said, laughing, aiming a playful cuff at the child, "I will make you a knight and you shall ride out to conquer giants and evil raiders, and rescue fair ladies."

"Oh no, my lord Arthur," said the child, his eyes still fastened on the white horse which Lancelet was riding up and down. "The lord Lancelet shall make me a knight, and we will go on a quest together."

Ectorius chuckled and said, "Young Achilles has found his Patroclus, so it would seem."

"I am quite in the shade," Arthur said good-naturedly. "Even my new-made wife cannot take her eyes from Lancelet, and begs him to call her by her Christian name, and now little Gareth would rather be made knight by *him!* If Lance were not my closest friend, I should be mad with jealousy."

Pellinore was watching the rider cantering up and down. He said, "That damnable dragon is still hiding in a lake on my lands, and coming out to kill my tenants or their cows. Perhaps if I had a horse like that, who would stand to fight . . . I think I will train a battle horse and go after it again. Last time I barely got away with my life."

"A dragon, sir?" asked little Gareth. "Did it breathe fire?"

"No, lad, but it had an almighty stench and a noise like sixty packs of hounds all baying together from his belly," said Pellinore, and Ectorius said, "Dragons do not breathe fire, my lad. That comes from the old way of calling a shooting star a dragon, for they have a long tail of fire—there may have been dragons *once* who breathed fire, but not in the memory of any living man."

Morgaine was not listening, though she wondered how much of Pellinore's tale was true, and how much exaggerated to impress the child. Her eyes were on Lancelet, putting the horse through its paces.

Arthur said to Gwenhwyfar, "I could never train a horse like that— Lancelet is training it to battle for me. Look, two months ago that one was wild as one of Pellinore's dragons, and now look at him!"

"He seems still wild to me," said Gwenhwyfar. "But then, I am afraid even of the gentlest horses."

"A horse to be ridden in battle must not be meek as a lady's palfrey," said Arthur. "He must have spirit—God in heaven!" he cried out, rising up suddenly. From somewhere there was a blur of white; a bird of some kind, a goose perhaps, had suddenly flapped upward, right under the horse's hooves. Lancelet, riding at ease, his vigilance relaxed, started as the horse reared upright with a frantic whicker; fought for control, slid off almost under the hooves; half senseless, managed to roll away.

Gwenhwyfar screamed. Morgause and the other ladies echoed the scream, while Morgaine, quite forgetting she was supposed to have an injured ankle, leaped up and ran toward Lancelet, dragging him out from under the horse's hooves. Arthur too dashed for the horse's bridle, grabbing it, wrestling the horse by main force away from where Lancelet sprawled unconscious. Morgaine knelt beside him, quickly feeling his temple, where a bruise already darkened and a trickle of blood mingled with the dust.

"Is he dead?" Gwenhwyfar cried. "Is he dead?"

"No," Morgaine said with asperity. "Bring some cold water, and there ought to be some of that bandage linen left. He's broken his wrist, I think; he broke his fall with it so as not to break his neck! And the clout on his head—" She bent down, laying her ear against his chest, feeling the warm rise and fall of it. She took the basin of cold water Pellinore's daughter handed her, sponging his brow with a bit of linen. "Someone catch that goose and wring its neck—and give the goose boy a good thrashing. The lord Lancelet could have broken his head, or damaged the High King's horse."

Gawaine came and led the horse back to the stables. The near tragedy had dampened the festivities, and one by one the guests began to drift away to their own pavilions and quarters. Morgaine bound up Lancelet's head and his broken wrist, mercifully completing the work of splinting the wrist before he stirred and moaned and clutched at it in agony; then, in conference with the housekeeper, sent Cai for some herbs which would make him sleep and had him carried to bed. She stayed with him, though he did not know her, only moaned and stared about with eyes that refused to stay in focus.

Once he stared at her, and muttered "Mother—" and her heart sank. After a while he fell into a heavy, restless sleep, and when he woke, he knew her.

"Morgaine? Cousin? What happened?"

"You fell off a horse."

"A horse? What horse?" he asked, confused, and when she told him he said positively, "That's ridiculous. I don't fall off horses," and dropped off to sleep again.

Morgaine sat beside him, letting him clutch at her hand, and felt that her heart would break. The mark of his kisses was still on her mouth, on her aching breasts. Yet the moment had passed, and she knew it. Even if he should remember, he would not want her; he had never wanted her, except to dull the agony of thinking of Gwenhwyfar and of his love for his king and cousin.

It was growing dark; far away in the castle she heard sounds of music again—Kevin was harping. There was laughter, singing, festivity. Suddenly the door opened, and Arthur himself, carrying a torch in his hand, came in.

"Sister, how does Lancelet?"

"He'll live; his head's too hard to break," she said with a hard flippancy.

"We wanted you among the witnesses when the bride was put to bed, as you witnessed the marriage contract," said Arthur. "But I suppose he should not be left alone, and I wouldn't want him left to a chamberlain, not even to Cai. He's fortunate he has you with him. You are his foster-sister, are you not?"

"No," said Morgaine, with unexpected anger.

Arthur came to the bedside and picked up Lancelet's limp hand. The injured man moaned, stirred, and looked up, blinking. "Arthur?"

"I'm here, my friend," said Arthur, and Morgaine thought she had never heard a man's voice so tender.

"Is your horse—all right?"

"The horse is fine. Damn the horse," Arthur said. "If you'd been killed, what good would a horse be to me?" He was almost weeping.

"How did it—happen?"

"A damned goose flew up. The goose boy's in hiding. I think he knows he'll be beaten within an inch of his life!"

"Don't do that," Lancelet said. "He's only a poor stupid creature without all his wits. He's not to blame that the geese are cleverer than he is, and one wandered loose. Promise me, Gwydion." She was astonished that he used the old name. Arthur pressed his hand, and bent down to kiss

Lancelet on the cheek, carefully avoiding the bruised side.

"I promise, Galahad. Sleep, now."

Lancelet gripped his hand hard. "I came close to wrecking your wedding night, didn't I?" he said, with something Morgaine recognized as her own hard irony.

"Believe you did—my bride has wept so hard over *you,* I wonder what she would do if *I* had broken my head?" Arthur demanded, laughing.

Morgaine said fiercely, "Arthur, even if you are the King, he must be kept quiet!"

"Right." Arthur straightened. "I will send the Merlin to look in at him tomorrow; he should not be left alone tonight, though—"

"I'll stay with him," she said angrily.

"Well, if you are sure—"

"Go you back to Gwenhwyfar! Your bride is waiting for you!"

Arthur sighed, subdued. After a moment he said, "I don't know what to say to her. Or what to do."

This is ridiculous—does he expect me to instruct him, or to instruct his bride? At the look in his eyes she lowered her own. She said, very gently, "Arthur, it is simple. Do as the Goddess prompts you."

He looked like a stricken child. At last he said, hoarsely, fighting the words, "She—she isn't the Goddess. She's just a girl, and she's—she's frightened." After a moment he blurted out, "Morgaine, don't you know that I still—"

She could not bear what he might be going to say. *"No!"* she said violently, holding up her hand, commanding silence. "Arthur, remember one thing at least. To her you will always be the God. Come to her as the Horned One. . . ."

Arthur crossed himself and shivered. He whispered at last, "God forgive me; this is the punishment . . ." and fell silent. They stood, looking at each other, unable to speak. Finally he said, "Morgaine, I have no right —will you kiss me once?"

"My brother—" She sighed, stood on tiptoe and kissed his forehead. Then she signed his head with the sign of the Goddess. "Bless you," she whispered. "Arthur, go to her, go to your bride. I promise you, I promise in the name of the Goddess, it will be well, I swear it to you."

He swallowed—she saw the muscles in his throat move. Then he broke away from her eyes and muttered, "God bless you, sister." The door closed behind him.

Morgaine dropped down on a chair, and sat, unmoving, staring at Lancelet's sleep, tormented by pictures in her mind. Lancelet's face, smiling at her in sunlight on the Tor. Gwenhwyfar, water-draggled, her skirts soaked, clinging to Lancelet's hand. The Horned God, his face smeared with deer's blood, drawing aside the curtain at the mouth of the cave. Lancelet's mouth frantic on her breasts—had it been only a few hours ago?

"At least," she muttered aloud fiercely, "he will not spend Arthur's bridal night dreaming of Gwenhwyfar." She laid herself down along the edge of the bed, pressing her body carefully against the hurt man's body; she lay there silent, not even weeping, sunk in a despairing misery too deep for tears. But she did not close her eyes that night, fighting the Sight, fighting dreams, struggling for the silence and the numb absence of thought she had been taught in Avalon.

And far away, in the furthest wing of the castle, Gwenhwyfar lay awake, looking in guilty tenderness at Arthur's hair shining in the moonlight, his chest that rose and fell with his quiet breathing. Tears trickled slowly down her cheeks.

I want so much to love him, she thought, and then she prayed. "Oh, God, holy Mary Virgin, help me to love him as I ought to do, he is my king and my lord and he is so good, he deserves someone who will love him more than I can love." All around her, it seemed, the night breathed sadness and despair.

But why, she wondered. *Arthur is happy. He has nothing with which to reproach me. Whence comes this sorrow in the very air?*

7

On a day in late summer, Queen Gwenhwyfar, with several of her ladies, sat in the hall at Caerleon. It was afternoon and very hot; most of them were making a pretense of spinning, or of carding the last of that spring's wool for spinning, but the spindles moved sluggishly, and even the Queen, who was the best needlewoman among them, had ceased to set stitches in the fine altar cloth she was making for the bishop.

Morgaine laid aside the carded wool for spinning and sighed. At this season of the year she was always homesick, longing for the mists that crept in from the sea over the cliffs at Tintagel . . . she had not seen them since she was a little child.

Arthur and his men, with the Caerleon legion, had ridden out to the southern coast, to examine the new fort that the Saxons of the treaty troops had built there. This summer had brought no raid, and it might well be that the Saxons, except for those who had made treaty with Arthur and were living peacefully in the Kentish country, would give up Britain for lost. Two years of Arthur's horse legion had reduced the Saxon fighting to a

sporadic summer exercise; but Arthur had taken this season of quiet to
fortify all the defenses of the coasts.

"I am thirsty again," said Pellinore's daughter, Elaine. "May I go, my
lady, and ask for more pitchers of water to be sent?"

"Call Cai—he will attend to it," Gwenhwyfar said.

Morgaine thought: *She has grown a great deal; from a scared and timid
child she has become a queen.*

"You should have married Cai when the King wished for it, lady
Morgaine," said Elaine, returning from her errand and sitting down on the
bench beside Morgaine. "He is the only man under sixty in the castle, and
his wife will never lie alone for half a year at a time."

"You are welcome to him, if you want him," Morgaine said amiably.

"I still wonder that you did not," Gwenhwyfar said, as if it were an
old grievance. "It would have been so suitable—Cai, the King's foster-
brother and high in his favor, and you, Arthur's sister and Duchess of
Cornwall in your own right, now that the lady Igraine never leaves her
nunnery!"

Drusilla, daughter of one of the petty kings to the east, snickered. "Tell
me, if the King's sister and brother marry, how is it other than incest?"

"Half-sister and foster-brother, you goose," said Elaine. "But tell me,
lady Morgaine, was it only his scars and lameness that deterred you? Cai
is no beauty, certainly, but he would be a good husband."

"I am not deceived by you," Morgaine retorted, pretending a good
humor she did not feel—did these women think of nothing but marriages?
"You care nothing for my wedded happiness with Cai, you merely wished
for a wedding to break the monotony of the summer. But you should not
be greedy. Sir Griflet was married to Meleas last spring, and that should be
weddings enough for now." She glanced at Meleas, whose dress had already
begun to grow tight over her pregnant body. "You will even have a babe
to fuss and coo over this time next year."

"But you are long unmarried, lady Morgaine," said Alienor of Galis.
"And you could hardly have hoped for a better match than the King's own
foster-brother!"

"I am in no great haste to be wed, and Cai had no more mind to me
than I to him."

Gwenhwyfar chuckled. "True. He has a tongue near as waspish as your
own, and no sweet temper—his wife will need more patience than the
saintly Brigid, and you, Morgaine, are ever ready with a sharp answer."

"And besides, if she should marry, she would have to spin for her
household," Meleas said. "As usual, Morgaine is shirking her share of the
spinning!" Her own spindle began to twirl again, and the reel sank slowly
toward the floor.

Morgaine shrugged. "It is true I had rather card wool, but there is no more to card," she said, and reluctantly took up the drop spindle.

"You are the best spinner among us, though," said Gwenhwyfar. "Your thread is always even and never breaks. Mine breaks if one looks at it."

"I have always been neat-handed. Perhaps I am simply tired of spinning, since my mother taught me when I was so young," Morgaine conceded, and began, reluctantly, to turn the thread in her fingers.

True—she hated spinning and shirked it when she could . . . twisting, turning the thread in her fingers, willing her body to stillness with only her fingers twisting as the reel turned and turned, sinking to the floor . . . down and then up, twist and twist between her hands . . . all too easy it was to sink into trance. The women were gossiping over the little affairs of the day, Meleas and her morning sickness, a woman who had come from Lot's court with scandalous tales of Lot's lechery . . . *I could tell them much if I would, not even his wife's niece escaped his lecherous hands. . . . It took me all my thought and sharp tongue to keep out of his bed; he cares not, maiden or matron, duchess or dairy maid, so it wears a skirt* . . . twist the thread, twist again, watch the spindle turning, turning. Gwydion must be a great boy by now, three years old, ready for a toy sword and wooden knights such as she had made for Gareth, instead of pet kittens and knucklebones. She remembered Arthur's weight on her lap when she was a little girl here at Caerleon in Uther's court . . . how fortunate it was that Gwydion did not resemble his father; a small replica of Arthur at Lot's court would have made tongues wag indeed. Soon or late, someone would still put together reel and spindle and spin the right thread to the answer. . . . Morgaine jerked her head up angrily. It was all too easy to fall into trance at the spinning, but she must do her share, there must be thread to weave this winter, and the ladies were making a cloth for banquets. . . . Cai was not the only man under fifty in the castle; there was Kevin the Bard, who had come here with news from the Summer Country . . . how slowly the spindle moved toward the floor . . . twist, twist the thread, as if her fingers had life of their own, apart from her own life . . . even in Avalon she had hated to spin . . . in Avalon among the priestesses she had tried to take more than her share of the work among the dye pots, to avoid the hated spinning, which sent her mind roaming as her fingers moved . . . as the thread turned, it was like the spiral dance along the Tor, round and round, as the world turned round the sun in the sky, though ignorant folk thought it was the other way. . . . Things were not always as they seemed, it might be that the reel went round the thread, as the thread went round itself over and over, spinning like a serpent . . . like a dragon in the sky . . . if she were a man and could ride out with the Caerleon legion, at least she need not sit and spin, spin, spin, round and round . . . but even

the Caerleon legion went round the Saxons, and the Saxons went round
them, round and round, as the blood went round in their veins, red blood
flooding, flooding . . . spilling over the hearth—
    Morgaine heard her own shriek only after it had shattered the silence
in the room. She dropped the spindle, which rolled away into the blood
which flooded crimson, spilling, spurting over the hearth. . . .
    "Morgaine! Sister, did you prick your hand on the reel? What ails
you?"
    "Blood on the hearth—" Morgaine stammered. "See, there, there, just
before the King's high seat, slain there like a slaughtered sheep before the
King . . ."
    Elaine shook her; dizzied, Morgaine passed her hand before her eyes.
There was no blood, only the slow crawl of the afternoon sun.
    "Sister, what did you see?" asked Gwenhwyfar gently.
    Mother Goddess! It has happened again! Morgaine tried to steady her
breathing. "Nothing, nothing . . . I must have fallen asleep and dreamed for
a moment."
    "Didn't you see anything?" Calla, the fat wife of the steward, peered
avidly at Morgaine. Morgaine remembered the last time, more than a year
ago, when she had gone into trance over her spinning and foreseen that Cai's
favorite horse had broken its leg in the stables and must have its throat cut.
She said impatiently, "No, nothing but a dream—I dreamed last night of
eating goose and I have not tasted it since Easter! Must every dream be a
portent?"
    "If you are going to prophesy, Morgaine," teased Elaine, "you should
tell us something sensible, like, when will the men be home so we may have
the wine warmed, or whether Meleas is making swaddling bands for a girl
or a boy, or when the Queen will get pregnant!"
    "Shut up, you beast," hissed Calla, for Gwenhwyfar's eyes had filled
with tears. Morgaine's head was splitting with the aftermath of unsought
trance; it seemed that little lights were crawling before her eyes, pale shining
worms of color that would grow and spread over her whole field of vision.
She knew she should let it pass, but even as that knowledge crossed her mind,
she exploded, "I am so weary of that old jest! I am no village wise-woman,
to meddle with birth charms and love potions and foretellings and spells.
I am a priestess, not a witch!"
    "Come, come," Meleas said peacefully. "Let Morgaine be. This sun is
enough to make anyone see things that are not there; even if she did see
blood spilt on the hearth, it is just as like that some lack-witted serving-man
will overset a half-roasted joint here, and the red gravy spill down! Will
you drink, lady?" She went to the bucket of water, dipped the ladle and
held it out, and Morgaine drank thirstily. "I never heard that most prophecy

came to aught—one might as well ask her when Elaine's father will finally catch and slay that dragon he goes off to pursue, in and out of season."

Predictably, the diversion worked. Calla jested, "If there was ever a dragon at all, and he was not merely seeking an excuse to go abroad from home when he was weary of the hearth!"

"If I were a man, and wedded to Pellinore's lady," Alienor said, "I might well prefer the company of a dragon I could not find, to the company of one in my bed."

"Tell me, Elaine," asked Meleas, "is there truly a dragon, or does your father follow it because it is simpler than seeing to his cows? Men need not sit and spin when there is war, but when there is peace, they may grow weary of the fowlyard and the pastures, I suppose."

"I have never seen the dragon," Elaine said. "God forbid. But *something* takes the cows from time to time, and once I did see a great slime trail in the fields, and smell the stench; and a cow lay there quite eaten away, and covered with a foul slime. Not the work of a wolf, that, nor even a glutton."

"Cows vanishing," jeered Calla. "The fairy folk are not, I suppose, too good Christians to steal a cow now and then, when the deer are not to be found."

"And speaking of cows," Gwenhwyfar said firmly, "I think I must ask Cai whether there is a sheep or a kid for slaughter. We need meat. Should the men come home this night or tomorrow, we cannot feed them all on porridge and buttered bread! And even the butter is beginning to fail in this heat. Come with me, Morgaine. I would that your Sight could tell me when we shall have rain! All of you, clear the thread and wool from the benches here, and put the work away. Elaine, child, take my embroidery work to my chamber and see that nothing spots it."

As they went toward the hallway, she said, low, "Did you truly see blood, Morgaine?"

"I dreamed," repeated Morgaine stubbornly.

Gwenhwyfar looked at her sharply, but there was real affection between them sometimes, and she did not pursue the subject. "If you did, God grant it be Saxon blood, and spilt far from this hearth. Come, let us ask Cai about the stock kept for meat. It is no season for hunting, and I have no wish to have the men about and hunting here when they come again." She yawned. "I wish the heat would break. We might yet have a thunderstorm—the milk was soured this morning. I should tell the maids to make clabber cheese with what's left of it, not throw it to the pigs."

"You are a notable housewife, Gwenhwyfar," Morgaine said wryly. "I would not have thought of that, so that it was out of my sight; but the smell of curd cheese clings so to the dairies! I would rather have the pigs well fattened."

"They are fat enough in this weather, with all the acorns ripe," said Gwenhwyfar, looking at the sky again. "Look, is that a flash of lightning?"

Morgaine followed her eyes, seeing the streak of glare across the sky. "Aye. The men will come home wet and cold, we should have hot wine ready for them," she said absentmindedly, then started, as Gwenhwyfar blinked.

"Now do I believe, indeed, that you have the Sight—certainly there is no sound of hooves nor no word from the watchtower," Gwenhwyfar said. "I will tell Cai to be sure there is meat, anyway." And she went along the yard, while Morgaine stood, pressing her aching head with one hand.

This is not good. At Avalon she had learned to control the Sight, not let it slip upon her unawares, when she was not attending. . . . Soon she would be a village witch indeed, peddling charms and prophesying boy- or girl-children and new lovers for the maidens, from sheer boredom at the pettiness of life among the women. The gossip bored her to spinning, the spinning beguiled her into trance. . . . *One day, no doubt, I would sink low enough to give Gwenhwyfar the charm she wants, so that she may bear Arthur a son . . . barrenness is a heavy burden for a queen, and only once in these two years has she shown any sign of breeding.*

Yet she found Gwenhwyfar's company, and Elaine's, endurable; most of the other women had never had a single thought beyond the next meal or the next reel of thread spun. Gwenhwyfar and Elaine had had some learning, and occasionally, sitting at ease with them, she could almost imagine herself peacefully among the priestesses in the House of Maidens.

The storm broke just before sunset—there was hail that clattered in the courtyard and bounced on the stones, there was drenching rain; and when the watchtower called down the news of riders, Morgaine never doubted that it was Arthur and his men. Gwenhwyfar called for torches to light the courtyard, and shortly after, the walls of Caerleon were bulging with men and horses. Gwenhwyfar had conferred with Cai and he had slaughtered not a kid, but sheep, so there was meat roasting and hot broth for the men. Most of the legion camped all through the outer court and the field, and like any commander, Arthur saw to the encampment of his men and the stabling of their horses before he came into the courtyard where Gwenhwyfar awaited him.

His head was bandaged under his helmet, and he leaned a little on Lancelet's arm, but he brushed away her anxious query.

"A skirmish—Jute raiders along the coast. The Saxons of the treaty troops had already cleaned most of them away before we came there. Ha! I smell roast mutton—is this magic, when you did not know we were coming?"

"Morgaine told me you would come, and there is hot wine as well," said Gwenhwyfar.

"Well, well, it is a boon to a hungry man to have a sister who is gifted with the Sight," said Arthur, with a jovial smile at Morgaine which rasped on her aching head and raw nerves. He kissed her, and turned back to Gwenhwyfar.

"You are hurt, my husband, let me see to it—"

"No, no, I tell you it is nothing. I never lose much blood, you know that, not while I bear this scabbard about me," he said, "but how is it with you, lady, after these many months? I had thought . . ."

Her eyes filled slowly with tears. "I was wrong again. Oh, my lord, this time I was so sure, so sure . . ."

He took her hand in his, unable to express his own disappointment in the face of his wife's pain. "Well, well, we must certainly get Morgaine to give you a charm," he said; but he watched, his face momentarily setting into grim lines, as Meleas welcomed Griflet with a wifely kiss, holding her young swollen body proudly forward. "We are not yet old folk, my Gwenhwyfar."

But, Gwenhwyfar thought, *I am not so young either. Most of the women I know, save for Morgaine and Elaine who are yet unwedded, have great boys and girls by the time they are twenty; Igraine bore Morgaine when she was full fifteen, and Meleas is fourteen and a half, no more!* She tried to look calm and unconcerned, but guilt gnawed within her. Whatever else a queen might do for her lord, her first duty was to give him a son, and she had not done that duty, though she had prayed till her knees ached.

"How does my dear lady?" Lancelet bowed before her, smiling, and she held him out her hand to kiss. "Once again we return home and find you only more beautiful than ever. You are the only lady whose beauty never fades. I begin to think God has ordered it so, that when all other women age and grow old and thick and worn, you shall be ever beautiful."

She smiled at him and felt comforted. Perhaps it was just as well that she was not pregnant and ugly . . . she saw that he looked on Meleas with a faint scornful smile, and she felt that she could not bear to be ugly before Lancelet. Even Arthur looked shabby, as if he had slept in the same crumpled tunic all through the campaign, and wrapped himself, in mud and rain and weather, in his fine, much-worn cloak; but Lancelet looked as crisp and new, his cloak and tunic as well brushed, as if he had dressed himself for an Easter feast—his hair trimmed and combed smooth, his leather belt polished, and even the eagle feathers in his cap standing up dry and unwilted. He looked, Gwenhwyfar thought, more like a king than Arthur himself did.

As the serving-maidens carried round platters of meat and bread, Arthur drew Gwenhwyfar to his side.

"Come sit here between Lancelet and me, Gwen, and we will talk—
it seems long since I heard a voice that was not rough and male, or smelled
the scent of a woman's gown." He passed his hand over her braid. "Come
you too, Morgaine, and sit by me—I am weary of campaigning, I want to
hear small gossip, not the talk of the camp!" He bit into a chunk of bread
with eager hunger. "And it is good to eat new-baked bread; I am tired of
hard-baked army bread, and meat gone bad by keeping!"

Lancelet had turned to smile at Morgaine.

"And you, how is it with you, kinswoman? I suppose there is no news
from the Summer Country, or from Avalon? There is another here who is
eager to hear it, if there is—my brother Balan rode with us."

"I have no news from Avalon," said Morgaine, feeling Gwenhwyfar
watching her—or was she looking at Lancelet? "But I have not seen Balan
for many years—I suppose he would have later news than mine?"

"He is there," Lancelet said, gesturing toward the men in the hall.
"Arthur bid him to dine here as my kinsman, and it would be a kindness
in you, Morgaine, to take him a cup of wine from the high table. Like all
men, he too is eager for a welcome from some woman, even if it be a
kinswoman and not a sweetheart."

Morgaine took one of the drinking cups, horn bound with wood, that
sat on the high table, and beckoned a servant to pour wine into it; then she
raised it between her hands and went around the table among the knights.
She was pleasantly conscious of their regard, even though she knew they
would look like this at any well-bred, finely dressed woman after so many
months of campaign; it was not a particular compliment to her beauty. At
least Balan, who was a cousin, almost a brother, would not eye her so
hungrily.

"I greet you, kinsman. Lancelet, your brother, sent you some wine
from the King's table."

"I beg you to sip it first, lady," he said, then blinked. "Morgaine, is
it you? I hardly knew you, you have grown so fine. I think of you always
in the dress of Avalon, but you are like to my mother, indeed. How does
the Lady?"

Morgaine set the cup to her lips—mere courtesy at this court, but
perhaps stemming from a time when gifts from the King were tasted before
a guest, when the poisoning of rival kings was not unknown. She handed
it to him, and Balan drank a long draught before looking up at her again.

"I had hoped to have news of Viviane from you, kinsman—I have not
returned to Avalon for many years," she said.

"Aye, I knew that you were in Lot's court," he said. "Did you quarrel
with Morgause? I hear that is easy done by any woman. . . ."

Morgaine shook her head. "No; but I wished to be far enough away to stay out of Lot's bed, and that is *not* easy done. The distance between Orkney and Caerleon is hardly far enough."

"And so you came to Arthur's court to be waiting-woman to his queen," said Balan. "It is a more seemly court than that of Morgause, I dare say. Gwenhwyfar guards her maidens well, and makes good marriages for them, too—I see Griflet's lady is already big with her first. Has she not found you a husband, kinswoman?"

Morgaine forced herself to say gaily, "Are you making an offer for me, sir Balan?"

He chuckled. "You are all too close kin to me, Morgaine, or I should accept your offer. But I heard some gossip that Arthur had intended you for Cai, and that seemed a good match to me, since you have left Avalon after all."

"Cai had no more mind to me than I to him," said Morgaine sharply, "and I have never said I would not return to Avalon, but only on that day when Viviane sends for me to come thither."

"When I was but a lad," Balan said—and for a moment, his dark eyes resting on Morgaine, she thought that indeed she could see the resemblance to Lancelet even in this great coarse man—"I thought ill of the Lady—of Viviane, that she did not love me as it was fit for a mother to do. But I think better of it now. As a priestess, she could not have had leisure to rear a son. And so she gave me into the hands of one who had no other work than that, and she gave me my foster-brother Balin. . . . Oh, yes, as a lad I felt guilty about that too, that I cared more for Balin than for our Lancelet, who is of my own flesh and blood. But now I know Balin is truly my own heart's brother, and Lancelet, though I admire him for the fine knight he is, will always be a stranger to me. And too," Balan said seriously, "when Viviane gave me up to Dame Priscilla for fostering, she put me into a household where I would come to know the true God and Christ. It seems to me strange, that if I had dwelt in Avalon with my own kin, I should be a heathen, even as Lancelet is. . . ."

Morgaine smiled a little. "Well," she said, "there I cannot share your gratitude, for I think it ill done of the Lady that her own son should abandon her Gods. But even Viviane has often said to me that men should have such manner of religious and spiritual counsel as liked them best, that which she could give, or other. Had I been truly pious and Christian at heart, no doubt, she would have let me live by the faith which was strong in my heart. Yet, though I was reared till I was eleven by Igraine, who was as good a Christian as any, I think perhaps it was ordained that I should see the things of the spirit as they come to us from the Goddess."

"Balin would be able to argue that with you better than I," said Balan, "for he is more pious than I and a better Christian. I should probably say to you what no doubt the priests have said, that there is only one true faith in which man and woman may trust. But you are my kinswoman, and I know my mother to be a good woman, and I have faith that even Christ will take her goodness into account on the last day. As for the rest, I am no priest and I see not why I should not leave all those matters to the priests who are schooled in them. I love Balin well, but he should have been a priest, not a warrior, if he is so tender of faith and conscience." He looked toward the high table and said, "Tell me, foster-sister, you know him better than I—what lies so heavy on our brother Lancelet's heart?"

Morgaine bent her head and said, "If I knew, Balan, it is not my secret to tell."

"You are right to bid me mind my own affairs," said Balan, "but I hate seeing him miserable, and miserable he is. I thought ill of our mother, as I said, because she sent me so young from home, but she gave me a loving foster-mother, and a brother of my own age, reared at my side and as one with me in all things, and a home. She did less well by Lancelet. He was never at home—neither in Avalon nor yet at the court of Ban of Benwick, where he was dragged up as just another of the king's unregarded bastards. . . . Viviane did ill by him indeed, and I wish Arthur would give him a wife, so he might have a home at last."

"Well," said Morgaine lightly, "if the King wishes me to wed Lancelet, he need only name the day."

"You and Lancelet? Are you not too close kin for that?" Balan asked, then thought for a moment. "No, I suppose not—Igraine and Viviane were but half-sisters, and Gorlois and Ban of Benwick are not in any way akin. Though some of the church folk say foster-kin should be treated as blood kin for marriage . . . well, Morgaine, I will drink to your wedding with pleasure on that day Arthur gives you to my brother, and bids you love him and care for him as Viviane never did! And neither of you need leave court—you the Queen's favorite lady and Lancelet our King's dearest friend. I hope it comes to pass!" His eyes dwelt on her with kindly concern. "You too are well past the age when Arthur should give you to some man."

And why should it be for the King to give me, as if I were one of his horses or dogs? Morgaine wondered, but shrugged; she had lived long in Avalon, she forgot at times that the Romans had made this the common law, that women were the chattels of their menfolk. The world had changed and there was no point in rebelling against what could not be altered.

Soon after she began to skirt the edges of the great mead table which had been Gwenhwyfar's wedding gift to Arthur. The great hall here in Caerleon, large as it was, was not really large enough; at one point she had to clamber over the benches because the table pushed them so close to the wall, to get by the great curve of it. The pot boys and kitchen boys, too, had to sidle past with their smoking platters and cups.

"Is Kevin not here?" asked Arthur. "Then we must have Morgaine to sing for us—I am hungry too for harps and all the things of civilized men. I am not surprised the Saxons spend all their time in making war. I have heard the dismal howling of their singers, and they have no reason to stay home!"

Morgaine asked one of Cai's helpers around the castle to fetch her harp from her chamber. He had to climb around the curve of the bench, and lost his footing; only the quickness of Lancelet, reaching out to steady boy and harp, kept the instrument from falling.

Arthur frowned. "It was good of my father-in-law to send me this great round mead table," he said, "but there is no chamber in Caerleon large enough for it. When the Saxons are driven away for good, I think I must build a hall just to hold it!"

"Then will it never be built." Cai laughed. "To say 'when the Saxons are driven away for good' is like to saying 'when Jesus shall come again' or 'when Hell freezes' or 'when raspberries grow on the apple trees of Glastonbury.' "

"Or when King Pellinore catches his dragon," Meleas giggled.

Arthur smiled. "You must not make fun of Pellinore's dragon," he said, "for there is word it has been seen again, and he is off to find it and slay it this time—indeed, he asked the Merlin if he knew any dragon-catching spells!"

"Oh, aye, it has been seen—like a troll on the hills, turned to stone by daylight, or the ring stones dancing on the night of the full moon," Lancelet gibed. "There are always people who see whatever vision they will —some see saints and miracles, and some see dragons or the old fairy folk. But never did I know of living man or woman who had seen either dragon or fairy."

Morgaine remembered, against her will, the day in Avalon when she had gone searching for roots and herbs and strayed into the strange country where the fairy woman had spoken with her and had sought to foster her child . . . what, indeed, had she seen? Or had it been only the sick fantasy of a breeding woman?

"You say that, when you were yourself fostered as Lancelet of the Lake?" she asked quietly, and Lancelet turned round to her. He said, "There are times when that seems unreal to me—is it not so for you, sister?"

She said, "It is true indeed, but at times I am homesick for Avalon. . . ."

"Aye, and I too, kinswoman," he said. Never since that night of Arthur's marriage, by word or look had he implied that he had ever felt anything more for her than for a childhood companion and foster-sister. She had thought she had long accepted the pain of that, but it struck her anew as his dark, beautiful eyes met hers in such kindness.

Soon or late, it must seem even as Balan said: we are both unmarried, the King's sister and his best friend. . . .

Arthur said, "Well, when the Saxons are driven away for good—and do not laugh as if that were a fabulous event! It can be done, now, and I think they know it—then I shall build myself a castle, and a great hall big enough for even this table. I have already chosen the site—it is a hill fort which was there long before Roman times, looking down on the Lake itself, and near to your father's island kingdom, Gwenhwyfar. You know the place, where the river flows into the Lake—"

"I know," she said. "When I was a small child I went there one day to pick strawberries. There was an old ruined well, and we found elf bolts there. The old folk who lived on the chalk had left their arrows." How strange, Gwenhwyfar thought, to remember that there had been a time when she had liked to go abroad under the wide, high sky, not even caring whether there was a wall or the safety of an enclosure; and now she grew sick and dizzy if she went out from the walls, where she could not see or touch them. Sometimes now she felt the lump of fear in her belly even when she walked across the courtyard, and had to hurry to touch the safety of the wall again.

"It is an easy place to fortify," Arthur said, "though I hope, when we are done with the Saxons, we may have leisure and peace in this island."

"An ignoble wish for a warrior, brother," said Cai. "What will you do in time of peace?"

"I will call Kevin the Bard to make songs, and I will break my own horses and ride them for pleasure," Arthur said. "My Companions and I will raise our sons without putting a sword in every little hand before it is full grown to manhood! And I need not fear they will be lamed or slain before they are full grown. Cai—would it not be better if you need not have been sent to war before you were old enough to guard yourself? Sometimes I feel it wrong that it was you, not I, who was lamed, because Ectorius wanted me kept safe for Uther!" He looked with concern and affection at his foster-brother, and Cai grinned back at him.

"And," said Lancelet, "we will keep the arts of war alive by holding games, as they did in the days of the ancients, and crown the winner of the games with laurel wreaths—what is laurel, Arthur, and does it grow in these islands? Or is it only in the land of Achilles and Alexander?"

"The Merlin could tell you that," Morgaine said, when Arthur looked perplexed. "I know not either, but whether or no we have laurel, there are plants enough to make wreaths for the victors at your games."

"And we will give garlands to harpers too," Lancelet said. "Sing, Morgaine."

"I had better sing for you now," Morgaine said, "for I do not suppose, when you men hold your games, you will let women sing." She took up the harp and began to play. She was sitting nearly where she had been sitting this afternoon when she saw blood spilled forth on the King's hearth . . . would it truly come to pass, or was it fantasy? Why, indeed, should she think she still possessed the Sight? It never came upon her now save in these unwelcome trances. . . .

She began to sing an ancient lament which she had heard at Tintagel, a lament of a fisherwoman who had seen the boats swept out to sea. She knew that she held them all with her voice, and in the silence of the hall she fell to singing old songs of the islands, which she had heard at Lot's court: a legend of the seal woman who had come out of the sea to find a mortal lover, songs of the solitary women herders, songs for spinning and for carding flax. Even when her voice grew weary they called for more, but she held up her hand in protest.

"Enough—no, truly, I can sing no more. I am hoarse as any raven."

Soon after, Arthur called the servants to extinguish the torches in the hall and light the guests to bed. It was one of Morgaine's tasks to see that the unmarried women who waited on the Queen were safely put to sleep in the long loft room behind the Queen's own chamber, at the opposite end of the building from the soldiers and armsmen. But she lingered a moment, her eyes on Arthur and Gwenhwyfar, who were bidding Lancelet good night.

"I have told the women to prepare the best spare bed for you, Lancelet," said Gwenhwyfar, but he laughed and shook his head.

"I am a soldier—it is my duty to see horses and men bedded safe for the night before I sleep."

Arthur chuckled, his arm around Gwenhwyfar's waist. "We must get you married, Lance, then you will not spend your nights so cold. I made you my captain of horse, but you need not spend your nights lying down among them!"

Gwenhwyfar felt a pain within her breast as she met Lancelet's eyes. It seemed to her that she could almost read his thoughts, that he would say aloud again, as he had said once, *My heart is so full of my queen I have no room there for any other lady.* . . . She held her breath, but Lancelet only sighed and smiled at her, and she thought, *No, I am a wedded wife, a Christian woman, it is sin even to think such thoughts; I must do penance.* And then, feeling her throat so tight she could not swallow, she felt the thought come unbidden. *Penance enough that I must be apart from the one I love* . . . and she gasped aloud, so that Arthur turned startled eyes on her.

"What is it, love, have you hurt yourself?"

"A—a pin pricked me," she said, and turned her eyes away, pretending to hunt for the pin at the folds of her dress. She saw Morgaine watching her, and bit her lip. *She is always watching me . . . and she has the Sight; does she know all my sinful thoughts? Is that why she looks on me so scornfully?*

Yet Morgaine had never shown her anything but a sister's kindness. And when she had been pregnant, in the first year of their marriage—when she had taken a fever and miscarried the child within five months—she could not bear to have any of her ladies about her, and Morgaine had cared for her almost like a mother. Why, now, was she so ungrateful?

Lancelet bade them good night again, and withdrew. Gwenhwyfar was almost painfully conscious of Arthur's arm around her waist, the frank eagerness in his eyes. Well, they had been apart a long time. But she felt a sudden, sharp resentment. *Not once, since that time, have I been pregnant —can he not even give me a child?*

Oh, but surely that was her own fault—one of the midwives had told her it was like a sickness in cattle when they cast their calves unborn, time after time, and sometimes women took that sickness too, so they could not carry a child more than a month or two, three at the most. Somehow, through carelessness, she must have taken that illness, gone perhaps into the dairy at the wrong time, or drunk of milk from a cow who had cast her calf, and so the life of her lord's son and heir had been forfeit, and it was all her doing. . . . Torn with guilt, she followed Arthur into their chamber.

"It is more than a jest, Gwen," said Arthur, sitting to draw off his leather hose. "We must get Lancelet married. Have you seen how all the lads run to him, and how good he is with them? He should have sons of his own. I have it, Gwen! We will marry him to Morgaine!"

"No!" The word was torn from her before she thought, and Arthur looked at her, startled.

"What is the matter with you? Does it not seem perfect, the right choice? My dear sister and my best friend? And their children, mark you, would be next heirs to our throne in any case, if it should be that the Gods send us no children. . . . No, no, don't cry, my love," he begged, and Gwenhwyfar knew, humiliated and shamed, that her face had twisted with weeping. "I meant not to reproach you, my dearest love, children come when the Goddess wills, but only she knows when we will have children, or if we will ever have them at all. And although Gawaine is dear to me, I have no will to put a son of Lot on the throne if I should die. Morgaine is my own mother's child, and Lancelet my cousin—"

"Surely it cannot matter to Lancelet whether or no he has sons," said Gwenhwyfar. "He is fifth—or is it sixth—son to King Ban, and bastard-born at that."

"I never thought to hear you, of all people, reproach my kinsman and dearest friend with his birth," Arthur said. "And he is no ordinary bastard, but son to the grove and the Great Marriage—"

"Pagan harlotries! If I were King Ban, I would clean all such sorcerous filth from my kingdom—and so should you!"

Arthur shifted uneasily, clambering under the bed cover. "Lancelet would have little cause to love me if I drove his mother from this kingdom. And I am sworn to honor Avalon, by the sword they gave me at my kingmaking."

Gwenhwyfar looked at the great sword Excalibur, where it hung over the edge of the bed in its magical scabbard covered with mystical symbols that seemed to shine with pale silver and mock at her. She put out the light and lay down beside Arthur, saying, "Our Lord Jesus would safeguard you better than any such wicked enchantments. *You* did not have to do with any of their vile Goddesses and sorcery before you were made King, did you? I know such things were done in Uther's day, but this is a Christian land!"

Arthur shifted uneasily and said, "There are many folk in this land, the Old People who dwelt here long before Rome came to us—we cannot take their Gods from them. And—what befell before my crowning—well, that touches you not, my Gwenhwyfar."

"Men cannot serve two masters," said Gwenhwyfar, surprised at her own daring. "I would have you altogether a Christian king, my lord."

"I owe allegiance to all my people," said Arthur, "not those alone who follow Christ—"

"It seems to me," said Gwenhwyfar, "that those are your enemies, not the Saxons. The true warfare for a Christian king is only against those who do not follow Christ."

Arthur laughed uneasily at that. "Now do you sound like the bishop Patricius. He would have us Christianize the Saxons rather than putting them to the sword, so that we may live at peace with them. For my part I am like to the priests who were here in the older days, who were asked to send missionaries to the Saxons—know you what they said, my wife?"

"No, I have never heard—"

"They said, they would send no missionaries to the Saxons, lest they be forced to meet them in peace, even before God's throne." Arthur laughed heartily, but Gwenhwyfar did not smile, and after a time he sighed.

"Well, think on it, my Gwenhwyfar. It seems to me the best possible marriage—my dearest friend and my sister. Then would he be my brother and his sons my heirs. . . ."

In the darkness his arms went round her, and he added, "But now we must strive to make it come to pass that we will need no other heirs, you and I, my love, but those you can give to me."

"God grant it," whispered Gwenhwyfar, moving into his arms, and tried to close away everything out of her mind but Arthur, here in her arms.

MORGAINE, lingering after she had seen the women to bed, stood near the window, restless. Elaine, who shared her bed, murmured to her, "Come and sleep, Morgaine; it is late, you must be weary."

She shook her head. "I think it is the moon that has gotten into my blood tonight—I am not sleepy." She was unwilling to lie down and close her eyes; even if she had not the Sight, it was her imagination which would torment her. All round her the newly returned men joined with their wives —she thought, with a wry smile in the darkness, it is like to Beltane in Avalon . . . even the soldiers who were not wedded, she was sure, had somehow found women for this night. Everyone, from the King with his wife down to the stablemen, lay in someone's arms tonight, except for the Queen's maidens; Gwenhwyfar thought it her duty to guard their chastity, even as Balan had said. *And I am guarded with the Queen's maidens.*

Lancelet, at Arthur's wedding . . . that had come to nothing, through no fault of their own. *And Lancelet has stayed away from the court as often as he might . . . no doubt, so that he need not see Gwenhwyfar in Arthur's arms! But he is here now* . . . and like herself, he was alone this night, among soldiers and horsemen, no doubt dreaming of the Queen, of the one woman in the kingdom he could not have. For surely every other woman at court, wedded or maiden, was as willing to have him as she herself. Save for bad fortune at Arthur's wedding, she would have had him; and honorable as he was, if he had made her pregnant, he would have married her.

❡ *Not that it is likely I would have conceived, with the harm I suffered at Gwydion's birth . . . but I need not have told him that. And I could have made him happy, even if I could not bear him a son. There was a time he wanted me, before ever he saw Gwenhwyfar, and after too . . . save for mischance, I would have made him forget her in my arms. . . .*

And I am not so undesirable as that . . . when I was singing tonight, many of the knights looked on me with desire. . . .

I could make Lancelet desire me. . . .

Elaine said impatiently, "Will you not come to bed, Morgaine?"

"Not yet awhile . . . I think I will walk a little out of doors," said Morgaine, though this was forbidden to the Queen's women, and Elaine shrank back, with that timidity which so exasperated Morgaine. She wondered if Elaine had caught it from the Queen like a fever, or a new fashion in wearing veils.

"Are you not afraid with all the men encamped about?"

Morgaine laughed. "Well, think you not I am weary of lying alone?" But she saw that the jest offended Elaine and said, more gently, "I am the King's sister. None would touch me against my will. Do you really think me so tempting no man could resist me? I am six-and-twenty, not a dainty young virgin like yourself, Elaine."

Morgaine lay down, without undressing, beside Elaine. In the darkness and silence, as she had feared, her imagination—or was it the Sight?—made pictures: Arthur with Gwenhwyfar, men with women all round her throughout the castle, joined in love or simple lust.

And Lancelet, was he alone too? Memory attacked her again, more intense than imagination, and she remembered that day, bright sunlight on the Tor, Lancelet's kisses running that first awakening knife-sharp through her body; and the bitterness of regret that she was pledged elsewhere. And then, when Arthur was wedded to Gwenhwyfar, and he had come near to tearing off her clothes and having her there in the stables—he had wanted her then. . . .

Now, sharp as the Sight, the picture came to her mind, Lancelet walking in the courtyard, alone, his face empty with loneliness and frustration . . . *I have not used the Sight nor my own magic to draw him to me in selfish purpose . . . it came to me unsought. . . .*

Silently, moving quietly so as not to waken the younger girl, she freed herself from Elaine's arm, slid gently from the bed. She had taken off only her shoes; she stooped now to draw them on, then silently went from the room, moving as noiselessly as a wraith from Avalon.

If it is a dream born of my own imagination, if he is not there, I will walk a little in the moonlight to cool my fever and then go back to my bed, there will be no harm done. But the picture persisted in her mind and she knew that Lancelet was there alone, like herself wakeful.

He too was of Avalon . . . *the sun tides run in his blood too. . . .* Morgaine, slipping quietly out of the door past the drowsing watchman, cast a glance at the sky. The moon, a quarter full, flooded down brightly into the stone-flagged space before the stables. No, not here; around to the side. . . . For a moment Morgaine thought, *He is not here, it was a dream, it was my own fantasy.* She almost turned about to go back to her bed, suddenly flooded with shame; suppose the watchman should come upon her here, and all would know that the King's sister crept about the house after all honest folk were asleep, no doubt bent on harlotries—

"Who is it? Stand, show yourself!" The voice was low and harsh; Lancelet's voice. Suddenly, for all her exultation, Morgaine was afraid; her Sight had shown truly, but what now? Lancelet's hand had gone to his sword; he looked very tall and thin in the shadows.

"Morgaine," she said softly, and he let his hand fall from his sword. "Cousin, is it you?"

She came out of the shadows, and his face, keen and troubled, softened as he looked at her.

"So late? Did you come to seek me—is there trouble within? Arthur —the Queen—"

Even now he thinks only of the Queen, Morgaine thought, and felt it like a tingling in her fingertips and the calves of her legs, anger and excitement. She said, "No, all is well—as far as I know. I am not privy to the secrets of the royal bedchamber!"

He flushed, just a shadow on his face in the darkness, and looked away from her. She said, "I could not sleep . . . how is it you ask me what I am doing here when you yourself are not in your bed? Or has Arthur made you his night watchman?"

She could sense Lancelet smile. "No more than you. I was restless when all around me slept—I think perhaps the moon has gotten into my blood."

It was the same phrase she had used to Elaine, and somehow it struck her as a good omen, a symbol that their minds worked in tune and that they responded one to the call of the other as a silent harp vibrates when a note on another is struck.

Lancelet went on, speaking softly into the darkness at her side, "I am restless these nights, thinking of so many nights of battle—"

"And you wish yourself back in battle like all soldiers?"

He sighed. "No. Although perhaps it is unworthy of a soldier to dream early and late of peace."

"I do not think so," Morgaine said softly. "For what do you make war, except that peace may come for all our people? If a soldier loves his trade overmuch, then he becomes no more than a weapon for killing. What else brought the Romans to our peaceful isle, but the love of conquest and battle for its own sake?"

Lancelet smiled. "Your father was one of those Romans, cousin. So was mine."

"Yet I think more of the peaceful Tribes, who wanted no more than to till their barley crops in peace and worship the Goddess. I am of my mother's people—and yours."

"Aye, but those mighty heroes of old we spoke of before—Achilles, Alexander—they all felt war and battle the proper business of a man, and even now, in these islands, it has come to be that all men think of battle first and peace as no more than a quiet and womanly interlude." He sighed. "These are heavy thoughts—it is no wonder sleep is far from us, Morgaine. Tonight I would give all the great weapons ever forged, and all the gallant songs of your Achilles and Alexanders for an apple from the branches of

Avalon. . . ." He turned his head away. Morgaine slipped her hand within his own.

"So would I, cousin."

"I do not know why I am homesick for Avalon—I did not live long there," Lancelet said, musing. "And yet I think it is the fairest place on all earth—if indeed it is on this earth at all. The old Druid magic, I think, took it from this world, because it was all too fair for us imperfect men, and must be like a dream of Heaven, impossible . . ." He recalled himself with a little laugh. "My confessor would not like to hear me say these things!"

Morgaine chuckled, low. "Have you become a Christian then, Lance?"

"Not a good one, I fear," he said. "Yet their faith seems to me so simple and good, I wish I could believe it—they say: believe what you have not seen, profess what you do not know, that is more virtuous than believing what you have seen. Even Jesus, they say, when he rose from the dead, chided a man who would have thrust his hands into the Christ's wounds to see that he was not a ghost or a spirit, for it was more blessed to believe without seeing."

"But we shall all rise again," said Morgaine, very low, "and again and again and again. We do not come once and go to Heaven or their Hell, but live again and again until we are even as the Gods."

He lowered his head. Now that her eyes were accustomed to the dimness of the moonlight, she could see him clearly, the delicate line of temple curving inward at the eye, the long, narrow sweep of the jaw, the soft darkness of his brows and his hair curling over it. Again his beauty made a pain in her heart. He said, "I had forgotten you were a priestess, and you believe. . . ."

Their hands were clasped lightly; she felt his stir within her own and loosed it. "Sometimes I do not know what I believe. Perhaps I have been too long away from Avalon."

"Nor do I know what I believe," he said, "but I have seen so many men die, and women and little children in this long, long war, it seems that I have been fighting since I grew tall enough to hold a sword. And when I see them die, I think faith is an illusion, and the truth is that we all die as the beasts die, and are no more ever—like grass cut down, and last year's snow."

"But these things too return again," Morgaine whispered.

"Do they? Or is this the illusion?" His voice sounded bitter. "I think perhaps there is no meaning in any of it—all the talk of Gods and the Goddess are fables to comfort children. Ah, God, Morgaine, why are we talking like this? You should go to your rest, cousin, and so should I—"

"I will go if you wish it," she said, and even as she turned away, happiness surged through her because he reached for her hand.

"No, no—when I am alone I fall prey to these fancies and wretched doubts, and if they must come I would rather speak them aloud so I can hear what folly they are. Stay with me, Morgaine—"

"As long as you wish," she whispered, and felt tears in her eyes. She reached out and put her arms around his waist; his strong arms tightened about her, then loosened, remorsefully.

"You are so little—I had forgotten how little you are—I could break you with my two hands, cousin. . . ." His hands strayed to her hair, which she had bundled loose under her veil. He stroked it; twined an end of it around his fingers. "Morgaine, Morgaine, sometimes it seems to me that you are one of the few things in my life which is all good—like one of those old fairy folk they tell of in legends, the elf-woman who comes from the unknown land to speak words of beauty and hope to a mortal, then departs again for the islands of the West and is never seen again—"

"But I will not depart," she whispered.

"No." At one side of the flagged yard there was a block where sometimes men sat waiting for their horses; he drew her toward it and said, "Sit here beside me—" then hesitated. "No, this is no place for a lady—" and started to laugh. "Nor was the stable that day—do you remember, Morgaine?"

"I thought you had forgotten, after that devil horse threw you—"

"You should not call him devil. He has saved Arthur's life in battle more than once, and Arthur would think him guardian angel instead," Lancelet said. "Ah, that was a day of wretchedness. I would have wronged you, cousin, to take you like that. I have often longed to beg your pardon and hear you grant me forgiveness and say you bore me no malice—"

"Malice?" She looked up at him and felt suddenly dizzied by the rush of intense emotion. "Malice? Only, perhaps, to those who interrupted us—"

"Is it so?" His voice was soft. He took her face between his hands and bent, deliberately, laying his lips against hers. Morgaine let herself go soft against him, opening her mouth beneath his lips. He was clean-shaven, in the Roman fashion, and she felt the prickly softness of his face against her cheek, the warm sweetness of his tongue probing her mouth. He drew her closer, almost lifting her from her feet, making a soft murmuring sound. The kiss went on until she finally, reluctantly, had to move her mouth to breathe, and he laughed softly, a sound of wonder.

"So here we are again . . . it seems we have been here before . . . and this time I will cut off the head of any that interrupts us . . . but we stand here kissing in the stable yard like serving-man and kitchen wench! What now, Morgaine? Where do we go?"

She did not know—there was not any place, it seemed, secure for them. She could not take him to her room where she slept with Elaine and four of Gwenhwyfar's maidens, and Lancelet himself had said he preferred to sleep among the soldiers. And something at the back of her mind told her that this was not the way; the King's sister and the King's friend should not go seeking a hayloft. The proper way, if truly they felt this about each other, was to wait until dawn and ask Arthur's permission to marry. . . .

Yet in her heart, hidden away so that she need not look at it, she knew that this was not what Lancelet wanted; in a moment of passion he might desire her indeed, but no more. And for a moment of passion, would she entrap him into a lifelong pledge? The way of the tribal festivals was more honest, that man and woman should come together with the sun tides and moon tides in their blood, as the Goddess willed; and only if they wished, later, to share a home and rear children was marriage thought upon. She knew in her heart, too, that she had no real wish to marry Lancelet or any other—even though she felt, for his own sake, and Arthur's, and even for Gwenhwyfar's, it would be best to remove him from the court.

But that was a fleeting thought. She was dizzy with his closeness, the sound of his heart pounding against her cheek—he wanted her; there was not, now, in his heart, any thought of Gwenhwyfar or anyone but herself.

Let it be with us as the Goddess wills, man and woman—

"I know," she whispered, and caught at his hand. Around behind the stables and the forge there was a path leading to the orchard. The grass was thick and soft and sometimes the women sat there on a bright afternoon.

Lancelet spread his cloak in the grass. Around them was the indefinable scent of green apples and grass, and Morgaine thought, *Almost, we might be in Avalon.* With that trick he had of catching up her thoughts, he murmured, "We have found ourselves a corner of Avalon this night—" and drew her down beside him. He took off her veil, stroking her hair, but he seemed in no haste for more, holding her gently, now and again leaning down to kiss her on cheek or forehead.

"The grass is dry—no dew has fallen. Like enough there will be rain before morning," he murmured, caressing her shoulder and her small hands. She felt his hand, sword-callused and hard, so hard that it startled her to remember he was full four years younger than she was herself. She had heard the story—he had been born when Viviane thought herself well beyond childbearing. His long fingers could encircle her whole hand and conceal it there; he toyed with her fingers, playing with her rings, moving his hand to the breast of her gown, and unlacing it there. She felt dizzied, shaken, passion sweeping through her like the tide surging in and covering a beach, so that she went under and drowned in his kisses. He murmured something that she could not hear, but she did not ask what he had said, she was beyond listening to words.

He had to help her out of her gown. The dresses worn at court were more elaborate than the simple robes she had worn as a priestess, and she felt clumsy, awkward. Would he like her? Her breasts seemed so soft and limp, they had been so since Gwydion's birth; she remembered how they had been when he first touched her, tiny and hard.

But he seemed to notice nothing, fondling her breasts, taking the nipples between his fingers and then, gently, between his lips and his teeth. Then she lost thought altogether, nothing existing in the world for her except his hands touching her, the pulse of awareness in her own fingers running down the smoothness of his shoulders, his back, the fine dark softness of the hair there . . . somehow she had thought the hair on a man's chest would be wiry and coarse, but it was not so with him, it was soft and silky as her own hair, curling so fine and close. In a daze she remembered that the first time for her had been with a youth no more than seventeen who scarce knew what he was about, so that she had had to guide him, to show him what to do . . . and for her that had been the only time, so that she came almost virgin to Lancelet. . . . In a rush of grief she wished that for her it *was* the first time, so that it might have been so blissful for her to remember; it should have been like this, this was how it should have been. . . . She moved her body against his, clinging in entreaty, moaning, she could not bear, now, to wait any longer. . . .

It seemed he was not yet ready, though she was all alive to him, her body flowing with the pulse of life and desire in her. She moved against him, hungry, her mouth avid, entreating. She whispered his name, begging now, almost afraid. He went on kissing her gently, his hands moving to stroke and soothe her, but she did not want to be soothed now, her body was crying out for completion, it was starvation, agony. She tried to speak, to beg him, but it came out a sobbing whimper.

He held her gently against him, still stroking her. "Hush, no, hush, Morgaine, wait, no more now—I do not want to hurt or dishonor you, never think that—here, lie here by me, let me hold you, I will content you . . ." and in despair and confusion she let him do what he would, but even while her body cried out for the pleasure he gave her, a curious anger was growing. What of the flow of life between their two bodies, male and female, the tides of the Goddess rising and compelling them? Somehow it seemed to her that he was stemming that tide, that he was making her love for him a mockery and a game, a pretense. And he did not seem to mind, it seemed to him that this was the way it should be, so that they were both pleasured . . . as if nothing mattered but their bodies, that there was no greater joining with all of life. To the priestess, reared in Avalon and attuned to the greater tides of life and eternity, this careful, sensuous, deliberate lovemaking seemed almost blasphemy, a refusal to give themselves up to the will of the Goddess.

And then, in the depths of mingled pleasure and humiliation she began to excuse him. He had not been reared as she was in Avalon, but thrown about from fosterage to court to military camp; he had been a soldier almost as long as he had been old enough to lift a sword, his life had been spent in the field, perhaps he did not know, or perhaps he was accustomed only to such women as would give him no more than a moment's ease for his body, or such women as wanted to toy with lovemaking and give nothing . . . he had said, *I do not want to hurt or dishonor you,* as if he truly believed there could be something wrong or dishonorable in this coming together. Spent, now, he was turned a little away from her, but he was still touching her, toying with her, drawing his fingers through the fine hair at her thighs, kissing her neck and breasts. She closed her eyes, holding herself to him, angry and desolate—well, well, perhaps it was no more than she deserved, she had played the harlot in coming to him like this, perhaps it was no more than her due that he should treat her as one . . . and she was so besotted that she had let him take her like this, she would have let him do whatever he would, knowing that if she asked for more she would lose even this, and she longed for him, she still hungered for him with an intolerable ache that would never be wholly slaked. And he wanted her not at all . . . still in his heart he hungered for Gwenhwyfar, or for some woman he could have without giving more of himself than this empty touching of skins . . . a woman who could be content to give herself and ask nothing more of him than pleasure. Through the ache and hunger of her love, a faint strain of contempt was threading, and it was the greatest agony of all—that she loved him no less, that she knew she would love him always, no less than at this moment of hunger and despair.

She sat up, drawing her gown toward her, fastening it over her shoulders with shaking fingers. He sat silent, watching her, stretching out his hands to help her adjust it. After a long time he said sorrowfully, "We have done wrong, my Morgaine, you and I. Are you angry with me?"

She could not speak; her throat was too tight with pain. At last she said, straining her voice to form the words, "No, not angry," and she knew that she should raise her voice and scream at him, demand what he could not give her—nor any woman, perhaps.

"You are my cousin, my kinswoman—but there is no harm done—" he said, and his voice was shaking. "At least I have not that to blame myself—

that I could bring you to dishonor before all the court—I would not do so for the world—believe me, cousin, I love you well—"

She could not keep back her sobs now. "Lancelet, I beg you, in the name of the Goddess, speak not so—what harm is done? It was in the way of the Goddess, what we both desired—"

He made a gesture of distress. "You speak so, of the Goddess and such heathen things. . . . Almost you frighten me, kinswoman, when I would keep myself from sin, and yet I have looked on you with lust and wickedness, knowing it was wrong." He drew on his clothes with trembling hands. At last he said, almost choking, "The sin seems to me more deadly, I suppose, than it is—I would you were not so like to my mother, Morgaine—"

It was like a blow in the face, like a cruel and treacherous blow. For a moment she could not speak. Then, for an instant, it seemed that the full rage of the Goddess angered possessed her and she felt herself rising, towering, she knew it was the glamour of the Goddess coming upon her as it had done in the Avalon barge; she felt herself, small and insignificant as she was, looming over him, and saw the powerful knight, the captain of the King's horse, shrink away small and frightened, as all men are small in the sight of the Goddess.

"You are—you are a contemptible fool, Lancelet," she said. "You are not even worth cursing!" She turned and fled from him, leaving him sitting there with his breeches half-fastened, staring after her in astonishment and shame. She felt her heart pounding. Half of her had wanted to scream at him, shrewish as a skua gull; the other half wanted to break down and weep in agony, in despair, begging for the deeper love he had denied her and rejected, refusing the Goddess in her. . . . Fragments of thought flickered in her mind, an old tale of the Goddess surprised and refused by a man and how the Goddess had had him torn to shreds by the hounds who ran hunting with her . . . and there was sorrow that she had what she had dreamed of all these long years and it was dust and ashes to her.

A priest would say this was the wages of sin. I heard such, often enough, from Igraine's house priest before I went to be fostered in Avalon. At heart am I more of a Christian than I know? And again it seemed to her that her heart must break from the wreck and disaster of her love.

In Avalon this could never have come to pass—those who came to the Goddess in this way would never have so refused her power. . . . She paced up and down, a raging fire unslaked in her veins, knowing that no one could possibly understand how she felt except for another priestess of the Goddess. Viviane, she thought with longing, Viviane would understand, or Raven, or any of us reared in the House of Maidens . . . *what have I been doing all these long years, away from my Goddess?*

Morgaine speaks . . .

Three days later I got leave from Arthur to depart from his court and ride to Avalon; I said only that I was homesick for the Isle and for Viviane, my foster-mother. And in those days I had no speech with Lancelet save for the small courtesies of every day when we could not avoid meeting. Even in those I marked that he would not meet my eyes, and I felt angry and shamed, and went out of my way that I might not come face to face with him at all.

So I took horse, and rode eastward through the hills; nor did I return to Caerleon for many years, nor knew I anything of what befell in Arthur's court . . . but that is a tale for another time.

8

In the summer of the next year, the Saxons were massing off the coast, and Arthur and his men spent all the year in gathering an army for the battle they knew must come. Arthur led his men into battle and drove the Saxons back, but it was not the decisive battle and victory for which he had hoped; they were damaged indeed, and it would take them more than a year to recover, but he had not enough horses and men to defeat them firmly and for all time, as he hoped to do. At this battle he took a wound, which seemed not serious; but it festered and inflamed and he had to spend much of the autumn bedfast—the first snow flurries were coming over the walls of Caerleon before he could walk a little about the courtyard, leaning on a stick, and he would bear the scars to his grave.

"It will be full spring before I can sit a horse again," he observed gloomily to Gwenhwyfar, who stood close to the courtyard wall, her blue cloak wrapped tight around her.

"It may well be," Lancelet said, "and longer, my dear lord, if you take cold in your wound before it is full healed. Come within doors, I beg you —look, there is snow on Gwenhwyfar's cloak."

"And in your beard, Lance—or is that only the first grey?" Arthur asked, teasing, and Lancelet laughed.

"Both, I suppose—there you have the advantage of me, my king, your beard is so fair the grey will not show when it comes. Here, lean on my arm."

Arthur would have waved him away, but Gwenhwyfar said, "No, take his arm, Arthur, you will undo all our fine leechcraft if you fall—and the stones are slippery underfoot, with this snow melting as it comes down."

Arthur sighed and leaned on his friend's arm. "Now have I had a taste of what it must be like to be old." Gwenhwyfar came and took his other arm, and he laughed. "Will you love me and uphold me like this when indeed there is grey in my beard and hair and when I go on a stick like the Merlin?"

"Even when you are ninety, my lord," said Lancelet, laughing with him. "I can see it well, Gwenhwyfar holding you by one arm and I by the other as our ancient steps totter toward your throne—we will all be ninety or thereabout!" Abruptly he sobered. "I am troubled about Taliesin, my lord, he grows feeble and his eyes are failing. Should he not go back to Avalon and rest his last years in peace?"

"No doubt he should," said Arthur. "But he says he will not leave me alone, with only the priests for councillors—"

"What better councillors than the priests could you have, my lord?" Gwenhwyfar flared. She resented the unearthly word *Avalon;* it frightened her to think that Arthur was sworn to protect their heathenish ways.

They came into the hall where a fire was burning, and Arthur made a gesture of annoyance as Lancelet eased him into his chair. "Aye, set the old man by the fire and give him his posset—I marvel that you let me wear shoes and hose instead of a bedgown!"

"My dear lord—" Gwenhwyfar began, but Lancelet laid a hand on her shoulder.

"Don't fret yourself, kinswoman, all men are so, peevish when they are ill—he knows not when he is well off, being nursed by fair women and tended with dainty foods and clean linen and those possets he scorns. . . . I have lain with a wound in a field camp, nursed by a sour old man too lame to fight, and lying in my own shit because I could not shift myself and no one came near to help me, with nothing brought but some sour beer and hard bread to soak in it. Stop grumbling, Arthur, or I shall try to see to it that you nurse your wound in manly fashion as befits a true soldier!"

"Aye, and he would do it, too," said Arthur, with an affectionate smile at his friend. "You go not in much fear of your king, Prince Galahad—" He took the horn spoon from his wife's hand and began to eat the concoction of warmed wine with bread and honey soaked in it. "Aye, this is good and warming—it has spices in it, has it not, those same spices you bade me send for from Londinium. . . ."

Cai came to them, when Arthur had finished, and said, "So, how goes the wound after an hour of walking on it, my lord? Is there still much pain?"

"Not as much as the last time, and that is all I can say," Arthur said. "It is the first time I have known what real fear was, fear I might die with my work still undone."

"God would not have it so," Gwenhwyfar said.

Arthur patted her hand. "I told myself that, but a voice within kept saying to me that this was the great sin of pride, fearing that I or any man could not be spared from what God wishes to be done—I have thought long about such things while I lay unable to set foot to the ground."

"I cannot see that you have so much undone, save for the final victory over the Saxons, my lord," said Cai, "but now you must go to your bed, you are weary with the out of doors."

When Arthur was stretched out on the bed, Cai took his clothes away and examined the great wound which still, faintly, oozed matter through the cloths. Cai said, "I will send for the women, and you must have hot cloths on this again—you have strained it. It is well you did not break it open while you were walking." When the women had brought steaming kettles and mixed the compresses of herbs and hot water, laying folded cloths upon the wound so hot that Arthur winced and roared, Cai said, "Aye, but you were lucky even so, Arthur. Had that sword struck you a hand span to one side, Gwenhwyfar would have even more cause to grieve, and you would be known far and wide as the gelded king . . . as in that old legend! Know you not the tale—the king wounded in the thigh and as his powers fade, so fades the land and withers, till some youth comes who can make it spring fertile anew. . . ."

Gwenhwyfar shuddered, and Arthur said testily, shifting in pain under the heat of the compress, "This is no tale to tell a wounded man!"

"I should think it would make you more aware of your good fortune, that your land will not wither and be sterile," Cai said. "By Easter, I dare say, the Queen's womb could be quick again, if you are fortunate—"

"God grant it," Arthur said, but the woman winced and turned away. Once again she had conceived, and once again all had gone awry, so quickly that she had scarce known she had been with child—would it be so always with her? Was she barren, was it the punishment of God on her that she did not strive early and late to bring her husband to be a better Christian?

One of the women took away the cloth and would have replaced it; Arthur reached for Gwenhwyfar. "No, let my lady do it, her hands are gentler—" he said, and Gwenhwyfar took the steaming hot cloth—so hot it was she burned her fingers, but she welcomed the pain as penance. It was her fault, all her fault; he should put her away as barren, and take a wife who could give him a child. It was wrong that he should ever have married her—she had been eighteen, and already past her most fruitful years. Perhaps . . .

If only Morgaine were here, I would indeed beseech her for that charm which could make me fruitful. . . .

"It seems to me now that we have need of Morgaine's leechcraft," she said. "Arthur's wound goes not as it should, and she is a notable mistress of healing arts, as is the Lady of Avalon herself. Why do we not send to Avalon and beseech one of them to come?"

Cai frowned at her and said, "I do not see that there is need of that. Arthur's wound goes on well enough—I have seen much worse come to full healing."

"Still, I would be glad to see my good sister," said Arthur, "or my friend and benefactor, the Lady of the Lake. But from what Morgaine has told me, I do not think I will see them together. . . ."

Lancelet said, "I will send a message to Avalon and beg my mother to come, if you will have it, Arthur," but it was at Gwenhwyfar he looked, and their eyes met for a moment. In these months of Arthur's illness, it seemed he had been ever at her side, and such a rock of strength to her that she knew not what she would have done without him; in those first days, when none believed that Arthur could live, he had watched with her, tireless, his love for Arthur making her ashamed of her thoughts. *He is Arthur's cousin, even as Gawaine, he stands as near to the throne, the son of Igraine's own sister; if aught came to Arthur, then would he be as much a king as we have need of . . . in the old days the king was naught but the husband of the queen. . . .*

"Shall we send, then, for the Lady Viviane?" Gwenhwyfar asked.

"Only if you have a wish to see the Lady," said Arthur, with a sigh. "I think now, all I need is a greater share of that patience to which the bishop counselled me when I spoke last with him. God was good to me indeed, that I lay not thus disabled when the Saxons first came, and if he goes on showing me his grace, I will be able to ride when they come again. Gawaine is off gathering the men to the north, is he not, for Lot and Pellinore?"

"Aye." Lancelet laughed. "He has told Pellinore that his dragon must wait till we have dealt with the white horse . . . he must bring all his men and come when we summon him. And Lot will come too, though he grows old—he will not let pass any chance that the kingdom might still go to his sons."

It will go to his sons indeed, if I give Arthur no son, Gwenhwyfar thought; it seemed that every word anyone spoke, of whatever matter, was an arrow, a taunt aimed into her heart for failing the first duty of a queen. Arthur liked her well, they could have been happy, could she only have felt free for one moment of the guilt of her childlessness. Almost, for a time, she had welcomed this wound, for he could not think of lying with any woman, and there was no reproach to her; she could care for him and cosset him, have him to herself as a wife could so seldom do when her husband belonged not to her but to a kingdom. She could love him, and not think always of her guilt; when he touched her, think of their love, not only of her fear and her desperate hope, *This time will he at last get me with child; and if he does, will it go well with me or will I cast forth the precious hope of the kingdom?* She had cared for him, nursed him night and day as a mother nurses a sickly child, and when he began to grow strong she had sat beside him, talked to him, sung to him—though she had not Morgaine's sweet voice for singing —gone herself to the kitchens and cooked for him such things as a sick man might be tempted to eat, so that he would put on flesh after the ghastly sickness and wasting away of the early summer.

Yet what good is all my care if I do not ensure that there will be an heir to his kingdom?

"I would that Kevin were here," Arthur said. "I would like to hear some music—or Morgaine; we have no fitting minstrels at court now!"

"Kevin has gone back to Avalon," Lancelet said. "The Merlin told me he had gone for some priestly doings there, so secret he could tell me no more—I wonder the priests allow these Druid mysteries to go on in a Christian land."

Arthur shrugged. "I command no man's conscience, King or no."

Gwenhwyfar said sternly, "God will be worshipped as he wills, Arthur, not as men choose, and therefore he sent the Christ to us."

"But he sent him not to this land," Arthur said, "and when the holy Joseph came to Glastonbury, and thrust his staff there in the earth and it bloomed, then the Druids welcomed him and he did not scorn to share their worship."

"Bishop Patricius says that is an evil and heretical tale," Gwenhwyfar insisted, "and the priests who worship in common with the Druids should be stripped of their priesthood and driven forth as he drove the Druids themselves!"

"He will not do it during my time," said Arthur firmly. "I have sworn my protection to Avalon." He smiled and stretched out his hand to where the great sword Excalibur hung in its crimson-velvet scabbard. "And you have reason to be grateful for that magic, Gwenhwyfar—had I not had this scabbard about me, nothing could have saved me. Even as it was, I came near to bleeding to death, and only its magic stanched the bleeding. Would I not be worse than an ingrate if I betrayed their goodwill?"

"You believe that?" Gwenhwyfar asked. "You would put magic and sorceries above God's will?"

"Why, sweetheart," Arthur said, and touched her fair hair, "do you believe that anything man can do is in despite of God's will? If this scabbard kept me indeed from bleeding to death, then it could not have been God's will that I should die. It seems to me that my faith is closer to God than yours, if you fear that some wizard could undo what God wishes. We are all in God's hands."

Gwenhwyfar looked quickly at Lancelet; there was a smile on his face, and it seemed for a moment that he was mocking them, but it passed and the woman thought it must have been no more than a little shadow. "Well, if you wish for music, Arthur, Taliesin will come and play for you, I suppose; though he grows old and his voice is nothing for singing, his hands still have great skill at harping."

"Call for him, then," said Arthur, and laughed. "In Scripture we are told that the old King Saul called for his young harper to play and ease his mind, but here I am, a young king who has need of his old harper to play and cheer his soul!"

Lancelet went in search of the Merlin, and when he came with his harp, they sat for a long time in the hall listening to the music.

Gwenhwyfar thought of Morgaine, playing there. *Would that she were here, to give me a charm—but not before my lord recovers* . . . and then, looking across the fire at Lancelet, she felt sinking in her body. He sat on a bench, leaning back and listening to the music, his hands tucked behind his head, his long legs stretched out to the fire. The other men and women had gathered close to listen to the music; Elaine, Pellinore's daughter, had been bold enough to come and crowd onto the bench beside Lancelet, but he sat without paying any heed to her.

Lancelet would be the better for a wife. I should bestir myself and write to King Pellinore, that he should give Elaine to Lancelet; she is my cousin and not unlike me, she is marriageable—but she knew she would not; she told herself it would be time enough for that on the day Lancelet told them that he was seeking to be wedded.

If Arthur should not recover . . .

Oh, no, no, never will I think of that. . . . She crossed herself in secret. But, she thought, it was long since she had been in Arthur's arms, and it was likely he could not give her a child anyway. . . . She found herself wondering what it would be like to lie with Lancelet—could *he* give her the child she wished for? Suppose she took Lancelet as lover? She knew there were women who did such things . . . Morgause now made no secret of it; now that she was past childbearing, her harlotries were as scandalous as Lot's wenching. She felt the color creeping up in her cheeks and hoped no one had seen as she looked at Lancelet's hands lying quiet in his lap and wondered what it would be like to feel them caressing her—no, she dared not think of that.

When women took lovers they must take care not to be made pregnant, not to bear a child who could disgrace them or bring shame on their husbands, so if she was barren then it would not matter . . . it would be her good fortune. . . . In God's name, how could she, a chaste and Christian woman, have such evil thoughts? Once before she had thought this, and

when she told it in confession, the priest had said only that it was no more
than reason that with her husband so long sick, her thoughts should turn
to such things; she must not feel guilty, but pray much and care for her
husband and think only that it was harder still for *him*. And Gwenhwyfar
had known that this was good and sensible and kindly counsel, but she felt
he had not understood it in full, just how sinful a woman she was and how
evil and foul her thoughts. Otherwise, surely, he would have berated her,
and given her heavy penance, and then she would have felt better and more
free. . . .

Lancelet would never reproach her that she was barren—

She became aware that someone had spoken her name, and raised her
head in confusion as if her thoughts were open to all.

"No, no more music, my lord Merlin," Arthur said. "Look, it grows
dark, and my lady is asleep where she sits. She is worn out with nursing
me, most likely. . . . Cai, have the men set the dinner, but I will go to my
bed and have some meat there."

Gwenhwyfar rose, went to Elaine, and asked her to take her place in
the hall; she would stay with her lord. Cai went to see to the servants, and
Lancelet stayed to give Arthur a hand as he limped, with the help of his
stick, to his chamber. Lancelet helped to settle Arthur in bed as tenderly as
any nurse.

"If he needs anything in the night, see that you have them call for me,
you know where I sleep," he said low, to Gwenhwyfar. "I can lift him more
easily than any other—"

"Oh, no, no, I think there will be no need now," she said, "but I thank
you."

He was so tall as he stood next her; he laid his hand gently on her cheek.
"If you want to go and sleep among your women, I will stay and watch
with him—you look as if you were wanting a long night of unbroken sleep.
You are like a nursing mother who has no rest till her babe can sleep through
the night without stirring. I can care for Arthur—there is no need for you
to watch with him now! I can stay in the room within earshot."

"You are so good to me," she said, "but I would rather be near him."

"But send for me if he needs me. Do not try to lift him yourself,"
Lancelet said, "promise me, Gwenhwyfar."

How sweet her name sounded on his lips; sweeter than when he said
my queen or *my lady*. . . . "I promise you, my friend."

He bent, gave her just the flicker of a light kiss on her forehead. "You
look so overwearied," he said. "Go you to bed and sleep well." His hand
lingered still a moment on her cheek and when he took it away she felt as
if her cheek would be cold and ache as if she had a toothache there. She
went and laid herself down beside Arthur.

For a time she thought he slept. But at last he said into the darkness, "He has been a good friend to us, has he not, my wife?"

"No brother could have been kinder."

"Cai and I were reared as brothers, and I love him well, but it is true what they say, blood is thicker than water, and blood kin brings a closeness I had not imagined till I came to know some of my own blood. . . ." Arthur shifted in bed, uneasily, sighing. "Gwenhwyfar, there is something I would say to you—"

She was frightened, her heart pounding—had he seen Lancelet kiss her, would he charge her with unfaithfulness?

He said, "Promise me that you will not weep again, I cannot bear it. I swear it to you, I have no thought of reproaching you—but we have been wedded now for many years, and only twice in that time have you had even the hope of a child—no, no, I beg you, do not cry, let me speak," he pleaded. "It may be that it is not your fault, but mine. I have had other women, as do all men. But though I never made any attempt to conceal who I was, not in all these years has any woman come to me, nor her kinfolk, and said, such and such a woman bore you a bastard child. It may be that it is I whose seed has no life, so that when you conceive, the child comes not even to quickening. . . ."

She lowered her head, letting the curtain of her hair hide her face. Did he reproach himself as well?

"My Gwenhwyfar, listen to me—a child there must be for this kingdom. If it should come about at any time that you give a child to the throne, be assured that I will never question. So far as I am concerned, any child you bear, I will acknowledge it mine and bring it up as my heir."

She thought that the burning in her face would make her burst into flame. Could he think her capable of betraying him? "Never, never could I do so, my lord and my king—"

"You know the ways of Avalon—no, my wife, do not interrupt me, let me speak—where when a man and woman come together in this wise, the child is said even to be born of the God. Gwenhwyfar, I would like it well if God sent us a child, whoever should work God's will in fathering him—do you understand me? And if it should so happen that the one who so did the will of heaven were my dearest of friends and the closest of kinsmen to me, then would I bless him, and the child you bore. No, no, do not weep, I will say no more," he said, sighing, reaching out his arms to her, letting her lie against his shoulder. "I am not worthy that you should love me so well."

After a time he slept, but Gwenhwyfar lay awake, tears rolling down her face. *Oh, no,* she thought, *my dear love, my dearest lord, it is I who am not worthy of your love, and now you have all but given me leave that I should betray you.* Suddenly and for the first time in her life she envied both Arthur and Lancelet. They were men, they lived lives of activity, they must go out into the world and risk death or worse in battle, but men were free of these terrifying decisions. Whatever thing she did, whenever she made any decision, however small, if it was of more weight than kid or dried beef for dinner, then was that weight on her soul, that from what she should decide the fate of kingdoms could rest. Now it was her own choice, and not simply the will of God, that she should give an heir to the kingdom or no; one who was of Uther Pendragon's blood or—or otherwise. How could she, a woman, make that decision? Gwenhwyfar pulled the fur coverlet over her head and curled herself into a ball and lay there.

Only this evening she had sat there and watched Lancelet listening to the harper, and the thought had come stealing into her mind. She had loved him long, but now she began to know it was that she desired him; in her heart she was no better than Morgause, who played the whore when she would, with her husband's knights and even, the story was whispered in scandal, with handsome pages or servant men. Arthur was so good, and she had come to love him well; she had found safety here in Caerleon. It was not to be borne that the folk about the castle and countryside might come to whisper scandal of her as they did of Morgause.

Gwenhwyfar wished to be good, to keep her soul clean and her virtue whole, but also it meant much to her that people should see her virtue and think of her as a good and spotless queen; she herself knew nothing evil of Morgaine, for instance, she had lived at her side for three years, and Morgaine was, so far as she knew, as virtuous as herself. Yet it was rumored that Morgaine was a witch because she had lived in Avalon, and had some wisdom and knowledge of healing herbs and of sendings, and so the people of the court and of the country roundabout had whispered that Morgaine was in league with the fairy folk or the Devil; and even she herself, knowing Morgaine as she did, sometimes wondered how what so many people said could be all untrue.

And tomorrow she must face Lancelet and go about her work by Arthur's side, knowing that he had all but given her leave—how could she ever again look into Lancelet's eyes? He was of the blood of Avalon, he was son to the Lady of the Lake, it could be that he too could read thoughts a little, that he could see into her eyes and know what she was thinking.

And then anger, so violent that it frightened her, swept through her trembling body like a flood. Gwenhwyfar, lying there angry and afraid, thought that she would never dare to go out of doors again for fear of what she might choose to do. Every woman in the court wanted Lancelet—yes, even Morgaine herself; she had seen her sister-in-law looking at him, and for that reason, when once a long time ago Arthur had said they should

marry, she had been distressed—Lancelet would surely find Morgaine too
bold. And perhaps they had quarrelled, for the last day or two before
Morgaine had departed for Avalon, she noted that they spoke less to each
other than usual, and did not turn their eyes to each other.

She missed Morgaine, yes . . . but all in all she was glad Morgaine was
not at court, and she would not send to Tintagel to hear news of her if she
was there. She fancied herself repeating to Morgaine what Arthur had just
said; she would die of shame, and yet she suspected that Morgaine would
laugh at her: Morgaine would surely say it was for her to choose whether
or no she would take Lancelet as a lover; or perhaps, even, that it was for
Lancelet to say.

Then it was as if a burning flame passed through her, like the fires of
hell, that she might offer herself to Lancelet and he might say to her no.
Then, surely, she would die of shame. She did not know how she could ever
bear to look at Lancelet again, or at Arthur, or at any of her ladies who
had never been so tempted. Even to the priests she would think it shame
to speak about this, for they would know Arthur was less a Christian than
he ought to be. How could she ever bear to go out of doors again, or to
leave the safe, protected space of this very room and this very bed? *Here,*
nothing wrong could come to her or harm her.

She did feel somewhat ill. Tomorrow she would tell her ladies that,
and they would think only, as Lancelet would think, that she was overwearied with nursing Arthur night and day. She would continue to be, as
she was always, a good and virtuous queen and a Christian woman—she
could never even think of being anything else. Arthur was distressed from
his wound and his long inactivity, that was all; when he was well and sound
he could never think such a thing, and no doubt he would be grateful to
her that she had not listened to his folly and had saved them both from a
fearful sin.

But just as she was about to drop into an exhausted sleep, she remembered something that one of her women had said, long ago—it was a few
days before Morgaine left the court. She had said that Morgaine should give
her a charm. . . . Well, and so she should; if Morgaine enchanted her so that
she had no choice but to love Lancelet, then she would be freed of that
fearful choice. . . . *When Morgaine returns,* she thought, *I will speak of it to
her.* But Morgaine had not been at court now for almost two years, and
it might be that she would never return.

9

I GROW *too old for these journeys,* Viviane thought as she rode through the late-winter rain, head bowed, her cloak wrapped tight around her body. And then resentment surged through her: *This should now be Morgaine's task, it is she who was to be Lady after me in Avalon.*

Taliesin had told her, four years ago now, that Morgaine had been in Caerleon for Arthur's wedding, and had been given to Gwenhwyfar for one of her ladies, and had tarried there. *The Lady of the Lake, waiting-woman to a queen?* How dared Morgaine forsake her true and appointed path in this way? And yet when she had sent a message to Caerleon with word that Morgaine should return to Avalon, the messenger had returned to say that Morgaine had left the court . . . they thought for Avalon.

But she is not in Avalon. Nor is she in Tintagel with Igraine, nor yet at the court of Lot in Orkney. Where then has she gone?

Some harm could have come to her on one of her solitary journeys. She might have been captured by one of the marauders or masterless men who throng the country—she might have lost her memory or have been raped, murdered, flung into a ditch somewhere and her bones never been found. . . . *Oh no,* Viviane thought, *if harm had come to her, I would surely have seen it in the mirror . . . or with the Sight. . . .*

Yet she could not be certain. The Sight was erratic in her now, and often when she sought to see beyond, nothing came but a maddening grey fog before her eyes, the veil of the unknown which she dared not try to pierce. And Morgaine's fate was concealed somewhere within that veil.

Goddess, she prayed as she had done so often before, *Mother, I have given you my life, bring back my child to me while I yet live . . .* but even as she spoke, she knew that there would be no answer, only grey rain like the veil of the unknown, the answer of the Goddess hidden in the unyielding sky.

Had it wearied her so much as this when last she made this journey, half a year ago? It seemed now to her that she had always ridden, before this, as lightly as a girl, and now the jolting of her donkey seemed to rattle every bone in her thin body, while the cold crept into her and gnawed at her with little icy teeth.

One of her escort turned back and said, "Lady, I can see the farmstead below. We will be there before nightfall, it seems."

Viviane thanked the man, trying not to sound as grateful as she felt. She could not betray weakness before her escort.

Gawan met her in the narrow barnyard as she was dismounting from her donkey, steadying her so that she did not step into the midden. "Wel-

come, Lady," he said, "as always, it is my pleasure to see you. My son Balin
and your son will be here with the morrow—I sent to Caerleon that they
might be here."

"Is it as grave as that, old friend?" Viviane asked, and Gawan nodded.
He said, "You will scarcely know her, Lady. She is fallen away to nothing
now, and if she eats or drinks ever so little, she says it is as if a fire were
lighted in her vitals. It cannot be much longer now, for all your medicines."

Viviane nodded and sighed. "I feared as much," she said. "When this
illness once has hold on anyone, it never lets loose its claw. Perhaps I can
give her some ease."

"God grant it," said Gawan, "for the medicines you left us when you
were last here do little now. She wakes and cries in the night like a little
child, when she thinks the serving-women and I do not hear. I have not even
the heart to pray that she shall be spared to us for any more suffering, Lady."

Viviane sighed again. When last she had come this way, half a year
ago, she had left her strongest drugs and medicines, and she had half
wished that Priscilla might take a fever in the autumn and die quickly,
before the medicines lost their effect. There was little more that she could
do. She let Gawan lead her into the house, seat her before the fire, and the
serving-woman dished her up a hot bowl of soup from a kettle near the
fire.

"You have been riding long in the rain, Lady," he said. "Sit and rest,
and you shall see my wife after the evening meal—sometimes she sleeps a
little at this time of day."

"If she can rest even a little, it is blessed, and I shall not disturb her,"
Viviane said, folding her chilled hands around the soup bowl, and letting
herself slump down on the backless bench. One of the serving-women drew
off her boots and cloak, another came with a warmed towel to dry her feet,
and Viviane, turning her skirts back so that her bony knees felt the fire,
rested for a moment in mindless comfort, forgetting her grim errand. Then
a thin wailing cry was heard from an inner room, and the serving-woman
started and trembled. She said to Viviane, "It is the mistress, poor thing—
she must be awake. I hoped she would sleep till we had set the night meal.
I must go to her."

"I will come too," said Viviane, and followed the woman to the inner
chamber. Gawan was seated by the fire, and she saw the look of dread on
his face as that thin cry died away.

Always before, since Priscilla had fallen ill, Viviane had found some
trace in the woman of her old buxom prettiness, some resemblance to the
jolly young woman who had fostered her son Balan. Now face and lips and
faded hair were all the same yellowed grey, and even the blue eyes seemed
faded, as if the sickness had leached all the color from the woman. When

last she had come, too, Priscilla had been up and about a part of every day; now she could see that this woman had been bedfast for months . . . half a year had made this much change. And always before, Viviane's medicines and herb potions had given ease and comfort and partial recovery. Now, she knew, it was too late for any further help.

For a moment the faded eyes drifted unfocused around the room, the lips moving faintly over the fallen-in jaw. Then Priscilla saw Viviane, blinked a little, and said in a whisper, "Is it you, Lady?"

Viviane went to her side and carefully took her withered hand. She said, "I am sorry to see you so ill. How is it with you, my dear friend?"

The faded, cracked lips drew back in a grimace which Viviane, for a moment, thought to be a movement of pain; then she realized it was meant for a smile. "I hardly know how it could be more ill," she whispered. "I think God and his Mother have forgotten me. Yet I am glad to see you again, and I hope to live long enough to look again on my dear sons and bless them. . . ." She sighed wearily, trying to shift her body a little. "My back aches so with lying here, and yet whenever I am touched, it is like knives thrusting into me. And I am so thirsty, yet I dare not drink for fear of the pain. . . ."

"I will make you as comfortable as I can," Viviane said, and, telling the servants what she wanted, she dressed the sores that came from lying in the bed and washed out Priscilla's mouth with a cooling lotion, so that even though she did not drink, her mouth would not torment her so with dryness. Then she sat near her, holding her hand, not troubling the sick woman with words. Some time after dark, there was a sound in the courtyard, and Priscilla, starting up again, her eyes feverish in the lamplight, cried out, "It is my sons!"

And indeed, after a little time, Balan and his foster-brother, Balin, Gawan's son, came into the room, stooping under the low ceiling.

"Mother," Balan said, and stooped to kiss Priscilla's hand, only then turning to Viviane to bow before her. "My lady."

Viviane reached out and touched her elder son's cheek. He was not as handsome as Lancelet, this one; he was a huge burly man, but his eyes were dark and fine like her own, or Lancelet's. Balin was smaller, a sturdy, grey-eyed man. He was, she knew, just ten days older than her own son. He looked as Priscilla had once looked, fair-haired and red-cheeked.

"My poor mother," he murmured, stroking Priscilla's hand, "but now the Lady Viviane has come to help you, then you will be well again very soon, will you not? But you are so thin, Mother, you must try to eat more and be strong and well again. . . ."

"No," she whispered, "I shall never be strong more until I sup with Jesus in Heaven, dear son."

"Oh, no, Mother, you must not say so—" Balin cried, and Balan, meeting Viviane's eyes, sighed.

He said in so low a tone that neither Priscilla nor her son could hear, "He cannot see that she is dying, my lady—my mother. Always he insists that she can recover. I had truly hoped that she would go in the autumn, when we all took the fever, but she has always been so strong—" Balan shook his head, and his thick neck was flushed. Viviane saw that tears were standing in his eyes; he dashed them quickly away. And after a little, she said that they must all go out and let the sick woman rest again.

"Say farewell to your sons, Priscilla, and bless them," she said, and Priscilla's eyes brightened a little. "I would it should truly be farewell, before it grows worse—I would not have them see me as I was this morning," she murmured, and Viviane saw the terror in her eyes. She bent over Priscilla and said gently, "I think I can promise you no more pain, my dear, if that is how you wish it to end."

"Please," whispered the dying woman, and Viviane felt the clawlike hand tighten on hers in entreaty.

"I will leave you here with your sons, then," Viviane said gently, "for they are both your sons, my dear, even though you bore but one of them." She went out into the other room and found Gawan there.

"Bring me my saddlebags," she said; and when this had been done, she searched in a pocket for a moment. Then she turned to the man. "She is at ease for a moment now, but I can do little more, save to put an end to her suffering. I think this is what she wishes."

"There is no hope then—none at all?"

"No. There is nothing left for her but suffering, and I cannot think that your God wills it that she should suffer more."

Gawan said, shaken, "She has said often—that she wished she had had courage to throw herself into the river while she could still walk thither—"

"It is time, then, that she should go in peace," Viviane said quietly, "but I wanted you to know that whatever I do, it is by her own will—"

"Lady," Gawan replied, "I have trusted you always, and my wife loves you well and trusts you. I ask no more. If her sufferings end here, I know she will bless you." But his face was drawn with grief. He followed Viviane into the inner room again. Priscilla had been speaking quietly to Balin; now she released his hand, and he went, weeping, to his father. She held out her thin hand to Balan and said in her shaking voice, "You too have been a good son to me, my lad. Always look after your foster-brother, and I beg you to pray for my soul."

"I will, my mother," said Balan, and bent to embrace her, but she gave a little trembling cry of pain and fear as he moved toward her, and so he only picked up her withered hand and pressed his fingers to it.

"Now I have your medicine for you, Priscilla," said Viviane. "Say good night, and sleep. . . ."

"I am so weary," the dying woman whispered, "I shall be glad to sleep . . . bless you, Lady, and your Goddess too. . . ."

"In her name, who gives mercy," Viviane murmured, and held Priscilla's head up so that she could swallow.

"I am afraid to drink—it is bitter, and whenever I swallow anything there is pain—" Priscilla whispered.

"I swear to you, my sister, that when you have drunk this, there will be no more pain at all," Viviane said steadily, and tipped the cup. Priscilla swallowed and raised her weak hand to touch Viviane's face.

"Kiss me in farewell, too, Lady," she said, with that ghastly smile again, and Viviane pressed her lips to the skull-like brow.

I have brought life and now I come as the Death-crone. . . . Mother, I do for her only what I would that one might do for me one day, Viviane thought, and shivered again, raising her eyes to meet Balin's frowning gaze.

"Come," she said quietly, "let her rest."

They went out into the other room. Gawan remained behind, his hand in his wife's; it was only fitting, Viviane thought, that he should remain with her.

The serving-women had set the evening meal and Viviane went to her place and ate and drank, for she was weary after the long ride.

"Have you ridden from Arthur's court at Caerleon all in this day, my boys?" she asked, then smiled—these "boys" were men!

"Aye, from Caerleon—" Balan said, "and a wretched ride it was, in cold and rain!" He helped himself to salt fish and spread butter on his bread, then handed the wooden dish to Balin. "You are eating nothing, my brother."

Balin shuddered. "I have not the heart to eat when our mother lies like that. But God be thanked now you have come, Lady, she will soon be all well again, will she not? Your medicines did her so much good last time, it was like a miracle, and now again she will be better, will she not?"

Viviane stared at him—was it possible that he did not understand? She said quietly, "The best end of all is that she might go to join her God in the hereafter, Balin."

He looked up at her, his ruddy face stricken. "No! She must not die," he cried. "Lady, tell me that you will help her, that you will not let her die—"

Viviane said severely, "I am not your God, and life and death are not in my keeping, Balin. Would you have her linger in such misery for much longer?"

"But you are skilled in all manner of magic lore," Balin protested angrily. "Why came you here, if not to cure her again? I heard you say but now, that you could put an end to her pain—"

"There is only one cure for such an illness as has taken your mother," Viviane said, laying a compassionate hand on Balin's shoulder, "and that is merciful."

"Balin, have done," Balan said, going to put his big callused hand on his foster-brother's. "Would you truly have her suffer more?"

But Balin jerked up his head and glared at Viviane. "So you used your sorcery tricks to cure her when it was honor to your evil fiend-Goddess," he shouted, "and now when you can get no more good of it you will let her die—"

"Be still, man," Balan said, and now his voice was rough and strained. "Marked you not—our mother blessed and kissed her farewell, it was what she wished for—"

But Balin was staring at Viviane, and then he raised his hand as if to strike her. "Judas!" he shouted. "You too betrayed with a kiss—" And he whirled and ran toward the inner room. "What have you done? Murderess! Foul murderess! Father! Father, here's murder and evil sorcery—!"

Gawan, white-faced, appeared in the chamber door, anxiously gesturing for silence, but Balin shoved him aside and burst into the room. Viviane followed, and she saw that Gawan had closed the dead woman's eyes.

Balin saw also, and he turned on her, shouting incoherently, "Murder! Treachery, sorcery—! Foul, murdering witch—!"

Gawan wrapped restraining arms around his son. "You will not speak so over your mother's very body to one she trusted and loved!"

But Balin raved and shouted, straining to come at Viviane. She tried to speak, to quiet him, but he would not hear. At last she went out into the kitchen and sat by the fire.

Balan came and took her hand and said, "I'm sorry he is receiving it in this way, my lady. He knows better, and when the shock is past he'll be grateful to you as I am—poor little mother, she suffered so, and now 'tis ended, and I bless you too." He lowered his head, trying not to sob aloud. "She was—was like mother to me too—"

"I know, my son, I know," Viviane murmured, patting his head as if he were the clumsy little boy he had been more than twenty years ago. "It's only right you should weep for your foster-mother, you would be heartless if you did not—" and he broke down and sobbed, kneeling at her side, his face buried in her lap.

Balin came and stood over them, his face drawn with fury. "You know she killed our mother, Balan, and yet you come to her for comfort?"

Balan raised his head, snuffling back sobs. "She did our mother's will. Are you such a fool you could not see—even with God's help our mother could not have lived another fortnight, do you grudge her that last pain she was spared?"

But Balin only cried desolately, "My mother, my mother is dead!"

"Be still, she was my foster-mother, my mother too," said Balan angrily, and then his face softened. "Ah, brother, brother, I grieve too, why should we quarrel? Come now, drink some wine, her suffering is ended and she is with God—better we should pray for her than be all at odds this way. Come, brother, come and eat and rest, you are weary too."

"No," cried Balin, "I will not rest under the roof that shelters the foul sorceress who slew my mother!"

Gawan came, pale and angry, and struck Balin across the mouth. He said, "Peace! The Lady of Avalon is our guest and our friend! You shall not sully the hospitality of this roof with such blasphemous words! Sit down, my son, and eat, or you will speak words we shall all regret!"

But Balin stared about him like a wild animal. "I will neither eat nor rest under this roof while it holds that—that woman."

Balan demanded, "Dare you offer insult to my mother?"

And Balin cried, "You are all against me, then—I shall go forth from this roof which shelters my mother's slayer!" He turned his back and ran from the house. Viviane sank down in a chair, and Balan came to offer his arm and Gawan to pour her a cup of wine.

"Drink, Lady—and accept my apologies for my son," he said. "He is beside himself; he will come soon enough to sanity."

"Shall I go after him, Father, for fear he should do himself some hurt?" Balan asked, but Gawan shook his head.

"No—no, son, stay here with your mother. Words will do him little good now."

Trembling, Viviane sipped at her wine. She, too, was overcome with sorrow for Priscilla, and for the time when they had been young women together, each with her baby son in her arms. . . . Priscilla had been so pretty and merry, they had laughed together and played with their babies, and now Priscilla lay dead after a wasting illness, and Viviane's own hand had held the cup of her death. That she had done Priscilla's own will only eased her conscience, it did not blunt her sadness.

We were young together, and now she lies dead and I am old, old as the Death-crone's very self; and those pretty babies who played about our feet, one has grey in his own hair, and the other would kill me if he could, as a foul sorceress and murderer. . . . It seemed to Viviane that her very bones rattled with an icy grief. She stood near to the fire, but still she shivered and could not get warm. She clutched her shawl about her, and Balan came and led her to the best seat, tucked a cushion behind her back, set a cup of heated wine in her hands.

"Ah, you loved her too," he said. "Don't trouble yourself about Balin, Lady, he will regain his reason in time. When he can think clear again, he'll know that what you did was great mercy to our mother—" He broke off, slow red creeping up his heavy jowls. "Are you angry with me, Lady, that still I think of my mother as she who died but now?"

"It is no more than reason," said Viviane, sipping at the hot wine, and caressing her son's hardened hand. Once, she thought, it had been so little and tender that she could enfold it within her own, like a curled rosebud, and now her own hand was quite lost within his. "The Goddess knows, she was more mother to you than ever I was."

"Aye, I should have known that you would understand that," said Balan. "Morgaine said as much to me when I saw her last at Arthur's court."

"Morgaine? Is she at Arthur's court now, my son? Was she there when you came away?"

Balan shook his head regretfully. "No, I saw her last—it was years gone, Lady. She left Arthur's court, let me think . . . it was before Arthur had his great wound . . . why, 'tis three years come Midsummer. I thought she was with you in Avalon."

Viviane shook her head and steadied herself against the arm of the high seat. "I have not seen Morgaine since Arthur's wedding." And then she thought, perhaps she is gone over the seas. She asked Balan, "What of your brother Lancelet? Is he at court or has he gone back to Less Britain?"

"He will not do that, I think, while Arthur lives," Balan said, "though he is not often at court now . . ." and Viviane, with a fragment of the Sight, heard the unspoken words Balan bit back, unwilling to speak gossip or scandal: *When Lancelet is at court, men mark how he never takes his eyes from Queen Gwenhwyfar, and twice he has refused Arthur when Arthur would have had him wedded.* Balan went on hastily, "Lancelet has said he will set all things in order in Arthur's kingdom, and so he is always out and about the lands, he has killed more marauding brigands and raiding bands than any other of Arthur's Companions. They say of him that he is an entire legion in himself, Lady—" and Balan raised his head and looked ruefully at Viviane. "Your younger son, Mother, is a great knight, such a knight as that old Alexander of the legends. There are those who say, even, that he is a better knight than Arthur's self. I have brought no such glory on you, my lady."

"We all do such things as the Gods give us to do, my son," Viviane said gently. "I am only glad to see that you do not bear malice toward your brother for that he is a better knight than you."

Balan shook his head. "Why, that would be like bearing malice toward Arthur that I am not the King, Mother," he said. "And Lancelet is modest and good to all men, and pious as a maiden too—knew you not that he had become a Christian, Lady?"

Viviane shook her head. "It surprises me not," she said, with a trace of scorn she did not know would be in her voice until she had spoken. "Always your brother fears those things he cannot understand, and the faith of Christ is a fitting faith for slaves who think themselves sinners and humble—" Then she stopped herself and said, "I am sorry, my son. I meant not to belittle. I know it is your faith too."

Balan blinked and smiled. "Now has a miracle come to pass, madam, that you ask pardon of any for any word you ever spoke!"

Viviane bit her lip. "Is that truly how you see me, my son?"

He nodded. "Aye, ever you have seemed to me the proudest of women—and it seemed to me right that you should be exactly as you are," he said. And Viviane mocked herself that she had come to this, seeking a word of approval from her son! She cast about to find something new to speak of.

"You told me Lancelet has twice refused to marry? For what, do you think, is he waiting? Does he want more of a dowry than any maiden can bring him?"

Again it seemed that she heard Balan's unspoken thoughts: *He cannot have the one he would have, for she is wedded to his king* . . . but her son said only, "He says he has no mind to marry any woman, and jests that he is fonder of his horse than he could be of any woman who could not ride with him into battle—he says in jest that one day he will take one of the Saxon shield maidens to wife. None can match him at arms, either, nor in the games Arthur holds at Caerleon. Sometimes he will take some handicap, ride without a shield, or change horses with another, so he will not have too much of the advantage. Balin challenged him once and won a course against him, but he refused a prize for it, because he found out it was because Lancelet's saddle girths broke."

"So Balin too is a courteous and good knight?" Viviane said.

"Oh, yes, Mother, you must not judge my brother by tonight," Balan said eagerly. "When he rode against Lancelet, truly I knew not which of them to cheer on. Lancelet offered him the prize, saying he had won it fairly, since he should not have lost control of his horse—so he said! But Balin would not take it, and they stood disputing with one another in courtesy like two heroes from the ancient sagas Taliesin used to tell us when we were lads!"

"So you can be proud of both your brothers," Viviane said, and the talk passed to other things, and after a little time she said she should go and

help with the laying-out. But when she went into the chamber, she saw that
the women were all in awe of her, and a priest had come, too, from the
village. He welcomed her courteously indeed, but Viviane could tell by his
words that he thought her one of the sisters from the nunnery nearby—
indeed, her dark travel dress made her look so, and she had no wish to
confront him this night. So, when they entreated her to go to the best guest
bed, she went, and at last she slept. But all that she had spoken of with Balan
seemed to come and go in her head, through her dreams, and at one moment
it seemed that she saw Morgaine through grey and thinning mists, running
away into a wood of strange trees and crowned with flowers such as never
grew in Avalon, and she said in her dreams, and again to herself when she
woke, I must delay no longer, I must seek for her with the Sight, or what
remains to me of the Sight.

The next morning she stood by while Priscilla was laid in earth. Balin
had returned and stood weeping by the graveside, and after the burial was
done and the other folk had gone into the house to drink ale, she approached
him and said gently, "Will you not embrace me and exchange forgiveness
with me, foster-son? Believe me, I share your grief. We have been friends
all our lives, Dame Priscilla and I, or would I have given her my own son
to nurse? And I am your foster-brother's mother." She held out her arms,
but Balin's face drew hard and cold, and he turned his back on her and
walked away.

Gawan besought her to stay for a day or two and rest there, but
Viviane asked for her donkey to be brought; she must return to Avalon, she
said, and she saw that Gawan, though his hospitality had been sincere, was
relieved—if someone had told the priest who she was, there might have been
awkwardness he had no mind to, during his wife's funeral feast. Balan, too,
asked, "Will you have me to ride with you to Avalon, madam? There are
sometimes brigands and evil folk on the road."

"No," she said, giving him her hand and smiling. "I look not as if I
had gold about me, and the men who ride with me are of the Tribesmen
—we could hide in the hills, should we be attacked. Nor am I any temptation to any man who might seek to take a woman." She laughed and said,
"And with Lancelet questing to kill all the brigands in this country, it will
soon be as it was said once it was, that a virgin of fifteen bearing a purse
of gold might ride from one end of the land to the other with no man to
offer her insult! Stay here, my son, and mourn your mother, and make peace
with your foster-brother. You must not quarrel with him for my sake,
Balan." And then she shuddered suddenly as if with cold, for a picture had
come into her mind, and it seemed to her as if there was the clash of swords
and her son bleeding from a great wound. . . .

"What is it, Lady?" he asked her softly.

"Nothing, my son—only promise to me that you will not break the peace with your brother Balin."

He bent his head. "I will not, Mother. And I will tell him that you have said this, so he will not think you bear him any grudge, either."

"By the Lady, I do not," said Viviane, but still she felt icy cold, though the winter sun was warm on her back. "May she bless you, my son, and your brother too, though I doubt he wishes for the blessing of any God but his own. Will you take the Lady's blessing, Balan?"

"I will," he said, bending to kiss Viviane's hand, and he stood looking after her as she rode away.

She told herself, as she rode toward Avalon that surely what she had seen had come of her own weariness and fear; and in any case Balan was one of Arthur's Companions, and it could not be looked for, in this war with the Saxons, that he should escape a wound. But the picture persisted in her mind, that Balan and his foster-brother should somehow quarrel in her name, until at last she made a stern banishing gesture and willed to see her son's face no more in her mind till she should look on it again in the flesh!

She was troubled too about Lancelet. He was long past the age when a man should marry. Yet there were men enough who had no mind to women, seeking only for the companionship of their brothers and comrades under arms, and she had wondered often enough if Ban's son were one of them. Well, Lancelet should take his own road; she had consented to that when he left Avalon. If he professed great devotion to the Queen, no doubt, it was only that his comrades should not mock at him as a lover of boys.

But she dismissed her sons from her mind. Neither of them was as near to her heart as Morgaine, and Morgaine . . . where was Morgaine? She had been disquieted before this, but now, hearing Balan's news, she feared for Morgaine's very life. Before this day was ended, she should send out messengers from Avalon to Tintagel, where Igraine dwelt, and northward to Lot's court where Morgaine might have gone to be with her child. . . . She had seen the young Gwydion, once or twice, in her mirror, but had paid him little heed, as long as he grew and thrived. Morgause was kindly to all little children, having a brood of her own, and there would be time enough to look to Gwydion when he came of an age for fostering. Then should he come to Avalon. . . .

With the iron discipline of years, she managed to put even Morgaine from her mind and to ride home to Avalon in a mood befitting a priestess who had just taken the part of the Death-crone for her oldest friend— sobered indeed, but without great grief, for death was only the beginning of new life.

Priscilla was a Christian. She believed she would now be with her God in Heaven. *Yet she too will be born again on this imperfect world, to seek the perfection of the Gods, again and yet again. . . . Balan and I parted as strangers, and so it must be. I am no more the Mother, and I should feel no more grief than when I ceased to be the Maiden for her . . .* yet her heart was filled with rebellion.

Truly, the time had come for her to give up her rulership of Avalon, that a younger woman might be Lady of the Lake and she herself no more than one of the wise-women, offering counsel and advice, but carrying no more that fearsome power. She had long known that the Sight was leaving her. Yet she would not lay down her power until she could place it in the hands of that one she had prepared to take it from her. She had felt that she could wait until Morgaine had outgrown her bitterness and returned to Avalon.

Yet if anything has befallen Morgaine . . . and even if it has not, have I the right to continue as Lady when the Sight has left me?

For a moment, when she came to the Lake, she was so cold and wet that when the boat's crew turned to her to call down the mists, she could not force herself to remember the spell. *Indeed it is time and more than time that I should lay down my powers. . . .* Then the words of power came back into her mind and she spoke them, but much of that night she lay wakeful, in dread.

When the morning had come, she studied the sky; the moon was darkening, and it would do no good to consult the mirror at this time. *Will it ever profit me anything to look into that mirror again, now the Sight has departed from me?* With iron discipline, she forced herself to say nothing of any of this to her attendant priestesses. But later that day she met with the other wise-women and asked them, "Is there anyone in the House of Maidens who is still virgin and has never yet gone to the grove or to the fires?"

"There is Taliesin's little daughter," said one of the women.

For a moment Viviane was confused—surely Igraine was grown and wedded and widowed, mother of the High King in Caerleon, and Morgause too was wedded and the mother of many sons. Then she recalled herself and said, "I knew not that he had a daughter in the House of Maidens." A time had been, she thought, when no girl had been taken into the Maiden House without her own knowledge, and it had been her hand that had tested each one for the Sight and for her fitness for the Druid lore. But in the last years, she had let this slip from her.

"Tell me. How old is she? What is her name? When did she come to us?"

"Her name is Niniane," said the old priestess. "She is the daughter of Branwen—do you remember? Branwen said that Taliesin had fathered this child at Beltane fire. It seems it was only a little while ago, but she must be eleven or twelve, perhaps more. She was fostered away in the North somewhere, but she came to us five or six seasons ago. She is a good child and biddable enough, and there are not now so many maidens who come to us that we can afford to pick and choose among them, Lady! There are none now like Raven or your fosterling Morgaine. And where is Morgaine now, Lady? She should return to us!"

Viviane said, "She should return to us indeed," and felt ashamed to say that she did not even know where Morgaine was, or even whether she was alive or dead. *How have I the insolence to be Lady of Avalon when I know not even the name of my successor, nor who dwells in the House of Maidens?* But if this Niniane was daughter to Taliesin and to a priestess of Avalon, surely she must have the Sight. And even if she had it not herself, Viviane could compel her to see, if she was a maiden still.

She said, "See that Niniane is sent to me before dawn, three days from now," and, although she saw a dozen questions in the eyes of the old priestess, she marked with a certain satisfaction that she was still unquestioned Lady of Avalon, for the woman asked her nothing.

NINIANE CAME TO HER an hour before dawn, at the end of the moon-dark seclusion; Viviane, sleepless, had spent much of the night in restless self-questioning. She knew herself reluctant to set aside her own position of authority, yet if she could lay it into Morgaine's hands, she would do so without regrets. She turned over in her hand the little sickle knife which Morgaine had abandoned when she fled from Avalon, then put it aside and raised her face to look at Taliesin's daughter.

The old priestess, even as I myself, loses track of time; surely she is more than eleven or twelve. The girl was trembling in awe, and Viviane recalled how Morgaine too had trembled when she first saw her as Lady of Avalon. She said gently, "You are Niniane? Who are your parents?"

"I am Branwen's daughter, Lady, but I do not know my father's name. She said only that I was Beltane-gotten." Well, that was reasonable enough.

"How old are you, Niniane?"

"I shall have finished fourteen winters this year."

"And you, have you been to the fires, child?"

The girl shook her head. She said, "I have not been called thither."

"Have you the Sight?"

"Only a little, I think, Lady," she said, and Viviane sighed and said, "Well, we shall see, child; come with me," and she led the way out of her isolated house, upwards along the hidden path to the Sacred Well. The girl was taller than she herself, slender and fair-haired, with violet eyes—she was not unlike Igraine at that age, Viviane thought, though Igraine's hair had been nearer red than golden. Suddenly it seemed that she could see this Niniane crowned and robed as the Lady, and she shook her head impatiently, to clear it of unwanted vision. Surely this was only wandering daydream. . . .

She brought Niniane to the pool, then stopped for a moment to look at the sky. She handed her the sickle knife which had been given to Morgaine when she had been made priestess, and said to her quietly, "Look into the mirror, my child, and see where she who held this dwells now."

Niniane looked at her hesitantly and said, "Lady, I told you—I have little of the Sight—"

Viviane suddenly understood—the girl was frightened of failure. "It does not matter. You will see with the Sight that once was mine. Be not afraid, child, but look for me into the mirror."

Silence, while Viviane watched the girl's bent head. In the surface of the pool it seemed only that wind came and ruffled the surface, as always. Then Niniane said in a quiet, wandering voice, "Ah, see . . . she sleeps in the arms of the grey king . . ." and was still.

What can she mean? Viviane could make nothing of the words. She wanted to cry out to Niniane, to force the Sight upon her undesired, yet she compelled herself, by the greatest effort of her life, to keep still, knowing that even her restless thoughts could blur the Sight for the maiden. She said, hardly above a whisper, "Tell me, Niniane, do you see that day when Morgaine shall return to Avalon?"

Again the empty silence. A little breeze—the dawn wind—had sprung up, and again the riffle of wind came and went across the glassy surface of the water. At last Niniane said softly, "She stands in the boat . . . her hair is all grey now . . ." and again she was still, sighing as if with pain.

"Do you see more, Niniane? Speak, tell me—"

Pain and terror crossed the girl's face and she whispered, "Ah, the cross . . . the light burns me, the cauldron between her hands—Raven! Raven, will you leave us now?" She gave a sharp indrawn breath of shock and dismay, and crumpled fainting to the ground.

Viviane stood motionless, her hands clenched, and then, with a long sigh, she bent to raise the girl. She dipped her hand in the pool, sprinkled water on Niniane's slack face. After a moment the girl opened her eyes, stared at Viviane in fright, and began to cry.

"I am sorry, Lady—I could see nothing," she whimpered.

So. She spoke, but she remembers nothing of what she saw. I might well have spared her this, for all the good it has done. It was pointless to be angry with her—she had done no more than she was commanded. Viviane stroked the fair hair back from Niniane's forehead and said gently, "Don't cry; I am not angry with you. Does your head ache? So—go and rest, my child."

The Goddess bestows her gifts as she will. But why, Mother of all, do you send me to do your will with imperfect instruments? You have taken from me the power to do your will; why, then, have you taken from me the one who should serve you when I am no longer here? Niniane, her hands pressed to her forehead, went slowly down the path toward the House of Maidens, and after a time, Viviane followed.

Had Niniane's words been nothing but raving? She did not think so —she was sure the girl had seen *something*. But Viviane could make nothing of what Niniane had seen, and the girl's few attempts to put it into words meant nothing to Viviane. And now Niniane had forgotten it all, so that she could not be questioned further.

She sleeps in the arms of the grey king. Did that mean Morgaine was lying in the arms of death?

Would Morgaine return to them? Niniane had said only, *She stands in the boat . . .* so Morgaine would return to Avalon. *Her hair is all grey now.* So the return would not come soon, if at all. That, at least, was unequivocal.

The cross. The light burns me. Raven, Raven, the cauldron between her hands. That was certainly no more than delirium, an attempt to put some tenuous vision into words. Raven would bear the cauldron, the magical weapon of water and of the Goddess . . . yes, Raven was empowered to handle the Great Regalia. Viviane sat staring at the wall of her chamber, wondering if this meant that now Morgaine was gone from them, Raven should bear the power of the Lady of the Lake. It seemed to her that there was no other way to interpret the girl's words. And even so, they might mean nothing.

Whatever I do now, I am in the dark—I might better have gone to Raven, who would have answered me only with silence!

But if Morgaine had indeed gone into the arms of death, or was lost to Avalon forever, there was no other priestess fit to carry the weight. Raven had given her voice to the Goddess in prophecy . . . was the place of the Goddess to go unserved because Raven had chosen her silent path?

Viviane sat alone in her dwelling, staring at the wall, pondering Niniane's cryptic words again and again in her heart. Once she rose and went alone up the silent path to stare again into the unmoving waters, but they were grey, grey as the unyielding sky. Once indeed it seemed to her that something moved there, and Viviane whispered, "Morgaine?" and looked deep into the silence of the pool.

But the face that looked out at her was not Morgaine's face—it was still, dispassionate as the Goddess herself, crowned with bare wicker-withes. . . .

. . . Is it my own reflection I see, or the Death-crone? . . .

At last, weary, she turned away.

This I have known since first I trod the path—a time comes when there is only despair, when you seek to tear the veil from the shrine, and you cry out to her and know that she will not answer because she is not there, because she was never there, there is no Goddess but only yourself, and you are alone in the mockery of echoes from an empty shrine. . . .

There is no one there, there was never anyone there, and all the Sight is but dreams and delusions. . . .

As she trudged wearily down the hill, she saw that the new moon stood in the sky. But now it meant nothing to her save that this ritual silence and seclusion were done for the time.

What have I to do with this mockery of a Goddess? The fate of Avalon lies in my hands, and Morgaine is gone, and I am alone with old women and children and half-trained girls . . . alone, all alone! And I am old and weary and my death awaits me. . . .

Within her dwelling the women had lighted a fire, and a cup of warmed wine sat steaming beside her usual chair so that she might break the moon-dark fast. She sank down wearily, and one of her attendant priestesses came silently to draw off her shoes and put a warm shawl about her shoulders.

There is no one but I. But I have still my daughters, I am not wholly alone. "Thank you, my children," she said, with unaccustomed warmth, and one of the attendants bowed her head shyly without speaking. Viviane did not know the girl's name—*why am I thus neglectful?*—but she thought she must be under a vow of silence for the time. The second said softly, "It is our privilege to serve you, Mother. Will you go to rest?"

"Not yet awhile," Viviane said, and then on an impulse said, "Go and ask the priestess Raven to attend me."

It seemed a long time before, with silent step, Raven came into the room. Viviane greeted her with a bending of the head, and Raven came and bowed, then, following Viviane's gesture, went to the seat across from Viviane's own. Viviane handed her the cup, still half filled with the hot wine, and Raven sipped, smiling thanks, and put it from her.

At last Viviane said in entreaty, "My daughter, you broke your silence once before Morgaine left us. Now I seek for her and she cannot be found. She is not in Caerleon, nor in Tintagel, nor with Lot and Morgause in Lothian . . . and I grow old. There is none to serve. . . . I ask of you as I would inquire of the oracle of the Goddess: will Morgaine return?"

Raven was silent. At last she shook her head and Viviane demanded, "Do you mean that Morgaine will not return? Or do you mean that you do not know?" But the younger priestess made an odd gesture of helplessness and questioning.

"Raven," said Viviane, "you know that I must lay down my place, and there is no other to bear it, none who has the old training of a priestess, none who has gone so far—only you. If Morgaine does not return to us, you must be Lady of the Lake. Your oath was given to silence, and you have borne it faithfully. Now it is time to lay it aside, and take from my hands the guardianship of this place—there is no other way."

Raven shook her head. She was a tall woman, slightly built, and, Viviane thought, no longer young; she was certainly ten years older than Morgaine—she must be nearing her fortieth year. *And she came here as a little maiden with her breasts not yet budded.* Her hair was long and dark, and her face dark and sallow, her eyes large beneath dark, thick brows. She looked worn and austere.

Viviane covered her face with her hands and said in a hoarse voice, through tears she could not shed, "I—cannot, Raven."

After a moment, her face covered, she felt a gentle touch on her cheek. Raven had risen and was bending over her. She did not speak, only took Viviane into a close embrace and held her for a moment, and Viviane, feeling the warmth of the younger woman pressed against her, began to sob, and felt that she would weep and weep with no will ever to cease. And at last, when in sheer exhaustion Viviane was silent, Raven kissed her on the cheek and went silently away.

10

ONCE Igraine had said to Gwenhwyfar that Cornwall was at the world's end. So it seemed to Gwenhwyfar—there might never have been such things as marauding Saxons or a High King. Or a High Queen. Here in this distant Cornish convent, even though on a clear day she could look out toward the sea and see the stark line of Tintagel castle, she and Igraine were no more than two Christian ladies. Gwenhwyfar thought, surprising herself, *I am glad I came.*

Yet when Arthur had asked her to go, she had been afraid to leave the enclosing walls of Caerleon. The journey had seemed a long nightmare to her, even the swift and comfortable ride along the Roman road south; when they left the Roman road and began to travel across the high, exposed moors, Gwenhwyfar had huddled in panic within her litter, hardly able to tell which was more of a terror to her, the high open sky or the long, long vistas of grass, treeless, where the rocks thrust up stark and cold like the very bones of the earth. Then for a time no living creature could be seen except the ravens that circled high, waiting for something to die, or, far away, one of the wild moorland ponies, stopping to throw up a shaggy head before bolting away.

Yet here in this distant Cornish convent, all was still and peaceful; a soft-toned bell rang the hours, and roses grew in the enclosed cloister garden and twined into crannies of the crumbling brick wall. Once it had been a Roman villa. The sisters had taken up the floor of one big room, they said, because it had portrayed some scandalous pagan scene—Gwenhwyfar was curious as to what it was, but no one told her and she was ashamed to ask. All around the edges of the room were lovely little tiled dolphins and curious fish, and at the center, common bricks had been laid. She sat there with the sisters sometimes in the afternoons and stitched at her sewing, while Igraine was resting.

Igraine was dying. Two months since, the message had come to Caerleon. Arthur had had to travel north to Eboracum to see to the fortification of the Roman wall there and could not go, nor was Morgaine there. And since Arthur could not go, and it could not be looked for that Viviane, at her age, could make the long journey, Arthur had begged Gwenhwyfar to go and stay with his mother; and after much persuasion she had agreed.

Gwenhwyfar knew little about tending the sick. Whatever illness had seized on Igraine, at least it was painless—but she was short of breath and could not walk far without coughing and gasping. The sister who cared for her said it was congestion in the lungs, yet there was no coughing of blood and she had no fever and flushing. Her lips were pale and her nails blue, and her ankles were swollen to where she could hardly walk on them; she seemed almost too weary to speak and kept her bed most of the time. She seemed not so very ill to Gwenhwyfar, but the sister said she was dying indeed, and now it could not be more than a week at most.

It was the fairest part of the summer, and this morning Gwenhwyfar brought a white rose from the convent garden and laid it on Igraine's pillow. Igraine had struggled to her feet last night to go to evensong, but this morning she had been so weary and without strength she could not rise. Yet she smiled up at Gwenhwyfar and said in her wheezing voice, "Thank you, dear daughter." She put the flower to her face, sniffing delicately at the petals. "Always I wanted roses at Tintagel, but the soil there was so poor, little would grow. . . . I dwelt there five years and never did I cease from trying to make some sort of garden."

"When you came to take me to be wedded, you saw the garden at my home," Gwenhwyfar said, with a sudden twinge of homesickness for that faraway walled garden.

"I remember how beautiful it was—it put me in mind of Avalon. The flowers are so beautiful there, in the courts of the House of Maidens." She was silent for a moment. "A message *was* sent to Morgaine at Avalon?"

"A message was sent, Mother. But Taliesin told us Morgaine had not been seen in Avalon," said Gwenhwyfar. "No doubt she is with Queen Morgause in Lothian, and in these times it takes forever for a messenger to come and go."

Igraine drew a heavy sigh and began to struggle with a cough again, and Gwenhwyfar helped her to sit upright. After a time Igraine murmured, "Yet the Sight should have bidden Morgaine to come to me—you would come if you knew your mother was dying, would you not? Yes, for you came, and I am not even your own mother. Why has Morgaine not come?"

It is nothing to her that I have come, Gwenhwyfar thought, *it is not me she wants here. There is no one who cares whether I am here or elsewhere.* And it seemed as if her very heart was bruised. But Igraine was looking at her expectantly, and she said, "Perhaps Morgaine has received no message. Perhaps she has gone into a convent somewhere and become a Christian and renounced the Sight."

"It may be so. . . . I did so when I married Uther," Igraine murmured. "Yet now and again it thrust itself on me undesired, and I think if Morgaine was ill or dying I would know it." Her voice was fretful. "The Sight came upon me before you were married . . . tell me, Gwenhwyfar, do you love my son?"

Gwenhwyfar shrank from the sick woman's clear grey eyes; could Igraine see into her very soul? "I love him well and I am his faithful queen, lady."

"Aye, I believe you are . . . and you are happy together?" Igraine held Gwenhwyfar's slender hands in her own for a moment and suddenly smiled. "Why, so you must be. And will be happier yet, since you are bearing his son at last."

Gwenhwyfar's mouth dropped open and she stared at Igraine. "I—I —I did not know."

Igraine smiled again, a tender and radiant smile, so that Gwenhwyfar thought, *Yes, I can believe it, that when she was young, she was beautiful enough for Uther to cast aside all caution and seek her with spells and charms.*

Igraine said, "It is often so, though you are not really so young—I am surprised you have not already had a child."

"It was not for lack of wanting, no, nor praying for it either, lady," Gwenhwyfar said, so shaken that she hardly knew what she was saying. Was the old Queen falling into delirium? This was too cruel for jesting. "How —what makes you think I am—am with child?"

Igraine said, "I forgot, you have not the Sight—it has deserted me for long and long I renounced it, but as I say, it steals upon me unawares, and never has it played me false." Gwenhwyfar began to weep, and Igraine, troubled, reached out her thin hand and laid it over the younger woman's.

"Why, how is this, that I give you good news and you weep, child?"

Now she will think I do not want a child, and I cannot bear to have her think ill of me. . . . . Gwenhwyfar said shakily, "Only twice in all the years I have been married have I had any cause to think myself pregnant, and then I carried the child only a month or two. Tell me, lady, do you—" Her throat closed and she dared not speak the words. *Tell me, Igraine, shall I bear this child, have you seen me then with Arthur's child at my breast?* What would her priest think of this compromise with sorcery?

Igraine patted her hand. "I wish I might tell you more, but the Sight comes and goes as it will. God grant it come to a good end, my dear; it may be that I can see no more because by the time your child is born, I shall not be here to see—no, no, child, do not weep," she begged. "I have been ready to leave this life ever since I saw Arthur wedded. I would like to see your son, I would like to hold a child of Morgaine's in my arms, should that day ever come, but Uther is gone and it is well with my children. It may be that Uther waits for me beyond death, or the other children I lost at birth. And if they do not—" She shrugged. "I shall never know."

Igraine's eyes closed, and Gwenhwyfar thought, *I have wearied her.* She sat silent until the older woman slept, then rose and went quietly into the garden.

She felt numbed; it had truly not seemed to her that she might be pregnant. If she had thought anything at all about it, it was that the stress of travel had delayed her courses . . . for the first three years of her marriage, every time it had been late, she had thought herself with child. Then, in the year in which Arthur had been, first, away for the battle of Celidon Wood and the long campaign before it, then wounded and too weak to touch her, the same pattern had persisted. And finally she had realized that her monthly rhythms were inconstant—there was no way to keep track of them by the moon, for sometimes two or three months might pass with no sign.

But now that Igraine had spoken, she wondered why she had not thought of this before; it never occurred to her to doubt the Queen. Something inside Gwenhwyfar said, *Sorcery,* and there was a small voice that persisted in reminding her, *All these things are of the Devil, and have no place in this house of holy women.* But something else said, *How could it be wicked to tell me this?* It was more, she thought, as when the angel was sent to Mary the Virgin to tell her of the birth of her son . . . and then for a moment Gwenhwyfar was struck with awe at her own presumption; and then she began softly to giggle, at the incongruity of Igraine, old and dying, as an angel of God.

At that moment the bell rang in the cloister for prayers, and Gwenhwyfar, though here as a guest, and without obligation, turned and went into the sisters' chapel, kneeling in her accustomed place among the visitors.

But she heard little of the service, for her whole heart and mind were caught up in the most fervent prayer of her entire life.

It has come, the answer to all my prayers. Oh, thank you, God and Christ and our Blessed Lady!

Arthur was wrong. It was not he who failed. There was no need . . . and once again she was filled with the paralyzing shame she had felt when he had said that thing to her, all but giving her leave to betray him . . . *and what a wicked woman I was then, that I could even have considered it. . . .* But now in the very midst of her wickedness God had rewarded her when she deserved it now. Gwenhwyfar raised her head and began to sing the Magnificat with the rest, so fervently that the abbess raised her head and looked sharply at her.

They do not know why I am thankful . . . they do not know how much I have to be thankful for. . . .

But they do not know how wicked I was either, for I was thinking here in this holy place of the one I love. . . .

And then, even through her joy, suddenly it was like pain again: *Now he will look upon me big with Arthur's child, and he will think me ugly and gross and never look on me again with love and longing.* And even through the joy in her heart, she felt small and cramped and joyless.

Arthur gave me leave, and we could have had each other, at least once, and now never . . . never . . . never. . . .

She put her face into her hands and wept behind them, silently, and no longer cared that the abbess was watching her.

THAT NIGHT IGRAINE'S BREATHING was so labored that she could not even lower her head to rest; she had to sit bolt upright, propped up on many cushions, to breathe at all, and she wheezed and coughed without end. The abbess gave her a draught of something which would clear the lungs, but it only made her queasy, she said, and she could take no more of it.

Gwenhwyfar sat beside her, drowsing a little now and then, but alert whenever the sick woman stirred, to give her a sip of water, to shift her pillows so that she could find a little ease. There was only a small lamp in the room, but there was brilliant moonlight, and the night was so warm that the door stood open into the garden. And through it all there was the ever-present muffled sound of the sea beyond the garden, beating at the rocks.

"Strange," Igraine murmured at last in a faraway voice, "never would I have thought I would come here to die. . . . I remember how dreary I felt, how alone, when first I came to Tintagel, as if I had come to the very end of the world. Avalon was so fair, so beautiful, so filled with flowers . . ."

"There are flowers here," Gwenhwyfar said.

"But not like the flowers of my home. It is so barren here, so rocky," she said. "Have you been in the Island, child?"

"I was schooled in the convent on Ynis Witrin, madam."

"It is beautiful on the Island. And when I travelled here over the moors, it was so high and barren and deserted, I was afraid—"

Igraine made a weak movement toward her, and Gwenhwyfar took her hand and was alarmed by its coldness. "You are a good child," Igraine said, "to come so far, when my own children could not. I remember how you dread travelling—and now to come so far, when you are pregnant."

Gwenhwyfar rubbed the icy hands between her own. "Do not tire yourself with talking, Mother."

Igraine made a little sound like a laugh, but it got lost in a fit of wheezing. "Do you think it makes any difference now, Gwenhwyfar? I wronged you—even on the very day you were wedded, I went to Taliesin and asked him, was there any honorable way for Arthur to get out of this marriage."

"I—did not know. Why?"

It seemed to her that Igraine hesitated before answering, but she could not tell, perhaps it was only that the other woman struggled for speech. "I know not . . . perhaps it was that I thought you would not be happy with my son." She struggled again with a fit of coughing so heavy that it seemed she would never get her breath.

When she had quieted a little, Gwenhwyfar said, "Now you must talk no more, Mother—will you have me bring you a priest?"

"Damn all priests," said Igraine clearly. "I will have none of them about me—oh, look not so shocked, child!" She lay still for a moment. "You thought me so pious, that I retired to a convent in my last years. But where else should I have gone? Viviane would have had me at Avalon, but I could not forget it was she who had married me to Gorlois. . . . Beyond that garden wall lies Tintagel, like a prison . . . a prison it was to me, indeed. Yet it was the only place I could call my own. And I felt I had won it by what I endured there. . . ."

Another long, silent struggle for breath. At last she said, "I wish Morgaine had come to me . . . she has the Sight, she should have known I was dying. . . ."

Gwenhwyfar saw that there were tears in her eyes. She said gently, rubbing the icy hands which now felt as taut as cold claws, "I am sure she would come if she knew, dear Mother."

"I am not so sure . . . I sent her from me into Viviane's hands. Even though I knew well how ruthless Viviane could be, that she would use Morgaine as ruthlessly as she used me, for the well-being of this land and for her own love of power," Igraine whispered. "I sent her from me because I felt it better, if it came to be a choice of evils, that she should be in Avalon and in the hands of the Goddess, than in the hands of the black priests who would teach her to think that she was evil because she was a woman."

Gwenhwyfar was deeply dismayed. She chafed the icy hands between her own and renewed the hot bricks at Igraine's feet; but the feet too were cold as ice, and when she rubbed them Igraine said she could not feel them.

She felt she must try again. "Now with your end near, do you not want to speak with one of Christ's priests, dear Mother?"

"I told you, no," said Igraine, "or after all these years when I kept silent to have peace in my home, I might tell them at last what I truly felt about them. . . . I loved Morgaine enough to send her to Viviane, that she at least might escape them. . . ." She began wheezing again. "Arthur," she said at last. "Never was he my son . . . he was Uther's—only a hope of the succession, no more. I loved Uther well and I bore him sons because it meant so much to him that he should have a son to follow him. Our second son —he that died soon after his navel string was cut—him, I think, I might have loved for my own, as I loved Morgaine. . . . Tell me, Gwenhwyfar, has my son reproached you that you have not yet borne him an heir?"

Gwenhwyfar bent her head, feeling her eyes stinging with tears. "No, he has been so good . . . never once has he reproached me. He told me once that he had never fathered a son by any woman, though he had known many, so that perhaps the fault was not mine."

"If he loves you for yourself, then he is a priceless jewel among men," said Igraine, "and it is all the better if you can make him happy. . . . Morgaine I loved because she was all I had to love. I was young and wretched; you can never know how unhappy I was that winter when I bore her, alone and far from home and not yet full-grown. I feared she would have become a monster because of all the hate I felt when I was bearing her, but she was the prettiest little thing, solemn, wise, like a fairy child. She and Uther only have I loved . . . where is she, Gwenhwyfar? Where is she that she would not come to her mother when she is dying?"

Gwenhwyfar said compassionately, "No doubt she knows not that you are ill—"

"But the Sight!" Igraine cried, moving restlessly on her pillow. "Where can she be, that she does not see that I am dying? Ah, I saw she was in deep trouble, even at Arthur's crowning, and yet I said nothing, I did not want to know, I felt I had had enough grief and said nothing when she needed me. . . . Gwenhwyfar, tell me the truth! Did Morgaine have a child somewhere, alone and far from anyone who loved her? Has she spoken of this to you? Does she hate me then, that she will not come to me even when I am dying, only because I did not speak out all my fears for her at

Arthur's crowning? Ah, Goddess . . . I put aside the Sight to have peace in my home, since Uther was a follower of the Christ. . . . Show me where dwells my child, my daughter. . . ."

Gwenhwyfar held her motionless and said, "Now you must be still, Mother . . . it must be as God wills. You cannot call upon the Goddess of the fiends here—"

Igraine sat bolt upright; despite her sick swollen face, her blue lips, she looked on the younger woman in such a way that Gwenhwyfar suddenly remembered, *She too is High Queen of this land.*

"You know not what you speak," Igraine said, with pride and pity and contempt. "The Goddess is beyond all your other Gods. Religions may come and go, as the Romans found and no doubt the Christians will find after them, but she is beyond them all." She let Gwenhwyfar lower her to her pillows and groaned. "I would my feet could be warmed . . . yes, I know you have hot bricks there, I cannot feel them. Once I read in an ancient book which Taliesin gave me of some scholar who was forced to drink hemlock. Taliesin says that the people have always killed the wise. Even as the people of the far southlands put Christ to the cross, so this wise and holy man was forced to drink hemlock because the rabble and the kings said he taught false doctrine. And when he was dying, he said that the cold crept upward from his feet, and so he died. . . . I have not drunk of hemlock, but it is as if I had . . . and now the cold is reaching my heart. . . ." She shivered and was still, and for a moment Gwenhwyfar thought she had ceased to breathe. No, the heart was still sluggishly beating. But Igraine did not speak again, lying wheezing on her pillows, and a little before dawn the rasping breaths finally ceased.

11

IGRAINE was buried at midday, after a solemn service of mourning; Gwenhwyfar stood beside the grave, tears sliding down her face as the shrouded body was lowered into the open earth. Yet she could not properly mourn her mother-in-law. *Her living here was all a lie, she was no true Christian.* If it was true what they believed, then Igraine was even now burning in hell. And she could not bear that, not when she thought of all Igraine's kindness to her.

Her eyes burned with sleeplessness and tears. The lowering sky echoed her vague dread; heavy, as if at any moment rain would fall on them. Here within convent walls she was safe, but soon she must leave the safety of this place and ride for days over the high moors with the brooding menace of that open sky everywhere, hanging over her and over her child. . . . Gwenhwyfar, shivering, clasped her hands across her belly, as if in a futile wish to protect the dweller there from the menace of that sky.

Why am I always so frightened? Igraine was a pagan and lost to the tricks of the Devil, but I am safe, I call upon Christ to save me. What is there under God's Heaven to be afraid of? Yet she was afraid, with the same reasonless fear that seized on her so often. *I must not fear. I am High Queen of all Britain; the only other to bear that title sleeps here beneath the earth . . . High Queen, and bearing the son of Arthur. Why should I be afraid of anything in God's world?*

The nuns finished their hymn, turning from the grave. Gwenhwyfar shivered again, clutching her cloak. Now she must take very good care of herself, eat well, rest much, make certain that nothing went amiss as it had done before. Secretly she counted on her fingers. If it had been that last time before she left . . . but no, her courses had not come upon her for more than ten Sundays, she simply was not certain. Still, it was sure that her son would be born sometime about Eastertide. Yes, that was a good time; she remembered when her lady Meleas had born her son, it had been the darkest of winter, and the wind had howled outside like all the fiends waiting to snatch the soul of the newborn child, so nothing would suit Meleas but that the priest must come down to the women's hall and baptize her babe almost before it cried. No, Gwenhwyfar was just as well pleased that she would not lie in at the darkest days of winter. Yet to have the longed-for child, she would be content to bear it even at Midwinter-night itself!

A bell tolled, and then the abbess came to Gwenhwyfar. She did not bow—temporal power, she had once said, was nothing here—but Gwenhwyfar was, after all, the High Queen, so she inclined her head with great courtesy and said, "Will you be staying on with us here, my lady? We would be deeply honored to keep you as long as you wish."

Oh, if only I could stay! It is so peaceful here. . . . Gwenhwyfar said, with visible regret, "I cannot. I must return to Caerleon."

She could not delay telling Arthur her good news, the news of his son. . . .

"The High King must hear of—of his mother's death," she said. Then, knowing what the woman wanted to hear, she added quickly, "Be sure I will tell him how kindly you treated her. She had everything she could wish for in the last days of her life."

"It was our pleasure; we all loved the lady Igraine," said the old nun. "Your escort shall be told, and be ready to ride with you early in the morning, God willing and send good weather."

"Tomorrow? Why not today?" Gwenhwyfar asked, then stopped— no, that would be insulting haste indeed. She had not realized she was so eager to tell her news to Arthur, to end for all time the silent reproach that she was barren. She laid her hand on the abbess' arm. "You must pray for me much now, and for the safe birth of the High King's son."

"Is it so, lady?" The abbess' lined face wrinkled up in pleasure at being the confidante of the Queen. "Indeed we shall pray for you. It will give all the sisters pleasure to think we are the first to say prayers for our new prince."

"I shall make gifts to your convent—"

"God's gifts and prayers may not be bought for gold," the abbess said primly, but she looked pleased nevertheless.

In the room near Igraine's chamber, where she had slept these last nights, her serving-woman was moving about, putting garments and gear into saddlebags. As Gwenhwyfar entered, she looked up and grumbled, "It suits not well with the dignity of the High Queen, madam, to travel with only one servant! Why, any knight's wife would have as much! You should get you another from one of the houses here, and a lady to travel with you as well!"

"Get one of the lay sisters to help you, then," said Gwenhwyfar. "But we shall travel all the more quickly if we are but few."

"I heard in the courtyard that there were Saxons landing on the Southern Shores," the woman grumbled. "It soon will not be safe to ride anywhere in this country!"

"Don't be foolish," Gwenhwyfar said. "The Saxons on the Southern Shores are bound fast by treaty to keep peace with the High King's lands. They know what Arthur's legion can do, they found it out at Celidon Wood. Do you think they want more work for ravens? In any case we will soon be back at Caerleon, and at the end of summer, we shall move the court to Camelot in the Summer Country—the Romans defended that fort against all the barbarians. It has never been taken. Even now Sir Cai is there, building a great hall fit for Arthur's Round Table, so that all the Companions and kings may sit at meat together."

As she had hoped, the woman was diverted. "That is near your own old home, is it not, lady?"

"Yes. From the heights of Camelot, one may look a bowshot across the water and see my father's island kingdom. Indeed, I went there in childhood once," she said, remembering how, when she was a little girl, even before she went to school with the nuns on Ynis Witrin, she had been taken up to the ruins of the old Roman fort. There had been little there then, except for the old wall, and the priest had not stinted to make this a lesson on how human glories faded away. . . .

She dreamed that night that she stood high on Camelot; but the mists drew in around the shore, so that the island seemed to swim in a sea of cloud.

Across from them, she could see the high Tor of Ynis Witrin, crowned with ring stones; although she knew well that the ring stones had been thrown down by the priests a hundred years ago. And by some trick of the Sight it seemed that Morgaine stood on the Tor and laughed at her and mocked her, and she was crowned with a wreath of bare wicker-withes. And then Morgaine was standing beside her on Camelot and they looked out over all the Summer Country as far as the Isle of the Priests, looking down over her own old home where her father Leodegranz was king, and over Dragon Island shrouded in mist. But Morgaine was wearing strange robes and a high double crown, and she stood so that Gwenhwyfar could not quite *see* her, but only knew she was there. She said, *I am Morgaine of the Fairies, and all these kingdoms will I give to you as their High Queen if you will fall down and worship me.*

Gwenhwyfar woke with a start, Morgaine's mocking laughter in her ears. The room was empty and silent except for the heavy snores of her serving-woman in a pallet on the floor. Gwenhwyfar made the sign of the cross and lay down to sleep again. But on the very edge of sleep it seemed to her that she looked into the clear and moonlit waters of a pool, and instead of her own face, Morgaine's pale face was reflected back at her, crowned with wicker-withes like the harvest dolls some of the peasant folk still made, and very far away. And again Gwenhwyfar had to sit up and make the sign of the cross before she could compose herself to sleep.

It seemed all too soon that she was wakened, but then she had been so insistent they should set forth at the first light. She could hear the rain pounding on the roof as she put on her gown by lamplight, but if they stayed for rain in this climate they should be here a year. She felt dull and queasy, but now she knew there was a good reason for that, and secretly patted her still-flat stomach as if to reassure herself it was real. She had no desire to eat, but dutifully swallowed some bread and cold meats . . . she had a long ride before her. And if she had no mind to riding in the rain, at least it was likely that any Saxons or marauders would stay within doors as well.

She was fastening the hood of her warmest cloak when the abbess entered. After a few formal words of thanks for the rich gifts made by Gwenhwyfar on her own behalf and on Igraine's, the abbess came to the real business of this farewell visit.

"Who now reigns in Cornwall, lady?"

"Why—I am not sure," said Gwenhwyfar, trying to remember. "I know the High King gave Tintagel to Igraine when he married, so that she might have a place of her own, and I suppose, after her, the lady Morgaine, daughter of Igraine by the old Duke Gorlois. I know not even who is there now as castellan."

"Nor I," said the abbess. "Some serving-man or knight of the lady

Igraine, I suppose. That is why I came to speak with you, madam . . . the castle Tintagel is a prize, and it should be tenanted, or there will be war in this countryside too. If the lady Morgaine is married and comes here to live, all will be well, I suppose—I do not know the lady, but if she is Igraine's daughter, I suppose she is a good woman and a good Christian."

You suppose wrong, Gwenhwyfar thought, and again it was as if she heard the mocking laughter from her dream. But she would not speak ill of Arthur's kinswoman to a stranger.

The abbess said, "Bear my message to Arthur the King, lady—that someone should come to dwell in Tintagel. I have heard something of a rumor that ran about the countryside when Gorlois died—that he had a bastard son and some other kinfolk, and some of them might strive to conquer this country again. While Igraine dwelt here, all folk knew it was under Arthur's dominion, but now it would be well if the High King sent one of his best knights hither—perhaps married to the lady Morgaine."

"I will tell Arthur," Gwenhwyfar said, and as she set out, she pondered this. She knew little of statecraft, but she remembered that there had been chaos before Uther came to the crown and again when he died leaving no heir; she supposed something like that might befall if Cornwall was left with none to rule or keep good laws. Morgaine was Queen of Cornwall and should come hither to reign. And then she remembered what Arthur had once said that his dearest friend should wed with his sister. Since Lancelet was not wealthy and had no lands of his own, it would be the right thing that they should come to reign together in Cornwall.

And now I am to bear Arthur's son, it would be best to send Lancelet far from court, that I might never again look on his face and think of him such thoughts as no wedded woman and no good Christian should think. And yet she could not bear to think of Lancelet wedded to Morgaine. Had there ever been so wicked a woman as she on the face of this wicked world? She rode with her face hidden in her cloak, not listening to the gossip of the knights who were her escort, but after a time she realized that they were passing by a village which had been burned. One of the knights asked her leave to stop a while, and went away to look for survivors; he came back looking grim.

"Saxons," he said to the others, and bit the words off when he saw that the Queen was listening.

"Don't be frightened, madam, they are gone, but we must ride as fast as we may and tell Arthur of this. If we find you a faster horse, can you keep our pace?"

Gwenhwyfar felt her breath catch in her throat. They had come up out of one of the deep valleys, and the sky arched high and open over them, filled with menace—she felt as some small thing must feel in the grass when the shadow of a hawk swoops over it. She said, and heard her voice thin and trembling like the voice of a very little girl, "I cannot ride faster now. I bear the child of the High King and I dare not endanger him."

Again it seemed as if the knight—he was Griflet, husband of her own waiting-woman, Meleas—bit off his words, setting his jaw with a snap. He said at last, concealing his impatience, "Then, madam, it were as well we should escort you to Tintagel, or to some other great house in this area, or back again to the convent, so that we may ride at speed and reach Caerleon before the dawn of tomorrow's day. If you are with child you certainly cannot ride through the night! Will you let one of us escort you and your woman back to Tintagel or to the convent again?"

I would like it well to be within walls again, if there are Saxons in this country . . . but I must not be such a coward. Arthur must have the news of his son. She said stubbornly, "Cannot one of you ride on toward Caerleon, and the rest of you travel at my pace? Or cannot a messenger be hired to bear the word quickly?"

Griflet looked as if he wanted to swear. "I could not trust to any hired messenger in this country now, madam, and there are few of us even for a peaceful country, barely enough to protect you. Well, it must be as it will, no doubt Arthur's men have received the word already." He turned away, his jaw white and set, and looked so angry that Gwenhwyfar wanted to call him back and agree to all he said; but she told herself firmly not to be so cowardly. Now when she was to bear the royal son, she must behave herself like a queen and ride on with courage.

And if I was at Tintagel and the countryside was filled with Saxons, there would I remain until the war had ended and all the country at peace again, and it might be long . . . and if Arthur did not even know I was with child, he might be content to let me dwell there forevermore. Why should he want to bring back a barren queen to his new palace at Camelot? Like enough he would listen to the counsel of that old Druid who hates me, Taliesin, who is his grandsire, and put me away for some woman who could bear him a bouncing brat every ten moons or so. . . .

But all will be well, once Arthur knows. . . .

It seemed as if the icy wind was sweeping across the high moors and into her very bones; after a time she begged them to stop again and get out the litter so that she might ride within it . . . the horse's motion jolted her so. Griflet looked angry, and for a moment she thought he would forget his courtesy and swear at her, but he gave the orders, and she huddled gratefully inside the litter, glad of the slow pace and the closed flaps which closed out the frightening sky.

Before dusk the rain stopped for a while, and the sun came out, low and slanting over the dismal moor. "We will set up the tents here," Griflet said. "Here on the moor at least we can see a long way. Tomorrow we should strike the old Roman road, and then we can travel faster—" and then he dropped his voice and said something to the other knights which Gwenhwyfar could not hear, but she cringed, knowing he was angry at the slow pace at which they must travel. Yet everyone knew a breeding woman was more like to miscarry if she rode a fast horse, and already twice she had miscarried a child—did they *want* her to lose Arthur's son this time too?

She slept poorly within the tent, the ground hard beneath her thin body, her cloak and blankets all damp, her body aching from the unaccustomed riding.

But after a time she slept, despite the pouring rain that leaked through the tent, and was wakened by the sound of riders and a call: Griflet's voice, harsh and rough.

"Who rides there! Stand!"

"Is it you, Griflet? I know your voice," came a cry out of the dark. "It is Gawaine, and I seek for your party—is the Queen with you?"

Gwenhwyfar threw her cloak over her nightdress and came out from the tent. "Is it you, cousin? What do you here?"

"I hoped to find you still at the convent," said Gawaine, sliding from his horse. Behind him in the darkness were other forms—four or five of Arthur's men, though Gwenhwyfar could not distinguish their faces. "Since you are here, madam, I suppose Queen Igraine has departed this life—"

"She died the night before last," Gwenhwyfar said, and Gawaine sighed.

"Well, it is God's will," he said. "But the land is under arms, madam —since you are here and so far on your way, I suppose you must continue on to Caerleon. Had you still been at the convent I was under orders to escort you, and such of the sisters as wished to seek protection, to Tintagel castle, and bid you remain there until there was safety in the land."

"And now you may spare the journey," said Gwenhwyfar irritably, but Gawaine shook his head. He said, "Since my message is useless, and I suppose the sisters will wish to take shelter within their convent walls, I must ride on to Tintagel with news for all men sworn to Arthur to come at once. The Saxons are massing near the coast with more than a hundred ships— beacon signals were sent from the lighthouses. The legion is at Caerleon, and all men are gathering. When the word came to Lothian, I rode at once to join Arthur; and Arthur sent me to Tintagel to bear word thither." He drew breath. "Not the Merlin's self is more a messenger than I these ten days."

"And I told the Queen," said Griflet, "that she should remain at Tintagel, but now it is too late to return there! And with armies gathering on the roads—Gawaine, perhaps you should escort the Queen back to Tintagel."

"No," said Gwenhwyfar clearly. "I must return now, I am not afraid to travel where I must." Even more, if he was facing war again, Arthur would wish for the good news she bore. Gawaine had already shaken his head impatiently.

"I cannot delay for any woman's riding, unless it were the Lady of the Lake herself, who can ride a day's journey with any man a-horse! And you are but a sorry rider, madam—nay, I spoke not to anger you, no one expects that you should ride like a knight, but I cannot delay—"

"And the Queen is breeding and must travel at the slowest pace of all," Griflet told him with equal impatience. "Can some of your slowest riders be told to escort the Queen, Gawaine, and I ride on with you to Tintagel?"

Gawaine smiled. "No doubt you wish to be at the heart of things, Griflet, but you have been given this task and no one envies you," he said. "Can you find me a cup of wine and some bread? I will travel on through the night, to be in Tintagel at sunrise. I have a message for Marcus, who is war duke of Cornwall and is to bring his knights. This may be the great battle Taliesin foretold, where we perish or we drive the Saxons once and for all from this land! But every man must come and fight at Arthur's side."

"Even some of the treaty troops will stand with Arthur now," said Griflet. "Ride on if you must, Gawaine, and God ride with you." The two knights embraced. "We will meet again when God wills, friend."

Gawaine bowed to Gwenhwyfar. She reached out a hand to him and said, "A moment—is my kinswoman Morgause well?"

"As ever, madam."

"And my sister-in-law Morgaine—she is safe in Morgause's court, then?"

Gawaine looked startled. "Morgaine? No, madam, I have not seen my kinswoman Morgaine for many years. Certainly she has not visited Lothian, or so my mother said," he replied, courteous despite his impatience. "Now I must be off."

"God ride with you," she said, and stood watching as the men's hoofbeats thundered away in the night.

"It is now so near dawn," she said, "is there any reason to try to sleep more, or should we break camp and ride on for Caerleon?"

Griflet looked pleased. "True, there will be little sleep for any, in this rain," he said, "and if you can travel, lady, it would please me well to be on the road. God knows what we shall have to pass through before we reach Caerleon."

But as the sun rose over the moors it was as if they rode through a land already struck silent by the war. It was the season when the farmers should be out in their fields, but although they passed several isolated hill farms, no sheep grazed, not a dog barked, nor any child came to watch them;

and even along the Roman road there was not a single traveller. Gwenhwy-far, shivering, realized that the word had gone out to raise the countryside for war, and such as could do nothing had crept behind closed doors to hide from the armies of either side.

Will it endanger my child, to travel at this pace? Yet now it seemed a choice of evils—endanger herself and her child and Arthur's by this forced travel, or delay on the road and perhaps fall into the hands of the Saxon armies. She resolved that Griflet should have no further cause to complain that she had delayed them. Yet as she rode, unwilling to take refuge within her litter lest he accuse her again of delaying him, it seemed that fear was hovering everywhere around her.

It was near to sunset, and it had been a long day, when they caught sight of the watchtower which Uther had built at Caerleon. The great crimson banner of the Pendragon floated from the heights, and Gwenhwyfar crossed herself as they passed beneath it.

Now all Christian men are to make a stand against the barbarians, is it fitting that this sign of an ancient Devil-faith should serve to rally the armies of a Christian king? Once indeed she had spoken of it to Arthur and he had answered that he had sworn to his people that he would rule over them as the Great Dragon, Christian and non-Christian alike without favor, and had laughed, stretching out his arms with the barbarian serpents tattooed all along their length. She felt loathing for those serpents, symbols that no Christian man should bear, but he had been stubborn.

"I bear them in sign of the kingmaking when I was given Uther's place in this land. We will speak no more of this, lady." And nothing she had said could force him to discuss it with her or to listen to what a priest might say on the subject.

"Priestcraft is one thing and kingcraft is another, my Gwenhwyfar. I would that you should share all things with me, but you have no wish to share this, and so I may not speak of it to you. And as for the priests, it is none of their affair. Leave it, I say." His voice had been firm, not angry, but still she had bent her head and said no more. Yet now, as she rode beneath the Pendragon banner, she trembled. *If our son is to rule in a Christian land, is it fitting that Druid banner should fly above his father's castle?*

They rode slowly through the encamped armies in the plain before Caerleon. Some of the knights, who knew her well, came out and set up a cheer for their queen, and she smiled and waved to them. They rode beneath the banner of Lot and through the men of Lothian, Northmen with pikes and long axes, wrapped in the crudely dyed clothes they wore; over their camp flew the banner of the Morrigán, the Great Raven of war.

Gawaine's brother Gaheris came out from that camp and bowed to her, and walked beside Griflet's horse as they rode up toward the castle.

"Did my brother find you, Griflet? He had a message for the Queen—"

"He met us when we were already a day on the road," Gwenhwyfar said, "and it was easier to continue here."

"I will come with you to the castle—all of Arthur's chosen Companions are bidden to dine with the King," said Gaheris. "Gawaine was angry at being sent with messages, yet no one can ride so swiftly as my brother when he must. Your lady is here, Griflet, but she is readying herself and the child to go to the new castle—Arthur says all the women must go, they can be more easily defended there, and he can spare but few to defend them."

To Camelot! Gwenhwyfar's heart sank—she had ridden all the way from Tintagel to give Arthur news of their child, and now would he pack her up and send her to Camelot?

"I do not know that banner," said Griflet, looking at a golden eagle sculptured lifelike on a pole. It seemed very ancient.

"It is the standard of North Wales," said Gaheris. "Uriens is here, with Avalloch his son. Uriens claims his father took this standard from the Romans, more than a hundred years ago. It may even be the truth! The men from Uriens' hills are strong fighters, though I'd not say so in their hearing."

"And whose banner is *that?*" asked Griflet, but this time, though Gaheris turned to speak, it was Gwenhwyfar herself who answered.

"That is the banner of my father, Leodegranz, the blue banner with the cross worked in gold." She herself, as a young maiden in the Summer Country, had helped her mother's women to embroider it for the king. It was said that her father had chosen this device after hearing a tale that one of the emperors of Rome had seen the sign of the cross in the sky before one of his battles. *We should now be fighting beneath that sign, not the serpents of Avalon!* She shivered, and Gaheris looked at her sharply.

"Are you cold, lady? We must ride on to the castle, Griflet, no doubt Arthur will be awaiting his queen."

"You must be weary of riding, my queen," said Griflet, looking up kindly at her. "Now will you soon be in the hands of your women."

And as they came closer to the doors of the castle, there were many of Arthur's Companions whom she knew, who waved to her and called to her in friendly, informal fashion. *Next year at this time,* she thought, *they will come out to cheer their prince.*

A big, lurching man, huge and clumsy-footed, in leather armor and a steel cap, came into the path of her horse—it was as if he stumbled, though he bowed to Gwenhwyfar and she could see that it was deliberate, that he had put himself in her way like this.

"Madam, my sister," he said, "do you not know me?"

Gwenhwyfar frowned and stared at him, then after a moment recognized him. "Is it you—"

"Meleagrant," he said. "I have come here to fight at our father's side and your husband's, my sister."

Griflet said, with a friendly smile, "I knew not that your father had a son, my queen. But all are welcome to fight under Arthur's standard—"

"Perhaps you will speak for me to your husband the King, my sister," said Meleagrant. Gwenhwyfar, looking at him, felt a faint distaste run through her. He was an enormous man, almost a giant, and like so many huge men, he looked misshapen, as if one side of his body were somehow grown larger than the other. One eye was certainly larger than the other, and had a squint; yet, trying to be fair, Gwenhwyfar thought the man's deformity was no fault of his, and she really knew nothing against him. Yet it was arrogance, that he should call her sister before all these men, and now he had grasped her hand without leave and made as if to kiss it. She clenched it into a fist and pulled it away.

Trying to make her voice firm, she said, "No doubt when you merit it, Meleagrant, my father will speak for you to Arthur and he will make you one of his knights. I am only a woman and I have no authority to promise you that. Is my father here?"

"He is with Arthur within the castle," said Meleagrant sullenly, "and I am like a dog out here with the horses!"

Gwenhwyfar said firmly, "I cannot see that you have any claim to more than this, Meleagrant. He has given you a post at his side, for your mother was once a favorite of his—"

Meleagrant said harshly, "All men in the country know as well as my mother that I am the king's son, his only living son! Sister, speak to our father for me!"

She pulled away her hand from his repeated effort to seize it. "Let me go, Meleagrant! My father claims you are not his son, and how can I say anything else? I never knew your mother—this is between you and my father!"

"But you must listen," said Meleagrant urgently, tugging at her hand, and Griflet thrust himself between them and said, "Here, here, fellow, you can't talk to the Queen like that, or Arthur will have your head on his platter at dinnertime! I'm sure our lord and king will grant you what's right, and if you fight well for him at this battle, no doubt he'll be glad to have you among his Companions. But you mustn't trouble the Queen this way!"

Meleagrant turned to face him, towering over Griflet until the latter, though he was a tall, athletic young man, looked like a child. The giant said,

"Are you going to tell me what I can say to my own sister, you little popinjay?"

Griflet put his hand on his sword and said, "I was given the task of escorting my queen, fellow, and I'll do the task Arthur's given me to do. Get out of my path or I'll force you to!"

"You with who else?" sneered Meleagrant, bracing himself with an ugly sneer.

"I, for one," said Gaheris, standing quickly at Griflet's side. Like Gawaine, he was a big, sturdy man who would have made two of the slender Griflet.

"And I," said Lancelet from the darkness beyond them, striding quickly toward Gwenhwyfar's horse, and she could have wept with relief. Never had he looked more handsome to her than now; and though he was slender and slightly built, something in his presence made Meleagrant draw back. "Is this man annoying you, lady Gwenhwyfar?"

She swallowed and nodded, and found to her dismay that she had no voice to speak. Meleagrant blustered, "Who may you be, fellow?"

"Take care," said Gaheris, "don't you know the lord Lancelet?"

"I am Arthur's captain of horse," said Lancelet, in his lazy amused voice, "and the Queen's champion. Have you anything to say to me?"

"My business is with my sister," said Meleagrant, but Gwenhwyfar said, high and shrill, "I am no sister of his! This man claims to be my father's son because his mother was for a time one of the king's women! He is no son of my father's, but a baseborn clown who belongs in a farmyard, though my father has been kind enough to give him a place in his household!"

"You had best get out of our way," said Lancelet, surveying Meleagrant with contempt, and it was easy enough to see that Meleagrant knew who Lancelet was and had no desire to try conclusions with him.

He edged backward, saying in a surly voice, "You will be sorry for this some day, Gwenhwyfar," but he gave ground, glowering, and let them pass.

Lancelet was dressed with his usual fastidious taste, in crimson tunic and cloak; his hair was carefully trimmed and combed, his face clean-shaven. His hands looked smooth and white as Gwenhwyfar's own, although she knew that they were hard and steel-strong. He was handsomer than ever. And he had come just in time to save her from an ugly encounter with Meleagrant. She smiled—she could not help herself; it was as if something turned over, deep inside her.

No, I must not look at him this way now, I am to be the mother of Arthur's son. . . .

Lancelet said, "You do not want to pass through the great hall, lady, in your draggled riding clothes. . . . Has it been raining most of your journey? Let me take you and your servant to the side door, and you can go directly to your chamber and refresh yourself, then greet my lord Arthur in the hall when you are freshly dressed and warm and dry—you are shivering! Is the wind cold on you, Gwenhwyfar?"

He long had the privilege of calling her by her name, without the formal "my queen" or "lady," but never had it sounded so sweet on his lips. "You are, as ever, thoughtful of me," she said, and let him lead her horse.

Lancelet said, "Griflet, go now and tell our king that the lady is safe in her chambers. And you too, Gaheris, you are longing to be back among the Companions. I will see my lady safe."

At the door he helped her to dismount, and she was only aware of the touch of his hands. She lowered her eyes and would not look at him.

"The great hall is filled with Arthur's Companions," he said, "and all is confusion—the Round Table has gone but three days ago, on three carts to Camelot, and Cai with it to set it in its place in the new hall. Now a rider has gone out in haste to summon Cai back, and such men as can ride from the Summer Country—"

She looked up at him, frightened. "Gawaine told us of the Saxon landing—is this truly the war Arthur feared?"

"It is what we have all known for years must come, Gwen," he said quietly. "For this Arthur has been training his legions, and I working with his horse troops. When this is over, perhaps, we shall have the peace we have longed for, all my life and all Uther's."

Suddenly she flung her arms around him. "You could be killed," she whispered. It was the first time she had had courage to do such a thing. She stood pressed against him, holding her face against his shoulder, and his arms went around her. Even through her fear she felt the sweetness that he would hold her so. He said, and his voice shook, "We all knew that it must come some day soon, my dear. By our good fortune, we have had years to prepare for it, and Arthur to lead us—do even you know what a great leader of men he is, and how dear we all hold him? He is young, but he is the greatest of the High Kings we have had since long before the time of the Romans, and with Arthur to lead us, we will certainly drive the Saxons hence—and for the rest, it's as God wills, Gwenhwyfar." He patted her shoulder gently, saying, "Poor girl, you are so wearied, let me take you to your women." But she could feel his hands trembling, and was suddenly shamed that she had thrown herself into his arms as if she were a camp follower!

IN HER OWN CHAMBERS all was confusion, Meleas putting garments into boxes, Elaine supervising the serving-women. Elaine came and took Gwenhwyfar in her arms, crying out, "Kinswoman, we have been so worried about you, on the roads—we had hoped that you had the message before leaving the convent, and would stay safe in Tintagel—"

"No," said Gwenhwyfar, "Igraine died. Gawaine met with us when we had already been a whole day on the road, and besides, my place is at my husband's side."

Meleas asked, "Lady, did Griflet return with you?"

Gwenhwyfar nodded. "He escorted me here. You will see him at dinner, I suppose—I heard Gaheris say that all of Arthur's Companions had been bidden to dine with the King—"

Meleas said, "If you can call it dining. It is more like gobbling soldier's rations—this place is like an armed camp, and it will be worse before it is better. But Elaine and I have done our best to keep all things in order." She was a usually smiling, plump young woman who now looked worried and tired. "I have put all your gowns and such things as you shall need for this summer into boxes, so that you may be ready to ride for Camelot in the morning. The King said we were all to go at once, and it is all but ready for occupancy, with the work that Cai has done. But we never thought we would go there like this, in haste and almost under siege."

No, thought Gwenhwyfar. *I have been riding these days and now I will not ride forth again! My place is here and my son has a right to be born in his father's own castle. I will not again be sent hither and thither like any bit of luggage or saddlery!* She said, "Be at ease, Meleas, perhaps there is no such haste as all this. Send someone for washwater and fetch me some gown which is not soaked and bedraggled by mud and travel. And who are all these women?"

These women, it turned out, were wives of some of the Companions and of certain of Arthur's subject kings, who would be sent with them to Camelot; it was easier if they all travelled in convoy, and there they would be safe from the Saxons. "It is near to your home," Elaine said, as if that should settle all Gwenhwyfar's unwillingness. "You can visit your father's wife, and your little brothers and sisters. Or while Leodegranz is at war, your stepmother will dwell with us at Camelot."

That would be no pleasure to either of us, Gwenhwyfar thought, and then was ashamed of herself. She felt like ending all this with a few words, *I am pregnant, I cannot travel,* but she shrank from the excited flurry of questions she knew would follow. Arthur should know it first.

12

When Gwenhwyfar came into the great hall, which looked barren and empty without the great Round Table and all the splendor of banners and tapestries and hangings gone, Arthur was sitting at a trestle table halfway down the hall near the fires, surrounded by half a dozen of his

Companions, others clustered near. She had been so eager to tell her news, but now she could not blurt it out before the whole court! She must wait until tonight when they were alone in bed—that was the only time she ever had him to herself at all. But when he looked up from his Companions and saw her, he rose and came to embrace her.

"Gwen, my dearest!" he said. "I had hoped Gawaine's message would keep you safe in Tintagel—"

"Are you angry that I have come back?"

He shook his head. "No, of course not. So the roads are still safe, then, and you were lucky," he said. "But I suppose this must mean that my mother . . ."

"She died two days ago, and was buried within the convent walls," Gwenhwyfar said, "and I set out at once to bring you the news. And now you have nothing but reproach for me that I did not stay safely at Tintagel because of this war!"

"Not reproach, my dear wife," he said gently, "concern for your safety. But sir Griflet cared well for you, I can see. Come and sit with us here." He led her to a bench and seated her at his side. The silver and pottery dishes had vanished—she supposed they too had been sent to Camelot, and she wondered what had happened to the fine red dish of Roman make which her stepmother had given her at her wedding. The walls were bare and the place stripped, and they ate their food out of plain wooden bowls, the crude carved stuff of the markets. She said, dipping a piece of bread into the dish, "Already this place looks as if a battle had swept over it!"

"It seemed as well to me that everything should be sent ahead to Camelot," he said, "and then we had the rumors of the Saxon landings and all's confusion. Your father is here, my love—no doubt you will want to greet him."

Leodegranz was seated near, though not in the inner ring of those around Arthur. She came and kissed him, feeling his bony shoulders under her hands—always her father had been a big man to her, big and imposing, and now suddenly he seemed old and wasted.

"I told my lord Arthur he should not have sent you travelling about the countryside at this time," he said. "Ah, yes, no doubt it was well done of Arthur that he wished to send you to his mother's deathbed, but he had a duty to his wife too, and Igraine has an unwedded daughter who should have been with her mother—where is the Duchess of Cornwall that *she* did not go?"

"I do not know where Morgaine is," said Arthur. "My sister is a woman grown, and her own mistress. She need not seek my leave to be here or there."

"Aye, it is ever so with a king," said Leodegranz querulously, "he is lord of all save his womenfolk. Alienor is the same, and I have three daughters, not even old enough to marry, and they think they rule my household! You will see them at Camelot, Gwenhwyfar. I have sent them there for safekeeping, and the oldest, Isotta, is old enough—you might wish to make her one of your ladies, your own half-sister? And since I have no sons living, I want you to ask Arthur to marry her to one of his best knights when she is old enough."

Gwenhwyfar shook her head in amazement at the thought of Isotta, her half-sister—old enough to come to court? Well, she had been almost seven years old when Gwenhwyfar was married—now she must be a great girl of twelve or thirteen. Elaine had been no older when she was brought to Caerleon. No doubt, if she asked, Arthur would give Isotta to one of his best knights, Gawaine perhaps, or possibly—since Gawaine would be king of Lothian some day—to Gaheris, who was the King's own cousin. She said, "I am certain that Arthur and I together will find someone for my sister."

"Lancelet is still unwed," suggested Leodegranz, "and so is Duke Marcus of Cornwall. Though no doubt it would be more suitable if Marcus married the lady Morgaine and they combined their claims, then would the lady have someone to keep her castle and defend her lands. And, though I understand the lady is one of the damsels of the Lady of the Lake, no doubt Duke Marcus could tame her."

Gwenhwyfar smiled at the thought of Morgaine being tamely married to someone they thought suitable. And then she grew angry. Why should Morgaine please herself? No other woman was allowed to do her own will, even Igraine who was mother to the King had been married as her elders thought good. Arthur should exert his authority and get Morgaine properly married before she disgraced them all! Conveniently Gwenhwyfar stifled the memory that when Arthur had spoken of marrying Morgaine to his friend Lancelet, she had objected. *Ah, I was selfish . . . I cannot have him myself, and I grudge him a wife.* No, she told herself, she would be happy to see Lancelet married if the girl was suitable and virtuous!

Leodegranz asked, "I thought the Duchess of Cornwall was among your ladies—?"

"She was," Gwenhwyfar said, "but she left us some years ago to dwell with her kinswoman and has not returned." And it occurred to her once again: where was Morgaine? Not in Avalon, not in Lothian with Morgause, not in Tintagel with Igraine—she might be in Less Britain, or on a pilgrimage to Rome, or in the fairy country, or in Hell itself for all Gwenhwyfar knew to the contrary. This could not go on—Arthur had a right to know where dwelt his nearest kinswoman, now that his mother was dead! But surely Morgaine would have come to her mother's deathbed if she could?

She went back to her place beside Arthur. Lancelet and the King were drawing with the tips of their daggers on the wooden boards before them, while they ate absentmindedly out of the same dish. Biting her lip—indeed she might as well have stayed in Tintagel for all the difference it made to Arthur that she was there or not—she would have withdrawn to a bench with her ladies, but Arthur looked up at her and smiled, holding out his arm to her.

"Nay, my dear one, I meant not to drive you away—I must indeed talk with my captain of horse, but there is room for you here, too." He beckoned to one of the servers. "Bring another plate of meat for my lady. Lancelet and I have made a wreck of this dish—there is fresh-baked bread too, somewhere, if any of it is left, though with Cai not here the kitchens are in chaos."

"I think I have eaten enough," Gwenhwyfar said, leaning a little against his shoulder, and he patted her absently. She could feel Lancelet, warm and solid, on the other side, and she felt secure and safe between them. Arthur leaned forward, one hand still stroking her hair, the other holding the dagger where he was sketching.

"Look, can we bring the horses up this way? We can travel fast, and leave the wagons with provisions and baggage to come around on the flat country, but men with horses can cut across country and march light and fast—Cai has had men baking hard journey-bread for the armies and stock-piling it these three years since Celidon Wood. It is likely they will land here—" He pointed to a spot on the rough map he had made. "Leodegranz, Uriens, come here and look at this—"

Her father came, and with him another man, slight and dark and dapper, though his hair was greying and his face lined.

"King Uriens," Arthur said, "I greet you as my father's friend and mine. Have you met my lady Gwenhwyfar?"

Uriens bowed. His voice was pleasant and melodious. "My pleasure to speak with you, madam. When the country is more settled, I will bring my wife, if I may, to present to you at Camelot."

"I shall be pleased," Gwenhwyfar said, feeling that her voice was insincere—never had she learned how to speak these polite platitudes so that they carried any conviction.

"It will not be this summer, we have other work to do," said Uriens. He bent over Arthur's rough map. "In Ambrosius' time we led an army up country this way—we had not so many horses, save with the baggage wagons, but one could bring them up and cut across ground here. You must keep out of swamps as you go to the south of the Summer Country—"

"I had hoped not to climb the fells," said Lancelet.

Uriens shook his head. "With that great body of horse, it is better."

"On those hills, horses slip on stone and break their legs," Lancelet argued.

"Better even that, sir Lancelet, than have men and horses and wagons all bemired—better fells than swamps," said Uriens. "Look, here lies the old Roman wall . . ."

"I cannot see where so many have scribbled," said Lancelet impatiently. He went to the fireplace and plucked out a long stick, shook out the fire on the end, and began drawing on the floor with the charcoaled stick. "Look, here lies the Summer Country and here the Lakes and the Roman wall. . . . We have, say, three hundred horse, and here two hundred—"

"So many indeed?" Uriens demanded incredulously. "The legions of Caesar had no more!"

"Seven years we have been training them, and training mounted soldiers in their use," said Lancelet.

"Thanks to you, dear cousin," Arthur said.

Lancelet turned and smiled. "Thanks to you, my king, who had vision to see what we could do with them."

"Some soldiers still know not how to fight on horseback," said Uriens. "As for me, I fought well enough leading men on foot—"

"And that is as well," said Arthur good-naturedly, "for we have not horses for every man who wishes to fight mounted, nor saddles and stirrups and harness for all, though I have had every harnessmaker in my kingdom working as fast as he might, and hard enough work I've had to levy enough money to pay for all this, and men thinking me a greedy tyrant." He chuckled, patting Gwenhwyfar on the back and saying, "All this time I have had hardly enough gold of my own to buy my queen silks for her embroidery! It has all gone to horseflesh and smiths and saddlers!" Suddenly the gaiety was gone and he was serious, almost frowning. "And now is the great test of all that we have done and all that we can do—the Saxons this time are a flood, my friends. If we cannot stop them, with less than half their numbers, there will be none fed in this country but ravens and wolves!"

"That is the advantage of horse troops," said Lancelet gravely. "Armed and mounted men can fight five, ten—it may be twenty times their number. We shall see, and if we have guessed right, we shall stop the Saxons once and for all time. If we have not—well, we shall die defending our own homes and the lands we love, and our women and little children."

"Aye," said Arthur softly, "that we would. For what else have we worked since we were tall enough to hold a sword, Galahad?"

He smiled, his rare, sweet smile, and Gwenhwyfar thought, with a stab of pain, *Never does he smile at me like that. Yet, when he hears what news I bear him, why then . . .*

For a moment Lancelet answered the smile, then he sighed. "I had a dispatch from my half-brother Lionel—Ban's eldest son. He said he would set sail in three days—no"—he stopped, counting on his fingers—"he is already at sea—the messenger was delayed. He has forty ships and he hopes to drive the Saxon ships, or as many as he may, onto the rocks, or south to the Cornish coast, where they cannot land their troops aright. Then when he lands he will march his men to where we are gathering. I should send a messenger with a place for rendezvous." He pointed to the improvised map on the stones.

Then there was a little stirring of voices at the door of the room, and a tall, thin, greying man strode in through the scattered benches and trestle tables. Gwenhwyfar had not seen Lot of Lothian since before the battle of Celidon Wood.

"Why, I see Arthur's hall as I never thought to see it, bare without his Round Table—what, Arthur, cousin, playing at knucklebones on the floor with all your schoolfellows?"

"The Round Table is already gone to Camelot, kinsman," said Arthur, rising, "with all my other furniture and women's gear—you see here an armed camp, waiting only for daybreak to send the last of the women to Camelot. Most of the women and all of the children are already gone."

Lot bowed to Gwenhwyfar and said, in his smooth voice, "Why, then, Arthur's hall will be barren indeed. But is it safe for women and children to travel with the land rising for war?"

"The Saxons have not yet come so far inland," said Arthur, "and there is no danger if they go at once. I must tell fifty of my men—and a thankless job it is—to stay out of the field, and guard Camelot. Queen Morgause is well where she is, in Lothian—I am glad my sister is with her!"

"Morgaine?" Lot shook his head. "She has not been in Lothian these many years! Well, well, well. I wonder where she may have gone? And with whom? I thought always there was more to that young woman than I ever could see! But why to Camelot, my lord Arthur?"

"It is easily defended," said Arthur. "Fifty men can hold it till Christ should come again. If I left the women at Caerleon here, I would need to hold back two hundred men or more from the battle. I know not why my father made Caerleon his stronghold—I had hoped before the Saxons came again we would be gone with all our court to Camelot, and then they would have to march across Britain's width to come at us, and we could give them battle on a field of our own choosing. If we led them into the swamps and lakes of the Summer Country, where the land is never the same two years in a row, why then mud and swamps could do some of the work of bow and arrow and axe for us, and the little folk of Avalon finish them off with their elf-arrows."

"They will come to do that anyway," said Lancelet, rising on his knees from studying the map on the stones. "Avalon has already sent three hundred, and more will come, they say. And the Merlin said when last I spoke with him that they had sent riders into your country too, my lord Uriens, so that all the Old People who dwell in your hills may come to fight at our side. So we have the legion, horse soldiers fighting on the flat ground, every horseman armored and armed with spears, good for a dozen or more Saxons. Then we have multitudes of foot soldiers, bowmen and swordsmen, who can fight in the hills and valleys. And then we have many of the men of the Tribes, with pikes and axes, and the Old People, who can fight from ambush and drop men with their elf-arrows unseen. I think we could thus meet every Saxon from all of Gaul and the shores of the continent!"

"And we will have to do just that," said Lot. "I have fought the Saxons since the days of Ambrosius—so has Uriens here—and never have we had to face anything like the army coming against us now."

"Since I was crowned, I have known this day was coming—the Lady of the Lake told me this when she gave me Excalibur. And now she is sending for all the folk of Avalon to rally beneath the banner of the Pendragon."

"We will all be there," said Lot, but Gwenhwyfar shuddered, and Arthur said solicitously, "My dear one, you have been riding all the day, and the day before, and you must set forth again at daybreak. May I call your women to take you away to bed?"

She shook her head, twisting her hands together in her lap. "No, I am not weary, no—Arthur, it seems no proper thing for the pagans of Avalon, ruled by sorcery, to fight on the side of a Christian king! And when you rally them under that pagan banner—"

Lancelet asked gently, "My queen, would you have the folk of Avalon sit and watch their homes fall into the hands of the Saxon? Britain is their land too—they will fight even as we do, to hold our land against the barbarians. And the Pendragon is their sworn king."

"It is that I do not like," said Gwenhwyfar, trying to make her voice steady so that she did not sound like a little girl raising her voice in the men's council. *After all,* she told herself, *Morgause is accepted as one of Lot's councillors, and Viviane never stinted to speak of matters of state!* "I like it not that we and the folk of Avalon should fight on the same side. This battle shall be the stand of civilized men, followers of Christ, descendants of Rome, against those who know not our God. The Old People are of the enemy, as much as the Saxons, and this will not be a proper Christian land until all those folk are dead or fled into their hills, and their demon gods with them! And I like it not, Arthur, that you should raise a pagan banner for your standard. You should fight, like Uriens, under the cross of Christ so that we may tell friend from foe!"

Lancelet looked shocked. "Am I also your enemy, Gwenhwyfar?"

She shook her head. "You are a Christian, Lancelet."

"My mother is that same wicked Lady of the Lake you condemn for her witchcraft," he said, "and I myself was fostered in Avalon, and the Old People are my own people. My own father, who is a Christian king, made also the Great Marriage with the Goddess for his land!" He looked hard and angry.

Arthur laid his hand on the hilt of Excalibur, in its scabbard of crimson velvet and gold. The sight of his hand laid on the magical symbols of that scabbard, and the serpents twined round his wrist, made Gwenhwyfar turn her eyes away. She said, "How will God give us the victory, if we will not put away from us all the symbols of sorcery and fight beneath his cross?"

"Why, there's something to what the Queen says," Uriens said, conciliating, "but I bear my eagles in the name of my fathers and of Rome."

Leodegranz said, "I offer to you the banner of the cross, my lord Arthur, if you will. You bear it rightly for your queen's sake."

Arthur shook his head. Only the high flush in his cheekbones told Gwenhwyfar that he was angry. "I swore to fight beneath the royal banner of the Pendragon, and so shall I do or die. I am no tyrant. Whoever wishes to do so may bear the cross of Christ on his shield, but the Pendragon banner stands in token that all the folk of Britain—Christian, Druid, Old People too—shall fight together. Even as the dragon is over all the beasts, so the Pendragon is over all the people! All, I say!"

"And the eagles of Uriens and the Great Raven of Lothian shall fight beside the dragon," said Lot, rising. "Is Gawaine not here, Arthur? I would have a word with my son, and I thought he was ever at your side!"

"I miss him as much as you, Uncle," said Arthur. "I know not where to turn without Gawaine at my back, but I had to send him on a message to Tintagel, for none can ride so swiftly."

"Oh, you have plenty to guard you," said Lot sourly. "I see Lancelet never more than a step or three from your side, ready to fill the empty place."

Lancelet flushed, but he said smoothly, "It is always so, kinsman, all of Arthur's Companions strive with one another for the honor of being the closest to the King, and when Gawaine is here, even Cai who is Arthur's foster-brother and I who am Queen's champion must take a place further off."

Arthur turned back to Gwenhwyfar and said, "Now indeed, my queen, you must go to rest. This council may go on far into the night, and you must be ready to ride at daybreak."

Gwenhwyfar clenched her hands. *This one time, this one time let me have courage to speak. . . .* She said clearly, "No. No, my lord, I do not ride at daybreak, not to Camelot or to anywhere else on the face of this earth."

Arthur's cheeks flushed again with that high color which told her he was angry. "Why, how's this, madam? You cannot delay when there is war in the land. I would willingly give you a day or two of rest before you ride, but we must make haste to get you all to safety before the Saxons come. I tell you, Gwenhwyfar, when the morning comes, your horse and gear will be ready. If you cannot ride you may travel in a litter or be carried in a chair, but ride you shall."

"I shall not!" she said fiercely. "And you cannot force me, not unless you set me on my horse and tie me there!"

"God forbid I should have to do so," Arthur said. "But what is this, lady?" He was troubled, yet trying to keep his voice light and humorous. "Why, all those legions of men out there obey my word, am I to have mutiny at my own hearth fire and from my own wife?"

"Your men may all obey your word," she said desperately. "They have not my reason for staying here! I will stay with no more than one waiting-woman and a midwife, my lord, but I will ride nowhere—not so far as to the banks of the river—before our son is born!"

There, I have said it . . . here before all these men. . . .

And Arthur, hearing, understood, and instead of looking overjoyed, seemed only dismayed. He shook his head, then said, "Gwenhwyfar—" and stopped.

Lot chuckled and said, "Are you breeding, madam? Why, congratulations! But that need not stop you from travelling. Morgause was every day in the saddle, till she was too big for her horse to carry her, while no one would know as yet that you were with child. Our midwives say that fresh air and exercise are healthy for a breeding woman, and when my own favorite mare is in foal, I ride her till six weeks before she drops the foal!"

"I am not a mare," said Gwenhwyfar coldly, "and twice I have miscarried. Would you expose me again to that, Arthur?"

"Yet you cannot stay here. This place cannot be properly defended," said Arthur distractedly, "and we may march out with the army at any time! Nor is it fair to ask your women to stay with you and risk being caught by the Saxons. I am certain it will not harm you, dear wife, there were pregnant women with those who left for Camelot last week—and you cannot stay here with all your women gone, it will be an armed soldier's camp, no more, my Gwen!"

Gwenhwyfar looked at her ladies. "Will not one of you stay with her queen?"

"I will stay with you, cousin, if Arthur permits," said Elaine. And

Meleas said, "I will stay, if my lord does not mind, though our son is already at Camelot—"

"No, Meleas, you must go to your child," Elaine said. "I am her kinswoman and I can endure anything Gwenhwyfar can endure, even to live in an armed camp with the men." She came and stood beside Gwenhwyfar, holding her hand. "But could you not travel in a litter? Camelot is so much safer."

Lancelet got up and came to Gwenhwyfar. He bent over her hand and said in a low voice, "My lady, I beg you to go with the other women. This countryside may all be in ruin within a matter of days, when the Saxons come. In Camelot you are near to your father's country. My own mother dwells in Avalon, within a day's journey—she is a notable healer woman and midwife, and I am sure she would come to you and care for you, or even stay to be with you when the babe is born. If I send to my mother with a message to come to you, will you go?"

Gwenhwyfar bent her head, fighting not to cry. *Once again I must do as I am bid, like any woman, no matter what I want!* Now even Lancelet had joined in to get her to do what she was told. She remembered the journey here from the Summer Country—even with Igraine at hand she had been terrified, and all this day she had ridden across the dreadful moors from Tintagel—now she was safe within walls and it seemed to her that she would never again be willing to leave their shelter.

Perhaps, when she was stronger, when her son was safe in her arms . . . then, perhaps she could dare that journey, but not now . . . and Lancelet could offer her as a gift the company of that evil sorceress his mother! How could he think she would let such a sorceress near her son? Arthur might contaminate himself with vows and links to Avalon, but her son should never be touched by that pagan evil.

"It is kind of you, Lancelet," she said stubbornly, "but I shall go nowhere until my son is born."

"Even if you were to be taken to Avalon itself?" Arthur asked. "You and our son would be safer there than anywhere in this world."

She shivered and crossed herself. "God and Mary Virgin forbid!" she whispered. "I would as soon go into the fairy country itself!"

"Gwenhwyfar, listen to me—" he began urgently, then sighed in defeat, and she knew she had won. "Have it as you will. If the danger of travel seems greater to you than the danger of remaining here, then God forbid I should force you to travel. . . ."

Gaheris said wrathfully, "Arthur, will you let her do this? I say to you, you should bundle her on to her horse and send her forth whether she will, or not! My king, will you listen like this to a woman's raving?"

Arthur shook his head wearily. "Peace, cousin," he said, "it is easy to see you are no married man. Gwenhwyfar, do as you will. Elaine may remain with you, and one serving-woman and a midwife and your priest, but no more. Everyone else must ride at daybreak. And now you must go to your chamber, Gwen, I have no more time for this!"

And Gwenhwyfar, dutifully raising her cheek for his dutiful kiss, had no sense that she had won a victory.

THE OTHER WOMEN set forth at daybreak. Meleas begged to stay with the Queen, but Griflet would not have it. "Elaine has neither husband nor child," he said. "Let her stay. Yet if I were King Pellinore I would not let my daughter remain, queen or no. You *shall* go, my lady." And Gwenhwyfar fancied that the look he gave her was one of scorn.

And Arthur made it clear to her that the main part of the castle was now the army camp, and she must keep to her chambers with Elaine and the serving-women. Most of her furniture had been sent to Camelot; a bed was brought up from the guest chamber, and she slept in it with Elaine. Arthur spent his nights in the camp with the men, sending to inquire for her once a day, but she rarely saw him.

At first she thought every day that she would see them march out to do battle with the Saxons, or that the battle would sweep over them here, but day followed day and then week came after week and she heard no news. Solitary riders and messengers came and went, and Gwenhwyfar could see more armies gathering, but immured in her chamber and the tiny garden behind it, she heard only such scattered bits of news as her servant and the midwife could bring, much garbled and mostly gossip. The time hung heavy over her; she was queasy in the morning and wished for nothing but to lie in bed, though later she felt well and would pace the garden restlessly, with nothing to do but make pictures in her mind of the marauding Saxons off the coast, and think of her child. . . . She would have liked to sew on baby clothes, but she had no wool to spin and the big loom had gone already.

However, she had the small loom, and the silks and spun wool and embroidery gear which had gone with her to Tintagel, and she began to plan the weaving of a banner. . . . Once Arthur had promised her that when she gave him a son she might ask him for whatever gift was in his power to give, and she had it in mind that on that day she would ask him to put aside the pagan banner of the Pendragon and raise Christ's cross. That would make all this land under the High King a Christian land, and Arthur's legion a holy army under the protection of Mary the Virgin.

It was most beautiful as she planned it—blue, with gold thread, and her priceless crimson-dyed silks for the mantle of the Virgin. She had no other occupation, so she sewed at it from morning to night, and with Elaine to help her, it grew swiftly under her fingers. *And into every stitch of this banner shall I weave my prayers that Arthur shall be safe, and this a Christian land from Tintagel to Lothian. . . .*

One afternoon the Merlin came to visit her, Taliesin the venerable. She hesitated—was it right she should have that old pagan and demon worshipper near to her at such a time as this, when she bore Arthur's son, who would one day be the king of this Christian land? But looking at the old man's kindly eyes, she recalled that this was Igraine's father and would be great-grandfather to her babe.

"May the Eternal bless you, Gwenhwyfar," he said, spreading out his arms in blessing. She made the sign of the cross, then wondered if he would be offended, but he seemed to take it simply as an exchange of blessings.

"How do you, lady, in this close confinement?" he said, looking around the room. "Why, you might be dungeoned here! You would be better in Camelot, or in Avalon, or on the isle at Ynis Witrin—you went to school there with the nuns, did you not? And there, at least, you would have had fresh air and exercise! This room is like to a byre!"

"I have air enough in the garden," said Gwenhwyfar, resolving that the bedding should be aired that very day and that the serving-woman should air and sweep the room which was littered with their possessions—it was too small for four women.

"Then make certain, my child, that you walk every day in the fresh air, even if it is raining—air is medicine for all ills," he said. "I can well believe that you are dull here. No, child, I did not come to reproach you," he added gently. "Arthur told me your happy news, and I rejoice for you, as do we all. And I especially—not many men live so long as to look on the face of their great-grandchildren." His creased old face seemed to glow with benevolence. "If there is anything I can do for you, you must command me, lady. Are they sending you suitable fresh food, or only soldier's rations?"

Gwenhwyfar assured him that she had everything she could wish for—every day a basket of the finest provisions to be had reached her—though she did not tell him she had little wish for food.

She told him of Igraine's death and that she lay buried in Tintagel, and that Igraine's last act had been to tell her of her child. Of the Sight she said little, but she did ask, looking at the old man with troubled eyes, "Sir, do you know where dwells Morgaine, that she did not come even to her mother's deathbed?"

He shook his head slowly. "I am sorry, I know not."

"But this is scandalous, that Morgaine should not let her kin know whither she has gone!"

"It may be that—as some of the priestesses of Avalon do—she has gone on some magical quest, or secluded herself to seek vision," Taliesin ventured, and he too looked troubled. "In that case I would not have been told, but I think, if she were in Avalon, where my own daughter dwells with the priestesses, I would have known. I know not." He sighed. "Morgaine is a woman grown, and she need not seek leave of any man to come and go."

It would serve Morgaine right, thought Gwenhwyfar, if she came to grief for her own stubbornness and the godless way in which she did her own will! She clenched her fists and did not answer the Druid, looking down so that he would not see her anger . . . he thought well of her, she would not have him think otherwise of her. Nor did he notice, for Elaine was showing him the banner.

"See, this is how we spend our prisoned days, good father."

"It grows swiftly," said the Merlin, smiling. "I see well that there is no time—what is it your priests say, the Devil finds work for the idle— you have left no place for the Devil to do his work here, you are as busy as a hive of bees, you two. Already I can see the beautiful design."

"And as I wove it, I prayed," said Gwenhwyfar defiantly. "With every stitch I wove a prayer that Arthur and the cross of Christ may triumph over the Saxons and their pagan Gods! Will you not rebuke me then, Lord Merlin, that I do this when you bid Arthur fight under their pagan banner?"

The Merlin said mildly, "Prayer is never wasted, Gwenhwyfar. Do you think we know nothing of prayer? When Arthur was given his great sword Excalibur, it was sheathed in a scabbard into which a priestess worked prayers and spells for safety and protection, and she fasted and prayed for five days all the time she worked upon it. And no doubt you have taken note that even though he is wounded, he sheds but little blood."

"I would have him protected with Christ, not sorcery," said Gwenhwyfar hotly, and the old man smiled and said, "God is one and there is but one God—all else is but the way the ignorant seek to put Gods into a form they can understand, like the image of your Virgin there, lady. Nothing befalls on this world without the blessing of the One, who will give us victory or defeat as God shall ordain. Dragon and Virgin alike are the signs of man's appeal to what is higher than we."

"But would you not be angry if the Pendragon banner was torn down and the standard of the Virgin raised over our legion?" asked Gwenhwyfar scornfully.

He stood close to her, reaching out a wrinkled hand to caress the brilliant silks. "Such a thing of beauty as this is," he said gently, "and made with such love, how could I possibly condemn it? But there are those who love their Pendragon standard as you love the cross of Christ—would you deny them their holy things, madam? Those of Avalon—Druid, priest and priestess—would know that the banner is but a symbol, and the symbol is nothing, while the reality is all. But the little folk, no, they would not understand, and they must have their dragon as a symbol of the King's protection."

Gwenhwyfar thought of the little people of Avalon and the far hills of Wales who had come bearing bronze axes and even little arrows of flint, their bodies smeared crudely with paint. She shuddered in horror that a folk so wild and savage should fight at the side of a Christian king.

The Merlin saw her shivering and mistook its cause. "It is dank and chill here," he said. "You must go out more into the sunlight." But then understanding touched him and he put his arm around the woman at his side and said gently, "Dear child, you must remember—this country is for all men, whatever their Gods, and we fight against the Saxons not because they will not worship our Gods but because they wish to burn and ravage our lands and take all that we have for themselves. We fight to defend the peace of these lands, lady, Christian and pagan alike, and that is why so many have flocked to Arthur's side. Would you have him a tyrant who put the souls of men in slavery to his own God, as not even the Caesars dared to do?"

But she only shivered, and Taliesin said he must go, but that she should send him word if she had need of anything.

Elaine asked, "Is Kevin the Bard in the castle, Lord Merlin?"

"Yes, I think so—I should have thought of that. I shall send him to come and play his harp for you ladies while you are cloistered here."

"We would willingly have him," said Elaine, "but what I was asking is, might we borrow his harp . . . or yours, Lord Druid?"

He hesitated, and said, "Kevin would not lend his harp—My lady is a jealous mistress." He smiled. "And as for mine, it is consecrated to the Gods and I may let no other touch it. But the lady Morgaine did not take her harp with her when she went away; it is in her rooms. Shall I have it sent here, lady Elaine? Can you play it?"

"Not well," said Elaine, "but I know enough of harp music to do it no harm, and it would give our hands something to do when we are weary of stitching."

"Yours," said Gwenhwyfar. "I have always thought it unseemly for a woman to play on the harp."

"So be it, unseemly then," said Elaine, "but I think I shall go mad shut away here if I have nothing to do, and there is none to see me, even if I dance naked like Salome before Herod!"

Gwenhwyfar giggled, then looked scandalized—what would the Merlin think? But the old man laughed heartily. "I will send you Morgaine's harp, lady, and you may indulge in your unseemly pastime—though indeed I see nothing unseemly in the making of music!"

That night Gwenhwyfar dreamed that Arthur stood beside her, but that the serpents on his wrists came alive and crawled to her banner, leaving it all cold with their slime, and fouled. . . . She woke gasping and retching, and that day she had no strength to leave her bed. Arthur came that afternoon to see her, and stood distraught beside her.

"I cannot see that this confinement does you any good, lady," he said. "I wish you were safe in Camelot! I have had word from the kings of Less Britain—they have driven thirty Saxon ships on to the rocks, and we will be marching out in ten days more." He bit his lip. "I would this were over, and we all safe at Camelot. Pray to God, Gwen, that we come safe there." He sat on the bed beside her, and she took his hand, but one of her fingers touched the serpents on his wrist and she drew it back with a gasp of dismay.

"What is it, Gwen?" he whispered, drawing her into his arms. "My poor girl, being shut up here has made you ill . . . I was afraid of this!"

She fought to control her tears. "I dreamed—I dreamed—oh, Arthur," she begged, sitting bolt upright in bed and throwing back the covers, "I cannot bear to think of it, that you would let that foul dragon cover all, as it was in my dream. . . . Look what I have made for you!" Barefoot, she drew him with both hands to the loom. "See, it is near finished, in three days I could have it ready—"

He put his arm round her and held her close. "I wish it did not mean so much to you, Gwenhwyfar. I am sorry. I will carry it to battle beside the Pendragon banner, if you will, but I cannot abandon the vow I have sworn."

"God will punish you if you keep a vow you have made to pagan folk and not to him," she cried. "He will punish us both—"

He put away her clinging hands. "My poor girl, you are sick and wretched, and no wonder, in this place. And now, alas, it is too late to send you away even if you would go, there may be Saxon bands between here and Camelot. Try to be calm, my love," he said, and went toward the door. She ran after him, holding to his arm.

"You are not so angry—?"

"Angry? When you are ill and overwrought?" He kissed her brow. "But we will not speak of this again, Gwenhwyfar. And now I must go, I am expecting a messenger who may come at any instant. I will send Kevin to play for you. His music will cheer you." He kissed her again and went away, and Gwenhwyfar went back to the banner and began to work at it in a frenzy.

Kevin came late the next day, dragging his misshapen body on a stick; his harp was hitched over one shoulder, giving him more than ever the look of some monstrous hunchback in silhouette against the door. It seemed to Gwenhwyfar that his nose wrinkled in distaste, and suddenly she could see the room through his eyes, cluttered with the daily things of four women, the air not overfresh. He raised his hand in the Druid blessing and Gwenhwyfar flinched—she could accept this from the venerable Taliesin, but from Kevin it filled her with dread, as if he would bewitch her and her babe with pagan sorcery; secretly she signed herself with the cross, and wondered if he saw.

Elaine went to him and said courteously, "Let me help you with the harp, Master Harper."

He shrugged as if to ward her away, though his smooth singer's voice was perfectly civil. "I thank you, but no one may touch My Lady. If I carry her with my own hands when I can hardly drag myself along on a stick, do you not think there is a reason, madam?"

Elaine bent her head like a scolded child and said, "I meant no harm, sir."

"Of course not, how could you know?" he said, and twisted painfully, or so it seemed to Gwenhwyfar, to unsling his harp and set it on the floor.

"Are you comfortable, Master Harper? Will you have a cup of wine to soothe your throat before you sing?" Gwenhwyfar asked, and he accepted politely enough. Then, noting the banner of the cross on the loom, he said to Elaine, "You are King Pellinore's daughter, are you not, madam? Are you weaving a banner for your father to carry into battle?"

Gwenhwyfar said quickly, "Elaine's hands worked as skillfully as mine, but the banner is for Arthur."

His rich voice was as detached as if he were admiring a child's first attempts to spin. "It is beautiful, and will make a fair wall-hanging for Camelot when you go there, madam, but I am sure Arthur will carry the Pendragon banner as did his father before him. But ladies love not to speak of battles. Shall I play for you?" He set his hands to the strings and began to play; Gwenhwyfar listened, spellbound, and her serving-woman crept to the door to listen too, aware of sharing a royal gift. He played for a long time in the gathering dusk, and as she listened, Gwenhwyfar was borne away into a world where pagan or Christian made no difference, war or peace, but only the human spirit, flaming against the great darkness like an everburning torch. When the harp notes finally stilled, Gwenhwyfar could not speak, and she saw that Elaine was weeping softly in the silence.

After a time she said, "Words cannot say what you have given us, Master Harper. I can say only that I will remember it always."

Kevin's crooked smile seemed for a moment to mock her emotion and his own as he said, "Madam, in music he who gives receives as much as he who hears." He turned to Elaine and added, "I see you have the lady Morgaine's harp. You, then, know the truth of what I say."

She nodded, but said, "I am only the worst of beginners at music. I

love to play, but no one could find pleasure in hearing me—I am grateful
to my companions for their forbearance while I struggle with the notes."

"That is not true, you know we enjoy hearing you," said Gwenhwyfar,
and Kevin smiled and said, "Perhaps the harp is the one instrument which
cannot sound evil no matter how badly played—I wonder if that is why
it is dedicated to the Gods?"

Gwenhwyfar's lips tightened—must he spoil the delight of this hour
by speaking of his infernal Gods? The man was, after all, a misshapen toad;
without his music he would never be allowed to sit at any respectable board
—somewhere she had heard that he was no more than a peasant's foundling
brat. She would not offend him when he had come to give them pleasure,
but she looked away; let Elaine chatter with him if she would. She stood
up and went to the door. "It is as hot in here as the breath of Hell," she
said irritably and flung it open.

Across the sky, darkening now, flamed spears of light, darting out of
the north. Her cry brought Elaine and the serving-woman, and even Kevin,
folding his harp tenderly into its covering, dragged himself heavily to the
door.

"Oh, what is it, what does it portend?" she cried.

Kevin said quietly, "The Northmen say it is the flashing of spears in
the country of the giants; when it is seen on earth, it portends a great battle.
And sure enough, that is what we face now—a battle where Arthur's legion,
madam, may determine, with the help of all the Gods, whether we live as
civilized men or go into the darkness forever. You should have gone to
Camelot, lady Gwenhwyfar. It is not right that the High King should be
concerned now with women and babes."

She turned on him and flared, "What would you know of women or
babes—or of battles, Druid?"

"Why, this would not be my first battle, my queen," he said equably.
"My Lady was from a king who gifted me for playing his war harps to his
victory. Would you think I should have gone to safety with the maidens
and the skirted eunuchs of the Christian priests? Not I, madam. Not even
Taliesin, old as he is, will run from battle." Silence, and above them the
northern lights flamed and flared. "By your leave, my queen, I must go to
my lord Arthur and speak with him and the Lord Merlin of what these lights
portend for the battle which comes upon us."

Gwenhwyfar felt it like a sharp knife run through her belly. Even this
malformed heathen might be with Arthur now, yet she, his wife, must lurk
here out of sight, although she bore the hope of his kingdom! She had
thought, if ever she bore Arthur's son, then he must give her place and show
her great respect, not treat her still as that useless woman he had been forced
to take as part of a dowry of horses! Yet here she was, packed off into a

corner again because he could not be rid of her, and even her gallant banner thrust back at her unwanted.

Kevin said with swift concern, "Are you ill, my queen? Lady Elaine, assist her!" He held out a hand to Gwenhwyfar, but it was misshapen, a twisted wrist, and she saw the serpent coiling around it, tattooed there in blue . . . she recoiled sharply and struck out at him, hardly knowing what she did, so that Kevin, who was none too steady on his feet, lost his balance and fell heavily to the stone floor.

"Keep away from me," she cried out, gasping. "Don't touch me, with your evil serpents—pagan, hell-bound, lay not your foul serpents on my babe—"

"Gwenhwyfar!" Elaine hurried to her, but instead of supporting Gwenhwyfar she bent solicitously over Kevin and gave him her hand to rise. "Lord Druid, do not curse her—she is ill and she does not know what she does—"

"Oh, do I not?" Gwenhwyfar shrieked. "Do you think I do not know how you all look at me—like a fool, as if I were deaf and dumb and blind? And you would calm me with kind words while you go behind the back of the priests to claim Arthur for pagan wickedness and heathendom, you who would give us over to the hands of the evil sorcerers. . . . Go from here, lest my babe be born deformed because I have looked on your vile face. . . ."

Kevin shut his eyes and the twisted hands clamped, but he turned quietly away and began laboriously hoisting his harp over his shoulder. He fumbled for his stick; Elaine handed it to him, and Gwenhwyfar heard her whisper, "Forgive her, Lord Druid, she is ill and knows not—"

Kevin's musical voice was harsh. "I know that well, lady. Think you I have never heard such sweet words from women before this? I am sorry, I wished only to give you pleasure," he said, and Gwenhwyfar, her head hidden in her hands, heard the dragging hitch of his stick and his stumbling feet as he hauled himself painfully from the room. But even when he had gone she went on huddling with her arms over her head—ah, he had cursed her with those vile serpents, she could feel them stabbing and biting into her body, the spears of the flaring lights overhead were impaling her, the lights flaring in her brain. . . . She screamed and hid her face with her hands and fell, writhing, as the spears went through her . . . she came to herself a little as she heard Elaine cry out.

"Gwenhwyfar! Cousin, look at me, speak to me! Ah, may the holy Virgin help us. . . . Send for the midwife! Look, the blood—"

"Kevin," Gwenhwyfar screamed, "Kevin has cursed my child—" and she drew herself up frantically, pain lashing through her, beating with her fists against the stone wall. "Ah, God help me, send for the priest, the priest, perhaps he can take away this curse—" and, ignoring the gushing of water and blood that now she could feel drenching her thighs, she dragged herself to the banner she had woven, signing herself with the cross again and again in a frenzy, before it all vanished in darkness and nightmare.

IT WAS DAYS LATER that she understood she had been dangerously ill, that she had come near to bleeding to death when she miscarried the four-months child which was too small and weak to breathe.

Arthur. Now for certain he must hate me, I could not even bring his son to birth. . . . Kevin, it was Kevin who cursed me with his serpents. . . . She wandered in evil dreams of serpents and spears, and once when Arthur came to her side and tried to hold her head, she started away in terror from the serpents which seemed to writhe on his wrists.

Even when she was out of danger, she did not recover her strength, but lay in a dreary apathy, unmoving, tears sliding down her face. She had not even the strength to wipe them away. No, it was folly to think Kevin had cursed her, that must have been a madness of her delirium . . . this was not the first child she had miscarried, and if there was any fault it was her own, for staying here where she could not have fresh air and fresh food and exercise and the company of her ladies.

Her house priest came to her, and he too agreed that it was madness to think that Kevin had cursed her. . . . God would not use the hands of a pagan priest to chastise her. "You must not be so quick to assign blame to others," he said severely. "If there is fault, it must be your own. Is there any unconfessed sin on your conscience, lady Gwenhwyfar?"

Unconfessed? No. For long ago she had confessed her love for Lancelet and been absolved, and she had striven to keep her thoughts only on her lawful lord. No, it could not be that . . . and yet she had failed.

"I could not persuade—I was not strong enough to persuade Arthur to lay aside his pagan serpents and the Pendragon banner," she said weakly. "Would God punish my child for that?"

"Only you know what lies on your conscience, lady. And speak not of punishment for the child . . . *he* is in the bosom of Christ . . . but it is you and Arthur being punished, if there is punishment, which," he added primly, "I must not presume to say."

"What can I do to atone? What can I do that God may send Arthur a son for Britain?"

"Have you truly done all you may to assure that Britain shall have a Christian king? Or do you hold back the words you know you must speak, because you wish to please your husband?" the priest asked austerely. And when he had gone away, she lay looking at the banner. Every night now, she knew, the northern lights burned in the sky, in portent of the great battle that was to come; yet once, a Roman emperor had seen the sign of the cross in the sky, and the fate of all Britain had been changed. Could she but bring such a sign to Arthur . . .

"Come, help me get up," she said to her woman. "I must finish the banner for Arthur to carry into battle."

Arthur came that night to her chambers, just as she set the last stitches to it, and the women were lighting the lamps.

"How is it with you now, my dear one? I am glad to see you up again, and well enough to work," he said, and kissed her. "Dearest, you must not grieve so . . . no woman could bring a healthy child to birth under this strain, with the battle impending at any moment—I should have sent you to Camelot, indeed. We are young still, my Gwenhwyfar, God may yet send us many children." But she saw the vulnerable look on his face, and knew he shared her sorrow.

She clasped his hand and drew him down beside her on the bench where she sat before the banner. "Is it not fair?" she said, and thought she sounded like a child begging for praise.

"It is very beautiful. I thought I had never seen so fine work as this" — and he laid his hand on the crimson-worked scabbard of Excalibur that never left his side—"but this is finer still."

"And I have woven prayers for you and your Companions into every stitch," she said, in entreaty. "Arthur, listen to me—do you think, could it not be, God has punished us because he feels we are not fit to give this kingdom another king, you and I, unless we will vow ourselves to serve him faithfully, not in pagan ways but in the new way under Christ? All the forces of pagan evil are allied against us, and we must fight it with the cross."

He laid his hand over hers and said, "Come, dear love, this is folly. You know I serve God as best I may. . . ."

"But you still raise that pagan banner of serpents over your men," she cried, and he shook his head in distress.

"Dear love, I cannot break faith with the Lady of Avalon who set me on my throne—"

"It was God, and no other, who set you on your throne," she said earnestly. "Ah, Arthur, if you love me, do this, if you wish for God to send us another child! Do you not see how he has punished us by taking our son to himself?"

"You must not speak so," he said firmly. "To think God would do so is superstitious folly. I came to tell you at last the Saxons are massing, and we shall move to give them battle at Mount Badon! I would now that you were well enough to ride to Camelot, but it cannot be—not yet—"

"Ah, I know it well, I am only an encumbrance to you," she cried out bitterly. "I was never more to you—it is a pity I did not die with my babe."

"No, no, you must not speak so," he said tenderly. "I have every confidence that with my good sword Excalibur and all my Companions, we shall triumph. And you must pray for us night and day, my Gwenhwyfar." He rose and added, "We will not march till daybreak. I will try to come and take leave of you this night before we march, and your father too, and Gawaine and perhaps Lancelet—he sent you greetings, Gwenhwyfar, he was very troubled when he heard you were so ill. Can you speak to them if they come?"

She bent her head and said bitterly, "I will do my king and my lord's will. Yes, let them come, though I wonder you trouble to ask my prayers —I cannot even persuade you to put away that pagan banner and raise the cross of Christ. . . . And no doubt God knows your heart, since God will not let you ride forth into battle believing that any son of yours shall rule this land, because you have not yet resolved to make this a Christian land. . . ."

He stopped and let her hand go, and she could feel him looking down at her. At last he bent and put his hand under his chin and raised her face to look at his. He said quietly, "My dear lady, my own dear love, in God's name, believe you that?"

She nodded, unable to speak, wiping her nose like a child on the sleeve of her gown.

"I tell you, dear lady, before God, I believe it not, that God works in such ways, nor that it matters so much what banner we carry. But if it matters thus to you—" He paused and swallowed. "Gwenhwyfar, I cannot bear to see you in such distress. If I bear this banner of Christ and the Virgin into battle over my troops, will you cease to mourn, and pray to God for me with your best heart?"

She looked up at him, transformed, her heart lifting with a wild joy. Would he indeed do this for her? "Oh, Arthur, I have prayed, I have prayed—"

"Then," said Arthur, with a sigh, "I swear it to you, Gwenhwyfar— I shall carry only your banner of Christ and the Virgin into battle, and no other sign shall be raised above my legion. So be it, amen." He kissed her, but Gwenhwyfar thought he looked very sad. She clasped his hands and kissed them, and for the first time, it seemed that the serpents on his wrists were nothing, mere faded pictures, and that she had indeed been mad to think they could have power to harm her or her child.

He called to his squire, who stood at the door of the room, to come and take the banner carefully and to raise it above their camp. "For we march at dawn tomorrow," he said, "and all must see my lady's banner with the Holy Virgin and the cross flying above the legion of Arthur."

The squire looked startled. "Sir—my lord—what of the Pendragon banner?"

Arthur said, "Take it to the steward, and bid him lay it somewhere away. We march under the standard of God."

The squire did as Arthur said, and Arthur smiled at Gwenhwyfar, but there was little gladness in the smile. "I will come to see you at sunset, with your father and some of our kin. We will dine here, and I will have my stewards bring food for us all. Elaine shall not be troubled with providing for so many. Until then, my dear wife," and he went away.

In the end the small dinner was held in one of the little halls, for Gwenhwyfar's chamber would not hold so many in comfort. Gwenhwyfar and Elaine put on the best gowns which had remained here at Caerleon and did their hair with ribbons; it was exciting to have some kind of festival after the grim confinement of the last weeks. The feast—though indeed it was not much better than army rations—was spread on trestle tables. Most of Arthur's older councillors had been sent to Camelot, including Bishop Patricius, but Taliesin the Merlin had been bidden to dine, and King Lot, and King Uriens of Wales, and Duke Marcus of Cornwall, and Lancelet's older half-brother, Lionel of Less Britain, Ban's oldest son and heir. Lancelet was there too, and he found a moment to come to Gwenhwyfar's side and kiss her hand, looking into her eyes with hopeless tenderness.

"Are you recovered, my lady? I was troubled for you." Under cover of the shadows, he kissed her, only a feather-brushing of soft lips against her temple.

King Leodegranz came too, scowling and fussing, to kiss her brow. "I am sorry for your illness, my dear, and sorry you lost your child, but Arthur should have bundled you off to Camelot in a litter—that is how I would have handled Alienor, if she had gainsaid me," he scolded. "And now, see, you have gained nothing by staying!"

"You must not rebuke her," said Taliesin gently, "she has suffered enough, my lord. If Arthur does not reproach her, it is not for her father to do so."

Elaine tactfully changed the subject. "Who is yonder Duke Marcus?"

"He is a cousin of Gorlois of Cornwall, who died before Uther took the throne," said Lancelet, "and he has asked Arthur that if we win the day at Mount Badon, he shall have Cornwall by marrying our kinswoman Morgaine."

"That old man?" said Gwenhwyfar, shocked.

"I think it would be as well to give Morgaine to an older man—she has not the kind of beauty to attract a younger one," said Lancelet. "But she is clever and learned, and as it happens, Duke Marcus wants her not for himself but for his son Drustan, who is one of Cornwall's best knights. Arthur has made him one of his Companions now, on the eve of this battle. Though it's likely, if Morgaine returns not to court, that Drustan will wed with the daughter of the old Breton king Hoell—" He chuckled. "Court gossip of the making of marriages—is there nothing else to speak of?"

"Well," said Elaine boldly, "when will you tell us of *your* marriage, sir Lancelet?"

He inclined his head gallantly and said, "On the day when your father offers you to me, lady Elaine, I will not refuse him. But it is likely your father will have you wed a wealthier man than I, and since my lady here is already wedded"—he bowed to Gwenhwyfar but she saw the sadness in his eyes—"I am in no haste to marry."

Elaine colored and cast down her eyes. Arthur said, "I bade Pellinore to join us, but he would stay in the field with his men, seeing to the order of march. Some of the wagons are moving out already. Look—" He pointed to the window. "The northern spears blaze over us again!"

Lancelet asked, "Is Kevin the Harper not to be with us?"

"I bade him come if he would," said Taliesin, "but he said he would rather not offend the Queen with his presence. Have you quarrelled, Gwen-hwyfar?"

She cast down her eyes and said, "I spoke harshly to him while I was ill and in great pain. If you see him, Lord Druid, will you say I would gladly beg his pardon?" With Arthur at her side and her banner flying above Arthur's camp, she felt love and charity for everyone, even for the bard.

"I think he knows you spoke in the bitterness of your own ordeal," said Taliesin gently, and Gwenhwyfar wondered what the younger Druid had told him.

Abruptly the door was thrust open and Lot and Gawaine strode into the room.

"Why, what's this, my lord Arthur?" demanded Lot. "The Pendragon banner we pledged ourselves to follow, it flies no more over the camp, and there is great unrest among the Tribes—tell me, what have you done?"

Arthur looked pale in the torchlight. "No more than this, cousin— we are a Christian folk, and we fight under the banner of Christ and the Virgin."

Lot scowled at him. "The archers of Avalon are talking of leaving you, Arthur. Fly your banner of Christ, if your conscience so bids you, but raise the Pendragon banner at its side with the serpents of wisdom, or you will see your men scattered and not all of one heart as they have been through all this dreary waiting! Would you toss all that goodwill away? And the Pict folk with their elf-bolts have killed many a Saxon before this, and will again. I beg you, don't take away their banner and their allegiance like this!"

Arthur smiled uneasily. "Even as that emperor who saw the sign in the sky and said, '*In this sign shall we conquer*,' so shall we. You, Uriens, who raise the eagles of Rome, you know that tale."

"I do, my king," said Uriens, "but is it wise to deny the folk of Avalon? Even as I, my lord Arthur, you wear the serpents at your wrists, in token of a land older than the cross."

"But it will be a new land if we win the victory," said Gwenhwyfar, "and if we do not, it will not matter."

Lot turned as she spoke and looked on her with loathing. "I might have known this was your doing, my queen."

Gawaine strode restlessly to the window and looked down at the camp. "I see them moving about their fires, the little folk—from Avalon, and from your country, King Uriens. Arthur, cousin"—and he went to the King— "I beg of you, as the oldest of your Companions, put the Pendragon banner into the field for those who wish to follow it."

Arthur hesitated, but a glance at Gwenhwyfar's shining eyes and he smiled at her and said, "I have sworn it. If we survive the battle, our son shall reign over a land united under the cross. I shall compel no man's conscience, but as it is written in Holy Writ—'as for me and my house, we will serve the Lord.' "

Lancelet drew a deep breath. He stepped away from Gwenhwyfar. "My lord and king, I remind you, I am Lancelet of the Lake, and I honor the Lady of Avalon. In her name, my king, who was your friend and benefactor, I beg this favor of you—let me carry the Pendragon banner into battle myself. Then your vow will be kept, and yet you will not be forsworn to Avalon."

Arthur hesitated. Gwenhwyfar shook her head imperceptibly, and Lancelet glanced at Taliesin. Taking the silence for consent, Lancelet was about to stride out of the room when Lot said, "Arthur, no! There is enough talk now about Lancelet being your heir and favorite! If he bears the Pendragon into battle, then will they think you have appointed him to bear your banner and there will be division in the kingdom, your party under the cross and Lancelet's under the Pendragon."

Lancelet turned on Lot violently. "*You* carry your own banner—so does Leodegranz, so does Uriens, so does Duke Marcus of Cornwall—why should I not bear a banner of Avalon?"

"But the Pendragon banner is the banner of all Britain united under one Great Dragon," said Lot, and Arthur sighed and nodded. "We must fight under *one* standard, and that standard is the cross. I am sorry to refuse you anything, cousin," Arthur said, and reached for Lancelet's hand, "but this I may not allow."

Lancelet stood with his mouth taut, visibly holding in his anger, then went to the window. Lot, behind him, said, "I heard it among my Northmen —they say these are the spears of the Saxons which we will face, and the wild swans are crying, and the ravens await us all. . . ."

Gwenhwyfar stood with her hand tightly clasped in Arthur's. She said quietly, "In this sign you shall conquer . . ." and Arthur squeezed her hand.

"Though all the forces of Hell, and not the Saxons alone, were ranged against us, lady, with my Companions I cannot fail. And you at my side, Lancelet," Arthur said, and moved to draw him close to them both. A moment Lancelet stood unmoving, his face still set in angry lines, and then he said, with a deep sigh, "So be it, King Arthur. But—" He hesitated, and Gwenhwyfar, standing very close to him, could feel the shudder which ran through his limbs. "I know not what they will say when they hear of it in Avalon, my lord and my king."

And for a moment there was total silence in the chamber, while the lights, the spears of the flames from the north, flared over them.

And then Elaine jerked the curtains shut, closing out the portents, and cried merrily, "Come and sit to your dinner, my lords! For if you ride forth to battle at daybreak, you shall not set forth unfeasted, and we have done our best for you!"

But again and again, as they sat at meat, while Lot and Uriens and Duke Marcus spoke of strategy and troop placement with Arthur, Gwenhwyfar caught Lancelet's dark eyes, and they were filled with sorrow and dread.

13

W hen Morgaine left Arthur's court at Caerleon, asking leave only to pay a visit to Avalon and her foster-mother, she kept her thoughts on Viviane—that way she need not think of what had befallen her and Lancelet. Whenever she let her mind wander to it, it was like being burnt with a hot iron of shame; she had offered herself to him in all honesty, in the old way, and he had wanted nothing of her but childish toyings that made a mockery of her womanhood. She did not know whether it was at him or herself that she was angered, that he could have so played with her, or that she could have hungered for him. . . .

Now and again she regretted her harsh words to him. Why had she flung insults at him? He was as the Goddess had made him, no worse and no better. But at other times, while she rode eastward, she felt herself to blame; the old taunt of Gwenhwyfar, *little and ugly as one of the fairy folk,* scalded her mind. Had she had more to give, had she been beautiful as Gwenhwyfar was beautiful . . . had she been content with what he had to give . . . and then her mind would swing the other way again, he had insulted her and the Goddess through her. . . . So tormented, she rode through the green country of the hills. And after a time her thoughts began to turn to what awaited her at Avalon.

She had left the Holy Isle unpermitted. She had renounced her state as priestess, leaving behind her even the little sickle knife of her initiation; and in the years since, always she had dressed her hair low on her brow, so that none might see the blue crescent tattooed there. Now in one of the villages she bartered away a little gilt ring she had for some of the blue paint the Tribeswomen used, and painted the faded mark afresh.

All that has befallen me has come because I forswore the vows I had given the Goddess . . . and then she recalled what Lancelet had said in his despair, that there were neither Gods nor Goddess, but these were the shapes mankind gives, in terror, to what they cannot make into reason.

But even if this were true, it would not lessen her guilt. For whether the Goddess took the form they thought, or whether the Goddess was only another name for the great unknowns of nature, still she had deserted the temple and the way of life and thought to which she was pledged, and she had forsaken the great tides and rhythms of the earth. She had eaten foods forbidden to a priestess, had taken the life of animal or bird or plant without giving thanks to that part of the Goddess being sacrificed for her good, she had lived unmindful, had given herself to a man without seeking to know the will of the Goddess in her sun tides, for mere pleasure and lechery— no, it was not to be looked for, that she could return and all should be as before. And as she rode through the hills, through ripening harvest and fertilizing rain, she was aware, with greater and greater pain, of how far she had come from the teachings of Viviane and of Avalon.

The difference is deeper than I thought. Even those who till the earth, when they are Christians, come to a way of life which is far from the earth; they say that their God has given them dominion over all growing things and every beast of the field. Whereas we dwellers in hillside and swamp, forest and far field, we know that it is not we who have the dominion over nature, but she who has dominion over us, from the moment lust stirs in the loins of our fathers and desire in the womb of our mothers to bring us forth, under her dominion, to when we quicken in the womb and are brought forth in her time, to the lives of plant and animal which must be sacrificed to feed and swaddle and clothe us and give us strength to live . . . all, all of these things are under the domain of the Goddess and without her beneficent mercy none of us could draw a living breath, but all things would be barren and die. And even when the time comes for barrenness and death, so that others may come to take our place on this earth, that is her doing too, she who is not only the Green Lady of the fruitful earth, but also the Dark Lady of the seed lying hidden beneath the snows, of the raven and the hawk who bring death to the slow, and of the worms who work in secret to destroy that which has served its time, even Our Lady of rot and destruction and death at the end. . . .

In the memory of all these things, Morgaine came at last to see that what had happened with Lancelet, after all, was but a little thing; the greatest sin was not with Lancelet but in her own heart, that she had turned away from the Goddess. What did it matter what the priests thought was good, or virtuous, or sinful, or shameful? The wound to her pride was only a healthful cleansing.

The Goddess will deal with Lancelet in her own time and her way. It is not for me to say. At the moment Morgaine thought it the best thing that could happen, should she never set eyes again on her cousin.

No; it was not to be looked for that she could return to her place as chosen priestess . . . but Viviane might have pity on her and let her amend her sins against the Goddess. At the moment she felt she could be content to dwell in Avalon, even as servant or humble worker-woman in the fields. She felt like a sick child, hurrying to lay her head in her mother's lap and weep there . . . she would send for her son and have him fostered in Avalon, among the priests, and never depart again from the way she had been taught. . . .

And so when first she saw the sight of the Tor, thrusting itself up, green and unmistakable, over the hills lying in between, the tears streamed down her face. She was coming home, home to her own place and to Viviane, she would stand within the ring stones and pray to the Goddess that her faults might be healed, that she might return to that place from which her own pride and self-will had thrust her.

It seemed that the Tor was playing hide-and-seek with her, now visible, thrusting itself up between the hills like an erect phallus, now hiding between smaller hills, now disappearing in the damp fogs; but at last she came to the shores of the Lake where she had come with Viviane so many years ago.

The greying waters, in late-evening sunlight, lay empty before her. Against the red light in the sky, the reeds were dark and barren, and the shores of the Island of the Priests just visible, rising in the sunset mist. But nothing stirred, nothing moved on the water, even though she thrust forth her whole heart and mind in a passionate effort to reach the Holy Isle, to summon the barge. . . . An hour she stood there unmoving, and then the darkness closed down, and she knew she had failed.

No . . . the barge would not come for her, this night or ever again. It would come for a priestess, for Viviane's chosen, cherished fosterling; it would not come for a runaway who had lived in secular courts and done her own will for four years. Once before, at the time of her initiation, she had been cast forth from Avalon, and the test of whether or no she might be called priestess was only this—that she should return without aid.

She could not call the barge; she feared within her very soul to cry aloud the word of power that would summon it through the mists. She could not command it, who had forfeited the right to be called a child of Avalon. As the color left the water and the last remnants of the sunlight faded into twilight mist, Morgaine looked mournfully toward the distant shore. No, she dared not call the boat; but there was another way into Avalon, around at the other side of the Lake, where she could cross by the hidden path through the swamp and there find her way into the hidden world. Aching with loneliness, she began to skirt the shore, leading her horse. The looming presence of the big animal in the dusk, his snorting breaths behind her, were a vague comfort. If all failed she could spend the night on the shores of the Lake; it would not be the first night she had spent alone in the open. And in the morning she would find her way. She remembered that solitary journey, disguised, to Lot's court far in the north, years ago. She had grown soft with the good living and luxury of the court, but she could do it again if she must.

But it was so still: no sound of bells from the Isle of the Priests, no chantings from the convent, no bird cries; it was as if she moved through an enchanted country. Morgaine found the place she was looking for. It was growing dark, and each bush and tree seemed to take on a sinister shape, some strange thing, some monster, some dragon. But Morgaine was recovering the habits of mind she had possessed when she dwelt in Avalon; there was nothing here that would harm her, if she meant it no harm.

She began to take her way along the hidden path. Halfway she must move through the mists; otherwise the path would but bring her to the monks' kitchen garden behind their cloister. She admonished herself firmly to stop thinking of the growing darkness and set her mind into meditative silence, fixing it on where she longed to go. Thus, then, with each step as if she wound a spell, treading out the spiral dance as if the way wound up the Tor toward the ring stones . . . she moved silently, her eyes half-closed, placing each foot with care. She could feel the mists cold about her now.

Viviane had not thought it any such great ill, that she should lie with her half-brother and bear him a child . . . a child born of the old royal line of Avalon, more a king than Arthur's self. Had she borne such a child to Lancelet, then could that child have been fostered here in Avalon and reared to become one of the greatest of the Druids. Now what would become of her son? Why did she leave Gwydion in the hands of Morgause? Morgaine thought, *I am an unnatural mother; I should have sent for my son.* But she had not been willing to look Arthur in the face and tell him of his child's existence. She would not want the priests and ladies at court to look on her and say, *This is the woman who bore a child to the Horned One in the old pagan way of the tribes who paint their faces and wear horns and run with the deer like animals* . . . the boy was well enough where he was, Arthur's court was no place for him, and what would she do with a little boy of three running at her heels? Arthur's?

But there were times when she thought of him, remembered nights when he had been brought to her full-fed and sweet-smelling, when she had sat holding him and crooning to him, thinking of nothing, her whole body filled with mindless happiness . . . when else had she been so happy? *Only once,* she thought, *when Lancelet and I lay in the sunshine on the Tor, when we hunted waterfowl by the shores of the Lake* . . . and then, blinking, she realized that by this time she should have come further than this, she should be past the mists and on the solid ground of Avalon.

And indeed the boggy places were gone—there were trees around her, and the path was firm underfoot, and she had not come to the priests' kitchen garden and outbuildings either. She should now be in the field behind the House of Maidens, leading into the orchard; now she must think of what she would say when she was found here, of the words she would speak to prove to the folk of Avalon that she had the right to be here. Or did she? Somehow it seemed that it was a little less dark; perhaps the moon was rising —it was three or four days after the full, soon there would be light enough to find her way. It was not to be looked for that every tree and bush should be the same as when she had dwelt here and known every step of every path. Morgaine clung to her horse's bridle, suddenly afraid of losing her way on the once-familiar paths.

No, it was actually growing brighter, she could see the bushes and trees quite plainly now. If the moon was rising, why could she not see it above the trees? Had she somehow gotten turned round, while she was walking with her eyes half-closed, treading out the path that led through the mists and between the worlds? If only she might see some familiar landmark! There were no clouds now—she could see the sky and even the mists had gone, but she could make out no star.

Perhaps she had been away too long from such things? She could see no sign of rising moon, though it should have been long since in the sky. . . .

And then it was as if cold water flooded down her back and set her blood to moving like ice inside her. That day when she had gone to seek roots and herbs, when she would have cast forth the child within her . . . had she wandered again into that enchanted country which was neither the world of Britain nor the secret world where the magic of the Druids

had taken Avalon, but that older, darker country where there was neither
star nor sun . . . ?

She bade her beating heart to still itself; she gripped the horse's bridle
and leaned against the warm, sweaty flank, feeling the solidity of muscle and
bone, hearing the soft snorting breaths real and definite under her cheek.
Surely if she stood still for a little and took thought, she would find her
way. . . . But fear was rising in her.

*I cannot go back. I cannot go back to Avalon, I am not worthy, I cannot
make my way through the mists. . . .* On the day of the ordeal of initiation
she had felt this for a moment, but she had firmly put her fear aside.

*But I was younger then and innocent. Never then had I betrayed the Goddess
or the secret teachings, never had I betrayed life. . . .*

Morgaine fought to control the rising tides of panic. Fear was the
worst thing. Fear would put her at the mercy of whatever misfortune came.
Even the wild beasts could smell fear on your body and would come and
attack, while they would flee from the courageous. This was why the bravest
man could run among the deer with safety, so long as fear was not smelled
on his skin . . . was this, she wondered, why they smeared their bodies with
the acrid blue dye of woad, because it covered the smell of fear? Perhaps
the truly brave man or woman was the one whose mind made no pictures
of what *might* happen if things went awry.

There was nothing here to harm her, even if it might be that she had
strayed into the fairy country. Once before she had found herself there, but
the woman who had mocked her had offered no harm or threat. They were
older even than the Druids, but they too lived by the will and rule of the
Goddess in their life and ways, and it might even be that one could guide
her to her proper path. So, either way, there was nothing to fear: at worst
she would meet no one and spend a lonely night among the trees.

Now she saw light—was it one of the lights that burned in the court
of the House of Maidens? If it was so, well, then she would soon be home,
and if not, then she could ask her way of whatever folk she met. If she had
strayed into the Isle of the Priests, then if she met with some strange priest
he might fear that she was one of the fairy women. She wondered if, from
time to time, these women did come to tempt the priests; it was only
reasonable that here, in the very shrine of the Goddess, some priest with
more imagination than others might feel the pulse of this place, come to
know that his way of life was a denial of the forces of life which ran within
the very pulse beat of the world. They denied life rather than affirming it,
from the life of the heart and the life of nature to the life that ran at root
between man and woman. . . .

*If I were Lady of Avalon, on the nights when the moon was new and
springing, I would send the maidens into the cloister of the priests, to show them*

that the Goddess cannot be mocked or denied, that they are men and that women are not evil inventions of their pretended Devil, but that the Goddess will have her way with them . . . aye, at Beltane or Midsummer. . . .

Or would these mad priests bid the maidens be gone and think them demons, come to tempt the faithful? And for a moment it seemed she could hear the voice of the Merlin: *Let all men be free to serve what God they best like. . . .*

Even, she wondered, *one which denied the very life of the earth?* But she knew Taliesin would have said, *Even so.*

Now through the trees she made out clearly the shape of a torch, flaring up yellow and blue from a long pole. The glare of it blinded her eyes for a moment, and then she saw the man who held the torch. He was small and dark, and neither priest nor Druid. He wore a loincloth of spotted deerskin and some sort of dark cloak over his bare shoulders; he was like to one of the little Tribesmen, only taller. His hair was dark and long, and he wore a garland of colored leaves in it; autumn leaves, though the leaves had not yet turned. And somehow that frightened Morgaine. But his voice was mellow and soft, as he spoke in an ancient dialect. "Welcome, sister; are you benighted? Come this way. Let me lead your horse—I know the paths." It was for all the world, she thought, as if she were expected.

As if she had fallen into a dream, Morgaine followed. The path grew harder underfoot and easier to follow, and the light of the torch blurred away the misty dimness. He led the horse, but now and then he turned toward her and smiled. Then he reached out and took her by the hand, as if he were leading a young child. His teeth were very white, and his eyes, dark in the torch glow, were merry.

There were more lights now; at some point, she did not know when, he had given over her horse to another, and led her within a ring of lights —she did not remember coming within walls, but she was in a great hall where there were men and women feasting, with garlands on their heads. Some bore garlands of the autumn leaves, but at the same time there were women who bore garlands of early spring flowers, the little pale arbutus that hides under the leaves even before the snow is gone. Somewhere, a harp was playing.

Her guide was still at her side. He led her toward the high table and there, somehow without surprise, she recognized the woman she had seen before, wearing in her hair a garland of bare twined wicker-withes. The woman's grey eyes seemed ageless and knowing, as if she could read and see all things.

The man set Morgaine on a bench and put a tankard in her hand. It was of some metal she did not know . . . the liquor in it was sweet and smooth and tasted of peat and heather. She drank thirstily, and realized she had drunk too quickly after her long fast; she felt dizzied. Then she recalled the old tale—should you blunder into the fairy country, you must never drink nor eat of their food . . . but that was only an old tale, no more; they would not harm her.

She asked, "What is this place?"

The lady said, "This is the Castle Chariot, and you are welcome here, Morgaine, Queen of Britain."

She shook her head. "No, no, I am no queen. My mother was High Queen, and I am Duchess of Cornwall, but no more. . . ."

The lady smiled. "It is all one. You are weary and have travelled long. Eat and drink, little sister, and tomorrow one shall guide you wherever you wish to go. Now is the time for feasting."

There were fruits on her plate, and bread, a dark soft bread of some unknown grain, but it seemed she had tasted it somewhere before this . . . she saw that the man who had led her hither had bracelets of gold about his wrists, twining like live snakes . . . she rubbed her eyes, wondering if she had fallen into a dream, and when she looked again it was only a bracelet, or perhaps a tattoo, like the one Arthur bore from his kingmaking. And at times when she looked at him, the torches flared so, it seemed there was the shadow of antlers above his brow; and the lady was crowned and hung about with gold, but now and again it seemed it was only a crown of wicker, and she had a necklace of shells about her throat, the little shells which were halved like a woman's private parts, and sacred to the Goddess. She sat between them and somewhere a harp was playing, a sweeter music than even the harps of Avalon. . . .

She was no longer wearied. The sweet-tasting drink had cleared her mind of fatigue and sorrow. Later someone put a harp in her hand and she too played and sang; never had her voice sounded so soft and clear and sweet. She fell into a dream as she played, where it seemed all the faces around her wore the semblance of someone she had known elsewhere. . . . It seemed she walked on the shores of a sunny island and played a curious bowed harp; and then there was a time when she sat in a great stone courtyard and a wise Druid in strange long robes taught them with compasses and a star finder, and there were songs and sounds that would open a locked door or raise a circle of ring stones and she learned them all, and was crowned with a golden serpent over her brow. . . .

The lady said it was time to go to rest—on the morrow one would guide her and her horse. She slept that night in a cool room hung about with leaves—or were they tapestries that now seemed to twist and change, telling stories of all the things that had been? She saw herself too, woven into the tapestry, with her harp in her hand, with Gwydion on her lap, and she saw herself woven into the tapestry with Lancelet—he played with her hair and held her hand, and she thought there was something she should remember, some reason she should be angry with Lancelet; but she could not remember what it was.

When the lady said that this night was festival and she should stay here a day or two more and dance with them, she let it be . . . it was so long, it seemed, since she had danced and been merry. But when she took thought to what festival it might be, she could not quite remember . . . surely the Equinox had not come yet, nor could she see moon or sun to reckon it for herself as she had been taught.

They put a garland of flowers in her hair, bright summer flowers, for, said the lady, you are no untried maiden. It was a starless night, and it troubled her that she could not see the moon, as she had not seen the sun by day. Had it been one day, or two or three? Somehow time seemed not to matter; she ate when she was hungry, slept where she was when she felt weary, alone, or lying on a bed, soft as grass, with one of the lady's maidens. Once, to her surprise, she found the maiden—yes, she looked somewhat like Raven—twining her arms round her neck and kissing her, and she returned the kisses without surprise or shame. It was as it is in a dream, where strange things seem wholly possible, and she was surprised at this, just a little, but somehow it did not seem to matter, she lived in an enchanted dream. Sometimes she wondered what had happened to her horse, but when she thought of riding forth, the lady said she must not think of it yet, they willed that she should stay with them . . . once years afterward when she was trying to recall all that had befallen her within the Castle Chariot, she remembered that she had lain in the lady's lap and suckled at her breast, and it did not seem strange to her at all that she, a grown woman, should lie in her mother's lap, and be kissed and dandled like an infant. But surely that had been no more than a dream, when she was dizzied with the sweet-tasting strong wine. . . .

And sometimes it seemed to her that the lady *was* Viviane, and she wondered: *Have I fallen sick, am I lying in a fever and dreaming all these curious things?* She went out with the lady's maidens and searched with them for root and herb, and the season seemed not to matter. And at the festival— was it that same night or another?—she danced to the harps, and again she took a turn at the harps for the dancing, and the music she made sounded both melancholy and merry.

Once when she was searching for berries and flowers for garlands, her feet stumbled over something: the white bleached bones of some animal. And round its neck was a fragment of leather, and on that a scrap of red cloth—it was something like to the bag in which she had borne her gear when she rode from Caerleon. What, she wondered, had happened to her own horse, was it safe in the stables here? She had not seen stables at all in the fairy castle, but she supposed they were somewhere. For now it was enough to dance, to sing, to let time pass, enchanted. . . .

Once the man who had brought her there led her aside from the dancing ring. She was never to know his name. How, when she could see neither sun nor moon, could the tides of moon and sun beat in her so fiercely?

"You have a dagger about you," he said, "you must put it from you, I cannot bear it near."

She unfastened the leather thongs that bound it to her waist and cast it away, not knowing where it fell. Then he came to her, his dark hair falling about hers; his mouth tasted sweet, of berries and of the strong heather drink. He undid her clothing. She had grown used to the cold—it did not matter to her that it was cold on the grass here, that she was naked under his body. She touched him; he was warm, his body warm, his strong male member hot and strong, his hands opening her thighs were strong and eager. Her whole body welcomed him as hungrily as a virgin; she moved with him and she felt the rhythm of the pulsing tides of the earth around her.

Then she was afraid . . . she did not want him to get her with child, it had gone so ill with her when Gwydion was born, another child would surely kill her. But when she would have spoken, he laid a hand gently over her lips and she knew he could read her thoughts.

"No fear of that, sweet lady, the tides are not right for that . . . this is the time for pleasure and not for ripening," he said softly, and she gave herself up to it, and yes, there were antlers shadowing his brow, she lay again with the Horned One, and it was as if stars were falling in the wood all round them, or was it but fireflies and glowworms?

Once she was wandering in the woods with the maidens and she came to a pool and bent over it, and looking deep there, she saw Viviane's face looking out at her from the waters. Her hair was greying now, strands of white all through it, and there were lines she had never seen before. Her lips opened; it seemed she was calling, and Morgaine wondered, *How long have I been here? Surely, I have been here four or five days, maybe even a week. I must surely go. The lady said one would guide me to the shores of Avalon. . . .*

And she made her way to the lady and told her that she must surely go. But night was falling—surely tomorrow would be time enough. . . .

Once again, in the water, it seemed she saw Arthur, his armies massing. . . . Gwenhwyfar looked weary and somehow older; she held Lancelet by the hand as he bade them farewell, and he kissed her lips. *Yes,* Morgaine thought in bitterness, *such games as he likes well to play. Gwenhwyfar would wish it so, to have all his love and devotion and never endanger her honor. . . .* But it was easy to put them away from her, too.

And then one night she woke with a start, hearing from somewhere a great cry, and for a moment, it seemed to her as if she stood on the Tor at the center of the ring stones, hearing the terrifying cry ringing through the worlds—the voice she had heard but once since she grew to womanhood, that harsh rusty voice, grown dull with unuse, the voice of Raven, who broke her silence only when the Gods had a message they dared not leave to any other. . . .

Ah, the Pendragon has betrayed Avalon, the dragon has flown . . . the banner of the dragon flies no more against the Saxon warriors . . . weep, weep, if the Lady should set foot from Avalon, for surely she will return no more . . . and a sound of weeping, of sobbing in the sudden darkness . . .

And silence. Morgaine sat upright in the greyish light, her mind suddenly clear for the first time since she had come into this country.

I have been here all too long, she thought, *winter has come. Now I must depart, now, before this day is over . . . no, I cannot even say so, the sun does not rise or set here . . . I must go now, at once.* She knew she should call for her horse, and then, remembering, she knew: her horse was long since dead in these woods. In a sudden fright, she thought, *How long have I been here?*

She searched for her dagger, and remembered that she had cast it away. She bound her dress about her—it seemed faded. She could not remember washing it, nor her underlinen, yet they seemed not dirtied much. She wondered suddenly if she were mad.

If I speak to the lady, she will beseech me again not to go. . . .

Morgaine tied her hair up in plaits . . . why had she let it hang free, she, a grown woman? And she set off down the path which, she knew, would bring her to Avalon.

MORGAINE SPEAKS . . .

To this very day I have never known how many nights and days I spent in the fairy country—even now my mind blurs when I try to reckon it up. Try as I may I can make it no fewer than five and no more than thirteen. Nor am I certain how much time passed in the world outside, nor in Avalon, while I was there, but because mankind keeps better records of time than the fairy folk, I know that some five years passed.

Perhaps, and I think this more as I grow older, what we speak of as time passing happens only because we have made it a habit, in our very blood and bones, to count things—the fingers of a newborn child, the rising and returning of the sun, we think so often of how many days must pass or how many seasons before our corn will ripen or our child grow in the womb and come to birth or some longed-for meeting take place; and we watch these by the turning of the year and the sun, as the first of the priestly secrets. Within the fairy country I knew nothing

of the passing of time, and so for me it did not pass. For when I came out of the
country I found that already there were more lines in Gwenhwyfar's face, and
Elaine's exquisite youthfulness had begun to blur a little; but my own hands were
no thinner, my face was untouched by line or wrinkle, and though in our family
white comes early to the hair—in his nineteenth year Lancelet had had already
a few grey strands—my hair was black and untouched by time as the wing of a
crow.

I have come to think that once the Druids had taken Avalon away from the
world of constant counting and reckoning it began to happen there, too. Time does
not flow in Avalon unreckoned like the passing of a dream, as it does in the fairy
country. Yet truly time has begun to drift a little. We see the moon and sun of
the Goddess there, and reckon the rites within the ring stones, and so time never
wholly leaves us. But it runs not even with time elsewhere, though one would think
that if the motion of sun and moon were known at all, it would move like to that
in the world outside . . . yet it is not so. Toward these last years I could bide a
month in Avalon and discover when I came away that an entire season had sped
by outside. And often, toward the end of those years, I did so, for I had no patience
to see what happened in the world outside; and when folk marked that I stayed
ever young, then more than ever did they call me fairy or witch.

But that was long, long afterward.

For when I heard Raven in that terrifying cry which moved into the spaces
between the worlds, reaching my mind even where I stayed in the timeless dream
of the fairy world, I set forth . . . but not to Avalon.

14

In the world outside, the light of the sun shone bright through fickle
cloud shadows over the Lake, and far away the sound of church bells rang
through the air. Against that sound, Morgaine dared not raise her voice to
cry the word of power which would summon the barge, nor take upon her
the form of the Goddess.

She looked at herself in the mirrored surface of the Lake. How long,
she wondered, had she tarried in the fairy country? With her mind free of
enchantments, she knew—even though she could reckon only two or three
days—that she had dwelt there long enough for her fine dark gown to wear
away ragged where it dragged on the ground; somewhere she had lost her
dagger or cast it away—she was not sure which. Now she remembered some
of the things which had befallen her there as dreams or madness, and her
face was stung with shame. Yet mingled with all this were memories of

music sweeter than she had heard in the world or in Avalon, or anywhere else, save when she had been at the borders of the country of Death when her child was born . . . almost, then, she had longed to cross over, if only to hear the music there. She remembered the sound of her own voice singing with the fairy harp—never had she sung or played so sweetly. *I would like to go back there, and stay there forever.* And she almost turned about to return, but the memory of Raven's fearful cry troubled her.

Arthur, betraying Avalon and the oath by which he had received the sword and been taken into the holiest place of the Druids. And danger to Viviane should she set forth from Avalon—slowly, trying to put things together in her mind, Morgaine remembered. She had set forth from Caer- leon—it seemed only a few days ago, in the late summer. She had never come to Avalon, and now it looked as if she never would come there . . . she looked sadly at the church atop the Tor. If she could steal into Avalon behind the island—but the paths had carried her only into the fairy country.

Somewhere, then, she had lost both dagger and horse; and now she remembered seeing bleached bone, and shuddered. And now she came to take note, the church on the Tor seemed different, the priests must have been building on it, and surely they could not have built it so big in a month or even two. . . . *Somehow,* she thought, gripping her hands together in sudden fright, *I must find out how many moons have sped by while I wandered with the maidens of the lady, or took my pleasure with the fairy man who led me there. . . .*

But no, it could not have been more than two or at most three nights . . . she thought wildly, not knowing it was the beginning of a confusion which would grow endlessly and never be wholly settled in her mind. And now when she thought of those nights she was frightened and ashamed, trembling with the memory of a pleasure she had never known, lying in the arms of the fairy man—and yet now she was away from the enchant- ment it seemed like something shameful, done in a dream. And the caresses she had given and received from the fairy maidens, something she could never have dreamed without such an enchantment—there had befallen something, too, with the lady . . . and now she thought of it, the lady was much like Viviane, and Morgaine was shamed too . . . in the fairy country it had been as if she had hungered all her life for such things, and yet in the outside world she would never have dared it, or even dreamed of it.

Despite the warm sun, she had begun to shiver. She did not know what time of year it might be, but there were patches of unmelted snow on the edge of the Lake, hiding in the reeds. *In the name of the Goddess, can the winter have passed and spring be at hand again?* And if enough time had gone by in the outside world so that Arthur could have planned betrayal of Avalon, then it must have been longer than she dared to think.

She had lost horse and dagger and everything else she had had with her. Her shoes, too, were worn, she had no food with her, and she was alone on the shores of unfriendly country, far from any place where she was known as the King's sister. Well, she had gone hungry before this. A flicker of a smile passed over her face. There were great houses and nunneries where she would perhaps be given bread as a beggar. She would make her way to the court of Arthur—perhaps somewhere she would come on a village where someone would need the services of a midwife, so that she could barter her skill for bread.

She gave one last longing look at the shores across the Lake. Dared she make a final attempt to speak the word of power which would bring her into Avalon? If she could speak with Raven, perhaps she could know precisely what danger threatened . . . she opened her mouth to cry out the word and drew back. She could not face Raven, either; Raven who had kept the laws of Avalon so meticulously, who had done nothing to shame her priestess garb. How could she face Raven's clear eyes with the memories of what she had done in the outside world and in the fairy country? Raven would have them from her mind in a moment . . . at last, the shores of the Lake and the spire of the church blurring through tears, she turned her back on Avalon to find the Roman road that led away south, past the mines and at last to Caerleon.

SHE HAD BEEN three days on the road before she met with another traveller. The first night she had slept in an abandoned herder's hut, supperless, sheltering from the wind, but no more. On the second day she had come to a farmstead where the folk were all from home except for a half-witted goose boy; but he had let her sit to warm herself by the banked fire inside, and she had taken a thorn from his foot, so that he gave her a hunk of his bread. She had walked farther with less to eat.

But then she came nearer to Caerleon and was shocked to find two burned-out houses, and crops rotting in the field . . . it was as if Saxons had passed this way! She went into one of the houses, which looked as if it had been sacked, for there was little left; but lying in one of the rooms she found an old and faded cloak, too ragged, she supposed, even for the raiders to take, abandoned by someone when they fled the place. It was warm wool, though, and Morgaine wrapped it round herself, though it made her look more than ever like a beggar woman; she had suffered more from the cold than from hunger. Near dusk some fowls clucked in the abandoned court; hens were creatures of habit, they had not yet learned that they could not come here to be fed. Morgaine caught one of them and wrung its neck, and in the ruined fireplace kindled a small fire; if she was lucky, no one would see smoke coming from the ruins, or if they did would think it was but ghosts. She spitted the chicken and roasted it on a green stick of wood over her fire. It was so old and tough that even her strong teeth had trouble chewing it, but she had been hungry so long that she did not care, and sucked the bones as if it were the daintiest of roast birds. She found some leather, too, in one of the outbuildings which had been some sort of forge or smithy; they had carried off every tool and every last scrap of metal, but there were some bits of leather lying about, and Morgaine wrapped what was left of the hen in it. She would have mended her shoes too, but she had no knife. Well, perhaps she would come to a village where she might get the loan of one for a few minutes. What madness had prompted her to cast her dagger away?

It was several days after full moon, and when she set forth from the ruined farm, there was frost on the stone doorstep, and a gibbous day moon lingered in the sky. As she crossed the door sill with her leather bag of cold meat and a thick stick clenched in her hand—some shepherd, no doubt, had cut it and left it here—she heard a hen clucking somewhere in wild announcement, and she sought out the nest and ate the egg raw and still warm from the hen's body, so she felt full fed and comfortable.

The wind was brisk and cold, and she walked at a good pace, glad of the cloak, threadbare and torn though it was. The morning was far advanced, and she was beginning to think of sitting herself down by the road and eating some of the cold fowl, when she heard hooves behind her on the road, overtaking her.

Her first thought was to continue on her way—she was bent on her own affairs and had as good a right to the road as any other traveller. Then, remembering the ruin of the farm, she took thought and went to the side of the road, concealing herself behind a bush. There was no way to tell what manner of folk travelled the roads now, with Arthur too busy keeping the peace against the Saxons to have much time to create peace in the countryside and protection along the roads. If the traveller seemed harmless, she might ask him what news; if not, well, she would lie here hidden until he was out of sight.

It was a solitary horseman, wrapped in a grey cloak and riding on a tall, lean horse; riding alone, with no servant or pack horse. No, but he bore a great pack behind him—no, not that either; it was that his body was hunched over in the saddle—and then she knew who the man must be, and stepped out from her place of concealment.

"Kevin Harper!" she said.

He drew up his horse; it was well trained and did not rear or sidle. He looked down at her, scowling, his mouth twisted in a sneer—or was it but the scars he bore?

"I have nothing for you, woman—" and then he broke off. "By the

Goddess! It is the lady Morgaine—what do you here, madam? I had heard last year that you were in Tintagel with your mother before she died, but when the High Queen went south to her burying, she said no, you had not been there—"

Morgaine reeled and put out a hand to steady herself on her stick. "My mother—dead? I had not heard—"

Kevin dismounted, steadying himself against the horse's flank until he got his stick under him. "Sit you down here, madam—you had not heard? Where, in the name of the Goddess, have you been? The word came even to Viviane in Avalon, but she is now too old and too frail to go forth."

But where I was, Morgaine thought, *I heard it not. It may be that when I saw Igraine's face in the forest pool, then was she calling to me with the news, and I never knew.* Pain wrenched at her heart; she and Igraine had grown so far from each other—they had parted soon after she was eleven years old and gone forth to Avalon—yet now it tore at her with anguish, as if she were that same little girl who had wept when she left Igraine's house. *Oh, my mother, and I knew nothing of it. . . .* She sat at the edge of the road, tears streaming down her face. "How did she die? Have you heard?"

"Her heart, I believe; it was a year ago in the spring. Believe me, Morgaine, I heard nothing but that it was natural and expected for her years."

For a moment Morgaine could not control her voice enough to speak; and with the grief, there was terror, for clearly she had dwelt out of the world longer than she had thought possible. . . . Kevin said, *a year ago in the spring.* So more than one spring had gone by while she lingered in the fairy country! For in the summer when she left Arthur's court, Igraine had not even been ailing! It was not a question of how many months she had been gone, but how many years!

And could she get Kevin to tell her, without revealing where she had been?

"There is wine in my saddlebag, Morgaine—I would offer it to you, but you must get it for yourself. . . . I walk not well at the best of times. You look thin and pale, are you hungry too? And how is it that I find you on this road, clothed"—Kevin wrinkled his brow in fastidious distaste—"worse than any beggar woman?"

Morgaine cast about in her mind for what she could say.

"I have dwelt . . . in solitude, and away from the world. I have not seen nor spoken with any man for I know not how long. I had lost count even of the seasons." And this much was true, for whatever the folk of the fairy country might be, they were not mankind.

"I can well believe it," said Kevin. "I could believe even that you had not heard of the great battle—"

"I see that this country has been all burned over."

"Oh, *that* was three years ago," said Kevin, and Morgaine started back. "Some of the treaty troops broke their vows and came all through this country, looting and burning. Arthur took a great wound at that battle and lay abed for half a year." He saw Morgaine's troubled face and mistook her concern. "Oh, he does well enough now, but all that time he did not set foot to the ground—I imagine he felt the want of your healing skills, Morgaine. Then Gawaine led down all of Lot's men from the North and we had peace for three years. And then this summer past there was the great battle at Mount Badon—Lot died in that battle—aye, *there* was a victory, such as bards will sing for a hundred years," Kevin said. "I do not think there is a Saxon chief left unkilled in all this land from Cornwall to Lothian, save those who call Arthur their king. There has been nothing like it since the days of the Caesars. And now all this land lies under the peace of Arthur."

Morgaine had risen and gone to the saddlebags. She found the flask of wine, and Kevin said, "Bring the bread and cheese too. It is near noon and I will eat here with you." When she had served him and opened her roll of leather with the remains of the chicken, offering it, he shook his head.

"Thank you, but I eat no flesh food now, I am under vows. . . . I marvel to see you eat meat, Morgaine, a priestess of your rank—"

"That or go fasting," said Morgaine, and told him how the chicken had come to her. "But I have not observed that prohibition since I left Avalon. I eat such things as are set before me."

"For myself, I think it makes little matter, flesh or fish or grain," Kevin said, "though the Christians make much of their fasting—at least this Patricius who is Arthur's bishop now. Before that, the brethren who dwelt with us upon Avalon used to repeat a saying of their Christ, that it was not what went into a man's mouth that defiled him, but what came out of it, and therefore man should eat humbly of all the gifts of God. And so I have heard Taliesin say. But for myself—no doubt you know that at a certain level of the Mysteries, what is eaten has so much effect on the mind—I dare not eat meat now, it makes me drunker than too much wine!"

Morgaine nodded—she had had that experience too. When she had been drinking the sacred herbs, she could eat nothing but a little bread and fruit; even cheese or boiled lentils were too rich and made her ill.

"But where do you go now, Morgaine?" And when she told him, he stared as if she were mad. "To Caerleon? Why? There is nothing there—or perhaps you did not know, though I find that hard to believe. . . . Arthur gave it to one of his knights who served him well at that battle. But on the day of Pentecost he moved his whole court to Camelot—it will be a year this summer that he has dwelt there. Taliesin liked that not, that he opened his court upon the Christian holy day, but he did it to please his queen—he listens to her in all things." Morgaine surprised a faint grimace on his face. "But then if you had not heard of the battle, it is likely you had not heard how Arthur betrayed the folk of Avalon and the Tribes."

Morgaine stopped the cup halfway to her lips. She said, "It is for that I came, Kevin. I heard that Raven had broken her silence and prophesied some such thing as that. . . ."

"It was more than prophecy," said the bard. He stretched his leg uneasily, as if sitting for long in one position on the ground hurt him.

"Arthur betrayed—what did he do?" Morgaine's breath caught. "He did not give them into the hands of the Saxons . . .?"

"You have *not* heard, then. The Tribes were sworn to follow the banner of the Pendragon, as they swore at his kingmaking, and Uther's before him . . . and the little folk of the days before the Tribes, they came too, with their bronze axes and flint hatchets and elf-arrows—no more than the fairy folk can they bear cold iron. All, all sworn to follow the Great Dragon. And Arthur betrayed them . . . he put away the dragon standard, even though we begged him that he should let Gawaine or Lancelet bear it into the field. But he swore that he would raise only his banner of the cross and the Holy Virgin into the field at Mount Badon. And so he did."

Morgaine stared in horror, remembering Arthur's kingmaking. Even Uther had not so pledged himself to the folk of Avalon! And he had betrayed *that* pledge? She whispered, "And the Tribes did not desert him?"

Kevin said in great anger, "Some of them came near to it; some of the Old People from the Welsh hills did indeed go home when the cross was raised—King Uriens could not stop them. As for the rest—well, we knew that day that the Saxons had us between the hammer and the anvil. We might follow Arthur and his knights into battle, or live thereafter under Saxon rule, for this was the great battle that had been prophesied. And he bore the sacred sword Excalibur from the Holy Regalia. Like enough the Goddess herself knew that she would be the worse if the land was ruled by the Saxons. So he fought, and the Goddess gave him victory." Kevin offered the wine flask to Morgaine, and when she shook her head, he drained it.

"Viviane would have come from Avalon to charge him with oathbreaking," he said, "but she is reluctant to do so before all his people. And so I am for Camelot, to remind him of his vow. If he heeds not that, then Viviane has sworn she will come to Camelot herself, on the day when all people present their petitions, and Arthur has sworn he himself will hear and judge them, at Pentecost. And then, she said, she would stand before him as a common petitioner, and claim his oath, and remind him of what must befall him who forswears his word."

Morgaine said, "The Goddess grant that the Lady of the Lake need never humble herself so far."

"I too would speak to him with wrath, not soft words, but it is not mine to choose," said Kevin. He held out his hand. "Will you help me to rise? I think my horse will bear two, and if not, when we come to a town we must get you a horse. I should be gallant even as the great Lancelet, and let you ride mine, but"—he pointed to his crippled body.

Morgaine pulled him to his feet. "I am strong, I can walk. If we must barter anything in the town, we should find shoes for me and a knife. I have not a single coin with me, but I will repay you when I can."

Kevin shrugged. "You are my vowed sister in Avalon—what I have is yours, so runs the law. There is no talk of payment between us."

Morgaine felt herself coloring in shame, that Kevin should so remind her of what she had sworn. *I have been out of the world, in truth.* "Let me help you to mount your horse. Will she stand, so?"

He smiled. "If she would not, she would be little use to me in travelling such roads as I go alone! Let us go—I would like to reach Camelot tomorrow."

In a town nestled in the hills, they found a cobbler to mend Morgaine's broken shoes, and an old bronze dagger; the man who had these things for sale said there was no dearth of them in this country since the great battle. Kevin bought her a decent cloak too, saying the ragged one she had found in the farmhouse would scarce make a saddle blanket. But the stop had delayed them, and once on the road again, it began to snow heavily, and the dark closed in early.

"We should have stayed in that town," said Kevin. "I could have bartered harp music for supper and bed for us both. Alone, I could sleep under a hedge or in the shelter of a wall, wrapped in my cloak. But not a lady of Avalon."

"What makes you think I have never slept so?" Morgaine asked.

He laughed. "You look to me, Morgaine, as if you had slept so all too often of late! But no matter how swiftly we press the horse, we cannot come to Camelot this night—we must look somewhere for shelter."

After a time, through the fast-falling snow, they could make out the dark shape of an abandoned building. Not even Morgaine could enter it walking upright; likely it had been a cattle byre, but the beasts had been gone so long that there was not even a smell, and the thatch-and-daub roof was mostly in place. They tethered the horse and crawled in, Kevin directing her with a gesture to lay the old ragged cloak on the filthy floor, and they each wrapped themselves in their cloaks and lay down side by side. But it was so cold that at last, hearing Morgaine's teeth chattering, Kevin said they must spread the two cloaks over them both and lie close together for warmth. "If it will not sicken you to be so close to this misshapen body of mine," he said, and she could hear the pain and anger in his voice.

"Of what is misshapen about you, Kevin Harper, I know only that with your broken hands you make more music than I, or even Taliesin, with hands that are whole," Morgaine said, and moved gratefully into his warmth. And at last she felt she could sleep, her head resting in the curve of his shoulder.

She had been walking all day and was weary; she slept heavily, but wakened when the light began to steal through the cracks in the broken wall. She felt cramped from the hard floor, and as she looked around the mud-daubed walls she felt a surge of horror. She, Morgaine, priestess of Avalon, Duchess of Cornwall, lying here in a beast shelter, cast out from Avalon . . . would she ever return? And she had come from worse places, from the Castle Chariot in the fairy country, out of all knowledge of Christendom and heathendom alike, out of the very doors of this world . . . she who had been so delicately reared by Igraine, she who was sister to the High King, schooled by the Lady of the Lake, accepted by the Goddess . . . now had she cast it all away. But, no, she had not cast it away, it had been taken from her when Viviane sent her to the kingmaking and she had come away with child by her own brother.

Igraine is dead, my mother is dead, and I cannot come again to Avalon, never in this world . . . and then Morgaine was weeping hopelessly, muffling her sobs in the coarse stuff of the cloak.

Kevin's voice was soft and husky in the half-light.

"Do you weep for your mother, Morgaine?"

"For my mother—and for Viviane—and perhaps most of all for myself." Morgaine was never certain whether she had spoken the words aloud. Kevin's arm circled her, and she let her head fall against his chest and wept and wept until she could weep no more.

He said, after a long time, still stroking her hair, "You spoke truth, Morgaine—you do not shrink from me."

"How could I," she said, nestling closer, "when you have been so kind?"

"All women think not so," he said. "Even when I came to the Beltane fires, I heard—for some folk think that because my legs and hands are lame, I am also deaf and dumb—I heard more than one, even of the maidens of the Goddess, whisper to their priestess that she should place them afar from me, so that there would be no chance I would look upon them when the time came to go apart from the fires. . . ."

Morgaine sat straight up in dismay. "Were I that priestess, I would drive such a woman forth from the fires, because she dared to question the form in which the God might come to her . . . what did you do, Kevin?"

He shrugged. "Rather than interrupt the ritual or put any woman to such a choice, I went away so quietly that none knew. Even the God could never change what they see or think of me. Even before I was forbidden by the Druid vows to couple with women who barter their bodies for gold, I could pay no woman to accept me. Perhaps I should seek to be a priest among the Christians, who, I have heard, teach their priests the secret of living without women. Or perhaps I should wish that when the raiders broke my hands and body they had gelded me too, so that I should not care one way or the other. I am sorry—I should not speak of it. But I wonder if you consented to lie at my side because you thought this crooked body of mine was not a man's, and did not think of me so . . ."

Morgaine listened to him, appalled at the agony of bitterness in his words, the wounds dealt to his manhood. She knew the awareness that lived in his hands, the quick emotion of the musician. Even before the Goddess, could women look only at a broken body? She remembered how she had flung herself into Lancelet's arms, and the wound to her pride which, she knew, would never cease to bleed.

Quite deliberately she bent down and kissed him on the lips, pulled his hand to her and kissed the scars there. "Never doubt it, to me you are a man, and the Goddess has prompted me to do this." She lay down again, turning toward him.

He looked sharply at her in the growing light. For a moment she flinched at what she saw in his face—did he think she pitied him? No: she shared the awareness of his suffering, which was another thing. She looked him directly in the eyes . . . yes, if his face had not been so drawn with bitterness, so twisted with suffering, he might have been handsome; his features were good, his eyes very dark and gentle. Fate had broken his body, but not his spirit—no coward could have endured the ordeals of the Druids.

Under the mantle of the Goddess, as every woman is my sister and my daughter and my mother, so must every man be to me as father and lover and son. . . . My father was dead before I could remember him, and I have not seen my son since he was weaned . . . but to this man I will give what the Goddess prompts me. . . . Morgaine kissed one of the scarred hands again and laid it inside her gown, against her breast.

He was inexperienced—which seemed to her strange for a man of his age. *But how,* Morgaine wondered, *could he possibly have been anything else?* And then she thought, *This is the first time, really, that I have done this of my free will, and had the gift taken simply, as it was offered.* It healed something in her. Strange, that it could have been so with a man she scarcely knew, and for whom she felt only kindness. Even in his inexperience he was

generous and gentle with her, and she felt, welling up within her, a great
and unspeakable tenderness.

"It is strange," he said at last, in a quiet, musing voice. "I had known
you were wise and a priestess, but somehow I had never thought you were
beautiful."

She laughed harshly. "Beautiful? Me?" But she was grateful that, to
him, at that moment, she seemed so.

"Morgaine, tell me—where have you been? I would not ask, but that
whatever it is, it lies heavy on your heart."

"I do not know," she blurted out. She had never thought she would
tell him. "Out of the world, perhaps—I was trying to reach Avalon—and
I could not come there, the way is barred to me, I think. Twice now, I have
been—elsewhere. Another country, a country of dreams and enchantments—a country where time stands still and is not, and there is nothing
but music—" And she fell silent; would the harper think her a madwoman?

He traced a finger along the corner of her eye. It was cold, and they
had thrown the covers off them; he tucked the cloaks gently round her again.
"Once I too was there, and heard their music . . ." he said, in a distant
brooding voice, "and in that place I was not near so crippled, and their
women did not mock me. . . . Some day, perhaps, when I have lost my fear
of madness, I shall go to them once again . . . they showed me the hidden
ways and said I might come because of my music . . ." and again, his soft
voice dropped into a long silence.

She shivered and looked away from him. "We had better get up. If
our poor horse has not quite frozen in the night, we will arrive at Camelot
this day."

"And if we arrive together," Kevin said quietly, "they may believe that
you have come with me from Avalon. It is none of their affair where you
have dwelt—you are a priestess, and your conscience is not in the keeping
of any man alive, not even of their bishops, or of Taliesin himself."

Morgaine wished she had a decent dress to put on; she would arrive
at Arthur's court in the garb of a beggar woman. Well, it could not be
helped. Kevin watched as she arranged her hair, then held out his hand, and
she helped him to his feet, matter-of-factly; but she saw that the bitter look
was in his eyes again. He was guarded behind a hundred fences of reserve
and anger. Yet just as they were crawling out the door he touched her hand.

"I have not thanked you, Morgaine—"

She smiled. "Oh—if there are thanks, they are to be spoken both ways,
my friend—or could you not tell that?"

For a moment the scarred fingers tightened on hers . . . and then it was
like a blaze of fire, she saw his ravaged face circled with a ring of fire,

contorted with shrieking, and all about and all around him fire . . . fire
. . . she stiffened and snatched her hand away, staring at him in horror.

"Morgaine!" he cried. "What is it?"

"Nothing, nothing—a cramp in my foot—" she lied, and avoided his
hand when he would have put it out to steady her. *Death! Death by burning!*
What did it mean? Not even the worst of traitors died that death . . . or had she
seen only what had befallen him when he was lamed as a boy? Brief as the
moment of Sight had been, it left her shaken, as if she herself had spoken
the word that would deliver him to his death.

"Come," she said, almost brusquely. "Let us ride."

15

Gwenhwyfar had never wished to meddle with the
Sight; did it not say in Holy Writ that no man knew what a day might
bring forth? Yet she had hardly thought of Morgaine in the last year, not
since they had moved the court to Camelot, but this very morning she had
wakened remembering a dream she had had of Morgaine—a dream in which
Morgaine had taken her hand, leading her to the Beltane fires and bidding
her lie with Lancelet there. When she was well awake she could laugh at
the madness of that dream. Surely dreams were sent from the Devil, for in
all of hers that gave her such evil counsel that no Christian wife could heed,
oftenest it was Morgaine who spoke it.

Well, she is gone from this court, I need never think of her again . . . no,
I do not wish her ill, I wish she might repent of her sins, and find peace in a
nunnery . . . but one very far from here. Now that Arthur had given over his
pagan ways, Gwenhwyfar felt that she would even be happy if it were not
for these dreams in which Morgaine led her into shameful things. And now
the dream haunted her while she sat working at the altar cloth she was
making for the church, haunted her so deeply that it seemed wicked to sit
working a cross in gold thread while she thought of Lancelet. She put down
her thread and whispered a prayer, but her thoughts went on, relentless.
Arthur, when she begged him at Christmas, had promised her that he would
put down the Beltane fires in the countryside; she thought he would have
done it before this, except that the Merlin had forbidden him. It would be
hard for any, Gwenhwyfar thought, not to love the old man—he was so
gentle and good; if only he were Christian, he would be better than any
priest. But Taliesin had said it was not fair to the countryfolk, either, to
take from them a simple awareness of a Goddess who cared for their fields

and their crops and the fertility of their beasts and their own wombs. Surely there was little that such folk could do in the way of sin, they had all they could do to toil in the fields and till their crops for enough bread to keep them out of death's reach; it was not to be looked for that the Devil should trouble himself with such people, if there was a Devil at all. But Gwenhwyfar said, "I suppose you think they do no sin, when they go to the Beltane fires and there do lewd and heathen rites and lie with other than their husbands—"

"God knows they have little enough joy in their lives," Taliesin responded tranquilly. "I cannot think it very wrong that four times in a whole year, when the seasons turn, they should make merry and do what pleasures them. I could not find much reason to love a God who took thought about such things and would call them wicked. Do *you* call them wicked, my queen?"

And she did; any Christian woman must think so, to go into the fields and dance naked and lie there with the first man sent to her . . . immodest and shameful and wicked. Taliesin shook his head, sighing.

"Still, my queen, none can be the master of another's conscience. Even if you think it wicked and shameful, would you pretend to know what is right for another? Even the wise cannot know everything, and perhaps the Gods have more purposes than we, in our little knowledge, can see."

"If I knew right from wrong—as I do and as the priests have taught us, and as God has taught us in Holy Writ—then should I fear God's punishment if I did *not* make such laws as would keep my people from sin?" Gwenhwyfar demanded. "God would require it at *my* hands, I think, if I allowed evil to take place in my realm, and if I were king I should already have put it down."

"Then, lady, I can say only that it is the good fortune of this land that you are not king. A king must protect his people from outsiders, from invaders, and lead his people to defend themselves—a king must be the first to thrust himself between the land and all danger, just as a farmer stands to defend his fields from any robber. But it is not his duty to dictate to them what their innermost hearts may do."

But she had debated with him hotly. "A king is the protector of his people, and what good is it to protect their bodies if he lets their souls fall into evil ways? Look you, Lord Merlin, I am a queen, and mothers in this land send their daughters to wait upon me and be schooled in courtly ways —understand you? Well, what manner of queen should I be, if I let another woman's daughter behave immodestly and get herself with child, or—as did Queen Morgause, I have heard—let her maidens go to the king's bed, if he wished to have his way with them? Mothers entrust me with their daughters because they know I will protect them—"

"It is different, that you should be entrusted with maidens too young to know their own will, and be even as a mother to bring them up rightly," Taliesin said. "But a king rules over grown men."

"God has not said there is one law for the court and one other for the country folk! He wishes all men to keep his commandments—and suppose the laws were not there? What do you think would happen to this land if I and my ladies went out into the fields and behaved so immodestly? How can such things be allowed to go on within the very sound of the church bells?"

Taliesin smiled. He said, "I do not think, even if there was no law against it, that you would be very likely to go into the fields at Beltane, my lady. I have marked it—that you like not to go out of doors much at all."

"I have had the good of Christian teaching and priestly counsel and I choose not to go," she said sharply.

"But Gwenhwyfar," he said very gently, his faded blue eyes looking at her out of the network of lines and patches on his face, "think of this. Suppose a law was made against it, and your conscience told you that it was the right thing to do, to give yourself to the Goddess, in acknowledgment that she is over us all, body and soul? If your Goddess wished for you to do so—then, dear lady, would you let the passing of a law forbidding the Beltane fires stop you from it? Think, dear lady: not more than two hundred years ago—has Bishop Patricius not told you of this?—it was strictly against the laws here in the Summer Country that any should worship the Christ, for so they should defraud the Gods of Rome of their just and righteous due. And there were Christians who died rather than do such a little thing, cast a pinch of incense before one of their idols—aye, I see you have heard the story. Would you have your God be as great a tyrant as any Roman emperor?"

"But God is real, and they are but idols fashioned by men," Gwenhwyfar said.

"Not so, no more than the picture of Mary Virgin which Arthur bore into battle . . ." said Taliesin, "a picture to give comfort to the minds of the faithful. It is strictly forbidden to me, a Druid, that I may have any representation of any God, for I have been so taught, in many lives, that I need none—I can think upon my God and he is with me. But the once-born cannot do that, and so they need their Goddess in round stones and pools, as your simple people need the picture of Mary Virgin and the cross which some of your knights bear on their shields, so that men may know they are Christian knights."

Gwenhwyfar knew there was a flaw in this argument, but she could not debate with the Merlin; and in any case, he was only an old man, and a heathen.

*When I have borne Arthur a son—once he said to me that then I might
ask of him anything he could give, and at that time I will ask him to forbid the
Beltane fires and the harvest fires.*

Gwenhwyfar remembered this conversation, months after, on the
morning of her dream. No doubt Morgaine would have counselled her so,
that she should go with Lancelet to the fires . . . Arthur had said he would
ask her no question if she should bear a child, he had all but given her leave
to have Lancelet as a lover . . . she felt her face flaming as she bent over
the cross; she was not fit to touch such stuff. She put the altar cloth from
her and wrapped it in a piece of coarser cloth. She would work on it when
she was more tranquil.

Cai's uneven step sounded at the door of the room. "My lady," he said,
"the King has sent to ask if you would come down to the arms field to
watch. There is something he would show you."

Gwenhwyfar nodded to her ladies. "Elaine, Meleas, come with me,"
she said. "You others, you may come or stay here and work, as you like."

One of the women, who was elderly and somewhat shortsighted, chose
to stay and go on with her spinning; the others, eager for a chance to get
out into the sunlight, flocked after Gwenhwyfar.

In the night there had been snow, but the strength of the winter was
past, and now the snow lay melting quickly in the sun. Little bulbs were
poking leaves through the grass; in another month, this would be a wilder-
ness of flowers. When she had come here to Camelot, her father Leodegranz
had sent her his favorite gardener, so that he could decide what vegetables
and pot herbs would grow best in this site. But this hilltop had been fortified
long before Roman times and there were some herbs growing; Gwenhwyfar
had had him transplant them all into her kitchen garden, and when they
found a patch where flowers were growing wild, Gwenhwyfar begged
Arthur that she should be left it for her own lawns, and he had built the
arms field further along the hilltop.

She looked up timidly, as they moved across the lawns. It was so open
here, so near to the sky; Caerleon had nestled close to the earth. Here at
Camelot, on rainy days, it was like being on an island of fog and mist—
like Avalon—but on clear days of sunlight, such as this one, it lay high and
exposed, so that it could command all the country round, and standing
at the edge of the hilltop she could see miles and miles of hill and
forest. . . .

It was like being too near to Heaven; surely it was not right that human
beings, mere mortals, should see so far—but Arthur said, even though there
was peace in the land, the King's castle should be difficult to come at.

It was not Arthur who came to meet her, but Lancelet. He had grown
even handsomer, she thought. Now that he need not keep his hair always

hacked short for the war helmet, he had let it grow long, and it curled around his shoulders. He wore a short beard—she liked the fashion on him, though Arthur teased him about it and said he was vain; Arthur himself kept his hair clipped short like a soldier, and had himself shaved every day by his chamberlains, as carefully and as closely as he combed his hair.

"Lady, the King is waiting for you," said Lancelet, and took her arm to escort her to the set of seats Arthur had had built close to the wooden railings of the exercise field.

Arthur bowed to her, thanking Lancelet with a smile as he took Gwenhwyfar's hand. "Here, Gwen, sit beside me—I brought you here because I want to show you something special. Look there—"

She could see that a group of the younger knights and some of the youngsters who served in the King's house were working at a mock battle in the yard: divided into two groups, they were fighting with wooden battens and big shields. "Look," said Arthur, "the big one in the ragged saffron shirt. Does he not put you in mind of someone?"

Gwenhwyfar looked at the boy, following his skillful work with sword and shield—he broke away from the others, attacked like a fury, toppling them over, caught one lad so hard a blow on his head that he left him stretched senseless, sent another reeling with a fierce blow on the shield. He was only a youngster—his rosy face was fuzzed with the first beginnings of beard, so that he still looked like a cherub—but he was near to six feet tall, and big and broad-shouldered as an ox.

"He fights like the fiend," Gwenhwyfar said, "but who is he? I seem to have seen him about the court—"

"He is that young lad who came to court and would not give his name," Lancelet said at their elbow, "so you gave him to Cai to help in the kitchens. He's the one they called 'Handsome' because his hands were so fine and white. Cai made all sorts of rude jokes about spoiling them by turning the spit and scrubbing vegetables. Our Cai has a rough tongue."

"But the boy never answered him back," said Gawaine gruffly at Arthur's other side. "He could break Cai with his two hands, but when the other lads urged him on to strike Cai—once Cai made some kind of wicked joke about his parentage, saying he must be base-born and the son of scullions, since he came so naturally to such things—Handsome only looked right over the top of his head and said it would not be well done to strike a man who had lamed himself in the service of his king."

Lancelet said wryly. "That would be worse to Cai than being beaten senseless, I think. Cai feels he is fit for nothing but to turn the spit and serve the plates. One day, Arthur, you must find a quest for Cai, even if it is no more than to go and find traces of old Pellinore's dragon."

Elaine and Meleas giggled behind their hands. Arthur said, "Well,

well, I will. Cai is too good and too loyal to be soured this way. You know
I would have given him Caerleon, but he would not take it. He said his
father had bidden him to serve me with his own hands so long as he lived,
and he would come here to Camelot to keep my house. But this boy—
Handsome, you called him, Lance? Does he not put you in mind of someone,
my lady?"

She studied the boy, charging now against the last of the opposing
group, his long, fair hair flying in the wind. He had a high, broad forehead
and a big nose, and his hands, gripped on the weapon, were smooth and
white—then she looked past Arthur at just another such nose and blue eyes,
though these were hidden in a shock of red hair, and said, "Why, he is like
Gawaine," as if it were something shocking.

"God help us, why, so he is," said Lancelet, laughing, "and I never saw
it—and I have seen much of him. I gave him that saffron shirt, he had not
a whole shirt to his name—"

"And other things, too," Gawaine said. "When I asked him if he had
all that was fitting to his station, he told me of your gifts. It was nobly done
of you to help the boy, Lance."

Arthur turned to him and said in surprise, "Is he, then, one of your
brood, Gawaine? I knew not you had a son—"

"Nay, my king. It is my—my youngest brother, Gareth. But he would
not let me tell."

"And you never told me, cousin?" Arthur said reproachfully. "Would
you keep secrets from your king?"

"Not that," protested Gawaine uncomfortably, and his big, slab-sided
face flushed red, so that he and his hair and his brick-red cheeks seemed all
one color; it seemed strange to Gwenhwyfar that so big and rough a man
could blush like a child. "Never that, my king, but the boy begged me to
say nothing—he said you have favored me because I was your cousin and
your kinsman, but if he won favor at Arthur's court and from the great
Lancelet—he said that, Lance, *the great Lancelet*— he wished it to be for what
he had done, not for his name and his birth."

"That was foolish," said Gwenhwyfar, but Lancelet smiled.

"Nay—it was honorably done. Often I have wished I had had wit and
courage to do the same, rather than being tolerated because, after all, I was
Ban's own bastard and needed not to win anything by merit—it was for
that I strove so fiercely always to be valorous in battle, so that none might
say I had not earned my favors—"

Arthur laid his hand gently on Lancelet's wrist. "You need never fear
that, my friend," he said, "all men know you are the best of my knights,
and closest to my throne. But, Gawaine"—he turned to the red-haired man
—"I favored not you, either, because you were my kinsman and heir, but

only because you were loyal and staunch, and have saved my life a dozen times over. There were those who told me my heir should never be my bodyguard, for if he did his duty too well, then would he never come to the throne, but many and many a day I have had occasion to be glad of so loyal a kinsman at my back." He put his arm across Gawaine's shoulders. "So this is your brother, and I knew it not."

"I knew it not either when he came to court," Gawaine said. "When last I had seen him, at your crowning, he was a little lad no taller than my sword hilt, and now—well, you see." He gestured. "But once I saw him in the kitchens and thought, perhaps, he was some bastard of our kin. God knows, Lot has enough of them—I recognized him, and then it was that Gareth begged me not to reveal who he was, that he might win fame on his own."

"Well, a year under Cai's harsh teachings would make a man of any mother's poppet," Lancelet said, "and he has borne himself manly enough, God knows."

"I wonder that you knew him not, Lancelet—he came near to getting you killed at Arthur's wedding," Gawaine said amiably. "Or do you not remember that you handed him over to our mother, and bade her beat him soundly to keep him from under the horses' feet—"

"And I came near to knocking out my brains soon after—aye, I remember now," Lancelet said, laughing. "So that is the same young rascal! But he has far outstripped the other boys, he should practice at arms with the men and knights. It looks now as if he would be among the best of them. Give me leave, my lord?"

"Do what you like, my friend."

Lancelet unbuckled his sword. He said, "Keep this for me, lady," and handed it to Gwenhwyfar. He leaped the fence, caught up one of the wooden battens kept for the boys to practice with, and ran toward the big, fair-haired boy.

"You are too big for those fellows, sirrah—come here now, and try conclusions with someone nearer your own size!"

Gwenhwyfar thought, in sudden dread, *Nearer to your own size?* But Lancelet was not so big a man, not much taller than herself, and young Handsome towered almost a full head over him! For a moment, facing the King's captain of horse, the boy hesitated, but Arthur gestured encouragement, and the boy's face lit up with a fierce joy. He charged at Lancelet, raising his mock weapon for a blow, and was startled when the blow descended and Lancelet was not under it; Lancelet had evaded him, spun round and caught him a blow on the shoulder. He had pulled back on the weapon as it came down so that it only touched the boy, but it tore his shirt. Gareth recovered himself quickly, caught Lancelet's next blow before it landed, and for a moment Lancelet's foot slipped on the wet grass and it looked as if he would go down, skidding to his knees before the boy.

Handsome stepped back. Lancelet got to his feet, yelling, "Idiot! Suppose I had been a great Saxon warrior!" and caught the boy a great blow on the back with the flat of his sword, which hurled him, his sword flailing wildly, halfway across the yeard; he went down and lay half-stunned.

Lancelet hurried to him and bent over him, smiling. "I did not want to hurt you, lad, but you must learn to guard yourself better than that." He held out his arm. "Here, lean on me."

"You have honored me, sir," said the boy, his fresh face coloring, "and indeed it did me good to feel your strength."

Lancelet clapped him on the shoulder. "May we always fight side by side and not as foemen, Handsome," he said, and returned to the King. The youngster picked up his sword and went back to his playmates, while they clustered around and teased him. "So, Handsome, you came close to knocking down the King's captain of horse in a fight—"

Arthur smiled as Lancelet climbed back over the fence. "That was courteously done, Lance. He will make a bonny knight—like to his brother," he added, nodding at Gawaine. "Kinsman, do not tell him that I know who he is—his reasons for concealing his name were honorable. But tell him I have seen him, and I will make him a knight at Pentecost, when any petitioner may come before me, if he will come before me and ask me for a sword befitting his station."

Gawaine's face lighted. Now, Gwenhwyfar thought, anyone who had seen them both should have known the relationship, for their smiles were the same. "I thank you, my lord and king. May he serve you as well as have I."

"He could hardly do that," Arthur said affectionately. "I am fortunate in my friends and Companions."

Gwenhwyfar thought that, indeed, Arthur inspired love and devotion in everyone—it was the secret of his kingship, for though he was skilled enough in battle, he was no great fighter himself; more than once, in the mock battles with which they amused themselves and kept themselves fit for fighting, she had seen Lancelet, and even old Pellinore, unseat him or knock him from his feet. Arthur was never angry or wounded by pride, but always said good-naturedly that he was glad he had such fine fighters to guard him, and better friends than foemen.

Soon after, the boys picked up their practice weapons and departed. Gawaine went off to have a word with his brother, but Arthur drew Gwenhwyfar out toward the fortified wall. Camelot sat on a broad, high hill, flat at the top as a large town, and all over the hill, inside the wall, they had built their castle and city. Now Arthur led Gwenhwyfar up to his favorite vantage point, where he could stand atop the wall and look out over all the broad valley. She felt dizzy, and clung to the wall. From where they stood she could see the island home of her childhood, the country of King Leodegranz, and a little to the north of it, the island that coiled, from where they stood, like a sleeping dragon.

"Your father grows old, and he has no son," said Arthur. "Who will rule after him?"

"I know not—like enough he will have it that you should appoint someone to reign as regent for me," Gwenhwyfar said; one of her sisters had died in childbirth, far away in Wales, and another had died in a siege of their castle. And her father's second wife had borne him no living son, either, so that Gwenhwyfar was heir to that kingdom. But how could she, a woman, keep it from those who were greedy for land? She looked beyond her father's lands and asked, "Your father—the Pendragon—was he too made king on Dragon Island, I wonder?"

"So the Lady of the Lake told me, and so he pledged his faith always to shelter the old religion, and Avalon—as did I," said Arthur moodily, and stood staring at Dragon Island. She wondered what pagan nonsense was filling his head.

"But when you turned to the one true God, then did he give you that greatest of victories, so that you drove the Saxons forth from this island for all of time."

"It is foolish to say so," said Arthur. "Never, I think, can any land be secure for all time, but only as God wills—"

"And God has given you all this land, Arthur, so that you may rule as a Christian king. It is like to the prophet Elijah—the bishop told me the tale—when he went out with the priests of God, and met the priests of Baal, so that they each called on their God, and the One God was the greatest and Baal but an idol, so that he answered them not. If there was anything of power in the ways of Avalon, would God and the Virgin have given you such a victory?"

"My armies drove off the Saxons, but I may be punished hereafter for oathbreaking," Arthur said. She hated it when the lines of sorrow and dread came into his face.

She went a little toward the south, straining her eyes—from here, if you looked hard, you could see the very tip of the church of Saint Michael which rose on the Tor—the church which had been built because Michael was lord of the underworld, fighting to keep down the gods of the heathen in Hell. Only there were times when it blurred before her eyes, so that she saw the Tor crowned with ring stones. The nuns on Glastonbury had told her that it had been so, in the bad old heathen days, and the priests had labored to take down the ring stones and haul them away. She supposed it

was because she was a sinful woman that she had this glance into heathendom. Once she had dreamed that she and Lancelet were lying together
beneath the ring stones, and he had had of her what she had never given
him. . . .

Lancelet. He was so good, never did he press her for more than a
Christian woman and a wedded wife could give him without dishonor
. . . yet it was written that the Christ had said himself, *whoever looks upon
a woman with lust has committed adultery already with her in his heart* . . . so
she had sinned with Lancelet, and there was no mitigation, they were both
damned. She shivered and turned her eyes away from the Tor, for it seemed
that Arthur could read her thoughts. He had spoken Lancelet's name—

"Don't you think so, Gwen? It's more than time Lancelet should
marry."

She forced her voice to stay calm. "On the day when he asks you for
a wife, my lord and my king, you should give him one."

"But he will not ask," Arthur said. "He has no will to leave me.
Pellinore's daughter would make him a good wife, and she is your own
cousin—don't you think it would suit? Lancelet is not rich, Ban had too
many bastards to give much to any one of them. It would be a good match
for both."

"Aye, no doubt you are right," Gwenhwyfar said. "Elaine follows him
about with her eyes as the lads in the play yard do, eager for a kind word
or even a look." Though it hurt her heart, perhaps it would be best if
Lancelet should marry, he was too good to be tied to a woman who could
give him so little; and then she could amend her sin with a firm promise
to sin no more, as she could not do when Lancelet was near.

"Well, I will speak of it again with Lancelet. He says he has no mind
to marry, but I will make him understand it means not exile from my court.
Would it not be good for me and mine, if our children, some day, might
have Lancelet's sons to follow them?"

"God grant that day may come," said Gwenhwyfar, and crossed herself. They stood together at the height, looking out over the Summer
Country, which lay spread before them.

"There is a rider on the road," said Arthur, looking down the road
which led toward the castle; then, as the rider drew nearer, "It is Kevin the
Harper, come here from Avalon. And at least this time he has had sense
enough to travel with a serving-man."

"That is no serving-man," said Gwenhwyfar, her sharp eyes resting on
the slender form riding behind Kevin on his horse. "That is a woman. I am
shocked—I had thought the Druids were like to priests, and stayed far from
women."

"Why, some of them do, sweetheart, but I have heard from Taliesin that all those who are not in the highest rank may marry, and frequently they do," he said. "Perhaps Kevin has taken him a wife, or perhaps he has only travelled with someone coming this way. Send one of your women to tell Taliesin that he is here, and another to the kitchens—if we shall have music this night, it is only fitting we have something like a feast to celebrate it! Let us walk this way and welcome him—a harper of Kevin's skill is worthy of welcome from the King himself."

By the time they reached the great gates, they had been opened, and Cai himself had stepped forward to welcome the great harper to Camelot. Kevin bowed to the King, but Gwenhwyfar's eyes were on the slender, ill-clad form behind.

Morgaine bowed and said, "So I have returned to your court, my brother."

Arthur went and embraced her. "Welcome back, my sister—it has been so long," he said, his cheek lingering against hers. "And now that our mother has gone from us, we who are kinfolk should be together. Do not go from me again, sister."

She said, "I had no thought of it."

Gwenhwyfar came and embraced her too, feeling the other woman's body sharp-boned and thin against her arms. She said, "You look as if you had been long on the road, my sister."

"True—I have come very far," Morgaine said, and Gwenhwyfar kept her hand as they walked within.

"Where have you been? You were so long away—almost I thought you would never return," Gwenhwyfar said.

"Almost I thought so myself," said Morgaine. But, Gwenhwyfar noticed, she did not say, either, where she had been.

"Such gear as you left with us—your harp, your gowns, all these things—they were left at Caerleon. Tomorrow I will send for them as swiftly as a messenger can ride," Gwenhwyfar said, as she took her to the room where her women slept. "Till then, if you will, I will lend you a gown —you have been travelling long, sister, and you look as if you had been sleeping within a cow byre. Were you attacked by robbers and your gear stolen?"

"I had ill fortune indeed on the road," Morgaine said, "and if you will send someone to me that I may bathe, and dress myself clean, I will bless you. I would ask the loan of a comb too, and pins for my hair, and a shift."

"My gown will be too long for you," said Gwenhwyfar, "but no doubt you can pin it up somehow until your own clothes have come. Combs and veils and shifts I will give you gladly, and shoes as well—those look as if you had walked in them from here to Lothian and back!" She beckoned to one of her waiting-women and said, "Bring the red gown, and the veil that goes with it, and a shift and my other indoor shoes and hose—choose everything so that my lord's sister is dressed as is fitting to her station. And send for a bath and a bath-woman too." She looked disdainfully at the gown Morgaine was taking off, and said, "If that one cannot be fitly aired and cleaned, give it to one of the dairy-women!"

When Morgaine appeared at the King's table she wore the red gown, which lent color to her dark skin and became her well; they besought her to sing, but she would not, saying that as Kevin was at hand, no one would listen to a robin's chirping when a nightingale was near.

The next day Kevin sought private audience with Arthur, and he and the King and Taliesin, too, were closeted for many hours, and even had supper brought to them there; but Gwenhwyfar never knew what they spoke of—Arthur told her little of affairs of state. No doubt, they were angered with him that he had chosen to renounce his vows to Avalon, but soon or late they must accept it—that he was a Christian king. As for Gwenhwyfar, she had other things to think of.

THAT SPRING THERE WAS fever at the court, and some of her women fell sick of it, so that until Easter was past she had no leisure to think of anything else. She had never thought she would be glad of Morgaine's presence, but Morgaine knew much of herb lore and of healing, and she thought it was due to Morgaine's wisdom that there were no deaths in the court—in the country round, she heard, many died, though mostly little children and old folk. Her little half-sister Isotta took the fever, but her mother heard and would not have her stay at court, so that she was sent back to the island, and later in that month Gwenhwyfar heard that she had died. She mourned for the girl—she had come to be fond of her, and had hoped to marry her to one of Arthur's Companions when she was older.

Lancelet fell sick of the fever too, and Arthur gave orders that he should be quartered in the castle and nursed by her own women. While there was still danger that she might take the fever she did not go near him— she had hoped herself pregnant again, but it turned out not to be so; only her own hopes and illusions. When he began to recover she went often and sat by his side.

Morgaine came too, to play the harp, while he was unable to leave his bed. One day, watching them when they spoke of Avalon, Gwenhwyfar caught the look in Morgaine's eyes, and thought, *Why, she still loves him!* She knew Arthur still hoped for this—a match between Morgaine and Lancelet and she watched, sick with jealousy, as Lancelet listened to Morgaine's harp.

Her voice is so sweet; she is not beautiful, but she is so wise and learned

—*beautiful women are so many, Elaine is beautiful, and Meleas, and the daughter of King Royns, and even Morgause is beautiful, but why should Lancelet care for that?* And she marked the gentleness of Morgaine's hands as she lifted him and gave him her herb medicines and cooling drinks. She, Gwenhwyfar, was not good at all with the sick, she had no skills, she sat dumb while Morgaine talked and laughed and amused him.

It was growing dark, and at last Morgaine said, "I can no longer see the harp strings, and I am hoarse as a crow—I can sing no more. You must drink your medicine, Lancelet, and then I will send your man to you, to get you settled for the night—"

With a wry smile Lancelet took the cup she put in his hand. "Your drinks are cooling, kinswoman, but ugh! The taste of them—"

"Drink it," Morgaine said, laughing. "Arthur has put you under my command when you are sick—"

"Aye, and I do not doubt, if I refused you should beat me and put me supperless to bed, while if I drink my medicine like a good lad I shall have a kiss and a honey cake," Lancelet said.

Morgaine chuckled. "You cannot have a honey cake yet, you can have your nice gruel. But if you drink up your potion, you shall have a good-night kiss and I will bake you a honey cake when you are well enough to eat it."

"Yes, Mother," Lancelet said, wrinkling up his nose. Gwenhwyfar could see that Morgaine did not like the jest, but when he had emptied the cup she bent over him and kissed him lightly on the brow, and drew up the covers under his chin as a mother smooths a child's cradle. "There, now, good child, go to sleep," she said, laughing, but the laughter sounded bitter to Gwenhwyfar, and Morgaine went away.

Gwenhwyfar stood by Lancelet's bed, and said, "She is right, my dear, you should sleep."

"I am weary of Morgaine being always right," said Lancelet. "Sit you here by me for a little, dear love—"

It was seldom he dared speak so to her, but she sat herself on his bed and let him hold her hand. After a little he pulled her down beside him and kissed her; she lay along the edge of his bed and let him kiss her again and again, but after a long time he sighed, weary, and did not protest when she rose from his side. "My dearest love, this cannot go on like this. You must give me leave to depart from the court."

"What? To chase Pellinore's favorite dragon? Why, what will Pellinore do in holidaytime, then? It is his favorite hunting," Gwenhwyfar said, jesting, but it was like a pain in her heart.

He seized both her arms, pulling her down. "No, make this not a jest, Gwen—you know it and I know it, and God help us both, I think even

Arthur knows it, that I have loved none but you, or ever will, since first I set eyes on you in your father's house. And if I am to remain a true man to my king and my friend, then I must depart from this court and never set eyes on you again—"

Gwenhwyfar said, "I would not hold you, if you feel that you must go—"

"As I have gone before," he said violently. "Every time I rode forth to war, half of me longed that I should fall at Saxon hands and return no more to hopeless love—God forgive me, there were times when I hated my king, whom I have sworn to love and serve, and then I thought, no woman should part the friendship that was between us two, and I have sworn I would think of you no more, save as the wife of my king. But now there are no more wars, and I must sit here day by day and look upon you at his side in his high seat, and think of you in his bed, his happy and contented wife—"

"Why do you think I am any more happy or contented than you?" she demanded, her voice shaking. "At least you can choose whether to stay or to go, but I was given into Arthur's hands without even so much as 'will you or no?' Nor can I rise and ride forth from court when things go not to my will, but must stay here within walls and do what is expected of me . . . if you must go, I cannot say, Stay; and if you stay, I cannot say to you, Go! At least you are free to go or to stay as makes you happiest!"

"Do you think there is happiness for me, either in staying or going?" Lancelet demanded, and for a moment she thought that he would weep. Then he mastered himself and said, "Love, what do you want me to do? God forbid I should give you more unhappiness. If I am gone from here, then is your duty plain, to be a good wife to Arthur, no more and no less. If I stay here—" He broke off.

"If you feel it is your duty to go," she said, "then you must go." And tears flooded down her face, blurring her sight.

He said, and his voice was strained as if he had had a mortal wound, "Gwenhwyfar—" He so seldom spoke her formal name, it was always *my lady* or *my queen,* or when he spoke to her in play it was always *Gwen.* When he spoke it now, it seemed to her she had never heard a sweeter sound. "Gwenhwyfar. Why do you weep?"

Now she must lie, and lie well, because she could not in honor tell him the truth. She said, "Because—" and stopped, and then, in a choking voice, she said, "because I do not know how I shall live if you go away."

He swallowed hard and took her hands between his own and said, "Why, then—why, love—I am not a king, but my father has given me a small estate in Brittany. Would you come with me away from this court? I—I know not, perhaps it would be the more honorable way, than stay here at Arthur's court and make love to his wife—"

He loves me, then, Gwenhwyfar thought, *he wants me, this is the honorable way* . . . but panic flooded through her. To go forth alone, so far, even with Lancelet . . . and then the thought of what everyone would say of her, should she be so dishonored. . . .

He lay clasping her hand in his. He said, "We could never return, you know—never. And it's likely we should be excommunicated, both of us— that would mean little to me, I am not so much a Christian as all that. But you, my Gwenhwyfar—"

She put up her veil over her face and wept, knowing what a coward she was.

"Gwenhwyfar," he said, "I would not lead you into sin—"

She said bitterly, "We have sinned already, you and I—"

"And if the priests are right we will be damned for it," Lancelet said bitterly, "and yet have I never had more of you than these kisses—we have had all the evil and the guilt, and none of the pleasure which is said to come from sin. And I am not so sure I believe the priests—what sort of God goes about every night like a night watchman, peeping here and prying there like an old village gossip to see if any man beds with his neighbor's wife—"

"The Merlin said something like that," Gwenhwyfar said, low. "And sometimes it seems to me sensible, and then again I wonder if it is the Devil's work to lead me into evil. . . ."

"Oh, talk not to me of the Devil," he said, and pulled her down beside him again. "Sweetheart, my own, I will go away if you want me to, or I will stay, but I cannot bear to see you so unhappy. . . ."

"I do not know what I want," she wept, and let him hold her, sobbing. At last he murmured, "We have paid for the sin already . . ." and his mouth covered hers. Trembling, Gwenhwyfar let herself surrender to the kiss, his eager hands searching at her breast. She almost hoped that this time he would not be content with that, but there was a sound in the hallway and Gwenhwyfar drew herself upright, in sudden panic. She sat on the edge of the bed as Lancelet's esquire came into the room. He coughed and said, "My lord? The lady Morgaine told me you were ready to go to your rest. By your leave, my lady—?"

Morgaine again, damn her! Lancelet laughed and let go of Gwenhwyfar's hand. "Yes, and I doubt it not, my lady is weary. Will you promise to come and see me tomorrow, my queen?"

She was both grateful and angry that his voice sounded so calm. She turned away from the light the serving-man carried; she knew her veil was crushed and her dress rumpled, her face smeared with crying and her hair coming down. How she must look—what would the man think they had been doing? She put her veil over her face and rose. "Good night, sir Lancelet. Kerval, care you well for my king's dear friend," and went out, hoping forlornly that she could get down the hall to her own room before she burst into weeping again. *Ah God, how—how dare I pray to God that I may sin further? I should pray to be free of temptation, and I cannot!*

16

a day or two before Beltane-eve, Kevin the Harper came again to Arthur's court. Morgaine was glad to see him; it had been a long and weary springtime. Lancelet had recovered from the fever and gone north to Lothian, and Morgaine had thought she should ride to Lothian too, to see how it was with her son; but she did not want to go in Lancelet's company, nor would he have wished for her as a travelling companion; she thought, *My son is well where he is, another time I will go and see him.*

Gwenhwyfar was sorrowful and silent; in the years Morgaine had been absent, the Queen had altered from a lighthearted, childish woman to a silent, thoughtful one, more pious than was reasonable. Morgaine suspected that she pined after Lancelet, and knowing Lancelet, Morgaine thought with a touch of contempt that he would neither leave the woman in peace nor lead her wholeheartedly into sin. And Gwenhwyfar was a good match for him—she would neither give in to him nor give him up. She wondered what Arthur thought, but it would have taken a braver woman than she to ask him.

Morgaine welcomed Kevin to court, and to herself she thought it not unlikely that they would keep Beltane together—the sun tides ran hot in her blood, and if she could not have the man she wanted (and she knew it was still Lancelet to whom she was drawn), it might be as well to take a lover who found delight in *her;* it was good to be cherished and sought after. And, as neither Arthur nor Lancelet would do, Kevin spoke with her freely of affairs of state. She thought, with a moment of bitter regret, had she stayed in Avalon, by now, she would be consulted in all the great affairs of her time.

Well, it was too late for that; done was done. So she greeted Kevin in the great hall and had him served food and wine, a task Gwenhwyfar gladly gave over to her—Gwenhwyfar liked well enough to hear Kevin play on the harp, but she could not bear the sight of him. So Morgaine served him, and spoke to him of Avalon.

"Is Viviane well?"

"Well, and still resolved to come to Camelot at Pentecost," said Kevin, "and it is well, for Arthur would scarce listen to me. Though he has promised not to forbid the Beltane fires this year, at least."

"It would do him little good to forbid them," said Morgaine. "But Arthur has trouble nearer home, too." She gestured. "Beyond that window, almost within sight from the heights of the castle, lies the island kingdom of Leodegranz—had you heard?"

"A chance-come traveller told me he was dead," Kevin said, "and he left no son. His lady Alienor died with her last child, a few days after his death. The fever was cruel in that country."

"Gwenhwyfar would not travel thither for the burying," Morgaine said. "She had little to weep for—hers was not a loving father. Arthur will have consulted her about setting a regent there—he says that now the kingdom is hers, and if they should have a second son, that son shall have it. But it seems not likely now that Gwenhwyfar will have even one."

Kevin nodded slowly. "Aye, she miscarried of a child before Mount Badon, and was very ill. Since then I have not heard even a rumor that she was pregnant," said Kevin. "How old is the High Queen?"

"I think she is at least five-and-twenty now," said Morgaine, but she was not certain, she had dwelt so long in the fairy country.

"That is old for a first child," said Kevin, "though, I doubt not, like all barren women, she prays for a miracle. What ails the Queen that she does not conceive?"

"I am no midwife," said Morgaine. "She seems healthy enough, but she has worn out her knees in prayer, and there is no sign."

"Well, the Gods will have it as they will," Kevin said, "but we will need their mercy on this land if the High King dies with no son! And now there are no threats from the Saxons outside to keep the rival kings of Britain from falling one upon the other and tearing this land to shreds. I never trusted Lot, but he is dead, and Gawaine is Arthur's staunchest man, so there is little to fear from Lothian, unless Morgause finds herself a lover with ambition to be High King on his own."

"Lancelet has gone there, but he should return quickly," said Morgaine, and Kevin added, "Viviane, too, would ride to Lothian for some reason, though we thought, all of us, that she was too old for such a journey."

Why, then, she will see my son. . . . Morgaine's heart leapt, and there was a tightness like pain, or weeping, in her throat. Kevin seemed not to see.

"I met not with Lancelet on the road," he said. "No doubt he took another road, or stayed to greet his mother, or perhaps"—he grinned slyly —"to keep the Beltane feast. That would give joy to every woman in Lothian, if he tarried there. Morgause would not let such a tender morsel escape her clutches."

"She is his mother's sister," Morgaine said, "and I think Lance is too good a Christian for that. He has courage enough to face the Saxons in battle, but small courage for *that* battle."

Kevin raised his eyebrows. "Oh ho, is it so? I doubt not you speak from knowledge," he said, "but for politeness' sake we will say it is from the Sight! But Morgause would like well to see Arthur's best knight brought low by scandal—then would Gawaine stand nearer to the throne. And the lady is liked well by all men—she is not so old, either, but still beautiful, her hair still red as ever without a line of grey—"

"Oh," said Morgaine caustically, "they sell henna from Egypt in the markets of Lothian."

"And her waist is slim, and they say she practices magic arts to spellbind men to her," Kevin said, "but this is gossip and no more. I have heard she has ruled well enough in Lothian. Do you dislike her so much, Morgaine?"

"No. She is my kinswoman and has been good to me," Morgaine said, and started to say, *She fostered my child,* and that would open the way to ask if he had heard news of Gwydion . . . then she stopped herself. Even to Kevin she could not confess that. She said, instead, "But I like it not that my kinswoman Morgause should be the common talk of Britain as a bawd."

"It is not so bad as that," Kevin said, laughing, and put away his wine cup. "If the lady has an eye to handsome men, she would not be the first or last. And now Morgause is widowed, no man can call her to account for who lies in her bed. But I must not keep the High King waiting. Wish me fortune, Morgaine, for I must bring ill news to my king, and you know the doom meted of old to him who brought the king news he had no mind to hear!"

"Arthur is not that sort," said Morgaine. "But if it is not secret, what ill news do you bring?"

"Not news at all," said Kevin, "for it has been said more than once that Avalon will not have it that he rule as a Christian king, whatever his private faith may be. He shall not allow the priests to put down the worship of the Goddess, nor touch the oak groves. And if he does so, then am I to say to him from the Lady: the hand which gave him the sacred sword of the Druids can turn it in his hand to smite him."

"That will not be pleasant hearing," said Morgaine, "but perhaps it will call his oath to mind."

"Aye, and Viviane has still one other weapon she can use," said Kevin, but when Morgaine asked what, he would tell her no more.

When he had gone from her, Morgaine sat thinking of the night to come. There would be music at dinner, and later—well, Kevin was a pleasant lover, gentle and eager to please her, and she was wearied of sleeping alone.

She was still sitting in the hall when Cai came to announce that another rider had come—"A kinsman of yours, lady Morgaine. Would you greet him and serve him wine?"

Morgaine agreed—had Lancelet returned so soon already?—but the rider was Balan.

She hardly knew him at first—he was heavier, so big now that she supposed it must take an oversized horse to carry his weight. But he recognized her at once.

"Morgaine! Greetings, kinswoman," he said, and sat beside her, taking the cup she offered. She told him that Arthur was speaking with Kevin and the Merlin, but would see him at dinner, and asked him for the news.

"Only that a dragon has been sighted again in the North," Balan said, "and no, this is no fantasy like old Pellinore's—I saw the track where it had been, and talked with two of the people who had seen it. They were not lying, nor telling a tale to amuse or give themselves importance; they were in terror of their lives. They said it had come out of the lake and taken their serving-man—they showed me his shoe."

"His—shoe, kinsman?"

"He lost it when he was taken, and I did not like touching the—slime —that besmeared it," Balan said. "I am going to ask Arthur for half a dozen knights to ride with me and put an end to it."

"You must ask Lancelet, if he returns," Morgaine said, as lightly as she could. "He will need some practice with dragons. I think Arthur is trying to make a match between Lancelet and Pellinore's daughter."

Balan looked at her sharply. "I do not envy the girl who has my little brother for husband," he said. "I have heard his heart is given—or should I not say—"

"You should not say it," said Morgaine.

Balan shrugged. "So be it. Arthur then has no special reason for wishing to find Lancelet a bride well away from court," he said. "I had not heard that you had come back to court, kinswoman. You look well."

"And how is it with your foster-brother?"

"Balin is well enough, when last I saw him," said Balan, "though he still has no love for Viviane. Still, there is no reason to believe he bears grudge for our mother's death. He raved and swore revenge then, but he would have to be a madman indeed to think still of such things. In any case, if such was his thought, he spoke not of it when he was here at Pentecost a year ago. That is Arthur's newest custom, you may not know—that wherever we may travel in all of Britain, every one of his old Companions should gather at Pentecost and dine at his table. At that time, too, he makes new Companions in the order of knighthood, and he will accept any petitioner, however humble—"

"Yes, I had heard of that," said Morgaine, and a flicker of unease passed over her. Kevin had spoken of Viviane—she told herself it was only disquiet at the idea that a woman of the Lady's years might come here as a common petitioner. As Balan said, it would take a madman to harbor thoughts of revenge after all this time.

That night there was music, Kevin's fine playing and singing; and later still that night, Morgaine slipped from the chamber where she slept with Gwenhwyfar's unwedded ladies, as noiselessly as a ghost—or as a priestess trained in Avalon—and made her way to the chamber where Kevin slept. She left there before daylight, well contented, but one thing Kevin had said —though they had had other things to speak of than Arthur—troubled her mind.

"Arthur would not listen to me," he said. "He told me that the folk of England were a Christian people, and while he would not persecute any man for following what Gods he liked, still he would stand with the priests and the church, as they had stood by his throne. And he sent word to the Lady of Avalon that if she would have back the sword, she could come and take it."

Even after she had crept back into her own bed, Morgaine lay wakeful. It was the legendary sword which had bound so many of the Tribesmen and Northmen to Arthur; and it was his allegiance to Avalon which had bound the dark pre-Roman people. Now, it seemed, Arthur was further from that allegiance than he had ever been.

She could speak with him—but no, he would not listen to her; she was a woman and his sister—and always, between them, lay the memory of that morning after the kingmaking, so that never could they speak freely as they might have done before. And she did not carry the authority of Avalon; with her own hands had she cast that away.

It might be that Viviane could make him see the importance of keeping to his oath. But tell herself this as she would, it was long before Morgaine could close her eyes and sleep.

17

Even before she rose from her bed, Gwenhwyfar could feel the bright sunlight through the bed-curtains—*Summer is here.* And then, *Beltane.* The very fullness of pagandom—she was sure that many of her serving-men and women would be slipping away from the court tonight, when the Beltane fires were lighted on Dragon Island in honor of their Goddess, there to lie in the fields . . . *some of them, no doubt, to come home again with their wombs quickened with the child of the God . . . and I, a Christian wife, cannot bear a son to my own dear lord. . . .*

She turned over in bed and lay watching Arthur's sleep. Oh, yes, he was her dear lord, and she loved him well. He had taken her as part of a dowry and sight unseen; yet he had loved her, cherished her, honored her —it was not her fault that she could not do the first duty of a queen and bear him a son for his kingdom.

Lancelet—no, she had sworn to herself, when last he went from court, she would think no more of him. She still hungered for him, heart and soul and body, but she had vowed that she would be a loyal and a faithful wife to Arthur; never again should Lancelet have from her even these games and toyings which made them both ache for more . . . it was playing at sin, even if there was nothing worse.

Beltane. Well, perhaps, as a Christian woman and queen of a Christian court, it was her duty to make such feastings and play this day as all the people of the court should enjoy without harm to their souls. She knew that Arthur had sent out word of games and arms practice to be held for prizes, at Pentecost—as he had done each year since the court came here to Camelot; but there were enough of his people here that some sport could be had this day too—she would offer a silver cup. And there should be harping and dancing, too, and she would do for the women what sometimes they did in play, offer a ribbon for the woman who could spin the most yarn in an hour, or work the largest piece of tapestry—yes, there should be innocent sport so that none of her people should regret the forbidden play on Dragon Island. She sat up and began to dress herself; she must go and talk to Cai.

But, although she busied herself all the morning, and Arthur when she spoke of it was pleased, thinking it the best of devices, so that he and Cai spent the morning in talking of the prizes they would offer for the best sword play and horsemanship, yes, and there should be a prize, perhaps a cloak, for the best among the boys—still, inside her heart, the thought gnawed. *It is the day on which the ancient Gods demand that we honor fertility, and I, I am still barren.* And so, an hour before high noon, at which hour the trumpets would be blown to gather men before the arms field to begin their sport, Gwenhwyfar sought out Morgaine, yet not quite certain what she would say to her.

Morgaine had taken charge of the dyeing room for the wool they spun, and was also in charge of the Queen's brew-women—she knew how to keep ale from spoiling when it was brewed, and how to distill strong spirit for medicines, and make perfumes of flower petals which were finer than those brought from over the seas and more costly than gold. There were some women in the castle who believed this was magic art, but Morgaine said no, it was only that she had been taught about the properties of plants and grains and flowers. Any woman, Morgaine said, could do what she did, if she was neat-handed and willing to take the time and trouble to see to it.

Gwenhwyfar found her with her holiday gown tied up and her hair covered with a cloth, sniffing at a batch of beer which had spoilt in the vats. "Throw it away," she said. "The barm must have got cold, and it has soured. We can start with another batch tomorrow—there is plenty for this day, even with the Queen's feasting, whatever put it into her head."

Gwenhwyfar asked, "Have you no mind to feasting, sister?"

Morgaine turned. "Not truly," she said, "but I marvel that *you* have, Gwen—I thought on Beltane you would be all for pious fasting and prayer, if only to show you were not one of those who made merry in honor of the Goddess of the crops and fields."

Gwenhwyfar colored—she never knew if Morgaine was making fun of her. "Perhaps God has ordained it, that people shall make merry in honor of the coming of the summer, and there is no need to speak of the Goddess . . . oh, I know not what I think—believe *you* that the Goddess gives life to crops and fields and the wombs of ewes and heifers and women?"

"I was so taught in Avalon, Gwen. Why do you ask this now?" Morgaine took off the headcloth with which she had covered her hair, and Gwenhwyfar thought suddenly that Morgaine was beautiful. Morgaine was older than Gwenhwyfar—she must be past thirty; but she looked no older than when Gwenhwyfar had first seen her . . . it was no wonder all men thought her a sorceress! She wore a fine-spun gown of dark blue wool, very plain, but colored ribbons were braided into her dark hair, which was looped about her ears and fastened with a gold pin. Next to her, Gwenhwyfar felt dull as a hen, a simple homekeeping woman, even though she was High Queen of Britain and Morgaine only a heathen duchess.

Morgaine knew so much, and she herself was so unlearned—she could do no more than write her name and read a little in her Gospel book. While Morgaine was skilled in all the clerkly arts, she could read and write, and yes, she knew the housewifely arts too—she could spin and weave and do fine embroideries, and dyeing and brewing, yes, and herb lore and magic as well. At last Gwenhwyfar faltered, "My sister—they have said it as a jest, but is it—is it true, that you know—all manner of charms and spells for fertility? I—I cannot live with it any longer, that every lady at court watches every morsel I eat to see if I am breeding, or takes note of how tight I tie my girdle! Morgaine, if indeed you know these charms they say you know—my sister, I beg you—will you use those arts for me?"

Moved and troubled, Morgaine laid a hand on Gwenhwyfar's arm. "In Avalon, it is true, it is said that such and such things can help if a woman does not bear when she should—but Gwenhwyfar—" She hesitated, and

Gwenhwyfar felt her face flooding with shame. At last Morgaine went on. "I am not the Goddess. It may be that it is her will that you and Arthur should have no children. Would you really try to turn the will of God with spells and charms?"

Gwenhwyfar said violently, "Even Christ in the garden prayed, 'If it be thy will, let this cup pass from me—' "

"But he said also, Gwen—'Not my will, Lord, be done, but thine,' " Morgaine reminded her.

"I wonder that you know such things—"

"I dwelt in Igraine's household for eleven years, Gwenhwyfar, and I heard the gospel preached as often as you."

"Yet I cannot see how it should be God's will that the kingdom be torn again by chaos if Arthur should die," Gwenhwyfar said and heard her own voice rise, sharp and angry. "All these years I have been faithful—yes, I know you do not believe it, I suppose you think what all the women in the court think, that I have betrayed my lord for the love of Lancelet—but it is not so, Morgaine, I swear it is not so—"

"Gwenhwyfar, Gwenhwyfar! I am not your confessor! I have not accused you!"

"But you would if you could, and I think you are jealous," Gwenhwyfar retorted at white heat, and then cried out in contrition, "Oh, no! No, I do not want to quarrel with you, Morgaine, my sister—oh, no, I came to beg you for your help—" She felt the tears break from her eyes. "I have done no wrong, I have been a good and loyal wife, I have kept my lord's house and strove to bring honor to his court, I have prayed for him and tried to do the will of God, I have failed no whit of my duty, and yet— and yet—for all of my loyalty and duty—I have not even had my part of the bargain. Every whore in the streets, every soldier's camp follower, they go about flaunting their big bellies and their fruitfulness, and I—I have had nothing, nothing—" She was sobbing wildly, her hands over her face.

Morgaine's voice sounded puzzled but tender, and she put out her arms and drew Gwenhwyfar to her. "Don't cry, don't cry—Gwenhwyfar, look at me, is it so much a sorrow to you that you have no child?"

Gwenhwyfar struggled to control her weeping. She said, "I can think of nothing else, day and night—"

After a long time, Morgaine said, "Aye, I can see it is hard for you." It seemed she could actually hear Gwenhwyfar's thoughts:

If I had a child, I would not think night and day of this love which tempts my honor, for all my thoughts would be given to Arthur's son.

"I would that I could help you, sister—but I am unwilling to have doings with charms and magic. We are taught in Avalon that simple folk may need such things, but the wise meddle not with them, but bear the lot the Gods have sent them." And as she spoke she felt herself a hypocrite; she was remembering the morning when she had gone out to find roots and herbs for a potion which would keep her from bearing Arthur's child. *That had not been surrendering herself to the will of the Goddess!*

But in the end she had not done it, either—

And then Morgaine wondered, in sudden weariness: *I who did not want a child, and who came near to death in bearing it, I bore my child; Gwenhwyfar, who longs night and day for one, goes with empty womb and empty arms. Is this the goodness of the will of the Gods?*

Yet she felt compelled to say, "Gwenhwyfar, I would have you bear this in mind—charms often work as you would not that they would do. What makes you believe the Goddess I serve can send you a son when your God, who is supposed to be greater than all the other Gods, cannot?"

It sounded like blasphemy, and Gwenhwyfar was ashamed of herself. Yet she found herself thinking, and saying aloud in a voice that choked as she spoke, "I think perhaps God cares nothing for women—all his priests are men, and again and again the Scriptures tell us that women are the temptress and evil—it may be that is why he does not hear me. And for this I would go to the Goddess—God does not care—" And then she was weeping stormily again. "Morgaine," she cried, "if you cannot help me, I swear I will go tonight to Dragon Island in the boat, I shall bribe my serving-man to take me there, and when the fires are lighted I too shall entreat the Goddess to give me the gift of a child . . . I swear it, Morgaine, that I will do this. . . ." And she saw herself in the light of the fires, circling the flames, going apart in the grip of a strange and faceless man, lying in his arms—the thought made her whole body cramp tight with pain and a half-shamed pleasure.

Morgaine listened in growing horror. *She would never do it, she would lose her courage at the last moment . . . I was frightened, even I, and I had always known my maidenhead was for the God.* But then, hearing the utter despair in her sister-in-law's voice, she thought, *Aye, but she might; and if she did, she would hate herself all her life long.*

There was no sound in the room but Gwenhwyfar's sobbing. Morgaine waited until it quieted a little, then said, "Sister, I will do for you what I can. Arthur can give you a child, you need not go to the Beltane fire, or seek one elsewhere. You must never say aloud that I have told you this, promise me that, and ask me no questions. But Arthur has indeed sired a child."

Gwenhwyfar stared at her. "He told me he had no children—"

"It may be that he does not know. But I have seen the child myself. He is being fostered at Morgause's court."

"Why, then, he has already a son and if I do not bear him one—"

"No!" said Morgaine quickly, and her voice was harsh. "I have told you—you must never speak of this, the child is not such a one as he could acknowledge. If you give him no child, then must the kingdom go to Gawaine. Gwenhwyfar, ask me no more, for I will not tell you more than this—if you do not bear, it is not Arthur's fault."

"I have not even conceived since last harvesttime—and only three times in all these years—" Gwenhwyfar swallowed, wiping her face on her veil. "If I offer myself to the Goddess—she will be merciful to me—"

Morgaine sighed. "It might be so. You must not go to Dragon Island. You can conceive, I know—perhaps a charm could help you to carry a child to birth. But I warn you again, Gwenhwyfar: charms do not their magic as men and women would have it, but by their own laws, and those laws are as strange as the running of time in the fairy country. Do not seek to blame me, Gwenhwyfar, if the charm acts other than you think it should."

"If it gives me even a slight chance of a child by my lord—"

"That it should do," Morgaine said, and turned, Gwenhwyfar following after her like a child being led by her mother. What would the charm be, Gwenhwyfar wondered and what would it do, and why did Morgaine look so strange and solemn—as if she were that Great Goddess herself? But, she told herself, taking a deep breath, she would accept whatever came, if it might give her what she desired most.

An hour later, when the trumpets were blown and Morgaine and Gwenhwyfar were sitting side by side at the edge of the field, Elaine leaned over to them and said, "Look! Who is that riding into the field at Gawaine's side?"

"It is Lancelet," said Gwenhwyfar breathlessly. "He has come home."

He was handsomer than ever. Somewhere he had gotten a red slash on his cheek, which should have been ugly, but it gave him the fierce beauty of a wild cat. He rode as if he were part of the horse's self, and Gwenhwyfar listened to Elaine's chatter, not really hearing, her eyes fixed on the man.

Bitter, bitter, the irony of this. Why now, when I am resolved and pledged to think no more of him but to do my sworn duty by my lord and king . . . Round her neck, beneath the golden torque Arthur had given her when they had been wedded a full five years, she could feel the weight of Morgaine's charm, sewn into a little bag between her breasts. She did not know, had not wanted to know, what Morgaine had put into it.

Why now? I had hoped that when he came home for Pentecost, I should be already bearing my lord's child, and he would look no more on me, since it was so clear I was resolved to honor my marriage.

Yet against her will, she remembered Arthur's words: *Should you bear me a child, I would not question . . . do you know what I am saying to you?* Gwenhwyfar had known what he meant all too well. Lancelet's son could be heir to the kingdom. Was this new temptation offered her, now, because she had already fallen into grievous sin by meddling with Morgaine's sorcery, and making wild and unchaste threats, hoping to force Morgaine into helping her . . .?

I do not care, if so be it I can bear my king a son . . . if a God would damn me for that, what have I to do with him? She was frightened at her own blasphemy, yet it had been blasphemy, too, to think of going to the lighted Beltane fires. . . .

"Look, Gawaine is down, even he could not stand against Lancelet's riding," Elaine said eagerly. "And Cai, too! How could Lancelet strike down a lame man?"

"Don't be more of a fool than you *must,* Elaine," said Morgaine. "Do you think Cai would thank Lancelet for sparing him? If Cai went into these games, surely he is able to risk whatever hurt he could take! No one bade him compete."

It had been foreordained from the moment Lancelet took the field who would win the prize. There was some good-natured grumbling among the Companions when they saw it. "There is no use in any of us entering the lists at all, while Lancelet is here," Gawaine said, laughing, his arm around his cousin. "Couldn't you have stayed away another day or so, Lance?"

Lancelet was laughing too, a high color in his face. He took the golden cup and tossed it in the air. "Your mother, too, besought me to stay in her court for Beltane. I came not here to defraud you of the prize—I have no need of prizes. Gwenhwyfar, my lady," he cried, "take this, and give me instead the ribbon you wear about your neck. The cup may go to the altar or to the Queen's high table!"

Embarrassed, Gwenhwyfar's hand flew to her throat and the ribbon on which she had tied Morgaine's charm. "*This* I may not give you, my friend—" But she fumbled at the sleeve which she had embroidered with small pearls. "Take this for a kindness to my champion. As for the prize— well, I will give prizes to all of you—" She gestured to Gawaine and Gareth, who had come in after Lancelet in the riding.

"Graciously done," Arthur said, rising in his place, while Lancelet took the embroidered silk and kissed it, then fastened it around his helm. "But my most valiant fighter must still be honored. You will sit with us at the high table, Lancelet, and tell us all that has befallen you since you left my court."

Gwenhwyfar excused herself with her ladies, the better to prepare for the feast. Elaine and Meleas were chattering about Lancelet's valor, his riding, his generosity in giving up all claim to the prize. Gwenhwyfar could think only of the look he had given her when he begged her for the ribbon about her throat. She looked up and met Morgaine's dark, enigmatic smile.

I cannot even pray for peace of mind. I have forfeited the right to pray.

For the first hour of the feast she was moving about, making sure that all of the guests were properly seated and served. By the time she took her seat at the high table they were drunk, most of them, and it was very dark outside. The servants brought lamps and torches, fastening them into the wall, and Arthur said jovially, "See, my lady, we are lighting our own Beltane fire within walls."

Morgaine had come to sit close to Lancelet. Gwenhwyfar's face throbbed with heat and with the wine she had drunk; she turned away so that she might not see them. Lancelet said, with a great yawn, "Why, it is Beltane indeed—I had forgotten."

"And Gwenhwyfar had it that we must have a feast so that none of our folk would be tempted to slip away into the old rites," Arthur said. "There are more ways to skin a wolf than chasing him out of his fur—if I forbade the fires, then would I be a tyrant—"

"And," Morgaine said, in her low voice, "faithless to Avalon, my brother."

"But if my lady makes it more pleasant for my people here to sit at our feast instead of going out into the fields to dance by the fires, then is our purpose achieved more simply!"

Morgaine shrugged. To Gwenhwyfar it seemed that she was secretly amused. She had drunk but little—perhaps she was the only wholly sober person at the King's table. "You have been travelling in Lothian, Lancelet —do they keep the Beltane rites there?"

"So says the Queen," Lancelet said, "but for all I know, she may have been jesting with me—I saw nothing to suggest that Queen Morgause is not the most Christian of ladies." But it seemed to Gwenhwyfar that he glanced uneasily at Gawaine as he spoke. "Mark what I say, Gawaine, I said nothing against the lady of Lothian, I have no quarrel with you or yours. . . ."

But only a soft snore answered him, and Morgaine's laughter was brittle. "Look, yonder lies Gawaine asleep with his head on the table! I too would ask news of Lothian, Lancelet . . . I do not think anyone reared there could so quickly forget the Beltane fires. The sun tides run in the blood of anyone reared on Avalon, like me, like Queen Morgause—is it not so, Lancelet? Arthur, do you remember the kingmaking on Dragon Island? How many years ago—nine, ten—"

Arthur looked displeased, though he spoke gently enough. "That is many years past and gone, as you say, sister, and the world changes with every season. I think the time for such things is past, save, perhaps, for those who live with fields and crops and must call on the Goddess for their blessing —Taliesin would say so, and I will not gainsay it. But I think those old rites have little to do with such as we who dwell in castles and cities and have heard the word of Christ." He raised his wine cup, emptied it, and spoke with drunken emphasis. "God will give us all we desire—all that is right for us to have—without need to call upon the old Gods, is it not so, Lance?"

Gwenhwyfar felt Lancelet's eyes on her for a moment before he said, "Which of us has all things he may desire, my king? No king, and no God, can grant that."

"But I want my—my subjects to have all they need," repeated Arthur thickly. "And so does my queen, giving us our own Bel-Beltane fires here—"

"Arthur," said Morgaine gently, "you are drunk."

"Well, and why not?" he asked her belligerently. "At my own feast and my own—own fire, and what else did I fight the Saxons for, all those years? Sit here at my own Round Table and enjoy the—the peace—good ale and wine, and good music—where is Kevin the Harper? Am I to have no music at my feast?"

Lancelet said, laughing, "I have no doubt he has gone to worship the Goddess at her fires, and to play his harp there, on Dragon Island."

"Why, this is treason," said Arthur thickly. "And another reason to forbid the Beltane fires, so I may have music—"

Morgaine laughed and said lightheartedly, "You cannot command the conscience of another, my brother. Kevin is a Druid and has the right to offer his music to his own Gods if he will." She leaned her chin on her hands, and Gwenhwyfar thought she looked like a cat licking cream from her whiskers. "But I think he has already kept Beltane in his own way—no doubt he has gone to his bed, for all the company here is too drunken to tell the difference between his harping and mine and Gawaine's howling pipes! Even as he sleeps he plays the music of Lothian," she added, as a particularly raucous snore from the sleeping Gawaine cut the silence, and she gestured to one of the chamberlains, who went and persuaded Gawaine to his feet. He bowed groggily to Arthur and staggered from the hall.

Lancelet raised the cup in his hand and drained it. "I too have had enough of music and feasting, I think—I have ridden since before daylight, since I would come to your games this day, and soon, I think, I will beg leave to be away to my bed, Arthur." Gwenhwyfar gauged his drunkenness by that offhanded *Arthur;* in public he was always very careful to speak formally to Arthur as "my lord," or "my king," and only when they were alone did he say "cousin" or "Arthur."

But indeed, so late in the feast, there were few sober enough to notice—they might as well have been alone together. Arthur did not even answer Lancelet; he had slipped down a little in his high seat, and his eyes were half closed. Well, Gwenhwyfar thought, he had said it himself—it was his own feast and his own fireside, and if a man could not be drunken in his own house, why had he fought so many years to make their feasts safe and secure?

And if Arthur should be too drunk tonight to welcome her to his bed, after all . . . she could feel the ribbon about her neck, where the charm hung, and its weight heavy and hot between her breasts. *'Tis Beltane; could he not keep sober for that? Had he been bidden to one of those old pagan feasts, he would have remembered,* she thought, and her cheeks burned with the immodesty of the thought. *I must be drunk too!* She looked angrily at Morgaine, cool and sober, toying with the ribbons of her harp. Why should Morgaine smile like that?

Lancelet leaned toward her and said, "I think our lord and king has had enough of feasting and wine, my queen. Will you dismiss the servants and Companions, madam, and I'll find Arthur's chamberlain to help him to his bed."

Lancelet rose. Gwenhwyfar could tell he was drunk, too, but he carried it well, moving with only a little more carefulness than usual. As she began to pass among the guests to bid them good night, she felt her own head swim and her steps unsteady. Seeing Morgaine's enigmatic smile, she could still hear the words of the damnable sorceress: *Do not seek to blame me, Gwenhwyfar, if the charm acts other than you think it should.* . . .

Lancelet came back through the guests streaming out of the hall. "I can't find my lord's body servant—someone in the kitchens said they were all away to Dragon Island for the fires . . . is Gawaine still here, or Balan? They are the only ones big and strong enough to carry our lord and king to his bed. . . ."

"Gawaine was too drunk to carry himself," Gwenhwyfar said, "and I saw not Balan at all. And for sure *you* cannot carry him, for he is taller and heavier than you—"

"Still, I'll have at it," said Lancelet, laughing, and bent beside Arthur. "Come, cousin—Gwydion! There's none to carry you to bed—I'll give you my arm. Here, come up, there's my brave fellow," he said, as if he spoke to a child, and Arthur opened his eyes and staggered to his feet. Lancelet's steps were none too steady, either, thought Gwenhwyfar as she followed the men, nor for that matter were her own . . . a fine sight they must look, if any servants were sober enough to notice, High King and High Queen and the King's captain of horse all staggering to bed on Beltane-eve too drunk for their feet to carry them. . . .

But Arthur sobered a little when Lancelet hauled him over the threshold of their room; he went to a ewer of water in the corner, splashed some on his face, and drank more.

"Thank you, cousin," he said, his voice still slow and drunken. "My lady and I have much for which to thank you, that is certain, and I know you love us both well—"

"God is my witness to that," said Lancelet, but he looked at Gwenhwyfar with something like despair. "Shall I go and find one of your servants, cousin?"

"No, stay a moment," Arthur said. "There is something I would say to you, and if I find not the courage for it now in drink, I shall never say it sober. Gwen, can you manage without your women? I have no mind that this should be carried beyond this chamber by idle tongues. Lancelet, come here and sit by me," and sitting on the edge of the bed, he stretched out his hand to his friend. "You too, sweeting—now listen to me, both. Gwenhwyfar has no child—and do you think I have not seen how you two look at each other? I spoke of this once to Gwen, but she is so modest and pious, she would not hear me. Yet now at Beltane, when all life on this earth seems to cry out with breeding and fertility . . . how can I say this? There is an old saying among the Saxons, a friend is one to whom you will lend your favorite wife and your favorite sword. . . ."

Gwenhwyfar's face was burning; she could not look at either of the men. Arthur went on, slowly, "A son of yours, Lance, would be heir to my kingdom, and better that than it should go to Lot's sons. . . . Oh, yes, Bishop Patricius would call it grievous sin, no doubt, as if his God were some elderly chaperone who went about at night looking to see who slept in whose bed . . . I think it greater sin to make no provision for a son to inherit my kingdom. Then should we fall into such chaos as threatened before Uther came to the throne—my friend, my cousin—what do you say?"

Gwenhwyfar saw Lancelet moisten his lips with his tongue, and she felt the dryness of her own mouth. At last he said, "I know not what to say, my king—my friend—my cousin. God knows—there is no other woman on this earth—" and his voice broke; he looked at Gwenhwyfar and it seemed she could not endure the naked longing in his eyes. For a moment she thought she would swoon away, and put out a hand to steady herself on the bed frame.

I am still drunk, she thought, *I am dreaming this, I cannot have heard him say what I thought I heard.* . . . and she felt an agonizing burst of shame. It seemed she could not live and let them speak of her like this.

Lancelet's eyes had not moved from hers.

"It is for my—for my lady to say."

Arthur held out his arms to her. He had drawn off his boots and the rich robe he had worn at the feast; in his undertunic he looked very like the boy she had wedded years ago. He said, "Come here, Gwen," and drew her down on his knee. "You know I love you well—you and Lance, I think, are the two I love best in the world, save for—" He swallowed and stopped, and Gwenhwyfar thought suddenly, *I have thought only of my own love, I have had no thought for Arthur. He took me unseen, unwanted, and he has shown me love and honored me as his queen. But I never thought that as I love Lancelet, there may well be one whom Arthur loves and cannot have . . . not without sin and betrayal. I wonder if that is why Morgaine mocks me, she knows Arthur's secret loves . . . or his sins . . .*

But Arthur went on deliberately, "I think I would never have had the courage to say this, were it not Beltane. . . . For many hundreds of years, our forefathers have done these things without shame, in the very faces of our Gods and by their will. And—listen to this, my dearest—if I am here with you, my Gwenhwyfar, then should a child come of this, then you may swear without any untruth that this child was conceived in your marriage bed, and none of us need ever know for certain—dear love, will you not consent to this?"

Gwenhwyfar could not breathe. Slowly, slowly, she reached out her hand and laid it in Lancelet's. She felt Arthur's touch on her hair as Lancelet leaned forward and kissed her on the mouth.

I have been married many years and I am as frightened now as any virgin, she thought, and then she remembered Morgaine's words when she laid the charm about her neck. *Beware what you ask for, Gwenhwyfar, for the Goddess may grant it to you. . . .*

At the time, she had thought Morgaine meant only that if she prayed for a child, then she might well die in childbirth. Now she knew it was more subtle than that, for it had come about that she should have Lancelet, and without guilt, with her husband's own will and permission . . . and in a flash of awareness, she thought, *It was this I wanted, after all; after all these years it is certain that I am barren, I will bear no child, but I will have had this at least. . . .*

With shaking hands she undid her gown. It seemed that the whole world had dwindled down to this, this perfect awareness of herself, of her own body aching with desire, a hunger she had never believed she could feel. Lancelet's skin was so soft—she had thought all men were like Arthur, sunburnt and hairy, but his body was smooth as a child's. Ah, but she loved them both, loved Arthur all the more that he could be generous enough to give her this . . . they were both holding her now, and she closed her eyes and put up her face to be kissed, not knowing for certain which man's lips closed over hers. But it was Lancelet's hand that stroked her cheek, moved down to her naked throat where the ribbon clung.

"Why, what's this, Gwen?" he asked, his mouth against hers.

"Nothing," she said, "nothing. Some rubbish Morgaine gave me." She pulled it free and flung it into a corner, sinking back into her husband's arms and her lover's.

BOOK THREE

The King
Stag

1

at this season in Lothian, it seemed the sun hardly went to rest; queen Morgause wakened as the light began to steal through the hangings, yet it was so early the gulls were hardly astir. But there was already light enough to make out the hairy, well-muscled body of the young man who slept at her side . . . a privilege he had enjoyed most of the winter. He had been one of Lot's esquires, and had cast longing eyes on the queen even before Lot's death. And in the deathly darkness of this winter past, it was too much to ask that she should sleep alone in the king's cold chamber.

It was not that Lot had been so good a king, she thought, slotting her eyes against the growing light. But his reign had been long—he had reigned since before Uther Pendragon took the throne, and his people were used to him; there were people well into their middle years who had known no other king. He had been on the throne, she thought, when young Lochlann was born . . . for that matter, so had she. But that thought was less comfortable, and she flinched away from it.

Gawaine would have succeeded his father, but Gawaine had hardly visited his native land since Arthur's crowning, and the people did not know him. Here in Lothian, the Tribes were quite content, since there was peace in the land, to be ruled by their queen, with her son Agravaine at hand should they need a leader in war. From time out of mind, a queen had ruled over the people, as a Goddess had ruled over the Gods, and they were content to have it so.

But Gawaine had not left Arthur's side . . . not even when Lancelet had come north before Beltane—he said, to see that the lighthouses had been put in order on the coast so that ships would not be driven on to the rocks. But Morgause supposed, rather, that he came so that Arthur's eyes could see what went on in Lothian, whether there was anyone there at odds with the rule of the High King.

She had heard, then, of Igraine's death—before that, word had not come north to Lothian. She and Igraine had not been friends when she was younger; she had always envied her older sister her beauty, and had

453

never forgiven her that Viviane had chosen her for Uther Pendragon; she would have made a better High Queen than that ninny, so pliant and pious and loving. And when all was said and done, when the lamp was out, one man was not so different from any other, and all of them were ridiculously easy to manage, foolishly dependent on that thing a woman could offer to them. She had ruled well behind Lot's throne; she would have done better yet with Uther, for she would not have become so stupidly entangled with the priests.

Yet when she heard of Igraine's death she had mourned her sincerely and wished she had made the time to ride to Tintagel before she died. She had so few woman friends now. . . .

Her waiting-women had mostly been chosen by Lot for their beauty or their availability to the king, and he cared most for such women as did not think very much or talk very intelligently; she was, he said once, quite enough in that line. He took her counsel in all things and respected her wit, but when she had borne him four royal sons, he went back to what he naturally preferred for his bed—pretty women with little of sense. Morgause had never begrudged him his pleasures and was just as well pleased to be spared further childbearing. And if she craved babes to play with, there was her fosterling Gwydion, and Lot's women had always been breeding —Gwydion had playmates enough of royal blood!

Lochlann stirred at her side, muttered, and sleepily drew her into his arms, and she gave over thinking for the moment. She had missed him— while Lancelet was at court she had sent Lochlann to sleep among the young men. Though for all the difference it had made to Lancelet, she might have kept Lochlann in her bed, or slept with the house dog! Well, he was here again; Lot had never begrudged her amusement, any more than she had begrudged him his women.

But when the excitement had subsided, and Lochlann had trundled down the stairs to the privy outside, Morgause thought suddenly that she missed Lot. Not that he had ever been particularly good at this kind of sport . . . he had been old when she married him. But when that was done, he could talk with her intelligently, and she found that she missed the years when they would wake together, and lie in bed and talk of all that was to be done or what befell in the kingdom, or all of Britain.

By the time Lochlann came back, the sun was already strengthening and the air was alive with the crying of gulls. She could hear small sounds down the stairs, and somewhere there was a smell of bannock baking. She pulled him to her for a quick kiss and said, "You must be off, my dear. I want you out of here before Gwydion comes—he is a big boy now, he is beginning to notice things."

Lochlann chuckled. "*That* one, he has been noticing everything since he was out of his nurse's arms. While Lancelet was here he noticed every move he made—even at Beltane. But I do not think you have to worry —he's not old enough to think of *that.*"

"I'm not so certain," Morgause said, and patted his cheek. Gwydion's way was to do nothing until he was sure he would not be laughed at as too young. Self-possessed as he was, he could never bear to be told he was too young for anything—even when he was four years old he had flown into a rage at being told he could not go birds-nesting on the cliffs, and had nearly fallen to his death trying to keep up with the older boys. She remembered that occasion, and other similar ones, when she had told him never to do so or so again, and he had set his small dark face and told her, "Aye, but I shall, and you cannot stop me." Her only reply to that had had to be, "You shall not, or I will myself beat you." Not that it mattered whether she beat him or not—it only made him more defiant, unless she was prepared to beat him insensible; and once, losing her temper, she had frightened herself with how hard she had struck the harmless child. None of her own sons, even the strong-willed Gareth, had ever been so defiant. Gwydion took his own way and did what he would, and so as he got older she had taken to subtler methods: "You shall not, or I shall have your nurse take off your breeks and beat you with a heather switch before all the house folk as if you were a babe of four or five." That had been effective, for a time—very conscious of his dignity was young Gwydion. But now he did as he would and there was no stopping him; it would have taken a harsh man to thrash him as hard as was needful, and he had a way of making anyone who offended him sorry for it, soon or late.

She supposed that he would be more vulnerable when he began to care what the maidens thought of him. Fairy-born he was and dark, like Morgaine, but handsome enough, even as Lancelet was handsome. And it might be that his outward indifference to the maidens would be the same as Lancelet's. She thought about that for a moment, knowing the sting of humiliation. Lancelet . . . there was the handsomest man she had seen in many a long year, and she had made it clear to him that even the queen was not beyond his reach . . . but Lancelet had professed not to understand, had meticulously called her "Aunt" early and late—one would have thought from Lancelet's manner that she was elderly indeed, Viviane's twin, not young enough to be Viviane's daughter!

She had begun taking her breakfast in bed while she talked with her women about what must be done that day. While she lingered, propped up on the cushions—they had brought her some of the fresh hot bannock, and there was, at this time of year, plenty of butter from the dairy—Gwydion came into the room.

"Good morning, foster-mother," he said. "I have been out and brought you some berries. And there is cream in the pantry. If you want it, I will run down and fetch it for you."

She looked at the berries, dew-fresh in a wooden bowl. "That was thoughtful of you, foster-son," she said, and sat up in bed to take him close in a great hug. When he was only a little younger he had crawled in beside her into the blankets at such occasions, while she fed him hot bannock and honey, and in winter snuggled him into her furs, like any pampered youngest; she missed the feel of the small warm body burrowing against her, but she supposed he was really too old now.

He straightened himself, smoothing his hair into place—he hated to be mussed. Like Morgaine, who had always been a tidy little thing.

"You are out early, my love," she said, "and you did all this just for your old foster-mother? No, I do not want any cream. You do not want me fat as the old sow, do you?"

He tilted his head to one side like a small precise bird and looked, considering, at Morgause. "It wouldn't matter," he said. "You would still be beautiful even if you were fat. There are women at this court—Mara, for instance—she is no bigger than you, but all the other women, and the men, call her Fat Mara. But somehow you do not look as big as you are, because when anyone looks at you, all they see is that you are beautiful. So have the cream if you want it, foster-mother."

So precise an answer for a child! But after all he was beginning to grow into a man. Though he would be like Agravaine, never very tall—one of the Old People, a throwback. And of course, next to the giant Gareth he would always look like a child, even when he was twenty! He had washed his face and brushed his hair very carefully; yes, and it had been trimmed freshly too.

"How nice you look, my love," she said, as his small fingers swooped precisely to appropriate a berry from the dish. "Did you cut your hair yourself?"

"No," he said, "I made the steward do it; I said I was tired of looking like the house dog. Lot was always clean-trimmed and clean-shaven, and so was Lancelet all the time he stayed here. I like to look like a gentleman."

"And so you always do, my dear," she said, looking at the small dark hand holding the berry. It was bramble-scratched and the knuckles grimed and grubby like any active boy's hand, but she noted, too, that he had scrubbed it long and hard and that the nails were not dirty and broken but carefully pared short. "But why have you put on your holiday tunic this morning?"

"Did I put on my holiday tunic?" he asked, his small dark face innocent. "Yes, I suppose I did. Well—" He paused, and she knew that whatever his reason, and of course he would have a good one, she would never know it. At last he said calmly, "I soaked my other one in the dew picking your berries, madam." Then, suddenly, he said, "I thought I should hate sir Lancelet, Mother. Gareth talked of him early and late as if he were a God," and Morgause remembered that, though he would not weep before her, Gwydion had been heartbroken when Gareth had gone south to King Arthur's court. Morgause had missed him too—Gareth had been the only person alive who had real influence with Gwydion and could make him do as he would with only a light word. Since Gareth had gone there was no one alive to whose counsel Gwydion would listen.

"I thought he would be a fool full of his own importance," Gwydion said, "but he is nothing of the sort. He told me more about lighthouses than even Lot knew, I think. And he said when I was older I should come to Arthur's court and be made a knight, if I was good and honorable." His deep-set dark eyes considered that. "All the women said I look like him— and they asked, and I was angry that I did not know how to answer them. Foster-mother"—he leaned forward, his dark, soft hair falling loose over his forehead, lending the composed small face an unusual vulnerability— "tell me true—is Lancelet my father? I thought that might be why Gareth was so fond of him. . . ."

And you are not the first to ask that question, my love, she thought, stroking the boy's soft hair. The unusual childishness in his face as he asked made her voice gentler than usual.

"No, my little one. Of all the men in the kingdom, Lancelet could not be your father—I made it my business to ask. All that year you were begotten, Lancelet was in Less Britain, fighting at the side of his father, King Ban. I thought so too, but you look like him because Lancelet is your mother's nephew, as he is mine."

Gwydion surveyed her skeptically, and Morgause could almost read his thoughts; that she had told him exactly what she would have told him if she had known Lancelet *was* his father. He said at last, "Perhaps one day I shall go to Avalon, rather than to Arthur's court. Does my mother dwell now in Avalon, foster-mother?"

"I know not." Morgause frowned . . . once again, this oddly adult foster-son of hers had led her on to speak to him as if he were a grown man; he did that so often. It came to her that now Lot was gone, Gwydion was the only person in this household with whom she spoke from time to time as one adult to another! Oh, yes, Lochlann was man enough in bed at night, but he never had much more to say than one of the shepherds or even the housemaids!

"Go out now, Gwydion my love, I am going to be dressed—"

"Why should I go?" he asked. "I have known well enough what you look like, ever since I was five years old."

"But you are older now," she said, with that old sense of helplessness. "It is not fitting you should be here while I dress."

"Do you care that much what is fitting, foster-mother?" he said ingenuously, his eyes resting on the depression in the cushion where Lochlann had lain, and Morgause felt the sudden upward rush of frustration and wrath—he could entangle her in these arguments as if he were a grown man and a Druid! She said sharply, "I need not account to you for my doings, Gwydion!"

"Did I say you must?" His eyes were all injured innocence. "But if I am older, then I will need to know more about women than I did when I was a baby, will I not? I want to stay and talk."

"Oh, stay, stay if you want to," she said, "but turn your back, I'll not have you staring at me, sir Impudence!" Obediently he turned away, but as she rose and signalled her woman to bring her gown, he said, "No, put on your blue gown, foster-mother, the new one from the looms, and your saffron cloak."

"And now you will be giving me advice on what I should wear? What's this, what's this?"

"I like to see you dressed like a fine lady and a queen," he said, persuasively. "And tell them to dress your hair high with your gold coil, will you not, foster-mother? To please me?"

"Why, you would have me fine as a Midsummer feast, so that I should sit and card wool in all my best gear—my women would laugh, child!"

"Let them laugh," Gwydion coaxed. "Will you not dress in your finest to please me? And who knows what may happen before the day is done? You might be glad of it."

Morgause, laughing, gave way. "Oh, as you wish—if you will have it that I dress myself for a festival, let it be so . . . we will have our own festival here, then! And now I suppose the kitchen must bake honey cakes for this imaginary festival—"

A child, after all, she thought, *he thinks in this way to tease for sweets. But then, he brought me berries, why not?* "Well, Gwydion, shall I have them bake a honey cake for supper?"

He turned around. Her gown was still unlaced, and she saw his eyes linger for a moment on her white breasts. *Not such a child, then.* But he said, "I am always happy to have a honey cake, but perhaps there will be some fish to bake, too, for dinner."

"If we are to have fish," she said, "you will have to change your tunic again and go fishing for it yourself. The men are busy with the sowing."

He answered quickly, "I will ask Lochlann to go—it will be like a holiday for him. He deserves one, doesn't he, foster-mother, you are pleased with him, aren't you?"

Idiotic! Morgause thought. *I will* not *blush before a boy his age!* "If you would like to send Lochlann fishing, love, do so. He can be spared today, I suppose."

And she thought, she would like well to know what was really in Gwydion's mind, with his holiday tunic and his insistence that she should wear her finest gown and provide a good dinner. She called her housekeeper and said, "Master Gwydion would like a honey cake. See to it."

"He shall have his cake," said the housekeeper, with an indulgent look at the boy. "Look at his sweet face, like one of those angels, he is."

Angel. That is the last thing I would call him, thought Morgause; but she directed her woman to do her hair up with the gold coil. She would probably never learn what was on Gwydion's mind.

The day wore slowly along in its accustomed way. Morgause had wondered at times whether Gwydion had the Sight, but he had never shown any of the signs, and when once she asked him point-blank he had acted as if he did not know what she was talking about. And if he had, she thought, at least once she would have caught him bragging of it.

Ah, well. For some obscure child's reason, Gwydion had wanted a festival and had coaxed her into it. No doubt, with Gareth gone, he was lonely all the time—he had little in common with Lot's other sons. Nor did he have Gareth's passion for arms and knightly things, nor so far as she could tell, Morgaine's gift for music, though his voice was clear, and sometimes he would bring out a little set of pipes like those the shepherd lads played and make strange, mournful-sounding music. But it was not a passion as it had been with Morgaine, who would have sat happy all day at her harp if she could.

Still, he had a quick and retentive mind. For three years, Lot had sent for a learned priest from Iona to dwell in their house and teach the boy to read; he had said the priest was to teach Gareth too while he was about it, but Gareth had no mind to his book. He struggled obediently with letters and Latin, but no more than Gawaine—nor Morgause herself, for that matter—could he keep his mind fixed on written symbols or the mysterious tongue of those old Romans. Agravaine was quick enough—he kept all the tallies and accounts of the estate, he had a gift for numbering things; but Gwydion soaked up every bit of learning, it seemed, as quickly as it was put before him. Within a year he could read as well as the priest himself and speak in Latin as if he were one of those old Caesars reborn, so that for the first time Morgause wondered might there not be something, after all, in what the Druids said—that we were reborn again and again, learning more and more in each life.

He is such a son as should make his father proud, Morgause thought. *And Arthur has no son at all by his queen. One day—yes, one day, I shall have a secret to tell Arthur, and then I can hold the King's conscience in my hand.* The thought amused her vastly. She was surprised Morgaine had never used that hold she had on Arthur—she could have forced him to negotiate a marriage for her with the richest of his subject kings, could have had jewels, or power . . . but Morgaine cared nothing for such things, only for her harp and for the nonsense the Druids talked. At least she, Morgause, would make better use of this unexpected power thrust into her hand.

She sat in her hall, dressed in her unaccustomed finery, carding the wool from the spring shearing, and making decisions: Gwydion must have a new cloak—he grew so fast, his old one was about his knees already and no good to him in the winter cold, and no doubt he would grow faster yet this year. Should she, perhaps, give him Agravaine's cloak, cut down a little, and make a new one for Agravaine? Gwydion, in his saffron holiday tunic, came and sniffed appreciatively as the scent of the honey cake, rich with spices, began to drift through the room, but he did not hang about to tease that it should be cut and that he should have a slice early, as he would have done only a few months ago. At midday he said, "Mother, I will have a piece of bread and cheese in my hand and I will be off to walk the boundaries —Agravaine said I should go and see if all the fences are in good order."

"Not in your holiday shoes," said Morgause.

"Certainly not. I will go barefoot," Gwydion said, unfastening his sandals and leaving them beside her near the hearth; he tucked up his tunic through his belt so that it was well above his knees, took up a stout stick, and was off, while Morgause frowned after him—this was not a task Gwydion ever took upon himself, no matter what Agravaine wanted! What was with the lad this day?

Lochlann came back after midday with a fine large fish, so heavy Morgause could not lift it; she surveyed it with pleasure—it would feed everyone who ate at the high table and there would be cold baked fish for three days. Cleaned, scented with herbs, it lay ready for the baking oven when Gwydion came in, his feet and hands scrubbed clean, his hair combed, and slipped his feet into his sandals again. He looked at the fish and smiled.

"Yes, indeed, it will be like a festival," he said with satisfaction.

"Have you done walking all the fences, foster-brother?" Agravaine asked, coming in from one of the barns where he had been doctoring a sick pony.

"I have, and they are mostly in good order," said Gwydion, "but at the very top of the north fells where we had the ewes last fall, there is a great hole in the fences where all the stones have fallen down. You must send men to fix it before you put any sheep to pasture there, and as for goats, they'd be away before you could speak to them!"

"You went all the way up there alone?" Morgause frowned at him in dismay. "You are not a goat—you could have fallen and broken a leg in the ravine and no one would have known for days! I have told you and told you, if you go up on the fells, take one of the shepherd lads with you!"

"I had my reasons for going alone," retorted Gwydion, with that stubborn set of his mouth, "and I saw what I wanted to see."

"What could you possibly see that would be worth risking some injury and lying there all alone for days?" demanded Agravaine crossly.

"I have never fallen yet," Gwydion said, "and if I did, it is I who would suffer for it. What is it to you, if I take my own risks?"

"I am your elder brother and ruler in this house," said Agravaine, "and you will show me some respect or I will knock it into you!"

"Perhaps if you knocked your head open, you could shove some sense inside it," Gwydion said pertly, "for sure, it will never grow there on its own—"

"You wretched little—"

"Aye, say it," Gwydion shouted, "mock me with my birth, you—I do not know my father's name, but I know who fathered *you*, and between the two I would rather be in my situation!"

Agravaine took a heavy step toward him, but Morgause quickly rose and thrust Gwydion behind her. "Don't tease the boy, Agravaine."

"If he always runs to hide behind your skirts, Mother, is it any wonder I cannot teach him to obey?" demanded Agravaine.

"It would take a better man than you to teach me that," Gwydion said, and Morgause drew back at the bitterness in his voice.

"Hush, hush, child—don't speak so to your brother," she admonished, and Gwydion said, "I am sorry, Agravaine—I should not have been rude to you."

He smiled up, his eyes big and lovely under dark lashes, the picture of a contrite child. Agravaine grumbled, "I am only thinking of your welfare, you young rascal—do you think I want you to break every bone in your body? And why would you take it into your head to climb the fells alone?"

"Well," said Gwydion, "otherwise you would not have known of the hole in the fences, and you might have pastured sheep there or even goats, and lost all of them. And I never tear my clothes—do I, Mother?"

Morgause chuckled, for it was true—Gwydion was easy on his clothes. There were some boys like that. Gareth had only to put on a tunic and it was crumpled, stained, and dirty before he had worn it an hour, while Gwydion had climbed the high fells in his saffron holiday tunic and it looked as if he had that moment taken it from the washing-woman. Gwydion looked at Agravaine in his working smock and said, "But you are not fit to sit at table with Mother in her fine clothes. Go and put on your fine tunic, brother. Would you sit down to dinner in your old smock like a farmer?"

"I won't be ruled by a young knave like you," Agravaine growled, but he did go off toward his chamber, and Gwydion smiled with secret satisfaction. He said, "Agravaine should have a wife, Mother. He is bad-tempered as a bull in spring, and besides, you should not have to weave his clothes and mend them."

Morgause was amused. "No doubt you are right. But I want no other queen beneath this roof. No house is big enough for the rule of two women."

"Then you should find him a wife who is not too well-born and very stupid," said Gwydion, "so that she will be glad you can tell her what to do, because she will be afraid of making a mistake among gentlefolk. The daughter of Niall would be about right—she is very pretty, and Niall's folk are rich but not too rich, because so many of their cattle and sheep died in the bad winter six years ago. She would have a good dowry, because Niall is afraid she will not marry. The girl had the measles when she was six years old, and her eyesight is not good, and she is not too broad in the wit, either. She can spin and weave well enough, but she has neither the eyesight nor the cleverness for much more, so she will not mind much if Agravaine keeps her always breeding."

"Well, well, well, what a statesman you are already," said Morgause caustically. "Agravaine should appoint you one of his councillors, you are so wise." But she thought, aye, he is right, I will speak to Niall tomorrow.

"He could do worse," said Gwydion seriously, "but I shall not be here for that, Mother. I meant to tell you, when I went up on the fells, I saw —no, but here is Donil the hunter, he can tell you." And indeed, the big hunter was already coming into the hall, bending low before Morgause.

"My lady," he said, "there are riders on the road, nearing the great house—a sedan chair draped like the Avalon barge, and with them a hunchbacked man with a harp, and servants in the garb of Avalon. They will be here in half an hour."

Avalon! Then Morgause saw Gwydion's secret smile and knew that he had been ready for this. *But he has never spoken of having the Sight! What child would not brag of it, if he did?* And suddenly, the thought that he could conceal it, enjoy it yet more that his knowledge was secret, seemed uncanny to her, so that for a moment she shrank away, almost afraid of her foster-son. And she knew he saw it, and was not displeased.

All he said was, "Now isn't it lucky that we have a honey cake, and baked fish, and that we have all dressed in our best clothing, so we may do honor to Avalon, Mother?"

"Yes," Morgause said, staring at her foster-son. "Very lucky indeed, Gwydion."

As SHE stood in the front yard to welcome the riders, she found herself remembering a day when Viviane and Taliesin had come to the faraway castle of Tintagel. Taliesin, she supposed, was long past such journeys, even if he was still alive. She would have heard if he had died. And Viviane rode no longer in boots and breeches like a man, travelling at speed, a law unto herself.

Gwydion stood quietly at her side. In his saffron tunic, his dark hair neatly combed from his face, he looked very like Lancelet.

"Who are these visitors, Mother?"

"I suppose it is the Lady of the Lake," Morgause said, "and the Merlin of Britain, the Messenger of the Gods."

"You told me my own mother was a priestess of Avalon," said Gwydion. "Does their coming have anything to do with me?"

"Well, well, do not tell me there is anything you do not know!" said Morgause sharply, then relented. "I do not know why they have come, my dear; I have not the Sight. But it may well be. I want you to hand the wine about, and to listen and to learn, but not to speak unless you are spoken to."

That, she thought, would have been hard for her own sons—Gawaine, Gaheris, and Gareth were noisy and inquisitive, and it had been difficult to school them to courtly manners. They were, she thought, great friendly dogs, while Gwydion was like a cat, silent, sleek, fastidious, and watchful. Morgaine as a child had been like that . . . *Viviane did not well when she cast Morgaine aside, even if she was angry with her for bearing a child . . . and why should it matter to her? She herself bore children, including that damnable Lancelet, who has set Arthur's kingdom so much at havoc that even here we have heard how the Queen favors him.*

And then she wondered, why did she assume that Viviane had not wanted Morgaine to bear this child? Morgaine had quarrelled with Avalon, but perhaps that had been Morgaine's doing and not the Lady's.

She was deep in thought; and Gwydion touched her arm and murmured in an undertone, "Your guests, Mother."

Morgause sank in a deep curtsey before Viviane, who seemed to have shrunk. Always before this, she had been ageless, but now she looked withered, her face lined, her eyes sunk into her face. But she had the same lovely smile, and her voice was low and sweet as ever.

"Ah, it is good to see you, little sister," she said, drawing Morgause into an embrace. "How long has it been? I like not to think of the years! How young you look, Morgause! Such pretty teeth, and your hair as bright as ever. You met Kevin Harper at Arthur's wedding, before he was the Merlin of Britain."

It seemed that Kevin too had grown older, stooped and gnarled, like an ancient oak tree; well, that was fitting, she thought, for one of those who consorted with oaks, and felt her mouth move in a little ripple of secret mirth. "You are welcome, Master Harper—Lord Merlin, I should say. How is it with the noble Taliesin? Is he yet in the land of the living?"

"He lives," said Viviane as another woman stepped from the sedan chair. "But he is old and fragile now, he will not make such a journey as this again." And then she said, "This is a daughter of Taliesin, a child of the oak groves—Niniane. So she is your half-sister, Morgause."

Morgause was a little dismayed as the younger woman stepped forward and embraced her, saying in a sweet voice, "I am glad to know my sister." Niniane seemed so *young!* She had fair reddish-gold hair and blue eyes beneath silky long lashes. Viviane said, "Niniane travels with me, now I am old. She is the only one except myself dwelling upon Avalon who is of the old royal blood." Niniane was dressed as a priestess; her fair hair was braided low across her forehead, but the blue crescent mark of a priestess, freshly painted with blue dye, could be clearly seen. She spoke with the trained voice of a priestess, filled with power; but she herself seemed young and powerless as she stood next to Viviane.

Morgause sought to recapture her sense that she was hostess and these were her guests; she felt like a kitchen girl before the two priestesses and the Druid. Then she reminded herself angrily that both these women were her own half-sisters, and as for the Merlin, he was only an old hunchback! "Be welcome to Lothian and to my hall. This is my son Agravaine, who reigns here while Gawaine is away at Arthur's court. And this is my foster-son, Gwydion."

The boy bowed gracefully to the distinguished guests, but made only a polite murmur of acknowledgment.

"He is a handsome lad and well grown," said Kevin. "This, then, is Morgaine's son?"

Morgause lifted her eyebrows. "Would it avail anything to deny it to one who has the Sight, sir?"

"Morgaine herself told me, when she heard that I rode north to Lothian," Kevin said, and a shadow crossed his face.

"Then Morgaine dwells again in Avalon?" asked Morgause, and Kevin shook his head. Morgause saw that Viviane too looked distressed.

"Morgaine is at Arthur's court," said Kevin. Viviane said, pressing her lips together, "She has work to do in the world outside. But she will return to Avalon at the appointed time. There is a place awaiting her which she must take."

Gwydion asked softly, "Is it of my mother that you speak, Lady?"

Viviane looked straight at Gwydion and suddenly she seemed tall and imposing—the old priestess-trick, thought Morgause, but Gwydion had never seen it before. And the Lady said, her voice suddenly filling the courtyard, "Why do you ask me, child, when you already know the answer perfectly well? Would you mock at the Sight, Gwydion? Take care. I know you better than you think, and there are still a few things in this world that you do not know!"

Gwydion backed away, his mouth open, suddenly only a precocious child again. Morgause raised her eyebrows; so there was still someone and something which could frighten him! For once he did not try to excuse or explain himself in his usual glib manner.

She took the initiative again, saying, "Come in. All things are prepared to welcome you, my sisters, Lord Merlin." And as she looked at the red cloth she had set upon the high table, the goblets and fine ware standing there, she thought, *Even here at the end of the world, our court is no pigsty!* She conducted Viviane to her own high seat and set Kevin Harper next to her. As Niniane was stepping up on the dais she stumbled, and Gwydion was swiftly there, with a ready hand and a polite word.

Well, well, at last our Gwydion is beginning to take notice of a pretty woman. Or is it just good manners or a wish to ingratiate himself because Viviane chided him? She was perfectly well aware that she would never know the answer.

The fish was baked to perfection, the red fish flaking lightly away from the bones, and there was enough of the honey cake for most of the house people to have some; and she had sent for extra barley beer so that each of the people in the lower hall might have something extra to their meal as well. There was plenty of fresh-baked bread and an abundance of milk and butter, as well as cheese made with ewe's milk. Viviane ate as sparingly as ever, but she was ready in praise of the food.

"You set a queenly table indeed. I would not be better guested in Camelot. I had not looked for such welcome, coming without warning as I did," she said.

"Have you been to Camelot? Have you seen my sons?" Morgause asked, but Viviane shook her head and her forehead ridged in a scowl.

"No, not yet. Though I shall go thither at what Arthur now calls Pentecost, like to the church fathers themselves," she said, and for some reason Morgause felt a slight icing of her back; but with her guests she had no leisure to think of it.

Kevin said, "I saw your sons at court, lady. Gawaine had a small wound at Mount Badon, but it healed clean and is hidden by his beard . . . he has begun wearing a small beard like to the Saxons, not because he wishes to be like them, but he cannot shave daily without slicing the top from the scar. He may start a new fashion at court! I saw not Gaheris—he is away to the south, fortifying the coast. Gareth is to be made a Companion at Arthur's high feast at Pentecost. He is one of the biggest, and one of the trustiest men at court, though sir Cai still bullies him and calls him 'Handsome' for his pretty face."

"He should have been made one of Arthur's Companions already!" said Gwydion jealously, and Kevin looked more kindly on the boy. "So, you are jealous for your kinsman's honor, my lad? Indeed he well deserves to be a Companion, and he is treated as one now his rank is known. But Arthur wished to show him honor at his first high feast in Camelot, so he will be made Companion with all the ceremony the King can manage. Rest you content, Gwydion, Arthur well knows his worth, even as he knows Gawaine's. And he is one of Arthur's youngest Companions."

Then, even more shyly, Gwydion asked, "Know you my mother, Master Harper? The lady M-Morgaine?"

"Aye, lad, I know her well," said Kevin gently, and Morgause thought that the ugly little man had at least a speaking voice that was rich and beautiful. "She is one of the fairest ladies at Arthur's court, and one of the most gracious, and she plays the harp as well as a bard."

"Come, come," said Morgause, her lips crinkling up in a smile, and amused at the obvious devotion in the harper's voice. "It is well to tell a tale to amuse a child, but truth must be served too. Morgaine, fair? She is plain as a raven! Igraine was beautiful when she was young, all men knew that, but Morgaine resembles her not at all."

Kevin's voice was respectful but also amused. "There is an old saying in the wisdom of the Druids . . . beauty is not all in a fair face, but lies within. Morgaine is indeed very beautiful, Queen Morgause, though her beauty resembles yours no more than a willow tree resembles a daffodil. And she is the only person at court to whose hands I will ever trust My Lady." He gestured to his harp which had been unwrapped and set at his side, and picking up her cue, Morgause asked Kevin if he would favor them with a song.

He took up the harp and sang, and for a time the hall was perfectly still except for the harp notes and the bard's voice, and as he sang, the people in the lower hall crept as close as they could to listen to the music. But when he had done, and Morgause had dismissed the house-folk—although she allowed Lochlann to stay, sitting quietly near the fire—she said, "I too love music well, Master Harper, and you have given us a pleasure I shall long remember. But you did not travel all this long journey from Avalon to the Northlands so that I might have feasting with a harper. I beg of you, tell me why you come here so unexpectedly."

"Not so unexpected," said Viviane, with a little smile, "for I found you all dressed in your best and ready to greet us with wine and baked fish and honey cakes. You had warning of my coming, and since you had never more than a glimmering of the Sight, I can only imagine it was another not far from here who warned you." She cast an ironic glance at Gwydion, and Morgause nodded.

"But he told me not why, only bade me prepare all things for a festival, and I thought it was a child's whim, no more."

Gwydion was hanging over Kevin's seat as he began to wrap his harp, and he asked, putting his hand out hesitantly, "May I touch the strings?"

"You may," said Kevin mildly, and Gwydion plucked a string or two, saying, "I have never seen so fine a harp."

"Nor will you ever. I think there is no finer one here, nor even in Wales, where there is a whole college of bards," said Kevin. "My Lady was a king's gift to me, and she never leaves my side. And like many women," he added, with a courtly bow to Viviane, "she grows but more beautiful with the years."

"Would that my voice had grown sweeter as I grew old," said Viviane good-humoredly, "but the Dark Mother has not willed it so. Only her immortal children sing more sweetly as the years grow longer. May My Lady never sing less beautifully than now."

"Are you fond of music, master Gwydion? Have you learned anything of the harp?"

"I have not a harp to play," said Gwydion. "Coll, who is the only harper at court, has now such stiff fingers that he seldom touches the strings. We have had no music for two years now. I play a little upon the small pipe, though, and Aran—he that was Lot's piper at war—taught me to play a little upon the pipe of elk-horn . . . it hangs yonder. He went with King Lot to Mount Badon, and like Lot, he came not back."

"Bring me the pipe," said Kevin, and when Gwydion brought it from where it hung on the wall, he rubbed it clean with a cloth, blew the dust from inside it, then put it to his lips and set his twisted fingers to the neat row of holes bored in the horn. He played a little dancing tune, then set it aside, saying, "I have small skill for this—my fingers are not quick enough. Well, Gwydion, if you love music, they will teach you at Avalon —let me hear you play a little upon this horn."

Gwydion's mouth was dry—Morgause saw him wet his lips with his tongue—but he took the wood-and-horn thing in his hands and blew carefully into it. Then he began to play a slow melody, and Kevin, after a moment, nodded.

"That will do," he said. "You are Morgaine's son, after all—it would be strange if you had no gift at all. We may be able to teach you much. You may have the makings of a bard, but more likely of a priest and Druid."

Gwydion blinked and almost let the pipe fall from his hand; he caught it in the skirt of his tunic.

"Of a bard—what do you mean? Tell me clear!"

Viviane looked straight at him, "It is the appointed time, Gwydion. You are Druid-born, and of two royal lines. You are to be given the ancient teachings and the secret wisdom in Avalon, that one day you may bear the dragon."

He swallowed—Morgause could see him absorbing this. She could well imagine that the thought of secret wisdom would attract Gwydion more than anything else they might have offered. He stammered, "You said —*two* royal lines—"

Viviane shook her head faintly when Niniane would have answered, so Niniane said only, "All things will be made clear to you when the proper time comes, Gwydion. If you are to be a Druid, the first thing you must learn is when to be silent and ask no questions."

He looked up at her mutely, and Morgause thought, *It was worth all the trouble of this day to see Gwydion for once impressed even to speechlessness!* Well, she was not surprised; Niniane was beautiful—she looked very much as Igraine had looked as a young girl, or she herself, only with fair hair rather than red.

Viviane said quietly, "This much I can tell you at once—the mother of your mother's mother was the Lady of the Lake, and from a long line of priestesses. Igraine and Morgause also bear the blood of the noble Taliesin, and so do you. Many of the royal lines of these islands, among the Druids, have been preserved in you, and if you are worthy, a great destiny awaits you. But you must be worthy—royal blood alone makes not a king, but courage, and wisdom, and farsightedness. I tell you, Gwydion, that he who wears the dragon may be more of a king than he who sits on a throne, for the throne may be won by force of arms, or by craft, or as Lot won it, by being born in the right bed and begot by the right king. But the Great Dragon can be won only by one's own efforts, not in this life alone, but those which have gone before. I tell you a mystery."

Gwydion said, "I—I do not understand!"

"Of course you do not!" Viviane's voice was sharp. "Even as I said —it is a mystery, and wise Druids have sometimes studied for many lifetimes to understand less than that. I did not mean that you should understand, but that you should listen and hear, and learn to obey."

Gwydion swallowed and lowered his head. Morgause saw Niniane smile at him, and he drew a long breath, as if reprieved, and sat down at her feet, listening quietly, for once without trying to make any pert answer or explanation. Morgause thought, *Perhaps the training of the Druids is what he needs!*

"So you have come to tell me I have fostered Morgaine's son long enough, and the time is come when he shall be taken to Avalon and schooled in the learning of the Druids. But you would not have travelled yourself by this long road to tell me that—you could have sent any lesser Druid to take the boy into his custody. I have known for years that it would not befit Morgaine's son to end his days among shepherds and fisherfolk. And where else than Avalon would his destiny be laid? I beg you, tell me the rest— oh, yes, there is more, I see in your faces that there is more."

Kevin opened his mouth to speak, but Viviane said sharply, "Why should I tell you all my thoughts, Morgause, when you seek to turn all things to your advantage and that of your own sons? Even now, Gawaine is nearest the High King's throne not only because of blood, but also in Arthur's love. And I foresaw when Arthur was wedded to Gwenhwyfar that she would bear no child. I thought it only likely that she might die in breeding, so I wished not to meddle with what happiness Arthur might have —then could we have found him, afterward, a more suitable wife. But I let it go on too long, and now he will not put her away, even though she is barren—and you see in that no more than an opportunity for your own son's advancement."

"You should not assume she is barren, Viviane." Kevin's face was set in bitter lines. "She was pregnant before Mount Badon, and she carried this child a full five months—she might well have brought it to birth. I think she miscarried because of the heat, and the close confinement in the castle, and her own fear of the Saxons . . . and it was pity for her, I think, which caused Arthur to betray Avalon and put aside the dragon banner."

Niniane said, "So it was not only her childlessness, Queen Morgause, by which Gwenhwyfar did Arthur such great harm. She is a creature of the priests, and already she has influenced him too well. If some day it should happen that she bear a child that might live to grow up . . . that would be the worst of all."

Morgause felt as if she would stifle. "Gawaine—"

Viviane said harshly, "Gawaine is Christian as Arthur. He longs only to please Arthur in all things!"

Kevin said, "I know not whether Arthur has any great commitment to the Christian God or whether it is all Gwenhwyfar's doing, to please her and pity her—"

Morgause said scornfully, "Is that man fit to rule who would forswear his oath for a woman's sake? Is Arthur forsworn, then?"

Kevin said, "I heard him say that since Christ and Mary the Virgin gave him the victory at Mount Badon, he will not put them aside now. And

I heard him say more, when he spoke with Taliesin—that Mary the Virgin was even as the Great Goddess, and it was she had given him the victory to save this land . . . and that the banner of the Pendragon was that of his father Uther, and not his own. . . ."

"Still," said Niniane, "he had no right to cast it all aside. We in Avalon set Arthur on his throne, and he owes it to us—"

Morgause said impatiently, "What matters it what banner flies over a king's troops? The soldiers need something to inspire their imagination—"

"As usual, you ignore the point," said Viviane. "It is what lives in their dreams and imagination that we must control from Avalon, or this struggle with Christ will be lost and their souls lie in slavery to a false faith! The symbol of the dragon should be always before them, that mankind seek to accomplish, not to think of sin and do penance!"

Kevin said slowly, "I know not—perhaps it would be as well that there should be these lesser mysteries for the fools, and then could the wise be shown the inner teaching. Perhaps it has been made all too easy for mankind to come to Avalon, and so they value it not."

Viviane said, "Would you have it that I should sit by and see Avalon go further into the mists, even as the fairy country?"

"I am saying, Lady," said Kevin, deferentially, but firmly, "that it may even now be too late to prevent it—Avalon will always be there for all men to find if they can seek the way thither, throughout all the ages past the ages. If they cannot find the way to Avalon, it is a sign, perhaps, that they are not ready."

"Still," said Viviane, in that hard voice, "I shall keep Avalon within the world, or die in attempting it!"

There was a silence in the hall, and Morgause realized that she was icy cold. She said, "Build up the fire, Gwydion—" and passed the wine. "Drink, will you not, sister? And you, Master Harper?"

Niniane poured the wine, but Gwydion sat still, as if dreaming or entranced. Morgause said, "Gwydion, do as I bade you—" but Kevin put out a hand and bade her be still. He said, in a whisper, "The boy's in trance. Gwydion, speak—"

"It is all blood—" he whispered, "blood, poured out like the blood of sacrifice on the ancient altars, blood spilt on the throne—"

Niniane stumbled and tripped, and the rest of the wine, blood red, went cascading over Gwydion where he sat, and across Viviane's lap. She rose, startled, and Gwydion blinked and shook himself like a puppy. He said, confused, "What—I am sorry—let me help you," and took the wineskin from Niniane's hand. "Ugh, it looks like spilt blood, let me fetch a cloth from the kitchens," and streaked away like any active lad.

"Well, there's your blood," said Morgause with disgust. "Is my Gwyd-ion, too, to be lost in dreams and sickly visions?"

Mopping the sticky wine from her gown, Viviane said, "Disparage not another's gift because you have not the Sight, Morgause!"

Gwydion came back with the cloth, but as he bent to mop it away, he faltered, and Morgause took the cloth from his hand and beckoned one of the serving-women to come and dry the table and the hearth. He looked ill, but where normally he would have tried to make more of it for her attention, she saw that he turned quickly away as if ashamed. She ached to take him in her arms and rock him, this child who had been her last baby when the others were grown and gone, but she knew he would not thank her for it and held her peace, staring down at her linked hands. Niniane put out a hand to him, too, but it was Viviane who beckoned him, her eyes stern and unflinching.

"Speak the truth to me: how long have you had the Sight?"

He lowered his eyes and said, "I know not—I did not know what to call it." He fidgeted, refusing to look at her.

She said quietly, "And you concealed it for pride and love of power, did you not? Now it has mastered you, and you must master it in turn. We came none too soon here—I hope we have not come too late. Are you unsteady on your feet? Sit here, then, and be still."

To Morgause's astonishment, Gwydion sank down quietly at the feet of the two priestesses. After a moment Niniane put her hand on his head and he leaned against her.

Viviane turned again to Morgause and said, "As I told you before, Gwenhwyfar will bear Arthur no son, but he will not put her aside. All the more because she is a Christian, and their religion forbids a man to put his wife away—"

Morgause shrugged and said, "What of that? She has miscarried once, or it may be, more than once. And she is not so young a woman, not now. Life is uncertain for women."

"Aye, Morgause," said Viviane, "once before you sought to trade on that uncertainty of life, so that your son might stand near to the throne—did you not? I warn you, my sister—meddle not in what the Gods have decreed!"

Morgause smiled. "I thought, Viviane, that you lectured me long—or was it Taliesin?—that nothing comes about save by the will of the Gods. If Arthur had died ere he came to Uther's throne, why then, I doubt not the Gods would have found another to serve their turn."

"I came not here to argue theology, you miserable girl," said Viviane angrily. "Do you think, if I had my will, that I would have entrusted you with life or death for the royal line of Avalon?"

Morgause said with silky wrath, "But the Goddess willed it not that you should do your own will, so it seems to me, Viviane. I am weary of this talk of old prophecy . . . if there be any Gods at all, of which I am not even certain, I cannot believe they would stoop to meddle in the affairs of men. Nor will I wait upon the Gods to do what I see clearly must be done—who's to say that the Goddess cannot work through my hand as well as another." She saw that Niniane was shocked—aye, she was another such ninny as Igraine, believing all this talk of Gods. "As for the royal line of Avalon, you see I have fostered it well."

"He seems strong and well, a healthy boy," said Viviane, "but can you swear you have not flawed him within, Morgause?"

Gwydion raised his head and said sharply, "My foster-mother has been good to me. The lady Morgaine cared not much for the fostering of her son—not once has she come hither to ask whether I lived or died!"

Kevin said severely, "You were bade speak only when spoken to, Gwydion. And you know nothing of Morgaine's reasons or purposes."

Morgause looked sharply at the crippled little bard. *Has Morgaine confided in this wretched abortion, when I had to force her secret from her by spells and the Sight?* She felt a surge of wrath, but Viviane said, "Enough. You fostered him well while it suited you, Morgause, but I mark you have not forgotten he stands one step nearer the throne than did Arthur at his age, and two steps nearer than your own son Gawaine! As for Gwenhwyfar, I have seen that she is to play some part in the fate of Avalon—she cannot be wholly without the Sight or the vision, for once she broke through the mists and stood upon the shores of Avalon. Perhaps if she were given a son, and it was made clear that it was by Avalon's arts and will—" She glanced at Niniane. "She is capable of conception—with a strong sorceress at her side to keep her from casting forth the child."

"It is too late for that," Kevin said. "It was all her doing that Arthur betrayed Avalon and set aside the dragon banner. The truth is, I suppose, that her wits are not in the right place."

"The truth is," said Niniane, "that you bear her a grudge, Kevin. Why?"

The harper cast his eyes down and stared at his scarred and twisted hands. He said at last, "True. I cannot even in my thoughts deal fair with Gwenhwyfar—I am no more than human. But even if I loved her well, I would say she is no queen for a king who must rule from Avalon. I would not grieve, should she suffer some accident or mischance. For if she gave Arthur a son, she would think it only the goodness of Christ, though the Lady of the Lake herself stood by her bed. I cannot help but pray she has no such good fortune."

Morgause smiled her cat smile. "Gwenhwyfar may seek to be more

Christian than Christ's self," she said, "but I know something of their Scriptures, for Lot had a priest here from Iona to teach the lads. The Holy Writ runs thus, that he is damned who shall put his wife away *save for adultery*. And even here in Lothian we have heard—the Queen is hardly so chaste as all that. Arthur is away often at the wars, and all men know how she looks with favor upon your son, Viviane."

"You do not know Gwenhwyfar," Kevin said. "She is pious more than reason, and Lancelet is so much Arthur's friend that I think Arthur would not move against them unless he took the two of them together in his bed before all of the court."

"Even that might be arranged," said Morgause. "Gwenhwyfar is too beautiful to think that other women would love her much. Surely someone around her could make an open scandal, to force Arthur's hand—"

Viviane made a grimace of distaste. "What woman would betray a fellow woman like that?"

Morgause said, "I would, if I were convinced it was for the good of the kingdom."

"I would not so," said Niniane, "and Lancelet is honorable, and Arthur's closest friend. I doubt he would betray Arthur for Gwenhwyfar. If we wish Gwenhwyfar set aside, we must look elsewhere."

"And there is this," said Viviane, and she sounded tired. "Gwenhwyfar has done nothing wrong that we know—we cannot set her down from Arthur's side while she keeps the bargain she has made, to be a dutiful wife to Arthur. If a scandal is made, there must be truth in it. Avalon is sworn to uphold the truth."

"But if there were a true scandal?" Kevin said.

"Then she must take her chances," Viviane said, "but I will not be party to any false accusations."

"Yet she has at least one other enemy," said Kevin thoughtfully. "Leodegranz of the Summer Country has just died, and his young wife and her last child with her, Gwenhwyfar is queen there now; but Leodegranz had a kinsman—he claims to be a son, but I believe it not—and I think he would like it well if he could claim to be king in the old manner of the Tribes, by bedding with the queen."

Gwydion said, "It is well they have no such custom at Lot's most Christian court, is it not?" But he spoke softly, so that they could affect not to hear him. And Morgause thought: *He is angry because he is being ignored, that is all. Am I to be angry because a puppy bites me with his little teeth?*

"By the old custom," said Niniane, her pretty brow ridging into little lines, "Gwenhwyfar is not wedded to any unless she has borne him a son, and if another man can take her from Arthur—"

"Aye, there's the question," said Viviane, laughing. "Arthur can keep his wife by force of arms. And he would do it, too, I doubt not." Then she sobered. "The one thing we can be certain of is that Gwenhwyfar shall remain barren. Should she conceive again, there are spells to make certain she carries not the child to birth, or past the first few weeks. As for Arthur's heir . . ." She paused, and looked at Gwydion, still sitting like a sleepy child, his head resting on Niniane's lap. "There sits a son of the royal line of Avalon—and son to the Great Dragon."

Morgause caught her breath. Never once, in all these years, had it occurred to her that it was anything other than the gravest mischance that Morgaine had gotten herself with child by her half-brother. Now she saw the complexity of Viviane's plan and was awe-stricken by the audacity of it—to set a child of Avalon and of Arthur on the throne after his father.

What of the King Stag when the young stag is grown . . . ? For a moment Morgause did not know whether the thought had been her own or had come into her head as an echo from one of the two Avalon priestesses before her; always she had had these disturbing, incomplete moments of the Sight, though she could never control when they would come or go, and, truth to tell, had not cared to do so.

Gwydion's eyes were wide; he leaned forward, his mouth open. "Lady—" he said breathlessly, "is it true—that I, I am the son of the—of the High King?"

"Aye," said Viviane, her mouth tight, "though the priests will never acknowledge it. To them it would be sin of all sins, that a son should get a son on his mother's daughter. They have set themselves up holier than the Goddess herself, who is mother to us all. But it is so."

Kevin turned; slowly, painfully, with his crippled body, he knelt down before Gwydion.

"My prince and my lord," he said, "child of the royal line of Avalon, and son to the son of the Great Dragon, we have come to take you to Avalon, where you may be prepared for your destiny. On the morrow you must be ready to depart."

2

O n the *morrow you must be ready to depart. . . ."*
It was like to the terror of a dream that they should speak thus openly of what I had kept secret all these years, even during that time when none thought I could live after his birth. . . . I could have gone to my death with none knowing I had borne a child to my own brother. But Morgause had got the secret from me,

and Viviane knew . . . it was an old saying, three could keep a secret if but two of them lay in their graves. . . . Viviane had planned this, she had used me as she had used Igraine!

But the dream was beginning to break up now and shift and ripple as if it were all underwater. I fought to keep it, to hear, but it seemed that Arthur was there and he drew a sword and advanced on Gwydion, and the child caught Excalibur from its scabbard. . . .

Morgaine sat bolt upright in her room at Camelot, catching at the blanket. No, she told herself, no, it was a dream, only a dream. *I do not even know who sits next to Viviane in Avalon, no doubt it is Raven, not this fair-haired woman so like to my mother that I have seen again and again in my dreams. And who knows if such a woman walks the face of this earth or Avalon, or whether she is a confused dream of my mother? I do not remember anyone even a little like her in the House of Maidens. . . .*

I should be there. It is I should be at Viviane's side, and I cast it away of my free will. . . .

"Look," Elaine called from the window. "Already there are riders coming in, and it is three full days till Arthur's great feast!"

The other women in the chamber crowded around Elaine, looking down at the field before Camelot; already there were tents and pavilions pitched there. Elaine said, "I see my father's banner. There he rides, with my brother, Lamorak, at his side—he is old enough to be one of Arthur's Companions now. I wonder if Arthur will choose him as one."

"He was not old enough to fight at Mount Badon, was he?" Morgaine asked.

"He was not old enough, but he fought nevertheless, as did every man old enough to hold a sword, and every young boy too," said Elaine proudly.

"Then I doubt not that Arthur will make him one of his Companions, if only to please Pellinore," said Morgaine. The great battle of Mount Badon had been fought a year ago on the day of Pentecost, and Arthur had vowed always to keep this day as a time of high feasting and to greet all his old Companions; on Pentecost, too, he would welcome all petitioners and give out justice. And all the subject kings from the outlying kingdoms would come before the High King to renew their allegiance.

"You must go to the Queen and help her dress," Morgaine said to Elaine, "and I must be off as well. I have much to do if there is to be a great feast in only three days!"

"Sir Cai will see to all that," Elaine remonstrated.

"Aye, he will see to the feeding and housing of the multitudes," said Morgaine cheerfully, "but it is I must provide flowers for the hall, and see to the polishing of the silver cups, and it is likely I must make the almond cakes and sweets too—Gwenhwyfar will have other things on her mind."

And indeed, Morgaine was glad to have so much to do for the three days of feasting; it took her mind away from the dread and terror of her dream. In these days, whenever Avalon came into her mind in a dream, she shut it out with desperation . . . she had not known that Kevin rode north to Lothian. *No,* she told herself, *and I do not know it now, it was only a dream.* But once during that day, when she encountered the elderly Taliesin in the courtyard, she bowed to him, and when he put out a hand to bless her, she said shyly, "Father—"

"Yes, dear child?"

Ten years ago, Morgaine thought, *I would have been angry that Taliesin speaks to me always as if I were still a child of seven who might crawl into his lap and tug at his beard.* Now, obscurely, it comforted her. "Is Kevin the Merlin bound here for Pentecost?"

"Why, I know not, child," said Taliesin, with a kindly smile. "He has ridden north to Lothian. But I know that he loves you well and that he will return to you when he can. I think nothing would keep him from this court while you were here, little Morgaine."

Does everyone at this court know that we have been lovers? Surely I have been more discreet than that. Morgaine said waspishly, "Is it common gossip at this court that Kevin the Harper comes and goes at my bidding—when it is not even true?"

Taliesin smiled again and said, "Dear child, never be ashamed to love. And it has meant everything to Kevin, that one so kindly and gracious and beautiful as you—"

"Do you mock me, Grandsire?"

"Why should I so, little one? You are the daughter of my dear daughter, and I love you well, and you know I think you the most beautiful and gifted of women. And Kevin, I have no doubt, thinks you so even more, and you are the only one at this court save myself, and the only woman ever, who can speak to him of music in his own language. If you know not that for Kevin the sun rises and sets where you come and go, then you are the only one at this court who knows it not. You deserve it well that he should turn to you as the starshine of his days and nights. It is not even forbidden to the Merlin of Britain that he should marry, if he chooses. Royal he is not, but he is noble in heart, and will one day be High Druid if his courage fails him not. And on the day when he seeks your hand, I do not think either Arthur or myself would say him no."

Morgaine lowered her face and stared at the ground. Ah, she thought, how fitting it would be if I could care so for Kevin as he for me. I value him, I love him well, I take pleasure even in sharing his bed, but marriage? No, she thought, no, no, not for all his devotion. "I have no mind to be married, Grandsire."

"Well, you must do your own will, child," Taliesin said gently. "You are lady and priestess. But you are not so young, either, and since you have forsaken Avalon—no, I do not reproach you, but I thought it might well be that you wished to marry and have a home of your own. I would not see you spend all your days as Gwenhwyfar's waiting-woman. As for Kevin the Harper, no doubt he will be here if he can, but he cannot ride as swiftly as other men. It is good that you do not despise him for his body's infirmity, dear child."

When Taliesin had gone, Morgaine went on toward the brew house, thinking deeply. She wished she could indeed love Kevin as Taliesin thought she did.

Why am I cursed with this feeling for Lancelet? All the time she prepared scented rose water for washing guests' hands and flavoring confections, she thought about that. Well, when Kevin was here, at least she had no reason to desire Lancelet—not that it would do her any good, she thought wryly, to desire him. *Desire must go two ways or it is worthless.* She resolved that when Kevin came back again to court, she would give him such a welcome as he could wish.

No doubt, I could do worse than wed with him . . . Avalon is lost to me . . . I will think of it. And indeed my dream saw true so far, that he was in Lothian . . . and I thought the Sight had forsaken me. . . .

KEVIN RETURNED to Camelot on the eve of Pentecost; all that day folk had been streaming into Camelot and the surrounding country, as if it were twice over harvest fair and spring-trading fair. It was the greatest festival ever to be held in this countryside. Morgaine welcomed Kevin with a kiss and embrace which made the harper's eyes glow, and led him to a guest chamber, where she took his cloak and travelling shoes and sent them with one of the boys to be cleaned, and brought him ribbons to make his harp fine.

"Why, My Lady will be brave as the Queen," said Kevin, laughing at her. "Do you not bear grudge to your only rival, Morgaine, love?"

He had never called her so before, and she came and stood close to him, her arm around his waist. He said softly, "I have missed you," and laid his face for a moment against her breast.

"And I you, my dear," she said, "and when all have gone to rest this night, I shall prove it to you . . . why, do you think, have I arranged that you shall have a guest chamber to yourself, when even Arthur's dearest Companions have had to be housed four to a room and sometimes two to a bed?"

He said, "I thought it was so that none other need share quarters with me."

"And so it shall be for the dignity of Avalon," said Morgaine, "though even Taliesin shares his chamber with the bishop—"

"I do not admire his taste," said Kevin. "I would sooner be housed in the stable with the other donkeys!"

"I would have it that the Merlin of Britain should be lodged in a chamber to himself, even if it is no bigger than a stall for one of those donkeys," said Morgaine. "But it is large enough for you and for My Lady, and"—she smiled and looked pointedly at the bed—"and for me, I dare say."

"You will always be welcome, and if My Lady is jealous I will turn her face to the wall." He kissed her, holding her tight for a moment with all the strength in his wiry arms. Then, letting her go, he said, "I thought you would like to hear—I rode with your son to Avalon. He is a well-grown lad, and a clever one, and has some of your gift for music."

"I dreamed of him the other night," she said. "In my dream, I think he played on a pipe—like Gawaine's."

"Then you dreamed truly," said Kevin. "I like him well, and he has the Sight. He will be schooled in Avalon for a Druid."

"And then?"

"Then? Ah, my dear," said Kevin, "things must go as they will. But I doubt not he will make a bard and a notable wise man—you need have no fear for him upon Avalon." He touched her shoulder gently. "He has your eyes."

She would have liked to ask more, but turned to something else. "The feast will not be till tomorrow," she said, "but tonight the closest of Arthur's friends and Companions have been bidden to dine. Gareth is to be made a knight upon the morrow, and Arthur, who loves Gawaine like a brother, has chosen to honor him at a family party."

"Gareth is a good man and a good knight," said Kevin, "and I will gladly do him honor. I like not Queen Morgause greatly, but her sons are fine men and good friends to Arthur."

Even though it was a family party, there were many close kinsmen to sit at Arthur's table here on the eve of Pentecost: Gwenhwyfar and her kinswoman Elaine, and Elaine's father, King Pellinore, and her brother, Lamorak; Taliesin and Lancelet, and three of Lancelet's half-brothers—Balan, son of the Lady of the Lake, and Bors and Lionel, both of whom were sons of Ban of Less Britain. Gareth was there, and as always, Gawaine stood behind Arthur at table. Arthur had protested, as they came into the hall. "Sit here beside us tonight, Gawaine—you are my kinsman, and king in your own right in Orkney, and I like it not that you should stand like a serving-man behind my place!"

Gawaine said roughly, "I am proud to stand and serve my lord and king, sir," and Arthur bent his head.

"You make me feel like those old Caesars," he complained. "Need I be guarded night and day even in my own hall?"

"For the dignity of your throne, sir, you are even as those Caesars, and more," insisted Gawaine, and Arthur laughed helplessly.

"I can deny nothing to those of you who were my Companions."

"So," Kevin said in an undertone to Morgaine, where they sat side by side, "it is not *hubris* then or arrogance, but he wishes only to please his Companions—"

"I think, truly, it is so," Morgaine said in an undertone. "This he loves best, I think, to sit in his own hall and look upon the peace he has wrought; whatever his faults, Arthur truly loves the rule of order and the kingdom of law."

Later, Arthur gestured them all to silence, calling young Gareth to him. "Tonight you will watch in the church by your arms," he said, "and in the morning before mass, whichever knight you choose shall make you one of my Companions. You have served me well and honorably, young as you are. If you wish for it, I will myself make you knight, but I will understand if you wish that your brother should give you this honor."

Gareth wore a white tunic; his hair was like a golden halo curling around his face. He looked almost like a child, a tall child towering to a good six feet high, with shoulders like a young bull. His face was fuzzy with soft golden down too fine to be shaven. He said, stammering a little in his eagerness, "Sir, I beg you—I mean no offense to you nor to my brother, but I—if he will—could I be made knight by Lancelet, my lord and my king?"

Arthur smiled. "Why, if Lancelet will have it so, I have no objection."

Morgaine remembered a little child prattling of Lancelet to a painted wooden knight she had carved for him. How many people, she wondered, saw such a childhood dream come true? Lancelet said gravely, "I should be honored, cousin," and Gareth's face lighted as if a torch had been set to it. Then Lancelet turned to Gawaine and said, with punctilious courtesy, "But it is for you to give me leave, cousin—you stand in a father's place to this lad, and I would not usurp your right—"

Gawaine looked awkwardly from one to the other of them, and Morgaine saw Gareth bite his lip—only now, perhaps, did he understand that this might be seen as an offense to his brother, and that the King had done him the honor of offering to make him a knight—an honor he had refused. What a child he was, despite his great strength and height and precocious skill at arms!

Gawaine said gruffly, "Who would be made knight by me when Lancelet would consent to do it?"

Lancelet flung an exuberant arm around each of them. "You do me too much honor, both of you. Well, go, lad," he said, releasing Gareth, "go to your arms, I will come and watch with you after midnight."

Gawaine watched as the boy loped away, with his long awkward stride, and then said, "You should be one of those old Greeks, as it was told in that saga we read when we were boys. How was he called—Achilles—whose true love was the young knight Patroclus, and neither cared anything for all the fine dames of the court of Troy—God knows every lad in this court worships you as their hero. Pity you have no mind to the Greek fashion in love!"

Lancelet's face turned dusky red. "You are my cousin, Gawaine, and can say such things to me—I would not hear such things from any other, even in jest."

Gawaine laughed loudly again. "Aye, a jest—for one who professes devotion only to our most chaste Queen—"

"You dare!" Lancelet began, turning on him, and gripped his arm with strength enough to break his wrist. Gawaine struggled, but Lancelet, though he was the smaller man, bent his arm backward, growling with rage like an angry wolf.

"Here! No brawling in the King's hall!" Cai thrust himself awkwardly between them, and Morgaine said quickly, "Why, Gawaine, what then will you say to all those priests who profess devotion to Mary the Virgin beyond all things on earth? Would you have it they all have a scandalous carnal devotion to their Christ? And indeed, we hear of the Lord Jesus that he never married, and that even among his chosen twelve there was one who leaned on his bosom at supper—"

Gwenhwyfar gave a shocked cry. "Morgaine, hush! Such a blasphemous jest!" Lancelet let go of Gawaine's arm; Gawaine stood rubbing the bruise, and Arthur turned and frowned at them.

"You are like children, cousins, squabbling and bickering—shall I send you to be beaten by Cai in the kitchens? Come now, be friends again! I heard not the jest, but whatever it was, Lance, it cannot have been so serious as all that!"

Gawaine laughed roughly and said, "I jested, Lance—all too many women pursue you, I know, for what I said to have anything at all of truth," and Lancelet shrugged and smiled, like a bird with ruffled feathers.

Cai chuckled. "Every man at court envies you your handsome face, Lance." He rubbed the scar that pulled his mouth up tight into a sneer, and said, "But it may not be all that much of a blessing, eh, cousin?"

It dissolved into good-natured laughter, but later Morgaine, crossing the court, saw Lancelet still pacing, troubled, feathers still ruffled.

"What is it, kinsman, what ails you?"

He sighed. "I would that I might leave this court."

"But my lady will not let you go."

"Even to you, Morgaine, I will not talk of the Queen," he said stiffly, and it was Morgaine's turn to sigh.

"I am not the keeper of your conscience, Lancelet. If Arthur does not chide you, who am I to speak a word of reproach?"

"You don't understand!" he said fiercely. "She was given to Arthur like something bought at market, part of a purchase in horses because her father would have kinship with the High King as part of the price! Yet she is too loyal to murmur—"

"I spoke no word against her, Lancelet," Morgaine reminded him. "You hear accusations from yourself, not from my lips."

She thought, *I could make him desire me,* but the knowledge was like a mouthful of dust. Once she had played that game, and beneath the desire he had feared her, as he feared Viviane herself; feared her to the edge of hatred *because* of that desire. If his king commanded he would have her, but would soon come to hate.

He managed to look directly at her. "You cursed me, and—and believe me, I am cursed."

And suddenly the old anger and contempt melted. He was as he was. She clasped his hand between her own. "Cousin, don't trouble yourself about that. It was many, many years ago, and I don't think there is any God or Goddess who would listen to the words of an angry young girl who thought herself scorned. And I was no more than that."

He drew a long breath and began to pace again. At last he said, "I could have killed Gawaine tonight. I am glad you stopped us, even with that blasphemous jesting. I—I have had to deal with that, all my life. When I was a boy at Ban's court, I was prettier than Gareth is now, and in the court of Less Britain, and like enough in other places, such a boy must guard himself more carefully than any maiden. But no man sees or believes any such thing unless it touches him, and thinks it only a slightly vulgar joke made about other people. There was a time when I thought it so too, and then a time when I thought I could never be otherwise. . . ."

There was a long silence, while he stared grimly at the flagstones of the courtyard.

"And so I flung myself into experiment with women, any woman—God help me, even with you who were my own mother's fosterling and pledged maiden to the Goddess—but there were few women who could rouse me even a little, till I saw—her." Morgaine was glad he did not speak Gwenhwyfar's name. "And since that moment there has been no other. With her, I know myself all man."

Morgaine said, "But she is Arthur's wife—"

"God! God!" Lancelet turned and struck his hand against the wall. "Do you think that does not torment me? He is my friend; if Gwenhwyfar were wedded to any other man who dwells this earth, I would have had her away with me and to my own place—" Morgaine saw the muscles of his throat move as he tried to swallow. "I do not know what will become of us. And Arthur must have an heir to his kingdom. The fate of all Britain is more important than our love. I love them both—and I am tormented, Morgaine, tormented!"

His eyes were wild; for a moment it seemed to Morgaine that she saw some hint of madness. Ever after, she wondered, *Was there anything, anything I could have said or done that night?*

"Tomorrow," Lancelet said, "I shall beg Arthur to send me out on some difficult quest—to go and make an end forever of Pellinore's dragon, to conquer the wild Northmen beyond the Roman wall—I care not what, Morgaine, anything, anything to take me away from here—" and for a moment, hearing in his voice a sadness beyond tears, Morgaine wanted to hold him in her arms and rock him at her breast like a babe.

I think I came near to killing Gawaine tonight, had you not stopped us," Lancelet said. "Yet he was only jesting, he would have died with horror if he knew—" Lancelet turned his eyes away and at last said in a whisper, "I know not if what he said is true. I should take Gwenhwyfar and be gone from here, before it becomes a scandal to all the courts of the world, that I love the wife of my king, and yet . . . yet it is Arthur I cannot leave . . . I know not but what I love her only because I come close, thus, to *him.*"

Morgaine put out her hand to stop him. There were things she could not bear to know. But Lancelet did not even see.

"No, no, I must tell someone or I shall die of it—Morgaine, know you how first I came to lie with the Queen? I had loved her long, since first I saw her on Avalon, but I thought I would live and die with that passion unspent—Arthur was my friend and I would not betray him," he said. "And she, she—you must never think that she tempted me! But—but it was Arthur's will," he said. "It came about at Beltane—" and then he told her, while Morgaine stood frozen, thinking only, *So this is how the charm worked . . . I would that the Goddess had stricken me with leprosy before ever I gave it to Gwenhwyfar!*

"But you do not know all," he whispered. "As we lay together— never, never had anything so—so—" He swallowed and fumbled to put into words what Morgaine could not bear to hear. "I—I touched Arthur —I touched him. I love her, oh, God, I love her, mistake me not, but had she not been Arthur's wife, had it not been for—I doubt even *she*—" He choked and could not finish his sentence, while Morgaine stood utterly still, appalled beyond speech. Was this then the revenge of the Goddess—that she who loved this man without hope, should become the confidante of both him and the woman he loved, that she should be the repository of all the secret fears he could speak to no one else, the incomprehensible passions within his soul?

"Lancelet, you should not say these things to me, not to me. Some man —Taliesin—a priest—"

"What can a priest know of this?" he demanded in despair. "No man, I think, has ever felt such—God knows I hear enough of what men desire, they talk of nothing else, and now and then some man reveals something strange he may desire, but never, never, nothing so strange and evil as this! I am *damned*," he cried out. "This is my punishment for desiring the wife of my king, that I should be held in this terrible bondage —even Arthur, if he knew, would hate and despise me. He knows I love Gwenhwyfar, but this not even he could forgive, and Gwenhwyfar—who knows if she, even she, would not hate and despise me—" His voice choked into silence.

Morgaine could only say the words she had been taught in Avalon. "The Goddess knows what is in the hearts of men, Lancelet. She will comfort you."

"But this is to spurn the Goddess," Lancelet whispered, in frozen horror. "And what of the man who sees that same Goddess in the face of the mother who bore him . . . I cannot turn to *her*. . . . Almost I am tempted to go and throw myself at the feet of the Christ. His priests say he can forgive any sin, however damnable, as he spoke words of forgiveness to those who crucified him. . . ."

Morgaine said sharply that she had never seen any sign that his priests were so tender and forgiving with sinners.

"Aye, no doubt you are right," said Lancelet, staring bleakly at the flagstones. "There is no help anywhere, till I am slain in battle or ride forth from here to throw myself in the path of a dragon. . . ." He poked with his shoe at a little clump of grass that was growing up through the stones in the courtyard. "And no doubt sin and good and evil are all lies told by priests and men, and the truth is only that we grow and die and wither even as this grass here." He turned on his heel. "Well, I will go and share Gareth's vigil, as I promised him . . . he at least loves me in all innocence, like a younger brother or my son. I should fear to kneel before that altar, if I believed one word of what their priests say, damned as I am. And yet— how I wish there were such a God as could forgive me and let me know myself forgiven. . . ."

He turned to go, but Morgaine caught at the embroidered sleeve of the festival gown he had put on. "Wait. What is this of a vigil in the church? I knew not that Arthur's Companions had grown so pious."

"Arthur thinks often of his kingmaking on Dragon Island," said Lancelet, "and he said once that the Romans with their many Gods, and the old pagan folk, had something which was needed in life, that when men took on some great obligation, they should do it prayerfully, and be in mind of its great meaning and dedication. And so he spoke with the priests, and they have made it so in ritual, that when any new Companion, not seasoned by battle—where he is tried by the very confrontation with death—when an unblooded man joins with the Companions, there is this special testing, that he shall watch and pray all night by his arms, and in the morning confess all his sins and be shriven, and then be made knight."

"Why, then, it is a kind of initiation into the Mysteries that he would give them. But he is no maker of Mysteries, he has no right to confer the Mysteries on another or give initiation, and all garbled in the name of their Christ God. In the name of the Mother, will they even take over the Mysteries?"

Lancelet answered defensively, "He consulted with Taliesin, who gave countenance to it," and Morgaine was startled that one of the highest Druids would so compromise the Mysteries. Yet there had been a time, so Taliesin said, when Christian and Druid worshipped in common.

"It is what happens in the soul of the man," said Lancelet, "not whether it is Christian or pagan or Druid. If Gareth faces the mystery in his heart, and it makes him a better man in his soul, does it matter whence it comes, from the Goddess or from Christ or from that Name the Druids may not speak—or from the very goodness within himself?"

"Why, you argue like Taliesin's very self!" said Morgaine sourly.

"Aye, I know the words." His mouth twisted with terrible bitterness. "Would to God—any God—I could find something in my heart which believed them, or some such comfort as that!"

Morgaine could only say, "I would that you might, cousin. I will pray for you."

"But to whom?" Lancelet asked and went away, leaving Morgaine sorely troubled.

It was not yet midnight. In the church she could see the lights where Gareth and now Lancelet kept vigil. She bent her head, remembering the night when she herself had kept watch, her hand automatically going to her side for the touch of a little crescent knife that had not hung there for many years.

And I cast it away. Who am I to speak of profaning the Mysteries?

Then the air suddenly stirred and swirled like a whirlpool before her, and she felt she would sink down where she stood, for Viviane stood before her in the moonlight.

She was older and thinner. Her eyes were like great burning coals set beneath her level brows, her hair almost all white now. She looked on Morgaine, it seemed, with sorrow and tenderness.

"Mother—" she stammered, not knowing whether she spoke to Viviane or to the Goddess. And then the image wavered and Morgaine knew that Viviane was not there; a Sending, no more.

"Why have you come? What do you want of me?" Morgaine whispered, kneeling, feeling the stir of Viviane's robes in the night wind. About her brow was a crown of wicker-withes like to the crown of the queen of the fairy country. The apparition stretched forth her hand, and Morgaine could feel the faded crescent burning on her brow.

The night watchman strode through the court, the light of his lantern flaring; Morgaine knelt alone, staring at nothing. Hastily she scrambled to her feet before the man could see.

She had lost, suddenly, all desire to go to Kevin's bed. He would be waiting for her, but if she did not come, he would never think of reproaching her. She stole quietly through the hallways to the room she shared with Gwenhwyfar's unmarried maidens, and into the bed she shared with young Elaine.

I thought the Sight forever gone from me. Yet Viviane came to me and stretched out her hand. Is it that Avalon has need of me? Or does it mean that I, like Lancelet, am going mad?

3

When Morgaine woke, all around her the castle was already waking to the noise and confusion of a holiday. Pentecost. In the courtyard there were banners flying, and people were streaming in and out of the gates, servants were setting up lists for the games, pavilions were sprouting all over Camelot and on the slopes of the hill like strange and beautiful flowers.

There was no time for dreams and visions. Gwenhwyfar sent for her to dress her hair—no woman in all Camelot was so deft with her hands as Morgaine, and Morgaine had promised her that this morning she would braid the Queen's hair in the special plaits with four strands which she herself used on high festivals. While she was combing out and separating Gwenhwyfar's fine silky hair for braiding, Morgaine glanced sidewise at the bed from which her sister-in-law had risen. Arthur had already been dressed by his servants and gone out. The pages and chamberlains were spreading the covers, taking away soiled clothes to be cleaned and washed, laying out fresh gowns for Gwenhwyfar's approval.

Morgaine thought: *They shared that bed, all three of them, Lancelet, Gwenhwyfar, Arthur*—no, such a thing was not wholly unknown; she remembered something in the fairy country that would not come clear in her mind. Lancelet was tormented, and she could have no idea how Arthur regarded all this. As her small quick hands moved on Gwenhwyfar's hair, she wondered what her sister-in-law felt. Suddenly her own mind was flooded with erotic images, memory of that day on Dragon Island when Arthur, waking, had drawn her into his arms, of the night she had lain in Lancelet's arms in the field. She lowered her eyes and went on twisting the fine hair.

"You are pulling it too tight," Gwenhwyfar complained, and Morgaine said stiffly, "I am sorry," and forced her hands to relax. Arthur had been only a boy then, and she a maiden. Lancelet—did he give to Gwenhwyfar what he had withheld from her, or was the Queen content with those childish caresses? Try as Morgaine would, she could not turn her mind from the hateful pictures that haunted it, but she went on calmly braiding, her face a mask.

"There, that will hold—hand me the silver pin," she said, fastening up the braids. Gwenhwyfar surveyed herself, delighted, in the copper mirror which was one of her treasures. "It is beautiful, dear sister—thank you so much," she said, turning and impulsively embracing Morgaine, who stiffened in her arms.

"You owe me no thanks—it is easier to do on another's head than my own," Morgaine said. "Wait, that pin is slipping—" and she refastened it. Gwenhwyfar was glowing, beautiful—and Morgaine put her arms around her, laying her cheek for a moment against Gwenhwyfar's. It seemed enough, for a moment, to touch that beauty, as if something of it could penetrate her and give her some of that glow and loveliness. Then she remembered again what Lancelet had told her, and thought, *I am no better than he. I too nurse all manner of strange and perverse desires, and who am I to mock at any?*

She envied the Queen, laughing happily as she directed Elaine to go to her chests and seek out cups for prizes for the winners of the games. Gwenhwyfar was simple and open, she was never tortured by these dark thoughts; Gwenhwyfar's griefs were simple, the griefs and troubles of any woman, fear for her husband's safety, grief over her childlessness—for all the charm's working, there had been no sign of pregnancy. *If one man could not get her with child, it is likely that two could not,* Morgaine thought wickedly.

Gwenhwyfar was smiling. "Shall we go down? I have not greeted the guests—King Uriens is here from North Wales, with his grown son. How would you like to be Queen of Wales, Morgaine? I have heard that Uriens will ask the King for a wife among his wards—"

Morgaine laughed. "You think I would make him a good queen because I am not likely to give him a son to challenge Avalloch's claim to the throne?"

"It is true you would be old to bear a first child," Gwenhwyfar said, "yet I still have hope that I may give my lord and king an heir." Gwenhwyfar did not know that Morgaine had a child, and she should never know.

Yet it nagged at her.

Arthur should know that he has a son. He blames himself that he can give Gwenhwyfar no child—for his own peace of mind he should know. And if it should come to pass that Gwenhwyfar never bears a child, then at least the King has a son. None need know that it is his own sister's. And Gwydion bears the royal line of Avalon. And now he is old enough to be sent to Avalon and be made a Druid. Truly I should have gone to look upon his face, long before this day. . . .

"Listen," said Elaine, "the trumpets are blowing in the courtyard—someone important is here, and we must make haste—they will serve mass in the church this morning."

"And Gareth is to be knighted," said Gwenhwyfar. "It is a pity Lot did not live to see his youngest son made knight—"

Morgaine shrugged. "He took no great joy in Arthur's company, nor Arthur in his." So, she thought, Lancelet's protégé would be made one of the Companions; and then she remembered what Lancelet had told her about the ritual watch and vigil of knighthood—the mockery of the Mysteries. *Is it my task to speak to Arthur about his duty to Avalon? He bore the image of the Virgin into battle at Mount Badon; he laid aside the dragon banner; and now he has turned one of the greater Mysteries over to the Christian priests. I will seek counsel of Taliesin. . . .*

"We must go down," said Gwenhwyfar, and tied on her pockets at her waist, fastening her keys to her girdle. She looked fine and stately with the braided headdress, in her gown of saffron color; Elaine wore a dress dyed green, and Morgaine her red gown. They went down the stair, gathering before the church. Gawaine saluted Morgaine, saying, "Kinswoman," and bowed to the Queen. Beyond him she saw a familiar face, and frowned a little, trying to remember where she had seen that knight before: tall, burly, bearded, almost as blond as a Saxon or a Northman, then she remembered, Balan's foster-brother Balin. She bowed to him coldly. He was a stupid, narrow-minded fool, yet even so he was bound by the sacred ties of foster-kin to Viviane, who was her nearest and dearest kinswoman.

"I greet you, sir Balin."

He scowled a little but remembered his manners. He was wearing a frayed and ragged surcoat; clearly he had been travelling long and had not yet had time to dress and refresh himself. "Are you going to mass, lady Morgaine? Have you renounced the fiends of Avalon and left that evil place, and accepted our Lord and Saviour Christ, lady?"

Morgaine found the question an offense, but did not say so. With a careful smile, she said, "I am going to mass to see our kinsman Gareth knighted." As she hoped, it changed Balin's direction.

"Gawaine's little brother. Balan and I knew him less well than the others," he said. "It is hard to think of him as a man—in my mind he is always the little lad who frightened the horses at Arthur's wedding, and came near to having Galahad killed." Morgaine recalled that was Lancelet's real name—no doubt the pious Balin was too proud to use any other. Balin bowed to her and went on into the church; Morgaine, following with Gwenhwyfar, watched him, frowning. There was the light of fanaticism about his face, and she was just as well pleased that Viviane was not here, although both the Lady's sons were here—Lancelet and Balan—and they could certainly prevent any real trouble.

The church had been decorated with flowers, and the people too, in their brilliant holiday dress, looked like massed flowers. Gareth had been dressed in a white linen robe, and Lancelet, in crimson, knelt beside him, beautiful and grave, Morgaine thought, the fair and the dark, the white and the crimson—and then another comparison occurred to her: Gareth happy and innocent, joyous at this initiation, and Lancelet sorrowful and tormented. Yet as he knelt, listening to the priest reading the Pentecost story, he looked calm and altogether unlike the tortured man who had poured out his soul to her.

". . . and when the day of Pentecost was done, they were all gathered together in one place; and suddenly out of the sky came the sound of a violent wind, which filled the whole house where they were staying. And there appeared tongues as of fire, which divided and sat on them, one to each. And they all were filled with the Holy Breath, and they began to speak in other languages, as the Spirit gave them to utter. Now there were living in Jerusalem Jews of the strict observance, from every race under the sky; and when this sound happened, the whole multitude came together and were confused, because every one of them heard these men speaking in his own language. And they were as men driven out of their minds, saying to one another, 'Look! Are all these preachers not Galileans? And how are we hearing them, each one of us, in our own native languages? Parthians and Medes and Elamites and men out of Mesopotamia, both Judea and Cappadocia, Asia, both Phrygia and Pamphylia, and visitors from Rome, Jews and Cretans and Arabs; but we all hear them talking in our own languages.' And they were all astounded, asking one another, 'What does this mean?' But others said, mockingly, 'These men have drunk too much of sweet new wine, so early in the day.' Then Peter the Apostle raised his voice and said to them, 'Men of Judea, and all of you, listen to my words; these men are not drunk as you imagine, since it is only the third hour; but it is as the prophet Joel has written; God says, in the last days of the world, I will send out my Spirit into all flesh, and your daughters shall prophesy, and your young men shall see visions and your old men shall dream dreams.' "

Morgaine, kneeling quietly in her place, thought, *Why, it was the Sight that came upon them and they did not understand it. Nor had they cared to understand; to them it only proved that their God was greater than other Gods.* Now the priest was talking of the last days of the world, how God would pour out his gifts of vision and prophecy, but she wondered if any of these Christians knew how commonplace all these gifts were, after all? Anyone could master these powers when he had demonstrated that he could use them suitably. But that did not include trying to astonish the common people with silly miracles! The Druids used their powers to do good privately, not to collect crowds!

When the faithful approached the rail for their shared bread and wine in commemoration, Morgaine shook her head and stepped back, though Gwenhwyfar tried to draw her forward; she was not a Christian and she would not pretend.

Afterward, outside the church, she watched the ceremony where Lancelet drew his sword and touched Gareth with it, his strong and musical voice clear and solemn. "Arise now, Gareth, Companion of Arthur, and brother now to all of us here, and to every knight of this company. Forget not to defend your king, and to live at peace with all knights of Arthur and all peaceful people everywhere, but remember always to make war against evil and to defend those who are in need of protection."

Morgaine recalled Arthur receiving Excalibur at the hands of the Lady. She glanced at him and wondered if he remembered too, and if this was why he had instituted this solemn pledge and ceremonial, so that the young men made knights in his company might have some such rite to remember. Perhaps this was not, after all, a mockery of the holy Mysteries, but an attempt to preserve them as best he could . . . but why must it take place in the church? Would a day come when he would refuse it to any who were not pledged Christian? During the service, Gareth and his cousin and sponsor Lancelet had been first to receive holy communion, even before the King. Was this not putting this order of knighthood into the church as a Christian rite, one of their sacraments? Lancelet had no right to do this; he was not himself qualified to confer the Mysteries on any other. Was this a profanation or an honest attempt to bring the Mysteries into the hearts and souls of all the court? Morgaine did not know.

After the service, there was an interval before the games. Morgaine greeted Gareth and gave him her gift, a fine dyed-leather belt on which he could carry sword and dagger. He bent down to kiss her.

"Ah, you have grown, little one—I doubt if your mother would know you!"

"It happens to all of us, dear cousin," Gareth said, smiling. "I doubt you would know your own son!" Then he was surrounded by the other knights, jostling and crowding to welcome and congratulate him; Arthur clasped his hands and spoke to him in a way that made Gareth's fair skin glow.

Morgaine saw that Gwenhwyfar was watching her sharply. "Morgaine—what was it Gareth said—*your son?*"

Morgaine said sharply, "If I have never told you, sister-in-law, it is because I respected your religion. I bore a son to the Goddess, from the Beltane rites. He is being fostered at Lot's court; I have not seen him since he was weaned. Are you content, or will you spread my secret everywhere?"

"No," said Gwenhwyfar, turning pale. "What sorrow for you, to be parted from your babe! I am sorry, Morgaine; and I will not tell even Arthur—he is Christian too and he would be shocked."

You do not know how shocked he would be, Morgaine thought grimly. Her heart was pounding. Could Gwenhwyfar be trusted with her secret? There were too many now who knew it!

The trumpet had been blown for the beginning of the games; Arthur had agreed not to take the lists, for no one wanted to attack his king, but one side of the mock battle was to be led by Lancelet as the King's champion and the other fell by lot to Uriens of North Wales, a hearty man well past middle age, but still strong and muscular. At his side was his second son, Accolon. Morgaine noted that as Accolon drew on his gloves his wrists were revealed; around them coiled blue tattooed serpents. He was an initiate of Dragon Island!

Gwenhwyfar had been jesting, no doubt, about marrying her to old Uriens. But Accolon—*there* was a proper man; perhaps, except for Lancelet, the handsomest young man on the field. Morgaine found herself admiring his skill at arms. Agile and well built, he moved with the natural ease of a man to whom such exercises come readily and who has been handling weapons since boyhood. Sooner or later, Arthur would wish to give her in marriage; if he should offer her to Accolon, would she say no?

After a time her attention began to wander. Most of the other women had long since lost interest and were gossiping about feats of prowess they had heard of; some were playing at dice in their sheltered seats; a few were watching with animation, having wagered ribbons or pins or small coins on their husbands or brothers or sweethearts.

"It is hardly worth wagering," said one discontentedly, "for we all know that Lancelet will win the day—he always does."

"Are you saying he does so unfairly?" Elaine asked with a flare of resentment, and the strange woman said, "By no means. But he should, at these games, stay on the sidelines, since no one can stand against him."

Morgaine laughed. "I have seen young Gareth there, Gawaine's brother, throw him ass-over-head in the dirt," she said, "and he took that in good part, too. But if you want sport, I will wager you a crimson silk ribbon that Accolon wins a prize, even over Lancelet."

"Done," said the woman, and Morgaine rose in her seat. She said, "I have no taste for watching men batter each other for sport—there has been enough of fighting that I am weary even of the sound of it." She nodded to Gwenhwyfar. "Sister, may I go back to the hall and see that all is in order for the feasting?"

Gwenhwyfar nodded permission, and Morgaine slid down at the back of the seats and made her way toward the main courtyard. The great gates were open and guarded only by a few who had no wish to attend the mock battles. Morgaine started toward the castle and never knew what intuition it was that sent her back toward the gates, or why she stood watching a pair of approaching riders who were arriving late for the first festivities. But as they came nearer, her skin began to prickle with foreboding, and then she began to run, as they rode through the gates, and now she was weeping. "Viviane," she cried out, and then stopped, afraid to throw herself into her kinswoman's arms; instead she knelt on the dusty ground and bent her head.

The soft, familiar voice, unchanged, just as she had heard it in dreams, said gently, "Morgaine, my darling child, it is you! How I have longed to meet with you all these years. Come, come, darling, you need not ever kneel to me."

Morgaine raised her face, but she was trembling too hard to rise. Viviane, her face shrouded in grey veils, was bending over her; she put out a hand, and Morgaine kissed it, and then Viviane pulled her close into an embrace. "Darling, it has been so long—" she said, and Morgaine struggled helplessly not to cry.

"I have been so troubled about you," Viviane said, holding tight to Morgaine's hand as they walked toward the entrance. "From time to time I would see you, a little, in the pool—but I am old, I can use the Sight but seldom. Yet I knew you lived, you were not dead in childbirth, nor far over the seas . . . I longed to look on your face, little one." Her voice was as tender as if there had never been any quarrel between them, and Morgaine was flooded by the old affection.

"All the people of the court are at the games. Morgause's youngest son was made knight and Companion this morning," she said. "I think I must have known that you were coming—" and then she recalled the moment of the Sight, last night; indeed, she *had* known. "Why have you come here, Mother?"

"I thought you had heard how Arthur betrayed Avalon," Viviane said. "Kevin has spoken to him in my name, but without avail. So I have come to stand here before his throne and demand justice. In Arthur's name the lesser kings are forbidding the old worship, sacred groves have been despoiled, even on the land where Arthur's queen rules by inheritance, and Arthur has done nothing—"

"Gwenhwyfar is overpious," Morgaine murmured, and felt her lip cruel in disdain; so pious, yet taking her husband's cousin and champion to her bed, with the sanction of that too-pious King! But a priestess of Avalon did not babble the secrets of the bedchamber if they came into her keeping.

It seemed that Viviane read her thoughts, for she said, "Nay, Morgaine, but a time might come when some secret knowledge might give me a weapon to force Arthur to his sworn duty. *One* hold, indeed, I have over him, though for your sake, child, I would not use it before his court. Tell me—" She glanced around. "No, not here. Take me where we may talk together in secret, and let me refresh myself and make myself seemly to stand before Arthur at his great feast."

Morgaine took her to the room she shared with Gwenhwyfar's ladies, who were all at the games; the servants were gone too, so she herself fetched Viviane water for washing, and wine to drink, and helped her to change her dusty, travel-worn clothing.

"I met with your son in Lothian," Viviane said.

"Kevin told me." The old pain clutched at her heart—so Viviane had gotten what she wanted of her, after all: a son of the doubled royal lines, for Avalon. "Will you make him a Druid, then, for Avalon?"

"It is too soon to know what stuff he has in him," said Viviane. "Too long, I fear, was he left in Morgause's keeping. But whether or no, he must be reared in Avalon, and loyal to the old Gods, so that if Arthur is false to his oath, we may remind him that there is a son of the Pendragon's blood to take his place—we will have no king turned apostate and tyrant, forcing that god of slaves and sin and shame down the throats of our people! We set him on Uther's throne, we can bring him down if we must, and all the more readily if there is one of the old royal line of Avalon, a son of the Goddess, to take his place. Arthur is a good king, I would be reluctant to make such threats; but if I must, I will—the Goddess orders my actions."

Morgaine shuddered; would her child be the instrument of his father's death? She turned her face resolutely from the Sight. "I do not think Arthur will be this false to Avalon."

"The Goddess grant he may not," Viviane said, "but even so, the Christians would not accept a son gotten in that rite. We must keep a place near the throne for Gwydion, so that he may be his father's heir, and one day we will have a king born of Avalon again. The Christians, mark you,

Morgaine, would think your son born out of sin; but before the Goddess he is of the purest royalty of all, mother and father born of her lineage—sacred, not evil. And he must come to think himself so, not be contaminated by priests who would tell him his begetting and birth were shameful." She looked Morgaine straight in the eye. "*You* still think it shameful?"

Morgaine lowered her head. "Always you could read my heart, kins-woman."

"Igraine's is the fault," said Viviane, "and mine, that I left you at Uther's court seven years. The day I knew you priestess-born, I should have had you from there. You are priestess of Avalon, darling child, why came you never back?" She turned, the comb in her hand, her long faded hair falling along her face.

Morgaine whispered, tears forcing themselves through the barrier of her tight eyes, "I cannot. I cannot, Viviane. I tried—I could not find the way." And all the humiliation and shame of that washed over her, and she wept.

Viviane put down the comb and caught Morgaine to her breast, holding her, rocking and soothing her like a child. "Darling, my own darling girl, do not cry, do not cry . . . if I had known, child, I would have come to you. Don't cry now—I shall myself take you back, we will go together when I have given Arthur my message. I will take you with me and go, before he gets it into his head to marry you off to some braying Christian ass . . . yes, yes, child, you shall come back to Avalon . . . we will go together. . . ." She wiped Morgaine's wet face on her own veil. "Come, now, help me to dress myself to stand before my kinsman the High King—"

Morgaine drew a deep breath. "Yes, let me braid your hair, Mother." She tried to laugh. "This morning I did the Queen's hair."

Viviane held her away and said, in great anger, "Has Arthur put you, priestess of Avalon and princess in your own right, to waiting hand and foot on his queen?"

"No, no," said Morgaine quickly, "I am honored as high as the Queen herself—I dressed Gwenhwyfar's hair this day out of friendship; she is as likely to do mine, or to lace my gown, as sisters do."

Viviane sighed with relief. "I would not have you dishonored. You are the mother of Arthur's son. He must learn to honor you as such, and so must the daughter of Leodegranz—"

"No!" Morgaine cried. "No, I beg of you—Arthur must not know, not before the whole court—listen to me, Mother," she pleaded, "all these folk are Christian. Would you have me shamed before them all?"

Viviane said implacably, "They must learn not to think shame of holy things!"

"But the Christians have power over all this land," Morgaine said, "and you cannot change their thinking with a few words—" And in her heart she wondered, had advancing age driven Viviane out of her wits? There was no way simply to proclaim that the old laws of Avalon should be set up again and two hundred years of Christianity be overthrown. The priests would drive her out of the court as a madwoman and go on as before. Viviane must know enough of practical ruling to know this! And indeed, Viviane nodded and said, "You are right, we must work slowly. But Arthur at least must be reminded of his promise to protect Avalon, and I will speak to him in secret, one day, about the child. We cannot proclaim it aloud among the ignorant."

Then Morgaine helped Viviane to arrange her hair and to dress herself in the stately robes of a priestess of Avalon, dressed for high ceremonial. And it was not long before they heard sounds telling them that the mock games were over. No doubt the prizes would be given indoors this time, at the feast; she wondered if Lancelet had won them all again in honor of his king. *Or,* she thought sourly, *his queen? And could one call that honor?*

They turned to leave the chamber, and as they left the room, Viviane touched her hand gently. "You will return to Avalon with me, will you not, dear child?"

"If Arthur will let me go . . ."

"Morgaine, you are a priestess of Avalon, and you need not ask leave, even of the High King, to come and go as it pleases you. A High King is a leader in battle—he does not own the lives of his subjects, or even of his subject kings, as if he were one of those Eastern tyrants who thinks the world is his and the life of every man and woman in it. I will tell him I have need of you in Avalon and we will see what he answers to that."

Morgaine felt herself choking with unshed tears. *Oh, to return to Avalon, to go home* . . . but even as she held Viviane's hand she could not believe she was truly to go there after this day. Later she was to say, *I knew, I knew,* and recognize the despair and foreboding that struck her at the words, but at the moment she was certain it was only her own fear, the sense that she was not worthy of what she had cast away.

Then they went down into Arthur's great hall for the Pentecost feasting.

It was Camelot, Morgaine thought, as she had never seen it before, and perhaps would never see it again. The great Round Table, Leodegranz's wedding gift, was now set in a hall worthy of its majesty; the halls had been hung with silks and banners, and a trick of the arrangement made it so that all eyes were drawn to where Arthur sat, at the high seat at the far end of the hall. For this day he had brought Gareth to sit beside him and his queen, and all the knights and Companions were ringed together, the Companions in fine clothing, their weapons gleaming, the ladies garbed brightly as flowers. One after another, the petty kings came, knelt before Arthur and brought him gifts; Morgaine watched Arthur's face, grave, solemn, gentle. She looked sidewise at Viviane—surely she must see that Arthur had grown into a good king, not one to be lightly judged, even by Avalon or the Druids. But who was she to weigh causes between Arthur and Avalon? She felt the old tremor of disquiet, as in the old days at Avalon when she was being taught to open her mind to the Sight that would use her as its instrument, and found herself wishing, without understanding why, *Would that Viviane were a hundred leagues from here!*

She looked around the Companions—Gawaine, sandy and bulldog-strong, smiling at his newly knighted brother; Gareth, shining somehow like new-minted gold. Lancelet looked dark and beautiful, and as if his thoughts were somewhere at the other end of the world. Pellinore, greying and gentle, his daughter, Elaine, waiting on him.

And now one came to Arthur's throne who was not one of the Companions. Morgaine had not seen him before, but she saw that Gwen-hwyfar recognized him and shrank away.

"I am the only living son of King Leodegranz," he said, "and brother to your queen, Arthur. I demand that you recognize my claim to the Summer Country."

Arthur said mildly, "You do not make demands in this court, Melea-grant. I will consider your request and take counsel of my queen, and it may be that I will consent to name you her regent. But I cannot deliver you judgment now."

"Then it may be I shall not wait for your judgment!" shouted Melea-grant. He was a big man, who had come to the feast wearing not only sword and dagger, but a great bronze battle-axe; he was dressed in ill-tanned furs and skins, and looked savage and grim as any Saxon bandit. His two men-at-arms looked even more ruffianly than he did himself. "I am the only surviving son of Leodegranz."

Gwenhwyfar leaned forward and whispered to Arthur. The King said, "My lady tells me that her father always denied he had begotten you. Rest assured, we shall have this matter looked into, and if your claim is good we will allow it. For the moment, sir Meleagrant, I ask you to trust to my justice, and join me in feasting. We will take this up with our councillors and do you such justice as we can."

"Feasting be damned!" said Meleagrant angrily. "I came not here to eat comfits and look at ladies and watch grown men making sport like boys! I tell you, Arthur, I am king of that country, and if you dare dispute my claim it will be the worse for you—and for your lady!"

He laid his hand on the hilt of his great battle-axe, but Cai and Gareth were immediately there, pinioning his arms behind him.

"No steel's to be drawn in the King's hall," said Cai roughly, while Gareth twisted the axe out of his hand and set it at the foot of Arthur's chair. "Go to your seat, man, and eat your meat. We'll have order at the Round Table, and when our king has said he'll do you justice, you'll wait on his good pleasure!"

They spun him roughly round, but Meleagrant struggled free of their hands and said, "To hell with your feast and to hell with your justice, then! And to hell with your Round Table and all your Companions!" He left the axe and turned his back, stamping down all the length of the hall. Cai took a step after him, and Gawaine half rose, but Arthur motioned him to sit down again.

"Let him go," he said. "We will deal with him at the proper time. Lancelet, as my lady's champion, it may well fall to you to deal with that usurping churl."

"It will be my pleasure, my king," said Lancelet, starting up as if he had been half asleep, but Morgaine suspected he had not the slightest idea what he had agreed to. The heralds at the door were still proclaiming that all men should draw near for the King's justice; there was a brief, comical interlude, when a farmer came in and told how he and his neighbor had quarreled over a small windmill on the borders of their property.

"And we couldn't agree, sir," he said, twisting his rough woolen hat between his hands, "so him and me, we made it out that the King had made all this country safe to have a windmill in, and so I said I'd come here, sir, and see what you say and we'd listen to it."

Amid good-natured laughter, the matter was settled; but Morgaine noticed that Arthur alone did not laugh, but listened seriously, gave judgment, and when the man had thanked him and gone away, with many bows and thanks, only then did he let his face break into a smile. "Cai, see that they give the fellow something to eat in the kitchens before he goes home, he had a long walk here." He sighed. "Who is next to ask justice? God grant it be something fitter my solving—will they come next to ask my advice in horse breeding, or something of that sort?"

"It shows what they think of their king, Arthur," said Taliesin. "But you should make it known that they should go to their local lord, and see that your subjects are also responsible for justice in your name." He raised his head to see the next petitioner. "But this may be more worthy of the King's attention after all, for it is a woman, and, I doubt not, in some trouble."

Arthur motioned her forward: a young woman, self-assured, haughty, reared to courtly ways. She had no attendant except for a small and ugly dwarf, no taller than three feet, but with broad shoulders and well muscled, carrying a short and powerful axe.

She bowed to the King and told her story. She served a lady who had been left, as had so many others after the years of war, alone in the world; her estate was northward, near to the old Roman wall which stretched mile after mile, with ruined forts and mile-castles, mostly now decrepit and falling down. But a gang of five brothers, ruffians all, had refortified five of the castles and were laying the whole countryside to waste. And now one of them, who had a fancy to call himself the Red Knight of Red Lands, was laying siege to her lady; and his brothers were worse than he was.

"Red Knight, hah!" said Gawaine. "I know that gentleman. I fought with him when I came southward from my last visit to Lot's country, and I barely got away with my life. Arthur, it might be well to send an army to clean out those fellows—there's no law in that part of the world."

Arthur frowned and nodded, but young Gareth rose from his seat.

"My lord Arthur, that is on the fringes of my father's country. You promised me a quest—keep the promise, my king, and send me to help this lady defend her countryside against these evil fellows!"

The young woman looked at Gareth, his shining beardless face and the white silk robe he had put on for his knighting, and she broke into laughter. "You? Why, you're a child. I didn't know the great High King was taking overgrown children to serve at his table!" Gareth blushed like a child. He had indeed handed Arthur's cup to the King—it was a service young well-born boys, fostered at court, all performed at high feasts. Gareth had not yet remembered it was no longer his duty, and Arthur, who liked the boy, had not reproved him.

The woman drew herself up. "My lord and king, I came to ask for one or more of your great knights with a reputation in battle which would daunt this Red Knight—Gawaine, or Lancelet, or Balin, one of those who is known as a great fighter against the Saxons. Are you going to let your very kitchen boys mock me, sire?"

Arthur said, "My Companion Gareth is no kitchen boy, madam. He is brother to sir Gawaine, and he promises to be as good a knight as his brother, or better. I did indeed promise him the first quest that I could honorably give him, and I will send him with you. Gareth," he said gently, "I charge you to ride with this lady, to guard her against the dangers of the road, and when you come to her country, to help her lady to organize her country in defense against these villains. If you need help, you may send me a messenger, but no doubt she has fighting men enough—they need only someone with knowledge and skill at strategy, and this you have learned from Cai and Gawaine. Madam, I give you a good man to help you."

She did not quite dare to answer the King, but she scowled at Gareth fiercely. He said formally, "Thank you, my lord Arthur. I will put the fear of God into these rascals who are troubling the countryside there." He bowed to Arthur and turned to the lady, but she had turned her back and stormed out of the hall.

Lancelet said in a low voice, "He is young for all that, sir. Shouldn't you send Balan, or Balin, or someone more experienced?"

Arthur shook his head. "I truly think Gareth can do it, and I prefer that no one of my Companions is favored over another—it should be enough for the lady to know that one of them is coming to help her people."

Arthur leaned back and signalled to Cai to serve his plate. "Giving justice is hungry work. Are there no more petitioners?"

"There is one, my lord Arthur," said Viviane quietly, and rose from her place among the Queen's ladies. Morgaine began to rise and attend her, but Viviane gestured her back. She looked taller than she was, because she held herself so straight. And part of it was glamour, the glamour of Avalon . . . her hair, all white, was braided high on her head; at her side hung the little sickle-shaped knife, the knife of a priestess, and on her brow blazed the mark of the Goddess, the shining crescent moon.

Arthur looked at her for a moment, in surprise, then recognized her and gestured her to come forward.

"Lady of Avalon, it is long since you honored this court with your presence. Come sit beside me, kinswoman, and tell me how I may best serve you."

"By showing honor to Avalon, as you are sworn to do," said Viviane. Her voice was very clear and low, but, the trained voice of a priestess, it could be heard to the farthest corners of the hall. "My king, I bid you look now on that sword you bear, and think on those who laid it in your hand, and what you swore—"

In later years when all that had befallen that day was talked of far and wide, no two of the hundreds in that hall could agree on what had happened first. Morgaine saw Balin rise in his place and rush forward, she saw a hand snatch up the great axe Meleagrant had left leaning against the throne, then there was a scuffle and a cry, and she heard her own scream as the great axe came whirling down. But she did not see the blow, only Viviane's white hair suddenly red with blood as she crumpled and fell without even a cry.

Then the hall was full of shouts and screams; Lancelet and Gawaine had Balin, struggling in their grasp; Morgaine had her own dagger in her hand and rushed forward, but Kevin gripped at her hard, his twisted fingers clutching at her wrist.

"Morgaine. Morgaine, no, it is too late—" he said, and his voice was roughened with sobs. "Ceridwen! Mother Goddess—! No, no, look not on her now, Morgaine—"

He tried to turn her away, but Morgaine stood frozen, as if turned to stone, listening to Balin howling obscenities at the top of his voice.

Cai said abruptly, "Look to the lord Taliesin!" The old man had slithered down fainting in his seat. Cai bent and steadied him, then, murmuring a word of apology to Arthur, seized the King's own cup and poured the wine down the old man's throat. Kevin let Morgaine go and stumbled awkwardly to the side of the ancient Druid, bending over him. Morgaine thought, *I should go to him,* but it was as if her feet were frozen to the floor, she could not take a single step. She stared at the fainting old man so that she need not look back at that horrible red-stained pool on the floor, soaking through robes and hair and long cloak. In that last instant Viviane had seized her own small sickle knife. Her hand lay on it now, stained with her own blood—there was so much blood, so much. Her skull—her skull had been cloven in half, and there was blood, *blood on the throne poured out like an animal for sacrifice, here at the foot of Arthur's throne. . . .*

Arthur finally found his voice. "You wretched man," he said hoarsely, "what have you done? This is murder, cold murder before the very throne of your king. . . ."

"Murder, you say?" Balin said in his thick, harsh voice. "Yes, she was the most foul murderess in this kingdom, she deserved death twice over— I have rid your kingdom of a wicked and evil sorceress, my king!"

Arthur looked more angry than grieved. "The Lady of the Lake was my friend and my benefactor! How dare you speak so of my kinswoman, she who helped to set me on my throne?"

"I call the lord Lancelet himself to witness if she did not compass the death of my mother," Balin said, "a good and pious Christian woman, Priscilla by name, and foster-mother to your own brother Balan! And she murdered my mother, I tell you she murdered her by her evil sorceries—" His face worked; the big man was weeping like a child. "She murdered my mother, I tell you, and I have avenged her as a knight should do!"

Lancelet closed his eyes in horror, his face contorted, but he did not weep. "My lord Arthur, this man's life belongs to me! Let me here take vengeance for my mother—"

"And my mother's sister," said Gawaine.

"And mine—" Gaheris added.

Morgaine's frozen trance broke. She cried, "No, Arthur! Let *me* have him! He has murdered the Lady before your throne, let a woman of Avalon avenge the blood of Avalon—look yonder how the lord Taliesin lies stricken, it is like that he has murdered our grandsire too—"

"Sister, sister—" Arthur held out his hand to Morgaine. "No, no, sister —no, give me your dagger—"

Morgaine stood shaking her head, her dagger still in her hand. Taliesin suddenly rose to take it from her with his own trembling old fingers. "No, Morgaine. No more bloodshed here—the Goddess knows, it is enough— her blood has been spilled as sacrifice to Avalon in this hall—"

"Sacrificed! Yes, sacrificed to God, as God shall strike down all these evil sorceresses and their Gods!" cried Balin in a frenzy. "Let me have that one too, my lord Arthur, purge this court of all their evil wizard line—" He struggled so violently that Lancelet and Gawaine could hardly hold him and signalled to Cai, who came and helped them cast Balin down, struggling still, before the throne.

"Quiet!" Lancelet said, jerking his head around. "I warn you, one hand laid on the Merlin or Morgaine, and I'll have your head whatever Arthur may say—yes, my lord Arthur, and die at your hands for it afterward if you will have it so!" His face was drawn with anguish and despair.

"My lord King," Balin howled, "I beg you, let me strike down all these wizards and sorcerers in the name of the Christ who hates them all—"

Lancelet struck Balin heavily across the mouth; the man gasped and was silent, blood streaming from a broken lip.

"By your leave, my lord." Lancelet unfastened his rich cloak and gently covered the ghastly, drained corpse of his mother.

Arthur seemed to breathe easier now that the corpse was out of sight. Only Morgaine went on staring wide-eyed at the lifeless huddle now covered with the crimson cloak Lancelet had worn for the holiday.

Blood. Blood on the foot of the King's throne. Blood, poured out on the hearth . . . Somewhere it seemed to Morgaine that she could hear Raven shrieking.

Arthur said quietly, "Look to the lady Morgaine, she will faint," and Morgaine felt hands gently helping her into a seat and some- one holding a cup to her lips. She started to push it away, and then it seemed she heard Viviane's voice saying, *Drink it. A priestess must keep her strength and will.* Obediently she drank, hearing Arthur's voice, stern and solemn.

"Balin, whatever your reasons—no, no more, I heard what you said —not a word—you are either a madman, or a cold-blooded murderer. Whatever you may say, you have slain my kinswoman and drawn steel before your High King at Pentecost. Still, I will not have you murdered where you stand—Lancelet, put up your sword."

Lancelet slid his sword back into its scabbard. "I will do your will, my lord. But if you do not punish this murder, then I beg leave to depart from your court."

"Oh, I will punish it." Arthur's face was grim. "Balin, are you sane enough to listen to me? Then this is your doom: I banish you forever from this court. Let this lady's body be made ready and put on a horse bier, and I charge you to take it to Glastonbury, and tell all your tale to the Archbishop and do such penance as he shall lay on you. You spoke but now of God and Christ, but no Christian king allows private vengeance to be taken by the sword before his throne of justice. Do you hear what I say, Balin, once my knight and Companion?"

Balin bent his head. His nose had been broken by Lancelet's blow; his mouth was streaming blood, and he spoke thickly through a broken tooth. "I hear you, my lord King. I will go." He sat with his head bowed.

Arthur gestured to the servants. "I beg you, bring someone to remove her poor body—"

Morgaine broke away from the hands that held her and knelt beside Viviane. "My lord, I beg you, allow me to ready her for burial—" and struggled to hold back the tears she dared not shed. This was not Viviane, this broken dead thing, the hand like a shrunken claw still clutching the sickle dagger of Avalon. She took up the dagger, kissed it, and slid it into her own belt. This, and only this, would she keep.

Great merciful Mother, I knew we could never go together to Avalon. . . .

She would *not* weep. She felt Lancelet close beside her. He muttered, "God's mercy Balan is not here—to lose mother and foster-brother in one moment of madness—but if Balan had been here it might not have happened! Is there any God or any mercy?"

Her heart ached for Lancelet's anguish. He had feared and hated his mother, but he had worshipped her, too, as the very face of the Goddess. A part of her wanted to pull Lancelet into her arms, comfort him, let him weep; yet there was rage too. He had defied his mother, how dared he grieve for her now?

Taliesin was kneeling beside them, and he said, in his broken old voice, "Let me help you, children. It is my right—" and they moved aside as he bowed his head to murmur an ancient prayer of passage.

Arthur rose in his place. "There will be no more feasting this day. We have had too much tragedy for a feast. Those of you who are hungry, finish your meal and go quietly." He came slowly down to where the body lay. His hand rested gently on Morgaine's shoulder; she felt it there, through her numb misery. She could hear the other guests quietly leaving the hall, one after another, and through the rustle she heard, softly, the sound of a harp; only one pair of hands in Britain played such a harp. And at last she melted and tears streamed from her eyes as Kevin's harp played the dirge for the Lady, and to that sound, Viviane, priestess of Avalon, was slowly borne from the great hall of Camelot. Morgaine, walking beside the bier, looked back only once at the great hall and the Round Table, and the solitary, bowed figure of Arthur, standing alone beside the harper. And through all her grief and despair, she thought, *Viviane never gave to Arthur the message of Avalon. This is the hall of a Christian king, and now there is no one who will say otherwise. How Gwenhwyfar would rejoice if she knew.*

His hands were outstretched; she did not know, perhaps he was praying. She saw the serpents tattooed about his wrists and thought of the young stag and the new-made king who had come to her with the blood of the King Stag on his hands and face, and for a moment it seemed to her that she could hear the mocking voice of the fairy queen. And then there was no sound but the anguished lamenting of Kevin's harp and Lancelet weeping at her side as they bore Viviane forth to rest.

MORGAINE SPEAKS . . .

I followed the body of Viviane from the great hall of the Round Table, weeping for only the second time that I could remember.

And yet later that night I quarrelled with Kevin.

Working with the Queen's women, I prepared Viviane's body for burial. Gwenhwyfar sent her women, and she sent linen and spices and a velvet pall, but she did not come herself. That was just as well. A priestess of Avalon should be laid to rest by attendant priestesses. I longed for my sisters from the House of Maidens; but at least no Christian hands should touch her. When I was done, Kevin came to watch by the body.

"I have sent Taliesin to rest. I have that authority now, as the Merlin of Britain; he is very old and very feeble—it is a miracle that his heart did not fail this day. I fear he will not long outlive her. Balin is quiet now," he added. "I think perhaps he knows what he did—but it is sure that it was done in a fit of madness. He is ready to ride with her body to Glastonbury, and serve such penance as the Archbishop shall decree."

I stared at him in outrage. "And you will have it so? That she shall fall into the hands of the church? I care not what happens to that murderer," I said, "but Viviane must be taken to Avalon." I swallowed hard so that I would not weep again. We should have ridden together to Avalon. . . .

"Arthur has decreed," said Kevin quietly, "that she shall be buried before the church at Glastonbury, where all can see."

I shook my head, unbelieving. Were all men mad this day? "Viviane must lie in Avalon," I said, "where all the priestesses of the Mother have been buried since time began. And she was Lady of the Lake!"

"She was also Arthur's friend and benefactor," said Kevin, "and he will have it that her tomb shall be made a place of pilgrimage." He put out his hand that I should not speak. "No, hear me, Morgaine—there is reason in what he says.

Never has there been so grave a crime in Arthur's reign. He cannot hide away her burial place out of sight and out of mind. She must be buried where all men may know of the King's justice, and the justice of the church."

"And you will allow this!"

"Morgaine, my dearest," he said gently, "it is not for me to allow or to refuse. Arthur is the High King, and it is his will that is done in this realm."

"And Taliesin holds his peace? Or is this why you have sent him to his rest, so that he might be out of the way while you do this blasphemy with the King's connivance? Will you have Viviane buried with Christian burial and Christian rites, she who was Lady of the Lake—buried by these folk who imprison their God within stone walls? Viviane chose me after her to be Lady of the Lake, and I forbid it, I forbid it, do you hear me?"

Kevin said quietly, "Morgaine. No, listen to me, my dear. Viviane died without naming her successor—"

"You were there that day she said she had chosen me—"

"But you were not in Avalon when she died, and you have renounced that place," Kevin said, and his words fell on my head like cold rain, so that I shivered. He stared at the bier and Viviane's body which lay covered there; nothing I could do could make that face fit to be seen in death. "Viviane died with no successor named to her place, and so it falls to me, as the Merlin of Britain, to declare what will be done. And if this is Arthur's will, only the Lady of the Lake—and, forgive me, my dear, that I say it, but there is now no Lady in Avalon—could speak out against what I say. I can see that the King has reason for what he wishes. Viviane spent all her life to bring about a peaceful rule of law in this land. . . ."

"She came to reprove Arthur that he had forsaken Avalon!" I cried in despair. "She died with her mission unfinished, and now you would have it that she should lie in Christian ground within the sound of church bells, so that they should triumph over her in death as in life?"

"Morgaine, Morgaine, my poor girl!" Kevin held out his hands to me, the misshapen hands which had so often caressed me. "I loved her too, believe me! But she is dead. She was a great woman, she spent her life for this land—do you think it matters to her where her empty shell shall lie? She has gone to whatever awaits her beyond death, and, knowing her, I know that it can only be good that awaits her. Do you think she would grudge it, that her body should lie where it can best serve those purposes she spent her life to accomplish—that the King's justice should triumph over all the evil in this land?"

His rich, caressing, musical voice was so eloquent that I hesitated for a moment. Viviane was gone; it was only those same Christians who made much of consecrated or unconsecrated ground, as if all the earth which is the breast of the Mother was not holy. I wanted to fall into his arms and weep there for the only mother I had ever known, for the wreck of my own hopes that I might return

to Avalon at her side, weep for all I had cast away and the breaking of my own
life. . . .

But what he said then made me start away in horror.

"Viviane was old," he said, "and she had dwelt in Avalon, sheltered from
the real world. I have had to live, with Arthur, in the world where battles are won
and real decisions made. Morgaine, my dearest, listen to me. It is too late to demand
that Arthur keep his pledge to Avalon in that same form he gave it. Time passes,
the sound of church bells covers this land, and the people are content to have it
so. Who are we to say that this is not the will of the Gods that lie behind the Gods?
Whether we wish it or no, my dearest love, this is a Christian land, and we who
honor Viviane's memory will do her no good by making it known to all men that
she came hither to make impossible demands of the King."

"Impossible demands?" I wrenched my hands away. "How dare you?"

"Morgaine, listen to reason—"

"Not reason but treason! If Taliesin heard this—"

"I speak as I have heard Taliesin himself speak," he said gently. "Viviane
did not live in order to undo what she has done, to create a land at peace—whether
it is called Christian or Druid does not matter; the will of the Goddess will be done
over all, whatever name men may call her. Who are you to say that it was not
the will of the Goddess that Viviane was struck down before she could spread strife
again in a land that has come to peace and successful compromise? I tell you, it
shall not be torn again by strife, and if Viviane had not been struck down by Balin,
I would myself have spoken against what she asked—and I think Taliesin would
have said as much."

"How dare you speak for Taliesin?"

"Taliesin himself named me the Merlin of Britain," said Kevin, "and he
must therefore have trusted me to act for him when he could not speak for himself."

"Next you will say you have become a Christian! Why wear you not beads
and a crucifix?"

He said, in such a gentle voice that I could have wept, "Do you truly think
it would make such a great difference, Morgaine, if I did so?"

I knelt before him, as I had done a year ago, pressed his broken hand to my
breast. "Kevin, I have loved you. For that I beg you—be faithful now to Avalon
and to Viviane's memory! Come with me now, tonight. Do not this travesty, but
accompany me to Avalon, where the Lady of the Lake shall lie with the other
priestesses of the Goddess. . . ."

He bent over me; I could feel the anguished tenderness in his misshapen
hands. "Morgaine, I cannot. My dearest, will you not be calm and listen to the
voice of reason in what I am saying?"

I stood up, flinging off his weak grip, and raising my arms, summoned the
power of the Goddess. I heard my voice thrumming with the power of a priestess.
"Kevin! In her name who came to you, in the name of the manhood she has given

you, I lay obedience on you! Your allegiance is not to Arthur nor to Britain, but only to the Goddess and to your vows! Come now, leave this place! Come with me to Avalon, bearing her body!"

I could see in the shadows the very glow of the Goddess around me; for a moment Kevin knelt shuddering, and I know that in another moment he would have obeyed. And then, I know not what happened—perhaps it crossed my mind, No, I am not worthy, I have no right . . . I have forsaken Avalon, I cast it away, by what right then do I command the Merlin of Britain? The spell broke; Kevin made a harsh, abrupt gesture, awkwardly rising to his feet.

"Woman, you do not command me! You who have renounced Avalon, by what right do you presume to give orders to the Merlin? Rather should you kneel before me!" He thrust me away with both hands. "Tempt me no more!"

He turned his back and limped away, the shadows making wavering mis-shapen movements on the wall as he moved from the room; I watched him go, too stricken even to weep.

And four days later Viviane was buried, with all the rites of the church, on the Holy Isle in Glastonbury. But I did not go thither.

Never, I swore, should I step foot upon that Isle of the Priests.

Arthur mourned her sincerely, and built for her a great tomb and a cairn, swearing that one day he and Gwenhwyfar should lie there at her side.

As for Balin, the Archbishop Patricius laid it upon him that he should make a pilgrimage to Rome and the Holy Lands; but before he could go into exile, Balan heard the tale from Lancelet and hunted him down, and the foster-brothers fought, one with another, and Balin was killed at once with a single stroke; but Balan took cold in his wounds and did not survive him a whole day. So Viviane—so they said when a song was made of it—was avenged; but what of that, when she lay in a Christian tomb?

And I . . . I did not even know whom they had chosen as Lady of the Lake in her place, for I could not return to Avalon.

. . . I was not worthy of Lancelet, I was not worthy even of Kevin . . . I could not tempt him to do his true duty to Avalon. . . .

. . . I should have gone to Taliesin and begged him, even on my knees, to take me back to Avalon, that I might atone for all my faults and return again to the shrine of the Goddess. . . .

But before the summer was ended, Taliesin was gone too; I think he never knew for certain that Viviane was dead, because even after she was buried, he spoke as if she would come soon and return with him to Avalon; and he spoke of my mother, too, as if she lived and was a little girl in the House of Maidens. And at summer's end he died peacefully and was buried at Camelot, and even the bishop mourned him as a wise and learned man.

*And in the winter after that, we heard that Meleagrant had set himself up
to rule as king in the Summer Country. But when spring came, Arthur was away
on a mission to the South, and Lancelet too had ridden out to see to the King's
castle at Caerleon, when Meleagrant sent a messenger under a flag of truce, begging
that his sister Gwenhwyfar should come and speak with him about the rule of that
country over which they both had a claim.*

4

I would feel safer, and I think my lord the king would like it better,
if Lancelet were here to ride with you," Cai said soberly. "At Pentecost
yonder fellow would have drawn steel in this hall before his king, and he
would not await the King's justice. Brother of yours or no, I like it not that
you ride alone with only your lady and your chamberlain."

"He is not my brother," Gwenhwyfar said. "His mother was the king's
mistress for a time, but he put her away because he found her with another
man. She claimed, and perhaps told her son, that Leodegranz was his father.
The king never acknowledged it. If he were an honorable man, and such
as my lord would trust, perhaps he could be regent for me as well as any
other. But I will not allow him to profit by such a lie."

"Will you trust yourself then in his hands, Gwenhwyfar?" asked
Morgaine quietly.

Gwenhwyfar looked at Cai and Morgaine, shaking her head. Why did
Morgaine look so calm and unafraid? Was Morgaine never afraid of anything, never touched by any emotion behind that cool, unreadable face?
Rationally she knew that Morgaine, like all mortal flesh, must sometimes
suffer from pain, fear, grief, anger—yet only twice had she actually seen
emotion in Morgaine, and that long ago; once when Morgaine had fallen
into trance and dreamed of blood on the hearth—then she had cried out in
fear—and once when Viviane was slain here before her eyes and she had
sunk down fainting.

Gwenhwyfar said, "I trust him not at all, except to be the greedy
impostor he is. But think, Morgaine. All his claim is based upon the fact that
he is my brother. Should he offer me the slightest insult, or treat me as
anything less than his honored sister, his claim is proved a lie. So he dares do
nothing else than welcome me as his honored sister and queen, do you see?"

Morgaine shrugged. "I would not trust him even so far as that."

"No doubt, like the Merlin, you have sorcery to give you knowledge
of what may come if I do."

Morgaine said indifferently, "It needs no sorcery to know that a villain is a villain, and no supernatural wisdom that bids me not let the nearest rogue hold my wallet for me."

Whatever Morgaine said, Gwenhwyfar always felt compelled to do precisely other; always she felt that Morgaine thought her a fool without the wit to lace her own shoes. Did Morgaine think that she, Gwenhwyfar, could not settle a matter of state when Arthur was absent? Yet she had hardly been able to face Morgaine since that ill-starred Beltane a year ago when she had begged her sister-in-law for a charm against her barrenness. Morgaine had told her that charms often work as you would not have them work . . . now whenever she looked on Morgaine, she thought her sister-in-law must be remembering it, too.

God punishes me; perhaps for meddling with sorcery, perhaps for that wicked night. And as always when she allowed the faintest memory of that time to come into her mind, she felt her whole body flushing with mingled delight and shame. Ah, it was easy to say they had all three been drunken, or to excuse herself that what was done that night was done with Arthur's consent, indeed, at his urging. Still it was grievous sin, adultery.

And since that night she had hungered for Lancelet, night and day; yet they had hardly been able to face each other. She could not look him in the eyes. Did he hate her as a shameful, adulterous woman? He must despise her. Yet she longed for him with terrible despair.

After that Pentecost, Lancelet had hardly been at court. She had never thought he had cared so much for his mother, nor yet for his brother Balan, yet he had mourned them both deeply. He had been away from court all this time.

"I wish," said Cai, "that Lancelet were here. Who should accompany the Queen on a mission of this sort, except that knight Arthur has named as his queen's champion and protector?"

"If Lancelet were here," said Morgaine, "many of our troubles would be over, for he would settle Meleagrant with a few words. But there is no good talking of what cannot be. Gwenhwyfar, shall I ride with you and protect you?"

"In God's name," said Gwenhwyfar, "I am not a child who cannot stir forth without a nurse! I will take my chamberlain, sir Lucan, and I will take Bracca to dress my hair and lace my gown if I am there for more than a night, and to sleep at the foot of my bed; what do I need more than that?"

"Still, Gwenhwyfar, you must have an escort fitting your rank. There are still some of Arthur's Companions here at court."

"I will take Ectorius," said Gwenhwyfar. "He is Arthur's foster-father, and nobly born, and a veteran of many of Arthur's wars."

Morgaine shook her head impatiently. "Old Ectorius, and Lucan who lost an arm at Mount Badon—why do you not take Cai and the Merlin with you as well, so that you may have all the old and the lame? You should have an escort of good fighting men who can protect you, Gwenhwyfar, in case it is in this man's mind to hold the Queen to ransom, or worse."

Gwenhwyfar repeated patiently, "If he does not treat me as his sister, then his claim is worthless. And what man would offer any threat to his sister?"

"I do not know if Meleagrant is so good a Christian as all that," Morgaine said, "but if you are not afraid of him, Gwenhwyfar, you know him better than I do. No doubt you can find an escort of old bumbling veterans to ride with you—so be it. You might offer to wed him to your kinswoman Elaine, to make his claim of kinship even more valid, and set him as regent in your place—"

Gwenhwyfar shuddered, remembering the great coarse man dressed in ill-tanned skins and furs. "Elaine is a gently reared lady; I would not give her to such a one," she said. "I will talk with him—if he seems to me an honest fighting man and such a one as will keep the peace in this kingdom, then if he will swear loyalty to my lord Arthur, he may reign upon the island—I like not all of Arthur's Companions either, but a man may be an honest king without being a good one to sit with ladies and talk in hall."

"I marvel to hear you say so," said Morgaine. "To hear you sing my kinsman Lancelet's praises, I thought you believed no man could be a good knight unless he were handsome and full of this kind of courtly matters."

Gwenhwyfar would not quarrel again with Morgaine. "Come, sister, I love Gawaine well, yet he is a rough Northman who trips over his own feet and has hardly a word to say to any woman. For all I know, Meleagrant too may be such a jewel in the wrappings of a knucklebone, and that is why I go thither—to judge for myself."

So the next morning Gwenhwyfar set forth, with her escort of six knights, Ectorius, the veteran Lucan, her waiting-woman, and a nine-year-old page boy. She had not visited her childhood home since that day she left it with Igraine, to be married to Arthur. It was not far: a few leagues down the hill, and to the shores of the lake, which at this season was drying up into boggy marshes, with cattle grazing in the summer fields and lush grasses filled with buttercup and dandelion and primrose. At the shore two boats were waiting, hung with her father's banners. This was arrogance, that Meleagrant should bear these unpermitted, but after all, it was possible that the man genuinely believed himself Leodegranz's heir. It might even be true; perhaps her father had lied about it.

She had landed at these very shores, bound for Caerleon, so many years ago . . . how young she had been, and how innocent! Lancelet had been at her side, but fate had given her to Arthur—God knows, she had tried to be a good wife to him, though God had denied her children. And then despair washed over her again as she looked at the waiting boats. She might give her husband three or five or seven sons, and a year might come of plague, or smallpox, or the throat fever, and all her sons would be gone . . . such things had happened. Her own mother had borne four sons, yet none of them had lived to be as much as five years old, and Alienor's son had died with her. Morgaine . . . Morgaine had borne a son to their evil God of witches, and for all she knew, *that* son lived and thrived, while she, a faithful Christian wife, could not bear any child, and now she might soon be too old.

Meleagrant himself was at the landing, bowing, welcoming her as his honored sister, gesturing her toward his own boat, the smaller of the two. Gwenhwyfar never knew even afterward how it had happened that she was separated from all of her escort except for the little page. "My lady's servants may go in the other boat, I myself will be your escort here," said Meleagrant, taking her arm with an overfamiliarity she did not like; but after all, she must bear herself with diplomacy and not anger him. At the last moment, with a momentary sense of panic, she gestured to sir Ectorius.

"I will have my chamberlain with me, as well," she insisted, and Meleagrant smiled, his great coarse face reddening.

"As my sister and queen desires," he said, and let Ectorius and Lucan step on to the smaller boat with her. He fussed about spreading a rug for her to sit on, and the oarsmen pulled out into the lake. It was shallow, grown heavily with weeds; in some seasons it was dry here. And suddenly, as Meleagrant seated himself beside her, Gwenhwyfar was seized with an attack of the old terror; her stomach heaved, and for a moment she thought she would vomit. She clung to the seat with both hands. Meleagrant was too near her; she moved as far away as the dimensions of the seat would allow. She would have felt more comfortable if Ectorius had been near; his presence was serene and fatherly. She noted the great axe Meleagrant wore through his belt—it was like the one he had left near the throne, the one Balin had seized to murder Viviane. . . . Meleagrant said, leaning so close that his heavy breath sickened her, "Is my sister faint? Surely the motion of the boat does not trouble you, it is so calm—"

She edged away from him, struggling for self-control. She was alone here except for two old men, and she was out in the middle of the lake, with nothing around her but weed and water and the reedy horizon . . . why had she come? Why was she not in her own walled garden at home, in Camelot? There was no safety here, she was out under the wide-open sky, so that she felt sick and naked and exposed. . . .

"We will be on shore soon," Meleagrant said, "and if you wish to rest before we conduct our business, sister, I have had the queen's apartments prepared for you—"

The boat scraped on shore. The old path was still there, she noted, the narrow winding way up to the castle, and the old wall, where she had sat that afternoon watching Lancelet run among the horses. She felt confused, as if it might have been only the day before and she was that shy young girl. She reached out surreptitiously and touched the wall, feeling it firm and solid, and stepped through the gate with relief.

The old hall seemed smaller than when she had lived there; she had grown used to great spaces in Caerleon and later at Camelot. Her father's old high seat was spread with skins like those Meleagrant wore, and a great black bearskin lay at the foot of the seat. The whole looked uncared-for, the skins ragged and greasy, the hall unswept, with a sour, sweaty smell; she wrinkled her nose, but it was so much a relief to be within walls that she did not care. She wondered where her escort had gone.

"Will you rest and refresh yourself, sister? Shall I show you to your apartments?"

She smiled and said, "I shall hardly be here long enough to call them mine, though it is true I would like to wash the dust off my hands and take off my cloak. Will you send someone to find my serving-woman? You should have a wife if you are to think of being regent here, Meleagrant."

"There is time enough for that," he said, "but I will show you to the apartments I have prepared for my queen." He led the way up the old stairs. They were also ill-kept and neglected; Gwenhwyfar, frowning, thought less well of choosing him as regent. If he had moved into the castle and restored it, had installed a wife and good servants to keep it well, with fresh hangings and good cleaning, and smart men-at-arms, well—but his soldiers looked more villainous than he did himself, and she had not yet seen any woman about the place. A faint qualm was beginning to steal over her; maybe she had not been too wise to come here alone, not to insist on her escort accompanying her every step of the way—

She turned on the stairs and said, "I will have my chamberlain accompany me, if you please, and I want my woman sent for at once!"

"As my lady wishes." He grinned. His teeth seemed very long, yellow and stained. She thought, *He is like a wild beast* . . . and edged against the wall in terror. Yet it was from some inner reserve of strength she drew to say firmly, "Now, please. Call sir Ectorius, or I will go right down into the hall again until my serving-woman is here. It is not seemly for Arthur's queen to go alone with a strange man—"

"Not even with her brother?" asked Meleagrant, but Gwenhwyfar, ducking beneath his outstretched arm, saw that Ectorius had come into the hall after her and called, "Foster-father! Accompany me, if you will! And send sir Lucan to find my servant!"

The old man came slowly up the stairs after them, passing Meleagrant, and Gwenhwyfar put out her arm to lean on him. Meleagrant looked but ill pleased at this. They came to the head of the stairs, to the chamber where Alienor had once dwelt; Gwenhwyfar had been in a little room behind hers. Meleagrant opened the door. It smelled stale and dank inside, and Gwenhwyfar hesitated. Perhaps she should insist on going at once downstairs and to business; she could hardly refresh herself or rest well in a room as dirty and neglected as this—

"Not you, old man," said Meleagrant, turning suddenly and pushing Ectorius down the stairs hard. "My lady does not need your service now." Ectorius stumbled, off balance, and at that moment Meleagrant pushed her into the room and slammed the door hard behind her. She heard the bar thrown down and stumbled to her knees; by the time she got up she was alone in the room, and no amount of hammering on the door brought any sound at all.

So Morgaine's warning had been right. Had they murdered her escort? Had they killed Ectorius and Lucan? The room where Alienor had borne her children and lived and later died was cold and dank; there were only some old rags of linen sheets across the great bed, and the straw smelled foul. Alinor's old carved chest was there, but the wood carving was greasy and smeared with dirt, and it was empty. The hearth was clogged with ash as if there had been no fresh fire lighted there for years. Gwenhwyfar beat on the door and shouted until her hands and her throat were sore; she was hungry and exhausted, and sickened by the smell and the dirt of this place. But she could not budge the door, and the window was too small to climb out—and there was a twelve-foot drop outside. She was imprisoned. Through the window she could see only a neglected barnyard with a single mouldy-looking cow wandering and bellowing at intervals.

The hours dragged by. Gwenhwyfar had to accept two things, that she could not get out of the room by her own efforts, and that she could not attract the attention of any person who would be likely to come and let her out. Her escort was gone—dead or imprisoned, in any case unable to come to her aid. Her waiting-woman and page were probably dead, certainly well out of reach. She was here, and alone, at the mercy of a man who would probably use her as a hostage to exact some kind of concession from Arthur.

Her own person was probably safe from him. As she had pointed out to Morgaine, all his claim rested on the fact that he was the only surviving son of her father; bastard, but still of the royal blood. However, when she thought of his rapacious grin and huge presence, she was terrified; he might

easily abuse her or try to force her to acknowledge him as regent of this
country.

The day dragged on; the sun moved slowly from the small crack of
window, across the room, and away again, and at last it began to grow dark.
Gwenhwyfar went through into the little chamber behind Alienor's that had
been her own when she was a child; once her mother had dwelt in Alienor's
chamber. The dark confined space, no more than a closet, felt comfortingly
secure; who could hurt her in here? No matter that it was dirty and stale,
the bedstraw mildewed; she crept into the bed and wrapped herself in
her cloak. Then she went back into the outer room and tried to shove
Alienor's heavy carved chest against the door. She had discovered that she
was very much afraid of Meleagrant, and even more afraid of his ruffianly
men-at-arms.

Certainly he would not let them hurt her—the only bargaining power
he had was her safety. *Arthur would kill him,* she told herself, Arthur would
kill him if he offered her the slightest insult or harm.

But, she asked herself in her misery, would Arthur really care? Although he had been kind and loving to her all these years and treated her
with all honor, still he might not be sorry to be quit of a wife who could
not bear him a child—a wife who was, furthermore, in love with another
man and could not conceal it from him.

*If I were Arthur I would make no move against Meleagrant; I would tell
him that now he had me, he might keep me, for all the good it would do him.*

What did Meleagrant want? If she, Gwenhwyfar, were dead, there
would be no one else with the shadow of a claim on the Summer Country's
throne; there were some young nephews and nieces by her sisters, but they
dwelt far away and probably did not know or care about this land. Perhaps
he simply meant to murder her or leave her here to starve. The night dragged
on. Once she heard some men and horses moving about in the barnyard
below; she went to the small window and peered out, but she saw only a
dim torch or two, and although she yelled and shouted through her sore
throat, no one raised his eyes or took the slightest notice.

Once, far into the night, when she had fallen into a brief, nightmare-
ridden doze, she started up, thinking she heard Morgaine calling her name;
she sat bolt upright on the dirty straw of the bed, staring into the thick
darkness, but she was alone.

*Morgaine, Morgaine. If you can see me with your sorcery, say to my lord
when he comes home that Meleagrant is false, that it was a trap . . .* and then
she wondered, would God be angry with her for calling on Morgaine's
sorcery to deliver her? And she fell to praying softly until the monotony
of her prayers put her to sleep again.

She slept heavily, this time, without dreams, and when she woke, her mouth dry, she realized it was full day and she was still prisoner in the empty and filthy apartment. She was hungry and thirsty, and sickened with the smell of the place, not only the stale straw and mould, but the smells from one corner she had had to use as a latrine. How long were they going to leave her here alone. The morning wore away and Gwenhwyfar no longer even had the strength or courage to pray.

Was she being punished, then, for her guilt, for not valuing enough what she had had? She had been a faithful wife to Arthur, yet she had hungered after another man. She had meddled with Morgaine's sorcery. *But, she thought in despair, if I am being punished for my adultery with Lancelet, for what was I being punished while I was yet a faithful wife to Arthur?*

Even if Morgaine could see, with her magic, that she was imprisoned, would she trouble to help her? Morgaine had no reason to love her; indeed, Morgaine almost certainly despised her.

Was there anyone who really cared? Why should anyone care what happened to her?

It was past noon when at last she heard a step on the stairs. She sprang to her feet, wrapping herself tightly in her cloak, and backed away from the door. It was Meleagrant who came in, and at sight of him she drew back even farther.

"Why have you done this to me?" she demanded. "Where is my woman, my page, my chamberlain? What have you done with my escort? Do you think Arthur will allow you to rule this country when you have offered insult to his queen?"

"His queen no longer," Meleagrant said quietly. "When I am done with you, he will not have you back. In the old days, lady, the consort of the queen was king of the land, and if I hold you and get sons on you, no man will gainsay my right to rule."

"You will get no sons from me," Gwenhwyfar said with a mirthless laugh. "I am barren."

"Pah—you were married to a damned beardless boy," he said, and added something more, which Gwenhwyfar did not completely understand, only that it was unimaginably foul.

"Arthur will kill you," she said.

"Let him try. It is harder than you would think to attack an island," said Meleagrant, "and by that time, perhaps, he will not care to try, since he would have to take you back—"

She said, "I cannot marry you, I have a husband."

"No man in my kingdom will care one way or the other," said Meleagrant. "There were many who chafed at the rule of the priests, and I have cast forth every damned priest of them! I rule by the old laws, and I will make myself king by that law, which says your man rules here—"

She whispered, "No," and backed away, but he sprang at her and pulled her toward him.

"You're not to my taste," he said brutally. "Skinny, ugly, pale wenches —I like better a woman who's some flesh to her bones! But you're old Leodegranz's daughter, unless your mother had more blood to her than I think she could have had! And so—" He pulled her to him. She struggled, got her arm loose, and struck him hard across the face.

He shouted as her elbow struck his nose, grabbed her arm and shook her, hard; then hit her with his clenched fist across the jaw. She felt something snap and tasted blood bursting in her mouth. He hit her again and again with his fists; she put her arms up, terrified, to ward off his blows, but he went on beating her. "Now," he yelled, "there'll be no more of that, you'll find out who's your master—" He seized her wrist and wrenched at it.

"Oh, no—no—please, please, don't hurt me—Arthur, Arthur will kill you—"

He answered her only with an obscenity, wrenched at her wrist, flung her down on the dirty straw of the bed, knelt beside her, hauling at his clothing. She writhed, shrieking; he hit her again and she lay still, crouched on a corner of the bed.

"Take off your gown!" he ordered.

"No!" she cried, huddling her clothes about her. He reached out, twisting her wrist, and held her while he ripped her gown deliberately down to the waist.

"Now will you take it off, or shall I tear off every rag of it?"

Shaking, sobbing, with trembling fingers, Gwenhwyfar pulled her gown over her head, knowing that she should fight, but too terrified of his fists and blows to resist. When she had done he pulled her down, held her down on the dirty straw, pushing her legs open with a rough hand. She struggled only a little, frightened of his hands, sickened by his foul breath, his huge hairy body, the big meaty phallus that thrust painfully into her, pushing and pushing till she felt she would break in two.

"Don't pull away from me like that, damn you!" he shouted, thrusting violently; she cried out with pain and he hit her again. She lay still, sobbing, and let him do what he would. It seemed to go on forever, his big body straining and pumping on and on, till finally she felt him convulse, thrust agonizingly hard; then he was gone from her, rolled a little away, and she gasped for breath, struggling to pull her clothes around her. He stood up, wrenching at his belt, and gestured to her.

"Won't you let me go?," she begged. "I promise you—I promise you—"

He grinned fiercely. "Why should I?" he asked. "No, here you are and here you'll stay. Is there anything you need? A gown to put in the place of that one?"

She stood weeping, exhausted, shamed, sickened. At last she said shakily, "I—can I have some water, and—and something to eat? And"—She began to cry harder than ever, with shame—"and a chamber pot?"

"Whatever my lady desires," said Meleagrant sarcastically, and went away, locking her in again.

Later in the day a crook-backed old crone brought her some greasy roast meat and a hunk of barley bread, and jugs of water and beer. She also brought some blankets and a chamber pot.

Gwenhwyfar said, "If you will bear a message to my lord Arthur, I will give you this—" and she took the gold comb from her hair. The old woman's face brightened at the look of the gold, but then she looked away, scared, and sidled out of the room. Gwenhwyfar burst into tears again.

At last she regained some calm, ate and drank, and tried to wash herself a little. She felt sick and sore, but worse than that was the sense of being used, shamed, ineradicably dirtied.

Was it true what Meleagrant had said—that Arthur would not have her back now, that she had been spoilt beyond redemption? It might be so . . . if she were a man she would not want anything Meleagrant had used either. . . .

No, but it was not fair; this was not anything she had done wrong, she had been trapped and tricked, used against her will.

Oh, but it is no more than I deserve . . . I who am not a faithful wife, but love another. . . . She felt sick with guilt and shame. But after a time she began to recover her composure and to consider her predicament.

She was here in Meleagrant's castle—her father's old castle. She had been raped and was held captive, and Meleagrant had proclaimed his intention of holding this island kingdom by right of being her consort. It was not to be considered that Arthur would let him do so; no matter what he thought of her personally, for his own honor as High King he would have to make war on Meleagrant. It would not be easy, but it should not be impossible to recapture an island. She knew nothing of Meleagrant as a fighter—except, she thought with a rare flash of grim humor, against a helpless woman, whom he had beaten into submission. But it was not to be considered, either, that he could stand against the High King who had driven the Saxons into utter rout at Mount Badon.

And then she must face him and tell him what had happened to her. It might be simpler to kill herself. Come what might, she could not imagine herself facing Arthur, telling him how Meleagrant had treated her . . . *I should have fought against him harder; Arthur, in battle, has faced very death, once he took a great wound which kept him abed half a year, and I—I stopped fighting after a few slaps and blows. . . .* She wished she had some of Morgaine's sorcery; she would turn him into a pig! But Morgaine would never have fallen into his hands, she would have guessed it was a trap; and she would have used that little dagger of hers, too—she might not have killed him, but he would have lost his desire, and perhaps his ability, to ravish any woman!

She had eaten and drunk what she could, washed herself, and brushed her filthy dress clean.

Again the day had begun to wane. It could not be hoped for—that she would be missed, that anyone would come for her until Meleagrant began to boast of what he had done, proclaim himself the consort of King Leodegranz's daughter. She had gone of her own free will, and properly attended by two of Arthur's Companions. Not until Arthur returned from the Southern Shores, and perhaps not for a week or ten days after that, when she did not return at the appointed time, would he begin to suspect that all was not well.

Morgaine, why did I not listen to you? You warned me he was a villain. . . . For a moment it seemed that she could see her sister-in-law's pale, passionless face—calm, slightly mocking—so clearly that she rubbed her eyes; Morgaine, laughing at her? No, it was a trick of the light, it was gone.

Would that she could see me through her magic . . . perhaps she could send someone . . . no, she would not, she hates me, she would laugh at my ill fortune . . . and then she remembered: Morgaine laughed and mocked, but when it was a real trouble, no one could be kinder. Morgaine had tended her when she miscarried; she had, against her own protest, been willing to try and help her with a charm. Perhaps Morgaine did not hate her after all. Perhaps all Morgaine's mockery was a defense against Gwenhwyfar's own pride, her scorn of the sorceresses of Avalon.

Twilight was beginning to blur the furniture in the room. She should have thought to ask for some sort of light. Now it seemed she would spend a second night as prisoner here, and it might be that Meleagrant would return . . . and at the thought she felt sick again with terror; she was still sore from his brutal treatment, her mouth swollen, bruises darkening on her shoulders and, she supposed, on her face. And although, when she was alone here, she could think quite calmly about ways to fight him and perhaps drive him away, she knew, with a sick sinking of terror in her body, that when he touched her, she would shrink away in dread and let him do whatever he would, to avoid more blows . . . she was so afraid, so afraid that he would hurt her again. . . .

And how could Arthur forgive her for this, that she had not been beaten entirely into submission, but had given way like a coward, after the threat of a few blows and slaps . . . how could he take her back as his queen and continue to love and honor her, when she had allowed another man to have her . . . ?

He had not minded when she and Lancelet . . . he had been a part of that . . . if there was sin it was not all hers, she had done as her husband wished. . . .

Oh, yes, but Lancelet was his kinsman and dearest friend. . . .

There was a commotion in the courtyard; Gwenhwyfar went to the window, peering out, but she could see only that same corner of the barnyard, and that same bellowing cow. Somewhere there was noise, shouting and yelling and the clash of weapons, but she could not see and the sound was muffled by the walls and stairs; it might be no more than those villains of Meleagrant's, fighting or brawling in the courts, or even—*oh, no! God forbid it!*—murdering her escort. She tried to crane her neck so she could see further from the slit of window, but there was nothing to see.

There was a sound outside. The door flew open and Gwenhwyfar, turning apprehensively, saw Meleagrant, a naked sword in hand. He gestured with it. "Get within—into that inner chamber," he ordered. "In with you, and not a sound from you, madam, or it will be the worse for you."

Does this mean someone has come to rescue me? He looked desperate, and Gwenhwyfar knew that she could get no information from him. She backed away, slowly, into the little inner room. He followed her, his hand on the sword, and Gwenhwyfar flinched, her whole body cringing in anticipation of the stroke . . . would he kill her now, or hold her as hostage for his own escape?

She never knew his plan. Meleagrant's head suddenly exploded in a spray of blood and brains; he crumpled with a weird slowness, and Gwenhwyfar sank down, too, half fainting, but before she reached the floor, she was in Lancelet's arms.

"My lady, my queen—ah, my beloved—" He caught her against him, holding her, and then, half senseless, Gwenhwyfar knew he was covering her face with kisses. She made no protest; it was like a dream. Meleagrant lay in his blood on the floor, the sword lay where it had fallen. Lancelet had to lift her over the body before he could set her on her feet.

"How—how did you know?" she stammered.

"Morgaine," he said tersely. "When I came to Camelot, Morgaine said she had tried to bid you delay till I was there. She felt it was a trap—I took horse and came after you, with half a dozen men. I found your escort imprisoned in the woods near here, tied and gagged—once I had freed them, it was not hard—no doubt he thought himself secure." Now Lancelet let her go long enough to see the bruises on her face and body, her torn gown, the cut lip where it was swollen. He touched them with shaking fingers.

"Now do I regret he died so quickly," he said. "It would give me delight to make him suffer as you have suffered—ah, my poor love, my darling, you have been so cruelly used—"

"You don't know," she whispered, "you don't know—" and she was sobbing again, clinging to him. "You came, you came, I thought no one would come, that no one would want me now, that no one would ever touch me again—now when I am so shamed. . . ."

He held her, kissing her again and again in a frenzy of tenderness. "Shamed? You? No, the shame is his, his, oh, and he has paid for it . . ." he muttered through his kisses. "I thought I had lost you forever, he might have killed you, but Morgaine said no, you lived—"

Even then, Gwenhwyfar spared a moment of fear and resentment— did Morgaine know how she had been humiliated, violated? Ah, God, if only Morgaine need not have known! She could not bear it, that Morgaine should know of this!

"Sir Ectorius? Sir Lucan—"

"Lucan is well enough; Ectorius is not young, and he has suffered grave shock, but there is no reason to think he will not live," Lancelet said. "You must go down, my beloved, and show yourself to them; they must know that their queen lives."

Gwenhwyfar looked at her torn gown, touched her bruised face with hesitant hands. She said, her voice catching in her throat, "Can I not have a little time to make myself proper? I do not want them to see—" and she could not go on.

Lancelet hesitated, then nodded. He said, "Yes; let them think he dared offer you no insult. It is better that way. I came alone, knowing I could match Meleagrant; the others are downstairs. Let me look in the other chambers—a man of his kind would not dwell here without some woman or other." He left her for a moment, and she could barely endure to see him out of her sight. She edged away from the body of Meleagrant on the floor, looking down at the man as if he were a wolf's carcass killed by some shepherd, without even distate for the blood.

After a moment Lancelet returned. "There is a room yonder which is clean, and chests there with some garments laid away—I think it was the old king's room. There is even a mirror." He led her down the hall. This room had been swept, and the bed straw on the big bed was fresh and clean, and there were sheets and blankets, and fur comforters—not too clean, but not disgusting, either. There was a carved chest she recognized, and inside it she found three gowns, one of which she had seen Alinor wear, and the others made for someone taller. Handling them, through a mist of tears, she thought, *These must have been my own mother's. I wonder that my father never gave them to Alienor.* And then she thought, *I never knew my father well. I have no idea what manner of man he was, he was only my father.* And that seemed so sad to her that she wanted to weep again.

"I will put this on," she said, and then she broke into a weak laugh. "If I can manage without a woman to dress me—"

Lancelet touched her face gently. "I will dress you, my lady." He began to help her off with her gown. And then his face twisted, and he lifted her up in his arms, half-dressed as she was.

"When I think of that—that animal, touching you—" he said, with his face muffled against her breast, "and I who love you barely dare to lay a hand on you—"

And for all her faithfulness, she had only come to this; God had rewarded her for her virtue and self-restraint by betraying her into Meleagrant's hands for rape and brutality! And Lancelet, who had offered her love and tenderness, who had scrupulously stepped aside that he might not betray his kinsman—he had to witness it! She turned in his arms, embracing him.

"Lancelet," she whispered, "my love, my dearest—take away from me the memory of what was done to me—let us not go from here yet for a little while—"

His eyes overflowed with tears; he laid her down gently on the bed, caressing her with shaking hands.

God did not reward me for virtue. What makes me think he could punish me? And then a thought which frightened her, *perhaps there is no God at all, nor any of the Gods people believe in. Perhaps it is all a great lie of the priests, so that they may tell mankind what to do, what not to do, what to believe, give orders even to the King.* She raised herself, pulling Lancelet down to her, her bruised mouth searching for his, her hands wandering all over the beloved body, this time without fear and without shame. She no longer cared, nor felt restraint. Arthur? Arthur had not protected her from ravishment. She had suffered what she had had to suffer, and now, at least, she would have this much. It had been by Arthur's doing that she had first lain with Lancelet, and now she would do what she would.

THEY RODE out of Meleagrant's castle two hours later, side by side, their hands reaching out between their horses to touch as they rode, and Gwenhwyfar no longer cared; she looked straight at Lancelet, her head held high with joy and gladness. This was her true love, and never again would she trouble herself to hide it from any man.

O n the *shores of Avalon the priestesses wound slowly along the reedy shore, torches in hand. . . . I should have been among them, but there was some reason I could not go. . . . Viviane would have been angry with me that I was not there, yet I seemed to stand on a far shore, unable to speak the word that would have brought me to them. . . .*

Raven paced slowly, her pale face lined as I had never seen it, a long streak of white at the side of her temple . . . her hair was unbound; could it be that she was still maiden, untouched save by the God? Her white draperies moved in the same wind that made the torches flare. Where was Viviane, where was the Lady? The sacred boat stood at the shore of the eternal lands, but she would come no more to the place of the Goddess . . . and who was this in the veil and wreath of the Lady?

I had never seen her before, save in dreams. . . .

Thick, colorless hair, the color of ripe wheat, was braided in a low coronal over her brow; but hanging at her waist where the sickle knife of a priestess should have hung . . . ah, Goddess! Blasphemy! For at the side of her pale gown a silver crucifix hung; I struggled against invisible bonds to rush forward and tear away the blasphemous thing, but Kevin stepped between us and held my hands in his own, which twisted and writhed like misshapen serpents . . . and then he was writhing between my hands . . . and the serpents were tearing at me with their teeth . . .

"Morgaine! What is it?" Elaine shook her bedfellow's shoulder. "What is it! You were crying out in your sleep—"

"Kevin," she muttered, and sat up, her unbound hair, raven-dark, moving about her like dark water. "No, no, it wasn't you—but she had fair hair like yours, and a crucifix—"

"You were dreaming, Morgaine," Elaine said. "Wake up!"

Morgaine blinked and shuddered, then drew a long breath and looked up at Elaine with her customary composure. "I am sorry—an evil dream," she said, but her eyes still looked haunted. Elaine wondered what dreams pursued the King's sister; for sure they must be evil, for she had come here from that evil island of witches and sorceresses . . . yet somehow Morgaine had never seemed to her an evil woman. How could any woman be so good when she worshipped devils and refused Christ?

She turned away from Morgaine and said, "We must get up, cousin. The King will return this day, so last night's messenger said."

Morgaine nodded and got out of bed, pulling off her shift; Elaine modestly averted her eyes. Morgaine seemed to be without shame—had she never heard that all sin came into this world through the body of a woman?

Now she stood shamelessly naked, rummaging in her chest for a holiday shift, and Elaine turned away and began to dress.

"Make haste, Morgaine, we must go to the Queen—"

Morgaine smiled. "Not too much haste, kinswoman, we must give Lancelet time to be well away. Gwenhwyfar would not thank you for making a scandal."

"Morgaine, how can you say such a thing? After what has happened, it is no more than reason that Gwenhwyfar should be afraid to be alone at night and should wish her champion to sleep at her very door . . . and indeed, it was fortunate Lancelet came in time to save her from worse—"

"Don't be more of a fool than you *must*, Elaine," said Morgaine with weary patience. "Do you believe that?"

"You, of course, know better by your magic," flared Elaine, so loudly that the other women who slept in the room turned their heads to hear what the Queen's cousin and the King's sister were quarrelling about. Morgaine lowered her voice and said, "Believe me, I want no scandal, no more than you. Gwenhwyfar is my sister-in-law and Lancelet is my kinsman too. God knows, Arthur should not chide Gwenhwyfar for what befell with Meleagrant—poor wretch, it was none of her doing, and no doubt it must be given out that Lancelet came in time to rescue her. But I have no doubt Gwenhwyfar will tell Arthur, at least in secret, how Meleagrant used her —no, Elaine, I saw how she was when Lancelet brought her back from the island, and I heard what she said, her terror that that damned hellhound might have managed to get her with child!"

Elaine's face went dead white. "But he is her brother," she whispered. "Is there any man alive would do such sin as *that?*"

"Oh, Elaine, in God's name, what a ninny you are!" Morgaine said. "Is *that* what you think the worst of it?"

"And you are saying—Lancelet has shared her bed while the King was away—"

"I am not surprised, nor do I think it the first time," said Morgaine. "Have sense, Elaine—do you begrudge it? After what Meleagrant did to her, I would not be surprised if Gwenhwyfar would never again wish any man to touch her, and for her sake I am glad, if Lancelet can heal that hurt for her. And now, perhaps, Arthur will put her away, so that he may get him a son somewhere."

Elaine said, staring at her, "Perhaps Gwenhwyfar will go into a convent—she told me once she was never happier than in her convent at Glastonbury. But would they have her, if she had been paramour to her husband's captain of horse? Oh, Morgaine, I am so ashamed of her!"

"It has nothing to do with *you*," Morgaine said. "Why should you care?"

Elaine said, surprising herself with her outburst, "Gwenhwyfar has a husband, she is wife to the High King, and her husband is the most honorable and kindly king ever to rule these lands! She has no need to look elsewhere for love! Yet how can Lancelet turn away to seek any other lady, if the Queen stretches out her hand?"

"Well," said Morgaine, "perhaps now she and Lancelet will go forth from this court. Lancelet has lands in Less Britain, and they have loved one another long, though I think that till this mishap, they had lived as Christian man and woman." Silently she absolved herself for the lie; what Lancelet had told her in his agony was to be held forever in the depths of her heart.

"But then would Arthur be the laughingstock of every Christian king in these islands," said Elaine shrewdly. "If his queen should flee out of his lands with his best friend and his captain of horse, they would call him cuckold or worse."

"I do not think Arthur will care what they say of him," Morgaine began, but Elaine shook her head.

"No, Morgaine, but he must care. The lesser kings must respect him so that they will rally to his standard when there is need. How can they do so when he allows his wife to live in open sin with Lancelet? Yes, I know you speak of these few days. But can we be certain it will stop at that? My father is Arthur's friend and vassal, but I think even he would mock at a king who could not rule his wife, and wonder how such a one could rule a kingdom."

Morgaine shrugged and said, "What can we do, short of murdering the guilty pair?"

"What talk!" said Elaine with a shudder. "No, but Lancelet must leave the court. You are his kinswoman, cannot you make him see that?"

"Alas," said Morgaine, "I fear I have but little influence with my kinsman in that way." And inside it was as if some cold thing seized her with its teeth.

"If Lancelet were married," said Elaine, and suddenly it seemed as if she wrenched at her own courage. "If he were married to me! Morgaine, you are wise in charms and spells, cannot you give me a charm which will turn Lancelet's eyes from Gwenhwyfar to me? I am a king's daughter too, and I am certainly as beautiful as Gwenhwyfar—and I at least have no husband!"

Morgaine laughed bitterly. "My spells, Elaine, can be worse than useless—ask Gwenhwyfar one day how such a spell rebounded upon her! But Elaine," she said, suddenly serious, "would you truly travel that road?"

"I think that if he married me," Elaine said, "he would come to see that I am no less worthy of love than Gwenhwyfar."

Morgaine put her hand under the young woman's chin and turned up her face. "Listen, my child," she began, and Elaine felt that the dark eyes of the sorceress were searching into her very soul. "Elaine, this would not be easy. You have said you love him, but love when a maiden speaks so is no more than a fancy. Do you truly know what kind of a man he is? Is this a fancy which could endure for all the years of a marriage? If you wanted only to lie with him—*that* I could arrange easily enough. But when the glamour of the spell had worn off, he might well hate you because you had tricked him. And what then?"

Elaine said, stammering, "Even that . . . even that I will risk. Morgaine, my father has offered me to other men, but he has promised me that he will never force my will. I tell you, if I cannot marry Lancelet, I shall go behind convent walls for all of my life, I swear it. . . ." The girl's whole body trembled, but she did not weep. "But why should I turn to you, Morgaine? Like all of us, like Gwenhwyfar herself, *you* would have Lancelet, whether as husband or paramour, and the King's sister may choose for herself. . . ."

Then, for a moment, Elaine thought her eyes tricked her, for in the cold eyes of the sorceress it seemed that tears gathered. Something in her voice made Elaine's eyes sting too. "Ah, no, child, Lancelet would not have me, even if Arthur bade him. Believe me, Elaine, you would have small happiness with Lancelet."

Elaine said, "I do not think women have ever much happiness in marriage—only young girls think so, and I am not so young. But a woman must marry some time or other, and I would rather have Lancelet." Then she burst out, "I do not think you can do anything of the sort! Why do you mock me? Are your charms and spells all moonlight rubbish, then?"

She had expected Morgaine to flare up at her, to defend her own craft, but Morgaine sighed and shook her head and said, "I put not much faith in love charms and spells, I told you that when first we spoke. They are for concentrating the will of the ignorant. The craft of Avalon is a very different thing, and not lightly to be invoked because a maiden would rather lie with one man than another."

"Oh, it is ever so with the craft of the wise," Elaine burst out scornfully. "I could do thus or thus, but I will not because it would not be right to meddle in the work of the Gods, or the stars are not right, or what have you. . . ."

Morgaine sighed, a heavy sound. "Kinswoman, I can give you Lancelet for husband, if that is truly what you desire. I do not think it will make you happy, but you are so far wise, you have said that you expect not happiness in marriage . . . believe me, Elaine, I want nothing more than to see Lancelet well wedded and away from this court and from the Queen. Arthur is my brother, and I would not see shame brought upon him, as soon or late it must be. But you are to remember that you asked me for this. See that you do not whimper when it turns to bitterness."

"I swear I will abide whatever comes, if I can have him for husband," Elaine said. "But why would you do this, Morgaine? Is it simply out of spite for Gwenhwyfar?"

"Believe that if you will, or believe I love Arthur too well to see scandal destroy what he has wrought here," Morgaine said steadily, "and bear in mind, Elaine, charms seldom work as you expect they will. . . ."

When the Gods had set their will, what did it matter what any mortal did, even with charms and spells? Viviane had set Arthur on the throne . . . yet the Goddess had done her own will and not Viviane's, for she had denied Arthur any son by his queen. And when she, Morgaine, had sought to remedy what the Goddess had left undone, the rebound of that charm had thrown Gwenhwyfar and Lancelet together into this scandalous love.

Well, *that* at least she could remedy, by making it sure that Lancelet made an honorable marriage. And Gwenhwyfar too was trapped; she would be glad, perhaps, of something to break this deadlock.

Her mouth twitched a little in something that was not quite a smile. "Beware, Elaine, there is a wise saying: Have a care what you pray for, it might be given you. I can give you Lancelet for husband, but I will ask a gift in return."

"What can I give you that you would value, Morgaine? You care not for jewels, that I have seen. . . ."

"I want neither jewels nor riches," Morgaine said, "only this. You will bear Lancelet children, for I have seen his son . . ." and she stopped, feeling her skin prickle all the way up her spine, as when the Sight came upon her. Elaine's blue eyes were wide with wonder. She could almost hear Elaine's thought, *So it is true then, and I will have Lancelet for husband and give him children. . . .*

Yes, it is true, though I did not know it until I spoke . . . if I work within the Sight, then I am not meddling with what should be left to the Goddess, and so the way will be made clear for me.

"I will say nothing of your son," Morgaine said steadily. "He must do his own fate. . . ." She shook her head to clear it of the strange darkness of the Sight. "I ask only that you give me your first daughter to be schooled at Avalon."

Elaine's eyes were wide. "In sorcery?"

"Lancelet's own mother was High Priestess of Avalon," Morgaine said. "I will bear no daughter for the Goddess. If through my doing you give Lancelet the son which every man craves, you must swear to me—swear by your own God—that you will send me your daughter for fostering."

The room seemed full of a ringing silence. At last Elaine said, "If all this comes to pass, and if I have Lancelet's son, then I swear you shall have his daughter for Avalon. I swear it by the name of Christ," she said, and made the sign of the cross.

Morgaine nodded. "And in turn I swear," she said, "that she shall be as the daughter I shall never bear to the Goddess, and that she shall avenge a great wrong. . . ."

Elaine blinked. "A great wrong—Morgaine, what are you speaking of?"

Morgaine swayed a little; the ringing silence in the room was broken. She was aware of the sound of rain outside the windows, and of a chill in the chamber. She frowned and said, "I do not know—my mind wandered. Elaine, this thing cannot be done here. You must beg leave to go and see your father, and you must make certain that I am invited to go and bear you company. I will see to it that Lancelet is there." She drew a long breath, and turned to take up her gown. "And as for Lancelet, we must by now have given him time to be gone from the Queen's chamber. Come, Gwenhwyfar will be awaiting us."

And indeed when Elaine and Morgaine reached the Queen, there was no sign of the presence there of Lancelet, or any other man. But once, when Elaine was for a moment beyond earshot, Gwenhwyfar met Morgaine's eyes, and Morgaine thought she had never seen such awful bitterness.

"You despise me, do you not, Morgaine?"

For once, Morgaine thought, *Gwenhwyfar has voiced the question that has been in her thoughts all these weeks.* She felt like hurling back a sharp answer —*If I do so, is it not because you have first despised me?* But she said as gently as she could, "I am not your confessor, Gwenhwyfar, and you, not I, are the one who professes belief in a God who will damn you because you share your bed with a man who is not your husband. My Goddess is gentler with women."

"He should have been," Gwenhwyfar burst out, then stopped herself and said, "Arthur is your brother, in your eyes he can do no wrong—"

"I said not that." Morgaine could not bear the wretchedness in the younger woman's face. "Gwenhwyfar, my sister, none has accused you—"

But Gwenhwyfar turned away. She said between clenched teeth, "No, and I want not your pity either, Morgaine."

Want it, or want it not, it is yours, Morgaine thought, but she did not put the thought into words; she was not a healer, to probe old wounds and make them bleed. "Are you ready to break your fast, Gwenhwyfar? What will you choose to eat?"

More and more, in this court, since there is no war, it is as if I were her servant, and she nobler than I. It was, Morgaine thought dispassionately, a game they all played, and she did not begrudge it to Gwenhwyfar. But there were in this kingdom noblewomen who might; and she liked it not, either, that Arthur accepted this, that now there were no wars to be fought, Arthur assumed that his old Companions should now be his personal attendants, even though they might be kings or lords in their own right. At Avalon she had willingly served Viviane because the old woman was the living representative of the Goddess, and her wisdom and magical powers put her almost beyond the human. But she had known, too, that the same powers were available to her, if she would work seriously to attain them; and a day could come when she would have the reverence, too, if she took on the power of the Goddess.

But for a war leader of the land, or for his consort—no, such powers were not suitable except in war itself, and it angered her that Arthur should keep his court in such state, assuming a power which should belong only to the greatest Druids and priestesses. *Arthur bears the sword of Avalon still, and if he keeps not his oath to Avalon, they will require it at his hands.*

And then it seemed to Morgaine that the room grew still all around her and seemed to open itself out as if everything were very far away; she could still see Gwenhwyfar, her mouth half opened to speak, but at the same time it seemed she could see *through* the woman's body, as if she were in the fairy kingdom. Everything seemed, all at once, distant and small and looming over her, and there was a deep silence within her head. In that silence she saw the walls of a pavilion, and Arthur sleeping with Excalibur naked in his hand. And she bent over him—she could not take the sword, but with Viviane's little sickle knife she cut the strings that bound the scabbard to his waist; it was old now, the velvet frayed and the precious metal of the embroideries dulled and tarnished. Morgaine took the scabbard in her hand, and then she was on the shores of a great lake, with the sound of reeds washing around over her. . . .

"I said, no, I do not want any wine, I am weary of wine for breakfast," Gwenhwyfar remarked. "Perhaps Elaine could find some new milk in the kitchens—Morgaine? Have you gone into a swoon?"

Morgaine blinked and stared at Gwenhwyfar. Slowly she came back, trying to focus her eyes. None of it was true, she was not riding madly along the shores of a lake with the scabbard in her hand . . . yet all this place had the look of the fairy world, as if she saw everything through rippling water, and it was somehow like a dream she had had once, if she could only remember . . . and even while she assured the other women that she was quite all right, promising to go herself to the dairy for fresh milk if there was none in the kitchen, still her mind led her through the labyrinths of the dream . . . if she could only remember what it was that she had dreamed, all would be well. . . .

But as she went down into the fresh air, cool even in summer, she felt no longer as if this world might melt at any moment into the world of fairy. Her head ached as if it had been split asunder, and all that day she was held captive by the strange spell of her waking dream. If only she could remember . . . she had flung Excalibur into the Lake, that was it, so that the fairy queen might not have it . . . no, that was not it, either . . . and her mind would begin again to try and unreel the strange obsessive path of her dream.

But past noon, when the sun was falling toward evening, she heard the horns announcing Arthur's arrival, and felt the stir which ran all through Camelot. With the other women she ran out to the earthworks at the edge of the heights and watched the royal party riding toward them, banners flying. Gwenhwyfar was trembling at her side. She was taller than Morgaine, but somehow, with her slender pale hands and the fragility of her narrow shoulders, it seemed to Morgaine that Gwenhwyfar was only a child, a tall, lanky child, nervous at some imaginary mischief which must be punished. She touched Morgaine's sleeve with her trembling hand.

"Sister—must my lord know? It is done and Meleagrant is dead. There is no reason for Arthur to make war on anyone. Why should he not think that my lord Lancelet reached me in time—in time to prevent—" Her voice was only a thin treble, like a little girl's, and she could not speak the words.

"Sister," said Morgaine, "it is for you to tell or not."

"But—if he heard it elsewhere—"

Morgaine sighed; could not Gwenhwyfar have said for once what she meant? "If Arthur hears aught to distress him, he will not hear it from me, and there is no other has the right to speak. But he cannot lay it to your charge that you were trapped and beaten into submission."

And then she knew, as if she had heard it, the voice of a priest speaking to the trembling Gwenhwyfar—was it now or when Gwenhwyfar was a child?—saying that no woman was ever ravished save she had tempted some man to it, as Eve led our first father Adam into sin; that the Holy Virgin martyrs of Rome had willingly died rather than lay down their chastity . . . it was *this* made Gwenhwyfar tremble. Somewhere in her mind, dismiss it how she might or try to smother the knowledge in Lancelet's arms, she truly believed it was her fault, that she merited death for the sin of having lived to be ravaged. And since she had not died first, Arthur had the right to kill her for it . . . no reassurances would ever quiet that voice in Gwenhwyfar's mind.

She feels this guilt over Meleagrant so that she need feel none for what she has done with Lancelet. . . .

Gwenhwyfar was shivering at her side, despite the warm sun. "I would he were here, that we might go indoors. Look, there are hawks flying in the sky. I am afraid of hawks, always I am afraid they will swoop down on me. . . ."

"They would find you too big and tough a mouthful, I am afraid, sister," Morgaine said amiably.

Servants were heaving at the great gates, opening them for the royal party to ride through. Sir Ectorius still limped heavily from the night he had spent imprisoned in the cold, but he came forward at Cai's side, and Cai, as keeper of his castle, bowed before Arthur.

"Welcome home, my lord and king."

Arthur dismounted and came to embrace Cai.

"This is an overly formal welcome to my home, Cai, you rascal—is all well here?"

"All is well here *now,* my lord," said Ectorius, "but once again you have cause to be grateful to your captain."

"True," said Gwenhwyfar, coming forward, her hand laid lightly in Lancelet's. "My lord and king, Lancelet saved me from a trap laid by a traitor, saved me from such a fate as no Christian woman should suffer."

Arthur laid one hand in his queen's and the other in that of his captain of horse. "I am, as always, grateful to you, my dear friend, and so is my wife. Come, we shall speak about this in private." And, moving between the two of them, he went up the steps into the castle.

"I wonder what manner of lies they will hurry to pour into his ears, that chaste queen and her finest of knights?" Morgaine heard the words, spoken low and very clear, from somewhere in the crowd; but she could not tell from where they came. She thought, *Perhaps peace is not an unmixed blessing: without a war, there is nothing for them to do at court, with their usual occupation gone, but pass on every rumor and bit of scandal.*

But if Lancelet were gone from the court, then would the scandal be quieted. And she resolved that whatever she could do to accomplish that end, would be done at once.

THAT NIGHT at supper Arthur asked Morgaine to bring her harp and sing to them. "It seems long since I heard your music, sister," he said, and drew her close and kissed her. He had not done this in a long time.

"I will sing gladly," she said, "but when will Kevin return to court?" She thought with bitterness of their quarrel; never, never should she forgive him his treason to Avalon! Yet, against her will, she missed him and thought regretfully of the time when they had been lovers.

I am weary of lying alone, that is all. . . .

But this made her think of Arthur, and her son at Avalon . . . if Gwenhwyfar should leave this court, then surely Arthur would marry again;

but it looked not like that at this moment. And should Gwenhwyfar never bear a son, then should not *their* son be acknowledged as his father's heir? He was doubly of royal blood, the blood of the Pendragon and of Avalon . . . Igraine was dead and the scandal could not harm her.

She sat on a carven and gilded stool near the throne, her harp on the floor at her feet; Arthur and Gwenhwyfar sat close together, hand in hand. Lancelet sprawled on the floor at Morgaine's side, watching the harp, but now and again she saw his eyes move to Gwenhwyfar and she quailed at the terrible longing there; how could he show his heart like this to any onlooker? And then Morgaine knew that only she could see his heart—to all other eyes he was only a courtier looking respectfully at his queen, laughing and jesting with her as a privileged friend of her husband.

And as her hands moved on the strings, the world again seemed to fall into the distance, very small and far and at the same time huge and strange, things losing their shapes so that her harp seemed at once a child's toy and something monstrous, a huge formless thing smothering her, and she was high on a throne somewhere peering through wandering shadows, looking down at a young man with dark hair, a narrow coronet around his brow, and as she looked on him, the sharp pain of desire ran down her body, she met his eyes and it was as if a hand touched her in her most private part, rousing her to hunger and longing. . . . She felt her fingers falter on the strings, she had dreamed something . . . a face wavering, a young man's smile at her, no, it was not Lancelet but some other . . . no, it was all like shadows—

Gwenhwyfar's clear voice broke through. "See to the lady Morgaine," she said, "my sister is faint—!"

She felt Lancelet's arms supporting her and looked up into his dark eyes —it was like her dream, desire running through her, melting her . . . no, but she had dreamed that. It was not real. She put her hand confusedly to her brows. "It was the smoke, the smoke from the hearth—"

"Here, sip this." Lancelet held a cup to her lips. What madness was this? He had barely touched her and she felt sick with desire for him; she thought she had long forgotten that, had had it burned out of her over the years . . . and yet his touch, gentle and impersonal, roused her to fierce longing again. Had she dreamed about him, then?

He does not want me, he does not want any woman save the Queen, she thought, and stared past him at the hearth, where no fire burned in this summer season, and a wreath of green bay leaves twined to keep the empty fireplace from gaping too black and ugly. She sipped at the wine Lancelet held for her.

"I am sorry—I have been a little faint all the day," she said, remembering the morning. "Let some other take the harp, I cannot. . . . "

Lancelet said, "By your leave, my lords, I will sing!" He took the harp and said, "This is a tale of Avalon, which I heard in my childhood. I think it was written by Taliesin himself, though he may have made it from an older song."

He began to sing an old ballad, of Arianrhod the queen, who had stepped over a stream and come away with child; and she had cursed her son when he was born, and said he should never have a name till she gave him one, and how he tricked her into giving him a name, and later how she cursed him and said he should never have a wife, whether of flesh and blood, nor yet of the fairy folk, and so he made him a woman of flowers. . . .

Morgaine sat listening, still twined in her dream, and it seemed to her that Lancelet's dark face was filled with terrible suffering, and as he sang of the flower woman, Blodeuwedd, his eyes lingered for a moment on the queen. But then he turned to Elaine, and sang courteously of how the blossom woman's hair was made of fine golden lilies, and how her cheeks were like the petals of the apple blossom, and she was clad in all the colors of the flowers that bloom, blue and crimson and yellow, in the fields of summer. . . .

Morgaine sat quietly in her place, cushioning her aching head in her hand. Later Gawaine brought out a pipe from his own northern country, and began to play a wild lament, filled with the cries of sea birds and sorrow. Lancelet came and sat near to Morgaine, taking her hand gently.

"Are you better now, kinswoman?"

"Oh, yes—it has happened before," Morgaine said. "It is as if I had fallen into a dream and saw all things through shadows—" And yet, she thought, it was not quite like that either.

"My mother said something like that to me once," said Lancelet, and Morgaine gauged his sorrow and weariness by that; never before had he spoken to her, nor to any other as far as she knew, of his mother or of his years at Avalon. "She seemed to think it was a thing which came of itself with the Sight. Once she said it was as if she were drawn into the fairy country and looking out from there as its prisoner, but I know not if she had ever been within the fairy country or if this was but a way of speaking. . . ."

But I have, Morgaine thought, and it is not like that, not quite . . . it is like trying to remember a dream that has faded. . . .

"I myself have known it a little," Lancelet said. "It comes at a time when I cannot see clearly, but only as if all things were very far away and not real . . . and I could not quite touch them but must first cross a weary distance . . . perhaps it is something in the fairy blood we bear—" He sighed and rubbed his eyes. "I used to taunt you with that, when you were only

a little maiden, do you recall, I called you Morgaine of the Fairies and it
made you angry?"

She nodded. "I remember well, kinsman," she said, thinking that for
all the weariness in his face, the new lines there, the touch of grey in the
crisp curls of his hair, he was still more beautiful to her, more beloved, than
any other man she had ever known. She blinked her eyes fiercely; so it was
and so it must be: he loved her as kinswoman, no more.

Again it seemed to her that the world moved behind a barrier of
shadows; it mattered nothing what she did. This world was no more real
than the fairy kingdom. Even the music sounded faraway and distant—
Gawaine had taken up the harp and was singing some tale he had heard
among the Saxons, of a monster who dwelled in a lake and how one of their
heroes had gone down into the lake and ripped off the monster's arm, then
faced the monster's mother in her evil den. . . .

"A grim and grisly tale," she said under her breath to Lancelet, and
he smiled and said, "Most Saxon tales are so. War and bloodshed and heroes
with skill in battle and not much else in their thick noddles. . . . "

"And now we are to live at peace with them, it seems," Morgaine said.

"Aye. So it shall be. I can live with the Saxons, but not with what
they call music . . . though their tales are entertaining enough, I suppose,
for a long evening by the hearth." He sighed, and said, almost inaudibly,
"I think perhaps I was not born for sitting by a hearth, either—"

"You would like to be out in battle again?"

He shook his head. "No, but I am weary of the court." Morgaine saw
his eyes go to where Gwenhwyfar sat beside Arthur, smiling as she listened
to Gawaine's tale. Again he sighed, a sound that seemed ripped up from the
very deeps of his soul.

"Lancelet," she said, quietly and urgently, "you must be gone from
here or you will be destroyed."

"Aye, destroyed body and soul," he said, staring at the floor.

"About your soul I know nothing—you must ask a priest about
that—"

"Would that I could!" said Lancelet with suppressed violence; he
struck his fist softly on the floor beside her harp, so that the strings jangled
a little. "Would that I could believe there is just such a God as the Christians
claim. . . ."

"You *must* go, cousin. Go on some quest like Gareth's, to kill ruffians
who are holding the land to ransom, or to kill dragons, or what you will,
but you must go!"

She saw his throat move as he swallowed. "And what of *her?*"

Morgaine said quietly, "Believe this or no, I am her friend too. Think
you not, she has a soul to be saved as well?"

"Why, you give me counsel as good as any priest." His smile was bitter.

"It takes no priesthood to know when two men—and a woman as well —are trapped, and cannot escape from what has been," said Morgaine. "It would be easy to blame her for all. But I, too, know what it is to love where I cannot—" She stopped and looked away from him, feeling scalding heat rise in her face; she had not meant to say so much. The song had ended, and Gawaine yielded up the harp, saying, "After this grim tale we need something light—a song of love, perhaps, and I leave that to the gallant Lancelet—"

"I have sat too long at court singing songs of love," said Lancelet, rising and turning toward Arthur. "Now that you are here again, my lord, and can see to all things yourself, I beg you to send me forth from this court on some quest."

Arthur smiled at his friend. "Will you be gone so soon? I cannot keep you if you are longing to be away, but where would you go?"

Pellinore and his dragon. Morgaine, her eyes cast down, staring and seeing the flicker of the fire past her lids, formed the words in her mind with all the force she could manage, trying to thrust them into Arthur's mind. Lancelet said, "I had it in mind to go after a dragon—"

Arthur's eyes glinted with mischief. "It might be well, at that, to make an end of Pellinore's dragon. The tales grow daily greater, so that men are afraid to travel into that country! Gwenhwyfar tells me Elaine has asked for leave to visit her home. You may escort the lady thither, and I bid you not return until Pellinore's dragon is dead."

"Alas," protested Lancelet, laughing, "would you exile me from your court for all time? How can I kill a dragon who is but a dream?"

Arthur chuckled. "May you never meet a dragon worse than that, my friend! Well, I charge you to make an end for all time of that dragon, even if you must laugh it out of existence by making a ballad of it!"

Elaine rose and curtseyed to the King. "By your leave, my lord, may I ask that the lady Morgaine visit me for a time as well?"

Morgaine said, not looking at Lancelet, "I would like to go with Elaine, my brother, if your lady can spare me. There are herbs and simples in that country about which I know little, and I would learn of them from the country wives. I need them for medicines and charms."

"Well," said Arthur, "you may go if you will. But it will be lonely here without you all." He smiled his rare, gentle smile at Lancelet. "My court is not my court without my best of knights. But I would not hold you here against your will, and neither would my queen."

I am not so sure of that, Morgaine thought, watching Gwenhwyfar struggling to compose her face. Arthur had been long away; he was eager to be reunited with his wife. Would Gwenhwyfar tell him honestly that she loved another, or would she go meekly to his bed and pretend again?

And for a bizarre moment Morgaine saw herself as the Queen's shadow . . . *somehow her fate and mine have gotten all entangled* . . . she, Morgaine, had had Arthur and borne him a son, which Gwenhwyfar longed to do; Gwenhwyfar had had Lancelet's love for which Morgaine would willingly have given her soul . . . *it is just like the God of the Christians to make such blunders—he does not like lovers. Or is it the Goddess who jests cruelly with us?*

Gwenhwyfar beckoned to Morgaine. "You look ill, sister. Are you still faint?"

Morgaine nodded. *I must not hate her. She is as much victim as I.* . . . "I am still a little weary. I will go to rest soon."

"And tomorrow," Gwenhwyfar said, "you and Elaine are to take Lancelet from us." The words were spoken lightly, as a jest, but Morgaine seemed to see very deep into Gwenhwyfar, where the woman was fighting rage and despair like her own. *Ah, our fates are entangled by the Goddess, and who can fight her will* . . . but she hardened her heart against the other woman's despair and said, "What is the good of a queen's champion, if he is not away fighting for what seems good to him? Would you hold him at court and away from the winning of honor, my sister?"

"Neither of us would want that," Arthur said, coming up behind Gwenhwyfar and laying his arm around her waist. "Since by the goodwill of my friend and champion, my queen is here and safe when I return. Good night to you, my sister."

Morgaine stood and watched them move away from her, and after a moment she felt Lancelet's hand on her shoulder. He did not speak, but stood silent, watching Arthur and Gwenhwyfar. And as she stood there, silent, she knew that if she made a single move, she could have Lancelet this night. In his despair, now when he saw the woman he loved returning to her husband, and that husband so dear to him that he could not lift a hand to take her, he would turn to Morgaine if she would have him.

And he is too honorable not to marry me afterward. . . .

No. Elaine would have him, perhaps, on those terms, but not I. She is guileless; he will not come to hate her, as he would certainly come to hate me.

Gently she removed Lancelet's hand from her shoulder. "I am weary, my kinsman. I am also for my bed. Good night, my dear. Bless you." And, knowing the irony of it, said, "Sleep well," knowing he would not. Well, so much the better for the plan she had made.

But much of that night she too lay unsleeping, bitterly regretting her own foreknowledge. Pride, she thought drearily, was a cold bedfellow.

6

In **Avalon** *the Tor rose, crowned with the ring stones, and on the night of the darkened moon, the procession wound slowly upward, with torches. At their head walked a woman, pale hair braided in a crown over a broad, low forehead; she was robed in white, the sickle knife hanging at her girdle. By the light of the flaring torches, it seemed that she sought out Morgaine where she stood in the shadows outside the circle, and her eyes demanded. Where are you, you who should stand here in my place? Why do you linger? Your place is here. . . .*

Arthur's kingdom is slipping from the Lady's grasp, and you are letting it go. Already he turns for all things to the priests, while you, who should stand in the place of the Goddess to him, will not move. He holds the sword of the Holy Regalia; is it you who will force him to live by it, or you who will take it from his hand and bring him down? Remember, Arthur has a son, and his son must grow to maturity in Avalon, that he may hand the kingdom of the Goddess down to his son. . . .

And then it seemed that Avalon faded away and she saw Arthur in desperate battle, Excalibur in his hand, and he fell, run through by another sword, and he flung Excalibur into the Lake that it might not fall into the hands of his son. . . .

Where is Morgaine, whom the Lady prepared for this day? Where is she who should stand in the place of the Goddess for this hour?

Where is the Great Raven? And suddenly it seemed to me that a flight of ravens wheeled overhead, diving and pecking at my eyes, circling down at me, crying aloud in Raven's own voice, "Morgaine! Morgaine, why have you deserted us, why did you betray me?"

"I cannot," I cried, "I do not know the way . . ." but Raven's face melted into the accusing face of Viviane, and then into the shadow of the Old Death-crone. . . .

And Morgaine woke, knowing she lay in a sunlit room in Pellinore's house; the walls were white with plaster, painted in the old Roman fashion. Only outside the windows, far off and distant, she could hear the cry of a raven somewhere, and shivered.

Viviane had never scrupled to meddle with the lives of others, when it meant the good of Avalon or of the kingdom. Nor should she. Yet she herself had delayed as the sunny days sped by. Lancelet spent the days on the hills by the Lake, searching for the dragon—*as if there actually were a dragon,* Morgaine thought scornfully—and the evenings by the fire, exchanging songs and tales with Pellinore, singing to Elaine while sitting at her feet. Elaine was beautiful and innocent, and not unlike her cousin

Gwenhwyfar, though five years younger. Morgaine let day after sunny day slide by, sure that they all must see the logic of it, that Lancelet and Elaine should marry.

No, she told herself bitterly, if any of them had had any wit to see logic or reason, then should Lancelet have married me years ago. Now it was time to act.

Elaine turned over in the bed they shared and opened her eyes; she smiled and curled up next to Morgaine. *She trusts me,* thought Morgaine painfully; *she thinks I am helping her to win Lancelet out of friendship. If I hated her I could do her no worse harm.* But she said quietly, "Now Lancelet has had enough time to feel the loss of Gwenhwyfar. Your time has come, Elaine."

"Will you give Lancelet a charm or a love potion . . . ?"

Morgaine laughed. "I put small trust in love charms, though tonight he shall have something in his wine which will make him ready for any woman. Tonight you shall not sleep here, but in a pavilion near the woods, and Lancelet shall have a message that Gwenhwyfar has come and has sent for him. And so he will come to you, in the darkness. I can do no more than that—you must be ready for him—"

"And he will think I am Gwenhwyfar—" She blinked, swallowing hard. "Well, then—"

"He may think you are Gwenhwyfar for a short while," Morgaine said, steadily, "but he will know soon enough. You are a virgin, are you not, Elaine?"

The girl's face was crimson, but she nodded.

"Well, after the potion I have given him, he will not be able to stop himself," said Morgaine, "unless you should panic and try to fight him away from you—I warn you, it will not be all that much pleasure, since you are a virgin. Once I begin I cannot turn back, so say now whether you wish me to begin."

"I will have Lancelet for my husband, and God forbid I should ever turn back before I am honorably his wife."

Morgaine sighed. "So be it. Now—you know the scent Gwenhwyfar uses . . ."

"I know it, but I do not like it much, it is too strong for me."

Morgaine nodded. "I make it for her—you know I am schooled in such things. When you go to bed in the pavilion, you must scent your body and your bedclothes with it. It will turn his mind to Gwenhwyfar and arouse him with that memory—"

The younger woman wrinkled her nose in distaste. "It seems unfair—"

"It *is* unfair," said Morgaine. "Make up your mind to that. What we are doing is dishonest, Elaine, but there's good to it too. Arthur's kingdom cannot long stand if the King is known a cuckold. When you are wedded a while, since you and Gwenhwyfar are so much alike, no doubt it will be put round that it was you Lancelet loved all this time." She gave Elaine the flask of scent. "Now, if you have a servant you can trust, have him put up the pavilion somewhere Lancelet will not see it till this night. . . ."

Elaine said, "Even the priest would approve, I doubt it not, since I am taking him away from adultery with a married woman. I am free to marry. . . ."

Morgaine felt her own smile thin and strained. "Well for you, if you can quiet your conscience so . . . some priests say so, that the end is all, and whatever means be used, they are for the best . . ."

She realized that Elaine was still standing, like a child at lessons, before her. "Well, go, Elaine," she said, "go and send Lancelet away another day to hunt the dragon. I must prepare my charm."

She watched them as they shared cup and plate at breakfast. Lancelet was fond of Elaine, she thought—fond as he might be of a friendly little dog. He would not be unkind to her when they were married.

Viviane had been just as ruthless as this, she had not scrupled to send a brother to the bed of his own sister. . . . Morgaine worried the memory painfully, like a sore tooth. This too is for the good of the kingdom, she thought, and as she went to hunt out her herbs and medicines, to steep them in wine for the potion she would give Lancelet, she tried to form a prayer to the Goddess who joined man and women in love, or in simple lust like the rutting of beasts.

Goddess, I know enough of lust . . . she thought, and steadied her hands, breaking the herbs and dropping them into the wine. *I have felt his desire, though he would not give me what I would have had from him.* . . .

She sat watching the slow simmering of the herbs in the wine; small bubbles rose, lazily broke, and spat bittersweet essences which fumed around her. The world seemed very small and far away, her brazier but a child's toy, each bubble that rose in the wine large enough that she could have floated away inside it . . . her whole body aching with a desire she knew would never be slaked. She could sense that she was moving into the state where powerful magic could be made. . . .

It seemed she was both within and without the castle, that a part of her was out on the hills, following the Pendragon banner which Lancelet sometimes carried . . . twisting, a great red dragon . . . but there were no dragons, not this kind of dragon, and Pellinore's dragon, it was surely only a jest, a dream, as unreal as the banner which flew somewhere, far to the southward, over the walls of Camelot, a dragon invented by some artist for the banner, like the designs Elaine drew for her tapestry. And Lancelet surely knew this. Following the dragon, he was but enjoying a pleasant ride over the summer hills, following a dream and a fantasy, leaving him leisure for daydreaming of Gwenhwyfar's arms. . . . Morgaine looked down at the bubbling liquid in her little brazier, drop by drop added a little more wine to the mixture, that it would not boil away. He would dream of Gwenhwyfar, and that night there would be a woman in his arms, wearing Gwenhwyfar's perfume. But first Morgaine would give him this potion which would put him at the mercy of the rut in him, so that he would not stop when he found he held not an experienced woman and his paramour, but a shrinking virgin. . . . For a moment Morgaine stopped to pity Elaine, because what she was cold-bloodedly arranging was certainly something like rape. Much as Elaine longed for Lancelet, she was a virgin and had no real idea of the difference between her romantic dreams of his kisses, and what really awaited her—being taken by a man too drugged to know the difference. Whatever it was for Elaine, and however bravely she endured it, it would hardly be a romantic episode.

I gave up my maidenhood to the King Stag . . . yet that was different. From childhood I had known what awaited me, and I had been taught and reared in the worship of that Goddess who brings man and woman together in love or in rut. . . . Elaine was reared a Christian and taught to think of that very life force as the original sin for which mankind was doomed to death. . . .

For a moment she thought she should seek out Elaine, try to prepare her, encourage her to think of this as the priestesses were taught to think of it: a great force of nature, clean and sinless, to be welcomed as a current of life, sweeping the participant into the torrent . . . but Elaine would think that even worse sin. Well, then, she must make of it what she would; perhaps her love for Lancelet would carry her through it undamaged.

Morgaine turned her thoughts back to simmering the herbs and the wine, and at the same time, somehow, it seemed she was riding on the hills . . . neither was it a fair day for a ride; the sky was dark and clouded, a little wind blowing, the hills bleak and bare. Below the hills the long arm of the sea which was the lake looked grey and fathomless, like fresh-smithied metal; and the surface of the lake began to boil a little, or was it but the water in her brazier? Dark bubbles rose and spilled a foul stench, and then, slowly, rising from the lake, a long, narrow neck crowned with a horse's head and a horse's mane, a long sinuous body, writhing toward the shore . . . rising, crawling, slithering its whole length onto the shore.

Lancelet's hounds were running about, darting down to the water, barking frenziedly. She heard him call out to them in exasperation; stop dead and look down toward the water, paralyzed, only half believing what he saw with his eyes. Then Pellinore blew his hunting horn to summon the others, and Lancelet put spurs to his horse, his spear braced on the saddle, and rode at a breakneck speed down the hill, charging. One of the hounds gave a pitiful scream; then silence, and Morgaine, from her strange distant watch, saw the curiously slimed trail where half the dog's broken body lay eaten away with the dark slime.

Pellinore was charging at it, and she heard Lancelet's shout to warn him back from riding directly at the great beast . . . it was black and like a great worm, all but that mockery of a horse's head and mane. Lancelet rode at it, avoiding the weaving head, thrusting his long spear directly into the body. A wild howl shook the shore, a crazed banshee scream . . . she saw the great head weaving wildly back and forth, back and forth . . . Lancelet flung himself from his rearing, bucking horse, and ran on foot toward the monster. The head weaved down, and Morgaine flinched, as she saw the great mouth open. Then Lancelet's sword pierced the eye of the dragon, and there was a great gush of blood and some black foul stuff . . . and it was all the bubbles rising from the wine. . . .

Morgaine's heart jumped wildly. She lay back and sipped a little of the undiluted wine in the flask. Had it been an evil dream, or had she actually seen Lancelet kill the dragon in which she had never really believed? She rested there for some time, telling herself that she had dreamed, and then forced herself to rise, to add some sweet fennel to the mixture, for the strong sweetness would conceal the other herbs. And there should be strong salted beef for dinner, so that everyone should thirst and drink a great deal of the wine, especially Lancelet. Pellinore was a pious man—what would he think if all his castle folk went to rutting? No, she should make sure that only Lancelet drank the spiced mixture, and perhaps, in mercy, she should give some to Elaine too. . . .

She poured the spiced wine into a flask and put it aside. Then she heard a cry, and Elaine rushed into her room.

"Oh, Morgaine, come at once, we need your work with simples— Father and Lancelet have slain the dragon, but they are both burned. . . ."

"Burned? What nonsense is this? Do you believe truly that dragons fly and belch fire?"

"No, no," Elaine said impatiently, "but the creature spat some slime at them and it burns like fire—you must come and dress their wounds. . . ."

Disbelieving, Morgaine glanced at the sky outside. The sun was hovering, a bare hand span above the western horizon; she had sat here most of the day. She went quickly, calling to the maids for bandage linen.

Pellinore had a great burn along one arm—yes, it looked very much like a burn; the fabric of his tunic was eaten away by it, and he roared with anguish as she poured healing salve on it. Lancelet's side was burned slightly, and on one leg the stuff had eaten through his boots, leaving the leather only a thin jellylike substance covering his leg. He said, "I should clean my sword well. If it can do that to the leather of a boot, think what it would have done to my leg . . ." and shuddered.

"So much for all those who thought my dragon only a fantasy," said Pellinore, raising his head and sipping the wine his daughter gave him. "And thanks be to God that I had the wit to bathe my arm in the lake, or the slime would have eaten my arm as it dissolved my poor dog—did you see the corpse, Lancelet?"

"The dog? Yes," said Lancelet, "and hope never to see that kind of death again. . . . But you can confound them all when you hang the dragon's head over your gate—"

"I cannot," said Pellinore, crossing himself. "There was no proper bone to it at all, it was all soft like a grub or an earthworm . . . and it has already withered away to slime. I tried to cut the head and the very air seemed to eat away at it. . . . I do not think it was a proper beast at all, but something straight from hell!"

"Still it is dead," Elaine said, "and you have done what the King bade you, made an end once and for all of my father's dragon." She kissed her father, saying with tender apology, "Forgive me, sir, I thought, too, that your dragon was all fancy—"

"Would to God it had been," Pellinore said, crossing himself yet again. "I would rather be a mockery from here to Camelot than face any such *thing* again! I wish I thought there were no more such beasts . . . Gawaine has told tales of what lives in the lochs yonder." He signaled to the potboy for more wine. "I think it would be well to get drunk this night, or I shall see that beast in nightmares for the next month!"

Would that be best? Morgaine wondered. No, if all about the castle were drunk, it would not fit her plans at all. She said, "You must listen to what I say, if I am to care for your wounds, sir Pellinore. You must drink no more, and you must let Elaine take you to bed with hot bricks at your feet. You have lost some blood, and you must have hot soup and possets, but no more wine."

He grumbled but he listened to her, and when Elaine had taken him away, with his body servants, Morgaine was left alone with Lancelet.

"So," she said, "how would you best celebrate your killing of your first dragon?"

He lifted his cup and said, "By praying that it will be my last. I truly thought my hour had come. I would rather face a whole horde of Saxons with no more than my axe!"

"The Goddess grant you have no more such encounters, indeed," Morgaine said, and filled his cup with the spiced wine. "I have made this for you, it is medicinal and will soothe your hurts. I must go and see that

Elaine has Pellinore safely tucked away for the night—"

"But you will come back, kinswoman?" he said, holding her lightly by one wrist; she saw the wine beginning to burn in him. *And more than the wine,* she thought; *an encounter with death sends a man ready for rutting. . . .*

"I will come back, I promise; now let me go," she said, and bitterness flooded her.

So, am I fallen so low that I would have him drugged, not knowing? Elaine will have him that way . . . why is it better for her? But she wants him for husband, for better or worse. Not I. I am a priestess, and I know this thing that burns in me is not of the Goddess, but unholy . . . am I so weak that I would have Gwenhwyfar's castoff garments and her castoff paramour also? And while her scorn cried no, the weakness through her whole body cried yes, so that she was sick with self-contempt as she went along the hall to the chamber of King Pellinore.

"How does your father, Elaine?" She wondered that her voice was so steady.

"He is quiet now, and I think he will sleep."

Morgaine nodded. "Now you must go to the pavilion, and sometime this night Lancelet will come to you. Forget not the scent Gwenhwyfar wears. . . ."

Elaine was very pale, her blue eyes burning. Morgaine reached out and caught her by the arm; she held out a flask with some of the drugged wine in it. She said, and her own voice was shaking, "Drink this first, child."

Elaine raised it to her lips and drank. "It is sweet with herbs . . . is it a love potion?"

Morgaine's smile only stretched her mouth. "You may think it so, if you will."

"Strange, it burns my mouth, and burns me within. . . . Morgaine, it is not poison? You do not—you do not hate me, Morgaine, because I will be Lancelet's wife?"

Morgaine drew the girl close and embraced and kissed her; the warm body in her arms somehow roused her, whether to desire or tenderness she could not tell. "Hate you? No, no, cousin, I swear it to you, I would not have sir Lancelet for husband if he begged me on his knees . . . here, finish the wine, sweeting . . . scent your body here, and here . . . remember what he wants of you. It is you who can make him forget the Queen. Now go, child, wait for him in the pavilion there. . . . " And again she drew Elaine close to her and kissed her. "The Goddess blesses you."

So like to Gwenhwyfar. Lancelet is already half in love with her, I think, and I but complete the work. . . .

She drew a long, shaking breath, composing herself to return to the hall and to Lancelet. He had not hesitated to pour himself more of the drugged wine, and raised fuddled eyes as she came in.

"Ah, Morgaine—kinswoman—" He drew her down beside him. "Drink with me . . ."

"No, not now. Listen to me, Lancelet, I bear a message for you. . . ."

"A message, Morgaine?"

"Yes," she said. "Queen Gwenhwyfar has come hither to visit her kinswoman, and she sleeps in the pavilion beyond the lawns." She took his wrist and drew him along to the door. "And she has sent you a message: she does not wish to disturb her women, so you must go to her very quietly where she is in bed. Will you do that?"

She could see the haze of drunkenness and passion in his dark eyes. "I saw no messenger—Morgaine, I did not know you wished me well. . . ."

"You do not know how well I wish you, cousin."

I wish that you may marry well and cease this hopeless, wretched love for a woman who can only bring you to dishonor and despair. . . .

"Go," she said gently, "your queen awaits you. If you doubt me, this token was sent you." She held out a kerchief; it was Elaine's, but one kerchief is like to another, and it had been all but drenched in the scent associated with Gwenhwyfar.

He pressed it to his lips. "Gwenhwyfar," he whispered. "Where, Morgaine, where?"

"In the pavilion. Finish the wine—"

"Will you drink to me?"

"Later," she said with a smile. His steps faltered a little; he caught at her for support, and his arms went round her. His touch roused her, light as it was. *Lust,* she told herself fiercely, *animal rut, this is nothing blessed by the Goddess. . . .* She struggled for calm. He was drugged like an animal, he would not care, he would take her now mindlessly, as he would have taken Gwenhwyfar, Elaine. . . . "Go, Lancelet, you must not keep your queen waiting."

She saw him disappear in the shadows near the pavilion. He would go in quietly. Elaine would be lying there, the lamp falling on her golden hair so like the Queen's, but so dim he could not distinguish her features, her body and bed smelling of Gwenhwyfar's scent. She tormented herself by imagining, as she turned to pace the long empty room, how his slender naked body would slide under the covers, how he would take Elaine in his arms and cover her with kisses. *If the little fool has but the wit to keep her mouth shut and say nothing till he is done. . . .*

Goddess! Shut away the Sight from me, let me not see Elaine in his arms . . . writhing, racked, Morgaine did not know whether it was her own imagination or the Sight that tortured her with the awareness of Lancelet's naked body, of the touch of his hands . . . how clearly she felt them in memory. . . . She went back into the hall where the servants were clearing the tables and said roughly, "Give me some wine."

Startled, the man poured her a cup. *Now they will think me a sot as well as a witch.* She did not care. She drank down the wine and asked for more. Somehow it cut away the Sight, freed her from her awareness of Elaine, frightened and ecstatic, pinned down under his rough, demanding body. . . .

Restlessly, like a prowling cat, she paced the hall, flickers of the Sight coming and going. When she judged the time was ripe, she drew a long breath, steeling herself for what she knew she must do now. The body servant who slept across the king's door started awake as Morgaine bent to rouse him.

"Madam, you cannot disturb the king at this hour—"

"It concerns his daughter's honor." Morgaine took a torch from the wall bracket and held it aloft; she could sense how she looked to him, tall and terrible, feeling herself merge into the commanding form of the Goddess. He drew aside in terror, and she moved smoothly past.

Pellinore lay in his high bed, tossing restlessly in pain from his bandaged wound. He, too, started awake, looking up at Morgaine's pale face, the torch held high.

"You must come quickly, my lord," she said, her voice smooth and taut with her own controlled passion. "This is betrayal of hospitality . . . I felt it right that you must know. Elaine—"

"Elaine? What—"

"She is not asleep in our bed," Morgaine said. "Come quickly, my lord." She had been wise not to let him drink; she could not have roused him had he slept heavily with wine. Pellinore, startled, incredulous, threw on a garment, shouting for his daughter's women. It seemed to Morgaine that they followed her down the stairs and out the doors as smoothly as the writhing of a dragon, a procession with herself and Pellinore at the serpent's head, and she thrust back the silken flap of the pavilion, holding the torch high and watching with cruel triumph as Pellinore's outraged face was lighted by the torch. Elaine lay with her arms wound around Lancelet's neck, smiling and blissful; Lancelet, coming awake in the torchlight, stared around in shock and awareness, and his face was agonized with betrayal. But he did not say a word.

Pellinore shouted, "Now you will make amends, you lecherous wretch, you who have betrayed my daughter—"

Lancelet buried his face in his hands. He said through them, strangled, "I will—make amends—my lord Pellinore." Then he raised his face and looked straight into Morgaine's eyes. She met them, unflinching; but it was like a sword through her body. Before this, at least, he had loved her as a kinswoman.

Well, better that he should hate her. She would try to hate him, too. But before Elaine's face, shamed and yet smiling, she wanted to cry instead, and beg for them to pardon her.

MORGAINE SPEAKS . . .

Lancelet was married to Elaine on Transfiguration; I remember little of the ceremony save Elaine's face, joyous and smiling. By the time Pellinore had arranged the wedding, she knew already that she bore Lancelet's son in her belly, and although he looked wretched, thin and pallid with despair, he was tender with Elaine, and proud of her swelling body. I remember Gwenhwyfar too, her face drawn with long weeping, and the look of ineradicable hatred that she turned on me.

"Can you swear that this was not your doing, Morgaine?"

I looked her straight in the eye.

"Do you begrudge your kinswoman a husband of her own, as you have one?"

She could not face me at that. And again I told myself, fiercely: Had she and Lancelet been honest with Arthur, had they fled from the court together, to live beyond Arthur's kingdom, so that Arthur could have taken him another wife to get an heir for the kingdom, then I would not have meddled.

But from that day, Gwenhwyfar hated me; and that I regretted most, for in a strange way I had loved her. Gwenhwyfar never seemed to hate her kinswoman; she sent Elaine a rich gift and a silver cup when her son was born, and when Elaine had the boy christened Galahad, for his father, she named herself his godmother and swore that he should be heir to the kingdom if she did not give Arthur a son. Sometime that year she indeed announced she was pregnant, but nothing came of it, and I think, indeed, it was only her desire for a child, and her fancy.

The marriage was no worse than most. That year Arthur had to face war on the northern coast, and Lancelet spent little time at home. Like many husbands, he spent his time at war, coming home two or three times a year to see to their lands—Pellinore had given them a castle near his own—to receive the new cloaks and shirts Elaine wove and embroidered for him—after he married Elaine, Lancelet always dressed as fine as the King himself—to kiss his son, and later his daughters, to sleep with his wife once, or maybe twice, and then he was off again.

Elaine always seemed happy. I do not know whether she was truly happy, being one of those women who can find their best happiness in home and babes, or whether she longed for more than this and yet abode bravely by the bargain she had made.

As for me, I dwelt at court for two more years. And then, at Pentecost of the second year, when Elaine was pregnant with her second child, Gwenhwyfar had her revenge.

7

as with every year, the day of Pentecost was Arthur's high festival. Gwenhwyfar had been awake since earliest daylight. On this day, all of those Companions who had fought at Arthur's side should be at court, and this year Lancelet would be here too . . .

. . . last year he had not come. Word had been sent that he was in Less Britain, answering a call from his father, King Ban, who sought to settle trouble in his kingdom; but Gwenhwyfar knew in her heart why Lancelet had not come, why he had chosen to stay apart.

It was not that she could not forgive his marriage to Elaine. Morgaine and her spite had brought that about—Morgaine, who would have had Lancelet for herself and would stop at nothing to part him from the one he truly loved. Rather than see him in Gwenhwyfar's arms, Gwenhwyfar supposed, Morgaine would have seen him in hell, or in his grave.

Arthur, too, missed Lancelet sorely, that she had seen. Although he sat in his high seat at Camelot, and dealt justice to all manner of men—he was loved, loved far more than any king Gwenhwyfar had heard tell of before this—she could see that always he looked back to the days of battle and conquest; she supposed all men were like that. Arthur would bear to his grave the scars of the wounds he had taken in his great battles. When they had fought year after year to bring peace to the land, he had spoken as if he wished for nothing more than leisure to sit at home in Camelot and enjoy his castle. Now he was never so happy as when he could get some of his old Companions about him, and fall to talking of those old evil days when there were Saxons and Jutes and wild Northmen on every hand.

She looked at Arthur where he lay sleeping. Yes, and he was still the handsomest and goodliest of all his old Companions; at times she thought he was fairer of face and better to look at even than Lancelet, though it was unfair to compare them, one so dark, one so blond. And after all they were cousins, they were of one blood . . . how, she wondered, had Morgaine come into that kindred? Perhaps indeed she was a changeling, nothing human at all, but left by the evil fairy folk to do wickedness among mankind . . . a sorceress schooled in un-Christian ways. Arthur too was tainted by that background, though she had gotten him to go often to mass and to speak of himself as Christian. Morgaine liked not that, either.

Well, she would fight to the last to save Arthur's soul! She loved him well, he was the best husband a woman could ever have had, even had he been no High King but a simple knight. Surely the madness that had seized her was long gone. It was right and fitting she should think kindly of her husband's cousin. Why, it was at Arthur's own will that she had first lain in Lancelet's arms. And now it was all past and over, and she had confessed it and been absolved; her priest had told her it was as if the sin had never been, and now she must strive to forget it.

Yet she could not help remembering, a little, on this morning when Lancelet would be coming to court with his wife and son . . . he was a married man, married to her own cousin. Now he was not only her husband's kinsman but her own kinsman as well. She could greet him with a kiss, and it would be no sin.

Arthur turned over, as if her thoughts could disturb him, and smiled at her.

"It is Pentecost day, sweetheart," he said, "and all of our kinfolk and friends will be here. Let me see you smile."

She smiled at him and he drew her down against him, kissing her and letting his fingers circle her breasts.

"You are certain what we do this day will not offend you? I would not have anyone think you were less to me," he said anxiously. "You are not old, God may yet bless us with children if it is his will. But the lesser kings have demanded it of me—life is never certain, so I must name an heir. When our first son is born, sweet, then it will be as if this day had never been, and I am sure young Galahad will not begrudge the throne to his cousin, but serve and honor him as Gawaine has done for me. . . ."

It might yet be true, Gwenhwyfar thought, surrendering herself to her husband's gentle caresses. There were such things told of in the Bible: the mother of John the Baptizer, who had been cousin to the Virgin—God had opened her womb long after she was past the age of bearing, and she, Gwenhwyfar, was not yet thirty . . . why, Lancelet had said once that his mother was older than this when he was born. Perhaps this time, after all these years, she would arise from her husband's bed bearing again the seed of his son in her body. And now that she had learned not only to submit to him as a good wife must, but to take pleasure in his touch, his manhood filling her, surely she was softened and all the more ready to conceive and bear. . . .

No doubt it was all for the best, when for a time three years ago she had thought she bore Lancelet's child, but something had gone amiss . . . three months she had not had her moon-blood and she had told one or two of her ladies that she was with child; and then, after three more months, when she should have felt the first quickening, it had proved to be nothing after all . . . but now, surely, with this new warmth she had known since she had been all wakened, *this* time it would come about as she wished. And Elaine would not gloat and triumph over her again. . . . She might, for a little time, have been the mother of the King's heir, but Gwenhwyfar would be the mother of the King's son. . . .

She said something like that later, when they were dressing, and Arthur looked at her, troubled. "Is Lancelet's wife unkind or scornful to you, Gwen? I had thought you and your cousin were good friends. . . ."

"Oh, we are," said Gwenhwyfar, blinking back tears, "but it is always so with women . . . those women who have sons think ever they are the betters of any woman who is barren. The wife of the swineherd, in her childbed, no doubt thinks with scorn and pity of the Queen who cannot give her lord so much as a single son."

Arthur came and kissed the back of her neck. "Don't, sweeting, don't cry. I would rather have you than another woman who could have given me a dozen sons already."

"Truly?" Gwenhwyfar said, a hint of scorn in her voice. "Yet I was only something my father gave you with a hundred horsemen, just a part of the bargain—and you took me dutifully to get the horses—but I was a bad bargain—"

He raised his eyes and stared at her with a blue incredulous gaze. "Have you been thinking of that and holding it against me all these years, my Gwen? But surely you must know that since the first moment that I looked on your face, no one could be dearer to me than you!" he said and wound his arms around her. She was rigid, blinking back tears, and he kissed her at the corner of her eye. "Gwenhwyfar, Gwenhwyfar, could you think— you are my wife, beloved, my own dear wife, and nothing on earth could part us. If I wanted only a brood mare to get me sons, God knows I could have had enough of them!"

"But you have not," she said, still stiff and cold in his arms. "I would willingly take your son to foster, and bring him up as your heir. But you thought me not worthy to foster *your* son . . . and it was you who pushed me into Lancelet's arms—"

"Oh, my Gwen," he said, and his face was rueful like a punished child. "Do you hold it against me, that old madness? I was drunk, and it seemed to me that you loved Lancelet well . . . I thought to give you pleasure, and if it might truly be so, that it was my fault you did not bear, then you could have a child by one so close to me that I could in good conscience call whatever child came of that night, my own heir. But mostly it was that I was drunk—"

"At times," she said, her face set like stone, "it has seemed to me that you loved Lancelet more than me. Can you say in truth that it was to give me pleasure, or was it for the pleasure of him you loved best of all——?"

He dropped his arm from her neck as if he were stung. "Is it a sin, then, to love my kinsman and think, too, of his pleasure? It is true, I love you both——"

"In Holy Writ it speaks of that city that was destroyed for such sins," said Gwenhwyfar.

Arthur was as white as his shirt. "I love my kinsman Lancelet with all honor, Gwen; King David himself wrote of his cousin and kinsman Jonathan, *Thy love to me was wonderful, passing the love of woman,* and God smote him not. It is so with comrades in battle. Dare you to say that such a love is a sin, Gwenhwyfar? I will avow it before the throne of God——" He stopped, unable to force further sound through his dry throat.

Gwenhwyfar heard her own voice cracking with hysteria.

"Can you swear that when you brought him to our bed . . . I saw it then, you touched him with more love than ever you have given the woman my father forced on you—when you led me into this sin, can you swear it was not your own sin, and all your fine talk no more than a cover for that very sin that brought down fire from Heaven on the city of Sodom?"

He stared at her, still deathly white. "You are certainly mad, my lady. On that night you speak of—I was drunk, I know not what you may have thought you saw. It was Beltane, and the force of the Goddess was with us all. I think all your prayers and thoughts of sin have turned your mind, my Gwen."

"No Christian man would say so!"

"And that is one reason why I like not to call myself a Christian!" he shouted back at her, losing patience at last. "I am tired of all this talk of sin! If I had put you away from me—aye, and I was counselled to do so, and would not because I loved you too well—and taken another woman——"

"No! Rather would you share me with Lancelet, and have him too——"

"Say that again," he said very low, "and wife or no, love or no, I will kill you, my Gwenhwyfar!"

But she was sobbing hysterically now and could not stop herself. "You say you wished for a son, and so you led me into such sin as God cannot pardon—if I have sinned, and God has punished me with barrenness, was it not you who led me into that sin? And even now, it is Lancelet's son is your heir. Can you dare say it is not Lancelet you love best, when you make his son your heir and not your own son, when you will not give me your son to foster for you——"

"Let me call your women, Gwenhwyfar," he said, with a deep breath. "You are beside yourself. I swear to you, I have no son, or if I do, it is some chance-gotten child from my days in battle, and the woman knew me not, nor who I was. No woman anywhere near my own station has ever come to me and said she bore my child. Priests or no, sin or no, I cannot believe any woman would be ashamed to admit that she had borne the son of a childless High King. I have taken no unwilling woman, nor played at adultery with any man's wife. What is this mad talk of a son of mine you would foster as my heir? I tell you, I have none. I have often wondered if some sickness in boyhood, or that wound I took, might have gelded me . . . I have no son."

"No, but that is a lie!" Gwenhwyfar said angrily. "Morgaine bade me not speak of it, but long ago I went to her, I begged her for a charm to help my barrenness. I was in despair, I said I would give myself to another man, since it was likely you could not father a son. And at that time Morgaine swore to me that you *could* father a child, that she had seen a son of yours, fostered at the court of Lot of Lothian, but she made me promise not to speak of it—"

"Fostered at the court of Lothian . . ." said Arthur, and then he caught at his chest, as if in dreadful pain there. "Ah, merciful God!" he said in a whisper, "and I never knew. . . ."

Gwenhwyfar felt sudden terror striking through her. "No, no, Arthur, Morgaine is a liar! No doubt it was but her malice, it was she who contrived Lancelet's marriage to Elaine, because she was jealous . . . no doubt she was lying to plague me. . . ."

Arthur said in a distant voice, "Morgaine is a priestess of Avalon. She does not lie. I think, Gwenhwyfar, that we must ask of this. Send for Morgaine—"

"No, no," Gwenhwyfar begged. "I am sorry I spoke—I was beside myself and raving as you said—oh, my dear lord and husband, my king and my lord, I am sorry for every word I said! I beg you to forgive me—I beg you."

He put his arms around her. "There is need for you to forgive me too, my dear lady. I see now I have done you great wrong. But when you have unloosed the winds, then must you abide by their blowing, whatever they may tear down. . . . " He kissed her very gently on the forehead. "Send for Morgaine."

"Oh, my lord, oh, Arthur, I beg you—I promised to her that I would never speak of it to you—"

"Well, then, you have broken your promise," Arthur said. "I besought you not to speak, but you would have it so, and now what has been said cannot be unsaid." He stepped to the door of the chamber and called to his chamberlain, "Go to the lady Morgaine and command that she attend me and my queen as quickly as she may."

When the man had gone, Arthur called Gwenhwyfar's servant, and Gwenhwyfar stood like a stone as the woman put on her holiday robe and braided her hair. She sipped at a cup of hot water and wine, but her throat was tight. She had spoken the unforgivable.

But if it is true that this morning he has given me his child to bear . . . and a strange pain struck inward through her body even into her womb. *Could anything take root and grow in such bitterness?*

After a time Morgaine came into the room in a dark-red gown, her hair braided with crimson silk ribbons; she had dressed well for the festival and looked alive and glowing.

And I am but a barren tree, Gwenhwyfar thought; *Elaine has Lancelet's son; even Morgaine, who has no husband and no wish for one, has played the harlot and borne a son to somebody or other, and Arthur has fathered a son on some unknown woman, but I—I have none.*

Morgaine came and kissed her; Gwenhwyfar stood rigid within her arms. Then Morgaine turned to Arthur and said, "You commanded me to come, my brother?"

Arthur said, "I am sorry to disturb you so early, sister. But, Gwenhwyfar," he said, "now must you repeat in my presence and Morgaine's what you have said. I will have no secret slanders repeated within my court."

Morgaine looked at Gwenhwyfar and saw the marks of tears around her reddened eyes. "Dear brother," she said, "your queen is ill. Is she pregnant again? As to whatever she has said, well, it's a true saying, hard words break no bones."

Arthur looked coldly at Gwenhwyfar, and Morgaine drew back; this was not the brother she knew well, this was the stern face of the High King as he sat in his hall to dispense justice.

"Gwenhwyfar," he said, "not only as your husband, but as your king, I command you: Repeat before Morgaine's face what you have said behind her back, and what she told you, that I had a son in fosterage at the court of Lothian—"

It is true, Gwenhwyfar thought in that split second. *Never before, save when Viviane was murdered before her eyes, have I seen Morgaine's face other than calm, serene, the face of a priestess. . . . It is true, and somehow it touches her deeply . . . but why?*

"Morgaine," Arthur said. "Tell me—is this true? Have I a son?"

What is it to Morgaine? Why should she wish it to be concealed, even from Arthur? She might wish her own harlotries to be hidden, but why should she conceal it from Arthur that he has a son? And then some inkling of the truth struck her, and she gasped aloud.

Morgaine thought: *A priestess of Avalon does not lie. But I am cast out of Avalon, and for this, and unless it is all to be for nothing, I must lie, and lie well and quickly. . . .*

"Who was it?" demanded Gwenhwyfar angrily. "One of the whore priestesses of Avalon who lies with men in sin and lustfulness at their demon festivals?"

"You know nothing of Avalon," said Morgaine, fighting to keep her voice steady. "Your words are like the wind, without meaning—"

Arthur took her by the arm. He said, "Morgaine—my sister—" and she thought that in another moment she would weep . . . as he had wept in her arms, that morning when first he knew how Viviane had trapped them both. . . .

Her mouth was dry and her eyes burned. She said, "I spoke—of your son—only to comfort Gwenhwyfar, Arthur. She feared you could not give her a child—"

"Would you had spoken so to comfort *me*," said Arthur, but his smile was only a grimace stretching his mouth. "All these years have I thought I could beget no son, even to save my kingdom—Morgaine, now you must tell me the truth."

Morgaine drew a long breath. In the dead silence inside the room she could hear a dog barking somewhere beyond the windows, and some small insect chirping somewhere. At last she said, "In the name of the Goddess, Arthur, since you will have it said at last—I bore a son to the King Stag, ten moons after your kingmaking on Dragon Island. Morgause has him in her keeping, and she swore to me that you should never hear it from her lips. Now you have had it from mine. Let it end here."

Arthur was white as death. He caught her into his arms, and she could feel how he was trembling. Tears were streaming down his face and he made no effort to check them or wipe them away. "Ah, Morgaine, Morgaine, my poor sister—I knew I had done you a great wrong, but I dreamed never that it was so great a wrong as this—"

"You mean this is true?" Gwenhwyfar cried out. "That this unchaste harlot of a sister of yours, she is such a one as would practice her whore's arts on her own brother—!"

Arthur swung round to her, his arm still around Morgaine. He said in a voice she had never heard before, "Be silent! Speak not one word against my sister—it was neither her doing nor her fault!" He drew a long, shaking breath, and Gwenhwyfar had time to hear the echo of her own ugly words.

"My poor sister," Arthur said again. "And you have borne this burden alone, nor ever laid the fault rightly at my door—no, Gwenhwyfar," he said earnestly, turning to her again, "it is not what you think. It was at my kingmaking, and neither of us knew the other—it was dark, and we had not seen one another since I was so small that Morgaine could carry me about in her arms. She was to me no more than the priestess of the Mother, and I was no more to her than the Horned One, and when we knew one another, it was too late and the harm was done," he said, and it was as if he forced his voice past tears. And he held Morgaine close to him, crying out, "Morgaine, Morgaine, you should have told me!"

"And again you think only of her!" Gwenhwyfar cried. "Not of your own greatest of all sins—she is your own sister, the child of your own mother's womb, and for such a thing as this God will punish you—"

"He has punished me indeed," said Arthur, holding Morgaine close. "But the sin was unknowing, with no desire to do evil."

"Maybe it is for this," Gwenhwyfar faltered, "that he has punished you with barrenness, and even now, if you repent and do penance—"

Morgaine pulled herself gently free of Arthur. Gwenhwyfar watched, with a rage she could not speak, as Morgaine dried his tears with her own kerchief, almost an absentminded gesture, the gesture of a mother or older sister, with nothing in it of the harlotry she wished to see. She said, "Gwenhwyfar, you think too much of sin. We did no sin, Arthur and I. Sin is in the wish to do harm. We came together by the will of the Goddess, for the forces of life, and if a child came to birth, then it was made in love, whatever brought us together. Arthur cannot acknowledge a son begotten on his sister's body, it is true. But he is not the first king to have a bastard son whose very existence he cannot admit. The boy is healthy and well, and safe in Avalon. The Goddess—for that matter, your God—is not a vindictive demon, looking about to punish somebody for some imagined sin. What happened between Arthur and me, it should not have happened, neither he nor I would have sought it, but done is done—the Goddess would not punish you with childlessness for the sins of another. Can you blame your own childlessness on Arthur, Gwen?"

Gwenhwyfar cried, "I do so! He has sinned, and God has punished him—for incest, for fathering a son on his own sister— for serving the Goddess, that fiend of foul abominations and lechery. . . . Arthur," she cried, "tell me you will do penance, that you will go on this holy day and tell the bishop how you have sinned, and do such penance as he may lay on you, and then perhaps God will forgive you and he will cease to punish us both!"

Arthur, troubled, looked from Morgaine to Gwenhwyfar. Morgaine said, "Penance? Sin? Do you truly believe that your God is an evil-minded old man, who snoops around to see who lies in bed with another's wife?"

"I have confessed *my* sins," Gwenhwyfar cried, "I have done penance and been absolved, it is not for *my* sins that God punishes us! Say you will do so too, Arthur! When God gave you the victory at Mount Badon, you swore to put aside the old dragon banner, and rule as a Christian king, but you left this sin unconfessed. Now do penance for this too, and let God give you the victory of this day as he did at Mount Badon—and be freed of your sins, and give me a son who can rule after you at Camelot!"

Arthur turned and leaned against the wall, covering his face with his hands. Morgaine would have moved toward him again, but Gwenhwyfar cried, "Keep away from him, you—! Would you tempt him into sin further than this? Have you not done enough, you and that foul demon you call your Goddess, you and that evil old witch whom Balin rightly killed for her heathen sorceries—?"

Morgaine shut her eyes, and her face looked as if she were about to weep. Then she sighed and said, "I cannot listen to you curse at my religion, Gwenhwyfar. I cursed not yours, remember that. God is God, however called, and always good. I think it sin to believe God can be cruel or vindictive, and you would make him meaner than the worst of his priests. I beg you to consider well what you do before you put Arthur into the hands of his priests with this." She turned, her crimson draperies moving silently around her, and left the room.

Arthur turned back to Gwenhwyfar as he heard Morgaine go. At last he said, more gently than he had ever spoken to her, even when they lay in each other's arms, "My dearest love—"

"Can you call me so?" she said bitterly, and turned away. He followed her, laying a hand on her shoulder and turning her round to face him.

"My dearest lady and queen—have I done you such a wrong?"

"Even now," she said shaking, "even now all you can think of is the wrong you have done to Morgaine—"

"Should I be happy at the thought of what I have brought on my own sister? I swear to you, I knew her not until the thing was done, and then, when I recognized her, it was she who comforted me, as if I had been the little boy who used to sit in her lap. . . . I think if she had turned on me and accused me, as she had every right to do, I would have gone away and drowned myself in the Lake. But I never thought what might come to her . . . I was so young, and there were all the Saxons and all the battles—" He spread his hands helplessly. "I tried to do as she bade me—put it behind us, remember that what we had done was done in ignorance. Oh, I suppose it was sin, but I did not choose to sin. . . ."

He looked so wretched that for a moment Gwenhwyfar was tempted to say what he wanted to hear, that indeed he had done no wrong; to take him in her arms and comfort him. But she did not move. Never, never had Arthur come to her for comfort, never had he acknowledged that he had done her any wrong; even now, all he could do was to insist that the sin which had kept them childless was no sin; his concern was only for the wrong he had done that damned sorceress of a sister of his! She said, crying again and furious because she knew he would think she wept from sorrow and not from rage, "You think it is only Morgaine you have wronged?"

"I cannot see I have harmed any other," he said stubbornly. "Gwenhwyfar, it was before ever I set eyes on you!"

"But you married me with this great sin unconfessed, and even now you cling to your sin when you might be shriven and do penance, and freed of your punishment—"

He said wearily, "Gwenhwyfar mine, if your God is such a one as would punish a man for a sin he knew not he committed, would he then abate that punishment because I tell a priest, and mouth such prayers as he gives me, and I know not what all—eat bread and water for a space, or what have you—?"

"If you truly repent—"

"Oh, God, do you think I have not repented?" Arthur burst out. "I have repented it every time I looked on Morgaine, these twelve years past! Would it make my repentance stronger to avow it before one of these priests who wants nothing more than to have power over a king?"

"You think only of your pride," Gwenhwyfar said angrily, "and pride too is a sin. Would you but humble yourself, God would forgive you!"

"If your God is such a God as that, I want not his forgiveness!" Arthur's fists were clenched. "I must rule this kingdom, my Gwen, and I cannot do that if I kneel before some priest and accept whatever he chooses to lay on me for penance! And there is Morgaine to think of—already they call her sorceress, harlot, witch! I have no right to confess to a sin which will call down scorn and public shame to my sister!"

"Morgaine too has a soul to be saved," said Gwenhwyfar, "and if the people of this land see that their king can put aside his pride and take thought for his soul, repent humbly for his sins, then it will help them to save their souls too, and it will be to his credit even in Heaven."

He said, sighing, "Why, you argue as well as any councillor, Gwenhwyfar. I am not a priest, and I am not concerned with the souls of my people—"

"How dare you say so?" she cried. "As a king is above all his people and their lives are in his hand, so are their souls too! You should be foremost in piety as you are in bravery on the battlefield! How would you think of a king who sent his soldiers to fight, and sat safe out of sight and watched them from afar?"

"Not well," said Arthur, and Gwenhwyfar, knowing she had him now, said, "Then what would you think of a king who saw his people pursue ways of piety and virtue, and said he need have no thought to his own sins?"

Arthur sighed. "Why should you care so much, Gwenhwyfar?"

"Because I cannot bear to think that you will suffer hellfire . . . and because if you free yourself of your sin, God may cease to punish us with childlessness."

She choked at last and began to cry again. He put his arms around her and stood with her head against his shoulder. He said gently, "Believe you this truly, my queen?"

She remembered; once before, when he had first refused to bear the banner of the Virgin into the battle, he had spoken to her like this. And then she had triumphed and brought him to Christ, and God had given him the victory. But then she had not known he had this sin unconfessed on his soul. She nodded against him and heard him sigh.

"Then I have done you wrong too, and I must somehow amend it. But I cannot see how it is right that Morgaine should suffer shame for this."

"Always Morgaine," said Gwenhwyfar, in a blaze of white rage. "You will not have her suffer, she is perfect in your eyes—tell me then, is it right that I should suffer for the sin that she has done, or you? Do you love her so much better than me that you will let me go childless all my days so that sin may be kept secret?"

"Even if I have done wrong, my Gwen, Morgaine is blameless—"

"Nay, that she is not," Gwenhwyfar flared, "for she follows that ancient Goddess, and the priests say that their Goddess is that same old serpent of evil whom our Lord drove from the Garden of Eden! Even now Morgaine clings to those filthy and heathenish rituals of hers—God tells us, yes, that those heathen who have not heard the word of the Lord may be saved, but what of Morgaine, who was brought up in a Christian household, and afterward turned to the filthy sorcerous ways of Avalon? And all these years at this court, she has heard the word of Christ, and do they not say that those who hear the word of Christ and do not repent and believe in him, they shall surely be damned? And women especially have need of repentance, since through a woman sin came first into the world—" Gwenhwyfar was sobbing so hard that she could hardly speak.

At last Arthur said, "What do you want me to do, my Gwenhwyfar?"

"This is the holy day of Pentecost," she said, wiping her eyes and trying to control her sobs, "when the spirit of God came down to Man. Will you go to the mass and take the sacrament with this great sin on your soul?"

"I suppose—I suppose I cannot," said Arthur, his voice breaking. "If truly you believe this, Gwenhwyfar, I will not deny it to you. I will repent as far as it is in me to repent for something I cannot think a sin, and I will do what penance the bishop lays on me." His smile was only a thin, harried grimace. "I hope, for your sake, my love, that you are right about God's will."

And Gwenhwyfar, even as she put her arms around him, crying with thankfulness, had a moment of shattering fear and doubt. She remembered when she had stood in the house of Meleagrant, and known that all her prayers could not save her. God had not rewarded her for her virtue, and when Lancelet came to her, had she not sworn to herself that never again would she hide or repent, because a God who had not rewarded her virtue would surely not punish her sin. God could not care either way. . . .

But God had punished her indeed; God had taken Lancelet from her and given him to Elaine, so for all that perilling of her soul she had won nothing . . . she had confessed and done penance, but God punished her still. And now she knew it might not be all her fault, but that she was bearing the weight of Arthur's sin too, the sin he had done with his sister. But if they were both freed of sin, if he did penance for that great sin unconfessed, and humbled himself, then no doubt God would forgive him too. . . .

Arthur kissed the top of her head and stroked her hair. Then he moved away, and she felt cold and lost when he took his arms away from her, as if she were not safely within walls but out under the huge open sky, bewildering, huge, filled with terror. She moved toward him again, to take refuge in his arms, but he had dropped into a chair and sat there, exhausted, beaten, a thousand leagues away from her.

At last he raised his head, and said, with a sigh that seemed ripped from the very depths of his being, "Send for Father Patricius."

8

When Morgaine left Arthur and Gwenhwyfar in their chamber, she snatched a cloak and fled out into the weather, uncaring of the rain. She went to the high battlements and walked there, alone; the tents of Arthur's followers and Companions, of the lesser kings and the guests, crowded the level space at the brow of the hill that was Camelot, and even in the rain, all the banners and flags fluttered brightly. But the sky was dark, and thick low clouds almost touched the brow of the hill; pacing, restless, Morgaine thought that the Holy Ghost could have chosen a finer day to descend on his people—and especially on Arthur.

Oh, yes. Gwenhwyfar would give him no peace until he had given himself into the hands of the priests. And what of his vow to Avalon?

And yet if it should be Gwydion's fate that one day he should sit on his father's throne, if *that* was what the Merlin planned . . . no man could escape fate. Morgaine thought mirthlessly, *No woman either.* Taliesin, who knew all manner of music and old tales, had once told her a story from the ancients who dwelt to the south in the Holy Land or somewhere near to there, of a man who was born under a curse that he should slay his father and wed with his mother. So the parents listened to the curse and cast him out to die, and he was reared by strangers, and one day, meeting with his father, unknowing, he quarrelled with him, killed him, and wedded with his widow; so that the very means they had taken to prevent the falling of the curse had brought it to pass—had he been reared in his father's house, he would not have done what he did in ignorance. . . .

She and Arthur had done what they did in ignorance, too, yet the fairy woman had cursed her son: *Cast forth your babe, or kill it as it comes from the womb; what of the King Stag when the young stag is grown?* And it seemed to her that all round her the world grew grey and strange, as if she had wandered into the mists of Avalon, and there was a strange humming in her brain.

There seemed a terrible clanging and banging in the air all round her, deafening her . . . no, it was the church bells, ringing for the mass. She had heard, too, that the fairy folk could not abide the sound of the church bells, and it was for that reason they had taken to the far hills and hollows . . . it seemed to her that she could *not* go and sit quietly, as she usually did, listening with polite attention because the Queen's waiting-women should set an example to all the others. She thought that the walls would stifle her and the mumbling of the priests and the smoke of the incense would drive her mad; better to stay out here in the clean rain. Now she thought to draw up the hood of the woolen cloak over her head; the ribbons in her hair were all wet, likely they were spoilt. She fumbled with them and the red came off on her fingers; poorly dyed they were, for materials so costly.

But the rain was slowing a little, and people were beginning to move about in the spaces between the tents.

"There will be no mock battle games today," said a voice behind her, "or I would ask you for one of those ribbons you are casting about, and carry it into battle as a flag of honor, lady Morgaine."

Morgaine blinked, trying to collect herself. A young man, slender and dark-haired, with dark eyes; something familiar about him, but she could not quite remember. . . .

"You do not remember me, lady?" he said reproachfully. "And I was told you had wagered a ribbon on my success in just such a mock battle a year or two ago—or was it three?"

Now she remembered him; he was the son of King Uriens of North Wales. Accolon, that was his name; and she had wagered with one of the Queen's ladies who claimed that no man could stand in the field against Lancelet. . . . She had never known how her wager came off; that was the Pentecost when Viviane had been murdered.

"Indeed I remember you, sir Accolon, but that Pentecost feast, you may remember, ended in such brutal murder, and it was my foster-mother who was slain—"

He was at once contrite. "Then I must beg your pardon for calling such a sad occasion to your mind. And I suppose there will be enough mock battles and combats before we leave here again, now that there is no war in the land—my lord Arthur wishes to know that his legions are still skilled to defend us all."

"The need seems not too likely," she said, "even the wild Northmen turn elsewhere these days. Do you miss the days of battle and glory?"

He had, she thought, a nice smile. "I fought at Mount Badon," he said. "It was my first battle, and came near to being my last. I think I prefer mock battles and tourneys. I will fight if I must, but it is better to fight in play against friends who have no real desire to kill, with pretty ladies looking down and admiring us—in real battle, lady, there is none to admire gallantry, and indeed, little of gallantry, for all they talk of courage. . . . "

They had moved, as they spoke, nearer to the church; and now the sound of the bells nearly drowned his voice—a pleasant, musical voice, she thought. She wondered if he played upon the harp. She turned abruptly away from the sound of the bells.

"Are you not going to the holy day mass, lady Morgaine?"

She smiled and looked down at his wrists, where the serpents twined. She ran a light finger over one of them. "Are you?"

"I do not know. I thought I might go to see the faces of my friends —no, I think not," he said, smiling at her, "when there is a lady to talk to. . . ."

She said, tingeing her voice with irony, "Do you not fear for your soul?"

"Oh, my father is pious enough for both of us . . . he has no wife now, and no doubt he wishes to study out the land and see how it lies for his next conquest. He has listened well to the Apostle and knows it is better to marry than to burn, and he burns oftener than I would think dignified for a man of his years. . . . "

"You have lost your mother, sir Accolon?"

"Aye, before I was weaned; and my stepmothers one, two, and three," Accolon said. "My father has three sons living, and it is certain he can have no further need of heirs, but he is too pious only to take a woman to his bed, so he must marry again. And even my oldest brother is married, and has a son."

"You were the son of his old age?"

"Of his middle age," Accolon said, "and I am not so young as all that. If there had not been war when I was younger, I might have been destined for Avalon and the lore of the priests. But my father has grown Christian in his old age."

"Yet you wear the serpents."

He nodded. "And know something of their wisdom, yet not enough to content me. In these days there is not much for a younger son to do. My father told me he would also seek a wife for me at this gathering," he said with a smile. "I would that you were the daughter of some lesser man, lady."

Morgaine felt herself blushing like a girl. "Oh, I am too old for you," she said, "and I am only the King's half-sister by his mother's first marriage. My father was Duke Gorlois, the first man Uther Pendragon killed as a traitor. . . ."

There was a brief silence before Accolon said, "In these days it is dangerous, perhaps, to wear the serpents—or will be, if the priests grow more powerful. When Arthur came to the throne, I heard he had the support of Avalon, that the Merlin gave him the sword of the Holy Regalia. But now he has made this so Christian a court . . . my father told me that he feared Arthur would move this land back to the Druid rule, but it seems he has not. . . . "

"True," she said, and for a moment anger stifled her. "Yet still he wears the Druid sword. . . ."

He looked at her closely. "And you bear the crescent of Avalon." Morgaine blushed. All the people had gone into the church now, and the doors were shut. "It has begun to rain harder—lady Morgaine, you will be drenched, you will take cold. You must go inside. But will you come and sit beside me at the feast this day?"

She hesitated, smiling. It was certain that Arthur and Gwenhwyfar would not seek her company at the high table this day of all days.

She who must remember what it was like to fall prey to Meleagrant's lust . . . should she blame me, she that comforted herself in the arms of her husband's dearest friend? Oh, no, it was not rape, nothing like to it, but still I was given to the Horned One without anyone's asking if it was what I wished . . . it was not desire brought me to my brother's bed, but obedience to the will of the Goddess. . . .

Accolon was still waiting for her answer, his face turned to her, eagerly. *If I willed it, he would kiss me, he would beg me for the favor of a single touch.* She knew it and the thought was healing to her pride. She smiled at him, a smile that dazzled him.

"I will indeed, if we can sit far off from your father."

And it struck her suddenly: Arthur had looked at her like that. *That is what Gwenhwyfar fears. She knows what I did not know, that if I stretched my hand to Arthur, I could make him ignore anything she said; Arthur loves me best. I have no desire for Arthur, I would have him only as a dear brother, but she does not know that. She fears that I will beckon with my hand, and with the secret arts of Avalon I will seduce him to my bed again.*

"I beg you, go inside and change your—your gown," said Accolon earnestly, and Morgaine smiled at him again and pressed his hand in her own.

"I will see you at the feast."

ALL THROUGH the holy day service, Gwenhwyfar had sat alone, striving to compose herself. The Archbishop had preached the usual Pentecost sermon, telling of the descent of the Holy Spirit, and she thought, *If Arthur has at last repented all his sins and become a Christian, then I must give thanks to the Holy Spirit for coming on us both today.* She let her fingers stray unseen to her belly; today they had lain together, it might be that at Candlemas she would hold in her arms the heir to the kingdom . . . she looked across the church to where Lancelet knelt at Elaine's side. She could see, jealously, that Elaine's waist was already swelling again. Another son, or a daughter. *And now Elaine flaunts herself, beside the man I loved so long and so well with the son I should have borne . . . well, I must bend my head and be humble a while, it will not hurt me to pretend that I believe her son will follow Arthur on his throne. . . . Ah, I am a sinful woman, I spoke to Arthur of humbling his pride, and I am full of pride.*

The church was crowded, as always at this holy day mass. Arthur looked pale and subdued; he had spoken with the bishop, but there had been no time for extended talk before the mass. She knelt beside him and felt that he was a stranger, far more of a stranger than when she had first lain in his bed, terrified of the unknown things ahead of her.

I should have held my peace with Morgaine. . . .

Why do I feel guilty? It was Morgaine who sinned . . . I have repented my sins and confessed them and been absolved. . . .

Morgaine was not in the church; no doubt, she had not had the brazenness to come unshriven to holy services when she had been exposed for what she was—incestuous, heathen, witch, sorceress.

The service seemed to last forever, but at last the blessing was given and the people began to move out of the church. Once for a moment she found herself crushed against Elaine and Lancelet; he had his arm protectively around his wife, that she should not be jostled. Gwenhwyfar raised her eyes to them, so that she need not look at Elaine's swollen belly.

"It is long since we have seen you at court," she said.

"Ah, there is much to do in the North," Lancelet said.

"No more dragons, I trust?" Arthur asked.

"God be thanked, no," Lancelet said, smiling. "My first sight of a dragon was like to be my last. . . . God forgive me that I mocked at Pellinore when he spoke of the beast! And now that there are no more Saxons to slay, I suppose our Companions must go against dragons and bandits and reavers, and all manner of ill things that plague the people."

Elaine smiled shyly at Gwenhwyfar. "My husband is like to all men —they would rather go into battle, even against dragons, than stay home and enjoy that peace they fought so hard to win! Is Arthur so?"

"I think he has battle enough, here at court where all men come to him for justice," said Gwenhwyfar, dismissing that. "When will this one come?" she added, looking at Elaine's swelling body. "Do you think it will be another son, or a daughter?"

"I hope it is another son, I do not want a daughter," Elaine said, "but it shall be as God wills. Where is Morgaine? Did she not come to church? Is she ill?"

Gwenhwyfar smiled scornfully. "I think you know how good a Christian Morgaine is."

"But she is my friend," Elaine said, "and no matter how bad a Christian she may be, I love her and I will pray for her."

Well you might, thought Gwenhwyfar bitterly. *She had you married to spite me.* It seemed that Elaine's sweet blue eyes were cloying, her voice false. It seemed to her that if she stood there a moment more listening to Elaine she would turn on her and strangle her. She made an excuse, and after a moment Arthur followed her.

He said, "I had hoped we would have Lancelet with us for some weeks, but he would be off to the North again. But he said Elaine might stay, if you would like to have her. She is near enough to her confinement that he would rather she did not return alone. Perhaps Morgaine is lonely for her friend, too. Well, you women must arrange that among yourselves—" He turned, and his face was bleak as he looked down at her. "I must go to the Archbishop. He said he would speak with me immediately after mass."

She wanted to clutch at him, keep him back, hold him with her by both hands, but it had gone too far for that.

"Morgaine was not in church," he said. "Tell me, Gwenhwyfar, did you say anything to her—"

"I spoke not one word to her, good or bad," she said shrilly. "As for where she is, I care not—I wish she were in hell!"

He opened his mouth and for a moment she thought he would chide her, and in a perverse way she longed for his wrath. But he only sighed and lowered his head. She could not bear to see him so beaten, like a whipped dog. "Gwen, I beg you, do not quarrel further with Morgaine. She has been hurt enough already—" And then, as if he was ashamed of his pleading, he turned abruptly and went away from her, toward where the Archbishop was standing and greeting his flock. As Arthur came toward him he bowed, spoke a few words of excuse to the others, and the King and the Archbishop moved away together through the crowds.

Inside the castle there was much to do—welcoming guests to the hall, speaking to men who had been Arthur's Companions in years gone by, explaining to them that Arthur had business with one of his councillors— that was no lie, Patricius was indeed one of Arthur's advisers—and would be late. For a time everyone was so busy greeting old friends, exchanging stories of what had befallen in their homes and villages, of what marriages had been made and daughters betrothed and sons grown to manhood, of what babies had been born and robbers slain and roads built, that the time went on and the absence of King Arthur was hardly noticed. But at last even reminiscences palled, and the people in the hall began to murmur. The food would be cold, Gwenhwyfar knew; but you could not start the King's feast unless the King was there. She gave orders for wine and beer and cider to be served, knowing that by the time the food was served now, many of the guests would be too drunk to care. She saw Morgaine far down the table, laughing and talking with a man she did not recognize, save that he had the serpents of Avalon around his wrist; would she practice her priestess- harlotries to seduce him too, as she had seduced Lancelet before him, and the Merlin? Morgaine's whorish ways were so great, she could not let any man slip beyond her grasp.

When Arthur finally came, walking slowly and heavily, she was overwhelmed with distress; she had never seen him look like that except when he was wounded and near to death. She felt suddenly that he had taken a deeper wound than she could know, in his very soul, and for a moment wondered, had Morgaine been right to spare him this knowledge? No. As his devoted wife, what she had done was to secure the health of his soul and his eventual salvation; what was a little humiliation against that?

He had taken off his holiday gown and wore a simple tunic, un- adorned; nor had he put on the coronet he wore on such occasions. His golden hair looked dull and greyed. As they saw him enter, all his Compan- ions had broken into wild applause and cheering; he stood solemnly, accept- ing it, smiling, then finally raised a hand.

"I am sorry to have kept you all waiting," he said. "I beg you forgive me, and go to your meat." He sat down at his place, sighing. The servants began to go around with the smoking pots and platters, the carvers to wield their knives. Gwenhwyfar let one of the butlers lay some slices of roast duck on her plate, but she only played with her food. After a time she dared to raise her eyes and look toward Arthur. Among the abundance of festival meats, he had nothing on his plate but a bit of bread, without even butter, and in his cup was only water.

She remonstrated, "But you are eating nothing—"

His smile was wry. "It is no insult to the food. I am sure it is fine as always, my love."

"It is not well done, to fast on a feast day—"

He grimaced. "Well, if you must have it," he said impatiently, "the bishop would have it that my sin was so grievous that he cannot absolve it with ordinary penance, and since that was what you wished of me, well—" He spread his hands wearily. "And so I come to Pentecost holiday in my shirt and without my fine clothing, and I have many fastings and prayers till I have done full penance—but you have had your wish, Gwenhwyfar." He picked up his cup and drank water, resolutely, and she knew he did not want her to say more.

But she had not wanted it like *this*. . . . Gwenhwyfar tightened her whole body so that she would not weep again; all eyes were on them, and surely it was scandal enough that the King sat fasting at his own highest festival. Outside the rain beat and battered on the roof. There was a strange silence in the hall. At last Arthur raised his head and called for music.

"Let Morgaine sing for us—she is better than any minstrel!"

Morgaine! Morgaine! Always Morgaine! But what could she do? Morgaine, she noticed, had put off the bright gown she had worn that morning and was wearing dark sober stuff like a nun's. She looked not so much like a harlot, now, without her bright ribbons; she came and took the harp, and sat near the King's table to sing.

Because it seemed to be what Arthur wished, there was some laughing and gaiety, and when Morgaine had finished, another took the harp, and another. There was much moving from table to table, talking, singing, drinking.

Lancelet came toward them and Arthur gestured to him to sit beside them, as in the old days, on the bench. The servants were bringing great plates of sweets and fruit, baked apples in cream and wine, all manner of delicate and subtle pastries. They sat talking of nothing in particular, and Gwenhwyfar felt happy for a moment: it was like old times, when they had all been friends, when there was love among them all . . . why could it not always have stayed like that?

After some time, Arthur rose and said, "I think I will go and talk to some of the older Companions . . . my legs are young, and some of them are getting so old and grey. Pellinore—he looks not as if he could fight a dragon. I think a good stiff fight with Elaine's little lapdog would be hard for him now!"

Lancelet said, "Since Elaine is married, it is as if he has nothing more to do in life. Such men often die soon after they have decided such a thing.

I hope it may not be so with him—I love Pellinore and hope he will be long with us." He smiled shyly. "I never felt I had a father—though Ban was good to me in his way—and now, for the first time, I have a kinsman who treats me as a son. Brothers I had not either, till I was grown and Ban's sons Lionel and Bors came to the court. I grew to manhood hardly speaking their language. And Balan had other concerns."

Arthur had hardly smiled since he had come from the bishop's rooms, but he was smiling now. "Does a cousin count for so much less than a brother, then, Galahad?"

Lancelet reached out and gripped his wrist. "God strike me if I could forget that, Gwydion—" He raised his eyes to Arthur, and for a moment, Gwenhwyfar thought Arthur would embrace him; but then Arthur drew back and let his hand drop. Lancelet gazed at him, startled, but Arthur got quickly to his feet.

"There is Uriens, and Marcus of Cornwall—he too grows old. . . . They shall see that their king is not too proud to come and speak to them today. Stay here by Gwenhwyfar, Lance, let it be like old times today."

Lancelet did as he was asked, sitting on the bench beside Gwenhwyfar. At last he asked, "Is Arthur ill?"

Gwenhwyfar shook her head. "I think he has penance to do and is brooding about it."

"Well, surely Arthur can have no great sin on his soul," Lancelet said, "he is one of the most spotless men I know. I am proud that he is still my friend—I do not deserve it, I know, Gwen." He looked at her so sadly that again Gwenhwyfar almost wept. Why could she not have loved the two of them without sin, why had God ordained that a woman must have only one husband? She was grown as bad as Morgaine, that she could think such a thing!

She touched his hand. "Are you happy with Elaine, Lancelet?"

"Happy? What man alive is happy? I do as best I can."

She looked down at her hands. For a moment she forgot that this man had been her lover and remembered only that he had been her friend. "I want you to be happy. Truly, I do."

His hand closed for a moment over hers. "I know, my dear. I did not want to come here today. I love you, and I love Arthur—but the day is past when I can be content to be his captain of horse and—" His voice broke. "And the champion of the Queen."

She said suddenly, looking up, her hand in his, "Does it seem sometimes to you that we are no longer young, Lancelet?"

He nodded and sighed. "Aye—it does so."

Morgaine had taken the harp again and was singing. Lancelet said, "Her voice is as sweet as ever. I am put in memory of my mother singing—she sang not so well as Morgaine, but she had the same soft, low voice—"

"Morgaine is as young as ever," said Gwenhwyfar jealously.

"It is so with those of the old blood, they seem ever young until the day they are suddenly old," Lancelet said; then, bending down to touch her cheek in a light kiss, he said abruptly, "Never think you are less beautiful than Morgaine, my Gwen. It is a different beauty, that is all."

"Why do you say this?"

"Love, I cannot bear it if you are unhappy. . . ."

She said, "I do not think I know what it means, to be happy."

How is Morgaine so untouched? That which wrecked my life and Arthur's, it lies lightly on her, there she sits laughing and singing, and yonder knight with the serpents about his wrists, is glamoured by her.

Soon after, Lancelet said he must go back to Elaine, and left her; and when Arthur returned, there were Companions and old followers coming to him for concessions, to give him gifts and recall their service. After a time Uriens of North Wales came, portly now and greying, but he still had all his own teeth, and he led his men into the field when he must.

He said, "I have come to ask you a favor, Arthur. I want to marry again, and I would like to be allied with your house. I have heard that Lot of Lothian is dead, and I ask your permission to marry his widow, Morgause."

Arthur had to stifle a laugh. "Ah, for that, my friend, you must ask leave of sir Gawaine. Lothian is his now, and no doubt he would be glad to marry his mother away, but no doubt, the lady is old enough to have a mind of her own. I cannot order her to marry—it would be like ordering my mother to marry!"

Gwenhwyfar was struck by sudden inspiration. This would be the perfect solution—Arthur himself had said that if it became known at court, Morgaine could be scorned or shamed. She reached out and touched Arthur's sleeve. She said in a low voice, "Arthur, Uriens is a valuable ally. You have told me that the mines of Wales are valuable as they were to the Romans, for iron and lead . . . and you have a kinswoman whose marriage is in your keeping."

He looked at her, startled. "Uriens is so old!"

"Morgaine is older than you," she said, "and since he has grown sons and grandsons, he will not mind too much if Morgaine does not give him children."

"That is true," said Arthur with a frown, "and this seems a good match." He raised his head to Uriens and said, "I cannot order lady Morgause to marry again, but my sister, the Duchess of Cornwall, is not married."

Uriens bowed. "I could not presume to ask so high, my king, but if your sister would be queen in my country—"

"I will compel no woman to marry unwilling," said Arthur, "but I will ask her." He beckoned one of the pages. "Ask the lady Morgaine if she will come to me when she has finished singing."

Uriens' eyes were on Morgaine where she sat, her dark gown lending fairness to her skin. "She is very beautiful, your sister. Any man would think himself fortunate to have such a wife."

As Uriens went to his seat, Arthur said thoughtfully, watching Morgaine come toward them, "She is long unmarried—she must wish for a home of her own where she will be mistress, rather than serving another woman always. And she is too learned for many young men. But Uriens will be glad that she is gracious and will rule his home well. I wish, though, that he were not quite so old. . . ."

"I think she will be happier with an older man," Gwenhwyfar said. "She is not a giddy young thing."

Morgaine came and curtseyed to them. Always, in public, she was smiling and impassive, and Gwenhwyfar was for once glad of it.

"Sister," said Arthur, "I have had an offer of marriage for you. And after this morning"—he lowered his voice—"I think it well you should not live at court for a time."

"Indeed I would be glad to be gone from here, brother."

"Why, then—" Arthur said, "how would you like to live in North Wales? I hear it is desolate there, but no more than Tintagel, surely—"

To Gwenhwyfar's surprise, Morgaine blushed like a girl of fifteen. "I will not try to pretend I am as surprised as all that, brother."

Arthur chuckled. "Why, he did not tell me he had spoken to you, the sly fellow."

Morgaine colored and played with the end of her braid. She did not, Gwenhwyfar thought, look anywhere near her age. "You may tell him I should be happy to live in North Wales."

Arthur said gently, "Does the difference in age not bother you?"

Her face was rosy. "If it does not bother him, it does not bother me."

"So be it," said Arthur, and beckoned to Uriens, who came, beaming. "My sister has told me that she would like it well to be Queen of North Wales, my friend. I see no reason we cannot have the wedding with all speed, perhaps on Sunday." He raised his cup and called out to the assembled company, "Drink to a wedding, my friends—a wedding between the lady Morgaine of Cornwall, my dear sister, and my good friend King Uriens of North Wales!"

For the first time that day it sounded like a proper Pentecost feasting, as the applause, cries of congratulation, acclaim, all stormed up. Morgaine stood still as a stone.

But she agreed to this, she said he had spoken to her . . . Gwenhwyfar thought, and then she remembered the young man who had been flirting with Morgaine. Was that not Uriens' son—Accolon, Accolon, that was it. But surely she could not have expected him to offer for her; Morgaine was older than he was! *It must have been Accolon—will she make a scene?* Gwenhwyfar wondered.

And then, with another surge of hatred, *Now let Morgaine see what it is like to be given in marriage to a man she does not love!*

"So you will be a queen, too, my sister," she said, taking Morgaine's hand. "I shall be your bride-woman."

But for all her sweet words, Morgaine looked her straight in the eye, and Gwenhwyfar knew that she had not been deceived.

So be it. We will at least be rid of one another. And no more pretense of friendship between us.

MORGAINE SPEAKS . . .

For a marriage destined to end as mine did, it began well enough, I suppose. Gwenhwyfar gave me a fine wedding, considering how she hated me; I had six bride-women and four of them were queens. Arthur gave me some fine and costly jewelry—I had never cared a great deal for jewelry, having not been accustomed to wear it in Avalon and never having learned since, though I had a few pieces that had been Igraine's. Now he gave me many more of our mother's gems, and some that had been plunder of the Saxons. I would have protested, but Gwenhwyfar reminded me that Uriens would expect to see his wife finely dressed as befitted a queen, and I shrugged and let her deck me out like a child's doll. One piece, an amber necklace, I remembered seeing Igraine wear when I was very young but never since; once I had seen it in her jewel chest when I was but small, and she said Gorlois had given it her and one day it should be mine, but before I was old enough to wear it I was priestess in Avalon and had no need of jewels. Now it was mine, with so many other things that I protested I would never wear them.

The one thing I asked of them—to delay the wedding till I could send for Morgause, who was my only living kinswoman—they would not do. Perhaps they thought I might come to my senses and protest that when I agreed to marry into North Wales, I had Accolon in mind, not the old king. I am sure Gwenhwyfar knew, at least. I wondered what Accolon would think of me; I had all but pledged myself to him, and before that night fell I had been publicly promised to his father! I had no chance to ask.

But after all, I suppose Accolon would want a bride of fifteen, not one of four-and-thirty. A woman past thirty—so women mostly said—must content herself with a man who had been often married and wanted her for her family connections, or for her beauty or possessions, or perhaps as a mother for his children. Well, my family connections could hardly be better. As for the rest—I had jewels enough, but I could hardly imagine myself as a mother to Accolon and whatever other children the old man might have. Grandmother to his son's children perhaps. I reminded myself with a start that Viviane's mother had been a grandmother younger than I was now; she had borne Viviane at thirteen, and Viviane's own daughter had been born before Viviane was fourteen.

I spoke but once alone with Uriens, in the three days which elapsed between Pentecost and our bridal. Perhaps I hoped that he, a Christian king, would refuse when he knew; or perhaps even now he wanted a young wife who could give him children. Nor did I want him to take me under false pretenses and reproach me later, and I knew what a great thing these Christians made of an untouched wife; I suppose they had it from the Romans, with their pride of family and worship of virginity.

"I am long past thirty years old, Uriens," I said, "and I am no maiden." I knew no gracious or polite way to say such things.

He reached forward and touched the small blue crescent between my brows. It was fading now; I could see it in the mirror which had been one of Gwenhwyfar's gifts. Viviane's had faded, too, when I came to Avalon, but she had used to paint it with blue dye.

"You were priestess of Avalon, one of the maidens of the Lady of the Lake, and you went as a maiden to the God, is it so?"

I assented.

Uriens said, "Some of my people still do so, and I make no great effort to put it down. The peasants feel that it is all very well for kings and great folk, who can afford to pay priests and the like to pray them out of Hell, to follow the way of Christ, but it would be hard on them if the Old Ones, who had been worshipped in our hills since time out of mind, should not have their due. Accolon thinks much the same, but now so much of power is going into the hands of the priests, it is needful I too must not offend them. As for me, I care not what God sits on the throne in Heaven, or what God is worshipped by my people, so that my kingdom is at peace. But once I wore the antlers. I swear I will never reproach you, lady Morgaine."

Ah, Mother Goddess, I thought, this is grotesque, this is madness, you jest with me . . . I might well have made a happy marriage with Accolon, after all. But Accolon was young and would wish for a young wife. . . . I said to Uriens, "One more thing you must know. I bore a child to the Horned One. . . ."

"I have said I will not reproach you with anything that is past, lady Morgaine—"

"You do not understand. It went so ill with me when that child was born *that I will certainly never bear another." A king, I thought, a king would want a fertile bride, even more than his younger son. . . .*

He patted my hand. I think he actually meant to comfort me. "I have sons enough," he said. "I have no need of others. Children are a fine thing, but I have had my share and more."

I thought: He is foolish, he is old, . . . but he is kind. If he had professed a madness of desire for me, I would have been sickened by him, but kindness I can live with.

"Do you grieve for your son, Morgaine? If you wish, you may send for him and have him fostered at my court, and I swear to you that neither he nor you shall ever hear a word of reproach, and he shall be decently reared as befits the son of the Duchess of Cornwall and the Queen of North Wales."

This kindness brought tears to my eyes. "You are very kind," I said, "but he is well where he is, in Avalon."

"Well, if you decide otherwise, tell me," he said. "I would be glad of another boy about the house, and he would be the right age, I suppose, for a playmate to my youngest son, Uwaine."

"I thought Accolon was your youngest, sir."

"No, no, Uwaine is only nine years old. His mother died when he was born . . . you wouldn't think an old fellow like me could have a boy as young as nine, would you?"

Why, yes, I would, I thought with an ironic smile, men are as proud of their ability to father sons as if it took a great skill. As if any tomcat could not do the same! At least a woman must bear a child in her body for most of a year and suffer to bring it forth, and so she has some reason for pride; but men accomplish their trick with no thought or trouble at all!

But I said, trying to make a jest of it, "When I was a young girl, sir, there was a saying in my country: a husband of forty may not become a father, but a husband of sixty surely will do so."

I had done this deliberately. If he had gone stiff and offended by the ribaldry of that, I would have known how I must treat him in the future, and taken great care always to speak him modest and quiet. Instead he laughed heartily and said, "I think you and I may agree well enough, my dear. I have had enough of being married to young girls who don't know how to laugh. I hope you will be content, marrying an old fellow like me. My sons laugh at me because I married again after Uwaine was born, but to tell the truth, lady Morgaine, a man gets used to being married, and I do not like living alone. And when my last wife died of the summer fever—well, it is true that I wished to be akin by marriage to your brother, but also, I am lonely. And it comes to me that you, who are unmarried so many years beyond the women of your age, you may not like it so ill to have a home and a husband, even if he is not young and handsome. I know you were not consulted about this marriage—but I hope you will not be too unhappy."

At least, I thought, he does not expect me to be madly excited about the great honor of being married to him. I could have said that it would be no change— I had not truly been happy since I left Avalon, and since I would be unhappy wherever I was, at least it would be better to be away from Gwenhwyfar's malice. I could no longer make pretense to be her loyal kinswoman and friend, and that saddened me somewhat, because there had been a time when we had truly been friends, and it was not I who had changed. I certainly had no wish to rob her of Lancelet; but how could I explain to her that, though I had once desired him, I despised him, too, and would not have had him for husband as a gift. Oh, yes, if Arthur had married us to each other before he was wed to Gwenhwyfar—but even then it was too late. It was always too late after that afternoon beneath the ring stones. If I had let him take me then, none of this would have come about . . . but done is done, and I had not known what other plans Viviane had had for me; and they had brought me in the end to this wedding with Uriens.

Our first bedding was about what I expected. He stroked me and fussed and pumped away atop me for a little while, snorting and breathing hard, and then was suddenly done and away from me and asleep. Having expected no better, I was not disappointed, nor particularly sorry to curl up in the curve of his arm; he liked having me there, and although after the first few weeks he lay with me but seldom, still he liked having me in his bed and would sometimes hold me in his arms for hours, talking of this and that, and what was more, listening to what I said. Unlike the Romans of the South, these men of the Tribes never scorned to listen to a woman's advice, and for that, at least, I was grateful, that he would hear what I said and never put it aside as being but a woman's counsel.

North Wales was a beautiful country, great hills and mountains that re-minded me of the country of Lothian. But where Lothian was high and barren, Uriens' country was all green and fertile, lush with trees and flowers, and the soil was rich and the crops good. Uriens had built his castle in one of the finer valleys. His son Avalloch, and Avalloch's wife and children, deferred to me in all things, and his youngest son, Uwaine, called me "Mother." I came to know what it might have been to have a son to bring up, to look after all the little daily concerns of a growing child, climbing trees and breaking bones, outgrowing his clothes or tearing them in the woods, being rude to his tutors or taking dog's leave to go hunting when he should have been at his book; the priest who taught Uwaine his letters despaired, but he was the pride and joy of the arms master. Troublesome as he was, I loved him well; he waited on me at dinner, and often sat in hall to listen to me when I played the harp—like all the folk of that country he had an ear for music and a clear and tuneful voice; and like all of that court, Uriens' family would rather make music themselves than listen to paid minstrels. After a year or two I began to think of Uwaine as my own son, and of course he could not remember his own mother. Wild as he was, he was always gentle with me; boys that age are not easy to control, but there were endearing moments, after days of rudeness *or sullenness, when he would suddenly come and sit by me in the hall and sing to my harp, or bring me wild flowers or a clumsily tanned hareskin, and once or twice, awkward and shy as a young stork, he would bend and brush my cheek with his mouth. Often I wished, then, that I had had children of my own that I could rear myself. There was little enough else to do at this quiet court, far away from the wars and troubles to the south.*

And then, when I had been married to Uriens for a year, Accolon came home.

9

S UMMER on the hills; the orchard in the queen's garden covered with pink and white blossoms. Morgaine, walking beneath the trees, felt an aching homesickness all through her blood, remembering the Avalon spring and the trees covered with those white and rosy clouds. The year was swinging toward the summer solstice; Morgaine reckoned it up, realizing ruefully that at last the effects of half a lifetime in Avalon were wearing away—the tides no longer ran in her blood.

No, need I lie to myself? It is not that I have forgotten, or that the tides no longer run in my blood, it is that I no longer let myself feel them. Morgaine considered herself dispassionately—the somber costly gown, suitable for a queen . . . Uriens had given her all the gowns and jewels which had belonged to his late wife, and she had her jewels from Igraine as well; Uriens liked to see her decked out in jewels befitting a queen.

Some kings kill their prisoners of state, or enslave them in their mines; if it pleases the King of North Wales to hang his with jewels and parade her forth at his side, and call her queen, why not?

Yet she felt full of the flow of the summer. Beneath her on the hillside she could hear a plowman encouraging his ox with soft cries. Tomorrow would be Midsummer.

Next Sunday a priest would carry torches into the field and circle it in procession with his acolytes, chanting psalms and blessings. The richer barons and knights, who were all Christian, had persuaded the people that this was more seemly in a Christian country than the old ways, where the people lighted fires in the fields, and called the Lady in the old worship. Morgaine wished—and not for the first time—that she had been only one of the priestesses, not one of the great royal line of Avalon.

I would still be there, she thought, *one of them, doing the work of the Lady . . . not here, like any shipwrecked sailor, lost in an alien land. . . .* Abruptly she turned and walked through the blossoming garden, her eyes downcast, refusing to look any further at the apple blossoms.

Spring comes again and again, and the summer follows, with its fruitfulness. But I am as alone and barren as one of those locked-up Christian virgins within convent walls. She set her will against the tears which seemed somehow always beneath the surface these days, and went inside. Behind her the setting sun spread crimson over the fields, but she would not look at it; all was grey and barren here. *As grey and barren as I.*

One of her women greeted her as she stepped inside the door.

"My lady, the king has returned and would see you in his chamber."

"Yes, I suppose so," said Morgaine, more to herself than to the woman. A tight band of headache settled around her forehead, and for a moment she could not breathe, could not force herself to walk inside the darkness of the castle which, all this cold winter, had closed round her like a trap. Then she told herself not to be fanciful, set her teeth, and went to Uriens' chamber, where she found him half-clad and lying on the flagstones, stretched out with his body servant rubbing his back.

"You have tired yourself again," she said, not adding, *you are no longer young enough to go about your own lands like this.* He had ridden to a nearby town to hear about some disputed lands. She knew that he would want her to sit beside him and listen to his tales of all that he had heard in the countryside. She sat down in her own chair nearby and listened with half an ear to what he told her.

"You can go, Berec," he told the man. "My lady will fetch my clothes for me." When the man had gone he asked, "Morgaine, will you rub my feet? Your hands are better than his."

"Certainly. But you will have to sit in the chair."

He stretched out his hands and she gave him a tug upward. She placed a footstool under his feet and knelt beside it, chafing his thin, callused old feet until the blood rose to the surface and they looked alive again; then she fetched a flask and began to rub one of her herbal oils into the king's gnarled toes.

"You should have your man make you some new boots," she said. "The crack in the old ones will make a sore there—see where it is blistered?"

"But the old ones fit me so well, and boots are so stiff when they are new," he protested.

Morgaine said, "You must do as you like, my lord."

"No, no, you are right, as always," he said. "I will tell the man tomorrow to come and measure my feet for a pair."

Morgaine, putting away her flask of herbal oil and fetching a pair of shapeless old soft shoes, thought: *I wonder if he knows that this may be his last pair of boots, and that is why he is reluctant?* She would not think about what the king's death would mean to her. She did not want to wish him dead —he had never been anything but kind to her. She slid the soft indoor slippers on his feet and stood up, wiping her hands on a towel. "Is that better, my lord?"

"Wonderful, my dear, thank you. No one can look after me the way you do," he said. Morgaine sighed. When he had the new boots he would have more trouble with his feet; they would, as he had rightly foreseen, be stiff, and that would make his feet just as sore as they were now. Perhaps he should stop riding and stay at home in his chair, but he would not do that.

She said, "You should have Avalloch ride out to hear these cases. He must learn to rule over his people." His oldest son was the same age as she. He had waited long enough to rule, and Uriens looked like living forever.

"True, true—but if I do not go, they will think their king does not care for them," Uriens said. "But perhaps when the roads are bad next winter I will do so. . . ."

"You had better," she said. "If you have chilblains again, you could lose the use of your hands."

"The fact is, Morgaine," he said, smiling his good-natured smile at her, "I am an old man, and there is nothing that can be done about it. Do you think there is roast pork for supper?"

"Yes," she said, "and some early cherries. I made sure of that."

"You are a notable housekeeper, my dear," he said, and took her arm as they went out of the room. She thought, *He thinks he is being kind to say so.*

The household of Uriens was assembled already for the evening meal: Avalloch; Avalloch's wife, Maline, and their young children; Uwaine, lanky and dark, with his three young foster-brothers and the priest who was their tutor; and below them at the long table the men-at-arms and their ladies, and the upper servants. As Uriens and Morgaine took their seats and Morgaine signalled to the servants to bring food, Maline's younger child began to clamor and shout.

"Granny! I want to sit on Granny's knee! Want Granny to feed me!"

Maline—a slender, fair-haired, pale young woman, heavily pregnant —frowned and said, "No, Conn, sit down prettily and be quiet!"

But the child had already toddled to Morgaine's knee, and she laughed and lifted him up. *I am an unlikely grandmother,* she thought; *Maline is almost as old as I.* But Uriens' grandsons were fond of her, and she hugged the little boy close, taking pleasure in the feel of the small curly head digging into her waist, the grubby little fingers clutching at her. She sliced bits of pork with her knife and fed them to Conn from her own plate, then cut him a piece of bread in the shape of a pig.

"See, now you have more pork to eat . . ." she said, wiping her greasy fingers, and turned her attention to her own meal. She ate but little meat, even now; she soaked her bread in the meat juices, but no more. She was quickly finished, while the rest were still eating; she leaned back in her chair and began to sing softly to Conn, who curled up contentedly in her lap. After a time she grew aware that they were all listening to her, and she let her voice drop away.

"Please go on singing, Mother," Uwaine said, but she shook her head.

"No, I am tired—listen, what did I hear in the courtyard?" She rose and signalled to one of the serving-men to light her to the doorway. Torch held high, he stood behind her, and she saw the rider come into the great courtyard. The serving-man stuck his torch into one of the wall brackets and hurried to help the rider dismount. "My lord Accolon!"

He came, his scarlet cape swirling behind him like a river of blood. "Lady Morgaine," he said, with a deep bow, "or should I say—my lady mother?"

"Please do not," Morgaine said impatiently. "Come in, Accolon, your father and brothers will be happy to see you."

"As you are not, lady?"

She bit her lip, suddenly wondering if she would weep. She said, "You are a king's son, as I am a king's daughter. Do I have to remind you how such marriages are made? It was not my doing, Accolon, and when we spoke together, I had no idea—" She stopped, and he looked down at her, then stooped over her hand.

He said so softly that even the serving-man did not hear, "Poor Morgaine. I believe you, lady. Peace between us, then—Mother?"

"Only if you do not call me Mother," she said, with a shred of a smile. "I am not *so* old. It is well enough for Uwaine—" and then, as they came back into the hall, Conn started upright and began to cry out again for "Granny!" Morgaine laughed, mirthlessly, and went back to pick up the toddler. She was aware of Accolon's eyes on her; she cast her own down at the child in her lap, listening silently as Uriens greeted his son.

Accolon came formally to embrace his brother, to bow before his brother's wife; he knelt and kissed his father's hand and then turned to Morgaine. She said shortly, "Spare me further courtesies, Accolon, my hands are all pork fat, I have been holding the baby, and he is a messy feeder."

"As you command, madam," said Accolon, going to the table and taking the plate one of the serving-women brought to him. But while he ate and drank, she was still conscious of his eyes.

I am sure he is still angry with me. Asking my hand in the morning, and in the evening, seeing me promised to his father; no doubt he thinks I succumbed to ambition—why marry the king's son if you can have the king?

"No," she said firmly, giving Conn a little shake, "if you are to stay in my lap you must be quiet and not paw at my dress with your greasy hands. . . ."

When he saw me last I was clad in scarlet and I was the king's sister, reputed a witch . . . now I am a grandmother with a dirty child in my lap, looking after the housekeeping and nagging my old husband not to ride in mended boots which make his feet sore. Morgaine was acutely aware of every grey hair, every line in her face. *In the name of the Goddess, why should I care what Accolon thinks of me?* But she did care and she knew it; she was accustomed to having young men look at her and admire her, and now she felt that she was old, ugly, undesirable. She had never thought herself a beauty, but always before this she had been one of the younger people, and now she sat among the aging matrons. She hushed the child again, for Maline had asked Accolon what news of Arthur's court.

"There is no news of great doings," Accolon said. "I think those days are over for our lifetime. Arthur's court is quiet, and the King still does penance for some unknown sin—he touches no wine, even at high feast days."

"Has the Queen yet shown any signs of bearing him an heir?" Maline asked.

"None," said Accolon, "though one of her ladies told me before the mock games that she thought the Queen might be pregnant."

Maline turned to Morgaine and said, "You knew the Queen well, did you not, mother-in-law?"

"I did," said Morgaine, "and as for that rumor, well, Gwenhwyfar always thinks herself pregnant if her courses come a day late."

"The King is a fool," said Uriens. "He should put her away and take some woman who would give him a son. I remember all too well what chaos ruled the land when they thought Uther would die with no son. Now the succession should be firmly established."

Accolon said, "I have heard that the King has named one of his cousins for his heir—the son of Lancelet. I like that not—Lancelet is the son of Ban of Benwick, and we want no foreign High Kings reigning over our own."

Morgaine said firmly, "Lancelet is the son of the Lady of Avalon, of the old royal line."

"Avalon!" said Maline disdainfully. "This is a Christian land. What is Avalon to us now?"

"More than you think," said Accolon. "I have heard that some of the country people, who remember the Pendragon, are not happy with so Christian a court as Arthur's, and remember that Arthur, before his crowning, took oath to stand with the folk of Avalon."

"Yes," said Morgaine, "and he bears the great sword of the Holy Regalia of Avalon."

"The Christians seem not to hold that against him," Accolon said, "and now I remember some news from the court—King Edric of the Saxons has turned Christian and came to be baptized, with all his retinue, at Glastonbury, and he knelt and took oath before Arthur in token that all the Saxon lands accepted Arthur as High King."

"Arthur? King over Saxons? Will wonders never cease!" Avalloch said. "I always heard him say he would deal with the Saxons only at the point of his sword!"

"Yet there he was, the Saxon king, kneeling in Glastonbury church, and Arthur hearing his oath and taking him by the hand," said Accolon. "Perhaps he will marry the Saxon's daughter to the son of Lancelet and have done with all this fighting. And there sat the Merlin among Arthur's councillors, and one would have said he was as good a Christian as any of them!"

"Gwenhwyfar must be happy now," said Morgaine. "Always she said God had given Arthur the victory at Mount Badon because he bore the banner of the Holy Virgin. And later I heard her say that God had spared his life that he might bring the Saxons into the fold of the church."

Uriens shrugged and said, "I do not think I would trust a Saxon behind me with an axe, even if he wore a bishop's miter!"

"Nor I," said Avalloch, "but if the Saxon chiefs are praying and doing penance for their souls' sake, at least they are not riding to burn our villages and abbeys. And as to penance and fasting—what, think you, can Arthur have on *his* conscience? When I rode with his armies, I was not among his Companions and knew him not so well, but he seemed an uncommon good man, and a penance of such length means some sin greater than common. Lady Morgaine, do you know, you who are his sister?"

"His sister, not his confessor." Morgaine knew her voice was sharp, and fell silent.

Uriens said, "Any man who waged war for fifteen years among the Saxons must have more on his conscience than he cares to tell; but few are so tender of conscience as to think of it when the battle is past. All of us have known murder and ravage and blood and the slaughter of the innocent. But the battles are over for our lifetime, God grant, and having made our peace with men, we have leisure to make peace with God."

So Arthur does penance still, and that old Archbishop Patricius still holds the mortgage on his soul! How, I wonder, does Gwenhwyfar enjoy that?

"Tell us more of the court," Maline begged. "What of the Queen? What did she wear when she sat at court?"

Accolon laughed. "I know nothing of ladies' garments. Something of white, with pearls—the Marhaus, the great Irish knight, brought them to her from the Irish king. And her cousin Elaine, I heard, has borne Lancelet a daughter—or was that last year? She had a son already, I think, that was chosen Arthur's heir. And there is some scandal in King Pellinore's court —it seems that his son, Lamorak, went on a mission to Lothian, and now speaks of marrying Lot's widow, old Queen Morgause—"

Avalloch chuckled. "The boy must be mad. Morgause is fifty, at least, maybe more!"

"Five-and-forty," Morgaine said. "She is ten years older than I." And she wondered why she thus turned the knife in her own wound . . . *do I want Accolon to realize how old I am, grandmother to Uriens' brood. . . ?*

"He is mad indeed," Accolon said, "singing ballads, and carrying about the lady's garter and such nonsense—"

"I should think that same garter would make a horse's halter by now," said Uriens, and Accolon shook his head.

"No—I have seen Lot's lady and she is a beautiful woman still. She is not a girl, but she seems all the more beautiful for that. What I wonder is, what can the woman want with a raw boy like that? Lamorak is not more than twenty."

"Or what can a boy like that want with the old lady?" Avalloch insisted.

"Perhaps," said Uriens, with a ribald laugh, "the lady is well learned at sport among the cushions. Though one would hardly think she could have learned it, married all those years to old Lot! But no doubt she had other teachers. . . ."

Maline flushed and said, "Please! Is this talk seemly in a Christian household?"

Uriens said, "If it were not, daughter-in-law, I doubt your girdle would be grown so wide."

"I am a married woman," said Maline, crimson.

Morgaine said sharply, "If to be a Christian household means not to speak of what one is not ashamed to do, then the Lady forbid I should ever call myself Christian!"

"Still," said Avalloch, "perhaps it is ill done to sit here at meat and tell ugly stories about lady Morgaine's kinswoman."

Accolon said, "Queen Morgause has no husband to be offended, and the lady is of age, and her own mistress. No doubt her sons are well pleased that she contents herself with a paramour and does not marry the boy! Is she not also the Duchess of Cornwall?"

"No," said Morgaine, "Igraine was Duchess of Cornwall after Gorlois was set down for his treason to Pendragon. Gorlois had no son, and since Uther gave Tintagel to Igraine for bride-gift, I suppose now it belongs to me." And Morgaine was suddenly overcome with homesickness for that half-remembered country, the bleak outline of castle and crags against the sky, the sudden dips into hidden valleys, the eternal noise of the sea below the castle . . . *Tintagel! My home! I cannot return to Avalon, but I am not homeless . . . Cornwall is mine.*

"And under the Roman law," said Uriens, "I suppose, as your husband, my dear, I am Duke of Cornwall."

Again Morgaine felt the surge of violent anger. *Only when I am dead and buried,* she thought. *Uriens cares nothing for Cornwall, only that Tintagel, like myself, is his property, bearing the mark of his ownership! Would that I could go there, live there alone as Morgause at Lothian, my own mistress with none to command me. . . .* A picture came in her mind, the queen's chamber at Tintagel, and she seemed very small, she was playing with an old spindle on the floor. . . . *If Uriens dares to lay claim to an acre of Cornwall, I will give him six feet of it, and dirt between his teeth!*

"Tell me now your news of this country," said Accolon. "The spring was late—I see the plowmen are just getting into the fields."

"But they have nearly done with plowing," said Maline, "and Sunday they will go to bless the fields—"

"And they are choosing the Spring Maiden," said Uwaine. "I was down in the village, and I saw them choosing among all the pretty girls . . . you were not here last year, Mother," he said to Morgaine. "They choose the prettiest of all for the Spring Maiden, and she walks in the procession around the fields when the priest comes to bless it . . . and there are dancers who dance round the fields . . . and they carry an image made from the last harvest, made from the barley straw. Father Eian does not like that," he said, "but I don't know why not, it is so pretty. . . ."

The priest coughed and said self-consciously, "The blessing of the church should be enough—why should we need more than the word of God to make the fields grow and blossom? The straw image they carry is a memory of the bad old days when men and animals were burned alive so that their lives should make the fields fertile, and the Spring Maiden a memory of—well, I will not speak before children of *that* evil and idolatrous custom!"

"There was a day," said Accolon, speaking directly to Morgaine, "when the queen of the land was the Spring Maiden, and the Harvest Lady as well, and *she* did that office in the fields, that the fields might have life and fertility." Morgaine saw at his wrists the faint blue shadow of the serpents of Avalon.

Maline made the sign of the cross and said primly, "God be thanked that we live among civilized men."

Accolon said, "I doubt you would be asked to do that office, sister-in-law."

"No," said Uwaine, tactless as any boy, "she is not pretty enough. But our mother is, isn't she, Accolon?"

"I am glad you think my queen is handsome," said Uriens hastily, "but the past is past—we do not burn cats and sheep alive in the fields, nor kill the king's scapegoat to scatter his blood there, and it is no longer needful that the queen should bless the fields in that way."

No, thought Morgaine. *Now all is sterile, now we have priests with their crosses, forbidding the lighting of the fires of fertility—it is a miracle the Lady does not blight the fields of grain, since she is angry at being denied her due. . . .*

Soon after, the household went to rest; Morgaine, the last to rise from her seat, went to supervise the locks and bars, and then went, with a small lamp in her hand, to make sure Accolon had been given a good bed—Uwaine and his foster-brothers were now occupying the room that had been his when he lived here as a boy.

"Is all well with you here?"

"Everything I could desire," said Accolon, "except a lady to grace my chamber. My father is a fortunate man, lady. And you well deserve to be the wife of a king, not of a king's younger son."

"Must you always taunt me?" she burst out. "I have told you; I was given no choice!"

"You were pledged to *me!*"

Morgaine knew that the color was leaving her face. She set her lips like stone. "Done is done, Accolon."

She lifted her lamp and turned away. He said behind her, almost a threat, "This is not done between us, lady."

Morgaine did not speak; she hurried along the corridor to the chamber she shared with Uriens. Her lady-in-waiting was ready to unlace her gown, but she sent the woman away. Uriens sat on the edge of the bed, groaning.

"Even those slippers are too hard on my feet! Aaah, it is good to go to rest!"

"Rest well, then, my lord."

"No," he said, and pulled her down at his side. "So tomorrow the fields are to be blessed . . . and perhaps we should be grateful we live in a civilized land, and the king and the queen need no longer bless the fields by lying together in public. But on the eve of the blessing, dear lady, perhaps we should have our own blessing, private in our chamber—what would you say to that?"

Morgaine sighed. She had been scrupulously careful of her aging husband's pride; never did she make him feel less than a man for his occasional and clumsy use of her body. But Accolon had roused in her an anguished memory of her years in Avalon—the torches borne to the top of the Tor, the Beltane fires lighted and the maidens waiting in the plowed fields . . . and tonight she had had to hear a shabby priest mocking what was, to her, holy beyond holiness. Now even Uriens, it seemed, made a mockery of it.

"I would say that such blessing as you and I might give the fields would be better left undone. I am old and barren, and you are not such a king as can give much life to the fields, either!"

Uriens stared at her. In all the year of their marriage she had never spoken a harsh word to him. He was too startled even to reproach her.

"I doubt it not, you are right," he said quietly. "Well, then, we will leave that to the young people. Come to bed, Morgaine." But when she lay down beside him, he lay quiet, and after a moment, he put a shy arm across her shoulders. Now Morgaine was regretting her harsh words . . . she felt cold and alone, she lay biting her lip so that she would not cry, but when Uriens spoke to her, she pretended she was asleep.

MIDSUMMER DAWNED brilliant and beautiful; Morgaine, waking early, realized that, however much she might say to herself that the sun tides ran no longer in her blood, there was something within her that ran heavy with the summer. As she dressed, she looked dispassionately at the sleeping form of her husband.

She had been a fool. Why should she have accepted compliantly Arthur's word, fearing to embarrass him before his fellow kings? If he could not keep his throne without a woman's help it might be he did not deserve to hold it. He was a traitor to Avalon, an apostate; he had given her into the hands of another apostate. Yet she had meekly agreed to what they had planned for her.

Igraine let her life be used for their politics. And something in Morgaine, dead or sleeping since the day she fled forth from Avalon, bearing Gwydion within her womb, suddenly woke and stirred, moving sluggishly and slow like a sleeping dragon, a movement as secret and unseen as the first movements of a child in the womb; something that said, clear and quiet within her, *If I would not let Viviane, whom I loved, use me this way, why should I bow my head meekly and let myself be used for Arthur's purposes? I am queen in North Wales, and I am duchess in Cornwall, where Gorlois's name still means something, and I am of the royal line of Avalon.*

Uriens groaned, heaving himself stiffly over. "Ah, God, I ache in every muscle and there is a toothache in every toe of my foot—I rode too far yesterday. Morgaine, will you rub my back?"

She started to fling back furiously, *You have a dozen body servants, and I am your wife, not your slave,* then stopped herself; instead she smiled and said, "Yes, of course," and sent a pageboy for her vials of herbal oil. Let him think her still compliant to everything; healing was a part of a priestess's work. If it was the smallest part, still, it gave her access to his plans and his thoughts. She rubbed his back and kneaded salve into his sore feet, listening to the small details of the land dispute he had ridden out yesterday to settle.

For Uriens, any woman could be queen, he wants only a smiling face and kind hands to cosset him. Well, he shall have them while it suits my purpose.

"And now it looks as if we would have a fine day for the blessing of the crops. We never have rain at Midsummer-day," Uriens said. "The Lady shines on her fields when they are consecrated to her—that is what they used to say when I was young and a pagan, that the Great Marriage could not be consummated in the rain." He chuckled. "Still, I remember once when I was very young, when the fields had been rained on for ten days, and the priestess and I might have been pigs wallowing in the mud!"

Against her will, Morgaine smiled; the picture he made in her mind was ludicrous. "Even in ritual, the Goddess will have her joke," she said, "and one of her names is the Great Sow, and we are all her piglets."

"Ah, Morgaine, those were good times," he said, then his face tightened. "Of course, that was long ago—now what the folk want in their kings is dignity. Those days are gone, and forever."

Are they? I wonder. But Morgaine said nothing. It occurred to her that Uriens, when he was younger, might have been a king strong enough to resist the tide of Christianity washing over the land. If Viviane had tried harder to put a king on the throne who was not bound hard and fast to the rule of the priests . . . but of course, who could have foreseen that Gwenhwyfar would be pious beyond all reason? And why had the Merlin done nothing?

If the Merlin of Britain and the wise folk at Avalon had done nothing to stem this tide that was drowning the land and washing away all the old ways and the old Gods, why should she blame Uriens, who was after all only an old man, and wanted peace? There was no reason to make him an enemy. If he was content, it would not matter to him what she did . . . she did not know yet what she meant to do. But she knew that her days of silent compliance were over.

She said, "I wish I had known you then," and let him kiss her on the forehead.

If I had been married to him when first I became marriageable, North Wales might never have become a Christian land. But it is not too late. There are those who have not forgotten that the king still wears, however faded, the serpents of Avalon about his arms. And he has married one who was a High Priestess of the Lady.

I could have done her work better here than all those years at Arthur's court, in Gwenhwyfar's shadow. It occurred to Morgaine that Gwenhwyfar would have been content with a husband like Uriens, whom she could keep within her own sphere, rather than one like Arthur, living an entire life in which she had no part.

And there had been a time, too, when Morgaine had had influence with Arthur—the influence of the woman he had first taken in coming to manhood, who wore, for him, the face of the Goddess. Yet, in her folly and pride, she had let him fall into the hands of Gwenhwyfar and the priests. Now, when it was too late, she began to understand what Viviane had intended.

Between us, we could have ruled this land; they would have called Gwenhwy-far the High Queen, but she would have had Arthur only in body; he would have been mine in heart and soul and mind. Ah, what a fool I was. . . . He and I could have ruled—for Avalon! Now Arthur is the priests' creature. And he bears, still, the great sword of the Druid Regalia, and the Merlin of Britain does nothing to hinder him.

I must take up the work that Viviane let fall. . . .

Ah, Goddess, I have forgotten so much. . . .

And then she stopped, shaking at her own daring. Uriens had reached a pause in his tale; she had ceased rubbing his feet, and he looked down questioning at her, and she said hastily, "I am quite sure you did the right thing, my dear husband," and spread some more of the sweet-smelling salve on her hands. She had not the slightest idea what she had agreed to, but Uriens smiled and went on with his tale, and Morgaine slid off into her own thoughts again.

I am a priestess still. Strange how I am suddenly sure of that again, after all these years, when even the dreams of Avalon are gone.

She pondered what Accolon had told them. Elaine had borne a daughter. She herself could not give Avalon a daughter, but as Viviane had done, she would bring her a fosterling. She helped Uriens to dress, went down with him, and with her own hands fetched him fresh new-baked bread from the kitchen and some of the foaming new beer. She served him, spreading honey on his bread. Let him think her the most doting of his subjects, let him think her only his sweet compliant wife. It meant nothing to her, but one day it might mean much to have his trust, so that she could do what she chose.

"Even with the summer my old bones ache—I think, Morgaine, that I will ride south to Aquae Sulis and take the waters there. There is an ancient shrine to Sul—when the Romans were here they built a huge bathhouse, and some of it is still there, unfallen. The great pools are choked, and when the Saxons came they carried off much of the fine work, and threw down the statue of the Goddess, but the spring is still there, undamaged—boiling up in clouds of steam, day after day and year after year, from the forges at the center of the earth. It is awesome to behold! And there are hot pools where a man can soak all the weariness from his bones. I have not been there for two or three years, but I shall go again, now the countryside is quiet."

"I see no reason you should not," she agreed, "now there is peace in the land."

"Would you care to go with me, my dear? We can leave my sons to care for everything here, and the old shrine would interest you."

"I would like to see the shrine," she said, sincerely enough. She thought of the cold unfailing waters of the Holy Well on Avalon, bubbling up inexhaustible, forever, sourceless, cool, clear. . . . "Still, I do not know if it would be well to leave all things in your sons' hands. Avalloch is a fool. Accolon is clever, but he is only a younger son—I do not know if your people would listen to him. Perhaps if I were here, Avalloch would take counsel of his younger brother."

"An excellent idea, my dear," Uriens said sunnily, "and in any case it would be a long journey for you. If you are here I will not have the slightest hesitation in leaving all things to the young men—I will tell them they must come to you for good advice in all things."

"And when will you set forth?" It would not be at all a bad thing, Morgaine thought, if it were known that Uriens did not hesitate to leave his kingdom in her hands.

"Tomorrow, perhaps. Or even after the blessing of the crops this day. Will you have them pack my things?"

"Are you sure you can travel that long a road? It is not an easy ride even for a young man—"

"Come, come, my dear, I am not yet too old to ride," he said, frowning a little, "and I am sure the waters will do me good."

"I am sure they will." Morgaine rose, leaving her own breakfast almost untasted. "Let me call your body servant and have everything made ready for you to depart."

She stood at his side during the long procession around the fields, standing on a little hill above the village and watching the capering dancers, like young goats . . . she wondered if any of them so much as knew the significance of the phallic green wands wound about with red and white garlands, and the pretty girl with her hair streaming, who walked, serene and indifferent, among them. She was fresh and young, not fourteen, and her hair was coppery gold, streaming halfway between her waist and knees; and she had on a gown, dyed green, that looked very old. Did any of them know what they were watching, or see the incongruity of the priest's procession, following them, two boys in black carrying candles and crosses, and the priest intoning the prayers in his bad Latin; Morgaine spoke better Latin than he!

These priests hate fertility and life so much, it is a miracle their so-called blessing does not blast the fields sterile—

It was like an answer from her own mind when a voice spoke softly behind her. "I wonder, lady, if any here save ourselves truly know what they are watching?"

Accolon took her arm for a moment to help her over a rough clump of the plowed land, and she saw again the serpents, fresh and blue along his wrists.

"King Uriens knows and has tried to forget. That seems to me a worse blasphemy than not to know at all."

She had expected that would make him angry; had, in a way, been inviting it. With Accolon's strong hands on her arm, she felt the strong hunger, the inner leap . . . he was young, he was a virile man, and she— she was the aging wife of his old father . . . and the eyes of Uriens' subjects were on them, and the eyes of his family and his house priest! She could not even speak freely, she must treat him with cold detachment: her stepson! If Accolon said anything kind or pitying, she would scream aloud, would tear at her hair, at her face and flesh with her nails. . . .

But Accolon only said, in a voice that could not have been overheard three feet away, "Perhaps it is enough for the Lady that *we* know, Morgaine. The Goddess will not fail us while a single worshipper gives her what is due."

For a moment she looked round at him. His eyes were dwelling on her, and although his hands on hers were careful, courteous, detached, it seemed that heat ran upward from them into her whole body. She was suddenly frightened and wanted to pull away.

I am his father's wife and of all women I am the one most forbidden to him. I am more forbidden to him, in this Christian land, than I was to Arthur.

And then a memory from Avalon surfaced in her mind, something she had not thought of for a decade; one of the Druids, giving instruction in the secret wisdom to the young priestesses, had said, *If you would have the message of the Gods to direct your life, look for that which repeats, again and again; for this is the message given you by the Gods, the karmic lesson you must learn for this incarnation. It comes again and again until you have made it part of your soul and your enduring spirit.*

What has come to me again and again . . . ?

Every man she had desired had been too close kin to her—Lancelet, who was the son of her foster-mother; Arthur, her own mother's son; now the son of her husband . . .

But they are too close kin to me only by the laws made by the Christians who seek to rule this land . . . to rule it in a new tyranny; not alone to make the laws but to rule the mind and heart and soul. Am I living out in my own life all the tyranny of that law, so I as priestess may know why it must be overthrown?

She discovered that her hands, still tightly held in Accolon's, were trembling. She said, trying to collect her scattered thoughts, "Do you truly believe that the Goddess would withdraw her life from this earth if the folk who dwell here should no longer give her her due?"

It was the sort of remark that might have been made, priestess to priest, in Avalon. Morgaine knew, as well as anyone, that the true answer to that question was that the Gods were what they were, and did their will upon the earth regardless of whether man regarded their doing one way or the other. But Accolon said, with a curious animal flash of white teeth in a grin, "Then must we make it sure, lady, that she should always be given her due, lest the life of the world fail." And then he addressed her by a name never spoken except by priest to priestess in ritual, and Morgaine felt her heart beating so hard she was dizzy.

Lest the life of the world fail. Lest my life fail within me . . . he has called on me in the name of the Goddess. . . .

"Be still," she said, distracted. "This is neither the time nor the place for such talk."

"No?" They had come to the edge of the rough ground. He let go of her hand and somehow her own felt cold without it. Ahead of them the masked dancers shook their phallic wands and capered, and the Spring Maiden, her long hair buffeted and tangled by the breeze, was going around the circle of the dancers, exchanging a kiss with each—a ritualized, formal kiss, where her lips barely touched each cheek. Uriens beckoned Morgaine impatiently to his side; she moved stiffly and cold, feeling the spot on her wrists where Accolon had held her as a spot of heat on her icy body.

Uriens said fussily, "It is your part, my dear, to give out these things to the dancers who have entertained us this day." He motioned to a servant, who filled Morgaine's hands with sweets and candied fruits; she tossed them to the dancers and the spectators, who scrambled for them, laughing and pushing. *Always mockery of the sacred things . . . a memory of the day when the folk scrambled for bits of the flesh and blood of the sacrifice. . . . Let the rite be forgotten, but not mocked this way!* Again and yet again they filled her hands with the sweets, and again and again she tossed them into the crowd. They saw no more in the rite than dancers who had entertained them; had they all forgotten? The Spring Maiden came up to Morgaine, laughing and flushed with innocent pride; Morgaine saw now that although she was lovely, her eyes were shallow, her hands thick and stubby with work in the fields. She was only a pretty peasant girl trying to do the work of a priestess, without the slightest idea what she was doing; it was folly to resent her.

Yet she is a woman, doing the Mother's work in the best way she has ever been told; it is not her fault that she was not schooled in Avalon for the great work.

Morgaine did not quite know what was expected of her, but as the girl knelt for a moment before the Queen, Morgaine took on the half-forgotten stance of a priestess in blessing, and felt for an instant the old awareness of something shadowing her, above her, beyond . . . she laid her hands for a moment on the girl's brow, felt the momentary flow of power between them, and the girl's rather stupid face was transfigured for a moment. *The Goddess works in her, too,* Morgaine thought, and then she saw Accolon's face; he was looking at her in wonder and awe. She had seen that look before, when she brought down the mists from Avalon . . . and the awareness of power flooded her, as if she were suddenly reborn.

I am alive again. After all these years, I am a priestess again, and it was Accolon who brought it back to me. . . .

And then the tension of the moment broke, and the girl backed away, stumbling over her feet, and dropping a clumsy curtsey to the royal party. Uriens distributed coins to the dancers and a somewhat larger gift to the village priest for candles to burn in his church, and the royal party went homeward. Morgaine walked sedately at Uriens' side, her face a mask, but inwardly seething with life. Her stepson Uwaine came and walked beside her.

"It was prettier than usual this year, Mother. Shanna is so lovely—the Spring Maiden, the daughter of the blacksmith Euan. But you, Mother, when you were blessing her, you looked so beautiful, you should have been the Spring Maiden yourself—"

"Come, come," she chided the boy, laughing. "Do you really think I could dress in green with my hair flying, and dance all round the plowed fields that way? And I am no maiden!"

"No," said Uwaine, surveying her with a long look, "but you looked like the Goddess. Father Eian says that the Goddess was really a demon who came to keep the folk from serving the good Christ, but do you know what I think? I think that the Goddess was here for people to worship before they were taught how to worship the holy mother of Christ."

Accolon was walking beside them. He said, "Before the Christ, the Goddess was, and it will not hurt if you think of her as Mary, Uwaine. You should always do service to the Lady, under whatever name. But I would not advise you to speak much about this to Father Eian."

"Oh no," said the boy, his eyes wide. "He does not approve of women, even when they are Goddesses."

"I wonder what he thinks of queens?" Morgaine murmured. Then they had arrived back at the castle and Morgaine had to see to King Uriens' travelling things, and in the confusion of the day, she let the new insights slide into the back of her mind, knowing that later she would have to consider all this most seriously.

Uriens rode away after midday, with his men-at-arms and a body
servant or two, taking leave of Morgaine tenderly with a kiss, counselling
his son Avalloch to listen to Accolon's counsel and that of the queen in all
things. Uwaine was sulking; he wanted to go with his father, whom he
adored, but Uriens would not be troubled with a child in the party.
Morgaine had to comfort him, promise some special treat for him while his
father was away. But at last all was quiet, and Morgaine could sit alone
before the fire in the great hall—Maline had taken her children off to bed
—and think of all that had befallen her that day.

It was twilight outside, the long evening of Midsummer. Morgaine
had taken her spindle and distaff in her hand, but she was only pretending
to spin, twirling it once in a while and drawing out a little thread; she
disliked spinning as much as ever, and one of the few things she had asked
of Uriens was that she might employ two extra spinning women so that she
would be free of that detested task; she did twice her share of the household
weaving in its stead. She *dared* not spin; it would throw her into that strange
state between sleep and waking, and she feared what she might see. So now
she only twirled the spindle now and again, that none of the servants would
see her sitting with her hands idle . . . not that anyone would have the right
to reproach her, she was busy early and late. . . .

The room was darkening, a few slashes of crimson light from the
setting sun still brilliant, darkening the corners by contrast. Morgaine narrowed her eyes, thinking of the red sun setting over the ring stones on the
Tor, of the priestesses walking in train behind the red torchlight, spilling
it into the shadows . . . for a moment Raven's face flickered before her, silent,
enigmatic, and it seemed that Raven opened her silent lips and spoke her
name . . . faces floated before her in the twilight: Elaine, her hair all unbound
as the torchlight caught her in Lancelet's bed; Gwenhwyfar, angry and
triumphant at Morgaine's wedding; the calm, still face of the strange woman
with braided fair hair, the woman she had seen only in dreams, Lady of
Avalon . . . Raven again, frightened, entreating . . . Arthur, bearing a candle
of penitence as he walked among his subjects . . . oh, but the priests would
never dare force the King to public penance, would they? And then she saw
the barge of Avalon, draped all in black for a funeral, and her own face like
a reflection on the mists, mirrored there, with three other women draped
all in black like the barge, and a wounded man lying white and still in her
lap—

Torchlight flared crimson across the dark room, and a voice said, "Are
you trying to spin in the dark, Mother?"

Confused by the light, Morgaine looked up and said peevishly, "I have
told you not to call me that!"

Accolon put the torch into a bracket, and came to sit at her feet. "The

Goddess is Mother to us all, lady, and I acknowledge you as such. . . ."

"Are you mocking me?" Morgaine demanded, agitated.

"I do not mock." As Accolon knelt close to her, his lips trembled. "I saw your face today. Would I mock *that*—wearing *these?*" He thrust out his arms, and by a trick of the light, the blue serpents dyed on his wrists seemed to writhe and thrust up their painted heads. "Lady, Mother, Goddess—" His painted arms went out around her waist, and he buried his head in her lap. He muttered, "Yours is the face of the Goddess to me. . . ."

As if she moved in a dream, Morgaine put out her hands to him, bending to kiss the back of his neck where the soft hair curled. Part of her was wondering, frightened, *What am I doing? Is it only that he has called on me in the name of the Goddess, priest to priestess? Or is it only that when he touches me, speaks to me, I feel myself woman and alive again after all this time when I have felt myself old, barren, half dead in this marriage to a dead man and a dead life?* Accolon raised his face to her, kissed her full on the lips. Morgaine, yielding to the kiss, felt herself melting, opened, a shudder, half pain half pleasure, running through her as his tongue against hers shot waking memories through her whole body . . . so long, so long, this long year when her body had been deadened, never letting itself wake lest it be aware of what Uriens was doing. . . . She thought, defiant, *I am a priestess, my body is mine to be given in homage to her! What I did with Uriens was the sin, the submission to lust! This is true and holy. . . .*

His hands trembled on her body; but when he spoke, his voice was quiet and practical.

"I think all the castle folk are abed. I knew you would be here waiting for me. . . ."

For a moment Morgaine resented his certainty; then she bowed her head. They were in the hands of the Goddess and she would not refuse the flow that carried her on, like a river; long, long, she had only whirled about in a backwater, and now she was washed clean into the current of life again. "Where is Avalloch?"

He laughed shortly. "He is gone down to the village to lie with the Spring Maiden . . . it is one of our customs that the village priest does *not* know. Ever, since our father was old and we were grown men, it has been so, and Avalloch does not think it incompatible with his duty as a Christian man, to be the father of his people, or as many of them as possible, like Uriens himself in his youth. Avalloch offered to cast lots with me for the privilege, and I had started to do so, then I remembered your hands blessing her, and knew where my true homage lay. . . ."

She murmured half in protest, "Avalon is so far away . . ."

He said, with his face against her breast, "But she is everywhere."

Morgaine whispered, "So be it," and rose. She pulled him upright with her and made a half turn toward the stairs, then stopped. No, not here; there was not a bed in this castle that they could honorably share. And the Druid maxim returned to her, *Can that which was never made nor created by Man, be worshipped under a roof made by human hands?*

Out, then, into the night. As they stepped into the empty courtyard, a falling star rushed downward across the sky, so swiftly that for an instant it seemed to Morgaine that the heavens reeled and the earth moved backward under her feet . . . then it was gone, leaving their eyes dazzled. *A portent. The Goddess welcomes me back to herself. . . .*

"Come," she whispered, her hand in Accolon's, and led him upward to the orchard, where the white ghosts of blossom drifted in the darkness and fell around them. She spread her cloak on the grass, like a magic circle under the sky; held out her arms and whispered, "Come."

The dark shadow of his body over her blotted out the sky and the stars.

MORGAINE SPEAKS . . .

Even as we lay together under the stars that Midsummer, I knew that what we had done was not so much lovemaking as a magical act of passionate power; that his hands, the touch of his body, were reconsecrating me priestess, and that it was her will. Blind as I was to all at that moment, I heard around us in the summer night the sound of whispers and I knew that we were not alone.

He would have held me in his arms, but I rose, driven on by whatever power held me now at this hour, and raised my hands above my head, bringing them down slowly, my eyes closed, my breath held in the tension of power . . . and only when I heard him gasp in awe did I venture to open my eyes, to see his body rimmed with that same faint light which edged my own.

It is done and she is with me. . . . Mother, I am unworthy in thy sight . . . but now it has come again. . . . I held my breath to keep from breaking out into wild weeping. After all these years, after my own betrayal and my faithlessness, she has come again to me and I am priestess once more. A pale glimmer of moonlight showed me, at the edge of the field where we lay, though I saw not even a shadow, the glimmer of eyes like some animal in the hedgerow. We were not alone, the little people of the hills had known where we were and what she wrought here, and come to see the consummation unknown here since Uriens grew old and the world had turned grey and Christian. I heard the echo of a reverent whisper and returned it in a tongue of which I knew less than a dozen words, just audible where I stood and where Accolon still knelt in reverence.

"It is done; so let it be!"

I bent and kissed him on the brow, repeating, "It is done. Go, my dear; be thou blessed."

He would have stayed, I know, had I been the woman with whom he had come into that garden; but before the priestess he went silent away, not questioning the word of the Goddess.

There was no sleep for me that night. Alone, I walked in the garden till dawn, and I knew already, shaking with terror, what must be done. I did not know how, or whether, alone, I could do what I had begun, but as I had been made priestess so many years ago and renounced it, so must I retrace my steps alone. This night I had been given a great grace; but I knew there would be no more signs for me and no help given until I had made myself, alone, unaided, again the priestess I had been trained to be.

I bore still on my brow, faded beneath that housewifely coif Uriens would have me wear, the sign of her grace, but that would not help me now. Gazing at the fading stars, I did not know whether or no the rising sun would surprise me at my vigil; the sun tides had not run in my blood for half a lifetime, and I no longer knew the precise place on the eastern horizon where I should turn to salute the sun at its rising. I knew not, anymore, even how the moon-tides ran with the cycles of my body . . . so far had I come from the training of Avalon. Alone, with no more than a fading memory, I must somehow recapture all the things I had once known as part of myself.

Before dawn I went silently indoors, and moving in the dark, found for myself the one token I had of Avalon—the little sickle knife I had taken from Viviane's dead body, a knife like the one I had borne as priestess and had abandoned in Avalon when I fled from there. I bound it silently around my waist, beneath my outer garments; it would never leave my side again and it would be buried with me.

I wore it thus, hidden there, the only memory I could keep of that night. I did not even paint the crescent anew on my brow, partly because of Uriens—he would have questioned it—and partly because I knew I was not, yet, worthy to bear it; I would not have worn the crescent as he wore the faded serpents about his arms, an ornament and a half-forgotten reminder of what once he had been and was no more. Over these next months and as they stretched into years, one part of me moved like a painted doll through the duties he demanded of me—spinning and weaving, making herbal medicines, looking to the needs of son and grandson, listening to my husband's talk, embroidering him fine clothes and tending him in sickness . . . all these things I did without much thought, with the very surface of my mind and a body gone numb for those times when he took brief and distasteful possession of it.

But the knife was there to touch now and again for reassurance as I learned again to count sun tides from equinox to solstice and back to equinox again . . . count them painfully on my fingers like a child or a novice priestess; it was years before I could feel them running in my blood again, or know to a hairline's difference where on the horizon moon or sun would rise or set for the salutations I learned again to make. Again, late at night while the household lay sleeping round me, I would study the stars, letting their influence move in my blood as they wheeled and swung around me until I became only a pivot point on the motionless earth, center of the whirling dance around and above me, the spiraling movement of the seasons. I rose early and slept late so that I might find hours to range into the hills, on pretext of seeking root and herb for medicines, and there I sought out the old lines of force, tracing them from standing stone to hammer pool . . . it was weary work and it was years before I knew even a few of them near to Uriens' castle.

But even in that first year, when I struggled with fading memory, trying to recapture what I had known so many years ago, I knew my vigils were not unshared. I was never unattended, though never did I see more than I had seen that first night, the gleam of an eye in the darkness, a flicker of motion out of the corner of my eyes . . . they were seldom seen, even here in the far hills, anywhere in village and field; they lived their own life secretly in deserted hills and forests where they had fled when the Romans came. But I knew they were there, that the little folk who had never lost sight of Her watched over me.

Once in the far hills I found a ring of stones, not a great one like that which stood on the Tor at Avalon, nor the greater one which had once been Temple of the Sun on the great chalk plains; here the stones were no more than shoulder-high even on me (and I am not tall) and the circle no greater than the height of a tall man. A small slab of stone, the stains faded and overgrown with lichens, was half-buried in the grass at the center. I pulled it free of weed and lichen, and as I did whenever I could find food unseen in the kitchens, left for her people such things as I knew seldom came to them—a slab of barley bread, a bit of cheese, a lump of butter. And once when I went there I found at the very center of the stones a garland of the scented flowers which grew on the border of the fairy country; dried, they would never fade. When next I took Accolon out of doors when the moon was full, I wore them tied about my brow as we came together in that solemn joining which swept away the individual and made us only Goddess and God, affirming the endless life of the cosmos, the flow of power between male and female as between earth and sky. After that I went never unattended beyond my own garden. I knew better than to look for them directly, but they were there and I knew they would be there if I needed them. It was not for nothing that I had been given that old name, Morgaine of the Fairies . . . and now they acknowledged me as their priestess and their queen.

I came to the stone circle, walking by night, when the harvest moon sank low in the sky and the breath of the fourth winter grew cold on the eve of the Day of the Dead. There, wrapped in my cloak and shivering through the night, I kept the vigil, fasting; snow was drifting out of the sky when I rose and turned my steps homeward, but as I left the circle I turned my foot on a stone which had not been there when I came thither, and, bending my head, I saw the pattern of white stones arranged.

. . .
. .
. .

I bent, moving one stone to make the next in sequence of the magical numbers —the tides had shifted and now we were under the winter's stars. Then I went home, shivering, to tell a story of being benighted in the hills and sleeping in an empty shepherd's hut—Uriens had been frightened by the snow, and sent two men to seek me. Snow, lying deep on the mountainsides, kept me within doors much of the winter, but I knew when the storms would lift and risked the journey to the ring stones at Midwinter, knowing the stones would be clear . . . snow lay never within the great circles, I knew, and I guessed that it would be so here in the smaller circles, where magic was still done.

And there at the very center of the circle I saw a tiny bundle—a scrap of leather tied with sinew. My fingers were recapturing their old skill and did not fumble as I untied it and rolled the contents into my palm. They looked like a couple of dried seeds, but they were the tiny mushrooms which grew so rarely near Avalon. They were no use as food, and most folk thought them poison, for they would cause vomiting and purging and a bloody flux; but taken sparingly, fasting, they could open the gates to the Sight . . . this was a gift more precious than gold. They grew not in this country at all, and I could only guess how far the little folk had wandered in search of them. I left them what food I had brought, dried meats and fruits and a honeycomb, but not in repayment; the gift was priceless. I knew that I would lock myself within my chamber at Midwinter, and there seek again the Sight I had renounced. With the gates of vision thus opened I could seek and dare the very presence of the Goddess, begging to repronounce what I had forsworn. I had no fear that I would be cast forth again. It was she who sent me this gift that I might seek again her presence.

And I bent to the ground in thanksgiving, knowing that my prayers had been heard and my penance done.

10

the snow was beginning to melt off the hills and a few of the earliest wild flowers showed in sheltered valleys when the Lady of the Lake was summoned to the barge to greet the Merlin of Britain. Kevin looked pale and worn, his face haggard, his twisted limbs dragging more reluctantly than ever, and he braced himself with a stout stick. Niniane noticed, her eyes hiding the pity she felt, that he had been forced to put My Lady from him into the hands of a serving-man, and she pretended not to see, knowing what a blow that must have been to his pride. She slowed her own steps on the path toward her dwelling place, and there she welcomed him, summoned her women to build up the fire, and sent for wine, of which he took only a token sip, and bowed gravely in thanks.

"What brings you here so early in the year, Venerable?" she asked him. "Have you come from Camelot?"

He shook his head. "I was there for a part of the winter," he said, "and I spoke much with Arthur's councillors, but early in the spring I went southward on a mission to the treaty troops—I should say now, I suppose, the Saxon kingdoms. And I take it you know whom I saw there, Niniane. Was that Morgause's doing, or yours, I wonder?"

"Neither," she said quietly. "It was Gwydion's own choice. He knew he should have some experience in battle, Druid teaching or no—there have been warrior Druids ere this. And he chose to go south to the Saxon kingdoms—they are allied with Arthur, but there he would not come under Arthur's eyes. He did not—for reasons known as well to you as to me—wish for Arthur to set eyes on him." After a moment she added, "I would not swear that Morgause did not influence his choice. He takes counsel of her, when he will seek the counsel of any."

"Is it so?" Kevin raised his eyebrows. "Aye, I suppose so—she is the only mother he has ever known. And she ruled Lot's kingdom as well as any man, and still rules, even with her new consort."

"I heard not that she had a new consort," said Niniane. "I cannot see as well what happens in the kingdoms as did Viviane."

"Aye, she had the Sight to aid her," Kevin said, "and maidens with the Sight when her own Sight failed her. Have you none, Niniane?"

"I have—some," she said hesitating. "Yet it fails me now and again—" and she was silent a moment, staring at the flagstones of the floor. At last she said, "I think—Avalon is—is drifting further from the lands of men, Lord Merlin. What season was it in the world outside?"

"Ten days have passed since the equinox, Lady," said Kevin.

Niniane drew a long breath. "And I kept that feast but seven days since. It is as I thought—the lands are drifting. As yet no more than a few days in every moon, but I fear soon we shall be as far from sun tide and moon tide as that fairy kingdom they tell of . . . it is ever harder to summon the mists and to pass forth from this land."

"I know," said Kevin. "Why, think you, I came at the slack of the tide?" He smiled his twisted grin and said, "You should rejoice—you will not age as women in the outer world are prone to age, Lady, but remain younger."

"You do not comfort me," said Niniane with a shudder. "Yet there is none in the outer world whose fate I follow, save—"

"Gwydion's," said Kevin. "I thought as much. But there is one with whose fate you should be concerned as well—"

"Arthur in his palace? He has renounced us," said Niniane, "and Avalon lends him no more help—"

"It is not of Arthur I spoke," said Kevin, "nor does he seek help from Avalon, not now. But—" He hesitated. "I heard it from the folk of the hills —there is a king again in Wales, and a queen."

"Uriens?" Niniane laughed, a scoffing laugh. "He is older than those same hills, Kevin! What can he do for those folk?"

"Nor did I speak of Uriens," said Kevin. "Had you forgotten? Morgaine is there, and the Old People have accepted her as their queen. She will protect them, even against Uriens, while she lives. Had you forgotten that the son of Uriens had teaching here, and wears the serpents about his wrists?"

Niniane was silent for a moment, motionless. At last she said, "I had forgotten that. He was not the elder son, so I thought he would never reign—"

"The elder son is a fool," said Kevin, "though the priests think him a good successor to his father, and from their view, he is so—pious and simple and he will not interfere with their church. The priests trust not the second son—Accolon—because he wears the serpents. And, since Morgaine has come there, he has remembered it, and serves her as his queen. And for the folk of the hills she is queen, too, whoever may sit on the throne in the Roman fashion. For them, the king is he who dies yearly among the deer, but the queen is eternal. And it may be that in the end Morgaine will do what Viviane left undone."

Niniane could hear, with a detached surprise, the bitterness in her own voice. "Kevin, not for one day since Viviane died and they came to set me here, have I been allowed to forget that I am not Viviane, that after Viviane I am nothing. Even Raven follows me with her great silent eyes that say always, *You are not Viviane, you cannot do the work Viviane spent her life to do.* I know it well—that I was chosen only because I am the last of Taliesin's blood and there was no other, that I am not of the royal line of the Queen of Avalon! No, I am not Viviane, and I am not Morgaine, but I have served faithfully here in this place when I sought it never and when it was thrust upon me because of Taliesin's blood. I have been faithful to my vows— is this nothing to anyone?"

"Lady," said Kevin gently, "Viviane was such a priestess as comes not into this world more than once in many hundreds of years, even in Avalon. And her reign was long—she ruled here for nine-and-thirty years, and very few of us can remember before her time. Any priestess who must follow in her steps would feel herself less in comparison. There is nothing for which you must reproach yourself. You have been faithful to your vows."

"As Morgaine was not," said Niniane.

"True. But she is of the blood royal of Avalon, and she bore the heir to the King Stag. It is not for us to judge her."

"You defend her because you were her lover—" Niniane flared, and Kevin raised his head. She had not realized; set within the dark and twisted face, his eyes were blue, like the very center of flame. He said quietly, "Would you try to pick a quarrel with me, Lady? That is over and gone years since, and when last I saw Morgaine, she called me traitor and worse, and drove me from her presence with harsh words such as no man with blood in his veins could forgive. Do you think I love her too well? But it is not my place to judge her, nor yours. You are the Lady of the Lake. Morgaine is my queen, and Queen of Avalon. She does her work in the world as you do yours here—and I where the Gods lead me. And they led me this spring into the fen country, where, at the court of a Saxon who calls himself king under Arthur, I saw Gwydion."

Niniane had been schooled in her long training to keep her face impassive; but she knew that Kevin, who had had the same teaching, could see that she must do so with an effort, and felt that somehow those sharp eyes could read within her. She wanted to ask news of him, but instead she said only, "Morgause told me that he has some knowledge of strategy and is no coward in battle. How fared he, then, among those barbarians who would rather batter out brains with their great clubs than make use of them at their courts? I knew he went south to the Saxon kingdoms because one of them wished for a Druid at court who could read and write and knew something of figures and mapmaking. And he said to me that he wished to be seasoned in war without coming under the eye of Arthur, so I suppose he had his wish. Even though there has been peace in the land, there is always fighting among yonder folk—is the Saxon God not one of war and battles?"

"Mordred, they call Gwydion, which means "Evil Counsel" in their tongue. It is a compliment—they mean it is evil for those who would harm them. They give every guest a name, as they call Lancelet Elf-arrow."

"Among the Saxons, a Druid, even a young one, might seem wiser than he is, in contrast to all their thick heads! And Gwydion is clever! Even as a boy he could think of a dozen answers for everything!"

"Clever he is," said Kevin slowly, "and knows well how to make himself loved, I have seen that. Me, he welcomed as if I had been his favorite uncle in childhood, saying how good it was to see a familiar face from Avalon, embracing me, making much of me—all as if he loved me well."

"No doubt he was lonely and you were like a breath from home," said

Niniane, but Kevin frowned and drank a little wine, then set it down and forgot it again. He demanded, "How far did Gwydion go in the magical training?"

"He wears the serpents," Niniane said.

"That may mean much or little," Kevin said. "You should know that—" And although the words were innocent, Niniane felt their sting; a priestess who bore the crescent on her brow might be a Viviane— or no more than she herself. She said, "He is to return at Midsummer to be made King of Avalon, that state Arthur betrayed. And now he is grown to manhood—"

Kevin warned, "He is not ready to be king."

"Do you doubt his courage? Or his loyalty—"

"Oh—courage," said Kevin, and made a dismissing gesture. "Courage, and cleverness—but it is his heart I trust not and cannot read. And he is not Arthur."

"It is well for Avalon that he is not," Niniane flared. "We need no more apostates who swear loyalty to Avalon and forsake their oath to the folk of the hills! The priests may set a pious hypocrite on the throne, who will serve whatever God he finds expedient at the moment—"

Kevin raised his twisted hand, with such a commanding gesture that Niniane fell silent. "Avalon is not the world! We have neither strength, nor armies, nor craft, and Arthur is loved beyond measure. Not in Avalon, I grant you, but all the length and breadth of these islands, where Arthur is the hand that has created the peace they value. At this moment, any voice arising against Arthur would be silenced within months, if not within days. Arthur is loved—he is the very spirit of all Britain. And even if it were otherwise, what we do in Avalon has little weight in the world outside. As you marked, we are drifting into the mists."

"Then all the more must we move quickly, to bring Arthur down and set a king on the throne of Britain who will restore Avalon to the world and the Goddess. . . ."

Kevin said quietly, "I wonder, sometimes, if that can ever be done— if we have all spent our lives within a dream without reality."

"You say that? You, the Merlin of Britain?"

"I have been at Arthur's court, not sheltered in an island that moves ever further from the world outside," said Kevin gently. "This is my home, and I would die, as I am sworn . . . but it was with Britain I made the Great Marriage, Niniane, not with Avalon alone."

"If Avalon dies," said Niniane, "then Britain is without her heart and will die, for the Goddess has withdrawn her soul from all the land."

"Think you so, Niniane?" Kevin sighed again, and said, "I have been all up and down these lands, in all weathers and all times—Merlin of Britain, hawk of the Sight, messenger of the Great Raven—and I see now another heart in the land, and it shines forth from Camelot."

He was silent. After a long while Niniane said, "Was it when you said such words as this to Morgaine that she called you traitor?"

"No—it was something else," he said. "Perhaps, Niniane, we do not know the ways of the Gods and their will as well as we think we do. I tell you, if we move now to bring Arthur down, this land will fall into a chaos worse than that when Ambrosius died and Uther had to fight for his crown. Do you think Gwydion can fight as Arthur did to take the land? Arthur's Companions would all be ranged against any man who rose against their king and their hero—he is like a God to them and can do no wrong."

"It was never our wish," said Niniane, "that Gwydion should face his father and fight him for his crown—only that one day, when Arthur knows he has no heir, he must turn to the son who comes of the royal line of Avalon and is sworn to loyalty to Avalon and the true Gods. And to that end he must be proclaimed King Stag in Avalon, so that there may be voices, when Arthur seeks an heir, to speak for him. I have heard that Arthur has chosen Lancelet's son for his heir, since the Queen is barren. But Lancelet's son is but a young child, and Gwydion already a man grown. If anything happened to Arthur now, do you not think they would choose Gwydion—a grown man, a warrior and a Druid—over a child?"

"Arthur's Companions would not follow a stranger, were he twice over warrior and Druid. Most likely they would name Gawaine regent for Lancelet's son till he came of age. And the Companions are Christian, most of them, and would reject Gwydion because of his birth—incest is a grave sin among them."

"They know nothing of sacred things."

"Granted. They must have time to accustom themselves to the idea, and that time is not yet. But if Gwydion cannot now be acknowledged as Arthur's son, it should be known that the priestess Morgaine, who is Arthur's own sister, has a son, and that this son is closer to the throne than Lancelet's child. And this summer there will be war again—"

"I thought," said Niniane, "that Arthur had made peace."

"Here in Britain, yes. But there is one in Less Britain who would claim all of Britain as his empire—"

"Ban?" asked Niniane in astonishment. "He was sworn long ago—he made the Great Marriage before our Lancelet was born. He would be all too old to go to war against Arthur—"

"Ban is old and feeble," said Kevin. "His son Lionel rules in his place, and Lionel's brother Bors is one of Arthur's Companions, and worships Lancelet as his hero. Neither of them would trouble Arthur's rule. But there is one who will. He calls himself Lucius, and he has somehow gotten the ancient Roman eagles and proclaimed himself emperor. And he will challenge Arthur—"

Niniane's skin prickled. She asked, "Is that the Sight?"

"Morgaine said to me once," Kevin said with a smile, "that it needed not the Sight to know a rogue will be a rogue. It needs not the Sight to know that an ambitious man will challenge where the challenge will further his ambition. There are those who may think Arthur is growing old because his hair shines not all gold as it did and he flies the dragon no more. But do not rate him low, Niniane. I know him, you do not. He is not a fool!"

"I think," said Niniane, "that you love him too well for a man you are sworn to destroy."

"Love him?" Kevin's smile was mirthless. "I am Merlin of Britain, messenger of the Great Raven, and I sit at his side in council. Arthur is an easy man to love. But I am sworn to the Goddess." Again the short laugh. "I think my sanity depends on this—that I know that what benefits Avalon must in the long years benefit Britain. You see Arthur as the enemy, Niniane. I see him still as the King Stag, protecting his herd and his lands."

Niniane said in a trembling whisper, "And what of the King Stag when the young stag is grown?"

Kevin leaned his head on his hands. He looked old and ill and weary. "That day is not yet, Niniane. Do not seek to push Gwydion so swiftly he will be destroyed, merely because he is your lover." And he rose and limped out of the room without looking back, leaving Niniane sullen and angry.

How did that wretched man know that?

And she told herself, *I am under no vows like the Christian nuns! If I choose to take a man to my bed, that is for me to say . . . even if that man should be my pupil, and only a boy when he came here!*

In the first years, he had twined himself around her heart, a lonely boy, lost and bereft, with none to love him or care for him or wonder how he did. . . . Morgause was the only mother he had known, and now he was parted from her too. How could Morgaine have found it in her heart to give up a fine son like this, clever and beautiful and wise, and never send to inquire how he did, or come to set eyes on him? Niniane had never borne a child, though she had thought, sometimes, that if she had come from Beltane with her womb filled she would have liked to bear a daughter to the Goddess. But it had never gone thus with her, and she had not rebelled against her lot.

But in those first years she had let Gwydion find his way into her heart. And then he had gone from them, as men must do, grown too old for the teachings of the priestesses, to be taught among the Druids and schooled in the arts of war. And he had returned, one year at Beltane, and she thought it was by craft that he had come near to her in the fire rites and she had gone apart with him. . . .

But they had not parted when that season was over; and whenever, after that, in his comings and goings, anything had brought him to Avalon, she made it clear that she wanted him, and he had not said her no. *I am closest to his heart,* she thought, *I know him best—what does Kevin know of him?*

And now the time has come when he shall return to Avalon, and shall have his trial as King Stag. . . .

And she turned her thoughts to that: where should she find a maiden for him? *There are so few women in the House of Maidens who are even halfway fit for this great office,* she thought, and there was sudden pain and dread in her thoughts.

Kevin was right. Avalon is drifting, dying; few come here for the ancient teachings, and there are none to keep the rites . . . and one day there will be no one at all . . . and again she felt that almost painful prickling in her body which came to her, now and again, in lieu of the Sight.

GWYDION CAME HOME to Avalon a few days before Beltane. Niniane greeted him formally at the boat, and he bowed to her in reverence before the maidens and the assembled folk of the Island, but when they were alone he caught her in his arms and kissed her, laughing, until they were both breathless.

His shoulders had broadened, and there was a red seam on his face. He had been fighting, she could tell; he no longer had the untroubled look of a priest and scholar.

My lover and my child. Is this why the Great Goddess has no husband, after the Roman fashion, but only sons, as we are all her children? And I who sit in her place must feel my lover as my son too . . . for all those who love the Goddess are her children. . . .

"And the lands are astir with it," he said, "here in Avalon and among the Old People of the hills, that on Dragon Island the Old People will be choosing their king again. . . . It was for this that you summoned me there, was it not?"

Sometimes, she thought, he could be as infuriating as an arrogant child. "I do not know, Gwydion. The time may not be ripe, and the tides may not be ready. Nor can I find anywhere within this house anyone to play for you the part of the Spring Maiden."

"Yet it will be this spring," he said quietly, "and this Beltane, for I have seen it."

Her mouth curved a little as she said, "And have you then seen the priestess who will admit you to the rite when you have won the antlers, supposing that the Sight does not mislead you to your death?"

She thought as he faced her that he had but grown more beautiful, his face cold and set, dark with hidden passion. "I have, Niniane. Do you not know that it was you?"

She said, suddenly chilled to the bone, "I am no maiden. Why do you mock me, Gwydion?"

"Yet I have seen you," he said, "and you know it as well as I. In her the Maiden and the Mother and the Crone meet and blend. She will be old and young as it shall please her, Virgin and Beast and Mother and the face of Death in the lightning, flowing and filling and returning again to her virginity. . . ."

Niniane bent her head and said, "Gwydion, no, it cannot be—"

"I am her consort," he said implacably, "and shall win it there . . . it is not the time for a virgin—the priests make much of that nonsense. I call upon her as the Mother to give me my due and my life. . . ."

Niniane felt as if she were trying to stand against some relentless tide that would sweep her away. She said, hesitating, "So it has always been, that in the running of the deer, though the Mother sends him forth, he returns again to the Maiden. . . ."

Yet there was reason in what he said. Surely it was better to have a priestess for the rites who knew what she was doing, rather than some half-trained child new come to the temple, whose only qualification was that she was not yet old enough to feel the call to the Beltane fire. . . . Gwydion spoke truth: the Mother ever renews herself, Mother and Crone and again the Maiden, even as the moon who hides herself in the dark sky.

She bent her head and said, "Let it be so. You shall make the Great Marriage with the land and with me in her name."

But when she was alone again she was frightened. How had she come to agree to this? What, in the name of the Goddess, was this power in Gwydion, that he could make all men do his will?

Is this, then, his heritage from Arthur, and the blood of the Pendragon? And ice flooded her again.

What of the King Stag . . . Morgaine was dreaming . . .

Beltane, and the deer running on the hills . . . and the life of the forest running through her body, as if every part of the forest was a part of the life within her . . . he was down among the deer, the running stag, the naked man with the antlers tied on his brow, and the horns thrust down and down, his dark hair matted with blood . . . but he was on his feet, charging, a knife flashing in the sunlight through the trees, and the King Stag came crashing down and the sound of his bellowing filled the forest with cries of despair.

And then she was in the dark cave, and the signs painted there were painted on her body, she was one with the cave, and all around her the Beltane fires flared,

sparks crashing skyward—there was the taste of fresh blood on her mouth, and now
the cave mouth was shadowed with the antlers . . . it should not be full moon, she
should not see so clearly that her naked body was not the slender body of a virgin,
but that her breasts were soft and full and pink as they had been when her child
was born, almost as if they were dripping with milk, and surely she had been tested
that she came virgin to this rite . . . what would they say to her, that she came
not as the Spring Maiden to the King Stag?

He knelt at her side and she raised her arms, welcoming him to the rite and
to her body, but his eyes were dark and haunted. His hands on her were tender,
frustrating, toying with pleasure as he denied her the rite of power . . . it was not
Arthur, no, this was Lancelet, King Stag, who should pull down the old stag,
consort of the Spring Maiden, but he looked down at her, his dark eyes tormented
by that same pain that struck inward through her whole body, and he said, I would
you were not so like to my mother, Morgaine. . . .

Terrified, her heart pounding, Morgaine woke in her own room,
Uriens sleeping at her side and snoring. Still caught up in the frightening
magic of the dream, she shook her head in confusion to ward the terror
away.

No, Beltane is past . . . she had kept the rites with Accolon as she had
known she would do, she was not lying in the cave, awaiting the King Stag
. . . and why, she wondered, why should this dream of Lancelet visit her
now, why did she dream not of Accolon, when she had made him her priest
and Lord of Beltane, and her lover? Why, after so many years, should the
memory of refusal and sacrilege strike inward at her very soul?

She tried to compose herself for sleep again, but sleep would not come,
and she lay awake, shaken, until the sun thrust the rays of early summer into
her chamber.

11

Gwenhwyfar had come to hate the day of Pentecost,
when each year Arthur sent out word that all his old Companions should
come to Camelot and renew their fellowship. With the growing of peace
in the land, and the scattering of the old Companions, every year there were
fewer to come, more who had ties to their own homes and families and
estates. And Gwenhwyfar was glad, for these Pentecost reunions put her too
much in mind of those days when Arthur had not been a Christian king
but bore the hated Pendragon banner. At Pentecost court he belonged to
his Companions and she had no part at all in his life.

She stood behind him now as he sealed the two dozen copies his scribes had made, for every one of his fellow kings and many of his old Companions. "Why do you send out a special call for them to come this year? Surely all those who have no other business will come without your calling."

"But that is not enough this year," said Arthur, turning to smile at her. He was going grey, she realized, though he was so fair-haired that none could see unless they were standing quite close. "I wish to assure them of such games and mock battles as will make all men aware that Arthur's legion is still well able to fight."

"Do you think any will doubt this?" Gwenhwyfar asked.

"Perhaps not. But there is this man Lucius in Less Britain—Bors has sent me word, and as all my subject kings came to my aid when the Saxons and Northmen would have overrun this island, so I am pledged to come to theirs. Emperor, he calls himself, of Rome!"

"And has he any right to be emperor?" Gwenhwyfar asked.

"Need you ask? Far less than I, certainly," Arthur said. "There has been no Emperor of Rome for more than a hundred years, my wife. Constantine was emperor and wore the purple, and after him Magnus Maximus, who went abroad over the channel to try and make himself emperor; but he came never back to Britain, and God alone knows what befell him or where he died. And after him, Ambrosius Aurelianus rallied our people against the Saxons, and after him Uther, and I suppose either of them could have called himself emperor, or I, but I am content to be High King of Britain. When I was a boy I read something of the history of Rome, and it was nothing new that some upstart pretender should somehow get the loyalty of a legion or two, and proclaim himself to the purple. But here in Britain it takes more than an eagle standard to make an Imperator. Else would Uriens be emperor in this land! I have sent for him to come—it seems long since I have seen my sister."

Gwenhwyfar did not answer that, not directly. She shuddered. "I do not want to see this land touched by war again, and torn apart by slaughter—"

"Nor do I," said Arthur. "I think every king would rather have peace."

"I am not so certain. There are some of your men who never cease speaking of the old days when they fought early and late against the Saxons. And now they begrudge Christian fellowship to those same Saxons, no matter what their bishop says—"

"I do not think it is the days of war they regret," Arthur said, smiling at his queen, "I think it is the days when we were all young, and the closeness that was between us all. Do you never long for those years, my wife?"

Gwenhwyfar felt herself coloring. Indeed, she remembered well . . . those days when Lancelet had been her champion, and they had loved

. . . this was no way for a Christian queen to think, and yet she could not stop herself. "Indeed I do, my husband. And, as you say, perhaps it is only longing for my own youth . . . I am not young," she said, sighing, and he took her hand and said, "You are as beautiful to me, my dearest, as the day when we were first bedded," and she knew that it was true.

But she forced herself to be calm, not to blush. *I am not young,* she thought, *it is not seemly that I should think of those days when I was young and regret them, because in those days I was a sinner and an adulteress. Now I have repented and made peace with God, and even Arthur has done penance for his sin with Morgaine.* She forced herself to practicality, as befitted the Queen of all Britain. "I suppose we shall have more visitors than ever, then, at Pentecost—I must take counsel with Cai, and sir Lucan, as to where we shall bestow them all, and how we shall feast them. Will Bors come from Less Britain?"

"He will come if he can," Arthur said, "although Lancelet sent me a message earlier in this week, asking leave to go and aid his brother Bors if he is besieged there. I sent him word to come here, for it might be that we will all go. . . . Now that Pellinore is gone, Lancelet is king there as Elaine's husband, while their son is a little child. And Agravaine will come for Morgause of Lothian, and Uriens—or perhaps one of his sons. Uriens is marvelously well preserved for his years, but he is not immortal. His elder son is something of a fool, but Accolon is one of my old Companions, and Uriens has Morgaine to guide and counsel him."

"That seems not right to me," Gwenhwyfar said, "for the Holy Apostle said that women should submit themselves to their husbands, yet Morgause rules still in Lothian, and Morgaine would be more than helpmeet to her king in North Wales."

"You must remember, my lady," said Arthur, "that I come of the royal line of Avalon. I am king, not only as Uther Pendragon's son, but because I am son of Igraine, who was daughter to the old Lady of the Lake. Gwenhwyfar, from time out of mind, the Lady ruled the land, and the king was no more than consort in time of war. Even in the days of Rome, the legions dealt with what they came to call *client queens,* who ruled the Tribes, and some of them were mighty warriors. Have you heard never of the Queen Boadicea?—she who, when her daughters were raped by the men of the legions, and the queen herself flogged as a rebel against Rome, raised an army and nearly drove all the Romans from these shores."

Gwenhwyfar said bitterly, "I hope they killed her."

"Oh, they did, and outraged her body . . . yet it was a sign that the Romans could not hope to conquer without accepting that in this country, the Lady rules. . . . Every ruler of Britain, down to my father, Uther, has borne the title the Romans coined for a war leader under a queen: *dux bellorum,* duke of war. Uther, and I after him, bear the throne of Britain as *dux bellorum* to the Lady of Avalon, Gwenhwyfar. Forget not that."

Gwenhwyfar said impatiently, "I thought you had done with that, that you had professed yourself a Christian king and done penance for your servitude to the fairy folk of that evil island. . . ."

Arthur said, with equal impatience, "My personal life and my religious faith are one thing, Gwenhwyfar, but the Tribes stand by me because I bear *this!*" His hand struck against Excalibur, belted at his side, inside its crimson scabbard. "I survived in war because of the magic of this blade—"

"You survived in war because God spared you to Christianize this land," said Gwenhwyfar.

"Some day, perhaps. That time is not yet, lady. In Lothian, men are content to live under the rule of Morgause, and Morgaine is queen in Cornwall and in North Wales. If the time were ripe for all these lands to fall to the rule of Christ, then would they clamor for a king and not for a queen. I rule this land as it is, Gwenhwyfar, not as the bishops would have it to be."

Gwenhwyfar would have argued further, but she saw the impatience in his eyes and held her peace. "Perhaps in time even the Saxons and the Tribes may come to the foot of the cross. A day will come, so Bishop Patricius has said, when Christ will be the only king among Christian men, and kings and queens his servants. God speed the day," and she made the sign of the cross. Arthur laughed.

"Servant to Christ will I be willingly," he said, "but not to his priests. No doubt, though, Bishop Patricius will be among the guests, and you may feast him as fine as you will."

"And Uriens will come from North Wales," Gwenhwyfar said, "and Morgaine too, no doubt. And from Pellinore's land, Lancelet?"

"He will come," said Arthur, "though I fear, if you wish to see your cousin Elaine again, you must journey thither to make her a visit: Lancelet sent word that she is in childbed again."

Gwenhwyfar flinched. She knew that Lancelet spent little time at home with his wife, but Elaine had given Lancelet what she could not—sons and daughters.

"How old now is Elaine's son? He is to be my heir, he should be fostered at this court," Arthur said, and Gwenhwyfar replied, "I offered as much when he was born, but Elaine said that even if he was to be king one day, he must be brought up to a simple and modest manhood. You too were fostered as a plain man's son, and it did you no harm."

"Well, perhaps she is right," said Arthur. "I would like, once, to see Morgaine's son. He would be grown to manhood now—it has been seventeen years. I know he cannot succeed me, the priests would not have it, but he is all the son I have ever fathered, and I would like, once, to set eyes on the lad and tell him . . . I know not what I would like to tell him. But I would like to see him once."

Gwenhwyfar struggled against the furious retort that sprang to her lips; nothing could be gained by arguing this again. She said only, "He is well where he is." She spoke the truth, and after she said it she knew it was the truth; she was glad Morgaine's son was being reared on that isle of sorceries, where no Christian king could go. Schooled *there,* it was more certain than ever that no sudden swing of fortune would set him on the throne after Arthur—more and more, the priests and people of this land distrusted the sorcery of Avalon. Reared at court, it might be that some unscrupulous person would begin to think of Morgaine's son as a successor more legitimate than Lancelet's.

Arthur sighed. "Yet it is hard for a man to know he has a son and never set eyes on him," he said. "Perhaps, one day." But his shoulders went up and then down in resignation. "No doubt you are right, my dear. What of the Pentecost feast? I know you will make it, as always, a memorable day."

AND SO SHE HAD DONE, Gwenhwyfar thought on that morning, looking out over the expanse of tents and pavilions. The great war-gaming field had been cleared and lined with ropes and banners, and the flags and banners of half a hundred petty kings and more than a hundred knights were moving briskly in the summer wind on the heights. It was like an army encamped here.

She sought out the banner of Pellinore, the white dragon he had adopted after the killing of the dragon in the lake. Lancelet would be there . . . it had been more than a year since she had seen him, and then formally before all the court. It had been many years since she had been alone with him even for a moment; the day before he had married Elaine, he had come to seek her out alone and to say farewell.

He had been Morgaine's victim too; he had not betrayed her, they had both been victim of the cruel trick Morgaine had played on them. When he told her about it, he had wept, and she cherished the memory of his tears as the highest compliment he had ever given her . . . who had seen Lancelet weep?

"I swear to you, Gwenhwyfar, she trapped me—Morgaine sent me the false message, and a kerchief with your scent. And I think she drugged me, too, or put some spell upon me." He had looked into her eyes, weeping, and she had wept too. "And Morgaine told Elaine some lie too, saying I was sick with love of her . . . and we were there together. I thought it was you at first, it was as if I were under some enchantment. And then when I knew it was Elaine in my arms, still I could not stop myself. And then

they were all there with torches . . . what could I do, Gwen? I had taken
the virgin daughter of my host, Pellinore would have been within his rights
to kill me then and there in her bed . . ." Lancelet cried out, and then, his
voice breaking, he had ended, "Would to God that I had rushed on his
sword instead. . . ."

She had asked him, *You do not care at all for Elaine, then?* She had
known it was an inexcusable thing to say, but she could not live without
that reassurance . . . but while Lancelet might uncover his own misery to
her, he would not speak of Elaine; he had only said, stiffly, that none of
this was Elaine's fault, and that he was bound in honor to try to make her
as happy as he could.

Well, it was done, Morgaine had had her will. So she would see
Lancelet and welcome him as her husband's kinsman, no more. The other
madness was past and gone, but she would see him and that was better than
nothing. She tried to banish all this with thoughts of the feast. Two oxen
were being roasted, would it be enough? And there was a huge wild boar
taken in hunting a few days ago, and two pigs from the farms nearby, being
baked in a pit yonder; already it smelled so good that a group of hungry
children were hanging around sniffing the good smell. And there were
hundreds of loaves of barley bread, many of which would be given away
to the countryfolk who came to crowd around the edges of the field and
watch the doings of the nobles, the kings and knights and Companions; and
there were apples baked in cream, and nuts by the bushel, and confectionery
for the ladies, honey cakes, and rabbits and small birds stewed in wine
. . . if this feast was not a success, certainly it would not be for the want
of good and abundant food!

Some time after the noon hour they gathered, a long line of richly
dressed nobles and ladies coming into the great hall and being ushered to
their proper places. The Companions, as always, were shown to their places
at the great round mead-hall table; but huge as it was, it would no longer
place all the assembled company.

Gawaine, who was always closest to Arthur, presented his mother,
Morgause. She was leaning on the arm of a young man Gwenhwyfar did
not for a moment recognize; Morgause was slender as ever, her hair still
thick and rich, braided with gems. She sank in a curtsey before Arthur, who
motioned her to rise and embraced her.

"Welcome, Aunt, to my court."

"I have heard that you ride only white horses," said Morgause, "and
so I have brought you one from the Saxon country. I have a fosterling there
who sent it as a gift."

Gwenhwyfar saw Arthur's jaw tighten, and she too could guess who
the fosterling must be. But he only said, "A kingly gift truly, Aunt."

"I will not have the horse led into the hall, as I am told is the custom in the Saxon countries," Morgause said gaily. "I do not think the lady of Camelot would like having her high hall, garnished for guests, turned into a byre! And, no doubt, your stewards have enough to do, Gwenhwyfar!" She embraced the Queen; the younger woman was enveloped in a warm wave, and close by she could see that Morgause's face was painted, her bright eyes lined with kohl; but she was beautiful no less.

Gwenhwyfar said, "I thank you for your forbearance, lady Morgause —it would not be the first time a fine horse or dog had been led before my lord and king here in his hall, and I know 'tis meant as courtesy, but I have no doubt your horse will be waiting outside quite content—I do not think the hospitality of Camelot means much even to the finest of horses. He would rather dine in his stall! Though Lancelet used to tell us a tale of some Roman who had his horse fed on wine in a golden trough and gave him honors and laurel wreaths—"

The handsome young man at Morgause's side laughed and said, "I remember, Lancelet told that story at my sister's wedding. It was the Emperor Gaius the God, who made his favorite horse one of his senators, and when he died, the next emperor said something like, at least the horse had given no evil counsel and done no murder. But do not the same, my lord Arthur—we have no chairs fit to hold such a Companion, should you see fit to name your stallion as one of them!"

Arthur laughed heartily and took the young man by the hand, saying, "I will not, Lamorak," and with a start, Gwenhwyfar realized who the young man at Morgause's side must be: he was Pellinore's son. Yes, she had heard some rumor of this—that Morgause had taken the young man as her favorite, even before her whole court—how could the woman share her bed with a man young enough to be her son? Why, Lamorak was only five-and-twenty, even now! She looked with fascinated horror and secret envy at Morgause. *She looks so young, she is still so beautiful despite all her paint, and she does what she will and cares not if all men criticize her!* Her voice was chill as she said, "Will you come and sit beside me, kinswoman, and leave the men to their talk?"

Morgause pressed Gwenhwyfar's hand. "Thank you, cousin. I come so seldom to court, I am happy to sit for once among ladies and gossip about who is married and who has taken a paramour and all the new fashions in gowns and ribbons! I am kept so busy in Lothian with the ruling of the land that I have small time for women's matters, and it is a luxury and a pleasure for me." She patted Lamorak's hand and, when she thought no one noticed, brushed his temple with a surreptitious kiss. "I leave you to the Companions, my dear."

Her ample fragrance, the warm scent of her ribbons and the folds of her gown, almost dizzied Gwenhwyfar as the Queen of Lothian sat beside her on the bench. Gwenhwyfar said, "If you are kept so busy with affairs of state, cousin, why do you not find a wife for Agravaine, and let him rule in his father's place, and give over the ruling of Lothian? Surely the folk there cannot be happy without a king—"

Morgause's laugh was warm and merry. "Why, then I should have to live unwedded, since in that country the queen's husband is king, and my dear, that would not suit me at all! And Lamorak is overyoung to rule as king, though he has other duties, and I find him most satisfactory—"

Gwenhwyfar listened with fascinated distaste; how could a woman Morgause's age make a fool of herself with so young a man? Yet his eyes followed Morgause as if she were the most beautiful and fascinating woman in the world. He hardly looked at Isotta of Cornwall, who was bending before the throne now at the side of her elderly husband, Duke Marcus of Cornwall. Isotta was so beautiful that a little murmur went all down the hall; tall and slender, with hair the color of a new-struck copper coin. But no doubt Marcus had thought more of the Irish gold she wore at her throat and at the clasp of her cloak, and the Irish pearls braided into her hair, than the treasure of her beauty. Isotta was, Gwenhwyfar thought, the most beautiful woman she had ever seen. Next to Isotta Morgause looked raddled and overblown, but still Lamorak's eyes followed her.

"Aye, Isotta is very beautiful," Morgause said, "but it is told in the court of Duke Marcus that she has more of an eye for his heir, young Drustan, than for old Marcus himself, and who can blame her? But she is modest and discreet, and if she has sense enough to give the old man a child —though, heaven knows, she might fare better at such craft with the young Drustan, at that." Morgause chuckled. "She looks not like a woman overhappy in her marriage bed. Still, I do not suppose Marcus wants much more of her than a son for Cornwall. Marcus wants only for that, I think, before he declares that Cornwall belongs to him who keeps it, not to Morgaine, who has it from Gorlois—where is my kinswoman Morgaine? I am eager to embrace her!"

"She is there with Uriens," said Gwenhwyfar, looking to where the King of North Wales waited to approach the throne.

"Arthur would have done better to marry Morgaine into Cornwall," Morgause said. "But I think he felt Marcus was too old for her. Though he might well have married her to yonder young Drustan—his mother was kindred to Ban of Less Britain, and he is a distant cousin to Lancelet, and handsome almost as Lancelet himself, is he not, Gwenhwyfar?" She smiled merrily and added, "Ah, but I had forgotten, you are so pious a lady, you look never on the beauty of any man save your own wedded husband. But then, it is easy for you to be virtuous, married to one so young and handsome and gallant as Arthur!"

Gwenhwyfar felt that Morgause's chatter would drive her mad. Did the woman think of nothing else? Morgause said, "I suppose you must speak a word or two of courtesy to Isotta—she is newcome to Britain. I have heard she speaks little of our tongue, only that of her Irish homeland. But I have heard, too, that in her own country she was a notable mistress of herbs and magic, so that when Drustan fought with the Irish knight the Marhaus, she healed him when none thought he could live, and so he is her faithful knight and champion—or at least he *said* that was his reason," Morgause chattered on, "though she is so beautiful, I would not wonder . . . perhaps I should make her known to Morgaine, she too is a great mistress of herb lore and spells of healing. They would have much to speak of, and I think Morgaine knows a little of the Irish tongue. And Morgaine, too, is married to a man old enough to be her father—I think that was ill done of Arthur!"

Gwenhwyfar said stiffly, "Morgaine married Uriens with her own consent. You do not think Arthur would marry away his dear sister without asking her!"

Morgause almost snorted, "Morgaine is full enough of life that I do not think she would be content in an old man's bed," she said, "and if I had a stepson as handsome as yonder Accolon, I know well *I* would not!"

"Come, ask the lady of Cornwall to sit with us," Gwenhwyfar said, to put an end to Morgause's gossip. "And Morgaine, too, if you will." Morgaine was safely married to Uriens; what was it to Gwenhwyfar if she made a fool of herself or put her immortal soul at hazard by playing the harlot with this man or that?

Uriens, with Morgaine and his two younger sons, had come to greet Arthur, who took the old king by both hands, calling him "Brother-in-law," and kissed Morgaine on either cheek.

"But you have come to offer me a gift, Uriens? I need no gifts from kinsmen, your affection is enough," he said.

"Not only to offer you a gift but to ask a boon of you," said Uriens. "I beg you to make my son Uwaine a knight of your Round Table and receive him as one of your Companions."

Arthur smiled at the slender, dark young man who knelt before him. "How old are you, young Uwaine?"

"Fifteen, my lord and king."

"Well, then, rise, sir Uwaine," said Arthur graciously. "You may watch this night by your arms, and tomorrow one of my Companions shall make you knight."

"By your leave," said Gawaine, "may I be the one to confer this honor on my cousin Uwaine, lord Arthur?"

"Who better than you, my cousin and friend?" Arthur said. "If that is agreeable to you, Uwaine, let it be so. I receive you willingly as my Companion for your own sake, and because you are stepson to my dear sister. Make him a place at table there, you men, and you, Uwaine, may fight in my company tomorrow in the mock battles."

Uwaine stammered, "I thank you, my k-king."

Arthur smiled at Morgaine. "I thank you for this gift, my sister."

"It is a gift to me as well, Arthur," Morgaine said. "Uwaine has been like a true son to me."

Gwenhwyfar thought, cruelly, that Morgaine looked her age; her face was touched with subtle lines, and there were streaks of white in the raven hair, though her dark eyes were as fine as ever. And she had spoken of Uwaine as her son, and she looked at him with pride and affection. *Yet her own son must be older yet. . . .*

And so Morgaine, damn her, has two sons, and I not so much as a fosterling!

Morgaine, seated at Uriens' side down the table, was conscious of Gwenhwyfar's eyes on her. *How she hates me! Even now when I can do her no harm!* Yet she did not hate Gwenhwyfar; she had even ceased to resent the marriage to Uriens, knowing that in some obscure way it had brought her back to what she had once been—priestess of Avalon. *Still, but for Gwenhwyfar, I would have been married to Accolon at this moment, and as it is, we are at the mercy of some servant who might spy on us, or blab to Uriens for a reward . . .* here in Camelot they must be very discreet. Gwenhwyfar would stop at nothing to make trouble.

She should not have come. Yet Uwaine had wished for her to see him knighted, and she was the only mother Uwaine had ever known.

Uriens could not, after all, live forever—though sometimes, in the dragging years, she felt that he had decided to rival old King Methuselah —and she doubted that even the stupid pig farmers of North Wales would accept Avalloch as king. If she could only bear Accolon a child, then no one would question that Accolon, at her side, would reign rightly.

She would have risked it—Viviane, after all, had been nearly as old as she was now when Lancelet was born, and she had lived to see him grown. But the Goddess had not sent her even the hope of conception, and to be honest, she did not want it. Uwaine was son enough for her, and Accolon had not reproached her for childlessness—no doubt he felt that no one would seriously believe it was Uriens' son, though Morgaine doubted not she could persuade her old husband to acknowledge the child his own; he doted on her in everything, and she shared his bed often enough—too often, for her taste.

She said to Uriens now, "Let me fill your plate. That roast pig is too rich for you, it will make you ill. Some of those wheaten cakes, perhaps, sopped in the gravy, and here is a fine fat saddle of rabbit." She beckoned to a serving-man carrying a tray of early fruits and chose some gooseberries and cherries for her husband. "Here, I know you are fond of these."

"You are good to me, Morgaine," he said, and she patted his arm. It was worth it—all the time she spent in cosseting him, caring for his health, embroidering him fine cloaks and shirts, and even now and then, discreetly, finding a young woman for his bed and giving him a dose of one of her herb medicines which would allow him something like normal virility; Uriens was convinced that she adored him, and never questioned her devotion or denied her anything she asked.

The feasting was breaking up now—people moving about the hall, nibbling at cakes and sweets, calling for wine and ale, stopping to speak to kinsmen and friends whom they saw only once or twice a year. Uriens was still munching his gooseberries; Morgaine asked leave to go and speak to her kinswomen.

"As you like, my dearest," he mumbled. "You should have cut my hair, my wife, all the Companions are wearing their hair shorn—"

She patted his scanty locks and said, "Oh, no, my dear, I think it is better suited to your years. You do not want to look like a schoolboy, or a monk." And, she thought, there is so little of your hair that if you cut it short, your bald spot would shine through like a beacon! "Look, the noble Lancelet still wears his hair long and flowing, and Gawaine, and Gareth— no one could call them old men!"

"You are right, as always," Uriens said smugly. "I suppose it is fitted to a mature man. It is all very well for a boy like Uwaine to clip his hair short." And Uwaine, indeed, had shorn his hair close to the nape of his neck in the new fashion. "I mark there is gray in Lancelet's hair as well—we are none of us young anymore, my dear."

You were a grandsire when Lancelet was born, Morgaine thought crossly, but she only murmured that none of them was as young as they had been ten years ago—a truth with which no one could possibly argue—and moved away.

Lancelet was still, she thought, the finest-looking man she had ever seen; next to him even Accolon seemed too perfect, his features too precise. There was grey in his hair, yes, and in the smoothly trimmed beard; but his eyes twinkled with the old smile. "Good day to you, cousin."

She was surprised at his cordial tone. Yet, she thought, it is true what Uriens said, we are none of us so young anymore, and there are not many of us who remember that time when we were all young together. He embraced her, and she felt his curly beard silky against her cheek.

She asked him, "Is Elaine not here?"

"No, she bore me another daughter but three days since. She had hoped the child would be already born, and she well enough to ride to Pentecost, but it was a fine big girl and she took her own time in coming. We had hoped to have her three weeks ago!"

"How many children have you now, Lance?"

"Three. Galahad is a big lad of seven, and Nimue is five years old. I do not see them very often, but their nurses say they are clever and quick for their age, and Elaine would name the new little one Gwenhwyfar, for the Queen."

"I think I shall ride north and visit her," Morgaine said.

"She will be glad to see you, I am sure. It is lonely there," said Lancelet. Morgaine did not think Elaine would be glad to see her at all, but that was between her and Elaine. Lancelet glanced toward the dais where Gwenhwyfar had taken Isotta of Cornwall to sit at her side while Arthur spoke with Duke Marcus and his nephew. "Know you yonder Drustan? He is a fine harper, though not like to Kevin, of course."

Morgaine shook her head. "Is Kevin to play at this feast?"

"I have not seen him," Lancelet said. "The Queen likes him not—the court is grown too Christian for that, though Arthur values him as a councillor and for his music as well."

She asked him bluntly, "Are you grown a Christian too?"

"I could wish I were," he said, sighing from the bottom of his heart. "That faith seems too simple to me—the idea that we have only to believe that Christ died for our sins once and for all. But I know too much of the truth . . . of the way life works, with life after life in which we ourselves, and only we, can work out the causes we have set in motion and make amends for the harm we have done. It stands not in the realm of reason that one man, however holy and blessed, could atone for all the sins of all men, done in all lifetimes. What else could explain why some men have all things, and others so little? No, that is a cruel trick of the priests, I think, to coax men into thinking that they have the ear of God and can forgive sins in his name—ah, I wish it were true indeed. And some of their priests are fine and sincere men."

"I never met with one who was half so learned or so good as Taliesin," said Morgaine.

"Taliesin was a great soul," Lancelet said. "Perhaps one lifetime of service to the Gods cannot create so much wisdom, and he is one of the great ones who has served them for hundreds of years. Next to him, Kevin seems no more fit to be the Lord Merlin than my little son to sit on Arthur's throne and lead his troops into battle. And Taliesin was big enough to make no quarrel with the priests, knowing they served their God as best they could, and perhaps after many lives they would learn that their God was bigger than they thought him. And I know he respected their strength to live chastely."

"That seems to me blasphemy and a denial of life," said Morgaine, "and I know Viviane would have thought it so." *Why, she wondered, do I stand here arguing religion with Lancelet, of all men?*

"Viviane, like Taliesin, came from another world and another time," said Lancelet. "They were giants in those days, and now we must make do with such as we have. You are so like her, Morgaine. *He smiled, a rueful half-smile, and it wrenched her heart; she remembered that he had said something like this to her . . . nay, she had dreamed it too, but she could not remember all . . .* but he went on, "I see you here with your husband and your fine stepson—a credit he will be to the Companions. I always wished you happiness, Morgaine, and for so many years you seemed so unhappy, but now you are queen in your own country, and you have a good son. . . ."

Surely, she thought, *what more could any woman want . . . ?*

"But now I must go and pay my respects to the Queen—"

"Yes," she said, and could not keep the bitterness from her voice. "You would be eager to do *that.*"

"Oh, Morgaine," he said, dismayed, "we have known each other so long, we are all kin, cannot we let the past die? Do you despise me so much, do you still hate her as much as that?"

Morgaine shook her head. "I don't hate either of you," she said. "Why should I? But I thought, now you were wedded—and Gwenhwyfar too deserves to be left in peace."

"You have never understood her," said Lancelet hotly. "I well believe you have disliked her since you were both young girls! It is not well done of you, Morgaine! She has repented her sin, and I—well, I am wedded, as you say, to another. But I will not shun her as if she were a leper. If she wants my friendship as her husband's kinsman, it is hers!"

Morgaine knew he spoke sincerely; well, it was nothing to her. She had now from Accolon what she had so long desired from him . . . and strangely even that was painful, like the space left by an aching tooth after it was drawn; she had loved him so many years that now when she could look on him without desire, she felt hollow inside. She said softly, "I am sorry, Lance, I had no wish to make you angry. As you say, it is all past."

I dare say he really believes that he and Gwenhwyfar can be no more than friends . . . maybe for him it is so, and Gwenhwyfar has grown so pious, I doubt it not at all. . . .

"So there you are, Lancelet, as always, chattering with the court's most beautiful ladies," said a merry voice, and Lancelet turned and caught the newcomer in a bear hug.

"Gareth! How goes it with you in the North country? And so you too are a married man and a householder . . . is it two children your lady has given you now, or three? Handsome, you are better-looking than ever —even Cai could not mock you now!"

"I would like it well to have him back in my kitchens," laughed Cai, coming up to clap Gareth on the shoulder. "Four sons, is it not? But the lady Lionors has twins, like one of the wildcats of your country, does she not? Morgaine, I think you grow ever younger with the years," he added, bending over her hand; he had always liked her.

"But when I see Gareth grown, and such a man, I feel older than the hills themselves." Morgaine too laughed. "A woman knows she is getting old when she looks at every tall young man and says to herself, I knew him before he was breeched. . . ."

"And, alas, 'tis true of me, cousin." Gareth bent to hug Morgaine. "I remember, you used to carve me wooden knights when I was no more than a babe—"

"You remember still those wooden knights?" Morgaine was pleased.

"I do—one of them Lionors keeps with my treasures still," Gareth said. "It is bravely painted in blue and red, and my oldest son would gladly have it, but I treasure it too greatly. Did you know I called it Lancelet when I was a babe, cousin?"

The older man laughed too, and Morgaine thought she had never seen Lancelet so carefree and merry as he was now among his friends. "Your son —he is almost as old as my Galahad, I think. Galahad is a fine boy, though he looks not much like my side of the family. I saw him but a few days ago, for the first time since he was out of breechclouts. And the girls are pretty, or they seem so to me."

Gareth turned back to Morgaine and said, "How does my foster-brother Gwydion, lady Morgaine?"

She said shortly, "I have heard he is in Avalon. I have not seen him," and turned away, leaving Lancelet to his friends. But Gawaine joined them, bending to give Morgaine an almost filial embrace.

Gawaine was a huge man now, monstrously heavy, with shoulders that looked—and probably were—strong enough to throw down a bull; his face was hacked and bitten with many scars. He said, "Your son Uwaine seems a fine lad. I think he will make a good knight, and we may need such— have you seen your brother Lionel, Lance?"

"No—is Lionel here?" asked Lancelet, glancing around, and his eyes fell on a tall, sturdy man, wearing a cloak of a strange fashion. "Lionel! Brother, how goes it with you in your foggy kingdom beyond the seas?"

Lionel came and greeted them, speaking with so thick an accent that Morgaine found it hard to follow his speech. "All the worse for you not being there, Lancelet—we may have some trouble there, you have heard? You have heard Bors's news?"

Lancelet shook his head. "I heard nothing later than that he was to marry King Hoell's daughter," he said, "I forget her name—"

"Isotta—the same name as the Queen of Cornwall," said Lionel. "But there has been no marriage as yet. Hoell, you must know, is one who can say never yea or nay to anything, but must ponder forever the advantage of alliance with Less Britain or Cornwall—"

"Marcus cannot give Cornwall to any," said Gawaine dryly. "Cornwall is yours, is it not, lady Morgaine? I seem to remember Uther gave it to the lady Igraine when he came to the throne, so that you have it of both Igraine and Gorlois, though Gorlois's lands were forfeit to Uther, if I mind the tale aright —it all befell before I was born, though you were a child then."

"Duke Marcus keeps the land for me," said Morgaine. "I knew never that he claimed it, though I know once there was talk I should marry Duke Marcus, or Drustan his nephew—"

"It would have been well if you had," said Lionel, "for Marcus is a greedy man—he got much treasure with his Irish lady, and I doubt it not, he will try to swallow up all of Cornwall and Tintagel too, if he thinks he can get away with it, as a fox gets away with a barnyard fowl."

Lancelet said, "I liked better the days when we were all but Arthur's Companions. Now I am reigning in Pellinore's country, and Morgaine queen in North Wales, and you, Gawaine, should be king in Lothian, if you had your rights—"

Gawaine grinned at him. "I have neither talent nor taste for kingship, cousin, I am a warrior, and to dwell always in one place and live at court would weary me to death! I am happy enough that Agravaine shall rule at my mother's side. I think the Tribes have the right of it—women to stay home and rule, and men to wander about and make war. I will not be parted from Arthur, but I admit I grow weary of life in court. Still, a mock battle is better than none."

"I am sure you will win honor and credit," said Morgaine, smiling at her cousin. "How does your mother, Gawaine? I have not yet spoken with her." She added, with a touch of malice, "I have heard she has other help than Agravaine in ruling your kingdom."

Gawaine chuckled broadly. "Aye, 'tis all the fashion now—it is your doing, Lancelet. After you married Pellinore's daughter, I suppose Lamorak thought no knight could be great and courtly and win great renown unless he had first been the para—" He stopped himself at Lancelet's grim face, and amended hastily, "the chosen champion of a great and beautiful queen. I think it is not just a pose—I think Lamorak truly loves my mother, and I begrudge it not. She was wedded to old King Lot when she was not yet fifteen, and even when I was a little fellow I used to wonder how she could live at peace with him and be always kind and good."

"Kind and good is Morgause indeed," said Morgaine, "nor had she any very easy life with Lot. He may have sought her counsel in all things, but the court was so full of his bastards he had no need to hire men-at-arms, and any woman who came into the court was his lawful prey, even I who was his wife's niece. Such behavior is thought manly in a king, and if any criticize it in Morgause, I will have a word to say to them myself!"

Gawaine said, "I know well you are my mother's friend, Morgaine. I know too Gwenhwyfar does not like her. Gwenhwyfar—" He glanced at Lancelet, shrugged, and held his peace. Gareth said, "Gwenhwyfar is so pious, and no woman has ever had anything to complain about at Arthur's court—perhaps Gwenhwyfar finds it hard to understand that a woman may have cause for wanting more of life than her marriage gives her. As for me, I am fortunate that Lionors chose me of her own free will, and she is always so busy breeding, or lying-in, or suckling our youngest, that she has no leisure to look at any other man even if she would. Which," he added, smiling, "I hope she has no desire to do, for if she wished for it I think I could deny her nothing."

Lancelet's face lost its grimness. He said, "I cannot imagine that a dame married to you, Gareth, would wish to look elsewhere."

"But you must look elsewhere, cousin," said Gawaine, "for there is the Queen looking for you, and you should go and pay your respects as her champion."

And indeed at that moment one of Gwenhwyfar's little maidens came and said in her childish voice, "You are sir Lancelet, are you not? The Queen has asked that you will come and speak with her," and Lancelet bowed to Morgaine, said, "We will speak later, Gawaine, Gareth," and went away. Gareth watched him, frowning, and muttered, "Ever he runs when she stretches out her hand."

"Did you expect anything else, brother?" Gawaine said in his easygoing way. "He has been her champion since she was wedded to Arthur, and if it were otherwise—well, so Morgaine said: such things are considered manly in a king, why should we criticize them in a queen? Nay, 'tis all the fashion now—or have you not heard the tales about yonder Irish queen, married to old Duke Marcus, and how Drustan makes songs for her and follows her about . . . he is a harper, they say, as fine as Kevin! Have you yet heard him play, Morgaine?"

She shook her head. She said, "You should not call Isotta Queen of Cornwall—there is no queen in Cornwall but I. Marcus reigns there only as my castellan, and if he does not know it, it is time he found it out."

"I do not think Isotta cares what Marcus may call himself," said Gawaine, turning to look at the long table where the ladies sat. Morgause had joined Gwenhwyfar and the Irish queen, and Lancelet had come to speak with them; Gwenhwyfar was smiling at Lancelet, and Morgause making some jest which made them laugh, but Isotta of Cornwall was staring at nothing, her exquisite face pale and drawn. "I never saw any lady who looked so unhappy as yonder Irish queen."

Morgaine said, "If I were married to old Duke Marcus, I doubt I should be happy," and Gawaine gave her a rough hug.

"Arthur did not well when he married you to that grandsire old Uriens, either, Morgaine—are you unhappy too?"

Morgaine felt her throat tighten, as if Gawaine's kindness would make her weep. "Perhaps there is not much happiness for women in marriage after all. . . ."

"I would not say that," Gareth said. "Lionors seems happy enough."

"Ah, but Lionors is married to you," Morgaine said, laughing. "And I could not have that good fortune, I am only your old cousin."

"Still," said Gawaine, "I criticize not my mother. She was good to Lot all his life long, and while he lived she never flaunted her lovers in his face. I begrudge her nothing, and Lamorak is a good man and a good knight. As for Gwenhwyfar—" He grimaced. "It's God's pity that Lancelet did not take her away from this kingdom while there was still time for Arthur to find him another wife—still, I suppose young Galahad will be a good king in his day. Lancelet is of the old royal line of Avalon, and royal, too, in his blood from Ban of Less Britain."

"Still," said Gareth, "I think *your* son closer to the throne than his, Morgaine," and she remembered that he had been old enough to remember Gwydion's birth. "And the Tribes would give allegiance to Arthur's sister —in the old days, the sister's son was the natural heir, in the days when rule passed through the blood of the woman." He frowned and thought for a moment, then asked, "Morgaine, is he Lancelet's son?"

She supposed the question was natural enough—they had been friends from childhood. But she shook her head, trying to make a jest instead of showing the irritation she felt. "No, Gareth, if it had been so I would have told you. It would have pleased you so, anything to do with Lancelet. Forgive me, cousins, I should go and speak with your mother—she was always good to me." She turned away, making her way slowly toward the dais where the ladies sat; the room was growing more and more crowded as everyone greeted old friends and little knots of people collected.

She had always disliked crowded places, and she had lately spent so much time on the green Welsh hills that she was no longer used to the smell of bodies crowded together and the smoke from the hearth fire. Moving to one side, she collided with a man who staggered under her light weight and caught at the wall to steady himself, and she found herself face to face with the Merlin.

She had not spoken with Kevin since the day of Viviane's death. She looked him coldly in the face and turned away.

"Morgaine—"

She ignored him. Kevin said, in a voice as cold as her glance, "Will a daughter of Avalon turn her face away when the Merlin speaks?"

Morgaine drew a long breath and said, "If you bid me hear you in the name of Avalon, I am here to listen. But that suits you not, you who gave Viviane's body to Christian rule. That I call a traitor's deed."

"And who are you to speak of traitor's deeds, lady, who sits as queen in Wales when Viviane's high seat is empty in Avalon?"

She flared, "I sought once to speak in Avalon's name and you bade me hold my peace," and bowed her head, not waiting for his reply. *No, he is right. How dare I speak of treachery when I fled from Avalon, too young and too foolish to know what Viviane planned? Only now do I begin to know that she gave me a hold on the King's conscience: And I cast it aside unused and let Gwenhwyfar lead him into the hands of the priests.* "Speak, Merlin. Avalon's daughter listens."

For a moment he said nothing, but only looked at her, and she remembered, sorrowfully, the years when he had been her only friend and ally at this court. At last he said, "Your beauty, like Viviane's, ripens with the years, Morgaine. Next to you every woman at this court, including that Irishwoman they call so beautiful, is a painted doll."

She smiled faintly and said, "You did not stop me in my tracks with the thunders of Avalon to make me pretty compliments, Kevin."

"Did I not? I spoke ill, Morgaine—you are needed in Avalon. She who sits there now is—" He broke off, troubled. "Are you so much in love with your elderly husband that you cannot tear yourself away?"

"No," she said, "but I do the work of the Goddess there too."

"This much I know," he said, "and so I have told Niniane. And if Accolon can succeed his father, the worship of the Goddess will grow there . . . but Accolon is not his father's heir, and the older son is a priest-ridden fool."

"Accolon is not king, but Druid," Morgaine said, "and Avalloch's death would avail nothing—they follow Roman ways in Wales now, and Avalloch has a son." *Conn,* she thought, *who sat in my lap and called me Granny.*

And Kevin said, as if he had heard her unspoken words: "The lives of children are uncertain, Morgaine. Many come not to manhood."

"I will do no murder," she said, "even for Avalon, and you may tell them so for me."

"Tell them yourself," said Kevin. "Niniane said to me that you would be coming there after Pentecost." And now Morgaine felt the empty, cold sickness strike at her stomach and was glad she had eaten but little of the rich food of the feast.

Do they know all, then? Do they watch, judging me, as I betray my old and trusting husband with Accolon? She thought of Elaine, trembling and shamed in the light of the torches that had caught her naked in Lancelet's arms. *Do they know even what I plan before I am certain of it myself?* But she had done only what the Goddess gave her to do.

"What is it that you came to tell me, Merlin?"

"Only that your place in Avalon is empty still, and Niniane knows it as well as I. I love you well, Morgaine, and I am no traitor—it pains me that you think me so, when you have given me so much." He held out his twisted hands. "Peace, then, Morgaine, between us?"

She said, "In the Lady's name, peace, then," and kissed his scarred mouth.

For him too the Goddess wears my face . . . and pain struck through her. *The Goddess is the giver of life and manhood . . . and of death.* As her lips touched his, the Merlin recoiled, and on his face was naked fear.

"Do you recoil from me, Kevin? I swear it on my life, I will do no murder. You have nothing to fear—" she said, but he put out his twisted fingers to stop the words.

"Make no oath, Morgaine, lest you pay the penalty of the forsworn . . . none of us knows what the Goddess may demand of us. I too have made the Great Marriage, and my life was forfeit on that day. I live only at the will of the Goddess, and my life is not so sweet that I would begrudge to lay it down," he said. Years later Morgaine would remember these words and feel them sweeten the bitterest task of her life. He bent to her, in the salute given only to the Lady of Avalon or to the High Druid, and then, swiftly, turned away. Morgaine stood trembling, watching him go. Why had he done that? And why did he fear her?

She moved on through the crowds; when she reached the dais, Gwen-hwyfar gave her a chilly smile, but Morgause rose and took her into an ample, warm embrace.

"Dearest child, you look tired—I know you have little love for crowds!" She held a silver cup to Morgaine's lips, and Morgaine sipped the wine, then shook her head. She said, "You seem to grow ever younger, Aunt!"

Morgause laughed gaily and said, "Young company does that for me, my dear—saw you Lamorak? While he thinks me beautiful, I think myself so, and so I am . . . it is the only sorcery I need!" She traced with her smooth finger a little line beneath Morgaine's eye, and said, "I recommend it to you, my dear, or you will grow old and cross . . . are there no handsome young men at Uriens' court with an eye for their queen?"

Over her shoulder Morgaine saw Gwenhwyfar's frown of distaste, even though she certainly believed Morgause was joking. *At least the tale of my behavior with Accolon is not common gossip here.* Then she thought angrily, *In the Lady's name, I am not ashamed of what I do, I am not Gwenhwyfar!*

Lancelet was talking with Isotta of Cornwall. Yes, he would always have an eye for the most beautiful woman in the room, and Morgaine could tell Gwenhwyfar liked it not; Gwenhwyfar said now, with nervous haste, "Lady Isotta, know you my husband's sister, Morgaine?"

The Irish beauty raised her eyes listlessly to Morgaine, and smiled. She was very pale, her chiselled features white as new cream, her eyes that blue that is almost green. Morgaine saw that although she was tall, her bones were so small that she looked like a child hung with jewels and pearls and golden chains which seemed too heavy for her. Morgaine had sudden pity for the girl and withheld the first words that came into her mind, which were, *So they call you queen in Cornwall now? I must have words with Duke Marcus!* She said only, "My kinsman told me you are skilled in herbs and medicines, lady. Some day, if we have leisure before I return to Wales, I would like to speak of them with you."

"It would be a pleasure," said Isotta courteously. Lancelet looked up and said, "I have told her also that you are a musician, Morgaine. Are we to hear you play this day?"

"With Kevin here? My music is nothing to his," said Morgaine, but Gwenhwyfar shuddered, and interrupted.

"I wish Arthur would listen to me and send that man from his court. I like it not, to have wizards and sorcerers here, and such an evil face must portend evil within! I know not how you can bear to touch him, Morgaine —I should think any fastidious woman would be ill if he touched her, yet you embraced and kissed him as if he were a kinsman—"

"Clearly," said Morgaine, "I am altogether lacking in proper feelings —and I rejoice at it."

Isotta of Cornwall said in her soft, sweet voice, "If what is without is like to that which is within, then the music Kevin makes must be a sign to us, lady Gwenhwyfar, that the soul within him is indeed that of the highest angels. For no evil man could play as he plays."

Arthur had come to join them, and had heard the last few words. He said, "Yet I will not affront my queen with the presence of one distasteful to her—nor will I have the insolence to command the music of such an artist as Kevin for one who cannot receive him with grace." He sounded displeased. "Morgaine, will you play for us, then?"

"My harp is in Wales," she said. "Perhaps, if someone can lend me a harp, at another time. The hall is so crowded and noisy, the music would be lost. . . . Lancelet is as much a musician as I."

Lancelet, standing behind him, shook his head. "Oh, no, cousin. I know one string from another, because I was reared in Avalon and my mother set a harp in my hand for a plaything as soon as I could hold one. But I have not the gift of music as Morgaine has, nor the nephew of Marcus—have you heard Drustan play, Morgaine?"

She shook her head, and Isotta said, "I will ask him to come and play for us."

She sent a page for him, and Drustan came, a slight young man, dark-eyed and dark-haired; he was indeed, Morgaine thought, not unlike Lancelet. Isotta asked him to play, and he called for his harp and sat on the steps of the dais, playing some Breton tunes. They were plaintive and sad, in a very old scale, and they made Morgaine think of the ancient land of Lyonnesse, far away and sunk past the coastline of Tintagel. He had, indeed, a gift beyond Lancelet's; even, she thought, beyond her own. Though he was not Kevin, nor near to it, he was the finest player, otherwise, that she had heard. His voice, too, was sweet and musical.

Under cover of the music Arthur said softly to Morgaine, "How is it with you, sister? It is long since you came to Camelot—we have missed you."

"Oh, indeed?" said Morgaine. "I thought that was why you married me away into North Wales—that my lady"—an ironic bow to Gwenhwy-far—"might not be affronted with the sight of anything distasteful to her, neither Kevin nor me."

"Why, how can you say that?" demanded Arthur. "I love you well, you know that, and Uriens is a good man, and he seems to dote on you —certainly he hangs on your every word! I sought to find you a kind husband, Morgaine, one who had sons and would not reproach you should you not give him children. And it was my pleasure this day to make your fine young stepson one of my Companions. What could you ask more than this, my sister?"

"What, indeed?" said Morgaine. "What more could a woman desire than a good husband old enough to be her grandsire, and a kingdom to rule at the far end of the world—I should bow down and thank you on my knees, my brother!"

Arthur sought to take her hand. "Indeed I did what I thought would please you, sister. Uriens is too old for you, but he will not live forever. Truly, I thought it would make you happy."

No doubt, thought Morgaine, he was telling the exact truth as he saw it. How could he be so good and wise a king, and have so little imagination? Or was this the secret of his kingship, that he held to simple truths and sought for no more? Was this why the Christian faith had lured him, that it was so simple, with a few simple laws?

"I like that everybody be happy," Arthur said, and she knew that this was really the key to his nature; he did indeed seek to see everyone happy, down to the least of his subjects. He had allowed what went on between Gwenhwyfar and Lancelet because he knew it would make his queen unhappy if he parted them, nor would he hurt Gwenhwyfar by taking another wife or a mistress to give him the son she could not.

He is not ruthless enough to be High King, she thought, while she tried to listen to Drustan's sorrowful songs. Arthur turned to speaking of the lead and tin mines of Cornwall—she should ride to see to them, Duke Marcus should know that he was not ruler over all that country, and, no doubt, she and Isotta would be friends, they both cared for music—see how intently she listened to Drustan.

It is not love of music which makes it impossible to take her eyes from him, Morgaine thought, but she did not say so. She considered the four queens who sat at this table, and sighed; Isotta could not take her eyes from Drustan, and who could blame her? Duke Marcus was old and stern, with quick, darting, ill-natured eyes that reminded her of Lot of Orkney. Morgause had beckoned to her young Lamorak and was whispering to him; well, who could blame her? She had been wedded to Lot—and he was no prize—when she was but fourteen, and all the while Lot lived she had been mindful of his pride and never flaunted her young lovers in his face. *And I am no better than any of them, cosseting Uriens with one hand and slipping away to Accolon's bed with the other, and justifying myself by calling Accolon my priest. . . .*

She wondered if any woman ever did otherwise. Gwenhwyfar was High Queen, and she had first taken a lover . . . and it seemed to Morgaine that her heart hardened like stone. She and Morgause and Isotta were married to old men, and such was their life. But Gwenhwyfar had been married to a man who was handsome, and no more than her own age, and High King as well—what had *she* to be discontented with?

Drustan put the harp aside, bowing, and took up a horn of wine to cool his throat. "I can sing no more," he said, "but if the lady Morgaine would like to take my harp, she is welcome. I have heard of the lady's skill as a musician."

"Yes, sing for us, child," said Morgause, and Arthur added his entreaty.

"Yes, it is long since I heard your voice, and it is still the sweetest voice I have ever heard . . . perhaps because it is the first voice I remember hearing," Arthur said. "I think you sang me to sleep with lullabies before I could talk plain, and you were no more than a child yourself. Always I remember you best like that, Morgaine," he added, and before the pain in his eyes, Morgaine bent her head.

Is this what Gwenhwyfar cannot forgive, that I bear for him the face of the

Goddess? She took Drustan's harp and bent her head over the strings, touching them one by one.

" 'Tis tuned differently than mine," she said, trying a few strings, and then looked up as there was a commotion in the lower hall. A trumpet blew, harsh and shrill inside the walls, and there was a tramp of armed feet. Arthur half rose, then sank back into his seat as four armed men, bearing sword and shield, strode into the hall.

Cai came to meet them, protesting—it was not allowed to bear weapons into the King's hall at Pentecost. They shoved him roughly to one side.

The men wore Roman helmets—Morgaine had seen one or two of those preserved in Avalon—and short military tunics and Roman armor, and thick red military cloaks streamed out behind them. Morgaine blinked —it was as if Roman legionaries had walked out of the past; one man bore, at the end of a pike, the carved and gilded figure of an eagle.

"Arthur, Duke of Britain!" cried out one of the men. "We bear you a message from Lucius, Emperor of Rome!"

Arthur rose from his seat and took a single step toward the men in legionary dress. "I am not Duke of Britain, but High King," he said mildly, "and I know of no Emperor Lucius. Rome has fallen and is in the hands of barbarians—and, I doubt not, impostors. Still, one does not hang the dog for the impertinence of the master. You may say your message."

"I am Castor, centurion of the Valeria Victrix legion," said the man who had spoken before. "In Gaul, the legions have been formed again, behind the banner of Lucius Valerius, Emperor of Rome. The message of Lucius is this—that you, Arthur, Duke of Britain, may continue to rule under that style and designation, provided that you send him, within six weeks, imperial tribute consisting of forty ounces of gold, two dozens of the British pearls, and three wagonloads each of iron, tin, and lead from your country, with a hundred ells of woven British wool and a hundred slaves."

Lancelet rose from his place, leaped forward into the space before the King.

"My lord Arthur," he cried, "let me flay these impudent dogs and send them yelping back to their master, and tell this idiot Lucius that if he wants tribute from England he may come and try to take it—"

"Wait, Lancelet," said Arthur gently, smiling at his friend, "that is not the way." He surveyed the legionaries for a moment; Castor had half drawn his sword, and Arthur said grimly, "No steel may be drawn on this holy day in my court, soldier. I do not expect a barbarian from Gaul to know the manners of a civilized country, but if you put not your sword back into its sheath, then, I swear, Lancelet may come and take it from you as best he can. And no doubt you have heard of sir Lancelet, even in Gaul. But I want no blood shed at the foot of my throne."

Castor, baring his teeth with rage, thrust his sword back into his sheath. "I am not afraid of your knight Lancelet," he said. "His days were long gone in the wars with the Saxons. But I was sent as a messenger with orders to shed no blood. What answer may I take the emperor, Duke Arthur?"

"None—if you refuse me my proper title in my own hall," said Arthur. "But say this to Lucius: that Uther Pendragon succeeded Ambrosius Aurelianus when there were no Romans to aid us in our death struggle against the Saxons, and I, Arthur, succeeded my father Uther, and my nephew Galahad will succeed me on the throne of Britain. There is none who can lawfully lay claim to the purple of the emperor—the Roman Empire rules no more in Britain. If Lucius wishes to rule in his native Gaul and the people there accept him as king, I will surely not come to contest his claim; but if he lays claim to a single inch of Britain or Less Britain, then he shall have nothing from us but three dozen good British arrowheads where they will do him most good."

Castor, pale with fury, said, "My emperor foresaw some such impudent answer as this, and this is what he bade me say: that Less Britain is already in his hands, and he has imprisoned King Ban's son Bors, in his own castle. And when the Emperor Lucius has laid all of Less Britain waste, then he will come to Britain, as did the Emperor Claudius of old, and conquer that country again, in despite of all your painted savage chiefs smeared with woad!"

"Tell your emperor," said Arthur, "that my offer of three dozen British arrowheads holds good, only now will I raise my offer to three hundred, and he gets no tribute from me but one of them through his heart. Tell him, too, that if he harms a single hair on the head of my Companion sir Bors, I shall give him to Lancelet and Lionel, who are Bors's brothers, to skin him alive and hang his flayed corpse from the castle walls. Now go back to your emperor and give him that message. No, Cai, don't let anyone lay a hand on him—a messenger is sacred to his Gods."

There was an appalled silence as the legionaries strode out of the hall, turning crisply on their heels and letting their mailed boots stamp and ring on the stones. When they had gone a clamor arose, but Arthur raised his hand and quiet fell again.

"There will be no mock battles on the morrow, for we will have real ones soon," he said, "and for prizes I can offer the plunder of this self-styled emperor. Companions, I would have you ready to ride at daybreak for the coast. Cai, you can handle the provisioning. Lancelet"—a faint smile as he looked at his friend—"I would leave you here to guard the Queen, but since your brother is prisoned, I know you will wish to ride with us. I shall ask the priest to say holy service for those of you who wish to be shriven of

any sins before you ride into battle, tomorrow at dawn. Sir Uwaine"—his
eyes sought out his newest Companion where he sat among the younger
knights—"now I can offer you glory in battle instead of war games. I beg
you, as my sister's son, to ride at my side and cover my back against
treachery."

"I am honored, m-my king," Uwaine stammered, his face glowing,
and in that moment Morgaine saw something of how Arthur had inspired
such great devotion.

"Uriens, my good brother-in-law," said Arthur, "I leave the Queen
in your care—remain at Camelot and guard her till I return." He bent to
kiss Gwenhwyfar's hand. "My lady, I beg you to excuse us from further
feasting—there is war upon us again."

Gwenhwyfar was white as her shift. "And you know it is welcome
to you, my lord. God keep you, dear husband." And she leaned forward
to kiss him. He rose and went down from the dais, beckoning.

"Gawaine, Lionel, Gareth—all of you—Companions, attend me!"

Lancelet delayed for a moment before following him. "Bid me also
God's blessing as I ride, my queen."

"Oh, God—Lancelet—" Gwenhwyfar said, and, regardless of the eyes
on her, she flung herself into his arms. He held her, gently, speaking so softly
that Morgaine could not hear, but Morgaine saw that she was weeping. But
when she raised her head her face was dry and tearless. "God speed you, my
dearest love."

"And God keep you, love of my heart," Lancelet said very softly.
"Whether I return or no, may he bless you." He turned to Morgaine. "Now
indeed do I rejoice that you are to pay a visit to Elaine. You must bear my
greetings to my dear wife, and tell her I have gone with Arthur to the rescue
of my kinsman Bors from this knave who calls himself the Emperor Lucius.
Tell her I pray God to keep her and care for her, and send my love to our
children."

He stood for a moment silent, and for a moment Morgaine thought
he would kiss her too; instead, smiling, he laid his hand against her cheek.
"God bless you too, Morgaine—whether or no you want his blessing." He
turned to join Arthur where the Companions were gathering in the lower
hall.

Uriens came to the dais and bowed to Gwenhwyfar. "I am at your
service, my lady."

If she laughs at the old man, Morgaine thought with a sudden, fierce
protectiveness, *I will slap her!* Uriens meant well, and the duty was no more
than ceremonial, a minor tribute to kinship; Camelot would be very well
in the hands of Cai and Lucan, as always. But Gwenhwyfar was accustomed
to diplomacy at court. She said gravely, "I thank you, sir Uriens. You are

most welcome here. Morgaine is my dear friend and sister, and I will be happy to have her near me at court again."

Oh, Gwenhwyfar, Gwenhwyfar, what a liar you are! Morgaine said sweetly, "But I must ride forth and visit my kinswoman Elaine. Lancelet charged me to bear his news."

"You are always kind," said Uriens, "and since the war is not in our countryside, but across the channel, you shall go when you wish. I would ask Accolon to escort you, but it is likely he must ride with Arthur to the coast."

He really would leave me in Accolon's care; he thinks good of everyone, Morgaine thought, and kissed her husband with real warmth. "When I have paid my visit to Elaine, my lord, may I have leave to visit my kinswoman in Avalon?"

"You may do your own will, my lady," said Uriens, "but before you go, will you unpack my things? My valet can never do it so well as you. And will you leave some of your herbal salves and medicines for me?"

"To be sure," she said, and as she went to make all ready for her journey, she thought with resignation that no doubt, before they parted, he would want to sleep with her this night. Well, she had endured it before this, she could do so again.

What a whore I have grown!

12

MORGAINE knew that she dared make this journey only if she made it one step at a time, one league at a time, one day at a time. Her first step, then, was to Pellinore's castle; bitter irony, that her first mission was a kindly message to Lancelet's wife and his children.

All that first day she followed the old Roman road northward through rolling hills. Kevin had offered to escort her, and she had been tempted; the old fear gripped her, that she would not find the way to Avalon this time either, not dare to summon the Avalon barge; that she would wander again into the fairy country and be lost there forever. She had not dared go after Viviane's death. . . .

But now she must meet this test, as when she had first been made priestess . . . cast out of Avalon alone, with no test save this, that she must be able somehow to return . . . by her own strength, not Kevin's, she must win entry there again.

Still she was frightened; it had been so long.

On the fourth day she came within sight of Pellinore's castle, and at noon of that day, riding along the marshy shores of the lake which now bore no trace of the dragon which once had lurked there (though her serving-man and woman shivered and clung together and told each other horrible tales of dragons), she caught sight of the somewhat smaller dwelling which Pellinore had given to Elaine and Lancelet when they were wedded.

It was more villa than castle; in these days of peace there were not many fortified places in that countryside. Broad lawns sloped down toward the road, and as Morgaine rode up toward the house, a flock of geese sent up a great squawk.

A well-dressed chamberlain greeted her, asking her name and business.

"I am the lady Morgaine, wife of King Uriens of North Wales. I bear a message from the lord Lancelet."

She was taken to a room where she could wash and refresh herself, then conducted to the great hall, where a fire burned and wheat cakes were set before her, with honey and a flask of good wine. Morgaine found herself yawning at the ceremoniousness of this—she was, after all, a kinswoman, not a state visitor. After a time, a small boy peered into the room, and when he saw that she was alone, came in. He was fair, with blue eyes and a splashing of golden freckles on his face, and she knew at once whose son he was, though he was nothing like his father.

"Are you the lady Morgaine that they call Morgaine of the Fairies?"

Morgaine said, "I am. And I am your cousin, Galahad."

"How do you know my name?" he asked suspiciously. "Are you a sorceress? Why do they call you Morgaine of the Fairies?"

She said, "Because I am of the old royal line of Avalon, and fostered there. And I know your name, not from sorcery, but because you look like your mother, who is also my kinswoman."

"My father's name is Galahad too," said the child, "but the Saxons call him Elf-arrow."

"I came here to bear your father's greetings to you, and to your mother, and to your sisters too," Morgaine said.

"Nimue is a silly girl," said Galahad. "She is a big girl, five years old, but she cried when my father came and would not let him pick her up and kiss her, because she did not recognize him. Do you know my father?"

"Indeed I do," said Morgaine. "His mother, the Lady of the Lake, was my foster-mother and my aunt."

He looked skeptical and frowned. "My mother told me that the Lady of the Lake is an evil sorceress."

"Your mother is—" Morgaine stopped and softened the words; he was, after all, only a child. "Your mother did not know the Lady as I did. She was a good and wise woman, and a great priestess."

"Oh?" She could see Galahad struggling with this concept. "Father Griffin says that only men can be priests, because men are made in God's image and women are not. Nimue said that she wanted to be a priest when she grew up, and learn to read and write and play upon the harp, and Father Griffin told her that no woman could do all these things, or any of them."

"Then Father Griffin is mistaken," said Morgaine, "for I can do them all and more."

"I don't believe you," Galahad said, surveying her with a level stare of hostility. "You think everyone is wrong but you, don't you? My mother says that little ones should not contradict grown-ups, and you look as if you were not so much older than I. You aren't much bigger, are you?"

Morgaine laughed at the angry child and said, "But I am older than either your mother or your father, Galahad, even though I am not very big."

There was a stir at the door and Elaine came in. She had grown softer, her body rounded, her breasts sagging—after all, Morgaine told herself, she had borne three children and one was still at the breast. But she was still lovely, her golden hair shining as bright as ever, and she embraced Morgaine as if they had met but yesterday.

"I see you have met my good son," she said. "Nimue is in her room being punished—she was impertinent to Father Griffin—and Gwennie, thank Heaven, is asleep—she is a fussy baby and I was awake with her much of the night. Have you come from Camelot? Why did my lord not ride with you, Morgaine?"

"I have come to tell you about that," Morgaine said. "Lancelet will not ride home for some while. There is war in Less Britain, and his brother Bors is besieged in his castle. All of Arthur's Companions have gone to rescue him and put down the man who would be emperor."

Elaine's eyes filled with tears, but young Galahad's face was eager with excitement. "If I were older," he said, "I would be one of the Companions and my father would make me a knight and I would ride with them, and I would fight these old Saxons—and any old emperor too!"

Elaine heard the story and said, "This Lucius sounds to me like a madman!"

"Mad or sane, he has an army and claims it in the name of Rome," Morgaine said. "Lancelet sent me to see you, and bade me kiss his children —though I doubt not this young man is too big to be kissed like a babe," she said, smiling at Galahad. "My stepson, Uwaine, thought himself too big for that when he was about your size, and a few days ago he was made one of Arthur's Companions."

"How old is he?" asked Galahad, and when Morgaine said fifteen, he scowled furiously and began to reckon up on his fingers.

Elaine asked, "How looked my dear lord? Galahad, run away to your tutor, I want to speak with my cousin," and when the child had gone, she said, "I had more time to speak with Lancelet before Pentecost than in all the years of our marriage. This is the first time in all these years that I have had more than a week of his company!"

"At least he did not leave you with child this time," said Morgaine.

"No," said Elaine, "and he was very considerate and did not seek my bed during those last weeks while we waited together for Gwen's birth—he said that I was so big, it would be no pleasure to me. I would not have refused him, but to tell the truth I think he cared not at all . . . and *there's* a confession for you, Morgaine."

"You forget," said Morgaine with a grim little smile, "I have known Lancelet all my life."

"Tell me," Elaine said, "I swore, once, I would never ask you this— was Lancelet your lover, did you ever lie with him?"

Morgaine looked at her drawn face and said gently, "No, Elaine. There was a time when I thought—but it came never to that. I did not love him, nor did he love me." And to her own surprise, she knew the words were true, though she had never known it before.

Elaine stared at the floor, where a patch of sunlight came in through an old, discolored bit of glass that had been there since Roman days. "Morgaine—while he was at Pentecost, did he see the Queen?"

"Since Lancelet is not blind, and since she sat on the dais beside Arthur, I suppose he did," Morgaine said dryly.

Elaine made an impatient movement. "You know what I speak of!"

Is she still so jealous? Does she hate Gwenhwyfar so much? She has Lancelet, she has borne his children, she knows he is honorable, what more does she want? But before the younger woman's nervously twisting hands, the tears which seemed to hang on her eyelashes, Morgaine softened. "Elaine, he spoke with the Queen, and he kissed her in farewell when the call to arms came. But I vow to you, he spoke as courtier to his queen, not as lover to lover. They have known one another since they were young, and if they cannot forget that once they loved in a way that comes not twice to any man or woman, why should you begrudge them that? You are his wife, Elaine, and I could tell when he bade me bear you his message, he loves you well."

"And I swore to be content with no more, did I not?"

Elaine lowered her head for a long moment, and Morgaine saw her blinking furiously, but she did not cry, and at last she raised her head. "You who have had so many lovers, have you ever known what it is to love?"

For a moment Morgaine felt herself swept by the old tempest, the madness of love which had flung her and Lancelet, on a sun-flooded hill in Avalon, into each other's arms, which had brought them together again and again, until it all ended in bitterness . . . by main will she forced away the memory and filled her mind with the thought of Accolon, who had roused again the sweetness of womanhood in her heart and body when she had felt old, dead, abandoned . . . who had brought her back to the Goddess, who had made her again into a priestess . . . she felt bands of crimson rising in quick successive waves over her face. Slowly, she nodded. "Yes, child. I have known—I know what it is to love."

She could see that Elaine wanted to ask a hundred other questions, and she thought how happy it would be to share all this with the one woman who had been her friend since she left Avalon, whose marriage she had made —but no. Secrecy was a part of the power of a priestess, and to speak of what she and Accolon had known would be to bring it outside of the magical realm, make her no more than a discontented wife sneaking to the bed of her stepson. She said, "But now, Elaine, there is something more to speak of. Remember, you made me a vow once—that if I helped you to win Lancelet, you would give me what I asked of you. Nimue is past five years old, old enough for fostering. I ride tomorrow for Avalon. You must make her ready to accompany me."

"No!" It was a long cry, almost a shriek. "No, no, Morgaine—you cannot mean it!"

Morgaine had been afraid of this. Now she made her voice distant and hard.

"Elaine. You have sworn it."

"How could I swear for a child not yet born? I knew not what it meant —oh, no, not my daughter, not my daughter—you cannot take her from me, not so young!"

Again Morgaine said, "You have sworn it."

"And if I refuse?" Elaine looked like a spitting cat ready to defend her kittens against a large and angry dog.

"If you refuse," Morgaine's voice was as quiet as ever, "when Lancelet comes home, he shall hear from me how this marriage was made, how you wept and begged me to put a spell on him so that he would turn from Gwenhwyfar to you. He thinks you the innocent victim of my magic, Elaine, and blames me, not you. Shall he know the truth?"

"You would not!" Elaine was white with horror.

"Try me," Morgaine said. "I know not how Christians regard an oath, but I assure you, among those who worship the Goddess, it is taken in all seriousness. And so I took yours. I waited till you had another daughter, but Nimue is mine by your pledged word."

"But—but what of her? She is a Christian child—how can I send her from her mother into—into a world of pagan sorceries . . . ?"

"I am, after all, her kinswoman," Morgaine said gently. "How long have you known me, Elaine? Have you ever known me do anything so dishonorable or wicked that you would hesitate to entrust a child to me? I do not, after all, want her for feeding to a dragon, and the days are long, long past when even criminals were burnt on altars of sacrifice."

"What will befall her, then, in Avalon?" asked Elaine, so fearfully that Morgaine wondered if Elaine, after all, had harbored some such notions.

"She will be a priestess, trained in all the wisdom of Avalon," said Morgaine. "One day she will read the stars and know all the wisdom of the world and the heavens." She found herself smiling. "Galahad told me that she wished to learn to read and write and to play the harp—and in Avalon no one will forbid her this. Her life will be less harsh than if you had put her to school in some nunnery. We will surely ask less of her in the way of fasting and penance before she is grown."

"But—but what shall I say to Lancelet?" wavered Elaine.

"What you will," said Morgaine. "It would be best to tell him the truth, that you sent her to fosterage in Avalon, that she might fill the place left empty there. But I care not whether you perjure yourself to him—you may tell him that she was drowned in the lake or taken by the ghost of old Pellinore's dragon, for all care."

"And what of the priest? When Father Griffin hears that I have sent my daughter to become a sorceress in the heathen lands—"

"I care even less what you tell him," Morgaine said. "If you choose to tell him that you put your soul in pawn for my sorceries to win yourself a husband, and pledged your first daughter in return—no? I thought not."

"You are hard, Morgaine," said Elaine, tears falling from her eyes. "Cannot I have a few days to prepare her to go from me, to pack such things as she will need—"

"She needs not much," said Morgaine. "A change of shift if you will, and warm things for riding, a thick cloak and stout shoes, no more than that. In Avalon they will give her the dress of a novice priestess. Believe me," she added kindly, "she will be treated with love and reverence as the granddaughter of the greatest of priestesses. And they will—what is it your priests say—they will temper the wind to the shorn lamb. She will not be forced to austerities until she is of an age to endure them. I think she will be happy there."

"Happy? In that place of evil sorcery?"

Morgaine said, and the utter conviction of her words struck Elaine's heart, "I vow to you—I was happy in Avalon, and every day since I left, I have longed, early and late, to return thither. Have you ever heard me lie? Come—let me see the child."

"I bade her stay in her room and spin in solitude till sunset. She was rude to the priest and is being punished," said Elaine.

"But I remit the punishment," said Morgaine. "I am now her guardian and foster-mother, and there is no longer any reason to show courtesy to that priest. Take me to her."

THEY RODE FORTH the next day at dawn. Nimue had wept at parting with her mother, but even before they were gone an hour, she had begun to peer forth curiously at Morgaine from under the hood of her cloak. She was tall for her age, less like Lancelet's mother, Viviane, than like Morgause or Igraine; fair-haired, but with enough copper in the golden strands that Morgaine thought her hair would be red when she was older. And her eyes were almost the color of the small wood violets which grew by the brooks.

They had had only a little wine and water before setting out, so Morgaine asked, "Are you hungry, Nimue? We can stop and break our fast as soon as we find a clearing, if you wish."

"Yes, Aunt."

"Very well." And soon she dismounted and lifted the little girl from her pony.

"I have to—" The child cast down her eyes and squirmed.

"If you have to pass water, go behind that tree with the serving-woman," said Morgaine, "and never be ashamed again to speak of what God has made."

"Father Griffin says it is not modest—"

"And never speak to me again of anything Father Griffin said to you," Morgaine said gently, but with a hint of iron behind the mild words. "That is past, Nimue."

When the child came back she said, with a wide-eyed look of wonder, "I saw someone very small peering out at me from behind a tree. Galahad said you were called Morgaine of the Fairies—was it a fairy, Aunt?"

Morgaine shook her head and said, "No, it was one of the Old People of the hills—they are as real as you or I. It is better not to speak of them, Nimue, or take any notice. They are very shy, and afraid of men who live in villages and farms."

"Where do they live, then?"

"In the hills and forests," Morgaine said. "They cannot bear to see the earth, who is their mother, raped by the plow and forced to bear, and they do not live in villages."

"If they do not plow and reap, Aunt, what do they eat?"

"Only such things as the earth gives them of her free will," said Morgaine. "Root, berry and herb, fruit and seeds—meat they taste only at the great festivals. As I told you, it is better not to speak of them, but you may leave them some bread at the edge of the clearing, there is plenty for us all." She broke off a piece of a loaf and let Nimue take it to the edge of the woods. Elaine had, indeed, given them enough food for ten days' ride, instead of the brief journey to Avalon.

She ate little herself, but she let the child have all she wanted, and spread honey herself on Nimue's bread; time enough to train her, and after all, she was still growing very fast.

"You are eating no meat, Aunt," said Nimue. "Is it a fast day?"

Morgaine suddenly remembered how she had questioned Viviane. "No, I do not often eat it."

"Don't you like it? I do."

"Well, eat it then, if you wish. The priestesses do not have meat very often, but it is not forbidden, certainly not to a child your age."

"Are they like the nuns? Do they fast all the time? Father Griffin says—" She stopped, remembering she had been told not to quote what he said, and Morgaine was pleased; the child learned quickly.

She said, "I meant you are not to take what he says as a guide for your own conduct. But you may tell me what he says and one day you will learn to separate for yourself what is right in what he says, and what is folly or worse."

"He says that men and women must fast for their sins. Is that why?"

Morgaine shook her head. "The people of Avalon fast, sometimes, to teach their bodies to do what they are told without making demands it is inconvenient to satisfy—there are times when one must do without food, or water, or sleep, and the body must be the servant of the mind, not the master. The mind cannot be set on holy things, or wisdom, or stilled for the long meditation which opens the mind to other realms, when the body cries out 'Feed me!' or 'I thirst!' So we teach ourselves to still its clamoring. Do you understand?"

"N-not really," said the child doubtfully.

"You will understand when you are older, then. For now, eat your bread, and make ready to ride again."

Nimue finished her bread and honey and wiped her hands tidily on a clump of grass. "I never understood Father Griffin either, but he was angry when I did not. I was punished when I asked him why we must fast and pray for our sins when Christ had already forgiven them, and he said I had been taught heathendom and made Mother send me to my room. What is heathendom, Aunt?"

"It is anything a priest does not like," said Morgaine. "Father Griffin is a fool. Even the best of the Christian priests do not trouble little ones like you, who can do no sin, with much talk about it. Time enough to talk about sin, Nimue, when you are capable of doing it, or making choices between good and evil."

Nimue got on her pony obediently, but after a time she said, "Aunt Morgaine—I am not such a good girl, though. I sin all the time. I am always doing wicked things. I am not at all surprised that Mother wanted to send me away. That is why she is sending me to a wicked place, because I am a wicked girl."

Morgaine felt her throat close with something like agony. She had been about to mount her own horse, but she hurried to Nimue's pony and caught the girl in a great hug, holding her tight and kissing her again and again. She said, breathlessly, "Never say that again, Nimue! Never! It is not true, I vow to you it is not! Your mother did not want to send you away at all, and if she had thought Avalon a wicked place she would not have sent you no matter what I threatened!"

Nimue said in a small voice, "Why am I being sent away, then?"

Morgaine still held her tight with all the strength of her arms. "Because you were pledged to Avalon before you were born, my child. Because your grandmother was a priestess, and because I have no daughter for the Goddess, and you are being sent to Avalon that you may learn wisdom and serve the Goddess." She noted that her tears were falling, unheeded, on Nimue's fair hair. "Who let you believe it was punishment?"

"One of the women—while she packed my shift—" Nimue faltered. "I heard her say, Mother should not have sent me to that wicked place— and Father Griffin has told me often I am a wicked girl—"

Morgaine sank to the ground, holding Nimue in her lap, rocking her back and forth. "No, no," she said gently, "no, darling, no. You are a good girl. If you are naughty or lazy or disobedient, that is not sin, it is only that you are not old enough to know any better, and when you are taught to do what is right, then you will do so." And then, because she thought this conversation had gone far for a child so young, she said, "Look at that butterfly! I have not seen one that color before! Come, Nimue, let me lift you on your pony now," she said, and listened attentively as the little girl chattered on about butterflies.

Alone she could have ridden to Avalon in a single day, but the short legs of Nimue's little pony could not make that distance, so they slept that night in a clearing. Nimue had never slept out of doors before, and the darkness frightened her when they put out the fire, so Morgaine let the child creep into the circle of her arms and lay pointing out one star after another to her.

The little girl was tired with riding and soon slept, but Morgaine lay awake, Nimue's head heavy on her arm, feeling fear stealing upon her. She had been so long away from Avalon. Step by slow step, she had retraced all her training, or what she could remember; but would she forget some vital thing?

At last she slept, but before morning it seemed that she heard a step in the clearing, and Raven stood before her. She wore her dark gown and spotted deerskin tunic, and she said, "Morgaine! Morgaine, my dearest!" Her voice, the voice Morgaine had heard but once in all her years in Avalon, was so filled with surprise and joy and wonder that Morgaine woke suddenly and stared around the clearing, half expecting to see Raven there in the flesh. But the clearing was empty, except for a trace of mist that blotted out the stars, and Morgaine lay down again, not knowing if she had dreamed, or whether, with the Sight, Raven knew that she was approaching. Her heart was racing; she could feel the beat of it, almost painful inside her chest.

I should never have stayed away so long. I should have tried to return when Viviane died. Even if I died in the attempt, I should have made it. . . . Will they want me now, old, worn, used, the Sight slowly going from me, with nothing to bring them. . . ?

The child at her side made a small sleepy sound and stirred; she shifted her weight slightly and moved closer into Morgaine's arms. Morgaine put an arm round her, thinking, *I bring them Viviane's granddaughter. But if they let me return only for her sake it will be more bitter than death. Has the Goddess cast me out forever?*

At last she slept again, not to waken until it was broad daylight, misty drizzle beginning to fall. With this bad start the day went badly; toward midday Nimue's pony cast a shoe, and, although Morgaine was impatient and would have taken the child up to ride before her—she herself was the lightest of burdens for a horse, who could have carried two her size without trouble—she did not want to lame the pony, so they must turn aside for a village and a blacksmith. She did not want it known or rumored in the countryside that the King's sister rode for Avalon, but now there was no help for it. There was so little news in this part of the land that whatever happened here seemed to fly on wings.

Well, it could not helped; the wretched little animal was not to blame. They delayed and found a small village off the main road. All day the rain fell; even though it was high summer, Morgaine was shivering, and the child was damp and fretful. Morgaine paid little attention to her fussing; she was sorry for her, especially when Nimue began to cry softly for her mother, but that could not be helped either, and one of the first lessons of a priestess in the making was to endure loneliness. She would simply have to cry until she found her own comfort or learned to live without it, as all the maidens in the House had had to learn to do.

It was now long past noon, although the overcast was so thick that they could get no hint of the sun. Still, at this time of year, the light lingered late, and Morgaine did not want to spend another night on the road. She resolved to ride as far as they could see their way and was encouraged to see that as soon as they began to ride again, Nimue stopped whimpering and began to take an interest in what they rode past. Now they were very near Avalon. Nimue was so sleepy that she swayed in her saddle and at last Morgaine lifted the little girl from her pony and held her in front of her on the saddle. But the child woke when they came to the shores of the Lake.

"Are we there, Aunt?" she asked, as she was set on her feet.

"No, but it is not far now," Morgaine said. "Within half an hour, if all goes well, you will be ready for supper and bed."

And if all does not go well? Morgaine refused to think of that. Doubt was fatal to power, and to the Sight. . . . Five years she had spent, laboriously retracing her steps from the beginning; now it was as it had been before, cast out of Avalon, with no test save this, *Have I the power to return . . . ?*

"I don't see anything at all," Nimue said. "Is *this* the place? But there is nothing here, Aunt." And she looked fearfully at the dismal dripping shore, the solitary reeds murmuring to the rain.

"They will send us a boat," said Morgaine.

"But how will they know we are here? How can they see us in this rain?"

"I will call it," said Morgaine. "Be quiet, Nimue." Within her echoed the fretful child's cry, but now, when she stood at last on the shores of home, she felt the old knowledge welling up, filling her like a cup overrunning its brim. She bent her head for an instant in the most fervent prayer of her life, then drew a long breath and raised her arms in invocation.

For an instant, heartsick with failure, she felt nothing; then, like a slowly descending line of light running down her, it struck through her, and she heard the little girl at her side gasp in sudden wonder; but she had no time for that, she felt her body like a bridge of lightning between Heaven and Earth. She did not consciously speak the word of power, but felt it throbbing like thunder through her whole body . . . silence. Silence, Nimue white and dumb at her side. And then in the dim, dull waters of the Lake there was a little stirring, like mist boiling . . . and then a shadow, and then, long and dark and shining, the Avalon barge moving slowly out of the patch of mist. Morgaine let her breath go in a long sigh that was half a sob.

It glided noiseless as a shadow to the shore, but the sound of the boat scraping on the land was very real and solid. Several of the little dark men scrambled out and took the horses' heads, bowing low to Morgaine, saying, "I will lead them by the other path, lady," and vanishing into the rain. Another drew back so that Morgaine could first step into the boat, lift the staring child in after her, give a hand to the frightened servants. Still in silence, except for the muttered words of the man who had taken the horses, the boat glided out into the Lake.

"What is that shadow, Aunt?" Nimue whispered, as the oars shoved out from shore.

"It is Glastonbury church," said Morgaine, surprised that her voice was so calm. "It is on the other island, the one we can see from here. Your grandmother, your father's mother, is buried there. Someday, perhaps, you will see her memorial stone."

"Are we going there?"

"Not today."

"But the boat is going straight toward it—I have heard there is a convent on Glastonbury too—"

"No," said Morgaine, "we are not going there. Wait and see, and be quiet."

Now would come the true test. They might have seen her from Avalon, with the Sight, and sent the boat, but whether she could open the mists to Avalon . . . that would be the test of all she had done in these years. She must not try and fail, she must simply arise and do it, without stopping to think. They were now in the very center of the Lake, where another stroke of the oars would take them into the current which ran toward the Isle of Glastonbury. . . . Morgaine rose swiftly, the flow of her draperies around her, and raised her arms. Again she remembered . . . it was like the first time she had done this, with a shock of surprise that the tremendous flow of power was silent, when it should blast the sky with thunders . . . she dared not open her eyes until she heard Nimue cry aloud in fear and wonder. . . .

The rain was gone, and under the last brilliance of a setting sun, the Isle of Avalon lay green and beautiful before them, sunlight on the Lake, sunlight striking through the ring stones atop the Tor, sunlight on the white walls of the temple. Morgaine saw it through a blur of tears; she swayed in the boat and would have fallen, except for a hand laid on her shoulder.

Home, home, I am here, I am coming home. . . .

She felt the boat scrape on the pebbled shore and composed herself. It seemed not right that she should not be wearing the garb of a priestess, though beneath her gown, as always, Viviane's little knife was belted close around her waist. It seemed not right . . . her silken veils, the rings on her narrow fingers . . . Queen Morgaine of North Wales, not Morgaine of Avalon . . . well, that could be changed. She lifted her head proudly, drawing a long breath, and took the child by the hand. However she had changed, however many the years that lay between, she was Morgaine of Avalon, priestess of the Great Goddess. Beyond that Lake of mists and shadows, she might be queen to an elderly and laughable king, in a country far away . . . but here she was priestess, and born of the old royal line of Avalon.

She saw without surprise, as she stepped on land, that before her stood a line of bowing servants and behind them, awaiting her, the dark-robed forms of priestesses . . . they had known and had come to welcome her home. And through the line of priestesses, she saw a face and form she had seen only in a dream, a tall woman, fair-haired and queenly, her golden hair braided low on her forehead. The woman came to Morgaine quickly through the line of the other priestesses, and took her into an embrace.

"Welcome, kinswoman," she said softly. "Welcome home, Morgaine."

And Morgaine spoke the name she had heard only in dreams till Kevin spoke it to her, confirming the dream. "I greet you, Niniane, and I bring you Viviane's granddaughter. She shall be fostered here, and her name is Nimue."

Niniane was studying her curiously; what had she heard, Morgaine wondered, in all these years? But then she looked away and stooped to look at the little girl.

"And this is Galahad's daughter?"

"No," said Nimue, "Galahad is my brother. I am the daughter of the good knight Lancelet."

Niniane smiled. "I know," she said, "but here we do not use the name the Saxons gave your father, and he has the same name as your brother, you see. Well, Nimue, have you come to be a priestess here?"

Nimue looked around at the sunset landscape. "That is what my aunt Morgaine told me. I would like to learn to read and write and play the harp, and know about the stars and all kinds of things as she does. Are you really evil sorceresses here? I thought a sorceress would be old and ugly, and you are very pretty." She bit her lip. "I am being rude again."

Niniane laughed. "Always speak out the truth, child. Yes, I am a sorceress. I do not think I am ugly, but you must decide for yourself whether I am good or evil. I try to do the will of the Goddess, and that is all anyone can do."

"I will try to do that, if you will tell me how," Nimue said.

The sun dropped below the horizon, and suddenly the shore was all grey twilight. Niniane signalled; a servant holding a single torch reached out to another, and the light passed swiftly from hand to hand until the shore was all ablaze with torchlight. Niniane patted the little girl on the cheek. She said, "Until you are old enough to know her will for yourself, will you obey the rules here, and obey the women who have you in charge?"

"I will try," Nimue said, "but I am always forgetting. And I ask too many questions."

"You may ask as many questions as you want to, when it is the proper time for such things," Niniane said, "but you have been riding all day and it is late, so for tonight the first command I give you is to be a good girl, and go and have supper and a bath and go to your bed. Say farewell to your kinswoman, now, and go with Lheanna to the House of Maidens." She gestured to a sturdy, motherly looking woman in the dress of a priestess.

Nimue sniffled a little and said, "Must I say goodbye now? Won't you come and tell me goodbye tomorrow, Aunt Morgaine? I thought I would be with you here."

Morgaine said, very gently, "No, you must go to the House of Maidens, and do what you are told." She kissed the petal-soft cheek. "The Goddess bless you, darling. We will meet again when she wills it." And as she spoke she *saw* this same Nimue grown to tall womanhood, pale and serious with the blue crescent painted between her brows, and the shadow of the Death-crone . . . she swayed, and Niniane put out a hand to support her.

"You are weary, lady Morgaine. Send the babe to her rest, and come with me. We can talk tomorrow."

Morgaine printed a final kiss on Nimue's brow and the little girl trotted away obediently at Lheanna's side. Morgaine felt a darkening mist before her eyes; Niniane gave her an arm and said, "Lean on me. Come with me to my quarters where you can rest."

Niniane brought her to the dwelling that had once been Viviane's, and to the little room where the priestesses in attendance on the Lady of the Lake slept in their turn. Alone, Morgaine managed to collect herself. For a moment she wondered if Niniane had brought her to these quarters to emphasize that she, not Morgaine, was Lady of the Lake . . . then stopped herself; that kind of intrigue was for the court, not for Avalon. Niniane had simply given her the most convenient and secluded of the rooms available. Once Raven had dwelt here, in her consecrated silence, so that Viviane might teach her. . . .

Morgaine washed the grime of travel from her weary body, wrapped herself in the long robe of undyed wool which she found lying across the bed, and even ate some of the food they brought, but did not touch the warmed and spiced wine. There was a stone water jar at the side of the fireplace, and she dipped out a ladleful, drinking, with tears in her eyes.

The priestesses of Avalon drink only water from the Sacred Well. . . . Again she was the young Morgaine, sleeping within the walls of her own place. She went to bed and slept like a child.

She never knew what woke her. There was a step in the room, and silence. By the last flicker of the dying firelight and the flooding light of the moon through the shutters, she saw a veiled form, and for a moment she thought that Niniane had come to speak with her; but the hair that flowed over the shoulders was long and dark and the dark face beautiful and still. On one hand she could see the darkened, thickened patch of an ancient scar . . . Raven! She sat up and said, "Raven! Is it you?"

Raven's fingers covered her lips, in the old gesture of silence; she came to Morgaine's side, bent over her and kissed her. Without a word, she threw off her long cloak and lay down at Morgaine's side, taking her in her arms. In the dimness Morgaine could see the rest of the scars running up along the arm and across the pale heavy breast . . . neither of them spoke a word, then, nor in the time that followed. It seemed that the real world and Avalon had both slipped away, and again she was in the shadows of the fairy country, held close in the arms of the lady. . . . Morgaine heard in her mind the words of the ancient blessing of Avalon, as Raven touched her slowly, with ritual silence and significance, and the sound seemed to shiver around her in the silence. *Blessed be the feet that have brought you to this place . . . blessed the knees that shall bend before her altar . . . blessed be the gate of Life. . . .*

And then the world began to flow and change and move around her, and for a moment it was not Raven in the silence, but a form edged in light, whom she had seen once, years before, at the time when she crossed the great silence . . . and Morgaine knew that she too was glowing in light . . . still the deep flowing silence. And then it was only Raven again, lying close to her with her hair perfumed with the herbs they used in the rites, one arm flung over her, her silent lips just touching Morgaine's cheek. Morgaine could see that there were long pale streaks of white in the dark hair.

Raven stirred and raised herself up. Still she did not speak, but she took from somewhere a silver crescent, the ritual ornament of a priestess. Morgaine knew, with a catch of breath, that it was the one she had left on her bed in the House of Maidens on that day when she had fled forth from Avalon with Arthur's child in her womb . . . silent, after a gasp of half-voiced protest, she let Raven bind it about her neck; but Raven showed her briefly, by the last glint of the setting moon, the flash of a knife blade bound about her own waist. Morgaine nodded, knowing that Viviane's ritual knife would never again while she lived leave her side; she was content that Raven should bear the one she herself had abandoned until one day she saw it bound about Nimue's waist.

Raven took the little razor-sharp knife, and Morgaine watched, stilled into a dream, as she raised it; *so be it, even if she wishes here to shed my blood before the Goddess I tried to flee* . . . but Raven turned the knife toward her own throat; from the breastbone she pricked a single drop of blood, and Morgaine, bowing her head, took the knife and made a slight cut over her heart.

We are old, Raven and I, we shed blood no longer from the womb but from the heart . . . and wondered afterward what she had meant. Raven bent to

her and licked the blood away from the small cut; Morgaine bent and
touched her lips to the small, welling stain at Raven's breast, knowing that
this was a sealing long past the vows she had taken when she came to
womanhood. Then Raven drew her again into her arms.

*I gave up my maidenhood to the Horned One. I bore a child to the God.
I burned with passion for Lancelet, and Accolon created me priestess anew in the
plowed fields which the Spring Maiden had blessed. Yet never have I known what
it was to be received simply in love. . . .* It seemed to Morgaine, half in a dream,
that she lay in the lap of her mother . . . no, not Igraine, but welcomed back
into the arms of the Great Mother. . . .

When she woke she was alone. Opening her eyes into the sunlight of
Avalon, weeping with joy, she wondered for a moment if she had dreamed.
Yet over her heart was a small stain of dried blood; and on the pillow beside
her lay the silver crescent, the ritual jewel of a priestess, which she had
left when she fled from Avalon. Yet surely Raven had bound it about her
throat. . . .

Morgaine tied it around her neck on its slender thong. It would never
leave her again; like Viviane, she would be buried with this about her neck.
Her fingers shook as she knotted the leather, knowing this was a reconsecra-
tion. There was something else on the pillow, and for a moment it shifted
and changed, an unopened rosebud, a blown rose, and when Morgaine took
it into her hand, it was the rose-hip berry, full and round and crimson,
pulsing with the tart life of the rose. As she watched, it shrank, withered,
lay dried in her hand; and Morgaine suddenly understood.

*Flower and even fruit are only the beginning. In the seed lies the life and
the future.*

With a long sigh, Morgaine tied the seed into a scrap of silk, knowing
that she must go forth again from Avalon. Her work was not completed,
and she had chosen the place of her work and her testing when she fled forth
from Avalon. One day, perhaps, she might return, but that time had not
yet come.

And what I am must be hidden, as the rose lies hidden within the seed. She
rose then and put on the garments of the queen. The robe of a priestess
should be hers again one day, but she had yet to earn again the right to wear
it. Then she sat and waited for Niniane to summon her.

WHEN SHE CAME into the central room where she had faced Viviane so often,
time swooped and circled and turned on itself so that for a moment it seemed
to Morgaine that she must see Viviane sitting where she had so often sat,
dwarfed by the high seat and yet impressive, filling the whole room
. . . then she blinked, and it was Niniane there, tall and slight and fair; it

seemed to Morgaine that Niniane was no more than a child, sitting in play in the high seat.

And then what Viviane had said to her when she stood before her, so many years ago, suddenly rushed over her: *you have reached a stage where obedience may be tempered with your own judgment* . . . and for a moment it seemed to her that her best judgment was to turn aside now, to say to Niniane only such words as might reassure her. And then the surge of resentment came over her at the thought that this child, this foolish and ordinary girl in the dress of a priestess, was presuming to sit where Viviane had sat and to give orders in the name of Avalon. She had been chosen only because she was of the blood of Taliesin. . . . *How does she dare sit here and presume to give orders to me. . . ?*

She looked down at the girl, knowing, without being certain how, that she had taken upon herself the old glamour and majesty, and then, with a sudden surge of the Sight, it seemed to her that she read Niniane's thoughts.

She should be here in my place, Niniane was thinking, *how can I speak with authority to Queen Morgaine of the Fairies* . . . and the thought was blurred, half with awe of the strange and powerful priestess before her, and half with simple resentment, *if she had not fled from us and forsworn her duty, I would not now be struggling to fill a place for which we both know I am not fit.*

Morgaine came and took her hands, and Niniane was surprised at her gentle voice.

"I am sorry, my poor girl, I would give my very life to return here and take the burden from you. But I cannot, I dare not. I cannot hide here and shirk my given task because I long for my home." It was no longer arrogance, nor contempt for the girl who had been thrust, unwilling, into the place which should have been hers, but simple pity for her. "I have begun a task in the West country which must be completed—if I leave it half done, it were better it had never been begun. You cannot take my place there, and so, may the Goddess help us both, you must keep my place here." She bent and embraced the girl, holding her tight. "My poor little cousin, there is a fate on us both, and we cannot escape it . . . if I had stayed here, the Goddess would have worked with me one way, but even when I tried to flee my sworn duty, she brought it upon me elsewhere . . . none of us can escape. We are both in her hands, and it is too late to say it would have been better the other way . . . she will do with us as she will."

Niniane held rigidly aloof for a moment, then her resentment melted and she clung to Morgaine, almost as Nimue had done. Blinking back tears, she said, "I wanted to hate you—"

"And I, you, perhaps . . ." Morgaine said. "But she has willed otherwise, and before her we are sisters. . . ." Hesitantly, her lips reluctant to speak the words which had been withheld for so long, she added something else, and Niniane bent her head and murmured the proper response. Then she said, "Tell me of your work in the West, Morgaine. No, sit here beside me, there is no rank between us, you know that. . . ."

When Morgaine had told her what she could, Niniane nodded. "Something of this I heard from the Merlin," she said. "In that country, then, men turn again to the old worship . . . but Uriens has two sons, and the elder is his father's heir. Your task then is to make certain that Wales has a king from Avalon—which means that Accolon must succeed his father, Morgaine."

Morgaine closed her eyes and sat with bent head. At last she said, "I will not kill, Niniane. I have seen too much of war and bloodshed. Avalloch's death would solve nothing—they follow Roman ways there now, since the priests have come, and Avalloch has a son."

Niniane dismissed that. "A son who could be reared to the old worship —how old is he, four years old?"

"He was so when I came to Wales," said Morgaine, thinking of the child who had sat in her lap and clung to her with his sticky fingers and called her Granny. "Enough, Niniane. I have done all else, but even for Avalon, I will not kill."

Niniane's eyes flamed blue sparks at her. She raised her head and said, warning, "Never name that well from which you will not drink!"

And suddenly Morgaine realized that the woman before her was priestess, too, not merely the pliant child she had seemed; she could not be where she was, she could never have passed the tests and ordeals which went into the making of a Lady of Avalon, if she had not been acceptable to the Goddess. With unexpected humility, she realized why she had been sent here. Niniane said, almost in warning, "You will do what the Goddess wills when her hand is laid upon you, and that I know by the token you bear . . ." and her eyes rested upon Morgaine's bosom as if she could see through the folds of the gown to the seed which lay there, or to the silver crescent on its leather thong. Morgaine bent her head and whispered, "We are all in her hands."

"Be it so," said Niniane, and for a moment it was so silent in the room that Morgaine could hear the splash of a fish in the Lake beyond the borders of the little house. Then she said, "What of Arthur, Morgaine? He bears still the sword of the Druid Regalia. Will he honor his oath at last? Can you make him honor it?"

"I do not know Arthur's heart," Morgaine said, and it was a bitter confession. *I had power over him, and I was too squeamish to use it. I flung it away.*

"He must swear again to honor his oath to Avalon, or you must get the sword from him again," said Niniane, "and you are the only person living to whom this task might be entrusted. Excalibur, the sword of the Holy Regalia, must not remain in the hands of one who follows Christ. You know Arthur has no son by his queen, and he has named the son of Lancelet, Galahad by name, to be his heir, since now the Queen grows old."

Morgaine thought, *Gwenhwyfar is younger than I, and I might still bear a child if I had not been so damaged in Gwydion's birth. Why are they so certain she will never bear?* But before Niniane's certainty she asked no questions. There was magic enough in Avalon, and no doubt they had hands and eyes at Arthur's court; and indeed the last thing they would wish would be that the Christian Gwenhwyfar should bear Arthur a son . . . not now.

"Arthur has a son," said Niniane, "and while his day is not yet, there is a kingdom he can take—a place to begin the recapture of this land for Avalon. In the ancient ways, the king's son meant little, the son of the Lady was all, and the king's sister's son was his heir . . . know you what I mean, Morgaine?"

Accolon must succeed to the throne of Wales. Morgaine heard it again, and then what Niniane did not say: *And my son . . . is the son of King Arthur.* Now it all made sense. Even her own barrenness after Gwydion's birth. But she asked, "What of Arthur's heir—Lancelet's son?"

Niniane shrugged and for a moment Morgaine wondered, horrified, whether it was intended to give Nimue the same hold on Galahad's conscience that she had been given on Arthur's.

"I cannot see all things," said Niniane. "Had you been Lady here— but time has moved on and other plans must be made. Arthur may yet honor his oath to Avalon and keep the sword Excalibur, and then there will be one way to proceed. And he may not, and there will be another way which she will prepare, to which end we each have our tasks. But whether or no, Accolon must come to rule in the West country, and that is your task. And the next king will rule from Avalon. When Arthur falls—though his stars say he will live to be old—then the king of Avalon will rise. Or else, the stars say, such darkness will fall over this land that it will be as if he had never been. And when the next king takes power, then will Avalon return into the mainstream of time and history . . . and then there will be a subject king over the western lands, ruling his Tribespeople. Accolon shall rise high as your consort—and it is for you to prepare the land for the great king from Avalon."

Again Morgaine bowed her head and said, "I am in your hands."

"You must return now," said Niniane, "but first there is one you must know. His time is not yet . . . but there will be one more task for you." She raised her hand, and as if he had been waiting in an anteroom, a door opened and a tall young man came into the room.

And at the sight Morgaine caught her breath, with a pain so great that it seemed for a moment that she could not breathe. Here was Lancelet reborn —young and slender as a dark flame, his hair curling about his cheeks, his narrow dark face smiling . . . Lancelet as he had been on that day when they lay together in the shadow of the ring stones, as if time had slipped and circled back as in the fairy country. . . .

And then she knew who it must be. He came forward and bent to kiss her hand. His walk was Lancelet's too, the flowing movements that seemed almost a dance. But he wore the robes of a bard, and on his forehead was the small tattoo of an acorn crest, and about his wrists the serpents of Avalon writhed. Time reeled in her mind.

If Galahad is to be king in the land, is my son then the Merlin, tanist and dark twin and sacrifice? For a moment it seemed she moved among shadows, king and Druid, the bright shadow who sat beside Arthur's throne as queen, and herself who had borne Arthur's shadow son . . . Dark Lady of power.

She knew anything she said would be foolish. "Gwydion. You are not like your father."

He shook his head. "No," he said, "I bear the blood of Avalon. I looked once on Arthur, when he made a pilgrimage to Glastonbury of the priests —I went there unseen in a priest's robe. He bows overmuch to the priests, this Arthur our king." His smile was fleeting, feral.

"You have no reason to love either of your parents, Gwydion," said Morgaine, and her hand tightened on his, but she surprised a fleeting look in his eyes, icy hatred . . . then it was gone and he was the smiling young Druid again.

"My parents gave me their best gift," Gwydion said, "the royal blood of Avalon. And one more thing I ask of you, lady Morgaine." Irrationally she wished he had called her, just once, by the name of Mother.

"Ask, and if I can give, it is yours."

Gwydion said, "It is not a great gift. Surely not more than five years hence, Queen Morgaine, you will lead me to look on Arthur and let him know that I am his son. I am aware"—a quick, disturbing smile—"that he cannot acknowledge me as his heir. But I wish him to look on the face of his son. I ask no more than that."

She bent her head. "Surely I owe you that much, Gwydion."

Gwenhwyfar might think what she liked—Arthur had already done penance for this. No man could be other than proud of this grave and priestly young Druid. Nor should she . . . after all these years, she knew it . . . feel shame for what had been, as now she knew she had felt it all these years since she fled from Avalon. Now that she saw her son grown, she bowed before the inevitability of Viviane's Sight.

She said, "I vow to you that day will come, I swear it by the Sacred

Well." Her eyes blurred, and angrily she blinked back the rebellious tears. This was not her son; Uwaine, perhaps, was her son, but not Gwydion. This dark, handsome young man so like the Lancelet she had loved as a girl, he was not her son looking for the first time on the mother who had abandoned him before he was weaned; he was priest and she priestess of the Great Goddess, and if they were no more to each other than that, at least they were no less.

She put her hands to his bent head and said, "Be thou blessed."

13

Queen Morgause had long ceased to repine that she had not the Sight. Yet twice, in the last days of falling leaves, when the red larch trees stood bare in the icy wind that blew over Lothian, she dreamed of her foster-son Gwydion; and she was not at all surprised when one of her servant folk told her that a rider was on the road.

Gwydion wore a strangely colored cloak, coarse and with a clasp of bone such as she had never seen, and when she would have wrapped him in her arms, he shrank away, wincing.

"No, Mother—" He put his free arm around her and explained, "I caught a sword cut there in Brittany—no, it is not serious," he reassured her. "It did not fester and perhaps I shall not even have a scar, but when it is touched it cries out to me!"

"You have been fighting in Brittany, then? I thought you safe in Avalon," she remonstrated, as she led him within and set him by the fire. "I have no southern wine for you—"

He laughed. "I am weary of it—barley beer is enough for me, or some of the firewater if you have it . . . with hot water and honey if there is any. I am stiff with riding." He let one of the women draw off his boots and hang his cloak to dry, leaning back at ease.

"So good it is to be here, Mother—" He set the steaming cup to his lips and drank with pleasure.

"And you came so far, riding in the cold with a wound? Was there some great tidings that needed to tell?"

He shook his head. "None—I was homesick, no more," he said. "It's all so green and lush and damp there, with fog and church bells . . . I longed for the clean air of the fells, and the gulls' cry, and your face, Mother . . ." He reached out for the cup he had set down, and she saw the serpents about his wrists. She was not greatly versed in the lore of Avalon, but she knew they were the sign of the highest rank of the priesthood. He saw her glance and nodded, but said nothing.

"Was it in Brittany you got you that ugly cloak, so coarse-woven and low, fit only for a serving-man?"

He chuckled. "It kept the rain from me. I took it from a great chief of the foreign lands, who fought under the legions of that man who called himself Emperor Lucius. Arthur's men made short work of that one, believe me, and there was plunder for all—I have a silver cup and a golden ring in my packs for you, Mother."

"You fought in the armies of Arthur?" Morgause asked. She had never thought he would do this; he saw the surprise in her face and laughed again.

"Yes, I fought under that great King who fathered me," he said, with a grin of contempt. "Oh, fear not, I had my orders from Avalon. I took care to fight among the warriors of Ceardig, the Saxon chief of the treaty men who loves me well, and to come not under Arthur's eyes. Gawaine knew me not, and I was careful not to let Gareth see me except when I was shrouded in a cloak like that—I lost my own cloak in battle, and feared if I was wearing a cloak of Lothian, Gareth would come to look on a wounded countryman, so I got this one. . . ."

"Gareth would have known you anywhere," said Morgause, "and I hope you do not think your foster-brother would ever betray you."

Gwydion smiled, and Morgause thought that he looked very like the little boy who had once sat in her lap. He said, "I longed to make myself known to Gareth, and when I lay wounded and weak, I came near to doing so. But Gareth is Arthur's man, and he loves his king, I could see that, and I would not put that burden on my best of brothers," he said. "Gareth—Gareth is the only one—"

He did not finish the sentence, but Morgause knew what he would have said; stranger as he was everywhere, Gareth was his brother and his beloved friend. Abruptly he grinned, chasing away the remote smile that made him look so young. "All through the Saxon armies, Mother, I was asked again and again if I was Lancelet's son! I cannot see the resemblance so much myself, but then I am not really familiar with my own face . . . I look into a mirror only when I shave myself!"

"Still," said Morgause, "anyone who had seen Lancelet, especially anyone who knew him in youth, could not look on you without knowing you his kinsman."

"Some such thing as that I said—I put on a Breton accent, sometimes, and said I too was kinsman to old King Ban," Gwydion said. "Yet I would think our Lancelet, with the face which makes him a magnet to all maids, would have fathered enough bastards that it would not be such a marvel to all men that one should go about wearing his face! Not so? I wondered," he said, "but all I heard of Lancelet was that it might be that he had fathered a son on the Queen and the child was spirited away somewhere to be fostered by that kinswoman of hers whom they married off to Lancelet. . . . Tales of Lancelet and the Queen are many, each wilder than the next, but all agree that for every other woman the Gods made, he has nothing but courtesy and fair words. There were even women who flung themselves at me, saying that if they could not have Lancelet, they would have his son. . . ." He grinned again. "It must have been hard for the gallant Lancelet. I have eye enough for a fair woman, but when they push themselves on me so, well . . ." He shrugged, comically. Morgause laughed.

"Then the Druids have not robbed you of that, my son?"

"By no means," he said. "But most women are fools, so that I prefer not to trouble myself making play with those who expect me to treat them as something very special, or to pay heed to what they say. You have spoilt me for foolish women, Mother."

"Pity the same could not have been said of Lancelet," said Morgause, "for never did anyone think Gwenhwyfar had more wits than she needed to keep her girdle tied, and where Lancelet was concerned, I doubt she had that much," and she thought, *You have Lancelet's face, my boy, but you have your mother's wit!*

As if he had heard her thoughts, he set down the empty cup, and waved away a serving-girl who would have scurried to refill it. "No more, I am so weary that I will be drunk at another taste! Supper I would have. I have had enough of hunter's fortune, I am sick of meat, and long for home food —porridge and bannock. . . . Mother, I looked on the lady Morgaine at Avalon before I left for Brittany."

Now why, Morgause wondered, *does he say this to me?* It could not be looked for that he should have much love for his mother, and then she felt sudden guilt. *I made sure he should not love any but me.* Well, she had done what she must, and she did not regret it.

"How looks my kinswoman?"

"She looks not young," said Gwydion, "it seemed to me that she was older than you, Mother."

"No," Morgause said, "Morgaine is younger than I by ten years."

"Still, she looks worn and old, and you . . ." He smiled at her, and Morgause felt the flood of sudden happiness. She thought, *None of my own sons have I loved as this one. Morgaine did well to leave him to my care.*

"Oh," she said, "I grow old too, my lad . . . I had a grown son when you were born!"

"Then you are twice the sorceress she is," said Gwydion, "for one could swear you had dwelt long in the fairy country with time never touching you . . . you look to me as you did the day I rode away for Avalon, Mother mine." He reached out his hand to hers and brought it to his lips and kissed it, and she came and put her arm round him, careful to avoid his wound. She stroked the dark hair. "So Morgaine is queen now in Wales."

"True," Gwydion said, "and high, I hear, in favor with the King . . . Arthur has made her stepson Uwaine a member of his own personal bodyguard, next to Gawaine, and he and Gawaine are close friends. Uwaine's not a bad fellow—not unlike Gawaine, I'd say—tough and staunch, both of them, and devoted to Arthur as if the sun rose and set where he pissed . . ." and Morgause noted the wry smile. "But then it's a fault many men have—and I came here to speak of this to you, Mother," he said. "Know you anything of Avalon's plan?"

"I know what Niniane said, and the Merlin, when they came to take you thither," said Morgause. "I know you are to be Arthur's heir, even though he believes he will leave the kingdom to that son of Lancelet's. I know you are the young stag who will bring down the King Stag . . ." she said in the old language, and Gwydion raised his brow.

"Then you know it all," he said. "But this, perhaps, you do not know . . . it cannot be done now. Since Arthur brought down this Roman who would be emperor, this Lucius, his star has never flamed higher than now. Anyone who raised a hand against Arthur would be torn in pieces by the mob, or by his Companions—never have I seen a man so loved. This, I think, is why I needed to look from afar on his face, to see what is it in a king which makes him so loved. . . ."

His voice fell away into silence and Morgause felt ill at ease. "And did you so?"

Gwydion nodded slowly. "He is a king indeed . . . even I who have no cause to love him felt that spell he creates around him. You cannot imagine how he is worshipped."

"Strange," said Morgause, "I for one never thought him so remarkable."

"No, be fair," said Gwydion. "There are not many—perhaps there is no other within this land who could have rallied all factions as he did! Romans, Welsh, Cornish, West-countrymen, East Anglians, men of Brittany, the Old People, the men of Lothian . . . all through this kingdom, Mother, all men swear by Arthur's star. Even those Saxons who once fought Uther to the death, stand and swear that Arthur shall be their king. He is a great warrior . . . no, not in himself, he fights no better than any other warrior, not half so well as Lancelet or even Gareth, but he is a great general. And it is something . . . something in himself," Gwydion said. "It is easy to love him. And while all worship him thus, I have no possible task."

"Then," said Morgause, "their love of him must somehow be made less. He must be discredited. He is no better than any other man, the Gods know that. He fathered you on his own sister, and it is well known here and abroad that he plays no very noble part with his queen. There is a name for a man who sits complacent while another man pays court to his queen, and not so pretty a name, after all."

"Something, I am sure, can be made of that," said Gwydion. "Though in these late years, it is said, Lancelet has stayed far from court and taken care never to be alone with the Queen, so that no shadow of scandal shall fall on her name. Yet they say she wept like a child, and so did Lancelet, when he took leave of her to go and fight at Arthur's side against this Lucius, and never did I see man fight as did Lancelet. One would think he longed to fling himself headlong into death. But he took never even a wound, as if his life was charmed. I wonder . . . he is the son of a High Priestess of Avalon," he mused. "It may be he bears supernatural protection of some sort."

"Morgaine would know that," said Morgause dryly, "but I would not suggest you ask her."

"I do know that Arthur's life is charmed," said Gwydion, "for he bears the sacred Excalibur, sword of the Druid Regalia, and a magical scabbard which guards him from shedding blood. Without it, so Niniane told me, he would have bled himself to death at Celidon Wood, and after that. . . . Morgaine has been given as her first task to get this sword again from Arthur, unless he will swear anew to be true to Avalon. And I doubt not my mother is wily enough to do so. I doubt she would stop at much, my mother. Of the two, I think I like my father better—he knew not what evil he had wrought when he got me, I think."

"Morgaine knew not that, either," said Morgause sharply.

"Oh, I am weary of Morgaine . . . even Niniane has fallen under her spell," said Gwydion sharply. "Do not *you* begin to defend her to me, Mother."

Morgause thought, *Viviane was even so, she could charm any man alive to do her will, and any woman either . . . Igraine went pliant at her bidding to wed with Gorlois and later to seduce Uther . . . and I to Lot's bed . . . and now Niniane has done what Morgaine wished.* And this foster-son of hers had, she suspected, something of that power, too. She recalled, suddenly and with unexpected pain, Morgaine with her head bent, having her hair combed like a child, on the night she bore Gwydion; Morgaine, who had been to her as the daughter she never bore, and now she was torn between Morgaine and Morgaine's son, who was even dearer to her than her own sons. "Do you hate her so, Gwydion?"

"I know not how I feel," said Gwydion, looking up at her with

Lancelet's dark mournful eyes. "It seems not to run with the vows of Avalon that I should so hate the mother who bore me and the father who got me. . . . I would that I had been reared at court as my father's son and his sworn follower, not his bitterest enemy. . . ."

He laid his head down on his arms and said through them, "I am weary, Mother. I am weary and sick of fighting, and I know Arthur is so, too . . . he has brought peace in these isles—from Cornwall to Lothian. I do not like to think that this great king, this great man, is my enemy and that for the sake of Avalon I must bring him down to nothing, to death or dishonor. I would rather love him, as all men do. I would like to look on my mother—not you, Mother, but lady Morgaine—I would like to look on her who bore me as my mother, not as the great priestess whom I am sworn to obey whatever she bids me. I would that she were my mother, not the Goddess. I wish that when Niniane lay in my arms she were no more than my own dear love, whom I love because she has your sweet face and your lovely voice. . . . I am so weary of gods and goddesses . . . I would that I had been your son and Lot's and no more than this, I am so weary of my fate. . . ." And he lay for a long moment quiet, his face hidden, his shoulders shaking. Tentatively, Morgause stroked his hair. At last he raised his head and said, with a bitter grin that defied her to make anything of his moment of weakness, "I will have now another cup of that strong spirit they brew in these hills, without the water and honey this time . . ." and when it was brought, he drained it, without even looking on the steaming porridge and bannock the girl had brought. "What was it said in those old books of Lot's, when the house priest beat Gareth and me until our backsides were bloody, trying to teach us the Roman tongue? Who was yonder old Roman who said, 'Call no man happy until he is dead'? My task, then, is to bring that greatest of all happinesses to my father, and why should I then rebel against that fate?" He signalled for another drink; when Morgause hesitated, he seized the flask and poured the cup full again.

"You will be drunk, my dear son. Eat your supper first, will you not?"

"So I will be drunk," said Gwydion bitterly. "So let it be. I drink to death and to dishonor . . . Arthur's and mine!" Again he drained the drinking horn and flung it into a corner, where it struck with a metallic sound. "So let it be as the fates have ordained—the King Stag shall rule in the forest until the day the Lady has ordained . . . *for all the beasts were born and joined with others of their kind and lived and worked the will of the forces of life and at last gave up their spirits into the keeping of the Lady again.* . . ." He spoke the words with a strange, harsh emphasis, and Morgause, untrained in Druid lore, knew that the words were those of ritual, and shivered as he spoke them.

He drew a deep breath. Then he said, "But for tonight I shall sleep in my mother's house and forget Avalon, and kings, and stags, and fates. Shall I not? Shall I not?" and, as the strong drink at last overpowered him, he fell forward into her arms. She held him there, stroking his fine dark hair, so much like Morgaine's own, as he slept with his head on her breast. But even in his dreams he twitched and moaned and muttered as if his dreams were evil, and Morgause knew it was not only the pain of his unhealed wound.

BOOK FOUR

The Prisoner in the Oak

1

In the far hills of North Wales, rain had been falling day after day, and the castle of King Uriens seemed to swim in fog and damp. The roads were ankle-deep mud, the fords swollen as rivers rushed down in spate from the mountains, and damp chill gripped the countryside. Morgaine, wrapped in cloak and heavy shawl, felt her fingers stiffening and slowing on the shuttle as she sent it through the loom; suddenly she started upright, the shuttle falling from her cold hands.

"What is it, Mother?" Maline asked, blinking at the sharp sound in the quiet hall.

"There is a rider on the road," Morgaine said. "We must make ready to welcome him." And then, observing her daughter-in-law's troubled look, she cursed herself; again she had let herself slip into the half-trance which women's work always brought upon her nowadays. She had long ago ceased to spin, but weaving, which she enjoyed, had seemed safe if she kept her wits about her and didn't succumb to the drowsy trancelike monotony of it.

And Maline was looking at her in the half-wary, half-exasperated way which Morgaine's unexpected seeings always evoked. Not that Maline believed there was anything wicked or even magical about them—it was just her mother-in-law's queer way. But Maline would speak of them to the priest, and he would come again and try to be subtle about asking her whence they came, and she would have to put on a meek-woman face and pretend she didn't know what he was talking about. Someday she would be too weary or too unguarded to care, and she would speak her mind to the priest. Then he would really have something to talk about. . . .

Well, done was done, and could not be helped now. She got along well enough with Father Eian, who had been Uwaine's tutor—he was an educated man for a priest. "Tell the Father that his pupil will be here at dinnertime," Morgaine said, and once again realized that her tongue had slipped; she had known Maline had been thinking of the priest and had responded to Maline's thought, not her words. She went out of the room leaving the younger woman staring.

All the winter, which had been heavy with rain and snow and repeated storms, not a single traveller had come. She dared not spin; it opened the gates too quickly to trance. Now, weaving was likely to do the same. She sewed industriously at making clothes for all the folk of the household, from Uriens down to Maline's newest baby, but it was hard on her eyes to do fine needlework; in the winter she had no access to fresh herbs and plants, and could do little with brewing simples and medicines. She had no companion—her waiting-women were the wives of Uriens' men-at-arms and duller than Maline; not one of them could spell out so much as a verse in the Bible and were shocked that Morgaine could read and write and knew some Latin and Greek. And she could not sit always at her harp. So she had spent the winter in a frenzy of boredom and impatience . . .

. . . the worse, she thought, because the temptation was always there to sit and spin and dream, letting her mind slide away, to follow Arthur at Camelot, or Accolon on quest—it had come to her, three years ago, that Accolon should spend enough time at court that Arthur should know him well and trust him. Accolon bore the serpents of Avalon, and that might prove a valuable bond with Arthur. She missed Accolon like a constant ache; in his presence she was what he always saw her—high priestess, confident of her goals and herself. But that was secret between them. In the long, lonely seasons, Morgaine experienced recurrent doubts and dreads; was she then no more than Uriens thought her, a solitary queen growing old, body and mind and soul drying and withering?

Still, she kept her hand firmly on this household, over countryfolk and castlefolk alike, so that all should turn to her for counsel and wisdom. They said in the country around: *The queen is wise. Even the king does nothing without her consent.* The Tribesmen and the Old Ones, she knew, came near to worshipping her; though she dared not appear too often at the ancient worship.

Now in the kitchen house she made arrangements for a festal dinner —or as near to it as they could come at the end of a long winter when the roads were closed. Morgaine gave from the locked cupboards some of her hoarded store of raisins and dried fruits, and a few spices for cooking the last of the bacon. Maline would tell Father Eian that Uwaine was expected at the hall for dinner. She herself should bear the tidings to Uriens.

She went up to his chamber, where he was lazily playing at dice with one of his men-at-arms; the room smelled frowsty and unaired, stale and old. *At least his long siege with the lung fever this winter has meant I need not be expected to share his bed. It has been just as well,* Morgaine thought dispassionately, *that Accolon has spent this winter in Camelot with Arthur; we might have taken dangerous chances and been discovered.*

Uriens set down the dice cup and looked up at her. He was thinner, wasted by his long struggle with the fever. There had been a few days when Morgaine thought he could not live, and she had fought hard for his life; partly because, in spite of everything, she was fond of him and did not want to see him die, partly because Avalloch would have succeeded to his throne the moment he died.

"I have not seen you all day. I have been lonely, Morgaine," Uriens said, with a fretful note of reproach. "Huw, here, is not half so good to look at."

"Why," Morgaine said, tuning her voice to the broad jesting Uriens liked, "I have left you purposely alone, thinking that in your old age you had taken a taste for handsome young men . . . if you do not want him, husband, does that mean that I can have him?"

Uriens chuckled. "You are making the poor man blush," he said, smiling with broad good nature. "But if you leave me alone all day, why, what am I to do but moon and make sheep's eyes at him, or at the dog."

"Well, I have come to give you good news. You shall be carried down to the hall for dinner tonight—Uwaine is riding hither and will be here before suppertime."

"Now God be thanked," Uriens said. "I thought this winter that I should die without seeing either of my sons again."

"I suppose Accolon will return for the Midsummer festivals." In her body Morgaine felt a stab of hunger so great that it was pain as she thought of the Beltane fires, now only two months away.

"Father Eian has been at me again to forbid the rites," Uriens said peevishly. "I am tired of hearing his complaints. He has it in mind that if we cut down the grove, then the folk would be content with his blessing of the fields, and not turn away to the Beltane fires. It is true that there seems more and more of the old worship every year—I had thought that as the old folk died off, year by year, it would grow ever less. I was willing to let it die out with the Old People who could not accustom themselves to new ways. But if the young people now are turning back to heathen ways, then we must do something—perhaps, even, cut down the grove."

If you do, I shall do murder, Morgaine thought, but schooled her voice to gentleness and reason. "That would be wrong. The oaks give pig food and food for the country people—even here we have had to use acorn flour in a bad season. And the grove has been there for hundreds of years—the trees are sacred—"

"You sound too much a pagan yourself, Morgaine."

"Can you say the oak grove is not the work of God?" she retorted. "Why should we punish the harmless trees because foolish men make a use of them that Father Eian does not like? I thought you loved your land."

"Well, and so I do," said Uriens fretfully, "but Avalloch, too, says I should cut it down, so that the pagans should have no place of resort. We might build a church or chapel there."

"But the Old Ones are your subjects too," Morgaine said, "and in your youth you made the Great Marriage with the land. Would you deprive the Old People of the grove that is their food and shelter, and their own chapel built by the very hands of God and not of man? Would you then condemn them to die or starve as they have done in some of the cleared lands?"

Uriens looked down at his gnarled old wrists. The blue tattoos there had almost faded and were no more than pale stains. "Well are you called Morgaine of the Fairies—the Old People could have no better advocate. Since you plead for their shelter, my lady, I will spare the grove while I live, but after me, Avalloch must do as he will. Will you fetch me my shoes and robe, so that I may dine in hall like a king, and not an old dodderer in bedgown and slippers?"

"To be sure," said Morgaine, "but I cannot lift you now. Huw will have to dress you."

But when the man had finished his work, she combed Uriens' hair and summoned the other man-at-arms who awaited the king's call. The two men lifted him, making a chair between their arms, and carried him into the hall, where Morgaine placed cushions about his high seat and watched as the thin old body was deposited there.

By that time she could hear servants bustling about, and riders in the courtyard . . . *Uwaine,* she thought, hardly raising her eyes as the young man was escorted into the hall.

It was hard to bear in mind that this tall young knight, with broad shoulders and a battle scar along one cheek, was the scrawny little boy who had come to her, like a wild animal tamed, in her first lonely, desperate year at Uriens' court. Uwaine kissed his father's hand, then bent before Morgaine.

"My father. Dear mother—"

"It's good to see you home again, lad," said Uriens, but Morgaine's eyes were on the other man who followed him into the hall. For a moment she did not believe it, it was like seeing a ghost—*surely if he were really here I would have seen him with the Sight* . . . and then she understood. *I have been trying so hard not to think of Accolon, lest I go mad* . . .

Accolon was slenderer than his brother, and not quite so tall. His eyes darted to Morgaine, one swift furtive look as he knelt before his father, but his voice was wholly correct when he turned to her. "It is good to be home again, lady—"

"It is good to have you here," she said steadily, "both of you. Uwaine, tell us how you got that dreadful scar on your cheek. Since the defeat of Emperor Lucius, I thought all men had pledged to Arthur to make no further trouble!"

"The usual," said Uwaine lightly. "Some bandit who moved into a deserted fort and amused himself by preying on the countryside and calling himself a king. Lot's son Gawaine went with me and we made short work of him, and Gawaine got himself a wife out of it—the lady is a widow with rich lands. As for this—" He touched the scar lightly. "While Gawaine fought the master I took the man—an ugly bastard who fought left-handed and got through my guard. Clumsy, too—I'd rather fight a good swordsman than a bad, any day! If you'd been there, Mother, I wouldn't have quite such a scar—the surgeon who stitched it up for me had hands like cabbages! Has it spoilt my looks as much as that?"

Morgaine reached out and gently touched her stepson's slashed cheek. "You will always be handsome to me, my son. But perhaps I can still do something—there is festering there and swelling; before I sleep I will make you a poultice for it, so that it will heal better. It must pain you."

"It does," Uwaine admitted, "but I thought myself lucky not to get the lockjaw from it, which one of my men did. Ai, what a death!" He shuddered. "When the wound swelled, I thought I was for it, too, and my good friend Gawaine said, as long as I could drink wine I was in no danger —and he kept me well supplied, too. I swear I was drunk for a fortnight, Mother!" He guffawed. "I would have given all the plunder of that bandit's castle for some of your soup—I couldn't chew bread or dried meat, and I nearly starved to death. I *did* lose three teeth. . . ."

She rose and peered at the wound. "Open your mouth. Yes," she said, and gestured to one of the servants. "Bring sir Uwaine some stew, and some stewed fruit, too," she said. "You must not even try to chew hard food for a while. After supper, I'll see to it."

"I won't say no to that, Mother. It still hurts like the devil, and besides, there's a girl at Arthur's court—I don't want her to shrink away as if I were a devil face." He chuckled. But for all the pain in his wound he ate hugely, telling tales of the court until they were all laughing. Morgaine dared not take her eyes from her stepson, but all through the meal she could feel Accolon's eyes on her, warming her as if she were standing in sunlight after the winter's chill.

It was a merry meal, but at last Uriens began to look weary and Morgaine summoned his body servants. "This is the first day you have left your bed, my husband—you must not weary yourself too much."

Uwaine rose and said, "Let me carry you, Father." He stooped and lifted the sick man as if he were a child. Morgaine, following, turned back before leaving the dining hall to say, "See to all things here, Maline—I will bandage Uwaine's cheek before I go to rest."

Soon Uriens was tucked into bed in his own chamber, Uwaine standing beside him while Morgaine went to the kitchens to brew a poultice for his cheek. She had to prod the cook awake and set him to heating more water over the kitchen fire . . . she should have a brazier and a cauldron in her own rooms if she was going to do this kind of work, why had she never thought of it before? She went up and sat Uwaine down so that she could poultice his cheek with the hot cloths wrung in steaming herb brew, and the young man sighed with relief as the poultice began to draw out the soreness from the festered wound.

"Oh, but that's good, Mother—that girl at Arthur's court wouldn't know how to do this. When I marry her, Mother, will you teach her some of your craft? Her name is Shana, and she's from Cornwall. She was one of Queen Isotta's ladies—how is it that Marcus calls himself king in Cornwall, Mother? I thought Tintagel belonged to you."

"So it does, my son, from Igraine and Duke Gorlois. I knew not that Marcus thought to reign there," Morgaine said. "Does Marcus dare to claim Tintagel as his own?"

"No, for the last I heard he had no champion there," Uwaine said. "Sir Drustan has gone into exile in Brittany—"

"Why? Was he one of the Emperor Lucius' men?" asked Morgaine. This talk of the court was a breath of life in the deadness of this isolated place.

Uwaine shook his head. "No . . . there was talk that he and Queen Isotta had been overfond of each other," he said. "One can hardly blame the poor lady . . . Cornwall is the end of the world, and Duke Marcus is old and peevish and his chamberlains say he is impotent too—hard life for the poor lady, while Drustan is handsome and a harper, and the lady fond of music."

"Have you no gossip of court save of wickedness and other men's wives?" demanded Uriens, scowling, and Uwaine laughed. "Well, I told the lady Shana that her father might send a messenger to you, and I hope, dear father, that when he comes you will not refuse him. Shana is not rich, but I have no great need of a dowry, I won goods enough in Brittany—I shall show you some of my plunder, and I have gifts for my mother, too." He raised his hand to stroke Morgaine's cheek as she bent over him, changing the poultice for a fresh one. "Well I know *you* are not such a woman as that lady Isotta, to turn your back on my good old father and play the harlot."

Her cheeks stung; she bent over the kettle of steaming herbs, wrinkling her nose at the bitter scent. Uwaine thought her the best of women, and his trust was sweet to her, yet there was the bitterness of knowing it unmerited.

At least I have never made Uriens look a fool, nor yet flaunted any other lover in his face. . . .

"But you should go to Cornwall, when my father is well enough to travel," Uwaine said seriously, flinching a little as the heat of the poultice touched a new spot on his festered cheek. "There should be a clear understanding, Mother, that Marcus cannot lay claim to what is yours. You have not shown your face in Tintagel for so long that the common people may forget they have a queen."

"I'm sure it will not come to that," said Uriens. "But if I am well again this summer, I will ask Arthur, when I ride to Pentecost, about this matter of Morgaine's lands."

"And if Uwaine marries into Cornwall," said Morgaine, "he shall keep Tintagel for me—would you like to be my castellan, Uwaine?"

"I would like nothing better," said Uwaine, "except, perhaps, to sleep tonight without forty separate toothaches in my jaw."

"Drink this," said Morgaine, pouring one of her medicines from a small flask into his wine, "and I can promise you sleep."

"I would sleep without it, I think, madam, I am so glad to be in my own home and my own bed, under my mother's care." Uwaine bent and embraced his father, and kissed Morgaine's hand. "But I will take your medicines willingly." He swallowed the medicined wine and beckoned to one of Uriens' men-at-arms to light him to his own room. Accolon came and embraced his father, and said, "I too am for my bed . . . lady, are there pillows there, or is the room empty and bare? I have not been home in so long, I expect to find pigeons roosting in that old room where I used to sleep and Father Eian tried to beat Latin into my head through the seat of my breeches."

"I told Maline to be sure you had everything you needed," said Morgaine, "but I will come and see. Will you need me again this night, my lord," she asked, turning to Uriens, "or shall I too go to my rest?"

Only a soft snore answered her, and his man Huw, settling the old man on the pillows, answered, "Go, lady Morgaine. If he wakes in the night I'll look after him."

As they went out, Accolon asked, "What ails my father?"

"He had the lung fever this winter," said Morgaine, "and he is not young."

"And you have had all the weight of caring for him," Accolon said. "Poor Morgaine—" and he touched her hand; she bit her lip at his tender voice. Something hard and cold inside her, frozen there since the winter, was melting and she thought she would dissolve into weeping. She bent her head and did not look at him.

"And you, Morgaine—not a word or a look for me—?" He reached out and touched her, and she said between clenched teeth, "Wait."

She called a servant to fetch fresh bolsters, a blanket or two from the store. "Had I known you were coming, I would have had the best linens and blankets, and fresh bed straw."

He said in a whisper, "It is not fresh straw I want in my bed," but she refused to turn her face to him while the serving-women were making the bed up, bringing hot water and light, and hanging up his armor and outer garments.

When they were all away for a moment he whispered, "Later, may I come to your room, Morgaine?"

She shook her head and whispered back, "I will come to you—I can have some excuse for being out of my chamber in the middle of the night, but since your father has been ill, often they come to fetch me—you must not be found there—" and she gave him a quick, silent pressure of her fingers. It was as if his hand burned her. Then she went with the chamberlain on the last rounds of the castle to make sure that all was locked and secure.

"God give you a good night, lady," he said, bowing, and went away. She tiptoed through the hall where the men-at-arms slept, moving on noiseless feet; along the stairs, past the room where Avalloch slept with Maline and the younger children, the room where young Conn had slept with his tutor and his foster-brothers before the poor lad had succumbed to the lung fever. In the farther wing were Uriens' own chamber, one she now kept for herself, another room usually allotted to guests of importance, and at the far end, the room where she had left Accolon. She stole toward his room, her mouth dry, hoping he had had the sense to keep his door ajar . . . the walls were old and thick and there would be no way he could hear her at his door.

She looked into her own room; went in, swiftly, and disarranged the bed clothing. Her own waiting-woman, Ruach, was old and deaf, and in the winter past Morgaine had cursed her for her deafness and stupidity, but now that would serve her . . . even so, she must not wake in the morning and find Morgaine's bed untouched; even old Ruach knew that King Uriens was not well enough to share his bed with the queen.

How often have I told myself, I am not ashamed of what I do . . . yet she must not bring scandal on her name, or she could accomplish nothing here. But she hated the need for secrecy and furtiveness.

He had left the door ajar. She slipped inside, her heart pounding, and pushed the door shut; felt herself seized in a hungry embrace that waked her body into fierce life. His mouth closed on hers as if he had starved for this as much as she . . . it seemed as if the whole winter's desolation and pain fell away and that she was like melting ice, that she would flood and overflow. . . . She pressed her body to Accolon's and fought to keep from crying.

All her resolve that Accolon was no more to her than priest of the Goddess, that she would not allow any personal tie between them, had gone for nothing in the face of this wild hunger in her. She had felt so much scorn for Gwenhwyfar, bringing the court to scandal and her king into contempt, because he could not keep his wife in order. But now, in Accolon's arms, all her resolve melted. She sank down in his embrace and let him carry her to his bed.

2

the night was far advanced when Morgaine slipped away from Accolon's side. He lay heavily asleep; she ran her fingers over his hair, kissed him softly, and stole from the room. She had not slept—she had feared to sleep too long and be surprised there by day. It was more than an hour before sunrise. Morgaine rubbed her burning eyes. Somewhere outside a dog barked, a child wailed and was hushed, birds chirped in the garden. Morgaine thought, looking out through a narrow slit in the stone wall, *In another moon it will be full daylight at this hour.* She leaned for a moment against the wall, overcome by memories of the night past.

I never knew, she thought, *I have never known what it was to be only a woman. I have borne a child and I have been married for fourteen years and I have had lovers . . . but I knew nothing, nothing. . . .*

She felt a sudden rough hand on her arm. Avalloch's hoarse voice said, "What are you doing sneaking around the house at this hour, girl?"

He had evidently mistaken her for one of the servant-women; some of them were small and dark with the blood of the Old Ones.

"Let me go, Avalloch," she said, looking at the dimly seen face of her older stepson. He was heavy and soft, his jowls blurred with fat, his eyes small and set close. Accolon and Uwaine were handsome men, and one could see that once Uriens had been good-looking in his own way. But not Avalloch.

"Well, my lady mother!" he said, stepping back and giving her an exaggerated bow. "I repeat, what were you doing at this hour?"

His hand remained on her arm; she picked it off as if it were a crawling bug. "Must I account for my movements to you? It is my house and I move in it as I will and that is my only answer." *He dislikes me,* she thought, *almost as much as I dislike him.*

"Don't play games with me, madam," said Avalloch. "Do you think I do not know in whose arms you spent the night?"

She said, contemptuously, "Now is it you who play with sorcery and the Sight?"

His voice dropped and took on a cozening sound. "Of course it must be dull for you, wed to a man old enough to be your father—but I would not hurt my father's feelings by telling him where his wife spends her nights, provided"—he put his arm round her and by main force drew her close to him. He bent his head and nibbled on her neck, his unshaven cheek scratching her—"provided you come and spend some of them with me."

She pulled away from him and tried to make her voice jocular. "Come now, Avalloch, why should you pursue your old stepmother when the Spring Maiden is yours, and all the pretty young maidens in the village—"

"But I have always looked on you as a beautiful woman," he said, and his hand stole out to caress her shoulder, sliding under the half-fastened front of her robe. She pulled away again and his face twisted into a snarl. "Why play the modest maiden with me? Was it Accolon or Uwaine, or both at once?"

She stared at him. "Uwaine is my son! I am the only mother he can remember!"

"Am I to think that would stop you, lady Morgaine? It was common talk at Arthur's court that you were Lancelet's paramour and tried to lure him from the Queen, and that you shared the Merlin's bed—that you had not stopped at making unlawful love to your own brother, and that was why the King sent you from court, that you might tempt him no more from Christian ways—why should you stop at your stepson? Does Uriens know what kind of incestuous harlot he took for his wife, madam?"

"Uriens knows everything about me that he has any need to know," said Morgaine, surprised that her voice was so steady. "As for the Merlin, we were then both unwed and neither of us cares anything for the laws of a Christian court. Your father knew and absolved me of that. None but he has any right to complain of my conduct since then, and when he does so I will answer to him, as I need not answer to you, sir Avalloch. And now I will go to my own room, and I bid you do the same."

"So you throw the pagan laws of Avalon at me," Avalloch said, his voice a sneering growl. "Harlot, how dare you claim you are so good—"
He grabbed her; his mouth crushed hers. Morgaine stabbed her stiffened fingers into his belly; he grunted and let her go with a curse. She said angrily, "I claim nothing. I need not answer to you for my conduct, and if you speak to Uriens, I will tell him that you laid hands on me in a fashion unseemly for your father's wife, and we will see whom he will believe."

Avalloch snarled, "Let me tell you, lady, you may cozen my father as you will, but he is old, and on the day I am made king in this land, be sure there will be no more grace extended to those who have lived on because my father cannot forget that once he wore the serpents!"

"Oh, rare," said Morgaine scornfully. "First you make advances to your father's wife, and then you boast of how good a Christian you will be when your father's land is yours!"

"You first bewitched me—harlot!"

Morgaine could not keep back her laughter. "Bewitch *you?* And why? Avalloch, if all men save you vanished from the earth, I would sooner share my bed with one of the puppies! Your father may be old enough to be my grandsire, but I would sooner lie with him than you! Do you think I am jealous of Maline, when every time you go down to the village at harvest or spring-plowing festival she sings? If I made such an enchantment, it would not be to enjoy your manhood but to wither it! Now get your hands off me, and go back to whoever will have you, for if you touch me again with one fingertip I swear I *will* blast your manhood!"

He believed she could do it; that was clear from the way he shrank from her. But Father Eian would hear of this, and then he would question her, and he would question Accolon, and he would question the servants, and then he would be at Uriens again to cut down the sacred grove and put down the old worship. Avalloch would not stop until he had set this whole court by the ears.

I hate Avalloch! Morgaine was surprised that her rage was physical, a scalding pain beneath her breastbone, a shaking through her whole body. *Once I was proud; a priestess of Avalon does not lie. And now there is something about which I must avoid the truth. Even Uriens would see me as a treacherous wife, creeping in secret to Accolon's bed for her own lusts. . . .* She was weeping with rage, feeling Avalloch's hot hands again on her arm and her breast. Now, soon or late, she would be accused, and even if Uriens trusted her, she would be watched. *Ah, I was happy for the first time in many years and now it is all spoilt. . . .*

Well, the sun was rising, soon the housefolk would be waking, and she must make arrangements for the work of the day. Had he been only guessing? Uriens must keep his bed, certainly Avalloch would not disturb his father this day. She must brew some more of the herb medicine for Uwaine's face wound, and the roots of one of his broken teeth must be dug out, too.

Uwaine loved her—surely he would not listen to any accusation Avalloch might make. And at that, she felt the flooding, surging fury again, remembering Avalloch's words: *Was it Accolon or Uwaine, or both at once. . . ? I am as much Uwaine's mother as if I had borne him! What kind of woman does he think me?* But was that rumor indeed in Arthur's court, that she had committed incest with Arthur, himself? *How, then, in the face of that, can I bring Arthur to acknowledge Gwydion his son? Galahad is Arthur's*

*heir, but my son must be acknowledged, and the royal line of Avalon. But there
must be no further scandal about me, certainly not any hint that I have committed
incest with my stepson. . . .*

And she wondered a little at herself. She had flown into a desperate
rage when she knew she was to bear Arthur's son and now it seemed trivial
to her; after all, she and Arthur had not even known themselves brother and
sister. But Uwaine—no blood kin to her—was far more her son than
Gwydion; she had mothered Uwaine. . . .

Well, there was nothing to be done about it now. Morgaine went to
the kitchen and heard the cook complain that all the bacon was gone, and
the storerooms were near enough empty to make it hard to feed all these
homecomers.

"Well, we must send Avalloch to hunt today," said Morgaine, and
stopped Maline on the stairs as she carried up her husband's morning drink
of hot wine.

Maline said, "I saw you talking with Avalloch—what did he have to
say to you?" She frowned a little, and Morgaine, reading her thoughts as
it was easy to do with a woman as stupid as Maline, realized that her
daughter-in-law feared and resented her; thought it unfair that Morgaine
should still be slim-bodied and hard when she, Maline, was heavy and worn
with childbearing, that Morgaine should have glossy dark hair when Maline
herself, busied with babies, never had time to comb and plait her own, and
make it shine.

Morgaine said truthfully, but also with a wish to spare her daughter-
in-law's feelings, "We spoke of Accolon, and of Uwaine. But the storerooms are nearly empty, and Avalloch must go hunting for boar." And
then what she must do flashed full-blown into her head, and for a moment
she stood frozen, hearing Niniane say in mind and memory, *Accolon must
succeed his father,* and her own voice replying. . . . Maline was staring at
her, waiting for her to finish what she was saying, and Morgaine quickly
collected herself. "Tell him that he must go out after boar, today if he
can, tomorrow at the latest, or we shall be eating the last of the flour too
soon."

"Certainly I will tell him, Mother," said Maline. "He will be glad to
have an excuse to be away." And through Maline's complaining voice,
Morgaine knew the younger woman was relieved that it had been nothing
worse.

Poor woman, married to that pig. She remembered, troubled, exactly
what Avalloch had said, *On the day I am made king in this land, there will
be no more grace extended to those who have lived on because my father cannot
forget that once he wore the serpents.*

This, then, was her task: to make certain that Accolon should succeed his father, not for her own sake or for revenge, but for the sake of the old worship which she and Accolon had brought back to this land. *If I had half an hour to tell Accolon all, he would go with Avalloch hunting, and I doubt not that would solve all.* And she thought, with cold calculation, *Shall I keep my hands clean of this, and leave it to Accolon?*

Uriens was old; but he might live another year, or another five years. Now that Avalloch knew all, he would work with Father Eian to undermine any influence Accolon and Morgaine might have, and all that she had done would be undone again.

If Accolon wants this kingdom, perhaps it is he who should make certain of it. If Avalloch dies of poison, it is I who will die for a sorceress. Yet if she left it to Accolon—then would it be all too much like that old ballad, the one which began, *Two brothers went a-hunting. . . .*

Shall I tell Accolon, and let him act in his rage? Troubled, still not certain what she would do, she went up to find Accolon in his father's room, and as she came in she heard him say, "Today Avalloch goes to hunt boar—the storeroom is near to empty. And I will ride with him. It is all too long since I have hunted in my own hills—"

"No," Morgaine said sharply. "Stay with your father today. He will need you, and Avalloch has all his huntsmen to help him."

She thought, *Somehow I must tell him what I mean to do,* and then she stopped herself. If he knew what she planned—though she was not yet sure herself what form her necessity would take—he would never accede to it, except perhaps in his first anger at hearing what Avalloch had said to her.

And if he did, she thought—*though I thought I knew him better than that, still my own hunger for his body might have deceived me, and he may be less honorable than I think him—if he were such a one as would consent to be party to this, then he would be kin slayer and under that curse, and not such a one as I could trust for what lies before us. Avalloch is kin to me by marriage alone; there is no blood tie to dishonor. Only if I had borne Uriens a son would there be blood guilt on me.* Now, she was glad she had given Uriens no son.

Accolon said, "Let Uwaine stay with father—if his cheek wound is being poulticed still, it is he that should stay indoors and keep to the fireside."

How can I make him understand? His hands must be clean; he must be here when the news comes . . . what can I say to him to make him understand that this is important, perhaps the most important thing I shall ever ask of him? Urgency, and the impossibility of voicing her inner thoughts, made her voice sharp.

"Will you do as I ask you without argument, Accolon? If I am to tend Uwaine's wound too, I shall have no leisure to tend your father as well, and he has been left to serving-folk all too often of late!" *And your father, if the*

Goddess is with me, shall have more need of you at his side than ever, before this day is ended. . . .

She slurred her words, hoping Uriens would not understand what she was saying. "As your mother I ask it," she said, but what she was saying to Accolon, with all the force of her thoughts, was, *From the Mother I command it. . . .* "Obey me," she said and, turning a little away from Uriens, so that Accolon alone could see, she touched the faded blue crescent on her forehead. Accolon looked at her—puzzled, questioning—but she turned away, shaking her head slightly, hoping that at least he would understand why she could not speak more freely.

He said, frowning, "Certainly, if you wish it so much. It is no hardship to stay with my father."

Morgaine saw Avalloch ride out at midmorning with four huntsmen, and while Maline was in the lower hall, she slipped into their bedchamber, searching through the untidy room and through the discarded baby clothes and still unwashed napkins of the youngest. At last she found a small bronze arm ring she had seen Avalloch wear. There were some gold things too in Maline's chest, but she did not dare to take anything of value which might be missed when Maline's servant came to sort out the room. As it was, the serving-woman found her there and asked, "What did you want, lady?"

Morgaine feigned anger. "I will not live in a house that is kept like a pig's byre! Look at all these unwashed napkins, they stink of baby shit! Take them down now, and give them to the washwoman, and then sweep and air this room—must I put on a clout and do all the sweeping myself?"

"No, madam," said the servant, cringing, and took the fouled cloths that Morgaine heaped in her arms. Morgaine tucked the bronze ring inside her bodice and went down to have the cook heat water for Uwaine's wound; that must be done first, and somehow she must order things in this house so that she would be idle and alone this afternoon. . . . She sent for the best surgeon to bring his tools and made Uwaine sit down and open his mouth so that she could help to find the broken root of his tooth. He endured the probing and pulling stoically (though the tooth broke off in his jaw and again had to be dug for; fortunately it was numb and swollen), and finally when all the tooth was out, she dropped some of her strongest numbing medicine into the wound and poulticed the sore swollen cheek again. Finally it was done and Uwaine sent to bed with a strong dram of liquor inside him; he protested, arguing that he had ridden and even fought when he was in worse case than this, but she firmly ordered him to go to his bed and let her medicines take their full effect. So Uwaine, too, was safely out of the way and beyond suspicion. And since she had sent the servants to do washing, there were none of these, either, so that Maline began to complain. "If we are to have new gowns for Pentecost, and if Avalloch is to have his cloak finished—you do not like to spin, Mother, but I must weave at Avalloch's cloak, and all the women are heating kettles of water for the washing and getting out their beating paddles—"

"Oh, dear, I had forgotten that," said Morgaine. "Well, there is no help for it, I must spin then—unless you would have me do the weaving." Better, she thought, even than the arm ring, a cloak made to his measure by his wife.

"Would you do that then, Mother? But you have the king's new cloak set up on the other loom—"

"Uriens does not need it so much as Avalloch," Morgaine said. "I will weave at Avalloch's cloak." *And when I am done,* she thought, a shudder running through her heart, *he will never need a cloak anymore. . . .*

"Then I will spin," said Maline, "and I will be grateful to you, Mother —you weave better than I." She came and pressed her cheek to her mother-in-law's. "You are always kind to me, lady Morgaine."

But you do not know what I shall be weaving today, child.

Maline sat down and picked up the distaff. She paused for a moment, pressing her hands to her back.

"Are you not well, daughter-in-law?"

Maline said, "It is nothing—my courses are four days late. I am afraid I have gotten with child again, and I had hoped I could nurse the baby another year—" She sighed. "Avalloch has women enough in the village, but I think he never loses hope I will give him another son to take Conn's place! He doesn't care anything for the girls—he did not even weep when Maeva died last year, just before I was brought to bed with the baby, and when she was another girl, he was really angry with me. Morgaine, if you truly know any charms, could you give me a charm so that I would bear a son next time I am brought to bed?"

Morgaine smiled, putting the shuttle to the threads. She said, "Father Eian will not like it, if you ask me for charms. He would tell you to pray to the Virgin Mother for a son."

"Well, her son was a miracle, and I am beginning to think that if I ever have another son it would be another miracle," said Maline. "But perhaps it is only this dismal chilly weather."

"I will make you some tea for that," said Morgaine. "If you are truly with child, I swear it will not disturb you, but if it is only delay from a chill, it will bring on your courses."

"Is this one of your magical spells from Avalon, Mother?"

Morgaine shook her head. "It is herb lore, no more," she said, went to the kitchen and made up the brew over the fire. She brought it to Maline and said, "Drink it as hot as you can, and wrap up in your shawl while you spin, try to keep warm."

Maline drank up the brew, emptying the little pottery cup, and grimaced at the taste. "Ugh, foul!"

Morgaine said, smiling, "I should have put honey in it, as I do with the brews I make for the children when they have fever."

Maline sighed, taking up the spindle and distaff again. She said, "Gwyneth is old enough to spin—I could spin when I was five years old."

"So could I," said Morgaine, "but I beg you, defer the lesson another day, for if I am to weave in here I do not want noise and confusion."

"Well then, I will tell the nurse to keep all the children out in the gallery," said Maline, and Morgaine dismissed her from her mind, beginning to run the shuttle slowly through the cloth and making sure of the pattern. It was a pattern of green and brown checkered cloth, not very demanding for a good weaver; so long as she counted the threads automatically, she need not keep her mind on it very long . . . spinning would have been better. But she had made her distaste for spinning so well known that if she volunteered to spin this day it would be remembered.

The shuttle slid through the cloth: green, brown, green, brown, picking up the other shuttle every tenth row, changing the color. She had taught Maline to dye this green color, which she had learned in Avalon . . . green of the new leaves coming into the spring, brown of the earth and of the fallen leaves where the boar rooted in the forest for acorns . . . shuttle sliding through the cloth, the comb to tighten each row of threads, her hands moving automatically, in and out and across, slide down the bar, pick up the shuttle from the other side . . . *would that Avalloch's horse would slip and fall and he would break his neck and save me from what I must do. . . .* She felt cold and shivered, and willed herself to ignore it, concentrating on the shuttle sliding in and out of the threads, in and out, letting images rise and go at will, seeing Accolon in Uriens' chamber playing with his father at draughts, Uwaine asleep, tossing and turning with the pain in his cheek wound even through his slumber, but now it would heal cleanly . . . *would that a wild boar would fight back and Avalloch's huntsman be too slow to come to his aid. . . .*

I said to Niniane that I would not kill. Never name that well from which you will not drink . . . an image rose in her mind of the Holy Well of Avalon, the water rising from the spring, flooding into the fountain. The shuttle flickered in and out, green and brown, green and brown, like the sunlight falling through the green leaves onto the brown earth, where the spring tides rising within the forest ran with life, sap running in the brown wood . . . the shuttle flashing now, faster and faster, the world beginning to blur before her eyes . . . *Goddess! Where you run in the forest with the running life of the deer . . . all men are in your hands, and all the beasts. . . .*

Years ago she had been the Virgin Huntress, blessing the Horned One and sending him forth to run with the deer and to conquer or die as the Goddess might decree. He had come back to her . . . now she was no longer that Virgin, holding all the power of the Huntress. As the Mother, with all the power of fertility, she had woven spells to bring Lancelet to Elaine's bed. But motherhood for her had ended in the blood of Gwydion's birth. Now she sat here with her shuttle in her hand and wove death, like the shadow of the Old Death-crone. *All men are in your hands to live or die, Mother. . . .*

The shuttle flickered, flashed in and out of her sight, green, brown, green like leaves and forest intertwined, where they ran, the beasts . . . the wild boar snuffling and grunting and rooting with his long tusks, the sow with the piglets bounding behind her, in and out of a copse . . . the shuttle raced in her hands and she saw nothing, only the snorting snuffle of the swine in the forest.

Ceridwen, Goddess, Mother, Death-crone, Great Raven . . . Lady of death and life . . . Great Sow, eater of your young . . . I call you, I summon you . . . if this is truly what you have decreed, it is for you to accomplish it . . . time slid and shifted around her, she lay in the glade with the sun burning her back while she ran with the King Stag, she moved through the forest, softly, snuffling . . . she sensed the life, the hunters trampling and shouting. . . . *Mother! Great Sow . . .*

Morgaine knew in a random corner of her mind that her hands continued to move, steadily, green and brown, brown and green, but beneath her lowered eyelids she saw nothing of the room or the threads, but only the new green springing beneath the trees, the mud and dead leaves brown from the winter, trampling, it was as if she rooted on all fours in the fragrant mud . . . *life of the Mother there beneath the trees . . .* behind her the little gruntings and squealings of the piglets, tusks tearing up the ground for hidden roots and acorns . . . *brown and green, green and brown . . .*

Like a shock to her nerves, as if it ripped through her body, she felt the sound of the trampling in the forest, the distant cries . . . her body sat motionless before the loom, weaving brown threads and changing for green, shuttle after shuttle, only her fingers alive, but with the starting thrill of terror and rush of rage, she charged, letting the life of the swine rush through her . . .

Goddess! Let not the innocent suffer . . . the huntsmen are nothing to you. . . . She could do nothing, she watched in dread, trembling, shuddering with the smell of blood, the smell of her mate's blood . . . blood spilled from the great boar, but this was nothing to her, like the King Stag he must die . . . when his time was come, then must his blood be shed on the earth . . . behind her she heard the squeals of frenzied piglings and suddenly the life of the Great Goddess rushed through her, not knowing whether she was

Morgaine or the Great Sow, heard her own high frenzied grunting—as when, in Avalon, she had raised her hands and brought down on her the mists of the Goddess, so she flung her head back, shivering, grunting, hearing the terror of her piglings, making short little rushes, flinging up her head, rushing in circles . . . green and brown under her eyes, an irrelevant shuttle in automatic fingers, unnoticed . . . then, maddened by the alien smells, blood, iron, strangeness, the enemy rising on two legs, steel and blood and death, she felt herself charge, heard cries, felt the hot stab of metal and red blurring her eyes through the brown and green of the forest, felt her tusks tearing, felt hot blood burst forth and gush as the life went out of her in searing pain and she fell and knew no more . . . and the shuttle went on, leaden, weaving brown and green and brown over the agony in her belly and the red bursting through her eyes and her pounding heart, the screams still in her ears in the silent room where there was no sound but the whisper of shuttle and warp and spindle and distaff . . . she swung silent, in her trance, exhausted . . . slumped forward at the loom and lay there, motionless. After a time she heard Maline speak, but she neither moved nor answered.

"Ah! Gwyneth, Morag—Mother, are you ill? Ah, heavens, she *will* weave, and always it brings these fits upon her—Uwaine! Accolon! Come, Mother has fallen at her loom—"

She felt the woman restlessly chafing her hands, calling her name, heard Accolon's voice, felt him lift and carry her. She did not, could not, move or speak—she let them lay her on her bed, bring wine to revive her, felt it trickle down her neck, and wanted to say, I am all right, let be, but she heard herself make a frightened little grunting sound and was still, agony ripping her, knowing that in death the Great Sow would release her, but first she must suffer the death throes . . . and even as she lay there, blind, tranced, agonized, she heard the hunting horn sound and knew that they were bringing Avalloch home, dead on his horse, slain by the sow which had attacked him within moments after he had killed the boar . . . and he in turn had slain the sow . . . death and blood and rebirth and the flow of life in and out of the forest, like the winding in and out of the shuttle. . . .

IT WAS hours later. She still could not move a muscle without griping, terrifying pain; almost she welcomed it. *I should not go wholly free of this death, but Accolon's hands are clean. . . .* She looked up into his eyes. He was bending over her with concern and dread, and they were alone for a moment.

"Are you able to speak now, my love?" he whispered. "What happened?"

She shook her head and could not speak. But his hands on her were tender, welcome. *Do you know what I have done for you, dear love?*

He bent and kissed her. He would never know how close they had come to being exposed and defeated.

"I must go back to Father," he said gently, troubled. "He weeps and says, if I had gone, my brother would not have died—he will blame me always." His dark eyes rested on her, a shadow of disquiet in them. "It was you who commanded me not to go," he said. "Did you know this with your magic, beloved?"

She found a shred of voice through the soreness in her throat. "It was the will of the Goddess," she said, "that Avalloch should not destroy what we have done here." She managed, with great pain, to move her finger, tracing out the line of the tattooed serpent on the hand that touched her face.

His expression changed, grew suddenly fearful. "Morgaine! Had you any part in this?"

Ah, I should have known how he would look at me if he knew . . .

"Can you ask?" she whispered. "I was weaving in the hall all this day in clear sight of Maline and the servants and the children . . . it was her will and her doing, not mine."

"But you knew, you knew?"

Slowly, her eyes filling with tears, she nodded, and he bent and kissed her lips.

"Be it so. It was the will of the Goddess," he said, and he went away.

3

tHERE was a place in the woods where a rushing stream broadened out between rocks into a deep pool; Morgaine sat there on a flat rock overlooking the water and made Accolon sit beside her. They would be unseen here, except by the little ancient folk, and they would never betray their queen.

"My dear, all these years we have worked together—tell me, Accolon, what is it you think we are doing?"

"Lady, I have been content to know you had a purpose," he said, "and not to ask questions of you. If you had sought only for a lover"—he raised his eyes to her and reached for her hand—"there would have been others than I for that, better suited to such games. . . . I love you well, Morgaine, and I have been—glad and honored—that you turned to me, even for companionship and the touch of tenderness, but it was not that which called me to you, priest to priestess." He hesitated, and sat stirring the sand at his feet with a booted foot. Finally he said, "It has come to me, too, that there was more of purpose in this than the wish of a priestess to restore the rites in this country, or your need to draw down upon us the moon tides—glad I have been to aid you in this and share the worship with you, lady. Lady of this land you have been indeed, especially to the ancient folk who see in you the face of the Goddess. For a time I thought it was only that we had been called to restore the old worship here. But now it comes to me, I know not why"—he touched the serpents which twined about his wrists —"that by *these,* I am bound to this land, to suffer and perhaps to die if need be."

I have used him, Morgaine thought, *as ruthlessly as ever Viviane did me. . . .*

He said, "I know it well—not once in a hundred years, now, is that old sacrifice exacted. Yet when *these"*— again he touched, with a brown fingertip, the serpents encircling his wrist—"were set here, it came to me that perhaps I should indeed be the one called by the Lady for that ancient sacrifice. In the years between, I had come to think of this as no more than a green boy's fancy. But if I am to die . . ." and his voice faded, like the ripples in the dying pool. It was very still; they could hear some insect making a small dry noise in the grass. Morgaine spoke no word, though she could feel his fear. He must pass the barriers of fear unaided, even as had she . . . or Arthur, or the Merlin, or any other facing that last testing. And if he was to face the final test he must go to it consenting.

At last he asked, "Is it exacted of me, then, lady, that I must die? I had thought—if blood sacrifice is demanded—then, when Avalloch fell prey to her . . ." and she saw the muscles in his face move; he tightened his jaw and swallowed hard. Still she said nothing, though her heart ached in pity. For some reason she heard Viviane's voice in her mind, *a time will come when you will hate me as much as you love me now . . .* and felt again the surge of love and pain. Still she hardened her heart; Accolon was older than Arthur had been when he faced his kingmaking. And while Avalloch had indeed been blood sacrifice, spilled to the Goddess, still another's blood could not redeem any other, nor could Avalloch's death free his brother of the obligation to face his own.

At last his breath went out in a harsh sigh. "So be it—I have faced death in battle often enough. I swore unto her, even to death, and I shall not be forsworn. Tell me her will, lady."

Then at last she stretched out her hand and clasped his. "I do not think it is death that will be demanded of you, and certainly not the altar of sacrifice. Still, testing is needed; and death lies always near to the doors of such testing. Would it reassure you to know that I too have faced death this way? Yet I am here at your side. Tell me: are you sworn, man to man, to Arthur?"

"I am not one of his Companions," Accolon said. "Uwaine you have seen sworn to him, but not I, though I have fought willingly enough among his men."

Morgaine was glad, though she knew that she would even have used the oath of a Companion against Arthur now. "Listen to me, my dear," she said. "Arthur has twice betrayed Avalon; and only from Avalon can a king reign over all this land. I have sought, again and again, to call to Arthur's mind that oath he gave. But he will not hear me, and he holds still, in his pride, the holy sword Excalibur, the sword of the Sacred Regalia, and with it the magical scabbard I fashioned for him."

She saw his face turn pale. "You mean it truly—that you will bring Arthur down?"

"Not so, not unless he refuses still to bring his oath to completion," Morgaine said. "I shall give him, still, every opportunity to become what he has sworn to be. And Arthur's son is not yet ripe to the challenge. You are no boy, Accolon, and you are trained to kingcraft, not Druid-craft, in spite of *these*—" and she laid a slender fingertip on the serpents encircling his wrist. "Say then, Accolon of Wales, if all other shifts fail, will you be champion of Avalon, and challenge the betrayer for that sword he holds by betrayal?"

Accolon drew a long breath. "To challenge Arthur? Fitly did you ask, Morgaine, if I am ready to die," he said. "And you speak to me in riddles. I knew not that Arthur had a son."

"His son is son to Avalon and to the spring fires," said Morgaine. She thought she had long outgrown shame for this—*I am priestess, I need make no accounting to any man for what I must do*—but she could not force herself to meet Accolon's eyes. "Listen, and I will tell you all."

He sat silent as she told him of the kingmaking on Dragon Island, and what had befallen after; but when she told how she had fled from Avalon and of Gwydion's birth, he put out his hand and encircled her small fingers in his own.

"He has passed his own testing," said Morgaine, "but he is young and untried: none thought that Arthur would betray his oath. Arthur was young too, but he came to his kingmaking when Uther was old and dying and men were seeking everywhere for a king of the Avalon line. Now Arthur's star is high and his renown great, and even with all the powers of Avalon at his back, Gwydion could never challenge Arthur for his throne."

"How is it that you think I can challenge Arthur and get the sword Excalibur from him and not be slain at once by his men?" said Accolon.

"And there is nowhere in this world that I can challenge him where he goes not so guarded."

"That is true," Morgaine said, "but you need not challenge him in this world. There are other realms which are not within this world at all, and within one of these realms you may get from him the sword Excalibur, to which he has forfeited all shadow of right, and the magical scabbard which protects him from all harm. Once disarmed, he is no more than any other man. I have seen his Companions—Lancelet, Gawaine, Gareth—disarm him in play at their mock battles. Without his sword, Arthur is easy prey. He is not the greatest of warriors, nor, with that sword and scabbard, did he ever need to be. And Arthur once dead—"

She had to stop and steady her voice, knowing she incurred the curse of kin slayer, that same curse she had hesitated to bring on Accolon when Avalloch died.

"Arthur once dead," she repeated firmly at last, "I am nearest his throne, and his sister. I shall rule as Lady of Avalon, and you as my consort and duke of war. True, in your time you too will be challenged and brought down as King Stag . . . but before that day comes you shall have your day as King at my side."

Accolon sighed. "I never thought to be King. But if you bid me, lady, I must do her will—and yours. Yet to challenge Arthur for his sword—"

"I did not mean that you shall do so without all the help I can give. For what else have I been schooled all these weary years in magic, and for what have I made you my priest? And there is one greater than I who shall help us both to your testing."

"Speak you of those magical realms?" Accolon asked her, almost in a whisper. "I do not understand you."

That surprises me not; I know not myself what I mean to do, nor what I say, Morgaine thought, but she recognized the strange dimness rising in her mind, clouding thought, as that state in which powerful magic was made. *I must trust to the Goddess now, and let her lead me. Not I alone, but he who stands at my side, who will take up the sword from Arthur's hand.*

"Trust me, and obey." She rose, moving through the woods on silent feet, looking for . . . what was she looking for? She asked, and heard her voice distant and strange, "Does hazelwood grow within this forest, Accolon?"

He nodded, and she followed him to the grove of trees, at this season just bursting into leaf and flower. The wild pigs who roamed here had eaten the last of the nuts; fragments of nut hulls lay scattered on the thick leaf mold of the forest floors. Yet new shoots were springing, too, toward the light, where new trees would rise, so that the life of the forest would never die.

Flower and fruits and seed. And all things return and grow and come to light and at the last give up their bodies into the keeping of the Lady again. But she who works, silently and alone, at the heart of nature, cannot work her magic without the strength of Him who runs with the deer and with the summer sun draws forth the richness of her womb. Beneath the hazel tree she looked across at Accolon, and while part of her mind was aware that this man was her lover, her chosen priest, she knew that now he had consented to a testing beyond what she alone could confer.

Before ever the Romans had come to these hills seeking for tin and lead, the hazel grove had been a sacred place. At the edge of the grove there was a pool, standing beneath three of the sacred trees, hazel and willow and alder—a magic older than the magic of the oak. The surface of the pool was somewhat obscured with dry sticks and leaves, but the water was clear and dark, brown with the clear brown of the forest, and she saw her own face reflected as she bent and dipped up the water in her hand, touching it to brow and lips. Before her eyes the reflected face shifted and changed, and she saw the strange deep eyes of the woman from that older world than this. And something in her crawled in terror at what she saw in those eyes.

The world had shifted subtly round them—she had believed this strange ancient land lay at the borders of Avalon, not here in the remote fastnesses of North Wales. Yet a voice said silently in her mind, *I am everywhere, and where the hazel reflects in the sacred pool, there am I.* She heard Accolon draw in a breath of wonder and awe, and turned to see that the lady of the fairy kingdom was with them, standing straight and silent in her shimmering garment, the crown of bare wicker-wither above her brow.

Was it she who spoke, or the lady?

There is other testing than the running of the deer . . . and suddenly it was as if a horn rang out, far and eerie, through the hazel grove . . . or was it the hazel grove? And then the leaves lifted and stirred, and there was the rushing of sudden winds, making the branches creak and sway, and a chill of fear rippled through Morgaine's body and blood.

He is coming . . .

Slowly, reluctant, she turned and saw that they were not alone in the grove. There at the edge between the worlds, he was standing . . .

Never did she ask Accolon what it was that *he* saw . . . she saw only the shadow of the antler crown, the bright leaves of gold and crimson where they stood in a wood gilded with the first buds of spring, the dark eyes . . . once she had lain with him on a forest floor like this, but he had not come for her this time, and she knew it. Now she, and even the lady, must step aside. His step, light on the leaves, still somehow raised the wind that kept thrusting floods of air through the grove, so that her hair blew about on her forehead and she felt her cloak flapping with it. He was tall and dark, and he seemed at once to be clothed in the richest garments, and in leaves, and at the same time she would have taken oath that his flesh gleamed smooth and naked before them. He gestured, raising one slender hand, and as if compelled, Accolon moved slowly forward, step by step . . . and at the same time it was Accolon that she could see crowned and robed with leaves and antlers, glimmering in the strange motionless light of fairy. Morgaine felt herself buffeted, struck and battered by the wind; in the grove, she knew, were forms and faces she could not clearly see; this testing was not for her, but for the man at her side. It seemed that there were cries and horn-calls; were the riders within the air, or did the beating of their hooves drum on the forest floor with this great noise that drowned out thought? She knew Accolon was no longer at her side. She stood clasping the bark of the hazel tree, her face hidden; she did not know, she would never know, it was not for her to know what form Accolon's kingmaking should take . . . that was not in her power to give or to know. She had invoked the powers of the Horned One through the Lady, and he had gone where she could not follow.

She never knew how long she stood there, clutching at the hazel bark, her brow pressed painfully against the bole of the tree . . . and then the wind died and Accolon was with her. They stood together, alone in the hazel grove, hearing only the beat of thunder from a dark and cloudless sky where the sun's rim glared like hot metal behind the moon's dark eclipse disk, and the stars burned against the unfallen night. Accolon's arm was around her. He whispered, "What is it, what is it?"

"It is the eclipse." Her voice was steadier than she could have believed. She felt her heartbeat quieting to normal at the touch of his arms, warm and alive, holding her. The ground was quite steady under her feet again, the solid earth of the hazel grove, and when she looked down into the pool she saw fragments of broken boughs from the uncanny wind that had ravaged the grove. Somewhere a bird complained at the sudden dark, and at their feet a small pink piglet rooted in the dead leaf mold. Then the light began to steal so brightly that she saw the shadow passing away from the sun. She saw Accolon staring at the brightness and said sharply, "Turn away your eyes—you can be blinded now the darkness is gone!"

He swallowed and lowered his face to hers. His hair was awry with a wind that was not of this world, and clinging to his hair was a crimson leaf which made Morgaine shiver as they stood beneath the just unfolding buds of the hazel.

He said in a whisper, "*He* is gone . . . and *she* . . . or was it you? Morgaine, did it happen, was any of it real?"

Morgaine, looking into his dazzled face, saw something in his eyes, something that had never been there before—the touch of the nonhuman. She reached out and plucked the crimson leaf from his hair, holding it out to him. "You who bear the serpents . . . need you question?"

"Ah—" She saw the shudder run right through him. He struck the crimson leaf from her hand with a savage gesture, letting it fall silent to the forest floor, and said, with a gasp, "It seemed that I rode high above the world and saw such things as come never to mortal man . . ." and then he reached for her, with blind urgency tearing at her dress and pulling her down to the ground. She let him do as he would and lay stunned on the damp ground as he thrust blindly into her, driven by a force he hardly understood. It seemed to her, as she lay silent beneath that driving strength, that his face was shadowed again with antlers or with crimson leaves; she had no part in this, she was only the passive earth beneath rain and wind, thunder and lightning bolt, and it was as if the lightning struck through her into the earth beneath. . . .

Then the darkness receded and the strange stars shining forth by day were all gone, and Accolon's hands, tender and apologetic, were helping her to rise, to arrange her disordered dress; he bent to kiss her, to stammer some half-explanation, some word of excuse, but she smiled and laid her hand across his lips. "No, no—it is enough—" The grove was silent again, and around them were only the normal sounds of the quiet day.

She said calmly, "We must go back, my love. We will be missed, and everyone will be shouting and crying out about the eclipse, as if it were some strange marvel of nature . . ." and smiled faintly; she had seen something far stranger than an eclipse this day. Accolon's hand was cold and solid in hers.

He whispered, as they walked, "I knew never that you . . . you look like *her*, Morgaine. . . ."

But I am she. However, Morgaine did not speak the words aloud. He was an initiate; he should have been better prepared, perhaps, for this testing. Yet he had faced it as he must, and he had been accepted by something beyond her own small powers.

Then cold struck at her heart and she turned to look at his smiling, beloved face. He had been accepted. But that did not mean he would triumph; it meant only that he might attempt the final testing for which this was only the beginning.

I felt not like this when as Spring Maiden I sent Arthur—whom I knew not to be Arthur—forth for his testing. Ah, Goddess, how young I was then, how young we both were . . . mercifully young, for we knew not what we did. And now I am old enough to know what it is that I do, how shall I have courage to send him forth to face death?

4

On the eve of Pentecost, Arthur and his queen had bidden those guests with family ties to the throne to dine with them privately. Tomorrow would be the usual great banquet for all of Arthur's subject kings and his Companions, but Gwenhwyfar, dressing herself carefully, felt that this would be the greater ordeal. She had long accepted the inevitable. Her husband and lord would by his act tomorrow make public and irrevocable what had long been known. Tomorrow, Galahad would be made knight and Companion of the Round Table. Oh, she had known it for years, yes, but then Galahad had been only a fair-haired little boy growing up somewhere in King Pellinore's lands. When she had thought of it, she had even been pleased; Lancelet's son, by her own cousin Elaine—now dead in childbed—was a reasonable heir for the King. But now she felt him a living reproach to an aging queen whose life had been without fruit.

"You are distressed," said Arthur, watching her face as she set the coronet about her hair. "I am sorry, Gwenhwyfar—I thought it would be the way to get to know the lad, as I must if he is to have my throne. Shall I tell them that you are ill? You need not appear—you can meet him at some other time."

Gwenhwyfar tightened her mouth. "As well now as later."

He took her hand. "I do not see Lancelet very often anymore—it will be good to speak with him again."

Her mouth moved in something she knew was not the smile she had intended. "I wonder you will have it so—do you not hate him?"

Arthur smiled uneasily. "We were all so much younger then. It seems as if it all was in another world, and Lance no more than my dearest and oldest friend, almost my brother, as much as Cai."

"Cai is your brother too," said Gwenhwyfar, "and his son Arthur is one of your most loyal knights. It seems to me that he would make a better heir than Galahad. . . ."

"Young Arthur is a good man and a trusty Companion. But Cai's blood is not royal. God knows, in all these years I have wished often enough that Ectorius had in truth been my own father . . . but he was not, and there's an end of it, Gwen." After a moment, hesitant—he had never spoken of this, not since that other dreadful Pentecost—he said, "I have heard that—the other lad, Morgaine's son—is in Avalon."

Gwenhwyfar put out a hand as if to avoid a blow. "No—!"

"I will arrange it so that you need never meet him," he said, not looking at her, "but royal blood is royal blood and something must be done for him. He cannot have my throne, the priests would not have it—"

"Oh," said Gwenhwyfar, "and if the priests *would* have it, I suppose you would proclaim Morgaine's son your heir—"

"There will be those who wonder that he is not," said Arthur. "Would you have me try to explain it to them?"

"Then you should keep him far from the court," said Gwenhwyfar, thinking, *I did not know my voice was so harsh when I was angry.* "What place at this court has one who has been reared in Avalon as a Druid?"

He said dryly, "The Merlin of Britain is one of my councillors and has always been so, Gwen. Those who look to Avalon are always my subjects too. It is written: *Other sheep have I which are not of this fold. . . .*"

"A blasphemous jest," Gwenhwyfar observed, making her voice gentler, "and hardly suitable for the eve of Pentecost—"

Arthur said, "Before Pentecost there was always Midsummer, my love. At least, now there are no Midsummer fires lighted, not even on Dragon Island, or, so far as I know, anywhere within three days' ride of Camelot —except on Avalon itself."

"The priests have set wards on Glastonbury Island, I am sure," said Gwenhwyfar, "so that there shall be no coming and going from that land. . . ."

"It would be a sad day if it should be lost forever," Arthur said. "As it is sad for the peasant folk to lose their own festivals . . . town folk, perhaps, have no need of the old rites. Oh yes, I know, there is only one name under Heaven by which we may be saved, but perhaps those who live in such close kinship with the earth need something more than salvation. . . ."

Gwenhwyfar started to speak, then held her peace. Kevin was no more than a misshapen old cripple, and a Druid, and the day of the Druids now seemed to her as far away as the time of the Romans. And even Kevin was less known at court as the Merlin of Britain than as a superb harper. The priests did not hold him in reverence as a good and kindly man, as once with Taliesin; Kevin's tongue was quick and ungentle in debate. Yet Kevin's knowledge of all the old ways and the common law was greater even than Arthur's, and Arthur had come into the way of turning to him when it was a question of old law and custom which could not be set aside.

"If this were not so strictly a family party, I would command that the Merlin perform for us tonight."

Arthur smiled and said, "I can send to ask of him, if you will, but such music as his is not to be commanded, even by a king. I can bid him dine at our table, and beg him to honor us with a song."

She smiled back and said, "So the King begs of a subject, rather than the other way around?"

"There must be a balance in all things," he said. "It is one of the things I have learned in my rule—in some matters, a king cannot command but must sue. Perhaps that was why the Caesars fell, because they fell into what my tutor used to call *hubris,* thinking they could command outside the legitimate sphere of a king. . . . Well, my lady, our guests are waiting. Are you sufficiently beautiful?"

She said, "You are making fun of me again. You know how old I am."

"You are scarcely older than I," said Arthur, "and my chamberlain tells me I am a handsome man still."

"Oh, but that is different. Men do not age as women do." She looked at his face, which was only faintly lined with the years—a man in the prime of his life.

He said, taking her hand, "It would little beseem me to have a maiden at my side for my queen. You are suited to me." They moved toward the door; the chamberlain approached and spoke in a low voice, and Arthur turned to Gwenhwyfar. "There will be other guests at our table. Gawaine sent word that his mother has come, and so we cannot but invite Lamorak as well, since he is her consort and travelling companion," said Arthur. "I have not seen Morgause in many years, God knows, but she is my kinswoman too. And King Uriens and Morgaine with their sons . . ."

"Then it will be a family party indeed."

"Yes, with Gareth and Gawaine—Gaheris is in Cornwall and Agravaine could not leave Lothian," said Arthur, and Gwenhwyfar felt pricked with an old grievance . . . Lot of Lothian had so many sons. "Well, my dear, our guests are assembled in the little hall. Shall we go down to them?"

The great hall of the Round Table was Arthur's domain—a man's place, where warriors and kings met. But the little hall with the hangings she had ordered from Gaul and the trestle tables and benches—that was where Gwenhwyfar felt most a queen. She was growing daily more short-sighted; at first, though there was still plenty of light, she saw only stripes of color from the ladies' gowns and the brilliant indoor robes worn by the men. That huge figure there, well over six feet with a great shock of sandy hair, that was Gawaine—he came to bow before the King and then, rising, to embrace his cousin in a great bear hug. Gareth followed him, more modestly, and Cai came to clap Gareth on the shoulder, to call him Handsome in the old way, and to ask after his brood of children, still too young to come to court—the lady Lionors was, he said, still abed after their latest, and had stayed in their castle northward by the Roman wall. Was that eight now, or nine? Gwenhwyfar had seen the lady Lionors only twice, because always, according to Gareth, she was breeding or lying-in or still suckling her latest. Gareth was no longer pretty-faced, but good-looking as ever, and as Arthur and Gawaine and Gareth grew older, the resemblance between them all grew ever stronger. Now Gareth was being embraced by a slender man with dark curling hair streaked with grey, and Gwenhwyfar bit her lip; Lancelet changed not at all with the years, save to grow yet more handsome.

Uriens had none of that magical immunity to time. He looked at last really old, though he was still upright and strong. His hair was all white, and she heard him explaining to Arthur that he had but recently recovered from the lung fever, and had that spring buried his oldest son, savaged by a wild pig.

Arthur said, "So you will be King of North Wales one day, sir Accolon? Well, so it shall be—God giveth and taketh, so it says in Holy Writ."

Uriens would have bent to kiss Gwenhwyfar's hand, but she leaned instead to kiss the old man on the cheek. He was foppishly dressed in green, with a handsome cloak of green and brown.

"Our queen grows ever younger," he said, smiling with good humor. "One would think you had dwelled in the fairy country, kinswoman."

Gwenhwyfar laughed. "Perhaps I should paint lines in my face then, lest the bishops and priests think I have learned spells unseemly for a Christian woman—but such jesting is uncanny on the eve of a holy day. Well, Morgaine"—for once she could greet her sister-in-law with a jest— "you seem younger than I, and I know you are older. What is your magic?"

"No magic," said Morgaine in her rich low voice. "It is only that there is so little to occupy my mind, in that country at the end of the world, that it seems to me that time does not pass there, and so, perhaps, that is why I grow no older."

Now she looked closer, Gwenhwyfar could indeed see the small traces of time in Morgaine's face; her skin was still smooth and unmarred, but there were tiny creases around her eyes and the eyelids drooped a little. The hand she gave Gwenhwyfar was thin and bony, so that her rings hung loose. Gwenhwyfar thought, *Morgaine is at least five years older than I.* And suddenly it seemed to her that they were not women in middle life, but those two young girls who had met in Avalon.

Lancelet had come first to greet Morgaine. Gwenhwyfar would not have believed that she could still be torn with this raging passion of jealousy . . . *now Elaine is gone . . . and Morgaine's husband is so old he surely cannot look to see another Christmas.* She heard Lancelet speak some laughing compliment, heard Morgaine's low sweet laughter.

But she does not look at Lancelet like a lover . . . her eyes turn to Prince

Accolon—he is a goodly man too . . . well, her husband is more than twice her age . . . and Gwenhwyfar felt a stab of self-righteous disapproval.

"We should go to table," she said, beckoning to Cai. "Galahad must go at midnight to watch by his arms; and perhaps, like many young men, he would like to rest a little beforehand so he will not be sleepy—"

"I shall not be sleepy, lady," the young man said, and Gwenhwyfar felt again the pain. She would so gladly have had this fair young man as her son. He was tall now, broad-shouldered and big as Lancelet had never been. His face seemed to shine with scrubbing and with a calm happiness. "This is all so new to me—Camelot is such a beautiful city, I can hardly believe it is real! And I rode here with my father—all my life my mother spoke of him as if he were a king or a saint, quite beyond mortal men."

Morgaine said, "Oh, Lancelet is mortal enough, Galahad, and if you come to know him well enough, you will know it too."

Galahad bowed politely to Morgaine. He said, "I remember you. You came and took Nimue from us, and my mother wept—is my sister well, lady?"

"I have not seen her for some years," Morgaine said, "but if it was not well with her, I would have heard."

"I remember only that I was angry with you for telling me I was wrong about everything—you seemed very certain, and my mother—"

"No doubt your mother told you I am an evil sorceress." She smiled —*smug as a cat,* Gwenhwyfar thought—at the transparent blush that covered Galahad's face. "Well, Galahad, you are not the first to think me so." She smiled to Accolon too, who returned the smile so openly that Gwenhwyfar was shocked.

Galahad said bluntly, "And are you a sorceress, then, lady?"

"Well," said Morgaine, with that cat-claw smile again, "no doubt your mother had reason to think me so. Since now she is gone, I may tell you all—Lancelet, did Elaine never tell you how she begged and besought me for a charm that would turn your eyes on her?"

Lancelet turned to Morgaine, and it seemed to Gwenhwyfar that his face was stricken, tight with pain. "Why make jests about days that are long gone, kinswoman?"

"Oh, but I jest not," said Morgaine, and for a moment she raised her eyes to meet Gwenhwyfar's. "I thought it time you stopped breaking hearts all through the kingdoms of Britain and Gaul. So I made that marriage, and I do not regret it, for now you have a fine son who is heir to my brother's kingdom. If I had not meddled, you would have remained unwed, and still be breaking all our hearts—would he not, Gwen?" she added audaciously.

I knew it. But I did not know Morgaine would confess it so openly. . . . But Gwenhwyfar took a queen's privilege to change the subject. "How does my namesake, your little Gwenhwyfar?"

"She is pledged in marriage to Lionel's son," Lancelet said, "and will be Queen of Less Britain, one day. The priest said the kinship was overclose but a dispensation could be had—I paid a great fee to the church for that to be set aside, and Lionel paid one, too—the girl is but nine and the wedding will not be for another six years."

"And your elder daughter?" asked Arthur.

"Sire, she is in a nunnery," Lancelet said.

"Is that what Elaine told you?" Morgaine asked, and again there was the flash of malice in her eyes. "She is in your own mother's place in Avalon, Lancelet. Did you not know?"

He said peacefully, "It is all one. The priestesses of the House of Maidens are much like to the nuns of holy church, living lives of chastity and prayer, and serving God in their own way." He turned quickly to Queen Morgause, who was approaching them. "Well, Aunt, I cannot say you are unchanged by time, but the years have treated you kindly indeed."

She looks so like Igraine! I have heard only the jests and have laughed at her, but now I can well believe that young Lamorak is beglamoured by her for love and not ambition! Morgause was a big woman, and tall, her hair was still rich and red, flowing in loose braids, over her green gown—a vast expanse of brocaded silk, embroidered with pearls and golden threads. A narrow coronet set with shining topaz twinkled in her hair. Gwenhwyfar held out her arms and embraced her kinswoman, saying, "You look much like Igraine, Queen Morgause. I loved her well, and still I think often of her."

"When I was younger that statement would have had me frantic with jealousy, Gwenhwyfar—I was maddened that my sister Igraine was more beautiful than I, and had so many kings and lords at her feet. Now I remember only that she was beautiful and kind, and I am glad to know I resemble her still." She turned to embrace Morgaine, and Gwenhwyfar saw that Morgaine was lost in the bigger woman's embrace, that Morgause towered over her. . . . *Why did I ever fear Morgaine? She is just a little thing after all, and the queen of an unregarded kingdom.* . . . Morgaine's dress was a simple dark wool, and she wore no ornament but a silver torque about her throat and some kind of silver bracelet about her arms. Her hair, dark and rich as ever, was simply braided and wound around her head.

Arthur had come up to embrace his sister and his aunt. Gwenhwyfar took Galahad's hand in hers. "You shall sit by me, kinsman." *Ah, yes, this was the son I should have borne to Lancelet—or to Arthur.* . . . She said, as they sat down, "And now you have come to know your father, have you discovered, as Morgaine said, that he is no saint but merely a very lovable man?"

"Ah, but what else is a saint?" asked Galahad, his eyes shining. "I cannot think of him as only a man, lady, he is surely more than that. He is the son of a king too, and I am sure that if they chose the best rather than the eldest son, he would reign in Less Britain. I think that man is happy whose father is also his hero," he said. "I had some time to speak with Gawaine—he despised his father and thought little of him, but no man has ever spoken of my father save with admiration!"

"I hope, then, that you see him always as a hero untarnished," said Gwenhwyfar. She had placed Galahad between herself and Arthur, as befitted the adopted heir to the kingdom; Arthur had chosen to seat Queen Morgause next to him, with Gawaine beyond, and next to him, Uwaine, who was Gawaine's friend and protégé, as Gareth had been Lancelet's when they were younger.

At the table next to them were Morgaine and her husband, and other guests; they were all kin, but she could not see their faces clearly. She craned her neck and squinted to see, reproving herself—squinting would make her ugly—and rubbed at the tight wrinkle beneath her brows. She wondered suddenly whereby her old fear of open spaces when she was a girl had simply come from being so shortsighted? Had she feared what the world was like only because she could not really see?

She asked Arthur across Galahad, who was eating with the hearty appetite of a healthy boy still growing, "Did you bid Kevin dine with us?"

"Aye, but he sent a message that he could not come. Since he could not be in Avalon, perhaps he keeps the holy day in his own fashion. I bid Bishop Patricius as well, but he keeps the vigil of Pentecost in the church —he will see you there at midnight, Galahad."

"I think that being made a king must be a little like being made a priest," said Galahad clearly; there was a lull in the conversation that made his young voice audible from one end of the table to another. "They are both sworn to serve man and God and to do what is right—"

Gareth said, "I felt something like that, lad. God grant you see it always so."

"I have always wanted my Companions to be men dedicated to the right." said Arthur. "I do not demand that they be godly men, Galahad, but I have hoped they would be *good* men."

Lancelet said to Arthur, "Perhaps these youngsters may live in a world where it is easier to be good," and it seemed to Gwenhwyfar that he sounded sad.

"But you are good, Father," said Galahad. "All up and down this land it is told that you are King Arthur's greatest knight."

Lancelet chuckled, embarrassed. "Aye—like that Saxon hero who tore the arm from the Lake monster. My works and deeds have been made into song because the true tale is not exciting enough to tell by the fireside in winter."

"But you did slay a dragon, did you not?" Galahad said.

"Oh, yes—and it was a fearful beast enough, I suppose. But your grandsire did as much as I in killing it," said Lancelet. "Gwenhwyfar, my lady, we dine never so well as at your table—"

"Too well," said Arthur cheerfully, patting his middle. "If feasts like this came often, I would be as fat as one of those beer-guzzling Saxon kings. And tomorrow is Pentecost, and another feast for even more folk—I do not know how my lady does it!"

Gwenhwyfar felt a small glow of pride. "This feast is mine, that of tomorrow is sir Cai's pride—for that one the beeves are already roasting in their pit. My lord Uriens, you are eating no meat . . ."

Uriens shook his head. "A wing of one of those birds, perhaps. Since my son was slain, I have vowed never again to eat the flesh of swine."

"And your queen shares your vow?" said Arthur. "As always, Morgaine is all but fasting—no wonder you are so small and spare, my sister!"

"It is no hardship for me not to eat swine's flesh."

"Is your voice sweet as ever, my sister? Since Kevin could not join us, perhaps you would sing or play—"

"If you had told me you wished it, I would not have eaten so well. I cannot sing now. Later, perhaps."

"Then you, Lancelet," Arthur said.

Lancelet shrugged and gestured to a servant to bring the harp. "Kevin will sing this tomorrow—I am no match for him. I made the words from a Saxon poet. I said once I could live with the Saxons, but not with what they called music. Then, when I dwelt among them last year, I heard this song and wept when I heard it, and tried in my poor way to put it into our tongue." He left his seat to take the small harp. "It is for you, my king," he said, "for it speaks of what sorrow I knew when I dwelt far from court and from my lord—but the music is Saxon. I had thought, before this, that all their songs were of war and battle and fighting."

He began to play a soft, sorrowful melody; his fingers were not as skillful as those of Kevin, but the sad song had a power of its own, which gradually quieted them. He sang, in the husky voice of an untrained singer:

"What sorrow is like to the sorrow of one who is alone?
Once I dwelt in the company of the king I loved well,
And my arm was heavy with the weight of the rings he gave,
And my heart weighed down with the gold of his love.
The face of the king is like the sun to those who surround him,
But now my heart is empty
And I wander alone throughout the world.
The groves take on their blossoms,
The trees and meadows grow fair,

But the cuckoo, saddest of singers,
Cries forth the lonely sorrow of the exile,
And now my heart goes wandering,
In search of what I shall never see more;
All faces are alike to me if I cannot see the face of my king,
And all countries are alike to me
When I cannot see the fair fields and meadows of my home.
So I shall arise and follow my heart in its wandering
For what is the fair meadow of home to me
When I cannot see the face of my king
And the weight on my arm is but a band of gold
When the heart is empty of the weight of love.
And so I shall go roaming
Over the fishes' road
And the road of the great whale
And beyond the country of the wave
With none to bear me company
But the memory of those I loved
And the songs I sang out of a full heart,
And the cuckoo's cry in memory.

GWENHWYFAR BENT HER HEAD to hide tears. Arthur's head was lowered, his eyes covered by his hand. Morgaine was staring straight ahead and Gwenhwyfar could see the stripes of tears making wet streaks down her face. Arthur rose and came around the table; he put his arms round Lancelet and said in a voice that was not steady, "But you are again with your king and your friend, Galahad."

The old bitterness stabbed at Gwenhwyfar's heart. *He sang of his king, not of his queen and his love. His love for me was never more than a part of his love for Arthur.* She closed her eyes, unwilling to see them embrace.

"That was beautiful," said Morgause softly. "Who would ever think that a Saxon brute could write music like that—it must have been Lancelet, after all—"

Lancelet shook his head. "The music is theirs. And the words only a poor echo of their own. . . ."

A voice that was like an echo of Lancelet's said gently, "But there are poets and musicians among the Saxons, as well as warriors, my lady," and Gwenhwyfar turned toward the voice. A young man in dark clothing, slender, dark-haired, a blur beyond her sight; but the voice, accented softly with the tones of the North country, still sounded like Lancelet's, the very pitch and timbre of his.

Arthur beckoned him forward. "There sits one at my table I do not know—and at a family party, that is not right. Queen Morgause—?"

She stood up in her place. "I had meant to present him to you before we went to table, but you were busy talking with old friends, my king. This is Morgaine's son, who was fostered at my court—Gwydion."

The youth came forward and bowed. "King Arthur," he said, in the warm voice that was like an echo of Lancelet's. For a moment a dizzied joy struck through Gwenhwyfar; *this* was Lancelet's son, surely, not Arthur's —and then she recalled that Morgaine's aunt, Viviane, was Lancelet's mother too.

Arthur embraced the youth. He said, in a voice too shaken to be audible three yards distant, "The son of my dearly beloved sister shall be received as a son at my own court, Gwydion. Come and sit beside me, lad."

Gwenhwyfar looked at Morgaine. She had spots of crimson on her cheek, as bright as if they were painted, and she was worrying her lower lip between her small, sharp teeth. Had Morgause not prepared her, then, to see her son presented to his father—no, to the King, Gwenhwyfar reminded herself sharply; there was no reason to think the boy had any idea who his father was. Though if he had ever looked in a mirror, no doubt he would come to believe, whatever anyone might say, that he was Lancelet's son.

Not a boy, after all. He must be near enough to five-and-twenty; he was a man.

"Your cousin, Galahad," Arthur said, and Galahad impulsively put out his hand.

"You are closer kin to the King than I, cousin—you have a better right than I to be where I am now," he said, with boyish spontaneity. "I wonder you don't hate me!"

Gwydion smiled and said, "How do you know I do not, cousin?" and for a moment Gwenhwyfar was jolted, until she saw the smile. Yes, he was Morgaine's son, he had the cat-smile she could show sometimes! Galahad blinked, then decided the words were meant as a jest. Gwenhwyfar could follow Galahad's transparent thoughts—*Is this my father's son, is Gwydion my bastard brother by Queen Morgaine?* He looked hurt, too, like a puppy whose playful proffer of friendship has been rebuffed.

"No, cousin," Gwydion said, "what you are thinking is not true." Gwenhwyfar thought, her breath catching in her throat, that he even had Lancelet's sudden breathtaking smile that transformed a rather dark and somber face into an overwhelming brilliance, as if a ray of sun had come out and transformed it.

Galahad said defensively, "I was not—I did not—"

"No," said Gwydion, kindly, "you did not *say* anything, but it is all too obvious what you are thinking, and what everyone in this room must be thinking." He raised his voice, just a little, that voice so like Lancelet's, although overlaid with the soft North-country accent: "In Avalon, cousin, we take our lineage from the line of the mother. I am of the old royal line of Avalon, and that is quite enough for me. It would be arrogance for any man to claim to be father to the child of a High Priestess of Avalon. But of course, like most men, I would like to know who fathered me, and what you thought has been said before—that I am the son of Lancelet. That likeness has been remarked upon before this—especially among the Saxons where I spent three years learning to be a warrior," he added. "Your reputation among them, lord Lancelet, is still much remembered there! I could not count how many men said to me that it was no disgrace to be the bastard son of a man like you, sir!" His low chuckle was like an eerie echo of the man he faced, and Lancelet looked uneasy too. "But in the end I always had to tell them that what they thought was not true. Of all the men in this kingdom who could have fathered me, one I know is *not* my father. And so, I must inform them that it is only a family likeness, no more. I am your cousin, Galahad, not your brother." He leaned lazily back in his chair. "Will it embarrass you too much—that everyone who sees us will think so? After all, we cannot go around telling everyone the truth!"

Galahad looked confused. "I would not have minded if you were truly my brother, Gwydion."

"But then I should have been your father's son and perhaps the King's heir, too," Gwydion said, and smiled—and it struck Gwenhwyfar suddenly that he actually took pleasure in the discomfort of the people around the table; that he was Morgaine's son, if only in that touch of malice.

Morgaine said, in that low voice which carried so clearly without being loud, "It would not have been displeasing to me, either, if Lancelet had fathered you, Gwydion."

"No, I suppose not, lady," Gwydion said. "Forgive me, lady Morgaine. Always I have called Queen Morgause my mother—"

Morgaine laughed. "If I seem an unlikely mother to you, Gwydion, you seem just as unlikely a son to me. I am grateful for this family party, Gwenhwyfar," she said. "I might have been confronted with my son tomorrow at the great feast, without warning."

Uriens said, "I think any woman would be proud of such a son, and as to your father, whoever he may have been, young Gwydion, it is his own loss that he did not claim you for his own."

"Oh, I don't think so," Gwydion said, and Gwenhwyfar thought, watching the small flicker of his eyes toward Arthur, *He may say for some reason that he does not know who is his father, but he is lying.* Somehow that made her uncomfortable. Yet how much *more* uncomfortable it would be if he were to face Arthur and demand to know why he, the son, was not also the heir.

Avalon, that accursed place! She wished it would sink into the sea like the lost land of Ys in the old tale, and never be heard of again!

"But this is Galahad's special night," Gwydion said, "and I am taking attention away from him. Are you to watch by your arms this night, cousin?"

Galahad nodded. "It is the custom for Arthur's Companions."

"I was the first," Gareth said, "and it is a good custom. I suppose it is the nearest a layman can come to being a priest, to take vows that he will always serve his king and his land and his God with his arms." He laughed and said, "What a fool of a boy I was—my lord Arthur, have you ever forgiven me, that I refused your offer to knight me with your own hands, and instead asked that Lancelet might do so?"

"Forgiven you, lad? I envied you," Arthur said, smiling. "Do you think I did not know Lancelet was the greater warrior of us two?"

Cai spoke for the first time, his somber scarred face twisting in a smile. "I told the lad then that he was a good fighter and would make a good knight, but he was certainly no courtier!"

"And so much the better," said Arthur heartily. "God knows I had enough of those!" He added, leaning forward, speaking directly to Galahad, "Would you prefer that your father should knight you, Galahad? He has knighted enough of my Companions. . . ."

The boy bowed his head. "Sir, it is for my king to say. But it seems to me that this knighthood comes from God and it does not matter who bestows it. I—I do not mean that quite as it sounds, sir—I mean, the vow is made to you, but mostly to God—"

Arthur nodded, slowly. "I know what you mean, my boy. It is much the same with a king—he vows to rule over his people, but the vow is given not to the people but to God—"

"Or," said Morgaine, "to the Goddess, in her name, as token of the land the king shall rule." She looked directly at Arthur as she spoke and he shifted his eyes, and Gwenhwyfar bit her lip . . . Morgaine reminding Arthur again that his allegiance had been given to Avalon—*damn her!* But that was past and Arthur was a Christian king . . . under no authority but that of God.

"We will all be praying for you, Galahad, that you make a good knight, and that one day, you will make a good king," said Gwenhwyfar.

"So, as you make your vows, Galahad," said Gwydion, "you are making, in some form, the same kind of Sacred Marriage to the land that the King used to make in the old days. But you will not, perhaps, be so hard tested."

The color rose in the younger boy's face. "My lord Arthur came to the throne proved in battle, cousin, but there is no way I can now be so tested."

"I could think of a way," said Morgaine softly, "and if you are to rule over Avalon as well as the Christian lands, one day you must come to that, too, Galahad."

He set his mouth firmly. "May that time be far—surely, my lord, you will live many, many years—and by then all those old folk who still believe they must give allegiance to the pagan ways will have gone."

"I trust not," said Accolon, speaking up for the first time in that company. "The sacred groves still stand, and in them, the old ways are done as they have been done from the beginning of the world. We do not anger the Goddess by denying her worship, lest she turn upon her people and blight the harvests and darken the very sun that gives us life."

Galahad was startled. "But this is a Christian land! Have no priests come to you to show you that the evil old Gods among whom the Devil had sway have no more power now? Bishop Patricius has told me that all the sacred groves have been cut down!"

"Not so," said Accolon, "nor will be while my father lives, or I after him."

Morgaine opened her mouth to speak, but Gwenhwyfar saw Accolon lay his hand on her wrist. She smiled at him and said nothing. It was Gwydion who said, "Nor yet in Avalon, while the Goddess lives. Kings come and kings go, but the Goddess shall endure forever."

What pity, Gwenhwyfar thought, *that this handsome young man should be a pagan! Well, Galahad is a good and pious Christian knight, who will make a Christian king!* But as she reassured herself with that thought, a faint shiver went through her.

As if Gwenhwyfar's thoughts disturbed him, Arthur leaned forward to Gwydion, and his face was troubled. "Have you come to court to be one of my Companions, Gwydion? I need not tell you that the son of my sister is welcome among my knights."

"I admit I brought him here for that," said Morgause, "but I did not know that this was Galahad's great ceremonial. I would not steal the luster from this occasion. Surely another time will do as well for that."

Galahad said ingenuously, "I would not mind sharing my vigil and vows with my cousin."

Gwydion laughed. "You are too generous, kinsman," he said, "but you know little of kingcraft. The King's heir must be proclaimed without any to share that moment. If Arthur should knight us both at the same time, and I am so much the older, and resemble Lancelet so much more—well, there is gossip enough about my parentage; it should not shadow your knighthood as well. Nor," he added, laughing, "my own."

Morgaine shrugged. "They will gossip about the King's kin, whether or no, Gwydion. Let them have some morsel to chew on!"

"Yet another thing," Gwydion said lightly. "I have no intent ever to watch by my arms in any Christian church. I am of Avalon. If Arthur will admit me among his Companions for what I am, that will be well, and if not, that too will be well."

Uriens raised his knotty old arms so that the faded serpents could be seen. "I sit at the Round Table with no such Christian vow, step-son."

"Nor I," said Gawaine. "We won our knighthoods, all of us who fought in those days, and needed no such ceremonial. Some of us would have been hard put to it, had knighthood been fenced about by such courtly vows as now."

"Even I," Lancelet said, "would be somewhat reluctant to take such vows, such a sinful man as I am. But I am Arthur's man for life or death, and he knows it."

"God forbid I should ever doubt it," said Arthur, smiling with deep affection at his old friend. "You and Gawaine are the very pillars of my kingdom. If I should ever lose either of you, I think my throne would split and fall from the very top of Camelot!"

He raised his head as a door opened at the far end of the hall, and a priest in white robes, with two young men dressed in white, came in. Galahad rose, eagerly. "By your leave, my lord—"

Arthur rose too, and embraced his heir. "Bless you, Galahad. Go to keep your vigil."

The boy bowed and turned to embrace his father; Gwenhwyfar could not hear what Lancelet said to him. She reached out her hand and Galahad bent to kiss it. "Give me your blessing, lady."

"Always, Galahad," Gwenhwyfar said, and Arthur added, "We will see you to the church. You must keep your vigil alone, but we will come a little way with you."

"You do me too much honor, my king. Did you not keep vigil when you were crowned?"

"He did indeed," said Morgaine, smiling, "but it was far other than *this.*"

As the whole party moved toward the church, Gwydion dropped back until he was walking at Morgaine's side. She looked up at her son—he was not as tall as Arthur, who had the height of the Pendragons, but at her side he seemed tall.

"I had not expected to see you here, Gwydion."

"I had not expected to be here, madam."

"I heard that you had been fighting in this war, among Arthur's Saxon allies. I knew not that you were a warrior."

He shrugged. "You have had little opportunity to know much of me, lady."

Abruptly, not knowing what she was going to say until she heard herself saying it, she asked, "Do you hate me that I abandoned you, my son?"

He hesitated. "Perhaps—for a time when I was young," he said at last. "But I am a child of the Goddess, and this forced me to be so in truth, that I could look to no earthly parents. I bear you no grudge now, Lady of the Lake," he said.

For a moment the path blurred around her; it was as if the young Lancelet stood at her side . . . her son steadied her gently with his arm.

"Take care, the path here is not smooth—"

She asked, "How is it with all in Avalon?"

"Niniane is well," he said. "I have few ties with any other there, not now."

"Have you seen Galahad's sister there, the maiden called Nimue?" She frowned, trying to remember how old Nimue would be now. Galahad was sixteen—Nimue would be at least fourteen, almost grown.

"I know her not," said Gwydion. "The old priestess of the oracles—Raven, is it?—has taken her into the silence and into seclusion. No man may look upon her face."

I wonder why Raven did that? A sudden shudder went through her, but she said only, "How does Raven, then? Is she well?"

"I have not heard that she was otherwise," said Gwydion, "though when I last saw her at the rites she seemed older than the very oaks. Still, her voice was sweet and young. But I have never had private speech from her."

Morgaine said, "Nor has any man living, Gwydion, and few women. Twelve years I spent there as a maiden, and I heard her voice but half a dozen times." She did not wish to speak or to think of Avalon and said, trying to keep her voice commonplace, "So you have had battle experience with the Saxons?"

"True, and in Brittany—I spent some time at Lionel's court. Lionel thought me Lancelet's son and would have had me call him Uncle and I told him nothing contrary. It will do Lancelet no harm to be thought capable of fathering a bastard or so. And, even as with the good Lancelet, the Saxons around Ceardig gave me a name. Elf-arrow they called him—any man who accomplishes anything gets a name from those folk. *Mordred,* they called me —it means in our tongue something like to 'Deadly counsel' or even 'Evil counsel,' and I think not that they meant it as compliment!"

"It takes not much craft in counsel to be wilier than a Saxon," she said, "but tell me, then, what prompted you to come here before the time I had chosen?"

Gwydion shrugged. "I felt I might well see my rival."

Morgaine glanced fearfully around her. "Say that not aloud!"

"I have no reason to fear Galahad," he said quietly. "He looks not to me like one who will live long enough to rule."

"Is that the Sight?"

"I need not the Sight to tell me it would take one stronger than Galahad to sit on the throne of the Pendragon," Gwydion said. "But if it will ease your mind, lady, I will swear to you by the Sacred Well, Galahad will not die by my hand. Nor," he added after a moment, seeing her shiver, "by yours. If the Goddess does not want him on the throne of the new Avalon, I think we may leave it to her."

He laid his hand for a moment on Morgaine's; gentle as the touch was, she shivered again.

"Come," he said, and it seemed to Morgaine that his voice was as compassionate as a priest's giving absolution. "Let us go and see my cousin to his arms. It is not right that anything should spoil this great moment of his life. He may not have many more."

5

As often as Morgause of Lothian had come to Camelot, she never tired of the pageantry. Now, conscious that as one of Arthur's subject queens and the mother of three of his earliest Companions, she would have a favored place at the mock games which marked this day, she sat beside Morgaine in church; at the end of the service, Galahad would be knighted, and he knelt now beside Arthur and Gwenhwyfar, pale and serious and shining with excitement.

Bishop Patricius himself had come from Glastonbury to celebrate the Pentecost mass here in Camelot; he stood now before them in his white robes, intoning: "Unto thee have we offered this bread, the body of the Only-begotten. . . ."

Morgause put a plump hand over her mouth, smothering a yawn. However often she attended Christian ceremonies, she never thought about them; they were not even as interesting as the rites at Avalon where she had spent her childhood, but she had thought, since she was fourteen or so, that all Gods and all religions were games which men and women played with their minds. None of them had anything to do with real life. Nevertheless, when she was at Pentecost, she dutifully attended mass, to please Gwenhwy-far—the woman was her hostess, and the High Queen, after all, and a close relative—and now, with the rest of the royal family, she went forward to receive the holy bread. Morgaine, attentive at her side, was the only one in the King's household who did not approach the communion table; Morgause thought lazily that Morgaine was a very great fool. Not only did she alienate the common people, but the more pious among the King's household called Morgaine witch and sorceress, and worse things, among themselves. And, after all, what difference did it make? One religious lie was as good as another, was it not? King Uriens, now, he had more sense of what was expedient; Morgause did not think Uriens had any more religion than Gwenhwyfar's pet house cat. She had seen the serpents of Avalon around his arms; yet, like his son Accolon, he went forward to take part.

But when the final prayer came, including one for the dead, she discovered that she had tears in her eyes. She missed Lot—his cynical cheerfulness, his steadfast loyalty to her; and he had, after all, given her four fine sons. Gawaine and Gareth knelt near her, among Arthur's own house-hold—Gawaine, as always, close to Arthur; Gareth side by side with his young friend Uwaine—Morgaine's stepson; she had heard Uwaine call Morgaine mother, heard a genuine maternal note in Morgaine's voice when she spoke to him, something she had never thought Morgaine capable of.

With a rustle of gowns and the small chink of scabbarded swords and such gear, Arthur's household arose and moved to the church porch. Gwen-hwyfar, though a little haggard, was still beautiful with the long bright golden braids over her shoulder and her fine gown belted in with a brilliant golden girdle. Arthur looked splendid, too. Excalibur hung in its scabbard at Arthur's side—the same old red velvet scabbard he had worn for more than twenty years now. She supposed that Gwenhwyfar could have embroi-dered him a handsomer one at any time in the past ten years.

Galahad knelt before the King; Arthur took from Gawaine a handsome sword and said, "For you, my dear kinsman and adopted son, this." He gestured to Gawaine, who belted it around the boy's slender waist. Galahad looked up with his boyish smile and said clearly, "I thank you, my king. May I bear it only and always in your service."

Arthur laid his hands on Galahad's head. He said, "I gladly receive you among the company of my Companions, Galahad, and confer on you the order of knighthood. Be always faithful and just, and serve the throne and the righteous cause always." He raised the youngster, embraced him and kissed him. Gwenhwyfar kissed him too, and the royal company went out toward the huge field, the others behind him.

Morgause found herself walking between Morgaine and Gwydion, with Uriens, Accolon, and Uwaine just behind them. The field had been decorated with green staves wound with ribbons and pennants, and the marshals of the games were pacing off the fighting areas. She saw Lancelet with Galahad, embracing him and giving him a plain white shield. Morgause said, "Will Lancelet fight today?"

Accolon said, "I think not—I heard he is to be master of the lists; he has won the field too many times. Between ourselves, he is no longer so young, and it would hardly suit the dignity of the Queen's champion to be unseated from his horse by some youth hardly made knight. I've heard that he's been beaten by Gareth more than once, and once by Lamorak—"

Morgause said smiling, "I think well of Lamorak that he forbore to boast of *that* conquest—few men could resist bragging that they had overcome Lancelet even in a mock battle!"

"No," said Morgaine quietly, "I think most young knights would be unhappy at the thought that Lancelet was no longer king of the field. He is their hero."

Gwydion chuckled. "Do you mean that the young stags forbear to challenge the knight who is King Stag among them?"

"I think none of the older knights would do so," said Accolon, "and of the young knights, there are few with enough strength or experience to challenge him. If they did, he would show them a trick or two still."

"I would not," said Uwaine quietly. "I think there is no knight at this court who does not love Lancelet. Gareth could overthrow him any time now, but he will not shame him at Pentecost, and he and Gawaine have always been evenly matched. Once at a Pentecost like this they fought for more than an hour, and once Gawaine knocked his sword from his hand. I do not know if I could best him in single combat, but he may stay champion while he lives, for all I will ever do to challenge it."

"Challenge him, someday," Accolon said, laughing, "I did so, and he took all the conceit out of me in five minutes! He may be old, but he has all his skill and strength."

He handed Morgaine and his father into the seats reserved for them. "By your leave, I will go and enter the lists before it is too late."

"And I," said Uwaine, bending to kiss his father's hand. He turned to Morgaine. "I have no lady, Mother. Will you give me a token to bear into the lists?"

Morgaine smiled indulgently and gave him a ribbon from her sleeve, which he tied about his arm, saying, "I have arranged to challenge Gawaine to a trial of strength."

Gwydion said with his charming smile, "Why, lady, you had better take back your favor—would you have your honor so easily disposed of as that?"

Morgaine laughed up at Accolon, and Morgause, watching her face come alight, thought, *Uwaine is her son, far more than Gwydion; but Accolon, it is plain to see, is more than that. I wonder if the old king knows—or cares?*

Lamorak was approaching them, and Morgause felt warmed and complimented—there were many pretty ladies on the field, he could have a favor from any of them, yet, before them all, before all Camelot, her dear young man would come and bow before her.

"My lady, may I wear a token into battle?"

"With pleasure, my dear." Morgause gave him the rose from the nosegay she wore at her bosom. He kissed the flower; she gave him her hand, pleasantly conscious that her young knight was one of the handsomest men there.

"Lamorak seems enchanted by you," said Morgaine, and although she had given her favor to him before the whole court, Morgause felt herself blush at Morgaine's detached voice.

"Do you think I have need of charms or spells, kinswoman?"

Morgaine laughed. "I should have used another word. Young men seem mostly to want a fair face and little more."

"Well, Morgaine, Accolon is younger than you, and you have certainly captivated him to the point where he has no desire for a younger woman—or a fairer one. I am not the one to reproach you, my dear. You were married against your will, and your husband could be your grandsire."

Morgaine shrugged. "Sometimes I think Uriens knows—perhaps he is glad that I have a lover who will not tempt me to leave him."

A little hesitantly—she had never asked Morgaine any personal question since Gwydion's birth—Morgause said, "You and Uriens are at odds, then?"

Morgaine gave again that indifferent shrug. "I think Uriens cares not enough for me to be at odds one way or the other."

"How like you Gwydion?" Morgause asked.

"He frightens me," said Morgaine. "Yet it would be hard not to be charmed by him."

"What do you expect? He has Lancelet's beauty and your powers of mind—and he is ambitious as well."

"How strange that you should know my son better than I do," Morgaine said, and there was so much bitterness in the words that Morgause, whose first instinct was to rap out a sharp reply—Morgaine had deserted her son, why should it surprise her?—patted the younger woman's hand and said, not unkindly, "Oh, my dear, once a son is grown out of your lap, I think anyone knows him better than his mother! I am sure that Arthur and his Companions, and even your Uwaine, all know Gawaine better than I do, and he is not even a hard man to understand—he's a perfectly simple man. If you had reared him from a babe you still would not understand Gwydion—I freely confess that I do not!"

Morgaine's only answer was an uneasy smile. She turned to look at the lists, where the first events were starting; Arthur's fools and clowns were dancing about in ridiculous mock battles, flapping pig's bladders for weapons and cloth banners, garishly painted, in the place of shields, until the watchers were guffawing at their capers. They bowed at last, and Gwenhwyfar, in an exaggerated parody of the gesture with which she would later bestow prizes to the real winners, flung them handfuls of sweets and cakes. They scrambled for them, to more laughter and applause, then capered away to the good dinner waiting for them in the kitchens.

One of the criers called out that the first match would be a trial combat between the Queen's champion, sir Lancelet of the Lake, and the King's, sir Gawaine of Lothian and the Isles. There was a tumult of applause as they came onto the field—Lancelet slender, dark, and still so handsome, despite the lines in his face and the grey in his hair, that Morgaine felt her breath catch.

Yes, thought Morgause, watching her younger kinswoman's face, *she loves him still, despite the years. Perhaps she does not know it herself, but there it is.*

The combat was like an elaborately choreographed dance, the two moving round one another, their swords and shields ringing loud. Morgause could not see that either of them had the slightest advantage, and when at last they lowered their swords, bowed to the King, and embraced each other, they were cheered impartially and applauded without the slightest favoritism.

Then came the horse games: demonstrations of fancy riding, a man riding an unbroken horse to master it—Morgause faintly remembered a time when Lancelet had done some such thing, perhaps at Arthur's wedding—it seemed very long ago. After that, there were individual duels on horseback, with blunted spears which could nevertheless unhorse a rider and give him a nasty spill into the field. One young rider fell twisted on his leg and was carried away screaming, the leg sticking out at an improbable angle. This was the only serious injury, but there were bruises, smashed fingers, men flung senseless to the ground, and one who barely escaped being kicked by a badly trained horse. Gwenhwyfar gave prizes at the end of all this, and Morgaine too was called by Arthur and asked to distribute several prizes.

Accolon had won one of the prizes for riding, and as he came to kneel and accept the prize from Morgaine's hands, Morgause was astonished to hear a low, but perceptible hiss of disapproval somewhere in the stands.

Someone softly but audibly whispered, "Witch! Harlot!"

Morgaine colored, but her hands did not falter as she handed Accolon the cup. Arthur said in a low voice to one of his stewards, "Find out who that was!" and the man slipped away, but Morgause was sure that in such a crowd, the voice would never be recognized.

When Morgaine came back to her seat at the start of the second half of the entertainment, she looked pale and angry; her hands, Morgause noted, were shaking, and her breath coming fast in her throat.

"My dear, don't worry about it," said Morgause. "What do you think they call *me,* when it is a year of poor crops, or when someone has had justice done to him and would rather have gotten away with his villainy?"

"Do you think I care what that rabble think of me?" Morgaine said scornfully, but Morgause knew her indifference was pretended. "I am loved well enough in my own country."

The second half of the games began with some Saxon churls demonstrating the art of wrestling. They were huge hairy men, hair not only on their faces but all over their near-naked bodies; they grunted and strained and heaved, with hoarse cries, grappling and wrenching with bone-cracking strength. Morgause leaned forward, shamelessly enjoying the sight of their male strength; but Morgaine turned her eyes away in squeamish distaste.

"Oh, come, Morgaine, you are growing as prudish as the Queen. What a face!" Morgause shaded her eyes with her hand and glanced down to the field. "I think the mock battle is about to begin—Look! Is that Gwydion? What can he be doing?"

Gwydion had leaped into the field, and waving away the crier who hurried to him, called out in a strong, clear voice which could be heard clearly from one end of the field to another, "King Arthur!"

Morgause saw that Morgaine had sunk back, white as death, and was clutching the rails with both hands. What was the lad about? Was he going to make a scene here before half of Arthur's people, demanding the acknowledgment that was his?

Arthur rose, and Morgause thought that he too looked uneasy, but his voice was ringing clear.

"Yes, nephew?"

"I have heard that it is customary at these games to allow a challenge, if the King is willing. I ask now if sir Lancelet will meet me for a challenge fight!"

Lancelet had once said—Morgause remembered this—that such challenges were the bane of his existence; every young knight wanted to master the Queen's champion. Arthur's voice was grave. "It is customary, but I cannot speak for Lancelet. If he agrees to this match, I cannot refuse him, but you must challenge him directly and abide by his answer."

Morgause said, "Oh, damn the boy! I had no idea this was what he had in mind . . ." but Morgaine somehow felt she was not so displeased, after all.

A wind had come up, and dust from the field was blowing, blurring the summer glare of the dry white clay of the field. Gwydion walked through the dust to the end of the lists, where Lancelet was sitting on a bench. Morgause could not hear what either of them said, but Gwydion turned angrily and shouted, "My lords! I heard always that a champion's duty is to meet with all comers! Sir, I demand that Lancelet now meet my challenge or yield up his high office to me! Does he hold his post because of his skill at arms, or for some other reason, my lord Arthur?"

"I wish," said Morgause, "that your son were still young enough to have his breeches well dusted, Morgaine!"

"Why blame him?" asked Morgaine. "Why not blame Gwenhwyfar for making her husband so vulnerable? Everyone in this kingdom knows she favors Lancelet, yet no one cries out 'witch' or 'harlot' when she comes before the people."

But Lancelet, below them, had risen and strode to Gwydion; he brought back his gloved hand and struck the younger man smartly across the mouth. "Now indeed you have given me cause to chastise your ungentle tongue, young Gwydion. We will see who refuses combat now!"

"I came here for that," said Gwydion, unmoved by blow or words, though there was a small trickle of blood on his face. "I will even grant you first blood, sir Lancelet. It is fitting that a man of your years should have some advantage."

Lancelet spoke to one of his marshals, who came to take his place as master of the lists. There was a considerable murmuring in the stands as Lancelet and Gwydion took swords and faced the King for the ritual bow which began the contest. Morgause thought, *If there is a man in that crowd who does not believe that they are father and son, he must have poor eyesight.*

The two men raised swords to each other, their faces now hidden by helmets. They were within an inch of the same height; the only difference between them was between Lancelet's battered old breastplate and armor, and Gwydion's newer, unstained gear. They circled one another slowly, then rushed in and for a moment Morgause lost track of the separate strokes, which were nearly too fast for the eye to follow. She could see that Lancelet was taking the younger man's measure, and after a moment he pressed hard and struck a mighty blow. Gwydion caught it on the side of his shield, but the force behind it was so enormous that he reeled, lost his balance, and measured his length on the field. He began to scramble up. Lancelet put his sword aside and went to help the young man to his feet. Morgause could not hear what he said, but the gesture was good-natured, something like, "Had enough, youngster?"

Gwydion pointed to the trickle of blood down Lancelet's wrist from a small cut he had managed to inflict. His voice was clearly audible.

"You drew first blood, sir, and I second. Shall we decide it with one more fall?"

There was a small storm of hissing and disapproval; first blood in these demonstration matches, since the contestants fought with sharp weapons, was supposed to end the fight.

King Arthur rose in his place. "This is a festival and a courtesy challenge, not a duel! I will have no settling of grudges here, unless you fight with fists or cudgels! Continue if you will, but I warn you, if there is a serious wounding, you will both be under my gravest displeasure!"

They bowed and moved apart, circling for their advantage; then they rushed together, and Morgause gasped, watching the fierceness of it. It seemed that at any moment one or the other might rush in under the shield and inflict a mortal wound! One of them had gone to his knees—a rain of blows on the shield, the swords locked together in a deadlock, and one was borne closer and closer to the ground . . .

Gwenhwyfar rose and cried out, "I will have this go no further!"

Arthur cast his baton into the lists; by custom, a fight was instantly stopped when that happened, but neither man saw, and the marshals had to pull them apart. Gwydion stood fresh and erect, smiling as he pulled off his helmet. Lancelet's squire had to help the older man to his feet; he was breathing hard, sweat and blood pouring down his face. There was a perfect storm of hissing, even from the other knights on the field; Gwydion had added nothing to his popularity by shaming the hero of the people.

But he bowed to the older knight. "I am honored, sir Lancelet. I came to this court a stranger, not even one of Arthur's Companions, and I am grateful to you for a lesson in swordplay." His smile was the very reflection of Lancelet's own. "Thank you, sir."

Lancelet managed to summon from somewhere his old smile. It exaggerated the resemblance between them almost to the point of caricature. "You bore yourself most bravely, Gwydion."

"Then," said Gwydion, kneeling before him in the dust of the field, "I beg of you, sir, grant to me the order of knighthood."

Morgause caught her breath. Morgaine sat as if she had been turned to stone. But from where the Saxons sat there was a burst of cheering. "Crafty counsel indeed! Clever, clever—how can they refuse you now, lad, when you have stood up well to combat with their own champion!"

Lancelet glanced at Arthur. The King sat paralyzed, seeming frozen, but after a moment, he nodded. Lancelet gestured to his squire, who brought a sword. Lancelet took it and belted it around Gwydion's waist. "Bear this always in the service of your king, and of the righteous cause," said the old knight. He was deadly serious now. All the mockery and defiance had gone from Gwydion's face; he looked grave and sweet, his eyes raised to Lancelet, and Morgause saw that his lips were trembling.

Sudden sympathy for him rose in Morgause—bastard, not even an acknowledged one, he was even more of an outsider than Lancelet had been. Who could blame Gwydion for the ruse by which he had forced his kinsmen to notice him? She thought, *We should have taken him long since to Arthur's court, had him privately acknowledged even if Arthur could not do so publicly. A king's son should not have to do this.*

Lancelet laid his hands on Gwydion's brow. "I confer on you the honor of a Companion of the Round Table, by permission of our king. Serve him always, and since you have won this honor by craft rather than brute strength—though indeed you have shown that too, well enough—I name you among this company, not Gwydion, but Mordred. Rise, sir Mordred, and take your place among the Companions of Arthur."

Gwydion—no, *Mordred,* Morgause remembered; for the naming of a Companion was a rite not much less serious than baptism—rose and heartily returned Lancelet's embrace. He seemed deeply moved, almost unhearing the cheers and applause. His voice broke as he said, "Now I have won the prize of the day, whoever is judged winner in these games, my lord Lancelet."

"No," Morgaine said quietly at Morgause's side, "I do not understand him. That is the last thing I would have expected."

THERE WAS a long pause before the Companions ranged themselves for the final mock battle. Some went to drink water or swallow a hasty bite of bread; some gathered in little knots, arguing about which side they should take in the final games; others went to see to their horses. Morgause went down to the field where a few of the young men lingered, Gareth among them—he towered over the others by half a head, making him easy to pick out. She thought he was talking to Lancelet, but when she came closer she discovered her sight had deceived her; he was facing Gwydion, and his voice sounded angry. She caught only the last few words.

"—what harm has he ever done you? To make a fool of him before the whole field—"

Gwydion laughed and said, "If our cousin needs protection before a whole field of his friends, God help Lancelet when he falls among the Saxons or the Northmen! Come, foster-brother, I doubt not he can protect his own reputation! Is that all you have to say to me after all these years, brother, to chide me that I have distressed someone you love so well?"

Gareth laughed and caught Gwydion into a great hug. He said, "Same reckless young one, you are—what put it into your head to do that? Arthur would have made you knight, if you had asked him!"

Morgause remembered: Gareth did not know all the truth about Gwydion's parentage; no doubt, he meant only, *because you are his sister's son.*

Gwydion said, "I am sure of it—he is always kind to his kinsmen. He would have made *you* knight, Gareth, for Gawaine's sake, but you took not that road either, foster-brother." He chuckled. "And I think Lancelet owes me something for all those years I have walked about wearing his face!"

Gareth shrugged ruefully. "Well, it seems he bears you no grudge, so I suppose I too must forgive you. Now you, too, have seen how great-hearted he is."

"Aye," said Gwydion softly, "he is so—" then raised his head and saw Morgause. "Mother, what do you here? How may I serve you?"

"I came only to greet Gareth, who has not spoken with me this day," said Morgause, and the big man bent to kiss his mother's hand. She asked him, "How will you fight in the mock battle?"

"As always," said Gareth, "I fight at Gawaine's side, in the King's men. You have a horse for fighting, do you not, Gwydion? Will you fight with the King's side, then? We can make a place for you."

Gwydion said, with his dark enigmatic smile, "Since Lancelet made me knight, I suppose I should fight with the army of sir Lancelet of the Lake, and at Accolon's side, for Avalon. But I will not take the field at all today, Gareth."

"Why not?" Gareth asked and laid his hand on the younger man's shoulder, looking down at him as he had always done—Morgause thought of a younger Gareth, smiling down at his little brother. "It is expected of those who have been made knight—Galahad will fight among us, you know."

"And which side will he take?" Gwydion asked. "His father Lancelet's, or that of the King who has made him heir to his kingdom? Is that not a cruel test of his loyalties?"

Gareth looked exasperated. "How then would you divide the armies for the mock battle, save by the two greatest knights among us? Do you think either Lancelet or Arthur believes it a test of loyalties? Arthur will not take the field himself, just so that no man will have to make the choice whether to strike at his king, but Gawaine has been his champion since he was crowned! Are *you* going to rake up old scandal? *You?*"

Gwydion shrugged. "Since I am not intending to join either force—"

"But what will they think of you? That you are cowardly, that you shrink from combat—"

"I have fought enough in Arthur's armies that I care not what they say," said Gwydion, "but if you wish, you may tell them that my horse is gone lame and I have no wish to risk more injury to him—that is an honorable excuse."

"I would lend you a horse of Gawaine," Gareth said, puzzled, "but if you wish for an honorable excuse, do what you will. But why, Gwydion? Or must I now call you Mordred?"

"You shall call me always what you will, foster-brother."

"But will you not tell me why you shirk the fight, Gwydion?"

"None other but you could speak that word unchallenged," said Gwydion, "but since you ask me, I will tell you. It is for your sake, brother."

Gareth scowled at him. "What, in God's name, do you mean?"

"I know little of God, or care to," said Gwydion, and stared down at his feet. "Since you will know, brother—you know from old—I have the Sight—"

"Aye, and what of it?" asked Gareth impatiently. "Have you had some ill dream that I will fall before your lance?"

"No, make not a jest of it," said Gwydion, and Morgause felt ice go through her veins as he turned up his face to Gareth. "It seemed to me—" He swallowed, as if his throat closed against the words he would speak. "It seemed to me that you lay dying—and I knelt at your side, and you would not speak to me—and I knew it was my doing you lay without the spark of life."

Gareth pursed his lips and whistled soundlessly. But then he clapped his foster-brother on the shoulder. "Nay, but I put small faith in dreams and visions, youngster. And fate, no man can escape. Did they not teach you that in Avalon?"

"Aye," Gwydion said softly. "And if you fell, even at my hand, in battle, fate then it would be . . . but I will not tempt that fate in play, my brother. Some ill chance might guide my hand to strike amiss. . . . Let it be, Gareth. I will not take the field this day, let them say what they will."

Gareth still looked distressed. "Well, do as you will, lad. Stay beside our mother, then, since Lamorak will take the field beside Lancelet." He bent to kiss his mother's hand, and went; Morgause, frowning, started to ask Gwydion what he had seen; but he was scowling, staring at the ground, and she forbore, saying only, "Well, if I am to have a young courtier to sit beside me, will you bring me a dipper of water before I go to my seat again?"

"Certainly, Mother," he said, and went off toward the water butts.

To Morgause, the final scrimmage battle was always something of a blur; her head had begun to ache with the sun and she was eager for it to be over. She was hungry, too, and could smell, from a distance, the meat roasting in the pits.

Gwydion sat beside her and explained it to her, though she knew little of the fine points of fighting, nor cared to. But she did note that Galahad acquitted himself well, unseating two riders; she was a little surprised, he seemed so gentle a boy. But then, Gareth too had seemed a gentle child to her, and he was the most fearsome of fighters. At the end, he took the prize on the King's side where Gawaine was at the head of the fighting. To no one's surprise, Galahad won the prize on Lancelet's side; this was customary for a young man who had been knighted that day, and she said so.

"You could have had a prize too, Gwydion," she said, but he laughed and shook his head. "I need it not, Mother. Why spoil this day for my cousin? And Galahad fought well—no one begrudges him the prize."

There were many smaller prizes, and when they were all given, the knights went to be sluiced with buckets of water from head to toe by their squires, and to put on fresh clothing. Morgause went with the ladies of the King's household to a room put at their disposal, where they could arrange their gowns and hair, and wash off the dust and sweat of the stands.

"How do you think?" Morgause asked. "Has Lancelet made himself an enemy?"

Morgaine said, "I think not. Did you see them embrace?"

"They looked like father and son," said Morgause. "Would that they were!"

But Morgaine's face was like stone. "It is many years too late to speak of that, Aunt."

Morgause reflected, *Perhaps she has forgotten that I know whose son he really is.* But before Morgaine's frozen calm she could only say, "Would you like me to help with your braids at the back?" and took up the comb as Morgaine turned. "Mordred," she said, as she worked. "Well, he showed crafty counsel here, God knows! Now he has won himself a place by valor and impudence, so he need not demand one from Arthur on the grounds of his parentage. The Saxons named him well. But I knew not he was so much of a fighter. He has certainly managed to carry away the luster of the day! Even though Galahad won the prize, no one will talk about anything but Mordred's daring gesture."

One of the Queen's ladies came up to them. "Lady Morgaine, is sir Mordred your son? I never knew you had a son—"

Morgaine said steadily, "I was very young when he was born, and Morgause fostered him. I had come near to forgetting it myself."

"How proud you must be of him! And isn't he handsome? As good-looking as Lancelet himself," the woman said, and her eyes glistened.

"He is, isn't he," agreed Morgaine, her tone so courteous that only Morgause, who knew her well, knew that she was angry. "It has been an embarrassment to them both, I dare say. But Lancelet and I are first cousins, and when I was a little girl, I was more like him than like my own brother. Our mother was tall and red-haired like Queen Morgause here, but Lady Viviane was of the old folk of Avalon."

"Who is his father, then?" asked the woman, and Morgause saw Morgaine's hands clench at her sides. But she said with a pleasant smile, "He is a Beltane child, and the God claims all children gotten in the groves. No doubt you remember that as a young girl I was one of the damsels of the Lady of the Lake."

Trying to be polite, the woman murmured, "I had forgotten—they still kept the old rites there, then?"

"As they do now," said Morgaine quietly. "And the Goddess grant they shall do so till the world end."

As she had intended, that silenced the woman, and Morgaine turned away, saying to Morgause, "Are you ready, kinswoman? Let us go down to the hall." As they left the room she drew a long breath of mingled exasperation and relief.

"Chattering fools—listen to them! Have they nothing better to do than gossip?"

"Probably not," said Morgause. "Their most Christian husbands and fathers make sure they shall have nothing else to occupy their minds."

The doors to the great chamber of the Round Table where the Pentecost feast would be held were shut, so that they might all enter at once.

"Arthur every year gives us more pageantry," said Morgause. "Now a grand procession and entrance, I suppose?"

"What do you expect?" Morgaine asked. "Now there are no wars, he must touch the imagination of his people somehow, and he is clever enough to do it by making great display for them—I have heard it was the Merlin who counselled him so. The common folk—yes, and the nobles too—like a fine show, and the Druids have known that since they lit the first Beltane fires. Gwenhwyfar has spent many years making this the greatest holiday anywhere in any Christian land." She gave the first real smile Morgause had seen on her face this day. "Even Arthur knows he cannot hold his people with a mass and a feast alone—if there is no great marvel to see, I doubt not Arthur and the Merlin will somehow arrange one! What a pity they could not arrange to hold the eclipse today!"

"Did you watch the eclipse in Wales? My folk were frightened," Morgause said, "and no doubt, those fools of Gwenhwyfar's ladies shrieked and shouted as if the world were coming to an end!"

"Gwenhwyfar has a passion for fools among her ladies," Morgaine said. "Yet she herself is not really a fool, though she likes to seem so. I wonder how she can tolerate it?"

"You should show more patience with them," Morgause warned, and Morgaine shrugged.

"I care not what fools think of me."

"I cannot imagine how you have dwelt in Uriens' kingdom as his queen so long, and not learned more of queencraft," said Morgause. "Whatever she is thought by men, a woman must depend on the goodwill of other women—what else did you learn at Avalon?"

Morgaine said, her voice hard, "The women in Avalon are not such fools." But Morgause knew her well enough to know that her angry tone concealed loneliness and suffering.

"Morgaine, why do you not return to Avalon?"

Morgaine bent her head, knowing that if Morgause spoke kindly again to her she would break and weep. "My time has not yet come. I have been ordered to stay with Uriens—"

"And Accolon?"

"Oh, aye, with Accolon," said Morgaine. "I might have known you would reproach me with that—"

"I am the last to speak," said Morgause. "But Uriens will not live long—"

Morgaine said, her face as frozen as her voice, "So I believed on that day years ago when we were wedded. He is like to live as long as Taliesin himself, and Taliesin was past ninety when he died."

Arthur and Gwenhwyfar had arrived and were slowly making their way to the head of the line—Arthur resplendently clad in white robes, Gwenhwyfar beside him, exquisite in white silk and jewels. The great doors were flung open, and they passed within, then Morgaine as the King's sister with her husband and his sons, Accolon and Uwaine; then Morgause with her household, as the King's aunt; then Lancelet and his household, and then the other knights one by one, proceeding around the Round Table to take their seats. A few years back, some craftsman had wrought in gold paint and crimson the name of every Companion over his customary chair. Now, as they entered, Morgause noticed that the seat nearest the King, reserved all these years for his heir, had been painted with the name Galahad. But she saw it only in a flicker of her eye. For at the great thrones where Arthur and Gwenhwyfar were to sit, two white banners, like the garish banners with which the battles of the clowns had been fought, had been draped, and across them were scrawled paintings, ugly caricatures—on one throne was a banner portraying a knight standing on the heads of two crowned figures, bearing a devilish likeness to Arthur and Gwenhwyfar; and across the other was a lewd painting which made even Morgause, who was by no means prudish, blush, for it depicted a small, dark-haired woman, stark naked, in the embrace of a huge horned devil, and all about her, accepting certain strange and disgusting sexual ministrations, were scrawled a group of naked men.

Gwenhwyfar cried out in a shrill scream, "God and Mary defend us!"

Arthur, stopped dead, turned on the servants in a voice of thunder. "How came this—this—" Words failed him and he waved his hand at the drawings. "—this here?"

"Sir—" the chamberlain stammered, "it was not here when we finished decking the hall—all was orderly, even to the flowers before the Queen's seat—"

"Who was last in this hall?" Arthur demanded.

Cai limped forward. "My lord and my brother, it was I. I came to be certain all was in good order, and I swear as God sees us all, everything was ready at that time to honor my king and his lady. And if ever I find the foul dog who sneaked in to put this thing here, I will have his head like this!" And he gestured as if he were wringing a chicken's neck.

"Look to your lady!" said Arthur sharply. The women were twittering and chattering as Gwenhwyfar began to sink down in a faint. Morgaine held her up, saying in a sharp, low voice, "Gwen, don't give them this satisfaction! You are a queen—what do you care what some fool scrawls on a banner? Control yourself!"

Gwenhwyfar was crying. "How can they—how could they—how could anyone hate me so?"

"There is no one alive who can live without offending some idiot or other," said Morgaine, and helped her toward her seat. But the more crudely sexual of the banners was still draped over it, and Gwenhwyfar shrank back as if she touched something filthy. Morgaine threw it on the floor. There were wine cups set; Morgaine gestured to one of Gwenhwyfar's waiting-women to fill one and give it to the Queen.

"Don't let it trouble you, Gwen—I imagine *that* one is meant for me," she said. "It is whispered indeed that I take devils to my bed, and what do I care?"

Arthur said, "Get this foulness out of here and burn it, and bring scented woods and incense to take away the stink of evil." Lackeys scurried to obey him, and Cai said, "We will find out who did this. No doubt it is some servant I dismissed, coming back to embarrass me because I had shown some pride in the decorations of the hall this year. Men, bring the wine round, and the ale, and we will have our first round of drinking shame and confusion to that stinking louse who tried to spoil our feast. Will we let him? Come! Drink to King Arthur and his lady!"

A thin cheer went up, which grew to a genuine cry of appreciation as Arthur and Gwenhwyfar bowed to them all. The feasters seated themselves, and Arthur said, "Now bring before me any petitioners."

Morgause watched as they brought up some man with a complaint which seemed stupid, about a boundary. Then came an overlord who complained that his vassal had taken a deer on his lands.

Morgause was near Gwenhwyfar; she leaned over and murmured to the Queen, "Why does Arthur hear these cases himself? Any of his bailiffs could handle this and not waste his time."

Gwenhwyfar murmured, "So I once thought. But he hears a case or two like this, every year at Pentecost, so that the common folk may not think he cares only for the great nobles or his own Companions."

Well, Morgause thought, that was wise enough. There were two or three more small petitions, then as the meat was brought round, jugglers and acrobats entertained the company, and a man did some conjuring trick of bringing small birds and eggs from the most unlikely places. Morgause thought that Gwenhwyfar seemed calm now, and wondered if they would ever catch the author of the drawings. One portrayed Morgaine as a harlot and that was bad enough; but the other, it seemed, was more serious—showing Lancelet trampling on both King and Queen. Something had happened today beyond a public humiliation for the Queen's champion, Morgause reflected. That could have been dispelled by the graciousness he had shown to young Gwydion—no, Mordred—and the obvious lack of any grudge between them after. But despite Lancelet's popularity with King and Companions, there were, no doubt, some who detested Gwenhwyfar's obvious partiality to her champion.

"What is happening now?" she asked Gwenhwyfar.

The Queen smiled; whatever it was, as the horns blew outside the hall, it was something which pleased her.

The doors were flung open; horns blared again, the crude horns of the Saxons. Then three great Saxons, wearing gold torques and bracelets about their arms, clad in garments of fur and leather, bearing great swords and their horned helmets and with circlets of gold about their heads, strode into the hall of the Round Table, each with his retinue.

"My lord Arthur," called out one of them, "I am Adelric, lord of Kent and Anglia, and these are my brother kings. We have come to ask that we may give tribute to you, most Christian of kings, and make permanent treaty with you and your court forever!"

"Lot would be turning in his grave." remarked Morgause, "but Viviane would be pleased at this day." But Morgaine did not answer.

Bishop Patricius rose and came toward the Saxon kings, welcoming them. He said to Arthur, "My lord, after the long wars, this gives me great joy. I urge you to welcome these men as your subject kings and take their oath, in token that all Christian kings should be brothers."

Morgaine was deathly white. She started to rise and speak, but Uriens looked at her with a stern frown and she sank back at his side. Morgause said good-naturedly, "I remember when the bishops refused even to send anyone to Christianize these barbarians. Lot told me they had vowed they

would not meet with the Saxons in fellowship even in Heaven, and that they
would not send missions to them—they felt it right that the Saxons should
all end up in Hell. But, well, that is thirty years gone!"

Arthur said, "Since I came to my throne, I have longed for an end to
the wars which have ravaged this land. We have dwelt in peace for many
years, Lord Bishop, and now I welcome you, good sirs, to my court and
to my company."

"It is our custom," said one of the Saxons—not Adelric, Morgause
noticed, for this one was wearing some kind of blue cloak, and Adelric's
had been brown—"to take oath on steel. May we take oath on the cross
of your sword, Lord Arthur, in token that we meet as Christian kings under
One God who rules us all?"

"Be it so," said Arthur quietly, and came down from the dais to stand
before them. In the light of the many torches and lamps, Excalibur flashed
like lightning as he drew it. He set it upright before him and a great
wavering shadow, the shadow of a cross, fell all the length of the hall, as
the kings knelt.

Gwenhwyfar looked pleased; Galahad was flushed with joy. But Morgaine was white with rage, and Morgause heard her whisper to Uriens. "He
has dared to put the sacred sword of Avalon to such uses! I will not, as
priestess of Avalon, sit and witness it in silence!" She began to rise, but
Uriens gripped her wrist. She struggled silently, but old as Uriens was, he
was a warrior, and Morgaine a little woman; for a moment Morgause
thought he would break the small bones of Morgaine's wrist, but she did
not cry out or whimper. She set her teeth, and managed to wrench her wrist
away. She said, loud enough that Gwenhwyfar could certainly hear, "Viviane died with her work unfinished. And I have sat idle while children
unconceived grew to manhood and were knighted, and Arthur fell into the
hands of the priests!"

"Lady," said Accolon, leaning over her chair, "even you cannot disrupt
this holy day, or they will serve you as the Romans served the Druids. Speak
in private with Arthur, remonstrate with him there if you must—I am sure
the Merlin will help you!"

Morgaine lowered her eyes. Her teeth bit into her lip.

Arthur embraced the Saxon kings one by one, welcoming them and
leading them to seats near his throne. "Your sons, if they show themselves
worthy, will be welcome among my Companions," he said, and had his
servants bring gifts—swords and fine daggers, a rich cloak for Adelric.
Morgause took up a cake, sticky with honey, and put it between Morgaine's
clenched lips.

"You are too fond of fasting, Morgaine," she said. "Eat this! You are
pale, you will swoon where you sit!"

"It is not hunger that makes me pale," said Morgaine, but she took the cake in her mouth. She drank a little wine too, and Morgause could see that her hands were shaking. On one wrist there were dark bruises left by Uriens' fingers.

Then Morgaine rose. She said quietly to Uriens, "Do not worry, my most beloved husband. I will say nothing to offend you or our king." Then, turning to Arthur, she said loudly, "My lord and brother! May I ask a favor of you?"

"My sister and the wife of my loyal subject king Uriens may ask what she will," said Arthur genially.

"The least of your subjects, sir, may ask for audience. I ask that you will grant me such an audience," she said. Arthur raised his eyebrows, but took his formal tone from her.

"Tonight before I sleep, if you will. I will receive you in my own room, with your husband if you wish."

I wish, thought Morgause, *that I could be a fly on the wall at that audience!*

6

In the chamber Gwenhwyfar had assigned King Uriens and his family, Morgaine combed her hair again with leaden fingers and had her waiting-woman lace her into a fresh gown. Uriens was complaining that he had eaten and drunk too well and was not looking forward to the audience.

"Go to bed then," she said. "It is I who has a thing to say to him, it has nothing to do with you."

"Not so," said Uriens. "I too was lessoned in Avalon. Do you think I take pleasure in seeing the holy things put to the service of the Christian God who would strip all other knowledge from the world? No, Morgaine, it is not you alone as priestess of Avalon who should show your outrage at this. It is the kingdom of North Wales, I myself as ruler, and Accolon, who is pledged to rule when I am gone."

"Father is right, madam." Accolon met her eyes as he said, "Our people trust us that we will not betray them, nor let church bells ring in their holy groves—" and for a moment it seemed, though she knew that neither she nor Accolon had moved, that they were standing together in one of the magical groves, joined before the Goddess. Uriens, of course, had seen nothing. He urged, "Let Arthur know, Morgaine, that the kingdom of North Wales will not fall meekly under the rule of the Christians."

Morgaine shrugged. "As you wish."

I was a fool, she thought. *I was priestess at his kingmaking, I bore Arthur a son, I should have used that hold I had on the King's conscience—made myself, not Gwenhwyfar, the ruler behind the throne. While I hid like an animal licking wounds, I lost my hold on Arthur. Where, at one time, I could have commanded, now I must beg, without even the power of the Lady!*

She had already turned toward the door when there was a knocking; a servant went to open it, and Gwydion came in. He was still wearing the Saxon sword that Lancelet had given him at his knighting, but he had taken off his armor and wore a rich gown of scarlet; she had not known he could look so fine.

He saw her eyes light on him. "Lancelet gave it me. We were drinking in the hall, and word came from Arthur that the King wished to see me in his chambers. . . . I said that my only tunic was bedraggled and blood-soaked and he said we were of a size and he would lend me a gown. When I had it on, he said it became me better than it did him and I should keep it—that I had had few enough gifts at my knighting, while the King had given Galahad many rich presents. Does he know Arthur is my father, that he said that?"

Uriens blinked and looked surprised, but said nothing. Accolon shook his head. "No, stepbrother. Lancelet is the most generous of men, that is all. When Gareth came first to court, unknown to his own kinsmen, Lancelet gave him clothes and weapons, so that Gareth should be dressed according to his station. And if you should ask if Lancelet likes it overmuch, seeing his gifts on the bodies of handsome young men, well, that has been said too before now, though I know of no man at this court, young or old, who has ever had a word from Lancelet beyond knightly courtesy."

"Is it so?" Gwydion asked, and Morgaine could see him taking this piece of information and putting it away like gold in a miser's chest. "Now I recall," he said slowly, "a tale that went about of some feast at Lot's court when Lancelet was no more than a youth—something of a ballad made when they thrust a harp into his hand and bade him play, and he sang some lay of Rome or the days of Alexander, I know not what, of the love of knightly companions, and they jeered at him for it. Since then, his songs are all of the beauty of our queen, or knightly tales of adventure and dragons."

Morgaine felt she could not bear the scorn in his voice. She said, "If you came to claim a gift for your knighting, I will speak with you when I have seen Arthur, but not now."

Gwydion looked down at his shoes. It was the first time she had ever seen him less than self-assured and confident. "Mother, the King has sent for me too—may I go in your company?"

She liked him a little better, that he should confess his own vulnerability this way. "Arthur means you no harm, my son, but if it will please you to go with us before him, he can do no worse than send you away and say he would rather speak to you separately."

"Come, then, stepbrother," said Accolon, taking Gwydion's arm in such a way that the younger man could see the serpents tattooed on Accolon's wrists. "The King shall go first with his lady, and you and I will follow. . . ."

Morgaine, at Uriens' side, thought that she liked it well that Accolon should befriend her son and acknowledge him brother. At the same time she felt herself shiver, and Uriens took her hand. "Are you cold, Morgaine? Take your cloak . . ."

IN THE KING'S apartments a fire burned, and Morgaine heard the sound of a harp. Arthur sat in a wooden chair heaped with cushions. Gwenhwyfar was setting stitches in a narrow band which twinkled with gilt thread. The servant announced ceremoniously, "The King and Queen of North Wales, and their son Accolon, and sir Lancelet—"

Gwenhwyfar looked up at Lancelet's name, then laughed and said, "No, though he is very like. Sir Mordred, is it not, that we saw knighted this day?"

Gwydion bowed to the Queen but did not speak. But in this family gathering Arthur was not one to stand upon ceremony.

"Sit down, all of you—let me send for wine—"

Uriens said, "I have had enough wine this day, Arthur, to float a ship down to the shore! None for me, thank you—perhaps the young men have better heads for it."

Gwenhwyfar moved toward Morgaine, and Morgaine knew that if she did not speak now, Arthur would begin his parley with the men and she would be expected to sit in a corner with the Queen and keep silence, or talk in whispers of women's things—embroidery, servants, who at the court was breeding . . .

She gestured to the servant with the wine. "I will have a cup," she said, remembering, like a pain within her, when as priestess of Avalon she had been proud to drink only of the Holy Well. She sipped and said, "I am deeply distressed at the welcome of the Saxon envoys, Arthur. No—" She silenced him as he would have spoken. "I do not speak as a woman meddling in affairs of state. I am Queen of North Wales, and Duchess of Cornwall, and what concerns the realm touches me too."

"Then you should be glad for peace," Arthur said. "I have worked all my lifetime, it seems, since I was old enough to hold a sword, to end the wars with the Saxons. At that time I believed the war would be ended by driving them back over the seas whence they came. But peace is peace, and if it comes by making treaty with them, let it be so. There are more ways to deal with a bull than roasting him for dinner. It is equally effective to geld him and make him pull your plow."

"Or save him to serve your cows at stud? Will you ask your subject kings to marry their daughters to Saxons, Arthur?"

"That too, perhaps," said Arthur. "Saxons are no more than men—do you call to mind that song Lancelet sang? They have the same longings for peace—they too have lived on lands ravaged and burned again and again. Will you say I should have fought on till the last of them was dead or driven out? I thought women longed for peace."

"I too long for peace, and welcome it, even with Saxons," Morgaine said, "but have you made them give up their Gods too, and accept your own, that you made them swear to you on the cross?"

Gwenhwyfar had been listening intently. "There *are* no other Gods, Morgaine. They have agreed to put aside the devils they worshipped and called Gods, that is all. Now they worship the one true God and the Christ sent in his name to save mankind."

Gwydion said, "If you truly believe that, my lady and queen, then for you it is truth—all the Gods are One God and all the Goddesses one Goddess. But would you presume to declare one truth for all of mankind throughout the world?"

"Call you that presumption? It *is* the one truth," Gwenhwyfar said, "and a day must come when all men everywhere will acknowledge it."

"I tremble for my people that you say so," said King Uriens. "I have pledged myself to protect the sacred groves, and my son after me."

"Why, I thought you a Christian, my lord of North Wales—"

"And so I am," said Uriens, "but I will not speak ill of another's God."

"But there are no such Gods," Gwenhwyfar began.

Morgaine opened her mouth to speak, but Arthur said, "Enough of this, enough—I did not bid you here to discuss theology! If you have the stomach for that, there are priests enough who will listen and argue. Go you and convert *them* if you must! What did you come here to say, Morgaine? Only that you are wary of the good faith of the Saxons, oaths on the cross or no?"

"No," Morgaine said, and as she spoke, she noted that Kevin was in the room, sitting in the shadows with his harp. Good; the Merlin of Britain could witness this protest in the name of Avalon! "I call the Merlin to witness, you had them swear an oath on the cross—and you transformed the holy sword of Avalon, Excalibur, the very sword of the Holy Regalia, into your cross for the oath! Lord Merlin, is this not blasphemy?"

Arthur said quickly, "It was only a gesture, to catch the imagination of everyone, Morgaine—such as the gesture Viviane made, when she bade me fight for peace in the name of Avalon with that selfsame sword."

The Merlin said in his rich low voice, "Morgaine, my dear, the cross is a symbol older than Christ and venerated before ever there were followers of the Nazarene. In Avalon there are priests brought here by the patriarch Joseph of Arimathea, who worship at the side of the Druids. . . ."

"But they were priests who did not try to say that their God is the only God," Morgaine said angrily, "and I doubt not that Bishop Patricius would silence them if he could, and preach only his own brand of bigotry!"

"Bishop Patricius and his beliefs are not at issue here, Morgaine," said Kevin. "Let the uninitiated think that the Saxons swore on the cross of Christ's sacrifice and death. We too have a sacrificed God, whether we see him in the cross, or in the sheaf of barley which must die to the earth and be raised again from the dead—"

Gwenhwyfar said, "Your sacrificed Gods, Lord Merlin, were sent only that mankind might be ready when the Christ came to die for man's sins—"

Arthur moved his hand impatiently. "Be quiet, all of you! The Saxons swore to peace on a symbol meaningful to them—"

But Morgaine interrupted him. "It was from Avalon you received the sacred sword, and to Avalon that you swore an oath to preserve and guard the Holy Mysteries! And now you would make the sword of the Mysteries into the cross of death, the gallows for the dead! When Viviane came to court, she came to demand of you that you fullfil your oaths to Avalon. Then she was struck down! Now I am come to finish that work she left undone, and to demand from you that holy sword of Excalibur which you have presumed to twist into the service of your Christ!"

Gwenhwyfar said, "A day will come when all false Gods shall vanish and all pagan symbols shall be put to the service of the one true God and his Christ."

"I did not speak to you, you canting fool," said Morgaine furiously, "and that day will come over my corpse! You Christians have saints and martyrs—do you think Avalon will have none?" And as she spoke she shuddered, knowing that, unaware, she had spoken through the Sight, and there was the body of a knight, draped in black with a cross banner over his body. . . . She wanted to turn, as she could not do here in this company, and throw herself into Accolon's arms.

"How you exaggerate all things, Morgaine!" said Arthur with an uneasy laugh, and that laugh maddened her, driving away both the fear and the Sight. She drew herself up to her full height, and knew that for the first time in many years she spoke mantled in all the power and authority of a priestess of Avalon.

"Hear me, Arthur of Britain! As the force and power of Avalon set you on the throne, so the force and power of Avalon can bring you down into ruin! Think well how you desecrate the Holy Regalia! Think never to put it to the service of your Christian God, for every thing of Power carries its own curse—"

"Enough!" Arthur had risen from his chair, and his frown was like a storm. "Sister or no, do not presume to give orders to the King of all Britain."

"I do not speak to my brother," she retorted, "but to the King! Avalon set you on the throne, Arthur, Avalon gave you that sword you have misused, and in the name of Avalon I now call on you to render it back again to the Holy Regalia! If you wish to treat it only as a sword, then call your smiths to make you another!"

There was a dreadful silence, and it seemed to her for a moment that her words were falling into the great echoing empty spaces between the worlds, that far away in Avalon the Druids must wake, that even Raven must stir and cry out against Arthur's betrayal. But the first sound she heard was nervous laughter.

"What nonsense you are talking, Morgaine!" It was Gwenhwyfar who spoke. "You know Arthur cannot do that!"

"Do not interfere, Gwenhwyfar," Morgaine said, with deadly menace. "It has nothing to do with you, except that if it was you who bade Arthur break oath to Avalon, beware!"

"Uriens," said Gwenhwyfar, "will you stand idle and let your unruly wife speak so to the High King?"

Uriens coughed; his voice when he spoke sounded as nervous as Gwenhwyfar's. "Morgaine, perhaps you are being unreasonable . . . Arthur made a dramatic gesture for political reasons, to catch the imagination of the crowd. If he did so with a sword of power, well, so much the better. The Gods can take care of their own worship, my dear—do you think the Goddess needs your help to protect her own?"

At that moment, if Morgaine had had a weapon, she would have struck Uriens down. He had come to support her, and now he deserted her this way?

Arthur said, "Morgaine, since you are so troubled, let me say this for your ears alone: I intended no desecration. If the sword of Avalon also serves as a cross for an oath, does it not mean that Avalon's powers are joined in the service of this land? So Kevin advised me—"

"Oh, aye, I knew him traitor when he had Viviane buried outside the Holy Isle—" Morgaine began.

"Be it so or otherwise," said Arthur, "I gave the Saxon kings the gesture they wanted, to swear on my sword!"

"But it is not *your* sword!" Morgaine retorted, at white heat. "It is the sword of Avalon! And if you bear it not as you have sworn, then shall it be given into the hands of one who will be true to his oath—"

"Sword of Avalon it may have been a generation ago," said Arthur, who was now as angry as Morgaine; he clenched his hand over the hilt of Excalibur, as if someone would take it from him that very moment. "A sword is his who uses it, and I have won the right to call it *mine* by driving forth all enemies from this land! I bore it in battle, and I won this land at Mount Badon—"

"And you have tried to subject it to the service of the Christian God," Morgaine retorted. "Now in the name of the Goddess I demand of you that it be returned to the shrine of the Lake!"

Arthur drew a long breath. Then he said in a voice of studied calm, "I refuse. If the Goddess wants this sword returned, then she herself will have to take it from my hands." Then his voice softened. "My dear sister, I beg of you, do not quarrel with me about the name by which we call our Gods. You yourself have said to me that all the Gods are the One God."

And he will never see why what he has said is wrong, Morgaine thought in despair. *Yet he has called on the Goddess, if she wants his sword to come and take it. Be it so, then; Lady, may I be your hand.* She bowed her head for a moment and said, "To the Goddess, then, I leave the disposal of her sword." *And when she has done with you, Arthur, you will wish you had chosen to deal with me instead. . . .* And she went to sit beside Gwenhwyfar. Arthur beckoned to Gwydion.

"Sir Mordred," he said, "I would have made you one of my Companions at any time you asked it of me. I would have done so for Morgaine's sake and for my own—you needed not to force knighthood from me by a trick."

"I thought if you made me knight without some good excuse such as this," Gwydion said, "there might be talk of a kind you did not wish. Will you forgive me the trick, then, sir?"

"If Lancelet has forgiven you, I have no reason to bear you any grudge," said Arthur, "and since he has gifted you richly, it would seem he cherishes no wrath. I wish it lay in my power to acknowledge you my son, Mordred. Until a few years ago, I knew not that you existed— Morgaine told me not what came of that kingmaking. You do know, I suppose, that to the priests and bishops, your very existence is sign of something unholy."

"Do you believe that, sir?"

Arthur looked his son directly in the eye. "Oh—times I believe one thing, times another, like all men. It does not matter what I believe. The facts are thus—I cannot acknowledge you before all men, though you are such a son as any man, let alone a childless king, would be glad and proud to own. Galahad must inherit my throne."

"If he lives," said Gwydion, and at Arthur's shocked look, added quietly, "No, sir, I am not making a threat to his life. I will swear any oath you will, by cross or oak, by the Sacred Well or by these serpents I bear" —he thrust out his wrists—"which you bore before me: may the Goddess send living serpents like these to take my life if ever I raise a hand against my cousin Galahad. But I have seen it—he will die, honorably, for the cross he worships."

"God save us from evil!" cried out Gwenhwyfar.

"Indeed, lady. But if he does not live to ascend your throne—my father and my king, he is a warrior and a knight, and no more than mortal, and you may live to be older than King Uriens. What then?"

"Should Galahad die before he comes to my throne—God stand between him and harm—" said Arthur, "I will have no choice. Royal blood is royal blood, and yours is royal, from the Pendragon and from Avalon. Should such an evil day come, I suppose even the bishops would rather see you on the throne than leave this land to such chaos as they feared when Uther died."

He rose and stood with his two hands on his son's shoulders, looking into his eyes. "Would that I could say more, my son. But done is done. I will say only that—I wish with all my heart that you had been the son of my queen."

"And so do I," said Gwenhwyfar, rising to embrace him.

"Still, I will not treat you as a baseborn churl," said Arthur. "You are Morgaine's son. Mordred, Duke of Cornwall, Companion of the Round Table, you shall go to be the voice of the Round Table among the Saxon kings. You shall have the right to do the King's justice, and to collect my taxes and revenues, keeping a suitable portion to maintain such a household as the King's chancellor should have. And, if you wish it, I give you permission to marry the daughter of one of the Saxon kings, which will give you a throne of your own, even if you come never to mine."

Gwydion bowed and said, "You are generous, sir."

Yes, Morgaine thought, *and this would keep Gwydion well out of the way, until and unless there was need of him.* Arthur was skilled at kingcraft! She raised her head and said, "You have been so generous to my son, Arthur, may I trespass again on your kindness?"

Arthur looked wary, but he said, "Ask me something I can grant, my sister, and it will be my pleasure to give it."

"You have made my son Duke of Cornwall, but he knows little of Cornwall's land as yet. I have heard that Duke Marcus now claims all that country. Will you come with me to Tintagel, and investigate this matter and this claim?"

Arthur's face relaxed; had he been braced for her to raise the matter of the sword Excalibur again? *No, my brother, not ever again before this court; when again I stretch forth my hand for Excalibur, it will be in my own country and in the place of the Goddess.*

"I have not been in Cornwall for more years than I can reckon," Arthur said, "and I cannot leave Camelot until Midsummer is past. But remain here in Camelot as my guest, and then we will go together to Tintagel, and see if Duke Marcus, or any other man God ever made, will dispute the claim of Arthur and of Morgaine, Duchess of Cornwall." He turned to Kevin. "And now enough of high matters—my lord Merlin, I would not command you to sing for me before my entire court, but in private within my own chambers, and in the company of my family alone, may I entreat you for a song?"

"It will be my pleasure," said Kevin, "if the lady Gwenhwyfar does not object." He glanced at the Queen, but she was silent, and so he set his harp to his shoulder and began to play.

Morgaine sat quietly beside Uriens, listening to the music. A royal gift indeed Arthur had commanded for his family, Kevin's music. Gwydion listened, his hands clasped about his knees, silent and spellbound; she thought, *In that at least he is my son.* Uriens listened with polite attention. Morgaine looked up for a moment, meeting Accolon's eyes, and thought; *Somehow this night we must manage to meet, even if I must give Uriens a sleeping potion; there is much I must say to him . . .* and then she cast down her eyes. She was no better than Gwenhwyfar. . . .

Uriens was holding her hand, fondling her fingers and wrists; she felt him touch the bruises he had made that day, and through the pain, she felt revulsion. She must go to his bed if he desired it; here in this Christian court she was his property, like a horse or dog he could fondle or beat at his own will!

Arthur had betrayed both her and Avalon; Uriens had played her false as well. Kevin, too, had betrayed her. . . .

But Accolon would not fail her. Accolon should rule for Avalon, the King Viviane had foreseen would come; and after Accolon, Gwydion, Druid King, King of Avalon and all Britain.

And behind the King, the Queen, ruling for the Goddess as in the days of old. . . .

Kevin raised his head and met her eyes, and Morgaine shivered, knowing she must conceal her thoughts. *He has the Sight, and he is Arthur's man. He is the Merlin of Britain, and nevertheless he is my enemy!*

But Kevin said mildly, "Since this is a family party, and I too would wish to hear music made, may I ask as my fee that the lady Morgaine will sing?" and Morgaine went to take his place, feeling the power of the harp in her hands.

I must charm them, she thought, *so they think no harm,* and set her hands to the strings.

7

URICΠS said, when they were alone in their chamber, "I knew not that your claim to Tintagel was being disputed again."

"The things you do not know, my husband, are as many as acorns in a pig meadow," she said impatiently. How had she ever thought she could suffer this fool? Kind, yes, he had never been unkind to her, but his stupidity grated on her like a rasp. She wanted to be alone, to consider her plans, to confer with Accolon, and instead she must placate this old idiot!

"I should know what you are planning." Uriens' voice was sullen. "I am angry that you did not consult with me if you were displeased at what was happening in Tintagel—I am your husband and you should have told me rather than appealing to Arthur!" The sulkiness in his voice held a hint of jealousy too, and she remembered now, stricken, that it had been brought out what she had concealed all these years—who had fathered her son. But could Uriens really think that after a quarter of a century she still held power of that sort over her brother, because of something only fools and Christians would think a sin? *Well, if he has not wit enough to see what is happening before his eyes, why should I explain it to him word by word like a child's lesson?*

She said, still impatient, "Arthur is displeased with me because he thinks a woman should not contend with him this way. Therefore I asked his help, so that he will not believe I am in rebellion against him." She said no more. She was priestess of Avalon, she would not lie, but there was no need to speak more truth than she wished. Let Uriens think, if he would, that she only wished to make up her quarrel with Arthur.

"How clever you are, Morgaine," he said, patting her wrist. She thought, flinching, that already he had forgotten that it was he who had inflicted the injury. She felt her lips trembling as if she were a child, thinking, *I want Accolon, I want to lie in his arms and be cherished and comforted, but in this place how can we contrive even to meet and speak in secret?* She blinked away angry tears. Strength was her only safety now; strength and concealment.

Uriens had gone out to relieve himself, and came back, yawning. "I heard the watchman cry midnight," he said. "We must to bed, lady." He began to take off his festal robe. "Are you very weary, dear one?"

She did not answer, knowing that if she did she would weep. He took her silence for consent and drew her close, nuzzling at her throat, then pulled her toward the bed. She endured him, wondering if she could remember some charm or herb to put an end to the old man's too-enduring virility —damn him, he should be long past this by his age, no one would even think it the result of sorcery. She lay wondering, afterward, why she could not simply turn to him with indifference, let him have her without even thinking, as she had done so often in these long years . . . what did it matter, why should she notice him any more than a stray animal sniffing round her skirts?

She slept fitfully, dreaming of a child she had found somewhere and must suckle, though her breasts were dry and ached terribly . . . she woke with the pain still in them. Uriens had gone to hunt with some of Arthur's men—it had been arranged days ago. She felt sick and queasy. *I ate more,* she thought, *than I usually do in three days, no wonder I am sick.* But when she went to fasten her gown, her breasts were still sore and aching. It seemed to her that the nipples, brown and small, looked pink and swollen.

She let herself collapse on the bed as if her knees had been broken. She was barren! She *knew* she was barren, they had told her after Gwydion's birth that she would probably never bear a child again, and in all the years since, never once from any man had she gotten with child. More than that, she was near to nine-and-forty, long past the childbearing years. But for all that, she was certainly pregnant now. She had thought herself long past the possibility. Her courses had grown irregular and were absent for months at a time, she had thought herself coming to the end of them. Her first reaction was fear; she had come so near to death when Gwydion was born. . . .

Uriens would certainly be delighted at this supposed proof of his manhood. But when this child was conceived, Uriens had been ill with the lung fever; there was small likelihood, after all, that it was Uriens' child. Had it been fathered by Accolon, on the day of the eclipse? Why, then, it was child to the God as he had come to them then in the hazel grove.

What would I do with a babe, old woman that I am? But perhaps it will be a priestess for Avalon, one to rule after me when the traitor has been tumbled from the throne where Viviane set him. . . .

It was grey and dismal outside, drizzling rain. The games field of yesterday was trampled and muddy, with scattered banners and ribbons trodden into the mud; one or two of the subject kings were making ready to ride out, and a few kitchen women, their gowns tucked up to their bare thighs, carrying washing paddles and sacks of clothing, were trudging down toward the shores of the lake.

There was a knock at the door; the servant's voice was soft and respectful. "Queen Morgaine, the High Queen has asked that you and the Queen of Lothian should come to break your fast with her. And the Merlin of Britain has asked that you will receive him here at noon."

"I will go to the Queen," said Morgaine. "Tell the Merlin I will receive him." She shrank from both confrontations, but she dared not deny herself to either, especially now.

Gwenhwyfar would never be anything but her enemy. It was her doing that Arthur had fallen into the hands of the priests and betrayed Avalon. *Perhaps,* Morgaine thought, *I am plotting the downfall of the wrong person; if I could somehow manage it that Gwenhwyfar left court, even to run away with Lancelet to his own castle, now that he is widowed and can lawfully take her . . .* but she dismissed that idea.

Probably Arthur has asked her to make up the quarrel with me, she thought cynically. *He knows, too, that he cannot afford to quarrel with subject kings, and if Gwenhwyfar and I are at odds, Morgause, as ever, will take my part. Too strong a family quarrel, and he would lose Uriens, and Morgause's sons too. He cannot afford to lose Gawaine, Gareth, the Northmen. . . .*

Morgause was in the Queen's room already; the smell of food made Morgaine sick again, but she controlled it with iron will. It was well known that she never ate much and it would not be particularly noticed. Gwenhwyfar came and kissed her, and for a moment Morgaine's real tenderness for this woman returned. *Why should we be enemies? We were friends once, so long ago. . . .* It was not Gwenhwyfar herself that she hated, it was the priests who had so much influence over her.

She came to the table, accepting but not eating a piece of new bread and honey. Gwenhwyfar's ladies were the kind of pious idiots with whom Gwenhwyfar always surrounded herself. They welcomed Morgaine with curious looks and a great outward display of cordiality and pleasure.

"Your son, sir Mordred—what a fine lad he is, how proud you must be of him," one of them said, and Morgaine, breaking the bread and crumbling it, remarked with composure that she had hardly seen him since he was weaned. "It is Uwaine, my husband's son, who is more truly my own son, and it is in his knightly accomplishments that I take pride," Morgaine said, "for I reared him from a little child. But you are proud of Mordred as your own son, are you not, Morgause?"

"But Uriens' son is not your own child?" someone else asked.

"No," she said patiently, "he was nine years old when I married my lord of North Wales."

One of the girls giggled that if she were Morgaine, she would pay more heed to that other handsome stepson of hers, Accolon was it not? Morgaine, clenching her teeth, thought, *Shall I kill this fool?* But no; the ladies of Gwenhwyfar's court had nothing to do but spend their time in mindless jests and gossip.

"Now tell me—" Alais, who had been waiting-woman when Morgaine was also at Gwenhwyfar's court, and whose bride-woman Morgaine had been when the girl was married, giggled. "Isn't he Lancelet's son, really?"

Morgaine raised her eyebrows and said, "Who? Accolon? King Uriens' late wife would hardly thank you for that imputation, lady."

"You know what I mean." Alais snickered. "Lancelet was the son of Viviane, and you were raised by her—and who could blame you? Tell me the truth now, Morgaine, who was that handsome lad's father? There is no one else it *could* have been, is there?"

Morgause laughed and said, trying to break the tension, "Well, we are all in love with Lancelet, of course—poor Lancelet, what a burden to bear."

"But you are eating nothing, Morgaine," said Gwenhwyfar. "Can I send to the kitchens, if this is not to your liking? A slice of ham? Some better wine than this?"

Morgaine shook her head and put a piece of bread into her mouth. Hadn't this all happened before? Or perhaps she had dreamed it . . . she felt a sick dizziness before her eyes, grey spots dancing. It would indeed give them gossip to enliven many a boring day if the old Queen of North Wales swooned away like a breeding woman! Her fingernails cut into her hands and somehow she managed to make the dizziness recede a little. "I drank too much at the feast yesterday—you have known for twenty years that I have no head for drinking wine, Gwenhwyfar."

"Ah, and it was good wine too," said Morgause, with a greedy smack of her lips, and Gwenhwyfar replied courteously that she would send a barrel of it to Lothian with Morgause when she left. But Morgaine, mercifully forgotten, the blinding headache clamping down over her brow like a torturer's band, felt Morgause's questioning eyes on hers.

Pregnancy was one thing that could not be hidden . . . no, and why should it be hidden? She was lawfully wedded; people might laugh if the old King of North Wales and his middle-aged Queen became parents at their advanced ages, but the laughter would be good-natured. Yet Morgaine felt that she would explode from the sheer force of the anger in her. She felt like one of the fire mountains of which Gawaine had told her, far in the countries to the north. . . .

When the ladies had all gone away and she was alone with Gwenhwyfar, the Queen took her hand and said in apology, "I am sorry, Morgaine, you do look ill. Perhaps you should return to your bed."

"Perhaps I shall," Morgaine said, thinking, *Gwenhwyfar would never guess what was wrong with me; Gwenhwyfar, should this happen to her, would welcome it, even now!*

The Queen reddened under Morgaine's angry stare. "I am sorry, I didn't mean for my women to tease you like that—I should have stopped them, my dear."

"Do you think I care what they say? They are like sparrows chirping, and have as much sense about them," Morgaine said, with contempt as blinding as the pain in her head. "But how many of your women really know who fathered my son? You made Arthur confess it—did you confide it to all your women as well?"

Gwenhwyfar looked frightened. "I do not think there are many who know—those who were there last night, when Arthur acknowledged him, certainly. And Bishop Patricius." She looked up at Morgaine, and Morgaine thought, blinking, *How kindly the years have treated her; she grows even more lovely, and I wither like an ancient briar. . . .*

"You look so tired, Morgaine," said Gwenhwyfar, and it struck Morgaine that in spite of all old enmities, there was love too. "Go and rest, dear sister."

Or is it only that there are so few of us, now, who were young together?

THE MERLIN HAD AGED, too, and the years had not been so kind to him as to Gwenhwyfar; he was more stooped, he dragged his leg now with a walking stick, and his arms and wrists, with their great ropy muscles, looked like branches of an ancient and twisted oak. He might indeed have been one of the dwarf folk of which tales told that they dwelt beneath the mountains. Only the movements of his hands were still precise and lovely, despite the twisted and swollen fingers, his graceful gestures making her think of the old days, and her long study of the harp and of the language of gesture and hand speech.

He was blunt, waving away her offer of wine or refreshment, dropping on a seat without her leave, by old habit.

"I think you are wrong, Morgaine, to harry Arthur about Excalibur."

She knew her own voice sounded hard and shrewish. "I did not expect you to approve, Kevin. No doubt you feel that whatever use he makes of the Holy Regalia is good."

"I cannot see that it is wrong," Kevin said. "All Gods are one—as even Taliesin would have said—and if we join in the service of the One—"

"But it is that with which I quarrel," Morgaine said. "Their God would be the One—and the only—and drive out all mention of the Goddess whom we serve. Kevin, listen to me—can you not see how this narrows the world, if there is one rather than many? I think it was wrong to make

the Saxons into Christians. I think those old priests who dwelt on Glastonbury had the right idea. Why *should* we all meet in one afterlife? Why
should there not be many paths, the Saxons to follow their own, we to
follow ours, the followers of the Christ to worship him if they choose,
without restraining the worship of others. . . ."

Kevin shook his head. "My dear, I do not know. There seems to be
a deep change in the way men now look at the world, as if one truth should
drive out another—as if whatever is not their truth, must be falsehood."

"But life is not as simple as that," Morgaine said.

"I know that, you know that, and in the fullness of time, Morgaine,
even the priests will find it out."

"But if they have driven all other truths from the world, it will be
too late," Morgaine said.

Kevin sighed. "There is a fate that no man, and no woman, may stop,
Morgaine, and I think we are facing that day." He reached out one of his
gnarled hands and took hers; she thought she had never heard him speak so
gently. "I am not your enemy, Morgaine. I have known you since you were
a maiden. And after—" He stopped, and she saw his throat twitch as he
swallowed. "I love you well, Morgaine. I wish you nothing but well. There
was a time—oh, yes, it was long ago, but I forget not how I loved you
and how privileged I felt that I could speak of love to you. . . . No man
can fight the tides, or the fates. Perhaps, if we had sent sooner to Christianize
the Saxons, it would have been done by those same priests who built a chapel
where they and Taliesin could worship side by side. Our own bigotry
prevented that, so it was left to fanatics like Patricius, who in their pride
see the Creator only as the avenging Father of soldiers, not also as the loving
Mother of the fields and the earth. . . . I tell you, Morgaine, they are a tide
that will sweep all men before them like straw."

"Done is done," Morgaine said. "But what is the answer?"

Kevin bent his head and it struck Morgaine that what he really wanted
was to lay that head down on her breast; not now as a man to a woman,
but as if she were the Mother Goddess who could quiet his fear and despair.

"Maybe," he said, his voice stifled, "maybe there is no answer at all.
It may be that there is no God and no Goddess and we are quarrelling over
foolish words. I will not quarrel with you, Morgaine of Avalon. But neither
will I sit idle and let you plunge this kingdom again into war and chaos,
wreck this peace that Arthur has given us. Some knowledge and some song
and some beauty must be kept for those days before the world again plunges
into darkness. I tell you, Morgaine, I have seen the darkness closing. Perhaps,
in Avalon, we may keep the secret wisdom—but the time is past when we
can spread it again into the world. Do you think I am afraid to die so that
something of Avalon may survive among mankind?"

Morgaine—slowly, compelled—put out her hand to touch his face, to wipe away tears; but she jerked her hand back in sudden dread. Her eyes blurred—she had laid her hand on a weeping skull, and it seemed her own hand was the thin, winter-blighted hand of the Death-crone. He saw it too, and stared at her, appalled, for a single terrified moment. Then it was gone again, and Morgaine heard her voice harden.

"So you would bring the holy things into the world, that the holy sword of Avalon may be the avenging sword of Christ?"

"It is the sword of the Gods," Kevin said, "and all the Gods are one. I would rather have Excalibur in the world where men may follow it, than hidden away in Avalon. So long as they follow it, what difference does it make which Gods they call on in doing so?"

Morgaine said, steadily, "It is *that* I will die to prevent. Beware, Merlin of Britain: you have made the Great Marriage and pledged yourself to die for the preservation of the Mysteries. Beware, lest obeying that oath be claimed of you!"

His beautiful eyes looked straight into hers. "Ah, my lady and my Goddess, I beg you, take counsel of Avalon before you act! Indeed, I think the time has come for you to return to Avalon." Kevin laid his hand over hers. She did not draw it away.

Her voice caught and broke with the tears that had laid heavy on her all this day. "I—I wish I might return—it is because I long so much for it that I dare not go thither," she said. "I shall go there never, until I may leave it never more—"

"You *will* return, for I have seen it," said Kevin wearily. "But not I. I know not how, Morgaine, my love, but it comes to me that never again shall I drink of the Holy Well."

She looked at the ugly misshapen body, the fine hands, the beautiful eyes, and thought, *Once I loved this man.* Despite all, she loved him still, she would love him till both of them were dead; she had known him since the beginning of time, and together they had served their Goddess. Time slid away and it seemed that they stood outside time, that she gave him life, that she cut him down as a tree, that he sprang up again in the corn, that he died at her will and she was taken in his arms and brought back to life . . . the ancient priest-drama played out before Druid or Christian set foot upon the earth.

And he would cast this away?

"If Arthur shall forswear his oath, shall I not require it at his hands?"

Kevin said, "One day the Goddess will deal with him in her own way. But Arthur is King of Britain by the will of the Goddess. Morgaine of Avalon, I tell you, beware! Dare you set your face against the fates that rule this land?"

"I do what the Goddess has given me to do!"

"The Goddess—or your own will and pride and ambition for those you love? Morgaine, again I say to you, beware. For it may well be that the day of Avalon is past, and your day with it."

Then the fierce control she had clamped upon herself broke. "And you dare call yourself the Merlin of Britain?" she shrieked at him. "Be gone, you damned traitor!" She picked up her distaff and flung it at his head. "Go! Out from my sight and damn you forever! Go from here!"

8

ten days later, King Arthur, with his sister, Queen Morgaine, and her husband, Uriens of Wales, set forth to ride to Tintagel.

Morgaine had had time to decide what she must do and had found a moment to speak alone with Accolon the day before. "Await me on the shores of the Lake—be certain that neither Arthur nor Uriens sees you." She reached her hand to him in farewell, but he caught her close and kissed her again and again.

"Lady—I cannot bear to let you go into danger this way!"

For a moment she leaned against him. She was so weary, so weary, of being always strong, of making certain that all things went as they must! But he must never suspect her weakness! "There is no help for it, my beloved. Otherwise there would be no answer but death. You cannot come to the throne with the blood of your father on your hands. And when you sit on Arthur's throne—with the power of Avalon behind you and Excalibur in your hand—then you can send Uriens back to his own land, there to rule as long as God wills."

"And Arthur?"

"I mean Arthur no harm, either," said Morgaine steadily. "I would not have him killed. But he shall dwell for three nights and three days in the land of Fairy, and when he returns, five years or more will have passed, and Arthur and his throne will be a tale remembered by the older men, and the danger of a priest rule long past."

"But if he somehow finds his way out—"

Morgaine's voice had trembled. *What of the King Stag when the young stag is grown? It must be with Arthur as the fates decree. And you will have his sword.*

Treachery, she thought, and her heart pounded as they rode through the dismal grey morning. Thin fog was rising from the Lake. *I love Arthur.*

I would not betray him, but he first betrayed the oath he swore to Avalon.

She still felt queasy, the motion of the horse making it worse. She could not remember that she had been sick as this when she carried Gwydion —Mordred, she reminded herself. Yet it might be, when he came to the throne, that he would choose to rule in his own name, the name that had been Arthur's and bore no taint of Christian rule. And when Kevin saw the thing already accomplished, no doubt he too would choose to support the new King of Avalon.

The fog was thickening, making Morgaine's plan even simpler to follow. She shivered, pulling her cloak tight around her. It must be done now, or, as they skirted the Lake, they would turn southward to Cornwall. The fog was so thick already that she could hardly make out the forms of the three men-at-arms who rode ahead of them; twisting in her saddle, she saw that the three men behind were almost equally dim. But the ground for a little way before and behind them was clear, though overhead the fog was like a thick white curtain with no hint of sun or daylight.

She stretched out her hands, raising herself high in her saddle, whispering the words of the spell she had never dared use before. She felt a moment of pure terror—she knew it was only the coldness that came from power draining out of her body—and Uriens, shivering, raised his head and said peevishly, "Such fog as this I have never seen—we will surely be lost and have to spend the night on the shores of the Lake! Perhaps we should seek shelter at the abbey in Glastonbury—"

"We are not lost," said Morgaine, the fog so thick that she could barely see the ground under her horse's hooves. *Oh, as a maiden in Avalon I was so proud that I spoke only truth! Is it queencraft, then, to lie, that I may serve the Goddess?* "I know every step of the way we are going—we can shelter this night in a place I know near the shores, and ride on in the morning."

"We cannot have come so far as that," said Arthur, "for I heard the bells in Glastonbury ring the Angelus—"

"Sounds carry a long way in the fog," Morgaine said, "and in fog such as this they carry further still. Trust me, Arthur."

He smiled lovingly at her. "I have always trusted you, dear sister."

Oh, yes; he had always trusted her, since that day when Igraine had placed him in Morgaine's arms. At first she had hated the squalling thing, and then she had come to know that Igraine had abandoned and betrayed them both, and she must care for him, and had wiped away his tears . . . impatient, Morgaine hardened her heart. That had been a lifetime ago. Since then Arthur had made the Great Marriage with the land and had betrayed it, giving the land he had sworn to protect into the hands of priests who would drive out the very Gods that fed the land and made it fertile. Avalon had set him on his throne, through her hand as priestess, and now

. . . Avalon, through her hand, would bring him down.

I will not hurt him, Mother . . . yes, I will take from him the sword of the
Holy Regalia and give it into the hands of one who will bear it for the Goddess,
but I will never lay hand on him. . . .

But what of the King Stag when the young stag is grown?

That was the way of nature and could not be amended for the sake
of her sentiment. Arthur would meet his fate unprotected by the spells he
bore, by the scabbard she herself had made for him after she had gone to
him in the Great Marriage, when she bore, still not knowing it, his child
within her body. She had often heard his knights speak of his charmed life,
of how he could take the worst of wounds and not lose blood enough to
kill. She would not lay a hand upon her mother's son and the father of her
child. But the spell she had put upon him in the aftermath of her lost
virginity, *that* she might withdraw from him, and then it must be with him
as the Goddess willed.

The magical fog had thickened so much around them that Morgaine
could hardly see Uriens' horse. His face, angry and sullen, swam out of the
mist. "Are you *sure* you know where you are leading us, Morgaine? I have
never been here before, I would swear to it, I know not the curve of that
hill . . ."

"I vow to you, I know every step of the way, fog or no fog." At her
feet Morgaine could see the curious little cluster of bushes unchanged from
that day when she sought entry into Avalon, that day when she had feared
to summon the boat . . . *Goddess,* she prayed to herself, not even a whisper,
grant that the church bells ring not while I seek to enter, lest it vanish back into
the fog and we find never our way into that country. . . .

"This way," she said, picking up her reins and digging her heels into
her horse. "Follow me, Arthur."

She rode swiftly into the fog, knowing they could not follow her so
fast in this absence of light. Behind her she heard Uriens cursing, his voice
cross and muffled, heard Arthur speak reassuringly to his horse. Suddenly
an image flashed into Morgaine's mind, of the skeleton of a horse bearing
her own riding gear . . . well, it must be as it must be. The fog had begun
to thin, and suddenly they were riding in full daylight through the dappled
trees. Clear green light spilled down, though they could see no sun, and she
heard Arthur's cry of surprise.

Out of the forest came two men who cried out in their clear voices,
"Arthur, my lord! It is a pleasure to welcome you here!"

Arthur drew up his horse swiftly, lest he trample the men. "Who are
you, and how do you know my name?" he demanded. "And what is this
place?"

"Why, my lord, this is the Castle Chariot, and our queen has long
desired to receive you as her guest!"

Arthur looked confused. "I did not know there was a castle in these parts. We must have ridden further than we thought in the fog." Uriens looked suspicious, but Morgaine could see the familiar spell of the fairy lands falling over Arthur, so that it never occurred to him to question; as in a dream, whatever happened simply happened, and there was no need to question. But she must keep her wits about her. . . .

"Queen Morgaine," said one of the men, the dark beautiful people who seemed like ancestors or dream versions of the little dark people of Avalon, "our queen awaits and will gladly receive you. And you, my lord Arthur, you shall be taken to feast with us. . . ."

"After all this riding in fog, a feast will be welcome," said Arthur good-naturedly, and let the man lead his horse into the woods. "Do you know the queen of these lands, Morgaine?"

"I have known her since I was a young girl."

And she mocked me . . . and offered to rear my babe in the fairy world. . . .

"It is surprising that she came never to Camelot to offer allegiance," Arthur said, frowning. "I cannot remember, but it seems to me that I heard something of the Castle Chariot a long, long time ago . . . but I cannot quite remember," he said, dismissing it. "Well, in any case these people seem to be friendly. Give my compliments to the queen, Morgaine, and no doubt I shall see her at this feast."

"No doubt," Morgaine said, and watched the men lead him away.

I must keep my wits about me; I will use the beat of my heart to count the time, I will not lose track, or I shall be carried away and entangled in my own spells . . . she braced herself to meet with the queen.

Unchanged she was, always the same, the tall woman who, nevertheless, had something of the look of Viviane about her, as if she and Morgaine were blood kin. And she embraced and kissed her as such.

"What brings you of your free will to our shores, Morgaine of the Fairies?" she asked. "Your knight is here, one of my ladies found him . . ." and she gestured, and Accolon was there. "They found him wandering along the reeds of the Lake, not knowing his way in the fog. . . ."

Accolon gripped Morgaine's hand; she felt it solid and real in hers . . . yet she knew not even now whether they were within or out-of-doors, whether the glass throne of the queen was within a magnificent grove or within a great vaulted hall, more magnificent than the hall of the Round Table at Camelot.

Accolon knelt before the throne, and the queen pressed her hands on his head. She raised one of his wrists and the serpents seemed to move and twine round his arms, crawled away and sat there in the queen's palm where she sat absently playing with them, petting their small blue darting heads. "Morgaine, you have chosen well," she said. "I think not that this one would

ever betray me. Look, Arthur has feasted well, and there he lies—" and she
gestured to where a wall seemed to open wide, and by pale light Morgaine
saw Arthur, sleeping with one arm under his head and the other across the
body of a young girl with long, dark hair, who seemed like a daughter of
the queen—or like Morgaine herself.

"He will, of course, think that it was you, and that it is a dream sent
him by the evil one," said the queen, smiling, "so far he has moved from
us that he will think shame to be given his dearest wish . . . did you not
know that, my Morgaine, my darling?" And it seemed to Morgaine that
she heard Viviane's voice, dreamlike, caressing her. But it was the queen who
said, "So sleeps the King, in the arms of one he will love until he dies
. . . and what when he wakes? Will you take Excalibur and cast him out
naked on the shores, seeking you always in the mists?"

Morgaine remembered suddenly the skeleton of a horse lying beneath
the fairy trees. . . . "Not that," she said, shivering.

"Then he shall remain here, but if he is truly as pious as you say and
thinks to say the prayers which will part him from illusion, it will vanish,
and he will call out for his horse and for his sword—what then shall we
do, lady?"

Accolon said grimly, "I will have the sword, and if he can get it again
from me, he is welcome to it."

The dark-haired maiden came to them, and in her hand she held
Excalibur in its scabbard. "I had it from him while he slept," she said, "and
with it he called me by your name—"

Morgaine touched the jewelled hilt of the blade.

"Bethink you, child," said the queen, "would it not be better to return
the Holy Regalia at once to Avalon, and let Accolon make his way as King
with only such a sword as he can get for himself?"

Morgaine trembled. It seemed very dark in the hall, or grove, or
whatever it was, and did Arthur lie sleeping at her feet, or was he far away?
But it was Accolon who reached out and grasped the sword.

"I will have Excalibur and the scabbard," he said, and Morgaine knelt
at his feet and belted it round his waist.

"Be it so, beloved—bear it more faithfully than he for whom I made
this scabbard—"

"The Goddess forbid I should ever be false to you, though I die for
it," he whispered, his voice shaking with emotion, and raised Morgaine to
her feet and kissed her; it seemed that they clung together till the shadow
of the night faded and the queen's sweet mocking smile seemed to shimmer
around them.

"When Arthur calls for a sword he shall have one . . . and something
like to the scabbard, though it will not keep him from spilling a single drop

of blood. . . . Give it to my smiths," she said to the maiden, and Morgaine stared as if in a dream—had it been in a dream that she had belted Excalibur round Accolon's waist? The queen was gone and the damsel, and it seemed that she and Accolon lay alone in a great grove and that it was the time of the Beltane fires, and he took her into his arms, priest to priestess. And then they were no more than man and woman, and it seemed to her that time stopped, that her body melted into his as if she were without nerve or bone or will, and his kiss was like fire and ice on her lips. . . . *The King Stag should challenge him, and I must make him ready. . . .*

Why, how was it that she lay with him in the grove, signs painted on her naked body, how was it that her body was young and tender, how was it that when he bore his body down into hers there was tearing pain as if he took again the maidenhead she had laid down to the Horned One half a lifetime gone, so that she came maiden to him, as if all her life had never been? Why did it seem that there was a shadow of the antlers over his brow? Who was this man in her arms, and what had time been between them? He lay heavy across her, spent, the sweetness of his breath like honey to her love; she caressed him and kissed him, and as he moved a little away from her, she hardly knew who he was, whether the hair that brushed her face was shining with gold or dark, and it seemed that the little snakes crawled gently down her breasts, which were pink and tender and almost childish, half-formed. The tiny blue serpents twined around her nipples and she felt a thrill of exquisite pain and pleasure at the touch.

And then she knew that if, indeed, she wished it, time would return, and twist upon itself, and she could go forth from the cave on that morning with Arthur, and use her power to bind him to her forever, and none of it would ever have been. . . .

And then she heard Arthur calling out for his sword, and crying out against these enchantments. Very far away and small, as if she were seeing him from midair, she watched him waken and she knew that their destiny, past and future, was in his hands. If he could face what had been between them, if he called her name and begged her to come to him, if he could admit to himself that it was only she that he had loved all these years and that none other had ever come between them . . .

Then should Lancelet have Gwenhwyfar and then should I be queen in Avalon . . . but queen with a child for a consort, and he would fall in his turn to the King Stag. . . .

This time Arthur would not turn from her in horror at what they had done, she would not thrust him away with childish tears . . . it seemed for a moment that all the world waited, echoing, for what Arthur would say. . . .

He spoke and it seemed to ring like the knell of doom through all the world of Fairy, as if the very fabric of time trembled and the weight of years fell.

"Jesus and Mary defend me from all evil," he said. "This is some wicked enchantment, wrought by my sister and her witchcraft!" He shuddered, and called out, "Bring me my sword!"

Morgaine felt it like a tearing pain in her heart. She reached out to Accolon, and again it seemed that there was the shadow of antlers above his brow, and once again Excalibur was belted about his waist—had it always been there?—and the serpents that had twined about her naked body were only fading blue stains about the man's wrists.

She said steadily, "Look, they are bringing him a sword which is like to Excalibur—the fairy smiths have made it this night. Let him go, if you can. But if you cannot—well, do what you must do, beloved. And the Goddess be with you. I will await you in Camelot when you come thither in triumph." And she kissed him and sent him from her.

Never till this moment had she faced it fully: one of them must die, brother or lover, the child she had held in her arms, the Horned One who had been lover and priest and king—

Whatever comes of this day, she thought, *never again, never again shall I know a moment's happiness, since one of those I love must die. . . .*

Arthur and Accolon had gone where she could not follow; there was still Uriens to be considered, and for a moment she considered abandoning him to the fairy realm. He would wander contentedly in the enchanted halls and woods till he died . . . *no. There has been enough death, whatever happens,* Morgaine thought, and turned her thoughts to watch Uriens, where he lay dreaming. Now he sat up as she approached him, looking happily drunken and befuddled. "The wine here is too strong for me," he said. "Where have you been, my dear, and where is Arthur?"

Even now, she thought, *the fairy maiden has brought Arthur the sword so like Excalibur that in enchantment he will believe it so . . . ah, Goddess, I should have sent the sword back to Avalon, why must anyone else die for it?* But without Excalibur, there was no way Accolon could reign as the new King from Avalon. . . *When I am Queen, this land shall be at peace, and the minds of men free, with no priests to tell them what they must do and believe. . . .*

"Arthur has had to go on ahead of us," she said gently. "Come, my dear husband, we must return to Camelot." Such was the enchantment of the fairy country, she realized, that he never questioned this. Horses were brought to them, and the tall, beautiful people escorted them to a place where one of them said, "You can surely find your way from here."

"How quickly the sunlight has gone," Uriens complained, as a grey fog and rain seemed to condense suddenly and fall about them. "Morgaine, how long were we in the queen's country? I feel as if I had been sick of a fever, or enchanted and wandering in a spell. . . ."

She did not answer him. He too, she thought, had had some sport with the fairy maidens, and why not? She cared not how he amused himself, so that he let her alone.

A sharp twinge of sickness reminded her that never once in the fairy country had she thought of the pregnancy which burdened her, and now, when all would be awaiting her word, when Gwydion took the throne and Accolon reigned . . . now she would be heavy of foot and sick, grotesque . . . certainly she was too old to bear a child without risk. Was it too late to find the herbs that would rid her of that unwanted burden? Yet, if she could bear Accolon a son, at this time when the reign went into his hands, how much more would he value her as his queen? Could she sacrifice that hold over him? *A child I could keep, a child I could hold in my own arms, a babe to love . . .*

She could still remember the sweetness of Arthur as a babe, his little arms around her neck. Gwydion had been taken from her, Uwaine had been nine years old when he learned to call her mother. It was a sharp pain and a sweetness beyond love, tugging at her body, the hunger to hold a child again . . . yet reason told her that she could not, at her age, survive the bearing of another child. She rode at Uriens' side as if in a dream. No, she could not survive the bearing of this child, and yet she felt she could not bear to take the irrevocable step that it should die unborn.

My hands will already be stained with the blood of one I love. . . . Ah, Goddess, why do you try me thus? And it seemed that the Goddess wavered before her eyes, now like the fairy queen, now like Raven, solemn and compassionate, now like the Great Sow who had torn out Avalloch's life *. . . and she will devour the child I bear. . . .* Morgaine knew that she was at the edges of delirium, of madness.

Later, I will decide it later. Now my duty is to get Uriens back to Camelot. She wondered how long she had been in the fairy world. Not, she supposed, more than a moon, or the child would make its presence more felt . . . she hoped it had been only a few days. Not too few or Gwenhwyfar would wonder how they had come and gone so swiftly; not too many, or it would be too late to do what she knew she *must* do: she could not bear this child and live.

They arrived in Camelot at midmorning; the journey was, in truth, not very long. Morgaine was grateful that Gwenhwyfar was nowhere to be seen, and when Cai asked after Arthur, she told him, lying this time without a moment's hesitation, that he had been delayed in Tintagel. *If I can kill, lying is no sin so great,* she thought, distracted, but somehow she felt contaminated by the lie, she was priestess of Avalon and she valued the truth of her words. . . .

She took Uriens to his room; the old man was looking weary now and confused. *He is growing too old to reign. Avalloch's death was harder for him than I can know. But he too was reared to the truths of Avalon—what of the King Stag when the young stag is grown?*

"Lie down here, my husband, and rest," she said, but he was fractious.

"I should set out for Wales. Accolon is too young to reign alone, the young puppy. My people need me!"

"They can spare you another day," she soothed him, "and you will be stronger."

"I have been too long away already," he fretted. "And why did we not go on to Tintagel? Morgaine, I cannot remember why we came away! Were we truly in a country where the sun shone always . . . ?"

She said, "I think you must have dreamed it. Why do you not sleep a little? Shall I send for some food for you? I do not think you have eaten this morning—"

But when the food came, the sight and smell of it turned her queasy again. She turned sharply away, trying to conceal it, but Uriens had seen.

"What is it, Morgaine?"

"Nothing," she said angrily. "Eat, and rest."

But he smiled at her, reaching out his hand to draw her to the bedside. He said, "You forget, I have been married before this—I know a breeding woman when I see one." Clearly, he was delighted. "After all these many years—Morgaine, you are pregnant! But that is wonderful—one son is taken from me, but I have another—shall we call this one Avalloch if it is a son, my darling?"

Morgaine flinched. "You forget how old I am," she said, and her face was like stone. "It is not likely I can carry this child long enough that it would live. Do not hope for a son of your old age."

"But we will take good care of you," said Uriens. "You must consult with one of the Queen's own midwives, and if the ride home would make you likely to miscarry, then you must stay here till the child is born."

She wanted to lash out at him, *what makes you think it would be* your *child, old man?* This was Accolon's child, certainly . . . but she could not dismiss the sudden fear that this was, indeed, Uriens' child . . . an old man's child, weakly, some monster like Kevin . . . no, she was surely mad! Kevin was no monster, but had suffered injuries—fire, burns, maiming in childhood, so that his bones had grown awry. But Uriens' child would surely be twisted, deformed, sickly, and Accolon's child would be healthy, strong . . . and she, she was old almost past childbearing; would *her* child be some monster? Sometimes, when women bore babies in their old age, it was so. . . . Was she mad, to let these fantasies turn and sicken her brain like this?

No. She did not want to die, and there was no hope she could bear this child and live. Somehow she must come by the herbs . . . but how? She had no confidante at court; none of Gwenhwyfar's women could she trust enough to get her these things, and if it somehow became court gossip that old Queen Morgaine was pregnant by her still-older husband, how they would laugh!

There was Kevin, the Merlin—but she herself had turned him away, flung his love and loyalty back in his face . . . well, there must be midwives at court, and perhaps she could bribe one of them well enough to stop her mouth. She would tell some pitiful tale of how hard Gwydion's birth had been, how she feared at her age to bear another. They were women, they would understand that well enough. And in her own bag of herbs she had one or two things—mixed with a third, harmless in itself, they would have the effect she wanted. She would not be the first woman, even at court, to rid herself of an unwanted child. But she must do it secretly, or Uriens would never forgive her . . . in the name of the Goddess, what did it matter? By the time it could come to light, she would be Queen here at Arthur's —no, at Accolon's—side and Uriens would be in Wales, or dead, or in hell—

She left Uriens sleeping and tiptoed from the room; she found one of the Queen's midwives, asked her for the third, and harmless, herb, and returning to her room, mixed the potion over her fire. She knew it would make her deathly ill, but there was no help for it. The herb mixture was bitter as gall; she drank it down, grimacing, washed the cup, and put it away.

If only she could know what was happening in the fairy country! If only she could know how her lover fared with Excalibur. . . . She felt nauseated, but she was too restless to lie down on her bed beside Uriens; she could not bear to be alone with the sleeping man nor could she bear to close her eyes for fear of the pictures of death and blood that would torment her.

After a time she took her distaff and spindle and went down into the Queen's hall, where she knew the women—Queen Gwenhwyfar and her ladies, even Morgause of Lothian—would be at their eternal spinning and weaving. She had never lost her distaste for spinning, but she would keep her wits about her, and it was better than being alone. And if it opened her to the Sight, well, at least she would be free of the torment of not knowing what befell the two she loved on the borders of the fairy country. . . .

Gwenhwyfar welcomed her with a chilly embrace and invited her to a seat near the fire and Gwenhwyfar's own chair.

"What are you working at?" Morgaine asked, examining Gwenhwyfar's fine tapestry work.

The Queen proudly spread it out before her. "It is a hanging for the altar of the church—see, here is the Virgin Mary, with the angel come to tell her she will bear the son of God . . . and there stands Joseph all in amazement—see, I have made him old, old with a long beard—"

"If I were old as Joseph, and my promised wife told me, after being closeted with such a handsome young man as yonder angel, that she were with child, I would ask myself some questions about the angel," Morgause said irreverently. For the first time Morgaine wondered how miraculous had that virgin birth been after all? Who knew but the mother of Jesus had been ready to conceal her pregnancy with a clever tale of angels . . . but after all, in all religions but that one, for a maiden to be pregnant by a God was nothing so strange. . . .

I myself, she thought, at the edge of hysteria, taking a handful of carded wool and beginning to twirl the spindle, *I myself gave up my maidenhood to the Horned One and bore a son to the King Stag . . . will Gwydion set me on a throne in Heaven as Mother of God?*

"You are so irreverent, Morgause," Gwenhwyfar complained, and Morgaine quickly complimented Gwenhwyfar on the fineness of her stitches and asked who had drawn the pattern for the picture.

"I drew it myself," said Gwenhwyfar, surprising Morgaine; she had never believed Gwenhwyfar had talents of this sort. "Father Patricius has promised, too, that he will teach me to copy letters in gold and crimson," the Queen said. "He says I have a good hand at it for a woman. . . . I never thought I could do so, Morgaine, and yet you made that fine scabbard Arthur wears—he told me that you broidered it for him with your own hands. It is very beautiful." Gwenhwyfar chattered on, as artlessly as a girl half her age. "I have offered to make him one, many times—I was offended that a Christian king should bear the symbols of heathendom, but he said it was made for him by his own dear, beloved sister and he would never lay it aside. And indeed it is beautiful work . . . did you have gold threads made for it in Avalon?"

"Our smiths do beautiful work," said Morgaine, "and their work in silver and gold cannot be bettered." The spindle's twirling made her sick. How long would it be before the wrenching sickness of the drug would seize on her? The room was close and seemed to smell of the stuffy, airless lives these women led, spinning and weaving and sewing, endless work so that men might be clothed . . . one of Gwenhwyfar's ladies was heavily pregnant and sat sewing on infant's swaddling cloths . . . another stitched an embroidered border to a heavy cloak for father or brother or husband or son . . . and there was Gwenhwyfar's fine stitchery for the altar, the diversion of a queen who could have other women to sew and spin and weave for her.

Round and round went the spindle; the reel sank toward the floor and she twisted the thread smoothly. When had she learned to do this work?

She could not even remember a time when she could not spin a smooth thread . . . one of her earliest memories was of sitting on the castle wall at Tintagel, beside Morgause, spinning; and even then, her thread had been more even than her aunt's, who was ten years her senior.

She said so to Morgause, and the older woman laughed. "You spun finer thread than I when you were seven years old!"

Round and round went the spindle, sinking slowly toward the stone floor; then she wound the thread up on her distaff and meanwhile twisted a fresh handful of wool. . . . As she spun out the thread, so she spun the lives of men—was it any wonder that one of the visions of the Goddess was a woman spinning . . . *from the time a man comes into the world we spin his baby clothes, till we at last spin a shroud. Without us, the lives of men would be naked indeed. . . .*

. . . It seemed to her that, as in the kingdom of Fairy, she had looked through a great opening and seen Arthur asleep at the side of a maiden with her own face, so now a great space opened out, as if it were before her; and as the reel sank to the floor and the thread twisted, it seemed to spin out Arthur's face as he wandered, sword in hand . . . and now he whirled, to see Accolon, bearing Excalibur . . . ah, they were fighting, she could not see their faces now, nor hear the words they flung at one another. . . .

How fiercely they fought, and it seemed strange to Morgaine, watching dizzied as the spindle sank, twirled, rose, that she could not hear the clashing of the great swords . . . Arthur brought down a great blow that would surely have killed Accolon had it struck him fair, but Accolon caught the blow on his shield and only took a wound in the leg—and the wound sliced without blood, while Arthur, taking a glancing blow on the shoulder, began suddenly to bleed, crimson streaks flowing down his arm, and he looked startled, afraid, one hand going in a swift gesture of reassurance to his side where the scabbard hung . . . but it was the sham scabbard, wavering even now in Morgaine's sight. Now the two were mortally locked together, struggling, their swords locked at the hilt as they grappled with their free hands for the advantage . . . Accolon twisted fiercely, and the sword in Arthur's hand, the false Excalibur made by fairy enchantments in a single night, broke off close below the hilt—she saw Arthur twist round in desperate avoidance of the killing blow and kick out violently. Accolon crumpled up in agony, and Arthur snatched the real Excalibur from his hand and flung it as far away as he could, then leaped on the fallen man and wrenched at the scabbard. As soon as he had it in his hand, the flow of blood from the great wound in his arm ceased to bleed, and in turn blood gushed forth from the wound in Accolon's thigh. . . .

Excruciating pain stabbed through Morgaine's whole body; she doubled up with the weight of it. . . .

"Morgaine!" said Morgause sharply, with a catch of breath; then called out, "Queen Morgaine is ill—come tend to her!"

"Morgaine!" Gwenhwyfar cried out. "What is it?"

The vision was gone. However she tried, she could not see the two men, nor which had prevailed, whether one of them lay dead—it was as if a great dark curtain had closed over them, with the ringing of church bells —in the last instant of the vision she had seen two litters carrying the wounded men into the abbey at Glastonbury, where she could not follow. . . . She clung to the edges of her chair as Gwenhwyfar came, with one of her ladies, who knelt to raise Morgaine's head.

"Ah, look, your gown is soaked with blood—this is not any ordinary bleeding."

Morgaine, her mouth dry with the sickness, whispered, "No—I was with child and I am miscarrying—Uriens will be angry with me—"

One of the women, a plump jolly one about her own age, said, "Tsk! Tsk! For shame! So His Lordship of Wales will be angry, will he? Well, well, well, and who chose him for God? You should have kept the old billy goat out of your bed, lady, it is dangerous for a woman to miscarry at your age! Shame on the old lecher to put you so at risk! So *he* will be angry, will he?"

Gwenhwyfar, her hostility forgotten, walked beside Morgaine as they carried her, rubbing her hands, all sympathy.

"Oh, poor Morgaine, what a sad thing, when you had hoped all over again. I know all too well how terrible it must be for you, my poor sister . . ." she repeated, holding Morgaine's cold hands, cradling her shaking head when she vomited in the ghastly sickness that overcame her. "I have sent for Broca, she is the most skilled of the court midwives, she will look after you, poor dear. . . ."

It seemed that Gwenhwyfar's sympathy would choke her. Racked by repeated, agonizing pains, she felt as if a sword had thrust through her vitals, but even so, even so, it was not so bad as Gwydion's birth had been, and she had lived through that . . . shaking, retching, she tried to cling to consciousness, to be aware of what was going on around her. Maybe she had been ready to miscarry anyhow—it was surely too quick for the drug to have worked. Broca came, examined her, smelled at the vomited stuff, and raised her eyebrows knowingly. She said in an undertone to Morgaine, "Lady, you should have taken more care—those drugs can poison you. I have a brew which would have done what you wanted more quickly and with less sickness. Don't worry, I won't speak to Uriens—if he has no more sense than to let a woman of your years try to bear him a child, then what he does not know will do him no harm."

Morgaine let the sickness take her. She knew, after a time, that she was

more gravely ill than they had thought . . . Gwenhwyfar was asking if at
last she wanted to see a priest; she shook her head and closed her eyes, lying
silent and rebellious, not caring now whether she lived or died. Since
Accolon or Arthur must die, she too would go into that shadow . . . why
could she not see them, where they lay within Glastonbury, which of them
would come forth? Surely the priests would tend Arthur, their own Christian king, but would they leave Accolon to die?

*If Accolon must go into the shades, let him go with the spirit of his son to attend
him,* she thought, and lay with tears sliding down her face, hearing in some
distant place the voice of the old midwife Broca. "Yes, it's over. I am sorry,
Your Majesty, but you know as well as I that she is too old to bear children.
Yes, my lord, come and see—" The voice was harsh with asperity. "Men
never think of what they do, and all the bloody mess women have for men's
pleasure! No, it was all too soon to tell whether it would have been a boy or
not, but she had had one fine son, I doubt not she would have borne you
another, had she been strong enough and young enough to carry it!"

"Morgaine—dearest, look at me," Uriens pleaded. "I am so sorry, so
sorry you are ill, but don't grieve, my darling, I still have two sons, I don't
blame you—"

"Oh, you don't, do you?" said the old midwife, still truculent. "You
had better not speak one word of blame to her, Your Majesty, she is still
very weak and sick. We will have another bed put in here so that she may
sleep in peace till she is quite well again. Here—" and Morgaine felt a
comforting woman's arm under her head; something warm and comforting
held to her lips. "Come, dear, drink this now, it has honey in it, and
medicines to keep you from bleeding anymore—I know you are sick, but
try to drink it anyhow, there's a good girl—"

Morgaine swallowed the bittersweet drink, tears blurring her vision.
For a moment it seemed that she was a child, that Igraine held her and
comforted her in some childish sickness. "Mother—" she said, and even as
she spoke knew it was delirium, that Igraine had been dead for half a
lifetime, that she was no child or maiden, but old, old, too old to lie here
in this ugly way and so near death. . . .

"No, Your Majesty, she doesn't know what she's saying—there, there,
dear, you just lie still and try to sleep, we've got hot bricks on your feet
and you'll be warm in a minute—"

Soothed, Morgaine floated away into dream. Now it seemed to her
that she was a child again in Avalon, in the House of Maidens, and that
Viviane was speaking to her, telling her something she could not quite
remember, something of how the Goddess spun the lives of men, and she
handed Morgaine a spindle and bade her spin, but the thread would not
come smooth, but tangled and knotted and at last Viviane, angry with her,

said, "Here, give it to me . . ." and she handed over the broken threads and the spindle; only it was not Viviane, either, but the face of the Goddess, threatening, and she was very small, very small . . . spinning and spinning with fingers too small to hold the distaff, and the Goddess bore the face of Igraine. . . .

She came to awareness a day or two later, cool-headed, but with a vast and empty ache in her body. She laid her hands over the soreness, and thought, grimly, *I might have saved myself some pain; I should have known that I was ready to miscarry anyway. Well, done is done, and now I must ready myself to hear that Arthur is dead, I must think what I will do when Accolon returns —Gwenhwyfar shall go into a nunnery, or if she wishes to go beyond the seas to Less Britain with Lancelet, I will not stop them. . . .* She rose and dressed herself, made herself beautiful.

"You should keep your bed, Morgaine, you are still so pale," said Uriens.

"No. There are strange tidings coming, my husband, and we must be ready for them," she said, and went on braiding her hair with scarlet ribbons and gems. Uriens stood at the window and said, "Look, the Companions are practicing their military games—Uwaine, I think, is the best rider. Come, my dear, does he not ride as well as Gawaine? And that is Galahad at his side. Morgaine, don't grieve for the child you lost. Uwaine will always think of you as his mother. I told you when we were wedded, I would never reproach you for barrenness. I would have welcomed another child, but since it was not to be, well, we have nothing to grieve for. And," he said shyly, taking her hand, "perhaps it is better so—I did not realize how near I had come to losing you."

She stood at the window, his arm about her waist, feeling at one and the same time a feeling of revulsion and a gratitude for his kindness. He need never know, she thought, that it had been Accolon's son. Let him take pride that in his old age he could father a child.

"Look," said Uriens, craning his neck to see further, "what is that, coming through the gate?"

A rider, together with a monk in dark habit on a mule, and a horse bearing a body—"Come," she said, pulling at his hand, "we must go down now." Pale and silent, she moved at his side into the courtyard, feeling herself tall and commanding as befitted a queen.

It seemed that time stopped; as if they were again in the fairy country. Why was not Arthur with them, if he had triumphed? But if this was Arthur's dead body, where was the ceremony and pomp on the death of a king? Uriens reached to support her with his arm, but she thrust it away and stood clinging to the wood-framed door. The monk put back his hood and said, "Are you Queen Morgaine of Wales?"

"I am," she said.

"I have then a message for you," he said. "Your brother Arthur lies wounded in Glastonbury, nursed by the sisters there, but he will recover. He sends you this"—he waved his hand at the shrouded figure on the pack horse—"as a present, and he bid me say to you that he has his sword Excalibur, and the scabbard." And as he spoke he twitched away the pall covering the body, and Morgaine, all the strength in her body running out of her like water, saw Accolon's sightless eyes staring at the sky.

Uriens cried out, a great cry like death. Uwaine thrust his way through the crowd around the steps, and as his father fell, stricken, across the body of his son, Uwaine caught and supported him.

"Father, dear Father! Ah, dear God, Accolon," he said with a gasp, and stepped toward the horse where Accolon's body lay. "Gawaine, my friend, give my father your arm—I must see to my mother, she is fainting—"

"No," said Morgaine. "No." She heard her own voice like an echo, not even sure what she wanted to deny. She would have rushed to Accolon, flung herself on his body shrieking in despair and grief, but Uwaine held her tight.

Gwenhwyfar appeared on the stairway; someone explained the situation to her in a whisper, and Gwenhwyfar came down the steps, looking at Accolon. "He died in rebellion against the High King," she said clearly. "Let there be no Christian rites for him! Let his body be flung to the ravens, and his head hung on the wall as a traitor!"

"No! Ah, no," cried out Uriens, wailing. "I beg of you, I beg—Queen Gwenhwyfar, you know me one of your most loyal subjects, and my poor boy has paid for his crimes—I beg you, lady, Jesus too died a common criminal between thieves, and even for the thief on the cross at his side there was mercy. . . . Show the mercy he would have shown. . . ."

Gwenhwyfar seemed not to hear. "How does my lord Arthur?"

"He is recovering, lady, but he has lost much blood," said the strange monk. "Yet he bade you have no fear. He will recover."

Gwenhwyfar sighed. "King Uriens," she said, "for the sake of our good knight Uwaine, I will do as you wish. Let the body of Accolon be borne to the chapel and there laid in state—"

Morgaine found her voice to protest. "No, Gwenhwyfar! Lay him in earth decently, if you can find it in your heart to do so much, but he was no Christian—do not give him Christian burial. Uriens is so filled with grief he knows not what he says."

"Be still, Mother," said Uwaine, gripping her shoulder hard. "For my sake and my father's, bring no scandal here. If Accolon served not the Christ, then has he all the more need of God's mercy against the traitor's death he should have had!"

Morgaine wanted to protest, but her voice would not obey her. She let Uwaine guide her indoors, but once within the door she threw off his arm and walked alone. She felt frozen and lifeless. Only a few hours gone, it seemed to her, she had lain in Accolon's arms in the fairy country, had belted the sword Excalibur at his waist . . . now she stood knee-deep in a relentless tide, watching it all swept away from her again, and the world was filled with the accusing eyes of Uwaine and his father.

"Aye, I know it was you who plotted this treachery," said Uwaine, "but I have no pity for Accolon, who let himself be led astray by a woman! Have decency enough, Mother, not to drag my father any further into your wicked schemes against our king!" He glared at her, then turned to his father, who stood as if dazed, clutching at some piece of furniture. Uwaine put the old man into a chair, knelt and kissed his hand. "Father dear, I am still at your side. . . ."

"Oh, my son, my son—" Uriens cried out, despairing.

"Rest here, Father, you must be strong," he said. "But now let me care for my mother. She is ill, too—"

"Your mother, you call her!" Uriens cried out, starting upright and staring at Morgaine with implacable wrath. "Never again let me hear you call that abominable woman Mother! Do you think I know not that by her sorcery she led my good son into rebellion against his king? And now I think by her evil witchcraft she must also have contrived the death of Avalloch —aye, and of that other son she should have borne to me—three sons of mine has she sent down into death! Look out that she does not seduce you and betray you with her witchcraft, into death and destruction—no, she is not your mother!"

"Father! My lord!" Uwaine protested, and held out a hand to Morgaine. "Forgive him, Mother, he does not know what he is saying, you are beside yourselves with grief, both of you—I beg you in God's name to be calm, we have had enough grief this day—"

But Morgaine hardly heard him. This man, this husband she had never wanted, he was all that was left of the wreck of her plans! She should have left him to die in the fairy country, but now he was doddering around in the fullness of his useless old life and Accolon was dead, Accolon who sought to bring back all that his father had pledged and forsworn, all that Arthur had vowed to Avalon and forsaken . . . and nothing was left but this ancient dotard. . . .

She snatched the sickle knife of Avalon from her girdle and thrust away Uwaine's restraining arms. Rushing forward, she raised the dagger high; she hardly knew what it was she meant to do as it flashed down.

An iron grip caught her wrist, wrenching at the dagger. Uwaine's hand came near to breaking her wrist as she struggled. "No, let it go . . . Mother!"

he pleaded. "Mother, is the Devil in you? Mother, look, it is only Father . . . ah, God, can you not show some pity for his grief? He does not mean to accuse you, he is so miserable he does not know what he is saying, in his right mind he will know that what he says is wild nonsense . . . I do not accuse you either . . . Mother, Mother, listen to me, give me the dagger, dear Mother. . . ."

The repeated cries of "Mother!" and the love and anguish in Uwaine's voice finally reached down through the mist that blurred Morgaine's eyes and mind. She let Uwaine wrench away the little knife, noticing, as if from a thousand leagues away, that there was blood on her fingers where the razor edge of the sickle had cut her as they struggled. His hand was cut too, and he put his finger in his mouth and sucked at it as if he had been ten years old.

"Father dear, forgive her," Uwaine begged, bending over Uriens, who lay white as death. "She is distraught, she loved my brother too—and remember how ill she has been, she should not have left her bed today at all! Mother, let me send for your women to take you back to bed—here, you will want this," he said, pressing the sickle back into her hand. "I know you had it from your own foster-mother, the Lady of Avalon, you told me that when I was just a little boy. Ah, poor little mother," he said, encircling her shoulders with his arms. She could remember when she had been taller than he, when he was a thin little boy with bones as small and green as a bird's, and now he towered over her, holding her gently against him. "Mother dearest, my poor little mother, come now, come, don't cry, I know you loved Accolon just as you loved me—poor Mother—"

Morgaine wished that she could cry indeed, that she could let all this terrible grief and despair rush out of her with tears, as she felt Uwaine's hot tears falling on her own forehead. Uriens too stood weeping, but she stood tearless and cold. The world seemed all grey, crumbling at the edges, and everything she looked on seemed to take on some giant menacing shape and yet to be very small and far away, as if she could pick it up like a toy . . . she dared not move lest it should fall to bits at her touch, she hardly knew it when her women came. They took her stiff and unresisting body and lifted her and carried her to bed, they took off the queenly crown and the gown she had put on for her triumph, and distantly she knew that her shift and underlinen were soaked again with blood, but it seemed not to matter. A long time after, she came to herself and knew that she was washed clean and dressed in a clean shift and lying in bed beside Uriens, with one of her women drowsing on a stool at her side. She raised herself a little and looked down at the sleeping man, his face sunken and reddened with weeping, and it was as if she looked on a stranger.

Yes, he had been good to her in his own way. *But now that is all past and my work in his land is done. I will never see his face again while I live, nor know where he lies in death.*

Accolon was dead and her plans in ruins. Arthur still bore the sword Excalibur and the enchanted scabbard which gave him a charmed life, and since the one to whom she had entrusted that task had failed her, escaping into death where she could not follow, then she herself must be the hand of Avalon to strike him down.

Moving so silently that she would not have wakened a sleeping bird, she put on her clothes and tied the dagger of Avalon at her waist. She left all the fine gowns and jewels that Uriens had given her, wrapping herself in her plainest dark robe, not unlike the dress of a priestess. She found her little bag of herbs and medicines, and in the dark, by touch, she painted her brow with the dark moon. Then she took the plainest cloak she could find —not her own, embroidered with gold thread and precious stones, but a servant's rough hooded wrap—and stole noiselessly down the stairs.

From the chapel she heard sounds of chanting; somehow Uwaine had arranged this over Accolon's body. Well, it did not matter. Accolon was free, what did it matter what mummery the priests made with the tenantless clay? Nothing mattered now but reclaiming the sword of Avalon. She turned her back on the chapel. One day she would have leisure to mourn him; now she must carry on where he had failed.

She went silently into the stable and found her horse, managing to bind on the saddle with clumsy hands. She led the animal to the small side gate.

She was almost too dizzy to climb into the saddle, and for a moment she sat swaying, wondering if she would fall. Should she wait, or try to summon Kevin to attend her? The Merlin of Britain was vowed to follow the will of the Lady. But she could not trust Kevin either, he had betrayed Viviane into the hands of those priests who now chanted their hymns over Accolon's helpless body. She whispered to the horse, felt him break into a trot beneath her, and from the foot of the hill turned back to look her last on Camelot.

I shall come here but once again in this life, and then there will no longer be a Camelot to which I might return. And even as she whispered the words, she wondered what they meant.

As OFTEN AS MORGAINE had travelled to Avalon, she had only once set foot upon the Isle of the Priests; Glastonbury Abbey, where Viviane lay buried and Igraine, too, had spent her last years, was a stranger journey to her than the crossing of the mists into the hidden lands. There was a ferry there, and she gave the ferryman a small coin to row her across the Lake, wondering what the man would do if she suddenly rose as she would do with the Avalon barge and cast the spell that would lead it into the mists and bring it forth in Avalon . . . but she did not. *Is it only that I cannot?* she asked herself.

The air was cool and fresh in the hour just before sunrise. Overhead, the sound of church bells was soft and clear, and Morgaine could see a long line of grey-robed forms pacing slowly toward the church. The brothers rose early to pray and chant their soft hymns, and for a moment Morgaine stood quiet, listening. Her mother, and Arthur's, lay buried there. Viviane, too, had been laid to rest within the sound of those hymns. The musician in Morgaine, always quickly moved, listened to the soft song, borne on the early-morning breeze, and for a moment she stood motionless, tears burning her eyes; was she planning outrage on this holy soil? *Let it go, let there be peace among you, children* . . . it seemed that it was Igraine's forgotten voice murmuring to her.

Now all the grey forms were within the church. She had heard much of the abbey here . . . she knew there was a brotherhood of monks, and at some distance from them, a house of nuns where women dwelt, vowed to be virgins of the Christ till they died. Morgaine wrinkled her face in distaste; a God who chose to keep men and women with their thoughts on Heaven rather than on this world, which had been given to them for learning and growing in spirit, seemed alien to her, and now that she actually saw men and women mingling this way in worship with no thought of any other touch or communication, she felt sickened. Oh yes, there were holy virgins in Avalon—she herself had been secluded that way till the proper time, and Raven had given not only her body but her very voice to the Goddess for her use. There was her own foster-daughter, Lancelet's daughter Nimue, who had been selected by Raven to dwell unseen in solitude . . . but the Goddess recognized that this was a rare choice, not one to be imposed on every woman who sought to serve her.

Morgaine did not believe what some of her companions in Avalon had said, that monks and nuns merely pretended holiness and chastity to impress the peasants with their purity and behind the closed doors of their monasteries did whatever wantonness they would. Yes, she would have despised that. Those who had chosen to serve spirit rather than flesh should do so in truth; hypocrisy was always disgusting. But the knowledge that they really lived that way, that any force calling itself divine could prefer barrenness to fruitfulness—*that* seemed to her a terrible betrayal of the very forces which gave life to the world.

Fools and worse, narrowing their lives and thus wishing to narrow all other lives to their own mean compass . . .

But she must not linger here. She turned her back on the church bells

and stole toward the guest house, her mind reaching out, calling on the Sight
to lead her to where Arthur lay.

There were three women in the guesthouse—one dozing beside the
door, another stirring a kettle of gruel in the kitchen at the back, and yet
a third at the door of the room where very dimly she could feel Arthur's
presence; he was deep in slumber. But the women in their somber robes and
veils stirred as she came; they were holy women in their own way, and they
had something very like the Sight—in her presence they could sense something inimical to their lives, the touch, perhaps, of the strangeness of Avalon.

One of them rose and confronted her, asking in a whisper, "Who are
you, and why have you come here at this hour?"

"I am Queen Morgaine of North Wales and Cornwall," Morgaine said
in her low, commanding voice, "and I am here to see my brother. Will
you dare to forbid me?"

She held the woman's gaze, then waved her hand in the simplest of
the spells she had been taught, to dominate, and the woman sank back,
unable to speak or forbid her. Later, she knew, the woman would tell a tale
of enchantments and of fear, but in truth it was no more than this: the simple
domination of a powerful will over one which had been given up, deliberately, to submission.

A soft light burned inside the room, and by its dimness Morgaine could
see Arthur, unshaven, haggard, his fair hair darkened with sweat. The
scabbard was lying on the foot of his bed . . . he must have anticipated some
such action on her part, he would not let it out of his reach. And in his hand
he held the hilt of Excalibur.

Somehow, somehow, his mind gave him warning. Morgaine was filled
with dismay. He had the Sight, too; though he looked so fair and unlike
the dark people of Britain, he too was of the ancient royal line of Avalon
and he could reach her thoughts. She knew that if she reached out to take
Excalibur from his hand, he would sense her intent, would wake—and he
would kill her; she had no illusions about that. He was a good Christian,
or so he thought himself, but he had been set on the throne to kill his
enemies, and in some mystical way Morgaine only half understood, the
sword Excalibur had grown entangled with the very soul and spirit of
Arthur's kingship. If it had not been so, if it had only been a sword, then
would he have been willing to render it back to Avalon and had another
made for himself, a stronger sword and a better . . . but Excalibur had
become for him the visible and ultimate symbol of what he was as King.

*Or perhaps it is the sword itself which has entangled itself with Arthur's soul
and kingship and will kill me of its own will, should I seek to take it from him
. . . and dare I set myself against the will of such a magical symbol?* Morgaine
started and told herself not to be fanciful. She laid her hand on her dagger;

it was razor sharp and she could move, when she must, as swiftly as a striking snake. She could see the small vein in his throat and knew that if she could cut swift and deep to where the great artery lay beneath it, he would be dead almost before he could cry out.

She had killed before this. She had sent Avalloch without hesitation to his death, and not three days since, she had slain the harmless child in her womb . . . he who lay sleeping before her was the greater traitor, surely. One stroke, swift and quiet . . . ah, but this was the child Igraine had placed in her arms, her first love, the father of her son, the Horned God, the King. . . . *Strike, fool! For this you came here!*

No. There has been too much death. We were born from a single womb and I could not face my mother in the country beyond death, not with the blood of my brother on my hands, and for a moment, knowing she moved at the very edge of madness, she heard Igraine calling impatiently, *Morgaine, I told you to take care of the baby . . .*

It seemed to her that he stirred in sleep, as if he too heard that voice; Morgaine slid the dagger back into its sheath, reached out her hand, and took the scabbard. This at least she had a right to take—with her own hands she had fashioned it, the spells she had woven into it were her own.

She hid the scabbard under her cloak and went swiftly out through the thinning darkness to the ferry. As the ferryman rowed her across, she felt the prickling of her skin and seemed to see, like a shadow, the barge from Avalon . . . on the far shore they were all around her, the crew of the Avalon barge. Now quickly, quickly, she must get back again to Avalon . . . but the sun was rising and the shadow of the church lay across the water, and suddenly the sun flooded the landscape and with the dawn a ringing of church bells was everywhere. Morgaine stood as if paralyzed; through that sound she could not summon the mists, nor speak the spell.

She said to one of the men, "Can you take us to Avalon? Quickly?"

He said, shivering, "I cannot, lady. It grows harder, without a priestess to speak the spell, and even so, at dawn and at noon and at sunset, when they ring the bells for prayer, there is *no* way to cross the mists. Not now. The spell no longer opens the way at these times, although, if we wait till the bells are silent, it may be that we can manage to return."

Why, Morgaine wondered, should this be so? It had to do with the knowledge that the world was as it was because of what men believed it was . . . year by year, these past three or four generations, the minds of men had been hardened to believing that there was *one* God, *one* world, *one* way of describing reality, and that all things which intruded on the realm of that great one-ness must be evil and of the fiends, and that the sound of the bells and the shadow of their holy places would keep the evil afar. And as more and more people believed this, it *was* so, and Avalon no more than a dream adrift in an almost inaccessible other world.

Oh yes, she could still call the mists . . . but not here, not where the shadow of the church's spire lay across the water and the clamor of the bells struck terror into her heart. They were trapped on the shores of the Lake! And now she was aware that a boat was pushing out from the shores of the priests' Isle, to cross the Lake and find her here. Arthur had wakened and found her scabbard gone from him, and now would pursue her. . . .

Well, let him follow her as he could, there were other ways into Avalon where the shadow of the church did not prevent her passage. She climbed quickly into her saddle and began to ride along the shores of the Lake, circling; she would come at last to a place where, at least in summer, she could cross through the mists; the place where she and Lancelet had once found Gwenhwyfar strayed from the nunnery. It was not Lake but swampland, and they could get into Avalon by the back way, behind the Tor.

She knew that the little dark men were running behind her horse, that they could run for half a day at her horse's tail if they must. But now she heard hoofbeats . . . she was pursued, Arthur was hard on her heels, and there were armed knights with him. She dug her feet into the horse's side, but this was a lady's horse, not intended for the chase. . . .

She slid down her horse's side, the scabbard in her hand. "Scatter," she whispered to the men, and one by one it was as if they melted into the trees and mists . . . they could move like shadows if they must, and no man alive could find them if they did not want to be found. Morgaine grasped the scabbard in her hand and began to run along the shores of the Lake. In her mind she could hear Arthur's voice, feel his rage. . . .

He had Excalibur; she could feel it, like a great shining in her mind, the holy thing of Avalon . . . but the scabbard he should never bear again. She took it in both hands, whirled it over her head, and flung it, with all her strength, far out into the Lake, where she saw it sink into the deep and fathomless waters. No human hand could ever reclaim it—there it would lie till leather and velvet rotted and the silver and gold thread tarnished and twisted and at last the spells woven into them vanished utterly from the world.

Arthur was riding in pursuit, Excalibur naked in his hand . . . but she and her escort were gone. Morgaine drew herself into silence, a part of shadow and tree as if some essential part of herself had gone into Fairy; while she stayed there motionless, covered in the silence of a priestess, no one from the mortal world could see so much as her shadow. . . .

Arthur shouted her name.

"Morgaine! Morgaine!" A third time he called, loud and angry; but the very shadows were still, and at last, confused from riding in circles—

once he came so close that Morgaine could feel the breath of his horse—
he wearied, and called to his escort, and they came to find him swaying in
his saddle, the bandages slowly soaking through with blood, and they led
him away the way they had come.

Then Morgaine raised her hand, and once again the normal sound of
bird and wind and tree came back into the world.

MORGAINE SPEAKS . . .

*In later years I heard the tale told of how I took the scabbard by sorcery,
and how Arthur rode after me with a hundred knights, and I too had a hundred
fairy knights all round me; and when Arthur's pursuit grew near, I turned myself
and my men into ring stones. . . . Someday, no doubt, they will add that when
I had done, I called for my chariot with the winged dragons, and flew away into
Fairy.*

*But it was not so. It was no more than this, that the little people can hide
in the forests and become one with tree and shadow, and that day I was one of
them, as I had been taught in Avalon; and when Arthur had been taken away by
his escort, near to fainting with the long pursuit and the cold in his wound, I said
farewell to the men of Avalon, and rode away to Tintagel. But when I came to
Tintagel it mattered little to me what they did in Camelot, for I was sick even
to death for a long time.*

*I know not, even now, what ailed me; I know only that summer faded and
the leaves began to fall while I lay in my bed, tended by the servants I had found
there, neither knowing nor caring whether I would ever rise. I know I had a low
fever, a weariness so great that I could not force myself to sit upright or to eat,
a heaviness of mind so great that I cared not whether I would live or die. My
servants—one or two of them I recalled from the days when I lived there as a little
child, with Igraine—thought me enchanted; and it may even have been true.*

*Marcus of Cornwall sent to me in homage, and I thought, Arthur's star rides
high, no doubt he believes that I have come here at Arthur's will, and he will not
—now—challenge Arthur even for these lands he believes his own. A year ago,
I might have laughed at this, or even made common cause with Marcus, promising
him lands here in return for leading a party of the disaffected against Arthur. And
even now it crossed my mind; but with Accolon dead, it seemed to matter nothing.
Arthur had Excalibur . . . if the Goddess wished that it should be taken from him,
she would have to come and take it herself, for I had failed, I was her priestess
no more. . . .*

*. . . I think it was that which hurt me worst, that I had failed, failed Avalon,
that she had not put forth her hand to help me do her will. The strength of Arthur
and the priests and of the traitor Kevin had been stronger than the magic of Avalon,
and there was no one left.*

No one left. No one. I mourned without ceasing for Accolon, and for the child whose life had barely begun before it was ended, cast aside like offal. I mourned too for Arthur, lost to me now, and my enemy, and, unbelievably, even for Uriens, and for the wreck of my life in Wales, the only peace I had ever known.

I had killed or thrust from me or lost to death everyone in this world I had ever loved. Igraine was gone, and Viviane lost to death, murdered and lying among the priests of their God of death and doom. Accolon was gone, the priest I had consecrated to do that last battle against the Christian priests. Arthur was my enemy; Lancelet had learned to hate and fear me, and I was not guiltless for that hate. Gwenhwyfar feared and loathed me, even Elaine was gone now . . . and Uwaine, who had been as my own son, hated me too. There was none to care whether I should live or die, and so I did not care either. . . .

The last of the leaves had gone and the fearful storms of winter had begun to beat over Tintagel when one day one of my women came to me and said that a man had come to seek me.

"At this season?" I looked out beyond the window, where unceasing rain beat down from skies as grey and bleak as the inside of my own mind. What traveller would come through this bitter weather, struggling through storms and darkness? No; whoever he might be, I cared not. "Say to him that the Duchess of Cornwall sees no man, and send him away."

"Into the rain on a night such as this will be, lady?" I was startled that the woman should protest; most of them feared me for a sorceress, and I was content to have it so. But the woman was right; Tintagel had never failed in hospitality when it was in the hands of my long-dead father, or of Igraine . . . so be it. I said, "Give the traveller hospitality fitting his rank, and food, and bed; but tell him that I am ill, and cannot receive him."

She went away and I lay watching the fierce rain and darkness, feeling its cold breath through the slit of the window and trying to find my way back into the peaceful blankness where now I felt most like myself. But after a very little, the door opened again and the woman returned, and I started upright, shaking with anger, the first emotion I had let myself feel in many weeks.

"I have not summoned you, and I did not bid you return! How dare you?"

"I am charged with a message for you, lady," she said, "a message I didn't dare say no to, not when one of the high ones speaks. . . . He said, 'I speak not to the Duchess of Cornwall but to the Lady of Avalon, and she cannot refuse the Messenger of the Gods when the Merlin seeks audience and counsel.'" The woman paused and said, "I hope I've got it right . . . he made me say it over twice to be sure I had it all."

Now, against my will, I felt the stirrings of curiosity. The Merlin? But Kevin was Arthur's man, surely he would not have come like this to me. Had he not aligned himself firmly with Arthur and with the Christians, traitor to Avalon? But perhaps some other man now held that office, Messenger of the Gods, Merlin of

Britain . . . and now I thought of my son Gwydion, or Mordred as I supposed I must now think of him; perhaps this was his office, for he alone would now think of me as Lady of Avalon. . . . After a long silence, I said, "Tell him I will see him, then." After a moment I added, "But not like this. Send someone to dress me." For I knew that I was too weak to put on my own clothes. But I would not receive any man this way, weak and ill and in my bedchamber; I, who was priestess of Avalon, would manage to stand on my feet before the Merlin, even if what he brought was sentence of death for all my failure . . . I am still Morgaine!

I managed to rise, to have my dress put on and my shoes, and my hair braided down my back and covered with the veil of a priestess; I even painted, after the woman's clumsy hands had twice botched it, the symbol of the moon on my forehead. My hands—I noted it incuriously, as if they belonged to someone else—were shaking, and I was weak enough that I let the woman give me her arm as I crawled down the steep stairs. But the Merlin should not see my weakness.

A fire had been built in the hall; the fire was smoking a little, as always here when it rained, and through the smoke I could see only a man's figure seated by the fire, turned away from me, draped in a grey cloak—but at his side stood a tall harp I could not mistake; from My Lady I knew the man. Kevin's hair was all grey now, but he dragged his stooped body upright as I came in.

"So," I said, "you call yourself still Merlin of Britain, when you serve only Arthur's will and defy that of Avalon?"

"I know not what to call myself now," said Kevin quietly, "save perhaps servant of those who serve the Gods, who are all One."

"Why have you come here, then?"

"Again, I know not," said the musical voice I had loved so well, "save perhaps in repayment of some debt laid down before these hills were raised, my dear." Then he raised his voice to the serving-woman.

"Your lady is ill! Get her to a seat!"

My head was swimming and a grey mist seemed to waver around me; the next thing I knew I was seated by the fire across from Kevin, and the woman was gone.

He said, "Poor Morgaine, poor girl," and for the first time since Accolon's death had turned me to stone, I felt that I could weep; and clenched my teeth against the weeping, for if I shed one tear, I knew that everything within me would melt, and I would cry and cry and cry and never cease crying until I melted into a very lake of tears. . . .

I said tightly, clenched, "I am no girl, Kevin Harper, and you have won your way to my presence falsely. Now say what you will say, and go your way."

"Lady of Avalon—"

"I am not," I said, and remembered that the last time I saw this man, I had driven him from my presence, shrieked at him, called him traitor. It seemed not to matter; perhaps it was fate that two traitors to Avalon should sit here before this *fire, for I too had betrayed my oath to Avalon . . . how dared I judge Kevin?*

"What then are you?" he asked quietly. "Raven is old, and silent now for years. Niniane will never have the power to rule. You are needed there—"

"When last we spoke," I interrupted him, "you said Avalon's day was done. Why then should there be any to sit in Viviane's place except a child half-fitted for that high office, waiting for the day when Avalon fades forever into the mists?" I felt a scalding bitterness in my throat. "Since you have forsaken Avalon for the banner of Arthur, will it not make your task easier if none reigns in Avalon save an ancient prophetess and a powerless priestess . . . ?"

"Niniane is Gwydion's love and his creature," said Kevin. "And it comes to me that your voice and your hands are needed there. Even if Avalon is fated to pass away into the mists, will you refuse to pass with it? I never thought you a coward, Morgaine." And then he raised his eyes to mine and said, "You will die here, Morgaine, die of grief and exile . . ."

I turned my face away and said, "For that I came here . . ." and for the first time I knew indeed that I had come here to die. "All I have tried to do is in ruin, I have failed, failed . . . it should be your triumph, Merlin, that Arthur has won."

He shook his head. "Ah, no, my dear, no triumph," he said. "I do what the Gods have given me to do, no more, and you do the same. And indeed if your doom shall be to see the end of the world we have known, why then, my dearest love, let that doom find us each in our appointed place, serving what our God has given us to serve. . . . It is laid on me to recall you to Avalon, Morgaine, I know not why. My task would be simpler with only Niniane there, but, Morgaine, your place is in Avalon, and mine where the Gods shall decree. And in Avalon you can be healed."

"Healed." I said it in contempt. I did not care.

Kevin looked at me sadly. "My dearest love," he had called me. It seemed to me now that he was the one person alive who knew me as I was; before every other person alive, even Arthur, I had worn a different face, seeking always to appear other and better than I was; even to Viviane, that she might find me more worthy to be a priestess. . . . For Kevin I was Morgaine, thus and no other. It came to me that even if I stretched forth my hand to him as the Death-crone he would see nothing but my own face, Morgaine. . . . I had always felt that love was other than this, was that burning I had felt for Lancelet, for Accolon. For Kevin I had felt little save for that detached compassion, friendship, kindness; what I had given him had meant but little to me, and yet . . . and yet he alone had taken thought to come to me, to care whether or no I died here of grief.

But how dared he break in upon my peace, when I had almost won through to that utter quiet which was beyond life? I turned away from him and said, "No." I could not come back to life again, could not struggle and suffer, and live with the hatred of those who had once loved me. . . . *If I lived, if I returned to Avalon, I must enter again into a death struggle with Arthur whom I loved, I must see Lancelet still in Gwenhwyfar's prison of love. I had ceased to care, I could endure no further the pain that was in my heart. . . .*

No. I was here, in silence and peace, and before long, I knew it now, I would pass even further into peace . . . the dizziness that was near to death was drawing closer and ever closer, and this Kevin, this traitor, would bring me back? I said, "No," again and turned away, my hands covering my face. "Leave me in peace, Kevin Harper. Hither I came to die. Leave me now."

He did not move, nor did he speak, and I sat very still, my veil over my face. After a little time, surely, now he would arise and leave me, for I had not the strength to go forth from him. And I . . . I would sit here until I was carried back to my bed by the women, and then I would never rise again.

And then, into the silence, I heard the soft sound of the harp. Kevin played, and after a moment he sang.

I had heard a part of this ballad, for he had sung it often at Arthur's court, of that bard in ancient times, sir Orfeo, who made the trees to dance and the stones on the plain to stand in a ring and dance, and all the beasts of the wood to come and lay themselves at his feet when they should have rent him with their claws. But beyond that, today, he sang the other part of the song, which was a Mystery, and which I had never heard before. He sang of how the initiate, Orfeo, had lost her that he loved, and had descended into the Afterworld and spoken there before the Lords of Death, and pleaded for her, and was given permission to go into the dark lands, and bring her forth, and then he had found her there on the Undying Plains. . . .

And then his voice spoke from the soul . . . and I heard what seemed my own voice pleading.

"Seek not to bring me forth, when I am resigned to stay here in death. Here within these undying lands all is at rest, with neither pain nor struggle; here can I forget both love and grief."

The room faded away around me; no longer could I smell the smoke from the fireplace, the chill breath of rain beyond the window, I was no longer conscious of my own body, ill and dizzy where I sat. It seemed to me that I stood in a garden filled with scentless flowers and eternal peace, with only the distant voice of the harp breaking unwillingly through the silence. And that harp sang to me, undesired.

It sang of the wind from Avalon, with the breath of apple blossom and the smell of ripened apples in their season; it brought to me the cool freshness of the mist over the Lake, and the sounds of the running deer deep in the forest where the little folk live still, and it brought me the sun-soaked summer where I lay in the sun beneath the ring stones, with Lancelet's arms round me and the blood of life rising like sap within my veins for the first time. Then I felt again in my arms *the heavy softness of my little son, his soft hair against my face, his milky breath sweet and soft . . . or was it Arthur himself in my lap, clinging to me, his little hands patting my cheek . . . again Viviane's hands touched my brow in blessing, and I felt myself a bridge between earth and sky as I stretched my own hands forth in invocation . . . high winds swirled through the grove where I lay with the young stag in the darkness of the eclipse, and Accolon's voice spoke my name. . . .*

And now it was not the harp alone but the voices of the dead and the living crying out to me: "Return again, return, life itself is calling you with all its pleasure and pain . . ." and then a new note came into the voice of the harp.

"It is I who calls you, Morgaine of Avalon . . . priestess of the Mother . . ."

And I raised my head, seeing not Kevin's twisted body and sorrowing features, but where he had stood was Someone, tall and shining, a sunlit glory about his face and in his hands the shining Harp and Bow. I caught my breath before the God, as the voice sang on . . . "Return to life, return again to me . . . you who have sworn . . . life awaits you beyond this darkness of death. . . ."

I struggled to turn away. "It is not the God who can command me, but the Goddess. . . ."

"But," said the familiar voice in the silence of that eternity, "you are the Goddess and it is I who call you . . ." and for a moment, as if in the calm waters of the mirror of Avalon, I saw myself robed and crowned with the high crown of the Lady of Life. . . .

"But I am old, old, I belong now to death, not to life . . ." I whispered, and in the silence, words heard again and again in ritual suddenly came to life on the lips of the God.

". . . she will be old and young as it shall please her . . ." and before my eyes my own mirrored face was again young and fair as the maiden who had sent forth the young stag to challenge the running deer . . . yes, and I had been old when Accolon came to me, yet I had sent him forth to the challenge heavy with his child . . . and even old and barren, yet life pulsed within me as within the eternal life of the earth and the Lady . . . and the God stood before me, the eternal One who summoned me forth to life . . . and I took one step and then another, and then I was climbing, climbing from the darkness, following the distant notes of the harp that sang to me of the green hills of Avalon, and the waters of life . . . and then I found I was on my feet, reaching for Kevin . . . and he put the harp gently aside and caught me, half-fainting, in his arms. And for a moment the shining hands of the God burned me . . . and then it was only Kevin's sweet, musical, half-mocking voice that said, "I cannot hold you, Morgaine, as well you know," and he placed me gently into my chair. "When did you eat last, Morgaine?"

"I cannot remember," I confessed, and suddenly I was aware of my deathly weakness; he called the serving-woman and said, speaking in the gently authorita-

tive voice of a Druid and a healer, "Bring your mistress some bread and some warmed milk with honey."

I raised a hand to protest, and the woman looked indignant, and now I remembered that twice she had tried to coax me to eat with these very things. But she went to do his bidding, and when she returned, Kevin took the bread and soaked it in the milk and fed it to me, gently, a few mouthfuls at a time.

"No more," he said. "You have been fasting too long. But before you sleep, you must drink a little more milk with an egg beaten into it . . . I will show them what to do. The day after tomorrow, perhaps, you will be strong enough to ride."

And suddenly I began to cry. I wept, at last, for Accolon lying dead on his pall, and for Arthur who hated me now, and for Elaine who had been my friend . . . and for Viviane, lying dead beneath a Christian tomb, and for Igraine, and for myself, for myself who had lived through all these things . . . and he said again, "Poor Morgaine, poor girl," and held me against his bony breast, and I cried and cried until at last I was quiet, and he called my women to carry me to my bed.

And for the first time in many days, I slept. And two days later, I rode to Avalon.

I remember little of that northward journey, sick in body and mind. I did not even wonder that Kevin left me before I came to the Lake. I came to those shores at sunset, when the waters of the Lake seemed to run crimson and the sky was all afire; and out of the flame-colored water and sky appeared the barge, painted and draped all in black, oars muffled to the silence of a dream. And for a moment it seemed to me that it was the Sacred Boat on that shoreless sea of which I may not speak, and that the dark figure at the prow was She, and that somehow I bridged the gap between earth and sky . . . but I do not know whether that was real or a dream. And then the mists fell over us, and I felt within my very soul that shifting which told me I was once again within my own place.

Niniane welcomed me at the shore, taking me in her arms, not as the stranger I had seen but twice, but as a daughter greets a mother she has not seen for many years; then she took me away to the house where once Viviane had dwelt. She did not, this time, send young priestesses to tend me, but cared for me herself, putting me to bed in the inner room of the house, bringing me water from the Sacred Well; and when I tasted it, I knew that although the healing would be long, I was not yet beyond healing.

I had known enough of power. I was content to lay down the burdens of the world; it was time to leave that to others, and to let my daughters tend me. Slowly, slowly, in the silence of Avalon, I recovered my strength. There at last I could mourn for Accolon—not for the ruin of my hopes and plans . . . I could see now what madness they had been; I was priestess of Avalon, not Queen. But I could mourn the brief and bitter summer of our love; I could grieve, too, for the child who had not lived long enough to be born, and suffer once again that it had been my own hand that had sent him into the shades.

It was a long season of mourning, and there were times when I wondered if I should mourn all my life and never again be free of it; but at last I could remember without weeping, and recall the days of love without unending sorrow welling up like tears from the very depths of my being. There is no sorrow like the memory of love and the knowledge that it is gone forever; even in dreams, I never saw again his face, and though I longed for it, I came at last to see that it was just as well, lest I live all the rest of my life in dreams . . . but at last there came a day when I could look back and know that the time for mourning was ended; my lover and my child were on the other shore, and even if I should somehow meet them beyond the gates of death, none of us would ever know . . . but I lived, and I was in Avalon, and it was my task now to be Lady there.

I do not know how many years I dwelt in Avalon before the end. I remember only that I floated in a vast and nameless peace, beyond joy and sorrow, knowing only serenity and the little tasks of every day. Niniane stood ever at my side; and I came, too, to know Nimue, who had grown to a tall, silent, fair-haired maiden, as fair as Elaine when first I knew her. She became to me the daughter I had never known, and day after day she came to me, and I taught her all those things I had learned from Viviane in my own early years in Avalon.

In those last days, too, there were some who had seen the tree of the Holy Thorn in its first flowering for the followers of Christ, and worshipped their Christian God in peace, seeking not to drive out the beauty of the world, but loving it as God made it. In those days they came in numbers to Avalon to escape the harsh and shrivelling winds of persecution and bigotry. Patricius had set up new forms of worship, a view of the world wherein there was no room for the real beauty and mystery of the things of nature. From these Christians who came to us to escape the bigotry of their own kind I learned something, at last, of the Nazarene, the carpenter's son who had attained Godhead in his own life and preached a rule of tolerance; and so I came to see that my quarrel was never with the Christ, but with his foolish and narrow priests who mistook their own narrowness for his.

I know not whether it was three years, or five, or even ten, before the end. I heard whispers of the outside world like shadows, like the echo of the church bells we heard sometimes even on that shore. I knew when Uriens died, but I did not mourn him; he had been dead to me for many years, but I could hope that in the end he had found some healing for his griefs. He had been kind to me as best he might, and so let him rest.

Now and again some rumor of Arthur's deeds and those of the knights would come to me, but in the serenity of Avalon it seemed not to matter; those deeds sounded like old tales and legends, so that I never knew whether they spoke of Arthur and Cai and Lancelet, or of Llyr and the children of Da'ana; or when tales were whispered of the love of Lancelet and Gwenhwyfar, or later, of Marcus' wife,

Isotta, and young Drustan, they were not after all retelling some old tale of Diarmid and Grainné from the ancient days. It seemed not to matter, it seemed that I had heard all these tales long ago in my childhood.

And then, one spring when the land lay beautiful before us and the first apple trees of Avalon were white with blossom, Raven broke silence with a cry, and perforce my mind returned to the things of that world I had hoped to leave forever behind.

9

t**he** sword, the sword of the Mysteries is gone . . . now look to the cup, now look to all of the Holy Regalia . . . it is gone, it is gone, taken from us. . . ."

Morgaine heard the cry out of sleep, and yet, when she tiptoed to the door of the room where Raven slept, alone and in silence as ever, the women who attended her slept; *they* had not heard that cry.

"But there is nothing but silence, Lady," they told her. "Are you certain it was not an evil dream?"

"If it was an evil dream, then it came to the priestess Raven as well," Morgaine said, staring at the untroubled faces of the girls. It seemed to her that with every passing year, the priestesses in the House of Maidens grew younger and more like children . . . how could little girls like this be entrusted with the holy things? Maidens whose breasts had scarcely formed . . . what could they know of the life of the Goddess which was the life of the world?

Again, it seemed, that shattering cry rang through Avalon, rousing alarm everywhere, but when Morgaine asked, "There—did you hear?" they looked at her again in dismay and said, "Do you dream now, Lady, with your eyes wide open?" and Morgaine realized that in the bitter cry of terror and grief there had been no actual sound.

She said, "I will go to her—"

"But you may not do that—"one of them began, then stepped back, her mouth open, as she realized the full meaning of who Morgaine was, and she bent her head as Morgaine stepped past her.

Raven was sitting up in bed, her long hair flung about her in mad disarray, and her eyes wild with terror; for a moment Morgaine thought that indeed her mind had overheard some evil dream, that Raven walked in the worlds of dream. . . .

But she shook her head and then she was wide awake and sober. She drew a long breath, and Morgaine knew that she was struggling to speak, to overcome the years of silence; now it was as if her voice would not obey her.

At last, trembling all over, she said, "I saw—I saw it . . . treachery, Morgaine, within the very holy places of Avalon. . . . I could not see his face, but I saw the great sword Excalibur in his hand . . ."

Morgaine put out a hand, quieting her. She said, "We will look within the mirror when the sun rises. Do not trouble yourself to speak, my dearest." Raven was still trembling; Morgaine put her hand firmly over Raven's, and by the flickering light of the torch, she saw that her own hand was lined and spotted with the dark spots of age, that Raven's fingers were like twisted ropes around the narrow, fine bones. *We are old,* she thought, *both of us, who came here maidens in attendance on Viviane . . . ah Goddess, the years that pass. . . .*

"But I must speak now," Raven whispered. "I have been silent too long . . . I kept silence even when I feared this would come . . . listen to the thunder, and the rain—a storm is coming, a storm to break over Avalon and sweep it away in the flood . . . and darkness over the land . . ."

"Hush, my dear! Be still," Morgaine whispered, and put her arms around the shaking woman, wondering if her mind had snapped, if this was all an illusion, a fever dream . . . there was no thunder, no rain, outside the moon was shining brilliantly over Avalon and the orchards white with blossom in the moonlight. "Don't be frightened. I will stay here with you, and in the morning we shall look into the mirror and see if any of this is real."

Raven smiled, a sad smile. She took Morgaine's torch and put it out; in the sudden darkness Morgaine could see, through the chinks in the wattle, a sudden flare of lightning in the distance. Silence; and then, very far away, a low thundering. "I do not dream, Morgaine. The storm will come, and I am afraid. You have more courage than I. You have lived in the world and known real sorrows, not dreams . . . but now, perhaps, I must go forth and break silence forevermore . . . and I am afraid. . . ."

Morgaine lay down beside her, pulling Raven's cover over them both, and took Raven in her arms to still her shaking. As she lay quiet, listening to the other woman's breathing, she remembered the night she had brought Nimue there, and how Raven had come to her then, welcoming her to Avalon . . . *why does it seem to me now that of all the love I have known, that is the truest . . .* but she only held Raven gently, the other woman's head on her shoulder, soothing her. After a long time there was a great clap of thunder, startling them, and Raven whispered, "You see?"

"Hush, my dear, it is only a storm." And as she spoke the rain came down, rushing and rattling, bringing a chilly wind within the room, drowning speech. Morgaine lay silent, her fingers just entwined with Raven's, and thought, *It is only a storm,* but something of Raven's terror communicated itself to her and she felt herself shivering too.

A storm that will drive down out of Heaven and smash into Camelot, and scatter the years of peace that Arthur has made in this land . . .

She tried to call the Sight to her, but the thunder seemed to drown thoughts; she could only lie close to Raven repeating to herself again and again, *It is only a storm, a storm, rain and wind and thunder, it is not the wrath of the Goddess. . . .*

AFTER A LONG TIME the storm subsided, and she woke to a world new-washed, the sky pallid and cloudless, water shimmering on every leaf and raining down from every blade of grass, as if the world had been dipped in water and not dried or shaken. If Raven's storm were to break in truth over Camelot, would it leave the world thus beautiful in its wake? Somehow she thought not.

Raven woke and looked at her, wide-eyed with dread. Morgaine said, quiet and practical as always, "We shall go to Niniane at once, then to the mirror before the sun rises. If the wrath of the Goddess is to descend on us, we must know how and why."

Raven gestured her silent assent, but when they were dressed and about to leave the house, Raven touched Morgaine's arm. "Go to Niniane," she whispered, with the racking struggle to make her unused voice do her bidding. "I will bring—Nimue. She too is part of this. . . ."

For a moment Morgaine was startled almost to protest; then, with a glance at the paling sky in the east, she went. It might be that Raven had seen, in the evil dream of prophecy, the reason that Nimue had been brought here and kept in seclusion. Remembering the day when Viviane had told her of her own mission, she thought, *Poor girl!* But it was the will of the Goddess, they were all in her hands. As she went silent and alone through the wet orchard, she could see that all was not so calm and beautiful after all . . . the wind had ravaged the blossoms and the orchard lay under a white drift like snow; there would be little fruit this autumn.

We may plant the grain and till the soil. But only her favor brings the fruit to harvest. . . .

Why then do I trouble myself? It will be as she wills. . . .

Niniane, roused from sleep, looked at her as if she were mad. She is no true priestess, Morgaine thought; the Merlin spoke the truth—she was chosen only because she was Taliesin's kin. *The time has come, perhaps, to stop pretending who is truly the Lady of Avalon and take my proper place.* She did not want to offend Niniane, or seem to strive for power and set the younger woman down, she had had enough of power . . . but no true priestess, chosen of the Goddess, could have slept through Raven's cry. Yet somehow this woman before her had passed through the ordeals which go to the making of a priestess; the Goddess had not rejected her. What would the Goddess have her do?

"I tell you, Niniane, I have seen it and so has Raven . . . we must look before sunrise into the mirror!"

"I put not much faith in such things, either," said Niniane quietly. "What must come, will surely come . . . but if you will, Morgaine, I will go with you—"

Silent, like spots of blackness in the white and watery world, they moved toward the mirror below the Sacred Well. And as they went Morgaine could see, like a shadow at the corner of her eyes, the tall silent form of Raven, veiled, and Nimue like a pale shadow, all blossom and pale flowers like the morning. Morgaine was struck at the girl's beauty—even Gwenhwyfar in the fullest flush of her youth had never been so beautiful. She felt a wild stab of pure jealousy and anguish. *I had no such gift from the Goddess in return for all I must sacrifice . . .*

Niniane said, "Nimue is a maiden. It is she who must look into the mirror."

Their four dark forms were reflected in the pallid surface of the pool, against the pale reflection of the sky, where a few pale-pink streaks were beginning to herald the sunrise. Nimue moved to the edge of the pool, parting her long fair hair with both hands, and Morgaine found herself seeing in her mind the surface of a silver bowl, and Viviane's stilled, hypnotic face. . . .

Nimue said in a low, wandering voice, "What would you that I should see, my mother?"

Morgaine waited for Raven to speak, but there was only silence. So Morgaine said at last, "Has Avalon been breached and fallen victim to treachery? What has befallen the Holy Regalia?"

Silence. Only a few birds chirped softly in the trees, and the soft sound of water rippled, falling from the channel which overflowed from the Well to make this still pool. Below them on the slopes Morgaine could see the white drifts of the ruined orchards, and high above, the pale shapes of the ring stones atop the Tor.

Silence. At last Nimue stirred and whispered, "I cannot see his face . . ." and the pool rippled, and it seemed that Morgaine could see a hunched form, moving slowly and with difficulty . . . the room where she had stood silent that day behind Viviane, when Taliesin laid Excalibur in Arthur's hand and she heard his voice forbidding . . .

"No—it is death to touch the Holy Regalia unprepared. . . ." For a moment Morgaine could hear the voice of Taliesin, not Nimue's voice . . . but he had the right, he was the Merlin of Britain, and he took them from the hiding place, spear and cup and dish, and hiding the holy things under his cloak, he went out and across the Lake to where Excalibur gleamed in the darkness . . . the Holy Regalia now reunited.

"Merlin!" whispered Niniane aloud. "But why?"

Morgaine knew her face was like stone as she said, "Once he spoke of this to me. He said that Avalon was now outside the world, and that the holy things must be within the world to the service of man and the Gods, by whatever name men called them. . . ."

"He would profane them," Niniane said hotly, "and put them to the use of that God who would drive out all other Gods. . . ."

In the silence, Morgaine heard the chanting of monks. Then the sunlight touched the mirror and turned it all to shooting fire which flooded her head and eyes, burning, blazing, and in the glare of the rising sun it seemed as if all the world burned in the light of a flaming cross. . . . She shut her eyes, covering her face with her hands.

"Let them go, Morgaine," whispered Raven. "The Goddess will certainly care for her own. . . ."

Again Morgaine could hear the chanting of the monks—*Kyrie eleison, Christe eleison . . . Lord, have mercy, Christ, have mercy. . . .* The Holy Regalia were but tokens, surely the Goddess had let this befall them as a sign that Avalon needed these things no more, that they should go into the world and be in the service of men. . . .

The flaming cross burned still before Morgaine's eyes; she covered them and turned away from the light. "Even I cannot abrogate the Merlin's vow. He swore a great oath and made the Great Marriage with the land in the King's stead, and now he is forsworn and his life forfeit. But before I deal with the traitor, I must deal with the treachery. The Regalia must be returned to Avalon, even if I must bring them hither again with my own hands. I will go forth to Camelot at dawn." And she suddenly saw her plan complete as Nimue whispered, "Must I go forth too? Is it mine to avenge the Goddess?"

She, Morgaine, would deal with the Holy Regalia. They had been left in her care, and if only she had taken her proper place here instead of revelling in sorrow and considering her own comfort, this could never have come to pass. But Nimue should be the instrument of the traitor's punishment.

Kevin had never seen Nimue. Of all those who dwelt on Avalon, the Merlin had never seen that one who dwelt in seclusion and silence. And as always transpires when the Goddess brings down punishment, it should be the Merlin's own undefended fortresses which should bring him to ruin.

She said slowly, clenching her fists . . . how had she ever softened to that traitor? . . . "You shall go forth to Camelot, Nimue. You are Queen Gwenhwyfar's cousin and the daughter of Lancelet. You will beg her that you may dwell among her ladies, and beg her to keep it secret, even from King Arthur, that you have ever dwelt in Avalon. Pretend even, if you must, that you have become a Christian. And there you will come to know the Merlin. He has a great weakness. He believes that women shun him because he is ugly and because he is lame. And for the woman who shows no fear or revulsion of him, for that woman who shows him again the manhood he craves and fears, he will do anything, he would give his very life. . . . Nimue," she said, looking straight into the girl's frightened eyes, "you will seduce him to your bed. You will bind him to you with such spells that he is your slave, body and soul."

"And then—" said Nimue, trembling, "what then? Must I kill him?"

Morgaine would have spoken, but Niniane spoke first.

"Such death as you could give would be all too swift for such a traitor. You must bring him, enchanted, to Avalon, Nimue. And there he shall die a traitor's cursed death within the oak grove."

Trembling, Morgaine knew what fate awaited him—to be flayed alive, then thrust living within the cleft of the oak, and the opening stopped with wattle and daub, leaving only enough space so that his breath would not fail, lest he die too quickly. . . . She bowed her head, trying to conceal her shudder. The blinding sun was gone from the water; the sky dripped with pale dawn clouds. Niniane said, "Our work is done here. Come, Mother —" but Morgaine pulled herself free.

"Not done—I too must go forth for Camelot. I must know to what use the traitor has put the Holy Regalia." She sighed; she had hoped never again to go forth from the shore of Avalon, but there was no other to do what must be done.

Raven put out her hand. She was shaking so terribly that Morgaine feared she would fall; and now she whispered, her ruined voice only a distant hiss and scratching like wind against dead branches, "I too must go . . . it is my fate, that I shall not lie where all those before me have lain in the enchanted country . . . I ride with you, Morgaine."

"No, no, Raven," Morgaine protested. "Not you!" Raven had never set foot off Avalon, not in fifty years . . . surely she could not survive the journey! But nothing she could say shook Raven's determination; shivering with terror, she was adamant: she had seen her destiny and must go with Morgaine at any cost.

"But I am not going as Niniane would travel, in the pomp of priestess garb, in the litter of Avalon, riding in state to Camelot," she argued. "I am going in disguise as an old peasant woman, as Viviane travelled so often in the old days." But Raven shook her head and said, "Any road you can travel, Morgaine, I too can travel."

Morgaine still felt a deadly fear—not for herself, but for Raven. But she said, "Be it so," and they made ready to ride. And later that day they took their secret ways out of Avalon, Nimue travelling in state as the kinswoman of the Queen, riding on the main roads, and Morgaine and Raven, wrapped in the somber rags of beggar women, out of Avalon by the back ways and side roads, making their way on foot toward Camelot.

Raven was stronger than Morgaine had believed; as they made their way, day by day, slow-paced and afoot, at times it seemed that she was the stronger. They begged broken meats at farm doors, they stole a bit of bread left for a dog at the back of a farmstead, they slept once in a deserted villa and one night beneath a haystack. And on that last night, for the first time on their silent journey, Raven spoke.

"Morgaine," she said, when they were lying side by side, wrapped in their cloaks, under the shadow of the hay, "tomorrow is Easter at Camelot, and we must be there at dawn."

Morgaine would have asked why, but she knew Raven could give her no answer but this—that she had seen it as their fate. And so she answered, "Then we shall leave here before dawn. It is no more than an hour's walk from here—we might have kept walking and slept in the shadow of Camelot, if you had told me this before, Raven."

"I could not," Raven whispered. "I was afraid." And Morgaine knew that the other woman was weeping in the darkness. "I am so frightened, Morgaine, so frightened!"

Morgaine said brusquely, "I told you that you should have remained in Avalon!"

"But I had the work of the Goddess to do," whispered Raven. "In all these years I have dwelt in the shelter of Avalon, and now it is Ceridwen, our Mother, who demands my all in return for all the shelter and safety I have had from her . . . but I am afraid, so afraid. Morgaine, hold me, hold me, I am so frightened—"

Morgaine clasped her close and kissed her, rocking her like a child. Then, as if they entered together into a great silence, she held Raven against her, touching her, caressing her, their bodies clinging together in something like frenzy. Neither spoke, but Morgaine felt the world trembling in a strange and sacramental rhythm around them, in no light but the darkness of the dark side of the moon—woman to woman, affirming life in the shadow of death. As maiden and man in the light of the spring moon and the Beltane fires affirmed life in the running of spring and the rutting which would bring death in the field to him and death in childbearing to her; so in the shadow and darkness of the sacrificed god, in the dark moon, the

priestesses of Avalon together called on the life of the Goddess and in the
silence she answered them. . . . They lay at last quiet in each other's arms,
and Raven's weeping was stilled at last. She lay like death, and Morgaine,
feeling her heart slowing to stillness, thought, *I must let her go even into the
shadow of death if that is the will of the Goddess. . . .*

And she could not even weep.

No ONE took the slightest notice of two peasant women, no longer young,
in the turmoil and tumult about the gates of Camelot this morning. Morgaine was used to this; Raven, who had lived so long in seclusion even on
quiet Avalon, turned white as bone and tried to hide herself under her
ragged shawl. Morgaine also kept her own shawl about her—there were
some who would recognize the lady Morgaine, even with her hair streaked
with white and in the garb of a peasant woman.

A drover striding through the yard with a calf ran into Raven and
came near to knocking her down, and he cursed her when she only stared
at him in dismay. Morgaine said quickly, "My sister is deaf and dumb," and
his face changed.

"Ah, poor thing—look, go up by there, they're giving everybody a
good dinner at the lower end of the King's hall. You two can creep in at
that door and watch them when they come in—the King's got some big
thing planned with one of the priests in the hall today. You'll be from
upcountry and not know his ways? Well, everyone in this countryside
knows that he makes it a custom—he never sits down to his great feasts
unless there's some great marvel arranged, and we heard today that there is
to be something truly marvelous."

I doubt it not, Morgaine thought disdainfully, but she only thanked the
man in the rough country dialect she had used before and drew Raven along
with her toward the lower hall, which was filling rapidly—King Arthur's
generosity on feast days was well known, and this would be the best dinner
many people had all year. There was a smell of roasting meat in the air, and
most of the people jostling round her commented greedily on it. As for
Morgaine, it only made her feel sick, and after one look at Raven's white
terrified face, she decided to withdraw.

*She should not have come. It was I who failed to see the danger to the Holy
Regalia; it was I who failed to see that the Merlin was traitor. And when I have
done what I must do, how will I manage to flee to Avalon with Raven in this
condition?*

She found a corner where they would be disregarded, but where they
could see reasonably well what was happening. At the higher end of the
room was the great mead-hall table, the Round Table which was already

almost legendary in the countryside, with the great dais for the King and Queen, and the painted names of Arthur's Companions over their customary places. On the walls hung brilliant banners. And after years spent in the austerity of Avalon, this all seemed gaudy and garish to Morgaine.

After a long time there was a stir, and then the sound of trumpets somewhere, and a whisper ran through the jostling crowd. Morgaine thought, *It will be strange to see the court from outside, after being a part of it for so long!* Cai was opening the great doors to the upper end of the hall, and Morgaine shrank—Cai would know her, whatever garb she wore! But why should he even look in her direction?

How many years had she spent quietly drifting in Avalon? She had no idea. But Arthur seemed even taller, more majestic, his hair so fair that no one could have told whether or no there were silver strands among the carefully combed curls. Gwenhwyfar, too, although her breasts sagged under the elaborate gown, bore herself upright and seemed slim as ever.

"Look how young the Queen looks," muttered one of Morgaine's neighbors, "yet Arthur married her the year I had my first son, and look at me." Morgaine glanced at the speaker, bent and toothless, stooped like a bent bow. "I heard that witch sister of the King, Morgaine of the Fairies, gave them both spells to keep their youth. . . ."

"Spells or no," mumbled another toothless crone tartly, "if Queen Gwenhwyfar had to muck out a byre night and morning, and bear a babe every year and suckle it in good times and bad, there'd be none of that beauty left, bless her! Things are as they are, but I wish some priest'ud tell me why she gets all the good in life and I get all the misery?"

"Stop grumbling," said the first speaker. "You'll have your belly full today, and get to see all the lords and ladies, and you know what the old Druids used to say about why things are what they are. Queen Gwenhwyfar up there gets fine gowns and jewels and a queen's business because she did good in her last lives, and the likes of you and me are poor and ugly because we were ignorant, and someday, if we mind what we do in this life, there's a better fortune for us too."

"Oh, aye," grunted the other old woman, "priests and Druids are all alike. The Druid says that, and the priest says if we do our duty in this life we'll go to Heaven and live with Jesus and feast with him there and never come back to this wicked world at all! It all winds up the same, whatever the lot of them say—some are born in misery and die in misery, and others have it all their own way!"

"But she's none so happy, I've heard," said another of the group of old women wedged in together. "For all her queening it, she's never borne a single babe, and I have a good son to work the farm for me, and one daughter married to the man at the next farm, and another who's servant to the nuns on Glastonbury. And Queen Gwenhwyfar has had to adopt sir Galahad there, who's the son of Lancelet and of her own cousin Elaine, for Arthur's heir!"

"Oh, aye, that's what they *tell* you," said a fourth old woman, "but you know and I know, when Queen Gwenhwyfar was absent from court in the sixth or seventh year of his reign—something like that—don't you think they were all counting on their fingers? My stepbrother's wife was a kitchen woman here at court, and he said it was common talk all round here that the Queen spent her nights in another bed than her husband's—"

"Keep quiet, old gossip," said the first speaker. "Just let one of the chamberlains hear you say that aloud, and you'll be ducked in the pond for a scold! I say Galahad's a good knight and he'll make a good king, long live King Arthur! And who cares who his mother is? I think meself he's one of Arthur's by-blows—he's fair like him. And look yonder at sir Mordred—everybody knows *he's* the King's bastard son by some harlot or other."

"I heard worse than that," said one of the women. "I heard Mordred's the son of one of the fairy witches and Arthur took him to court in pawn for his soul, to live a hundred years—you'll see, he'll not age, sir Mordred there. Just look at Arthur, he must be past fifty and he could be a man in his thirties!"

Another old woman spoke a barnyard obscenity. "What's it to me, all of that? If the Devil were about business like that, he could have made yonder Mordred in Arthur's own image so anyone could accept him as Arthur's son! Arthur's mother was of the old blood of Avalon—did you never see the lady Morgaine? She was dark too, and Lancelet, who's his kin, was like that. . . . I'd rather believe what they said before, that Mordred is Lancelet's bastard son by the lady Morgaine! You've only got to look at them—and the lady Morgaine pretty enough in her way, little and dark as she was."

"She's not among the ladies," one of the women remarked, and the woman who had known a kitchen woman at court said authoritatively, "Why, she quarreled with Arthur and went away to the land of Fairy, but everybody knows that on All Hallows Night she flies round the castle on a hazel twig annd anyone who catches sight of her will be struck blind."

Morgaine buried her face in her ragged cloak to smother a giggle. Raven, hearing, turned an indignant face to Morgaine, but Morgaine shook her head; they must keep still and not be noticed.

The knights were seating themselves in their accustomed places. Lancelet, as he took his seat, raised his head, looking sharply round the hall, and for a moment it seemed to Morgaine that he sought her out where she stood, that his eyes met hers—shivering, she ducked her head. Chamberlains were moving at both ends of the hall, pouring wine for the Companions and their ladies, pouring good brown beer from great leather jacks down among the peasants crowded in at the lower end. Morgaine held out her cup and Raven's, and when Raven refused, she said in a harsh whisper, "Drink it! You look like death, and you must be strong enough for whatever is coming." Raven put the wooden cup to her lips and sipped, but she could hardly swallow. The woman who had said that the lady Morgaine was pretty enough in her way asked, "Is she sick, your sister?"

Morgaine said, "She is frightened, she has never seen the court before."

"Fine, aren't they, the lords and ladies? What a spectacle! And we'll get a good dinner soon," said the woman to Raven. "Hey, doesn't she hear?"

"She is not deaf, but dumb," Morgaine said again. "I think maybe she understands a little of what I say to her, but no one else."

"Now you come to speak of it, she does look simpleminded, at that," said the other woman, and patted Raven on the head like a dog. "Has she always been like that? What a pity, and you have to look after her. You're a good woman. Sometimes when children are like that, their folks tie them to a tree like a stray dog, and here you take her to court and all. Look at the priest in his gold robes! That's the bishop Patricius, they say he drove all the snakes out of his own country . . . think of that! Do you think he fought them with sticks?"

"It's a way of saying he drove out all the Druids—they are called serpents of wisdom," Morgaine said.

"How'd the likes of you know a thing like that?" Morgaine's interrogator scoffed. "I heard for sure that it was snakes, and anyhow all those wise folk, Druids and priests, they hang together, they wouldn't quarrel!"

"Very likely," said Morgaine, not wanting to draw further attention to herself, her eyes going to Bishop Patricius. Behind him there was someone in the robes of a monk—a hunched figure, bent over and moving with difficulty—now what was the Merlin doing in the bishop's train? She said, her need to know overcoming the risk of attracting attention, "What's going to happen? I thought surely they would have heard their mass in the chapel this morning, all the lords and ladies—"

"I heard," said one of the women, "that since the chapel would hold so few, there would be a special mass here today for all the folk before meat —see, the bishop's men carrying in that altar with the white cloth and all. Ssssh—listen!"

Morgaine felt that she would go mad with rage and despair. Were they going to profane the Holy Regalia beyond any possibility of cleansing, by using it to serve a Christian mass?

"Draw near, all ye people," the bishop was atoning, "for today the old

order giveth way to the new. Christ has triumphed over all the old and
pretended Gods who shall now be subservient to his name. For the True
Christ said unto mankind, *I am the Way and the Truth and the Life.* Also he
said, *No man may come to the Father except he come in my name, for there is
no other name under Heaven in which you may be saved.* And by that token,
then, all those things which once were devoted to false Gods before mankind
had knowledge of the truth, now shall be devoted to Christ and newly
dedicated in service to the True God. . . ."

But Morgaine heard no more; suddenly she knew what they were
planning to do—*No! I am sworn to the Goddess. I must not allow this blasphemy!* She turned and touched Raven's arm; even here, in the midst of this
crowded hall, they were open one to the other. *They would use the Holy
Regalia of the Goddess to summon the Presence . . . which is One . . . but they
would do it in the narrow name of that Christ who calls all Gods demons, unless
they invoke in his name!*

*The cup the Christians use in their mass is the invocation of water, even as
the plate whereon they lay their holy bread is the sacred dish of the element of earth.
Now, using the ancient things of the Goddess, they would invoke their own narrow
God; yet instead of the pure water of the holy earth, coming from the clear crystal
spring of the Goddess, they have defiled her chalice with wine!*

*In the cup of the Goddess, O Mother, is the cauldron of Ceridwen, wherein
all men are nourished and from which all men have all the good things of this
world. You have called upon the Goddess, O ye willful priests, but will you dare
her presence if she should come?* Morgaine clasped her hands in the most
fervent invocation of her life. *I am thy priestess, O Mother! Use me, I pray,
as you will!*

She felt the rushing downward of power, felt herself standing taller,
taller, as the power flooded through her body and soul and filled her; she
was no longer conscious of Raven's hands holding her upright, filling her
like the chalice with the sacred wine of the holy presence. . . .

She moved forward and saw Patricius, stunned, draw back before her.
She had no fear, and though she knew it was death to touch the Holy
Regalia unprepared—*how,* she wondered in a remote corner of her waking
mind, *did Kevin manage to prepare the bishop? Had he betrayed that secret too?*
She knew with certainty that all her life had been preparation for this
moment when, as the Goddess herself, she raised the cup between her hands.

Afterward, she heard, some said that they saw the Holy Chalice borne
round the room by a maiden clothed in shimmering white; others said that
they heard a great rushing wind fill the hall, and a sound of many harps.
Morgaine knew only that she lifted the cup between her hands, seeing it
glow like a great sparkling jewel, a ruby, a living, beating heart pulsing
between her hands . . . she moved toward the bishop and he fell to his knees

before her as she whispered, "Drink. This is the Holy Presence. . . ."

He drank, and briefly she wondered what it was that he saw, but then he fell away behind her as she moved on, or the cup itself moved, drawing her with it . . . she could not tell. She heard a sound as of many wings, rushing before her, and she smelled a sweetness that was neither incense nor perfume. . . . The chalice, some said later, was invisible; others said that it shone like a great star which blinded every eye that looked on it. . . . Every person in that hall found his plate filled with such things as he liked best to eat . . . again and again later she heard *that* tale, and by that token she knew that what she had borne was the cauldron of Ceridwen. But for the other tales she had no explanation, and needed none. *She is the Goddess, she will do as she will.* . . .

As she moved before Lancelet she heard him whisper in awe, "Is it you, Mother? Or do I dream? . . ." and set the cup to his lips, filled with overflowing tenderness; today she was mother to them all. Even Arthur knelt before her as the cup briefly passed before his lips.

I am all things—Virgin and Mother and she who gives life and death. Ignore me at your peril, ye who call on other Names . . . know ye that I am One. . . . Of all those in that great hall, only Nimue, she thought, had recognized her, had looked up in astonished recognition; yes, Nimue too had been reared to know the Goddess, whatever form she might take. "You too, my child," she whispered with infinite compassion, and Nimue knelt to drink, and Morgaine felt somewhere through her the surging of lust and vengeance, and thought, *Yes, this too is a part of me.* . . .

Morgaine faltered, felt Raven's strength bearing her up . . . was Raven beside her, holding the cup? Or was it illusion, was Raven still crouching in her corner, holding her upright with a flow of strength which poured through them both into the Goddess bearing the cup . . . ? Later, Morgaine never knew whether in truth she had borne the chalice or whether that, too, had been part of the vast magic she had woven for the Goddess . . . yet it seemed to her, still, that she bore the cup around the great hall, that every man and every woman there knelt and drank, that the sweetness and the bliss flooded her, that she walked as if borne along on those great wings she could hear . . . and then Mordred's face was before her.

I am not your mother, I am the Mother of All. . . .

Galahad was white, overawed. Did he see it as the cup of life or as the holy chalice of Christ? Did it matter? Gareth, Gawaine, Lucan, Bedivere, Palomides, Cai . . . all the old Companions and many she did not recognize, and it seemed at the last that they walked somewhere beyond the spaces of the world, and all of those who had ever been among them, even those who had passed beyond this world, came to commune with them at the Round Table this day—Ectorius, Lot, dead years since at Mount Badon; young

Drustan, murdered in jealous rage by Marcus; Lionel; Bors; Balin and Balan
hand in hand, like brothers again past the gates of death . . . all those who
had ever gathered here around the Round Table, past and present, today
were gathered here in this moment beyond time, even at last before the wise
eyes of Taliesin. And then it was Kevin kneeling before her, the cup to his
lips . . .

*Even you. I forgive all this day . . . whatever may come in the times yet
to be seen. . . .*

At last she raised the chalice to her own lips and drank. The water of
the Sacred Well was sweet on her lips, and though she saw now all the others
in the hall eating and drinking, somehow it seemed, when she took a bite
of bread, that on her lips it was the soft honey bannock that Igraine had
baked for her when she was a child in Tintagel.

She replaced the cup on the altar, where it shone like a star. . . .

*Now! Now, Raven, the Great Magic! It took all the strength of all the
Druids to shift Avalon from this world, but now we need not do so much . . . the
cup and the dish and the spear must go . . . they must go from this world forever,
safely into Avalon, never again to be touched or profaned by mortal men. Never
again may they be used for our own magic among the ring stones, for they have
been defied by their moments on a Christian altar. But never again will they be
profaned by priests of a narrow God who would deny all other truths. . . .*

She felt Raven's touch, hands gripping hers, and it seemed to her that
beyond Raven's hands she felt other hands, she knew not whose . . . and
in the hall it seemed as if the great wings flapped for a final time and a great
rushing wind swept through the hall and was gone. White daylight broke
into the room, and the altar was bare and empty, and the white cloth was
crumpled and lying there untenanted. She could see the pale terrified face
of Bishop Patricius.

"God has visited us," he whispered, "and today we have drunk of the
wine of life by the Holy Grail. . . ."

Gawaine leaped to his feet. "But who has stolen away the holy vessel?"
he cried. "We have seen it veiled . . . I swear I shall go forth to find it and
bring it again to this court! And on this quest I shall spend a twelvemonth
and a day, till I see it more clearly than here. . . ."

Of course it would have to be Gawaine, thought Morgaine, *always first
to set himself face to face with the unknown!* Yet he had played into her hands.
Galahad stood up, pale and shining with excitement.

"A twelvemonth, sir Gawaine? I swear that I shall spend all my life,
if need be, till I see the Grail clear before me. . . ."

Arthur held out his hand and tried to speak, but the fever had caught
them all and they were crying out, pledging themselves, all talking at once.

There is now no other cause so dear to their hearts, Morgaine thought.

The wars have been won, there is peace in the land. Between wars, even the Caesars had the sense to set their legions to the building of roads and the conquest of new lands. Now this quest, they think, will unite them again in the old fervor. Once again they are the Companions of the Round Table, but this will scatter them to the four winds . . . in the name of that God you would set above Avalon, Arthur! The Goddess works as she will. . . .

Mordred had risen and was speaking, but Morgaine had eyes now only for Raven, fallen to the floor. All round her the old peasant women were still chattering about the fine foods and drink they had tasted under the spell of the cauldron.

"White wine it was, rich and sweet as fresh honey and grapes . . . I never tasted it but once, years ago . . ."

"Plum cake I had, stuffed with raisins and plums and a sauce of rich red wine . . . I never had anything so good . . ."

But Raven lay silent, white as death, and when Morgaine bent to her, she knew what she had already known when she first saw her lying there. The weight of that Great Magic had been too much for the terrified woman; she had held firm, buoyed by the Great Magic, until the Grail had gone away to Avalon, all her own strength poured out selflessly to strengthen Morgaine in the work of the Goddess; and then, that strength withdrawn, her life had gone with it. Morgaine held her close, in wild grief and despair.

I have killed her too. Truly, truly, now have I killed the last one I had to love. . . . Mother, Goddess, why could it not have been me? I have nothing more to live for, no one to love, and Raven has never harmed a living soul, never, never. . . .

Morgaine saw Nimue come down from her high seat beside the Queen and speak with the Merlin, her look warm and sweet, and lay a confiding hand on his arm. Arthur was speaking with Lancelet, the tears streaming down both their faces; she saw them embrace and kiss as they had not done since they were boys. Arthur left him then, and walked down into the lower end of the hall, moving among his subjects.

"Is all well, my people?"

All were speaking to him about the magical feast, but as he came nearer someone called out, "Here's an old deaf and dumb woman, my lord Arthur, dead—the excitement was just too much for her!"

Arthur walked to where Raven lay lifeless in Morgaine's arms. Morgaine did not raise her head. Would he recognize her, cry out, accuse her of witchcraft . . .?

His voice was gentle and familiar, but distant. *Of course,* she thought, *he is not speaking now to sister or priestess or equal, he sees no more than a crouching old peasant woman, white-haired, clad in rags.* "Your sister, my good woman? I am sorry this has come to you at a festival, but God has taken her at a blessed moment into the very arms of his own angel. Would you have her lie here for burial? She shall lie in the churchyard, if you wish."

The women around drew breath, and Morgaine knew this was, indeed, the highest charity he could offer. But her cloak still over her head, she said, "No." And then, as if compelled, looked up into his eyes.

They had changed so much, both of them . . . she was old and burdened, but Arthur, too, had changed from the young King Stag. . . .

Not then nor ever did Morgaine know whether Arthur had recognized her. Their eyes met for a moment, then he said gently, "Would you take her home then? Be it as you will, mother. Tell my stablemen to give you a horse—show them this." He put a ring into her hand. Morgaine bent her head, squeezing her eyes tight against tears, and when she raised it again, Arthur was gone.

"Here, I'll help ye carry her," said one of the women nearby, and then another, and they bore Raven's slight body from the hall. And Morgaine was tempted to look back into the hall of the Round Table, for she knew she would never see it again, nor ever set foot again upon Camelot.

Now her work was done, and she would return to Avalon. But she would return alone. Now she would always be alone.

10

Gwenhwyfar, watching the preparations in the hall, hearing Bishop Patricius' soft voice saying, *No man may come to the Father except he call upon my name,* looked on the cup with mixed emotions. Half of her said, *This beautiful thing should be dedicated, as Patricius wishes, to the service of Christ; even the Merlin has come at last to the cross.*

But the other half of her insisted, quite against her will, *No. It would have been better to destroy it, to melt down the gold if need be, and fashion from it another chalice dedicated, from its first making, to the true service of the true God. For this one is of the Goddess, as they call her, and that same Goddess is that great harlot who has from the beginning of time been the enemy of God. . . . Truly the priests say, with woman came evil into this world,* and then she was confused, for surely not all that is woman can be evil—even God chose a woman to bear his son, and Christ himself spoke of Heaven to his chosen disciples and their sisters and wives. . . .

One, at least, had forsaken that Goddess. She felt her face soften as she looked on Nimue—Elaine's daughter, and very like Elaine as a child, but even more beautiful, with something of the smiling gaiety and dancing grace of the younger Lancelet. So fair and sweet was Nimue, she could not believe anything of her was evil, yet this woman had served since childhood in the very house of the Goddess. And now she had repented of that evil service and come to Camelot, begging that no one should know that she had served in Avalon, not even Bishop Patricius. Not even Arthur. It would be hard, Gwenhwyfar thought, to refuse Nimue anything at all; she had willingly pledged herself to keep the young maiden's secret.

She looked past Nimue to where Patricius was standing, ready to take the cup with his hands. And then . . .

. . . and then it seemed to Gwenhwyfar that a great angel, wings falling away in shadow behind the shining form, raised between its hands a cup that glowed like a great shining star. It was crimson like a beating heart, a glowing ruby . . . no, but it was the very blue of the deepest heaven, and there was a scent like all the roses of every garden she had ever entered in all her life. And a great clean-scented wind seemed suddenly to blow through the hall, and though they were at holy service, Gwenhwyfar suddenly felt that she could rise from her seat and run out of doors on the hills, into the great spaces which belonged to God, under his great wide healing sky. She knew, knew deep within her heart, that she would never again be afraid to leave the prison of chamber and hall; she could walk under the open sky and on the hills without fear, because wherever she might go, God would be with her. She smiled; disbelieving, she heard herself laugh aloud, and the small, once-prisoned thing within her asked angrily, *At holy service?* but the real Gwenhwyfar said, still laughing, though no one heard, *If I may not take delight in God, then what is God to me?*

And then, through the sweet scents and joy, the angel was before her and the cup at her lips. Shaking, she drank, lowering her eyes, but then she felt a touch on her head and looked up, and she saw that it was not an angel but a woman veiled in blue, with great sad eyes. There was no sound, but the woman said to her, *Before Christ ever was, I am, and it was I who made you as you are. Therefore, my beloved daughter, forget all shame and be joyful because you, too, are of the same nature as myself.*

Gwenhwyfar felt that her whole body and heart were made of pure joy. She had not been as happy as this since she was a little child. Even in Lancelet's arms she had never known this absolute bliss. *Ah, could I only have brought this to my lover!* She knew that the angel, or whatever Presence had touched her, had moved on, and she was saddened that it had withdrawn, but the joy was still pulsing inside her, and she looked up, with love, as the angel held the burning cup to Lancelet's lips. *Ah, if only she can give you some of this joy, my sorrowing lover!*

The fiery flames and the rushing wind filled the hall and were silenced. Gwenhwyfar ate and drank, although she never knew what it was, only that it was sweet and savorous; and she gave herself up to the delight of it. *Surely whatever has come among us today, it is holy. . . .*

Silence fell on the hall; it seemed bare and empty in the pale noonday, and Gawaine had risen, crying out. And after him Galahad.

"I swear that I shall spend all my life, if need be, till I see the Grail clear before me. . . ."

Bishop Patricius looked faint, and she remembered that he was old; and the altar where the cup had lain was empty. She rose swiftly from her place and went to him.

"Father—" she said, and held a cup of wine to his lips. He sipped, and as the color began to come back into his lined face, he whispered, "Surely something holy has come among us. . . . I was fed truly at the Lord's Table by the very cup from which he drank on that last holy night before he went to his Passion. . . ."

Gwenhwyfar was beginning to know what had happened—whatever had come to them that day by God's will was a vision. The bishop whispered, "Did you see, my queen, the very cup of Christ . . ."

She said gently, "Alas no, dear Father, perhaps I was not worthy for that, but I saw an angel, I think, and I thought for a moment it was God's Holy Mother who stood before me. . . ."

"God has given us each a vision," said Patricius. "How I have prayed that something might come among us, to inspire all these men with the love of the true vision of Christ. . . ."

Gwenhwyfar thought of the ancient proverb, *Have a care what you pray for, it might be given you.* Surely something had inspired these men. One after another they were rising, pledging to spend a year and a day searching, and she thought, *All of the Round Table now is scattering to the four winds.*

She looked at the altar where the chalice had lain. *No,* she thought, *Bishop Patricius and Kevin the Merlin, you were wrong as Arthur was wrong. You cannot call down God to serve your own purposes this way. God blows through human purposes like a mighty wind, like the rush of angel's wings which I heard in this hall this day, and tears them asunder. . . .*

And then she wondered, *What is wrong with me, that I am thinking to criticize Arthur or even the bishop for what they did?* Yet then, with new strength, she thought, *By God, yes! They are not God, they are only men, and their purposes are not sacred!* She looked at Arthur, walking now among the peasants and subjects at the far end of the hall . . . down there something had happened, some peasant had fallen down dead, perhaps overfilled with the joy of the Holy Presence. He came walking back, looking sorrowful.

"Gawaine, must you go—Galahad—? Not you too, my son? Bors, Lionel—what, all of you?"

"My lord Arthur," called out Mordred. He wore, as always, the crimson which suited him so well and which exaggerated, almost to the point of caricature, his likeness to the young Lancelet.

Arthur's voice was gentle. "What is it, my dear boy?"

"My king, I ask your permission *not* to go on this quest," he said. "Though it may be laid on all your knights, someone must remain at your side."

Gwenhwyfar felt an overflowing tenderness for the young man. *Ah, this is Arthur's true son, not Galahad, all dreams and visions!* Had there ever been a time when she had disliked and distrusted Mordred? She said, heartfelt, "May God bless you, Mordred," and the young man smiled at her. Arthur bowed his head and said, "Be it so, my son."

It was the first time Arthur had called him so before other men; Gwenhwyfar gauged his disturbance by that. "God help us both, Gwydion —Mordred, I should say—with so many of my Companions scattered to the four corners of the world, and God alone can say whether or no they will ever return. . . ." He reached out and clasped Mordred's hands, and for a moment it seemed to Gwenhwyfar that he leaned on his son's strong arm.

Lancelet came to her side and bowed. "Lady, may I take my leave of you?"

It seemed to Gwenhwyfar that tears were as near the surface as joy. "Ah, love, must you go on this quest?" and cared not who heard her speak the words. Arthur too looked troubled, holding out his hand to his cousin and friend. "Will you leave us, Lancelet?"

He nodded; there was something rapt, otherworldly, shining in his face. So it had come to him, too, that great joy? But why, then, did he need to go forth to seek it? Surely it was within him as well?

"All these years, my love," she said, "have you told me that you are none so good a Christian as all that. Why then must you run away from me on this quest?"

She saw him struggling for words, and at last he said, "All those years, I knew not whether God was nothing but an old tale told by the priests to frighten us. Now I have seen—" He wet his lips again with his tongue, trying to find words for something beyond them. "I have seen . . . something. If a vision such as this can be shown, whether of Christ or of the Devil—"

"Surely," interrupted Gwenhwyfar, "surely it came of God, Lancelet—"

"So you say, for you have seen, you *know*," he said, holding her hand against his heart. "I am not sure—methinks my mother mocked at me, or all Gods are one as Taliesin used to say—I am torn now between the darkness of never knowing, and the light beyond despair, which tells me—" And again he fumbled for words. "It was as if a great bell called to me, far away, a light like to the faraway lights in the marsh, saying, *Follow* . . . and I know that the truth, the real truth, is there, *there,* just beyond my grasp, if I can only follow it and find it there and tear away that veil which shrouds it . . . it is there if only I can reach it, my Gwenhwyfar. Would you deny me the search, now that I know there is truly something worth the finding?"

It seemed as if they were alone in a room, not in the court before all men. She knew she could prevail on him in all else, but who can come between a man and his soul? God had not seen fit to give him this sureness and joy, and she did not wonder that he must now go seeking for it, for if she had sensed it was there, yet without the surety, she too would have spent the rest of her life in that seeking. She reached both hands to him, and said, feeling as though she embraced him before all men in the clear light of day, "Go then, my beloved, and God reward your search with the truth you seek."

And he said, "God remain with you always, my queen, and may he grant that someday I return to you."

Then he turned to Arthur, but Gwenhwyfar did not hear what they said, only that he embraced Arthur as he had done when they were all young and innocent.

Arthur stood, his hand on Gwenhwyfar's shoulder, watching him go. "I think sometimes," he said softly, "that Lance is the best of us," and she turned to him, her heart overflowing with love for this good man who was her husband, and said, "I think so too, my dearest love."

He said, surprising her, "I love you both, Gwen. Never think, never, that you are less to me than anything on earth. I am almost glad you have never borne me a son," he added, almost in a whisper, "for then you might think I loved you only for that, and now I can say to you, I love you beyond all else save only my duty to this land whereof God has given me the stewardship, and you cannot be jealous of that. . . . "

"No," she said softly. And then, for once meaning it absolutely, without reservation, she said, "And I love you too, Arthur, never doubt that."

"I have never for a moment doubted that, my own dear love." And he raised both her hands to his lips and kissed them, and Gwenhwyfar was filled again with that great and overflowing joy. *What woman alive has had so much of life, that the two greatest men within the borders of this world have loved me?*

All around them, the noises of the court were rising again, demanding notice for the things of everyday life. Everyone, it seemed, had seen something different—an angel; a maiden bearing the Grail; some, like herself, had seemed to see the Holy Mother; and many, many others had seen nothing, nothing but a light too bright to bear, and had been filled with peace and joy, and been fed with such meats and drinks as they liked best.

Now a rumor was going about that, by the favor of Christ, what they had seen was the very Grail from which Christ had drunk at the Last Supper among his disciples, where he broke the bread and shared the wine as if it were body and blood of the ancient sacrifice. Had Bishop Patricius chosen his moment to spread that tale, while they were all confused and no man knew precisely what he had actually seen?

There was a tale Morgaine had told her, Gwenhwyfar remembered, crossing herself: Jesus of Nazareth, they said in Avalon, had come here in youth to be educated among the wise Druids in Glastonbury, and after his death, his foster-father, Joseph of Arimathea, had come here and struck his staff into the ground where it had blossomed into the Holy Thorn. Did it not then seem reasonable that this same Joseph had brought hither the cup of the sacrifice? Surely, whatever passed, it was holy . . . surely this was a holy thing, since, if it had not come of God, it could not be anything but a most evil enchantment, and how could such beauty, such joy, be evil?

Yet whatever the bishop said, it had been an evil gift, Gwenhwyfar thought, shaking. One by one, the Companions had arisen and ridden forth on their quest, and now she looked on a hall which was all but empty. They were gone, all the Companions save for Mordred, who had vowed to remain, and Cai, who was too old and lame to ride forth. Arthur turned away from Cai—she knew he must be comforting Cai for not riding on this quest with the others—and he said, "Ah, I too should have ridden forth with them, but I could not. I would not shatter their dream."

She came and herself poured him some wine, and she wished suddenly that they were within their own rooms, not here where they were left alone in the hall of the Round Table. "Arthur, you planned what happened—you told me that something amazing was being planned for Easter—"

"Yes," he said, leaning back wearily in his chair, "but I swear to you that I knew not what was planned by Bishop Patricius or by the Merlin. I knew that Kevin had brought here the Holy Regalia from Avalon." He laid a hand on his sword. "I was given the sword at my crowning, and now it has been given to the service of this kingdom and of Christ. It seemed to me, as the Merlin said, that the holiest of Mysteries of the ancient world should be put to the service of God, since all the Gods are one, as Taliesin always told us. In the old days the Druids called their God by other names, but these things belonged to God and should be given to him. Yet I know not what happened in the hall this day."

"You know not? *You?* Does it not seem to you that we beheld a true miracle, that God himself came before us to show that the Holy Grail should be reclaimed for his service?"

"At times, I think so," said Arthur, slowly, "and then I wonder . . . was it not the magic of the Merlin which enchanted us, so that we should see a vision and think thus? For now are my Companions gone forth from me, and who knows whether they shall ever return?" He raised his face to her; she noticed, as from very far away, that his eyebrows were all white now, and that his fair hair was liberally silvered.

He said, "Knew you not that Morgaine was here?"

"Morgaine?" Gwenhwyfar shook her head. "No, I knew it not . . . why came she not to greet us?"

He smiled, "You ask that? She left our court under my great displeasure." His lips tightened and again his hand sought the hilt of Excalibur, as if to reassure himself that still it lay at his side. It hung now in a leather scabbard, a coarse and ugly thing; she had never dared to ask him what had become of the one Morgaine had made for him so many years ago, but now she guessed that was behind their quarrel.

"You knew it not—that she had rebelled against me. She would have put her paramour Accolon on the throne in my place . . ."

Gwenhwyfar had thought she would never again feel wrath at any living creature after the day's joyous vision; even now, what she mostly felt was pity for Morgaine, and pity too for Arthur, knowing how he had loved and trusted the sister who had betrayed him. "Why did you not tell me that? I never trusted her."

"That is why," said Arthur, pressing her hand. "I thought I could not bear it, to hear you say how you trusted her never, and how you had often warned me against her. But Morgaine was here this day, in the guise of an old peasant woman. She looked old, Gwenhwyfar, old and harmless and sick. I think that she had come in disguise for another look, perhaps, at that place where once she had held high state, and perhaps for another glimpse of her son. . . . She looked older than our mother looked when she died . . ." and he was silent, reckoning for a moment on his fingers, and saying at last, "Why, and so she is, as I am older than my father ever was, my Gwenhwyfar. . . . I think not that Morgaine came to do mischief, and if she did, why, for sure it was prevented by the holy vision . . ." and he was silent. Gwenhwyfar knew, with her sure instinct, that he did not want to say aloud that he loved Morgaine still and that he missed her.

As the years pass there are so many things I cannot say to Arthur, or he to me . . . but at least we both spoke today of Lancelet and of the love that was among us all. And it seemed to her for the moment that this love was the greatest truth in her life, and that love could never be weighed out or measured, so much for this one and so much for that, but was an endless and eternal flow, that the more she loved, the more love she had to give, as she gave it now to everyone, as it had been given her by her vision.

Even toward the Merlin, today, she felt that flow of warmth and tenderness. "Look how Kevin struggles with his harp. Shall I send someone to help him, Arthur?"

Arthur smiled and said, "He needs it not, for Nimue is ministering to him, see?"

And again she felt the flood of love, this time for Lancelet's daughter and Elaine's—child to two of those she had loved best. Nimue's hand under the Merlin's arm . . . like the old tale of the maiden who fell in love with a wild beast from the depths of the forest! Ah, but today she even felt love for the Merlin too, and was glad that he had Nimue's strong young hands to help him.

AND AS THE DAYS passed in the near-empty court at Camelot, Nimue came to seem more and more like the daughter she had never had. The girl listened with attentive courtesy when she spoke, flattered her subtly, was ever quick to wait upon her hand and foot. Only in one thing did Nimue displease Gwenhwyfar—she spent far too much time listening to the Merlin.

"He may now call himself Christian, child," the Queen warned, "but at heart he is an old pagan, sworn by the barbaric rites of the Druids, which you have renounced . . . you can see still the serpents he wears on his wrists!"

Nimue stroked her own satiny wrists. "Why, so does Arthur," she said gently, "and I too might have worn them, cousin, had I not seen the great light. He is a wise man, and there is no man in all Britain who can play more sweetly upon the harp."

"And there is the bond of Avalon to bind you," said Gwenhwyfar, a little more sharply than she intended.

"No, no," said Nimue, "I beg of you, cousin, say this never to him. He did not see my face at Avalon, he knows me not, and I do not wish him to think me an apostate from that faith to this. . . ."

She looked so troubled that Gwenhwyfar said lovingly, "Why, if you wish, I will not tell him. I have not told even Arthur that you came to us from Avalon."

"And I am so fond of music, and of the harp," Nimue pleaded. "May I not speak with him?"

Gwenhwyfar smiled indulgently. "Your father, too, was a fine musician—once he said that his mother had set a harp in his hand for a plaything before he was old enough even to hold a toy sword, and taught him to touch the strings. I would like Merlin the better if he stayed with his harp and sought not to be one of Arthur's councillors." Then she shuddered and said, "To me the man is a monster!"

Nimue said patiently, "I am sorry to see you so against him, cousin. It is not his doing—I am sure he would rather be as handsome as my father and as strong as Gareth!"

Gwenhwyfar bent her head. "I know it is not charitable of me . . . but from childhood I have had a revulsion for those who are so misshapen. I am not sure it was not the sight of Kevin which caused me to miscarry when last I had a chance to bear a son. And if God is good, does it not follow that what comes from God must be beautiful and perfect, and what is ugly and misshapen must be the work of the foul fiend?"

"No," said Nimue, "it seems not at all likely to me. God himself sent trials to the folk in Holy Writ, for he afflicted Job with leprosy and boils, and he caused Jonah to be swallowed up by a great fish. And again and again we are told he made his chosen people to suffer, and even Christ himself suffered. One might say that these people suffer because it is the will of God that they shall suffer more than others. It may be that Kevin suffers this affliction for some great sin he did in some life before this one."

"Bishop Patricius tells us that is a heathen notion and no Christian should believe that abominable lie—that we are born and reborn again. Or how should we ever go to Heaven?"

Nimue smiled, remembering Morgaine saying to her, *Never speak to me again of anything Father Griffin said to you.* She thought she would like to say it now to Gwenhwyfar, but she kept her voice gentle.

"Oh no, cousin, for even in Holy Scripture, it is told how men asked of John the Baptizer who he was. Some men said that Jesus Christ was Elijah come again, and he said instead, *I tell you that Elijah has come among you already and ye knew him not.* And men knew—so it says in Holy Writ— that he spoke of John. And so, if Christ himself believed that men were reborn, how can it be wrong for mankind so to believe?"

Gwenhwyfar wondered how so much knowledge of Scripture had come to Nimue, living upon Avalon. And she remembered that Morgaine, too, had known more, she sometimes thought, of the holy writings than she herself did.

Nimue said, "I think perhaps the priests do not want us to think of other lives because they wish us to be very good in *this* one. Many priests think there is not much time remaining before the world will end and Christ come again, and so they are afraid that men will wait for another life to be good, and will not have time to attain perfection before Christ comes. If men knew they would be reborn, would they work so hard to be perfect in this life?"

"That seems to me dangerous doctrine," Gwenhwyfar said, "for if people believed that all men must at last be saved in some life or other, what would keep them from committing sins in *this* one, in the hope that at last God's mercy would prevail?"

"I do not think that fear of the priests, or of God's wrath, or anything else, will ever keep mankind from committing sins," said Nimue, "but only when they have gained enough wisdom in all their lives that they know that error is useless and evil must be paid for, sooner or later."

"Oh! Hush, child," Gwenhwyfar said. "Suppose someone should hear you speaking such heresies! Although it is true," she said after a moment, "that since that day of Easter, it seems to me that there is infinite mercy in God's love, and perhaps God does not care so much about sin as some of the priests would have us believe . . . and now I am talking heresy too, perhaps!"

Nimue only smiled again, thinking to herself, *I did not come to court to bring enlightenment to Gwenhwyfar. I have a more perilous mission, and it is not for me to preach to her the truth, that all men, and all women too, must one day come to enlightenment.*

"Do *you* not believe Christ will come again, Nimue?"

No, thought Nimue, *I do not, I believe that the great enlightened ones, like Christ, come but once, after many lives spent in attaining wisdom, and then they go forth forever into eternity; but I believe the divine ones will send other great masters to preach the truth to mankind, and that mankind will always receive them with the cross and the fire and the stones.*

"What I believe does not matter, cousin, what matters is the truth. Some priests preach that their God is a God of love, and others that he is evil and vengeful. Sometimes I feel that the priests were sent to punish people; since they would not hear Christ's words of Love, God sent them the priests with their message of hatred and bigotry." And then she stopped short, for she did not want to anger Gwenhwyfar. But the Queen only said, "Well, Nimue, I have known priests like that."

"And if some priests are bad men," said Nimue, "I find it not wholly beyond reason that some Druids might be good ones."

There must, thought Gwenhwyfar, be some error in that reasoning, but she could not make it out. "Well, my dear, you may be right. But it makes me queasy to see you with the Merlin. Although I know Morgaine thought well of him . . . it was rumored here at court, even, that they were lovers. I wondered often how a woman so fastidious as Morgaine could have let him touch her."

Nimue had not known that and she thrust it away in her mind for reference. Was that how Morgaine had known of his undefended fortresses? She said only, "Of all I learned in Avalon, what most I loved was music, and what I have heard in Holy Writ that pleases me most was the psalmist who told us to praise God with the lute and the harp. And Kevin has promised me that he will help me to find a harp, for I came away without my own. May I send for him here, cousin?"

Gwenhwyfar hesitated, but she could not resist the sweet entreaty in the young girl's smile and said, "To be sure you may, my dearest child."

11

After a time, the Merlin came—*no,* thought Nimue, *I must remember; he is no more now than Kevin the Harper, traitor to Avalon*—and behind him a servant carrying My Lady. Nimue thought, *Now he is a Christian, there is no law that no other may touch his harp; it is simpler than keeping an initiated man about him to bear My Lady when his strength fails.*

He walked with two sticks, dragging his tortured body after them. But he smiled at the ladies and said, "You must consider, my queen and my lady Nimue, that somehow my spirit has made to you the courtly bow that my unruly body is no longer able to make."

Nimue whispered, "I beg you, cousin, ask him to sit—he cannot stand for long."

Gwenhwyfar waved permission, glad for once of her near sight that meant she need not clearly see the misshapen body. For a moment, Nimue was afraid that Kevin's man was from Avalon and would recognize and perhaps greet her, but he was only a servant in the dress of the court. How had Morgaine, or old Raven, been able to see so far ahead, to order her as a child into seclusion, so that when she came to womanhood, there would be one fully trained priestess in Avalon whom the Merlin would not know by sight? She understood that she was merely a pawn in the great work of the world, sent forth with no weapons but her beauty and her guarded virginity to work the vengeance of the Goddess on this man who had betrayed them all.

Nimue placed another cushion from her own chair under the Merlin's arm. His bones seemed to protrude through the skin, and when she barely touched his elbow, it seemed that there was so much heat in the swollen joints that it burned her. And she felt a moment's pity and rebellion.

Surely the Goddess already works her own vengeance! This man has surely suffered enough! Their Christ suffered a day on the cross; this man has been crucified in his broken body for a lifetime!

Yet others had been burned for their faith and had not broken, nor betrayed the Mysteries. She hardened her heart and said sweetly, "Lord Merlin, will you play your harp for me?"

"For you, my lady," Kevin said in his rich voice, "I will play what you will, and I could wish I were that ancient bard who could play till the trees danced!"

"Oh no," said Nimue with mocking laughter. "What would we do if they came dancing in here! Why, we would have earth all over the hall, and all our maids with mops and brooms would not be able to clean it! Leave the trees where they are, I beg you, and sing!"

The Merlin put his hands to the harp and began to play. Nimue sat beside him on the floor, her great eyes looking up, intent, into his face. The Merlin looked down on the maiden just as a great dog might watch its master—with humble devotion and utter preoccupation. Gwenhwyfar took such emotion almost for granted. She herself had been the object of intense devotion so often that she never thought twice about it—it was simply the homage that men paid to beauty. Perhaps, though, she should warn Nimue, lest her head be turned by it. Yet she could not imagine how Nimue could sit so close to his ugliness or look at him so attentively.

There was something about Nimue that puzzled Gwenhwyfar. Some-how, the girl's concentration was not quite what it seemed. It was not the delight taken by one musician in another's work, nor was it the artless admiration of a naïve maiden for a well-travelled and mature man. No, thought Gwenhwyfar, and it was not a sudden passion, either; *that* she could have understood and, in a sense, sympathized with—she herself had known that sudden overpowering love which sweeps away all obstacles. It had struck her like lightning and had ruined all her hopes that her marriage with Arthur could be a good and proper one. It had been a curse, yet she had known it was something that came of itself, over which neither she nor Lancelet had any power. She had come to terms with it, and she could have accepted that it had happened to Nimue—even though Kevin the Merlin seemed the most unlikely object for such a passion. But it was *not* that . . . she did not know how she knew, but she knew.

Simple lust? It might have been that on Kevin's part—Nimue was beautiful, and even though the Merlin had been most circumspect, she might have kindled any man; but Gwenhwyfar could not believe that Nimue had been likewise roused by such a one when she had remained courteous but cool and unattainable to all of Gwenhwyfar's handsomest young knights.

From where she sat at the Merlin's feet, Nimue sensed that Gwenhwy-far was watching her. But she did not turn her eyes away from Kevin. *In a way,* she thought, *I am enchanting him.* Her purpose demanded that she have him completely at her mercy—her slave and her victim. And again she stifled the flash of pity that she felt. This man had done worse than simply revealing the Mysteries or the secret teaching; he had given the holy things themselves into the hands of the Christians, to be profaned. Ruthlessly, Nimue refused to consider her next thought, that the Christians had not intended profanation but hallowing. The Christians knew nothing of the inner truths of the Mysteries. And in any case the Merlin had betrayed a sworn oath.

And the Goddess appeared to prevent that profanation. . . . Nimue had had enough training in the Mysteries to know what she had witnessed; even now a shiver went over her at the thought of what had passed among the Companions on that festival day. She had not wholly understood, but she knew that she had touched the greatest holiness.

And the Merlin would have profaned this. No, he must die like the dog he was.

The harp was silent. Kevin said, "I have a harp for you, lady, if you will accept it. It is one which I fashioned with my own hands when I was a lad on Avalon, and first come there. I have made others, and they are better, but this is a good one and I have carried it long. If you will accept it, it is yours." Nimue protested that such a gift was all too valuable, but inwardly she was overjoyed. If she should possess something so valuable to him personally, something he had fashioned with his own hands and labor, then would it bind him to her, just as if it were a lock of his own hair or a drop of his blood. There were not many, even in Avalon, who knew that the law of magic went so far, that something which had been so intimately intertwined with the mind and the heart and the passions—and Nimue grasped that music was his deepest passion—retained even more of the soul than hair clipped from the body retained the essence of the body.

She thought with satisfaction, *He himself, of his own free will, has put his soul into my hands.* When he sent for the harp, she caressed it; small and crudely made as it was, the post had been worn smooth with resting against his body, and his hands had touched the strings with love . . . even now they lingered on it tenderly.

She touched the strings, testing their music. In truth, the tone of the harp was good; he had somehow managed that perfect curve and structure that made the soundingboard echo the strings with the sweetest tone. And if he had done this as a boy, with those mutilated hands . . . again Nimue felt the surge of pity and pain, *Why did he not keep to his music and meddle not in the high affairs of state?*

"You are too kind to me." She let her voice tremble, hoping he would think it was passion instead of triumph . . . *with this, soon he will be mine, possessed body and soul.*

But it was too soon. The great tides of Avalon running in her blood told her that the moon was waxing; such great magic as this could be worked only in moon-dark, the slack time when the Lady sheds none of her light on the world, and her hidden purposes are made known.

She must not let his passion grow beyond bounds, nor her own sympathy with him.

He will desire me at full moon; this bond I am forging is a double-edged sword, a rope with two ends . . . I will desire him as well, I cannot prevent that. For an enchantment to be total, it must involve both enchanter and enchanted, and she knew, with a spasm of terror, that this spell she was weaving would work on her too, and rebound on her. She could not pretend passion and desire; she must *feel* them as well. She knew, with a fear that wrung her heart, that even as the Merlin would be helpless in her hands, so it might well be that she would come to be helpless in his. *And what of me, O Goddess, Mother . . . that is all too great a price to pay . . . let it not come on me, no, no, I am afraid. . . .*

"Well, Nimue, my dear," Gwenhwyfar said, "now that you have the harp in your hands, will you play and sing for me?"

She let her hair curtain her face as she looked timidly at the Merlin and murmured, "Shall I, then?"

"I beg you to play," he said. "Your voice is sweet and I can hear that your hands will bring enchantment from the strings. . . ."

They will indeed if I am favored of the Goddess. Nimue set her hands to the strings, remembering that she must not play any song of Avalon that he would remember and recognize. She began to play a drinking song she had heard at the court, with words none too proper for a maiden; she saw Gwenhwyfar looking scandalized, and thought, *Good, if she is shocked by my unmaidenly behavior, she will not inquire too deeply into my motives.* Then she played and sang a lament she had heard from a northern harper, the mournful song of a fisherman out on the sea, looking for the lights of his home on the shore.

At the end of the song she rose, looking shyly at him. "I thank you for the use of your harp—may I borrow it again, that my hands may keep their skill?"

"It is my gift to you," said Kevin. "Now that I have heard what music your hands can bring from it, it could belong to no other. Keep it, I beg you—I have many harps."

"You are too kind to me," she murmured, "but, I beg you, now that I can make music for myself, do not abandon me or deprive me of the pleasure of listening to yours."

"I will play for you whenever you ask me," Kevin said, and she knew that his heart was in the words. She contrived to brush against him as she leaned forward to take the harp.

She murmured, softly so Gwenhwyfar would not hear, "Words alone cannot express my gratitude to you. Perhaps a time will come when I can express it more fittingly."

He looked at her, dazed, and she discovered that she was returning his gaze with the same intensity.

A double-edged spell indeed. I am victim too. . . .

He went away, and she sat obediently by Gwenhwyfar and tried to turn her attention to her spinning.

"How beautifully you play, Nimue," said Gwenhwyfar. "I need not ask where you learned . . . I heard Morgaine sing that lament once."

Nimue said, averting her eyes, "Tell me something of Morgaine. She had departed from Avalon before I came there. She was married to a king in—Lothian, was it?"

"In the north of Wales," Gwenhwyfar began.

Nimue, who knew all this perfectly well, was still not completely false. Morgaine remained a puzzle to her, and she was eager to know how the lady Morgaine had appeared to those who knew her in the world.

"Morgaine was one of my ladies-in-waiting," Gwenhwyfar was saying. "Arthur gave her to me as such on our wedding day. Of course he had been fostered apart from her and hardly knew her, either. . . ."

As she listened attentively, Nimue, who had been trained to read emotions, realized that beneath Gwenhwyfar's dislike for Morgaine, there was something else: respect, awe, even a kind of tenderness. *If Gwenhwyfar were not so fanatically, mindlessly Christian, she would have loved Morgaine well.*

At least while Gwenhwyfar was talking of Morgaine, even though she condemned her as an evil sorceress, she was not mouthing the pious nonsense that bored Nimue almost to weeping. But she could not give Gwenhwyfar's tales her full attention. She sat in an attitude of passionate interest, she made the proper sounds of attention or astonishment, but within, her mind was in turmoil:

I am afraid; I can come to be the Merlin's slave and victim as I would have him mine. . . .

Goddess! Great Mother! It is not I who must face him, but you. . . .

The moon was waxing; four nights until full, and she could already feel the stirring of that tide of life. She thought of the Merlin's intent gaze, his magical eyes, the beauty of his voice, and knew that already she was deeply entangled in her own spell weaving. Already she had ceased to feel the slightest revulsion against his twisted body, feeling only the strength and life force flowing within it.

If I give myself to him at full moon, she thought, *then will the tides of life within us both be taken at the flood, then will my purposes become his own, then will we blend together as one flesh . . .* she felt an ache and agony of desire, longing to be caressed by those sensitive hands, feel his warm breath against her mouth. Everything in her ached together in hunger which, she knew, was at least partly an echo of his own desire and frustration; the magical link she had created between them meant that she too must be tormented with his torment.

When life runs full at the rounding of the moon, then shall the Goddess receive the body of her lover. . . .

It was not altogether beyond belief. She was the daughter of the Queen's champion and the King's closest friend. Kevin, the Merlin, unlike a Christian priest, was not forbidden to marry. The court would be pleased at a marriage so high-placed, even though some of the ladies would be shocked that she could yield up her delicate body to a man they considered a monster. Arthur surely knew that Kevin could not, after what he had done, return to Avalon, but he had a place at court as the King's councillor. Also, he was a musician of surpassing skill. *There would be a place for us, and happiness . . . when the moon is full, brimming with life, he will plant a child in my womb . . . and I will bear it joyfully . . . he is not monster born, his deformity is from childhood injuries . . . his sons would be handsome . . .* and then she stopped herself, disturbed by the power of her own fantasies. No, she must not become so deeply entangled in this spell. She must deny herself, even though the waxing moon made the surging blood in her veins a very agony of frustration. She must wait, wait . . .

As she had waited all those years. . . . There is a magic that comes with yielding to life. The priestesses of Avalon knew it when they lay in the fields at Beltane, invoking the life of the Goddess in their own bodies and hearts . . . but there is a deeper magic which comes from guarding the power, damming up the stream. The Christians knew something of this, when they insisted that their holy virgins live in chastity and seclusion, that they might burn with the darker flame of that harnessed force; that their chaste priests might pour all their contained power into their Mysteries, such as they were. Nimue had felt that power in the lightest word or gesture from Raven, who had never wasted words on anything trivial, so that her force, when she spent it, was tremendous. She had wondered often, alone in the temple at Avalon, when she was forbidden to mingle with the other maidens or to go to the rites, when she felt that life force in her veins with such power that she sometimes burst into hysterical crying or tore at her hair and her face . . . why had they set her aside for this, why must she bear the terrible weight of all this without relief? But she had trusted the Goddess and obeyed her mentors, and now they had entrusted this great work to her, and she must not fail them through her own weakness.

She was a charged vessel of power, like the Holy Regalia which it was death to touch unprepared, and all this power of her long preparation would be hers to bind the Merlin to her . . . but she must wait for the tide to slacken and fill again; at the dark moon she must take the other tide which came of the other side of the moon . . . not fertile but barren, not of life at all but of dark magic older than human life. . . .

And the Merlin knew these things; he knew of the old curse of the dark moon and the barren womb . . . he must be so wholly enspelled by her that he would not even wonder why she had refused him at the spring tide and sought him out at the slack. She had one advantage: he did not know that *she* knew these things, he had never seen her in Avalon. Yet the bond went between them both ways, and if she could read his thoughts, he might read hers; she must guard herself every moment lest he see within and guess her purposes.

I must so wholly blind him with desire that he will forget . . . forget all he has been taught in Avalon. And at the same time, she must not be overcome by his desire, she must contain her own. It would not be easy.

She began to frame in her mind the next wile she would use on him. *Tell me of your childhood,* she would say, *tell me how you were so hurt.* Sympathy would be a powerful bond; she knew just how she would touch him with the very tips of her fingers . . . and she knew, in despair, that she was seeking out ways to be near him and touch him, not for her work but for her own hunger.

Can I make this spell without bringing myself, too, to ruin?

"YOU WERE not at the Queen's feast," murmured the Merlin, looking into Nimue's eyes, "and I had made a new song for you. . . . It was the fulling of the moon, and there is great power in the moon, lady. . . ."

She looked at him, all intent. "Truly? I know so little of these things . . . are you a magician, my lord Merlin? I sometimes feel helpless, that you are working your magic on me. . . ."

She had hidden herself at the full moon, sure that if he looked into her eyes at that time he would be able to read her thoughts and perhaps divine her purposes. Now that the strength of that magical tide was past, she could, perhaps, guard herself from him.

"You must sing me your song now." She sat listening, feeling her whole body quiver as the harp strings quivered under his touch.

I cannot bear it, I cannot . . . I must act this time as soon as the moon is dark. Another of these tides, she knew, and she would succumb to the flood tide of hunger and desire she was building between them . . . *and I would never be able to betray him . . . I would be his forever, for this life and beyond. . . .*

She reached out and touched the twisted lumps that were his wrist bones, and the touch thrilled her with longing. She could only imagine from the sudden dilation of his pupils, the swift intake of his breath, what it had done to him.

Betrayal, she thought, under the inexorable laws of fate, betrayal would be punished a thousandfold by the Goddess, in life after life; betrayed and betrayer would be punished and bound together for love and hate for thousands of years. But she did this at the command of the Goddess, she had been sent to punish a traitor for betrayal . . . would she then be punished in turn? If it were so, then there was no justice even in the realms of the Gods. . . .

Christ said true repentance wipes out all sin. . . .

But fate and the laws of the universe cannot be so easily set aside. The stars in their courses do not stop because someone cries out to them, *Stop!*

Well, be it so; perhaps she betrayed the Merlin as part of a deed done by one of them before the ancient land beneath the waves had sunk into the sea. It was her fate, and she dared not question. He had stopped playing and closed his hand softly over hers; as if in a daze, she laid her lips to his. *Now, now it is too late to turn back.*

No. It had been too late to turn back when she had bowed her head and accepted the work Morgaine laid on her. It had been too late to turn back when she swore the oath to Avalon. . . .

"Tell me more of yourself," she whispered, "I want to know everything about you, my lord. . . ."

"Call me not so. My name is Kevin."

"Kevin," she said, and made her voice soft and tender, just brushing her fingers again over his arm.

Day by day she wove her spell, with touches and glances and whispered words, as the moon waned away toward darkness. After that first, swift kiss, she withdrew again, as if he had frightened her. *It is true. But it is more that I frightened myself . . .* never, never in all the years of seclusion had she suspected herself of being capable of such passion, such hunger; and she knew that her spells were enhancing it in herself as in him. At one point, teased beyond endurance by her whispered touches, the soft brushing of her hair against his face when she bent over him where he sat at his harp, he turned and seized her and crushed her to him, and she struggled in real, not pretended, fright this time.

"No—no, I cannot—you forget yourself—I beg you, let me go—" she cried out, and when he only clasped her closer, burying his face in her bosom and covering her breasts with kisses, she began to cry softly. "No, no, I am afraid, I am afraid—"

He let her go then and drew away, almost in a daze. His breath was hoarse and hard. He sat with his eyes closed, his twisted hands hanging limp.

After a moment he murmured, "My beloved, my precious white bird, my own sweetheart—forgive me—forgive me—"

Nimue realized that now she could use even her own very real fear for her own ends. She said, whimpering, "I trusted you. I trusted you—"

"You should not," he said hoarsely. "I am no more than a man, and certainly not less than one . . ." and she cringed at the bitterness as he added, "I am a man of flesh and blood, and I love you, Nimue, and you play with me as if I were a lapdog and expect me to be tame as a gelded pony . . . do you think because I am a cripple I am less than a man?"

In his mind Nimue could see, clear and mirrored, memory of a time when he had said this to the first woman who had ever come to him, and saw Morgaine reflected in his eyes and his mind, not the Morgaine *she* knew but a dark, bewitching woman, soft of voice, yet somehow terrible too, worshipped and also feared because through the daze of passion he could remember that suddenly the lightning would strike. . . .

Nimue reached her hands to him and knew they were trembling and that he would never know why. She guarded her thoughts carefully and said, "I never thought that. Forgive me, Kevin. I—I could not help myself—"

And it is all true. Goddess, it is all true. But not as he believes. What I say is not what he hears.

And yet for all her pity and desire there was a thread of contempt too. Otherwise I could not bear it, to do what I do . . . but a man so nakedly at the mercy of desire is contemptible. . . . I too tremble, I am torn . . . but I will not be at the mercy of my body's hunger. . . .

And that was why Morgaine had given her the key to this man, put him wholly into her hands. Now was the time to speak the words that would consolidate the spell, make him hers, body and soul, so that she might bring him to Avalon and the appointed doom.

Pretend! Pretend to be one of those feckless virgins Gwenhwyfar has about her, with their minds between their legs!

She said, faltering, "I am sorry—I know you are indeed a man—I am sorry I was afraid—" and she raised her eyes to his, a gaze aslant through her long hair, afraid that if he could look deep into her eyes she would blurt out all her duplicity. "I . . . I—yes, I wanted you to kiss me, but then you were so fierce, and I was frightened. This is neither the time nor the place, someone might come suddenly upon us, and then the Queen would be angry, and I am one of her maidens, and she has warned us that we must not run about with men . . ."

Is he fool enough to believe me when I speak such simpering nonsense?

"My poor darling!" Kevin covered her hands with contrite kisses. "Ah, I am a beast to frighten you, I love you so . . . I love you so much that I cannot bear it! Nimue, Nimue, are you so afraid of the Queen's anger? I cannot—" He stopped and breathed again, hard. "I cannot live like this—would you have it that I should be gone from this court? Never, never have I—" he stopped again and then, holding her hands between his, he said, "I cannot live without you. I must have you or die. Will you not have some pity on me, beloved?"

She lowered her eyes, with a long sigh, watching his contorted face, his dazed breathing. At last she whispered, "What can I say to you?"

"Say that you love me!"

"I love you." She knew that she sounded like a woman under a spell. "You know that I do."

"Say that you will give me all your love, say that—ah, Nimue, Nimue, you are so young and beautiful, and I am so twisted and ugly, I cannot believe you care for me, even now I think I am dreaming, that you have for some reason roused me like this that you might make fun of the beast grovelling at your feet like a dog. . . ."

"No," she said, and swiftly, as if she were afraid of her own daring, bent quickly down and laid the lightest of kisses against his eyes, two darting swallows that came and went.

"Nimue, will you come to my bed?"

She whispered, "I am frightened . . . we might be seen, and I dare not be so wanton—we might be discovered." She arranged her lips into a childish pout. "If we were caught, then the men would think you only all the more manly for it, and none would chide or shame you, but I, I am a maiden and they would point to me as a harlot or worse . . ." and she let tears slide down her cheek, but inward she was all triumph. *I have him now safe within my net. . . .*

"I would do anything, anything to protect you, to reassure you . . ." Kevin said, his voice trembling with sincerity.

"I know men like to boast of their conquest of maidens," she said. "How do I know you will not brag of it throughout Camelot, that you have the favor of the Queen's kinswoman and have taken her maidenhood?"

"Trust me, I beg you, trust me—what can I do? What proof can I give you of my sincerity? You know that I am yours, body and heart and soul—"

And for a moment she was angry, *I do not want your damned soul,* she thought, close to weeping with tension and fear. He held her between his hands and whispered, "How? When will you be mine? What can I do to prove that I love you beyond all things?"

She said, hesitating, "I cannot take you to my bed. I sleep in a room with four of the Queen's ladies, and any man who came there would be seized by the guards—"

He said, bending again to cover her hands with kisses, "My poor little love, I would never bring shame on you. I have a place of my own—a little chamber fit for a dog, mostly because none other of the King's men wishes to share quarters with me. I do not know if you would dare to come *there.*"

"Surely there must be some better way . . ." she whispered, keeping her voice soft and tender. *Damn you, how can I suggest it without dropping this pretense of maidenly innocence and stupidity . . . ?* "I cannot think of anywhere within the castle where we could be truly safe, and yet—" She stood and pressed herself against him, where he sat, her breasts just nudging his brow.

He flung his arms around her and buried his face in her body, his shoulders shaking. Then he said, "At this season—it is warm and fair and there is little rain. Would you dare to come out of doors with me, Nimue?"

She murmured as artlessly as she could, "I would dare anything to be with you, my love."

"Then—tonight . . . ?"

"Oh," she whispered, shrinking, "the moonlight is so bright, we should be seen . . . wait a few days, then there will be no moon. . . ."

"When the moon is dark—" Kevin flinched, and she knew that here was the moment of danger, the moment when the carefully played fish might slip off the hook and out of the net and be free. In Avalon the priestesses secluded themselves at moon-dark, and all magic was suspended . . . but he knew not that she was of Avalon.

Would his fear or his desire win out? She was motionless, just fluttering her fingers within his. He said, "That is an uncanny time—"

"But I am afraid to be seen. . . . You do not know how angry the Queen would be with me, if she knew I was such a wanton as to desire you . . ." she said, holding herself a little closer to him. "Surely you and I do not need a moon to see one another. . . ."

He held her tight, his face buried in her breasts, covering them with hungry kisses. And then he whispered, "My little love, let it be as you will, be the moon light or dark . . ."

"And you will take me away from Camelot afterward? I do not want to be shamed . . ."

"Anywhere," he said, "I swear it . . . I will swear it by your God, if you will."

She murmured, bending her head close to him, her hands moving through the sweet clean curliness of his hair, "The Christian God does not like lovers, and hates it when women lie with men . . . swear it by *your* God, Kevin, swear it by the serpents around your wrists. . . ."

He whispered, "I swear," and the meaning of the oath seemed to ripple the air around them both.

Oh, fool, you have sworn to your death. . . . Nimue shivered, but Kevin, his face still hidden against her breasts, his hot breath damping her gown, was oblivious to anything except her breasts under his lips. As a promised lover he took the privilege of touching, kissing, drawing her gown aside a little to cup them in his hands. "I do not know how I can bear to wait." And she murmured, "No, nor I," and meant it with all her heart,

I would that this was done. . . .

The moon would not be visible, but the moon tide would turn exactly two hours after sunset, three days from now; she could feel its ebbing like a great sickness in her blood, withdrawing life from her veins. Most of those three days she spent in her chambers, telling the Queen that she was ill, and it was not far from the truth. Much of her time alone she spent with her hands on Kevin's harp, meditating, filling the ether around her with the magical bond between them.

An ill-omened time, and Kevin knew it, as she did; but he was too blinded by the promise of her love to care.

The day dawned when the moon would darken; Nimue felt it through her body. She had made herself an herbal brew which would keep the moon-dark bleeding from coming on—she did not want to disgust him with the sight of her blood, nor frighten him to recalling the taboos of Avalon. She had to turn her mind away from the physical realities of the act; for all her training, she knew that in truth she was the nervous virgin she pretended to be. Well, so much the better, she need not try to pretend. She could simply be what she was—a girl giving herself for the first time to a man she loved and desired. And what would come after that, well, it was as the Goddess had bidden her.

She hardly knew how to make the day pass. Never had the chatter of Gwenhwyfar's ladies seemed so meaningless, so vapid. In the afternoon she could not turn her mind to spinning, so she brought the harp Kevin had given her and played and sang for them; but it was not easy, she must avoid all the songs of Avalon, and they were the ones which she found floating in her mind. But even the longest day wears to sunset. She washed herself and scented her body, and sat near Gwenhwyfar in the hall, merely picking at her food, sick and faint, disgusted by the grossness of the table manners, the dogs under the table. She could see Kevin seated among the King's councillors, near the house priest who confessed some of the ladies. He had been bothering her, asking why she did not seek spiritual advice, and when she said she was in no need of it, frowning as if she were the worst of sinners. Kevin. She could almost feel his hungry hands on her breast, and it seemed as if the look he sent toward her must be audible.

Tonight. Tonight, my beloved. Tonight.

Ah, Goddess, how can I do this to this man who loves me, who has put his

*whole soul into my hands. . . . I have sworn. I must keep my oath or be as much
a traitor as he.*

They met for a moment in the lower hall as the Queen's ladies went
away to their chambers. He said, swiftly and very low, "I have concealed
your horse and mine in the woods beyond the gate. Afterward"—and his
voice shook—"afterward I will take you away wherever you will, lady."

You do not know whither I shall lead you. But it was too late to turn
back. She said, through tears she could not control, "Ah, Kevin, I—I love
you—" and knew it was true. She had wound herself so deep in his heart
that she did not know, she could not even imagine, how she could bear to
be apart from him. It seemed to her that the whole air of the night was alive
with magic, that somehow others must see this great trembling in the air
and the darkness hovering over her.

She must let them think she had gone abroad on some likely errand.
She told the ladies who shared her chamber that she had promised one of
the chamberlain's wives to try a remedy for the toothache, and that she
would not be back for many hours. Then, taking her darkest, heavy cloak
and tying the small sickle of her initiation about her waist beneath her gown,
she slipped out. After a moment she turned into a dark corner and removed
the little sickle, slipping it into a tied pocket at her waist—whatever befell,
Kevin must not see it.

His heart would break if I failed to keep this tryst, she thought; he did
not know how fortunate he would be. . . .

Darkness. Not even shadows in the moonless courtyard. She found
herself trembling, picking her steps carefully by the dimmest of starlight.
After a little there was a deeper darkness and she heard his voice, a muted
hoarse mutter: "Nimue?"

"It is I, my beloved."

*Which is the greater falsity, to break my oath to Avalon, or to lie to Kevin
thus? Both are false . . . is a lie ever right?*

He took her arm and the touch of his hot hand made her own blood
heat. They were both deeply entangled now in the magic of the hour. He
led her outside the gate, down the steep slope that raised the ancient fort
of Camelot above the surrounding hills. In winter this ran a river and
swampy; now it was dry, thick with the rank growth of the damp lands.
He led her into a grove of trees.

*Ah Goddess, I always knew that on this day when I laid down my virginity,
that it would be within a grove . . . but I did not know it would be with all the
sorcery of the dark moon. . . .*

He took her close and kissed her. His whole body seemed to be
burning. He spread their cloaks together on the grass, and drew her down,
his twisted hands shaking so hard on the fastenings of her dress that she

had to take and loosen them herself. He said with a shred of his natural voice, "I am glad it is dark . . . that my misshapen body will not terrify you. . . ."

"Nothing about you could frighten me, my love," she whispered and reached out her hands for him. At the moment she meant it utterly, rapt in her own spell which had caught her too, knowing that this man, body and heart and soul, was in her hands. Yet, for all her magic, she was inexperienced, and she shrank away with real fear from the touch of his hardening manhood. He kissed and soothed and caressed her, and she felt the burning of the slack tide, the thick darkening of the hour of sorcery. At the very moment when it peaked she pulled him down to her, knowing that if she delayed until the new moon showed in the sky, she would lose much of her power.

He murmured, feeling her trembling, "Nimue, Nimue—my little love —you are a maiden—if you will, we can—pleasure one another and I need not take your virginity. . . ."

Something in that made her want to weep—that he, maddened by his desire, this heavy thing that twisted between them, could still so consider her . . . but she cried out, "No! No! I want you," and pulled him down fiercely to her, taking her hands and guiding him into her, almost welcoming the sudden pain; the pain, the sudden blood, the peaking of his frenzied desire, woke a like frenzy in her, and she clung to him, gasping, encouraging him with her fierce cries. And then at the very last moment she held him away, while he gasped and pleaded, and she whispered—"On your oath! You are mine?"

"I swear it! Ah, I cannot bear—I cannot—let me—"

"Wait! You swear it! You are mine! Say it!"

"I swear, I swear by my soul—"

"Yet a third time—you are mine—"

"I am yours! I swear!" And she felt his sudden spasm of fear, knowing what had happened, but now he was in the grip of his own frenzy, moving on her as if despairing, heaving and gasping, crying out as if in unendurable agony, and she felt the magical spell descending on her at the very moment of slack tide, as he cried out and fell heavily on her unresisting body, and she felt the spurting of his seed within her. He was still as death, and she trembled, feeling her breath charged as if with exhaustion. There was none of the pleasure she had heard spoken of, but there was something greater than pleasure—a vast triumph. For the spell was heavy around them both, and she had his spirit and soul and essence. She felt with her hands his sperm that had mingled with the blood of her virginity at the very moment of the moon's turning. She took it on her fingers and marked his brow, and at the touch the spell came on him and he sat up, slack and lifeless.

"Kevin," she said. "Get to your horse and ride."

He rose, his movements leaden. He turned toward the horse and she knew that with this spell she must be precise.

"Garb yourself first," she said, and mechanically he drew on his robe, tying it about his waist. He moved stiffly, and by starlight she saw the gleam of his eyes; he knew, now, behind the domination of the spell, that she had betrayed him. Her throat tightened with agony and a wild tenderness, she wanted to pull him down again and take away the spell and cover his broken face with kisses, and weep and weep for the betrayal of their love.

But I too am sworn and it is fate.

She covered herself with her robe and took her horse and they rode silently away, taking the road to Avalon. At dawn Morgaine would have the boat waiting for them on the shore.

SOME HOURS BEFORE DAWN, Morgaine waked from restless sleep, sensing that Nimue's work was done. Silently she robed herself, wakening Niniane and the attendant priestesses, who came slowly in her train down to the shore, wrapped in their dark robes and spotted deerskin tunics, hair braided in the single braid down their backs, and the black-handled sickle knives tied at their waists. They waited, silent, Niniane and Morgaine at their head, and as the sky began to flush pale pink with the first light, she motioned to the barge to cast off and watched it disappear in the mists.

They waited. The light strengthened, and just as the sun was rising, the boat appeared out of the mists again. Morgaine could see Nimue standing in the prow of the boat, her cloak pulled over her head, tall and straight; but her face was hidden in the darkness of the cloak. There was a slumped heap in the bottom of the boat.

What has she done to him? Is he dead or enspelled? Morgaine found herself wishing that indeed he was dead, that he had taken his life in despair or terror. Twice she had raged at this man and called him traitor to Avalon, and the third time he had truly been traitor beyond question, taking the Holy Regalia forth from their hiding place. Oh, yes, he deserved death, even such a death as he should this morning die. She had spoken with the Druids, and they had agreed, one and all, that he should die in the oak grove, and that he should not die the swift death of mercy. Treachery of this sort had not been known in all of Britain since the days of Eilan, who had secretly married a son of the Roman proconsul and put forth pretended oracles to keep the Tribes from rising against the Romans. Eilan had died in the fire, and three of her priestesses with her and Kevin's deed was not treachery alone, but blasphemy, as when Eilan had meddled with the voice of the Goddess. And it must be punished.

Two of the barge crew helped the Merlin to his feet. He was half-clad, his robe loosely tied around him, barely concealing his nakedness. His hair was disheveled, his face blank . . . drugged or enchanted? He tried to walk, but without his sticks he reeled and caught for balance at the nearest support. Nimue stood frozen, not looking at him, her face still hidden in her cloak; but as the first rays of the sun arose, she put back the hood, and at that moment, touched by the first sunlight, the enchantment slid off Kevin's face, and Morgaine saw startled comprehension come into his eyes; he knew where he was and what had happened.

Morgaine saw him look at Nimue, blinking at the sight of the Avalon barge. And then all at once the whole knowledge of his betrayal came over his face, and he lowered his head in shock and shame.

So now he knows not only what it is to betray but to be betrayed.

But then she looked at Nimue. The girl was pale, her face bloodless, her long hair in disarray, though she had hastily tried to braid it. Nimue was looking at Kevin, and her lips trembled as she hastily turned her eyes away again.

She loved him, too; the spell rebounded on her. I should have known, Morgaine thought, *that so powerful a spell would have rebounded on its maker.*

But Nimue bowed low as Avalon custom demanded.

"Lady and Mother," she said, her voice toneless, "I have brought you the traitor who betrayed the Holy Regalia."

Morgaine stepped forward and embraced the girl, who shrank from the embrace. She said, "Welcome back to us, Nimue, priestess, sister," and kissed the girl on her wet cheek. She could feel Nimue's misery through her whole body. *Ah, Goddess, has this destroyed her too? If so, we have bought Kevin's life at too dear a price.*

"Go now, Nimue," she added in compassion. "Let them take you back to the House of Maidens—your work is done. You need not witness what must come after this, you have done your part and you have suffered enough."

Nimue whispered, "What will become of—of him?"

Morgaine held her tight. "Child, child, that need concern you not. You have done your part with strength and courage, it is enough."

Nimue caught her breath as if she would weep, but she did not. She looked at Kevin, but he did not meet her eyes, and at last, shivering so hard she could hardly walk, she let two of the priestesses lead her away. Morgaine said in a low voice to them, "Don't torment her with questions. Done is done. Let her be."

When Nimue was gone, Morgaine turned back to Kevin. She met his eyes, and pain struck at her. This man had been her lover, but he had been more; he had been the only man who had never sought to entangle her in any political maneuvers, never sought to use her birth or high position, never asked anything of her save love. He had called her alive out of hell in Tintagel, he had come to her as the God, he had been perhaps her only friend, man or woman, in her entire life.

She forced her words through the tremendous pain in her throat. "Well, Kevin Harper, false Merlin, forsworn Messenger, have you anything to say to her before you meet her judgment?"

Kevin shook his head. "Nothing that you would consider important, Lady of the Lake." She remembered, through a haze of pain, that he had been the first to yield to her this title.

"Be it so," she said, and felt her face like stone. "Take him forth to judgment."

He took a single faltering step between his captors, then turned back and faced her, his head thrown back in defiance. "No, wait," he said. "I find I have a thing to say to you after all, Morgaine of Avalon. I told you once that my life was a small thing to forfeit for the Goddess, and I want you to know it is for her that I have done this."

"Are you saying it is for the sake of the Goddess that you betrayed the Holy Regalia into the hands of the priests?" Niniane demanded, and her voice cut with scorn. "Why then, you are mad as well as forsworn! Take the traitor away!" she commanded, but Morgaine signalled to them to wait.

"Let him be heard."

"It is even so," said Kevin. "Lady, I said it once to you before this— the day of Avalon is ended. The Nazarene has conquered, and we must go into the mists further and further until we are no more than a legend and a dream. Would you then take the Holy Regalia with you into that darkness, preserving it carefully against the dawning of a new day that now shall never be? Even if Avalon must perish, I felt it right that the holy things should be sent forth into the world in the service of the Divine, by whatever name God or the Gods may be called. And because of what I have done, the Goddess has manifested herself at least once in the world yonder, in a way that shall never be forgotten. The passing of the Grail shall be remembered, my Morgaine, when you and I are only legends for the fireside and tales for children. I do not think that wasted, nor should you, who bore that chalice as her priestess. Now do with me what you will."

Morgaine bent her head. The memory of that moment of ecstasy and revelation, when she had borne the Grail in the form of the Goddess, would remain with her until her death; and of those who had experienced the vision, whatever they might have seen, none of their lives would ever be the same. But now she must face Kevin in the person of the avenging Goddess, the Death-crone, the ravening sow who will devour her own young, the Great Raven, the Destroyer. . . .

Yet he had given the Goddess this much. She reached out her hand to him . . . and stopped, for under her hand again she saw what once before she had seen, a skull beneath her fingers. . . .

. . . now he is fey, he sees his own death, and I see it too. . . . Yet he shall not suffer nor be tortured. He spoke truth; he has done what the Goddess has given him to do, and now must I do the same. . . . She waited until her voice was steady before she spoke. In the distance she heard a soft thundering.

At last she said, "The Goddess is merciful. Take him to the oak grove, as is ordained, but there slay him swiftly with a single stroke. Bury him beneath the great oak, and let it henceforth be shunned now and forever by all men. Kevin, last of the Messengers of the Goddess, I curse you to forget all, to be reborn without priesthood and without enlightenment, that all you have done in your former lives be wiped away and your soul returned to the once-born. A hundred lifetimes shall you return, Kevin Harper, always seeking the Goddess and never finding her. Yet in the end, Kevin, once Merlin, I say to you—if she wants you, be very sure she will find you again."

Kevin looked straight at her. He smiled, that curious, sweet smile, and said, almost in a whisper, "Farewell, then, Lady of the Lake. Tell Nimue I loved her . . . or it may be that I will tell her myself. For I think it will be a long, long time before you and I shall meet again, Morgaine." And again soft thunder punctuated his words.

Morgaine shivered as he limped away without looking back, supported on the arms of his captors.

Why do I feel so shamed? I showed mercy; I could have had him tortured. They will call me, too, traitor and weakling, that he was not taken to the oak grove and there made to scream and pray for death till the very trees shrank from the sound. . . . Am I only a weakling, that I would not torture a man I once loved? Is his death to be so easy that the Goddess will then seek vengeance on me? So be it, even if I must meet the death I could not give him.

She flinched, looking into the grey storm clouds in the sky. *Kevin has suffered all his life long. I will add nothing more than death to his fate.* Lightning flared in the sky, and she thought, with a shiver—or was it only the cold wind that came with the sudden rush of the storm outside?—*So passes the last of the great Merlins, into the storm that breaks now over Avalon.*

She gestured to Niniane. "Go. See my sentence done to the letter, that they slay him with a single stroke, and leave not his body above ground for a single hour." She saw the younger woman's gaze rest on her face; was it known, then, to everyone, that once they had been lovers? But Niniane only asked, "And you?"

"I go now to Nimue. She will need me."

But Nimue was not in her room in the House of Maidens, nor

anywhere in the house, nor, when Morgaine hurried across the rain-swept courts, was she in the secluded house where she had dwelt with Raven. She was not anywhere in the temple, and one of the attendant priestesses told Morgaine that Nimue had refused food or wine or even a bath. Morgaine, terrible apprehension growing in her with every flash of lightning as the storm grew and raged, called for all the servants of the temple to search for her; but before they could Niniane came, her face white, attended by the men she had sent to see Kevin's death done as Morgaine had decreed.

"What is it?" Morgaine demanded, her voice cold. "Why was my sentence not done?"

"He was slain with a single stroke, Lady of the Lake," Niniane whispered, "but with the very stroke came lightning from the sky and struck the great oak—cleft it in twain. There is a great rift in the sacred oak, from the sky to the ground. . . ."

Morgaine felt steel clamp around her throat. *Nothing so strange, that with the storm should come the lightning flash, and ever the lightning strikes at the highest point. But that it should come in the same hour wherein Kevin prophesied the end of Avalon . . .*

She shivered again, wrapping her arms about herself under her cloak so that those who looked on her should not see her trembling. How could she turn this omen, for omen it surely was, aside from the impending destruction of Avalon?

"The God has prepared a place for the traitor. Bury him, then, within the cleft in the oak. . . ."

They bowed acquiescence and went away, through thunder and the sudden rattle of rain, and Morgaine, distraught, realized that she had forgotten Nimue. But a voice within her said, *Now it is too late.*

They found her at high noon, just as the sun came out after the storm, floating among the reeds of the Lake. Her long hair was spread out on the surface like water weeds, and Morgaine, stunned with grief, could not find it in her heart to regret that Kevin had not gone alone into the shadowed land beyond death.

12

MORGAINE thought often, in the bleak days which followed upon Kevin's death, now indeed the Goddess had taken it upon herself to destroy the Companions of the Round Table. But why had it been her will to destroy Avalon too?

I am growing old. Raven is dead and Nimue is dead, who should have been Lady after me. And the Goddess has laid her hand upon no other to be her prophetess. Kevin lies entombed within the oak. What of Avalon now?

It seemed that the world was shifting, that beyond the mists the world moved at an ever-accelerating pace. No one save herself and one or two of the oldest priestesses could open the gateway through the mists, and there was now little reason to try. And there were times when she walked abroad and could see neither sun nor moon, and she knew that she had strayed over the borders of the fairy country; but she saw only the rarest glimpses of the fairy folk among the trees, nor did she ever again have sight of the queen.

She wondered if indeed the Goddess had deserted them, for some of the maidens from the House of Maidens had gone again into the world, and others strayed into the fairy country and did not return again.

The Goddess came forth for the last time into the world when she bore the Grail through Arthur's hall at Camelot, Morgaine thought, and then, confused, she asked herself whether the Goddess had truly borne the Grail, or had it only been herself and Raven working illusion?

I have called on the Goddess and found her within myself.

And Morgaine knew that never again would she have the ability to seek beyond herself for comfort or counsel; she could look only within. No priestess, no prophetess, no Druid or councillor, no Goddess now to turn to; none but her unguided self. Now and again, when, as the habit of a lifetime bade her, she sought to call up the image of the Goddess to guide her, she saw nothing, or sometimes the face of Igraine—not the elderly, priest-ridden wife and widow of Uther, but the young and beautiful mother who had first laid these burdens on her, who had bidden her care for Arthur and given her into the hands of Viviane. And now and again she would see the face of Viviane, who had sent her to the bed of the Horned One, or Raven, who had stood at her side during that great moment of invocation.

They are the Goddess. And I am the Goddess. And there is no other.

She cared little to look into her magical mirror, but now and again when the moon was dark she went to drink of the spring and to look into the waters. But she saw only tantalizing glimpses: the Companions of the Round Table rode this way and that, following dreams and glimmers of vision and the Sight, but none found the true Grail. Some forgot the quest and rode openly in search of adventure; some met with more of adventure than they could manage, and so died; some did good deeds, and some evil. One or two, in piercing visions of faith, dreamed their own Grail and so died. Others, following the message of their own visions, went on pilgrimage to the Holy Lands; and others still, following a wind that was blowing all through the world in these days, withdrew into solitude and the hermit life, seeking, in crude caves and shelters, the life of silence and penitence—

but what visions came to them, whether of the Grail or of some other thing, Morgaine never knew nor cared.

Once or twice she had glimpses of a face she knew. She saw Mordred at Camelot, at Arthur's side. Galahad, too, she saw as he sought the Grail; but then she saw him no more, and wondered if the quest had claimed him to death.

And once she saw Lancelet, half naked, clad in animal skins, his hair long and ragged, without armor or sword, running in the forest, and the gleam of madness was in his eyes; well, she had guessed that this quest might lead him only to madness and despair. Still she sought him again in the mirror, from moon to moon, but for a long time she had no success. Then she saw him sleeping, ragged and naked, on straw somewhere, and the walls of a prison or dungeon rose about him . . . and then she saw him no more.

Ah, Gods, has he gone too . . . with so many of Arthur's men. . . .

Truly the Grail was no blessing to Arthur's court, but a curse. . . .

And rightly so, a curse to the traitor who would have profaned it . . .

And now is it gone forever from Avalon.

For a long time Morgaine believed that the Grail had been taken away by the Goddess into the realms of the Gods, so that mankind might never again profane it, and she was content that it should be so; for it had been defiled with the wine of the Christians, which somehow was blood as well as wine, and she had no notion of how to cleanse it.

Whispers came from the outside world to Morgaine through some of the old brotherhood of priests who came in these days to Avalon; Christians, some of them, of the old ones who had once worshipped beside the Druids, in their firm belief that their Christ had once lived here on Avalon and been taught wisdom. Now, fleeing from the enforced conformity of that new breed of Christians who would wipe out all other worship but their own, they came to Avalon, and from them Morgaine heard something of the Grail.

The priests were now saying that it was indeed the true cup from which Christ had drunk at his Last Supper, and that it had been taken away into Heaven whence it would never again be seen in the world. Yet also there were rumors that it had been seen on that *other* isle, Ynis Witrin, sparkling in the depths of their well, that well which on Avalon was the holy mirror of the Goddess; and therefore the priests on Ynis Witrin had begun to call it the Well of the Chalice.

And when the old priests had dwelt for a time upon Avalon, Morgaine began to hear rumors that now and again the Grail had been seen, for a moment, upon their altar. *That must be as the Goddess wills. They will not profane it.* But she knew not whether it was truly there in the ancient church of the Christian brotherhood . . . which was built on the very spot of the church on the other island, so that they said that, when the mists thinned, the ancient brotherhood on Avalon could hear the monks chanting in *their* church on Ynis Witrin. Morgaine remembered the day when the mists had thinned to let Gwenhwyfar through to Avalon.

Time ran strangely now upon Avalon. Morgaine did not know whether that twelvemonth and a day to which the knights were vowed had passed or not, and sometimes she thought that indeed years must have passed in the outside world. . . .

She thought long on the words Kevin had spoken: . . . *the mists are closing on Avalon.*

And then, one day, she was summoned to the shores of the Lake, but she needed no Sight to tell her who stood in the barge. Avalon had once been his home too. Lancelet's hair was all grey now and his face thin and haggard, but as he stepped from the boat, with only the shadow of his old light-footed grace, she stepped forward and took his hands, and she could see in his face no trace of madness.

He looked into her eyes, and suddenly it seemed that she was the Morgaine of the old days, when Avalon was a temple alive with priestesses and Druids and not a solitary land adrift in the mists with a bare handful of aging priestesses, a few elderly Druids, a handful of half-forgotten ancient Christians.

"How is it that you are so untouched by time, Morgaine?" he asked her. "All seems changed, even here in Avalon—look, even the ring stones are hidden in the mists!"

"Oh, they are still there," Morgaine said, "though some of us would lose our way if we sought them now." And like a pain in her heart she remembered a day—ah, it was a lifetime ago!—when she and Lancelet had lain together in the shadow of the stones. "I think perhaps they will one day go altogether into the mists, and thus never be torn down by human hands or the winds of time. There are none to worship at them now . . . even the Beltane fires are no longer lighted on Avalon, though I have heard that they keep the old rites still in the wildnesses of North Wales and in Cornwall. The little people will never let them die while any of them survive. I am surprised that you were able to come here, kinsman."

He smiled, and now she could see the traces of pain and grief—yes, even of madness—around his eyes. "Why, I hardly knew it was hither I came, cousin. My memory plays tricks on me, now. I was mad, Morgaine. I cast away my sword and lived like an animal in the forests, and then there was a time, I know not how long, that I was confined in a strange dungeon."

"I saw it," she whispered. "I knew not what it meant."

"Nor did I, nor do I yet," Lancelet said. "I remember very little of that time—it is God's blessing, I think, that I cannot remember what I might have done. I think it was not the first time—there were times, during those years with Elaine, that I hardly knew what I did. . . ."

"But you are well now," she said quickly. "Come and breakfast with me, cousin—it is too early for anything else, for whatever reason you came here."

He followed her, and Morgaine took him into her dwelling; except for her attendant priestesses, he was the first person who had entered it in years. There was fish from the Lake, this morning, and she served him with her own hands.

"Ah, this is good," he said, and ate hungrily—she wondered how long it had been since he had last remembered to eat. His hair was as fastidiously combed as ever, his curly hair—all grey now, and patches of white in his beard—neatly trimmed, and his cloak, though shabby and travel-worn, was neatly brushed and clean. He saw her glance at the cloak and laughed a little.

"In the old days I would not have used this cloak for a saddle blanket," he said. "I lost cloak and sword and armor, I know not where—it may be that I was robbed of them in some evil adventure, or cast them away in madness. I know only that one day I heard someone speak my name, and it was one of the Companions—Lamorak, perhaps, though it is still very hazy in my mind. I was too weak to travel, but though he rode on the next day, I began slowly to remember who I was, and they gave me a gown and let me sit to table to eat with my knife instead of throwing me scraps in a wooden piggin—" His laugh was shaky, nervous. "Even when I knew not that I was Lancelet, I had still my accursed strength, and I think I had done some of them harm. I think I lost the best part of a year out of my life. . . . I remember only little things, and the main thought in my mind was never to let them know I was Lancelet, lest I bring shame on the Companions or Arthur . . ." He fell silent, and Morgaine guessed at his torment by what he did not say. "Well, slowly I grew strong enough to travel, and Lamorak had left money for a horse and goods for me. But most of that year is darkness—"

He picked up the remaining bread on his plate and resolutely mopped up the scraps of fish. Morgaine asked him, "What of the quest?"

"What indeed? I have heard a little," he said, "here and there, here and there, as I rode in the land. Gawaine was the first to return to Camelot."

Morgaine smiled, almost against her will. "He was always fickle—to everything and everyone."

"Except to Arthur," Lancelet said. "He is more loyal to Arthur than any of his dogs! And I met with Gareth as I rode hither."

Morgaine said, "Dear Gareth, he is the best of Morgause's sons! What said he to you?"

"He said he had had a vision," Lancelet said slowly, "which bade him return to court and do his duty by his king and his lands, and not to delay, loitering about and seeking visions of holy things. And he talked a long time with me, begging me to lay aside the quest of the Grail and return to Camelot with him."

"I am surprised you did not," Morgaine said.

He smiled. "I am surprised too, kinswoman. And I have promised to return as soon as I can." Suddenly, his face grew grave. "Gareth told me," he said, "that Mordred is always about Arthur now. And when I would not return to court with him, he told me this—that what I could best do for Arthur was to find Galahad and bid him return at once to Avalon, for he mistrusted Mordred and his influence upon Arthur. . . . I am sorry to speak ill of your son, Morgaine."

Morgaine said, "He told me once that Galahad would not live to rule . . . yet he swore to me, by an oath I do not think he would dare break, that he would have no hand in his death."

Lancelet looked troubled. "I have seen many evil adventures that may befall on this accursed quest. God grant that I can find Galahad before he falls prey to one of them!" A silence fell between them, while Morgaine thought, *I knew it in my heart—this was why Mordred refused the quest.* She realized, quite suddenly, that she had ceased to believe that her son Gwydion —Mordred—would ever now be King from Avalon. She wondered when she had begun to accept that in her heart. Perhaps it had been when Accolon died and the Goddess did not stretch forth her hand to protect her chosen.

Galahad will be King, and he will be a Christian king.

And that may well mean that he will kill Gwydion. What of the King Stag, when the young stag is grown? But if the day of Avalon had ended, perhaps Galahad would take his throne in peace, without the need to kill his rival.

Lancelet laid down the remnant of a piece of bread and honey and looked past her at the corner of the room. "Is that Viviane's harp?"

"Yes," she said. "I left mine at Tintagel. But I suppose it is yours by right of inheritance if you want it."

"I play no longer, nor do I have any will to make music, Morgaine. By right it is yours, as are all other things which belonged to my mother."

Morgaine recalled words which had cut her to the heart—again, a lifetime ago!—*I would that you were not so much like my mother, Morgaine!* Now the memory held no pain, but warmth; Viviane was not gone entirely from the world if something survived in her. He said, stumbling, "There are now so few of us—so few who recall the old days at Caerleon—even at Camelot—"

"Arthur is there," she said, "and Gawaine, and Gareth, and Cai, and many more, my dear. And no doubt they ask one another with every day, *Where is Lancelet? Why are you here, and not there?*"

"I said, my mind plays me tricks—I hardly knew I came hither," Lancelet said. "Yet now I am here, I should ask—I heard Nimue was here," and she remembered: she had told him this, once, when he had thought his daughter at the convent where once Gwenhwyfar had been. "I should ask, what has become of her—is she well, does she thrive among the priestesses?"

"I am sorry," Morgaine said. "It seems I have nothing but ill news for you—Nimue died, a year ago."

More than this she would not say. Lancelet knew nothing of the Merlin's betrayal, or of Nimue's last visit to the court. It could only grieve him to know the rest. He asked no questions, only sighed heavily, and cast his eyes on the floor. At last he said without looking up, "And the baby —little Gwenhwyfar—she is married, and in Less Britain, and this quest has swallowed Galahad. I never knew any of my children. I never tried to know them—it seemed to me they were all I could give Elaine, and so I left them to her almost entirely, even the boy. I rode for a time with Galahad when first we departed from Camelot, and I knew more of him in the ten days and nights we rode together than in all the sixteen years he had lived. I think perhaps he would make a good king, if he lives. . . ."

He looked at Morgaine, almost pleading, and she knew he was longing for reassurance, but she had no comfort for him. At last she said, "If he lives, he will be a good king, but I think he will be a Christian king." It seemed that for a moment all the sounds of Avalon were hushed around her, as if the very waves of the Lake and the whispering sound of the reeds on the border were silent to hear her say it. "If he survives the quest of the Grail —or if he should abandon it—still his rule will be circled about by the priests, and through all the land there will be only one God and only one religion."

"Would that be such a tragedy, Morgaine?" Lancelet asked quietly. "All through this land, the Christian God is bringing a spiritual rebirth here —is that an evil thing, when mankind has forgotten the Mysteries?"

"They have not forgotten the Mysteries," she said, "they have found them too difficult. They want a God who will care for them, who will not demand that they struggle for enlightenment, but who will accept them just as they are, with all their sins, and take away their sins with repentance. It is not so, it will never be so, but perhaps it is the only way the unenlightened can bear to think of their Gods."

Lancelet smiled bitterly. "Perhaps a religion which demands that every man must work through lifetime after lifetime for his own salvation is too much for mankind. They want not to wait for God's justice, but to see it now. And that is the lure which this new breed of priests has promised them."

Morgaine knew that he spoke truth, and bowed her head in anguish.

"And since their view of a God is what shapes their reality, so it shall be —the Goddess was real while mankind still paid homage to her, and created her form for themselves. Now they will make for themselves the kind of God they think they want—the kind of God they deserve, perhaps."

Well, so it must be, for as man saw reality, so it became. While the ancient Gods, the Goddess, were seen as benevolent or life-giving, so indeed had nature been to them; and when the priests had taught men to think of all nature as evil, alien, hostile, and the old Gods as demons, even so they would become, surging up from within that part of man which he now wished to sacrifice or control, instead of letting it lead him.

She said, remembering at random something she had read when she had looked into the books of Uriens' house priest in Wales, "And so all men will become even as that apostle who wrote that they should become as eunuchs for the Kingdom of God . . . I think I care not to live within that world, Lancelet."

The weary knight sighed and shook his head. "I think I care not for it either, Morgaine. Yet perhaps it will be a simpler world than ours, and it will be easier to know what is right to do. So I came to seek Galahad, for though he will be a Christian king, I think he would be a better king than Mordred. . . ."

Morgaine clenched her hands under the edge of her sleeves. *I am not the Goddess! It is—it is not mine to choose!* "You came—here to seek him, Lancelet? He was never one of us. *My* son Gwydion—Mordred—he was reared at Avalon. If he left Arthur's court he might come here. But Galahad? He was as pious as Elaine—he would scorn to set foot in this world of witchcraft and fairy!"

"But as I told you, I knew not that I came here," said Lancelet. "I sought to reach Ynis Witrin and the Isle of the Priests, for I heard a rumor of a magical brightness which comes and goes in the church there, and they have renamed their Well, I have heard, the Well of the Chalice—I thought perhaps Galahad rode this way. Another old habit brought me here."

She asked him seriously then, face to face, "What do you think of this quest, Lancelet?"

"I know not, truly, cousin," said Lancelet. "When I took this quest on me, I went as once I went to kill old Pellinore's dragon—do you remember that, Morgaine? None of us believed in it then, and yet I did in the end find that dragon and slay it. Yet I know that something, something of great holiness, came into Camelot that day we saw the Grail." And when she would have spoken, he said vehemently, "No, tell me not that I imagined it, Morgaine—you were not there, you do not know what it was like! For the first time, I felt that there was a Mystery somewhere which was beyond this life. And so I went on this quest, though half of me felt it was mad

—and I rode awhile with Galahad, and it seemed that his faith mocked mine, because he was so pure and his faith so simple and good, and I was old and stained—" Lancelet stared down at the floor, and she saw him swallow hard. "That is why, in the end, I parted from him, lest I damage that shining faith . . . and then I know not where I went, for the fog came down over my mind, and the darkness, and it seemed that Galahad must—must know all the sins of my life and he must despise me for them."

His voice had risen in excitement, and for a moment Morgaine saw the unhealthy brightness returning to his eyes, as she had seen it in the naked man running in the forest. She said quickly, "Don't think of that time, my dear. It is over."

He drew a long, shuddering breath and she saw his eyes fade. "My quest now is to seek Galahad. I know not what he saw—an angel maybe —or why the call of the Grail came so strongly to some and so little to others. Of all the knights, I think only Mordred saw nothing, or if he did he kept it to himself."

My son was reared at Avalon; he would not have been deceived by the magic of the Goddess, Morgaine thought, and was about to speak and tell Lancelet what he had seen—he had been, in youth, an initiate of Avalon and he should not be allowed to think of it as some mystery of the Christians. But, hearing again that strange note in Lancelet's voice, she bent her head and said nothing. The Goddess had given him a vision of comfort; it was not for her to destroy it with a word.

She had sought this, she had worked for it. Arthur had forsaken the Goddess, and the Goddess had scattered his fellowship with a wind blowing from her holy place. And the final irony was this: that her holiest of visions should inspire the most passionate legend of Christian worship. Morgaine said at last, reaching out her hand to him, "Sometimes I believe, Lancelet, that it does not matter what we do. The Gods move us as they will, whatever it is that we think that we are doing. We are no more than their pawns."

"If I believed that," said Lancelet, "I should go mad once and for all."

Morgaine smiled sadly and said, "And if I did *not* believe it, I should perhaps go mad. I *must* believe that I had no power to do other than I have done."

. . . must believe that I never had a choice . . . a choice to refuse the king-making, a choice to destroy Mordred unborn, a choice to refuse when Arthur gave me to Uriens, a choice to hold back my hand from the death of Avalloch, a choice to keep Accolon at my side . . . a choice to spare Kevin Harper a traitor's death, and Nimue . . .

Lancelet said, "And I must believe that man has the power to know the right, to choose between good and evil and know that his choice has made a difference . . ."

"Oh, aye," Morgaine said, "if he knows what good is. But does it not seem to you, cousin, that ever, in this world, evil wears the face of good? Sometimes I feel it is the Goddess who makes the wrong appear the right, and the only thing we can do—"

"Why then, the Goddess would be just such a fiend as the priests say she is," said Lancelet.

"Lancelet," she said, leaning forward to plead with him, "never blame yourself. You did what you must! Believe only that it was your fate and ordained—"

"No, or I should slay myself at once, so that the Goddess could not make use of me to bring about more evil," said Lancelet vehemently. "Morgaine, you have the Sight, and I cannot—I cannot believe it is God's will that Arthur and his court shall fall into Mordred's hands! I told you I came hither because my mind played tricks on me. Without thinking, I called the Avalon barge to me and came here, but now, I think, perhaps I wrought better than I knew. You, who have the Sight, can look within the mirror and see for me where Galahad has gone! I will even brave his anger and demand that he leave this quest and return to Camelot—"

The ground seemed to quiver beneath Morgaine's feet. Once she had stepped unwary into a patch of quicksand and had felt the mud shiver and slip sidewise; it was like that, as if she must throw herself at once to safe ground . . . she heard herself say, as if very far away, "You will indeed return to Camelot with your son, Lancelet—" and wondered why the cold seemed to suck at her very vitals. "I will look into the mirror for you, kinsman. But I know Galahad not, I may not see anything which is of use to you."

"Yet tell me you will do what you can," Lancelet pleaded, and she said, "I have told you I will look into the mirror. But it will be with us as the Goddess wills. Come."

The sun was high now, and as they walked down the hill toward the Sacred Well, a raven croaked once overhead. Lancelet crossed himself against the evil omen, but Morgaine looked up and said, "What did you say, sister?"

Raven's voice said in her mind, *Be not afraid. Mordred will not kill Galahad. And Arthur will kill Mordred.*

She said aloud, "Arthur will be King Stag still. . . ."

Lancelet turned and stared at her. "What did you say, Morgaine?"

Raven said in her mind, *Not to the Holy Well, but to the chapel, and now. It is the time ordained.*

Lancelet asked, "Where are we going? Have I forgotten the way to the Holy Well?" and Morgaine, raising her head, realized that her steps had brought them, not to the Well, but to the little chapel where the ancient Christian brotherhood held their services. They said it had been built by the brotherhood when the ancient Joseph had thrust his staff into the ground on the hill called Wearyall. She put out her hand and took a sprig of the Holy Thorn; it pricked her finger to the bone, and hardly knowing what she did, she put out her hand and marked Lancelet's forehead with the streak of blood.

He looked at her, startled. She could hear the priests singing softly, *Kyrie eleison, Christe eleison.* She went in quietly and knelt down to her own surprise. The chapel was filled with mist, and it seemed to Morgaine that through the mist she could see that other chapel, the one on Ynis Witrin, and hear both sets of voices singing . . . *Kyrie eleison* . . . and there were women's voices too; yes, this must be on Ynis Witrin, for in the chapel on Avalon there were no women, these must be the nuns in the convent there. It seemed for a moment that Igraine knelt beside her and she heard her voice, clear and soft, singing *Christe eleison.* The priest was at the altar, and then it seemed to her as if Nimue was there, her golden hair hanging down her back, fair and lovely as Gwenhwyfar had been when she was a young maiden in the convent. But instead of the old jealous fury, Morgaine looked on her with the purest love for her beauty . . . the mists thickened; she could hardly see Lancelet kneeling at her side, but before her, kneeling at the altar in the *other* chapel, she could see Galahad with his face raised, shining, and on it was the reflected brightness . . . and she knew that he, too, saw through the mists, into the chapel here on Avalon, where the Grail stood. . . .

She heard from the other chapel a ring of tiny bells, and heard . . . she never knew which of the priests, the one here in Avalon, or the one on Ynis Witrin . . . but in her mind it was the gentle voice of Taliesin . . . murmuring, "For in that night in which the Christ was betrayed, our Master took the cup and blessed it, and said, *All of you drink of this, for this is my blood which will be shed for you. So often as ye drink of this cup, do it ever in remembrance of me.*"

She could see the shadow of the priest who lifted the cup of communion, yet it was the damsel of the Grail, Nimue . . . or was it she herself who set the cup to his lips? Lancelet rushed forward, crying out, "Ah—the light, the light—!" and dropped to his knees, his hands shielding his eyes, then slipped further forward and lay prone on the ground.

Under the touch of the Grail, the shadowed face of the young man became clear, solid, real, and the mists were gone; Galahad knelt and drank of the cup.

"For as the wine of many grapes was crushed to make a single wine, so as we unite in this bloodless and perfect sacrifice, then shall we all become One in the Great Light which is Infinite. . . ."

And even as the rapture glowed through his face, the light shining there, he drew a great breath of absolute joy, and looked full into the light. He reached out to grasp the cup in his hands . . . and fell forward, slithered to the floor of the chapel, and he too lay there without moving.

It is death to touch the holy things unprepared. . . .

Morgaine saw Nimue—or was it she herself?—cover Galahad's face with a white veil. And then Nimue was gone, and the cup was standing on the altar, only the gold cup of the Mysteries, without any trace of the unearthly light . . . she was not sure it was there . . . it was surrounded by mist. And Galahad lay dead on the floor of the chapel in Avalon, cold and still beside Lancelet.

IT WAS a long time before Lancelet stirred, and as he raised his head, Morgaine saw that his face was shadowed with tragedy. He whispered, "And I was not worthy to follow him."

"You must take him back to Camelot," Morgaine said gently. "He has won the quest of the Grail—but it was his final quest. He could not bear that light."

"Nor could I," Lancelet whispered. "Look, the light is still on his face. What did he see?"

Slowly, she shook her head, feeling the cold rise up her arms. "Neither you nor I will ever know that, Lancelet. I know only this—that he died with the Grail at his lips."

Lancelet looked up at the altar. The priests had gone quietly away, leaving Morgaine alone with the dead and the living; and the cup, surrounded in mist, still gleamed there, softly glowing.

Lancelet rose. He said, "Yes. And *this* shall come back with me to Camelot, that all men may know the quest is ended . . . and no more knights seeking the unknown to die or go mad . . ."

He took one step toward the altar where the Grail gleamed, but Morgaine flung her arms around him and held him back.

"No! No! It is not for you! The very sight of it struck you down! It is death to touch the holy things unprepared——"

"Then I shall die for it," he said, but she held him hard, and soon she felt him give way. He said, "Why, Morgaine? Why must this suicidal folly go on?"

"No," she said, "the quest of the Grail is ended. You were spared to return to Camelot and tell them that. But you cannot take it back to Camelot. No man can hold and confine it. Those who seek it in faith"— she heard her own voice, though she did not know what she was going to say until she said it—"will always find it—here, beyond the mortal lands. But if it should go back with you to Camelot, it would fall into the hands of the narrowest of the priests, and become a pawn for them. . . ." She could feel the tears thickening her voice. "I beg of you, Lancelet. Leave it here in Avalon. Let there be, in this new world without magic, one Mystery the priests cannot describe and define once and for all, cannot put within their narrow dogma of what is and what is not . . ." Her voice broke. "In the day which is coming, the priests will tell mankind what is good and what is evil, what to think, what to pray, what to believe. I cannot see to the end—perhaps mankind must have a time of darkness so that we will one day again know what a blessing is the light. But in that darkness, Lancelet, let there be one glimmer of hope. The Grail came once to Camelot. Let the memory of that passing never be sullied by seeing it captive on some worldly altar. Leave one Mystery and one source of vision for man to follow . . ." She heard her voice go dry until it seemed like the croaking of the last of ravens.

Lancelet bowed down before her. "Morgaine, or are you truly Morgaine? I think I do not know who or what you are. But what you say is true. Let the Grail remain forever in Avalon."

Morgaine raised her hand, and the little folk of Avalon came and lifted up Galahad's body, bearing it silently to the Avalon barge. Lancelet's hand still in her own, Morgaine walked down to the shore, where she looked at the body lying in the boat. For a moment it seemed that Arthur lay there, then the vision wavered and vanished, and it was only Galahad, with that uncanny peace and light on his face.

"Now you ride to Camelot with your son," said Morgaine quietly, "but not as I foresaw. I think the Sight is given to mock us—we see what the Gods give us to see, but we know never what it means. I think I will never use the Sight more, kinsman."

"God grant it." Lancelet took her hands in his own for a moment; then he bent and kissed them.

"And so at last we part," he said softly. And then, for all she had said of refusing the Sight, she saw in his eyes what he saw when he looked at her—the maiden with whom he had lain in the ring stones and from whom he had turned away from fear of the Goddess; the woman he had gone to in a frenzy of desire, trying to blot out the guilt of his love for Gwenhwyfar and Arthur; the woman he had seen pale and terrible, holding aloft the torch when they had taken him in Elaine's bed; and now the dark, quiet Lady, shadowed in lights, who had lifted his son from the Grail and pleaded with him to leave it forever outside the world.

She leaned forward and kissed him on the brow. There was no need for words; they both knew it was farewell and benediction. As slowly he turned from her and stepped into the magical barge, Morgaine watched the droop of his shoulders and saw the glint of the setting sun on his hair. It was all white now; and Morgaine, seeing herself again in his eyes, thought, *I too am old. . . .*

And now she knew why she had never again caught sight of the queen within the land of Fairy.

I am the queen now.

There is no Goddess but this, and I am she . . .

And yet beyond this, she is, as she is in Igraine and Viviane and Morgause and Nimue and the queen. And they live in me too, and she . . .

And within Avalon they live forever.

13

*f*AR to the north, in the country of Lothian, word came seldom and unreliably of the quest for the Grail. Morgause waited for the return of her young lover, Lamorak. And then, half a year later, word came to her that he had died on the quest. *He was not the first,* she thought, *and he will not be the last to die of this monstrous madness, leading men to seek for the unknown! Always I have thought that religions and Gods were a form of madness. Look what they have brought on Arthur! And now they have taken my Lamorak, still so young!*

Well, he was gone, and though she missed him and would always miss him in her own way—he had been at her side longer than any other, save only Lot—she need not resign herself to old age and a solitary bed. She scanned herself in her old bronze mirror, sponged away the marks of her tears, then surveyed herself again. If she no longer had quite the full-blown beauty that had brought Lamorak, dazzled, to her feet, she was still a good-looking woman; there were still enough men in the land, and not all of them could have been caught by this questing madness. She was rich, she was Queen of Lothian, and she had her woman's weapons—she was still handsome, with all her own teeth, though now she must blacken her fading eyebrows and eyelashes . . . they were such a pale-gingery color now. Well, there would always be men; they were all fools, and a clever woman could do with them what she liked. She was no fool like Morgaine, to fret over devotion or virtue, nor a whining idiot like Gwenhwyfar, to think always about her soul.

From time to time some tale of the quest, each one more fabulous than the last, would reach her. Lamorak, she heard, had come back at last to Pellinore's castle, drawn by an old rumor of a magical dish that was kept there in a crypt beneath the castle, and there he had died, crying out that the Grail floated before him in the hands of a maiden, in the hands of his sister, Elaine, as she had been in childhood . . . she wondered what he had really seen. Word came, too, from the country near the Roman wall that Lancelet was dungeoned somewhere in sir Ectorius' old country as a madman, and that no one dared send word to King Arthur; then she heard that his brother Bors had come and recognized him, and he had come to his wits and ridden away, whether to follow the quest further or to ride back to Camelot she neither knew nor cared. Perhaps, she thought, with luck he too would die on this quest; otherwise the lure of Gwenhwyfar would draw him back yet again to Arthur and his court.

Only her sensible Gwydion had not gone on the quest, but had remained at Camelot, close to Arthur's side. Would that Gawaine and Gareth had had the wit to do the same! Now at last *her* sons had come into the place that should always have been theirs with Arthur.

Yet she had another way to know what was happening. Viviane had told her, in her youth at Avalon, that she had not the patience nor the hardihood for initiation into the Mysteries, and Viviane—she knew it now —had been right; who would wish to forsake life for so long as that? For many years she had believed that the doors of magic and of the Sight were closed to her, save for such little tricks as she had mastered on her own. And then she had begun to understand, when first she had used her sorcery to discover Gwydion's parentage, that the magical art was *there,* awaiting her, needing nothing but her will; having nothing to do with the complex Druidical rules and limitations about its use, or lies about the Gods. It was simply a part of life, there and accessible, nothing to do with good or evil, but available to anyone who had the will and the ruthlessness to use it.

All those who pretend to religions, Morgause thought, *wish only to keep the sources of power in their own hands. But now I have them freely and of my own making, without binding myself by oaths about their use or direction.*

So now, on this night, shut away from her servants, she made her preparations. She felt a dispassionate sympathy for the white dog she had brought in, and a moment of genuine revulsion as she cut its throat and set forth the dish of hot blood she had caught; but, after all, it was her own dog, as much hers as a pig she might have slaughtered for the table, and the power of spilled blood was stronger and more direct than the power built up by the long prayers and disciplines of the Avalon priesthood. Before the fireplace, one of her servant-women was lying, drugged and ready, before the fireplace; not one, this time, for whom she had any affection or any real need. She had learned that lesson when last she had attempted this. She spared a regretful thought for the waste of a good spinning woman that time; at least this one would be no loss to anyone, not even the cook who had half a dozen more helpers than she needed.

She still felt a certain squeamishness at the preliminaries. The blood marking her hands and forehead was unpleasantly sticky, but it seemed to her that she could almost see, billowing forth from the blood like smoke, the thin streams of magical power. The moon had shrunk to the thinnest of glimmers in the sky, and she knew the one who awaited her call in Camelot would be ready. At the precise moment the moon moved into the proper quarter of the sky, she poured the rest of the blood into the fire and called three times aloud.

"Morag! Morag! Morag!"

The drugged woman by the fireside—Morgause vaguely recalled that her name was Becca, or something like that—stirred, her vague eyes taking on depth and purpose, and for a moment, as she arose, it seemed that she was wearing the elegant garb of one of Gwenhwyfar's waiting-women. Her voice, too, was not the rough dialect of the dim-witted country girl, but the careful speech of a southern court lady.

"I am here at your call. What would you have of me, Queen of the Darkness?"

"Tell me of the court. What of the Queen?"

"She is much alone since Lancelet has gone, but often calls young Gwydion to her. She has been heard to say that he is like the son she never had. I think she has forgotten that he is the son of Queen Morgaine," said the girl, the careful speech so incongruous from the empty-eyed, rough-handed kitchen girl in her shapeless smock of sacking.

"Do you still put the medicine in her wine at bedtime?"

"There is no need, my queen," said the alien voice which came through and *behind* the kitchen girl. "The Queen's courses have not come upon her now for more than a year, and so I have ceased to give her the drug. But in any case the King comes very seldom to her bed."

So Morgause's last fear could now be quieted—that somehow, against all odds, Gwenhwyfar would bear a belated child to endanger Gwydion's position at court. Besides, the King's subjects would never accept a child for king, after the long peaceful years of Arthur's reign. Nor, she supposed, would Gwydion have any scruples about making an end to a small, unwanted rival. But it was better not to chance it; Arthur himself, after all, had escaped all Lot's plotting and her own, and had lived to be crowned.

I have waited too long. Lot should have been King of these lands many years ago, and I Queen. Now there is none to stop me. Viviane is gone; Morgaine is old; Gwydion will make me Queen. I am the only woman living to whose word he will listen.

"What of sir Mordred, Morag? Is he trusted by the Queen, by the King?"

But the voice grew thick and heavy. "I cannot stay—Mordred is often with the King—once I heard the King say to him—*eh, my head aches, what am I doing here by the fire? Cook will skin me alive . . .*" It was the idiot voice of Becca, thick and sullen, and Morgause knew that far away in Camelot, Morag had sunk back into her bizarre dream in which she faced the faraway Queen of Lothian or the Queen of Fairy. . . .

Morgause seized the pan of blood, shaking the last remaining drops into the fire. "Morag, Morag! Hear me, stay, I command!"

"My queen," came the faraway ladylike voice, "sir Mordred has always at his side one of the damsels of the Lady of the Lake, they say that she is somehow kin to Arthur—"

Niniane, daughter of Taliesin. Morgause thought, *I did not know she had left Avalon. But why now should she stay?*

"Sir Mordred has been named captain of horse while Lancelet is gone from court. There are rumors . . . *Eh, the fire, my lady, will you set the whole of the castle afire?*" Becca was rubbing her eyes and whimpering on the hearth. Infuriated, Morgause gave her a savage push, and the girl fell screaming into the fire; but she was still bound and could not pull herself away from the flames.

"Damn her, she will wake the whole household!" Morgause reached out to pull the girl from the flames, but her dress had caught fire, and her shrieks were dreadful, striking Morgause's ears like red-hot needles. She thought, with a trace of pity, *Poor girl, there is nothing to be done for her now —she would be so burnt, we could not help her even if she should live!* She pulled the screaming, struggling girl out of the fire, not regarding the burns on her own hands, and leaned close for a moment, laying her head on the girl's brow as if to soothe her; then, with a single stroke, she cut her throat from ear to ear. Blood poured into the fire, and the smoke rushed high up into the chimney.

Morgause felt herself shaking with the unexpected power, as if she were spreading out through the whole of the room, through the whole of Lothian, through the whole of the world . . . she had never dared so much before, but now it had come to her, unsought. It seemed that she hovered bodiless over all the land. Again after years of peace there were armies on the road, and on the west coast hairy men in high-beaked dragon ships landed, plundering and burning cities, laying monasteries waste, carrying away women from the walled convents where they lived . . . like a crimson wind, sweeping down even to the borders of Camelot . . . she was not sure whether what she saw now was even at this moment moving in the land or was yet to come.

She cried out through the growing darkness, "Let me see my sons on the quest of the Grail!"

Darkness filled the room, sudden, black and thick, with a curious smell of burning, while Morgause crouched, beaten to her knees by the rush of power. The smoke cleared a little, with a small stirring and coiling in the darkness, like the boiling of a pot. Then Morgause saw, in the widening light, the face of her youngest son, Gareth. He was dirty and travel-worn, his clothing ragged, but he was smiling with the old gaiety, and as the light grew, Morgause could see what he was looking at—the face of Lancelet.

Ah, Gwenhwyfar would not fawn on him now, not this sickly and wasted man with grey in his hair and the traces of madness and suffering in the lines round his eyes . . . he looks indeed like something hung up in the field to scare birds from the grain! The old hatred surged through her: it was intolerable, that her youngest and best son should think kindly of this man, should love him and follow him as he had when he was a little child prattling to carved wooden knights. . . .

"No, Gareth"—she heard the voice of Lancelet, soft in the curdled silence in the room—"you know why it is that I will not return to court. I will not speak of my own peace of soul—nor yet of the Queen's—but I am vowed to follow the Grail for a year and a day."

"But this is madness! What the devil is the Grail, against the needs of our king? I was sworn to him, and so were you, years before any of us heard of the Grail! When I think of our King Arthur at court with none of his faithful men save such as are lame or infirm or cowardly . . . times, I wonder if perhaps it was the work of the fiend, masquerading as a work of God and come to scatter Arthur's Companions out of his hands!"

Lancelet said quietly, "I know that it came from God, Gareth. Do not try to deprive me of that." And for a moment it seemed that again the light of madness flickered in his eyes.

Gareth said, and his voice was oddly subdued when he spoke, "But when God does the same work as the Devil? I cannot think it is God's will that all Arthur has wrought in more than a quarter of a century should thus be cast aside! Do you know there are wild Northmen landing on the shores, and when the men of those lands cry out for Arthur's legions to come and help them, there are none to send to their aid? And so the Saxon armies are gathering again, while Arthur sits idle in Camelot and you seek for your soul—Lancelet, I beg you, if you will not return to court, at least seek for Galahad and make him return to Arthur's side! If the King is old and his will grows weak—and God forbid I should ever have to say so much— then perhaps your son may stand in his place, for all men know he is the King's adopted son and heir!"

"Galahad?" Lancelet's voice was somber. "Think you I have much influence with my son? You and the others swore to follow the Grail for a year and a day, yet I rode for a time with Galahad, and I know it is with him even as he said on that day, that if need be he would follow it lifelong."

"No!" Gareth leaned from his horse and gripped Lancelet by the shoulders. "That is what you must make him see, Lancelet, that at all costs he must return to Camelot! Ah, God, Gwydion would call me traitor to my own blood, and I love Gwydion well, but—how can I say this even to you, my cousin and my heart's brother? I trust not that man's power over our king! The Saxons who send to Arthur find themselves always speaking with him, they think of him as the sister's son of Arthur, and among them, know you not, the sister's son is heir—"

Lancelet said, with a gentle smile, "Recall then, Gareth, that it was even so with the Tribes before the Romans came—we are not Roman, you and I."

"But will you not fight for the rights of your own son?" demanded Gareth.

"It is for Arthur to say who shall follow him on his throne," said Lancelet, "if indeed there shall be any king after him at all. Sometimes, it seemed to me when I wandered among the visions of my madness—nay, I mean not to speak of that, but I think perhaps it was a little akin to the Sight—that a darkness would fall over this land when Arthur had gone."

"And then it should be as if Arthur had never been? What of your vow to Arthur?" Gareth demanded, and Lancelet sighed.

"If it is your will, Gareth, I will seek out Galahad."

"As quickly as you can," Gareth urged, "and you must persuade him that his loyalty to the King is beyond all quests and Grails and Gods—"

Lancelet said sadly, "And if he will not come?"

"If he does not," Gareth said slowly, "then perhaps he is not the King we will need after Arthur. In that case, we are in God's hands, and may he help us all!"

"Cousin, and more than brother," said Lancelet, embracing him again, "we are all in God's hands whatever comes. But I vow to you, I will seek for Galahad and bring him with me to Camelot, I swear it. . . ."

And then the stirring and the brightness were gone, Gareth's face faded and went into the dark, and for a moment it was only Lancelet's eyes, lustrous and so like Viviane's that for a moment Morgause felt that her sister and priestess was looking on her with frowning disapproval, as if to say, *Morgause, what have you done now?* Then that too was gone, and Morgause was alone with her fire, still belching smoke from which all the clouds of magical power had faded, and the limp, bloodless body of the dead woman lying on the hearth.

Lancelet! Lancelet, damn him, he could still play havoc with her plans! Morgause felt her hate like a pain that struck through, a tightness in her throat that travelled down her body to her very womb. Her head was aching, and she felt deathly sick with the aftermath of magic. She wanted nothing more than to sink down on the hearth and sleep for hours, but she must be strong, strong with the powers of sorcery she had called to herself; she was Queen of Lothian, Queen of Darkness! She opened the door and flung the body of the dog onto the midden heap there, disregarding the sickening stench.

She could not handle the body of the kitchen girl alone. She was about to call out for help, when she stopped, her hands to her face, still marked and sticky with blood; they must not see her like this. She went to the basin and ewer of water, poured it out and washed her face and hands and braided her hair afresh. There was nothing she could do about the bloodstains on her dress, but now that the fire was out, there was little light in the room. At last she called out for her chamberlain, and he came to the door, avid curiosity in his face.

"What is it, my queen? I heard shouts and screams—is anything amiss here?" He held up the light, and Morgause knew very well how she looked to him—beautiful, dishevelled—as if she could see herself through his eyes in the aftermath of the Sight. *I could stretch forth my hand now and have him over the girl's body,* she thought, feeling the strange cramping pain and pleasure of desire, and inwardly she laughed, but she put it willfully aside; there would be time enough for that.

"Yes, there is grave trouble. Poor Becca—" She indicated the limp corpse. "She fell into the fire, and when I would have helped her burns, she grabbed the knife from my hand to cut her throat—she must have been maddened with the agony, poor thing. See, her blood is all over me."

The man cried out in consternation and went to examine the lifeless form of the girl. "Well, well, the poor lass had not all her wits. You should not have let her in here, madam."

Morgause was disturbed at the hint of reproach she heard in the man's voice; had she actually thought of taking this one to her bed? "I did not call you hither to question my deeds. Take her out of here and have her decently buried, and send my women to me. I ride at dawn for Camelot."

NIGHT WAS falling, and a thick drizzling rain was blurring the road. Morgause was cold and wet, and it only annoyed her when her captain of horse came up and asked, "Are you sure, madam, that we are on the right road?"

She had had her eye on this one for months; his name was Cormac, and he was tall and young, with a hawklike face and strong shoulders and thighs. But it seemed to Morgause now that all men were stupid, she would have done better to leave Cormac at home and lead this party herself. But there were things even the Queen of Lothian could not do.

"I do not recognize any of these roads. Yet I know from the distance we have ridden this day that we must be near to Camelot—unless you have somehow lost your way in the fog and we are riding northward again, Cormac?"

Under ordinary conditions she would have welcomed another night on the road, in her comfortable pavilion, with all the comforts she could provide, and perhaps, when all her women slept, this Cormac to warm her bed.

Since I found the way to sorcery, all men are at my feet. Yet now, it seems, I care for none . . . strange, I have sought out no man since word came to me of Lamorak's death. Am I growing old? She recoiled from the thought, and resolved she would have Cormac with her tonight . . . but first they must reach Camelot; she must act there to protect Gwydion's interest and to advise him. She said impatiently, "The road must be here, dolt. I have made this journey more times than I have fingers on my two hands! Do you think me a fool?"

"God forbid, madam. And I too have ridden this road often, yet somehow, it seems, we are lost," Cormac said, and Morgause felt she would choke with her exasperation. Mentally she retraced the road she had travelled so often from Lothian, leaving the Roman road and taking the well-travelled way along the edge of the marshes to Dragon Island, then along the ridge till they should strike the road to Camelot, which Arthur had had broadened and resurfaced until it was almost as good as the old Roman road.

"Yet somehow you have missed the Camelot road, dolt, for there is that old fragment of Roman wall . . . somehow or other we are half an hour's ride past the turn to Camelot," Morgause scolded. There was no help for it now but to turn the whole caravan about, and already darkness was closing down. Morgause drew up her hood over her head and urged her plodding horse through the grey lowering twilight. At this time of year there should have been another hour of sunlight, but there was only the faintest glimmer of light in the west.

"Here it lies," said one of her women. "See, that clump of four apple trees—I came here one summer to take a graft of apples for the Queen's garden."

But there was no road, only a little track winding upward on a barren hill, where there should be a broad road, and above it, even through mist, there should have been the lights of Camelot.

"Nonsense," she said brusquely, "we have lost the way, somehow— are you trying to tell me that there is no more than one clump of four apple trees in Arthur's kingdom?"

"Yet that is where the road ought to be, I swear it," grumbled Cormac, but he got the whole line of riders, horses, and pack animals into motion again and they plodded on, rain coming down and down as if it had been coming down since the beginning of time and had forgotten how to stop. Morgause was cold and weary, longing for hot supper at Gwenhwyfar's table and hot mulled wine and a soft bed, and when Cormac rode up to her again she demanded crossly, "What now, dolt? Have you managed to lose us again, and miss a wide wagon road once more?"

"My queen, I am sorry, but somehow—look, we are back again where we paused to rest the horses after we turned off the Roman road—that bit of rag I dropped, I'd been using it to clean the muck off one of the packs."

Her wrath exploded. "Was ever a queen plagued with so many damnable fools about her?" she shouted. "Must we look for the biggest city north of Londinium all over the Summer Country? Or must we ride back and forth on this road all night? If we cannot see Camelot's lights in the dark, we could at least hear it, a castle with more than a hundred knights and serving-men, horses and cattle, Arthur's men patrolling all the roads about —everything that moves on this road is clearly in sight of his watchtowers!"

Yet in the end there was nothing to do but to have lanterns lighted and turn southward again; Morgause herself rode at the head of the line, next to Cormac. The fog and rain seemed to damp out all sound, even echoes, until, through the foggy rain, they found themselves again at the ruined patch of Roman wall where they had turned about before. Cormac swore, but he sounded frightened too.

"Lady, I am sorry, I cannot understand it—"

"Damnation seize you all!" Morgause shrieked at him. "Will you have us riding hither and thither on this road all night?" Yet she too recognized the ruined wall. She drew a long breath, exasperation and resignation in one. "Perhaps by morning the rain will have ended, and if we must we can retrace our steps to the Roman wall. At least we will know where we have come!"

"If indeed we have come anywhere and have not wandered somehow into the fairy country," murmured one of the women, surreptitiously crossing herself. Morgause saw the gesture, but she only said, "No more of that! It's bad enough to be lost in the rain and fog without such idiot nonsense! Well, why are you all standing about? We can ride no more tonight, make haste to camp here, and in the morning we will know what to do."

She had intended to call Cormac to her, if only that she might have no leisure for the fear that had begun to steal through her . . . had they indeed come out of the real world into the unknown? Yet she did not, lying alone and wakeful among her women, restless, mentally retracing all the steps of their journey. There was no sound in the night, not even the calling of frogs from the marshes. It was not possible to lose the whole city of Camelot;

yet it had vanished into nowhere. *Or was it she herself, with all her men and ladies and horses, who had vanished into the world of sorcery?* And every time she came to that point in her thoughts she would wish that she had not allowed her anger with Cormac to set him to watching over the camp; if he were lying here beside her, she would not have that terrifying sense of the world somehow insanely out of joint . . . again and again she tried to sleep and found herself restlessly staring, wide awake, into the dark.

Sometime in the night, the rain stopped; when day broke, although damp mist was rising everywhere, the sky was free of cloud. Morgause woke from a fitful doze, a dream of Morgaine, greying and old, looking into a mirror like her own, and went out of her pavilion, hoping that she would look up the hill and find that Camelot was, indeed, where it should have been, the broad road leading up to the towers of Arthur's castle, or else that they were on some unknown road clearly miles and miles from where they should have been. But they were camped by the ruined Roman wall, which she knew to be about a mile south from Camelot, and as horses and men prepared to ride, she looked up at the hill which should have been Camelot; but the hill was green and grass-grown and featureless.

They rode slowly along the road, muddy with the many tracks where they had ridden back and forth half the night. A flock of sheep grazed in a field, but when Morgause's man went to speak with the shepherd, the man hid behind a rock wall and would not be coaxed out.

"And this is Arthur's peace?" Morgause wondered aloud.

"I think, my lady," said Cormac with deference, "there must be some enchantment here—whatever it is, this is not Camelot."

"Then in God's name, what is it?" asked Morgause, but he only muttered, "In God's name, what indeed?" and had no further answer for her.

She looked upward again, listening to the frightened whimpering of one of her women. For a moment it was as if Viviane spoke again in her mind, saying what Morgause had never more than half believed, that Avalon had gone into the mists, and that if one set out there, either Druid or priestess, and not knowing the way, one would come only to the priests' Isle of Glastonbury. . . .

They could retrace their steps to the Roman road . . . but Morgause felt a curious growing fear: would they find that the Roman road too was gone, was Lothian gone, was she alone on the face of the earth with these few men and women? Shivering, she recalled a few words of Scripture she had heard preached by Gwenhwyfar's house priest, about the end of the world . . . *I say to you, two women will be grinding grain side by side, and one will be taken, and the other one will be left. . . .* Had Camelot and all those within it been taken up into the Christian Heaven, had the world ended, with a few stragglers like herself left to wander on the face of the stricken world?

But they could not stand staring at the empty track. She said, "We will retrace our steps toward the Roman road." *If,* she thought, *it is still there, if there is anything there at all.* It seemed, as she looked on the mists rising like magical smoke from the marshes, that the world had vanished and even the rising sun was unfamiliar. Morgause was not a fanciful woman; she told herself, it was better to move and try to make their way back, than to stand in that otherworldly silence. Camelot was real, a place in the real world, it could not vanish entirely away.

Yet if I had had my way, if Lot and I had been successful in our plotting against Arthur, perhaps the whole land would be like this, silent and desolate and full of fears. . . .

Why was it so quiet? It seemed in all the world there was no sound but their horses' hooves, and even these seemed to fall like stones dropped into water, muffled and dying away in ripples. They had nearly reached the Roman road—or where the Roman road should have been—when they heard hoofbeats on a hard road; a rider was coming, slow and deliberate, from Glastonbury. They could make out a dark figure through the fog, some kind of heavy-laden pack animal behind him. After a moment one of her men cried out, "Why, look there, it is sir Lancelet of the Lake—God give you good morning, sir!"

"Hallo! Who rides there?" It was indeed Lancelet's well-known voice, and as he came closer, the homely sound of the hooves of horse and pack mule seemed to release something in the world around them. Sounds carried a long way in the fog, and this was a simple sound, dogs barking somewhere, a whole pack of dogs, perhaps quarrelling over their food after a hungry night, but it broke the unworldly stillness with its simple, normal noise.

"It is the Queen of Lothian," called Cormac, and Lancelet rode toward them, halting his horse before her.

"Well, Aunt, I had not hoped to meet with you here—are my cousins with you, perhaps, Gawaine or Gareth?"

"No," she said, "I ride alone for Camelot." *If,* she thought irritably, *such a place still exists upon the face of this earth!* Her eyes rested intently on Lancelet's face as he said some polite words of greeting. He looked weary and travel-worn, his clothing ragged and not overly clean, a cloak of fustian worse than he would have given his groom. *Ah, the beautiful Lancelet, Gwenhwyfar will not find you so handsome now, even I would not stretch out my hand to invite him into my bed.*

And then he smiled, and she realized, *In spite of all, he is beautiful.*

"Shall we ride together then, Aunt? For indeed I come on the most sorrowful of missions."

"I had heard that you were on the quest of the Grail. Have you found it, then, or failed to find it that you are so long-faced?"

"It is not for such a man as I to find that greatest of Mysteries. Yet

I bring with me one who did indeed hold the Grail in his hands. And so I have come to say that the quest is ended, and the Grail gone forever out of this world."

And then Morgause saw that on the pack mule, covered and shrouded, was the body of a man, She whispered, "Who—?"

"Galahad," said Lancelet quietly. "It was my son who found the Grail, and now we know that no man may look on it and live. Would that it had been I—if only because I bear such bitter news to my king, that the one who should be King after him has gone before us into the world where he may forever follow his quest unspoilt—"

Morgause shuddered. *Now indeed will it be as if Arthur had never been, the land will have no king save for the king in Heaven, ruled over by those priests who have Arthur in their hands . . .* but angrily she dismissed those fancies. *Galahad is gone. Arthur must choose Gwydion to rule after him.*

Lancelet looked sorrowfully at the pack mule with Galahad's body, but he said only, "Shall we ride on? I had not intended to rest a night by the road, but the mists were thick, and I feared to lose my way. I would have thought it Avalon itself!"

"We could not find Camelot in the mists, no more than Avalon—" Cormac began, but Morgause interrupted him fretfully.

"Have done with that foolishness," she said. "We mistook the road in the darkness, and rode back and forth half the night! We too are in haste to come to Camelot, nephew."

One or two of her men present knew Lancelet and had known Galahad, and now they crowded close to the body, with soft expressions of sympathy and kindly words. Lancelet listened to all they had to say, his face sorrowful, then, with a few soft words, brought it to an end.

"Later, my lads, later, there will be time enough to mourn. I am in no haste, God knows, to bear such news to Arthur, but delaying will make it no kinder. Let us ride on."

The mist was thinning and burning away fast as the sun gained height. They set off down the road where Morgause and her men had ridden back and forth for hours in search of Camelot, but before they had gone very far there was another sound that broke the strange silence of the haunted morning. It was a trumpet call, clear and silver in the still air, from the heights of Camelot. And before her at the clump of four trees, broad and unmistakable in the growing sunlight, lay the wagon road built by Arthur's men for his legions to ride.

It seemed appropriate that the first man Morgause should see on the heights of Camelot was her son Gareth. He strode forth to challenge them at the great gates of Camelot; then, recognizing Lancelet, hurried to him. Lancelet flung himself headlong from his horse and took Gareth into a strong embrace.

"So, cousin, it is you—"

"Aye, it is that—Cai is too old and lame to be patrolling the walls of Camelot in these days. Ah, it is a good day in which you return to Camelot, my cousin. But I see that you found not Galahad, Lance?"

"Aye, but I did," said Lancelet sorrowfully, and Gareth's open face, still boyish despite his full beard, was struck with dismay as he looked at the outlines of the dead man under the pall.

"I must bear this news to Arthur at once. Take me to him, Gareth."

Gareth bowed his head, his hand resting on Lancelet's shoulder. "Ah, this is an evil day for Camelot. I said once before, it seemed to me that yonder Grail was the work of some devil, not of God at all!"

Lancelet shook his head, and it seemed to Morgause that something bright shone *through* him, as if his body were transparent; and through his sad smile there was hidden joy. "No, my dear cousin," he said, "you must put that from your mind forever. Galahad has had what God gave to him, and, God help us, so have we all. But his day is finished, and he is free of all human fate. Ours is still to come, dear Gareth—God grant us that we meet it with as much courage as he."

"Amen to that," said Gareth, and to Morgause's horrified surprise he crossed himself. Then, with a start, he looked up at her.

"Mother, is it you? Forgive me—yours is the last company in which I would expect to find Lancelet." He bent over her hand with a dutiful kiss. "Come, madam, let me summon a chamberlain and take you to the Queen. She will make you welcome among her ladies while Lancelet is with the King."

Morgause let herself be led away, wondering now why she had come. In Lothian she ruled as queen in her own right, but here in Camelot she could only sit among Gwenhwyfar's ladies, and know no more of what was going on than what one of her sons might see fit to tell her.

She said to the chamberlain, "Say to my son Gwydion—sir Mordred —that his mother has come, and bid him to wait upon me as soon as he can." But she wondered, sunk in despondency, if in this strange court he would even be troubled to pay her such respects as Gareth had done. And once again, she felt she had done wrong to come to Camelot.

14

fOR many years, Gwenhwyfar had felt that when the Companions of the Round Table were present, Arthur belonged not to her but to them. She had resented their intrusion into her life, their presence at Camelot; often she had felt that if Arthur were not surrounded by the court, perhaps they might have had a life happier than the one they led as King and Queen of Camelot.

And yet in this year of the Grail quest, she began to realize that she had been fortunate after all, for Camelot was like a village of ghosts with all the Companions departed, and Arthur the ghost who haunted Camelot, moving silently through the deserted castle.

It was not that she took no pleasure in Arthur's company when at last it was entirely hers. It was only that now she came to understand how much of his very being he had poured into his legions and the building of Camelot. He showed her ungrudging courtesy and kindness, and she had more of his company than ever she had had in all the long years of war or the years of peace that followed them. But it was as if some part of him was absent with his Companions, wherever they might be, and only a small fraction of the man himself was here with her. She loved Arthur the man no less than Arthur the King, but she realized now how much less was the man without the business of kingship into which he had put so much of his life. And she was ashamed that she could notice it.

They never spoke of those who were absent. In that year of the Grail quest, they lived quietly and in peace from day to day, speaking only of everyday things, of bread and meat, of fruits from the orchard or wine from the cellars, of a new cloak or the clasp of a shoe. And once, looking around the empty chamber of the Round Table, he said, "Should we have it put away until they return, my love? Even in this great chamber, there is small room to move, and now when it is all empty—"

"No," she said quickly, "no, my dear, leave it. This great room was built for the Round Table, and without it, it would be like an empty barn. Leave it. You and I and the household folk can dine in the smaller chamber." He smiled at her, and she knew he was glad she had said that.

"And when the knights return from the quest, we can once again make a great feast there," he said, but then fell silent, and she knew he was wondering how many would ever return.

Cai was with them, and old Lucan, and two or three of the Companions who were old or infirm or nursing old wounds. And Gwydion— Mordred as he was now called—was always with them, like a grown son;

often Gwenhwyfar looked on him and thought, *This is the son I might have borne to Lancelet,* and heat went scalding and flooding through her whole body, leaving her broken into a hot sweat as she thought of that night when Arthur himself had thrust her into Lancelet's arms. And indeed this heat came often now and went, so that she never knew whether a room was hot or cold, or whether it was this strange sudden heat from within. Gwydion was gentle and deferential to her, calling her always lady or, sometimes, shyly, Aunt; the very shyness with which he used this term of family closeness warmed her and made him dear to her. He was like to Lancelet, too, but more silent and less light of heart; where Lancelet had ever been ready with a jest or play on words, Gwydion smiled and was always ready with some wit like a blow or the thrust of a needle. His wit was wicked, but she could not but laugh when he made some cruel jest.

One night when their shrunken company was at dinner, Arthur said, "Until Lancelet comes back to us, nephew, I would have you take his post and be my captain of horse."

Gwydion chuckled. "Light enough will that duty be, my uncle and my lord—there are few horses in that stable now. The finest horses in your stables went with your knights and Companions, and who knows, indeed, whether or no some horse will be the one to find that Grail they seek!"

"Oh, hush," Gwenhwyfar said. "You must not make fun of their quest."

"Why not, Aunt? Again and again the priests tell us that we are the sheep of our Lord's pasture, and if a sheep may seek a spiritual presence, why, I have always thought a horse a nobler beast than any sheep. So who's to say whether or no the nobler beast may achieve the quest? Even some scarred old war horse may come at last to seek spiritual repose, as they say the lion shall one day lie down beside the lamb and never think it dinnertime."

Arthur laughed uneasily. "Will we need our horses again for war? Since Mount Badon, God be praised, we have had peace in the land—"

"Save for Lucius," Gwydion said, "and if I have learned one thing in my life, it is that peace is something which cannot last. Wild Northmen in dragon ships are landing on the coast, and when men cry out for Arthur's legions to defend them, the answer comes only that Arthur's Companions have ridden away to seek their souls' peace. And so they seek for help from the Saxon kings in the South. But no doubt when this quest is done, they will look once more to Arthur and to Camelot—and it seems to me that war horses might be in short supply when that day comes. Lancelet is so busy with the Grail and his other deeds that he has had little time to see to the King's stables."

"Well, I have told you I wished you to fill that place," said Arthur, and it struck Gwenhwyfar that his tone sounded peevish, and old, without the strength it once held. "As captain of horse you have authority to send for horses in my name. Lancelet used to deal with traders from somewhere to the south, beyond Brittany—"

"As I shall do also, then," said Gwydion. "There were no horses like the horses from Spain, but now, my uncle and my lord, the best horses come from further still. The Spaniards themselves buy horses from Africa, from a desert country there. Now these Saracens are beginning to overrun Spain itself—this I heard from yonder Saracen knight Palomides, who journeyed here and was guested for a time, then rode away to see what adventure there might be among the Saxons. He is not a Christian, and it seemed strange to him that all these knights should ride away after the Grail when there was war in the land."

"I spoke to Palomides," said Arthur. "He had a sword from that southern country of Spanish steel—I would gladly have had one like to it, though I think it is no finer than Excalibur. No sword in our country will hold such an edge, like a razor. I am glad I never had to face such a sword in the lists. The Northmen have great axes and clubs, but their weapons are not so good even as the Saxon weapons."

"They are fiercer fighters, though," said Gwydion. "They go into a madness of fighting, as sometimes the Tribesmen of Lothian used to do, casting away their shields in battle. . . . No, my king, we may have had peace for a goodly time, but even as the Saracens are beginning to overrun Spain, so the wild Northmen are on our coasts, and the wild Irishmen. In the end, no doubt, the Saracens will be good for Spain even as the Saxons have been good for this land—"

"Good for this land?" Arthur looked at the younger man in astonishment. "What do I hear you say, nephew?"

"When the Romans left us, my lord Arthur, we were isolated at the end of the world, alone with the half-savage Tribes. The war with the Saxons forced us to reach beyond ourselves," he said. "We had trade with Less Britain and with Spain and the countries to the south, we had to barter for weapons and horses, we built new cities—why, here's your own Camelot, sir, to show that. I do not even speak of the movement of the priests, who now have come among the Saxons and made them no longer wild Tribesmen with hair on their faces, worshipping their own barbarian Gods, but civilized men with cities and trade of their own, and their own civilized kings who are subject to you. For what else has this whole land been waiting? Now, even, they have monasteries and learned men writing books, and much more . . . without the wars against the Saxons, my lord Arthur, Uther's old kingdom would have been forgotten like that of Maximus."

Arthur said with a glimmer of amusement, "Then, no doubt, you think these twenty years and more of peace have endangered Camelot, and we need more wars and fighting to bring us into the world again? It is easy to see you are not a warrior, young man. I have no such romantic view of war as that!"

Gwydion smiled back. "What makes you think I am not a warrior, my lord? I fought among your men against Lucius who would have been emperor, and I had ample time to make up my own mind about wars and their worth. Without wars, you would be more forgotten than the least of those kings in Wales and in Eire—who now can call the roll of the kings of Tara?"

"And you think one day it may be so with Camelot, my boy?"

"Ah, my uncle and my king, would you have the wisdom of a Druid or the flattery of a courtier?"

Arthur said, laughing, "Let us have the crafty counsel of a Mordred."

"The courtier would say, my lord, that the reign of Arthur will live forever and his memory be forever green in the world. And the Druid would say that all men perish, and one day they will be, with all of their wisdom and their glories, like unto Atlantis, sunken beneath the waves. The Gods alone endure."

"And what would my nephew and my friend say, then?"

"Your *nephew*"—he put just enough emphasis on the word that Gwenhwyfar could hear that it should have been *your son*—"would say, my uncle and my lord, that we are living for this day, and not for what history may say of us a thousand years hence. And so your nephew would advise that your stables should once again reflect the noble days when Arthur's horses and his fighting men were known and fearful to all. No man should be able to say, the King grows old and with all his knights on quest, cares nothing to keep his men and horses in fighting trim."

Arthur gave him a friendly clap on the shoulder. "So let it be, dear boy. I trust your judgment. Send to Spain, or to Africa if you will, for horses such as best suit the reputation of Arthur's legion, and see to their training."

"I shall have to find Saxons for that," said Gwydion, "and the Saxons know little of our secrets of fighting a-horse—you have always said they should not. Is it your will that since the Saxons are our allies now, they should be trained in our fighting skills?"

Arthur looked troubled. "I fear I must leave that, too, in your hands."

"I shall try to do my best for you," Gwydion said, "and now, my lord, we have sat overlong in this talk, and wearied the ladies—forgive me, madam," he added, inclining his head to Gwenhwyfar with that winning smile. "Shall we have music? The lady Niniane, I am certain, would be happy to bring her harp and sing to you, my lord and my king."

"I am always happy to hear my kinswoman's music," said Arthur gravely, "if it is pleasing to my lady."

Gwenhwyfar nodded to Niniane, who fetched her harp and sat before them, singing, and Gwenhwyfar listened with pleasure to the music—Niniane played beautifully, and her voice was sweet, though not so pure or strong as Morgaine's. But as she watched Gwydion, his eyes on Taliesin's daughter, she thought, *Why is it that we, a Christian court, must always have here one of those damsels of the Lady of the Lake?* It worried her, although Gwydion seemed as good a Christian as anyone else at court, coming always to mass on Sunday, as did Niniane herself. For that matter she could not remember how Niniane had come to be one of her ladies, save that Gwydion had brought her to court and asked the Queen to extend her hospitality as a kinswoman of Arthur and as Taliesin's daughter. Gwenhwyfar had only the kindest memories of Taliesin, and had been pleased to welcome his daughter, but somehow it seemed now that, without ever putting herself forward, Niniane had assumed the place of the first among her ladies. Arthur always treated her with favor and often called to her to sing, and there were times when Gwenhwyfar, watching them, wondered if he looked on her as more than kinswoman.

But no, surely not. If Niniane had a paramour here at court it was more than likely to be Gwydion himself. She had seen him look at her . . . and yet her heart grew sore within her; this woman was fair, fair as she herself had been, and she was but an aging woman with her hair fading, the color gone from her cheeks, her body sagging. . . . And so when Niniane had put up her harp and withdrawn, she frowned as Arthur came to escort her from the hall.

"You look weary, my wife, what ails you?"

"Gwydion said you were old—"

"My own dear wife, I have sat on that throne of Britain for one-and-thirty years, with you at my side. Do you think there is anyone in this kingdom who can still call us young? Most of our subjects were not yet born when we came to the throne. Though indeed, my dear, I know not how it is that you look ever so young."

"Oh, my husband, I was not seeking to be praised," she said impatiently.

"You should be flattered, my Gwen, that Gwydion does not deal in empty flattery to an aging king, cozening me with lying words. He speaks honestly and I value him for it. I wish—"

"I know what you wish," she interrupted him, her voice angry. "You wish you could acknowledge him your son, so that he and not Galahad might have your throne after you—"

He colored. "Gwenhwyfar, must we always be so sharp with each other on this subject? The priests would not have him for King, and there's an end of it."

"I cannot but remember whose son he is—"

"I cannot but remember that he is *my* son," said Arthur gently.

"I trust not Morgaine, and you yourself have found that she—"

His face grew hard and she knew that he would not hear her on this one subject. "Gwenhwyfar, my son was fostered by the Queen of Lothian, and her sons have been the support and stay of my kingdom. What would I have done without Gareth and Gawaine? And now Gwydion stands fair to be like them, kindest and best of friends and Companions. It will not make me think the less of Gwydion that he stood beside me when all my other Companions forsook me for this quest."

Gwenhwyfar did not want to quarrel with him. She said now, sliding her hand into his, "Believe me, my lord, I love you beyond all else on this earth."

"Why, I believe you, my love," he said. "The Saxons have a saying —that man is blessed who has a good friend, a good wife, and a good sword. And all those have I had, my Gwenhwyfar."

"Oh, the Saxons," she said, laughing. "All those years you fought against them, and now you quote their sayings of wisdom—"

"Well, what is the good of war—as Gwydion says—if we cannot learn wisdom from our enemies? Long ago, someone—Gawaine, perhaps—said something about the Saxons and the learned men in their monasteries. He said it is like to a woman who is raped, and yet, after the invaders have left our coasts, bears a good son—is it better to have had only the evil, or, when the evil is done and there's no mending it, to take what good may come from that evil?"

Gwenhwyfar frowned and said, "Only a man, I think, could make such a jest as that!"

"No, I meant not to bring up old sorrows, dear heart," he protested, "but the harm was done for me and Morgaine years ago." She realized that for once he spoke his sister's name without that cold tightening in his face. "Would it be better that no good of any kind should come from the sin I did with Morgaine—for you will have it that it was sin—or should I be grateful that, since the sin was done and there's no going back to innocence, God has given me a good son in return for that evil? Morgaine and I parted not as friends, and I know not where she is or what has befallen her, nor do I suppose I will ever again look upon her face this side of the day of judgment. But her son is now the very stay of my throne. Should I mistrust him because of the mother who gave him birth?"

Gwenhwyfar would have said, *I do not trust him because he was reared in Avalon,* but she had no wish to, so she held her peace. But when, at her door, Arthur held her hand and asked softly, "Is it your will that I join you this night, lady?" she avoided his eyes and said, "No—no, I am tired." She tried not to see the look of relief in his eyes. She wondered if it were Niniane or some other who shared his bed these days; she would not stoop to question his chamberlain. *If it is not I, why should I care who it might be?*

The year moved on into the darkness of winter, and on toward spring. One day Gwenhwyfar said fiercely, "I wish this quest were done and the knights returned, Grail or no Grail!"

"Hush, my dear, they are sworn," said Arthur, but later that day, indeed, a knight rode up the track to Camelot, and they saw that it was Gawaine.

"Is it you, cousin?" Arthur embraced him and kissed him on either cheek. "I had no hope of seeing you till a year was done—did you not swear to follow the Grail for a year and a day?"

"I did so," said Gawaine, "but I am not false to my oath, Lord, and yonder priest need not look at me as if I were forsworn. For I last saw the Grail here in this very castle, Arthur, and I am just as like to see it here again as in this corner or that of the world. I rode up and down, hither and thither, and never did I hear word of it more, and one day it came to me that I might as well seek it where I had seen it already, at Camelot and in the presence of my king, even if I must look for it every Sunday on the altar at mass, and nowhere else."

Arthur smiled and embraced him, and Gwenhwyfar saw that his eyes were wet. "Come in, cousin," he said simply. "Welcome home."

And some days later, Gareth too came home. "I had a vision indeed, and I think it may have come from God," he said as they sat at supper in the hall. "I dreamed I saw the Grail uncovered and fair before me, and then a voice spoke to me from the light around the Grail and said, 'Gareth, Companion of Arthur, this is all you will ever see of that Grail in this life. Why seek further for visions and glories, when your king has need of you in Camelot? You may serve God when you reach Heaven, but while you live here on earth, return to Camelot and serve your king.' And when I woke, I remembered that even Christ had said that they should render unto Caesar those things which belonged to Caesar, and so I came home this way, and I met with Lancelet as I rode, and I bade him do the same."

"Do you think, then, that you truly found the Grail?" Gwydion asked.

Gareth laughed. "Perhaps the Grail itself is only a dream. And when I dreamed of the Grail, it bade me do my duty to my lord and king."

"I suppose we shall look to see Lancelet here among us soon, then?"

"I hope he can find it in his heart to come," said Gawaine, "for indeed we need him here. But Easter will be upon us soon, and then we can look to have them all come home."

Later Gareth asked that Gwydion would bring his harp and sing for them. "For," he said, "I have not heard even such rough music as I would hear at the court of the Saxons, and you who sit here at home have surely had time to perfect your songs, Gwydion."

Gwenhwyfar would not have been surprised had he stood aside for Niniane, but instead he brought out a harp Gwenhwyfar recognized.

"Is that not Morgaine's harp?"

"It is so. She left it at Camelot when she went from here, and if she wants it she can send for it, or come and take it from me. And until that day, well, it is surely mine, and I doubt she would begrudge me this when she has given me nothing else."

"Save only your life," said Arthur in a tone of mild reproof, and Gwydion turned on him a look of such bitterness that Gwenhwyfar was sorely distressed. His savage tone could not be heard four feet away. "Should I then be grateful for that, my lord and my king?" Before Arthur could speak, he set his fingers to the strings and began to play. But the song he sang shocked Gwenhwyfar.

He sang the ballad of the Fisher King, who dwelt in a castle at the middle of a great wasteland; and as the king grew ancient and his powers waned, so did the land fade and put forth no crops, till some younger man should come and strike the stroke of mercy which would pour out the blood of the ancient king upon the land. Then the land would grow young again with the new king, and bloom with his youth.

"Say you so?" demanded Arthur uneasily. "That the land where an old king rules can only be a land which fades?"

"Not so, my lord. What would we do without the wisdom of your many years? Yet in the ancient days of the Tribes it was even so, where the Goddess of the Land alone endures, and the king rules while he shall please her. And when the King Stag grew old, another would come from the herd and throw him down . . . but this is a Christian court, and you have no such heathen ways as that, my king. I think perhaps that ballad of the Fisher King is but a symbol of the grass which, even as it says in your Scriptures, is like to man's flesh, enduring but a season, and the king of the wasteland but a symbol of the world which yearly dies with the grass and is renewed with spring, as all religions tell . . . even Christ withered like the Fisher King when he died the death of the cross and returns again with Easter, ever new . . ." and he touched the strings and sang softly:

"For lo, all the days of man are as a leaf that is fallen and as the grass that withereth.

Thou too shalt be forgotten, like the flower that falleth on the grass, like the wine that is poured out and soaks into the earth.

And yet even as the spring returns, so blooms the land and so blooms life which will come again . . ."

Gwenhwyfar asked, "Is that Scripture, Gwydion? A verse perhaps of a psalm?"

Gwydion shook his head. "It is an ancient hymn of the Druids, and there are those who say it is older than that, brought perhaps from those lands which now lie beneath the sea. But each religion has some such hymn as that. Perhaps indeed all religion is One . . ."

Arthur asked him quietly, "Are you a Christian, my lad?"

Gwydion did not answer for a moment. At last he said, "I was reared a Druid and I do not break the oaths I have sworn. My name is not Kevin, my king. But you do not know all the vows I have made." Quietly he rose from his place and went forth from the hall. Arthur, staring after him, did not speak even to reprove his lack of courtesy, but Gawaine was scowling.

"Will you let him take leave with so little of ceremony, lord?"

"Oh, leave it, leave it," Arthur said. "We are all kinsmen here, I ask not that he should treat me always as if I were on the throne! He knows well that he is my son, and so does every man in this room! Would you have him always the courtier?"

But Gareth was frowning after him. He said softly, "I wish with all my heart that Galahad would return to court. God grant him some such vision as mine, for you need him more here than you need me, Arthur, and if he comes not soon, I shall go forth myself to seek him."

It was only a few days before Pentecost when Lancelet finally came home.

They had seen the approaching procession—men, ladies, horses and pack animals—and Gareth, at the gates, had summoned all men to welcome them, but Gwenhwyfar, standing at Arthur's side, paid little heed to Queen Morgause, except to wonder why the Queen of Lothian had come. Lancelet knelt before Arthur with his sorrowful news, and Gwenhwyfar too felt the pain in his eyes . . . always, always it had been like this, that what smote his heart was like a lash laid to her own. Arthur bent and raised Lancelet to his feet and embraced him, and his own eyes were wet.

"I have lost a son, no less than you, dear friend. He will be sorely missed." And Gwenhwyfar could bear it no more, and stepped forward to give Lancelet her hand before them all and say, her voice trembling, "I had longed for you to return to us, Lancelet, but I am sorry that you must come with such sad news."

Arthur said quietly to his men, "Let him be taken to the chapel where he was made knight. There let him lie, and tomorrow he shall be buried as befits my son and heir." As he turned away, he staggered a little, and Gwydion was quick to put his hand beneath his arm and support him.

Gwenhwyfar did not often weep now, but she felt she must weep at Lancelet's face, so marred and stricken. What had befallen him in this year when he followed the Grail? Long sickness, long fasting, weariness, wounds? Never had she seen him so sorrowful, even when he came to speak with her of his marriage to Elaine. Watching Arthur leaning heavily on Gwydion's arm, she sighed, and Lancelet pressed her hand and said softly, "I can even be glad now that Arthur came to know his own son and to value him. It will soften his grief."

Gwenhwyfar shook her head, not wanting to think of what this would mean for Gwydion and for Arthur. Morgaine's son! Morgaine's son, to follow after Arthur—no, there was no help for it now!

Gareth came and bowed before her and said, "Madam, my mother is here—" and Gwenhwyfar recalled that she was not free to stay among the men, that her place was with the ladies, that she could not speak a word of comfort to Arthur or even to Lancelet. She said coldly, "I am happy to welcome you, Queen Morgause," and it came to her mind, *Must I confess this then as a sin, that I lie to the queen? Would it somehow be more virtuous if I said to her, I welcome you as duty demands, Queen Morgause, but I am not glad to see you and I wish you had stayed in Lothian, or in hell for all I care!* She saw that Niniane was at Arthur's side, that Arthur was between her and Gwydion, and she frowned.

"Lady Niniane," she said coolly, "I think that the women will withdraw now. Find a guest room for the Queen of Lothian, and see that everything is made ready for her."

Gwydion looked angry, but there was nothing to be said, and Gwenhwyfar reflected, as she and her ladies left the courtyard, that there were advantages to being a queen.

ALL THAT DAY, the Companions and knights of the Round Table were riding back toward Arthur's court, and Gwenhwyfar was busy with the preparations for the feast on the morrow, which would be the funeral. On the day of Pentecost, such of Arthur's men as had returned from this quest would be reunited. She recognized many faces, but some, she knew, would never return: Perceval, and Bors, and Lamorak—she turned a gentler face on Morgause, who, she knew, sincerely mourned for Lamorak. She had felt that the older woman had made a fool of herself with her young lover, but grief was grief, and when at the funeral mass for Galahad the priest spoke of all those others who had fallen on this quest, she saw Morgause hiding tears behind her veil, and her face was red and blotched after the mass.

The night before, Lancelet had watched by his son's body in the chapel, and she had had no chance for private words with him. Now, after the funeral mass, she bade him sit beside her and Arthur at dinner, and when she filled his cup, she hoped that he would drink himself drunk and be past mourning. She grieved over his lined face, so drawn with pain and privation, and over the curls around his face, so white now. And she who loved him best, she could not even embrace him and weep with him in public. For many years she had felt it like a deep pain that she would never have any right to turn to him before other men, but must sit at his side and be only a kinswoman and his queen. And now it seemed to her more dreadful than ever, but he did not turn to her, he did not even meet her eyes.

Standing, Arthur drank to the knights who would never return from the quest. "Here before you all, I swear that none of their wives or children shall ever know want while I live and Camelot stands with one stone upon another," he said. "I share your sorrow. The heir to my throne died in the quest of the Grail." He turned, and held out his hand to Gwydion, who came slowly to his side. He looked younger than he was, in a plain white tunic, his dark hair caught in a golden band.

Arthur said, "A king cannot, like other men, indulge in long mourning, my Companions. Here I ask you to mourn with me for my lost nephew and adopted son, who now will never reign at my side. But even though our mourning is still green, I ask you to accept Gwydion—sir Mordred— the son of my only sister, Morgaine of Avalon, as my heir. Gwydion is young, but he has become one of my wise councillors." He raised his cup and drank. "I drink to you, my son, and to your reign when mine is done."

Gwydion came and knelt before Arthur. "May your reign be long, my father." It seemed to Gwenhwyfar that he was blinking back tears, and she liked him better for it. The Companions drank, and then, led by Gareth, broke out in cheering.

But Gwenhwyfar sat silent. She had known this must come, but she had not expected it to happen at Galahad's very funeral feast! Now she turned to Lancelet and whispered, "I wish he had waited! I wish he had consulted with his councillors!"

"Knew you not he intended this?" Lancelet asked. He reached out and took her hand, pressing it softly and holding on to it, stroking her fingers beneath the rings she wore. Her fingers seemed now so thin and bony, not young and soft as they had been; she felt abashed and would have drawn her hand away, but he would not let her. He said, still stroking her hand, "Arthur should not have done that to you without warning—"

"God knows, I have no right to complain, who could not give him a son, so he must make do with Morgaine's—"

"Still, he should have warned you," Lancelet said. It was the first time, Gwenhwyfar thought distantly, that he had ever, even for a moment, seemed to criticize Arthur. He raised her hand gently to his lips, then let it go as Arthur approached them with Gwydion. Stewards were bringing smoking platters of meat, trays of fresh fruits and hot breads, setting sweetmeats every few places along the table. Gwenhwyfar let her steward help her to some meat and fruits, but she barely touched her plate. She saw, with a smile, that it had been arranged that she shared her plate with Lancelet, as so often she had done at other Pentecost feasts; and that Niniane, on Arthur's other side, was eating from his dish. Once he called her daughter, which relieved Gwenhwyfar's mind somewhat—perhaps he accepted her already as his son's potential wife. To her surprise Lancelet seemed to follow her thought.

"Will the next festival at court be a wedding? I would have thought the kinship too close—"

"Would that matter in Avalon?" Gwenhwyfar asked, her voice harsher than she intended; the old pain was still there.

Lancelet shrugged. "I know not—in Avalon as a boy I heard of a country far to the south of here, where the royal house married always their own sister and brother that the royal blood might not be diluted by that of the common people, and that dynasty lasted for a thousand years."

"Heathen men," said Gwenhwyfar. "They knew nothing of God, and knew not that they sinned. . . ."

Yet Gwydion seemed not to have suffered from the sin of his mother and his father; why should he, Taliesin's grandson—no, his great-grandson—hesitate to wed with Taliesin's daughter?

God will punish Camelot for that sin, she thought suddenly. *For Arthur's sin and for mine . . . and Lancelet's . . .*

Beyond her she heard Arthur say to Gwydion, "You said once in my hearing that Galahad looked not like one who would live to his crowning."

"And you remember too, my father and my lord," said Gwydion quietly, "that I swore to you I would have no part in his death, but that he would die honorably for the cross he worshipped, and it was so."

"What more do you foresee, my son?"

"Ask me not, lord Arthur. The Gods are kind when they say that no man may know his own end. Even if I knew—and I say not that I know—I would tell you nothing."

Perhaps, thought Gwenhwyfar, with a sudden shiver, *God has punished us enough for our sin when he sent us this Mordred . . .* and then, looking at the young man, she was dismayed. How can I think so of the one who has been to Arthur as a son indeed? He is not to blame for his fathering!

She said to Lancelet, "Arthur should not have done this before Galahad was cold in his grave!"

"Not so, my lady. Arthur knows well the duties of a king. Do you think it would matter to Galahad, where he has gone, who sits on the throne he never wished for? I would have done better to make my son a priest, Gwenhwyfar."

She looked at Lancelet, brooding, a thousand leagues away from her, gone into himself where she could never follow, and she said, awkwardly, reaching for him in the best way she could, "And did you, then, fail to find the Grail?"

She saw him come slowly back through the long distance. "I came— nearer than any sinful man can come and live. But I was spared, to tell the men at Arthur's court that the Grail has gone forever beyond this world." Again he fell silent, then said across that vast distance, "I would have followed it beyond the world, but I was given no choice."

She wondered, *Did you not, then, wish to return to court for my sake?* And it seemed clear to her that Lancelet was more like Arthur than she had ever known, and that she had never been anything more, to either of them, than a diversion between war and quest; that the real life of a man was lived in a world where love meant nothing. All his life he had devoted to wars at Arthur's side, and now when there was no war he had given himself over to a great Mystery. The Grail had come between them, as Arthur had come between them, and Lancelet's own honor.

Now even Lancelet had turned to God, and thought, no doubt, only that she had led him into grave sin. The pain was unendurable. In all of life, she had had nothing more than this, and she could not keep herself from reaching out to him, clasping his hand. "I have longed for you," she whispered, and was shocked at the longing in her voice; *he will think me no better than Morgause, flinging myself at his head.* . . . He held her hand and said softly, "And I have missed you, Gwen." And then, as if he could read her whole hungry heart, he said in a low voice, "Grail or no Grail, beloved, nothing could have brought me back to this court but the thought of you. I would have remained there, spending the rest of my life in prayers that I might see again that Mystery that was hidden from my eyes. But I am no more than a man, my beloved. . . ."

And she knew what it was that he was saying, and pressed his hand. "Shall I send away my women, then?"

He hesitated a moment, and Gwenhwyfar felt the old dread . . . how dared she be so forward, so lacking in a woman's modesty? . . . Always, this moment was like death. Then he tightened his grip on her fingers and said, "Yes, my love."

BUT AS SHE awaited him, alone in the darkness, she wondered in bitterness if his "Yes" had been like Arthur's, an offer made from time to time out of pity, or a wish to save her pride. Now that there was no longer the slightest hope that she would bear to Arthur a belated child, he could have stopped coming to her, but he was too kind to give her women cause to smile behind her back. Still, it was like a knife in her heart that Arthur always seemed relieved when she sent him away; there were even times when she invited him in and they talked together or she lay for a time in his arms, content to be held and comforted, but demanding no more of him. Now she wondered if Arthur felt that his embraces would be unwelcome to her, so that he seldom offered them, or whether he truly did not desire her. She wondered if he ever had desired her, or had always come to her because she was the wife he had taken and it was his duty to give her children.

All men praised my beauty and desired me, save for the husband I was given. And now, she thought, perhaps even Lancelet comes to me because he is too kind to abandon me or turn me away. She grew feverish, and it seemed that even in her light bed gown she was overheated, her whole body breaking out in drops of sweat. She rose and sponged herself with the cold water in a jar on her dressing table, touching her sagging breasts with distaste. *Ah, I am old, surely it will disgust him, that this ugly old flesh is still as eager for him as if I were young and beautiful. . . .*

And then she heard his step behind her; and he caught her into his arms, and she forgot her fears. But after he had gone she lay wakeful.

I should not risk this. It was different, in the old days; now we are a Christian court and the eyes of the bishop are always on me.

But I have nothing else . . . and it occurred to her suddenly, *nor has Lancelet. . . .* His son was dead, and his wife, and the old closeness with Arthur was gone beyond recall.

Would that I were like Morgaine, who does not need a man's love to feel herself alive and real. . . . And yet Gwenhwyfar knew that even if she did not need this from Lancelet, it was he who needed her; and without her, he would be utterly alone. He had come to court because he needed her no less than she needed him.

And so, even if it was sin, it seemed the greater sin to leave Lancelet comfortless.

Even if we are both damned for it, she thought, *never shall I turn aside from him. God is a God of love,* she thought; how then could he condemn the one thing in her life that was born of love? And if he did, she thought, terrified at her blasphemy, he was not the God she had always worshipped, and she did not care what he thought!

15

that summer there was war again, the Northmen raiding the western coasts, and Arthur's legion rode forth to battle, this time riding at the head of the Saxon kings from the southern country, Ceardig and his men. Queen Morgause remained in Camelot; it was not safe to take the road alone to Lothian, and none could be spared to escort her.

They returned late in the summer. Morgause was in the women's hall with Gwenhwyfar and her ladies when they heard the trumpets from the heights.

"It is Arthur returning!" Gwenhwyfar rose from her seat. Immediately all of the women dropped their spindles and clustered around her.

"How do you know?"

Gwenhwyfar laughed. "A messenger brought me the news last night," she said. "Do you think I am dealing in sorcery at my age?" She looked around her at the excited girls—to Morgause it seemed that all of Gwenhwyfar's ladies were but little girls, fourteen and fifteen, who made every excuse to leave off spinning; and now the Queen said indulgently, "Shall we go and watch them from the heights?"

Chattering, giggling, gathering in groups of two and three, they ran off, leaving the dropped spindles where they had fallen. Good-naturedly, Gwenhwyfar called one of the serving-women to put the room to rights and, at Morgause's side, followed at a more dignified pace to the brow of the hill, where they could see the wide road leading up to Camelot.

"Look, there is the King—"

"And sir Mordred, riding at his side—"

"And there is the lord Lancelet—oh, look, he has a bandage round his head, and his arm is in a sling!"

"Let me see," said Gwenhwyfar and pushed them aside, while the girls stared. Morgause could make out Gwydion, riding at Arthur's side; he appeared unwounded, and she drew a sigh of relief. She could see Cormac back among the men, too—he had ridden to war with all the men, and he too seemed unhurt. Gareth was easy to find among them—he was the tallest man in Arthur's whole company, and his fair hair blazed like a halo. Gawaine, too, at Arthur's back as always, was upright in his saddle, but as they came nearer she could see a great bruise on his face, darkening his eyes, and his mouth swollen as if he had had a tooth or two knocked out.

"Look, sir Mordred is handsome—" one of the little girls said. "I have heard the Queen say that he looks exactly as Lancelet did when Lancelet was young," and then she giggled and dug her neighbor in the ribs. They clung together, whispering, and Morgause watched, sighing. They seemed so young, all of them, so pretty with their hair silky-soft and bound in plaits and curls, brown or red or golden, their cheeks soft as petals and smooth as a baby's, their waists so slim, their hands so smooth and white—she felt, suddenly, wild with jealousy; once she had been more beautiful than any of them. Now they were nudging one another, whispering about this knight and that.

"Look how the Saxon knights are all bearded—why do they want to look shaggy like dogs?"

"My mother says," one of the maidens said impudently—she was the daughter of one of the Saxon noblemen, her name was something barbarian which Morgause could hardly pronounce, Alfreth or something of that sort —"that to kiss a man without a beard is like kissing another maiden, or your baby brother!"

"Yet sir Mordred shaves his face clean, and there is nothing maidenly about him," said one of the girls, and turned laughing to Niniane, standing quietly among the women, "is there, lady Niniane?"

Niniane said, with a soft laugh, "All these bearded men seem old to me—when I was a little girl, only my father and the oldest Druids ever went bearded."

"Even Bishop Patricius now wears his beard," said one of the girls. "I heard him say that in heathen times men deformed their faces by cutting their beards and men should wear their beards as God made them. Maybe the Saxons think it so."

"It is but a new fashion," said Morgause. "They come and they go—when I was young, Christian and pagan alike shaved their faces clean, and now the fashion has changed—I think not it has anything to do with holiness either way. I doubt not, one day Gwydion will wear a beard—will you think less of him, Niniane?"

The younger woman laughed. "No, cousin. He is the same, bearded or shaven. Ah, look, there rides King Ceardig, and others—are they all to be guested here at Camelot? Madam, shall I go and tell the stewards?"

"Please do, my dear," Gwenhwyfar said, and Niniane moved toward the hall. The girls were shoving one another to get a better view, and Gwenhwyfar said, "Come, come—all of you, back to your spinning. It is unseemly to stare at young men this way. Have none of you anything better to do than talk so immodestly about the men? All of you now, be off with you, you will see them this night in the great hall. There is to be feasting, which means work for all of you."

They looked sulky, but they went obediently back to the hall, and Gwenhwyfar sighed and shook her head as she walked back at Morgause's side. "In Heaven's name, was there ever such a lot of unruly girls? And somehow I must keep them all chaste and under my guidance—it seems they spend all their time gossiping and giggling instead of minding their spinning. I am ashamed that my court should be so filled with empty-headed and immodest little hussies like this!"

"Oh, come, my dear," said Morgause lazily, "surely you too were fifteen once? Surely you were not such a model maiden as all that—did you never steal a look at a handsome young man and think and gossip about how it would be to kiss him, bearded or shaven?"

"I do not know what you did when you were fifteen," Gwenhwyfar flared at her, "but I was behind convent walls! It seems to me that would be a good place for these unmannerly maids!"

Morgause laughed. "When I was fourteen, I had an eye for everything that wore breeches. I recall that I used to sit in Gorlois's lap—he that was married to Igraine before Uther's eyes fell on her—and Igraine knew it well, for when she married Uther, her first act was to pack me off to be married to Lot, which was about as far from Uther's court as she could send me without crossing the ocean! Come, Gwenhwyfar, even behind your convent walls can you swear you never peeped out at any handsome young man who came to break your father's horses, or the crimson cloak of any young knight?"

Gwenhwyfar looked down at her sandals. "It seems so very long ago—" and then, recollecting herself, spoke briskly. "The hunters brought in a deer last night—I shall give orders that it be cut up and roasted for dinner, and perhaps we should have a pig killed too, if all these Saxons are to be guested here. And fresh straw must be spread in the rooms where they will sleep, there will never be enough beds for all these people!"

"Send the maidens to see to that too," said Morgause. "They must learn to manage guests in a great hall—for what other reason are they in your care, Gwenhwyfar? And it is the duty of a queen to welcome her lord when he returns from war."

"You are right." Gwenhwyfar sent her page to give the orders, and they walked toward the great gates of Camelot together. Morgause thought, *Why, it is exactly as if we had been friends all our lives.* And she thought, there were so few of them who had been young together.

She had much the same feeling when she sat that night in the great hall that was hung with decorations and brilliant with the fine clothes of the ladies and the knights. Almost it was like the great days of Camelot. Yet so many of the old Companions were gone in war, or on the Grail quest, and would never return. Morgause did not remember often that she was old, and it frightened her. Half the seats of the Round Table, it seemed, were filled now with hairy Saxons with their great beards and their rough cloaks, or with young men who seemed hardly old enough to hold weapons. Even her baby, Gareth, was one of the older knights of the Round Table, and the newer ones deferred to him amazingly, calling him sir, and asking his advice, or hesitating to argue with him if they differed. As for Gwydion —most of them called him sir Mordred—he seemed quite a leader among the younger men, new knights and the Saxons whom Arthur had chosen as his Companions.

Gwenhwyfar's ladies and stewards had done their task well; there was roast and boiled meat in plenty, and great meat pies with gravy, platters of early apples and grapes, hot bread and lentil porridge. At the high table, when the feasting was done and the Saxons were drinking and at their favorite game of asking riddles, Arthur called Niniane to sing for them. Gwenhwyfar had Lancelet at her side, his head bandaged and his arm in a sling—he had been wounded by a Northman's battleaxe. He could not use his arm, and Gwenhwyfar was cutting his meat for him. No one, Morgause thought, paid it the slightest attention.

Gareth and Gawaine were seated further down the table, and Gwydion close to them, sharing a dish with Niniane. Morgause went to greet them. Gwydion had bathed and combed his hair into curls, but one of his legs was bandaged, propped on a stool.

"Are you hurt, my son?"

"It does well enough," he said. "I am too big now, Mother, to run and climb into your lap when I stub my toe!"

"It looks worse than that," she said, looking at the bandage and the crusted blood at the edges, "but I will leave you alone, if you wish. Is that tunic new?"

It was made in a fashion she had seen many of the Saxons wearing, with sleeves so long that they came down past the wrist and half covered the knuckles of the hand. Gwydion's was of blue-dyed cloth, embroidered with crimson stitchery.

"It was a gift from Ceardig. He told me it was a good fashion for a Christian court, for it conceals the serpents of Avalon." His mouth twisted. "Perhaps I should give my lord Arthur such a tunic for a New Year's gift this winter!"

"I doubt if anyone would know the difference," said Gawaine. "No one, now, thinks of Avalon, and Arthur's wrists are so faded no one sees or would criticize if they did."

Morgause looked at Gawaine's bruised face and eyes. He had in truth lost more than one tooth, and his hands, too, looked cut and bruised.

"And you too are wounded, my son?"

"Not from the enemy," Gawaine growled. "This I got from our Saxon friends—one of the men in Ceardig's army. Damn them all, those unmannerly bastards! I think I liked it better when they were all our foes!"

"You fought him, then?"

"Aye, and will do so again, should he dare to open his clacking jaw about my king," Gawaine said angrily. "Nor did I need Gareth to come to my rescue, as if I were not big enough to fight my own battles without my little brother coming to my aid—"

"He was twice your size," said Gareth, putting down his spoon, "and he had you on the ground, and I thought he would break your back or crack your ribs—I am not sure yet that he did not. Was I to sit aside while that foul-tongued fellow beat my brother and slandered my kinsman? He will think twice and then thrice before he opens his evil mouth again with such words."

"Still," said Gwydion quietly, "you cannot silence the whole Saxon army, Gareth, especially when what they say is true. There's a name, and not a pretty one, for a man, even when that man's a king, who sits back and says nothing while another man does his husband's duty in his wife's bed—"

"You dare!" Gareth half rose, turning on Gwydion and gripping the Saxon tunic at the neck. Gwydion put up his hands to loosen Gareth's hold.

"Easy, foster-brother!" He looked like a child in the giant Gareth's grip. "Will you treat me as you treated yonder Saxon because here among kinsmen I speak truth, or am I too to keep to the pleasant lie of the court, when all men see the Queen with her paramour and say nothing?"

Gareth slowly relaxed his grip and eased Gwydion back to his seat. "If Arthur has nothing to complain of in the lady's conduct, who am I to speak?"

Gawaine muttered, "Damn the woman! Damn her anyhow! Would that Arthur had put her away while there was still time! I have no great love for so Christian a court as this has become, and filled with Saxons. When I was first knight at Arthur's side, there was not a Saxon in all this land with more of religion than a pig in his sty!"

Gwydion made a deprecating sound, and Gawaine turned on him. "I know them better than you. I was fighting Saxons while you were wetting your swaddling bands! Are we now to run Arthur's court by what these hairy grunters think of us?"

"You do not know the Saxons half so well as I do," Gwydion said. "You do not get to know a man at the business end of a battleaxe. I have lived in their courts and drunk with them and courted their women, and I venture to say that I know them well, which you do not. And this much is true: they call Arthur and his court corrupt, too pagan."

"That comes well from them," Gawaine snorted.

"Still," said Gwydion, "it is no laughing matter, that these men, unrebuked, can call Arthur corrupt—"

"Unrebuked, say you?" Gareth grumbled. "I think Gawaine and I did some rebuking!"

"Will you fight your way through the Saxon court? Better to amend the cause of slander," said Gwydion. "Cannot Arthur rule his wife better than this?"

Gawaine said, "It would take a braver man than I to speak ill of Gwenhwyfar to Arthur's face."

"Yet it must be done," said Gwydion. "If Arthur is to be High King over all these men, he cannot be a laughingstock. When they call him cuckold, will they take oath to follow him in peace and in war? Somehow he must heal the corruption in this court—send the woman to a nunnery perhaps, or banish Lancelet—"

Gawaine looked anxiously around. "For God's sake, lower your voice," he said. "Such things should not even be whispered in this place!"

"It is better that *we* should whisper them than that they should be whispered all the length and breadth of the land," Gwydion said. "In God's name, there they sit close by him, and he smiles on them both! Is Camelot to become a joke, and the Round Table a bawdy house?"

"Now shut your filthy mouth or I will shut it for you," Gawaine snarled, gripping Gwydion's shoulder in his iron fingers.

"If I were speaking lies, Gawaine, you might well try to shut my mouth, but can you stop the truth with your fists? Or do you still maintain that Gwenhwyfar and Lancelet are innocent? You, Gareth, who have all your life been his pet and minion, I might well believe that you will think no evil of your friend—"

Gareth said, gritting his teeth, "It is true I wish the woman at the bottom of the sea, or behind the walls of the safest convent in Cornwall. But while Arthur does not speak, I will hold my tongue. And they are old enough to be discreet. All men have known for years that he has been her champion lifelong—"

"If I only had some proof, Arthur might listen to me," Gwydion said.

"Damn you, I am certain Arthur knows what there is to know. But it is for him to allow it or to interfere . . . and he will hear no word against either of them." Gawaine swallowed and went on. "Lancelet is my kinsman, and my friend too. But—damn you—do you think I have not tried?"

"And what said Arthur?"

"He said that the Queen was above my criticism, and whatever she chose to do was well done. He was courteous, but I could tell that he knew what I was saying and was warning me not to interfere."

"But if it were drawn to his attention in a way he could not choose to ignore," Gwydion said quietly, considering, then raised his hand and beckoned. Niniane, seated at Arthur's feet, her hands still touching the strings of her harp, softly asked leave of Arthur, then rose and came to him.

"My lady," Gwydion said, "is it not true that she"— he inclined his head very slightly in Gwenhwyfar's direction—"often sends her women away for the night?"

Niniane said quietly, "She has not done so while the legion was away from Camelot."

"So at least we know the lady is loyal," said Gwydion cynically, "and does not distribute her favors wholesale."

"No one has ever accused her of common lechery," said Gareth angrily, "and at their ages—they are both older than you, Gawaine—whatever they are about cannot be much harm to anyone, I should think."

"No, I am serious," said Gwydion with equal heat. "If Arthur is to remain High King—"

"Mean you not," said Gareth angrily, "if you are to be High King after him—"

"What would you, brother? That when Arthur is gone I should turn over all this land to the Saxons?" Their heads were close together, and they were talking in furious whispers. Morgause knew they had forgotten not only her presence but her very existence.

"Why, I thought you loved the Saxons well," said Gareth, in angry scorn. "Would you not be content to have them rule, then?"

"No, hear me," said Gwydion in a rage, but Gareth grabbed at him again and said, "The whole of the court will hear you if you do not moderate your voices—look, Arthur is staring at you, he watched when Niniane came over here! Maybe Arthur is not the only one who should look to his lady, or—"

"Be silent!" Gwydion said, wrestling himself free of Gareth's hands.

Arthur called out to him, "What, do my loyal cousins of Lothian quarrel among themselves? I will have peace in my hall, kinsmen! Come, Gawaine, here's King Ceardig asking if you will have a game of riddles with him!"

Gawaine rose, but Gwydion said softly, "Here's a riddle for you— when a man will not mind his property, what's to be done by those who have an interest in it?"

Gawaine stalked away, pretending he did not hear, and Niniane bent over Gwydion and said, "Leave it for now. There are too many ears and eyes. You have planted the seed. Now speak to some of the other knights. Do you think you are the only one who saw—that?" and she moved her elbow just a little. Morgause, following the slight gesture, saw that Gwenhwyfar was bending with Lancelet over a game board on their laps; their heads were close together.

"I think there are many who think it touches the honor of Arthur's

Camelot," Niniane murmured. "You need only find some who are less—biased—than your brothers of Lothian, Gwydion."

But Gwydion was looking angrily at Gareth. "Lancelet," he muttered, "always Lancelet!" And Morgause, looking from Gwydion to her youngest son, thought of a small child prattling to a red-and-blue carved knight which he called Lancelet.

Then she thought of a younger Gwydion, following Gareth about like a puppy. *Gareth is his Lancelet,* she thought. *What will come of this?* But her disquiet was swallowed up in malice. *Surely it is time,* she thought, *that Lancelet should have to answer for all he has wrought.*

NINIANE STOOD at the crest of Camelot, looking down at the mists that surrounded the hill. She heard a step behind her, and said, without turning, "Gwydion?"

"Who else?" His arms came around her and held her tight, and she turned her face to kiss him. He demanded, without letting her go, "Does Arthur kiss you like that?"

She freed herself from his embrace to confront him. "Are you jealous of the King? Was it not you who told me to gain his confidence?"

"Already Arthur has had more than enough of what is mine—"

"Arthur is a Christian man—I will say no more than that," Niniane said, "and you are my dear love. But I am Niniane of Avalon, and I account to no man on this earth for what I do with what is mine—yes, mine and not yours. I am not Roman, to let some man tell me what I may do with what the Goddess gave me. And if you like that not, Gwydion, then I shall return to Avalon."

Gwydion smiled, the cynical smile she liked least about him.

"If you could find the way," he said. "You might find that not so easy any longer." Then the cynicism slipped from his face and he stood holding Niniane's hand lightly in his and said, "I care not what Arthur may do in the time remaining to him. Like Galahad, he may have his moments, for he will be a long time without them." He stared down at what looked like an ocean of mist surrounding Camelot. "When the mist clears we will see Avalon from here, perhaps, and Dragon Island." He sighed and said, "Did you know—some of the Saxons are moving into that country now, and there has been hunting of the deer on Dragon Island, though Arthur forbade it."

Niniane's face hardened in anger. "A stop must be put to that. The place is sacred, and the deer—"

"And the little folk who own the deer. But Aedwin the Saxon slaughtered them," Gwydion said. "He told Arthur that they shot at his men with poisoned elf-arrows, so he gave his men leave to kill as many of them as he could find. And now they hunt the deer—and Arthur will go to war against Aedwin, if he must. I wish Aedwin had a better cause—in honor I must fight to protect those who look to Avalon."

"And Arthur goes to war for their sakes?" Niniane was surprised. "I thought he had forsworn Avalon."

"Avalon, perhaps, but not the harmless folk from the island." Gwydion was silent, and Niniane knew he was remembering a day on Dragon Island. He slid his fingers along the tattooed serpents on his wrists, then pulled the sleeves of his Saxon tunic down over them. "I wonder, could I still pull down a King Stag with only my hands and a flint knife?"

"I doubt not that you could, if you were challenged," said Niniane. "The question is, could Arthur? For if he cannot . . ."

She left the question hanging in the air, and he said somberly, watching the enclosing mist, "I do not think it will clear. Mist hangs here always, so thickly now that some of the Saxon kings who send messengers cannot find their way. . . . Niniane! Will Camelot too go into the mists?"

She began to fling him back some careless word of jest or reassurance, then stopped and said, "I know not. Dragon Island is defiled, the folk dying or dead, the sacred herd prey to the Saxon hunters. Northmen raid the coast. Will they one day sack Camelot as the Goths overthrew Rome?"

"If I had known in time," Gwydion said with smothered violence, striking one fist against the other, "if the Saxons had brought word to Arthur, he could have sent me—or some other—to protect that holy ground where he was made King Stag and made the sacred marriage with the land! Now the shrine of the Goddess has been overthrown, since he did not die to protect it, his kingship is forfeit."

Niniane heard what he did not say: *And mine.* She said, "You knew not that it was endangered."

"And for that too I blame Arthur," Gwydion said. "That the Saxons could think of doing this without consulting him—does it not say to you how little they think now of his High Kingship? And why do they think so little of him? I will tell you, Niniane—they think little of any king who is cuckold, who cannot rule his women—"

"You who were reared in Avalon," she said angrily, "will you judge Arthur by the Saxon's standards, which are worse than those of the Romans? Will you let a kingdom rise or fall because of some notion of how a man should keep his women in bonds? You are to be King, Gwydion, because you bear the royal blood of Avalon and because you are the child of the Goddess—"

"Pah!" Gwydion spat and followed it with an obscenity. "Did it never occur to you, Niniane—perhaps Avalon fell as later Rome fell, because there was corruption at the heart of the realm? By Avalon's laws, Gwenhwy-far has done no more than is right—the lady shall choose who she will for her consort, and Arthur should be overthrown by Lancelet! Why, Lancelet is the son of the High Priestess herself—why not set him to be King in Arthur's place? But is our king to be chosen because some woman wants him in her bed?" Again he spat. "No, Niniane, that day is done—first the Romans and now the Saxons know how the world's to be. The world is no longer a great womb bearing men—now the movement of men and armies settles things. What people now would accept my rule because I was the son of this woman or that? Now it is the king's son who takes the land, and shall we turn away a good thing because the Romans did so first? We have better ships now—we will discover lands beyond the old lands that have sunk in the sea. Will a Goddess who is tied to this one patch of earth and its crops follow us there? Look at the Northmen who are raiding our coasts—will they be stopped with the Mother's curses? The few priestesses that are left in Avalon—no Saxons or wild Northmen will ever ravish them, because Avalon is no longer a part of the world in which these wild raiders live. Those women who live in the world that is coming will need men to guard them. The world now, Niniane, is not one of Goddesses, but of Gods, perhaps of one God. I need not try to bring Arthur down. Time and change alone will do that."

Niniane's back prickled as if with the Sight. "And what of you, King Stag of Avalon? What of the Mother who sent you forth in her name?"

"Do you think I mean to go into the mists with Avalon and Camelot? I mean to be High King after Arthur—and to do that, I must keep the glory of Arthur's court at full height. So Lancelet must go, which means that Arthur must be forced to banish him, and probably Gwenhwyfar as well. Are you with me, Niniane, or not?"

Her face was deathly white. She clenched her fists at her side, wishing that she had the power of Morgaine, the power of the Goddess, to rise like a bridge from earth to sky and strike him down with the lightning force of the outraged Goddess. The crescent moon on her brow burned with rage.

"Am I to help you by betraying a woman who has taken the right the Goddess has given to all women, to choose what man she will?"

Gwydion laughed mockingly. "Gwenhwyfar gave up that right when first she knelt at the feet of the slave's God."

"Nevertheless, I'll have nothing to do with betraying her."

"Then you will not send me word when she sends her women away again for the night?"

"No," said Niniane, "by the Goddess, I will not. And Arthur's treachery to Avalon is nothing to yours!" She turned her back on him and would have moved away, but he caught and held her there.

"You'll do what I command you!"

She struggled to free herself, at last wrenching her bruised wrists from him. "Command me? Not in a thousand years!" she said, breathless with fury. "Beware, you who have laid hands on the Lady of Avalon! Arthur shall know now what sort of viper he has taken to his breast!"

In a towering rage, Gwydion grabbed her other wrist and pulled her toward him, then struck her full force across the temple, and she fell to the ground without a cry. He was so full of wrath that he let her fall without a move to catch her.

"Well did the Saxons name you," said a low, savage voice from the fog. *"Evil counsel, Mordred—murderer!"*

He turned with a convulsive moment of fear and looked at the crumpled body of Niniane at his feet. "Murderer? No! I was only angry with her—I would not hurt her—" He stared around him, unable to make out anything in the thickening mist, yet knowing the voice.

"Morgaine! Lady—my mother!"

He knelt, panic clutching at his throat, raising Niniane up, searching for a heartbeat but she lay there without breath, without life.

"Morgaine! Where are you? Where are you? Damn you, show yourself!" But there was only Niniane, lifeless and unmoving at his feet. He clasped her to him, imploring. "Niniane! Niniane, my love—speak to me—"

"She will not speak again," said the bodiless voice, but as Gwydion turned this way and that in the fog, a woman's solid figure materialized out of it. "Oh, what have you done, my son?"

"Was it you? Was it you?" Gwydion demanded, his voice cracking in hysteria. "Was it you called me murderer?

Morgause stepped back, half afraid. "No, no, I came but now—what have you done?"

Gwydion flung himself at her, and she held him, stroking him as she had done when he was twelve years old. "Niniane angered me—she threatened me—as the Gods witness it, Mother, I meant her no harm, but she threatened to go to Arthur and tell him I plotted against his precious Lancelet," Gwydion said, almost babbling. "I struck her, I swear I meant only to frighten her, but she fell—"

Morgause let Gwydion go and knelt beside Niniane. "You struck an unlucky blow, my son—she is dead. There's nothing you can do now. We must go and tell Arthur's marshals and stewards."

His face had gone livid. "Mother! The marshals—what will Arthur say?"

Morgause felt a great melting within her heart. He was in her hands, as when he had been a little helpless child whom Lot would have killed, his life was hers, and he knew it. She folded him to her breast.

"Never mind, my love, you mustn't suffer for it, any more than for any other you killed in battle," she said, looking down with triumph at Niniane's lifeless body. "She could have fallen in the fog—it's a long way to the bottom of the hill," she said, looking over the brow of Camelot, where it descended steeply into the mist. "So, catch hold of her feet thus. Done is done, and nothing that happens to her now can make a difference." Her old hatred of Arthur surged up; Gwydion would bring him down, and he would do it with *her* help—and when it was done, she would be at his side, the lady who had set him on his throne! Niniane was no longer between them; she herself alone should be his support and his help.

Silently, in the fog, the slight body of the Lady of Avalon disappeared into the mists. Later Arthur would call for her and when she did not appear, send men to search; but Gwydion, staring as if hypnotized into the mists, thought for a moment that he saw the black shadow of the Avalon barge somewhere on the waters between Camelot and Dragon Island. It seemed to him for a moment that Niniane, robed in black as the Death-crone, beckoned to him from the barge . . . and then it was gone.

"Come, my son," said Morgause. "You spent this morning in my rooms and the rest of the day you must spend with Arthur in his hall. Remember, you have not seen Niniane this day—when you come to Arthur, you must ask for her, even seem a little jealous, as if you feared to find her in his bed."

And it was balm to her heart that he clutched at her and muttered, "I will. I will, my mother. Surely you are the best of all mothers, the best of all women!"

And she held him for a moment and kissed him again, savoring her power, before she let him go.

16

Gwenhwyfar lay wide-eyed in the darkness, waiting for the step of Lancelet, yet thinking of Morgause, smiling—almost leering —as she murmured, "Ah, I envy you, my dear! Cormac is a fine young man, and hearty enough—but he has none of the grace and beauty of *your* lover."

Gwenhwyfar had bent her head and said nothing. Who was she to scorn Morgause, when she was doing the same thing? But it was too dangerous. The bishop, on his last Sunday, had preached a sermon on the great commandment against adultery, saying that the chastity of wives lay at the very root of the Christian way of living, since only by married chastity did women redeem the sin of Eve. Gwenhwyfar recalled the tale of that woman taken in adultery, whom they had brought to Christ; he had said, *Let that one who has done no sin, cast at her the first stone.* There had been none guiltless to cast it—but here in *her* court, there were many who were sinless, with Arthur himself to cast that stone. Christ had said to the woman, *Go and sin no more.* And that was what she must do. . . .

It was not his body she desired. Morgause, sniggering over the lusty young man who was her lover, would never have believed how little difference *that* had made to either of them. Seldom, indeed, had he ever taken her in that way which was sin and dishonor—only in those first years, when they had had Arthur's acquiescence, to try and see if Gwenhwyfar could bear a son to the kingdom. There had been other ways to find pleasure, which she somehow felt less of a sin, less violation of Arthur's marriage rights in her body. And even so, it was not that she desired so much, only that she should be with him . . . it was a thing, she thought, almost more of the soul than the body. Why should a God of love condemn this? He might condemn the sin they had done, for which she had done penance over and over, but how could he condemn this, which was the truest love of the heart?

I have taken nothing from Arthur which he desired or needed of me. He must have a queen, a lady to keep his castle; for the rest, he wanted nothing of me save a son, and it was not I but God who denied him that.

There was a soft step in the darkness; she whispered, "Lancelet?"

"Not so." A glimmer of a tiny lamp in the darkness confused her; for a moment she saw what seemed a beloved face, grown young—then knew who it must be.

"How dare you? My women are not so far but that I can scream aloud, and there is none will believe that I summoned you here!"

"Lie still," he said. "There is a knife at your throat, my lady." And as she shrank away, clutching the bed clothing, "Oh, don't flatter yourself, madam, I came not here for rape. Your charms are too stale for me, my lady, and too well tasted."

"That's enough," said a husky voice in the dark behind Gwydion. "Don't mock her, man! This is a dirty business, snooping at bedchamber doors, and I wish I'd never heard of it! Quiet, all of you, and hide yourselves around the chamber!"

She recognized Gawaine's face as her eyes adapted to the dim light, and beyond them a familiar form. "Gareth! What do you here?" she asked, sorrowfully. "I thought you Lancelet's dearest friend."

"And so I am," he said grimly. "I came to see no worse done to him than justice. *That* one"—he flicked a contemptuous gesture at Gwydion—

"would cut his throat—and leave you to be accused of murder!"

"Be still," said Gwydion, and the light went out. Gwenhwyfar felt the pricking of the knife at her throat. "If you speak a syllable to warn him, madam, I will cut your throat and take my chances explaining why to my lord Arthur." The point dug in till Gwenhwyfar, flinching with pain, wondered if it had actually drawn blood. She could hear small noises—the rustle of garments, the clink of weapons hurriedly muffled; how many men had he brought to this ambush? She lay silent, twisting her hands in despair. If only she could warn Lancelet . . . but she lay like a small animal in a snare, helpless.

Minutes crawled by for the trapped woman silent between her pillows and the knife. After a long time, she heard a tiny sound, a soft whistle like a bird call. Gwydion felt the tensing of her muscles and asked in a rasping whisper, "Lancelet's signal?" He dug the knife again into the yielding skin at her throat, and she whispered, sweating in terror, "Yes."

She felt the straw beneath her rustle as he shifted his weight and moved away. "There are a dozen men in this room. Try to give him warning, and you will not live three seconds."

She heard sounds in the antechamber; Lancelet's cloak, his sword—ah, God, would they take him naked and weaponless? She tensed again, feeling in advance the knife driving into her body, but somehow she must warn him, must cry out—she opened her lips, but Gwydion—*was it the Sight, how did he know?*—thrust his hand cruelly over her face, smothering the cry. She writhed under his suffocating hand, then felt Lancelet's weight on the bed.

"Gwen?" he whispered. "What is the matter? Did I hear you crying, my beloved?"

She managed to writhe away from the concealing hand.

"Run!" she screamed. "It's a trick, a trap—"

"Hell's doors!" She could feel him, like a cat, springing back.

Gwydion's lamp flared; somehow the light went from hand to hand, until the room was filled with light, and Gawaine, Cai, and Gareth, with a dozen shadowy forms behind them, stepped forward. Gwenhwyfar huddled under the bedcover, and Lancelet stood still, quite naked, weaponless.

"Mordred," he said, in contempt. "Such a trick is worthy of you!"

Gawaine said formally, "In the King's name, Lancelet, I accuse you of high treason. Get me your sword."

"Never mind that," said Gwydion, "go and take it."

"Gareth! In God's name, why did you lend yourself to this?"

Gareth's eyes were glistening as if with tears in the lamplight. "I never believed it of you, Lancelet. I would to God I had fallen in battle before ever I saw this day."

Lancelet bent his head and Gwenhwyfar saw his eyes, panicky, move around the room. He muttered, "Oh, God, Pellinore looked at me so when they came with the torches to take me in Elaine's bed—must I betray everyone, everyone?" She wanted to reach out to him, to cry out with pity and pain, to shelter him in her arms. But he would not look at her.

"Your sword," said Gawaine quietly. "And dress yourself, Lancelet. I will not take you naked and disgraced into Arthur's presence. Enough men have witnessed your shame."

"Don't let him get at his sword—" some faceless voice in the darkness protested, but Gawaine gestured the speaker contemptuously into silence. Lancelet turned slowly away from them, into the tiny antechamber where he had left clothing, armor, weapons. She heard him drawing on his garments. Gareth stood, his hand on his sword, as Lancelet came into the room, dressed but weaponless, his hands in full view.

"I am glad for your sake that you will come with us quietly," said Gwydion. "Mother"—he turned into the shadows, and Gwenhwyfar saw, with consternation, Queen Morgause standing there—"see to the Queen. She shall be in your charge until Arthur may deal with her."

Morgause advanced on the bedside. Gwenhwyfar had never noticed before how large a woman Morgause was, and how ruthless her jaw line.

"Come along, my lady, get into your gown," she said. "And I will help you peg your hair—you do not want to go naked and shameless before the King. And be glad there was a woman here. These men—"she looked contemptuously at them—"meant to wait until they could catch him actually inside you." Gwenhwyfar shrank from the brutality of the words; slowly, with lagging fingers, she began to draw on her gown. "Must I dress before all these men?"

Gwydion did not wait for Morgause to answer. He said, "Don't try to cozen us, shameless woman! Dare you pretend you have anything left of decency or modesty? Put on that gown, madam, or my mother shall bundle you into it like a sack!"

He calls her mother. No wonder Gwydion is cruel and ruthless, with the Queen of Lothian to foster him! Yet Gwenhwyfar had seen Morgause so often as merely a lazy, jolly, greedy woman—what had brought her to this? She sat still, fastening the laces of her shoes.

Lancelet said quietly, "It is my sword you want, then?"

"You know it," Gawaine said.

"Why, then"—moving almost more swiftly than the eye could follow, Lancelet leaped for Gawaine, and in another catlike movement, had Gawaine's own sword in his hand—"come and take it, damn you!" He lunged with Gawaine's sword at Gwydion, who fell across the bed, howling, bleeding from a great slash in his backside; then, as Cai stepped forward, sword in hand, Lancelet caught up a cushion from the bed and pushed Cai backward with it so that he fell into the advancing men, who tripped over him. He leaped up on the bed and said, low and short to Gwenhwyfar, "Keep perfectly still and be ready!"

She gasped, shrinking back and making herself small in a corner. They were coming at him again; he ran one of them through, briefly engaged another, and over that one's body, lunged and slashed at a shadowy attacker. The giant form of Gareth crumpled slowly to the floor. Lancelet was already fighting someone else, but Gwydion, bleeding, cried out, "Gareth!" and flung himself across the body of his foster-brother. In that moment of horrified lull, while Gwydion knelt, sobbing, over Gareth's body, Gwenhwyfar felt Lancelet catch her up on his arm, whirl, kill someone at the door—she never knew who it was—and then she was on her feet in the corridor, and Lancelet was pushing her, with frantic haste, ahead of him. Someone came at him out of the dark and Lancelet killed him, and they ran on.

"Make for the stables," he gasped. "Horses, and out of here, fast."

"Wait!" She caught at his arm. "If we throw ourselves on Arthur's mercy—or you escape and I will stay and face Arthur—"

"Gareth might have seen justice done. But with Gwydion's hand in it, do you think either of us would ever reach the King alive? I named him well Mordred!" He hurried her into the stables, swiftly flung a saddle on his horse. "No time to find yours. Ride behind me, and hold on well—I'm going to have to ride down the guards at the gate." And Gwenhwyfar realized she was seeing a new Lancelet—not her lover, but the hardened warrior. How many men had he killed this night? She had no time for fear as he lifted her on his horse and sprang up before her.

"Hang on to me," he said. "I'll have no time to look after you." He turned then, and gave her one hard, long kiss. "This is my fault, I should have known that infernal bastard would be spying—well, whatever happens now, at least it's over. No more lies and no more hiding. You're mine forever—" and he broke off. She could feel him trembling, but he turned savagely to grip the reins. "And now we go!"

MORGAUSE LOOKED ON in horror as Gwydion, weeping, bent over her youngest son.

Words spoken in half earnest, years ago—Gwydion had refused to take the lists on the opposite side from Gareth, even in a mock battle. *It seemed to me that you lay dying,* he had said . . . *and I knew it was my doing you lay without the spark of life. . . . I will not tempt that fate.*

Lancelet had done this, Lancelet whom Gareth had always loved more than any other man.

One of the men in the room stepped forward and said, "They're getting away—"

"Do you think I care about that?" Gwydion winced, and Morgause realized that he was bleeding, that his blood was flowing and mingling with Gareth's on the floor of the chamber. She caught up the linen sheet from the bed, tore it, and wadded it against Gwydion's wound.

Gawaine said somberly, "No man in all of Britain will hide them now. Lancelet is everywhere outcast. He has been taken in treason to his king, and his very life is forfeit. God! How I wish it had not come to this!" He came and looked at Gwydion's wound, then shrugged. "No more than a flesh cut —see, the bleeding is slowed already, it will heal, but you will not sit in comfort for some days. Gareth—" His voice broke; the great, rough, greying man began to weep like a child. "Gareth had worse fortune, and I will have Lancelet's life for it, if I die myself at his hands. Ah God, Gareth, my little one, my little brother—" and Gawaine bent and cradled the big body against him. He said thickly, through sobs, "Was it worth it, Gwydion, was it worth Gareth's life?"

"Come away, my boy," said Morgause, through a tightness in her own throat—Gareth, her baby, her last child; she had lost him long ago to Arthur, but still she remembered a fair-haired little boy, clutching a wooden painted knight in his hand. *And one day you and I shall go on quest together, sir Lancelet* . . . always Lancelet. But now Lancelet had overreached himself, and everywhere in the land every man's hand would be against him. And still she had Gwydion, her beloved, the one who would one day be King, and she at his side.

"Come, my lad, come away, you can do nothing for Gareth now. Let me bind up your wound, then we shall go to Arthur and tell him what has befallen, so that he may send out his men to seek for the traitors—"

Gwydion shook her grip from his arm. "Get away from me, curse you," he said in a terrible voice. "Gareth was the best of us, and I would not have sacrificed him for a dozen kings! It was you and your spite against Arthur always urging me on, as if I cared what bed the Queen slept in— as if Gwenhwyfar were any worse than you, when from the time I was ten years old you had this one or that one in your bed—"

"Oh, my son—" she whispered, aghast. "How can you speak so to me? Gareth was my son too—"

"What did you ever care for Gareth, or for any of us, or for anything but your own pleasure and your own ambition? You would urge me to a throne, not for my sake but for your own power!" He thrust away her clinging hands. "Get you back to Lothian, or to hell if the devil will have you, but if ever I set eyes on you again, I swear I will forget all except that you were the murderer of the one brother I loved, the one kinsman—"

and as Gawaine urgently pushed his mother from the chamber, she could hear Gwydion weeping again. "Oh, Gareth, Gareth, I should have died first—"

Gawaine said shortly, "Cormac, take the Queen of Lothian to her chamber."

His strong arm was holding her upright, and after they had moved down the hall, after that dreadful sobbing had died away behind her, Morgause began to draw breath freely again. How could he turn on her this way? When had she ever done anything except for his sake? She must show decent mourning for Gareth, certainly, but Gareth was Arthur's man, and surely Gwydion would have realized it, sooner or later. She looked up at Cormac. "I cannot walk so fast—hold back a little."

"Certainly, my lady." She was very much aware of his arm enfolding her, holding her. She let herself lean a little on him. She had bragged to Gwenhwyfar of her young lover, but she had never yet actually taken him to her bed—she had kept him delaying, dangling. She turned her head against his shoulder. "You have been faithful to your queen, Cormac."

"I am loyal to my royal house, as all my people have ever been," the young man said in their own language, and she smiled.

"Here is my chamber—help me inside, will you? I can scarce walk—"

He supported her, eased her down on her bed. "Is it my lady's will that I call her women?"

"No," she whispered, catching at his hands, aware that her tears were seductive. "You have been loyal to me, Cormac, and now is that loyalty to be rewarded—come here—"

She held out her arms, half shutting her eyes, then opened them, in shock, as he pulled awkwardly away.

"I—I think you are distraught, madam," he stammered. "What do you think I am? What do you take me for? Why, lady, I have as much respect for you as for my own grandmother! Should I take advantge of an old woman like you when you are beside yourself with grief? Let me call your waiting-woman, and she will make you a nice posset and I will forget what you said in the madness of grief, madam."

Morgause could feel the blow in the very pit of her stomach, repeated blows on her heart—*my own grandmother . . . old woman . . . the madness of grief. . . .* The whole of the world had suddenly gone mad—Gwydion insane with ingratitude, this man who had looked on her so long with desire turning on her . . . she wanted to scream, to call for her servants and have him whipped till his back ran crimson with his blood and the walls rang with his shrieking for mercy. But even as she opened her mouth for that, the whole weight of her life seemed to descend on her in deadly weariness.

"Yes," she said dully, "I do not know what I was saying—call my women, Cormac, and tell them to bring me some wine. We will ride at daybreak for Lothian."

And when he had gone, she sat on the bed without the strength to lift her hands.

I am an old woman. And I have lost my son Gareth, and I have lost Gwydion, and I will never now be Queen in Camelot. I have lived too long.

17

CLINGING to Lancelet's back, her gown pulled up above her knees and her bare legs hanging down, Gwenhwyfar closed her eyes as they rode hard through the night. She had no idea where they were going. Lancelet was a stranger, a hard-faced warrior, a man she had never known. *There was a time,* she thought, *when I would have been terrified, out like this under the open sky, at night . . .* but she felt excited, exhilarated. At the back of her mind was pain too, mourning for the gentle Gareth who had been like a son to Arthur and deserved better of life than to be struck down so—she wondered if Lancelet even knew whom he had killed! And there was grief for the end of her years with Arthur, and all they had shared for so long. But from what had happened this night there could be no going back. She had to lean forward to hear Lancelet over the rushing of wind. "We must stop somewhere soon, the horse must rest—and if we ride in daylight, my face and yours are known all through this countryside."

She nodded; she had not breath enough to speak. After a time they came within a little wood, and there he pulled to a stop and lifted her gently from the horse's back. He led the horse to water, then spread his cloak on the ground for her to sit. He stared at the sword by his side. "I still have Gawaine's sword. When I was a boy—I heard tales of the fighting madness, but I knew not that it was within our blood—" and sighed heavily. "There is blood on the sword. Whom did I kill, Gwen?"

She could not bear to see his sorrow and guilt. "There was more than one—"

"I know I struck Gwydion—Mordred, damn him. I know I wounded him, I could still act with my own will then. I don't suppose"—his voice hardened—"that I had the luck to kill him?"

Silently she shook her head.

"Then who?" She did not speak; he leaned over and took her shoulders so roughly that for a moment she was afraid of the warrior as she had never been of the lover. "Gwen, tell me! In God's name—did I kill my cousin Gawaine?"

This she could answer without hesitation, glad it was Gawaine he had named. "No. I swear it, not Gawaine."

"It could have been anyone," he said, staring at the sword and suddenly shuddering. "I swear it to you, Gwen, I knew not even that I had a sword in my hand. I struck Gwydion as if he had been a dog, and then I remember no more until we were riding—" and he knelt before her, trembling. He whispered, "I am mad again, I think, as once I was mad—"

She reached out, caught him against her in a passion of wild tenderness. "No, no," she whispered, "ah, no, my love—I have brought all this on you, disgrace and exile—"

"You say that," he whispered, "when I have brought them on you, taken you away from everything that meant anything to you—"

Reckless, she pressed herself to him and said, "Would to God that you had done it before!"

"Ah, it is not too late—I am young again, with you beside me, and you—you have never been more beautiful, my own dear love—" He pushed her back on the cloak, suddenly laughing in abandon. "Ah, now there's none to come between us, none to interrupt us, my own—ah, Gwen, Gwen—"

As she came into his arms, she remembered the rising sun and a room in Meleagrant's castle. It was like that now; and she clung to him, as if there were nothing else in the world, nothing more for either of them, not ever.

They slept a little, curled together in the cloak, and wakened still in each other's arms, the sun searching for them through the green branches overhead. He smiled, touching her face.

"Do you know—never before have I wakened in your arms without fear. Yet now I am happy, in spite of all . . ." and he laughed at her, a note of wildness coming into the laughter. There were leaves in his white hair, and leaves caught in his beard, and his tunic was rumpled; she put up her hands and felt grass and leaves in her own hair, which was coming down. She had no way to comb it, but she caught it in handfuls and parted it to braid, then bound the end of the single braid with a scrap ripped from the edge of her torn skirt. She said, her voice catching with laughter, "What a pair of wild ragamuffins we are! Who would know the High Queen and the brave Lancelet?"

"Does it matter to you?"

"No, my love. Not in the least."

He brushed leaves and grass out of his hair and beard. "I must get up and catch the horse," he said, "and perhaps there will be a farm nearby where we can find you some bread or a drink of ale—I have not a single coin with

me, nor anything worth money, save my sword, and this—" He touched
a little gold pin on his tunic. "For the moment, at least, we are beggars,
though if we could reach Pellinore's castle, I still have a house there, where
I lived with Elaine, and servants—and gold, too, to pay our passage overseas.
Will you come with me to Less Britain, Gwenhwyfar?"

"Anywhere," she whispered, her voice breaking, and at that moment
she meant it absolutely—to Less Britain, or to Rome, or to the country
beyond the world's end, only that she might be with him forever. She pulled
him down to her again and forgot everything in his arms.

But when, hours later, he lifted her on the horse and they went on at
a soberer pace, she fell silent, troubled. Yes, no doubt they could make their
way overseas. Yet when this night's work was talked from one end of the
world to the other, shame and scorn would come down on Arthur, so that
for his own honor he must seek them out wherever they fled. And soon or
late, Lancelet must know that he had slain the friend who was dearest to
him in all the world save only Arthur's self. He had done it in madness, but
she knew how grief and guilt would consume him and in time he would
remember, when he looked on her, not that she was his love, but that he
had killed his friend, unknowing, for her sake; and that he had betrayed
Arthur for her sake. If he must make war on Arthur for her sake, he would
hate her. . . .

No. He would love her still, but he would never forget by whose
blood he had come to possess her. Never would one or the other—love or
hate—take power over him, but he would live with them both, tearing
doubly at his heart, and one day they would tear his mind to bits and he
would go mad again. She clung close to the warmth of his body, leaning
her head against his back, and wept. She knew, for the first time, that she
was stronger than he, and it cut at her heart with a deathly sword.

And so when they paused again, she was dry-eyed, though she knew
that the weeping had moved inward to her heart and never would she cease
to mourn. "I will not go overseas with you, Lancelet, nor will I bring strife
among all the old Companions of the Round Table. When—when Mordred has his way, they will all be at odds," she said, "and a day will come
when Arthur will need all his friends. I will not be like that lady of old
time—was her name Helen, that fair one in the saga you used to tell to me?
—who had all the kings and knights of her day at strife over her in Troy."

"But what will you do?" She tried not to hear that even through the
bewilderment and grief in his voice, there was a thread of relief.

"You will take me to the Isle of Glastonbury," she said. "There is a
nunnery there where I was schooled. There I will go, and I will tell them
only that evil tongues made a quarrel between you and Arthur for my sake.
When some time has passed, I will send word to Arthur so that he knows

where I am, and knows that I am not with you. And then he can with honor make his peace with you."

He protested, "No! No, I cannot let you go—" but she knew, with a sinking at her heart, that she would have no difficulty persuading him. Perhaps, against all odds, she had hoped that he would fight for her, that he would carry her off to Less Britain with the sheer force of his will and passion. But that was not Lancelet's way. He was as he was, and whatever he was, so and no other way he had been when first she loved him, and so he was now, and so she would love him for the rest of her life. And at last he strove no more with her, but set the horse's head on the road toward Glastonbury.

THE LONG SHADOW of the church lay across the waters when they set foot at last on the boat that would bring them to the island, and the church bells were ringing out the Angelus. Gwenhwyfar bent her head and whispered a word of prayer.

Mary, God's Holy Mother, have pity on me, a sinful woman . . . and then for a moment it seemed to her that she stood beneath a great light, as she had stood on that day when the Grail passed through the hall. Lancelet sat in the prow of the ferry, his head lowered. He had not touched her from the moment she had told him what she had decided, and she was glad; a single touch of his hand would have worn away her resolve. Mist lay on the Lake, and for an instant it seemed to her that she saw a shadow, like the shadow of their own boat, a barge draped in black, with a dark figure at the prow—but no. It was only a shadow, a shadow. . . .

The boat scraped on the shore. He helped her from it. "Gwenhwyfar —are you certain?"

"I am certain," she said, trying to sound surer than she felt.

"Then I will escort you to the doors of the convent," he said, and it suddenly struck her that this took, for him, more courage than all the killing he had done for her sake.

The old abbess recognized the High Queen, and was awed and amazed that she should return, but Gwenhwyfar told the tale she had decided on —that evil tongues had wrought a quarrel between Arthur and Lancelet for her sake, and she had chosen to take refuge here so they might amend their quarrel.

The old woman patted her cheek as if she were the little Gwenhwyfar who had been lessoned here when she was a child. "You are welcome to stay as long as you wish it, my daughter. Forever, if that is your will. In God's house we turn no one away. But here you will not be a queen," she warned, "only one of our sisters."

Gwenhwyfar sighed with utter relief. She had not known till this moment how heavy it was, the weight of being a queen. "I must say farewell to my knight, and wish him well, and bid him amend the quarrel with my husband."

The abbess nodded gravely. "In these days, our good King Arthur cannot spare a single one of his knights, and surely not the good sir Lancelet."

Gwenhwyfar went out into the anteroom of the convent. Lancelet was there, wandering restlessly. He took her hands. "I cannot bear to say farewell to you here, Gwenhwyfar—ah, my lady, my love, must it be this way?"

"It must be so," she said pitilessly, but knowing that for the first time she acted without thought of herself. "Your heart was always with Arthur, my dearest. I often think the only sin we did was not that we loved, but that I came between the love you had for each other." *If it could always have been among us three as it was on that Beltane night with Morgaine's love charm,* she thought, *there would have been less of sin. The sin was not that we lay together, but that there was strife, and less of love therefore.* "I send you back to Arthur with all my heart, dearest. Tell him for me that I loved him never the less."

His face was almost transfigured. "I know that now," he said. "And I know, too, that I loved him never the less, and I felt always that I wronged you by loving him. . . ." He would have kissed her, but it was not suitable here. Instead he bent over her hand. "While you are in God's house, pray for me, lady."

My love for you is a prayer, she thought. *Love is the only prayer I know.* She thought she had never loved him so much as at this moment, when she heard the convent door close, hard and final, and felt the walls shutting her in.

So safe, so protected, those walls had made her feel, in that day long past. Now she knew that she would walk between them all the rest of her life. *When I had freedom,* she thought, *I desired it not, and feared it. And now, when I have learned to love it and long for it, I am renouncing it in the name of my love.* Dimly she felt that this was right—the acceptable gift and sacrifice to bring before God. But as she walked through the nuns' cloister, she looked at the walls closing her in, trapping her.

For my love. And for the love of God, she thought, and felt a small seed of comfort stealing through her. Lancelet would go to the church where Galahad had died, and there he would pray. Perhaps he would remember a day when the mists of Avalon had opened, and she and he and Morgaine had stood together, lost, knee-deep in the waters of the Lake. She thought of Morgaine too, with a sudden passion of love and tenderness. *Mary, Holy Mother of God, be with her too, and bring her to you one day. . . .*

The walls, the walls, they would drive her mad, closing her in, she would never be free again. . . . No. For her love, and for the love of God, she would even learn to love them again one day. Folding her hands in prayer, Gwenhwyfar walked down the cloister to the sisters' enclosure, and went inside forever.

MORGAINE SPEAKS . . .

I thought I was beyond the Sight; Viviane, still younger than I, had renounced it, chosen another to be Lady in her place. But there was none to sit in the shrine of the Lady after me, and none to approach the Goddess. I saw it, helpless, when Niniane died, and I could not stretch forth my hand.

I had loosed this monster upon the world, and I had acquiesced in that move which should send him to throw down the King Stag. And I saw it from afar when, on Dragon Island, the shrine was thrown down and the deer hunted in the forest, without love, without challenge, without appeal to her who was giver of the deer; only arrows from afar and the edge of the spear, and her people hunted down like her deer. The tides of the world were changing. There were times when I saw Camelot too, drifting in the mist, and the wars raging up and down the land again, the Northmen who were the new foe plundering and burning . . . a new world, and new Gods.

Truly the Goddess had departed, even from Avalon, and I, mortal as I was, remained there alone. . . .

And yet, one night, some dream, some vision, some fragment of the Sight, drove me, at the hour of the dark moon, to the mirror.

At first I saw only the wars raging up and down the land. I never knew what came between Arthur and Gwydion, although, after Lancelet fled with Gwenhwyfar, there was enmity among the old Companions, blood feud declared between Lancelet and Gawaine. Later, when Gawaine lay dying, that great-hearted man begged Arthur, with his last breath, to make his peace with Lancelet and summon him to Camelot once more. But it was too late; not even Lancelet could rally Arthur's legion again, not when so many followed Gwydion, who now led half of Arthur's own men and most of the Saxons and even a few of the renegade Northmen against him. And in that hour before dawn, the mirror cleared, and in the unearthly light I saw the face of my son at last with a sword in his hand, circling slowly, in the darkness, seeking . . .

Seeking, as Arthur in his day had sought, to challenge the King Stag. I had forgotten what a small man Gwydion was, like Lancelet. Elf-arrow, the Saxons had called Lancelet; small, dark, and deadly. Arthur would have towered more than a head above him.

Ah, in the days of the Goddess, man went against King Stag to seek his kingship! Arthur had been content to await his father's death, but now a new thing *was coming upon this land—father and son enemies, and sons to challenge fathers for a crown . . . it seemed to me that I could see a land that ran red with blood, where sons were not content to await their crowning day. And now, in the circling dark, it seemed that I could see Arthur too, tall and fair and alone, cut off from his men . . . and Excalibur naked in his hand.*

But through and around the prowling figures I could see Arthur in his tent, restlessly asleep, Lancelet guarding him as he slept; and somewhere, too, I knew Gwydion slept among his own armies. Yet some part of them prowled restless on the shores of the Lake, seeking in the darkness, swords naked, against one another.

"Arthur! Arthur, stand to the challenge, or do you fear me too much?"

"No man can say that I ever ran from a challenge." Arthur turned as Gwydion came from the wood. "So," he said, "it is you, Mordred. I never more than half believed that you had turned against me till now when I see it with my own eyes. I thought those who told me so sought to undermine my courage by telling me the worst that could befall. What have I done? Why have you become my enemy? Why, my son?"

"Do you truly believe that I was ever anything else, my father?" He spoke the word with the greatest bitterness. "For what else was I begotten and born, but for this moment when I challenge you for a cause that is no longer within the borders of this world? I no longer even know why I am to challenge you—only that there is nothing else left in my life but for this hatred."

Arthur said quietly, "I knew Morgaine hated me, but I did not know she hated me as much as this. Must you do her will even in this, Gwydion?"

"Do you think I do her will, you fool?" Gwydion snarled. "If anything could bid me spare you, it is that—that I do Morgaine's will, that she wishes you overthrown, and I know not whether I hate more her or you . . ."

And then, stepping forth into their dream or vision or whatever it might be, I knew that I stood on the shores of the Lake where they challenged each other, stood between them clad in the robes of a priestess.

"Must this be? I call upon you both, in the name of the Goddess, to amend your quarrel. I sinned against you, Arthur, and against you, Gwydion, but your hate is for me, not for each other, and in the name of the Goddess I beg of you—"

"What is the Goddess to me?" Arthur tightened his fist on the hilt of Excalibur. "I saw her always in your face, but you turned away from me, and when the Goddess rejected me, I sought another God. . . ."

And Gwydion said, looking on me with contempt, "I needed not the Goddess, but the woman who mothered me, and you put me into the hands of one who had no fear of any Goddess or any God."

I tried to cry out, "I had no choice! I did not choose—" but they came at each other with their swords, rushing through me as if I were made of air, and it seemed that their swords met in my body . . . and then I was in Avalon again, staring in horror at the mirror where I could see nothing, nothing but the widening stain of blood in the sacred waters of the Well. My mouth was dry and my heart pounding as if it would beat a hole in the walls of my chest, and the taste of ruin and death was bitter on my lips.

I had failed, failed, failed! I was false to the Goddess, if indeed there was any Goddess except for myself; false to Avalon, false to Arthur, false to brother and son and lover . . . and all I had sought was in ruin. In the sky was a pale and reddening flush where, sometime soon, the sun would rise; and beyond the mists of Avalon, cold in the sky, I knew that somewhere Arthur and Gwydion would meet, this day, for the last time.

As I went to the shore to summon the barge, it seemed to me that the little dark people were all around me and that I walked among them as the priestess I had been. I stood in the barge alone, and yet I knew there were others standing there with me, robed and crowned, Morgaine the Maiden, who had summoned Arthur to the running of the deer and the challenge of the King Stag, and Morgaine the Mother who had been torn asunder when Gwydion was born, and the Queen of North Wales, summoning the eclipse to send Accolon raging against Arthur, and the Dark Queen of Fairy . . . or was it the Death-crone who stood at my side? And as the barge neared the shore, I heard the last of his followers cry, "Look—look, there, the barge with the four fair queens in the sunrise, the fairy barge of Avalon. . . ."

He lay there, his hair matted with blood, my Gwydion, my lover, my son . . . and at his feet Gwydion lay dead, my son, the child I had never known. I bent and covered his face with my own veil. And I knew that it was the end of an age. In the days past, the young stag had thrown down the King Stag, and become King Stag in his turn; but the deer had been slaughtered, and the King Stag had killed the young stag and there would be none after him . . .

And the King Stag must die in his turn.

I knelt at his side. "The sword, Arthur. Excalibur. Take it in your hand. Take it, and fling it from you, into the waters of the Lake."

The Sacred Regalia were gone out of this world forever, and the last of them, the sword Excalibur, must go with them. But he whispered, protesting, holding it tight, "No—it must be kept for those who come after—to rally their cause, the sword of Arthur—" and looked up into the eyes of Lancelet. "Take it, Galahad —hear you not the trumpets from Camelot, calling to Arthur's legion? Take it —for the Companions—"

"No," I told him quietly. "That day is past. None after you must pretend or claim to bear the sword of Arthur." I loosed his fingers gently from the hilt. "Take it, Lancelet," I said softly, "but fling it from you far into the waters of the Lake. Let the mists of Avalon swallow it forever."

Lancelet went quietly to do my bidding. I know not if he saw me, or who he thought I was. And I cradled Arthur against my breast. His life was fading fast; I knew it, but I was beyond tears.

"Morgaine," he whispered. His eyes were bewildered and full of pain. "Morgaine, was it all for nothing then, what we did, and all that we tried to do? Why did we fail?"

It was my own question, and I had no answer; but from somewhere, the answer came. "You did not fail, my brother, my love, my child. You held this land in peace for many years, so that the Saxons did not destroy it. You held back the darkness for a whole generation, until they were civilized men, with learning and music and faith in God, who will fight to save something of the beauty of the times that are past. If this land had fallen to the Saxons when Uther died, then would all that was beautiful or good have perished forever from Britain. And so you did not fail, my love. None of us knows how she will do her will—only that it will be done."

And I knew not, even then, whether what I spoke was truth, or whether I spoke to comfort him, in love, as with the little child Igraine had put into my arms when I was but a child myself; Morgaine, she had told me, take care of your little brother, and so I had always done, so I would always do, now and beyond life . . . or was it the Goddess herself who had put Arthur into my arms?

He pressed his failing fingers over the great cut at his breast. "If I had but —the scabbard you fashioned for me, Morgaine—I should not lie here now with my life slowly bleeding forth from me. . . . Morgaine, I dreamed—and in my dream I cried out for you, but I could not hold you—"

I held him close. In the first light of the rising sun I saw Lancelet raise Excalibur in his hand, then fling it as hard as he could. It flew through the air end over end, the sun glinting as if on the wing of a white bird; then it fell, twisting, and I saw no more; my eyes were misted with tears and the growing light.

Then I heard Lancelet: "I saw a hand rising from the Lake—a hand that took the sword, and brandished it three times in the air, and then drew it beneath the water . . ."

I had seen nothing, only the glimmer of light on a fish that broke the surface of the Lake; but I doubt not that he saw what he said he saw.

"Morgaine," Arthur whispered, "is it really you? I cannot see you, Morgaine, it is so dark here—is the sun setting? Morgaine, take me to Avalon, where you can heal me of this wound—take me home, Morgaine—"

His head was heavy on my breast, heavy as the child in my own childish arms, heavy as the King Stag who had come to me in triumph. Morgaine, my mother had called impatiently, take care of the baby . . . and all my life I had borne him with me. I held him close and wiped away his tears with my veil, and he reached up and caught at my hand with his own.

"But it is really you," he murmured, "it is you, Morgaine . . . you have come back to me . . . and you are so young and fair . . . I will always see the Goddess with your face . . . Morgaine, you will not leave me again, will you?"

"I will never leave you again, my brother, my baby, my love," I whispered to him, and I kissed his eyes. And he died, just as the mists rose and the sun shone full over the shores of Avalon.

epilogue

In the spring of the year after this, Morgaine had a curious dream.

She dreamed that she was in the ancient Christian chapel upon Avalon, built in the old times by that Joseph of Arimathea who had come here from the Holy Land. And there, before that altar where Galahad had died, Lancelet stood in the robes of a priest, and his face was solemn and shining. In her dream she went, as she had never done in any Christian church, to the altar rail for the sharing of their bread and wine, and Lancelet bent and set the cup to her lips and she drank. And then it seemed to her that he knelt in his turn, and he said to her, "Take this cup, you who have served the Goddess. For all the Gods are one God, and we are all One, who serve the One." And as she took the cup in her hands to set it to his lips in her turn, priestess to priest, he was young and beautiful as he had been years ago. And she saw that the cup in her hands was the Grail.

And then he cried out, as he had done when Galahad knelt before him, "Ah, the light—the light—" and fell forward and lay on the stones without moving; and Morgaine woke in her isolated dwelling on Avalon with that cry of rapture still ringing in her ears; and she was alone.

It was very early, and mist lay thick on Avalon. She rose quietly and robed herself in the dark garb of a priestess, but she tied her veil around her head so that the crescent tattoo there was invisible.

She went quietly out into the stillness of the dawn, taking the downward path beside the Sacred Well. Still as it was, she could sense noiseless footsteps, silent as shadows, behind her. She was never alone; the little dark people always attended her, though she seldom actually saw them—she was their mother and their priestess and they would never leave her. But when she came near the shadow of the ancient Christian chapel, the footsteps gradually ceased; they would not follow her on this ground. Morgaine paused at the door.

Inside the chapel there was a glimmer of light, the light they always kept in their sanctuary. For a moment, so real was the memory of her dream, Morgaine was tempted to step inside . . . she could hardly believe she would

not see Lancelet there, struck down by the magical brilliance of the Grail
. . . but no. She had no business there, and she would not intrude on their
God; and if indeed the Grail was there, it had gone beyond her reach.

Yet the dream remained with her. Had it been sent as a warning?
Lancelet was younger than she herself was . . . she knew not how time ran
in the outer world. Avalon, now, had gone so far into the mists that it might
be with Avalon as it had been with the fairy country when she was young
—while a single year passed within Avalon, three or five or even seven years
might have run by in the outer world. And so what it had come to her to
do should be done now, while she could still come and go between the
worlds.

She knelt before the Holy Thorn, whispering a soft prayer to the
Goddess, and asking leave of the tree; then she cut a slip for planting. It was
not the first time: in these last years, whenever one had come to Avalon and
returned to the outside world, wandering Druid or pilgrim priest . . . for
a few of them could still come to the ancient chapel on Avalon . . . she had
sent with him a slip of the Holy Thorn, so that it might still blossom in
the world outside. But this she must do with her own hands.

Never, except at Arthur's crowning, had she set foot on the *other* island
. . . except, perhaps, for that day when the mists had opened, and Gwenhwyfar had somehow fallen or wandered through. But now, deliberately, she
called the barge, and when it was out in the Lake, sent it into the mists, so
that when it glided forth into the sunlight again, she could see the long
shadow of the church lying over the Lake, and hear the soft tolling of a
bell. She saw her followers shrink from the sound, and knew that here, too,
they would not follow her, nor set foot. So be it, then; the last thing she
wished for was to have the priests on that isle staring in fear and dread at
the barge from Avalon. Unseen, they glided toward the shore and unseen
she stepped onto the land, watching the black-draped barge vanish again into
the mists. And then, the basket over her arm—*like any old market woman or
peddler come here on pilgrimage,* she thought—she went silently up the path
from the shore.

*Only a hundred years or less, certainly less in Avalon, that these worlds have
diverged; yet already the world here is different.* The trees were different, and
the paths, and she stopped, bewildered, at the foot of a little hill—surely
there was nothing like this on Avalon? She had somehow thought the land
would be the same, only the buildings different, for they were, after all, the
same island, separated only by some magical change . . . but now she saw
that they were very different.

And then she saw, winding down the hill toward the little church, a
procession of robed monks, and they bore with them, toward the church,
a body on its bier.

So I saw truly, then, even though I thought it a dream. She stopped, and as the monks brought the body to rest before taking it into the church, she went forward and drew back the pall from the dead face.

Lancelet's face was drawn and lined, far older than when they had parted . . . she did not want to think how much older. But she saw that only for a moment; then what she saw on his face was only the sweet and marvelous look of peace. He lay smiling, looking so far beyond her that she knew on what his dying eyes had rested.

She whispered, "So at last you found your Grail."

One of the monks who carried him said, "Perhaps you knew him in the world, sister?" and she knew that in her dark garb, he thought her one of them.

"He was a—a kinsman of mine."

Cousin, lover, friend . . . but that was long ago. At the end we were priestess and priest.

"I thought as much," said the monk, "for they called him Lancelet at the court of Arthur, in the old days, but here among us we called him Galahad. He had been with us for many years, and he was made priest but a few days ago."

So far you came in your search for a God who would not mock you, my cousin!

The monks who carried him raised him again to their shoulders. The one who had spoken with her said, "Pray for his soul, sister," and she bowed her head. She could not feel grief; not now, when she had seen the reflection of that faraway light on his face.

But she would not follow him into the church. *Here the veil is thin. Here Galahad knelt, and saw the light of the Grail in the* other *chapel, the chapel on Avalon, and reached for it, reached through the worlds, and so died. . . .*

And here at last Lancelet has come to follow his son.

Morgaine walked slowly along the path, half ready to abandon what she had come to do. What difference did it make now? But as she paused, irresolute, an old gardener, kneeling at one of the beds of flowers behind the path, raised his head and spoke to her. "I know you not, sister, you are not one of those who dwell here," he said. "Are you a pilgrim?"

Not as the man thought; but so she was, in a way. "I seek the burial place of my kinswoman—she was the Lady of the Lake—"

"Ah yes, that was many, many years ago, in the reign of our good King Arthur," he said. "It lies yonder, where pilgrims to the island may see it. And from it, the path leads up to the convent of the sisters, and if you are hungry, sister, they will give you something to eat there."

Has it come to this, that I look like a beggar? But the man had meant no harm, so she thanked him, and walked in the direction he had pointed out.

Arthur had built for Viviane a noble tomb indeed. But what lay there was not Viviane; nothing lay there but bones, slowly returning to the earth from which they had come . . . *and all things at last give up their body and their spirit into the keeping of the Lady again.* . . .

Why had it made so much difference to her? Viviane was not there. Yet when she stood with bent head before the cairn, she was weeping.

After a time, a woman in a dark robe not unlike her own, with a white veil over her head, approached her. "Why do you weep, sister? She who lies here is at peace and in God's hands, she has no need of mourning. But maybe she was one of your kin?"

Morgaine nodded, bending her head against the tears.

"We pray always for her," said the nun, "for, though I do not know her name, she was said to be the friend and benefactor of our good King Arthur in the days that were gone." She lowered her head and murmured some prayer or other, and even as she prayed, bells rang out, and Morgaine drew back. So, in place of the harps of Avalon, Viviane had only these clanging bells and doleful psalms?

Never did I think I would stand side by side with one of these Christian nuns, joining with her in prayer. But then she remembered what Lancelet had said in her dream.

Take this cup, you who have served the Goddess. For all the Gods are One . . .

"Come up to the cloister with me, sister," said the nun, smiling and laying a hand on her arm. "You must be hungry and weary."

Morgaine went with her to the gates of their cloister, but would not go in. "I am not hungry," she said, "but if I might have a drink of water—"

"Of course." The woman in black beckoned, and a young girl came and brought a pitcher of water, which she poured into a cup. And she said, as Morgaine lifted it to her lips, "We drink only the water of the chalice well—it is a holy place, you know."

It was like Viviane's voice in her ears: *The priestesses drink only the water of the Sacred Well.*

The nun and the young girl, robed in black, turned and bent their heads before a woman who came from the cloister, and the nun who had guided her said, "This is our abbess."

Morgaine thought, *Somewhere I have seen her.* But even as the thought crossed her mind, the woman said, "Morgaine, you do not know me? We thought you long dead . . ."

Morgaine smiled at her, troubled. "I am sorry—I do not—"

"No, you would not remember me," said the abbess, "though I saw you, now and again, at Camelot; I was so much younger. My name is Lionors. I was married to Gareth, and when all my children were grown,

I came here—here to end my days. Did you come to Lancelet's funeral, then?" She smiled and said, "I should indeed have said *Father Galahad*, but it is hard to remember, and now he is in Heaven it will not matter." She smiled again. "I know not now even who is King, or whether Camelot still stands—there is war in the land again, it is not as it was in Arthur's time. That all seems so very long ago," she added with detachment.

"I came here to visit Viviane's grave. She is buried here—do you remember?"

"I have seen the tomb," said the abbess, "but it was before ever I came to Camelot."

"I have a favor to beg of you," Morgaine said, and touched the basket on her arm. "This is the Holy Thorn that grows on the hills of Avalon, where it is said that the foster-father of Christ struck his staff into the ground and it blossomed there. I would plant a cutting of this thorn tree on her grave."

"Plant it if you will," said Lionors. "I cannot see how anyone could object to that. It seems right to me that it should be here in the world, and not hidden away in Avalon."

She looked at Morgaine, dismayed.

"Avalon! Have you come here from that unholy land?"

Morgaine thought, *Once I would have been angry with her.* "Unholy it is not, whatever the priests say, Lionors," she said gently. "Think—would the foster-father of Christ have struck his staff there if the land had seemed to him evil? Is not the Holy Spirit everywhere?"

The woman bowed her head. "You are right. I will send novices to help you with the planting."

Morgaine would sooner have been alone, but she knew it was a kindly thought. The novices seemed no more than children to Morgaine, girls of nineteen or twenty, so young that she wondered—forgetting that she herself had been made priestess when she was eighteen—how they could possibly know enough of spiritual things to choose lives like this. She had thought nuns in Christian convents would be sad and doleful, ever conscious of what the priests said about the sinfulness of being born women, but these were innocent and merry as robins, talking gaily to Morgaine of their new chapel and bidding her rest her knees while they dug the hole for the cutting.

"And it is your kinswoman who is buried here?" asked one of the girls. "Can you read what it says? I never thought I would learn to read, for my mother said it was not suitable, but when I came here, they told me I must be able to read in the mass book, and so now I can read in Latin! Look," she said proudly, and read: " 'King Arthur made this tomb for his kins-woman and benefactress, the Lady of the Lake, slain by treachery at his court in Camelot'—I cannot read the date, but it was a long time ago."

"She must have been a very holy woman," said another of the girls, "for Arthur, they say, was the best and the most Christian of all kings. He would never have had any woman buried here unless she was a saint!"

Morgaine smiled; they reminded her of the girls in the House of Maidens. "I would not call her a saint, though I loved her. In her day, there were those who called her a wicked sorceress."

"King Arthur would never have a wicked sorceress buried here among holy people," said the girl. "And as for sorcery—well, there are ignorant priests and ignorant people, who are all too ready to cry sorcery if a woman is only a little wiser than *they* are! Are you going to stay and take the veil here, Mother?" she asked, and Morgaine, for a moment startled at the word, realized that they were speaking to her with the same deference and respect as any of her own maidens in the House of Maidens, as if she were an elder among them.

"I am vowed elsewhere, my daughter."

"Is your convent as nice as this one? Mother Lionors is a kind woman," the girl said, "and we are all very happy here—once we had a woman among our sisters who had been a queen. And I know we will go to Heaven, all of us," said the girl with a smile, "but if you have taken vows elsewhere, I am sure that is a good place, too. Only I thought you might perhaps want to stay here, so that you could pray for the soul of your kinswoman who lies buried here." The girl rose and dusted off her dark dress. "Now you may plant your cutting, Mother . . . or would you like me to set it in the earth?"

"No, I will do it," said Morgaine, and knelt to press the soft soil around the roots of the plant. As she rose, the girl said, "If you wish, Mother, I will promise to come here and say a prayer every Sunday for your kinswoman."

For some absurd reason, Morgaine felt that tears were coming to her eyes. "Prayer is always a good thing. I am grateful to you, daughter."

"And you, in your convent, wherever it may be, you must pray for us too," said the girl simply, taking Morgaine's hand as she rose. "Here, Mother, let me brush the dirt from your gown. Now you must come and see our chapel."

For a moment Morgaine was inclined to protest. She had sworn when last she left Arthur's court that she would never again enter any Christian church; but this girl was so much like one of her own young priestesses that she would not profane the name by which the girl knew her God. She let the girl lead her inside the church.

In that other world, she thought, *that church where the ancient Christians worship must stand on this very spot; some holiness from Avalon must surely come through the worlds, through the mists . . .* she did not kneel or cross herself, but she bent her head before the high altar of the church; and then the girl tugged gently at her hand.

"Come," she said. "The high altar is of God and I am a little afraid here always . . . but you have not seen *our* chapel—the sisters' chapel . . . come, Mother."

Morgaine followed the young girl into the small side chapel. There were flowers here, armfuls of apple blossom, before a statue of a veiled woman crowned with a halo of light; and in her arms she bore a child. Morgaine drew a shaking breath and bowed her head before the Goddess.

The girl said, "Here we have the Mother of Christ, Mary the Sinless. God is so great and terrible I am always afraid before *his* altar, but here in the chapel of Mary, we who are her avowed virgins may come to her as our Mother, too. And look, here we have little statues of our saints, Mary who loved Jesus and wiped his feet with her hair, and Martha who cooked dinner for him and scolded her sister when she would not cook with her —I like to think of Jesus when he was a real man who would do something for his mother, when he changed the water into wine at that wedding, so she wouldn't be unhappy because there wasn't enough wine for everyone. And here is a very old statue that our bishop gave us, from his native country . . . one of their saints, her name is Brigid . . ."

Morgaine looked on the statue of Brigid, and she could feel the power coming from it in great waves that permeated the chapel. She bowed her head.

But Brigid is not a Christian saint, she thought, *even if Patricius thinks so. That is the Goddess as she is worshipped in Ireland. And I know it, and even if they think otherwise, these women know the power of the Immortal. Exile her as they may, she will prevail. The Goddess will never withdraw herself from mankind.*

And Morgaine bowed her head and whispered the first sincere prayer she had ever spoken in any Christian church.

"Why, look," said the novice, as she brought her out of doors into the daylight, "we have one of the Holy Thorn here too, not the one you planted on your kinswoman's grave."

And I thought I could meddle in this? Morgaine thought. Surely, the holy thing had brought itself from Avalon, moving, as the hallows were withdrawn from Avalon, into the world of men where it was most needed. It would remain hidden in Avalon, but it would be shown here in the world as well. "Yes, you have the Holy Thorn, and in days to come, as long as this land shall last, every queen shall be given the Holy Thorn at Christmas, in token of her who is queen in Heaven as in Avalon."

"I don't know what you are talking about, Mother, but thank you for your blessing," said the young novice. "The abbess is awaiting you in the guesthouse—she will take breakfast with you. But would you like, perhaps, to stay in the Lady's chapel first and pray awhile? Sometimes when you are alone with the Holy Mother, she can make things clear to you."

Morgaine nodded, unable to speak, and the girl said, "Very well. When you are ready, just come to the guesthouse." She pointed, and Morgaine went back into the chapel and bowed her head, and giving way at last, sank to her knees.

"Mother," she whispered, "forgive me. I thought I must do what I now see you can do for yourself. The Goddess is within us, yes, but now I know that you are in the world too, now and always, just as you are in Avalon and in the hearts of all men and women. Be in me too now, and guide me, and tell me when I need only let you do your will. . . ."

She was silent, kneeling, for a long time, her head bowed, but then, as if compelled, she looked up, and as she had seen it on the altar of the ancient Christian brotherhood in Avalon, as she had seen it when she bore it in Arthur's hall, she saw a light on the altar, and in the Lady's hands— and the shadow, only the shadow, of a chalice . . .

It is in Avalon, but it is here. It is everywhere. And those who have need of a sign in this world will see it always.

There was a sweet scent that did not come from the flowers; and for an instant it seemed to Morgaine that it was Igraine's voice that whispered to her . . . but she could not hear the words . . . and Igraine's hands that touched her head. As she rose, blinded by tears, suddenly it rushed over her, like a great light.

No, we did not fail. What I said to comfort Arthur in his dying, it was all true. I did the Mother's work in Avalon until at last those who came after us might bring her into this world. I did not fail. I did what she had given me to do. It was not she but I in my pride who thought I should have done more.

Outside the chapel, sunlight lay on the land, and there was a fresh scent of spring in the air. Where the apple trees moved in the morning breeze, she could see the blossoms that would bear fruit in their season.

She turned her face toward the guesthouse. Should she go there and breakfast with the nuns, speak perhaps of the old days at Camelot? Morgaine smiled gently. No. She was filled with the same tenderness for them as for the budding apple trees, but that time was past. She turned her back on the convent and walked down to the Lake, along the old path by the shore. Here was a place where the veil lying between the worlds was thin. She needed no longer to summon the barge—she need only step through the mists here, and be in Avalon.

Her work was done.

A NOTE ABOUT THE TYPE

The text of this book has been film set in a type face named Bembo. The roman is a copy of a letter cut for the celebrated Venetian printer Aldus Manutius by Francesco Griffo, and first used in Cardinal Bembo's *De Aetna* of 1495— hence the name of the revival. Griffo's type is now generally recognized, thanks to the researches of Mr. Stanley Morison, to be the first of the old face group of types. The companion italic is an adaption of the chancery script type designed by the Roman calligrapher and printer Lodovico degli Arrighi, called Vincentino, and used by him during the 1520's.

Composed by ComCom, a division of The Haddon Craftsmen, Inc., Allentown, Pennsylvania. Printed and bound by R. R. Donnelly & Sons, Harrisonburg, Virginia. Typography and binding design by Virginia Tan.